THE DARK WOMAN;

OR,

THE DAYS OF THE PRINCE REGENT.

BY THE AUTHOR OF "EDITH THE CAPTIVE."
MALCOLM J. ERRYM.
1862.

WITH FIFTY-TWO ILLUSTRATIONS.

DRAWN BY F. GILBERT, G. F. SARGENT, AND G. STANDFAST.

VOL. II.

LONDON:
PUBLISHED BY JOHN DICKS, 313, STRAND.

INDEX TO THE ENGRAVINGS.

INDEX TO VOL. II.

THE DARK WOMAN;

or,

THE DAYS OF THE PRINCE REGENT.

CHAPTER CXI.

SIR HINCKTON MOYS PAYS AN EARLY VISIT TO THE COUNTESS D'UMBRA'S HOUSE.

THE Dark Woman had reason enough left to be well aware of that; and after one look into

No. 53.—DARK WOMAN.

the face of the Regent, that made him shrink back from before her, she went to the door and flung it open.

Willes very nearly fell into the room.

"Seize that woman!" cried the Regent.

"Yes, your Highness."

Willes pretended to make a vigorous effort to

stop the Dark Woman; but in reality it was but a lumbering one, and intended to let her escape. He affected to fall, and she darted past him.

But she was in danger.

The repeated ringing of the bell from the private room of the Regent had been heard by some of the Yeomen of the Guard, who were on duty in the interior of the Palace, and they hastened towards the spot.

Lights began to flash in different directions about the galleries. There was the clash of arms, and the rapid tread of feet.

The Dark Woman began to feel that it was possible she might fall as a prisoner into the hands of the Regent, and what then could save her from another dismal incarceration in some asylum, from which she would never again emerge, except to her grave?

Fear of such a result added wings to her speed, and she fled from room to room, and from gallery to gallery, only intent upon baffling those who might be in search of her.

She could hear that the whole Palace was thoroughly alarmed.

Reaching, then, a door, she was about to open it, when she shrunk back upon hearing voices on the other side of it.

"It is quite impossible any one can escape now," said the voice, "since every avenue from both Carlton House and St. James's is guarded."

"Oh, we shall have her, my lord!" said another voice.

The Dark Woman turned at once and fled from the immediate vicinity of those persons who were so evidently in earnest in their endeavours to arrest her.

She had completely lost her way; for although the interior of the Palace was tolerably known to her, yet she required to go with deliberation from place to place in it to avoid confusion.

She passed through several apartments which had been evidently in the occupation during the day of some of the Court officials. There she stopped at a door and listened intently.

All was profoundly still on the other side of it.

The Dark Woman then ventured to place her hand upon the handle of the lock, and to open this door.

There was a faint illumination on the other side of it; and when she ventured to look out of the room, she knew at once whereabouts in the Palace she was.

The Titian Gallery was immediately before her.

The Dark Woman now had no difficulty whatever in regard to the topography of the Palace; but if every avenue of escape were guarded, what was she to do?

She paused a few moments to listen.

She could hear no sounds now of pursuit or of search.

At the further end of the gallery from where she was, she knew well of the existence of that short flight of steps which led to the little guard room, and thence into one of the open courts.

She asked herself if it would be safe to venture to try to leave by that one.

Even while so asking herself, the Dark Woman slowly traversed the Titian Gallery, and she had got about half-way down its entire length when she heard the measured tramp of feet on that very short flight of stairs that she was so dubiously approaching.

"Forward!" she heard a sharp voice cry.

Then some one in another moment cried, "Halt!"

There was the rattle of arms.

She then heard a loud, clear voice say, "You will keep this post, sentinel, until relieved, and allow no one to pass. Forward!"

The tramp of feet sounded again.

The Dark Woman felt confident that sentinels were being posted at all the staircases of the Palace.

Surely she was lost.

Her eyes fell upon a door. Above it was, in bold sculptured relief, the royal arms of England. And, strange to say, a key was in the lock of the door.

It was the door that led into the suite of deserted rooms where the interview had taken place between the Prince Regent and Allan Fearon. It was the fair Countess de Blonde, who, with her usual carelessness, had forgotten to remove the antique key from the lock.

And there it was, ready to the hand of the Dark Woman.

Another moment, and she must have been seen by the rapidly approaching guard; but as it was, she turned the key, and opened the door, with the speed of thought. Taking the key out of the outer side of the lock, then, she promptly transferred it to the inner, and closed and locked the door.

She was safe.

Safe, at all events, for a time; for the guard passed the door without the slightest observation of it, and she heard the whole process of another sentinel being posted in the actual gallery itself.

The adventure which Sir Hinckton Moys had had in St. James's Park, and those further proceedings which had been productive to him both of surprise and amusement within the garden of Carlton House, had dipped pretty deeply into the night; but he was not likely to allow himself to rest until he had thoroughly examined the mysterious document, which he had become possessed of through a serious encounter with the house-breaker.

It was in the quiet and security of his own lodgings, that Moys read with surprise and satisfaction that most compromising document which Shucks had extracted from the fears of the Dark Woman.

To read it and re-read it, many times over, was a work of positive pleasure to Sir Hinckton Moys; and then there shone quite a light of joy in his countenance, as he exclaimed, "My restoration now, to the full confidence and favour of the Regent is positive and certain. It is one of the dearest wishes of his heart to get rid at once, and for ever, of the persecutions he has endured from this troublesome woman."

Sir Hinckton Moys actually hummed a tune He felt as if he should like to sally out again into the night air and take a walk, if it were for no other purpose than to get rid of the excitement of his spirits.

"Yes," he added; "I shall now be the grand almoner of fortune. It seems to me that all my enemies are falling before me. Surely my lucky star is in the ascendant; for, although I have left St. James's Palace in defeat and disgrace, I shall return to it a conqueror."

He folded the paper carefully, smiling slightly as he did so, to see the spot of blood upon its surface, and the perforation right through it where the sword had passed.

"This is indeed," he added, "a passport to fame and fortune. I will play with this woman yet awhile—this Countess d'Umbra, as she calls herself. I will angle with her fears, and see if it be not possible to extract some wealthy advantage, as payment for silence and secrecy, that shall last but for so long as shall lull my victim into a false security, and then her fate shall be the greater."

Sir Hinckton Moys paced his rooms triumphantly.

"To be sure," he added. "She will expiate her crimes upon the scaffold — upon that same scaffold from which she rescued Allan Fearon; and I will take excellent care that it shall not for long want another temporary tenant in his person."

Little did Sir Hinckton Moys imagine, as he thus dimly pictured to himself some new and more successful villany, which should be the destruction of Allan, that his relation with the Prince Regent had so largely altered — little did he imagine that, for once and for ever, Allan was protected against every possible machination of his foes.

It might be that the Regent, inflamed by jealousy, might cast him off for ever, and crush, in his own mind, that lightly awakened feeling of affection which the presence of a new-found son had engendered in his heart; it might be that, believing Allan involved in the machinations of Buckingham House, the Regent might close the doors of St. James's against him; but as for his life or liberty, in relation to the law, were they not now the safest in all England? But Sir Hinckton Moys knew nothing of all this.

To his mind, after the destruction of the Dark Woman, came the gratification of his revenge against Allan.

Then he pictured to himself the disgrace of the Countess de Blonde.

Then the discharge of Willes.

And after that, the vindictive courtier had something else to do. He would involve his rival, Colonel Hanger, in some disreputable transaction, and he would set the policemen to work upon Astorath the Astrologer.

Sir Hinckton Moys's information was decidedly defective on several points.

He had yet to learn that Astorath and the Dark Woman were one and the same person; but his exultation was immense, and it was with difficulty he could persuade himself to retire to rest on that night, so intensely anxious was he for the morrow.

It was at a most unusual hour, for him, that Moys rose, and despatched a breakfast which said as much for his mental serenity as his health.

He felt as if his mind was wrapped in roses. A delightful feeling of security, and of power, was about his heart; and his step was proud and disdainful, as he made his way to Hanover Square, with something of the feeling of a sportsman, who, feeling sure of his game, was not unwilling to protract its tortures for his own special amusement.

"I will see this woman face to face," he said,—"this terror of the Regent. I will laugh at her threats—I will ridicule her tears—and, bit by bit, I will let her know how thoroughly aware I am of all her antecedents; and if she has riches, I will see what brilliant offers she will make me, for her life—yes, for her very life."

Little did Sir Hinckton Moys imagine that the Dark Woman, to whom he projected paying so triumphant a visit, was at that moment actually beneath the roof of St James's Palace, meditating an act which would, at all events, place her beyond the reach of his petty malice.

The number of the house was well indicated upon the blood-stained scrap of paper which Sir Hinckton Moys had in his possession; and so pleased was he, that he had some difficulty in schooling his countenance to an expression of ordinary indifference, as he stood on the door step of the Countess d'Umbra's mansion.

"No, sir," was the reply, in answer to Sir Hinckton Moys's request to know if the Countess were stirring,—"no, sir. Her ladyship has not yet appeared."

"I am an old friend," said Sir Hinckton Moys, "and will wait for her."

This was a request that the hall-porter could not very well refuse, for there was quite sufficient about the appearance of Sir Hinckton Moys to show that he belonged to the richer, if not to the better class of society.

He was shown into that very drawing-room, so splendid in its details, where the Dark Woman had passed through such a scene of agony and degradation with the two housebreakers, Shucks and Brads.

And well pleased was Sir Hinckton Moys to see those signs of wealth and magnificence about him—well pleased was he to believe that this woman, whom he intended to make so heartlessly a victim, possessed wealth enough to purchase what she might think would be a total silence, but which he would make so brief an one, that she would find herself doubly betrayed in the very act.

He waited a quarter of an hour with patience — half an hour with some growing impatience — three-quarters exhausted him, and he rung the bell.

It was the Countess's page who replied to the summons.

There was a look of intense anxiety about the face of this young girl, who, in her fanciful boy's dress, presented herself before Sir Hinckton Moys.

"I wish to see the Countess," he said. "Surely she is stirring now?"

"No, sir. We have none of us seen her this morning, and her dressing-room door continues locked."

A slight shade of suspicion came across the countenance of Sir Hinckton Moys. Could he have been watched entering the house, or seen by the Dark Woman, after he had entered it, and his errand suspected?

He looked keenly into the countenance of the page.

"My good boy," he said, "I have something of the greatest importance to say to your mistress

—of importance to her, mind you, and not to me."

"Yes, sir," said the page; "but my mistress has not yet left her dressing-room."

"So you say. Now here, my lad, is half a guinea."

"Sir?"

"Half a guinea, I say. Don't you know what half a guinea is?"

"Oh, yes—perfectly."

"Then it is for you, if you will go and tap at your mistress's door, and say that a gentleman must see her, to relate to her something she wishes particularly to know."

"I never take money, sir, but from my mistress, who gives me much more than I require; but I will tap at her door, and deliver the message."

The page left the drawing-room, after having thus added largely to the suspicions of Sir Hinckton Moys that he was known and avoided; for the rejection of half a guinea, by any one in such a position, was to him, upon any other supposition, a most inexplicable circumstance.

Hardly, however, had the page closed the door, when it was flung open again, and a footman announced a visitor.

At the moment, Sir Hinckton Moys made a half dart forward, for he thought it must surely be the Countess herself who was making her appearance.

Wonderfully and wofully disappointed was Sir Hinckton Moys when the footman announced Mr. Fearon, and no other than Allan himself appeared upon the threshold of the room.

It was a strange sight to see these two men confront each other.

The oppressor and the oppressed—the innocent and the guilty—the man who had been hunted almost to death, and he who had led the pursuit.

More willingly—much more willingly would Sir Hinckton Moys have met the arch-fiend himself in that drawing-room, than Allan Fearon. But he was a bold, fearless man, and there were few circumstances indeed which, amid the varying scenes of human life, he would shrink from.

Certainly, he would have much, very much preferred to be anywhere else than in the Countess d'Umbra's mansion in Hanover Square at that moment; but since it was so—since he was there, he put on as bold a front of defiance as he could.

The expression that came over the face of Allan was one of indignation and loathing.

Easy enough had it been for Fearon to combine in his own mind, and in conversations with his dear Marian, all the circumstances which pointed with irresistible force to the conclusion that it was to Sir Hinckton Moys he owed all the miseries and all the dangers he had passed through; and now to see him there, in that house, foreboded further evil to himself or to the Countess d'Umbra.

And be that self-styled Countess d'Umbra whom she might—Linda de Chevenaux, Dark Woman, or by whatever other title she chose to call herself, or was called by others—Allan could not forget that she was yet his mother.

No wonder, then, that he looked upon Sir Hinckton Moys with eyes of horror and aversion.

And how widely different were the errands of those two men to that splendid mansion in Hanover Square.

One came to bring what consolation he could to the poor, bruised heart of a long—nearly a life-long—sufferer.

The other came to inflict what agony it was possibly within his power to bring to bear upon the mind of one who should merit pity, if it were only from the world of persecution she had already endured.

If the maxim be true of human nature that a man never hates any one so much as he does him whom he has deeply injured, then the feeling of Sir Hinckton Moys against Allan Fearon must indeed have been compounded of gall and bitterness.

As for Allan, he shrunk from Moys as he would have done from some venomous reptile.

Sir Hinckton mistook that shrinking for fear, and he gathered boldness himself accordingly.

"You here!" was the exclamation of Allan Fearon,—"you here, villain!"

Sir Hinckton Moys stepped back a step; and the colour paled on his face as he replied, "Not hanged yet, eh? Ha! ha! Well, I fancy the time will yet come!"

Allan looked surprised, but it was at the desperate effrontery of the man who could address such words to him.

Again was Sir Hinckton Moys deceived, and thought that Allan feared him.

Nothing could well be wider from the truth than any such supposition.

Allan went at once to the side of the fire-place, past Sir Hinckton Moys, and rung the bell.

The page appeared.

"Is the Countess within?"

"We hardly now know, sir, since she makes no reply to applications at the door of her dressing-room."

Allan felt a strange pang at his heart.

What if the concurrence of all the circumstances that had so recently taken place, had been too much for the heated brain of his mother?

What if she had sought that peace in death, which this world, with all its jarring interests, appeared so pertinaciously to deny her?

Allan darted to the door.

"I will go to her," he said.

"You, sir?" said the page.

"You?" exclaimed Sir Hinckton Moys.

"Ah!" added Allan, suddenly. "I am glad you spoke. I had for the moment forgotten you."

"Forgotten me?"

"Yes. Speak, my pretty boy. Is there no one who will prevent this man from leaving the house until I have seen your mistress?"

"Prevent me from leaving!" cried Sir Hinckton Moys. "Ha! ha! I tell you, my gaol bird, that I come here to see the Countess d'Umbra, and I do not intend to leave until I have done so!"

"You heard me, boy," added Allan, without saying a word to Sir Hinckton, or appearing to pay the least attention to him. "I want to know if there is any one here who will undertake to prevent this man from leaving the house until I have seen your mistress, for he is one of the bitterest enemies she has?"

"Ah, yes," said the page; "there is one who, with that knowledge, will detain him."

"Fetch that one."

"Yes, sir."

"Hold!" cried Sir Hinckton Moys, as he

glanced at the clock, and saw that the morning was advancing, and that it would be a serious thing if he were prevented from keeping the appointment with the Regent, — "hold, boy! Beware of what you do. Obey only my orders here, and they will have the sanction of your mistress."

"Sir," said the page, "I know that this gentleman," indicating Fearon, "is in my mistress's confidence; but of you I know nothing."

"And so, my pretty page," said Allan, "you will do as I wish."

There was a slight flush of colour on the face of the apparent page-boy as Allan used the word "pretty," and he said, gently, "I will send some one, sir."

"Spare yourself the trouble," said Sir Hinckton Moys. "I have altered my mind, and will call again—probably in the evening."

"No," said Allan.

"You say no to me?"

"I do. You may possibly call again, but now that you are here I do not intend to let you go until I know what your errand is in this house, and with the Countess d'Umbra."

"You do not intend to let me go?—you—you?"

"Yes, Sir Hinckton Moys, even I; and I would by no means advise you to place yourself in such peril as to attempt to leave here without my good will that you should do so."

Sir Hinckton looked irresolute for a few seconds, and those few seconds had sufficed to enable the page to summon a most effectual assistant to the scene of action.

It was Binks who made his appearance, with a short pipe in his mouth, and looking curious and expectant.

"What's the row, eh?"

"This is the man," said the page, addressing Allan, "who will no doubt do what you desire."

"All right!" added Binks. "Who is it?"

"My good fellow," said Allan, "are you a friend as well as a servant to the Countess?"

"Rather!"

"Then this man, whom you see here, has come to the house on some errand that I feel assured is against her peace; and I want you to keep him from going away again until she sees him, and we know what it is."

"That's the dodge!"

"You will do it?"

"It's done!"

"I protest," said Sir Hinckton Moys,—"I protest against this outrage, which, if persevered in, you will all hear of it at another time, and in a manner which will be anything but agreeable to you!"

"You will keep him securely in this room?" added Allan.

Binks nodded, and lounged against the wall close to the door.

"My good fellow," said Sir Hinckton Moys, as he stepped a few paces closer to Binks,—"my good fellow, you are led into a very great error, indeed!"

"Don't be a palavering French to me!" said Binks.

"French? My good man, I speak plain English, when I tell you that it is I who am the friend of the Countess; and this man here, Fearon, who

was so nearly hanged the other day, and who will be hanged some day, who is her foe!"

"What's that to you?" said Binks.

"But I tell you he is a housebreaker—a—a—dishonest person!"

"What's that to you?" roared Binks again. "Eh? What's that to you?"

This was so unanswerable a plea, that Sir Hinckton Moys was brought completely to a stand-still; but as Binks took it suddenly into his head, from his crafty look, that he was about to make a spring upon him, he took the initiative by darting at Moys himself, exclaiming, as he did so, "Will you, then—will you? I should only like to see you try it!"

Binks's immense fist came so close to the eyes of Sir Hinckton Moys that he retreated most precipitately.

Allan left the room.

The page was lingering on the threshold of the door, and Allan said, "Show me the rooms of your mistress, and I will see if she will answer me."

"But, sir——"

"I know what you would say. Believe me, there will be no blame. Do you not know me?"

"I have seen you, sir."

"And do you not know who I am?"

"Scarcely, sir; although I have seen tears in the eyes of my mistress when you have left the house."

"I do not think any secrecy necessary," added Allan. "I am the son of your mistress."

"Ah, I thought so!"

"Then you will show me her rooms?"

"Oh, yes, sir! Follow me; and if—if——"

"If what?"

"Oh, sir, if you could only persuade her to leave at once and for ever the life of danger she leads, how happy, happy it would be."

"It is the wish that lies nearest to my heart," said Allan.

"Then God bless you ever, sir."

"You feel more than a common interest in her, I can see," rejoined Allan. "Has she been very good and kind to you?"

"She has, indeed."

"Then I thank heaven for that. I would fain have her good and kind to something human. But which is the door of her room?"

"This one, sir. This is the door of her dressing-room. The bed-room is beyond it. She always locks this door on retiring to rest, but I never knew her remain so long without opening it."

"Then you, too, have fears?"

"Alas, sir, I have."

"Of what?"

"Of some sudden illness, sir."

"Pray heaven it be nothing worse."

Allan rapped at the door—at first gently, and then sharply, and then so loudly that it would have been impossible for the soundest sleeper not to have been awakened by it.

There was no response.

Allan began to feel terribly anxious.

The face of the page paled perceptibly.

"Something has happened," said Allan. "I feel that something must have happened."

"Alas! alas! my poor mistress!"

Allan hesitated for a moment, and only for a moment. He was young and vigorous, and the door was but a slight one. He retreated a step or two. Then he made a rush forward. There was a slight crash, and the hasp of the lock gave way, and the door opened.

"That is well done," said the page.

Allan and the young Carlos, as the Dark Woman named her, at once entered the dressing-room.

CHAPTER CXII.

ALLAN FEARON TEACHES A WHOLESOME LESSON TO SIR HINCKTON MOYS

THE dressing-room of the Dark Woman, to which Allan Fearon, by the feeling that his near relationship to her had now penetrated, presented much which, under ordinary circumstances, would have attracted his attention.

But now his whole mind was too intent upon seeking her to permit any external objects to attract him.

"Countess—mother!" he cried. "Speak! It is I—it is your son who calls to you!"

Allan was in hope that some reply would come to him from the inner room, but all was still.

The page did not hesitate a moment, but passed onwards into the bed-chamber. Allan heard him utter a cry of satisfaction, as he thought, and he was right, for it was such; since no sooner was the young girl who played the part of the page Carlos satisfied that the bed had not been slept in, than she felt quite at ease about her mistress.

She returned to the dressing-room.

"All is well, sir!"

"Well? She sleeps?"

"Oh, no, no! She has been from home the whole night, and has not returned. That is all."

"All?"

"Yes, sir. It is too usual to excite any alarm in the minds of those who know the Countess as well as I do."

"I can see that you now feel quite at ease," said Allan; "but I am very far from being so, since she may be in great danger wherever she is gone."

"It has happened so often," replied the page, apologetically, "that I have ceased to think it possible anything amiss can take place. No doubt, though, she will very soon return."

"Then I will wait."

Allan cast his eyes now round the dressing-room much more observantly than he had done before, for the confidence of the page in the safety of the Dark Woman had begot something of the same feeling in himself.

It was a superb apartment, and contained everything which ease or luxury could suggest; but what most surprised Allan, considering that it was the dressing-room of a lady, was to see the many articles of male apparel which were in and about it.

In one corner, too, there were some half-dozen swords, of different sizes and patterns, and some walking-canes; so that, take it for all in all, that dressing-room might either have been taken to belong to an actress, or to be shared by one of the masculine gender.

"I will go down now to this man—Sir Hinckton Moys," said Allan; "for since the Countess is really not in the house, it will be needless to keep him any longer a prisoner."

Allan sought the drawing-room again, and there he found Moys still the prisoner of Binks, who was lounging close to the door, in the same attitude in which Fearon had left him.

Sir Hinckton Moys was close to one of the windows, looking excessively angry, and as if he was half inclined to open it, and call out for some help from the passers-by.

And probably he would have done so, but that he fancied he felt himself so strong in his power over the Dark Woman.

But for his possession of that little scrap of paper with the life-blood of Shucks, the burglar, upon it, he would, no doubt, have been only too well pleased to do something which would publicly compromise the Dark Woman, and all who felt in any way interested in her fortunes.

How far Allan Fearon was so interested he could not, as yet, make out.

But his own observations and reflections had told him that it was to the mock Countess d'Umbra that he owed the defeat of his most villanous scheme for the destruction of Allan by the hands of the hangman.

That he could comprehend well enough, although why she took so great an interest in the young man he could not conceive.

It was rather surprising that Sir Hinckton Moys did not, in fact, hit upon the true solution of the difficulty, by supposing that Allan was the long lost son of the Dark Woman; but the fact was, that he had treated the whole story about there being a son at all born to Linda de Chevenaux as an absurd myth.

Had he been asked why he doubted the matter so completely, he probably would have used the same argument as the Regent.

Was it likely, he would have said, that the claims upon the Prince's purse, which such a boy would have had, would have been let slumber for twenty years?

Taking the low pecuniary view of human nature, which such a man as Sir Hinckton Moys was sure to take, that would have been quite conclusive on the subject.

At the appearance of Allan, he now put on a blustering look, as he said, "Well, sir. How long are you and your silly myrmidons going to confine me a prisoner in this house? The consequences to yourselves, I fancy, increase with the duration of this outrage!"

"Sir Hinckton Moys," said Allan, with all the loathing and contempt that one man can possibly feel for another, "I now tell you that you are at liberty to go."

"Indeed!"

"You need not stay," added Allan, turning to Binks.

"All's right! That will do! If you want me again, just howl over the stairs-head, and I'll come! I don't like the looks of the fellow at all!"

"That feeling is perfectly mutual," said Sir Hinckton Moys; "for a more perfectly ugly ruffian I never saw in all my life!"

Binks laughed. His feelings did not lie so near the surface as to be hurt by any such remark as that which had just fallen from Sir Hinckton Moys.

"And now, sir," added Allan, "instead of detaining you, I order you out of this house!"

"You order me out?"

"I have said so."

"You?—you?"

"Even I; and I am quite prepared to enforce my order! Go, sir—go!"

"And by what right? By what possible pretence do you, as one visitor to the Countess d'Umbra, order out another? But I comprehend. Ha! ha! Her ladyship has not yet risen! Ha! ha! A certain gentleman feels himself at liberty to seek her even in her bed-chamber, while other visitors may wait below! I comprehend all now! The condemned Allan Fearon was, after all, under the protection of the Dark Woman! Ha! ha!"

Allan's face reddened with anger, but he was not unmindful that those words "Dark Woman" had passed the lips of Sir Hinckton Moys; and that they suggested his possession of the terrible secret of the identity of the Countess d'Umbra with the Dark Woman, whose deeds had rendered her so obnoxious to the law.

Moys saw the contest that was taking place in the mind of Allan. He made a mock bow of great respect, as he added, "Sir, I congratulate you upon your enviable position; particularly as Annie Gray, the Countess de Blonde, was induced to torment the Regent into granting you a pardon on account of your being the husband of her sister! Ha! ha! It will be a little bit of news to her that you are, at the same time, the paramour of the Dark Woman!"

"Villain!"

"Oh, sir! Hard words cannot prevent facts!"

"Worse than villain!"

"As you please! Ha! ha! I shall, I hope and trust, have an opportunity yet, before the close of this day, of informing the fair Countess de Blonde by some means of this little interesting fact!"

"You will lie, then, sir!"

"Sir!"

"I say, sir, you will lie! That there is love—that there is familiarity and tenderness between me and the Countess d'Umbra I will not deny; but you may add to whoever you speak to upon that subject, that it is the love of a mother to a son—of a son to a mother!"

Sir Hinckton Moys fairly staggered back, and was glad to hold a chair for support.

"Can this be possible?"

"I have said it, sir."

"You—the—the long lost—the doubtful—the son of——"

"The Regent!"

"Ah! Fool! fool! Oh, what a fool I have been to be sure!"

Sir Hinckton Moys clasped one hand over his eyes, and felt, at that moment, that all his air-built schemes had surely vanished into empty space, leaving him deserted and desolate.

Would it be at all safe now to pursue the desperate course that he had commenced with the Regent against his own son? Would it be possible to influence the Prince's mind sufficiently against him?—or would it be safe in any shape or way for him, Sir Hinckton Moys, to pursue any further his plans of revenge against Allan?

As these thoughts crowded to his mind in a moment.

He made a low bow to Allan.

"Sir," he said, "if such be the fact, it will give me pleasure to—to—that is to say, to advance your interests—to speak to the Regent."

"Sir Hinckton Moys, there is the door."

"But, sir——"

"There is the door."

"But——"

"Unless you prefer the window, from which I will fling you if you do not make a speedy exit."

Moys moved towards the door.

He stood upon the very threshold; and then, in a high voice of anger and menace, he said, "Beware, sir—beware! You send me from this house in possession of a secret which you would gladly purchase from me at any price—which your mother, the Countess d'Umbra, alias the Dark Woman, will find is her death warrant! It is your own act. The consequences be upon your own head! Beware, I say—beware!"

"Go, sir—go; and take with you my scorn, my defiance, and my contempt!"

"Be it so—be it so!"

Sir Hinckton Moys struck the breast of his coat as he spoke. "Be it so! I have a small scrap of paper here—a document that has been extorted from the Dark Woman by some one who has either had the art to prey upon her credulity, or upon her fears. I achieved possession of it at my sword's point. It is worth countless thousands to her, for it is her condemnation, in, no doubt, her own hand-writing. You send me away with such a document. Ha! ha! Wise youth! Be it so!"

"No," said Allan, as he sprung forward, and caught Sir Hinckton Moys by the collar,—"no! If you are not lying—if you really have such a document, I will take it from the centre of your heart, if it were hidden there."

"Ah, you would rob me!"

"I will have that paper you mention."

"Never!"

"I will have it."

"Help! Murder!"

"Call out as you will—I intend to have it."

"You are, then, the robber who so narrowly escaped death at Newgate. You rely upon the possible greater strength of youth to take from me by force that which you dare not fight for, like a man. I am a gentleman and an officer; and I challenge you to a fair combat, since you have presumed to lay hands upon me."

"Come back, sir," said Allan, as he half dragged Sir Hinckton Moys back into the drawing-room,—"come back, sir. Even you shall not say that I have done aught unbefitting the son of a prince."

Sir Hinckton drew a long breath.

"I ask you, sir, for the paper you mention," added Allan Fearon.

"It is to sell."

"No!"

"I say it is to sell!"

"That depends upon how you became possessed of it."

"I fought for it."

"Indeed!"

"You are incredulous, young sir. But, as a proof that I did fight for it, I am desirous—ay, and willing, too—to fight for its retention. I will meet you to-morrow morning at daybreak, when and where you will, as one gentleman should meet another; and if you conquer me, you shall have the document I have mentioned."

"You challenge me?"

"I do."

"Then that leaves me the choice of weapons."

"It does."

"And of time, and place."

"All that."

"Then I name swords."

"Agreed."

"And the present time, and the present place."

Sir Hinckton Moys turned pale. He had not, for a moment, intended to meet Allan. He had only affected to do so, in order to get out of the dilemma which his imprudent boasting about the possession of the document he had taken from Shucks had placed him in. His intention had been to tell the Regent that he had accidentally met with Allan, and been challenged, and to leave it to the Prince to put a stop to the duel, provided Allan were really his son.

"Well, sir," said Fearon, "what say you?"

"I cannot."

"Wherefore?"

"It is inconvenient. I have not the time to spare."

"Ten minutes."

"No, no! I mentioned to-morrow morning—you know that I mentioned to-morrow morning. You must recollect that I said to-morrow morning at an early hour."

"Yes; but you must likewise recollect that you admitted it was left to me to name weapons, and time, and place."

"But, on consideration, I know not if I ought to cross swords with one in such a position of life as yourself."

"I am the son of a prince."

"It might cost me my commission."

"If you live, I will speak to the Regent on that head."

"You—you will? You speak to the Regent?"

"Yes, to my father."

"But you have not—he has not—that is to say, you—he——Eh?"

Sir Hinckton Moys was swelling with curiosity to know if Allan Fearon had, or had not, had an interview with the Regent, and what had taken place at that interview; but it was not likely that Allan was going to gratify one whom he looked upon as such a deadly foe with any such particulars.

Allan had quite made up his mind that Sir Hinckton Moys should not leave that house in Hanover Square with the damaging document to the Dark Woman, he had declared himself to be in possession of.

It was with Allan now rather a romantic point of honour not to take the paper from him by main force, which he felt he had the power to do, but to give him a chance of its retention by a combat.

Allan remembered those swords which he had seen in the dressing-room of the Countess d'Umbra, and it was by the aid of two of them that he hoped to force Sir Hinckton Moys to a combat which should be a retribution for all his villanies.

And, by a strange combination of circumstances, it so happened that Allan Fearon was by no means so unaccustomed to the use of a sword as

from his lowly state so long might have been supposed.

Mr. Webber, in whose service he had been, was gold lace manufacturer, embroiderer, and military acoutrement-maker to the Court of St. James's; and among those matters which formed his stock in trade were swords of all sorts and patterns.

Many a time had Allan Fearon whiled away an hour by fencing with some of the officials of the establishment, and fortunately with an old pensioner from the guard, who was a porter to the house.

Hence had Allan come to know the use of the weapon to which he had to oppose himself in the hands of Sir Hinckton Moys.

CHAPTER CXIII.

SIR HINCKTON MOYS REACHES ST. JAMES'S IN A WOUNDED CONDITION.

PERHAPS there was in the mind of Sir Hinckton Moys an idea that he would obtain an easy victory over Allan Fearon, even if absolutely forced to the combat, in consequence of the want of skill of his opponent.

How was it likely he could suppose for a moment that one who had been educated and brought up in so humble a position, could be acquainted, even in the most limited sense, with the use of a weapon sacred as one might almost call it to the hands of a gentleman.

Seeing that there was no escape—feeling assured that Allan would be as good as his word, and force him to a personal contest—Sir Hinckton Moys's next effort was to endeavour to extract all the personal advantages possible from the transaction.

What a tale would he not have to tell the Regent! How he had encountered his son, and held him at his sword's point, and at his mercy, just because he had discovered his paternity.

Truly, if one portion of his scheme should fail, and the Regent should not incline to believe that Allan was a spy from Buckingham House, he had other resources and plans to fall back upon, which might yet avail him

Under these circumstances, then, Sir Hinckton thought it would be his best plan to assume an air of frankness and courage, and accept the combat.

"It is not for me," then he said, "holding his Majesty's commission, to shrink any longer from what you propose. Be it so, if you will have it; but whatever may happen to one or other of us, it is you alone who will be to blame, fighting, as we shall here, without witnesses or seconds."

"There you are wrong," said Allan. "I intend there should be a witness, since I am well aware that the man who could stoop so low in dissimulation as Sir Hinckton Moys has stooped, would not scruple to place any colour he chose upon this transaction."

Sir Hinckton Moys bit his lips with anger, but he restrained himself from the utterance of the passionate expressions he would fain have indulged in.

"Where are your witnesses?" he said. "Where are your seconds?"

No. 51.—DARK WOMAN.

"I will summon one of the household of the Countess; or two, if you prefer it; and they shall see exactly what happens, without knowing how or why it happens."

"I do not understand you."

"Then I will further explain to you. There are swords in this house, two of which I will send for. It may be assumed that we are about to have a trial of skill, in the way of a fencing match, and that we are desirous of an umpire being present to record the hits. A servant can perform that office perfectly, and at the same time will become an unconscious witness, who could be called upon at any time to depose to the circumstances of this real duel."

"As you please," cried Sir Hinckton Moys, impatiently. "I have an appointment at mid-day, and must settle this matter in time to keep it."

Allan Fearon rang for the page, who presently made an appearance; but it betrayed the principal anxiety which was upon the mind of Allan, when his first words were an inquiry if the Countess had come home.

"No, sir," said the page, "my mistress has not yet appeared."

There was an air of great sadness about the manner in which these words were spoken, so that Allan could not but perceive that the page was beginning to have some fears on account of the prolonged absence of the Dark Woman.

But he would say no more in the presence of the man with whom he was so soon to be at deadly strife. Turning to the page, he addressed him with carelessness in his tone and manner.

"Look you here, boy," he said. "This gentleman and I have a mind for a fencing match, to decide some question upon points of skill on which we differ. Fetch me a couple of swords, as nearly matched in point of length and size as you can, from your mistress's dressing-room."

"Ah, sir," said the page," I fear——"

"Fear nothing," said Allan, "but do as I bid you."

"Knowing who you are, sir, I feel bound to obey your orders; but I fear this is no trial of skill."

"Fear nothing, but do as I bid you. All will be well."

The page, with a look of sadness, left the drawing-room, and then Sir Hinckton Moys spoke.

"If we are to fight with one witness," he said, "let that boy suffice. I would rather he were present than some more vulgar servant of the house."

"I am content," replied Allan. "Be it so."

Since the page had learnt the exact relationship between Allan Fearon and the Countess d'Umbra, there was no hesitation in obeying his orders, and presently Carlos returned with two dress-swords, which very nearly matched each other.

The moment Allan Fearon took one in his hand, a suspicion began to grow up in the mind of Sir Hinckton Moys that he was by no means so ignorant of the use of the weapon as might fairly have been surmised. It never occurred to the courtier that accident had placed Allan in a position to acquire an accomplishment which otherwise would have been far beyond his reach.

"Carlos," said Allan, "will you remain here as a witness to this little trial of skill?"

"I will, sir."

The page closed the door.

A shade of anxiety came over the face of Sir Hinckton Moys.

"I am afraid," he said, "these swords are not sufficiently alike to make this a fair fight."

"Then do you take your choice," said Allan. "I will make myself content with the one you reject."

It was quite impossible to frame an excuse in objection to this mode of settling the difficulty, and Sir Hinckton Moys took one of the swords at once, poising it in his hand, and calculating the chances in his favour if, after all, by some accident, Allan Fearon should have had a few lessons in fencing.

The courtier was a very tolerable swordsman. It would never have done for a man like Sir Hinckton Moys to be greatly deficient in an accomplishment, any want of ordinary skill in which might have cost him his life.

Duelling was certainly fading away in England at that period, as one of the dying-out institutions of a more barbarous age, but still it was by no means extinct.

The rarity was when the sword was used, for the use of that weapon in settling the little honourable disputes of gentlemen had almost entirely gone out of fashion, being superseded by the long duelling-pistol, with its hair trigger, which, in the hands of the weakest, was as sufficient a weapon as it could possibly be in the hands of the strongest.

The page, with a look of deep interest, retired to the recess of one of the windows.

Allan slipped off his coat, and at once took up a position.

That position spoke volumes to Sir Hinckton Moys.

"Ah!" he cried. "You fence."

"And was it possible, sir," said Allan, "that you took that sword in your hand with the idea that I could not?"

"This little passage of arms," cried Sir Hinckton, "is your own act. Blame me not for its results."

"Ah, then," cried the page, "this is, indeed, a combat!"

The swords clashed together.

"Peace, Carlos," cried Allan; "and, if you love your mistress, give no alarm, but let us proceed.'

Sir Hinckton Moys set his teeth hard, and summoned all his skill; but, after the first pass or two, he felt that he had to deal with one who possessed considerable mastery of the sword.

But Moys was a man who had passed into the middle of life. He had been present at many contests, both as second and principal; and consequently in experience, and those tricks of fence which only experience can give, he was decidedly the superior of Allan Fearon.

But then Allan had youth and agility—a clear, piercing eye, which seemed to look into his opponent's soul, and he bore with him that heart which was not corrupted with injustice. He was a trifle taller, too, than Sir Hinckton Moys, and his reach of arm was a little greater.

But, take it for all in all, the advantages and disadvantages under which these two men laboured were pretty nearly balanced and counterbalanced on either side.

And so the fight went on.

The swords were thin and slender in the blades —they were constructed but for piercing and for that play of wrist and *finesse* of action which strips a combat of this kind of all noise and tumult.

To be sure, there was the ring of the blades one upon another, as in a serpentine manner they traversed from hilt to point—but that was all.

A flush of colour had come upon the face of Allan.

Sir Hinckton Moys had turned deadly pale.

With an attitude and an expression of deep interest, the page had come out from the recess in the window, and stood watching the combatants.

"One," said Allan.

Sir Hinckton uttered a sharp cry. There was blood upon his arm.

"You record that for me," called Allan, glancing towards the page.

"Ah, yes! Right willingly!"

That slight glance from his opponent's face nearly cost Allan Fearon his life, for Moys took advantage of it to make a savage and ferocious assault upon him.

Allan just succeeded in parrying the deadly thrust so that the sword passed over his shoulder, ripping up the skin in its progress.

For the moment, Sir Hinckton Moys thought that he had inflicted a serious wound upon Fearon, and at the same moment that thought came to his mind, he was ready to curse his own folly for allowing his passion to get the better of his judgment.

He would have thought nothing of taking the life of Allan Fearon; but the son of the Regent, illegitimate though he thought him, was quite another personage.

The two opponents were now so close together that it was only by shortening his arm considerably Allan could act upon the offensive; and that he did, for the next instant his sword passed through a portion of the neck of the courtier.

Sir Hinckton dropped his sword and staggered back.

"You may have killed me," he said; "but I fancy I have had my revenge!"

The blood flowed freely from his wound.

"Enough, enough!" cried the page, in an imploring attitude. "Surely this is enough."

"It should be enough," cried Allan, who still kept upon the defensive.

"Then you are content?" said Sir Hinckton Moys, faintly, as he staggered back, feeling with his hand until he came to a chair, into which he sank; "then you are content?"

"Not quite," said Allan, as, casting down the sword, he with three or four strides reached the wounded courtier; "not quite, Sir Hinckton Moys, as well you know."

At the commencement of the contest, Moys had buttoned his coat closely over the chest, and now with one rapid action Allan Fearon tore it open, and from a side-pocket from which it just peeped, to give assurance of its presence, Allan took that self-accusing document which the Dark Woman had been compelled to give Shucks the housebreaker, and which at his death had passed into the hands of Sir Hinckton Moys.

Moys had received the document stained with the blood of the man whom he had murdered in St. James's Park, and it was rather a singular circumstance that the wound Sir Hinckton had now received had sent a trickling stream right down upon that paper again.

The writing upon it was getting obliterated, bit by bit, by the blood of all who possessed it.

"Now, Sir Hinckton Moys," said Allan, "if you require assistance you shall have it; but if not, you are at liberty to depart from this house at your own good pleasure."

Moys by this time had found out that he was not seriously hurt. It was but a slight flesh wound in the neck, after all, that he had received; but he chose for his own purposes to put the worst complexion upon it that he could.

"I am hurt," he said; "but I will not remain in this house. The character of its inmates does not recommend it to me."

He affected to stagger to the door of the drawing-room.

"Help him," said Allan to the page.

"No," said Moys. "I will have no help from any one here—though sorely wounded, I will find my own way."

He passed out of the drawing-room, and down the grand staircase. It was nearly eleven o'clock, and his appointment with the Regent was at midday—that appointment upon which he had built such high hopes, but which he now hardly knew how to conduct, so changed were all the circumstances upon which he had originally based it.

But his first care was to see to his wound, which, trivial though it was, might, if neglected, lead to inconvenience.

That care taken, by the assistance [of a] surgeon in a neighbouring street, Sir Hinckton Moys had a hackney coach called, and proceeded at once to his lodgings in St. James's, where, with more assistance from his valet than he usually required, he made as elaborate a toilet as, under the circumstances, he could; but he took care to wrap up his neck, so as to give as much importance as possible to his wound; and then, for the first time since his disgrace, he fairly set out for St. James's Palace, to wait upon the Regent.

During this time the Dark Woman had remained beneath the roof of St. James's. Immediately upon penetrating into those disused apartments, which, indeed, would have had a most special interest in her eyes, could she have known that in them her son had had an interview with his father, the Regent, she felt that she was tolerably safe from pursuit.

What would become of the Regent for the remainder of the night was a question she did not ask herself; but she felt that there was so much alarm throughout the whole interior of the Palace, that any attempt again to force herself upon his attention would be only to place herself in the most imminent peril, without accomplishing her object.

The Dark Woman groped her way through the rooms in silence and darkness. Occasionally she touched some of the antique pieces of furniture, which had remained there for so many years, fading and rotting away.

"Till the morning—till the morning," she muttered to herself; "I will remain here till the morning, for I have yet something to do in the Palace of St. James's. Hitherto, all concerning me and mine has been involved in mystery and secrecy; but now the time for publicity has come, and the world shall ring with my wrongs. To-morrow—yes, to-morrow! Until then—the first time for many a weary year—I shall sleep beneath the roof of St. James's Palace.

With arms outstretched before her, to prevent any serious collision with any of the articles of furniture in the rooms, the Dark Woman passed through several of the apartments; and finally she came to a large and massive couch, on which she could feel that the dust was lying thickly.

But that she heeded not. Worn out, both in mind and body, she cast herself upon it; and under, perhaps, the most singular circumstances in which any human being ever sought repose, she fell into a deep sleep.

Every avenue of St. James's Palace was strictly guarded, but still the Regent had such an opinion of the mysterious powers of his persecutor, the Dark Woman, that he fully believed she had found some secret means of escaping.

When in the morning, then, he was informed that no person had attempted to pass out of the building, he consoled himself with the idea that, at all events, he had got rid of her for a time, and perhaps for ever.

"Why should she torment him any further?" he asked himself. "Had she not found her son, and had not he acknowledged him? And had she not heard, from his own lips, that that was all which could be done? Surely common sense would tell her now that she had arrived at the end of her career."

But there was an uneasy sensation on the mind of the Regent, which did not so much concern the Dark Woman as it concerned Allan. Over and over again he kept asking himself if it were possible that Allan had joined himself to the party at Buckingham House, and had become, politically and domestically, one of his enemies.

Probably, had there been nothing more than the mere letter of Sir Hinckton Moys—clever and unscrupulous as it was—to lead him to such a conclusion, he might have rejected it; but there was, in addition, that seemingly candid and open despatch from the Countess of Sunningham.

What could he say to that?

The one seemed to confirm the other so practically and essentially that the Regent was puzzled how to act, or how to think.

Then, perhaps, with still more force, and still more coherence—engendering much more anger, and much more bitterness—came the idea which had been suggested on more than one occasion, that Annie Gray was false to him, and that her wonderful interest in the preservation of Allan Fearon from death was on account of an intrigue between them, for which his marriage with her sister was but a convenient cloak.

Truly, George, Prince of Wales, and Regent of England, was very much disturbed in his mind on that eventful morning, which, however, was to produce more disturbance still than he had ever dreamed or thought of.

———

CHAPTER CXIV.

THE DARK WOMAN CARRIES OUT A TERRIBLE DETERMINATION.

It was at half-past eleven o'clock that the Regent sat in a small room which went by the name of Queen Anne's Cabinet, because it was believed to be the apartment in which that monarch was accustomed to hold her long, gossiping conferences with the celebrated and imperious Duchess of Marlborough.

It had become very much the habit of the Regent after breakfast to retire to this room, which was fitted up as a small writing-room, and in the desks and cabinets of which he was supposed to keep most of his private papers.

It will be necessary, considering the exigencies of our story, that the reader should understand precisely the position of this room in the Palace of St. James's.

It looked, then, into the Colour Court by one window, over which hung usually a green silk curtain, of great thickness and beauty.

A short flight of three steps from this small apartment led into a lower room, but of much larger dimensions, which had two windows likewise looking into the Colour Court; and from this larger room, several others might be reached, the next one to it being an ante-room, in which one of the pages on duty always sat, while the Regent was in Queen Anne's Cabinet.

It was to this small apartment, then, that the Regent retired as usual; and it was for the express purpose of reading over, still more carefully, Sir Hinckton Moys's letter, and the despatch from the Countess of Sunningham, be-because, as he fully expected to see Moys at mid-day, he wished, if possible, to be amply prepared for his presence, so far as making up his mind what precise questions he had to ask him was concerned.

The Regent had sat for about ten minutes, and had rapidly read over both the troublesome documents twice, when a slight tap at the door of the apartment let him know that some one had something to say of sufficient importance to excuse disturbing him.

It was one of the pages, who, with a low bow, advanced, and placed a small scrap of paper before the Regent.

On this piece of paper were the following words:—

"Colonel Hanger, the most humble servant of His Royal Highness the Prince of Wales, begs to state that he is quite certain a female, who may be described as *D. W.*, is still beneath the roof of the Palace, and waiting but an opportunity of being dangerous."

"By Jove!" cried the Regent, as he sprung to his feet; "am I never to be rid of this woman?"

Some one coughed on the other side of the door.

The Prince turned pale for a moment; but as the cough sounded again, he felt certain that it was of a masculine character.

He felt more composed.

There was a small silver bell upon the table

before the Regent, a touch upon which would at once summon one of the pages who were in attendance.

The bell was touched.

The royal page who made an appearance in answer to the summons bowed very low, and waited the Prince's commands.

"If Colonel Hanger is at hand, show him in here."

The page bowed again, and made his exit.

It was not etiquette in the Palace even to make any reply when a distinct order was given by one of the royal family. Even so much as "Yes, your Royal Highness," would have been considered a familiarity under ordinary circumstances.

In a few seconds there came another light tap at the small cabinet door.

"Come in," said the Regent.

Colonel Hanger made his appearance; and the Prince, holding up the scrap of paper that had been laid before him, said, "You sent this, Hanger?"

"I took that liberty, hoping that it was for the service of your Royal Highness."

"But what grounds have you for supposing that this woman is still in St. James's?"

"Ocular demonstration, your Highness."

"What? You have seen her?"

"Not I, your Royal Highness; but one upon whom I can depend. At an early hour this morning she has been seen."

"Where?—oh, where?"

"In the Titian Gallery."

"Close to the Countess's rooms?"

"Just so."

"This must be seen to. This must be put an end to. It amounts to such a persecution, that I should be something less or more than a man to put up with it. Leave me, Hanger, and let me think. Something must be done. Stop——"

Hanger was near the door.

"Send for Mr. Scott."

"The barrister?"

"Yes, yes. Send for him. He will be able to devise a something."

"Ah, your Highness, it was a thousand pities that on the occasion of the banquet the bullet that I fired failed to perform its duty. Some great prince of jugglery was at work on that occasion."

"That may or may not have been, but I want no violence, Hanger; and I only wonder that I have not yet taken more notice of your attempt to do a deed which I could never approve."

"Your Highness is ever indulgent to those who commit faults, when the motive is to do you the greatest possible service."

"Go, now—go! I will think of it. But send at once for Mr. Scott."

Colonel Hanger left the cabinet, but dark thoughts were at work in his brain.

"If I could only kill this woman," he said, "and make it look like an accident, I should have an everlasting claim upon the gratitude of the Regent."

But Hanger, although he was quite willing to do the deed, did not see any ready way of setting about it. He had been informed, and truly enough, too, by one of the under-servants of the Palace, that a figure, answering to the description that had been given of the Dark Woman, had been seen in the Titian Gallery.

The servant who had seen her had taken to flight in alarm; and then, as he owed his place to the Colonel, he took him the intelligence.

Hence the little scrap of paper which Hanger had been able to send to the Regent.

But the Prince was now alone again, and he sat for some few minutes in deep thought—in much deeper thought than he was in the habit of usually indulging in.

"What is to be done?" he said. "This mania of Linda's will last her life or mine. It will in time grow into such a scandal that something violent will have to be done in it. And then what will he say?—what will my son say? He will not be willing to forget that she is his mother."

At this moment, a strange, crackling noise came upon the ears of the Regent.

"What was it? and where was it?"

These were two questions he found it most difficult to answer.

It was with a sort of entranced fascination that the Regent listened to the odd noise, without thinking of giving any alarm in consequence of it.

At one moment, he thought it came from the floor beneath his feet; then from the ceiling over his head, and then from one of the walls.

It was a strange creaking sound.

But soon it localized itself; and the eyes of the Regent became fixed with a gaze, that for his life's sake he could not have withdrawn for a moment, upon a three-quarter length portrait of Queen Anne, which was in the room.

It was either a fact, or some freak of his fancy, but certainly, to all appearance, the face of the portrait actually moved.

The Regent now tried to cry out. Alarm stopped his utterance. He could only utter a faint sound—far too faint a sound to induce any one to come to his assistance.

The portrait certainly moved.

The face was agitated in a strange manner, and then he saw that there were other eyes gazing from that picture-frame than those that belonged to the portrait.

The eyes that he saw were those of some living person. A portion of the canvas of which the portrait was composed was torn aside; and, in place of the placid countenance of Queen Anne, the Regent saw another face, and another pair of eyes, that were less composed and serene.

The Prince knew who it was.

"The Dark Woman!" he gasped. "The Dark Woman—Linda de Chevenaux!"

He half rose from his chair.

He intended to touch the bell, and then call aloud for help.

But he was too late.

The Dark Woman spoke.

"George of Wales, if you desire instant death, you will raise your voice, so that others may hear as well as I; or you will give some alarm, that will bring others to this apartment."

The Regent had never for a moment withdrawn his fascinated gaze from the face that had protruded through the picture; and now, as that gaze seemed to be sharpened by apprehension, he saw the long, bright barrel of a pistol projecting from the wall, and pointing full upon him.

"Ah!" said the Regent.

"Hush!"

The Prince sank back into his chair.

But his eyes still remained riveted upon the face of the Dark Woman, and upon the bright and threatening barrel of the pistol.

"You will be silent?" she said.

"I—I—am silent."

"That is well. Last night, when pursued through St. James's by your creatures, I took refuge in a long disused suite of rooms, which communicate with this cabinet. At last I have managed to make a communication by laboriously working a way through the panel."

"Yes; I see—I see."

"It became necessary that I should yet speak a few more words to you."

"Words?"

"Yes, words. But words may stab—words may kill, if there be the heart to give them utterance, and the other heart to hear them."

"What—what do you want to say to me now?"

"This much. Can you on your conscience still deny that I am your lawful wife?"

"You know well that I can."

"On your oath? Will you call witnesses?"

"What witnesses?"

"Well, one will suffice. Will you use the name of your Creator?"

"I can truly say before heaven that there was no royal consent to our marriage."

"But you could as easily say that there was."

"Not with truth."

"Stop—stop! My brain burns."

"Take away that pistol. Surely you do not mean to murder me?"

"It is for my own defence. Alas! alas! For the first time my intellect in part abandons me, and I know not what I say."

"Mad!" said the Regent.

He had spoken in a low tone, but she heard him.

"No, no! I remember now—I remember now what I meant to say; and I am not mad. I have thought over it all in the long, weary, dead hours of the night, and it is all fresh in my mind now."

"What is all fresh?"

"Hush! Some one comes."

The Regent uttered a sound of congratulation.

"Yes," he said, "I hear some footstep approaching. You cannot say that I summoned any one. It is an accident: you see that. I am not to blame that you will be in danger now."

"You might be to blame."

A tap came at the door.

The Regent was on the point of saying, "Come in," when the Dark Woman interposed; and, speaking in a low, hissing whisper, which was quite distinct to the Prince, but could not be heard beyond the room, she said, "Your fate be on your own head! My finger is upon the trigger of this pistol. If you allow any one to come into this room, there will be a slight pressure, and then farewell, Regent!"

The countenance of the Prince turned pale.

"What is it you wish?" he said, faintly.

"Send away him who knocks."

The tap, in a quiet, respectful manner, came again at the door of the cabinet.

"Who is it?" cried the Prince.

That was not "Come in," so the handle of the door was not so much as touched.

"It is I, your Royal Highness; the page on duty."

"What do you want?"

"Sir Hinckton Moys, your Royal Highness, waits with pleasure for an audience."

"Let him wait in the ante-room."

The page left the door.

"There," said the Regent, "I have done as you wish. Now what is it that you have to say to me?"

"This. You consent to acknowledge that Allan Fearon, as he has been called, is your son?"

"I do."

"Well, upon condition that you admit you were really married to me, his mother, and that he is legitimate—— "

"I cannot—you know I cannot."

"Hear me out."

"Well, well."

"If you will do that, and let him have the rank and expectations of a prince, I will consent to be dead, and to have been long before your second marriage with the Princess Caroline of Brunswick."

"I do not comprehend you."

"You will when I speak more plainly. If you will receive and acknowledge my son, your son, as your legitimate child, I will die within the hour that you do so, and you may date my death when you please."

"You will die?"

"Yes. I will take my own life, and for once and for all rid you of myself and of all reproach concerning me, if you will consent to what I propose. All that the world can then say will be that the Prince of Wales had concealed his first marriage, and now chose to acknowledge its offspring in the person of his son."

"But——"

"Hear all. Consider that by such a course your daughter, the Princess Charlotte, still remains legitimate, because you can say that I died, if you please, even at the birth of our son."

"I cannot!"

"You cannot? Oh, yes, you can! What will be more easy? I tell you I will die—I am content to die! Nay, I will even go so far as to promise you—and be assured that I will keep my word—my death shall remove me utterly and entirely for ever—my body shall not appear to be a trouble to you or a speculation to others "

"What do you mean?"

"I will take passage in some ship to a foreign land, and in the dead hour of the night I will start up to the deck, and seek peace and oblivion in the ocean."

The Regent shuddered.

"You will do this," added the Dark Woman, still speaking in a low but imploring voice,— "you will do this, and I shall yet die blessing you. I give my own life for what has been the object of that life—the exaltation of my son and your son, too. Oh, tell me that you will consent to it!"

"And if I do not?"

"If you do not—oh, beware of me!"

"You aim at my life."

"No."

The Regent drew a long breath of relief.

"But you came here armed, as though that were your object," he said.

"I came here armed because it is necessary for me to protect myself. But if you refuse the terms I offer, I promise you more life than you have ever had; because life is publicity, and I will make the story of my wrongs so public, that the old walls of St. James's shall ring with it."

"You will never be so mad?"

"I shall be so mad. These windows—the windows of this room—and those adjoining, look into the Colour Court of the Palace. It is near to mid-day. The court is full of loungers, waiting the arrival of the guard. I will go down among all the people there assembled, and gathering them about me, I will tell them who and what I am, and who and what you are!"

"What will you tell them?"

"That I am your wife—that you are the royal bigamist, who would acknowledge your son in secret, but dare not do so in public. I will tell the whole tale of my wrongs and of my sufferings; of how, for years after my child had been torn from my heart, I was made a prisoner on pretence of insanity in a madhouse, my whole offence being that the capricious fancy of the Regent no longer cared for what he was once pleased to call the charms of Linda de Chevenaux!"

"You are indeed mad now!"

"Perhaps I am."

"And do you suppose for one moment that any one will believe the tale?"

"I think they will. But if they will not, then heaven pity their hard hearts!"

"But——"

The Regent was about to say something, and even while he was speaking he was wondering in his own mind what he had better do under the extraordinary and puzzling circumstances in which he was placed, when his words were cut short by a loud crash at the wall.

The Dark Woman, by a sudden force, had dashed the portrait of Queen Anne from the panel, and left a space sufficiently large to allow her to pass into the apartment.

The fears of the Regent now overcame every other consideration, and he called aloud for help.

The trampling of feet came plainly in the outer room.

"Help! help Guard!" cried the Regent.

The Dark Woman dashed past him, and herself flung open the door of the little cabinet, meeting, as she did so, the page on duty face to face. But the barrel of that long bright pistol, with which the Dark Woman was armed, touched the forehead of that official personage, and he retreated with so much quickness that he fell over a chair.

"Help! help!" again cried the Regent.

"Who touches me, dies!" said the Dark Woman.

A tall man, dressed in black, had darted forward, but at the sight of the pistol he recoiled again.

That was Colonel Hanger.

"Ah!" said the Dark Woman. "Villain, I know you well!"

The pistol was presented full at Hanger's head, and he, believing that the next moment would speed the possible bullet it contained to his destruction, flung himself backward on to the floor to save his life.

The page was just struggling to his feet from his fall as Colonel Hanger flung himself back, and they both rolled to the floor together.

"Cowards!" said the Dark Woman. "How much you fear the death which for me has no terrors! Cowards! cowards!"

"Seize her!" cried the Regent, again.

"No. They have not the courage to face death, even to obey you, George of Wales!"

The Dark Woman passed through the room, but she paused for a moment on the threshold, and then, by some impulse that came over her, she flung the pistol to the floor, saying, "I have no further need now of arms, for I am about to proclaim myself the Princess of Wales to the people."

———

CHAPTER CXV.

THE DARK WOMAN IS APPREHENDED AS A STATE PRISONER.

THE route from the few rooms that adjoined Queen Anne's Cabinet to the Colour Court of St. James's Palace was very simple and straightforward.

There was the room which we have before stated was just adjoining the cabinet, and from which it was reached by three steps. There was the pages' chamber, and then there was an ante-room, which might be made a guard chamber, and beyond that was a short flight of ten stairs that led to a door, which opened at once into the Colour Court.

All this route was well known to the Dark Woman, and as it could not take above two minutes to traverse the whole distance, she was actually in the Colour Court before any further alarm could be given by the Regent, or the page, or Colonel Hanger.

There was a strange, miscellaneous crowd of people in the court.

Guardsmen off duty—soldiers of all arms of the service on recruiting intentions—civilians, who made the Colour Court a daily lounge—servants with children, who came to neglect the children and to flirt with the soldiers.

Such was the character of the throng of persons among whom the Dark Woman dashed like an apparition.

Her appearance at once excited all the curiosity of the listless crowd; and when she went to the very centre of the court-yard, and, elevating her hands above her head, cried out, "Englishmen and Englishwomen, you see before you the persecuted Princess of Wales, the real wife of the Regent!" the excitement became intense.

"Hear me, all who have ears to drink in the story of my wrongs," she added. "My name was Linda de Chevenaux, and I lived in honour and in virtue at my father's house until the Prince of Wales, now the Regent of England, cast his eyes upon me. He sought me for his love in an unhallowed fashion, but I scorned to be the minion even of a prince; and then proffered marriage, and this poor heart was dazzled by the splendour of a crown. He brought to me the consent of his father, the old King."

Yells, shouts, and cries now began to come from the crowd.

"She's mad! Seize her! Call the constables! Guard! guard! It is high treason!"

"It is true," added the Dark Woman. "I am the wife of the Regent, and my son is a prince in England. It is true; and from you, Englishmen, and from you, Englishwomen, I ask for justice!"

There was a confused kind of rush made by some of the soldiery to seize her, but other persons who were present interposed. They wanted to hear more.

"Hear her out!" cried a voice. "We all know what the Prince of Wales is!"

But it is doubtful if the Dark Woman would have been allowed another moment of liberty but for a very singular occurrence, which rendered the immediate neighbourhood of where she stood not a very desirable post.

She had cast her eyes towards the window of Queen Anne's Cabinet, and stretching forth her arm in the same direction, she called out, "Even now the false, perjured Regent looks down upon the wreck that he has made! I can see his baleful eyes! There—there—there!"

All eyes were at once turned upwards in the direction to which the Dark Woman pointed, and at the moment that they did so there came a sharp flash of light and a puff of smoke from one of the windows.

The report of some fire-arm immediately succeeded, and a bullet whistled over the heads of the spectators and past the cheek of the Dark Woman.

The panic that took possession of the crowd was at once complete and ludicrous.

The rush to get out of the Colour Court was most tremendous, and it for a few moments confounded even the soldiers in the general scramble.

The Dark Woman looked up calmly to the window. She spread out her arms.

"Yes," she said; "consummate now your villany! You or your agents have only now to commit a murder, and all will be over!"

But the shot was not repeated.

The Dark Woman's eyes flashed with a strange light, and, in a screaming voice, she added, "I denounce George the Regent as a perjured bigamist! I denounce him! I denounce——Ah!"

A couple of men had run into the Colour Court from the gate entrance in St. James's Street, and one of them flung his arms round the Dark Woman, while the other seized her hands.

"Now, madam," said one of these men, "you will be so good as to come along with us, and the less trouble you give the better it will be for you."

The Dark Woman uttered a scream of despair. Death would have been at any moment more welcome to her than to be again the prisoner of the Regent.

She struggled desperately with the men who held her, but all was in vain. They were strong and practised officers; and the Dark Woman, securely tied, so that she could do no further mischief, was dragged through a small doorway into the Palace.

By the time the crowd came back, and had in some degree recovered from the fright into which they had been thrown, the Dark Woman was gone.

The whole episode had not lasted above five minutes, and they might almost have doubted the reality of it, but that upon a portion of the wall of the Colour Court, between two windows on the opposite side to the window of Queen Anne's Cabinet, there was an indented star-like mark.

It was the mark of the bullet from the pistol that had been fired at the Dark Woman.

How that pistol came at all to be fired at her it is now our business to relate.

The Dark Woman had left Colonel Hanger and the royal page in no small confusion, but that confusion lasted no longer than her presence.

The dissolute Hanger was the first to scramble to his feet, and when he did so, he at once possessed himself of the pistol which the Dark Woman had cast down on to the floor of the room.

The Regent was on the threshold of the next apartment, and from the pallid hue of his face, it was evident how greatly his fears had been excited.

When, however, absolute personal fear passed away, anger took its place.

He called out in a loud voice, "I will give any reward at all in reason to any one who captures that woman—or—or—rids me of her!"

Now those words "rids me of her" bore rather a wide signification. At least, Colonel Hanger was quite ready to translate them in the widest possible sense.

"The Regent's life has been attempted!" he called out. "It is a plot against the life of the Regent!"

As he spoke, he picked up the pistol again, which he had laid upon a chair, and running to the window, he opened it only just so far as to admit the exit of the muzzle of the pistol, and fired at the Dark Woman.

The Regent heard the report, and ran forward.

"Good heaven!" he said; "have you killed her?"

"I don't know," said Hanger; "the smoke is in my eyes."

The smoke was indeed in Colonel Hanger's eyes, for in his eagerness to take aim at the Dark Woman, and at the same time not expose himself to the observation of any one in the Colour Court below, he had placed his eyes so close down to the pistol that the priming scorched his face.

It was the Regent himself who looked through the small opening of the window, and saw that the shot had missed its mark; for there stood the Dark Woman in the centre of the Colour Court, evidently uninjured.

"Hanger! Hanger!" he said, "that was rather a foul shot; and it is as well for you as for me that it has missed."

"Then it has missed?" said Colonel Hanger, wiping the powder from his eyes.

"Yes, she is untouched, and is still haranguing the people."

"Your Highness may be assured that nothing but the death of that woman will leave you in peace."

The Regent made no reply to this observation, but turning round, said, "Where is Mr. Arrowsmith?"

WALL

This was the page who had been in waiting, and who, the moment that he had recovered his feet, had adopted the most practical mode he could of getting rid of the Dark Woman. It was not so romantic as shooting her through a window, but as it turned out, it was much more effectual, since it was Mr. Arrowsmith, the page in waiting, who brought the two constables into the Colour Court.

The Dark Woman was conducted into a very small room upon the ground floor of the Palace, and the page, after seeing her safely bestowed there, hurried to the Regent, for the purpose of taking his further instructions in regard to her.

But never had the Regent been more puzzled how to act, than upon the present occasion. The notoriety of the whole affair brought with it many serious considerations; but still the dominant idea in the mind of the Prince was to transfer Linda de Chevenaux once more to some

asylum, where every extra precaution would be taken to prevent her escaping.

There was but one objection to this course.

That objection was Allan Fearon. What would the Regent say to him, when, by virtue of the general invitation he had received, he should come to the Palace and ask for his mother?

Was the persecution, which the Regent had so long endured from the Dark Woman on account of her son, only to change its title, and to become a persecution from that son on account of his mother?

Truly the Regent was puzzled how to act, and it was in the midst of this emergency that he thought of his appointment with Sir Hinckton Moys.

And then came the recollection of all that Moys had insinuated in that letter which had procured the appointment.

" Surely, surely," said the Regent, to himself,

"If this new-found son of mine, be really the spy and intriguant that Moys and the Marchioness of Sunningham say he is, I need not consider what he will say or do under any such circumstances."

Then the Regent made up his mind that he would see Sir Hinckton Moys before he determined upon what he would do with his prisoner, the Dark Woman.

Turning to the page, he spoke rather abruptly.

"Let the officers," he said, "keep her in close and safe custody. In half an hour I shall know what to do with her."

The Regent knew very well where Moys would be waiting for him, and much to the chagrin of Colonel Hanger, he passed him without another word, and went to the meeting with the lately disgraced favourite, who certainly had a fair chance of a re-instalment in the Royal favour.

Moys was pacing the room in which he was waiting to see the Regent in great perplexity of mind. He felt that he was at fault—he wanted more information to make him feel perfect in the part he had to play.

He had been taken too much by surprise in the discovery of the close relationship between Allan Fearon and the Regent, to be able as yet to arrange in his own mind what it would be safe to do, say, or suggest.

And, if it be possible, all his old feelings of hatred against Allan Fearon were largely increased. He had another score to settle with him on account of the wound he had so recently received; and the more difficult it seemed to be to achieve revenge on Allan Fearon, the more passionately ardent became Sir Hinckton Moys in his desire for it.

And he could not but feel the circumstances were now widely different from what they were.

The poor, obscure Allan Fearon was a very different personage indeed from even the illegitimate son of the Regent.

It was this state of perplexity which had made Sir Hinckton Moys very tolerant indeed of the Regent's want of punctuality in meeting him at mid day as he had promised.

It was a great misfortune for Sir Hinckton Moys that the room in which he was placed to await the coming of the Prince commanded no view of the Colour Court; for if it had, he would have accumulated some more materials for thought and action.

To be sure, he could not but hear that there was some confusion, and the pistol-shot sounded strangely in his ears.

He would fain have made some inquiry, but having achieved so much beyond expectation in getting the Regent to make an appointment with him at all, he feared to lose that vantage-ground by any indiscretion.

So Sir Hinckton Moys waited.

And at length the door was flung open, and the page announced "His Highness, the Regent!"

Sir Hinckton Moys bowed almost to the buckles of his shoes.

"Well, Moys," said the Regent, "you're here again. Of course I had your letter, but I don't know what to say about it."

"If I might advise your Royal Highness," replied Moys, executing another bow, and throwing an air of great respect into his manner, "I would not believe a word of it."

"What?"

"Not a word of it, your Royal Highness."

"And yet you had the audacity to write it to me!"

"If your Royal Highness will graciously permit me to add why I would not believe a word of it, I am sure I shall be quite exonerated from the charge of audacity."

"Why, then?"

"Because I think that your Royal Highness ought not to believe anything half so serious without proof."

"Ah to be sure! You're right there!"

Sir Hinckton bowed again.

"It would indeed have been audacity to write such a letter, unless I felt quite certain that the proof would be forthcoming."

"Then you mean to say that you really can prove that this young man, this—this Allan Fearon, is all that you say?"

"I regret much, your Highness, to be placed in such a position that my desire for your service impels me to such proof, because—because——"

"Because what? Why do you hesitate, Sir Hinckton?"

"Because I cannot define it to myself, or say why; but I have quite an affection for the young man."

"Hem!"

"Yes, he has won upon my regard in a singular fashion; so much so, that had I stood upon the same terms with your Royal Highness as formerly, I should have liked to have recommended him to your service."

"Well, well; no more of that. Let me know distinctly what you charge him with?"

Sir Hinckton Moys spoke slowly and resolutely.

"He is in the pay of the people at Buckingham House, and——"

"And what?"

"He is on excellent terms with Annie, Countess de Blonde."

"And you mean to tell me you can prove those two things?"

"I can, and will, with your Highness's permission."

"Then," said the Regent, as he paced the room uneasily, "I cast him off for ever. I will not have another word to say to him. I will see him no more, and will forget that I have a—a——"

The Regent paused, turned abruptly upon Moys, saying while he looked into his eyes, "Do you know who this young man is? Have you no suspicion of who he is?"

Sir Hinckton Moys was certainly a most accomplished actor, for nothing could exceed the look of quiet, easy candour with which he gazed into the face of the Regent, as he said, "No."

"I thought not—I thought not. Very well, Sir Hinckton. We will have your proof. But mind you, nothing but absolute proof, such as I can convince myself of with my own senses, will suffice. You go to Buckingham House yourself."

"On your Highness's service?"

"Well, well! I suppose, come what may, we mustn't have you at St. James's. The Countess de Blonde is as bitter against you as ever."

"But," slowly insinuated Sir Hinckton Moys, "if your Royal Highness should really discover that the Countess is playing you false?"

"Why, then," said the Prince, as he shut his hands tightly, "she should go at once."

"And then?"

"Oh, then, you might come back, because of course there would be no difficulty."

"I don't think I could ever rest a night in St. James's Palace while so great a traitor to your Highness's feelings and wishes resided in it as that double-dealing trickster, Willes. He is the spy, go-between, and letter-carrier among all these people."

"Well, well, we will see to that. Bring me your proofs. You can have access when you like. And now I have some news for you."

"Before imparting that, will your Royal Highness promise me one thing?"

"What is it?"

"Secrecy."

"Ah, yes! I comprehend! These folks must not be put upon their guard. Trust to me for that. I am only too anxious to arrive at the truth, to do anything which might jeopardize such a consummation."

"Ah, your Highness, I had forgotten."

"What, now?"

"There is another one about you, who makes an infamous traffic of your confidence. I allude to Colonel Hanger."

"Moys, if you came back through one door, if there was but another in the whole Palace of St. James's, out at that other, I fancy Colonel Hanger would see the propriety of going. Are you content?"

"I am."

"Very well, then. Listen to me. The Dark Woman is a prisoner in my hands."

"Ah!" exclaimed Sir Hinckton Moys; "then that accounts for——"

He was going to add "for my not finding her at home in Hanover Square;" but as he had not thought proper to say anything to the Regent of that circumstance at all, he turned it off into the words—"that accounts for your Royal Highness looking somewhat pleased this morning."

"She came here," added the Regent, "and by dint of severe threats, secured an interview with me. She held a pistol to my head."

"Capital!"

"Capital say you?"

"Yes, your Royal Highness; for now there is but one way to deal with her. That is high treason. Let a warrant be issued, and send her to the Tower. She can go quietly and secretly, and need not be brought to trial for an indefinite period. It is probable, too, that any one who may take an interest in her fate may be easily convinced that their best plan will be to leave her there in peace."

"The Tower," said the Regent, musingly. "It might be done."

"Most easily, your Highness. A Council warrant would place her there in custody at once, and it is better than all the lunatic asylums in the world for such a person."

"I will consider," said the Regent. "Good morning, now, Sir Hinckton Moys. Believe me, I shall wait impatiently for the proofs of the facts you have alleged."

CHAPTER CXVI.

SIR HINCKTON MOYS MANUFACTURES PROOFS FOR THE REGENT.

IT was about the dusk of that same evening, that, in a small apartment at Buckingham House, two persons might have been seen, engaged in earnest conversation.

Their heads were very close together, and they spoke in whispers; for each had something to communicate to the other which was interesting.

These persons were none other than Sir Hinckton Moys and the Marchioness of Sunningham, who had entered into so complete an alliance, that they almost began to trust each other.

Moys was detailing the particulars of his interview with the Regent, and the Marchioness was giving the latest intelligence respecting the politics of Buckingham House.

"And now," said Sir Hinckton, "it will be necessary that no time be lost in providing the Regent with the proofs he requires. This young man, Allan Fearon, must be induced to pay a visit here to Buckingham House."

"That cannot be difficult," said the Marchioness.

"And," added Moys, "the Countess de Blonde must be induced to pay a visit to his lodgings."

"That will be a little more difficult, I'm afraid."

"I think not. I can manage the one, if you, Marchioness, can manage the other; and the Regent must see both. Nothing will satisfy him but demonstration of his own eyesight. And now, Marchioness, if you will write a note to this Allan Fearon, I will see that it be delivered."

"I will write from your dictation, Sir Hinckton. The little despatch which you worded to me on a former occasion was too clever for me not to have confidence in your powers on this occasion."

"Marchioness, you flatter me."

"Not at all. Now begin, I am ready."

"'Mr. Allan Fearon is particularly requested to call at Buckingham House at half-past ten o'clock this evening, and ask for the Marchioness of Sunningham. who has something of great interest to impart to him respecting his mother. The Marchioness, both on her own part, and on that of a higher personage, feels very earnestly the services rendered.'"

"Is that all?" said the Marchioness, as Sir Hinckton Moys ceased dictating.

"It will do."

"Rather ambiguous."

"I hope so, Marchioness. The first paragraph will bring him, the second will puzzle him; but should he ever produce the letter in a certain quarter, it will tally with already well-grounded suspicions."

The Marchioness of Sunningham was very well satisfied that Sir Hinckton Moys was doing the very best he could for their mutual interests, so the note was fairly copied and placed in his hands, and Moys set about one of the most despicable transactions which the ingenuity of a fiend could have produced.

In these cases the cunning intriguer would trust no one but himself; and attired in a shabby great coat, and a hat which came far over his brows, Moys left Buckingham House, and walked hastily to Martlett's Court, where he still believed Allan Fearon and Marian to reside.

The hour was early, and provided the note could have reached Allan's eyes any time within an hour or an hour and a half after it was written, there would have been ample time for him to comply with its directions.

Moys, however, met with a little disappointment upon being informed that Fearon had removed; but yet the distance was not great, and he took his way at once down to the street by the river, where Allan and Marian had found a home.

Of course, Sir Hinckton had no idea of appearing himself as the bearer of the note, and he looked anxiously about him for some person whom he could employ for that purpose

A man came lounging along in a lazy manner, and attired in such a costume that Moys thought he would be just the person who would be glad to earn a shilling, which, in the neighbourhood of the Strand, could be so readily converted into some strong potation.

"My good fellow," said Moys, "do you mind earning a shilling by a five minutes' job?"

"Not a bit," said the man, with a strange sort of laugh,—"not a bit! I'm cleaned out!"

"Very well. Then take this note, and deliver it to its address."

"Why, you see, I haven't the advantage of reading, so I don't think I can do it. And where's the odds; for if I am cleaned out to-night, don't I know where to go in the morning, and get a fresh supply?"

There was a thickness and hesitation about this man's utterance which left no question at all upon the mind of Moys that he was in a state of semi-inebriation.

But such a man suited Sir Hinckton quite as well, provided he really delivered the letter, since probably by the next morning he would forget all about it, and Moys was fully alive to the desirableness of not accumulating small evidences in regard to his little transactions.

"My good fellow, I will read the address to you—or, at all events, the name, for I can point out to you the house. It is the last house looking on to the river, and the person you are to ask for is Mr. Allan Fearon."

"Allan Fearon?" exclaimed the man.

"Ah! do you know him?"

"Not a bit. I thought you said Smith, because I know Jack Smith, you see, if it had been him."

"Drunken idiot!" muttered Sir Hinckton Moys; "but he will answer my purpose as well as any other. Take the letter, my man, and there's your shilling. I will wait for you at the corner of the street."

"All's right! I'll do it."

Sir Hinckton Moys watched the big burly figure of this man, as he went down towards the house now in the occupation of Fearon; but perhaps he would not have been quite so well pleased, if he had heard the muttered remarks of the semi-inebriated individual as he went on his errand.

"Who's he, I wonder? As sure as my name's Brads, I've seen him before! What a odd thing that he should give me a letter to carry to Mr. Fearon just as I was a going to see my little girl;

and what a odd thing it is that I can't find Shucks! There's no end of odd things in the world. I fancy we was both a little the worse for something to drink; and it seems like a dream, but I think we went into St. James's Park. What can have become of him? Well, I suppose he'll turn up some day. But I must go to the Countess again to-morrow morning, for I've got rid of all my money one way or another, and my fine clothes, too. I'm sure those fellows cheated us—those checkers, with their dice!"

Brads—for it was indeed our old acquaintance of that name—made his way in rather an erratic fashion down towards the house in the occupation of Allan Fearon.

The circumstances which made that house and its occupants interesting to Brads, are already well known to the reader.

There it was that that child resided who was the only being that really bound him by affectionate ties to the world, and who, by being in the care of the Fearons, had induced in his mind a transfer of some of the affection he had for her to them.

Little did Sir Hinckton Moys imagine that a duplicate of that very paper that he had wrenched from the dying Shucks, in St. James's Park, was actually at that moment in the breast-pocket of the man upon whom he had bestowed a shilling to take the letter to Allan Fearon.

It was strange that Brads became more sober to all appearance as he approached the house. The growing presence of the better feelings of his nature seemed to have this effect upon him; and by the time he reached Allan Fearon's door, there was nothing left of the appearance in him of the reckless man of crime he really was.

Even the knock with which he demanded admittance was gentle and submissive.

"Who knows?" he said. "Perhaps the little one's asleep; and it isn't for such a fellow as I am to go waking her up."

Allan was at home. He had waited more than half the day at the Countess of d'Umbra's house in Hanover Square, and then, despairing of her presence perhaps until nightfall, he had hurried home, after leaving word with Carlos, the page, to seek his mistress's permission to let him, Allan, know when she returned.

But still, notwithstanding all that Carlos had said, there was a very uneasy impression on the mind of Fearon in regard to the fate of that Dark Woman who was entitled to call him son.

That she was surrounded by many dangers he could well conceive, and an intense anxiety began to take possession of him in regard to what might be the ultimate fate of one so surrounded by dangerous circumstances.

It was as much as Marian could do to produce anything like a feeling of serenity or of patience for a time in the mind of Allan, and when he heard Brads knock at the door, he started to his feet.

"Surely that," he cried, "is some news of her?"

"Doubtless, Allan," said Marian; "for we have no visitors."

Allan flung the door open; but the night was too dark upon the river, and the one oil-lamp in that narrow street too far off, to enable him distinctly to see his visitor.

Brads spoke very gently.

"I don't want to wake the little one, if she's asleep, Mr. Fearon; but I thought I'd just call to ask how she was, and how you all were."

"Ah! I know you! The child sleeps; but come in—you are ever welcome."

"Well, you see, Mr. Fearon, I feels like a sort of acquaintance, because I'm an old pal of Sixteen-stringed Jack's. Bless you, Mr. Fearon, it seems to me as if about this house where the little one is there was a something—a something—well, I don't know what to call it; but it is something that makes me feel weak-hearted."

"Come in—come !"

"Yes, I'm a coming. Perhaps you haven't got such a thing as a drop of something to drink ?"

"Indeed, we have not."

"To be sure not. What a wretch I was to ask you, as if the thoughts of the little one wasn't meat and drink all in one to me ! How do you do, ma'am ? I hope you are all right, ma'am. I was just a saying to your young man here that I feel quite well myself, and if you would like a thousand pounds to-morrow to lay out in a few toys. you know, for the little one, why I know where to get them."

"What is that you have ?" said Fearon, as he saw the letter in the hands of Brads.

"Bless me !—to be sure ! I have a head and so has a hammer. It's a letter for you."

"For me ?"

"Oh, yes ! A cove gave it to me at the end of the street, and a shilling ; but that makes no difference, ma'am, to the thousand pounds, to-morrow. You see, ma'am, I have been cleared out at the Chequers, and I'm dead sure they cheated."

"Marian, read this," said Allan. "What can it mean ?"

Marian read the note that had been written by the Marchioness of Sunningham, on the dictation of Sir Hinckton Moys, with deep surprise.

"Buckingham House, Allan." she said, "is the residence of the Princess of Wales."

"It is. But yet it is possible that there they may know something of my mother. I will go at once."

"Do, Allan—do !"

"So do," said Brads. "Crack the crib at once !"

"Eh ?"

"Oh, I begs your pardon, ma'am! Bless us, I feel a want of something weak—I mean strong. Good night—God bless you all ! I will tell the cove at the end of the street that it's all right. He isn't the best looking cove in all the world, and I—I—good night—good—good night—crack the crib—crack—eh ?—good night !"

Brads slid off his chair, and, with his head and shoulders propped up against it fell fast asleep.

"What is to be done ?" said Marian.

Allan looked vexed.

"I must carry him out, Marian dear, for it is time, if I would obey the mandate in this letter, that I should make my way to Buckingham House."

"Let him remain," said Marian,—"let him remain, Allan, until you return. We will not forget that he is the father of that dear child who is committed to our care. Let him sleep, and by

the time you return he will probably be quite recovered."

"Be it so, then, Marian. Shut up the house, and you can sit in the upper room with the little one."

"Oh, yes, yes!"

Brads was evidently in a profound sleep; and Allan hurried on his hat, and sallied out with the note in his hand, to keep his appointment with the Marchioness of Sunningham at Buckingham House.

It was indeed fortunate for the plans of Sir Hinckton Moys that there was in the mind of Allan already a great anxiety about his mother, since the expression used in the letter just came to apply to it.

Moys was in a doorway at the end of the street.

He was waiting for his messenger; but he was better pleased to see Allan himself issue out of the street, and make his way with hurried steps down the Strand.

"That will do," said Moys. "I have him now. If I fairly house him at Buckingham House. the Marchioness will keep him either waiting or in some frivolous talk until I can bring the Regent into the Park to see him emerge from it again."

Thus, then, everything seemed to be turning out just as Sir Hinckton Moys wished.

Allan Fearon probably would have been much more thoughtful and suspicious about the note he had received in so mysterious a fashion, but for the real and deep anxiety he felt for the fate of his mother.

It was that one word "mother" which was the true invocation in the letter from Buckingham House, which swayed his feelings.

And so, without casting a single glance behind him to see if he were followed, and without, for one moment, the idea crossing his brain that he might be so, Allan turned towards St. James's Park, at the Pimlico end of which was situated the then well-known Buckingham House.

Sir Hinckton Moys dogged him like his shadow.

The entrance by the Horse Guards was the one most handy to Allan; and passing the sentinels on duty there, he made his way, in a slant direction, towards the grand mall.

The old trees were now in full leaf, and betrayed but little indication of the terrible winter that had just passed away.

The night was dark; and although Sir Hinckton Moys kept wonderfully close to Allan, even had the latter now turned, to see if any one was in the Park close to him, he could not have recognised the courtier.

And so Fearon sped onwards ; and young, agile, and fleet of foot as he was, he soon reached the gate of Buckingham House.

Orders had been given by the politic and unscrupulous Marchioness of Sunningham, that if a gentleman naming himself Fearon were to come to the house, he was to be shown into her own apartments.

Allan, therefore, was received in the hall of Buckingham House as an accredited visitor, and was at once taken up a flight of stairs, and shown into a handsome room which the Marchioness of Sunningham called her own while she favoured the Princess of Wales with her company.

Now a consultation had taken place in Buckingham House, regarding Allan Fearon, to which the Princess of Wales had not been admitted.

That consultation was specially in regard to Allan Fearon. The object of it was to decide whether it would not be sound and good policy to endeavour to make a real friend, spy, and partisan of Allan, instead of merely amusing him for a time in the mansion, so that the Regent might, to suit the purposes of Sir Hinckton Moys, believe him to be such.

They had as yet no real knowledge of who Allan was.

That secret, which he would not, as we have seen, take the trouble to keep as a secret at all, had not yet got to be sufficiently public to reach Buckingham House.

What these intriguing ladies, who so damaged the cause of the Princess of Wales, by crowding about her, thought, was that, in truth, Allan Fearon was the favoured lover of Annie Gray, the so-called Countess de Blonde.

Probably enough, from their own experiences, they thought it no such unlikely thing, that while the fair Countess de Blonde professed to be everything to the Regent, her real fancies were somewhere else.

They knew the favour that Annie enjoyed with the Prince, and they thought that it would be no bad plan to detach Allan from her in reality, and convert him into a real spy upon St. James's, while he was only to be thought one by the Regent.

The Marchioness of Sunningham was finally deputed by the little party to try all the arts she possessed to shake Allan's supposed allegiance to the Countess de Blonde.

Therefore was it that he was received by the Marchioness with an *empressement* of style and manner which she thought would go far towards fascinating him.

Besides, she was a real Marchioness, while his Countess de Blonde, as the Marchioness thought her, was but a theatrical dignity.

"Surely," she thought, "so young a man will easily fall before the artillery of such arts and such charms as I can bring into the field."

Allan had not waited many minutes before the fair and portly Marchioness made her appearance, with so fascinating a smile upon her face that it was evident she meant to conquer.

Allan, with the natural inborn grace of a gentleman, bowed low, and handed the Marchioness a chair.

She had made up her mind to play a certain part; and in order to get rid of a difficulty at the commencement, she had determined to entirely repudiate the letter which had been written by her from the dictation of Sir Hinckton Moys, and sent to Allan.

It would be much more convenient to do so, inasmuch as the mother, who was there mentioned, she, the Marchioness, knew nothing whatever about.

Allan waited for the elegant lady to commence the conversation; but as she put on an inquiring look, and only indulged in a few set smiles, he found himself compelled to say something.

"Madam," he said, "have I the honour of addressing the Marchioness of Sunningham?"

"Certainly."

"My name, then, is Fearon, madam."

The Marchioness looked gracious, but the sort of inclination of the head she bestowed upon Allan seemed to say quite plainly, "Well, what then?"

Allan was somewhat disconcerted.

"Madam," he said, "your note requesting me to call here, came duly to hand."

"My note?"

"Yes, madam; and I am here in consequence."

"This is surprising, sir."

"Surprising, madam?"

"Yes; for I thought you were here in consequence of a note which you had sent to me."

"I, madam?"

"Oh, yes! I received a note, signed Allan Fearon, requesting an interview with me, on some important matters in connexion with the Princess of Wales."

"Impossible!"

"Do you doubt my word, sir?"

"Oh, no, madam. I merely meant to say that it was impossible I could have anything to say to you about the Princess of Wales."

The Marchioness again bowed, and smiled.

"Here, madam, is the letter I received."

Allan produced and held out to her the letter, which the Marchioness glanced at, and then in a firm voice said, "A forgery, sir!"

"Indeed! Then, madam, I can say the same, without even so much as looking at it, for the letter you state you have received from me."

"Then, sir, we have both been deceived."

"Both, madam."

"We have been made the sport of some cruel jest."

"Or we have been brought together, madam, in furtherance of some wicked and sinister design."

"Can you think so?"

"From my heart, I believe it."

"Then you have an enemy?"

"Indeed, I have."

"And, I, too. Oh, sir! do you not feel that there is, after all, a something providential about our meeting?"

"There may be, madam; but since both the letters seem to be forgeries, I think the best way to disappoint their author is for me to respectfully take my leave."

Allan rose and bowed.

CHAPTER CXVII.

THE REGENT IS CONVINCED THAT HE CAN TRUST TO NO ONE.

As Allan Fearon bowed to go, the Marchioness of Sunningham approached closer to him, and laying her fair, plump, jewelled hand upon his arm, she said, "Oh, no, no, Mr. Fearon; there is surely another and a better way to disappoint our enemies."

"Is there, madam?"

"Yes. Does not your own heart point it out to you?"

Allan shook his head.

"It is, then, that we should really become friends from this auspicious moment."

Allan was silent for a moment.

It was a very difficult thing to reply to a pretty woman, with the perfect courtesy of a gentleman.

when she made such a speech, and yet to let her know that nothing was further from his intentions than to make friends with any one at Buckingham House.

"Madam," he said, " I am much honoured by your kindness, but—but——"

"Nay, I will take no denial. Come, sit down again, and let us converse like old friends."

"Pardon me, Lady Sunningham, but——"

"That odious, terrible 'but,' again. What can it mean? Ah, Mr. Fearon, is your heart so thoroughly the property of another, that there is no room in it for even a new sensation?"

"It is."

"I know that other well."

"You, madam?"

"Yes, quite well; and I can tell you that she is tottering to a fall, even at this present time; and such a fall, too, as will bring down, in her own destruction, all who cling solely to her and her fortunes."

"Really, madam," said Allan, with quite a puzzled look, "I do not in the least comprehend you."

"Artful man!" said the Marchioness, as she tapped the back of Allan's hand with a fan.

"No, madam. You mistake me much."

"Ah, no! I know your whole sex. It is a principle I am well aware of, with you men, never to acknowledge to one woman that you care in the least for another."

"It is no principle of mine, Lady Sunningham; for here, I at once assure you that my whole heart and affections are so completely engaged and absorbed, that, as you say, I have no room for a new sensation."

"Indeed!"

"It is the truth."

"Then you must suffer the most terrible of pangs."

"What pangs?"

"Of jealousy."

"I jealous! Oh, no, madam! I would scorn to nourish the vain and deadly passion. My love is a thing that has become a part of my existence— the fair, brighter, and happier part, and it is quite free from any sensations, or jealous pangs."

"You amaze me."

Allan bowed. He was beginning to have a cordial dislike to the woman, who, upon so short and so slight an acquaintance, sought to engage him in conversation upon such a subject.

But never were two people more at cross purposes than were Allan Fearon and the Marchioness of Sunningham.

It was Marian's image that was ever present to the mind of Fearon.

It was the Countess de Blonde to whom the Marchioness alluded.

"Can it be possible," she said, "that you love this woman as you say, and yet feel no pangs at the knowledge of her acquaintance with his Royal Highness the Regent?"

"Acquaintance with the Regent? She has no acquaintance with the Regent."

"What? The Countess de Blonde has no acquaintance with the Regent?"

"Madam, I was not talking or thinking of the Countess de Blonde."

"Of who, then?"

"Of my wife."

"Oh!"

There was so much pitying contempt about the tone of voice in which this " oh!" was uttered, that Allan, all unused as he was to the ways of such persons as the Marchioness, could not but feel that it was intended to express the utter contempt in which a man was held who had the slightest respect for his moral obligations.

Allan determined to go at once.

He moved towards the door.

"My lady," he said, "it seems that we have both been much mistaken, and that this whole interview is an inopportune blunder and mistake. I have the honour to take my leave."

"Oh, no, no! We shall soon understand each other better, I am sure "

"I am equally sure we shall not, madam On the contrary, I am of opinion that the longer we converse, the more we shall find that we misunderstand each other."

The Marchioness was piqued; but she did not like to give up the game quite so easily.

"Listen to me for a moment," she said. " By attaching yourself to the fortunes of the Princess of Wales, a brilliant future may await you."

"Madam, I respectfully decline."

"Ah, Mr. Fearon. is not all this acting? Are you so very insensible? No—no—no—no!"

At each of these utterances of the word no, the Marchioness approached closer and closer still to Allan, until he could feel her breath upon his cheek.

"Madam," he said, "you waste blandishments upon one who is indeed insensible to them. Good night!"

"Wretch!"

Allan bowed, and made towards the door.

"Monster!"

Allan laughed.

"Be it so, then," cried the Marchioness: "you have made a foe where you might have made a friend. Go, and remember that there is one thing which a woman never forgets."

Allan opened the door.

"And that," screamed the Marchioness, "is a slight when she—she——"

Allan was gone. He did not hear the last part of the sentence, so he failed to know how far, in her anger, the Marchioness would in words admit the part she had been playing.

It was with a sensation of immense relief that Allan found himself once more on the outside of Buckingham House, and with the free air of the Park blowing upon his face.

There was much that was confusing about the scene he had gone through, and Allan could not help thinking there was much more in it and in its consequences, than at once met the eye.

He was, indeed, as the reader is well aware, right in that idea.

Perhaps if Allan Fearon had been a vain man, he might have supposed that the whole affair had its origin in some fancy that the Marchioness had taken to him, owing to having accidentally seen him somewhere.

But no one in the world could be more free from personal vanity than Allan Fearon, and such an explanation of the eccentric conduct of her ladyship never occurred to him.

Little—as little did the real truth present itself to his imagination, and he was far indeed from supposing that he had been cajoled into a visit to Buckingham House in order that the Regent might, with his own eyes, see him emerge from it.

The night still continued very dark, and when Sir Hinckton Moys had fairly seen Allan Fearon housed in Buckingham House, he went as quickly as he could to Carlton House.

By the aid of that key of which he still held possession, he opened the garden gate and let himself in. He was prepared with a sealed-up note, on which were merely the following words:—

"The proof of one of the allegations of Sir Hinckton Moys awaits his Royal Highness the Regent."

Moys felt so certain that the time was rapidly approaching when he should be able to resume his old station at the Court, that he scarcely took the trouble to conceal himself in the garden of Carlton House.

He had had time to reflect fully upon the character of the relationship which he had found to subsist between the Regent and Allan Fearon, and instead of discouragement from the circumstance that they were father and son, he began to gather hope.

What could be a greater aggravation of the jealousy of the Regent, than to find, or fancy he found, it was his own son who was the favoured lover of his mistress?

If anything could barb the shaft, that knowledge surely would do so.

Therefore was it that Sir Hinckton Moys resolved to carry out his plans to the letter, so far as they regarded Allan Fearon, with the one exception that he could not help feeling now how inexpedient would be any attempt upon the life of Allan, since the Regent would never again allow him to stand in the mortal jeopardy from which he had been so narrowly rescued.

With that one exception, then, Moys was prepared to carry out his original plan.

Making his way towards a portion of Carlton House, where he knew he should find some of the servants, he, to the intense surprise of a couple of the royal footmen, walked coolly into a room where they were indulging in a pleasant hot supper.

They knew him instantly.

Moys did not give them time to make any remark about his presence in the Palace, but at once handed out the note he had prepared.

"You will let the Prince have this at once," he said. "It is his Royal Highness's orders that there should be no delay. You will likewise inform the Regent that I am in waiting in the Audience Chamber, to which I will now proceed."

The footman looked aghast. But still there was such an air of confidence and command about Moys that they dreaded to disobey him.

One of them took the note.

' Be quick, or the Regent will be angry," added Sir Hinckton.

"Yes, sir."

The point was gained. After once the letter had been respectfully received, and a reply of such a character given, it was too late to object to Sir Hinckton Moys's orders; and, at that moment, he could almost feel that he was in Carlton House upon his old footing as the confidant of the Regent, and a man whose orders were to be considered as almost of equal importance as those of the Regent himself.

But some change had taken place in the feelings of the Prince of Wales with regard to the whole transaction by this time; and if from the bottom of his heart he had told the exact truth, he would have declared that it would please him better if the proofs of Sir Hinckton Moys's statements were withheld from him.

He saw nothing but trouble in those proofs; and provided they fully came up to the conditions which Moys had specified, they would of necessity entail upon him some action, which, however justified it might be by the facts, would go a long way towards making him uncomfortable in his domestic affairs.

Even then he would have been only too glad to compound with the whole affair by giving Allan and the Dark Woman such a sum of money as would have assured to them ease and competence, always provided they would have left him in peace and ease, by going to some other country than England to enjoy it.

But that was a sort of compromise that his judgment told him Linda de Chevenaux would be the last person ever to enter into.

The Regent then kept his appointment practically with Sir Hinckton Moys, although it was some time before he appeared, during which Moys endured agonies of impatience.

Moys was most obsequious in his manner to the Prince, and he affected an air of blunt sincerity, which he thought that the occasion fully warranted him in using.

"Your Royal Highness," he said, "was good enough to require of me certain proofs of statements I had the honour of making."

"Well, well?"

Moys could see that the Regent was impatient, and he certainly did not keep him long in suspense.

"I have, then, one of those proofs, if your Highness will only choose to look upon it."

"What is it?"

"The proof that the young man named Allan Fearon is an accomplice with the party at Buckham House."

"That is all?"

"For the present, it is all. The other proof, that he is the favoured lover of the Countess de Blonde, shall be forthcoming."

The Regent paced the room uneasily.

"It is late, do you know, Moys?" he said.

"By daylight, your Highness, I should find it difficult to lay the proof before you, without too great a risk."

"Risk?—what risk?"

"To your Royal Highness's reputation."

"My reputation?"

"Yes. It would not do for your Highness to be observed watching a subject."

"No, no! Certainly not. And since you put it in that light, I don't think it will do for me to be seen at such an employment, or even to be known by any one to have undertaken it at any hour, whether of day or night."

"Am I, then, to understand that your Highness will not avail yourself of an opportunity to

put an end to all doubts at once by merely taking a walk in the Park."

"Can I do so?'

"It is all that will be required."

The Regent hesitated.

"And so, Moys, you say that I may be satisfied that my—that is, that this young man, Allan Fearon, is in league with those who are my avowed foes, by merely taking a walk in the Park?"

"Just so, your Highness."

"I will do it."

"It is well resolved. A cloak and a hat somewhat different to that which you usually wear, will be ample and sufficient disguise."

"Wait here. I will soon return to you."

The Regent was absent about ten minutes.

When he returned, he was attired in a cloak that completely covered him up from head to foot.

No. 56.—DARK WOMAN.

"Now, Moys," he said, "I am ready for you. I will, as the poet says, 'show my eyes if I grieve my heart.'"

If Sir Hinckton Moys had not happened to be aware of the close relationship between the Regent and Allan Fearon, these words would have been perfectly inexplicable, but as it was, they were easily understood.

Moys, however, took good care to make no remark upon them; and he and the Prince sallied out by a small side door in one of the wings of Carlton House into the garden.

It was scarcely to be supposed that the Regent was not seen by some of the servants of the Palace; but it was a point of etiquette which they all understood perfectly well that the Prince was never to be observed either in going out or coming into Carlton House when he evidently did not want to attract attention.

The cool air of the garden was grateful to the

Regent, and he seemed to breathe more freely. It was not to be supposed that, cold, callous, and selfish as that man was he yet had no human feeling; it was, no doubt, a heart-bitterness to him to think that he was about to have proof that his own son betrayed him.

Sir Hinckton Moys could not but be conscious that the Prince was not well pleased.

The silence that ensued after they had reached the Park for some minutes was rather an embarrassing one to the courtier, who but a short time before was so full of elated feelings. He almost began to suspect that it would have been better after all to have left Allan Fearon alone.

But it was too late now for retreat.

"If your Highness," he said, "will condescend to stand in the shadow of these elm trees, you will command a view of the gate of Buckingham House."

"Very well."

The tone in which the Regent spoke was short and curt.

It sounded uncomfortably upon the ears of Sir Hinckton Moys.

But not for many minutes was the patience of the Prince of Wales tried by waiting on that spot. Had the night vigil lasted much longer, he certainly would have given it up. As it was, he had just made a movement as though he were about to speak, when Moys spoke sharply, "There! There, your Highness!"

"Ah!"

"You see him?"

"I see some one"

"Coming out of the house?"

"Yes, yes!"

"It is the young man I have mentioned to your Royal Highness."

"I don't know that."

Sir Hinckton almost uttered an exclamation of anger; at that moment he would gladly have applied the well-known proverb to the Prince of "None so blind as those who will not see;" but he was saved all necessity of saying anything further on the subject of the identity of Allan by his own movements.

As if fate would have it that the Regent should have no doubt, whatever, on his mind in regard to his identity, Fearon crossed over from the gate of Buckingham House exactly to the clump of elm trees, in the deep shadow of which the Regent and Sir Hinckton Moys were hidden.

Then Allan paused a moment, and gazed back at Buckingham House.

He even spoke.

"Yes,' he said; "I must hurry back now, and hold a consultation with Marian; for I feel assured there is more in all this than meets the eye."

Then Allan hurried along the wall, and was soon lost to sight in the darkness of the night.

The Regent drew a long breath.

"Yes," he said. "There is no doubt now."

"Your Royal Highness is quite convinced?"

"I am!—I am!"

"That this young man is an emissary of Buckingham House?"

"It must be so."

Sir Hinckton Moys was delighted.

The Regent turned, to go back to Carlton House; and when they reached the little door in the garden wall, of which the Prince always had a key, he opened it himself; and then, turning to Sir Hinckton, he said, "Moys, you have only now to convince me that Annie—that is to say, that the Countess de Blonde is false to me, to make me the most miserable of men."

"Your Highness——"

"Good night!"

The Prince almost might be said to close the door in the face of Sir Hinckton Moys.

Rage swelled in the irascible heart of the courtier, and he lifted his foot, as though he intended to deal the door such a kick as would go near to its demolition; but he abstained.

"No, no! I won't do that," he said, "but I will remember the sort of thanks I have got for services to George the Regent. Ha! ha!"

"Ha! ha!" echoed a voice.

Moys started.

"What is that? Who is that?"

"Only an old acquaintance, my dear Sir Hinckton," said a mocking voice, which Moys had no difficulty in localising as coming from some one who was looking over the wall of the garden, close to the door.

"Ah, I know you!"

"Then there is no disguise," said the voice.

"You are Willes."

"Certainly."

"Well, my friend, I have some advice to give you."

"Thank you, Sir Hinckton."

"Buy some good, stout, large trunks."

"Indeed!"

"Yes; for you will want them to pack up your plunder in, when you are told to leave St. James's peremptorily."

"Oh, it's all well packed, Sir Hinckton; but I am not going yet. It is quite an odd thing that men like you, who are kicked out of every place, become quite maniacal upon the subject, and fancy that every one else is about to undergo the same process."

"Wait a bit, my dear Willes."

"I mean to do so."

"Ha! ha! You fancy now, because you are on the right side of the hedge——"

"The wall—the wall, my good sir! Really you seem to me to have taken leave of your senses; but I must go now and inform the Prince of the little remarks you were pleased to make about him a few moments since."

"You are a villain!"

"Ha! ha!"

"And as I happen to have my key of this door, I will come into the garden now, and at once put an end to your further powers of mischief."

"Ha! ha!"

Sir Hinckton Moys tried to open the door in the garden wall, but it was fast. He stamped with passion.

"There now," said Willes, "you are getting quite beside yourself again. I must advise the Prince, out of humanity towards an old servant to have you placed in some asylum, where you can neither hurt yourself nor any one else."

"Wretch, I will have your worthless life!"

Again Sir Hinckton Moys made an effort to open the door, and again did he find all his efforts frustrated.

"It's no use," said Willes; "I've put up the bar."

Moys dashed away from the spot in a state of frenzy; and as he went, he heard the low, triumphant, chuckling laugh of Willes on the night air.

CHAPTER CXVIII.

THE PRINCE REGENT OPENS HIS HEART AND MIND TO ANNIE THE COUNTESS.

THE Regent did a very sensible thing that night. He went at once to the apartments of the Countess de Blonde, after leaving Sir Hinckton Moys, and made up his mind to tell her all.

Perhaps in all the Palace of St. James's, and in all the various chambers of Carlton House, there was not to be found a really better heart than that which beat in the fair breast of Annie Gray.

For the head of the somewhat thoughtless Countess de Blonde we cannot say so much.

It was not, however, that Annie was at all deficient in sense or wit, but hers was one of those flighty intellects which want ballast to make them sail steadily over the wild seas of human life.

But still the Regent did a sensible thing when he went to the Countess's apartments with a determination to consult her.

Annie could see very well that all was not well with her royal lover. Perhaps she did not greatly care about it.

She received him with a pout.

"Annie," said the Prince, "I want to speak to you seriously."

"Then I don't want to hear you."

"Not hear me?"

"Certainly not. I never was serious—I never want to be."

"But it is now necessary. I want to speak to you about Allan Fearon."

"Allan Fearon? What of him? He is in no new danger, I hope and trust!"

"No, no! How is it possible—how can it be possible, that he should be? Annie—Annie, I want to ask you how you became acquainted with that young man?"

"Are you jealous of him still, George?"

"That is not an answer to my question."

"But I want you to tell me, for all that."

"No, then."

"At a hop."

"What?"

"At a hop."

"Are you mad?"

"No, George; but you asked me how I became acquainted with Allan Fearon, and I answer at a hop."

"Good heavens! What is a hop?"

"A dance, to be sure. You see he was in love with Marian, and so he followed us both about wherever we went on her account, and I got to be well acquainted with him, because he was so fond of my sister."

"And—and—did he—he—never—never make love to you, as well as to your sister?"

Annie shook her head.

"No, George—oh no! I was never good

enough for Allan Fearon. I do very well for you, but I am not good enough for Allan Fearon."

"Upon my life, Annie, you are flattering."

"It's true."

"Well, then, do you know, I have been told that he is your lover all the while, and that his pretended marriage with your sister is but a sham to blind my eyes."

"Then you have been told what is not true."

"And I have been told, likewise, that he is a sort of spy from Buckingham House, where you know all my enemies are to be found at some time or another within the four-and-twenty hours.'

"Some one has been telling you lies, George."

"You don't believe it?'

"I don't."

"But what, now, if I were to tell you I was sure of it?'

"Of what?"

"That he was in the habit of visiting at Buckingham House."

"I don't know, but I don't believe that there is anything false, or treacherous, or spy-like about Allan Fearon."

The Regent rose and paced the room with disordered steps. There was a something so quiet and so candid about the way in which Annie spoke, that he felt half-inclined to doubt the evidence of his own senses in regard to having seen Allan Fearon emerge from Buckingham House.

"Anything else?" said Annie.

"Yes—yes"

"Sit down, then."

"I will. I feel impelled, Annie, to tell you all—to make a confidant of you. Allan Fearon is my son."

Annie nodded.

"You know it?"

"Guessed it. He is your son, and the long lost son of that very odd person who calls herself the Dark Woman. I have been for some time thinking about it."

"Then as you know so much, Annie, I pray you advise me what had I better do."

"Make him a duke at once, and give the Dark Woman no end of money to go somewhere and be happy for the rest of her days. My sister Marian, who is so much better than I am, will be a duchess, while I am only a countess; but I shan't mind that a bit."

"How thoughtless you are, Annie."

"Thoughtful, you mean, George You have been jealous of Allan, I know. You could not believe that because my good, dear, kind sister Marian loved him, that I felt on that account, and that only, an interest in him. That bad man, Sir Hinckton Moys, tried to persuade you to the contrary, and that he was a lover of mine; but I thought that was all settled. You however begin again. What do you mean by it, George, eh?"

"No, Annie, I will not begin again. But you know when two bad things are alleged against any one, and upon careful investigation one of them is found to be true, it is a fair presumption that the other may be."

"Stuff!" said Annie. "Let us have some supper."

The Regent felt his heart somewhat more at ease; and it would have been better for him if he had carried out his full intention, and let Annie know that the Dark Woman was still a prisoner in the Palace.

Annie had heard that there had been some uproar and alarm about mid-day, but she was not aware of the actual fact that the Dark Woman was a prisoner.

She was soon to be aware of it, however.

The fair Countess de Blonde and the Regent sat down to one of those little *recherchè* repasts which he was so fond of, and which she, by association with him, was beginning to enjoy with a far greater zest than at first.

The Regent, as his appetite was gratified, began to grow almost amiable. He looked at Annie for a few moments in silence; and then he said, "Countess, I will take your advice."

"In what?"

"About that—that Dark Woman."

"Very well. Give her a heap of money, and let her go."

"Stop. You don't know all. Only this morning, there was a disturbance in the Palace on her account. She was here."

"I thought so."

"She is here now—here, and a prisoner."

"Here!" exclaimed Annie, as she glanced around, with a feeling that the words of the Regent might be literal.

"No, no! I don't mean here in these rooms, but here in the Palace. She is securely locked up What I want to know is, what I shall do with her?"

"Let her go."

"She has threatened me. I am advised to consign her to the Tower, and to make a case of treason of it."

Annie shook her head.

"No," she said; "that will not do. Let me see her, and speak to her. She will do me no harm, and who knows but I may be able to prevail upon her to go in peace, and trouble you no more? I fancy I know, well enough, the whole story."

"There is so little to know," said the Regent, "that any one who knows anything knows all. But it is late."

"No matter, George; let me see her—let me speak with her, and I will try to rid you once and for all of the annoyance of her visits. Poor thing! she can do herself no good by them."

"Not the least."

The Regent rose as he spoke, and touched a hand bell.

Willes was on the threshold of the room door in a moment.

"You know where the Dark Woman is imprisoned," said the Regent; "take a light, and conduct the Countess to her. Annie, I will wait here for you."

"Do so. It is much better that she should suppose I go to her alone than that you should be at hand. Now, Willes!"

The valet had rather an anxious look upon his face, but he took a light, and with a low bow preceded the Countess de Blonde.

The moment they got into the Titian Gallery, Annie said, in her sharp, short way, "Tell me all that happened this morning!"

"I will, Countess The Dark Woman, it appears, found a way to Queen Anne's Cabinet,

where his Royal Highness was writing, and presented a pistol at him."

"Is that all?'

"It is high treason!"

"High fiddlestick! If she presented a pistol at him, intending to shoot him, why did she not do so? I begin to pity this poor woman, now that bit by bit I know her history. Come on! Take me to her at once, and I will speak with her."

Willes led the way down several staircases, and along several corridors, until they came to a door at which stood on duty one of the Yeomen of the Guard.

The man knew the Regent's valet perfectly well, and made way for him to pass through the doorway.

On the other side was a long, narrow apartment, which was very dimly lighted by one oil lamp from the ceiling. In this apartment sat two men, who both rose up as the Countess and Willes appeared.

"This lady," said Willes, "is, by command of his Highness the Regent, to see the prisoner."

The two officers made some clumsy attempts at bows, and at once flung open a door at the further end of that room in which they had kept guard. There was a much smaller apartment beyond.

There, in the dim light that came from a lamp in one of the courts of the Palace, and which shone through a high window which was quite out of reach, sat the Dark Woman.

Her head was resting on her hands; and she was so perfectly still—so absolutely motionless—that one might have supposed her dead.

Annie regarded her for a few moments in silence; and then, in a low voice, she bade Willes leave her alone with the prisoner.

Willes hesitated.

"Go!" said Annie, imperiously.

The sharper sound of that one word spoken so commandingly aroused the Dark Woman, and she looked up.

"Ah, she is still alive!" said Willes—and he immediately left the room.

Annie approached the chair on which the unhappy woman sat, and placed her hand in a kindly manner on her arm.

The Dark Woman shuddered.

"I have come to see you," said Annie.

"You?—you?"

"Yes—why not I? Come, look up! I am sorry for you. I would fain do something, or say something, that would make you happier than you now are."

"Happier? Ha! ha! Happier!"

"Well, I will say not so unhappy. I am sure you have suffered much—very much; but I am sure, likewise, that you make yourself suffer much more, because you will not let the future be better to you than the past."

"What do you mean, girl?"

"This. You contend in vain with the Regent. You must feel that such is the case. You vex and annoy him. That, no doubt, for a time you will have the power to do, but into what terrible dangers do you not cast yourself at the same time? Why will you not be happy, as far as peace can give you happiness? I am but a young girl in comparison to you. I know nothing perhaps of the world as you know it; and at times, even my heart, that looks so light, and as if its brightness shone out of my eyes,—at times, I say, that poor heart is like to break!"

"You unhappy?" said the Dark Woman. "You, the child of luxury and of pleasure?"

"Yes, even I. But I do not make myself more unhappy still by cherishing discontents. I am now what you know I am. My slightest wishes are complied with. The Regent satisfies all my wildest caprices; but the time will come when I shall be cast aside like a faded flower, and then—then I shall be, perhaps, more desolate even than you are!"

The Dark Woman, in that dim light, fixed her eyes upon the fair face of the young girl who thus spoke to her, and deep sighs came from her labouring breast.

"Poor, poor, moth!" she said. "You have fluttered around the flame which looked to you so like a sun, and you will fall scorched and screaming to destruction! Heaven help you—heaven help you!"

"And you," said Annie.

A sob came from the Dark Woman.

"Come," said Annie, gently; and she stooped and left a soft kiss upon the brow of the Dark Woman. "Come! Be happier! Listen to me, and choose for yourself a better fate!"

The Dark Woman burst into an hysterical passion of tears.

"Oh, no, no! Do not—do not say that there is one human heart in all the world which feels a throb of affection or of pity for me! Oh, no, no! My own son—my own boy—he looks coldly on me; and when I would stir up in his heart the memory of his mother's wrongs, he talks of forgiveness and of peace! Oh, heaven, has it come to this—has it come to this?"

She wrung her hands and wept bitterly.

Annie let the tears have their way. She held one of the hands of the Dark Woman in both her own.

"Now," she said, "you will listen to me. There is no hope—there can be no hope of peace and happiness for you here in London—perhaps not even in England! Go far away, and try to forget as you try to forgive!"

"If I could—oh, if I could!"

"Will you try?"

"It is so cruel! You do not know, Annie Gray—you cannot know all! I am the wife of that man! He brought to me the consent even of the poor old King, whose maniac cries they now say alarm the solitary sentinel as he keeps his watch upon the ancient ramparts of Windsor Castle. It was a priest in orders who united us. I was, I am his wife; and now, laughing all ties of earth or of heaven to scorn, he casts me from him! Oh, wicked—wicked! Worse—worse than wicked!"

Annie shuddered.

"You were deceived, no doubt," she said; "and if so, of what avail are all your passionate complaints? Will you sacrifice yourself because another has been faithless?"

"Yes, yes!" cried the Dark Woman, as she hastily withdrew her hand from the grasp of Annie; and clasping both her hands together, she held them in a strange attitude above her head. "Yes—oh, yes;—most freely! Let him but

acknowledge my son, and I am content to die at his feet."

"Will he not do so? I thought, from all that I could hear, that the Prince did acknowledge that Allan Fearon was his son."

"His son, yes; but not a Prince."

"Ah, yes! I see now what you mean."

"Let him do that, and I will die."

"Alas, it cannot be! I have spoken with him of you."

"When? Where?"

"Even now, in my own apartments. He is disposed to arrange as best he may now your future fortunes. He will take care that both you and your son are placed far above all anxieties; and although it is hard to say such words to one who has suffered as you have, yet what else can be said or done? I implore you, in regard for yourself, to accept what good is offered to you, and to go somewhere in peace."

"Ah! You say that?"

"From my heart."

"No; from his head—he has no heart. You have talked to the Regent even now, and then you come to me."

"I do. Surely there is nothing wrong in that?"

"They fear me—they fear me still!"

"But you are a prisoner here. Do not delude yourself by an idea that you are feared now. Indeed—indeed it is to save you, not to mollify your anger, that I come."

"Girl," said the Dark Woman, "I have a little tale to tell you."

"To tell me?"

"Yes. Once upon a time, when in the midst of such despair that I knew not if my heart would break or not, I found, in the laboratory of a man whose reputation for good or for evil I found a means of proving, a small box of platinum. That, you know, is the hardest and purest metal in existence, and should, as a box, contain only some precious substance. You attend to me?"

"I do; but——"

"Hear me out. The little box of platinum contained a fine and subtle powder; and when I inhaled its fragrance, it was strange how it lightened the weight upon my heart, and how much brighter and happier appeared all things about me. The box is here."

The Dark Woman produced, from some secret receptacle about the breast of her apparel, a small box of white metal. She touched a spring, and the lid flew open.

"It harms no one," added the Dark Woman, as, in the most natural manner in the world, she held it towards the face of Annie, who, with the heedlessness of a child, smelt at it.

A dreamy look came over the eyes of the Countess de Blonde, and she smiled faintly as she spoke.

"It is a most—beautiful perfume, and—and—it is so strange that I—should feel so—so languid. Yes, George—yes! I sleep—I sleep—sleep—sleep——"

Slowly the Countess de Blonde slid down to the floor, with that same gentle smile upon her lips which had first sat upon them when she inhaled the delicate odour of the subtle powder in the platinum box.

She looked like some happy infant falling into

a deep and quiet slumber, which was likely to be full of pleasant visions.

The Dark Woman closed the platinum box, and replaced it in the breast of her apparel. She gently moved Annie to an attitude where she could rest easily, half on the floor, and half resting, in a sitting posture, against the chair.

"It is well," she said. "Astorath was a great chemist. This is one of the products of his skill, that I found, with a full and complete description of its use, upon searching his house and laboratory. It is well. Rest thou for a time, gentle and good heart. No evil will come to thee."

CHAPTER CXIX.

THE DARK WOMAN MEDITATES A TERRIBLE REVENGE UPON THE REGENT.

SOME new and terrible idea had evidently taken possession of the mind of the Dark Woman. She stood for a few minutes, watching the quiet slumber of Annie, and at the same time with her head bent aside in an attitude of intense listening.

The Palace appeared to be profoundly still.

"My time has come," she said. "Heaven above me, you know that I have tried all mortal means for justice! I claim now that last refuge of outraged humanity—revenge! revenge!"

There was something terrible about the eyes of the Dark Woman as she now glared about her in that small apartment, as though looking for some mode of egress

But there was none.

No secret panel—no hole in the floor—no casement, through which she might make her way to freedom, presented itself; but still the Dark Woman felt that she had a resource.

That resource was Willes, the valet.

She tapped lightly on the door that separated what might be called the prison-cell from the guard-chamber without.

Willes was there, and he thought that the Countess de Blonde, having said all she wished to say, was summoning him to accompany her back to her own apartments.

He glided into the room in a moment.

The Dark Woman seized his arm with a clutch of iron, and the door with the other hand.

"There is no occasion for alarm," she said, in a low, deep, earnest tone; "nor has anything happened at all disastrous to the Countess de Blonde."

"Oh, heaven!" said Willes.

He had caught sight of the recumbent form of Annie, and his first, and, indeed, natural enough impression was that she had fallen a victim to the mad jealousy of the Dark Woman.

"Hush, fool!" said Linda de Chevenaux. "There is no harm done, I tell you."

"No—no barm?'

"None. She does but sleep. Do you think I have not art enough to cast who I please into repose that, though it may look like death, has no kindred to it."

"You—you can do that?"

"In a moment. I could cast you, if I so pleased, down at my feet in a trance that would last for hours"

"Oh, do not—do not."

"I have need of you, and will not."

"Yes, yes, my lady; I am your very humble servant, as you know."

"I do know it. Where is the Regent?"

"In the Countess's apartments, no doubt, by this time, very impatient for her return."

"I will go to him.'

"You, my lady—you?"

"I have said it. You, Willes, will pass me through all obstacles that may impede my progress I have some last words to say to the Regent, before I go at once and for ever. You comprehend they wish that my persecutions of the Prince should cease, and that I should leave him to security and peace, and seek security and peace myself?"

"Indeed, it would be best."

"So I think, now, and I have resolved upon it.'

"I am rejoiced to hear those words, my lady. I am quite sure, too, that the Regent will be rejoiced to hear them.'

"Perhaps. Lead on, now."

"Ah, my lady, I don't know why you have thought proper to place the Countess in such a deep sleep. I can hear her breathing; but as it is so, if you will put over your head that silk scarf which you see she has, and which she cast over her hair when she left her own rooms to come with me here, the men in the outer room will, in the dim twilight that is there, think you are her, and you can pass along with me without question."

"That is well. It is done."

The Dark Woman lifted gently from the head and shoulders of Annie the scarf which Willes alluded to. It was one of those which Allan Fearon had had the use of when he came to the Palace as the pretended silk merchant She wound it about her own head and face; and as it had some very bright embroidered stars upon it, there was very little doubt but that the men on guard would at once fancy they recognised the Countess de Blonde.

Willes cast one more anxious glance at Annie, though, before he left the room, and in a tone of some anxiety he said, "Oh, my lady, I hope you are quite sure that she will come to no harm."

The Dark Woman stooped over the slumbering form of the fair young girl, and left a soft kiss upon her cheek.

"Am I a Judas?" she said. "Are you content? Do you think I could do that if I meditated or had done harm to her?'

"No, no," said Willes. "I—I don't think, my lady, you really could, and I feel more at ease."

"Lead on, then."

Willes was evidently nervous, notwithstanding he had said he felt more at his ease.

Preceding the Dark Woman by about half a pace, he went out into the guard chamber, and the two men who were there began, in their clumsy fashion, to execute more bows, which effectually prevented them from recognising any change of persons in the female figure that accompanied the Regent's valet.

The Dark Woman spoke not a word now until they had reached the Titian Gallery, and then, turning to Willes, she took from her finger an emerald ring of great value and beauty.

"Take this," she said, in a strange, low, constrained voice, such as he had never yet heard from her. "Take this. Keep it for the sake and remembrance of one who, if she has at times caused you some uneasiness, has not been an illiberal pay-mistress."

"Oh, madam!" said Willes, with more of emotion than any one could have thought him capable of —"oh, madam, I would much rather that you kept this jewel, and did not speak to me in such a way."

"Is this possible?" sighed the Dark Woman.

"What, madam?—oh, what?"

"That you feel for me?"

"Indeed I do! I do, really and truly; and if, madam, you will only now not look so despairingly, but take advantage of present opportunities, so as to escape from St. James's, you might soon be far enough off to be out of all danger."

"No," sighed the Dark Woman,—"no, it cannot—it may not be! Do you know that a shot was fired at me this morning from one of the windows that overlook the Colour Court?'

"I have heard so."

"Who fired it?"

Willes shook his head.

"That, madam, I have not yet been able to ascertain."

"Shall I tell you? It was the Regent!"

"I hardly think so, madam, for it is contrary to all his thoughts and habits to do so. I should fancy it came rather from Colonel Hanger's hand, or from some one of the royal pages."

"I shall know—I shall know; and now leave me, for I will compromise you no further. I will seek the Regent."

To the surprise of Willes, the Dark Woman did not attempt to enter the rooms in the occupation of the Countess de Blonde by the ordinary route from the Titian Gallery, but she made her way to that private secret door, which by the very narrow passage would lead to the innermost of the apartments.

The kind of calmness with which the Dark Woman had spoken to him had had the effect of somewhat reconciling Willes to her friendship. He could not continue to think that one who was so outwardly composed was on the eve of the commission of any act of desperation.

But still Willes thought that it would be well to take some precaution, and he thought that if he could only succeed in awakening the Countess de Blonde from the kind of trance into which she appeared to have fallen, that he might throw upon her all the responsibilities of the situation.

With this view the valet made his way back again to the small room in which the fair Countess still slept under the influence of the powerful odour which she had inhaled from the concentrated narcotic powder in the little platinum box.

Willes, however, took the Regent's dressing-room in his route, and, from among the costly scents and essences on the table there, he selected a powerful and fragrant one.

Armed with that, as a revivifying agent, he hastened onwards, and hoped that he would be able to restore Annie to consciousness.

Meanwhile, the Dark Woman opened the narrow private door, and at once plunged into the narrow passage that would lead, by a circular, segmental route, to the inner apartments of the gorgeous suite devoted to the Countess de Blonde.

The distance was but short, and soon the Dark Woman set foot in that splendid bed-chamber, in which one might suppose that care and anxiety could find no home.

But the Dark Woman had no eyes for the gorgeous glitter of that regal abode of beauty. Her mind was enveloped in the dull cloud of the terrible resolution which had taken possession of her—the resolution to die.

She passed out of the bed-chamber, from behind the gilt screen that shrouded its door, and she stood in the presence of the Regent.

The Prince slept.

The bright fire had burnt low on the hearth. The wax candles were burning short, and the Prince, after waiting some time the arrival of Annie from her self-imposed mission to the Dark Woman, had settled himself comfortably in his chair, and fallen asleep.

It was a wonder that the very flash of the eyes of the Dark Woman, as they lit upon him, did not awaken him.

But he was breathing heavily and regularly. His sleep was sound.

The Dark Woman saw the vacant chair opposite to him, which had so short a time before been in the occupation of Annie, and she gently seated herself upon it.

There, for a few minutes, she sat, and gazed upon the face of the Prince—of her destroyer.

A glass—a tall, elegant glass, with a spiral stem—was by the side of the Regent. It was still about two-thirds full of some wine, of a pale amber colour.

By the side of the Dark Woman, where the Countess de Blonde had sat, was a similar glass, but it had not so much wine in it, although it was of the same colour as that by the Regent.

The Dark Woman, then, for a moment, during which she seemed to suffer the sharpest pangs of mental agony that human nature could endure and live, clasped both her hands over her face and brow.

She uttered a low moan.

That sound of the very abandonment and bitterness of grief found its way faintly to the senses of the Regent.

He moved uneasily, and uttered almost an echo of the moan.

The Dark Woman again fixed her eyes upon him, and he slowly lapsed into the same deep slumber from which he had been slightly disturbed.

"I am warned!—I am warned!" she whispered, in so low a tone that it was not possible it could reach the ears of the sleeper. "The time has come—the time for action!"

Slowly and painfully—for it was tightly fixed there—the Dark Woman took from the middle finger of her left hand a large and antique ring.

Turning this ring, so that the inner surface of its massive golden hoop was visible, she touched a spring in it, and a small square opening started into sight in the gold.

It was as if some genii, from within the very substance of the gold, had opened a little door, by which to make an exit.

Compacted in the space within was a pasty-looking compound. There could not have been more in quantity than would have spread thinly over the smallest coin.

The Dark Woman, with the pin of a brooch,

which she took from the breast of her apparel, hooked out a small portion of the paste-like substance.

She immersed the point of the pin then in the wine that remained in the tall glass close to her.

At that moment she started to her feet. She was nearly uttering an exclamation, but she repressed it. She had heard, or she fancied she had heard, a noise.

Whence came it? Was it there in that room, or was it from the adjoining chamber?

She listened intently.

All was still—still as the grave—still as death—as the death which she expected to be in that chamber before many minutes more should pass away.

The Dark Woman made two steps from the chair, and she went so far towards the gilt screen that she was able to glance behind it, and into the bed-chamber beyond.

No one was visible. Surely she was alone—quite alone.

She returned to the chair, and to the table.

The pin of the brooch had remained resting about an inch in depth in the wine, and the brooch itself was hanging over the edge of the glass.

The pasty substance had completely dissolved, and the gold glitter of the brooch-pin was undimmed.

No alteration of colour or of clearness appeared in the wine.

"Twenty deaths," said the Dark Woman, in a panting whisper,—"twenty deaths linger in the one crystal vessel now."

From the side of the table at which she was, she could easily reach over to the glass which was by the elbow of the Regent. The table was a small one, which had been specially brought there for the accommodation only of two persons—the Regent and the Countess.

The Dark Woman lifted the tall glass with the spiral stem, and the amber-coloured wine in it, over towards her. She went through the same process with the pin's point of the brooch, and the pasty-looking substance in the ring, that she had done with the other glass.

Upon immersing the pin's point into the amber-coloured wine, there was, for a moment, a faint hissing noise in the liquid, and a cloudy precipitate began to settle downwards.

The Dark Woman slightly shook the glass.

The cloudy precipitate disappeared.

Slowly the wine assumed its former brightness. No one, to look at it, could suppose, for a moment, that it had been tampered with.

The Dark Woman shuddered.

With trembling hands now, she took from a secret pocket of her dress a small gold box, from which she extracted a scrap of old, yellow-looking paper.

"Let me be sure!—let me be sure!" she said. "This is the paper I found wound about the platinum box and the ring, when I made the discovery of both in the cabinet of Astorath, the chemist and astrologer. Oh, let me be quite sure!"

She read to herself, in a low voice:—

"The subtle powder in the box of platinum will, if inhaled even for a few seconds by any one, produce a profound repose. The pasty, yellowish substance in the ring is a concentrated fate—a death, speedy, complete, and perfect, to all human eyes."

The Dark Woman paused to think.

"I have pondered," she said, "over those words, and know not what they may mean. 'To all human eyes.' Is there a hidden meaning in them, or do they but express that the death is certain? It must be so!—it must be so! The one animal upon whom I essayed an experiment with this poison, fell dead upon the faintest taste of it, and the corpse was cast into the street. Yes—oh, yes!—it is death!—it is death!"

She slowly reached across the table again with the Regent's glass in her hand, but she did not place it exactly in the same spot from whence she had taken it. She kept it about half-way between her and the Regent, equally within her sudden reach as his.

The Dark Woman had a motive in so placing the glass.

Then she spoke in a low but distinct tone.

"George, Prince of Wales, awake! awake! awake!"

She touched the edge of an empty glass with the blade of a silver knife as she spoke, and the light, tinkling sound perhaps did more to arouse the Regent than even her voice.

He started awake.

"Yes, Annie, yes."

The Dark Woman's eyes were fixed upon him like two flaming orbs.

The Prince uttered a cry of surprise—there was something, too, of terror in it—as he made an effort to rise.

"Peace! Be still!" said the Dark Woman. "You sent one to me, with the olive branch of peace. I came to talk to you in such a strain that for your own dear life's sake I would have you listen to me. I am going soon far from you, for ever and for ever."

"Ah! indeed! Then Annie has seen you?"

"She has."

"Well, well? She told you how utterly impossible—how foolish it was to—to make me miserable and yourself likewise. Even now, I am willing—I am quite willing, if you will go away, to behave in the most liberal and handsome manner to you."

"Listen."

"One moment. Oh! I had some Tokay here."

"Wait. Hear me first. I, too, am willing to rid you for ever of my most unwelcome presence—on the one condition——"

"What condition?"

"I will die, if you will acknowledge my son."

"I have. I have done so."

"As a prince of the blood royal of England?"

"Impossible. You rave, as usual."

The Dark Woman uttered a gasping sob.

"It is over," she said,—"oh, heaven, it is over! If there be great guilt in this, oh, think of my great provocation! It is over! over!"

"What do you mean?" said the Regent, in a tone of alarm. "How did you get here? Where is the Countess? By heaven, woman, if she has met with any foul play at your hands, I will——"

"Ha! ha!" laughed the Dark Woman. "And what will you—what can you do, poor, trembling worm that you are?"

"Help! What ho, there? Who waits? Willes! I will no more endure this mad woman."

"Be still!" cried the Dark Woman

Across the table, she presented full in the face of the Regent another pistol, which was entirely, with the exception of those parts which were necessarily of steel, made of silver, richly chased. It was so small that it might almost have been hidden in the hollow of the hand. It looked almost a toy. But the Regent saw that it was a firearm.

He sank back into his chair.

"This little weapon," said the Dark Woman, "carries two small steel bullets, each not much larger than a pea."

"Stop! Don't! Take it away!"

"But they will reach the brain."

"No, no! You are mad—mad! What have I done to you that you should threaten my life?"

No. 57.—DARK WOMAN.

"Much."

"But—but—I say, Linda—Linda, an accident might happen! Take the pistol, if it be a pistol, further off."

"On condition."

"More conditions?"

"No, the same. Acknowledge my son, and your son, to be what he truly is, and not only is your own safety assured, but I will, by my death, give you the best possible security that I will trouble you no more."

"I cannot even speak to you while you threaten my life."

"There, then!"

She placed the tiny pistol on the table.

"Then," said the Regent, earnestly, "if you are not entirely bereft of reason—if you are not quite inaccessible to common sense, let me tell you that if I were fifty times over to say that Allan Fearon were my legitimate son, it would not make him so. The marriage that took place between you and me will never hold good."

"Stop! You produced the consent of the Crown."

"I am sorry now to say that it was written by a different person from the King."

"The King is insane, and his evidence in regard to any act can scarcely be received."

"That is true. But since it is on record in the regular way that he did give his consent to my marriage with Caroline of Brunswick, it will put an end to all your fancied claims."

"Fancied claims!" groaned the Dark Woman, "Oh, heaven! all the world—the earth—the trees—the bright flowers—the huge mountains, and the useless ocean, are but fancies, and we live but in a fevered dream!"

"Well, well, be reasonable. I am so thirsty that I can hardly speak to you; but if you have really done no harm to the Countess de Blonde, and will promise to leave England——"

"Oh, yes," interrupted the Dark Woman, "I will leave England."

"When?—when?"

"Now."

She placed her hand upon the glass with the small quantity of the amber-coloured wine in it.

The Regent saw the movement. He made a slight inclination of the head, as he said, "Imperial Tokay."

"This wine?"

"Yes, Linda; and if now, in truth, you will leave me and this country at once and for ever, I will settle upon you a competent sum."

"It is hard to leave you, too."

"Me?"

"Yes, George. In leaving England, I fancy, if I could only take you with me, I should be content."

"Me, with you! There, you rave again!"

The Prince looked over the table, as if searching for something, and he saw the tall glass with the spiral stem, and the Tokay in it, which he had been drinking.

He lifted it to his mouth.

"Linda," he said, "I seem to see some signs that you are getting much more reasonable; and be assured that so soon as you are so, and that you bring to an end all my trouble concerning you, your own troubles will likewise cease."

"I know it."

"Then——"

"Stop—oh, heaven!—one moment!"

The Prince paused, with the glass almost at his lips.

"You are about to drink?"

"Certainly, I am."

"Let me, too. In this glass there is some wine. I, too, will drink; and I will pledge you, George, Prince of Wales!"

"As you please."

The Dark Woman raised the other glass.

"Farewell!" she said.

"An odd toast!"

"A true one."

"As you please. I suppose you have made up your mind, and refer to your departure?"

"I have. I do."

"Then, so be it. Farewell!"

The Prince drank about half of the contents of the glass.

The Dark Woman drained hers to the dregs.

A shriek burst from some one at this moment in the inner chamber, close behind the screen; and then Annie, the Countess de Blonde, with her fair and beautiful hair all in disorder about her head and shoulders, darted into the room.

"Hold! hold! Good heaven!" she cried; "am I too late?"

"Too late?" said the Regent. "Too late for what, Annie?"

"Too late!" cried the Dark Woman, as she clasped her hands together, and looked, with an air of triumph, at the Regent. "Yes; too late!"

"What? What?" added the Prince. "What is it?"

"Oh, your Royal Highness! Oh, my poor royal master!' said another voice; and Willes, with a look of despair upon his face, appeared likewise from behind the screen.

"Ha! ha!" laughed the Dark Woman, "it is done!"

"What is done?" said the Regent. "Are you all mad? What is the meaning of this? Are you all out of your senses? Or is this some foolish jest you have on foot?"

"George! George!" said Annie, as she rushed forward, and holding him by the hands, looked in his face, "what have you taken?"

"Taken?'

"Yes; what wine?"

"Tokay."

"Alas! alas! Tell me again, Willes—tell me again!"

"I was hidden, and so horrified that——"

Willes was interrupted by the Regent, who now turned deadly pale as he said, faintly, "What—what is this? All mist—all—all fog about me! Where are the lights?"

"Help! help!" shrieked Annie. "He is dying! He is poisoned! Look in his face! Help! oh, help!"

Willes raised frantic yells of despair.

The Dark Woman fell heavily to the floor.

"Physicians!" cried Annie. "Oh! quick—quick! They may save him yet! Help! Ring all the bells! Give an alarm in the Palace! Heaven! she has poisoned him!"

"Yes," said the Dark Woman, faintly, "we leave England together."

She made a powerful effort to raise her head and one arm, and then fell flat upon her face, and appeared to be dead.

The Regent uttered one fierce cry of mortal fear, and then fell back into the arm-chair in which he had been sleeping.

A death-like colour spread over his face. He made strange movements with his hands; and then, just as there came a rush of footsteps into the apartments, and a crowd of officials of the Palace appeared, his head fell back, and Annie cried out, "He is gone!—he is gone! Oh, this is terrible, for now I find that I did love him!"

She burst into tears, and fell at the feet of the Regent in an agony of grief.

Yeomen of the Guard, pages, grooms of the chambers, and inferior servants, had all crowded to the spot. To all appearance, the Regent was no more.

A clerk of the Lord Chamberlain's was present,

and he looked in the face of the Prince, and shook his head.

"If his Royal Highness," he said, "be really dead, those who were with him must consider themselves in custody."

The Regent slipped slowly off the chair, and fell to the floor by the side of Annie.

"Dead! dead!" cried every one.

CHAPTER CXX.

SIXTEEN-STRINGED JACK COMES TO TOWN TO LOOK AFTER HIS OLD FRIENDS.

It was on the very night when these remarkable events were taking place at St. James's Palace, that a hackney carriage slowly made its way down the long, narrow, straggling street which leads from Hampstead Heath in the direction of London.

That hackney carriage was driven by a lad, who seemed rather proud of his occupation; and immediately following it, a few paces distant only, came a man on horseback.

The man was a stalwart specimen of humanity, and wore a cloak with a brass clasp at the neck, and a hat which nearly obscured the whole of the upper part of his face.

By the shape of the holsters to the saddle, it might well be conjectured that they carried a serviceable pair of pistols; and from the contiguity of this mounted man to the carriage, and his actions in regard to it, it seemed pretty evident that he held it in special charge, and considered himself as a sort of guard over it and its contents.

As the carriage emerged from the long narrow street, and made its way into the more open portion of the village of Hampstead, the mounted man allowed the distance between him and it to increase, so that until they had cleared the houses, it would not seem to any casual observer that he had any connexion with it. But no sooner had they got into a portion of the road with nothing but hedges on either side, than the mounted man galloped up to the door of the coach, and placing his hand upon it, spoke kindly to some one within.

The words he uttered will be sufficient to enable the reader to identify the persons whom we introduce to them on such an occasion, on the high road from Hampstead to London.

"Lucy," said the horseman, who was no other than our friend Sixteen-stringed Jack,—"Lucy, I have been thinking more than ever, as we rode along, that you are right in wishing to come to London. It was but a dull abode for you, in that gloomy cavern on the Heath."

"Yes, father," said Lucy; "and for you, too: it was dull for you to be with me, and you were anxious when away from me. But if we can only find out my old and dear friend, Marian Grey, whom I should now, though, call Marian Fearon, I am sure she will receive me; and then, you know, father, I can cease to be a burden to you, for I can still support myself as I did of old."

"A burden to me?" cried Jack. "Now, by the stars above us, Lucy, this is unkind of you

my child; but be assured we shall find your friend Marian; and I may add, too, that there was something of a necessity for leaving the cavern on the Heath. It is no secret to you now, Lucy, that my fortune has ever depended upon what I could help myself to upon the high road; and it is true that I should lead a life of greater action than I have been able to do up yonder on the common."

"Father, father, if you would only leave this dangerous employment."

"No, Lucy—impossible. I believe once a highwayman, always a highwayman; but I have another motive likewise in coming to London, which is that I am particularly anxious to know what has become of our acquaintances Shucks and Brads."

"I fear, father, some great evil has happened to them. Although rough in manner, they were not unkindly of heart."

"I will find them out, Lucy, you may depend, for I look upon them now as friends of yours, as well as friends of mine."

Sixteen-stringed Jack was able, by bending down his head, to hold this conversation with Lucy, as the coach sped its way towards London; and as Jack Singleton knew perfectly well that Allan Fearon had removed from Martlett's Court to the little picturesque house close to the river, he was able to direct his course accordingly.

Upon reaching the Strand, Jack stopped the coach, and having bestowed upon the boy a liberal gratuity, he assisted Lucy to alight, and they both waited somewhere near the corner of that narrow thoroughfare which led down to the abode of Allan Fearon, until the coach had taken its departure.

"Now, Lucy, my dear," said Jack, "walk on, and I will ride but a few paces behind you. You must stop at the last house you come to, for that, now, is the abode of your friend, where, I make no doubt, you will be much happier than amid the silence and gloom of our late home."

Lucy was elated with the idea of being soon again in association with Marian, for whom she entertained so sincere an affection. She paused at the house which had been indicated by her father, and then Sixteen-stringed Jack himself seeing that the street was quite deserted dismounted, and casting the bridle of his horse over his arm, he rapped smartly at the door of the house.

Marian was practically alone, for that was the time when Allan Fearon was paying that visit to Buckingham House, which he had been induced to make by the machinations of Sir Hinckton Moys and the Marchioness of Sunningham.

To be sure Shucks was there, but he was fast asleep. Little, however, did Sixteen-stringed Jack imagine that when bringing his daughter Lucy to town again for the companionship of her old friend Marian, he should at once light upon one of the two housebreakers, concerning whose fate he was getting anxious.

Marian heard the knock, but she was by no means solicitous to admit strangers to the house; and she repaired to an upper window in order to see who it was that claimed admittance to that humble residence, which in its obscurity saw so few visitors.

For a few moments the prospect of a man and a

horse was not encouraging, for owing to Lucy being close to the door, Marian was not able to observe her.

The voice, however, of Sixteen-stringed Jack soon dissipated all her fears, for he had been reconnoitring the house with sufficient vigilance to enable him to see that some one was performing the same office from within.

"Allan Fearon," he cried, "if you are here, let me tell you it is an old friend who waits at your door."

"Ah, yes!" cried Marian; "and well I know that old friend's voice."

She hurried to the door, as she thought, to admit Sixteen-stringed Jack, but was both delighted and surprised to find herself clasped in the arms of Lucy.

"Dear Marian, you must answer me at once. May I come and live in affectionate companionship with you, or is it not possible that you can let me do so?"

"A thousand welcomes, Lucy! I have longed for you, and believe me it is a happy moment in which I hear you talk of staying with me."

"And Allan," said Lucy, "will he, too?"

"He will only be too happy to know that when he is from home I have the companionship of one whom I love so truly; but here is your father waiting on the threshold, and we give him no welcome."

"The dearest welcome," said Jack; "but tell me is all well with Allan?"

"Yes—oh, yes! And such strange things have come to pass."

"I had a fancy that they would; and now, Marian—if you will permit me to call you so— let me tell you that my little girl here is not to be a burden to you. I will take good care of that."

"I can work," said Lucy.

"Work, my Lucy?" laughed Jack, although the laugh was a sad one. "No—no more work. Leave that to me."

It was at this moment that some one made a sudden rush from the house, and seizing Jack by the collar, called out, "I've got him!—I've got him! Run, all of you—you ain't nabbed yet!"

Jack was upon the defensive in a moment, and but that he recognised the voice of the person who had attacked him, he might have inflicted some injury upon his old acquaintance Shucks, who but half awake, and probably not yet perfectly recovered from the effect of his deep potations, had suddenly aroused himself, and hearing a man's voice, had taken it into his head that there was an attack of the officers of police.

"Why, Shucks," cried Jack, "can I believe my eyes and ears? Is it really you?"

"Bless us and save us!" cried Shucks. "If it isn't Jack Singleton! Have you got rid of them?"

"Rid of who?—rid of what?"

"Why, the traps, to be sure—and yet I suppose I was dreaming, for I don't feel quite clear in the attic story now. Why, Jack, I've got such a heap to tell you. Brads and me, you see, have come into our fortune. It's all right. The other fellows are dead—so you see we take all the shares except the Dark Woman's. Ha! ha! Why you'll kill yourself with laughing, Jack, when I tell you all about it; and you shall go

with me and Brads, too; and her ladyship—ha! ha!—her ladyship won't mind standing an odd thousand or two to you! And we'll have some eff-and eff too. Oh, Jack, that fellow with the eff-and-eff will be the death of you! He's worth any money, he is. 'Here's the eff-and-eff!'"

Shucks was so amused at the recollection of the scene which had taken place at the Countess d'Umbra's grand mansion in Hanover Square, that he was compelled to sit down on the step of the door to indulge in laughter.

"Why, you're mad, Shucks, I do believe," said Jack.

"No I ain't — no I ain't. 'Here's the eff-and-eff!'"

"What on earth does he mean?" said Jack to Marian.

"I cannot tell. He came here with a letter for Allan, and being not quite—that is to say, a little——"

"I understand," said Jack. "You let him stay to sleep off some 'drop too much' he had taken."

"To be sure she did," cried Shucks; "but it wasn't eff-and-eff. It was some prime stuff that the nobs drink—half a guinea a bottle, Jack, my boy; and all you've got to do is to knock off the neck, and out it comes. But where's Brads? Has anybody seen anything of Brads?"

"We should ask you that question," said Jack.

Shucks shook his head, and the look of confusion that came over his face showed what a very dim idea he had of the events of the last six and thirty hours.

"I will take him away with me," whispered Sixteen-stringed Jack, to Marian. "He's a harmless fellow enough; but still, as Allan appears to be out, I will take him away with me. Good night, Marian; and you, too, my dear child, good night; and heaven bless you both! You will hear of me soon!"

Lucy sprung forward to her father.

"Tell me—oh, tell me," she said, "that you are not going into danger?"

"Not the least," said Jack, with a smile, as he kissed her fondly. "Not the least."

Lucy was compelled to be satisfied. The door was closed; and Sixteen-stringed Jack, putting his right arm beneath the left of Shucks, and resting the bridle of his horse upon his other hand, spoke coaxingly to him. "Come, old comrade," he said. "I partly came to town to hunt you up, and am well pleased to find you. Tell me what you've been about since you and Brads left the old cavern?"

"To be sure I will, Jack," said Shucks, confusedly; "but I rather think I've been a bit of a fool! It's so hard, though, for a fellow to keep on the right side of his senses, when he has only to stretch out his hand to get thousands and thousands of pounds."

"You said something of that kind, Shucks, before: what on earth does it mean?"

"The Dark Woman, my boy!"

"What of her?"

"Why, bless you, Brads and I found her out! She's set up as a great lady, and calls herself the Countess d'Umbra, and lives in no end of a fine house in Hanover Square! We went to crack the crib all in the regular way of business, and who should we find mistress of it but the Dark

Woman. So we made up matters, you see, and got part of our shares down; but I'm afraid after that we got into bad company, do you know, Jack."

"The company of too many bottles, Shucks, I fancy!"

"Well, yes; but as we had turned gentlemen all at once, we thought we'd do as the other nobs do, and shake the ivory a little."

"Gambling?"

"You may call it gambling, Jack; but you see there are dishonest people in the world, and Brads and me got robbed. I wonder where Brads is? I seem at times to have a sort of an idea that I left him in St. James's Park."

Jack was silent for a few moments, and then he said, abruptly, "Is the career of that woman to commence again, with all the mysteries and crimes surrounding her?—is she again to become notorious under some other name, perhaps, with you and Brads as her assistants?"

Shucks looked perplexed.

"Well, Jack, I don't know; but you shall go with us to morrow."

"Hush! What is this?"

They had crossed the Strand; and taking their way towards Charing Cross, where, passing the door of an old public-house then known as the "Spanish Armada," but which has been long since swept away in modern improvements—quite a throng of persons were streaming in and out from the low doorway of this ancient hostel; and from the remarks and exclamations they uttered as they emerged, it was quite evident something that excited great curiosity was to be seen within.

"A sad sight!" said one. "A shocking sight! What will the inquest say to it?"

"A most foul murder, that's clear!" said another.

"And quite a gentleman, too, by his fine linen!" cried a third.

It was a sort of impulse that he did not care to resist, which induced Sixteen-stringed Jack to pause at the door of the public-house, and ask one of the persons who dived out from beneath its low porch, what was the matter.

"A dead body. A man found murdered, sir, in St. James's Park."

"St. James's Park?" cried Shucks, darting forward. "Who knows but it's——"

"Hush! Are you mad!" interrupted Jack.

Shucks was just saved from uttering the name of his companion; and after Jack had handed the bridle of his horse to a boy to hold, they both entered the little low public-house, and following the stream of visitors, they found themselves in a small room.

There was a fearful object lying upon a deal table in the centre of the apartment: ghastly in death, and dabbled in blood, they saw the unfortunate Brads. The rich apparel he had hastily bought with some of the money received from the Dark Woman, was torn and disordered; and there was such a look of mortal agony upon the face that at the first glance Shucks was sobered in an instant.

He clutched almost painfully the arm of Jack Singleton, as he whispered, "It is Brads—it is Brads! It is my old friend and companion—my comrade, my almost brother! Oh, Jack—Jack!

All is not gold that glitters! We found the Dark Woman, and we thought we had her at our mercy! It is but four and twenty hours, and there lies one of us! How soon shall I, too, be stretched in blood, as a spectacle for every idler who chooses to take a dram at the public-house bar?"

"This is, indeed, a sad sight," said Jack.

"Jack, one moment. Can we have the room to ourselves?"

"What for?"

"Brads has a paper. I have one likewise. I shall know in a moment if this be the work of the Dark Woman. Keep the people out for a moment. If his paper is safe, it is not her doing; but if it's gone, she has murdered him; and I shan't know a moment but some of her hellhounds may be upon my track! Keep the door, Jack; we're alone this moment."

Jack Singleton placed his back against the door of the room, and Shucks rapidly advanced to the dead body and tore open the vest.

Well he knew the small slit in the lining which Brads had made to contain that important document, which had been wrung from the fears of the Dark Woman.

It was gone.

The reader knows well its destination; and that, blood-stained and perforated by the sword which had taken the housebreaker's life, that important paper had found its way into the hands of the villanous Sir Hinckton Moys.

But Shucks only saw in all this an example of the implacable vengeance of the Dark Woman.

"It is gone, Jack," he said. "She has killed him—killed him at last! His blood is upon her head, and it's my turn next! I shan't know which way to turn—which way to look—how to eat, drink, or sleep! Jack, Jack, help me, for I'm a murdered man! Look at him there, how he glares at me! The dead mouth seems to tell me of it! 'Your turn next,' it says—'your turn next!' Stick by me, Jack—stick by me, or I shall never get out of this house alive!"

CHAPTER CXXI.

SIXTEEN STRINGED JACK AND SHUCKS PAY A VISIT TO HANOVER SQUARE AND THEN TO ST. JAMES'S PALACE.

THERE was so much genuine alarm about the manner of Shucks as he spoke to Jack Singleton that the latter began to think that he was somewhat deranged.

"Shucks, Shucks!" he cried, "what do you mean by all this? Are you the kind of man to give way to such shadowy fancies?"

The housebreaker trembled violently.

"Come away—come away, Jack; I cannot stay and look at him! Perhaps if I had staid by him it would not have happened! Who knows—who knows? Come away, Jack! I cannot stay here and look upon the dead face, and if I do stay I cannot turn my eyes from it!"

"Come, then," replied Sixteen-stringed Jack. "It is not a grateful sight to my eyes."

They were close to the door, when a violent rapping came from without.

"Open! open!" cried a voice. "Open, or I will find some means to make you!"

"They think I am still holding the door," said Jack, "when it will open now at a touch. Who hinders you, my friend, from opening the door?"

Jack uttered these last words aloud, and the door of the room was on the moment flung open, and a short, stout-built man made his appearance, with a smile upon his rather good humoured, rubicund countenance.

"Now, my fine fellows," he said, "I fancy I have you!'

"What do you mean?" asked Jack.

"My name is Billingham!"

Jack knew well that there was a Bow Street officer of that name, and he made no doubt but that he saw that very individual before him.

Shucks shrank back a little.

Billingham smiled.

"The game's up," he said. "I know you!"

"Me?" said Jack.

"To be sure; and a comrade of mine is now on your horse at the door of this public! Ha! ha! I have been looking for you a long time, Sixteen-stringed Jack!"

"Well," said Jack, "it will not come to much among so many of you."

"What do you mean?"

"The reward. I believe there is only a hundred offered for me, and when that comes to be divided among five or six, it really is not worth the while of such a man as you, Billingham."

The officer was taken off his guard for a moment.

"You are mistaken, Jack—you are mistaken. It will all go into one pocket. The man now in charge of your horse is only an odd man who helps me now and then. I shall have all! Ha! ha! What do you say to that, Mr. Jack? I shall have all!'

"Not yet!" said Jack.

Simultaneously with the utterance of the words, Sixteen-stringed Jack made one leap at the officer, and caught him by the throat with a grip of iron.

"Now, Mr. Billingham," he said. "Did you never read or hear the fable of the man who caught a Tartar?"

"Help! he ——"

The compression of Jack's hand upon the throat of the Bow Street officer cut short the second cry for help, and Billingham began to look black in the face.

This little scene had quite a magical effect upon Shucks It seemed at once to restore him to all his courage, all his coolness, and all that presence of mind which in sight of the dead body of his old companion, Brads, he appeared to have lost.

"That's the way to do it, Jack," he said. "I have him!"

Shucks produced a stout piece of cord from some pocket, and in an instant he had it round the neck of the officer in the form of a noose.

Billingham's eyes were by this time almost starting out of his head, and Jack, who had some compassionate feelings, spoke to him: "If I take off the pressure from your throat, will you be quiet?"

Billingham made a frantic effort to nod. Speak he could not.

Jack shifted his grasp from his throat to the back of the officer's neck.

Billingham began to recover his natural colour.

Shucks gave the cord he had round his neck a slight pull, which was the first intimation Billingham had of its presence; for when he had it first put round him, he was in by far too great a state of confusion to be conscious of it.

"Goodness gracious, gentlemen," he said, "you don't want to take my life!"

"It would serve you right for your impudence!" said Shucks.

"What—what? I am sure I was civil!"

"Your impudence in supposing that Jack Singleton would be so easily taken."

"Oh, well——"

"Be quiet!" said Jack.

"I am. I will."

"Come here," said Shucks.

Painfully persuaded by a good jerk at the cord, the captive officer followed Shucks, who, standing on a chair, tied the other end of the cord over a stout brass pole that was along the top of the window.

"Why—why, gentlemen both," said the officer, "you surely are not going to hang a fellow?"

"No," said Shucks; "but a fellow may hang himself if he likes. Will that do?"

"Murder!"

"Silence, on your life!" said Jack.

Shucks had drawn the cord so tight that it was only by standing on the extremity of his toes, and elongating his neck to an alarming degree, that the officer could save himself from actual strangulation.

Shucks then took off Mr. Billingham's hat, and placed it under his feet, so that frail as was that support it relieved him a little; but that was only for a moment, as Shucks drew the cord tighter and the unfortunate officer was within an ace of being hung—indeed, it was only his hat beneath his feet that saved him.

"There you are!" said Shucks.

"Stop!—the—the hat—it won't bear me! I can feel it even now bulging in!"

"You keep quiet, and you will do. And if you make the least row the hat will bulge in, and you will be hanged to a certainty. Good evening, old fellow!"

"Good evening, Mr. Billingham," said Jack; "I would advise you to keep quiet."

"I—I—oh, dear! Murder! Don't leave me in this way! A man might as well stand upon nothing as upon such a thing as a hat!"

"If you think so," said Shucks, "I will soon kick it away."

"No, no! Oh, no!"

"I thought not."

Shucks dived his hand into the coat-pocket of the officer, and drew forth the small brass staff which was the symbol of his authority as a constable.

"This may be of some use, Jack," he said.

"No doubt of it. Come on!"

"Good bye, poor Brads!—good bye, old pal! I little thought to see you in death in such a fashion! Good bye!"

Shucks and Jack went out of the room. A man and woman were waiting to go in and look at the corpse; but Jack turned the key in the lock of the door, as he said, "No more to-night. You must come to-morrow if you want to see him, good people."

"Yes, to-morrow," said Shucks, as he flourished the constable's staff in the faces of the man and woman.

They at once retreated to the bar of the public-house, and Shucks and Brads sallied out into the street.

"My horse," said Jack. "I am anxious about him."

"There he is!" said Shucks.

A man was mounted upon Sixteen-stringed Jack's horse, and slowly pacing about some distance down the street. They both approached him, and Shucks holding up the staff, said, "Now, my friend, you can get down. We won't trouble you any more."

"Do you come from Mr. Billingham?"

"Straight all the way?"

"Well, I would rather see him."

"Then seek him," said Jack; and as he spoke he took hold of the man's foot, and in a moment dislodged him from the back of the horse, sending him sprawling into the road.

The fellow began a series of yells and cries of murder, but Jack was in the saddle in a moment.

"Leap up on the crupper, Shucks," he said "The horse will carry double for some time. Leap up at once!"

"All's right, Jack!"

Shucks was on the horse instantly; and before any one could very well see which way to turn in order to assist the man who was lying in the road and crying "Murder!" Jack was off.

The horse at a hand gallop dashed up the Haymarket, and in a few moments all pursuit was at an end.

"Shucks," said Jack, "will you show me the paper you say you have, and which relates to the Dark Woman?"

"To be sure I will. Pull up."

There was a lamp close to the corner of old Swallow Street, at which Jack Singleton halted his horse. Jack's head was quite close to the lamp, so that when Shucks handed to him the paper which the Dark Woman had written, and the counterpart of which had found its way into the hands of Sir Hinckton Moys by the murder of Brads, he was easily able to read it.

"Ah," said Jack, when he had mastered the contents of the paper, "it is a most damaging document."

"It is, old pal."

"And I don't at all wonder that Brads lies dead at the 'Spanish Armada,' if he had a copy of it."

"That's what I say, Jack. She will settle me now."

"If she can."

"Yes, if she can. As soon as she can."

"No doubt."

Shucks whistled, but it was rather a lugubrious tune.

"Shucks," added Jack, after a few moments' consideration, "will you take my advice?"

"I may as well, Jack, while I can, for I feel quite sure it will be all over with me very soon."

"Will you come with me, then, to the Dark Woman's house, in Hanover Square?"

"Yes, Jack, with you."

"Come on, then."

"Shall I slip off the horse?"

"Oh, no! He will carry us both well that little distance, Shucks; so hold on. We shall be there in a few minutes."

Jack put his steed again to a good pace, and as he, with Shucks behind him, went towards Hanover Square, he could not help thinking back to the time when that same horse had carried him and the Dark Woman to St. James's Palace, in order to make the last effort to procure the pardon of Allan Fearon.

Hanover Square was soon reached, and Jack, turning to Shucks, said, "What number did you say it was?"

"Number ten, Jack."

"Then, here we are."

There was a good strong light reflected from the windows of the drawing-room floor, and when Jack alighted from his horse and knocked at the door of the house, he turned round to Shucks, saying, "I think you had better wait and take care of the horse. If I should want you, I will find a means of sending for you."

"All's right, Jack; only make some sort of bargain with her, if you can, for I don't like the idea of walking into the crib and knocking her on the head; although, in good truth, she deserves no less at my hands."

"Be patient," said Jack. "Give me that paper she wrote, Shucks: I may make better terms for you than even the fear of that will ever extort, to say nothing of its danger."

"There it is, Jack, and welcome. The fellow to it has been the death of poor Brads, that is quite clear."

The door of the house was flung open by the hall-porter.

"I want to see the Countess d'Umbra," said Jack.

"Dead!" said the man.

"What?"

"Dead!"

"Is that possible?"

"It's true, whether it's possible or not; and the authorities are in the house."

"What authorities?"

"Oh, a great man from the Court, and an officer. They are taking an inventory, you see, of all the things that belonged to the Countess. I was not to open the door to anybody; but I thought it was that horrid ruffian named Brads, and I want to have him taken up. Please to let me shut the door."

"No," said Jack.

"But I must."

"But I won't let you. I must see the authorities you speak of."

"What is all that?" cried a voice from the top of the first flight of the grand staircase. "What is all that about?"

"If you please sir, there is a man here who says he must and will come in, and I can't keep him out."

"I will soon settle that," said the voice, and no other than Sir Hinckton Moys himself ran down the stairs.

"Sir Hinckton Moys!" cried Jack, who knew him in a moment. "Are you here?"

"And who are you, pray?" asked Moys, with a loud manner of assumed authority. "Who are you, pray, who have the presumption to ask the question?"

Jack was rather puzzled to reply to this question; but he was relieved from the immediate necessity of doing so by the young girl who played the part of page to the Dark Woman.

This young creature appeared on the staircase some half-way up, and in loud and imploring accents, cried out, " If, sir, you are a friend to my poor mistress, oh, pray protect this house from that man, who I know to be an enemy, and find for me Mr. Allan Fearon, who, if my poor mistress be indeed dead, has alone the right of interference here."

" Officer !" cried Sir Hinckton Moys. " Secure that boy, and stop his mouth."

" Yes, sir," replied a man who came down the stairs behind the page; but the young girl darted right down to the hall, and clinging to Jack, she cried, " You will protect me—I am quite sure you will protect me !"

" To be sure I will," said Jack.

Sir Hinckton Moys was in the undress uniform of his military rank, which he was so fond of wearing, merely because it gave him the excuse to carry a sword.

That sword he now drew at once.

" I will soon clear the house of intruders," he said.

" Beware, sir !" said Jack.

The bright barrel of a pistol presented by Jack shone very uncomfortably into the eyes of Sir Hinckton Moys.

" Murder !" said the hall-porter. " I can see there will be murder done ! I will call the watch !"

He was close to the door; and if Jack and Sir Hinckton Moys both had wished to prevent him from opening it again, they would not have been able. He flung it open; but instead of darting out, as he had fully intended, right into the square, he rushed into the arms of some one, who it appeared had just arrived on the top of the steps.

" Hilloa !" cried the new arrival, " where are you a coming to, now, eh, stupid ?"

It was the herculean Binks, who, suiting action to words, gave the hall-porter such a lift with his shoulder and throw forward, that he flew the whole length of the hall, and was only brought up by the wall on the opposite side.

" Now, stupid," added Binks. " You will go on pushing a fellow !"

" Who is this ruffian ?" said Sir Hinckton Moys.

" That's the man, Sir Hinckton !—that's the man !" cried the one who had been called an officer by Moys; but was no other than his own valet. " That's the rascal, if you please, sir !"

" Who do you call a rascal ?" said Binks.

" You ! you ! you !"

The valet made a rush to get up the stairs, fully expecting that Sir Hinckton Moys would stand between him and harm; but his foot slipped, and he rolled right down to the hall.

Binks stepped forward and put one foot on the back of the valet, and then turning to Moys, he said, " Who the deuce are you ?"

Sir Hinckton Moys did not seem to be in a hurry to answer, and Jack spoke for him. " This man," he said, " states that the Countess d'Umbra is dead !"

" Dead ?—dead ? She dead ?"

Binks, in his astonishment at the possibility of such an event, put his other foot on the back of the valet.

" Murder ! murder ! He will tread me to death !"

" Get out !"

Binks stepped off the valet's back, and gave him a kick which sent him rolling over right into the ash-pan of the fire-place in the hall.

" Who says she is dead ? Who says it ?"

" I do," replied Sir Hinckton Moys,—" I do. The Countess d'Umbra now lies dead at St. James's Palace; and I have authority to take possession of this house and all it contains."

" No, no !" cried Carlos, the page; " I do not believe it ! Why does not the son of the Countess, Mr Allan Fearon, come ?"

" The son !" said Jack. " Ah !"

A new light broke in upon the mind of Jack Singleton in a moment. For the first time, he was now able to reconcile together many of the strange, seeming inconsistencies in the actions of the Dark Woman. Now he no longer had any difficulty in comprehending her extraordinary interest in the preservation of Allan from the hands of the executioner.

" Her son !" he said again. " Ah, yes, I see it all now. Her son is the proper person; and this man, who I know to be that son's most bitter enemy, cannot be in any authority here."

Sir Hinckton Moys bit his lips with passion. His presence at the house in Hanover Square may be easily explained. After his interview with the Regent, he had made his way into the Palace through the instrumentality of one of the female domestics, with whom he had an intrigue, and there he had staid quite long enough to hear the alarm of the death of the Regent, and of some mysterious woman who was found with him in the same room.

That this was the Dark Woman, and that she had brought her terrible course to a close by the murder of the Regent by poison, as well as her own death by the same means, appeared but too evident.

All Sir Hinckton Moys's hopes of a Court career appeared to be at an end. He was deeply in debt, and the idea struck him that if, with some show of authority, he could take possession of that costly house in Hanover Square, he might find in the course of a few hours booty sufficient to enable him to retire to the Continent a rich man.

He took his valet with him to play the part of an officer, and a five pound note to the hall-porter had won him over so that he was quite ready to believe anything.

Thus was it, then, that Sir Hinckton Moys was upon a purely piratical expedition at the Dark Woman's house in Hanover Square.

To be thus foiled, just at the moment when he thought all things would be successful, was one of those vexations which threw his temper completely off its balance.

With fury in his looks he made a rush upon Jack with his drawn sword, and it was only by great good luck that Jack was able with the barrel of the pistol he had in his hand to ward off the ferocious and sudden attack.

But Jack did successfully avoid the thrust, and in another moment Binks had hold of Sir Hinckton

Moys by the back of the neck, and half lifted him from the floor.

"What do you mean by that?" he said; "and what do you want here, I should like to know? Get out!"

"If the Countess is no more," said Jack, "I want nothing here."

"Oh, yes," said the page; "stay—do stay! I cannot—I do not think that she is dead. It seems so terrible and so incredible."

"Watch! Police!" cried Sir Hinckton Moys; and he made repeated attempts to wound Binks with his sword, until the latter snatched it out of his hand, and flung it into the square through the open door.

Now, the flinging of that sword through the open door attracted at once the full attention of Shucks, who thought it so out-of-the-way and extraordinary a circumstance, that he tied Jack's

No. 58.—DARK WOMAN.

horse to a lamp-post, and at once ran into the hall of the house.

"What's the row?" said Shucks.

"Hilloa!" shouted Binks; "hoorah! Why, is that you, my old pal? Hoorah! Who'd a thought o' seeing you here, old fellow?"

CHAPTER CXXII.

SIR HINCKTON MOYS IS FOILED IN HIS ATTACK UPON THE DARK WOMAN'S HOUSE.

BINKS had recognised at once in Shucks an old acquaintance, and if anything whatever had been wanting to induce him to look upon Jack Single-ton as the friend of his mistress, the Dark Woman, and Sir Hinckton Moys as her foe, the opportune appearance of Shucks would have supplied that one thing, and at once put an end to the question in the mind of Binks.

"Why, Binks," said Shucks, "is this possible? I thought you were hanged."

"Not at all—not at all. They wanted to, you see; but they didn't do it. How's business, old chap?"

"I'm here with a friend," replied Shucks, as he indicated Sixteen-stringed Jack; "and one you ought to know, too."

"A family man?" inquired Binks.

"To be sure, old comrade! What else?"

"Hush!" cried Sir Hinckton Moys at this moment. "Hush! what is it?"

There came a yelling voice in the square—one of those voices that shout out pieces of extraordinary intelligence, and which are not always particular about the authenticity of the news they bring.

But the words were of that import that they attracted general attention from even the discordant elements assembled in the hall of that magnificent mansion in Hanover Square.

The voice was hoarse with continued howling; but still the news was of that thrilling character that it seemed as if he who proclaimed it would not be likely to pause until physical exhaustion compelled him.

"Here you have the full, true, and particular account! Here you have it fresh from the press, and printed, by authority, in Little Peter Street, Seven Dials! Here you have the full, and harrowing, and heartrending particulars! All for one halfpenny!"

"What is it?" said Jack Singleton.

"What is it, indeed!" cried Sir Hinckton Moys. "I command you to release me. I will leave this house, since I must, at this present moment. But I have authority for what I do; and you will all repent interfering with me."

The man who was howling the intelligence approached nearer; and it was evident that what he said produced a degree of excitement in Hanover Square of the most extraordinary description.

Voices were heard calling from windows: the loud sound of doors being shut with violence after some person had emerged from them to purchase from the man his paper of intelligence, and the rushing of footsteps across the pavements, testified that something more than usual had taken place.

The man raised his voice again in howling accents, close to the Countess d'Umbra's house.

"Here you have the important and most extraordinary intelligence—for the small charge of one halfpenny—of the death of the Regent! The sudden and extraordinary death of his Royal Highness the Prince of Wales! The Regent's death for one halfpenny!"

"The Regent dead?" said Jack.

"Yes," said Sir Hinckton Moys, with something of an oratorical flourish of his arm, for Binks had released him from the firm clutch he had held at the back of his neck,—"yes; the man speaks truth: the Regent is no more; and his murderess

is she who chose to call herself the Countess d'Umbra, and to inhabit this mansion."

"My poor mistress!" cried the page.

"The poor Regent, rather!" added Sir Hinckton Moys, who spoke as though he felt himself to be the master of the situation,—"the poor Regent, rather, I should say! But as regards your mistress, boy, it is well that she has herself put an end to her existence, or she would die the death of a felon—accompanied by the execrations of a multitude."

The voice of the itinerant proclaimer of intelligence had nearly died away, for now they could hear but the faint echo of those words, which, on that eventful night, roused all London to excitement and attention, "The death of the Regent!—the death of the Regent!—the death of the Regent!"

The faintest echo died away in the far distance; and then Jack Singleton stepped a pace further forward, and spoke with an air of decision.

"If all this be true—if the Regent be indeed no more—and if the Countess d'Umbra, who has another name, which some of us here present know, is likewise with the dead, then the whole and sole claimant to this house and its contents must be that young man who has been in this hall proclaimed as her son. I mean Allan Fearon."

"Curses on him!" cried Sir Hinckton Moys. "His name or his presence meet me at every turn. Go where I will, do what I will, attempt what I may, I am ever confounded by the apparition of that Allan Fearon."

"Yes," said Jack Singleton; "and may you ever be so. He has good reason to know, and all his friends have good reason to believe, that you were the concoctor of the vile plot which so nearly consigned him to a felon's death. I tell you, Sir Hinckton Moys, that this house shall not hold you What your motive here may be I know not, but that it is one as base and criminal as your ordinary actions I cannot doubt."

"And who are you who speak so loud?"

"I am one that does not fear you. Let me speak now to those present, who, from attachment, or from gratitude or duty to her who is gone, will protect what she has left behind her for her son."

"I will do that," said Binks.

"And I," said the page.

There arose a tumultuous cry from the servants of the house, who had now collected in strong force close to the hall.

"We will all take care of the place for her ladyship's son," they said.

"Then turn these two men out," said Jack Singleton, pointing to Sir Hinckton Moys and his valet.

Moys saw that his position was no longer tenable, and that his intended plunder of that mansion in Hanover Square was foiled. A feeling compounded of rage and despair came over him. The Regent being dead, he might bid farewell, at once, to all that life of plunder, and dissipation, and evil-doing, which had become part and parcel of his existence at the Court of St. James's. There was no hope for him now but to fly a country which might well blush to call such a man one of its sons. Baulked of his revenge—in debt, difficulty and danger, without character, friends or expectations—Sir Hinckton Moys felt himself, at that moment, the veriest wretch that stood beneath the canopy of heaven.

It was with a yell of rage that he made a rush from the house, and would, at all events, have left the Dark Woman's mansion unscathed, but that, unfortunately for him, at that precise moment, his servant, who had accompanied him, to play the part of an officer of police, and so overawe the domestics of the house, was seized with a similar desire of getting quickly off the premises.

They met exactly in the doorway, with the force of two battering-rams; and, for two or three seconds, exchanged blows with each other, before they rolled together down the steps into the square.

"Close the door, Shucks," said Jack Singleton. Shucks did so.

Jack then turned to the servants.

"You may or you may not know, all of you—for I have not known it myself above half an hour—that a Mr. Allan Fearon is the son of your mistress; for now I find that I can identify her as the person whom he informed me was his mother. Keep house and home for him against all comers. We will seek him with the intelligence that must grieve his heart, and he will soon be with you."

Jack Singleton moved towards the door, and, as he did so, he placed his hand upon the arm of Shucks.

"Come," he said, "we've nothing further to do here now; but we must seek Fearon at once, and let him know what has happened, for I fancy he must be in ignorance of it, or he would surely have been here.'

"Good bye, Binks," said Shucks.

"Why, you're not a-going," said Binks. "There's lots of strong drink in the cellar; and as for me, I feel so poorly with grief, that I shall have to begin drinking, and keep it up for a fortnight, at least."

"I will call again," said Shucks. "Good night, now. I will call again."

Jack Singleton still kept his hand upon the arm of the housebreaker, so that he was, in a manner of speaking, compelled to leave the house with him; and the moment they got into the square, Jack released his horse from the lamp-post to which his bridle was tied.

"Shucks," he said, "I'm going down to see Allan Fearon, for he must know at once of these things. I don't know what you intend to do, but as for me, my means are getting low, and I'm for the road. I dare say we can always hear of each other somehow. But it seems to me, now, if it be true that the Dark Woman is no more, that we are both about to commence a new life.'

"It's sad for me," said Shucks. "I have cracked many a crib along with Brads, but I shall never crack another with him. And it will be many a long day indeed, Jack, before I forget how he looked as he lay on the table in that old public-house."

Jack tightened the girths of his horse, as he said, gently, "We all live till we die, Shucks—some sooner and some later; and he is the happiest fellow who can take things the easiest. Farewell!"

Jack sprung upon his horse, waved his hand, and in another moment was gone.

Shucks stood for a few moments irresolutely.

"If she killed him," he said, "why didn't she kill me too? What right had she to kill one of us, and leave the other alive, eh? But perhaps she didn't kill him, after all; and seeing that she's dead now herself, I begin almost to think she didn't; but if not, who did, I wonder? Ah, if I only knew that, it would be something worth living for. I'd hunt him up. If he got to the bottom of a well, I'd be down after him; or if he went up into the air in one of those new-fangled balloons they talk about, I'd hang on to the last rope, but I'd go with him. Poor Brads!—poor Brads! It's a wicked world, and I feels just now like the babes in the wood—that is to say, like one of them after the other's gone dead, and the sparrows are a covering of him up with blackberries. Ah!"

This exclamation of Shucks's was a loud one, for four men suddenly rushed upon him, and before he could make a movement in his own defence, had seized each a limb, and held him at their mercy.

"Now, my fine fellow," said one of the men, "I think we have you!"

Shucks made one violent effort to shake off his assailants, but he found it was in vain. The odds of four to one were too great for him to contend against. Perhaps it was a positive relief in the lonely and desolate condition of his mind, to find that he really had something to think about and struggle for.

"Well," he said, "I suppose you have nabbed me; and who are you when you're at home?"

"So you pretend you don't know me now, my beauty!" said another of the men.

"Yes I do, but you didn't speak before. You are Billingham, the officer."

"To be sure I am! Ha! ha! my clever chap! I thought I should have you!"

"How did you get the noose off your neck?"

"A great deal easier than you'll get it off yours. Bring him along, comrades; we won't trust him out of our sight for a moment, till he is within the walls of Newgate! He is Shucks, the notorious housebreaker; and this is a capture that will do good to all of you!"

Shucks made no remark by way of contradicting his identity. There was a feeling of depression on his mind, and the officers were rather surprised to hear him mutter to himself, "Well, it don't much matter; perhaps the Stone Jug's as good a place as any just at present."

Jack was far from supposing that he left Shucks in any danger, or it would have become a more primary object with him to rescue him than even to proceed to Allan Fearon's house, with the important information of which he was the bearer; and so, while surrounded by the officers until they could find a hackney coach in which they bestowed him, poor Shucks was being conveyed to Newgate, Sixteen-stringed Jack again reached the house by the Thames, and rapped hastily at the door.

Allan had returned some time from that ill-omened visit to Buckingham House, and himself replied to the summons for admission.

"Jack Singleton!" he cried, "is this you?"

"It is, Mr. Fearon. I have something to tell you.'

"Come in; come in."

"No, indeed, I would rather not. Give my best love to Lucy, and tell her that in about a week from now she shall see me; but it is on your account I come now, Allan, for I have something strange to tell you."

"It is calamitous, Jack, I can tell, by your tone."

"I fear it is."

"Then tell me at once; for I fancy I can bear anything better than suspense."

"Have you heard nothing, Allan, cried about the streets to-night—I mean in the way of news?"

"Nothing. We are almost out of the world down here, Jack; but my heart seems to tell me that what you have to say concerns my mother. If she is a prisoner, surely the Regent cannot—dare not sacrifice her——"

"I have been so bewildered," said Jack, "between the different *aliases* of the Dark Woman, that it is only to-night I seem fully to understand her, and that she is identical with the Countess d'Umbra of Hanover Square."

"I know it," said Allan, sadly.

"Then, Fearon, be a man when I tell you that there is a report about the town of the death of the Regent."

"Good heaven! Oh, no, not by her hand!"

"They say so, Allan."

"And has it come to this? Oh, why do I live to know it?"

"And it is stated by one who ought to know," added Jack, "that she is herself likewise no more. Some fearful catastrophe at the Palace of St. James's, to which you know she had strange and mysterious means of access, has alike destroyed the betrayer and the victim."

Allan Fearon clasped his hands over his face, and staggered back into the house.

"I can do nothing with this grief," said Jack; "it must wear itself out."

The highwayman gently closed the door and mounted his horse.

"Now for the road," he cried,—"now for the road! It is in the wild excitement of the moonlight heath, the shadowy lane, and the war against all comers, that I shall find relief from the strange oppression that wears me down. I will procure a certain sum for Lucy, and then farewell, my gallant horse, my trusty sword, and well-tried pistols—the mask, which at many a carriage window strikes with abject fear those who look upon it,—farewell, then, to all; and in some other clime, with the child who loves me, Sixteen-stringed Jack, the wild highwayman, may be forgotten in the sober, punctual citizen. But now to the road—to the road!"

Jack touched his horse lightly with the spur, and at a tremendous pace he took his way through the streets of London towards the Western Road.

The night was dark and gloomy, and one o'clock struck from several churches as Jack Singleton galloped past the corner of Edgeware Road and pulled up for a moment at the gate of Tyburn.

The gate was closed.

"Hilloa! Hoy, there!" cried Jack. "Shall I leap or pay?"

The turnpike-keeper rushed out with a nightcap on his head.

"Pay, pay, if you please," he said, "unless you're another express."

"Another what?" said Jack.

"Another express to Windsor. There's been one already, and he was in such a hurry that he left half-a-crown; so it's as good as cleared the gate for ever so many of you."

"Then it may be true," said Jack, "the strange news that's in the town."

"Lor' bless you, yes! The Regent's dead, and the Duke of Clarence has to be fetched from Eton Lodge."

"I've nothing to do with it," said Jack, as he threw the man a silver coin. "There's your toll, in case I should come back in a hurry. If I do, I'll call out 'Here I am again,' and you can fling the gate open."

"Don't say another word," said the toll-man. "Bless you, I know you; you're on the road. You're the sort of chaps that pay me well. Why, Sixteen-stringed Jack came through here one night, and paid me a guinea. To be sure, I shut the gate on two ugly fellows that were coming after him, and went dead off to sleep, and couldn't be roused up for twenty minutes. Ha! ha! I know how to do it. Good luck to you, Captain, and good night!"

"I suppose," said Jack, "all that means I'm to give you another guinea?"

"Another guinea? Why, bless me, no! Yes, surely you are! Can it be? I haven't seen you for an age! You are Sixteen-stringed Jack!"

"To be sure I am, and there's the guinea. Good night!"

Jack tossed the guinea into the man's ready palm, and spurred his horse down the Western Road.

"I'm glad of it," he said, as he galloped onward,—"I'm glad of it; and yet there seems a sort of fate in it. That was the last guinea I possessed in the world; but I've a good horse, two ounces of fine powder, a dozen pistol bullets, and a dusky night, with the Western Road before me,—some luck will surely come of it."

An immense bank of clouds here came up from the south-west, and the night was gathering additional darkness every moment; but the Western Road was so good a one that Sixteen-stringed Jack, although he could scarcely see his horse's length before him, galloped on for a couple of miles further with perfect confidence.

He passed through the village of Shepherd's Bush, dashed at speed down the little straggling street of Acton, and in the course of another quarter of an hour reined up his steed on Ealing Common.

CHAPTER CXXIII.

THE MYSTERY OF THE EARLY MORNING AT ST. JAMES'S PALACE.—AN EXPRESS FROM WINDSOR.

CONSTERNATION and alarm reigned triumphant in the old Palace of St. James's and in Carlton House, the special residence of the Regent.

Lights were flashing from window to window.

The tramp of the guests and the Yeomen on

duty resounded in the different passages and corridors.

Mounted men were despatched in hot haste to the Regent's two brothers, the Duke of Clarence and the Duke of York. The Dukes of Cumberland and Kent were on the Continent at that time.

The Cabinet Ministers were summoned by the Lord Chamberlain, who, residing in St. James's Street, was the first person in high authority who reached the Palace.

The Regent was placed upon that magnificent bed in the rooms of the Countess de Blonde, and such was the hurry and confusion that reigned throughout the whole establishment, that no one suggested there was a certain impropriety in leaving even the dead body of the Prince in charge of Annie, Countess de Blonde.

The corpse of the Dark Woman was removed to a small chamber at the end of the Titian Gallery, where, with the door merely left upon the latch, it was left, and utterly neglected by every one.

One of the King's physicians arrived at the Palace about half an hour after the alarm had been given.

Hastily opening the vest of the Prince, he laid his ear flat down upon the region of the heart.

All was still, or, if not still, the beat of life was too faint for any cognizance of mortal ears.

"Dead!" said the physician.

This was conclusive in the minds of all present.

Annie burst into tears.

"He did not love me! I often thought he did not love me, but I will shed tears for him. He was kind and good to me at times!"

"Madam," said the physician,—"it will be proper that some official personages should watch over the body of the Regent."

"No," said Annie, "it is more proper for me to do so, since, you see, sir, I have some tears to shed for him."

"But, madam——"

Annie controlled her tears for a moment, and looked in the face of the physician.

"Sir," she said, "by the grace and love of the Regent, this apartment is mine. He is here, and I will stay with him. Who will dare to oppose me?"

"We shall see and hear to-morrow, madam."

Annie was satisfied with this partial victory. She was not disposed to bring any considerations of the morrow to bear upon that night. She was left alone, and she sat down on the side of the bed and sobbed.

"It is all over," she said. "It is all past and over now! Oh, how like a dream it has been! Am I sure that I am awake now? Is it possible that I am here, and that he is dead? Annie! Annie! Awake! awake!"

She clasped her hands together—she pressed them over her eyes—but still, whenever she looked towards the bed, she saw lying on it the silent, motionless form of the Regent.

"Yes," she said—"oh, yes, I feel now, that, with all his—his selfishness, with all his caprices, I did love him! I did love him!—I feel it now that he has gone from me for ever—for ever! George! George! I would give half my poor life to see you alive again, to spend the other half with you!"

It was strange that, notwithstanding all the selfishness and all the want of heart which the Regent had so often exhibited to Annie, that she should love him.

But so it was.

Not from reason—not from reflection—not as a consequence of any of his own acts, did that fair girl love the Prince, but it was from the abundant affection of her own nature. It was not possible that Annie, who, with all her errors, had a kind, gentle, and affectionate heart, could avoid loving any one with whom she was thrown into association.

And so she, worthily and with all a woman's weakness and fondness, loved the unworthy Regent.

And she shed many and bitter tears for him.

Never, for one moment, did she think of herself, or what would become of her. It was all of him she thought—of him she spoke—and for him she wept.

Alas! poor Annie!

She leant her head gently upon the side of the coverlet of the bed. Her fair hair streamed down to the floor, and, overcome by her grief and fatigue, a deep sleep came over the Countess de Blonde.

The Palace clock struck four.

It wanted but one hour now to early twilight.

The Regent had been believed to be sleeping the sleep of death since some time after midnight.

The noises in the Palace had much decreased. By a sort of tacit common consent, all the official personages had put off, until the morning's light, further action and further investigation into the terrible catastrophe that had taken place.

The sound of the Palace clock did not disturb Annie. The sad heart had found temporary rest in deep repose. Now and then, only, there was a longer drawn breath than usual, and a slight half-sob from her breast—but her eyes were closed. Their long lashes were heavy with tears.

Annie slept soundly.

The dull vibrations of the turret clock, as it sounded that hour of four, passed away into the night air.

Then, with a long-drawn, faint sigh, the Regent opened his eyes.

The supposed subtle poison that the Dark Woman fancied she possessed from the laboratory of the alchemist was but an opiate, compounded so skilfully that it wrapped up those who partook of it in such a trance of seeming death that, to all observers, it would appear as if the King of Terrors had indeed claimed a victim.

The heart's pulsations had, in reality, never ceased, but they had been so slow and gentle that the ear of the physician had failed to catch them.

But the Prince still lived, and the opiate had filled his mind with serene, if confused, images; so that now, when its effects had passed away, and he opened his eyes with that deep and long-drawn sigh, a smile began to play around his lips.

Then something seemed to come across him that events had taken place which he had but a dim and painful recollection of, and he partially raised himself upon his elbow and looked curiously about him.

He saw in a moment where he was.

Of course, it was Annie's chamber. Each object was familiar to him, but he was rather surprised to find himself dressed.

He was still more surprised to see Annie in a deep sleep, with her head resting on the side of the bed and half sitting upon a small ottoman which was there.

A faint light only from one of the lustrous lamps with which that apartment of luxury was furnished, shone over the rich and glittering scene.

By that faint light the Regent saw a clock in the room. It pointed to five minutes past four.

The Regent put his hand to his head.

It was not that his head ached, but there was confusion in his perceptions and recollections.

"What was it?" he said faintly,—"what happened? I am certain there was something very unusual."

But memory had been baffled by the opiate, and as yet the Regent could not call to mind the circumstance that had preceded his finding himself lying on that bed in his clothes.

A dim suspicion came over him that possibly he might have indulged too deeply in some strong stimulant, but he did not recollect having done so.

He would awaken Annie; of course that would be the best thing to do, and the easiest way out of all the difficulty. She could tell him exactly what had happened, and then all would be well.

The Regent gently slid off the bed.

It is very odd that people always make as little noise as possible in their movements, even when they move to awaken a sleeper.

Is it that there is something mysterious in sleep which awes the senses?

The Regent was on the floor. He bent down his head, and looked at Annie. The traces of recent tears were only too evident to be mistaken.

"What can be the matter?" he said.

Annie began to sob gently in her sleep.

The Regent spoke to her.

"Annie! Annie! What is this? Annie, rouse yourself! Annie, awake!"

She started half to her feet; she dashed aside the long tresses of her fair hair, and through a mist of tears she looked at him.

The Regent, in slight alarm at the suddenness of her movement, had drawn himself back, with one arm that he had intended to cast around her, stretched out before him. The dim light threw his whole figure into dusky relief.

Annie thought in that moment, between sleeping and waking, that she saw a spectre.

With a loud cry, she fell fainting to the floor, and lay without sense or motion.

"Help! help! hilloa! Gracious heaven! what does all this mean?" said the Regent. "Annie! Annie! What has happened? What is the meaning of it all? Look up! Do you not know me? Look up, Annie! Look up!"

Annie was in a swoon, from which words would not be efficacious enough to arouse her.

The Regent ran to the door of the bedchamber, and tore it open. He passed at once into that small but magnificent apartment in which he was in the habit of supping with the Countess de Blonde, and striding over it, he opened another door, which would take him to the outer rooms, where surely some of Annie's attendants would be found.

A faint red light shone in the room into which the Regent made his way.

That red light came from a nearly expiring fire, by which sat an old woman dozing.

Annie's servants had all left the Palace, carrying with them whatever plunder they could lay their hands upon, for they had fully expected her career was over, and that she would be turned out the moment the Royal Dukes should arrive.

"Help! help!" cried the Regent. "Is there no one here?"

The old woman had not even been aroused by the scream of Annie when she had fainted, but the Prince of Wales shook her roughly by the shoulder.

"Who are you?" he cried, "and where are the attendants of the Countess de Blonde? She is ill, and wants assistance. Wake up! Who are you?"

"The Lord preserve us!" said the old woman, and then she opened her eyes; but the moment she saw the Regent, she fell off her chair, and with two gasps, which appeared as if they heralded her dissolution, she too fell in a swoon at his feet.

"Good heavens!" cried the Regent, "the women are all mad!"

He knew not what to do.

By the aid, however, of a little flickering light that shot up from the fading fire, he could see that the room was in a good deal of confusion, as though a general assault had been made upon its contents.

The fact was, that Annie's servants had carried off everything that was at all portable.

But there was no good to be done there, and the Prince knew that there was but another apartment to pass through, and he would be in the Titian Gallery. He hastily passed on, and opened the door that led into the gallery.

The usual oil lamp, that for the whole night was accustomed to lend some appearance of faint illumination to the air of the Titian Gallery, was upon this occasion burning more dimly than usual, so that it was but a faint twilight that pervaded the place.

As the Prince Regent emerged from Annie's apartments, he was certain that he heard the click of the lock of a door.

He paused to listen.

A strange fear began to creep over him. The Palace was so still; there was such a total absence of the usual obsequious attendance of the various functionaries, who at his call should have been so ready to show themselves; and Annie's apartments were left apparently in the keeping of an idiotic old woman only.

What could it all mean?

The Prince was beginning to feel decidedly and uncomfortably superstitious.

He stood close to the doorway, and looked the whole length of the Titian Gallery, in the direction where he had felt certain he heard a sound come from.

Did his eyes deceive him, or were they—like Macbeth's, when he saw the air-drawn dagger—worth all the other senses?

Did he really see a figure coming slowly towards him, gliding with solemn movements forward, as though it slid rather than walked along the floor of the gallery?

Yes! He felt certain of it. Some figure, such as would seem to be not of this earth, and yet upon it, was approaching him. Who? What could it be?

The Regent felt the cold dew of fear standing upon his brow.

The figure slowly approached.

It had to pass one spot, when from some capricious burning of the wick of the oil lamp in the gallery, there was a narrow ray of light projected on to the wall, which was manifestly brighter than the surrounding dim radiance.

The face of the figure passed that way.

"Linda!" gasped the Prince. "It is Linda!"

It was, in truth, the Dark Woman!

Had she not likewise partaken of that subtle opiate, with a full belief that by its deadly influence she and the Regent would meet together on the shores of eternity? Had she not, as he had done, fallen into that trance of seeming death, from which, even as he had done, she had awakened with a deep-drawn sigh, to wonder if she were still a denizen of this world or not?

And as the Prince had arisen, so had she risen, and like two spectres haunting the night air of the old Palace of St. James's, they both appeared in that long and dreary gallery.

But the Dark Woman's imagination was much more active and mystical than that of the Regent.

When she had opened her eyes, and found herself in the small apartment, whither, as a supposed corpse that was to be disposed of in some way on the morrow, she had been conveyed, she for a time believed, and found a kind of dreamy mystical satisfaction in the belief, that she had indeed passed through the portals of death, and that it was in the spirit that she now revisited the world.

Still confused by the action of the opiate—confused, and with all and much more of that bewildering feeling which was about the mind of the Regent, the Dark Woman arose and got off the table, on which her supposed dead body had been placed.

"Death! death!" she said, "I have not felt thy sting."

The faint rustle of her garments did more than any course of reasoning could have done to instil a suspicion into her mind that it was not death which, for a time, had sealed up her senses.

But the Dark Woman was more inclined to be pleased to think herself a supernatural being than otherwise, and she clung with a gloomy pertinacity to the insane notion that she was her own ghost.

With a slow and stately movement she crept across the floor. The door, as we have said, was on the latch, and she opened it at once, producing only that faint sound which, amid the stillness of the night, had reached the ears of the Regent.

And so the Dark Woman glided out into the Titian Gallery, looking, certainly, as spectral-like as any being of flesh and blood could look. Terror began to freeze up the faculties of the Regent. He would fain have cried for help; he would fain have fled from the spot, but a kind of sensible fascination kept him fixed and silent, with all his senses concentrated in one fixed gaze upon the Dark Woman.

Slowly she advanced.

At times she moaned slightly, and there was an aspect of great weakness about the mode in which she walked, which gave that dragging expression to her progress which had struck the Prince as the gliding movement popularly attributed to ghosts.

She reached the spot over which he stood.

Their eyes met.

"Ah!" said the Dark Woman, "it must then be so. We meet at last beyond the grave!"

The Regent was intensely terrified. His eyes seemed to protrude from his head, and his limbs shook.

"What—what is this?" he gasped. "What is this?"

"Do you not know me?"

"Yes, you are—you were—that is, your name was—is—Linda."

"Yes, George, Prince of Wales, as you were."

"Were?"

"When in life."

"When in life? No—no! Don't tell me I am not in life now? Help! help! Who dare say I am not in life! Help, I say! Guard! help! I feel quite—quite well! I am sure I live!"

The Dark Woman sighed deeply.

"It is in vain," she said. "You and I have passed away from mortal life—from earthly hopes and fears; and now, as a spirit may regret the acts done in the mortal frame, I do, with such bitterness as an ethereal nature may feel, regret that I gave you that potion which has made you what you are."

"Potion? What I am? What?—what?"

"Do you not remember? I poisoned the wine"

"Ah!"

The whole of the scene in the supper-room, when he drank the drugged Tokay, came like a flood of light to the memory of the Regent. For the moment, he almost believed that he was his own spectre.

"Now you remember all!" said the Dark Woman.

"Wretch, yes! I do remember all, but you shall not longer persuade me that I am dead. Help! help! Guard, there! Guard! Hilloa! hilloa!"

There was a gong in the Titian Gallery. It was there put as a curiosity from China; but the Regent's eyes fell upon it, and he rushed towards it. There was no means by which he could beat it, but he lifted it in his hands, and violently struck it against the back of a chair.

The sound was dull, and he changed his mode of operation by banging the gong against the uplifted hand of a statue of the Venus of the Shell, which was in the gallery.

That was probably the first time that a Grecian divinity had ever beaten a Chinese gong.

The sounds echoed fast and furiously through the Palace,—and each one, too, seemed, as he heard it, to remove a weight of alarm from the heart of the Regent.

That gong brought him back to the world, and to all worldly things; and by the time some half-dozen of its alarming vibrations had filled the air of the gallery with a perfect uproar of sounds, the Regent was himself again.

And the Dark Woman felt that she, too, was mortal.

For a few seconds she stood bewildered by the volley of alarming sounds.

Then she made but one rush, and reached that end of the gallery, where was the short flight of steps that led to the guard-room, where usually a sergeant's party of the Yeomen was stationed.

The echoes of the gong seemed to pursue her as she fled.

But the Dark Woman felt that she was alive—of earth, earthy, still.

CHAPTER CXXIV.

THE DARK WOMAN TAKES REFUGE IN THE OLD HOUSE IN FRITH STREET.

THE sounds of alarm still reverberated through St. James's Palace; and never, perhaps, in the dead hour of the night had such echoes been evoked as upon that occasion by the gong which the Prince Regent had set in motion.

All those who had sought repose from the excitements of the early part of the night, and who were looking forward to the morrow as a day which was to produce great events in the history of England, sprung up with disordered looks, and in the course of ten minutes the whole Palace was alive.

But those ten minutes had been sufficient to carry the Dark Woman to freedom.

So distinct and certain had been the impression of every one that looked upon her in the Palace that she was no more, that when she descended that little flight of stairs that led to the small guard-room where the Yeomen were on duty, they, who had each, in turn, visited the little chamber, and seen her, as they thought, lying in death, fled now at the sight of her in dire dismay.

Accompanied, too, as she appeared to be, by that hideous sound of a gong, she presented herself to their startled eyes with all the effect of a dramatic spectre.

The halberts were flung aside, and the sergeant's guard of Yeomen, too terrified to speak, or to place the slightest hindrance to her progress, allowed her to pass them unmolested.

And now that the Dark Woman felt that she, too, was in life—now, too, that she felt the act she had committed that night in the Palace was one which could never be overlooked, since it was a direct attempt upon the life of the Regent—she knew that moments were precious to her, if she would save herself from a dreary incarceration which, surely, would be worse than death.

The thought, perhaps, was not a bitter one that she had been deceived in regard to the potency of the drug concealed in the ring of the alchemist Astorath; but still the more she felt that life was before her, and that neither she nor the Regent had come to an end of that mortal career which was one of such great antagonism between them, she felt the necessity of escape.

She wanted to feel that she was in the open air again, for to breathe the atmosphere of St. James's Palace now was as if she lingered in the shadow of a dungeon.

She heard the alarm spreading from gallery to corridor—she heard the opening and shutting of doors—the sound of voices—the tramp of feet—the clash of arms.

Each moment the sensation of her own danger grew terrible and oppressive.

Then, with a gasp of satisfaction, she breathed the open air. The Ambassadors' Court was before her, and she felt that she was free. Well acquainted as she was with the Palace in most of its internal intricacies, and certainly in all its most quiet and secret modes of entrance and exit, she had no difficulty in soon finding her way into the Park; and there, exhausted, but exultant—for she felt that she was free—the Dark Woman sunk down to rest on that very bench in the Grand Mall, close to which Brads had met his death.

But what was she to do?

What was to become of her now that she had opened a gulf between her and the Regent which never could be crossed? Could she for a moment palter with the fact that she had attempted his life? And what even would Allan Fearon, her son and his son, say to such an occurrence?

The Dark Woman wrung her hands and groaned in agony of spirit, as this reflection crossed her imagination.

Then she asked herself if it would still be possible to carry on an existence in London under the assumed name of the Countess d'Umbra in that mansion in Hanover Square; and along with that question she asked herself again what would be the object of such an existence, since all that she had pictured to herself as its results had now faded away.

What had she to do with wealth and luxury? What to her were gorgeous equipages, and retinues of servants, and the false glitter of an assumed title? The dream of her existence had faded away, and she felt herself a wanderer in a world of cold and chill reality.

She felt now, and for the first time she seemed to feel it without a doubt, that the Regent would never acknowledge the reality of his marriage with her, and the legitimacy of her son.

How dark and drear was the prospect before her!

"What do I live for?" she cried. "Oh, what do I live for?"

Even as she uttered the words, there seemed to come, welling out from the depths of her heart, a terrible answer. It was couched in the one word "Revenge!"

"Yes," she cried, as she sprung to her feet, and looked upward at the black, drifting clouds which were careering over the night sky. "Yes, I that have to live for yet! I can still seek revenge! I can still be to this man, who has blighted by his crimes my whole existence, a retribution and a fate! I may yet cross him in his dearest hopes; and may be to him a shadowy Nemesis—baffling his grasp, eluding his vengeance, and yet ever present to his imagination in a thousand terrors! Yes, I can seek revenge!"

She was silent for a few moments, and then

she clasped her hands over her eyes, for they seemed to burn with some inward fire.

"They call me the Dark Woman," she muttered; "and from the moment that the sense of wrong fell with iron grasp upon my heart, my life has been a crime and a mystery; but, dark as it has hitherto presented itself, it shall bear no comparison with the career which is to come. They may still call me the Dark Woman, and truly will I earn the title. Farewell now all compunction—all shrinking—all human feeling and shuddering sympathies. I will seek revenge; and to him, and to all who oppose me, I will be a terror and a desolation."

There was a strange calmness about her tones and manner; and it was evident that this revulsion of feeling which had taken place in her breast, was one that sunk deeply.

From the time that she had discovered in the person of Allan Fearon her long lost son, the

No. 59.—DARK WOMAN.

tender human feeling which had been for a time quenched in her heart, had welled up again like a clear fountain unsealed in the desert.

Her hopes—wild and extravagant as they were—that the Regent would acknowledge Allan as his legitimate son, had for a time restored her to the fraternity of mankind; but now that those hopes were quenched for ever, the dark and evil spirit rose up again, and with the shadow of its pinions enveloped her soul.

With a slow and stately step she took her way from the Park. She moved like a thing of fate; and, to have looked upon the expression of her face, one would have imagined that she felt a consciousness of the power of evil, such as some bad spirit might exult in as he trod the fair earth.

"Revenge!" she muttered. "Yes, revenge! I can yet live for revenge!"

The Dark Woman was not cognisant of those

events which had taken place in Hanover Square since last she had crossed its threshold.

To be sure she was well aware of her liabilities of visits from the two housebreakers, Shucks and Brads (for of the death of the latter she knew nothing), but that was all; and in her new frame of mind, to sweep them from her path she felt would scarcely be an act of trouble or of difficulty; and certainly it would not be one about which she would hesitate for a moment.

Little did she imagine that a few short hours had made so remarkable a change in the position and prospects of the self-styled Countess d'Umbra.

Little could she dream that one of those important documents which had been wrung from her by the two housebreakers had reached the hands of the Court parasite, Sir Hinckton Moys; and completely in ignorance, likewise, was she of the fact that the whole of London had been alarmed by news of the supposed death of the Regent; and that along with that authentic intelligence had appeared to reach her own home in Hanover Square, that she, too, was no more.

And so she sought that mansion, believing, at all events, it afforded her a temporary refuge, since the Earl of Ilchester, whom she trusted, and Shucks and Brads, who sought to make profit by the secret, and her own son Allan, were the only depositories of the mystery of who she was.

The faint grey light of early morn was stealing over the housetops of mighty London, when the Dark Woman made her way into Hanover Square. She was within a few paces of her own house, when a light active figure, agile as a fawn, darted from the iron railings of the square garden, and clasped its arms about her.

"Oh, mistress! mistress! Is this possible? Do I, indeed, again see you in life? They said that you were dead; but, indeed—indeed I did not believe them. Something told me that you would still come home! Oh! how I have watched! What weary hours!—what long and weary hours! But you are here at last, and all is well again!"

"What means this, Carlos?" said the Dark Woman, in a cold and dreamy tone. "Whence all this emotion? Is it so entirely new a thing that I should be absent from my home for merely an hour."

"No—no; but they said that you were dead! And when that false and wicked man came to the house with the dreadful news that you had killed the Regent, and were yourself no more; and that he, in the name of the law, had authority to take possession of all things, I thought my heart would break!"

The Dark Woman fairly staggered back a pace or two.

"What is this you tell me?" she said. "Speak—speak again. How came the calamitous, but false, intelligence to reach Hanover Square?"

"Oh, mistress, it was cried loudly through the streets. They said the Regent was murdered —murdered in his Palace; and then Sir Hinckton Moys——"

"Ah! that fiend in human shape?"

"Yes, madam. He came and said that it was you who had done the deed, and that he must take possession of the house, and that he well knew who and what you were; and but for that Jack Single-

ton, I know not what would have happened. But he sent him away, and then he went himself to fetch Mr. Allan Fearon, who came here with distraction in his looks, and such despair!"

"Stop—stop!" cried the Dark Woman, as she clutched her hands convulsively. "Too much— too much! Why do you speak so fast? These tidings come in troops. Let me breathe a moment."

"Yes, mistress, yes! But I am so glad that I have met with you, because——"

"Because what?"

"It might not be well for you to go into the house again."

"Go on—go on; you had some more to say."

"Only that Mr. Fearon spoke distractedly, and gathered from me all I knew; and then he said that he would go to St. James's Palace; and he looked so pale and so sad, that I was filled with pity to look at him."

The Dark Woman considered for a few moments.

"Be it so," she said; and she cast her eyes up towards the house as one might look at an object with the certainty that it was for the last time. "Be it so. Farewell! Come with me, Carlos."

"Yes, madam; but——"

"But what? Do you, too, hesitate?"

"No—no; but I was going to ask you to let me put a question."

"What is it?"

"Is the Regent indeed no more?"

"The Regent lives, as I live."

"Ah! how much lighter my heart feels. Now, madam, I will go with you anywhere, and be as ever your humble friend and servant."

"We have but one place to go to, Carlos, which has about it even the sound of safety. I have still the key of the astrologer's house in Frith Street. We will go there."

"Yes, madam; most willingly."

The morning was now making so much progress that the Dark Woman feared to excite much more observation than she would wish, if she did not succeed in reaching Frith Street before the working population of London was on foot. It was quite a godsend to her to see a lumbering hackney coach turn into the square, and she saw the page to see if it was unoccupied.

No one was in the coach; but the coachman, with dogged obstinacy, refused the fare.

"I've been out all night, and I shan't go nowhere—no, not for five shillings—if it was only a mile."

"Here is four times the sum you have named," said the Dark Woman, stepping up; "and the distance is scarcely the mile. Take us quickly to Soho Square, and the money is yours."

"Bless your ladyship; get in, to be sure. I'm sure I'd be happy to drive your ladyship about all day—for nothing—that is, I mean for a guinea a mile."

A very short time sufficed to set down the Dark Woman and the page at the corner of Frith Street. A bright gleam of light was shining upon the trees in the square garden, but no one was about; and in two minutes more the Dark Woman stood upon the threshold of that mysterious house, to which the reader has been more than once conducted in the course of this eventful history.

Amid the various disguises she had assumed, and the rapid alterations of fortune that had taken place since last she crossed the threshold of the astrologer's house, the Dark Woman might well have lost or mislaid the key that would admit her to it, and probably she would have done so, had it not been in a place of much better security than as though she had taken it with her.

There was a small cleft or opening between the stone of the steps and the brickwork in front of the house. It was not larger than sufficient to receive the key, and the opening was rendered secure from observation by a small plaster of London mud, which shut it completely up.

But the Dark Woman knew the precise position of it, and pointed it out to the page, whose small nimble fingers very quickly got possession of the key.

"We are unobserved, I think," said the Dark Woman.

"Quite, madam; there is not a soul in the street, and the windows of the opposite houses are all closed."

"Come, then, thou faithful heart—come with me into the gloom of this house, which may well strike terror to thy young spirit."

"I will feel no fear, madam, with you."

The Dark Woman opened the door. The passage within was dull and gloomy as the entrance to a vault. A cold earthy smell was about the air, and there was a scampering noise in the passage, which indicated that the rats from the cellars deep down below had begun to consider the deserted mansion as their own.

The young girl who played so well the part of a page, shuddered, and clung to the dress of the Dark Woman.

"Fear nothing, Carlos; fear nothing. We are the most powerful creatures in this place, and in time to come I will be feared as well here as far beyond this mansion."

The page did not speak, and the Dark Woman, having closed the outer door, crept slowly forward in the intense darkness towards the staircase.

"Oh, madam," said the page. "I wonder that you will live in such a place as this. Do you not think that far away from London—from England, in some bright pretty spot, where all is peace and sunshine, you might——"

"Hush!" cried the Dark Woman vehemently. "Speak not to me of peace and sunshine; the war of fierce passions is in my breast. It is with the storms of human fate that I shall have to do. Come on—come on."

"The place is cold and chill!"

"We will soon have warmth. Do not tremble. Come on—come on."

They had reached the top of the staircase—that mysterious staircase up which so many persons had followed the starlike light which had led them to the large mystic chamber of Astorath; and the Dark Woman had her hand upon the handle of the door, when both she and the page were startled by a heavy knock upon the outer door of the house.

It was a dull, determined blow with the knocker, as though some one had used all his force to make the sound reverberate throughout the house.

The page clung closer to the Dark Woman.

They neither of them spoke for a few seconds, and then the knock was repeated with the same heavy vehemence as before.

"Oh, madam!" whispered the page,—"who can it be? Some one has dogged us to the house, and we are lost!"

"It is not possible!" said the Dark Woman. "It is, most probably, some idle piece of mischief. I will go down and reconnoitre. Wait for me here; or pass into the mystic chamber."

The knock came a third time.

The Dark Woman then glided down the staircase; and her eyes being by this time much better accustomed to the gloom of the house, she made her way without difficulty to the street-door, and, removing a small sliding panel, which enabled her to look forth, she was near uttering a cry of surprise, for it was Shucks, the housebreaker, who was thus hammering at the door of that mysterious house in Frith Street.

CHAPTER CXXV.

THE REGENT TAKES SIR HINCKTON MOYS FULLY INTO HIS CONFIDENCE AND MAKES HIM USEFUL.

WE left the Prince of Wales beating a Chinese gong furiously in the Titian Gallery at James's Palace.

His Highness seemed to be pleased by the noise he made, for the more he heard that the Palace echoed to the loud, sonorous sounds, the louder he struck the gong.

It brought him fully back to the realities of life, and was so far most intensely gratifying, as it convinced him he was not his own ghost, which had been insinuated as a fact by the Dark Woman.

And soon the Titian Gallery was crowded with all sorts of persons, in all sorts of costumes.

The Regent was delighted.

He lived, breathed, and was a prince again. He saw around him all the dependants upon his state and power. There were all the obsequious ministers to his pleasures; and that dim, and, to him, ugly future, upon the confines of which the Dark Woman had almost succeeded in persuading him he stood, vanished at once from his imagination.

But the Regent did not mean to let any one know how well pleased—how absolutely delighted he was.

He assumed an air of hauteur—of indignation, almost.

"What is the meaning of all this?" he cried. "Here I might have been assassinated, and no one at hand to aid me."

"Oh, your Royal Highness," cried twenty voices in chorus, "we thought your Royal Highness had been murdered!"

The Regent smiled.

"I might have been——"

"His Royal Highness the Duke of York!" cried one of the gentleman ushers of the Palace at this moment.

The crowd gave way; and the Duke of York, with looks of perplexity and concern upon his face, walked up the gallery.

"Why, George," he said, "they told me something serious had happened to you!"

"So it has."

"What?—oh, what?"

"A visit from my brother."

As he spoke, the Regent, who happened to be just then on bad terms with the Duke of York, turned abruptly on his heel, and opening the door that led to Annie's apartments, he at once dived into them, and closed the door behind him with a loud noise.

The Duke of York looked flushed and angry.

"What discreditable hoax is this?" he said. "Who spread the report that the Regent was no more?"

No one spoke.

"And how is it that at such an hour as this every one is astir in St. James's?"

A groom of the chambers approached, and bowed low.

"Your Royal Highness, it was imagined that the Regent had been poisoned in some Tokay."

"Poisoned?"

"Yes, your Royal Highness,—by a woman."

"Ah! indeed!"

"A woman, your Royal Highness, who, partaking of the same draught herself, lies dead in the Palace."

"What woman?—and where does she lie dead?"

"She goes by the name of the Dark Woman, your Royal Highness, and she lies dead in yonder room at the end of the gallery."

"I will see for myself," said the Duke of York.

He walked towards the end of the gallery, and pushed open the door of the room in which the supposed dead body of the Dark Woman had been deposited.

The apartment was empty.

"I thought as much!" said the Duke. "I guessed as much! I don't know what the motive of all this may be, but there is some design in it. Tell my brother that I shall be found at Vanburgh House."

"The Regent, your Highness?"

"No, no! I mean Clarence, when he arrives; for the courier who summoned me to London said that one had been sent to him likewise."

With anger in his eyes, the Duke of York left the Palace; but the Duke of Clarence did not arrive at all, inasmuch as he met with a little adventure which delayed him until he heard that the alarm was a false one.

That little adventure we shall relate in its proper place; and in the meantime we follow the Regent into the apartments of Annie, Countess de Blonde.

The Regent had never felt better in all his life.

The opiate that the Dark Woman had mistaken for a deadly poison, must have been most excellently and skilfully compounded by Astorath the alchemist, to do its work and leave no ill behind it.

But so it was. That medicament had the power to steep the senses in oblivion for some hours; and so to still the heart's action and the functions of life, that it looked like death itself.

But when gone—when the effect had passed away, the machinery of existence beat to as healthful a tune as before; and, perhaps, more so, from the rest it had obtained.

So the Regent felt calm and pleased when he made his way into Annie's apartments.

Now Annie had certainly been awakened by the beating of the gong in the Titian Gallery; but it was a confused kind of awaking; and so strongly was she impressed with the idea that the dead body of the Regent still lay upon the bed in that chamber where, by his side, she had sunk to sleep, that she made no effort, when the sound of the gong awakened her, to ascertain if he were there still, or not.

The lamp in the room was upon the point of expiring, and sent up only now and then an uncertain and flickering light, which was quite as confusing as absolute darkness.

Annie, therefore, did not attempt to cast more than a timid glance to the bed, where so assured was she, in her own mind, of the presence of the dead body of the Regent, that the slightly disordered bed-clothes shaped themselves to her mind's eye into his form.

Annie then ran from the bed-chamber into the adjoining room, and there she paused to listen.

What could be the meaning of all the sounds of alarm she heard in the Palace?

"Is it fire?" she said, to herself.

No, no! It could not be fire, for that word of fear would surely have been heard mingling with all other sounds, and, indeed, rising above them.

Annie remembered that there had been a fire close to her humble home in Martlett's Court, and that the cry of "Fire! Fire!" had made itself prominent above all the disturbance that ensued.

Annie then touched a bell—that bell which, at a touch, was wont to summon obsequious attendants to wait upon her lightest wish.

No one replied to it now.

Annie was alone in those apartments, with the sole exception of the old woman who had fallen into a swoon on sight of what she thought was the ghost of the Regent.

And Annie had got so far before she suddenly remembered that she had had what appeared to her—when it flashed across her mind—to be a fearful dream.

She clasped her hands over her eyes as a gush of memory came to her aid.

"What does all this mean?" she said. "What is this that half baffles recollection, and yet seems to grow each moment, with a something I ought to remember? Ah, yes! I recollect now. I thought that the Regent rose from the bed and spoke to me, and then something seemed to plunge my senses into forgetfulness."

Annie had in truth fainted, and the faint had in time subsided into a sleep.

She rang the bell again.

Again it remained unanswered, and a feeling of the most intense surprise took possession of her; for she could not imagine what had really happened—namely, that her obsequious attendants had all fled when they thought her protector, the Regent, was no more.

But Annie was not doomed to remain many minutes longer in such a state of doubt and anxiety.

She heard a door open and then close rather violently; then there came a hasty footstep.

Annie uttered a cry of joy—she knew well that footstep, for she had listened to it often.

It was the step of the Regent.

"Not dead! Oh heaven, no! He is not dead!" said Annie, as she flew forward, and in another moment was lying on the Regent's breast.

"Is this possible?" said the Regent. "Can these tears, these sobs, be genuine? Is there one who loves me really?"

"Oh, yes—yes!" sobbed Annie. "I thought you were dead; but now that you are alive, I—I ——See what a wretch you are, George!"

"A wretch?"

"Yes, to be sure. Did you not say you wondered if my tears were genuine?"

"Well, well; I see they are."

"No, they are not. I—no—no—they are all false—shams. Don't you see, George, I am laughing, not crying? Oh no, no! not crying; not cry—cry—crying!"

Annie burst into a flood of fresh tears, and sobbed like a child upon the breast of the Regent.

He was touched.

"My dear Annie, I had no idea—indeed I had not—I had no notion in the world that you had such an affection for me. I am alive enough, as you see, although I suppose I have passed through some great danger; but it is well worth while."

"Worth while, George?"

"Yes, Annie; because it has taught me that there is one true heart upon which I can rely."

"Ah! you think so now?"

"On my soul, I do so."

Annie looked up into his face. There was a sweet smile, shining like sunlight through her tears.

"I will not jest with you," she said gently. "I will not gainsay the real feelings of my heart now. I do love you; and when I thought you had gone from me, I felt very, very desolate indeed!"

"Annie, I will never doubt you."

"Did you ever doubt me?"

The Regent slightly flushed.

"No, no! That is, I can only truly say that other people have tried to make me do so."

"Never mind."

"You don't mind?"

"Not a bit now. I am too happy to mind. But you must not presume too much, do you know, George, upon knowing that I love you."

"What do you mean by that?"

"Only that I mean to have my own way just as much as ever, and to be as wilful, and as troublesome, and as capricious as I was before."

"Is that all?"

"Yes; and enough, too, is it not?"

"My dear Annie, you shall be as wilful as you like, only just answer me one question."

"Well, what is it?"

"Did you ever—that is to say, were you ever——"

"Go on. What now?"

"Is it true that Allan Fearon was ever your lover?"

"Allan—my sister's husband? Never! I am not good enough—as I said once before—for Allan; but I am for the Prince Regent."

Annie was hurt that the Regent should revert again to that subject; and he saw that she was. His heart and conscience smote him for any suspicions of one who had shown such genuine sorrow for his supposed death, and joy at his recovery.

"Annie," he said, "I will make to you a voluntary promise that never again will I revert to such a matter, or trouble you with suspicions."

"Very well," said Annie, as she dashed from her large eye-lashes the drops that were still congregating there,—"very well, then, we will not be unhappy! It is getting morning, George, and I shall soon want some breakfast."

"And I."

The Regent and Annie found that in those deserted rooms they were not likely to get anything, and the Prince himself went out into the Titian Gallery, at about seven o'clock, and called to one of the Yeomen of the Guard, who was on duty, "Send Willes to me."

"Yes, your Highness."

The Prince and Annie waited and waited in vain. No Willes made his appearance.

The fact was, that as soon as Willes found that the Regent was no more, as he and every one else in the Palace thought, he made his way to the dressing-room of the Prince, and at once loading himself with all the valuables he knew so well where to lay his hands upon, he had left the Palace, under the full impression that his occupation was gone.

And so, indeed, it would have been, if the death of the Regent had been a reality.

So the Prince found himself on that morning without a valet; and Annie, the Countess de Blonde, found herself without a waiting-maid.

"Come," said the Regent, "we must go and hunt for some attendance the best way we can."

They had not to proceed far, for the servants of the royal building were soon astir. The Regent, however, conducted Annie to the apartments which he usually lived in at Carlton House, and, for the first time, Annie sat down to a meal beneath the roof of that mansion.

The Princess Charlotte still occupied the wing that had been devoted to her; but she had retired to rest again, after being just told that her father was dead, and then, some few hours afterwards, that he was alive.

She had made no attempt, however, to see him on either of those two interesting occasions.

Now, the news of the resuscitation of the Regent came so quickly upon that of his death, that it reached Willes, in a lodging he had for himself, in Bury Street, St. James's, about eight o'clock in the morning.

Willes's position was perplexing.

He had absconded from the Palace, carrying with him the more valuable portion of the Regent's dressing apparatus.

What could he now do? He felt that he had been a great deal too precipitate: get back he must, if possible.

But how?—that was the question.

It would not exactly do coolly to walk back, saying, "I thought your Royal Highness was dead, and so plundered your dressing-table, and ran off; but since I find you are alive, here I am again, just as before."

That would have been too cool a transaction, even for the valet.

But Willes had a tolerably fertile and imaginative brain, and he soon thought of a plan.

He had still with him his private key, which would admit him to the gardens of Carlton House, so he at once hurried there, and opening a little door in the wall, he let himself in without observation.

Willes then flung himself on the ground, and rolled twice over in the mud, for there had been a slight rain early in the morning, and mud was to be had. He then lay flat upon his face, presenting a most deplorable spectacle, and waited in anxious expectation that some of the servants of Carlton House would pass that way.

The valet had not long to wait.

One of the gardeners soon espied him, and raised an alarm.

Willes uttered the most hideous groans as he was lifted from the ground, and any one would have thought every bone in his body was broken.

He was removed carefully into the house, and it was just as the Regent had finished breakfasting, at an unusually early hour for him, with the Countess de Blonde, that one of the attendants intimated most respectfully that he had something to say to his Royal Highness.

"Well, Jennings," said the Prince, "what is it? You can speak. What is it?"

"Your Royal Highness, I have to say that Mr. Willes has been found very badly hurt in the garden."

"Willes—my man?"

"Yes, your Highness."

"Ah! then that accounts for his absence."

This was just the remark that Willes wanted the Regent to make, and if he had put the words into the mouth of the Prince himself, they would have been about the same.

"Is he badly hurt?" said Annie.

"Very badly, we all think, my lady, for he groans and moans dreadfully."

"Where is he?" said the Regent.

"He is in the rooms of the lodge porter, your Highness."

"I will go and see him."

"So will I," said Annie. "Who knows but he may have something to tell?"

"He is sure to have something to tell," said the Regent, "and it may throw a light upon the events of the night."

The Regent was full of curiosity to know what had befallen Willes, for he made no doubt that it had some connexion with what had befallen him.

Above all things, too, he was most anxious to know if Willes had encountered the Dark Woman after that brief interview that he, the Prince, had himself with her in the Titian Gallery.

So the Regent, with Annie on his arm, condescended to pay a visit to the valet.

Willes was in an arm chair, and moving his head from side to side, as though in great pain, but the moment he saw the Regent, he made an effort to throw himself at his feet, as he exclaimed, "Oh! I am repaid for all—I am repaid for all, now that I see your Royal Highness alive and well."

"Don't stir! Don't stir!" said the Prince. "What has happened to you?"

"I will tell your Royal Highness—alone."

The Prince waved his hand, and all left the room but himself and Annie, who still hung upon his arm.

"Now speak, Willes."

"I will, your Royal Highness; but I cannot think of sitting down in your Royal Highness's presence—I will endeavour to stand, by holding the back of the chair."

"No, no," said the Prince, "never mind that; we will waive etiquette for once. Sit still, as you are badly hurt, and tell me all."

"Your Royal Highness is too good. When I was informed that something had happened to your Royal Highness, I flew to your dressing-room for the purpose of fetching a bottle of Hungary water, and the moment I got into the room, I saw two men standing by the toilet table. One had a bag in his hand which he was holding open, while the other was deliberately putting into it your Royal Highness's silver and gold dressing implements."

"The deuce!" said the Regent.

"I flew at them, but they turned, and both assailed me. I cried for help, but no one came to my assistance; and they ran into the bath-room and from there on to some leaden roofs, and finally got down by the small conservatory of Carlton House gardens."

"And you?"

"I followed them; but when in the garden, they both turned upon me savagely, and attacked me, and I fell senseless beneath their blows."

"Poor Willes!"

"Ah! your Royal Highness, one kind expression of sympathy from your lips compensates me for all. I feel wonderfully better even as it is."

"Tell me, though, did you see nothing of the Dark Woman?"

"Nothing, your Highness."

"Well, I was in hope you had some news of her to tell, but since you have not, why it cannot be helped. Keep yourself quiet, Willes—keep yourself quiet, and I will not forget you."

"Ah!" said Willes to himself, when he was once more alone; "I have managed that tolerably well, I fancy."

CHAPTER CXXVI.

SIXTEEN-STRINGED JACK MEETS A HIGH PERSONAGE ON THE WESTERN ROAD

SIXTEEN-STRINGED JACK reined up his steed on Ealing Common. It was long since he had felt himself so thoroughly upon the road as now, when, fully equipped, he went to seek his fortune in the dim and dusky air of that night upon the old common, which had been the scene of so many exploits of those who had earned their reputation as knights of the road.

A profound stillness reigned about the tolerably wide expanse around him—an expanse much wider then than at the present day, since houses and gardens have gradually encroached upon the limits of the heath, and curtailed it of much of its fair proportions.

Jack Singleton looked to the priming of his pistols; for—although to take life was not one of his objects, yet, if hard-pressed, a bullet—although he might purposely send it wide of doing any mischief—became an useful and startling argument.

His horse pawed the ground with impatience, for the gallop the creature had had the short distance from London, had served but to warm its blood and make it more ripe and ready for action.

"Peace! Peace!" said Jack, as he patted the horse's neck. "Who knows but we may have a good ride to-night for liberty, and perhaps for life? How profoundly still the heath is!"

Indeed the stillness was of that character, that one would have supposed that nothing possessing human life could have been found for many a mile around Jack Singleton and his horse. It was one of those accidental lulls both in the air and on the earth when all noises, as if by common consent, seem hushed, and a profound repose rests upon the face of nature.

"Ah!" said Jack, as he looked around him, —and he spoke in a whisper—for the influence of that intense quietude was upon him; "we shall have a breeze in answer to this more than natural stillness before long."

Even as Jack spoke there came a sighing sound over some tree-tops in the distance, and then a few light drops of rain fell upon him.

It was at that instant that the hard galloping of a horse, which seemed—from some of the crossroads of the surrounding country—to have just emerged from the heath, came upon his ears.

"So ho!" said Jack, "we're not quite alone in the world, it seems!"

There was a clump of bushes—within their centre, a thick, stunted-looking thorn-tree—close to where Jack had been standing; and now he walked his horse to the shadowy side of this little cover, and waited the approach of the horseman on the heath.

The sound of the horse's feet had at first proclaimed that it was proceeding at a brisk gallop; for Sixteen-stringed Jack was somewhat surprised to find that as the horseman, whoever he might be, neared that little clump of bushes, his speed sensibly decreased.

Then, in a half military fashion—upon reaching the precise spot which Sixteen-stringed Jack himself had so recently occupied—the horseman wheeled abruptly and took up his station, like a sentinel, on the common.

Jack had scarcely time to make a remark to himself upon the oddity of this manœuvre, when his attention was directed to the unmistakable sounds of another horse galloping upon the common; and in a few seconds, to Jack's still further surprise, this second horseman halted opposite the first, after exchanging a word of salutation with him.

It was well for Sixteen-stringed Jack that the thick stunted thorn-tree grew low down to the ground, or he must inevitably have been seen by one or other, if not both, of these men. Not that Jack really feared a couple of men, even in a close encounter; but all his curiosity was excited by their extraordinary presence at such a spot, and the determined manner in which they took up a post on each side of the narrow roadway across the heath.

Jack was about six or seven yards distant from them, and he stooped low in the saddle, as well to keep his head out of observation, as to listen to what they were saying to each other in low earnest tones.

"To-night or never," said one, in a slightly foreign accent, "we shall have one of them."

"Yes; our friend of the Order of Jesus has given us most timely intelligence," replied the other. "And it is well that we have couriers and King's messengers who belong to our fraternity."

"Blessed be that fraternity!" exclaimed the other, in somewhat louder accents,—"and blessed be the great Emperor, who has promised us reinstatement in France, with all its ancient dignities and properties, when once again he sits upon the throne he has carved into existence with his word."

There was a strange exultation about the tone and manner of these men that made Sixteen-stringed Jack suspect, for a moment or two, that he was listening to a couple of maniacs; but they soon convinced him that if they were indeed mad, there was a method in their madness which made it deeply interesting.

"Nothing can be better," said one of them, "than this plan of confusing and perplexing England by securing, one by one, as the hostages for the safety of the Emperor, the royal princes. The old, mad King, at Windsor, cannot live long; and if the succession is so disturbed in this country by the princes of the blood being in secret somewhere, the Parliament and the nobles will be only too glad to ransom them with the reinstatement of Napoleon on the throne of France."

"It is true! it is true!" said the other. "There are wild and solitary fastnesses about the Pyrenees where they can be held in safety; and, one by one, I would have these princes of the Royal House of England disappear like shadows, and no one shall know their whereabouts."

"You speak well, my friend and coadjutor," said the other. "And to-night, as we have intelligence from our friend of the holy order that the Duke of Clarence is sent for in hot haste from Windsor, we can secure him at this point as he passes, for he will, in all human probability, be without an escort, and without attendants."

"It shall be done!—it shall be done!"

"The saints will aid us."

Jack Singleton drew a long breath. He now perfectly understood what these men were about. Their hearts and minds were by far too full of their enterprise to permit them to keep silence concerning it; and it was evident, from the manner in which they spoke about it to each other, that it was an intense relief to their overwrought feelings to do so.

Jack felt certain, from the fidgetty movement of the horses, that these men were holding their bridles nervously; but whether to charge upon them at once, or wait the issue of what should take place, the highwayman was in doubt.

Not long, however, was Jack left to make up his mind what course to pursue, for both the horsemen suddenly uttered exclamations at the same moment that Jack himself heard the rapid grinding of carriage-wheels upon the common.

Some vehicle was evidently approaching; and Jack's practised ear let him know that the horses comprised only a pair, and that although they made good speed, they were suffering from fatigue and weariness.

The soil of the common was rather loose, and the wheels of the carriage grated deeply into it, so that the speed of the carriage sensibly diminished as the tired horses toiled and struggled through it.

"Now!" said one of the mounted men, in a tone that sounded half-frantic to Sixteen-stringed Jack.

"Yes, now!" said the other.

"Well, gentlemen," muttered Jack to himself, as he loosened his pistols in the holsters,—"now, if it must be so; and since you seem inclined for a little fray, I do not see a bit why I should not take part in it."

Jack heard the ringing sound of a couple of swords drawn from their scabbards, and he felt certain, although he could not see the weapons, that these men were armed.

Jack then flung the bridle upon his horse's neck, and drawing his holster pistols, was about to dash forward, when he heard one of the men say, "Beware, oh, comrade, beware, and inflict upon this English duke not the slightest injury. Look on him as you would a precious jewel, without a flaw, which is to be exchanged in full value for the dethroned Emperor of France."

"I will guard him with my life," said the other; "and should he even kill one of us, the other will take him prisoner, and seek not to revenge the death."

"That is agreed—that is agreed. The French sloop, by Southend, will be waiting for us."

"Hush, oh, my friend, he comes, he comes!"

"So, so!" said Jack, as he slowly returned his pistols to the holster,—"if that's the game, I fancy I should like to see a little more of it. Prevention is better than cure in most cases; but if this should be really the Duke of Clarence who is coming to town, I may have a better chance of serving him after these men have carried their enterprise a little further, since they mean him no personal harm; and if I now attack them, a stray shot might lay me low, and then he would be at their mercy. I will wait—I will wait."

Jack had not long to wait.

The carriage came toiling along. The express from St. James's had reached the Duke of Clarence at Windsor, and he had started at once, alone, in one of the Royal carriages, with only a pair of horses and a postilion.

A fresh pair of horses had been obtained at Richmond, but still it was a hard trot from there to London, especially as the postilion kept up the pace, and it was no wonder that the horses flagged a little on the loose soil of Ealing Common.

The carriage reached the spot of action, and both the horsemen cried out "Halt!" in such startling tones, that the postilion was sure to draw his rein tight, from a natural impulse, on hearing the word.

The man's impression was that he was accidentally driving over some one; and he guided his horses with a sudden lurch to the side of the road.

This placed the carriage completely at the mercy of its two assailants.

One of the men rushed to the horses' heads, and held them firmly.

The other made his horse give two vaults or springs, which brought him to the door of the carriage at the precise moment that a gentleman who was within, let down the window and looked out.

"What is this? what is this?" cried the gentleman.

"Have I the honour," said the horseman, "of speaking to his Highness the Duke of Clarence?"

"Certainly — certainly! Are you another courier? What else has happened?"

"That I'm not able to inform your Highness; but you are my prisoner."

"Prisoner?"

"Yes, for life or death."

It was almost after the manner of a salute that the horseman brought his sword down, until its point rested upon the glass window of the coach.

"Drive on!" cried the Duke of Clarence in a loud voice, as he flung himself back in the vehicle.

The sword glittered for an instant before his face, and the postilion, who was a bold and fearless man, laid his knotted whip sharply on the haunches of the horses.

They reared and plunged, seeming almost to lift the stranger's horse along with them.

All this was the work of a few moments; then there was an exclamation in the French language; and just as Sixteen-stringed Jack dashed his heels back upon his horse's flanks, with a view of rushing forward to the rescue, there came the sharp report of a pistol-shot.

A fearful cry awakened the echoes of the old common, and in another moment the carriage dashed forward at a furious pace.

But Jack had given his horse the impulse, and at a single bound it was in the road.

"On! on!" he cried, as he patted its mane. "Forward! to the rescue!"

But, to the surprise and astonishment of Jack, the horse reared, and, for a few moments, absolutely fought the air with its fore-feet, while it rested almost upon its haunches.

It was in vain that Jack used both spur and rein, and, with words of encouragement, urged the animal to proceed. A sudden panic seemed to have seized upon the creature, and when it did bring its fore-feet down to the ground again, it retreated backwards, snorting and pawing up the earth, till it fell about itself and Jack like rain.

The carriage was tearing along the common, and dimly the highwayman could just see that one of the mounted men was still by its side, and the other at the head of the horse.

Then Jack cast his eyes to the ground at his feet, and he saw at once the reason of the disturbed condition of his horse, and its reluctance to proceed.

The dead body of the postilion, who had been shot, lay upon its back right across the roadway—a ghastly spectacle enough in the dim night-light of that dreary common.

Jack knew in a moment that a horse having once taken fright at such an object, would suffer itself to be goaded to death rather than leap over it, or repass it; he did, therefore, what he would have done some few moments before, had he been at all aware of the true cause of the restiveness of his usually docile and obedient steed.

Jack turned at once in a contrary direction, and galloped towards the country.

The horse went willingly and freely.

Gradually, then, Jack bent upon the off-rein, and left the road for the green turf of the common. He made a wide circuit; but the horse, as if to make up for the loss of time that this occasioned, dashed along now at a tremendous pace.

The spot on which lay the dead body of the postilion was passed at some two or three hundred yards to the right, and Sixteen-stringed Jack leaped the horse over some low bushes, which brought him safely into the road again.

He had lost five minutes—certainly, not more; but he felt confident that the carriage-horses, tired as they were, could not make more than above half the speed at which he was proceeding. It was a race, and he was not unmindful of the nautical phrase, "That a stern chase is a long chase;" but, bending low upon the neck of his horse, and urging it forward by spur, voice, and hand, he tore along, as if upon the wings of the wind.

The carriage was not above a hundred yards ahead. It had not cleared the common, although it was rapidly nearing its confines. In the clatter of their own horses' feet and the grating rush of the carriage-wheels, neither of the men who had attacked the Duke of Clarence, to make him prisoner, seemed to be at all aware of the approach of Sixteen-stringed Jack.

But now, as the highwayman neared the carriage, a new phenomenon presented itself.

To all appearance, the horseman who had hitherto kept up his position close to the door of the carriage suddenly swerved to the right, and galloped over the common.

Jack could not understand the meaning of this manœuvre, but a little later it was fully explained to him. He did not relax his speed, however, for a moment; and he was within some two dozen paces of the vehicle before the mounted man who galloped abreast of the carriage-horses, and by some means seemed to guide them, became aware that there was a stranger upon the road.

Then this man halted. Abruptly, and with great apparent strength, bringing the post-horses to a stand-still, Jack heard the same exclamation, in French, which had preceded the pistol-shot so fatal to the poor postilion.

Bang! came a similar sound, and Jack felt his hat fly off his head as if it had been snatched from him by some invisible agency.

"That'll do!" cried Jack; "turn and turn about is fair play."

There was another sharp report, and that was from one of Singleton's holster pistols. There was another exclamation in French, but it was of a very different character from those Jack had already heard twice, and he saw the horseman fling up his arms, and then fall backward on his saddle, sliding over the side of the horse heavily to the ground.

"I think that'll do!" said Jack, as he quietly trotted up to the door of the carriage.

The moment, however, that the highwayman reached the open window of the vehicle, his horse uttered a sharp cry of pain, as though it had been stung or wounded; and then Jack saw that a long, bright sword-blade was dashed in and out from the carriage window, like the tongue of a serpent; and then Jack understood how one of the horsemen had appeared to gallop away: the fact being that he had got inside the carriage; and having succeeded, as he thought, in the important enterprise, had made light of letting his horse go at liberty.

The royal carriage was now at a standstill, and Jack called out, in a loud voice, "I don't like to fire, for fear of killing your Royal Highness; but if you can secure that rascal's sword-arm, I'll have him out in a moment!"

The door of the carriage was thrown violently open, and, as if propelled from a mortar, out flew the Frenchman with the sword, rolling over several times on the loose sandy soil of the common.

CHAPTER CXXVII.

JACK SINGLETON MAKES AN ACQUAINTANCE WHO PROMISES TO BE USEFUL.

THE state of affairs within the carriage of the Duke of Clarence, previous to the highwayman's arrival, may be summed up in a very few words.

The Duke had no means whatever, in the midst of the sudden attack that had been made upon him, of knowing the number or the force of his enemies.

When the postilion was shot, and when a man with a drawn sword in his hand opened the door of the vehicle and leaped, without the least ceremony, into it, for all he, the Duke, could say, he might be surrounded by a determined gang of desperadoes.

Resistance, then, would have been a Quixotic kind of madness which might only produce some catastrophe that, by a little patience, would probably be avoided.

The Duke, too, was quite unarmed.

The exigency, and the message that had been

brought him from St. James's, had not permitted him to think of anything but the quickest way of getting to London.

And now he found himself to all appearance stopped on the way by those who, if they did not seek his life, would detain him an indefinite period, for the purpose of making a profit of his capture.

"Your Royal Highness," said the man with the sword, "will have nothing to fear, if you are prudent."

"If I had been more prudent," said the Duke, "I should not now be placed in such awkward circumstances."

"That may be right; but we are determined men."

"What is your object?"

"To arrest a Royal Duke of the House of Hanover."

"You want to rob me, say rather. There is my purse, and the sooner you relieve me of your company, the better."

"Your Highness mistakes; I am a gentleman."

"You a gentleman, and stop people on the highway?"

"I am no plunderer. Your Highness can put up your purse. Our purposes are political."

"Oh!" said the Duke; "in that case I have fallen into the hands of some maniac."

The Duke had a strong idea then that he would like to fall upon this man with the sword at once, and wrest it from him, and leap out of the carriage, and take his chance of what might ensue.

It is possible enough that he might have done so, had not the fortunate arrival of Sixteen-stringed Jack altered the whole posture of affairs.

Then came the pistol shot, by which Jack had replied to the bullet which winged its way with such deadly intent towards his head, and then the Duke heard Jack's advice to hold the sword-arm of the man who was plunging the long keen rapier through the coach window.

The Duke improved upon the advice, for he put up his foot, and catching the Frenchman in the middle of the back, he shot him out of the carriage with a speed which produced the extraordinary rolling over and over on the loose sandy road, we have before mentioned.

Jack hastily dismounted, keeping, however, the bridle of his horse over his arm, and made several attempts to lay hold of the Frenchman, and make him a prisoner; but he could not do so in consequence of the extraordinary manner in which he dashed about upon the ground.

He accompanied that dashing about likewise with a series of such discordant yells that the horses of the carriage, as well as that of Sixteen-stringed Jack, began to show uneasiness.

All at once then, after a frantic kind of leap from the ground, the Frenchman lay upon his face profoundly still.

Jack then saw what was the matter.

When he was so unceremoniously ejected from the coach by the Duke of Clarence, he had that long bright rapier in his hand, with which he had slightly wounded Jack's horse; and as he fell, he had the ill-luck to double his hand and arm in some way under him, so that the long keen blade ran right through his body.

It was in consequence of that terrible wound that the Frenchman had behaved so eccentrically upon the heath, and now he lay in the brief agonies of death.

There was a slight, narrow, rugged break in the dark clouds overhead, and the young moon looked down upon that strange scene on Ealing Common.

The faint silvery radiance fell upon the carriage of the Duke of Clarence, upon Jack Singleton and his horse, and upon the upturned face of the dying Frenchman.

The Duke had by this time sprung out of the vehicle, and he looked rather irresolutely at Sixteen-stringed Jack, as though he hardly knew whether to consider him as a part of the plot—against probably his life as well as his liberty—or not

"He is dead, I think," said Jack, alluding to the Frenchman, who had so oddly fallen upon his own sword, the blade of which could be seen in a diagonal fashion protruding from his breast.

The dying man at this moment made a last convulsive effort to rise, and in that effort he drew his last breath.

The cold moonbeams fell upon the face of the corpse, the dead expression of which could not be mistaken.

Then Jack touched his hat, as he said, "I am rejoiced that I have been able to do your Royal Highness a service."

"Then they are all gone?"

"There were but two of them, your Highness, and I fancy that they both now lie dead on the common."

"This is, indeed, a pretty piece of business, to happen within five miles of London," said the Duke.

"It is, indeed."

"And who are you, my friend? By the by, I ought to, and do, thank you very much."

"I am a stranger."

"Yes; but you have a name! You are somebody! Are you in the King's service?'

"No, your Highness; but it has given me much pleasure this night to be in that of the Duke of Clarence."

"By Jove! that is well said; and I won't forget it. Is the postilion killed?"

"Yes, your Highness."

"Poor fellow!—poor fellow! How, then, am I to get to London?"

"If your Highness will permit me, I think I shall be able to direct the coach-horses until we reach some inn."

"Well, well, if you can——Yet, no; I ought not, perhaps, to permit a gentleman——"

"I will do it with pleasure for your Royal Highness. There is an inn close at hand—I fancy, we cannot be above half a mile from it—called 'The Old Hats.'"

"Ah, yes, I know it!"

"There will be no difficulty in getting there a postilion to drive the carriage to London."

"Very well! very well! Let us proceed there. I will walk the distance. Don't say a word about it. I will walk it, if you can lead the horses."

"With ease, your Highness."

"And the common must be cleared of the dead. We must not forget to send some people to pick up those fellows—who have no life in them, I suppose."

"I am certain, your Highness, that they are no more."

"And what became of the horses?"

"They fled across the common."

"I cannot make it out altogether. What do you think, sir,—were they highwaymen?"

"I think not."

"Well, then, they must have been something worse, I fancy."

"A good deal worse," said Jack.

"But you won't tell me who you are!"

"I shall have that honour when I bid your Royal Highness good night."

"Very well! very well! But you can tell me one thing, at all events, sir. Did you come from London?"

"Yes, your Highness."

"Was there, then, any report about my brother, the Regent?"

"The general report was that he had been poisoned by some one; and that a fearful catastrophe had taken place in the Palace of St. James's "

"Who did it? Who do they say did it?"

"Did your Highness never hear of one who was called the Dark Woman?"

"The Dark Woman? The Dark Woman?" said the Duke. "To be sure I have! Some one was telling me some long story about some mysterious personage who tormented George, and who went by that name."

"Then," added Jack, "it is supposed that it was that person who, in revenge for some real or fancied wrong, has contrived to send the Regent out of the world at the same time that, by suicide, she resolved to quit it herself."

"It is very, very sad. The whole country will be much convulsed. Political affairs are not just now in that condition to stand well shocks of this kind. They unhinge men's minds, and throw them off their balance. But here, if I mistake not, is the inn you mentioned."

Jack had had no difficulty, with his bridle cast over his left arm, in leading the carriage horses with his right; and the Duke of Clarence had walked on, conversing as we have recorded, about a couple of paces in advance.

The old inn so well known on the Western Road by the name of "The Old Hats" was reached, and the sound of carriage-wheels brought out an under ostler, who cried out, "Horses for'ard, gentlemen?"

"No, no," said the Duke; "we want a postilion."

"Yes, sir."

"And some men must go on to the common, where they will find three dead bodies."

"The Lord preserve us!" cried the ostler, as, with a full impression that Jack and the Duke of Clarence were two desperate assassins, he ran into the stable-yard and swung shut the gate at which he had come out.

The Duke laughed.

"It seems," he said, "that we are taken for suspicious characters."

"By that man certainly we are, your Highness, but I will arouse the inn."

Jack placed his left hand trumpet-wise to his mouth, and called out, "House! house! house!"

He then, with the butt-end of the pistol which he had discharged upon the common at the French conspirator, hammered loudly upon the shutters of one of the lower windows of "The Old Hats."

This appeal was effectual, and the landlord himself looked out from an upper window.

"A postilion," cried Jack, "for this gentleman, who wants to proceed at once to London."

"That gentleman, and you, too," said the landlord, in a surly tone, "may proceed to London or stay where you are, for all I care. We don't keep a relay of postilions, I can tell you."

"Then," said Jack, in a loud voice, "your Royal Highness will have to go further."

"What?" screamed a female voice at this moment, and the landlord's head was pulled in from the window by main force, and a female nightcap made its appearance; "what did you say, sir?"

"I said that his Royal Highness the Duke of Clarence, since he was treated so uncivilly at 'The Old Hats,' must go further."

"Oh, gracious, Samuel! you brute! you wretch! Get out of the window at once, and go down on your knees to the Duke of Clarence, do!"

"My dear, I——"

"You shall, you villain!—you brute!"

There was a scuffle at the window, which terminated in both the nightcaps being thrown out into the road. Then, as the landlord, probably, got free from the grasp of his infuriated better-half, loud screams and a drumming of heels upon the floor came from the room, the window of which was open.

Another moment, and the door of the inn was flung open, and the landlord appeared, with some clothes hastily thrown upon him.

"I beg your Royal Highness's pardon; but I thought it was only a joke. We are so often knocked up by some of the young gentlemen from Windsor and Eton."

"Never mind," said the Duke. "Be quick now, and find me some one to drive. The carriage has been attacked on the common, and three dead men lie there."

"Certainly, your Royal Highness, and very proper too. Here, Diggory, Jerry, Tom! Where are you, you idle set of rascals? Come here quick, one of you, and mount and drive the carriage of his Royal Highness the Duke of Clarence. Three dead men on the common! Certainly, your Highness; nothing can be more proper. I fancy one of them must be that notorious Sixteen-stringed Jack; for I may tell your Royal Highness that one of my men saw the rascal ride through Tyburn Gate some hours ago."

"Oh, no," said Jack; "I know him well. He is neither of the bodies."

"Indeed, your Grace? Is he not indeed? Well, I thought he might be; but since your noble lordship says he is not, why, of course, he can't be. Oh, you are here, Diggory, are you?"

"Yes, master!"

"Mount at once, and drive to London."

"Yes, master!"

Diggory was in the postilion's saddle in another moment, and then the Duke of Clarence got into the carriage.

"To St. James's. Stop one moment. Sir, will you now tell me who you are?"

"I would like to see your Royal Highness in safety a little nearer London first."

"Very well; let us go on then."

Off went the carriage, and Jack, remounting his horse, trotted by the side of it.

After reaching Shepherd's Bush, just as the carriage began more slowly the ascent of Notting Hill, Jack placed his hand upon the door of the vehicle, as he inclined his head downwards, and said, "Your Highness wishes to know who I am?"

"Most certainly I do. Are you a man of rank?"

"No, your Highness."

"An officer?"

"Oh, no! I am a highwayman."

"A what?"

"A highwayman; and I am generally known by the name of 'Sixteen-stringed Jack.'"

The Duke of Clarence was silent for a few moments, and then he said, "Well, Sixteen-stringed Jack, I suppose you were on the common professionally?"

"I was."

"And I have spoilt your night's work?"

"Not so, your Highness; for I have done a night's work, which will be a pleasant recollection to me when I want to banish from my mind more uncomfortable thoughts"

"Tell me one thing, Jack."

"I will answer any questions your Royal Highness may think proper to put to me."

"How came you to know that I was in danger?"

Jack at once related to the Duke all that he had heard the two mounted men say to each other, while he was hiding behind the clump of shrubs and the thorn tree.

"Well, they are foiled," said the Duke; "and now tell me another thing. Would you, in your vocation as a highwayman, have stopped me as I came across the common?"

"Yes," said Jack.

The Duke laughed.

"Well, Jack, you must fancy that you stop me now. It must be a case of 'Stand and deliver!' So there is my purse, which I am happy to say is better furnished to-night than it always is."

"It seems so strange now," said Jack, "after I have been in such communication with your Royal Highness, to take your purse."

"Never mind that, Jack. Take it, and if ever you want a friend, you can recollect that the Duke of Clarence does not consider a service like that which you have rendered to him, repaid by a chance couple of hundred pounds that happened to be in his purse."

"Ah! your Royal Highness," said Jack, "let me return the money, and keep in my remembrance your Highness's words."

"Keep both—keep both. And now good night, Jack."

Sixteen-stringed Jack lifted his hat, and bowed low on the saddle.

"Postilion!" cried the Duke, "make what speed you can now to St. James's."

The postilion flourished and cracked his whip; and as the horses had for the last few minutes reached the level on the brow of Notting Hill, they set off at a good round trot for London.

Jack was alone again.

"Well," he said, "this is at once the strangest and the most profitable adventure I could have looked for upon the Western Road. Two hundred pounds! Well, that will last my dear, darling little Lucy for some time; and it has the advantage, too, of being money freely given, so that Mrs. Fearon will have no scruple about taking it."

Jack was not disposed on that night now, or, rather, on that early morning, to seek any more adventures on the road, and he trotted quietly back to London.

There was an inn near to Bayswater, and down a narrow lane, where he knew he could put up his horse with safety; and then Jack strolled out into the highway, after having had a couple of hours' good rest, to intercept an early coach which would come from Wycombe.

Jack took an inside place, that happened to be vacant, and was soon whirled into London, where he took up his quarters at the White Horse, in Piccadilly, until the morning should be a little more advanced, when he meant to call upon the Fearons.

In the meantime, Allan had made haste to proceed to his mother's house, in Hanover Square, which he found in great confusion.

The servants were packing up their things to leave, for the report had spread among them that the Countess d'Umbra was dead.

The page had left the house, to watch for the possible arrival of the Dark Woman.

Binks was deep in a bowl of strong ale, with which he intended to fortify himself against all the ills of life that might beset him now that he had no longer the imperious will of the Dark Woman to rest upon.

Poor Allan could gather no satisfaction from any one at the mansion in Hanover Square, and he left it again with a heavy heart.

But he determined in the morning to try the virtue of the ruby ring that the Regent had given him, and see if it would procure him admittance to the Palace, and an interview with, perhaps, the Duke of York or Clarence.

———

CHAPTER CXXVIII.

THE DARK WOMAN RECOVERS ONE OF THE IMPORTANT DOCUMENTS SHE HAD GIVEN TO THE TWO HOUSEBREAKERS.

WE left the Dark Woman in that gloomy house in Frith Street, Soho, whither she had flown, as to a place of refuge which surely would not fail her in that extremity of her fortunes when the hands of all persons seemed lifted against her.

The strange, doubtful, and yet interesting reputation that the house of Astorath, the astrologer, possessed made it a habitation peculiarly fitted for the Dark Woman.

The name and the practices of Astorath, which she had assumed upon his death, constituted now, perhaps, the only *alias* which was unknown to her enemies.

As the Dark Woman, she had been obliged to confess herself; and as the Countess de Launy, and the Countess d'Umbra, and Linda de Chevenaux she had been compelled to appear concentrated in one bodily identity to those men who would now raise the readiest weapon to hurl her from the world.

But as Astorath, the astrologer, alchemist, and fortune-teller, of Frith Street, Soho, she seemed yet to be impregnable.

That house seemed to be gloomy as the tomb but it at the same time seemed to possess the same security.

Hence was it that the Dark Woman, when even she heard those threatening knocks which came to the outer door of the gloomy abode, did not feel the same sensation of alarm that might have been awakened for a moment in her breast, had a summons for admission been made by some stranger to her magnificent mansion in Hanover Square.

Hence had she, with a courage which grew out of the sense of security, taken her way to the outer door, in order to reconnoitre the visitor.

But it was a surprise, and something more than surprise, to her, to see Shucks; for at the moment she dreaded to think that even by taking refuge in that gloomy mansion, she should not escape the persecutions of the two housebreakers, who knew her so well as the mistress-in-chief of "Paul's Chickens."

But Shucks was evidently alone, and that house was gloomy, quiet, and fit for any deed of darkness.

Was it possible that he would venture there in an antagonistic spirit, to place his wit and his prowess against the Dark Woman's?

She hesitated to know what to do.

Her life had been one of so many plots, surprises, and strange encounters, that she scarcely looked upon anything to be what it seemed.

To observe Shucks standing upon the threshold of that house apparently alone—apparently unarmed, and no one within sight to support him in case of danger or emergency—only awakened in the mind of the Dark Woman an idea of the depth and profundity of the plot for her death and destruction.

But this was just the fault of a person who looked at a simple thing through the complexity of a tortured imagination.

Shucks's presence on the threshold of that house may be easily explained.

He had heard over and over again, while in the cavern on Hampstead Heath, from Sixteen-stringed Jack, of the prophetic powers of Astorath the astrologer; and bewildered by the death of Brads, and a sensation of his own danger from the Dark Woman—whose reported death he was as doubtful of as the page Carlos, although from very different feelings—he had resolved to call upon the fortune-teller, with the double object of endeavouring to discover who was the murderer of Brads, and what would be his own fate ultimately with reference to the Dark Woman.

Shucks's visit, then, was simply a credulous one to an astrologer and soothsayer; and the last thing that could possibly have occurred to his mind would certainly have been, that as he stood there, asking admission to the house of Astorath, the eyes of the greatest foe he had in the world were fixed upon him.

The Dark Woman did not open the door, but she glided along the passage, and flitted up the staircase like a shadow.

She could see dimly on the stair-head the figure of Carlos, the page.

"Listen," she said. "You know what you have to do. It will cost you but a few moments' trouble to arrange the silken cord, and light that star-like guide up the staircase, which you have so often superintended. See to it at once; our visitor must wait until all is ready."

The page was agile and active, and in a very few seconds the little simple apparatus—by which, amid the profound darkness of the hall and staircase of that house, a bright star led the way for those who were permitted to ascend—was all duly arranged.

"It is ready, madam," said the page.

"That is well—admit the visitor."

As the Dark Woman herself entered that large and gloomy chamber wherein she had been in the habit of receiving the dupes of her prophetic skill, Shucks knocked once more loudly at the outer door.

It was the last time he intended to knock for admission, for he began to think the house was deserted. He was indeed turning aside from the very step when the door opened noiselessly before him, and he saw his way into the deep, cavernous, and gloomy passage.

Shucks crossed the threshold.

The door closed behind him with an alarming clang.

"Look up, and fear not!" said the page, in those low, sweet accents, which she had so often before used amid the still air of that place, in order to establish contrasts in the minds of those who visited the supposed Astorath, the astrologer.

"A pretty enough voice!" said Shucks; "and sounds almost like Jack's little girl Lucy. Ah, what a pretty star!"

The little bright light shone above his head, and took its way in that strange half-dancing fashion which a slight vibration of the silken cord on which it ran would so easily give it up the staircase.

"Follow! follow! follow!" said the page.

"All's right!" said Shucks; "and I may as well say at once—as I've got thus far—that I've heard of the fortune-teller and wise man—Astorath, I think they call him—and I want to ask a question or two. I'm quite willing to pay gold for the information, but I can't say I've altogether much faith; and perhaps, before I go any further, it might make up my mind nicely if Mr. Astorath now would just say who I am, for I don't think it's likely he can really know me."

The words were scarcely out of the housebreaker's mouth, when he was startled by a loud yelling laugh—which appeared to come from a considerable height above his head; and then a voice which seemed to be conveyed through some tube—so strange and hollow did it sound—called out, "Advance, Shucks—housebreaker and criminal! Advance, evil-doer, and learn your doom!"

"That's me!" said Shucks, quite composedly.

"Advance, Paul's Chicken that was – denizen of Newgate—enemy of honest men— advance!"

"That's me, again!" said Shucks. "Well, you've hit it this time, Mr. Astorath, or whoever you are; so I'll follow this little star in the air, and ask you, truly, what I come about."

Shucks had no idea of danger; he had been accustomed to consider such people as Astorath to be easily accessible to any one who came with a few guineas in their hand; and he ascended the stairs without a thought that he was marching into the toils of his worst enemy.

The star halted at the stair-head; and then the soft low voice said again, "Follow! follow!"

A door opened which showed a bright glow of purple light beyond it. Shucks walked forward hurriedly; but he had scarcely time to cast a single glance around him in the room he entered, when the purple light at once disappeared, leaving him in the profoundest darkness.

Then there came upon the pent-up, close air that fearful, yelling scream with which the Dark Woman was wont to throw the nervous system of any one who visited her for her prophetic skill off its balance.

Shucks was not a very imaginative person, but even he started; and as the vibrations of that fearful cry seemed to search the innermost chambers of his brain, he was certainly better prepared than he had been before to lend credulous eyes and ears to whatever might happen in that place.

"Peace! peace!" said a voice. "Hence, malignant spirit! Away—to the deep-hidden lakes, in endless ebullition, where earth's centre holds all things in its solvent grasp! Away! Away!"

Shucks did not understand a word of this; but the exaltation of tone and the mysterious character of the words impressed him mightily.

"I'm afraid, Mr. Astorath," he said, "that two or three guineas will hardly get you to tell a man like me anything."

"Speak!" said a deep, hollow voice. "What would you?"

"Then I would ask, first, who is it that has been the death of an old comrade and pal of mine? He's dead now; and I never knew till I saw his body lying, ever so cold and rigid, and still with a splash of blood upon his face, how much I should miss him. I want to know who killed him."

Shucks heard an exclamation, which might be of surprise or pleasure, mingled with some slight tone of alarm.

"Did you speak, Mr. Astorath?" he said.

"Are you sure your companion Brads is dead?"

"Ah! you know his name, too?"

"I do."

"Well, then, he's dead enough, poor fellow!"

"And the paper—that document which he wrung from the fears of the Dark Woman."

"Why, you know everything!" said Shucks. "And since that's the case, I may as well say that my idea is that he was killed for that very paper,—and by the Dark Woman, too, who wanted to get it back; but I'm not sure—and I like to be quite sure in these cases; for, if she's yet above ground, and I find that poor Brads owes his death to her, I'll never crack another crib again, but just to get money enough to keep me going, and I'll hunt her up until I get my hand upon her throat, and I see her face looking something like poor Brads's as he laid dead upon that old table at the public-house."

"You say so?" muttered the voice.

"I do say so; and I mean it! Now, tell me, Astorath, did she do it? Was it her hand that slew the poor fellow, or by her contrivance? There—there's my money! I don't see where else to put it, so I fling it on the floor. One—two—three—four—five—good golden guineas. I found them in odd corners of my pockets, only an hour or two ago, when I thought I hadn't a farthing left. Tell me, now, did she do it?—did she do it?"

"She did not do it!"

"Ah!"

"She did not do it!"

Shucks drew a long breath.

"Are you sure of that, Mr. Astorath, or whatever you call yourself? Who but she would wish to do it?"

"You saw the body?"

"I did—I did—and may I never look upon such another sight again."

"Did you search for the paper?"

"The paper we each of us got from the Countess d'Umbra?"

"Ay, that paper."

"I did, and Jack Singleton was with me. He's on the road, is Jack Singleton. We both looked for it, but it was gone—gone!"

"Gone!" sighed the voice; "but you have such a paper?"

"I have; and I mean to keep it. You tell me, Astorath, that she didn't do the deed. Well, it may be so; and they say she's dead, too, but I don't believe that; but, however—however——" (Shucks was getting vehement, and emphasizing his words by striking his clenched right hand into the open palm of his left),—"however, since you say she did not do it, who did? and I want to know if she's alive or dead, too? Come, now, Astorath, tell me that—tell me that?"

"She lives."

"By heavens! I thought so. Now, Astorath, who killed Brads—was it man or woman? Out with the name—let me know it!"

"Peace!—I will ask it."

"Ask it?"

"Yes; it seems hidden in the many folds of mystery."

A sparkling scarlet flame shot up, apparently from the very floor, and for an instant dazzled the eyes of Shucks.

"Speak! speak!" said the voice again.

The flame went instantly out; but then, apparently, quite another voice—for the tones were very different—coming, too, as well as could be judged, from far off, since it had a low, wailing sound, like the distant wind, spoke—"I may not answer yet. There are powers of earth and air which control me; but the time will come—the time will come."

"You hear," said the Dark Woman, then, in the same tones which the conversation had been previously carried on in.

"You hear—the name may not yet be spoken."

The Dark Woman might have her suspicions, but she was as much puzzled as Shucks could be, to know positively who could have been the death of Brads—apparently for the sole object of stealing from him that documentary confession of the Countess d'Umbra.

"There!" cried Shucks in a defiant tone. "I don't believe a single word of all I've heard in this house; and all your tricks, and all your cries, and shrieks, and lights, I don't value a rush, Mr. Astorath."

"Beware! beware! You will do one thing before you leave this house, in order that your question may be answered, you will leave behind you the copy of that same document which you say your comrade was murdered for the possession

of. It shall pass into the hands of the spirit of flame, and to-morrow you will have your answer as to where the other copy is, that you say was torn from the breast of your murdered friend; and where that other copy is, you may look for the murderer."

"No," said Shucks; "no! Who knows? If the Dark Woman be still alive, I shall find her yet in some great, grand mansion, as a countess or a duchess. Oh, no! I will not part with it, except—except——"

"Except what?"

"Except with my life—like poor Brads!"

"You will part with it; you have said it."

A strange fear began to creep over the heart of Shucks, and he passed his hands hastily over his pockets, to feel if he had any weapon for self-defence. For the first time since he had come into that house, a sense of personal danger assailed him; and he turned round several times in an anxious endeavour to find his way to the door of the room.

But the darkness was so profound that not the slightest shadowy outline of walls, doors, or windows could be caught; and for all he knew, he might be in the middle of a heath, or in a cell not six feet square.

"I will go," he said—"I will go. Astorath, I've no more to say to you, and it is not likely I shall ever have again."

"Not likely?" said the voice.

"No; because, you see, I'm going. Where is the door? where is the door?"

"Going?" said the voice.

"What do you mean by that? Where's the door, I say? It is the door I look for. How strange I feel! What odd things I think of, that have not come to my mind for many a long year! All my life seems to come before me—old times, old words, and well-remembered faces—remembered now, but once forgotten. Let me out, I say!—let me out!—let me out!"

Shucks stretched his hands out before him, and moved along nervously for a few paces; then it was almost with a cry of satisfaction he saw the bright little star shining about six feet above his head, and in the direction of some four or five yards in advance of where he stood.

The housebreaker hastened in that direction, and before he could reach it a door opened, and he passed out on to the stair-head. The little star preceded him, and it seemed to send a ray right down towards his feet, so that he was saved from a precipitate rush over the stair-head.

"Farewell, Astorath," he said, "farewell! You may keep the guineas, and I will search out poor Brads's murderer for myself, for never will I set foot in this house again."

He turned to descend the stairs, and had placed a foot upon the second one beneath him, when, with a cry of pain and despair, he clutched nervously and accidentally by the balustrade, and wrenching his head round, looked with eyes of agony into the darkness behind him.

A sword blade had passed through his body, entering just beneath his shoulder and passing out at his breast.

The housebreaker awakened the echoes of that dreary mansion with his scream of pain.

The bright gleaming blade was withdrawn, and oh! the fearful agony of that withdrawal! It seemed to combine in itself a thousand deaths.

Shucks clasped his hands above his head, and with a shriek fell headlong down the stairs.

———

CHAPTER CXXIX.

ALLAN FEARON DEMANDS NEWS OF HIS MOTHER FROM THE REGENT.

WHILE these terrible events were taking place at that abode of mystery and of crime in Frith Street, Soho, poor Allan Fearon was in a state of the greatest anxiety and affliction.

The apparent death of the Dark Woman was a pang to him, such as, considering the really slight acquaintance and communication he had had with her, would scarcely have seemed possible, but that there was that principle of nature in his heart towards one who stood to him in the relation of mother, which comprehended in itself a world of love and tenderness.

He could weep for that poor belated spirit, and he could find in the sad story of her life many an excuse for its excesses.

So Allan wept in truth and sincerity bitter tears for the supposed death of his mother, and he resolved upon paying to her remains all the respect that was possible.

Bit by bit he had learnt what had happened, and he could make no doubt but that she had gone to the Palace on his account and there perished.

But Allan was not long in hearing that if she, his mother, was no more, it was a false report which stated the Regent was dead.

In fact, so soon had the Prince recovered from the death-like syncope into which he had been thrown, that the report of his death was quenched almost as quickly as it had been promulgated.

By the earliest hour that he could very well get abroad, the Prince Regent walked slowly up St James's Street and back again to the Palace, leaning on the arm of Colonel Knox, while Beau Brummell strolled on at his other side a few steps from him.

This was a sort of publication of the fact of the continued existence of the Regent.

The news spread through London like wildfire, and it was considered then that the cries that had resounded through the metropolis announcing his death, had been one of those hoaxes which the literary gentleman of Grub Street were at times guilty of.

It was about half-past ten o'clock when Allan Fearon, with a sad heart, entered the Palace.

Although he had the ring in his possession which the Regent had given him, as a passport to his presence, he had no very defined idea of how he was to make use of it.

He could not exactly consider it in the light of the magician's ring in the Arabian Nights, which had but to be rubbed to summon a subtle geni, who would in a moment have been able to convey Allan to the presence of the Prince Regent.

Unhappily we live in days when the matter of fact has put to flight the genii of the ring and of the lamp, so that all Allan Fearon could do was, when at St. James's Palace, to ask to see some one who was in attendance on the Regent.

That some one turned out to be Willes, the valet.

Allan's message passed through several hands until it reached the Regent's dressing-room, where Willes was in attendance.

The valet did not seem over-disposed to take the trouble to see any one, but certain circumstances had of late taken place that made him feel anything might be of importance.

Perhaps it was a message from the Dark Woman; for Willes no more believed in the apparent fact of her death than did others of our *dramatis personæ* who knew her well.

The valet, therefore, took the first opportunity he could of going to the room into which Allan had been shown by one of the servants of the Palace.

Now, Fearon had been wise enough not to ask to see the Regent—such a request at the gate of St. James's would have been considered to indicate some serious derangement of brain—but he had asked to see some person in attendance.

That was quite another affair, and so he was shown into one of the ordinary waiting-rooms, where he passed a quarter of an hour before Willes made his appearance.

It was no longer a secret now to the valet who Allan Fearon was.

A short conversation with the Countess de Blonde had put him quite right in regard to the relationship subsisting between Allan and the Regent.

He could then, if he had chosen, have told Annie, the Countess, some interesting particulars about Allan's mother, the Dark Woman, but he thought it wise to keep them to himself.

But to Allan even, illegitimate son of the Regent as he was, the valet was prepared to be perfectly respectful.

It was with a low bow, therefore, that Willes made his appearance before Allan Fearon.

And Willes was, in his way, quite a fine gentleman, as the valet of a Prince should be, so that Fearon returned the obeisance politely.

At the same moment the young man, who was always peculiarly straightforward and prompt in his actions and words, slid from his finger the valuable ring with its sparkling gem which the Prince had given him, and handing it to Willes, he said, "If, sir, you will be so good as to show that to the Regent, he will, no doubt, grant me an interview."

Willes knew the ring at a glance.

It was one that he was well aware the Regent had always highly valued; and so Willes jumped to the correct conclusion on the subject.

"His Royal Highness, sir," he said, "has given you this ring as a means of reaching his presence."

"That is so."

Willes bowed again.

"I think then, sir, if you will follow me it will save time, as I will take you to his Highness's morning room."

Allan signified his assent to this arrangement by a slight bow, and followed the valet.

Willes felt certain that the interview Allan sought would be at once accorded. He was not aware, however, of the cause which he, the Regent, thought he had to mistrust Allan Fearon, owing to having seen him come out of Buckingham House.

The Prince's colour changed a little when he

looked at the ring as Willes respectfully laid it before him, saying, "A young gentleman, your Royal Highness, has brought this, and is waiting your pleasure."

"Ah!" said the Regent, "what can I say to him?"

Willes did not think these words addressed to him, so he made no reply to them, but he listened with both his ears.

"What can I say to him?" added the Regent. "I cannot tell him what has become of his mother, for I know not myself, except that she has disappeared, if that be what he comes about; and what am I to think about that affair at Buckingham House? Is he, in truth, a traitor to me!"

But the Regent did not absolutely like to dismiss Allan without seeing him. He might have something to tell him of his mother, instead of anything to demand of him concerning her.

The Regent slid the ring on to one of his own

No. 61.—DARK WOMAN.

fingers, as he said to Willes, "Where is the—the —gentleman?"

"In your Royal Highness's morning room."

"Very well, I will go—I will go."

Willes flung open a door with elaborately gilt mouldings round the panels, and the Regent, attired for the next few hours of the morning, and carrying in his hand a highly perfumed handkerchief, walked slowly towards the apartment in which Allan was waiting.

Willes adroitly opened the door of it, so that the Prince had not to pause a moment; and then as Allan half darted forward, feeling only at the instant that it was his father he saw, and forgetting that he was Regent of England, the door was closed again.

But Willes listened from the outer side.

The Prince chilled the warm advance of Allan by making a side step, which partially interposed a chair between them.

Then Allan sighed and bowed.

"Well, well!" said the Regent. "You have availed yourself, I see, of your privilege."

"I have—I have; but it is not to annoy or harass you with my presence."

"And yet——"

"I know what you would say—'yet I am here;' but it is not on my own account that I seek you—father!"

Allan was much hurt at the cold reception he was getting from the Regent.

"Well, then, what's it about? Speak freely. I have said that I would listen to you, and I will."

"My mother."

"Well, your mother?"

"I have reason to believe—reason to know that she came here last night, or rather the night preceding. Oh, sir—Prince!—father!—remember that she is my mother!—remember that you must once have loved her!"

"Come to the point!" said the Regent. "What message does she now send by you?"

"Message? Oh, none—none. Since she left her own house——"

"Her own house? What house? Where?"

"My mother resided in Hanover Square, under the name of the Countess d'Umbra."

"Ah! ah! And now?"

"Alas! now none of her household nor I know what has become of her. I had a fancy—an idea that she came here. Oh, say—tell me—does she live—or have you again deprived her of what is dearer than life—liberty? Speak to me, father! Tell me what is the fate of my lost mother! Indeed and in truth I sought to do your bidding, and to speak to her of calmness and of patience; I spoke to her of your kindly intentions to her for the future; and I urged her to let the past fade from her mind as a vision that would return no more."

The Regent was softened a little.

"Well, what said she?"

"Mad! mad! I think that she was mad!"

"Ah! no doubt."

"Father! father! you will remember that she has suffered much, and is much to be pitied!"

The Regent paced the room in its entire length twice, and then he stopped close to Allan.

"I am to understand, then, that you have lost sight of Linda de Chevenaux?"

"Of my mother."

"Well, of your mother. I am to understand that you come to me for news of her, having none yourself?"

"It is so—it is so."

"Then I will tell you what I know. She did come here—she came to threaten—she made an offer."

"What offer."

"Of her life; provided I would acknowledge you to the world as my legitimate son."

"Her life?"

"Yes, she said that, on that condition, she was content to lie down and die—in fact, that she would take her own life."

"Oh, horror! horror!"

"But I did not consent—I could not consent. Not a million of lives could make that which is not. You are my son, but you are not legitimate."

"I know—I know! Oh, tell me all! And then? and then?"

"Then she threatened me with public exposure; and she went down into the Court Yard of St. James's, and spoke to a crowd upon the subject of her wrongs. She was arrested, but contrived some mode of escape in the Palace. She assailed me again, and by some means mixed in my wine a drug, which cast me into a sleep which those around me mistook for death. She had herself, too, partaken of the same drug, so that it was thought she was no more. I recovered, as you see; and I cannot, even now, make out the object of her actions in this particular; and when a search was made for her in a small room where she was conveyed as dead, she was not to be found; and that is all I can tell you of her."

"Then she lives?"

"I fancy so, since I live."

"And she is free?"

"I hold her not as a prisoner."

"Sir—Prince—father, I thank you for this much. It is all so—so very sad, father!"

Allan's tears came to his eyes, despite his utmost efforts to restrain them.

"It is sad," said the Regent, "to be harassed in this manner."

"And I cannot but think now," added Allan, "that my poor mother, from long suffering, is not exactly in her right mind."

"I am sure she is not," said the Prince rapidly; "and if you can find her and let me know, I will see that she is, with your assistance, properly taken care of."

"Oh, no—no—no! Not again, father: not again. She has already suffered enough of that. It shall be my care to find her, to watch over her safety, and to contribute, if I can, to her happiness. I will try to find her."

At this moment, the door of the apartment was flung open, and an usher announced—"Her Royal Highness the Princess Charlotte of Wales."

Fair and serene, the ill-fated young Princess Charlotte entered the room with that gliding motion which was so peculiar to her.

The Regent looked confused.

A deep flush of colour came over the face of Allan Fearon.

For the first time he was in the presence of his half-sister; and the Regent felt strongly as he looked from one to the other of his children.

"Oh, Georgy!" said the Princess—who was in the habit of thus irreverently addressing her father—"I thought you were alone, and came to see if you were really dead or alive. People kept coming all night—some to say one thing and some another."

Allan's eyes met those of the young Princess, and for a moment they regarded each other fixedly, and perhaps with some secret natural instinct which they could not have defined to themselves.

It might have been something of that

"Touch of Nature which makes the whole world kin,"

but which specially let them know that they were more to each other than strangers could ever be.

Allan did not speak.

Then, for once in his life, the Regent, who was such a stickler for etiquette, committed the wonderful mistake—for him—of speaking to the Princess of one who had not been introduced to her. It was in his natural confusion that he did so.

"This — this gentleman," he said, indicating Allan.

The Princess did not wait to hear any more; but with the haughtiest possible bow left the room.

"Very well," said the Regent; "very well. Then I have your promise, Allan—I think your name is Allan?"

"I will seek my mother! But will you, too, promise me, father, that nothing shall be done to injure her, or to deprive her of her liberty, without my knowing?"

"Certainly! certainly!—I promise. And now, Allan, tell me what is your opinion of my relations at present with the Princess Caroline of Wales and her party?"

"Her party, father?"

"Yes; the political and social party which she has congregated about her, in order to annoy, harass, and impede me and my Government?"

In truth, Allan Fearon had no opinion upon the subject; and he was far from suspecting that this question from the Regent was a leading one, and merely for the purpose of ascertaining if he would acknowledge to having paid a visit at Buckingham House.

"I know so little," said Allan, "of all these affairs—and suspect, too, that they would pain my feelings to know more of them—that I rather rejoice in not having an opinion upon the subject."

"Very well," said the Regent, with a slightly discordant laugh; "perhaps that is the wisest way, after all; and as for Linda de Chevenaux, your mother, I leave you to discover where she is; and for her sake, as well as for mine, to take some measures to keep her out of these dangerous freaks, which, otherwise, must end in her destruction!"

The Prince made one of those slight bows with which he usually terminated interviews, and then moved to the door of the apartment.

It would have been courtly etiquette for Allan Fearon to open the door for him, and the Regent seemed to think that Allan was about to do so, as the young man moved hastily forward; but it was not with that intention, and Allan said anxiously, "Ah, father, am I never more to see you, that you take with you the ring which has this day procured me admission to the Palace."

There was a certain air of reluctance on the part of the Regent, as he slowly slid the ring from his finger; and it was but too evident to Allan Fearon that the first gush of natural affection which had prompted the Regent on their former interview to be tender and regardful of him, had passed away.

It was but the passing tribute which human nature had paid to one of the closest of human relationships. It said no more than that this cold, selfish Prince was, after all, nothing more than a man; but a little familiarity with those first yearnings of affection had diluted them with worldliness and selfishness, until they scarcely existed.

The Regent handed him the ring in silence, and Allan took it without a word. Then when the Prince had passed away, and even his footsteps no

longer sounded upon the ears of his son, Allan sighed deeply, and as he cast his eyes upon the ring, he said, "Not often, indeed, not often, will I avail myself of this privilege. I have warmer hearts to cling to than even this princely one of my father's."

Then Allan saw that some one was at the door as if waiting for his departure, and he walked slowly out of the room, and left the Palace of St. James's.

He had received no satisfaction from his visit; and there had been an air of truthfulness about the narration that had been given him by the Regent, which convinced him that the fate of his mother was unknown in the royal residence.

Where, then, should he go to seek her? By what possible means, amid all the mysteries that surrounded her existence, could he hope to discover her, even were she still in life?

Was it not, indeed, more probable that, rendered desperate by the complete and utter failure of all her plans and schemes, her hopes and wishes, she had laid violent hands upon herself, and left a world which no longer presented to her an object worth living for.

Thus revolving sadly and painfully the events of the past four and twenty hours, Allan almost unconsciously bent his steps towards Hanover Square again.

The door of the house was open, and men were passing in and out, while, as Allan lingered for a moment, he saw an auctioneer's bill put up outside, to signify that the house was to let furnished.

The agent in Bond Street had received notice that his tenant had disappeared; and that costly establishment of the Countess d'Umbra's, which had sprung into existence as if by the wave of a magician's wand, scattered again, so to speak, into its elements, and silence and gloom reigned in the closed up apartments of the brilliant mansion.

CHAPTER CXXX.

THE DARK WOMAN IS SATISFIED OF THE SAFETY OF AN IMPORTANT DOCUMENT.

SHUCKS did not utter another word or cry after that fearful fall down that cavernous-looking, dark, and dismal staircase, at the house in Frith Street.

It had a fearful sound with it, the descent of that dead, or apparently dead, body down those stairs, which seemed in their dim and black profundity to be but the thoroughfare to some deep pit, dug to the very centre of the earth.

Down! down! with a hideous plunge, as though some powerful impulse induced the senseless clay to seek the lowest possible depth it could merit, went the housebreaker; and then, as if he had been swallowed up in the thick washing waters of some sea of ink, he disappeared from before the eyes of the Dark Woman.

She clung to the topmost balustrade of the staircase, and glared into the deep obscurity down which the housebreaker had plunged.

Could any mortal eyes have looked into her face at that moment, what a mass of terrible human passions would they have observed!

With her teeth clenched tightly, and lips so firmly compressed that no particle of colour and no remains of ordinary shape were left about them, the Dark Woman, with eyes that flamed with fiery passion, seemed as though she needed no light to enable her to pierce the deep darkness of that staircase and passage beyond.

But there was a more human and a more feeling heart than that of Linda de Chevenaux, which throbbed in unison with the terrible incident that had just lent a new stain of blood to that gloomy house.

That was the young girl who played the part of the page to the Dark Woman.

With screams, sobs, and cries of affright and sympathy, this young girl, now that she had recovered from the first stunning shock which the deliberate murder had given her, clung to the dress of the Dark Woman.

"Oh, mercy, madam! Mercy!—mercy! Save him! Oh, spare him, for the love of heaven! Mercy!—mercy!"

The Dark Woman heard her as though she heard her not. By not the least movement—by not the lightest word did she signify that she had any appreciation of that frantic appeal to her compassion.

Perhaps she really only heard the sound, without taking in the sense, of the page's words.

Perhaps she was really too much engrossed with a mental contemplation of the deed she had done to be capable just then of comprehending any external sight or sounds beyond it.

But the page still frantically hugged at the apparel of the Dark Woman, and still, with sobs, and moans, and cries, tried to awaken within her heart some human feeling.

"Oh, madam, madam! In mercy do something! You know so much—you possess such wonderful secrets, that even now, although that dreadful sword seemed to pass through his heart, surely you may save him! Help!—oh, help! In mercy, madam, help him!"

The Dark Woman shuddered.

All was still below.

There had come echoing up the staircase a strange faint sigh—such a sigh as might have heralded some poor soul to judgment; and then there had sounded much more lightly than before the fall down some lower depth still than to the passage of the house of some body.

The Dark Woman was puzzled.

"A light! a light!" she cried. "Carlos, a light!"

"Yes, madam—oh, yes! You will try to help him now, I am sure! Whatever he has done to you, you will try to save him!—forgiving him for any injury that he has committed, you are satisfied now, dear madam, by what he has suffered."

The Dark Woman, for the first time, seemed suddenly to be aware that the young page was pleading and entreating for the life of the housebreaker.

"Ah!" she cried; "what is all this? What can prompt you? What can you mean by talking to me in this strain?"

"Dear madam, I pity that poor wounded man—that poor dead man, it may be. I feel sure that he must have done something very wicked to you, or you would not have acted as you have; but

now, madam, now if you will be so good and so merciful——"

"What?" yelled the Dark Woman.

The page repeated the words with an air of shrinking apprehension.

"I said, dear mistress, if you would be so good and so merciful as to spare him now—as to try to help him—as to—to—to——"

"Peace!" interposed the Dark Woman; "you know not what you ask—you know not what you say!"

She struck her breast as she spoke.

"No, no," she added, "henceforth there is no mercy here—none! none! It is war—war to the death with all humanity! A light!—a light, I say!"

The trembling page made her way into the large room where the astrologer received his dupes; and from a deep closet within it—which was of material assistance in producing some of those magical effects which astonished and alarmed the visitors of the supposed Astorath—she soon procured a small wax taper, which was lit by chemical means then little understood, although now too common to be longer a mystery.

The little flame of the wax taper shed a dim halo of light about it.

The page's hand trembled so as to confuse this halo still more than it would naturally be confused and confusing. It took in the pale sad face of the young girl, and showed the tears, which were still upon her cheeks.

"Quick!" cried the Dark Woman. "Quick, I say!"

She snatched the light from the hands of the trembling girl, and then she glided down the staircase after the dead body.

The page stood at the top of the stairs, and with clasped hands and straining eyes strove to pierce the profound depths below.

To follow the Dark Woman, unless ordered so to do, would have been an offence that her courage was not equal to; and she could only fix her eyes upon the little sparkle of light which the wax taper gave forth as the Dark Woman descended lower and lower with it.

"Alas! alas!" she murmured. "What a terrible fate is mine, to be a witness to such deeds; and yet what can I do? What ought I to do? This mistress of mine was kind to me when I had not a friend in all the world beside. Can I—ought I to betray her? Oh, heaven, take this poor heart into your good keeping, and guide it what to do!"

The young girl knelt at the head of the stairs, and clasped her small, delicate hands over her face.

The Dark Woman descended to the hall.

Step by step as she went she held the little taper-light low down, lest she should come suddenly upon the body of the murdered man.

But she saw nothing but some dark spots here and there upon the stairs.

Well she could guess what they were, and she muttered her conviction upon the subject.

"Blood!—blood! I would that I could so tread upon the heart's blood of all my foes!"

She reached the hall, and then a sudden accession of fear came over her.

The body was not there!

The Dark Woman even went the length of uttering a short, sharp cry of dismay.

The page above heard that cry, and echoed it by a scream.

"Hush! hush!" then said the Dark Woman. "What is amiss?—whence that scream?"

"It was I, dear madam."

"Peace, then, or dread my displeasure! Peace, I say!"

The page was silent.

The Dark Woman went the whole length of the hall to the outer door; and as she did so, she held the taper-light low down—so low down, indeed, as almost to trail it along the floor.

There were no spots of blood there to be seen.

There was no trace of the passage of the wounded man in that direction.

A feeling of great relief came over the Dark Woman.

Now, there were two doors opening from that dismal hall into apartments, both of which were immediately under the large reception room above, but the doors were securely locked.

The Dark Woman stood in the middle of the passage; and now, instead of holding the light low down to look for the track of the murdered man, she elevated it above her head, so as to cast, although but faintly, as many rays around her as she could, and make them penetrate the darkness as far as possible.

Right away at the further end of the passage the Dark Woman heard a slight sound.

It was like the sound of a door that was closed, but not fastened, and which by the influence of some disturbed air would make a slight noise as it closed and opened, perhaps, through the space of a quarter of an inch.

The Dark Woman understood that noise in a moment.

There was a door at the further end of the passage which led deep down to the lower regions of the house—to a series of gloomy, dismal kitchens and cellars, into which she had never penetrated, and which for many a long year had been abandoned to the rat, the spider, and the toad.

It was the door at the top of the dark and narrow staircase that led down into this gloomy and deserted region that was moving slightly.

The Dark Woman turned towards it.

The door had been secured by a bolt on the side next to the passage, but it opened downwards to the staircase.

That bolt was wrenched from its place; the socket was torn away from its old, rusty fastenings; and the door was on the swing.

The Dark Woman lowered the light, and looked down at the topmost stair that led below. On it there was one broad plash of blood.

Then she knew all.

The dead, or dying, housebreaker had fallen with all his might against that door, and the old rusted bolt had given way.

He had had another terrible fall down those gloomy stairs that led to the long disused portion of the house.

Should she follow him there?

That was the question; and well might even the Dark Woman, with all her stern resolves, and with all her fearlessness, shrink from a descent into what looked like some fathomless and pestiferous pit inhabited by she knew not what.

Strange noises came up to her upon the damp and darksome air from below.

The rush of the feet of the rats—the noisy contention of the vermin one with another—and now and then a low, strange, half-croaking, half-hissing sound, as if from out the darkness and the neglect of that lower region there had evolved existences in the shape of loathsome reptile things, it would be a terror to encounter.

The Dark Woman drew back.

She closed the door.

"Be it so," she said. "Let him lie there and rot. Let him lie there and be food for the rat, and the toad, and the newt, since it must be so. And yet I would fain myself have become possessed of that paper which he has about him, and which was extorted from me at the house in Hanover Square; but let it rot on his heart. Let it rot and decay in the blood that oozes from his wound! He is dead—he is dead! and that document is dead with him!"

She opened the door again, and projected her head into the intense darkness.

She heard, or thought she heard, an odd noise, as if some one—man or beast—was sucking moisture from some fruit, or what else? Blood from some opened vein!

The Dark Woman even shuddered.

Then she stepped back, and again closed the door.

"Be it so!—be it so! Rest there and rot!"

She felt in a pocket of her dress, and produced a bunch of keys of various sizes. There was a lock on the door, but the keys she had with her were all too small to fit it. Then she went to the back of the street-door, where on a hook there hung various keys all encrusted with rust, and she tried them successively on the lock of the door she now wished to fasten—never to open again, if that were possible.

With a harsh, grating noise, she managed at last to turn one in the lock.

The door was fast.

The Dark Woman picked up the taper-light which she had placed on the floor, for she had been compelled to take two hands to the rusted key in the rusted lock, and she moved towards the staircase.

At that moment she thought she heard a slight rushing sound on the stairs, which was more like a gust of wind than anything else.

What could it be?

"Carlos! Carlos!" cried the Dark Woman. "Is that you upon the stairs?"

There was no answer.

The Dark Woman slowly ascended. She saw nothing of the page; but upon passing on, which she now did with a firm and stately step into the large reception-room, she saw lying on one of the deep window-seats the page.

"Sleeping!" said the Dark Woman, as she passed the taper-light across the eyes of the apparently slumbering girl. "Sleeping after so much terror! Oh, happy privilege of youth and—and innocence!"

The Dark Woman passed slowly on, and opening the small door at the extremity of that apartment, which was concealed by some of the heavy cloth hangings which lent such solemnity to the place, she passed away into the laboratory of the astrologer and alchemist.

Then the apparently slumbering page sprung to her feet, and, in a crouching attitude, listened intently.

'The bond is broken,' she whispered faintly to herself.—'the bond is broken. I can no longer love or serve this dreadful woman.'

There came a slight sound, like the sound of some metallic substance, against a vase of glass.

The page shrunk down in apparent sleep again.

In a moment more, the cloth curtain that shrouded the doorway through which the Dark Woman had passed was pushed aside, and she looked out into the large room.

Some bright red light was burning in the laboratory, which streamed into the reception-chamber, and presented the form of the Dark Woman, in bold and clear relief, to the half-opened eyes of the page.

"Carlos! Carlos!"

The page did not reply.

"She really sleeps!" added the Dark Woman, as she advanced to the window-seat on which the page was lying, and shook her by the shoulder.

"Carlos, awake! awake!"

"Ah!—help! Oh, it's you, dear mistress!"

"What is the matter! Why did you cry for help?"

"A dream! a dream! Oh, such a fearful dream!"

"Heed it not — heed it not. I would rest awhile; and it is for you to keep good and faithful watch, since we are alone in this house."

"Yes, madam."

"Bring me the drink I taught you how to compound from the two vials."

"Directly, madam."

The Dark Woman passed through the laboratory, and by a door opposite to that at which she had entered it, she made her way into a bed-chamber, in which—while inhabiting the astrologer's house previously—she had snatched such repose as her agitated mind would at times permit her to take.

There were two vials in the laboratory—one of blue glass and the other white—from which the page had, after instructions from the Dark Woman, been in the habit of pouring certain quantities into a glass of pure water for her.

The page was aware that some sleeping principle was resident in one of those liquids; and, at a guess, she thought that it was in the blue glass that it was to be found.

The young girl poured, then, double the usual quantity of liquid from that blue vial into the water, that she had been instructed by her imperious mistress to use.

The draught was not materially different in colour to what it usually was, and it was very improbable that, at night, it would look at all so

The young girl was very pale, but she shed no tears now; for she had made a determination, and she felt that tears would not assist her in carrying it out.

She had crept down the staircase after the Dark Woman when the latter was searching in the passage of the house for the dead body of the housebreaker.

It was the sudden and rapid flight of the page up these stairs again which had made the strange rushing sound that reached the ears of the Dark Woman just previous to her own ascent.

And the page had heard all and seen all.

She knew perfectly well what had become of the murdered man, and she had seen how the Dark Woman had closed and locked the door of the lower regions of that dismal house upon him.

But for all that—for all the dreadful wounds she had seen him receive, there was a something in the heart of the page which whispered that he might still be alive.

And so that young girl—almost a child as she was—had come to a determination.

It was that she would seek the man who had been so foully treated, and at all events satisfy herself if he were dead or alive.

The page, therefore, looked pale, but shed no more tears, as she made her way to the chamber in which the Dark Woman waited for the potion, without which, or some equally potent drug, she had not now, for a long time, tasted repose.

The bed-chamber was in a state of semi-darkness, for the lamp which the Dark Woman had lit was shaded by a green glass, which shed that colour about it upon any object.

"Here is the drink, madam."

"That is well. You have properly compounded it?"

"Yes, madam."

"I can trust you, Carlos?"

"Yes, madam."

The Dark Woman drank off the potion.

"And what did you dream, Carlos, that so attracted your young imagination?"

"Madam, it was a terrible dream, but so like reality, that even now I can almost cheat myself with a belief that it really happened."

"What was it?"

"I thought that some one came here with some evil intentions, madam, and that you murdered him at the head of the stairs!"

"Ah!"

"Yes, madam; and that then he fell—oh, with such a sickening sound!—right down—down——"

"Yes — down! down!" murmured the Dark Woman. "Be it so—lie there and rot, together with—with the paper—the paper. Oh, sleep, I bless thee!—sleep!—sleep!"

The page bent over her, and looked into her eyes. For a moment there was just a glisten through the eyelids, and then they closed completely.

The Dark Woman slept.

"Now!" said the page—"now, heaven! oh, good kind heaven, aid me and protect me, for surely I am about work which God will approve!"

She had seen the Dark Woman place the key of the door through which the housebreaker had fallen, in the pocket of her dress, and it was now the first object of the young girl to get quiet possession of that key.

CHAPTER CXXXII.

SIR HINCKTON MOYS CONCOCTS THE CONCLUSION OF HIS PLOT.

"My dear Lady Sunningham," said Sir Hinckton Moys, as he sat with the Marchioness of that name in one of the private apartments of Buckingham House,—"my dear Lady Sunningham, all goe-well, believe me; and you will, I feel assured, be soon again installed in St. James's Palace as the favourite and adviser of the Regent."

"I hope so; but now that by one means or another we all know who this young man Allan Fearon is, I own to some doubts."

"Doubt not, I beg of you."

"But listen, Sir Hinckton—do you think it possible that the Regent will ever believe anything amiss of his own son?"

"Yes, most assuredly."

"But even you tell me that, notwithstanding he saw him, with his own eyes, come out of Buckingham House, there was nothing like irritation about him on the subject."

"That is true, my dear Marchioness, but all who know anything of the Regent, know that public matters do not affect him nearly so much as private ones."

"Granted; but——"

"One word—pray hear me out. The Regent would think but little of Allan Fearon being engaged in all the intrigues of Buckingham House, provided he in no way interfered with his private pleasures and feelings, you see?"

"Well, well, I suppose I do."

"Then, my dear Marchioness, in order utterly to ruin Fearon, and Annie, Countess de Blonde, at one blow, we have only to carry out, now, the remainder of our scheme."

"Jealousy?"

"Exactly; and such abundant proof as shall be anything but

"'Light as air.'

It shall be tangible to the senses, I assure you; and upon it we shall found four conclusions."

"Four conclusions, Moys?"

"Yes. First, the disgrace of the fair Countess de Blonde!"

"Good!"

"Then the reinstatement of the fair Marchioness of Sunningham as favourite of the Regent."

"Better still!"

"Then a breach between the Prince and this illegitimate son of his, that shall never be repaired."

"Very well."

"And then the appointment of one Sir Hinckton Moys as Lord Chamberlain."

"Very fairly put, Moys, I must say; and you are revenged on Allan Fearon."

"I am. And you are revenged on Annie Gray."

"I shall be."

"Most assuredly; and I do but trouble you, upon this occasion, to write a note which should appear to be in a lady's hand. Our masculine formation of letters can never be converted into the delicate up and down strokes which are so truly feminine."

"I'm quite at your service, Sir Hinckton Moys, in this little affair. It would be absurd of me, now, to shrink from anything which would carry out our objects. We both go upon honour; and, as we neither of us possess any——"

Sir Hinckton Moys elevated his eyebrows as he said, "Really, Lady Sunningham, we are getting quite Arcadian in our simplicity, and candid to a fault."

"I was going to say," added Lady Sunningham, "only you will interrupt me so, that we neither of us possess any particular scruples in regard to the means by which we carry out desirable ends."

"I accept the correction," replied Sir Hinckton Moys, with a bow. "And now what I want are two letters, which are supposed to pass between two ladies who will know nothing of either of them."

"I am at your service. Now, what am I to say?"

The Marchioness of Sunningham took a pen and drew some writing materials towards her. She looked inquiringly into the face of Sir Hinckton Moys, who, after a few moments, during which he either was or pretended to be in profound thought, dictated as follows:—

"MY DEAR SISTER,

"Send Allan to me at once, for I am quite certain there is something amiss, and that the Regent no longer believes that he is your husband and not my—what shall I call him? Let him come to me on receipt of this. I think it safer to address you than him. Willes will let him in as usual, and our dear friend Hanger will keep watch over the Regent.

"Believe me to be,
"Your own,
"ANNIE."

The Marchioness of Sunningham looked up into the face of Sir Hinckton Moys when this precious epistle was concluded, and a faint smile played over the features of the villanous courtier.

"You excel the proverb very much," said the Marchioness.

"What proverb?"

"That which talks of killing two birds with one stone—for here you make a wholesale slaughter of four."

"Marchioness, you are as witty as you are wise; and I will trouble you now to address this letter to Annie's sister, Mrs. Allan Fearon. I will see to its safe delivery."

"It is done."

"That is well. And now for the second epistle."

The Marchioness drew another sheet of paper towards her, and again awaited the diabolical suggestions of Sir Hinckton Moys.

He dictated:—

"Sister!—sister! come to me at once, if you have any remembrance of our young days, or any feeling for one who has ever been kind and good to you, or striven to be so. Come to me at once. My home is the last house in Surrey Street, Strand, leading down to the river. Speak to no one! Show no one this letter, but come to me at once, promptly and secretly, if you have a particle of love left in your heart for your poor sister

"MARIAN."

"Is that enough?" said the Marchioness.

"It is, Marchioness; and, by this time to-morrow, I have not the least doubt I shall be able to bring you some amusing intelligence of a little game of cross purposes at St. James's Palace."

The Marchioness of Sunningham was well enough contented. She saw nothing more in all this plotting and contriving, and writing of villanous epistles in other people's names, than the ordinary practice of a Court where intrigue was the order of the day, and everything was considered fair for love and power.

It was about five o'clock in the afternoon when Sir Hinckton Moys possessed himself of these two precious epistles; but his plans were by no means completed, and he had yet something of importance to do before even he would venture to see the Regent.

Moys knew perfectly well that he could rely upon his valet, who, from some little circumstances connected with his character for probity, might well despair of ever getting any other place if he should uncouple his fortunes from those of his villanous master, Sir Hinckton Moys.

It was to this unscrupulous servitor that Moys now repaired for assistance; and without imparting to him more than was absolutely necessary, he engaged him thoroughly in his plot against the peace of the Regent, and the position and prospects of the two or three other persons against whom he felt such bitterness of hatred and animosity.

The valet thought that he was making great progress in his master's favour, when he was called, for the first time, very familiarly by his surname. To be sure, that surname was not a pleasant one, nor suggestive of agreeable ideas, for it happened to be Shambles. Nevertheless, the valet felt pleased when Sir Hinckton, flinging himself into an easy chair at his chambers, called out to him, "Shambles, I want to speak to you upon a matter of some consequence."

"Quite at your service, Sir Hinckton, as in duty bound."

"I shall want two letters delivered to-night, with certainty, secrecy, and despatch, and both at the same hour."

The valet shrugged his shoulders.

"And I may want a couple of men, who, for a few guineas, will not scruple to stop a lady in a carriage, or a man on foot. Come, now, Shambles, among all your old acquaintances, can you not find me a couple of fellows, who, when they have earned the money, will manage to hold their tongues?"

"I think, Sir Hinckton," said the valet, "that London is such a great and noble metropolis, that anything may be found you wish for, provided you—you——"

"Provided I like to pay for it, you mean?"

"Just so, sir."

"Then you will find me the persons you mention: and as to the delivery of the letters—one of them you will take yourself, and the other, I fear, must be trusted to a stranger."

"That is a pity, Sir Hinckton; and, perhaps, if I knew more, I might be able to suggest——"

The valet looked very humble and self-deprecatory, and Sir Hinckton, for a few moments, appeared to be thinking.

"Look you here," he then said, "Shambles! I want a lady to call on a gentleman while that gentleman is out; and I want a gentleman to call on a lady under the same circumstances; or I should not at all mind if it could be brought about that they should meet in some public place."

"Hem!" said the valet, as if considering. "Meet in some public place!"

"Yes, Shambles; and if I could be certain that the lady and gentleman would encounter—say in St. James's Park—I should be better pleased still.

In a word, if it could be so managed that Mr. Allan Fearon should arrive in the grand mall of the Park on foot—as he undoubtedly would be—at the same time that the private carriage of the Countess de Blonde should issue forth from St. James's Palace by the Park entrance, everything might be managed."

"Everything might be managed!" said the valet, in a dubious tone.

Sir Hinckton Moys was clear, in his own mind, about the little details of his plan; and he soon saw that the more perfect the information was which he gave to Shambles, the more likely he would be to get good service from him.

Bit by bit, then, Moys told him all—or nearly all—and the valet at once became master of the situation.

He put on a calculating look.

"Sir," he said, "it would just take Mr. Allan Fearon about the same time to walk from his house at the bottom of Surrey Street here to the Park, that it would take the Countess de Blonde to order one of her private carriages, and get fairly out of the Palace; and if you will leave the arrangement of that little part of the affair to me, I feel quite assured I shall give you satisfaction."

"I will leave it to you, then; but be sure you get me the two men, and have them stationed at some convenient place between the Horse Guards and the Palace, in order that I may call upon them for assistance, should I require them."

"That shall be done, sir; and they will be lounging about that long Turkish piece of ordnance, close to the gun-house in the Park. They shall understand that, when they hear a whistle sounded twice, they are wanted, and will place themselves under your direction."

"Be it so—be it so; and recollect I want all these things to happen between nine and ten to-night, during which period the Regent will be in my society, and, I hope, guided by me in all respects."

"It is half-past six," said the valet, "and I have much to do."

He held out his hand as he spoke, but Sir Hinckton Moys perfectly understood the mute appeal, and placed some twenty or thirty guineas in it.

"Go!" he said. "I think you quite understand your mission!"

The tactics of Sir Hinckton Moys were now quite plain enough. What he wanted to do—by any means whatever—was, to procure an apparently secret and confidential meeting between the Countess de Blonde and Allan Fearon, at some time and in some place where the Regent could be a spectator of it.

That done, he thought that all the jealous feelings of the Prince would be roused into activity, and that there would be no further difficulty in accomplishing the disgrace of Annie, and the abandonment, by the Regent, of Allan Fearon; and although this latter circumstance by no means came up to the full vengeful feelings of Moys against Allan,—yet, to cut him off from the succour and countenance of the Regent was certainly a step towards leaving him more completely at his mercy.

In order, then, that the events of the next few hours—curious and important as they were—should be duly understood, it will be necessary

that we should follow Shambles—the valet of Sir Hinckton Moys—in the means that he took for carrying out his villanous master's wishes.

In those pestiferous regions lying at the back of Westminster Abbey, where existed, and exists still, a nest of habitations and a population out-rivalling St. Giles's, at its worst, in squalor, poverty, and criminality, there was a low-built public-house, of most ancient pretensions and picturesque exterior.

This house was called the "Shippers' Arms;" and at one time had, probably, been the resort of seafaring men and others, from the old ferry at Westminster. It had long ceased, however, to be anything else than a place of meeting for footpads, housebreakers, area-lurchers, and all the mass of strangely-named criminal population, which, at the period of which we write, formed much more a distinct fraternity or family than at present.

It was to this place, then, that Sir Hinckton

Moys's valet made his way in search of the two unscrupulous gentlemen that were required to play the part of bravos of modern time, in St. James's Park.

The air and manner, and easy, graceful, at-home sort of feel, with which the valet stepped down from the street on to the lower level of the ground-floor of the "Shippers' Arms," sufficiently testified to the fact that he was no stranger in that locality.

A door about half-way down the passage was immediately banged shut, and a broad panel in the wall, to the right hand, was flung open, the latter displaying a goodly assortment of pewter flagons, and bottles of all shapes and sizes.

"Now, sir!" said a rather harsh voice—"give your honour's orders—what shall it be?" But the voice immediately then changed its tone, adding, "Bless us and save us! can I believe my eyes? Why, it's Shambles! as sure as we're all honest men at the 'Shippers' Arms!' Why, what's in the wind now, old pal? Anything that can be put up safely, eh? You get your regulars, of course."

"No, Bonus," said Shambles; "but I want a couple of our fellows who'll do a little job in the Park for a few guineas to-night!"

"To be sure! to be sure! Come on! come on! I didn't know you a bit, at the moment. I'll be out directly to you. Now, here we are! Open—it's all right!"

The landlord tapped at the door in the passage, which had been so abruptly closed, and it was immediately opened from the other side by a man with a rough hair cap on his head, and who, to the surprise of Shambles, was holding a horse by the bridle, the head and fore-feet of the animal just emerging from a sanded parlour, which was to the left of the passage.

"Why, Bonus," said Shambles, "have you turned your house into a stable?"

"Bless you! no, old fellow—not at all; but, you see, Captain Singleton—him we call Sixteen-stringed Jack, you know—was trotting down Whitehall, and who should he come face to face to but the High Bailiff of Westminster, who knew Jack in a moment; so he sung out, 'Catch this fellow!' says he; 'it's Sixteen-stringed Jack, the highwayman!' and all the idle lolloping fellows that were about made a grab at Jack; but he has taught his horse to kick—and it did so to some purpose—and off started Jack, catching the High Bailiff by the leg as he passed, and leaving him sprawling in the mud, opposite Lady Dover's house. But there was quite a hue-and-cry; so Jack took the back-way down King Street; and after upsetting half a-dozen apple-stalls, he dashed down past the Abbey, and got here just a few minutes before anybody could run into sight of him; so we took him in, horse and all; and he's up-stairs, taking a glass of strong waters with my missus, and here's his horse."

"A clever escape enough," said Shambles; "and I shouldn't wonder——"

"Wonder at what, old friend?"

"Why, that he might take in hand the little job I come about."

"It'll all depend. It'll all depend. If Jack's hard up, he may; but what he likes best, you see, is the open road or the heath: that's the kind of above-aboard business that suits Jack best. He likes to cry out 'Stand and deliver!' in your true high-flying knight of the road style, and he don't mind a stray shot or two whistling about his ears; but I don't say he won't do it."

"I will speak to him," said Shambles, "if you will give me the opportunity, for I think he's just the sort of man we want. Business is business: and I don't see why he need scruple about what 't is, any more than I do."

"Bless you, that's what I say; but there's no convincing your high-flying 'Stand and deliver!' kind of chaps, that all's fish that comes to the net. However, you shall see him, Shambles, and make your own bargain; and I'll put in a word, if I can, for old acquaintance sake."

Shambles patted the neck of Jack's horse, and then followed the landlord up a winding, gloomy staircase, which led to the first-floor of the old rambling inn.

The "Shippers' Arms" was quite a curiosity in its way. It was but one storey high, properly so called; although in the enormous old tiled roof above that storey there were some ten or a dozen odd-shaped recesses and rooms, if they might be so called, leading from one to another in such a tortuous fashion, and connected with each other by so many winding staircases, narrow passages, and, in some cases, ladders, that it would take a month for any one thoroughly to comprehend the topography of the ancient place.

It was in the second floor of the "Shippers' Arms" that Sixteen-stringed Jack was to be found after his perilous encounter with the High Bailiff of Westminster, in Whitehall.

That second floor might be called the domestic portion of the house, for there Mr. Bonus, the landlord, dwelt with his decidedly better half, who ruled the entire household, although, truth to say, with by no means a very harsh sway.

The landlord flung open a door which disclosed an apartment of some pretensions almost to elegance, and there sure enough was Sixteen-stringed Jack and the lady of the mansion, together with Miss Polly Bonus, aged thirteen, who was quite an adept at giving her opinion in regard to whether Jack this or Tom the other was the "prettier man."

Jack was laughing, for his heart was light.

The sense of security that he had felt in regard to his daughter Lucy, since he had succeeded in placing her in care of Marian Fearon, had removed the only weight that had ever rested seriously on the mind of the highwayman.

To be sure, a stray bullet, in the course of his vocation, might at any time lay him low; or he might fall into the hands of the Philistines, and be compelled to bid the world good bye some fine morning at Tyburn; but familiarity with danger, as some one says, somewhat blunts the edge of apprehension, and Jack's spirits were not to be cast down by the exigencies and possibilities of his professional pursuit.

"Mr. Shambles, an' it so please you," said the landlord, as he introduced the valet.

"Is it really Mr. Shambles?" exclaimed Mrs. Bonus. "Well, I declare, the sight of you is good for bad eyes."

"Not that yours, my dear madam," said Shambles, "require any amendment—for they shine as brightly as ever."

"Oh, you bad man, there you go at your compliments again! Don't, now—don't! If there's anything I dislike more than another, it's anybody saying anything about my eyes; because I can't help what they are, seeing as one's eyes are born with one; and if they'd been ever so bad, instead of being what they are—hem!—why, of course, I shouldn't expect to be abused!"

"Ah, that's all very well, marm," said Shambles; "but we know that old story of how poor Ball, the tinker, as he was called, and who afterwards suffered at Tyburn, ran after you in a hackney coach in St. Martin's Lane, swearing there was a lady with the finest diamonds he had ever seen, and he would have them, when it turned out to be nothing but your eyes, Mrs. Bonus!"

"I declare you get worse and worse, Mr. Shambles; but I suppose that's owing to you living among the quality, and going to the Palace! Polly, my dear, fetch a glass from the buffet, and give Mr. Shambles some strong waters."

"I shan't!" said Polly.

"You little viper, do as you're told directly!"

"I shan't!" added Polly. "He's ugly—he's very ugly, and you know he is, ma; and if he didn't go on about your eyes, you'd hate the sight of him; so I shan't, and there's an end of it!"

"Oh, was ever woman," exclaimed Mrs. Bonus, "troubled with such a hussy? But it will come home to you some day, that it will!"

"Well, Jack," said Polly, turning to Sixteen-stringed Jack, "tell us more about Lucy, and the cave on the heath. It's as good as a play; and as I mean to marry the first highwayman I can find, I ought to know all about it."

"Marry a highwayman, you odious little slut!" exclaimed Mrs. Bonus. "Why, what do you suppose becomes of highwaymen's wives—eh?"

"I don't know."

"Why, they leave them always, to be sure," chimed in Mr. Bonus, assuming, as he spoke, an oratorical attitude,—"they leave them, to be sure, you wretched, immoral girl. If you'd said, now, that you'd be a highwayman's mistress, there'd been something in it; but, oh, dear!—oh, dear! what a thing it is to bring up daughters, and then to hear them talk of going astray!"

Jack Singleton laughed in spite of himself at the morality of the "Shippers' Arms;" but he put on rather a stern look, when, with a sneaking air, Mr. Shambles leant over the corner of the table and whispered to him, "A word with you, Mr. Singleton—a word with you."

Jack did not like the looks of the fellow at all; and, moreover, he recollected having heard something not much to the advantage of Mr. Shambles.

"A word with you—a word with you, Mr. Singleton."

"What is it?"

"Oh, private—private!"

"No," said Jack; "speak out! I've no secrets from old friends here."

"But it's business."

"All the less need, then, of making any mystery of it. What is it?"

"Yes," cried Polly. "Speak out, ugly!"

"Then, if I must speak," said Shambles, "I have to propose to you, Mr. Singleton, a little affair. It won't take up half an hour, and I dare say ten or twelve guineas——"

"I won't do it," said Jack.

"But, my dear sir, you've not heard."

"Nor do I want to hear. I work on my own account, and with and for no one."

"Go away, ugly!" said Polly. "Don't you hear——"

"Take that!" said Mrs. Bonus; and at the moment Polly's eyes flashed fire from a sounding box on the ear, which her mother bestowed upon her; but that charming and precocious Polly showed fight, and ducking under the table, she made her way to the sideboard, from which she commenced a cannonade of glasses of all kinds and descriptions: tumblers, rummers, wine and ale glasses, flew through the air in rapid succession. Mrs. Bonus uttered screams of dismay, and the landlord swore lustily, as he dashed after Polly, who made her escape by a side-door into the upper regions of the house.

"Very well," said Shambles, as he turned away from Sixteen-stringed Jack. "If you won't do it, you won't, Mr. Singleton; but it would have been easy enough, and close at hand."

"I don't care a bit," said Jack, "whether it's easy or not, or where it is."

"Well, well, you'll keep quiet?"

"I may well do that, as I know nothing."

"No—little or nothing; but, Bonus, old fellow, here's one of two letters I shall want delivered punctually at nine o'clock, at the bottom of Surrey Street. It'll be a crown for one of your men to do it sharply and well."

"To be sure," said Bonus, as he took the letter and read the address—"To Mrs. Marian Fearon—important and with speed."

"Ah!" cried Jack, as he caught the sound of the name. "Stop, Mr. Shambles! Why is the letter not to be delivered till nine o'clock, if it be important and with speed?"

"That," said Shambles, "is part of the nice little affair; but as you won't help me, Mr. Singleton, I don't feel that I ought to say any more about it."

"But, upon taking second thoughts," said Jack, "suppose I do help you?"

"Ah!" cried Shambles, with a grateful look; "now you speak rationally."

CHAPTER CXXXIII.

SIR HINCKTON MOYS'S VALET MAKES A CAPITAL ERROR IN HIS ARRANGEMENTS.

THE moment that Sixteen-stringed Jack had caught the sound of the name of Marian Fearon, on the letter which Shambles was so desirous should be delivered at nine o'clock, as "part of his plan," notwithstanding it was marked "important and with speed," and there wanted two good hours to that time, his feelings in regard to the objects of the valet materially changed.

Jack was now as anxious to have something to do with "the little affair," as he had been before to repudiate all connexion with it.

"So you will help, after all?" said Shambles.

"Yes, I will!"

"Your hand on it."

"Well, I don't see the necessity at all of that," said Jack, with an invincible repugnance to shaking hands with the rascally valet.

"Very well. Mr. Singleton, as you please—as you please. I don't wish to force any man to shake hands; so if you will now step into another room with me, I will tell you all about it at once."

"Good!" said Jack, as he rose.

"This way," cried Bonus. "You had better come into the yellow room, close at hand here. Dear me! Dear me! That girl Polly will be the ruin of me. There's a pound's worth of as good flint glass broke as ever was on a sideboard."

"It's her high spirits," said Shambles.

"Confound her high spirits! Only let me catch her, that's all! I'll make her repent it."

"What is that you say, Mr. Bonus?" cried Mrs. Bonus.

"I said, my dear, that so soon as I could catch Miss Polly, I would make her remember breaking the glass."

"If you dare, Mr. Bonus, to lay hands on that

child, I will not leave eyes in your head, I can tell you."

"Why, my dear, it was at you she flung the glasses."

"And pray, Mr. B., what is that to you, I should like to know, and therefore humbly ask—eh? eh? eh?"

"Oh! well, well!"

Mr. Bonus beat a hasty retreat, but scarcely in time to avoid a bottle which followed him like a cannon-shot down the stairs.

Jack laughed, as he entered the yellow room with Shambles, and there found Polly quietly at work on some gold thread with which she was making a loop for her hat.

"There, Polly," said Jack; "you can go to your mother again, as she is taking your part now, and has just flung a quart bottle after your father, for blaming you."

"Oh," said Polly, "I don't care a bit what they say. I shall not stay here long; but as soon as I can settle, I mean to go."

"Pray, Polly," added Jack, "be advised, and do nothing rashly."

Polly only laughed, as she gathered up her work and left the room singing gaily—

"When the heart of a man is oppressed with care,
    The gloom is dispelled when a woman appears."

"Well, Mr. Shambles," said Jack, "what, now, is all this little affair about?"

"My master——"

"Well, your master?"

"Sir Hinckton Moys."

Jack started.

"Sir Hinckton Moys, the late favourite of the Regent? The scoundrel!—the—the——"

"Hilloa!"

"Is he your master?"

"He is, Mr. Singleton; but permit me to say that you are treating my master to some very bad names; and, if that is your opinion of him, I begin to be afraid that, after all, you won't be likely to do him any very good service to-night!"

"It is your opinion of him as well," said Jack; "and yet you profess to be going to do him good service to-night!"

The valet laughed.

"Well, well! there may be something in that; so I will say, at once, that all you will have to do is to stay for about an hour close to the gun-house in the Park; and if Sir Hinckton Moys should blow a whistle twice, you, or some one who will be with you, will place yourselves at his orders."

"Is that all?"

"That is all."

"But what is the meaning of it all?"

"Why, you see, Mr. Singleton, my master has had a sort of breeze with the Countess de Blonde, and another sort of breeze with Mr. Fearon."

"Ah, yes."

"Well, he wants to get the better of them both, in some way; and he thinks that if the Regent could only be brought to think that there is something—you comprehend?—more than there ought to be between Mr. Fearon and the Countess de Blonde, he will get rid of her, and turn his back on Fearon. You see, now, don't you?"

"I do."

"Well, that's all, then. You see, I should not have known one-half that I do know, but I have had a peep into both the letters since I had them in my possession."

"Both the letters? Then there is another?"

"To be sure. That is to go to the Countess de Blonde; and, as I make it out, the letters invite her to his house, in Surrey Street, and him to the Palace; and they will meet in St. James's Park, as I will take good care to manage."

"How? how?"

"I will be on the footsteps of Fearon, and so soon as I see the Countess's carriage, I will say to him, as if in passing, 'That is the Countess de Blonde.' Then he will be quite sure to stop her. And then the Regent—who will be dodging about with my master, Sir Hinckton Moys—will seem to see them have a private and most clandestine meeting. Capital! is it not?"

"Oh, capital!"

"Well done, eh?"

"Very well imagined."

"I thought you would say so."

"But what do you suppose I shall be called upon to do, eh?"

"Why—as I comprehend it—my master wants both the letters back again into his own possession; and you, and whoever you have with you, will have to cry 'Stand and deliver!' to both the Countess and Mr. Fearon."

"Ah, yes."

"That was why, you see, I thought it so much in your line, Jack!"

"Quite in my line!"

"You will do it, then?"

"My good sir, I would not fail being in this affair for I don't know how much—I quite take to it, and feel an unusual delight in it!"

"I am glad of that, sir—delighted at that. Then I may count upon you?"

"Indeed you may!"

"Sir Hinckton will be delighted."

"No, no! Of one thing I must be quite sure. You must not name me to him. You are a 'family man,' you know, Mr. Shambles, and dare not betray me; but you must not say to him that you have engaged Sixteen-stringed Jack. Say a highwayman, if you please, but no more."

"Well, well, I won't, then."

"Mind, that is a bargain."

"It is, Mr. Singleton." (The valet had found out by the expression of Sixteen-stringed Jack's countenance that he did not exactly relish being called Jack by him.) "It is, Mr. Singleton; and you will find my word is as good as my bond."

"I don't doubt that in the least," replied Jack.

The valet now set about considering who was to be the companion of Sixteen-stringed Jack on the little enterprise; and Jack himself wondered if by any means he could suddenly light upon his acquaintance, the housebreaker, who would have been just the sort of person he would have liked to have with him.

But Sixteen-stringed Jack had no ready means of finding out his old comrade of the cavern on Hampstead Heath, so he was compelled to leave that part of the affair in the hands of Mr. Bonus.

Shambles accordingly called the landlord into consultation, who at once made mention of a certain Tom Pebbles, who wanted a job to set himself up again, since he had been unfortunate with the cards lately.

This individual was found fast asleep in one of

the lower rooms of the "Shippers' Arms," but he was soon roused; and it was duly explained to him that there were ten guineas to be earned between then and midnight.

Tom Pebbles was very near that maudlin stage of intoxication which induces tears, and he shed a whole shower of them as he shook the landlord by the hand, and called him his best friend, and then went through the same process with Shambles, the valet, and with Sixteen-stringed Jack.

"Only to think, now," he said, "that all of you should think of a poor devil who had been choused out of his last copper by the sharps, while he was asleep, and bring him a little job to do! It's too kind!—by Jove, it's too kind!"

Shambles began, from all this demonstrative conduct on the part of Mr. Tom Pebbles, to have doubts whether he were sufficiently in his senses to be of any use at all. But Mr. Bonus, with a wink, set that to rights, as he said, "Bless you, you don't know Tom as I do! I'll give him half a pint of vinegar, and pump on his head for ten minutes, in the yard, and he will be all right, and as cool as twenty cucumbers!"

With this assurance the valet was satisfied; and after making an agreement with Sixteen-stringed Jack, that he was to be at the old gun-house in St. James's Park at a quarter before nine o'clock precisely, he left the "Shippers' Arms," tolerably well content with his evening's villanous work.

No sooner was he gone, however, than Jack sought a private interview with Mr. Bonus.

"I tell you what it is, Bonus," he said. "This is not a regular piece of family business at all, but some Court villany."

"Shouldn't wonder at it," said Bonus.

"But do you think, then, that it is right and fair for me to engage in it, old fellow?"

"Ten guineas for about half an hour's stroll in the Park," said Bonus—"I should say that was business, if anything was."

Jack saw that he could make nothing of the landlord of the "Shippers' Arms" in the way of sympathy, so he abstained from saying anything more on the subject; but he repaired again to the sitting-room of the amiable little family.

Polly was there alone.

"Ah," said Jack, "you have the room all to yourself, Polly! Where is your mother?"

"Gone to bed."

"Well, Polly, I want you to tell me if you happen to know what Tom Pebbles likes best."

"Me!" said Polly.

"I don't mean that; I want to know what he likes best to drink?"

"Oh, that is quite another thing!—it is old rum, that is."

"Then, my dear Polly, do you think you could get me a stone bottle of that enchanting liquor, that I can conveniently carry with me?"

"Of course I could."

"And you will?"

"To be sure I will, Jack; I will do anything for you, because you are on the road in a regular way; but I hate such men as that horrid old ugly Shambles. I suppose you want to make Tom Pebbles take enough to put him out of the way of something?"

"I do. Keep the secret, Polly, and I will tell you. There is a most beautiful young lady,

against whose peace of mind that rascal Shambles is contriving something; and I have only promised to go with him that I may thwart his plans; but as I shall have Tom Pebbles with me, I don't want him to thwart me."

"Charming!" said Polly. "I'll get the rum, and the best, too, in the cellar—not that with water in it, that father serves in the bar."

Polly was as good as her word; and, by half-past eight o'clock, Sixteen-stringed Jack and Tom Pebbles were quite ready to emerge from the public-house, and take up their appointed stations in the Park.

Tom Pebbles had gone through the sanitary course of vinegar and cold water, which had been prescribed by Mr. Bonus, and looked steady enough, although there was a wild look about his eyes, as if he hardly knew where he was.

CHAPTER CXXXIV.

JACK SINGLETON DEFEATS SIR HINCKTON MOYS IN THE PARK.

THE clock at the Horse Guards struck the chimes of three-quarters past eight, as Sixteen-stringed Jack and Tom Pebbles took up their position beneath the shade of a tree, about thirty paces from the gun-house in the Park, and that old Turkish piece of ordnance, which is still to be seen—rusting and decaying—as a trophy.

But we must there leave them, just as a light mist was gathering about them, while we attend to what was doing in relation to the plot of Sir Hinckton Moys.

The valet—when he had made, as he thought, so successful an arrangement for his master's interests and purposes at the "Shippers' Arms"—made the best of his way to the lodgings of Sir Hinckton Moys, and announced that all was ready.

"Do you mean to say," said Moys, "that you have found two men who will do what is required?"

"I have, sir; and the best men in all London for the purpose, you may depend."

"And the letters?"

"One I will deliver myself, and the other I have found a person to deliver who can be thoroughly trusted."

"You are a capital fellow, Shambles!"

"I have the honour to be energetic in the service of a good master."

"Well, you shall not repent it. If all goes well to-night, I shall, before four-and-twenty hours are over, be in the occupation of my old apartments in St. James's Palace, and then I will make it my first care to do something handsome for you."

"You are too good, sir. The fellows would not come for less than fifteen guineas each, and it will cost a couple more to get the letters delivered at the Palace. That one for Surrey Street I will take myself."

"That makes thirty-two guineas, then," said Sir Hinckton Moys, with rather a blank look.

Shambles pretended to consider for a few moments, and then, with an air of great candour, he admitted that "that did make thirty-two guineas."

"And you had about thirty of me."

"Eighteen, sir."

"Eighteen?"

"Not another guinea, sir!"

"Unconscionable rogue!" muttered Moys to himself, as he emptied his purse, and placed this time a duly counted twenty guineas in the hand of Shambles.

"There," he said, "that will cover all."

"More than all, sir," said the valet; "because you see, sir, I don't require anything for myself, as I am in your service and paid regular wages; so you may depend, sir, that if there should be any change, I will bring it back to you."

"Hypocritical scoundrel!" muttered Moys; and then he said aloud, "Well, well; we will see about that—we will see about that. Be off, now, and get to work. I am going to the Palace at once."

Nobody could be better informed than was Moys of the ingoings and outgoings of the Prince of Wales at St. James's.

On that particular day he knew that the Regent had to be at Windsor at four o'clock to meet the Committee of the Cabinet Council, who had legal charge of the poor old insane King.

That the Regent would be back at St. James's by about eight o'clock to dine with Annie, the Countess de Blonde, he, Sir Hinckton Moys, was well aware.

He had spies in the Palace who could, if he had wished it, have told him what exact dishes were to be placed on the table in Annie's apartments.

Moys, then, reached the Palace about a quarter before eight, and the only danger he thought he ran was in Annie becoming aware that he was there, and waiting for the Regent.

Provided, however, that he escaped the observation of Willes, he thought that that was a danger which he might easily avoid.

But fate would have it that, although Sir Hinckton Moys made his way into the Palace by one of the most obscure entrances, Willes did become aware of his approach.

The previous visits of Sir Hinckton Moys to the Regent had come to the knowledge of Willes, and he had taken such measures that it would be impossible for Moys to penetrate into the Palace again without his being aware of the fact.

There was no great difficulty in Sir Hinckton making good an entrance to the royal residence, because in fact the position he had occupied was so well known, that the minor officials could hardly make up their minds if he were really disgraced or not.

Moys then had taken up his position in a small room called the "Partizan Chamber," through which it was next thing to certain that the Regent would make his way, on his arriving from Windsor.

But no sooner was Sir Hinckton Moys fairly ensconced in that "Partizan Chamber," in an easy chair, than one of the servants, who was in the pay of Willes, ran off to tell him his old friend, but present enemy, was there.

Willes was vexed and angry.

He knew not what to do or how to act, since, for all he could possibly know to the contrary, Moys might be there upon the express invitation or authority of the Regent.

In this extremity, Willes thought his best way would be at all events to show his allegiance to the Countess de Blonde, by informing her of the circumstance.

Without, then, interfering with Sir Hinckton Moys, Willes made his way to Annie's apartments, and was soon in the presence of the capricious but warm-hearted Annie, the Countess.

"What now?" said Annie, with her usual impetuosity. "You look as if you had seen a ghost; but if you say you have, I shall not believe you, because I have no faith in them."

"Worse!" said Willes.

"Worse? What then?"

"That Sir Hinckton Moys is again in the Palace."

"Again?"

"Yes; I had the honour, Countess, to inform you that he had been here before, and now he is here again."

"So, George, then, is intriguing with him, is he?"

"It looks like it."

"Well, I cannot help it."

"But——"

"It is no use now worrying me about it, Willes. I have made up my mind."

"May I humbly and respectfully ask to what the fair and incomparable Countess has made up her mind?"

"Simply to this—that if George don't choose to trust me about anything, I will not ask him."

"Oh, oh!"

"Don't be crying out 'Oh!' there. I tell you I have made up my mind. What's o'clock?"

Eight at that moment struck by the Palace clock.

"Eight—eight!" said Willes; "and the Regent will be here within the next half-hour. He will find that rascally Sir Hinckton Moys in the Palace, who, of course, has some villanous scheme on foot. Oh, if I could only feel sure!"

"Of what?"

"That the Regent had not asked him to come."

"What then?"

"I would have him kicked out into Pall Mall!"

"Stop a bit," said Annie. "I will be with you in ten minutes."

"I assure you, my dear Countess, that I have so much to do, that—that——"

"You will wait my pleasure," said Annie, as she abruptly left the room and banged shut a door after her, in the lock of which Willes heard her turn a key abruptly.

"What on earth is she after now?" groaned Willes, to himself. "She is clever—wonderfully clever; and yet she keeps me at times in a state of great fright, because along with her cleverness she is rash—so very rash."

The ten minutes soon, however, flew away, notwithstanding the impatience of Willes, and then he was startled by the sudden appearance in the room, through the very same door by which Annie made her exit, of a young officer of the Guards in full regimentals, who running in, cried out, as he seized Willes by the arm, apparently much excited, "My good, kind sir, you must get me out of these rooms as quickly as you can, for I don't know a moment when the Regent may arrive from Windsor."

"Good heaven!" said Willes.

"Yes; of course, amen! and all that sort of

thing," added the young officer; "but you must, my dear fellow, be well aware that the Prince would be rather vexed to find me in the apartments of the Countess."

"Rather vexed? Oh! oh!"

"Yes. I have been assisting her to dress."

"Oh! oh! Don't! don't! How imprudent—how very—very——Oh, I feel faint! faint!"

"Ha! ha! ha!" laughed the young officer, as he dealt Willes so smart a blow between the shoulders that it nearly sent him on to his face, and gave him a fit of coughing. "Ha! ha! ha! So my disguise is good, then?"

"Disguise?"

"Yes. Don't you know me now?"

"The Countess?"

"To be sure! How do I look, eh?"

"Oh, gracious!—wonderful!—charming!"

"Of course."

"You terrified me, Countess."

"I know I did; but that was not my object in putting on these clothes, which I made George get for me, so that I might go to a review, you see. I mean to fight Sir Hinckton Moys."

"Fight him?"

"Yes."

"And—and——"

"Kill him, do you mean?"

"It's probable enough—I mean to try. I don't expect the Regent till half-past eight. It is now ten minutes past, so I have just twenty minutes to spare; and if in that time I cannot rid us all of that wretch Moys, ugly as he is, it will be a bad case."

"But, my dear madam——"

"Silence!"

"My dear Countess——"

"March!"

"March where? Now, Countess, I will march or hop on my head all the way along the Titian Gallery to please you; but if anything should happen to you in consequence of this mad freak, what would become of me?"

"Oh, then it's of yourself you are thinking?"

"No—no—no!"

"Stuff! I am going into the Titian Gallery. You will send some one to Moys to say that he is wanted there. Do not say who it is, and he will come. He will, perhaps, think that the Prince has arrived by some other entrance—possibly through Carlton House. Now go at once, Willes, and do as I bid you."

"And you will hold me harmless, Countess, with the Regent?"

"Quite—quite!"

Annie was herself buckling on her sword, and she sallied out of her own rooms into the Titian Gallery, while Willes, full of a thousand apprehensions, went in search of one of the inferior servants of the wardrobe, on whom he could depend.

"Jennings," he said, "you will go to the Partizan Chamber, where you will find Sir Hinckton Moys, and you will tell him he is wanted in the Titian Gallery."

"Yes, Mr. Willes."

"But, Jennings, if he should ask you who sent you, you must be mysterious, and decline to say anything further than that it is a gentleman whose commands you feel bound to obey."

"Yes, Mr. Willes."

Jennings went on his errand, which he got through tolerably well, so that Sir Hinckton Moys started to his feet with an impression that it was surely the Regent who had sent for him.

"Certainly, certainly!" he said. "I will go at once—at once."

The interior of St. James's Palace was known as well to Sir Hinckton Moys as it was, probably, to the well-salaried Palace-architect, whose duty it was to see that it was kept in repair; and he made the best of his way to the Titian Gallery, in the full expectation of there finding the Prince.

The gallery was just lighted, and the oil in the lamp had not yet got warm, so that the light was not at its best, and the shadows were rather confusing.

All that Sir Hinckton Moys could see was an officer in full-dress, pacing the gallery with an air of great importance.

Of course he did not for one moment mistake the thin and elegant figure of Annie the Countess for the Prince Regent, who, by that time, had become the "stout Adonis" mentioned by Leigh Hunt.

Moys would then have drawn back, but the moment Annie saw him she called out, in a very well-feigned voice — "Is that the scoundrel Moys?"

"Sir!" said Sir Hinckton, as his cheeks paled with anger; "how dare you, or any man, address me in such terms?"

"Oh, yes!" added Annie; "it is the rascal. Come on, sir! Come on, I say, and defend your worthless life!"

"Ah! An assassin!"

"No, sir. You are armed, I see."

Moys was in the half-dress of his military rank, and wore his sword. His first impression was, that in this young officer he was about to encounter Allan Fearon; but the moment he heard the voice he was convinced it was not Allan, whose voice was, rather deep and grave, having an air of contemplation and thought about it, while the short, sharp manner in which he was addressed by this seeming young officer were impetuous and sharp.

"Come on, sir, I say," added Annie. "As the brother of the fair Countess de Blonde, who, by the grace of the Prince Regent, has become an officer of the Guard, I shall be compelled to take your miserable life, as I would that of any other reptile."

"Ah indeed!—the brother of the Countess de Blonde?"

"Yes, sir. Do you dispute that?"

"Oh, no!"

"Then what have you to say against it?"

"Nothing, young sir. On the contrary, I congratulate you, and wish you joy of your relationship to so virtuous and distinguished a personage."

"Thank you," said Annie.

At the same moment, she drew her sword, and made such a dash at Sir Hinckton Moys, that it was only by stooping and making a terrible spring on one side, that he avoided being run through the body.

"Murder!" cried Willes. "It will surely end in some dreadful deed!"

CHAPTER CXXXV.

THE REGENT CROSSES SWORDS WITH THE DIS-
GRACED COURTIER AND ANNIE.

SIR HINCKTON MOYS was not a coward, but there
were many things connected with his present
position in St. James's Palace which made such a
contest as that into which he appeared to be forced
most inconvenient.

It would be inconvenient to be killed, or even
badly wounded, since such an event would not be
looked upon with much philosophy by such a
man as the worldly Sir Hinckton Moys.

It would be excessively inconvenient to commit
homicide within the walls of St. James's, especially if, in truth, the person upon whom it was
to be committed were really a brother to the
favourite of the Regent.

But what could he do?

Here was a young man, in the uniform of an
officer of the Guard, with a drawn sword in his
hand, and evidently, from the spring forward he
had just made, in possession of a remarkable
amount of agility.

If he, Moys, should attempt by flight to put an
end to the awkwardness of the whole affair, there
was every probability that he would be caught
and ignominiously killed.

There was no resource, then, but to stand upon
the defensive.

Sir Hinckton Moys then drew his sword, and
faced his young and handsome antagonist.

"Well, sir," he groaned out through his
clenched teeth; "it is you who will have to give
an account of this affair to the Regent, and not I."

"Of course," said Annie. "It is only the
survivor in an affair of this kind who can give any
account of it; and as that will not be you, it will
naturally fall to me to do so."

This was a construction of his words which
Moys had not at all intended. He felt at the
moment as if some prophecy had been uttered, the
fulfilment of which was disagreeably near at hand.

"Now!" cried Annie. "Are you ready?"

"No, no!"

"I don't mind whether you are or not, then."

"Hold! hold! Sir, for your own sake, as
well as for mine, if we must fight, let there
be some witness to the fairness of the duel. I am
sure I heard a voice just now, close at hand."

"So did I," said Annie. "But I advise no one
to interfere. This is my affair, and all I shall
have to do is to dispose of your dead body!"

"My dead body?"

"To be sure! The dust-bins of the Palace are
very large, and you can be put into one of them."

With these words Annie made a sudden and
furious onslaught upon Sir Hinckton Moys, who
stepped back cautiously, keeping on the defensive, for he did not fight with a good heart; and
he hoped that the inevitable noise of the combat
might bring some one to the spot who would
interfere.

The swords clashed together, and Annie pressed
Sir Hinckton Moys the whole length of the Titian
Gallery, and had just slightly touched his cheek
with the point of her sword once, when, even amid
the noise of the conflict, an unusual commotion
was heard below in the Palace.

The Regent had returned from Windsor.

Moys heard the rattle of the carriage-wheels as
it rolled into the court-yard of St. James's, and he
became more than ever anxious to bring the combat to an end, which had been so completely forced
upon him.

"This is folly, sir," he said. "At another time,
and in another place, I will meet you."

"No time like the present," said Annie. "I
don't like to keep these affairs on hand."

"Then your death be upon your own head,"
yelled Moys; and in an instant all his evil passions
were in full force, and anger flashed from his eyes.

He became the assailant now in turn, and Annie
found she had enough to do take care of herself.

"Help! help!" shouted Willes. "Guard!
Help! There will be murder in the Palace!"

"That will do!" said Annie.

Sir Hinckton Moys had slipped, and fell upon
one knee.

Annie dashed at him, and her sword was within
a couple inches of his throat, when its blade was
suddenly crossed by another, and a loud voice, in
great anger, called out, "What is the meaning of
all this? Who is it that dares to draw a sword
in our presence?"

"Ah, the Regent!" said Annie.

Sir Hinckton Moys had now struggled to his
feet, and he was too far gone with wild passion to
see whether the Regent was there or not. He
made a desperate attempt to plunge his sword into
the breast of the seeming young officer, but the
Regent, even as he had crossed blades with Annie,
now beat down the sword of Sir Hinckton Moys,
as he called out, "Guard! guard! secure these
persons!"

There was a rush into the gallery of several of
the Yeomen of the Guard, and Sir Hinckton
Moys was seized.

One of the Yeomen tried to lay hold of Annie,
but she slipped pass him, and advancing to the
Regent, she saluted him in military fashion, saying, in a whisper, as she did so, "George, don't
betray me!"

"Ah! it is——"

"Hush!"

The Regent smiled.

"What foolish mummery is this?" he said.

"Your Royal Highness," cried Sir Hinckton
Moys, "will, I am sure, hear me, and do justice.
I was here on business to your Royal Highness,
and was set upon by that gentleman, with an
intention to take my life."

"Sir Hinckton Moys," said the Regent, "I
think it a very strange thing to find you with a
drawn sword in this part of St. James's!"

"I will explain, your Royal Highness—I will
explain!"

"Perhaps," added the Regent, "the least said
in such a matter, is the soonest mended."

"I am the Countess de Blonde's brother," whispered Annie to the Regent.

"Foolish girl, how can you?"

"Don't betray me, George, or you will never
hear the last of this affair. You will find it in
every shop window as a caricature."

That one word—"caricature"—always had a
most uncomfortable effect upon the nerves of the
Regent. He had been caricatured, and each shaft
of ridicule so aimed at him sunk deeply, and
rankled in the wound it made.

"G) to your rooms," he said; "go to your rooms."

"Well!" said Annie, aloud; "if your Royal Highness is of opinion that at present I should not pursue this matter further, I will go to my sister, the Countess, and tell her what has put a stop to it."

"Do, do! Go!"

"Sir Hinckton Moys, we shall meet again."

"I hope so," replied Moys; "and then I shall have, I trust, an opportunity of punishing the insolence of a malapert boy."

"No more of this!" said the Regent; "no more! Sir Hinckton Moys, whatever business you have with me will keep until to-morrow."

"No, your Highness," said Moys, as in two steps he reached the ear of the Regent; "no, unless your Highness's honour will likewise keep till to-morrow."

"My honour?"

No 63.—DARK WOMAN.

"Yes, your Highness."

"What do you mean?"

"If I might be so bold as to speak two words to your Highness, strictly in private——"

"Step this way."

The Regent led Sir Hinckton Moys into the deep recess of one of the windows of the Titian Gallery.

"Now, what is it?"

"The Countess——"

"Ah, it is of her?"

"Allan Fearon——"

"And of him?"

"Mars and Venus in conjunction, your Highness. It is of them I wish to speak."

"What is it? Speak out, man! speak out!"

"I had the honour of pledging myself to your Royal Highness to prove the infidelity of the fair Countess de Blonde to you."

The Regent sighed.

He had hoped that he should escape that proof; and, like poor Othello, he would fain not have known his own misery. Well might he, then and there, have dismissed Sir Hinckton Moys; but yet there was a yearning in his heart to know if it could be true that Annie was false to him, after all the favours he had lavished upon her.

"Well, Moys—well, out with it! What is this proof that the devil has helped you to?"

"Your Highness is displeased."

"Of course I am, man; but out with it! What is it?"

Moys bit his lips with rage.

He could hardly command his voice to speak in terms of courtesy.

"Your Royal Highness, then, perhaps, will hardly believe that the Countess de Blonde has an appointment in St. James's Park, this evening, with Allan Fearon."

"No! no!"

"It is as I have the honour to state."

"Impossible!"

Moys bowed low.

"And this is the faith of woman!" said the Regent. "And yet I ought not—I cannot believe it! What proof have you of this statement?"

"None."

"Ah, you say that?"

"I do, your Highness. I did not trouble myself to bring any proof, because I felt certain that none I could bring would be sufficiently satisfactory to you."

"Then you expect me to believe this absurd story, just because you choose to assert it?"

"Not so, your Highness."

"Well, what then?"

"I propose that your Highness should see the writing."

"I—I see it?"

"Just so. I do not think that any other proof whatever would satisfy your Highness."

"Alas! alas! It's dinner-time, too!"

Sir Hinckton Moys could hardly refrain from laughing at this lamentation, which was so truly in character with the feelings of the Prince of Wales.

"I would advise your Royal Highness," he said, "to countermand dinner until ten o'clock; and in the meantime some slight refection will enable you to feel satisfied until that hour."

"Sir Hinckton Moys," said the Regent, with more firmness and dignity of tone and manner than the Countess had thought him capable of,—"it is quite out of the question that I can bring myself to sit down patiently and quietly to dinner with the woman who has an appointment with one who rivals me in her affections, and who—who——"

"Who," added Moys, "will only wait until she can get rid of your Royal Highness, to keep that appointment."

"I was not going to say that," said the Regent faintly.

"I humbly beg your Highness's pardon."

"No, no! I was going to say that this blow, if it be a real one, has about it circumstances peculiarly severe. It is as if—as if—a child should strike a parent."

"That would be too shocking, your Highness."

"Well, well! It has happened—heaven knows it has happened! It has happened here in St. James's Palace."

"So I have heard."

"Wait for me—wait."

"Oh, your Highness, do nothing rash!"

"Rash? Do you take me for some Eastern potentate who thinks of nothing but the death of the criminals, when he meets with a case like this?"

"No—no! But——"

"Peace, Moys! I am going to make but one trial of the faith or truth of the Countess. I will make an excuse not to dine with her."

Sir Hinckton Moys was intensely pleased.

"And I will ask her, to her face, if she is going out to-night?"

"Do so, your Highness"

"Ah! you agree to that?"

"I advise it. She will tell you 'No,' and yet she will go out as soon as she can get rid of your Highness. Pray excuse the common expression."

"I cannot think it! I cannot think it! But I will try her faith. Wait here, Moys—wait here."

"I am, as ever, entirely at your Highness's service."

The Regent went at once to Annie's apartments.

It wanted one quarter to nine o'clock now.

Annie was sitting on a table in her military uniform, and, in the adjoining apartment, the little *recherché* dinner—which, but for Sir Hinckton Moys, the Regent would so much have enjoyed—was being laid.

"Well, George," said Annie, "here you are at last."

"Yes, at last."

"Come to dinner?"

"I am afraid——"

"Afraid of what?"

"That some business will detain me at Carlton—no, I mean Marlborough House, till about ten o'clock. You can, for once in a way, dine alone, Annie."

"Now, that is unkind!"

"Is it?"

"It is indeed, George. I should have dined long ago, but you know very well that I waited for you. Well, go then, if you won't stay."

"I must go. By the bye, Annie, shall you be at home all the evening?"

"Yes."

"You are sure?"

"Quite sure."

"You have, then, nowhere to go to, and no intention of stirring out of the Palace?"

"Not the least; so you will come back as soon as your precious business is over?"

"Yes," said the Regent, huskily.

"Business!" added Annie; "how I do hate the horrid word!"

The fair Countess de Blonde was not alone in her hatred of the horrid word, for the Regent had as hearty a distaste to it as she had. He was about to leave the room, when Annie called out, "Hilloa! Is that the way you go?"

"No—yes—that is—oh, no!"

He went back and kissed her.

"George!" said Annie, as she buried one of her little delicate hands in his cravat; "there is something the matter with you."

"With me?—the—the matter?"

"Yes. What is it?"

"I don't know."

"You do know!"

"No, Annie. Let me go, that's a good girl; and I hope that we shall sit down to dinner—or we may call it supper, if you like—quite happy and contented, yet, to-night. You—you are sure you don't want to go out for anything?"

"Sure? Of course I am. When do I go out at night?"

"Never, that I know of. But still, Annie, if you had any—any appointment——"

"What are you talking about, George? What is the matter with your wits now, eh?"

"Nothing—oh, nothing! Good bye, Annie—good bye."

He kissed her again.

"How do you like me," she said, "in my officer's dress?"

"Charming!"

"Go along, then. Come back as soon as you can, for I am in low spirits to-night, and it is all your fault."

"My fault?"

"Yes; you break faith with me—you know you do! But be well assured of one thing, George, and that is, that Sir Hinckton Moys is a villain; and you will never have anything to do with him that won't be the worse for your own peace and happiness. Now go!"

The Regent left the room, without another word.

Sir Hinckton Moys was waiting in the recess of that window in the Titian Gallery to which the Prince had led him, to hear the whispered conversation which, as Annie truly said, was so distressful to his peace.

Moys quite congratulated himself upon the very remarkable success of everything up to that point. The fact of the Regent going to ask Annie if she had any intention of leaving the Palace that evening quite delighted him, for he knew perfectly well that the letter which would entice her so to do would not be delivered until nine o'clock.

Annie, then, would be as sure to tell the Regent that she was not going out, as she would be sure ~ ~, on receipt of the forged letter from her sister Marian.

But Sir Hinckton Moys did not at all like the humour in which the Prince returned to him.

There are many things of which people may convince us which do not in any degree add to our appreciation of the person who takes the trouble of bringing to us the unimpeachable and disagreeable evidence.

"Now, Moys," said the Regent, "I am at your service. Prove your statement, or never let me see your face again."

Sir Hinckton bit his lip.

"I can well perceive, your Highness," he said, "that he is but a bad courtier who comes to his Prince with unwelcome truths."

"No, no! Don't talk in that way. I want the proof!"

"Will your Royal Highness then condescend to be led by me?"

"Implicitly."

"Then, when your Highness has taken some refreshment—"

"I want none."

Sir Hinckton Moys bowed. It was a bad sign in regard to his temper when the Prince of Wales did not want any refreshment; and Moys would much rather have seen him indulge too freely than keep so calm and so cool.

But there was no help for that now. The hour had come, and Moys felt that his fortunes at the Court of the Regent must stand or fall upon the events of the next hour.

The wily courtier had no doubt, however, about the revulsion of feeling against Annie which would take place if he (the Regent) actually saw her meet Allan Fearon in the Park.

That such a sight would meet his eyes he made no doubt, for he had abundant faith in the villainous cleverness of his valet to bring about such a result.

Moys then preceded the Regent along the Titian Gallery, and down the short flight of steps that led to the small guard-room, where the Sergeant's Guard of Yeomen were on duty for the night.

The Palace clock struck nine.

The Yeomen of the Guard stood to their arms as the Regent passed, and he touched his hat slightly.

Sir Hinckton Moys still marched on; and at the moment they reached the door which led into the Ambassadors' Court, there came one heavy knock at it from without.

The door was in the act of being flung open for the Regent, and the person who had knocked nearly fell in.

This person had a letter in his hand, and the moment he could push it into any one else's he seemed satisfied, and ran off.

"For the Countess de Blonde," said the groom who took the letter.

"Ah!" exclaimed the Regent, as he paused a moment.

Sir Hinckton Moys, at that instant, felt cold and sick. If the Regent should take possession of that letter, all the scheme would be blown to the winds.

It was the forged letter which was to induce Annie to leave the Palace that night.

The servant respectfully waited the pleasure of the Regent.

The cold perspiration poured down the face of Sir Hinckton Moys.

He was in mortal fear.

"For the Countess!" said the Regent, as, without touching the letter with his hands, he looked down upon it.

"Yes, your Highness," said the groom.

Now if the groom had had a gold or silver salver there at hand, on which to place the letter, it is probable enough the Regent might have taken possession of it; but to take it out of the hands of the man was such a breach of etiquette, that the Prince could not think of such a thing for a moment.

"Very well," he said. "Take it to the Countess."

Sir Hinckton Moys drew a long breath of relief.

"Now, Moys," added the Prince, "I am with you."

Another moment, and they had passed out of the Palace, and the door was closed behind them.

Sir Hinckton was fast recovering from his fright, but he felt quite weak yet for a few minutes, and could not speak a word.

"What is the matter with you now?" asked the Prince of Wales. "You reel like a drunken man."

"No, no? A sudden spasm!"

"Spasm?—spasm? You must be in a bad way, Moys, to have such things."

"It has passed away—it is gone, your Highness. Whatever I may feel, or whatever I may suffer, I am sure I shall always, while I live, have health and strength to serve your Highness."

"Well, well! Now what are we to do?"

"If your Highness will pause in the shade of these trees——"

"Not very dignified, Moys."

"Alas, no! And yet what can be done? Treachery and faithlessness can only be fully discovered by bringing to bear upon them some such espionage as this."

There was, and there are still, the remains of a dense clump of elm trees close to the roadway taken by equestrians through the Park, and by those carriages that have the royal license to pass through the Horse Guards. This clump of elms stands just at the turn of the road from the Mall into that portion of it which leads direct to the Horse Guards.

At the period of our story, some ten or twelve tall trees stood there. They were now in full leaf, for time has progressed, along with the incidents of our tale, although we have not always paused to remark upon its flight, or to notify exactly how days assembled into weeks, and how weeks grew into months.

At that time in the evening, then, beneath the shadow of those trees, there was an excellent shelter for a dozen men, if they had felt disposed to avail themselves of it.

It was a spot that was always looked to as the military rounds were made during the night in the old royal park.

There, then, the Prince and Sir Hinckton Moys took up their post of observation.

CHAPTER CXXXVI.

ANNIE THE COUNTESS MEETS ALLAN FEARON IN ST. JAMES'S PARK.

JUST opposite to the clump of elms, beneath whose umbrageous branches the Regent and Moys waited the course of events, was the gun-house and the gigantic piece of Turkish ordnance.

Then, too, in the shadow of the one tall tree that was close to that spot, a curious observer might have seen two persons.

They were none other than Sixteen-stringed Jack and Tom Pebbles.

The sentinel at the gun-house had more than once looked curiously in that direction, seeing that there were some persons lurking about; but he was tired and sleepy, and thought probably that it would be less trouble to leave them alone than to interfere with them.

Besides, if they were on evil actions intent, he would be sure to hear some alarm given, and then would be time enough for him to trouble himself about them.

The Regent was fidgety and anxious. But Sir Hinckton Moys was far more fidgety and anxious than he, inasmuch as he began, almost for the first time, to feel for what a stake he was playing.

Since the whole affair had so very nearly broken down by the forged letter coming into the hands of the Regent, Sir Hinckton had felt weak and timid.

It was but the want of a salver that had prevented the Prince from taking that letter. What so easy or so natural for him than to take possession of it, and say that he would give it to the Countess.

It was then that little circumstance of the danger the letter had brought him into, that made Moys begin to think his plot was flimsy and delicate, and liable to a thousand sad mischances.

No wonder he was weak and timid.

"Well," said the Regent, "there is one thing I must mention, and that is, my patience will soon exhausted."

"I'm sorry to hear your Highness make such a remark," replied Moys, "since we have not been here yet ten minutes."

"But ten minutes is a long while when you are waiting, and more especially when you've been deprived of your dinner."

"Hush! Oh, your Royal Highness, I do not think your patience would be called upon for any very great exertion, for I fancy even now I hear the sound of carriage-wheels in the direction of the Palace."

"Carriage-wheels—carriage-wheels?" said the Prince, petulantly. "What need that have to do with the affair? There may be many carriage-wheels in the Park; numbers of people have the right of entré to it—Ministers, members of the Privy Council, and general officers."

"Yes, your Highness; but I feel so certain of the information I have had the honour to impart to you—information which, heaven knows, I wish had been of another character—that I could almost wager my head that when we do fairly hear the sound of carrriage-wheels it will herald the approach of one of those elegant female chariots which your Highness has placed at the disposal of the Countess de Blonde."

"You cannot say that!—you cannot be sure of that!"

"I will be content, your Highness, to wait the issue. Hark! You hear——"

"I do hear the sound of carriage-wheels on the gravel of the Park, but I see no carriage-lights."

"She would scarcely use them, coming on such an errand."

"Well, well; perhaps not! And yet I will not believe—I cannot yet believe—that it is the Countess. She assured me so distinctly—so very distinctly, and with such artlessness—that she would not leave the Palace to-night. If she deceive me, I tell you, Moys, there is no faith to be found in woman. No, no! It cannot be Annie!—it cannot be Annie!"

Dark and lumbering-like, some huge shadow, taking eccentric shapes amid the dim obscurity of the Park, a carriage certainly made its appearance from the back of the Palace; and now, as it approaches that clump of elm-trees where the Regent and Sir Hinckton Moys always lie in waiting, we may briefly state that the worst fears of the Prince, and the best hopes of Sir Hinckton, were about to be realized.

It was, indeed, Annie, Countess de Blonde, who was in that vehicle.

The forged letter which had passed the Regent, actually upon the threshold of the Palace, had reached its destination; and although most truly and sincerely had Annie told the Regent she had not the remotest intention of leaving St. James's that evening, such a letter at once created a new circumstance that altered her resolves.

Annie read the epistle with greatly excited feelings; for if there was one thing which still remained in her heart as a strong, and never to be eradicated feeling, amid all the pomp, and glitter, and fictitious rank of her present existence, it was the deep and earnest affection for her sister Marian.

She had had time in many weary and solitary hours which she had spent amid the gauds and glitters of those apartments which she called her own, to think back upon the untiring love and devotion of that sister, who, although but so few years her senior, had yet lavished upon her all the care and tenderness of a mother.

It was not to be supposed, then, for a moment, that such a missive as that which the artful villany of Moys had concocted would fail of having its immediate effect upon the impulsive and generous nature of Annie, Countess de Blonde.

She had scarcely read it sufficiently to comprehend its character, and the request it contained, before she gave immediate orders for a carriage to be at her disposal.

"Quick! quick!" she cried. "I must leave St. James's at once! Tell the Regent, when he comes, I was compelled to go out, but will return as quickly as possible. A carriage—a carriage, as soon as it can be got ready, or I must go on foot!"

The servants who were in attendance upon Annie had had ample experience of her kindliness and generosity, as well as of a certain rapidity and quickness of temper, which made it necessary her commands, when sharply issued, should be promptly obeyed.

The carriage, then, was at Annie's disposal exactly thirteen minutes after the forged letter had been placed in her hands.

As nearly as possible, too, at that same moment when the Regent and Sir Hinckton Moys had encountered the letter on its route to the Countess de Blonde, at St. James's Palace, a sharp knock had awakened the attention of the inhabitants of that humble, but peaceful abode, at the bottom of Surrey Street, where Allan Fearon and Marian had certainly found a refuge from, at least, some of the storms of fate.

Sir Hinckton Moys had calculated well that that was not an hour at which, without some strong inducement, Allan Fearon would abandon his home; so that the forged letter which was intended for him would be likely to meet his eyes as quickly as that which was sent to the Countess de Blonde would, assuredly, come under her observation at St. James's Palace.

It was Shambles himself who had undertaken the task of delivering the letter at Allan Fearon's house; and the moment Marian opened the door and presented herself before his eyes, he thrust the letter into her hand, crying out, as he did so, "Madam, I believe this is a matter almost of life and death! Pray let it be seen to at once!"

Marian uttered an exclamation of dismay at these words; but then, when she recollected that Allan was at home, she felt that, although she had affections elsewhere, the agony of even a mo-mentary idea that anything had happened to him was spared her.

Allan heard her exclamation, and was by her side in a moment.

"What is this, Marian?" he said. "What has alarmed you?"

"I scarcely know; but here is a letter which some messenger in haste has delivered. Read it, Allan — read it, and let us know at once the worst that it can contain."

Allan tore the letter open; and both he and Marian were soon in possession of those few half-incoherent words, from which they might well presume that Annie was in some great strait, and required the immediate presence of a friend and protector.

"Yes! yes!" cried Marian; "you will go to her at once, without a moment's delay!"

"On the instant!" said Allan, as he snatched up his hat.

"Tell her! oh, tell her!" sobbed Marian, "that she has a home with us, ever!—oh, ever! If she is suffering from unkindness—from slights—from anything—tell her to come to us! Say that my heart is open to her as ever, and that all this episode in her life shall be forgotten, and we will but look back upon the past, when we were happy in our poverty together."

"I will, I will; I will tell her all. I cannot conceive what has happened, but I will tell her all that. It may be that the Regent has tired of her, or that some indiscretion——"

"Oh, go! At once, please—go at once! Do not torture me with suppositions!"

Allan was out into Surrey Street, and thence into the Strand, before another minute had passed away.

"Whitehall and the Park," he said; "that will be my nearest route. Up to ten o'clock I know I can find a passage. The ring—the ring! Ah! yes; the Regent's ring. Heaven be praised, I have it still! Once again will I bring its powers and virtues upon the officials of St. James's; and since it has procured me admission to the Regent, it will surely suffice to open what door may be between me and Annie Grey."

The calculations of Sir Hinckton Moys were correct, or rather those of his valet, Shambles.

At the moment that Allan Fearon entered the Park by the Horse Guards—which was free to pedestrians until ten o'clock at night—the Countess de Blonde's carriage emerged from the stable entrance of St. James's.

Allan was light and agile, and he crossed the broad space in front of the Horse Guards at a rate that rapidly brought him near to that clump of trees where Sir Hinckton Moys had hidden the Regent, in order that he might be a spectator of the result of the plot he had taken such pains to elaborate.

It would have been a curious speculation for any one who might have been then present in St. James's Park, could they have had the power of watching, alternately, the progress of the Countess de Blonde's carriage, and then the flitting figure of Allan Fearon, as they rapidly approached each other.

There were, in fact, two persons who had some sort of appreciation of that state of things.

Sir Hinckton Moys and Shambles, his valet, had both calculated upon just such a conjunction of circumstances; but Moys was very busy with the Regent, whose whole attention was turned towards discovering if the carriage which had issued from St. James's really contained the Countess de Blonde, or not.

Shambles, after delivering the letter in Surrey Street, had taken some of the short cuts at the back of the Strand, and had lingered about the entrance of the Horse Guards until fleeting and sharply Allan Fearon had passed him—plunging through the archway at a speed which tested somewhat the powers of Shambles to keep up with.

And while all this was proceeding, let the reader suspend for a moment by his mental power the progress of that carriage and of that pedestrian, and accompany us to the broad, deep shadow which was cast by the tree and the Turkish piece of ordnance, close to the gun-house.

There was Sixteen-stringed Jack along with his associate for the time being, Tom Pebbles, who, notwithstanding the judicious treatment of the landlord of the "Shipper's Arms," was in a very dubious state of mental capacity.

Jack had made up his mind that that dubious state should not last for long; and armed with the stone bottle which contained something over a pint of that particularly good rum which the charming Polly, the landlord's daughter, had supplied him with, he commenced operations upon his companion first, about five minutes before Annie's carriage entered the Park in one direction, and Allan Fearon plunged into it in the other.

"How do you feel, Mr. Tom Pebbles?" he said. "It strikes me that that treatment of our friend, Bonus, was rather rough to a man, who, after all, had only perhaps taken an extra glass."

"Rough!" said Tom Pebble's, his teeth chattering as he spoke. "I'm as cold as an icicle! You might slide down my back with no greater run than my head and neck."

"I don't wonder at it."

"The idea of drenching a fellow with cold water outside, and with vinegar inside! I'm all of a shiver, I tell you—all of a shiver."

"You seem so."

"I seem, then, just what I am. The vinegar has got into my veins and is running about me, giving me a twitch here and a twitch there, as if I'd never known what it was to have a drop of good liquor in my life! It's killing a man—I say it's killing a man to heal him in such a fashion! Vinegar within, and cold water without!"

"I tell you what it is, Tom Pebbles," said Sixteen-stringed Jack; "what you want to put you to rights is a drop of fine old rum."

"Don't—don't."

"That splendid, rich, fine, old, pine-apple rum!"

"Now—now—don't be aggravating!"

"Not that sort, you know, that old Bonus sells at his bar, but what he keeps in his cellar."

"Will you be quiet?"

"Strong, oily, and fragrant, and clear as a bell."

"I tell you what it is, Mr. Jack Singleton, you know I'm as weak as a rat that has been in the claws of a tom-cat for half an hour, or you wouldn't go on aggravating a fellow in that kind of way. Of course I should like some of the old rum—of course I know all about it, and that it

would set me up and make a man of me; but of course I can't get it!"

"I don't know that?"

"Ha! ha!" cried Tom Pebbles, with a faint little shriek, "he don't know that—he says he don't know that! Is there a bar in the middle of St. James's Park? Is that old gun a rum-puncheon? Is that sentinel there a publican, with lots of samples in his cartridge-box? Ha! ha! Am I a fool?"

"You are if you make so much noise. But I can tell you one thing, Mr. Tom Pebbles, which is that I saw, before you left the 'Shipper's Arms,' you would want something to hold you up, and comfort you, after all that drenching and that odious vinegar, so I got the charming Polly to fill a stone bottle."

"A what?"

"A stone bottle, with the best old rum out of her father's cellar."

Tom Pebbles flung himself upon the breast of Sixteen-stringed Jack, and burst into tears.

"My friend—my only friend! My best friend in the world, where is that stone bottle?"

"Heave up," said Jack, "and don't smother me. It's in my pocket. There, take it to yourself, I don't want any of it."

"Gracious goodness!" said Tom Pebbles, as, dropping to the ground, he propped his back up against a tree, and flinging away the cork of the stone bottle, he placed it to his lips. "It is—it is the right sort, the very best! The most delightful! I'm a new man!—a new man!—a new—new—new—ah! quite a new man!"

Tom Pebbles only removed the stone bottle at intervals from his lips, in order to take breath; and Jack Singleton began to get quite alarmed at the depth and protracted character of his potation.

"Stop—stop!" he said; "you won't drink it all! A pint of strong raw rum, man! Why it would kill you!"

Tom Pebbles uttered a deep sigh, and the bottle rolled from his grasp. It was empty! He made two or three ineffectual attempts to speak, and then an insane sort of smile played upon his features for a moment. His head drooped upon his breast and Sixteen-stringed Jack felt that he would have no trouble in regard to what Tom Pebbles might think of saying or doing in relation to affairs that night in St. James's Park.

"I hear voices," said the Regent, "over towards the gun-house."

Sir Hinckton Moys had heard them likewise, and felt right glad so to do, inasmuch as he was thereby assured his man Shambles had carried out his instructions.

"There are always people about the Park, your Royal Highness," he said, in reply. "It is, very probably, the sentinel at the gun-house talking to some comrade."

"Perhaps so—perhaps so; but here comes the carriage!"

"Yes. Here comes the carriage!"

"Stop it, Moys, stop it! We will see who is within it, and then I will go at once back to the Palace."

Shambles was rather panting as he ran after Allan Fearon; and as they both neared the clump of elms, he, too, saw the carriage in which, he had not the shadow of a doubt, would be found the Countess de Blonde.

"Sir! sir!" he cried to Allan, "one moment, you please!"

Fearon paused, and half-turned in the direction of the speaker.

"What is it?" he said. "If you are a Park footpad, you will get nothing by assailing me. Moreover, I'm apt to defend myself. What do you wish?"

"Sir, a lady has placed me here, and I want to know if you are Mr. Allan Fearon?"

"I am."

"Then the Countess de Blonde, sir, wishes to see you here, in the open Park. That is her carriage you see approaching; and if you run up to the side of it and speak to her, she will stop and let you know why she sent for you."

All this was so feasible that Allan could not doubt its authenticity for a moment. He saw the carriage even as this man, who was a stranger to him, had pointed it out; and more than ever full of wonder and amazement as to what had happened, or what Annie could possibly have to say that induced so strange and earnest a note to her sister, he ran forward and met the carriage close to the clump of elms.

CHAPTER CXXXVII.

THE REGENT IS CONVINCED OF THE INFIDELITY OF WOMAN.

"It is he!" said the Regent. "It is he!"

"Allan Fearon!" said Sir Hinckton Moys, in an exultant tone.

"Alas! alas! This is more than sad!"

"Keep back, your Highness; keep back still. I pray you leave nothing in doubt now. Such an opportunity will not occur again, and your mind ought to be thoroughly satisfied."

The Regent sighed deeply.

Allan Fearon ran up to the side of the carriage, and placing his hand upon the door, he cried out, "Annie! Annie! is this indeed you?"

"Stop! stop!" said Annie, as she pulled the check-string violently. "Allan! that is you, by your voice!"

"Yes, yes. You have something to say to me?"

"And you to me. Come into the carriage, Allan, at once, and tell me all."

"I will; and likewise hear all. Oh, Annie, believe me, you are still loved, and loved deeply! There is one who will be ever true to you amid all circumstances and all perils—one unchanging heart!"

The door of the carriage was opened, and Allan sprung in.

"Round the Park!" cried Annie, to the coachman. "Round to those trees again."

The coach was off.

"Curses on them both!" cried the Regent. "Fool! dupe! idiot that I've been! Why, he made violent love to her before my very face. Good heavens! this transcends belief! I will discard her! Turn her out adrift with her shame and her disgrace. I will never look upon her face again To be treated thus by one whom I trusted—one whom I loved! The only one I think I ever really, truely loved; and my own son, too! No, no what am I saying?"

Sir Hinckton Moys coughed, while he rubbed his hands with glee in the darkness;—for everything had happened, not only just as he wished it, but by happy accident to him and his designs, Allan Fearon, intending to speak of Marian, and her feelings towards Annie, had used language, which to a listener converted him into the appearance of her most ardent lover.

"Henceforward!" added the Regent, in a high, excited tone of voice, which sounded almost tearful,—"henceforth there is no honour in man, nor faith in woman. I will trust no one—no one! This, I suppose, is the fate of Princes. Happy, happy, some low estate, where lip service belies not the feelings of the heart, and where faith, unbroken, gilds the happy hours! To the Palace —to the Palace! I will back again."

"Yes, your Highness, to the Palace. Forget her. There are many more fairer, much fairer than she."

"No, no, Moys; don't speak to me in that way."

"Shall I have the honour of conducting your Royal Highness to the Palace?"

The Regent had not yet moved from the clump of trees; but now there was nothing more that Sir Hinckton desired so earnestly as to get him out of the Park.

He longed to be able to blow those two whistles which would bring to his aid Shambles, the valet, and the two men he believed to be waiting his pleasure by the gun-house.

By their aid he intended to attack the carriage of the Countess de Blonde in its progress round the Park, and by main force take from her and from Allan Fearon the two forged letters which he calculated justly enough they would be sure to have with them.

One of those letters it would not do to have produced at all; but the other one might well be shown to the Regent, since it compromised Colonel Hanger and Willes, and he wished to involve them in the common destruction which he made sure now awaited Allan Fearon and the Countess de Blonde.

It was a terrible annoyance, then, to Sir Hinckton Moys to find that the Regent did not move from the clump of trees with that alacrity he had desired.

A feeling of alarm, almost similar to that which had given him so much food for reflection at the time when the letter to the Countess de Blonde reached St. James's Palace, began to come over the heart of Sir Hinckton Moys again.

"Your Royal Highness," he said, "will surely now not remain longer in the night air?"

"I will!"

"But your Highness, I am sure, will not fail to remember that you have not dined?"

"I want no dinner. Like the man in the play —who is it?—I have dined or supped full of horrors."

"But, your Highness?"

"Moys, it is of no use to urge me to return to the Palace at present. Perhaps I shall never return to it again—at all events, not until a certain person has left it. I have seen the tender meeting between Annie and her lover, and I will stay here and see the parting; for something tells me that that, too, will take place at this spot."

Sir Hinckton Moys was puzzled and perplexed

For the Regent to stay there was full of danger to him and to all his projects; in fact, it would never do.

But how to get him away? That was the question, and one most difficult to answer.

Moys wanted to have that chariot and the two occupants all to himself, when it should come round again to the clump of elms. How dared he whistle for the two men he thought were only waiting that signal from him to rush forward and obey his orders, whatever they were, while the Prince was on the spot?

The grinding of wheels began to notify that the carriage had nearly made its round of the Park, and was rapidly approaching the spot at which Allan Fearon had become one of the occupants.

Sir Hinckton Moys was getting desperate.

But still, amid the complicated transactions of the night in St. James's Park, we must allow him to get more desperate than human patience can well bear; and we must leave the Regent, too, for a few minutes in his grief, while we follow that chariot in its progress round the Park, conveying as it did Annie and Allan Fearon, who each believed that the other had a something important to communicate.

"Oh! tell me, Allan, at once," said Annie, with genuine emotion—"tell me, how is dear Marian, and what has happened to her?"

"Rather let me know what has happened to you, Annie," said Allan, "and in what way I can be of service to you, since Marian – thank heaven—is perfectly well and happy, with the exception of the anxiety which your rather mysterious letter has thrown her into."

"My letter!"

"Yes; that letter which brought me here, and would have conducted me through all obstacles to the Palace to see you, had not your messenger stopped me in the Park, and pointed out this carriage."

"Stop, stop!" said Annie. "Say all that again." Allan did say it again.

"Then, Allan," added Annie, "either you or I are mad, for I wrote no letter to you."

"No letter?"

"None; but I have received one from Marian, urging me to come to her with all possible speed and secresy."

"Impossible! Marian has written no letter to you, Annie."

"I have it here."

"And I have here your letter to Marian, requesting her to send me instantly to St. James's."

They each produced the letters; and, amid the darkness of the carriage, as it rolled round the Park, the two pieces of paper clashed against each other like two swords drawn in deadly conflict.

There was a moment's silence; and then it was Annie who half-shrieked out—"We are both deceived! There is some villany at work, and I am certain I can guess whose handiwork it is!"

"You can?"

"I can, indeed, Allan. It is Sir Hinckton Moys who is managing and arranging all this. I sent no letter to Marian at all."

"And she sent none to you."

"Yet here are two letters; and it has been well managed that we should meet in the Park."

"But for what object, Annie?"

"Ah! ah! ah!"

Annie seized the arm of Allan, and held it tightly for a few seconds.

"I know now—I know now," she said. "I know all about it."

"You do, Annie? Then, for the love of truth—of justice—and of heaven, explain it to me."

"It is to make the Regent jealous."

"Of you?"

"And of you."

"Of you in regard to me, Annie?"

"That is it."

"What! of me? Jealous of me! Your sister's husband, and his son!"

"Yes; I know that, too. You are the son of the Regent, and your mother is—is——"

"Alas! you know that, too; but, knowing it, you may well, Annie, believe that it is almost too monstrous a proposition to think for a moment that the Regent can be jealous of me."

"Allan," said Annie, "when people are jealous, it is a disease; and there is no proposition, however monstrous, that will not appear to them as true and clear as daylight."

Annie Gray had not read Shakspere, or she would, probably, have quoted him in his own words, instead of merely alighting upon much the same idea from the natural quickness of her own intellect.

"It is a diabolical plot, then," said Allan, "if it be as you suppose; and I fancy that if we grant for a moment that it may be so, some curious and mischievous eyes are upon us at this instant."

"There is not the smallest doubt upon that subject," replied Annie.

"I will see the Regent. I will see him at once, then, Annie. Late as the hour is, I will see him. He shall not sleep and I will not sleep under the influence of this monstrous delusion."

"You shall see him, Allan."

"To the Palace, then, at once!"

"Yes; to the Palace—to the Palace! We will both see him, and we will show him these two forged letters, and he shall be convinced at once that he is in the hands of a knave by the name of Moys"

The chariot had by this time gone the round of the Park, and had passed the stable-entrance to St. James's. It had, indeed, just reached the clump of elms again as Annie and Allan came to this suitable and practical determination to seek the Regent and explain all the plot that had been aimed at his peace.

Annie checked the driver. She let down one of the front windows, and was about to give the order to turn and proceed to the Palace, when she heard a voice cry out, "Now then, your Highness, here they are!"

A figure emerged from the shadow of the trees, and a hand was laid upon the coach-door.

The figure was that of the Regent; and the hand was the royal one.

"Farewell! Farewell!" said the Prince. "Farewell, now and for ever, false, fickle, deceitful girl. My eyes are opened to all your treachery—to all your mock affection—to all your daily courses of imposture, craft, and guile! Farewell, for ever! I cast you from me at once and for all! Never let me look upon your face again!"

"George!——"

"Away! I will hear nothing! I have seen and heard enough—more than enough!"

"Sir," said Allan, hurriedly—"sir, I——"

"Peace! Do not speak to me, viper—serpent! I do not wish to hear your voice, emissary as you are of your mother, and of any one who can be called an enemy of mine! You are now unmasked, and I know you to cast you off for ever—for ever!"

"You are deceived."

"I know it. I did not believe it; but I know it now. I am deceived most bitterly."

"George, you are mad!" said Annie; "and you don't know what you are saying."

"I know only too well; and have no more to say."

"No, you don't. There is a letter—it is that which brought me out to-night. Take it, and read it. You will then alter your opinion."

"No, no; I will not take it. Nothing can or will alter my opinion. I will not take it!"

"But you have."

No. 64.—DARK WOMAN.

"I have not."

The spot was very dark—much darker, indeed, than it had been when first the Regent and Sir Hinckton Moys reached the shadowy shelter of those trees—so that Annie did not from the coach see that another hand than that of the Regent had stretched forward from behind him, and taken possession of the letter she held from the chariot window.

Sir Hinckton Moys, to whom that other hand belonged, could hardly refrain from an exclamation of gratification at how fortune and chance was favouring him by putting him in possession of the very letter he wanted.

Allan Fearon was so resolved that the Prince should not go away without a full explanation of the events of the night, that he opened the door of the chariot himself next to which he had been sitting, and sprung out.

"Your Highnesss," he said, "will not, I am

sure, refuse to listen to me. You cannot refuse to hear what will restore you to yourself."

This sudden action on the part of Allan Fearon appeared to bring affairs to a crisis, for no sooner had he spoken in the words we have just recorded than he called out again, but in a very different voice. "I am wounded—I am wounded! Some villain assails me in the darkness! Fly!—oh, fly, your Highness, for there are assassins in the Park!"

Allan had no sooner reached the ground on alighting from the carriage, than, dim as the night light was about the spot, he saw a dusky figure come round the coach by the back wheels, and then there was the flash of a sword-blade, and a well-intentioned thrust was made to run him through the body.

Fearon just swerved sufficiently to avoid the fatal intention, and the blade of the sword wounded him in the arm.

The Regent, upon hearing the cry of Allan, at once started off towards the Palace.

The word 'assassins' was quite sufficient to awaken all his apprehensions, for he had never quite got rid of the idea that there were some persons connected with the old directory of Frome who wished to take his life.

The reader has no difficulty in guessing who it was that ran round the chariot to do Allan Fearon a mischief, nor whose sword it was that aimed at his heart. Sir Hinckton Moys thought that a tolerable opportunity for settling all scores with Allan Fearon.

Upon finding, however, that he had missed his aim, he at once placed the whistle to his lips which he had been provided with by Shambles, his valet, and blew the two sounds which were to summon to his service the men presumed to be in waiting for such a signal by the gun-house.

There was a swift pattering of feet upon the loose gravel of the Park on the instant, and two men did reach the carriage.

They came, however, from different parts of the Park.

One came from the gun-house. That was Sixteen-stringed Jack.

The other came from the shadow of the old dilapidated palings that were round the interior of the Park, which was then a waste piece of ground with a stagnant ditch in the middle of it. That was Shambles.

Sir Hinckton Moys had seen the flying figure of the Regent, as he made his way towards the Palace, and he felt that he had the game in his own hands now, and was master of the situation.

Glancing up at the coachman, he said, "You are a dead man if you don't keep your horses quiet!"

All that happened had so alarmed and astonished the driver, that he was ready to take orders from any one. There was such a confusion in his mind between the Countess de Blonde, and the Regent, and the person who had been taken into the chariot by the Countess, that he hardly knew if he were dreaming or not.

"Seize him!" cried Sir Hinckton Moys. "Seize that man, my fine fellows! Hold him tight; he is rather dangerous!"

Moys indicated Allan Fearon, who was at the instant pounced upon by Shambles. But the moment the valet laid hands upon Allan, who from his wound was not well able to resist him, any one on the spot could hear that the fist of somebody had come into rather instant contact with some other person's head, for there was the unmistakable sound of it, and the short, sharp cry that a man might give when knocked down.

It was Sixteen-stringed Jack who had taken the liberty of knocking down Mr. Shambles.

At the moment that he did so, he whispered close to the ear of Allan, "It is I, Jack Singleton—a friend—keep quiet! Don't speak yet!"

A glow of satisfaction came across the mind Allan, for now he felt that neither he nor Annie were abandoned to their foes.

"What is that, my man," said Sir Hinckton Moys, who had run round to the other side of the coach to prevent Annie's escape.

"He would play the villain," said Jack; "so I thought it was better to knock him down."

"You are quite right," said Moys, thinking that it was Allan who was referred to.

—————

CHAPTER CXXXVIII.

SIR HINCKTON MOYS TRIES TO SLEEP ANOTHER NIGHT AT ST. JAMES'S.

ANNIE had made an impetuous attempt to leave the coach, but she was met at the door of it by her enemy, Sir Hinckton Moys.

"No, fair Countess," he said,—"no. Not yet, if you please. You and I have something to say to each other first."

"So we have," cried Annie; "and I will say my say at once—which is, that you are the greatest villain, as well as the silliest, that ever I heard of."

"Indeed?"

"Yes, and in truth."

"And pray what are you, Countess—or, rather, dropping the ridiculous title—what are you Annie Gray, the workgirl? Ha, ha! What are you?"

"What I am is nothing to you, except that I don't allow any one to be impertinent."

A sounding box on the ears testified to Sir Hinckton Moys that his head was a little too close to Annie, and he started back, uttering an execration and a threat.

"I have half a mind," he said, "to order my men to pull you out of the coach, and give you a ducking in the pond over the paling yonder."

"You have said it now," cried Annie.

"Said what?"

"About the ducking in the pond. I shall never be happy till you have had it."

"Ha ha! You have quite a sharp wit, Countess. But I have to tell you now that our relative positions are reversed. It is I who this night will sleep in St James's Palace, and it is you who will be refused admission to it."

"Not so," said Annie. "I shall see the Regent, and explain all to him. He already has the letter which induced me to leave the Palace tonight, and that will in some degree open his eyes."

"No!"

"But I say yes!"

"He has not the letter. It is in my possession You kindly handed it in the darkness, as I stood behind the Regent. Ha, ha!"

"Then I will go to the Palace."

"You shall go the Palace. The Regent has had time to get there; and you shall go in order, now, that you shall be turned from its doors with disgrace. I intend to sleep to-night in St. James's, and it is your turn now to be told that there is no accommodation for you beneath the Palace roof."

"Coachman!" cried Annie. "Home, home!"

"Yes, my lady."

"Ay!" added Moys. "To the Palace, coachman—to the Palace!"

"Stop, sir," said Sixteen-stringed Jack, who was resolved to see the affair out before be declared what part he was playing in it,—"stop, sir, one moment."

"Ah, yes! Your prisoner?"

"Yes, sir."

"Where is he?"

"On the ground."

"That will do. Coachman, lend me you whip for a moment.

The coachman surrendered the whip.

"Don't speak a word," whispered Jack to Allan Fearon, "but scramble up if you can behind the chariot, and leave it to me."

"I will—I will!" said Allan, in the same low tones. "I will leave all to you, for well I know I may trust all to you, Jack."

It was not without some little difficulty that Allan, with the slight wound in the arm which he had received, could make his way up behind the coach; but he had such perfect faith in what Sixteen-stringed Jack was about, and in any advice tendered by him, that, even with some personal pain, he clambered up behind the chariot, and was safely there on the perch that would have been occupied by one of the royal footmen—if that expedition into the Park had not been so sudden and so secret—by the time Sir Hinckton Moys had run round the vehicle with the coachman's whip in his hand.

"Where is the rascal?" cried Moys.

"There," said Jack, as he pointed to the prostrate Shambles, who was but very slowly recovering from a knock-down blow he had received so recently.

Sir Hinckton Moys saw the dim and dusky outline of a human form lying upon the ground, and he concluded at once that his enemy, Allan Fearon, lay before him.

"Now," he cried,—"now the time has come which I had hardly dared to hope for, when I can repay with interest that assault which covered me with confusion and disgrace by St. Paul's Church, in Covent Garden. My time has come, and oh, how welcome! You, fellow, whoever you are, for I know not your name, although this night you are in my service, run round to the other door of the coach, and prevent the female you will find there from leaving it."

"Yes, your honour," said Jack.

"Stop a moment. Who is that behind the vehicle?"

"My comrade," your honour.

"Oh, of course. All's right, to be sure. Now, scoundrel—now, bragging heart, that has crossed me and given me more uneasiness and trouble in a short few months than ever I have passed through before—now it is my turn to pay my debt, and with interest."

Shambles was but half conscious of existence;

for Sixteen-stringed Jack had been far from sparing in the force with which he knocked him over, and put an end to his transactions of the evening. For a few minutes, probably, he would have made an attempt to scramble to his feet; but Sir Hinckton Moys now commenced so savage an attack upon him with the coachman's whip, that the valet was fairly bewildered, and rolled over and over upon the ground, as though he had a particular design in endeavouring to distribute the blows impartially about him.

Moys took a savage delight in thus, as he thought, avenging himself upon Allan Fearon, little dreaming that it was his own valet, Shambles, whom he was castigating.

And Allan himself, holding in the darkness by the back of the coach, had the satisfaction of seeing this little mistake in full progress,—for from what Sixteen-stringed Jack had whispered to him, he was well enough aware that the man who lay upon the ground, and who was mistaken for himself, formed one of those who were carrying out the nefarious plot against him, Annie, and the Regent.

It was singular how, in all these circumstances, complicated as they were on that eventful evening in St. James's Park, so many strange accidents occurred, and arrangements were suddenly made which appeared to favour one party or the other, according to the caprice of the moment.

There was nothing Sixteen-stringed Jack desired more than an opportunity of saying a few words to Annie Gray; and that opportunity was placed completely in his power by Sir Hinckton Moys requesting him to go round the coach and keep watch at the other door, while he supposed he was gratifying his feelings of vengeance upon Allan Fearon.

There was little need even to speak in whispers, for Moys was well occupied; yet Sixteen-stringed Jack subdued his voice as he looked in at the coach window and said, gently, "Madam, I've the pleasure to inform you that I'm a friend. My name is Jack Singleton, and chance has made me acquainted with one of the most villanous plots that the mind of even such a man as Sir Hinckton Moys could conceive. He fancies me in his service, but I am here to thwart his evil designs. I know all about the affair, and can put everything right with the Regent."

"Well, then, I know you quite well," said Annie. "You are Lucy Singleton's father."

"I am; and, believe me, you may trust me."

"I do trust you; but it is cruel to leave Mr. Fearon, if he be wounded, in the vengeful hands of Sir Hinckton Moys. That is not at all like all that I've heard of you, Jack Singleton."

"It is so unlike me," said Jack, "that it could not possibly happen."

"But what is that I hear?"

Jack laughed slightly.

"It is what will not displease you in the least; for Mr. Fearon is quite safe on the perch behind the coach, and Sir Hinckton Moys is giving his own valet—one of the greatest scoundrels that ever lived—a severe lashing with the coachman's whip, mistaking him for Mr. Fearon."

"Capital!" said Annie—"capital!"

"And," added Jack, "as soon as he has finished that little affair—and in which I do not wish to hurry him in the least,—I purpose taking him by the collar to the Palace, and putting things right with the Regent."

"No," said Annie. "Stop!—not yet. I feel quite easy now; but I want to know how far he will go. Let him rise high in his supposed triumph, and his fall will be all the greater. Let him still consider that you are in his service. I long to find out how he will conduct himself, and carry out this affair; and I want to know what the Regent will do likewise. Indulge me, Mr. Singleton, by letting it go on, and keeping Sir Hinckton Moys to the delusion that he is quite successful."

"That may be very easily done," said Jack, "for he supposes he has two men at his service; and as in the darkness he has mistaken his own valet for Qllan Fearon, so he mistakes Fearon for one of those men; therefore he and I have the conduct of the whole affair."

"Nothing could be better!' cried Annie. "Nothing could be better! Let him take his own course, for we can stop him at any moment."

"It shall be so. Hush! here he comes."

"I never could have dreamed," said Moys, as he came round the coach, "that the young fellow would have taken a horsewhipping so quietly."

"I rather think I half stunned him," said Jack Singleton, "by knocking him down as he attempted to escape."

"You have done good service."

"I hope so, sir."

"But I can't think what has become of my valet, Shambles."

"I dare say he is somewhere hereabouts," replied Jack.

"The rascal ought to be at hand, for we might have wanted him."

"Oh, sir, we'll manage very well without him."

"I do not doubt that in the least. You're a bold and clever fellow."

"Well, so folks say, your honour."

"Get up behind the coach, along with your comrade. I am not at all sure but I may want you still. As for me, I've a few words to say to this fair lady within. Coachman, there is your whip: it has done good service. Drive now to St. James's Palace, and we will see what reception the fair Countess de Blonde is likely to meet with."

Sir Hinckton Moys opened the carriage door for himself, and sprung in. He closed it then by reaching his hand out of the window; and just as the vehicle got into motion, with Sixteen-stringed Jack and Allan Fearon behind it, he turned with a smile of triumph to Annie.

"Well, Countess," he said.

"Well, ugly," said Annie.

"Ha! ha! He is handsome who wins. I trust you now perceive I have placed you in a dilemma."

"Not at all."

"You will find your confidence misplaced. We are now about to proceed to the Palace, whither the Regent, after becoming possessed of this little adventure in the Park—which does not appear to be creditable to you—has preceded us, and where, if I am not very much mistaken, you will be refused admission."

"Perhaps so," said Annie, quite calmly.

"And I shall be admitted."

"Very likely."

"So that, in that case, I shall sleep beneath the roof of St. James's, while you will be denied that little privilege. Thus, you see, reversing our position of some time ago, when you boasted of just the contrary state of things."

"I may not sleep at St. James's to-night," said Annie; "nor will you."

"Ha! ha! We shall see."

"No, we shall not see; but I feel quite certain about it. Wherever I go for the night I shall surely sleep, because I shall naturally want repose, and I know of nothing to keep me awake. But you—if under the roof of St. James's—will be so perplexed and worried for fear your villanies should be found out, that you will not close an eye this night. So you see, Sir Hinckton Moys, you won't sleep in St. James's."

Moys laughed a hollow, discordant laugh. It was dreadfully forced, and no one who heard it could have supposed otherwise for a moment than that he felt the full truth of what Annie Gray had said to him.

Nothing was more impossible than that scheming, plotting man, with his whole intellect an aggregate of evil passions, should taste the sweets of repose on that night.

He was silent for a few moments; and then, with a suddenness which seemed to imply that it was a new thought at the moment, although possibly not entirely a new idea, he spoke. "Annie Gray, or Countess de Blonde, whichever you please to call yourself, I have an idea that you and I have fought with each other long enough. I would fain make terms with you; and if you will consent to a treaty of peace, I who have found the means to dispossess you of the favour of the Regent, will find some other means to restore it to you. I am satisfied with the vengeance I have inflicted upon Allan Fearon; and if from this night forth you will act with me and for me, you shall still be Countess de Blonde, and the favourite of the Regent."

"You don't say so?" said Annie.

"I do say so; and I mean so. I will accomplish all that I promise you. I will throw over the person with whom I have been acting against you, and a long career of power and prosperity will open before you."

"I'm quite aware of that," said Annie; "but I don't chose to add you to my fortunes! To-morrow night, if not to-night, I sleep in St. James's Palace as usual; and then I shall set to work to see how soon I can get you hanged."

"You reject all terms, then?"

"Of course I do."

"One word more. I offer you my heart, then my hand——"

"There are plenty of monkeys at the Tower, any one of which I would rather have!"

"Then it is to be war?"

"Oh, no, it is defeat."

"You being defeated?"

"No—you."

"Ha! ha!"

"Do you know, Sir Hinckton Moys, your laugh is about the ugliest thing in the world, except yourself!"

"Look you here, Annie Gray," cried Moys, in a tone of bitter, suppressed passion. "Look you here. Clever and confident as you are—look you here,—I will lay you a wager of my head to your's, that you will never again be restored to the favour and affection of the Regent!"

"It is not a fair wager," said Annie, "because there's no comparison in the value of them. You might lay a cocoa-nut to the crown of England against something. But I'll take it—I'll take it!"

"You will?"

"Yes, ugly as it is; and here we are at St. James's Palace."

"It's a wager—it's a wager!" cried Moys, as he sprung from the carriage, and at the same moment some of those small doors which were at the back entrance of the Palace were flung open, and a blaze of light streamed out upon the chariot.

―――

CHAPTER CXXXIX.

THE COUNTESS DE BLONDE SETS UP AN INDE-PENDENT ESTABLISHMENT.

EXACTLY within the doorway, close to the threshold of which the carriage had driven up, stood a couple of the Yeomen of the Guard, and a Groom of the Chambers in his quiet in-door costume.

"The Countess de Blonde!" cried Sir Hinckton Moys, in a high sarcastic tone of voice.

The Groom of the Chambers stepped forward and spoke.

"I have the commands of his Royal Highness, the Regent, to refuse admittance to the Countess de Blonde to St. James's Palace; and I may add, to save the Countess trouble, that similar orders are given at every entrance."

Nothing could equal the expression of malignant triumph that was upon the countenance of Sir Hinckton Moys, as he turned fairly round upon his heel and faced Annie.

"I'm likewise ordered to state," added the Groom, "that the carriage which brings the Countess here, is at her disposal to carry her wherever she pleases to go."

"You hear?" said Moys, with a mock bow to Annie.

At the back of the chariot there was one of those small square windows, common in vehicles of that description, and in order thoroughly to comprehend what was going on within, Sixteen-stringed Jack had broken the glass as he stood with Allan Fearon on the perch behind.

He was thus enabled to speak to Annie without any one but herself and Allan being aware that he held any communication with her.

"If you wish," he said, "to carry this affair any further, order yourself to be driven to the Hanover Hotel, and try to take Sir Hinckton Moys with you."

"On one condition," said Annie, inclining her head backward in her reply to Jack.

"What is that?"

"That before you leave him you duck him in the canal in the centre of St. James's Park."

"It shall be done."

"To the Hanover Hotel!" cried Annie; "and, Sir Hinckton Moys, I think it will go against your gallantry if you allow me to go there unattended."

"Ah!" cried Moys," "the fair Countess relents?"

"A little."

He sprang into the carriage, and the Groom of the Chamber from the Palace closed the door.

"Tell the Regent," said Annie, "that I shall see him to-morrow."

The carriage drove off, and Sir Hinckton Moys turned again to Annie, saying, "Well, Countess, perhaps you now see the propriety of making some terms with me, since your little career at the Court is otherwise at an end. It is well now that you should be reasonable, and, if so, I will gratify you even by not sleeping to-night at St. James's, because I will give the whole night to a consideration of some means of quenching the jealousy of the Regent, and reinstating you in his favour."

"I never cry off a wager," said Annie. "It's my head or yours, you know."

"But that's absurd."

"Your head is; but mine, I beg to say, I think quite differently of."

"You are obdurate, I see, and will take your own course. Be it so. You're bent upon your own destruction; and since you will not have it that I and you both should rule the Regent for mutual interests, you see that you have fallen beneath the superior genius of the person you contended with."

"I see nothing of the kind."

The carriage stopped at this moment at the Hotel which had been mentioned by Sixteen-Jack; and as it was still but early in the evening the establishment was well lighted, and a throng of waiters immediately appeared on the threshold.

The appearance of the royal carriage, private and plain though it was, and with no emblazonment of arms upon its panels, was still sufficient to let the practised eyes of the people of the Hotel see that it could only belong to some person of distinction; and although the two men who hung on behind were by no means in the recognised attire of fashion, yet the superb horses and the general effect of the turn-out was impressive to the officials of the Hanover Hotel.

Allan Fearon, on the recommendation of Sixteen-stringed Jack, held his head in such a position as to avoid observation; and Jack himself got down from behind to open the door for Annie; but in that he was superseded by some of the waiters of the Hotel, and Annie, without a glance behind her, made her way into the establishment.

Sir Hinckton Moys looked after her with a malignant sneer.

"That will soon end," he muttered to himself. "I will take care that the Regent's jealousy is kept to the full boiling point. Poverty will come upon her; or she will be compelled to accept an offer from some one who will soon tire of her caprices and her extravagancies. She has now commenced the slippery, down-hill path of life. I have given her the first impetus on its glassy surface. Let her go; and I may live to see her yet beg her bread in the streets of London."

"Villain, that shall never be!" said Allan, from the back of the coach.

"To the Palace!" cried Moys. "I shall yet sleep in St. James's to-night! The Regent, no doubt, waits for me."

Jack stood by his elbow, and turning to him, Moys added, "I do not think I need detain you longer. You and your companion have done your night's work; and my valet, no doubt, as he had the means to do so, has settled with you. The affair is over, so you can both go."

"Very well, your honour," said Jack. "Mr

Shambles will know where to find us if he wants us again on any little occasion."

"Yes, yes. That will do."

Sir Hinckton Moys paid no sort of attention to Sixteen-stringed Jack after this, and he was not aware that he had clambered up again behind the coach by the side of Allan Fearon.

The coachman, who happened to be a very stupid fellow, and whose intellects were in a perfect fog the whole of the evening, had heard the order to drive back to St. James's Palace, which he was nothing loth to obey; and the coach was soon on its route from the Hanover Hotel to that destination.

Sixteen-stringed Jack then lightly and actively got upon the roof of the coach, and crawling silently towards the coachman's box, he suddenly seized the man by the back of the neck, and clapping the cold muzzle of a pistol to his cheek, he said, in whispered tones, "If you make the least outcry, or show any disposition to disobey the orders I am about to give you, you will find the next moment a couple of bullets in your brain."

"Goodness gracious! Have mercy upon me!" said the man.

"Hush! not so loud."

"No, sir—no, sir. Don't take a poor fellow's life, and I'll do anything!"

"You're in no danger unless you make it for yourself."

"No, sir; I won't—I won't!"

"Drive into St. James's Park, through the Horse Guards. This is one of the Regent's carriages, and will not be refused the passage."

"No, sir, it won't."

"That is well. You will then make your way to that clump of elms where you took up a gentleman who spoke to the Countess de Blonde. Now go on as fast as you can."

Sir Hinckton Moys was so full of self-congratulation about what he considered the wonderful success of the whole evening's proceedings, that he was some time before he noticed that the carriage was not going the nearest way to St. James's Palace.

Despite some uneasy feelings which would now and then obtrude themselves upon him, he could not help thinking that he had obtained a triumph over the Countess de Blonde, and for ever dispossessed her of the favour of the Regent.

Allan Fearon, from his post behind, could hear through that little shattered glass window that Sir Hinckton Moys was congratulating himself.

"Yes," he said, "despite all her pretended confidence she is absolutely ruined. For the first time in his life, perhaps, the feelings of the Regent have sustained a shock. Had this little seeming escapade in the Park occurred with any other person than his own son he might have looked over it; but human nature revolts at what he will now consider to be so unnatural a struggle. She is ruined!—she is ruined! And with her shall go Willes and Colonel Hanger. I shall soon reign supreme in St. James's as the *confidante* of the Regent. I shall know too much for him ever to part with me again upon light terms, and a career of prosperity is opening before me."

Sir Hinckton Moys had not noticed that the carriage was passing down Whitehall, and it was not until the vehicle fairly turned into the Horse Guards and was challenged by the sentinel, that he began to wonder why the coachman had taken so eccentric a route from Hanover Square to St. James's.

"What carriage?" cried the sentinel.

"His Highness, the Regent's," replied the coachman.

"Pass on, his Highness the Regent's carriage."

The chariot rumbled onwards under the gateway and emerged into the Park, the clock of the Horse Guards at that moment striking the hour of eleven.

Sir Hinckton Moys pulled the check-string violently, for he was angry at the coachman for taking so circuitous a route. The coach stopped, and then Sixteen-stringed Jack found that his time had come for active interference, and to throw off the mask to Sir Hinckton Moys.

He whispered to the coachman a few words of caution.

"Continue to obey my orders for your life' sake, and stop at the clump of trees according t the direction I have given you.

"Yes, sir—oh, yes!"

"What on earth made you come this way for, you villain!" cried Moys, from the carriage.

"Because I couldn't help it, Sir Hinckton."

"You couldn't help it, scoundrel! I will make a complaint against you to the comptroller of the household. Drive on, at once."

Jack had been upon the point of leaping from the roof of the coach and confronting Sir Hinckton Moys, but he now delayed his purpose for a few minutes, until the chariot should stop at the clump of elms, which it did abruptly.

Sir Hinckton Moys was so astonished at this extraordinary conduct of the coachman, that he put out his hand to open the door, and would have sprung out, but Sixteen-stringed Jack now appeared at the coach window, and in a stern, calm tone addressed him.

"Sir Hinckton Moys, you're a prisoner!"

"A prisoner! A prisoner to whom? A prisoner in St. James's Park, and in one of the Regent's carriages! You scoundrel, you've been drinking!"

Jack's reply was calmly and coolly to place the barrel of a pistol on the window edge.

"I do not wish to argue with you, Sir Hinckton Moys," he said; "but I will shoot you dead as you there sit, if you make any outcry or resistance!"

"I am betrayed," said Moys, as he sunk back into the further corner of the coach.

"Betrayers are sometimes betrayed!" said Jack. "Sit still, see, and stir not, on your life!"

Sixteen-stringed Jack fully relied upon the state of sudden fright in which he had placed Sir Hinckton Moys; for he ran round the coach now, and peered amongst the shadows of the elms until he saw what he was searching for, which was no other than the still, miserable body of Mr. Shambles, who, what with the knock-down blow he had received from Jack, and the heavy punishment from his master, had been in a swoon during the whole time the carriage had left that spot.

The reader has noticed that Sixteen-stringed Jack, on more than one occasion, has been able to make a powerful exertion of strength for the accomplishment of any special object, and he now did so by lifting Shambles bodily from the ground, and placing him firmly on the roof of the coach.

It added not a little to the alarm of Sir Hinckton Moys to hear the lumbering of so heavy a body on the roof just above him; and as for the unhappy coachman, he began to think he never should get through the terrors and excitements of that night.

"What do you intend to do?" whispered Allan Fearon.

"I mean to leave Moys in the canal in the centre of the Park: and this rascal Shambles I shall take to the 'Shipper's Arms,' in Westminster."

"Where is that?"

"You have but to ask for it at the back of the Abbey. And now, Mr. Fearon, as you've been slightly touched by Sir Hinckton Moy's sword, I would advise you to go home as quickly as possible, and in the morning I think that you might well pay a visit to Annie Gray, at the Hanover Hotel, to tell her that I'm in full possession of information that will clear her conduct entirely with the Regent. I will meet you there, if you please, at eleven o'clock, by which hour we shall, doubtless, find the Countess stirring, and then she can say what she wishes us to do in regard to the Regent."

"Then I will bid you good night, Jack Singleton, with many, many thanks, for I feel somewhat tired and weak, and yet I will stay to help you if you think I may be of service to you."

"No," said Jack, "I fancy I can manage Sir Hinckton Moys and his insensible valet."

Allan shook the hand of the highwayman warmly, and then made the best of his way home, to give an account to the anxiously-expecting Marian of the strange and varied events of that night of plots and surprises.

Jack stepped up to the coachman, and gave another order to him.

"You will drive as close as you can to the palings that enclose the centre of the Park."

"Yes, sir."

Jack again placed the pistol on the window-ledge of the chariot, for Sir Hinckton Moys was beginning a remonstrance.

The coach, in a few moments, was close to the old dilapidated railing, and then Jack spoke again to the driver.

"Will your cattle stand still for five minutes?"

"Yes, sir. Oh yes!"

"Then come with me. Sir Hinckton Moys, I will trouble you to alight, for I have promised the Countess de Blonde to give you a ducking in the canal in the centre of the Park; and I have promised myself that if you seriously object, I will blow out your brains instead."

———

CHAPTER CXL.

SIXTEEN-STRINGED JACK SECURES MR. SHAMBLES AT THE "SHIPPER'S ARMS."

IT would be difficult to say whether rage or terror predominated most in the breast of Sir Hinckton Moys as Sixteen-stringed Jack addressed these words to him.

The warning that Annie had given to him that she intended he should receive a ducking in the canal in the Park came with full face to his mind; and he bitterly cursed his own folly, that, in a moment of irritation, had induced him to make so foolish and so unmanly a threat against the fair but provoking Countess de Blonde.

Still Moys could hardly bring himself to believe that the man who enforced his orders with a pistol could be actually serious in his desire to inflict such an indignity upon him.

Sir Hinckton spoke to Jack Singleton in what he intended to be conciliatory tones.

"Come, come, my good fellow," he said, "you have carried the joke quite far enough."

"What joke?"

"About—about putting me into the canal."

"Well," said Jack, "I am glad you look upon it as a joke; but, in my opinion—and I feel certain that so accomplished a gentleman as yourself will agree with me,—no joke is complete without its climax."

"Pho! pho!"

"And, therefore, I will trouble you to come with me over this paling here."

"I cannot—I will not!"

Jack put the pistol upon full cock.

The sharp click of the spring sounded very jarringly upon the ears of Sir Hinckton Moys, who exclaimed, "If you are not mad, you will think a hundred pound note a very good recompense for not carrying out this too absurd whim of the Countess de Blonde."

"Over the paling!"

"But——"

"Over, I say, before I count three!"

"I really——"

"One!"

"Two hundred pounds!"

"Two!"

"You accept?"

"No! Three!"

Sir Hinckton Moys thought it safer to scramble over the dilapidated paling that shut in the bit of waste ground which the centre portion of St. James's Park then was, than to wait to receive a bullet in his brain.

"Come, coachman," said Jack, "follow me."

A faint hope had sprung up in the mind of Moys, that when he got over the paling he might make an effort to save himself by flight, but that was disappointed by the speed with which Sixteen-stringed Jack placed himself by his side.

As for the coachman, he was so completely under the dominion of fear, so far as regards Jack and his pistols, that if he had been ordered to stand on his head, or to take the horses out of the Regent's carriage and put them inside and draw the vehicle himself, he would have attempted the feat.

Sir Hinckton Moys therefore found himself a little further from hope, and a little nearer to his destination.

That destination was the lazy, stagnant ditch which was in the middle of the enclosed space where they were.

Jack Singleton fancied he heard the sound of horses' feet in the Park, and he clutched Sir Hinckton Moys by the arm.

Sir Hinckton, too, heard the sound; he knew well what it meant.

The cavalry patrol, which still at stated periods takes the round of the Park, was passing

An irresistible desire took possession of Sir Hinckton Moys to make one effort for safety.

"Help! help, patrol! Murder!" he shouted.

If Sixteen-stringed Jack had in reality had the remotest intention of taking the life of Moys, certainly that would have been the time to do so; but he had never had any such intention. The shooting any man under such circumstances, whatever might be his deserts, was not an act at all in accordance with Sixteen-stringed Jack's notions.

Had he but known it in time, Sir Hinckton Moys was safe enough.

"Help! help! Murder! Patrol! Murder!"

"Bring him along!" said Jack. "Take his feet."

Jack seized Moys by the back of the neck with a suddenness that flung him off his feet, and the coachman, in obedience to Jack, caught him by the ankles.

"Run!" cried Jack.

They ran forward twenty yards or so.

"Swing!" shouted Singleton. "One—two—three!—Away!"

Sir Hinckton Moys was helpless—they were on the brink of the stagnant canal, on the surface of which was so fine and thick a coating of duckweed that it almost looked like a grass-plat.

There was then a loud cry and as loud a splash—Sir Hinckton Moys had disappeared about the centre of the canal.

"That will do," said Jack; "good night."

The bewildered coachman was left alone by the banks of the canal, for Sixteen-stringed Jack immediately disappeared in the darkness.

Jack knew that in the direction towards the Horse Guards the canal did not go right to the paling, and he soon treaded it, and made his way to the other side, where he clambered over the paling that was next to the Birdcage Walk.

Jack meant to proceed to the "Shipper's Arms," and partake of the hospitality of Mr. and Mrs. Bonus, and the lovely Polly.

The cavalry patrol had been alarmed in the Park, and the officer in command had ordered a halt. A couple of troopers dismounted, and proceeded in the direction of the cries for help, and the first person they encountered was the royal coachman scrambling over the fence back to his coach and horses.

The terror and bewilderment of this man was so great, that when he was seized by the troopers he fancied that some other phase of the dangers and entanglements of that night was about to commence; and dropping on his knees he cried out, "Kill me at once! kill me at once! It's just as well to kill me at once as drive me out of my wits!"

It was then with no small difficulty that the officer of the patrol elicited from him sufficient information to comprehend something of what had occurred.

The presence of one of the Regent's carriages, and of this man in the livery of the Prince, together with his state of fright, might well induce a belief that he was himself the willing agent in the perpetration of some horrible crime.

The officer of the guard had just ordered the two dismounted troopers to get links at the Horse Guards, and make an examination of the enclosure of the Park, when a wretched-looking figure appeared at the palings, making endeavours to cross them.

Had the officer and his men been at all superstitious they might well have fled in dismay before the more than strange aspect of the being who now presented himself.

The face, hands, and the whole of the clothing were covered with a thick green slime, and which trailed out of the garments of the wretched-looking object, as, with groans and sighs, and a slow, tremulous motion, it rather rolled over the top of the paling than with any energy climbed it.

The night light was just sufficient to enable the patrol of the guard to see this strange apparition; and it was only the officer, who had presence of mind enough to cry out, "Good heavens! Who and what are you?"

"Murder! Seize him! Kill him! A hundred pounds—two hundred pounds—a thousand pounds reward!" gasped Sir Hinckton Moys; for it was he who presented so miserable a spectacle.

"Why," said the officer, "if I were not certain of the impossibility of such a thing, I should say that was the voice of Sir Hinckton Moys, the—the friend of his Highness the Regent."

"I am! I am!"

"You, sir!"

"I am! Save me! Oh, save me and kill him!"

"Who! This coachman?"

"Yes, and then the other."

"Murder!" shouted the coachman; and taking now fairly to his heels he fled towards the Palace, leaving the Regent's carriage and horses to take care of themselves.

But Sir Hinckton Moys was slowly recovering some of his presence of mind, and he felt a wild fury as he reflected upon the sort of story that his maladventures of that night would furnish for all the gossips of the Court.

Over and over again he condemned his own folly for appearing in the state he was until the coast was clear.

"Hark you, sir," he said to the officer, "I am Sir Hinckton Moys; and I have, as you say, the honour of being the friend of his Royal Highness the Regent. It is upon his business I have been to night. I found it necessary to pursue, even across the pond yonder, some of his enemies; and I am of opinion that his Royal Highness will not feel obliged to any one who makes mention of this matter."

The officer bowed.

"You may depend upon my discretion, Sir Hinckton Moys."

"And your men, sir?"

"An order will suffice. A real soldier knows nothing and sees nothing that his officer does not wish him to know and see."

"That is well, sir. You are a subaltern?"

"I am."

"Your captaincy will not be far off, sir."

The officer bowed again; and Sir Hinckton Moys, feeling some uncomfortable, cold shivering coming over him, started off at a quick pace towards his lodgings.

But as he went, it was with a deep and bitter malediction he muttered to himself, "She has triumphed over me, after all, so far, that I shall not sleep in St. James's Palace to-night; for how can I possibly present myself in this plight? Well, well, I have still a power over her from this night's walk which must keep her and the Regent separate. My more than fortunate letter

that Annie thought she handed from the coach window to the Prince, put it out of her power to exculpate herself. Ah! confusion! Where — where? Death, and despair! Where is it!"

Sir Hinckton Moys felt hurriedly from pocket to pocket of his drenched apparel for the letter, but it was gone.

He clasped his hand in despair.

"The villain has stolen it from me," he said; "and I am lost, lost, lost!"

Moys seemed, upon this discovery, to lose in a moment all his strength. He could hardly crawl to his lodgings; and when he reached them, he fell down twice on the door step before he could put his private pass-key in the lock and procure admittance.

Indeed, it was only upon the approach of the watch — with whom he was afraid that he would have another long and tedious explanation to

No. 65 — DARK WOMAN.

endure — that he summoned strength enough to let himself into his lodgings.

But when there a new perplexity awaited Sir Hinckton Moys — for no sooner had he made his way into the first apartment of the suite he occupied than he fell prostrate over some one who seemed to have taken a fancy of enjoying a nap upon the floor.

But if such was the case, indeed, the slumbers of this person were roughly and rudely disturbed by Moys, who, being glad to have some apparently living object upon whom to wreak his vengeance, commenced by a series of kickings and cuffings of the most alarming character.

There was evidently a limit to the presence of this unknown person, which Sir Hinckton Moys soon reached; and then, the battle raged on both sides, creating so much confusion that the occupant of some adjoining chamber made his appearance in a state of ridiculous dishabille with a light, and finding the door of Sir Hinckton Moys' apartments open, shed a sudden illumination upon a very strange scene.

Sir Hinckton, still in that dilapidated and unwholesome condition in which he had emerged from the canal in the centré of St. James's Park, was furiously fighting with his valet, Shambles.

When the light came, they recognised each other.

"Wretch!" cried Sir Hinckton Moys. "How came you to be in my way, upon the floor?"

"I'm a dead man!" said Shambles.

"I wish to heaven you were!"

"I've suffered more to-night than ever I did in all my life before. I was knocked down in the Park by somebody who had a fist that would have felled an ox, and then I was belaboured by a horsewhip as long as somebody could find strength to lay it on me."

Sir Hinckton Moys, at these words, raised almost a scream of disappointment and rage.

"Fooled—fooled!" he cried. "Most completely foiled and beaten in all directions! My revenge, then, is yet to come, if it shall ever come! It was you, idiot, and not Allan Fearon, to whom I administered that punishment with a coachman's whip in St. James's Park. He has escaped me still! Something seemed to tell me, even at the moment, that the manner in which he took my vengeful assault was unnatural. All is lost for the present! I must rest—rest—rest, and think."

Sir Hinckton Moys clasped his head with his hands; and Shambles, in a very woful condition indeed, just managed to gather strength enough to scramble to his feet, and, borrowing a light of the alarmed neighbouring lodger, he closed the door of the chambers, and propping himself up in a distant corner, as far away as possible from Sir Hinckton Moys, he glared at him with a hope that he would either go to sleep or become rationally conversant.

———

CHAPTER CXLI.

THE DARK WOMAN'S PAGE, CARLOS, PROCEEDS ON AN ERRAND OF RELIEF AND MERCY.

THE Dark Woman slept.

Twice did that young girl, whose mind was so full of terrors that she trembled at her own footfall, proceed to the side of the couch on which lay her imperious mistress, and look anxiously in the now calm face, behind which toiled a brain so full of wild excitements and disordered passions.

The double opiate was doing its work; and that young girl, who for love and the few words of kindness which were at times vouchsafed to her by the Dark Woman, had followed her fortunes with such docility and faithfulness in the character of a page, felt that she had some hours at her own disposal.

Her resolution was to devote those hours to charity and mercy.

Her gentle mind had received a shock from the recent proceedings of the Dark Woman which it could not recover; and terrible as seemed the outer world to that child of sad fortunes, she felt a kind of moral necessity to discontinue further association with one to whom crime had become habitual,

and human life a plaything, to be broken and destroyed at her own good pleasure.

"She sleeps! she sleeps!" sighed the young girl. "Surely she sleeps soundly, now; and even those wild dreams which at times sweep like a tempest over her mind will fail to awaken her. Often—often has she told me how powerful was that sleeping draught which she trusted me to prepare for her. Alas! she has trusted me once too often, and I have betrayed her! Heaven pardon me, it is for a life's sake! I cannot look tamely on and see murder done as though it were but a casual incident, making up the sum of a single day's events! That cry, that fearful cry, still rings in my ears. I will save that life, if possible, and then fly for ever!"

The Dark Woman moaned sadly in her sleep.

Carlos started, and, with bated breath and clasped hands, awaited the possible awakening of Linda de Cheveneux.

But she stirred not.

Some distressful fancy had passed across the half-slumbering brain, and now she was still again, and as placid as death to look upon.

"Farewell!" said the page. "I do not go to betray you, but to save you; for, by saving this life that you would fain sacrifice, I surely lift off from your soul one sin which might help to weigh it down to perdition. Farewell! Such secrets as I know of yours shall lie deep in the recesses of my heart; but there is murder and despair in the atmosphere of this house, and I cannot breathe it. Farewell!"

The young girl was now perfectly assured that the Dark Woman slept soundly, and with a light and agile step she sought one of the apartments on that same floor where such simple provisions as she herself cared for were to be found.

Some milk, a small portion of new bread, and then from the laboratory of Astorath a small phial, containing a pink-looking liquid, were all the medicaments and provisions which the young girl encumbered herself with on her route to the lower regions of that dismal house in search of the man who might be possibly with the dead, but who, if he still lived, she felt determined should not perish for want of such slender aid as she could render him.

The profound stillness in that house was depressing, and calculated to engender such mental influences as might well unnerve the strength and spirits of one so young and gentle as this page, who had seen so much to terrify and disorder an imagination of the acutest order during her residence with the Dark Woman.

It appeared to her fancy, likewise, that the neighbouring houses, the streets in the vicinity—nay, the whole great city itself—had hushed down into a state of profound repose since the Dark Woman had closed her eyes, and that powerful opiate had laid its tender influence upon her brain.

And the effect of all this stillness was, that the young girl trod as lightly as foot could fall.

It seemed to Carlos—for still we must call her Carlos for want of another name—that the very rustle of her garments, or a deeper inspiration of breath than usual, would be sufficient to awaken some disturbing influence, and turn her from her purpose.

As she reached the passage of that dreary abode, her agitation became extreme.

The powerful mental influence which the Dark Woman had for so long exercised over her made this first attempt at independent action on her part appear to be full of a thousand perils and a thousand audacities.

But the compassionate feeling in that young breast conquered all others. Gloom, darkness, and danger,—all succumbed to the powerfully-aroused feeling of pity.

Again and again the echoes of that dismal cry, which the housebreaker had uttered when he fell before the assassinating and vengeful arm of the Dark Woman, smote her heart.

Could she lie down to rest in that mansion, and believe for a single moment that there was one in its lower regions panting for the breath of life—one to whom each passing moment counted as a pulsation, the numbers of which were few, that lay between him and the grave?

"I will save him! I will save him!" she murmured. "I will save him yet, for something tells me that he lives."

Slowly the young girl took her way to the extremity of the passage.

Her young eyes were accustomed to the darkness and obscurity of that melancholy house in Frith Street, Soho; and she, too, remarked—not with the exultation that the Dark Woman had done, but with a feeling of profound pity—the blood-stains which were upon the floor.

To trace them to the door through which the unfortunate Shucks had plunged was an easy task.

But the door was locked.

The Dark Woman had the key.

The young girl clasped her hands despairingly, and, but for the small basket in which she carried the provisions, and the bottle with the pink liquid hung upon her arm, she must have dropped them, from the feeling of listlessness which came over her.

But this feeling was transient.

"I have dared already," she said, "much, and I will dare more still. The Dark Woman sleeps; surely I can take from her with safety and security the key which will enable me to pass this door."

Even as she spoke she placed the little basket of provisions at her feet, and, with a quicker step by far than she had descended the staircase that led to the first floor of the house, she took her way to the side of the couch on which slept the Dark Woman.

The page well knew that in the breast of her apparel her slumbering mistress had a secret pocket, in which she was wont to place everything she set great store by.

There, in all probability, was the key.

There was a flush upon the fair countenance of that young girl—in whose eyes the light of joy so seldom shone—as the cold touch of the key saluted her fingers.

"I shall be successful!" she murmured. "Heaven prospers and aids me! I shall save him yet!"

Floating down the staircase again like a vision, or like some wandering ray of light that had been betrayed by accident into that gloomy place, and in vain sought its way out again to mingle with the sunshine and the free air of heaven, the young girl made her way again to the hall, and with hands trembling with anxiety fitted the key to the lock.

It turned with difficulty.

The door creaked on its hinges.

One hand upon her heart and the other behind her ear, in an attitude of intense listening, the Dark Woman's page bent slightly forward towards the dark and dismal abyss that was before her.

"All still! All silent! Is it the stillness of death — the silence of extinction? Ah, no! What sound is that—so light, so gentle, that it scarcely moves the stagnant air, and would surely not have reached younger or less acute senses than those of the fair being who, amidst such profound silence, had watched for some response to the light beatings of her own heart?

A sigh—a moan—some faint sound compounded of both sigh and moan, but yet unmistakable in its presence, far down below from where she stood —spoke to her still of the presence of life in the man who had been left there to die.

Then came again the glow of pleasure and satisfaction into the face of the page.

"I shall save him! I shall save him!"

She clasped her hands over her face for a moment, and perhaps, for the first time, she asked herself to account, with any rationality, for the abundant interest she took in the life of one who, from the few words he had uttered to the Dark Woman, betrayed his connexion with not a very creditable class of society.

But the page was baffled when she asked herself such a question; and she was fain to think that the innate principles of pity and compassion which belonged to her nature moved her to action.

There was something likewise fascinating to the imagination in the adventurous character of the circumstances. She, as yet upon the threshold of existence herself, was about to save a life— perhaps a worthless one, but still a life—and, worthless though it might be in human judgment, since heaven had thought fit to endow it with vitality, surely she should think it worth the saving.

The sigh was not repeated.

The moan came not again.

Were they the last utterances of expiring nature?

"Am I too late?—am I too late?" was the exclamation of the young page.

She seized the basket containing the provisions, and descended some few decayed steps of the gloomy staircase. Then, and not till then, she uttered an exclamation of impatience.

"Oh, how foolish I am!" she cried. "I go in darkness from the semi-darkness of this upper house! I go to the more complete obscurity of the cellars and regions below, and think that I can see to do some good in a place where the mole and the bat would find no eyes! I am thoughtless— thoughtless, and heedless, and all unfit to carry out the pity my heart prompts me to! A light! a light! a light! A spirit-lamp burns in the laboratory of Astorath,—that will suffice to scatter the darkness of this place! Wait yet a moment, poor heart, if you have not ceased to beat!"

Another sigh, more mournful and more profound than that which had preceded it, came from the depths below.

"Help! oh, help!" said a faint voice. "Kill me, or save me!"

"You shall be saved!" cried the page. "Patience—patience, but for a moment. Cling yet to life, and I will come to you. You shall be saved! You shall be saved!"

A strange cry, that must have had in it some tones of hope, came from below. It but faintly reached the ears of the page, for swiftly she was flying to the old laboratory of Astorath in search of the spirit-lamp.

The page was not absent more than a minute. The sound of that faint voice from below had dissipated a thousand fears. It was joy and pleasure to seek the living with succour; but the possibility of encountering the dead had been a shrinking terror.

She was at the door again. The spirit-lamp sent its faint rays upon the damp, unwholesome-looking walls and staircase; and elevating the faint, flickering light above her head, while she carried the small basket in the other hand, the Dark Woman's page descended the damp, slippery staircase, which had not echoed to the sound of human footstep for many a year, to save him whom the Dark Woman had doomed to destruction.

There must have been some peculiarity about the structure of that particular house, for the staircase descended much deeper than could possibly have been expected from the size and the style of the building above.

And now, so pleased and so elated was that young girl with the progress and the apparent success of her mission, that, as she descended deeper and deeper into that gloomy place, she cried out cheerily, "Keep a good heart! I come to help you—to try to save you! I know that you have suffered much. I heard and felt it all. My heart bleeds for you I bring you what help I can. Let hope and cheerfulness do the rest."

There was a something more than heavenly, kind, cheerful, and considerate, in the voice of this young girl, as she then called down from the upper world, so to speak, to that poor wounded soul below, who, until he heard those soft, sweet accents, could, if he thought at all, have had no other idea than to die in that dismal place.

The wound Shucks had received was far too deep and serious to leave him any power to help himself. Death! death by terrible and slow degrees, accompanied by excruciating pains, appeared to be the only fate prepared for him.

But that voice came to him like a message from heaven; and although Shucks, the housebreaker, was neither a poetical nor an imaginative man, he could not resist calling out at once, "Are you an angel?"

He had heard of angels; and there must have been some obscure idea in his mind that they had at times a mission to visit and comfort those who were in suffering.

"Are you an angel?" added Shucks.

"Oh, no, no, no!"

The young girl who played the part of page to the Dark Woman reached the foot of the steep, dreary staircase. Shucks raised himself upon one arm, all bruised and bleeding as he was, and looked into the face of the seeming page.

"Ah!" he cried, with a shriek of agony; "now I know you! now I know you! Oh, spare me and forgive me!"

He raised his eyes imploringly. One hand was soaked in blood, for he had been pressing it tightly upon his wound to stem the life-current which slowly welled from his breast where the sword had passed out after the fearful thrust the Dark Woman had made at him.

As the page held up the little spirit lamp, the small uncertain flame shed a faint lustre upon the face of the wounded man, and betrayed the world of agony that now convulsed his features.

That agony was now, though, one-half mental.

Shucks appeared to be gasping for breath for a few seconds, and then, as he closed his hands in the attitude of prayer, perhaps for the first time for many a long day, he bowed his head, and in a moaning voice sobbed, "Mary! Mary! forgive—oh, forgive me!"

His head sunk lower and lower still, and then he spoke not—he moved not.

The page set the lamp and the basket upon the lowest stair of that slippery and perilous flight she had descended, and sprang towards the wounded man.

"Speak—oh, speak again!" she cried,—"to give me assurance that you yet live!"

Shucks was silent.

"Dead! dead! He is dead! I am indeed too late—too late even with the life-restoring balsam here in this vial, which I have so often heard my dark, mysterious mistress declare contains in every drop the revivifying power of many lives. He is dead, and I am too late! All is lost!"

She knelt by the side of the miserable man. Slowly and gently she removed, one by one, his hands from before his face. Oh, how pale it was!

But yet it did not look like the face of the dead!

There was an expression upon the poor pale face that was very different from that which would have sat there had life indeed fled.

The page shook with emotion—with hope—with a feeling of ecstatic joy that she might be the means of saving a human life.

There was something to her mind so full of exultant happiness in the idea, that tears gathered to her eyes—those tears which arise from excess of sentimental feeling—not tears of grief.

There are quite as many tears shed for joy as for sorrow in this world.

But still the fearfully-wounded man did not speak.

Still he did not move.

The page dashed aside the pearly drops of feeling from her long silken eyelashes, and bestirred herself to aid him; and most of all she had reliance upon the contents of that little vial she had brought from the old laboratory of Astorath.

That young girl had every possible reliance upon the skill and learning of the Dark Woman, although she had lost all dependence upon her humanity.

The liquid in the vial was of a pale pinkish colour, and very transparent. The odour of it when the young girl unwound the piece of leather which covered the stopper, and took out the stopper itself, was powerful and narcotic.

Yet that odour was grateful to the senses—so grateful indeed, that the page inhaled it herself with pleasure.

Then she placed the neck of the open vial close to the lips of the wounded man.

The effect was almost instantaneous.

The new vapour that arose so close to his nostrils reached his slumbering brain.

Shucks slowly opened his eyes.

He uttered a deep sigh.

"Ah!" cried the page; "he lives! he lives! he will speak again!"

She slightly decanted the vial upwards, so that one drop, certainly not more, of the limpid pink fluid rested on the lips of Shucks.

That was enough.

A faint flush of colour came back to his face, and he sighed deeply; but it was one of those sighs that seem indicative of relief.

The page was delighted.

"You are better," she said. "You will live. The wound you have received is not mortal, surely, or ere now it would have killed you. Does it still bleed?"

Shucks had again pressed one of his hands upon his wound—that orifice just above his breast on the left side where the keen sword had passed; and now, in comprehension of what the page said to him, he lifted his hand.

The wound had ceased bleeding.

"Ah," she said, "you will be well again."

Shucks looked earnestly in the fair young face bent so compassionately—so almost lovingly over him; and twice, thrice his lips quivered as he tried to speak. Then he burst into tears.

———

CHAPTER CXLI.

THE DARK WOMAN'S PAGE DISCOVERS THAT A KIND ACT BRINGS WITH IT A RICH REWARD.

IT was long since Shucks, the highwayman and housebreaker, had shed tears such as they were which now welled up from his heart.

Those tears, though, wonderfully relieved him. As they flowed, the anguish of his wound became less, and in a few minutes he was able to speak.

"What has happened?" he said; "and where am I?"

"Do you not remember?"

Shucks shook his head.

"You visited the astrologer, Astorath, to ask if the Dark Woman had been the cause of the death of a comrade of yours, named Brads."

"Ah!—ah, yes!"

"You remember now?"

"I do—I do!"

"And in the darkness, at the head of a flight of stairs, you were assailed."

"Yes—oh, yes, I was badly wounded: a red-hot iron entered my breast."

"Nay, it was a sword thrust."

"It felt red-hot."

"That was, no doubt, the anguish of the wound."

Shucks was silent for a few moments; and when he spoke again it was in much fainter accents, so that the page became again alarmed for his safety.

"You—you seem to be a young and gentle boy," said Shucks; "and you look so—so kind and full of pity for me, that I am sure you will tell me—tell me——"

"What—what should I tell you?"

Shucks's voice had failed him through weakness; but he made a motion with his right hand towards the little vial, the aromatic odour from which was slowly impregnating the whole air of that dismal underground place.

Again she placed it to his lips, and this time she permitted several drops to pass out of the narrow neck of the vial.

The effect upon the failing energies of the wounded man was wonderful.

Shucks was able fairly to look into the eyes of the young girl, and to say with some amount of firmness of voice, "God bless you!"

The page smiled quietly.

"Oh, do not—do not!" moaned Shucks as he clasped his hands over his eyes.

"Do not what? What have I done to hurt you?"

"Why do you smile like her?"

"Like whom?"

"Mary—Mary!"

I do not know who you mean. I know no one of that name. Ah, surely your mind wanders, from the pain of your wound!"

"It does wander—it wanders to the past. But tell me now, while I can ask you—who and what are you?"

The young girl hesitated a moment or two, and then she said, "I am the page and attendant of the personage who resides in this house."

"Astorath's page?"

"Be it so."

"Ah, I understand now. You saw me attacked, and you are compassionate enough to come here and try to save me."

"That is it."

"And where are we?"

"In the cellars and vaults beneath the house."

"God bless you, boy—God bless you! And so you could not leave a poor fellow to die here?"

"I would not."

Shucks reached out his hand and took one of the young girl's in it, and held it as tightly as he could; and then, while tears came again to his eyes, he said, "If ever, living or dying, I forget this kindness, may—may——Well, well! I know not what to say, but I feel it—I feel it here, boy."

Shucks pressed his other hand upon his heart.

"I am sure you do," said the page. "And now tell me, can you get up, do you think, and leave the house?—for if you can, I will now take you out of it in safety."

"I will try. Oh, heaven!"

Upon the first movement that Shucks made to gain his feet, the agony of the fearful wound he had received was so great that he was compelled to sink back again to the damp earth.

"You cannot yet—I see you cannot yet quit the place, and I am not strong enough to carry you; but be not alarmed. I will tend you until you gather more strength—I will bring you food; and perhaps in a few days you may be well enough to avail yourself of the liberty that I now give you."

"Thanks—oh, thanks! What shall I not owe to you!"

"Nothing—nothing. I feel so much happier than ever I did before, that you can scarcely owe me thanks."

"Do not say that, boy—do not say that. But—but there is one thing I would ask of you."

"What is it?"

"It is that—that you will not smile again."

"How strange a request! But since you ask it,

I will be careful not to do so. Alas! I do not smile often."

"And yet you are so young!"

"I am young."

"And no smiles?"

"Mine has been no smiling childhood. But will you not tell me why it is you object to my looking, even for a passing moment, happy?"

"I—I—will. I seem—I don't know why—but I feel as if I ought to tell you. Perhaps, after all, this bad wound will be my death, and it may be that it will be all the better for me in another world that I have told some one here how sorry—how very, very sorry I am, and how I repent. Will you listen to me, boy?"

"With all my heart."

"Well, then, you must know that—that some sixteen years ago there was one who loved me; the only one who ever did love me. But I was wild and reckless, and slighted the good heart that was all my own."

"Alas! alas! Why did you?"

"Because it was all my own. That, boy, was just the reason."

"I cannot understand that as a reason."

"No, no! Perhaps you cannot, but it was so."

"Of whom do you speak?"

"Of my wife—my poor wife!"

Shucks was now silent for a short time, and in tones of deep sadness he added, "I will tell you now why I asked you not to smile. It was because your smile is the picture of hers; and when I looked into your face I could fancy that I saw her back again in life."

"She is dead, then?"

"She is. I—I—Oh, heaven! I——"

"Whence this emotion? Why do you look so convulsed with grief? Why those tears?"

"I killed her!"

The young girl shrank back so as to be out of reach of Shucks, and an expression of horror and dislike came over her sweet face.

"You killed her? You, who I am saving at peril of my own life? You are the murderer of one who loved you and smiled upon you? Your hand deprived her of life—your own wife?"

"No, no! Oh, do not think that!"

"You said it."

"Not my hand. I never raised a hand against her; never—never! But—but I scorned her love; and one day—one night, rather, I should say—I left her to want—to bitter cold—to tears—to misery. When I returned she was no more."

"Dead?"

"Dead—dead!"

"And you—what did you do then?"

"The bitterness of grief came over me, and I called aloud for my child."

"What child?"

"My own little one. An infant rested upon the breast of the deserted one when I left her to want and to death. The door, when I returned, of the wretched house in which we lived was swinging on its hinges, and the snow was beating—beating into the place. It fell upon the body of my lost, murdered wife, but the child was gone. I fled in despair and remorse from the spot, and from that time to this I have led a life of crime."

"And your child?"

"I never saw her again."

"Her! It was a girl, then?"

"Yes—yes! A dear, sweet little one. But I should know her—I ought to say I shall know her if ever I am permitted to look upon the angels. It was a freak, a whim of mine, when the little one was but one month old, to make, with a small needle's point and some powdered gunpowder, a cross upon her arm."

The page of the Dark Woman uttered a shriek.

"Good heaven! What is amiss! You swoon, boy! Who has hurt you? Help! help!"

"No, no! This is heaven's goodness! Oh, thanks! thanks! a million thanks! Such boundless gratitude to heaven—I—I—I——"

The words the young girl would fain have uttered were choked in sobs. But she gently placed her arms around the wounded housebreaker, and rested her head upon his breast and cried like a child.

"What—what—what is all this, boy? You—you seem to—to——Oh, what am I to think?"

"Father! father! my own father!"

"Father? You—you——"

"Yes, I am your own child. I adopted this disguise to please an imperious mistress. The cross is on my arm. Oh, father, father! you have found me. I am your dear daughter!"

Shucks uttered a bewildering scream, and then fell back insensible.

The spirit lamp showed symptoms of extinction at this moment, and the agony of the page was intense at the idea that the father she had so recently found was possibly no more. She forgot at the moment where they were, and all the dangers of her situation in that house with the Dark Woman: she cried aloud for help, and screaming, she fled to the hall.

"Help! help! He is dying! My father is dying—my own father!"

The intense stillness of the house probably had more effect upon the alarmed imagination of that young girl than any words would have had; and after a few moments she paused, and crouching down to listen if any sounds came either from above or below in that house of terror, she was soon more calm and self-possessed.

"A light—a better light!" she said, as she darted up the staircase to the first floor.

The page knew well where to procure light in that house, and she was quickly in possession of one that would last some hours.

With all her intense desire, however, to revisit her wounded father in those gloomy regions below the level of the street, she could not control the irresistible desire to see if the Dark Woman still slept soundly.

Yes, all was still.

The slumbers of the Dark Woman appeared now to be more profound even than when the young girl had last looked upon her.

The powerful opiate had probably more time in which to do its work. It had, no doubt, now laid hold, with all its deadening power, of the nervous system of Linda de Chevenaux.

"That is well. The house is still my own," said the page.

She darted with speed into the hall again, and thence down the steep slippery stairs that led to the cellars and long disused vaults.

Shucks was still in a state of insensibility, but the wound in his breast had not given forth any more blood, so that she had hopes of soon restoring him to consciousness by the aid of that potent liquid in the little vial.

A few drops upon his lips caused a slight twitching of the muscles of the face, and then Shucks opened his eyes again.

"Father! father!"

"A dream—a dream!" murmured the house-breaker.

"No, father—it is no dream. I am here—your own child—your own daughter."

Shucks stretched out his arms, and held his daughter to his breast.

"Tell me—oh, tell me all!" he said. "Why are you here? How are you here? Am I dead or alive?"

"You are alive, father; but you are in danger."

"In this house? Yes, it is in this house I received so fearful a wound. What have I done to Astorath that he should seek my life?"

"It is not Astorath."

"Who then? You are silent—you do not speak to me, my own child. God bless you, it is not I who should command you to speak. Say to me what you will, or only look upon me, and I am too—too happy."

"Father, I ought to tell you all. The attempt that has been made against your life absolves me from all allegiance — from all obligation to another. And besides, in order that you should know how to be cautious, it is proper you should be aware from whom you received your supposed death wound."

"Yes, yes, my child—tell me."

"The Dark Woman!"

"Ah!"

"She it was who wielded the sword which has so narrowly escaped your heart."

"The Dark Woman here?"

"Even here."

"But how—how could she? How could Astorath permit her, or lend himself to such an act?"

"There is no Astorath, father. Linda de Chevenaux, the Dark Woman, is alone the inhabitant of this house; and it is she who plays the part of Astorath, the astrologer and fortune-teller."

Shucks drew a long breath.

"Then I put my head in the lion's mouth, indeed, by coming here."

"She was sure to try to kill you."

"Of course—of course. But you—you, dear—how came you here?"

"Friendless, forsaken, and destitute, she was kind to me in her strange way; and for a long time, now, out of my young life, I have been a faithful servant to her."

"Kind to you?"

"Oh, yes, very kind."

"Then—then I won't kill her. I forgive her, for that. But we must get away, my dear. God bless your sweet eyes! you shall not stay here. I am a bad—a very bad fellow; but there is Sixteen-stringed Jack and his daughter Lucy. You shall know them, and they will be kind to you. Oh, that I was but able to walk!—but this sword thrust has laid me up, my dear child."

"We will wait, father."

"Where is she now?"

"Above, in the house, asleep."

"Hush!"

The young girl started. A dull, heavy sound came from above. It was a knocking at the outer door of the house; and situated as Shucks and his daughter were in that dismal, underground portion of the premises, the sound only came to their ears in a strange, muffled fashion, as though it was much further off than in reality it was.

"It is some one demanding admission to the house," said the page.

"Who?—who, think you?"

"I cannot tell; but it will be safer and better for me to go to the door. You will have the light here, father, and you will be safe."

The dull, heavy knocking continued; and it was evident that whoever, in such a noisy fashion, demanded admittance to that dismal house in Frith Street, Soho, either had abundant authority, or was careless of the amount of noise he made.

"My dear child," said Shucks, "come to me again as soon as you can."

"I will—father, I will; but this knocking, which sounds, no doubt, much louder above than here, may awaken the Dark Woman, and you are too seriously wounded, and I am too weak, to cope with her."

"That is well thought of," said Shucks. "Here is a loaded pistol, my dear child. It is so small, you see, that you may easily carry it about with you. Take it, and defend yourself and me."

"I take it, father; but I will pray to heaven there may be no cause to use it."

The young girl lightly ran up the staircase to the hall, which, when she reached, she was alarmed to stay in; for the knocking at the street door seemed as if it had never ceased, and would never never cease until the door was opened.

The means of ascertaining the character, and number, and condition of any visitors to the house of Astorath, the astrologer, were full and complete; and although the night was dark, yet the interior of the house was darker still, so that dimly illumined as was Frith Street, Soho, by one of those wretched oil lamps which did duty in London at that period, it was quite possible to make an accurate observation through small squares of glass let into the intricate scroll-work at each side of the door.

Such observations had been too often made by the Dark Woman's page, since she had played the part of Astorath, the astrologer, to present any difficulties to the young girl, who now felt more interest than ever she had done in any visitors that might come to that gloomy and mysterious mansion.

Drawn up close to the kerb-stone was a coach, which, from its dark and sombre aspect, might be supposed to be one of those belonging to a mourning establishment.

Upon the doorstep was a man muffled in a cloak, who kept up the furious knocking at the door.

As the young girl-page of the Dark Woman made these observations, the man who was demanding admittance ceased his furious application on the door panel; and then, as if he had come to a second point in some duty which particularly devolved upon him that night, he began to speak in a drawling, monotonous tone of voice.

"I order this door to be opened," he said, "in the name of the law, and by warrant of the Privy Council, sitting in judgment upon sworn information; and upon contumacy, this door will be forced forthwith, and Linda de Chevenaux—falsely calling herself Princess of Wales — will be duly apprehended."

The page shrank back.

Here, then, was surely the end of the career of the Dark Woman. Here was the secret of her existence discovered, and of her abode in that house of Astorath, the astrologer.

What was to be done? A pang shot across the heart of the young girl; and notwithstanding the horror of the recent proceedings of the Dark Woman, she felt half inclined to rush up the staircase and warn her of her danger.

But the page recollected how deep was that unnatural slumber into which she had herself thrown the Dark Woman, by administering to her double the quantity of the opiate she had desired.

"I have destroyed her!" she cried. It will not be possible to awaken her from that unnatural sleep. I have destroyed her! She is lost!"

A strange, creaking noise came at the outer door, and then, with a sudden crash, it was burst open at the side nearest its hinges.

The page fled from the hall like some fleeting shadow through the darkness, and passing through the doorway which led to the vaults and cellars below, she placed her fragile form against it—for there was no fastening on the inner side—and listened to what might ensue.

CHAPTER CXLIII.

ANNIE CARRIES ON A DIPLOMATIC CORRESPONDENCE WITH THE REGENT.

THE excitement at the Hanover Hotel was very great; for before the next day after Annie's residence there had half passed away, there was not a soul in the establishment, from the hall porter to the proprietor, who was not perfectly well aware that the elegant and rather imperious young lady who occupied the best suite of apartments in the house, was none other than the Countess de Blonde, the well-known last favourite of the Regent.

Annie made herself quite at home.

That light-hearted gaiety of disposition—which really covered, as we know, a great amount of genuine feeling—always carried Annie, Countess de Blonde, triumphantly through any little circumstances like the present.

The same smile was on her lip, the same sparkle in her eyes, and the same easy air of nonchalant prosperity, as when she seemed to be the life-tenant of a suite of apartments in St. James's Palace.

Annie knew her position perfectly well. The Regent was all in the wrong, and she was all in the right; consequently she made up her mind to assume a dignity to which he would have to bow down, or for ever forego her really affectionate companionship.

Annie was extravagant, and Annie was vain. The value of money, as such, never presented itself to her imagination; but she was exceedingly single-hearted.

George, the Regent, had penetration enough to perceive that of all the mistresses who had graced and gratified his leisure, she was the only one who had never betrayed a grasping cupidity suggestive of the period of their separation.

If Annie wished for a new set of jewels, it was not for their intrinsic value, but in order that they might glitter in his presence, and just please a little fretful vanity of an hour.

The Regent had tested her frequently in this respect.

If the value of these commodities had been what Annie had sought after, what she called the "old ones"—in reference to, sometimes, a set of brilliants worth about a thousand pounds—would not have been surrendered with the carelessness of a child who throws away a toy of which it is tired for a new one, as she always gave up to him such matters when anything in the shape of novelty took their place.

If ever there was a human being who cast no thought upon the future, certainly that human being was Annie, Countess de Blonde.

This was certainly not, perhaps, very wise in respect to her association with the Prince of Wales; but Annie never asked herself if it were wise or not.

And now let us look at her, seated at the most elegant breakfast which the resources of the Hanover Hotel could possibly produce.

Every delicacy of the season that could adorn such a meal was placed before her; and then Annie, after surveying the whole, astonished the waiters and attendants by quietly breakfasting off a piece of bread and butter and one small cup of coffee.

Everybody in the hotel had managed, by some means or another, to obtain a glimpse of her.

How strange are the mutations of this great artificial world in which we live!

Over and over again had Annie, while working for the wardrobes of the theatres,—and earning by that wretched employment scarcely enough to keep life in her delicate and pretty structure—passed, shivering, through rain, snow, and tempest down different streets of the metropolis without a passing glance being cast on her.

Now, the waiters of the Hanover Hotel reaped a rich harvest of half-crowns from different persons for the opportunity of getting a peep at her.

At twelve o'clock Annie rung the bell, the silken cord of which, by her special direction, had been conducted over the arm of the sofa, just within her reach.

The landlord himself, upon this occasion, made his bowing appearance, for he thought the breakfast was over; and as it was the first meal the illustrous Countess de Blonde had partaken of in his house, he rather laid himself out for some expressions of approval upon its sumptuous character.

"Your ladyship was pleased to ring," he said.

"To be sure I was," said Annie. "What else is the bell for?"

The landlord found it difficult to answer this remark very readily, and he only rubbed his hands together, looking expectant and foolish.

"Yes, I rang the bell," added Annie: "dear me, what was it for?"

"Perhaps," said the landlord, brightening up, "it was to say that your ladyship approved of our humble exertions in the way of breakfast?"

"No, that wasn't it."

"But still I hope——"

The landlord gave a sweeping glance at the courtly equipage which glittered with silver and

cut-glass, so that Annie saw in a moment what he meant.

"Oh, you mean all this," she said. "Why didn't you send what I ordered? I've been forced to breakfast on bread and butter."

"Good gracious, your ladyship! Is it possible you ordered anything in my house that was not brought to you immediately?"

"To be sure."

"May I humbly ask what was it?"

"Perhaps I did not mention it; but, you see, I'm in the habit of having things brought to me, that I want, without speaking."

"Then, your ladyship, I—a—rather wonder how those who must always take a pleasure in serving your ladyship find out exactly what to do."

"That's their business."

The landlord bowed.

"I dare say I didn't say what I wanted, but

No. 66 —DARK WOMAN.

your people ought to have found out; but they are dreadfully stupid."

The landlord coughed slightly.

"And you don't seem to know."

"I must confess, your ladyship, that I have the singular misfortune to be at fault."

"Then you ought not to be. It's the most simple and natural thing in the world for breakfast."

"May I ask——"

"Well, I suppose I must take the trouble of saying it."

"If your ladyship graciously pleases."

"It is a stewed peacock, with pippin apples."

The landlord staggered back, aghast.

"Well, stupid," said Annie, "do you hear?"

"I'm afraid your ladyship——"

"Of course you are—you look as if you were. I believe I've more real courage than all the men put together. Why don't you get it? Come, I want it at once."

"But, your ladyship, a peacock has to be caught, and plucked, and stewed; and then the pippins——"

"Oh, I see!—of course. One can't get what one wants, so I won't have it at all. But you can tell the Regent, if he calls here, to wait. I won't see him till one o'clock."

The landlord bowed himself out backward from the room, and he was so utterly confounded by the order that Annie had given, that she burst out into a scream of laughter to hear him shout out at the top of the stairs, "The Countess wants a stewed Regent and pippins, and the peacock to wait till one o'clock."

It was at this moment that a horseman, attired in a quiet and gentlemanly suit of brown cloth, with violet-coloured gloves, and a cravat of great richness and elegance, halted at the door of the Hanover Hotel.

Alighting, he entered the hall with an easy air of confidence which bespoke immediate attention from the waiters.

"I wish to see the Countess de Blonde," said the visitor in courteous tones.

It was not at all probable that the occupant of the best suite of rooms in the Hanover Hotel, who had complained of not having a peacock and pippins for breakfast, and had ordered that the Regent himself should be told to wait till one o'clock should he happen to call, would allow herself to be intruded upon by a chance visitor on horseback.

But still there was something about the air and manner of the visitor that induced the landlord to think that it might be just as well to carry his name to the capricious Countess.

The visitor was quite prepared for this contingency, inasmuch as he was none other than our friend Sixteen-stringed Jack.

Jack had two errands to the Countess this morning, both of which he knew would afford her satisfaction.

One was, to assure her that her instructions in regard to the ducking of Sir Hinckton Moys in the canal of St. James's Park had been faithfully carried out; and the other was, to place in her hands the two letters—one for herself, purporting to be from Marian, her sister, and the other to Allan Fearon as if from the Countess de Blonde—both of which spurious and forged letters Jack Singleton was now in possession of, to the justification of Annie, and the confusion of her enemies.

One of these letters Sixteen-stringed Jack had procured from Allan Fearon himself, and the other he had adroitly managed to take from the pocket of Sir Hinckton Moys, previous to the immersion of that individual in the stagnant waters of the canal in St. James's Park.

Sixteen-stringed Jack was not at a loss when asked for a name to send up to the Countess de Blonde; and he had, in his own mind, arranged an *alias* for the occasion which would be sufficiently explicit to her, without compromising his own safety by a declaration of who he was.

"Be so kind as to tell her ladyship," he said, "that Sir Singleton John Stringer requests the honour of an audience."

Sixteen-stringed Jack believed that Annie had quite wit enough to transpose this name into its more true signification, and he was not at all surprised to be asked, in a few moments, to walk up.

The door of the elegant apartment in which Annie was seated was thrown open ostentatiously by the landlord, who, in favour of a guest who required stewed peacocks and pippins for breakfast, and sent down messages to Prince Regents to wait his leisure, thought it no derogation of his dignity to act the part of chief waiter himself.

"Sir Singleton John Stringer, my lady!"

"Come in, Jack!" said Annie.

"Good gracious!" said the landlord as he closed the door; "that's worse than the peacock. The first visitor she has she calls Jack. I suppose if the Regent should come she'd bawl over the stairs, 'Is that you, George?'"

Sixteen-stringed Jack smiled, and cast a rapid glance round the room.

"Alone, I suppose, Countess?" he said.

"Quite. I should only like to find anybody here! I know what you come to tell me, Jack Singleton. You ducked Moys in the canal."

"I did."

Annie clapped her hands together as she exclaimed, "I was sure you would. So that being settled, it leaves me quite at liberty to see to my little wager with him."

"Wager?" said Jack—"what wager?"

"Oh, he laid his head against mine that he would destroy me with the Regent, and reinstate himself in favour."

"He will lose, Countess."

"To be sure he will."

"But you will not succeed in getting his head, since, now-a-days, heads are a little more secure than they used to be."

"But I must have it," said Annie, pattering on the floor with both her feet. "A bet's a bet, and if I have to cut it off myself with a pair of scissors, I'll have it."

Jack smiled.

"I think, Countess," he said, "I can help you to everything short of the fellow's head."

"Does that mean his head, too? since he will be that the shorter."

"Countess, you have really as much wit as you have beauty, and that is a high compliment to both; and I may add, that I think you have as much real good-heartedness as wit and beauty."

"Dear me!" said Annie, making an affected rummaging in all her pockets; "what do you want for all that?"

"Nothing; but, in addition to it, I beg to hand to you these two letters."

"Ah!" cried Annie, as she clasped her hands in triumph.

"One of them is that which, in the darkness at the carriage door in St. James's Park, you fancied you handed to the Regent; while, in reality, it was the villain Moys who took it. The other is the forged epistle purporting to be from yourself to Allan Fearon, which induced him to be in the Park, on his route to St. James's Palace, at the time in question."

"Then I am doubly armed," said Annie.

"Your exculpation with the Regent will be as clear as day. You will see, by casting your eyes over it, the sort of letter that induced Allan Fearon to fall into the snare prepared for him and for you."

"Poor Allan, and poor sister Marian, too!" said

Annie, as she read the letter. "I feel that while they live I shall never want friends. This, indeed, will be a convincing proof of the entire and perfect innocence of last night's proceedings. Ah, George—George! you may love me in your way and in your fashion; but it is not that love which, as one of its prime elements, possesses trustfulness."

This was about one of the most serious speeches Annie had ever made in her life; and it rather surprised Sixteen-stringed Jack to find that so apparently careless and heedless a personage could have the depth of thought to utter the words.

"What will you do, Annie?" he said, after a pause; and then he added, quickly, "Pardon me; I call you Annie because I have been in the habit of thinking of you in connexion with my own little girl, Lucy, who is now happily at home with your sister Marian. But I will be more mindful, Countess."

"Then you're the greatest wretch I know," said Annie.

"Wretch? What have I done?"

"Why, talked about being mindful not to call me Annie. Do you know, I'll never speak to you again if you call me Countess? I am no Countess. You know what I am well enough—the toy and plaything of an hour to a man who will cast me off on the caprice of a moment."

There was a touch of sadness about the tone in which Annie, Countess de Blonde, uttered these words; and Sixteen-stringed Jack could not forbear the rejoinder to them which rose to his lips.

"If," he said, "you think it possible that such may be your fate, why wish to return to the society of such a man?"

"Because—because——"

"Because what?"

"It is too late."

"I do not comprehend you, Annie."

"Then I will tell you what I mean, if for no other reason than because you have remembered what I said to you and called me Annie. It is too late, then, to be other than what I am. What honest heart would have me now?"

Annie clasped her small, delicate hands over her face; and Sixteen-stringed Jack then felt a regret that he had called into existence the feelings which, in that heart of many changes and caprices, had far better have been let slumber for ever.

"Forgive me," he said; "I am afraid I have wounded your feelings."

"No, no! Oh, no! You did not intend to do so, and therefore it is nothing. I am much beholden to you, Jack; and if ever you should want a friend, you well know, that as long as I have any power to serve any one, that power shall be at your service."

"I thank you with all my heart. But there has been two taps at the door; I fancy some one is here."

"Ah! Perhaps——"

Annie paused; and Sixteen-stringed Jack, instead of crying out "Come in," or leaving Annie to do so, went to the door and flung it open.

The landlord met him with a low bow.

"Sir," he said, "there is another gentleman who asks to see the Countess. His name, he says, is Fearon."

"Admit him instantly," cried Annie.

Allan Fearon, pale and sad, stood on the threshold of the gorgeous apartment.

"My dear Allan!" cried Annie, "come in. Believe me, I am very, very glad to see you, for am I not your sister? Oh, Allan, pray own me for a sister!"

CHAPTER CXLIV.

THE REGENT BEGINS TO FEEL UNHAPPY IN HIS MIND ABOUT ANNIE.

It is necessary that we should request the kind and indulgent reader's company from the Hanover Hotel—where the Countess de Blonde seems to be holding a kind of levee—to the abode of the Regent.

Carlton House was not exactly an elysium, on the morning after the strange events that had taken place in St. James's Park, to those whose duty it was to come into immediate contact with the Regent.

The temper of that potentate was in anything but a satisfactory condition.

The order that the Regent had given, to refuse admission to the Palace to the Countess de Blonde, had been wrung from him in a moment of passion and irritation. It was anything but the real spontaneous result of his convictions.

It is a rule or law of the moral world, that let deceit or untruth be closed in what seductive or probable garbs they may, there is always a something about them which engenders a suspicion that all is not right.

The most artfully constructed lie that the perverse ingenuity of man ever produced is, after all, but a lie; and although it may bear so great a resemblance to truth as to make it difficult to distinguish its spurious character, yet, as it is not truth, there must be something about it which proclaims the counterfeit.

The Regent, then, thought that he ought to feel quite certain in regard to the faithlessness of Annie; but yet he had a painful lingering doubt in the depths of his heart upon the subject.

He thought he ought to entertain no doubt whatever of the fact that Allan Fearon was the favoured lover of the Countess de Blonde, and yet he could not altogether reconcile himself to a perfect and demonstrated conviction on the matter.

The Regent was, therefore, unhappy.

The Regent was, therefore, cross.

When illustrious personages are unhappy and cross, it is very likely to happen that those whose duties may bring them into the presence of such illustrious personages may find out the fact in an uncomfortable fashion.

It was found out that morning by all who came into the presence of George, Prince of Wales and Regent of England.

Snappish, exacting, disappointed, and bullying was the Regent; and the attendants at the royal breakfast might, and perhaps did, liken themselves, in the terms of the proverb, to a well-known domestic animal, who found himself in the regions where the blessed do not go, and at the same time destitute of claws.

It was twelve o'clock—just when Annie, at the Hanover Hotel, was promulgating her want of a peacock and pippins—that a groom of the chambers at the Palace ventured to intimate to the Regent that Sir Hinckton Moys waited his royal pleasure and his royal leisure.

It was almost with a bark like a dog who is out of humour that the Regent turned upon the groom of the chambers, and cried out, "Let him wait, then."

The Regent in another moment was alone again. Pacing one of the rooms of St. James's Palace —for he had removed immediately after breakfast from Carlton House to the old Palace by way of the private gardens—he muttered to himself his discontent.

"I wish—I wish I could find out it was all false—all a plan—all a mere scheme to separate me from Annie. Oh, if I could be only sure of that, and if I could but bring it home to the perpetrators of it, they should feel what it was to play such a game with me. And yet—yet I saw her— I saw her with these eyes, meet him in the Park. Why did I see her? Why—why? I had much better never have seen her."

The Regent flung himself into a chair, with a groan. The manner in which he had been pacing to and fro in rather a small room was beginning to confuse his brain.

"Willes, Willes!" shouted the Regent; for he felt his brain swimming and his stomach out of order.

The idea of being ill was to the Regent one of the most terrible that could enter his comprehension. He had a morbid terror of sick people—of death—of, indeed, anything in the shape of physical deterioration; and that he, the great, glorious, handsome Prince of Wales should ever be subject to any infirmity, appeared to him to be an outrage upon the due order of the world.

"Willes, Willes!" he cried again.

The valet took good care never to be far off from his royal master, and he appeared almost on the instant.

'Oh, you are there?"

'I have the honour to be here.'

'Brandy!'

'It is here, your Royal Highness.'

To the surprise of the Regent, Willes was able to hand to him, on a small gold salver, a liqueur glass of brandy.

The Regent drank it off at a draught.

"Your Highness is better?"

"Much. Another! Oh, Willes, you must never leave me."

"Never, your Royal Highness."

"You are useful to me, Willes."

"It is the highest honour and the highest ambition I could ever dream of, your Royal Highness."

"And I trust you, Willes."

Willes bowed to the ground.

"Come, come! Now tell me—truly, mind you —tell me what you think. You know that I am very angry, and justly so, with the—the—Countess——"

"De Blonde?"

"Yes, Willes, the Countess de Blonde. I have ample cause to be angry, and nothing on earth shall induce me ever to recall her to the Palace. I am quite convinced of her faithlessness, and therefore there is an end of all communication between her and me. And yet, Willes, believing you to be a faithful fellow, and far from a fool, I

should like to know what you think of the whole affair."

"May I humbly ask your Royal Highness for particulars?"

"Oh, they are few—they are few. The Countess assured me when I left her last evening, that she had no intention of leaving the Palace; but within ten minutes afterwards she ordered a carriage in haste, and went into the Park, and met some one close to the gun-house."

"May I humbly ask if that is all?" said Willis.

"I think it enough."

Willes coughed in a quiet, genteel sort of manner.

"What do you mean by that?"

"I shall offend your Royal Highness if I tell you."

"No, you won't."

"I feel that I shall, because my opinion is favourable to the Countess."

"Ah! indeed!"

"Yes, your Royal Highness. I do not think that she is guilty. I think she loves your Royal Highness, and has been, and is, faithful to you."

"But—but Willes, you are a rascal!"

The valet bowed.

"You are in the Countess's pay."

Willes was silent.

"Come, now. What grounds have you for your absurd belief in the innocence of Annie?"

The Regent was beginning to call her Annie again; and Willes noticed the change by the ghost of a smile.

"Speak! speak!" added the Regent. "Your reasons, Willes?"

"Firstly, your Royal Highness, Sir Hinckton Moys is a very great enemy of the Countess."

"Well? well?"

"And it was from him your Royal Highness got the news that this meeting in the Park was to take place."

"Well?"

"It seems very strange then, your Highness, that the Countess should have made a confidante of him."

"Of him!—of Moys?"

"Of her sworn foe."

"Ah!"

"Your Highness sees how strange that would be?"

"By Jove! I never thought of that before! And yet—yet, Willes, the fact remains the same. She did meet the person in the Park, you know, Willes. I should be *obleeged* to you to get over that fact if you can"

"And that person, your Royal Highness, was Mr. Fearon, whom your Royal Highness has seen, and from whose manner, and education, and sentiments, your Royal Highness may judge if he is likely to be a party to an intrigue with the sister of his wife."

The Regent was silent, and rested his head upon his hand for a few seconds. When he looked up again, Willes was holding on the gold salver, in a respectful attitude before him, a letter.

"What is that?"

"A letter for your Highness."

"Stuff! Throw it away!"

Willes bowed.

"Who is it from?"

"From Buckingham House, your Highness

and as it is always desirable to know what one's enemies have got to say, I would humbly suggest that your Highness should become aware of the contents of this note."

"Then you think it is from—from the Princess of Wales?"

"No, your Highness."

"No?"

"The seal does not bear the impress of her Highness's arms."

"Whose, then?"

"There is an earl's coronet."

"Open it, and read it to me."

Willis opened the letter. In a low, monotonous voice, which by no means rendered the contents of this letter more impressive, Willes read:—

"Buckingham House,
"Friday.

"DEAREST PRINCE,

"I am able to writ to you with a hope that the news I send you, since I am in the enemy's camp on your service, may be acceptable. The communications between St. James's and Buckingham House, by means of the young man, Fearon, who gets his intelligence from the Countess de Blonde, are more frequent than ever.

"A strange proposal has, however, been made to me by a certain high personage."

Willes had got thus far in the reading of the letter when the Regent burst into furious exclamations.

"Good gracious, Willes! Tell me who is that tirade of nonsense and wickedness from?"

"The letter, your Highness, is signed by the Marchioness of Sunningham."

"Ah!"

"Shall I finish it?"

"Do."

Willes read on:—

"A strange proposal has, however, been made to me by a certain high personage. It is that I should endeavour once again to possess myself of your Royal Highness's confidence and affections, and betray both to the coterie at Buckingham and Warwick Houses. If it should ever be my good fortune to entertain the leisure of your Royal Highness, I would turn the tables upon those parties who would fain make me false to my Prince and to my heart; and they would be the parties whose cabals, and treacheries, and treasons should be presented to the knowledge of the king of my affections and the Regent of England.

"Ah, George, George! you are still the one cherished idol of the fond heart of

"SARAH SUNNINGHAM."

The Regent looked in the face of Willes with a comical expression, and Willes almost ventured to smile.

"Well, Willes, what do you say to that?"

"Your Royal Highness, it only exemplifies the fact, that so soon as by any means a vacancy is caused at Court, some applicant who has early information offers for it."

"I see—I see!"

"Your Royal Highness was sure to see. What might escape ordinary penetration was sure to be quickly patent to your Royal Highness."

The Regent nodded. Such fulsome flattery as this by no means disgusted him. Use had made it sound quite natural to his ears, and he really believed the greater part of it.

"The Marchioness of Sunningham," he said, "thinks Annie dismissed, and would fain fill up her place. How has she come to know within a few short hours what has taken place in St. James's?"

"Sir Hinckton Moys, your Highness——"

"Ah, yes!"

"Waits your leisure."

The Regent laughed.

"I will see him. But you stay within hearing, Willes. Send him in here. I will see him."

Willes bowed himself out of the royal presence; and, to the great relief of Moys, he was informed by an attendant that the Regent would see him.

Moys looked pale and haggard. The events of the preceding night had told upon him. He had been half drowned in the canal in the Park; for when soused into it in the very unceremonious way adopted by Sixteen-stringed Jack, he had reached the bottom of it, where there was a plentiful supply of mud, before he could make use of either hands or feet to swim out of it.

Sir Hinckton Moys, therefore, had been compelled to gulp down considerable draughts of that not over salubrious ditch water; and he had come to the conclusion that the green slime that might be very wholesome food for ducks was anything but calculated for the human stomach.

But still, in the malignant intellect of Sir Hinckton Moys, there was a set-off against all these disagreeables.

He had triumphed over Annie!

The fair Marchioness had been turned from the door of St. James's Palace!

Sir Hinckton Moys kept telling himself this fact as a pendant to the qualms and disagreeables he felt; and so he sought the presence of the Regent, prepared to enjoy a certain amount of triumph.

Moys would have suggested to the Prince the re-establishment of the Marchioness of Sunningham as favourite if he found himself on terms to do so. The Marchioness's letter was written without his knowledge; and that epistle was sent by the intriguing and disreputable person with the hope that she should receive a favourable reply from the Prince, and be installed in St. James's without being further indebted to Moys in the matter.

Indeed she would have been quite ready to sacrifice Sir Hinckton if necessary; and she rather looked forward to doing so if she should find, on an interview with the Regent, that there were disagreeable associations connected with the name and presence of that person.

The Marchioness of Sunningham was not troubled with many scruples about throwing over one who had assisted her in her plans and projects.

But the Marchioness, although approaching those conditions which afterwards had charms for the Prince Regent—namely, "fat, fair, and forty"—had no idea of the sort of supremacy which the ingenuous mind and the youthful charms of Annie, Countess de Blonde, possessed over the heart of the Regent.

She was one of those women of "a certain age" who are too apt to underrate and undervalue the attractions of youth and unselfishness such as Annie's.

So the letter was ill-judged and ill-timed.

It lay on the floor when Sir Hinckton Moys was introduced to the Regent.

Moys was too good a courtier not to see that his reception was far from flattering. He bit his lip as he bowed, and was resolved that the Regent should speak first.

"Well, Moys—what now?"

"I hope your Highness rested well?"

"Never worse."

"I am sorry."

"So am I."

Moys was at a nonplus. What to do or what to say next he could not divine. The pause that ensued was decidedly awkward. It was broken however, by the Regent, who, with his eyes half closed, said in that cold, supercilious style which he could put on when he pleased, "Have you any business with us, Sir Hinckton Moys?"

"No, your Highness; but I had hoped that one who had toiled and suffered for your Highness would have received a somewhat more kindly reception."

"Eh?"

"I say a somewhat more kindly reception."

"Do you mean to reprove me?"

"Oh, no, no! But——"

"You would like to do so?"

"Still I reply no, your Highness. But I am at this present moment forcibly reminded of the fact that no one is thanked for ill news, and no one is more unpopular than he who has taken the trouble to remove the scales of some prejudice or deceit from our minds, which carried with it the elements of satisfaction and pleasure while it lasted."

There was a certain air of dignity about Sir Hinckton Moys as he uttered these words, which, even in his present state of mental irritation, had an effect upon the mind of the Regent.

It was quite impossible but that to a certain extent he must acknowledge their truthfulness.

It did not, or should not, lie with him to reproach Sir Hinckton Moys for the results of the very service he had employed him to render.

There was a latent feeling of generosity in the mind of the Regent, which gave Sir Hinckton's words of reproach all their effect. It perhaps depended upon the accident of a moment whether he would make an angry reply and dismiss Moys for ever from his presence, or, in a more liberal spirit, acknowledge his seeming services.

And the baffled courtier felt himself that he had played his last stake. It was a bold one; and perhaps, for that very reason, had a winning element about it.

"Hark you, Moys!" said the Prince; "there are some delusions so pleasant while they last, that although we may go through fire and water to prove them delusions, yet we feel ten times more unhappy in the knowledge. Perhaps I have been petulant to you."

"Oh, your Highness," said Moys, bowing low and clasping his hands, imparting at the same time a well-acted tremulousness to his voice,—"oh, your Highness! one word of conciliation—one word of regret, is far more than sufficient to obliterate all sense of—of—what shall I call it? despairing service."

"Say no more—say no more," said the Regent.

"I suppose I ought to thank you for making me this morning the most miserable man alive."

"And yet to see your Highness deceived—to see your kindly feelings and best affections wasted upon one who——"

"No more of that—no more of that! I know all about it! Tell me, Moys, did you part from her late last night?"

"I did, your Highness."

"And where did she go—eh, Moys?—where did she go?"

"To the Hanover Hotel, whither I conducted her with every possible respect."

"What did she say?"

"She made a wager with me."

"A wager—a wager! What was it?"

"She laid her head against mine that she would destroy my credit with your Highness, and reinstate herself in your favour."

"Your head, Moys—your head? You'd look funny without your head; but as this is not a despotic monarchy, I'm afraid I can't oblige Annie with it."

The heart of Sir Hinckton Moys sunk within him as he heard these words from the lips of the Regent. If the Prince had opened his whole soul to him, and spoken for an hour for the purpose of letting him understand what were really the thoughts passing through his mind, he could not more distinctly have made Moys understand that he would have been quite willing to make Annie, Countess de Blonde, a present of his head, provided he could have her again as a resident in that splendid suite of rooms in St. James's Palace that had been fitted up for her reception.

Again, and not for the first time, did the strong conviction come over the mind of Sir Hinckton Moys of the fatal mistake he had made in the beginning in not attaching his fortunes to the Countess de Blonde instead of opposing her, and, with the weak means at his command, attempting her ruin.

CHAPTER CXLV.

THE COUNTESS DE BLONDE ACHIEVES A GREAT TRIUMPH AT THE HANOVER HOTEL.

WRETCHED, sick, and downcast, Sir Hinckton Moys gazed into the face of the Regent. The pause that ensued was disagreeable, if it did not actually get the length of being painful on both sides.

In the mind of Moys there was the conviction of utter and complete failure in all that he had attempted to achieve.

The Regent felt a disagreeable sensation that he was ill-using the man who had suffered a good deal in his service, and who was only disagreeable to him because he had made him cognizant of some unwholesome truths.

"Moys," he said, "I can give you a little employment. Pick up that letter."

Sir Hinckton picked up with some surprise the Marchioness of Sunningham's epistle.

"Take it to Buckingham House as it is, and return it to her ladyship. Then, Moys, if you like to accept the Hanoverian Legation, it is at your service."

"I will take this letter as your Highness orders; but if it be permitted me respectfully to decline the Hanoverian Legation, I would rather do so."

"Very well. Good morning, Moys—good morning! We are very much *obleeged* to you—very much *obleeged* to you! Good morning! Willes! Willes!"

"Your Highness!"

"Wheel up that writing-table close to us. Come, quick, Willes, and find me a messenger to take me a note to the Hanover Hotel. It is not fitting that she who has been so long the friend and companion of the Regent of England should leave St. James's so totally unprovided for, as I know her to be. She was the most unselfish creature under the sun, and has taken nothing with her, and I dare say, has not a farthing. Good day, Moys—good day! We're *obleeged*—we're *obleeged*."

Sir Hinckton Moys staggered out of the room as though he had received a mortal blow. He clenched his hands and looked at Willes as he passed him, as though he would gladly have taken his life.

Willes smiled and bowed.

"Wait!" muttered Moys.

"I mean to do so," replied Willes; "while you do the other thing."

"What other thing, wretch?"

"Go, villain!"

"Beast!"

"Hyena!"

"Never mind!"

"Oh, I don't a bit!"

With a growl of rage, Sir Hinckton Moys rushed through a corridor and the Titian Gallery, muttering to himself, "She will be in the Palace again in less than an hour; and if this were indeed a despotic Government, she would have my head before dinner-time."

The Regent was calmly writing a letter. And as we will now request the reader's attention and good company to the Hanover Hotel again, we shall have there a better opportunity of scanning the contents of the royal epistle, since the letter is addressed to none other than Annie, Countess de Blonde, whose address in London Sir Hinckton Moys had kindly imparted to the Regent.

We left Annie at the moment that Allan Fearon had made his appearance at the hotel.

Allan had hastened to do so, with the conviction upon his mind that Annie was for ever divorced from the affections of the Regent.

It was not only in fair weather, and while Annie seemed likely for ever to bask in the smiles of royalty, and to be surrounded by all the luxuries the world could produce, that Marian proffered her the hand of sisterly affection.

Allan's mission now was to let her know that there was a home for her where she would be received welcomely and affectionately under any circumstances.

But poor Allan, with his simplicity of mind upon such matters, and Marian, with her ingenuous, kindly nature, were little aware of the light in which Annie viewed the whole transaction.

"Why, Allan!" she said, "you look as serious as if there was something the matter!"

"Annie, Annie! has there not always been something the matter since you left your home and Marian?"

"Now be quiet; it's no good preaching to me. I'm as bad as I can be, and I shall never be any better. How is Marian?"

"Well, but anxious."

"Poor Marian! She has suffered far more for me than ever I suffered for myself. Tell her, Allan, that I am very, very happy. Tell her not to waste a thought, a sigh, a tear upon me."

"That I should tell her in vain. But will you not remove from this place, Annie, and come to us?"

Annie shook her head.

"I can't," she said; "I'm going back to St. James's."

"Is that possible?"

"It's not only possible, but it's going to be."

"To my father! Oh, Annie, Annie! you bewilder me!"

"You look so, my dear Allan," said Annie; "so now sit down to breakfast, and you, Jack, too."

The door was flung open at this moment, and the landlord of the hotel, with a look of important consequence upon his countenance, announced in a loud voice, "A special messenger from his Royal Highness the Regent!"

Immediately following the landlord was one of those private couriers, three or four of whom were always on duty at the Palace, and who carried a despatch box covered with crimson leather, on which were the Regent's arms in gold.

"For the Countess de Blonde!" said the messenger, as he advanced, and opening his despatch box, he made use of one half of it as an extemporaneous salver, upon which he handed Annie a letter.

"I will wait your ladyship's answer in the hall, below."

"No, stop here!" said Annie; "I dare say I can give you an answer at once."

She opened the letter, which was the same the Regent had been so busily writing before Sir Hinckton Moys had fairly got out of the apartment.

An enclosure fell from the letter, to which Annie paid no attention for the present. The epistle itself contained the following words:—

"Annie, whatever you may think, it is impossible that I can be entirely unmindful of one trait in your character. You were never self-seeking, covetous, or grasping; and I feel quite confident that you must be in want of means to live with the comfort I would desire.

"Enclosed, you will find an order on Coutts's, which, if you present there on the first of every month, will produce you the sum of five hundred pounds on every occasion.

"I hope, Annie, that while you know yourself to have been single-minded and unselfish, you will not think me unjust or ungenerous.

"GEORGE."

A very few seconds sufficed to enable Annie to read this letter, and then she picked up the enclosure, which was an order on Coutts's bank to pay to her signature, on or after the first of each month, the sum of five hundred pounds.

Annie looked up at the special messenger, and said with calm indifference, "Is his Highness in town?"

"The Regent, madam, is at St. James's."

"Very well. Jack!"

Annie said this so sharply that the special messenger gave a jump; and as his name happened to be John, he was in doubt for a moment whether the Countess de Blonde had not lapsed into a sudden and absurd familiarity with him, which, however flattering it might be, was decidedly embarrassing.

Sixteen-stringed Jack, however, stepped forward and relieved his mind, by owning himself as the Jack in question.

"Yes, Countess—what can I do?"

"Cut me two thin slices of bread and butter."

Jack looked surprised, but he obeyed Annie's directions, who then, deliberately placing the Regent's order for five hundred pounds a month between the two pieces of bread and butter, took a childishly large bite, and then turning to the astonished messenger, with her mouth full, she said, "You can go and tell George I've got the money, and am eating it up as fast as I can. That 'll do. There now, be off and tell him!"

The messenger had backed to the door as he saw the Countess de Blonde thus demolishing an annuity of six thousand a-year between two slices of bread and butter, which somebody of the name of Jack had as coolly cut for her.

"Is there nothing more, madam?" he said.

"No. Yet, stop! Yes, yes, stop!"

The messenger paused.

Annie had her mouth full again in the most ungenteel way in the world as she called out, in imitation of the Regent, "Tell him I'm *obleeged*—I'm *obleeged*."

The messenger nearly fell down stairs, and never made such haste in his life with a counter-message to St. James's Palace as upon that occasion.

"Well, that's settled!" said Annie.

"But was it quite prudent?" said Jack Singleton.

"I don't know a bit; but if it wasn't prudent it's rather nasty, and I won't take any more of it."

Sixteen-stringed Jack laughed as he lifted one of the pieces of bread and butter from the other.

"Annie," he said, "you've eaten the signature, at all events, therefore the order is worthless."

"Very good!" said Annie. "Pour me out a cup of coffee; George sticks in my throat."

"Annie! Annie!" said Allan Fearon; "you have at least proved your disinterestedness. The common reproach can never cling to you, that you sold yourself to that man. Come, come, dear Annie, and be assured——"

"What a tiresome fellow you are!" interrupted Annie. "What do you mean by 'Come, come,' and all that sort of thing? I'm waiting for the next special messenger from the Regent!"

"Can you expect one, Annie, after the treatment you have given his first communication?"

Annie smiled and looked radiantly beautiful.

"By Jove, she's right!" said Sixteen-stringed Jack. "Her ingenuous simplicity, her haste, her carelessness, her very recklessness, takes the place of most consummate art; and I predict the Regent will be more violently in love with her than ever. In fact, she is so truly beautiful, so fascinating, so charming——"

"Bravo! bravo!" cried Annie clapping her hands. "Bravo! bravo! I must say, Jack, you are a man of the most excellent judgment I ever came near. Bravo! bra——"

The door was flung open again, and the landlord, almost out of breath, cried out, "Another special message from his Royal Highness the Regent!"

"Of course!" said Annie.

Another special messenger appeared, fully equipped with another crimson despatch box on which the royal arms were conspicuous.

"A letter for her ladyship the Countess de Blonde!"

"All right!" said Annie; "here you are. Don't stand there, man, looking like a fool!"

The messenger had rather a stupid, bewildered kind of look, and the scene—take it altogether—had so much of the elements of comedy about it that both Sixteen-stringed Jack and Allan Fearon were fain to retire into a recess of a window to hide their laughter.

"Well!" said Annie, "where is the letter?"

"Here, your ladyship!"

Again was one half the royal despatch box made to do duty as a salver for the purpose of handing a letter from the Regent to Annie Countess de Blonde.

The epistle contained the following words:—

"St. James's Palace.

"Annie, if you have any reasonable explanation to give me of the strange events of last night, do so. I ask you by the memory of the past, have you any such explanation to give? Answer this yourself, in writing.

"GEORGE."

"Pen and ink!" cried Annie.

Sixteen-stringed Jack and Allan Fearon both started round from the recess of the window into which they had retired. Jack Singleton saw on a side table some writing materials, and he brought them to Annie.

The capricious Countess de Blonde was in one of her wildest humours.

"Ah!" she said; "that is all very right. George asks a question, and he wants the answer in writing, which he shall have. Let me see—what does he say? 'I ask you, by the memory of the past, have you any such explanation to give?' Yes, that is it, and here is the reply."

Annie selected a large sheet of letter-paper, and wrote, in the very middle of it, the word "No." She then signed herself "De Blonde."

"There," she said, as she handed the note hastily folded to the messenger—"that is the answer."

"Will your ladyship not seal it?"

"Very well."

"His Royal Highness is so very particular."

"So am I. Wax!"

The messenger gave another jump as Annie pronounced the word "wax" with a sharpness of intonation that made it have almost the effect of a box on the ears.

"Here, Annie!" said Sixteen-stringed Jack, with a smile; "here is some sealing-wax among these pens."

"That will do."

Annie sealed the letter to the Regent, and stamped it with a ring she wore; and then, handing it to the messenger, she dismissed him with the uncourtly expression of "Be off!"

The messenger was glad to get out of the

presence of so singular a personage; and probably since royal messengers were in existence as a class, never had one of them borne so laconic an epistle to all but a crowned head as that one of Annie's to the Regent of England.

"Now," said Annie, "it's about lunch time, and you can both have what you like."

Allan shook his head.

"Nothing for me, Annie—nothing for me! But I would fain ask you a question."

"What is it?"

"Do you know anything of her whom I need not name to you?"

"The Dark Woman, Allan?"

"Yes. That is indeed and in truth the name by which you or any one may well feel justified in calling her."

Annie reflected for a few moments, and then she said, "She was at the Palace, there is no doubt; but I know nothing, as yet, of her fate. There

are two people there, though, who I think ought to know."

"And they?"

"They are, Colonel Hanger, for one, and the Regent's valet, Willes, for the other."

"I will find a way to question them both."

"I think you had better leave that to me, Allan, when I go back."

"Is it possible, Annie, that you contemplate going back to the Regent after all this?"

"That's just it!" said Annie, with a laugh. "It is because of what you call 'all this' that I am sure I shall go back. I have no doubt at all but that, by this time, Sir Hinckton Moys is in disgrace, and that George would give anything in his power to have me back again."

"She is right!" said Jack Singleton; "I, too, have no doubt on the subject."

"Then," said Allan, "if it should be so, Annie, I leave in your hands my sacred trust."

Annie nodded.

"Do not, if you know of it and can help it, let any harm come to—to——"

Allan was much affected, and paused a moment before he could add the word " mother."

During that pause he had turned again to the recess of the window, and then he uttered an exclamation, and facing round to Annie, he said, " We must go—Jack Singleton and I."

"What for ?"

"The Regent is crossing the road on foot, and making for the door of the hotel."

A triumphant smile came over the face of Annie; and she nodded her fair head several times, while a bright sparkle came to her eyes, and the colour deepened on her cheeks.

"No," she said; "don't go."

"But—but——"

"You shall not go! You have, both of you, witnessed my disgrace; you shall now witness my triumph."

Jack and Allan Fearon looked at each other, and then at Annie, and then at the door of the room, confusedly.

"You don't quite understand me," added Annie. "I don't mean the Regent to see you. Get behind that screen, both of you. I will not detain you many minutes; and I bid you both good-bye for the present now, because, if George properly apologises, I shall go back with him to St. James's."

"Mr. Smith!" announced the landlord of the hotel at this moment.

"Don't know him!" cried Annie.

"Mr. George Smith," said the Regent, as he appeared at the door of the room, attired in a plain blue surtout, which was buttoned up to the chin, while a hat was pulled down very low upon his brow.

Annie burst into a peal of loud and most uproarious laughter, and clapped her hands together.

CHAPTER CXLVI.

THE REGENT AND THE COUNTESS DE BLONDE MUTUALLY EXPLAIN THEMSELVES.

ALLAN FEARON and Sixteen-stringed Jack had only just had time to dart behind the screen which Annie had indicated, when the Prince of Wales appeared at the door of the magnificent room she occupied at the Hanover Hotel.

The somewhat lugubrious aspect of the Regent struck Annie as being very comical; and she laughed until the tears ran down her cheeks.

The Regent looked vexed.

"Is this, then, all a jest?" he said.

"Yes—yes; to be sure."

"Annie!"

"Georgey!"

"Come, come; you have played with my feelings too much and too long."

"Your feelings?"

"Yes; too much and too long. But since the human heart and the—the—a——"

"Come, come, George," said Annie; "I can very well see that you have been conning some fine speech over and over in your mind as you came here, but now you forget all of it."

"No—no."

"But I say yes, yes! Well, what is it?"

"What is what?"

"What do you want?"

"To give you, Annie, an opportunity of satisfactorily—if you can—explaining your extraordinary conduct; and to take away from you the power of saying that pride, passion, or prejudice hindered me from laying aside my rank, and, as a gentleman, seeking you with that feeling of concession which is always due from our sex to yours."

"Bravo! Bravo!"

"Annie! Annie!"

"But I say bravo! I never heard you make so sensible a speech in all my life. It was capital! First rate! You are not near so stupid, George, as—as——"

"As I look, you mean. Oh, pray add it!"

"No—no; you don't look stupid. I was going to say as your enemies would fain make out."

"Very well, Annie; what have you to say to me?"

"Nothing."

"Nay! nay! do not say that."

"George! George! What have you to say?"

"Something."

"Well, what is it?"

"Last night you informed me that you would wait supper for me, and then you went into St. James's Park and met a man."

"Do you think I would be fool enough to go into St. James's Park to meet a woman?"

"Annie! Annie! this levity——"

"George! George! this foolishness——"

"Will ruin you."

"Will choke you."

"I am choked already with rage, regret, and passion. Once more, Annie, I ask you what excuse can you make for your conduct?"

"None."

"That is enough."

"I am glad to hear it."

"You plead guilty?"

"Oh, no."

"Then what do you say? What do you assert? I have a right—no; well, you don't like me to say I have a right—but I put it to you as a matter of kindness—as a matter of feeling—after much affection that I have lavished upon you, to tell me if I have a complaint in truth against you or not?"

"No."

"No? You say no?"

"I say no!"

"Then you will explain."

"No, George, I will not explain. When you appeared at the door of the coach in the Park I offered to explain, and handed you a letter with that object."

"I did not get it."

"That was your fault. I have nothing further to say. I have given you no cause to suspect me. It is your vile—what shall I call him?—associate, demon, what you will, Sir Hinckton Moys, who can explain all."

"He declares you guilty."

"Very well."

"Annie! you know I love you."

"Trust me, then."

"In the face of all apparent proof to the contrary? Oh, Annie, you ask a great deal of human nature."

The Regent was, or pretended to be, affected, and put his handkerchief to his eyes.

"Stuff!" said Annie. "Don't pretend to be crying here. If you wanted to do so you should have brought an onion. Shall I ring for an onion?"

"Gracious powers! no."

"Then be quiet. I am going to lunch. Goodbye, if you have said all you came to say, though I can't say it has been very much to the purpose."

"You refuse me all explanation, then, Annie?"

"I do."

"But you declare your innocence, and that you are faithful to me?"

"I do."

"Then, Annie, I will not ask you another question on the subject; and if all the world were to say you were false, your word should outweigh them all; and I will never again injure you, or tamper with my own feelings and judgment, by allowing myself even to suspect you. As you like, and when you like, Annie, you shall go and come, where you like; and, in the faith I shall place in you, you will find a shield ever between you and all your enemies."

Annie turned her head on one side and pattered the floor with her foot.

"But," added the Regent, "you are justly, no doubt, angry, and so I bid you farewell. I shall always love you, Annie—always admire you; and let them say what they will of you, I can say that you have been an affectionate, gentle, generous and unselfish friend to your Prince, who will ever think of you with—with——"

"George!"

"Annie! Ah, Annie, now you want the odious onion."

"No, I don't."

The Regent stepped up to her and held out his hand. Annie placed hers in it, and looked up into his face with a smile.

"Bless you, Annie! I do love you."

"I almost begin to think you do, George."

"On my soul, I do!"

Annie rose from the couch, and placed both her hands on his shoulders, and gave him a little pert sort of kiss on the chin; and then, holding up one finger, she said, "But I did go to the Park to meet a man."

"Well, well?"

"And I love him."

"No, no!"

"I do—I do."

"My Annie!"

"And you don't mind—you will say nothing about it—but believe me, just simply on my own mere word, when I tell you that that love is innocent and sisterly, and has no element of wrong in it to you."

"Yes, I will—I do believe all that."

"Then, George, you shall have the proofs. Sit down by me, now, and you shall not have to trust to me or faith alone, but I will show you in black and white how all this came about. Sit down, I say."

"Yes, Annie, here I am. Now what is it?"

"You see this letter. It was brought to me only three minutes after you had left me last evening."

"By Jove, I saw it! It passed me at the very entrance of the Palace, to which some one brought it."

"Very well, read it."

The Regent read that letter which had been the inducement for Annie to leave the Palace on that eventful evening; and the moment he had finished it, before he could open his lips to make a remark about it, Annie, in her impetuous way, snatched it from him, and placed in his hands the other letter which had imposed on Allan Fearon, and lured him from his home by the suggestion that she, Annie, was in some danger.

The Regent read that letter likewise

"Well?" said Annie, with such startling abruptness in his ear that he really sprung up from the couch.

"My dear Annie, this has been an awful piece of wickedness."

"You see that, now?"

"I do, indeed."

"That will do. Now, George, we will have some lunch."

"I am full of horror and indignation."

"Never mind."

"It is a vile plot. But all's well that ends well, Annie, and this affair will have the effect of completely opening my eyes, once and for all, to the proceedings of certain people, who, for their own purposes, would fain make a quarrel between us."

"All's right, George."

Annie tore the two letters into twenty different pieces and let them fall to the floor.

"My dear Annie, you shall come home with me now. I will send for one of my own carriages, and all the world shall see that there is no one more valued, more truly beloved by the Regent of England, than yourself."

"No, no, no!"

"Do not say no, Annie. Let me please myself by giving you a triumph and your enemies a pang."

"No, again, George. You came here as Mr. Smith, and you shall leave by no other name. I will take your arm, and we will walk together home. I can, and do love you, George, but—but——"

Annie let her fair face fall gently on the breast of the Regent as she added, "I will not disgrace you."

"Generous, kind-hearted girl, when I forget you may heaven forget me."

"No, no! You may forget me, yet I will hope heaven will not forget you. But we will not talk in this way. If you do not wish to have lunch here, let us go home. I will take your arm. Come now, George, we shall look like Darby and Joan out for a walk!"

The Regent smiled.

Gallantly he offered his arm to Annie, who had on her hat and looked wondrously beautiful.

"I am ready, George."

"And I, dear Annie."

They reached the door arm-in-arm, and the Regent opened it. They passed a couple of waiters of the hotel and descended the grand staircase, which, with its soft carpeting and gilt balustrades, almost rivalled Carlton House or St. James's.

The landlord was in the hall, and he met the Countess de Blonde with a low bow.

"Does your ladyship dine here?"

"No," said Annie, "I shall not return."

"No," added the Regent, "the Countess will not return."

"Hem—hem——"

"What is it?"

"The—a—my—a—little bill."

"To be sure!" said Annie. "Pay him, Smith."

"Pay him! Oh, yes, certainly."

"Seven guineas," said the landlord, with another bow; "and two guineas for the apartments and wax-lights, and four guineas for the sleeping accommodation."

"Stop—stop!" said the Regent, as he felt first in one pocket and then in another. "I am afraid I have come out without any money!"

"And I have not a farthing!" said Annie with a loud laugh.

The landlord looked serious.

"You can send to the Comptroller of the Household of the Prince Regent for the money," said Annie.

The landlord shook his head. An idea had begun to find a place in his imagination that the Countess de Blonde was about to be off with this Mr. Smith, and that her connexion with the Regent was over.

"It is unusual," he said.

"What is?"

"To leave without paying."

"Get out of the way, rascal!" said the Regent, "or I will soon make you!"

"No, you won't, Mr. Smith, as you call yourself, —which, by the bye, is no more your name, I dare say, than it is mine. No, you won't make me. Here, police! Thomas! Samuel! run for a constable!"

Annie laughed uproariously.

"You may depend upon it, George," she said, "we shall end this affair by finding ourselves in the watch-house."

"Confusion to the fool!" said the Regent; "I will send for the money."

"Fetch Mr. Jackson, the constable!" cried the landlord. "Run, Thomas, run!"

Thomas was one of the waiters, and he did run in obedience to his master's orders, and in such a reckless fashion, too, that he projected his head right against the stomach of some one who, at that moment, opened the swinging glass door of the hotel from the street rather hastily.

"Idiot!" cried this person, "what do you mean by bolting out in such a fashion?"

"I beg pardon, sir."

Both the Regent and Annie uttered exclamation of surprise and vexation; for in this person who was entering the hall of the Hanover Hotel they had no difficulty—considering their intimate acquaintance with him—in recognising Sir Hinckton Moys.

Utterly and entirely failing with the Regent, and feeling that his fortunes were irretrievably lost, unless he made some bold and original stroke for their redemption, he had conceived the idea of throwing himself on the mercy of the Countess de Blonde.

Sir Hinckton Moys must have had a high idea of the charity which dwelt in Annie's heart to make him think for a moment such a course at all practicable or feasible.

Perhaps it might have succeeded to a certain extent, but he was too late.

It was quite impossible that either the Regent or Annie could avoid in the broad daylight which streamed into the hall of the hotel the observation of Sir Hinckton Moys; and he, the moment his eyes fell upon them, staggered back with so much dismay that the swinging doors behind him gave way at the pressure, and he fell backwards down the steps of the hotel.

But Sir Hinckton Moys had had time to utter four words, which produced a remarkable revulsion of feeling in the breasts of the landlord of the hotel and his waiters.

"His Highness the Regent!"

That was the announcement which produced so magical a transformation, and in a moment seemed as if it bowed down the landlord to the very dust, changing his aspect from that of a big and blustering bully to a crawling reptile, who would willingly have licked the feet that trod upon him.

The words seemed to fly round the hall with electric speed.

"His Highness the Regent! His Highness the Regent!" repeated everybody.

A couple of waiters held open the folding glass-doors; and while the landlord, after a yell of dismay, fell half-fainting into the arms of his wife, who had rushed out of the peculiar sanctum, surrounded by bottles of all sorts and sizes, in which she presided, Annie and the Regent, arm-in-arm, walked out into the street, and mingled with the mid-day crowd of the West End of London.

Sixteen-stringed Jack and Allan Fearon thought it likewise high time for them to leave the hotel; and amid the general excitement of the whole establishment, they passed out through the hall without observation.

It is probable enough, therefore, that beyond the honour and the excitement of the visit of the Regent to the Hanover Hotel the landlord got nothing for the accommodation he had given in his princely establishment to Annie, Countess de Blonde.

Sixteen-stringed Jack and Allan Fearon walked slowly together into Bond Street; and Jack said, in a half-laughing tone, "It is, you see, as I predicted: Annie has reinstated herself entirely in the good graces of the Regent; and is, I suppose, now the most powerful person in this country."

"It would seem so," said Allan, with much sadness in his tones,—"it would seem so; and I much fear that the anxieties of Marian will never come to an end on Annie's account. But I have done all I can, and she has done all she can, to withdraw her from this course of life."

"She is happy and content," said Sixteen-stringed Jack. "And, after all, there is not so much happiness and contentment in the world, that we need grudge any of it to such a butterfly existence as Annie's."

"We will not argue about it, Jack," replied Allan. "I will go home at once, with an account of all these strange proceedings, to Marian; and be assured Singleton, that, come what may, your daughter Lucy shall always find a home with us. Marian will be a mother—or, perhaps, I should more appropriately say, sister—considering their relative ages."

"My heart thanks you," said Jack; "I have no words in which to do so. But do not suppose, Allan, that I intend Lucy to be a burden to you.

No, thank heaven! I will always find a means of reimbursing you for the cost of her support. The kindness with which you have ministered those means I can never repay—*that* is quite another thing, you know; and my gratitude to you and Marian will not be the less because I do not allow myself to dig my hands into your pockets."

"It is not for me to dictate to you, Jack, what you may choose to do in that way; but whatever your resources may be, I only wish they came to you by some other means than your wild, adventurous, and dangerous life upon the highway."

"That can't be helped now, Fearon."

"Say not so!—say not so! I may have the power myself to help you to something better."

"What do you purpose doing yourself?"

"I have thought much of that. The Regent is my father by nature, although the laws, civil and ecclesiastical, will not acknowledge me as his son. He promises me to engage in no further persecution of my poor passionate and deluded mother. I do not see, therefore, that I am justified in refusing his bounty: it would be a false and poor pride to condemn myself and Marian to poverty because the father, who can support us, has been guilty of a great wrong. I shall, therefore, accept what he chooses to do for me."

"You speak rationally, Fearon, and are quite right."

"I feel that I am; yet am glad that you think so likewise."

"And your mother—what of her?"

"She is mad, Singleton—she is mad! But I have one thing to ask you in regard to her."

"What is it?"

"Whatever has passed between you and her of strife, or of opposition, let me beg of you to nourish no revenge against her."

"I promise."

"I was sure you would."

"With all my heart, I promise."

"Many—many thanks! I know, in her wild and frantic passion, she has attempted even your life."

"Think no more of it, Fearon. But where is she now?"

"In truth, I know not."

"Does the Regent know?"

"No; when that serious difference of opinion arose between myself and my mother, concerning the mode in which I was to meet and address the Regent, I lost her confidence and knew but little of her actions?"

"She wanted to make out her marriage legitimate, did she not?"

"She did; and wanted me wildly and passionately to declare myself a prince of the blood royal and legitimate heir to the Regent. But I am well convinced that the union between the ill-starred Linda de Chevenaux and the Regent can bear no such construction; so that whatever opinion I may really have of the morality of the transaction, the less I choose to waste my time in useless reproaches to the Regent. It is useless conversing more upon it; and I will accept his bounty, and accord to him such duty and affection as I can."

"You are quite right!" said Fearon,—"quite right! You are young, and have all your life before you; and whatever my own fate may be, I wish you every possible happiness."

They had now reached about the centre of Bond Street; and Sixteen-stringed Jack, as he glanced about him with a smile, added, "The air of London in broad daylight is not very wholesome for me, considering that the police authorities are so anxious for my society, that they are willing to pay a considerable sum to any one who will procure it for them; so I will bid you farewell! Adieu!"

"Stop, Jack!" said Fearon, as he laid his hand upon his arm.

"What is it?"

"I have noticed that those two men have walked before us all down Bond Street."

"Ah! say you so?"

Jack Singleton turned abruptly; but the moment he did so, two other men, it appeared, who had followed them, and who were in concert with the two who had preceded them, made a sudden spring upon Sixteen-stringed Jack.

CHAPTER CXLVII.

DETAILS HOW THE DARK WOMAN WAS PUT OUT OF THE WAY OF FURTHER MISCHIEF.

WHAT happened to Sixteen-stringed Jack and Allan Fearon in Bond Street we must leave for the matter of another chapter, since it is necessary, in order to bring our narrative in all its details up to a certain point, that we should repair with the reader to that large and pretentious house in Bedford Square, known as No. 6, which was then in the occupation of Sir John Scott, the confidential legal adviser of the Regent, and who was upon the next change of Ministry appointed Lord Chancellor, with the title of Earl of Eldon.

The Regent had made the best use of his time from that period when he last set eyes upon the Dark Woman in St. James's Palace, to that at which we saw him arm-in-arm with Annie, descending the doorsteps of the Hanover Hotel.

Two hours of that intervening period he had spent quietly and unostentatiously at Sir John's Scott's house, in consultation with that eminent legal personage in regard to what was to be done with the Dark Woman, *alias* Linda de Chevenaux.

There was a third person at this conference.

The notorious Colonel Hanger was admitted to it, simply because whatever course was determined upon, he would, in all probability, have the carrying it out.

It by no means followed that the Regent was particularly enamoured of the society of Colonel Hanger by the fact that he permitted him to be present at his conference with Sir John Scott; but having a shrewd suspicion that there would be some disagreeable and unscrupulous work to do, the Regent took the man with him who was most likely to be effective in its performance.

Moreover, Hanger, by the violent and audacious attempts he had already made to rid his royal master of the persecutions of the Dark Woman, was certainly entitled to any further confidences on the subject that might be requisite.

It was much safer and better likewise to employ an agent who already knew so much, than to open the whole affair to some one else; for now that the Regent had lost the prime mover in all his iniquities, and the suggester of many a one that would never have come into his own imagination, in the apparent necessity of getting rid of Sir Hinckton Moys, he had no one to turn to for the conduct of any little affair but Colonel Hanger.

Therefore was it that in the peculiarly private cabinet of the great Conservative lawyer, Hanger was permitted—not to occupy a chair—but to be present.

The Regent had promised Allan Fearon not to attempt anything against the life of his mother; and as we know the Prince of Wales, whatever might be his ordinary faults, was neither blood-thirsty nor cruel, he fully intended to keep his word, and had laid an interdict upon Hanger not to attempt or repeat any such violent means of ridding him of the Dark Woman's persecution as had already so nearly cost her her life.

Colonel Hanger, in his own mind, of course, thought this a needless refinement of humanity.

According to his ideas, if any one happened to be in the way, the easiest and shortest mode of putting them out of the way was to put them out of the world, and had he received a *carte blanche* from the Regent upon the subject, he would, probably enough, have found some means yet of compassing the destruction of the unhappy Linda de Chevenaux.

But there was no mistake about the interdict of the Regent; and Hanger felt perfectly well assured that if, after that, he tried any of his short and easy ways of completing the business, the Regent would have no scruple whatever in leaving him quietly to be hanged as a natural result.

And, besides, he had no particular wishes himself upon the subject: all he wanted was to be an useful confidential man to the Regent, for the Prince was in the possession of power; and empty though his purse most commonly was, the exchequer of England was at hand, and it was sure to be replenished sooner or later.

Sir John Scott, although then a much younger man than the present generation has been in the habit of considering him, was much the same creeping, wily-looking personage that for so many years was familiar to everybody on the judicial bench.

The divine right of kings and all the collateral branches of royalty to do just what they liked with their own—their own, in his estimation, being the resources of the kingdom, and every one in it was a fixed principle in the mind of the future Chancellor; and the moans and groans with which he heard the statement of the Regent in respect to Linda de Chevenaux were not upon her account, or on account of anything she had suffered or undergone, but because, as he feelingly expressed himself, "There is a dangerous party in the State ever ready to interfere with the prerogatives of monarchy, and to put the worst construction upon any little exercise of power essential to the peace and happiness of a royal personage."

This doctrine of the divine right of kings was not likely to be unpleasing to one who was a king all but in name.

The Regent was quite satisfied that Sir John

Scott was right in theory, and he was quite prepared to mourn with him that the practice could not be made consistent with it.

"You will understand, Scott," he said, "that I don't wish any harm to come to the woman, but I must be protected from her. She's mad—positively mad; and by some extraordinary means she makes her way either into St. James's Palace or Carlton House at her good will and pleasure"

The future Chancellor inclined his head on one side in a dreamy state of reflection; and Colonel Hanger thought it was time for him to put in a word.

"By Jove!" he said, "your Royal Highness,—and you, Mr. Scott,—I call it her bad will and pleasure; for I have not the slightest doubt that her object is to take your Highness's life."

"Can you make an affidavit of that?" said Sir John Scott, sharply.

"Certainly I can, with all the pleasure in life. It can never be said that Jack Hanger wasn't ready to make an affidavit to oblige a friend—and particularly when that friend is his most illustrious Prince."

"Nothing of the sort is required," said the Regent hastily. "She has attempted my life! My statement to that effect is sufficient; and there is no doubt she will attempt it again if she be not restrained and prevented."

"It's high treason!" said Sir John Scott. "Any attempt on your Highness's life became high treason from the moment you were invested with the Regency and exercised the functions of the Crown."

"But what can I do?" said the Regent. "I don't want to touch her life."

"And his Royal Highness don't want publicity!" cried Hanger. "Sink me, if this town isn't full of such a set of snobs and Jacobites, that there would be no end of talking, if all this story came to the public ear. There's the rascally newspapers, too! No, sink me! it mustn't come out!"

"A warrant," said Sir John Scott, laying his fore-finger upon the palm of his other hand, and, speaking sententiously as though he were giving judgment,—"a warrant signed by any three members of the Privy Council, and charging A, or B, or C, or Nokes, or Stokes, or Styles, or Giles with high treason, is good and sufficient for the incarceration of them, or any of them, in the Tower."

"The Tower?" exclaimed the Regent.

"Ay, the Tower!" said Sir John Scott, with an unconscious imitation of Richard the Third.

"But there is a disagreeable notion abroad," added the Regent, "that nobody can be imprisoned in England upon any charge whatever without being speedily brought to trial."

"I congratulate your Royal Highness," said Sir John Scott, "upon your knowledge of that grand principle of jurisprudence. It is the paladium of English freedom."

"Sink! the paladium!" said Colonel Hanger.

"But," added Sir John Scott, "when, without publicity, this Linda de Chevenaux is conveyed to the Tower, two eminent medical men—still without publicity—will state the fact that she is not in a state of mind to plead to any indictment, and, consequently, she remains in the Tower.'

"Good!" said Hanger.

"But still," said the Regent, with some anxiety, "that is like taking legal proceedings in a regular way, and may come out."

"Not above half a dozen persons, your Royal Highness," replied Sir John Scott, "need be at all concerned in the transaction; and those persons are all official, having a well-grounded knowledge that if they talk too much they cease to be official; and the plan has this advantage, that, whatever publicity may by any accident arise out of it, your Royal Highness is acting strictly and mercifully within the letter of the law."

"It shall be done," said the Regent. "Hanger, I think you will be just the man to carry this affair out."

"Yes, your Highness, if we can but find her."

"That, of course, I leave you to do."

"London is large, but I'll try; and I think I have a clue."

"Clue or no clue, it is your business. A Privy Council warrant will be placed in your hands; and if you have not the ingenuity to execute it, you're not the man I take you for."

"Sink me, your Highness! Don't say another word about it. It shall be done, if Jack Hanger loses his head in the doing it."

"It strikes me very forcibly," said Sir John Scott, "when I listen to you, and look at you this evening, Colonel Hanger, that you are inebriated."

"Sink me! inebriated!"

"So he is," said the Regent; "quite drunk. I did not observe it before. You're a pretty rascal, Hanger! When you knew you had particular business of mine on hand, to intoxicate yourself!"

"If your Highness says that I have had a bottle too much, Jack Hanger is not the man to be so insulting as to contradict his Prince; but I'm as secret as an oyster, and as ferocious as a dragon, for all that. I will find out the Dark Woman if she be above ground. It's romantic. Sink me, if it ain't romantic! The Tower! Ha! ha! The Tower! It's some time since any one was popped in there, Sir John."

"Don't be too sure of that," said Sir John Scott, drily. "All you have to do is to do your duty, and then hold your tongue."

"Then," said the Regent, rising, "I will look upon the affair as settled so far. Upon my information, Scott, you can get the warrant prepared. You're a Privy Councillor yourself, and can put the first signature to it."

"Sink me!" cried Colonel Hanger. "Make me a Privy Councillor, your Royal Highness, and I'll put the second."

"Beast!" said the Regent, as he left the house, and stepped into a private and plain chariot, which was waiting for him.

Colonel Hanger was left standing on the pavement, and, as a little drizzling rain began to fall, his position was none of the pleasantest.

Intoxication at that period was so popular a vice among all classes of society, that neither the Regent nor Sir John Scott were, in truth, very much shocked at the slightly unsteady condition of Colonel Hanger.

In this case, that slightly unsteady condition, and the unreflective character of the thoughts it induced, did more for Colonel Hanger and the plan for incarceration of the Dark Woman in the Tower, than any sober judgment and reflection would have effected.

The very common-place idea struck Colonel Hanger of going to Hanover Square, which he ascertained had been the late residence of the Dark Woman, under the *alias* of the Countess d'Umbra.

What sort of information he expected to get from an empty house, or by staring at it with his back against the railings of the square, it is hard to say, but thither he certainly went.

On the very doorstep of that number ten which, for so short a time, had been the magnificent abode of Linda de Chevenaux, reposed some one, either dead or in so profound a sleep that it looked like death.

Colonel Hanger was just in that state of mind to induce him to interfere without reflection with any one, and he accordingly commenced a series of kicks at the inanimate object on the doorstep, while he cried out, "Get up! get up, can't you? Get up, if you're a dead man; if only drunk, lie still, and be buried!"

"Go to the deuce!" said the person thus assailed. "Who are you?"

"You've said it," said Hanger.

"Said what?"

"The deuce, to be sure! That's me! And now, my friend, who are you?"

"Ha! ha! That's a good idea. Why, if you must know who I am, I'm Binks."

"Binks! That's a pretty name."

"Ain't it?"

"Well, I said it was. But what are you doing here on the doorstep of Linda de Chevenaux, *alias* Countess d'Umbra, *alias* the Dark Woman?"

"What?" cried Binks, whom the reader will now recognise as the unscrupulous ruffian who had been for some time in the employment of the Dark Woman. "What? Do you know her?"

"To be sure I do! I'm her most intimate friend. My purse, and my heart, and my cellar are always open to her. She conceals nothing from me—sink me!—nothing."

Binks seemed to cogitate for a few moments; and then, as he was far gone in intoxication, he thought he was wonderfully cunning by saying, "Then, if you know her so well, perhaps you know that she has left this house?"

"Of course I do."

"Perhaps you know, then, where she's gone? Frith Street, eh? Astrologer's house, eh? Astorath, eh? Perhaps you know that? and if you don't I'm not the man to tell you. Catch a weazel asleep! Binks may have had his drop, and may choose to sit down on a doorstep and sleep it off before he goes home, but he's not agoin' to blab for all that—not he! Hilloa! where is he? Why, he's off! A good thing I didn't tell him anything! Catch a weazel asleep! Now, if I'd been a fool, and not quite so deep when I've had a drop as I am without one, I might have told that fellow where to find the missus. Ha! ha!—catch a weazel asleep!"

Mr. Binks's head sunk again upon his breast, and he slowly reclined back upon the stone steps again in a deep slumber.

The information he had so suddenly and so unexpectedly received, quite sobered Colonel Hanger, and heedless now of the rapidly descending rain, he made his way back to Bedford Square, and demanded to see Sir John Scott.

Under the circumstances, the wily lawyer did not like actually to refuse the visit, although his own impression was that a demand upon his purse occasioned it.

"Sir John," said Colonel Hanger, in quite a different tone, and with quite a different manner to that which had sat upon him on his former visit—"Sir John, I've found the Dark Woman."

"No!"

"I have, sir; and as soon as I'm provided with the necessary warrant, I can execute it."

"You knew, then, where she was?"

"On my soul, no! When I left this house, within the hour, she might have been in the moon, for all I knew of her whereabouts."

"Well, Colonel, you've made good use of your time; and you either shammed drunkenness then, or you sham sobriety now."

Hanger smiled.

"Never mind about that, Sir John—only tell me when I can have the warrant."

"In two hours from now."

"And here?"

"Yes. I will order my carriage, and, if you like to wait, I will bring it back, signed. It will take me that time to hunt up a couple of Privy Councillors to put their signatures to the document after mine."

"I will wait, for the night is not inviting."

"Or will you come with me?"

"Ah! that will do. I can wait in the carriage while you get the signatures; for I am very anxious not to lose a moment in the execution of the warrant, since, whether it can be executed without a breeze and bloodshed depends upon whether a drunken man sleeps quietly or not for the next two hours upon a door-step."

"Come, then, Colonel, and I will do my part of the business as quickly as may be. It seems to me that you are supplanting Sir Hinckton Moys in favour with the Regent."

"Oh! he's a fool—a doll—an ass!—and, I fancy, will scarcely set foot again in St. James's Palace, or Carlton House. I worship the risen sun, the fair Countess de Blonde."

Sir John Scott coughed dubiously; and then this strangely assorted pair entered the lawyer's carriage, and in less than the two hours he had specified, the future Chancellor procured the signatures required for the purpose of legally consigning the Dark Woman to the Tower, where she was, very illegally, to be afterwards detained.

"Understand how this is to be done," said Sir John Scott, as he handed the warrant to Colonel Hanger. "You must send a Yeoman of the Guard at once with a copy of this to the Lieutenant at the Tower, intimating that you will probably be there during the night with your prisoner. But you will not be admitted at the Barbican Gate, on Tower Hill."

"Where then?"

"You must go by water. Traitors' Gate will receive you on production of this warrant."

"Ha! ha! On my soul, it is quite romantic! If I don't astonish the nerves of Linda de Chevenaux to-night, my name's not Colonel Hanger!"

CHAPTER CXLVIII.

THE MYSTERIOUS KNOCKING AT THE DOOR OF THE HOUSE IN FRITH STREET HAS AN OMINOUS MEANING.

THE girl-page of the Dark Woman, as she stood in the gloomy passage of the house of Astorath, in Frith Street, Soho, and heard the door, upon which so many unsuccessful assaults had been made, now at once yielding to those who, in the name of the law, summoned the Dark Woman to surrender, felt as if she herself had, in some direct manner, brought this danger on her mistress.

It seemed to the page as if now, from the moment that she had ceased to be faithful to the wishes and orders of the dark and mysterious woman she had served so long, that career of crime was at an end.

The spell which had hitherto preserved Linda de Chevenaux through so many dangers was surely over.

Her time of disaster had come.

The page wrung her hands, as she descended the dark and slippery stairs to the lower regions, where the wounded Shucks awaited her.

"Lost!" she said,—"all is lost now!"

"Ah!" moaned Shucks. "What new calamity, my dear, have you to speak of?"

"The Dark Woman!"

"She is coming here?"

"Oh, no! no! no!"

"I breathe again, then, although it is in pain. What do you mean, my child?"

"Do you not hear, father? The house is assailed by men, who seek the Dark Woman to her destruction. Perhaps they will kill her."

"And a good job too," said Shucks.

"Oh, no! no!—do not—do not say so! She has been kind to me!"

"Then, I won't say so, my dear! If it were not for this ugly wound, which feels for all the world now as if—as if——Oh! it is terrible!"

"As if what, father? Your voice fails you! Oh, for mercy, speak to me again!"

"Red-hot!" groaned Shucks. "I was going to say that I cannot get rid of the idea that the sword was red-hot, and had left two feet of its blade in my breast."

Shucks fell back exhausted, and the page ran to him and raised his head, while his tears fell plentifully upon his face.

"What!—oh, what have I done," said Shucks, "that any child of mine should cry for me?"

"You are my father."

"But so—so bad a father!"

"No, no! I do not want you to say that. This poor heart of mine has so yearned for a father, that—that——"

"That you would rather have such a desperate bad one as I am, than none at all?"

"I did not mean to say that. But hush!—oh, hush!—do you not hear?"

"What?"

"A noise above, father. They have found her."

"Ah!"

"They will drag her to a prison, if they do not kill her here. Ah! that cry!"

A fearful cry sounded through the house, and the young girl sprang to her feet.

"Father, let me go!—let me go to listen! There can be no—harm—no danger in listening!"

"Go, my dear—go! I would myself like to know what is going on. And yet, what does it matter to me? It cannot matter to me long, for this pain will kill me."

The page ran up the staircase, and crawling down just within the doorway, she listened.

Sounds of confusion, and the trampling of footsteps, were in the house; and then one loud voice exclaimed in coarse, harsh accents of exultation, "You have done your duty, my men, well. Don't smother her, but bring her along."

Then there was a stifled cry, as though some one had tried to scream through the covering that kept in the full volume of the sound over the mouth.

There was the scuffling of feet such as might ensue as people carried something heavy between

No. 68 —DARK WOMAN.

them, and then with a loud, careless kind of rush the door of the house was pulled shut.

A slight sound of the same character immediately afterwards came upon the ears of the page. It was the sudden and rather violent closing of a coach door.

Then came the grinding and rattle of wheels, and after that all was still in Frith Street, Soho, and in the house of the Dark Woman.

The page shuddered, and burst into tears.

"Farewell! Farewell for ever! I feel that it is for ever—farewell! It is strange that, with all your wi kedness, Linda de Chevenaux, I should love and regret you still!"

It was strange.

That young girl's mind must have been of that order which thinks more of a casual kindness from one habitually stern and harsh, than of the continued caresses which know no change.

There are thousands of such intellects—good,

kind, and amiable, and with that taint of weaknes in them.

The page was, however, aware that the outer door of the house had been found open; and she considered that, notwithstanding it had been pulled close again, the house must be at the mercy of any one who chose to come into it.

This was a state of things which gave her uneasiness, since there seemed to be no prospect of her father being able to move from his present quarter for some time to come.

Lightly and silently she moved towards the street door, and then she saw by the faint night-light that made its way into the hall, that the hinges were forced from their places, and she felt confident that a very slight push from the outside would send the disarranged door right into the passage.

What to do under such circumstances she knew not; and the very danger she dreaded and expected seemed in a few moments about to ensue.

With a heavy plunge, as though he had thrown himself against it, some one fell against the door.

Insecure as the door was, it gave way at once before this pressure, and fell right into the hall, with the intruder, whoever he was, above it.

The page could not control the impulse to utter a cry of fear.

"Confound it!" said a deep voice, the thick guttural accents of which sufficiently proclaimed the state of the speaker. "Confound it! Who would have thought you was agoing to open the door so quick as all that, eh? Perhaps you will try to make out that I'm drunk, eh?"

It was Binks.

A sensation of great relief came over the heart of the young girl. The great, strong, rough man had been in his way kind enough to her. He had always looked upon her in her page's dress as a kind of doll or fragile plaything, that had to be touched very tenderly for fear of breaking.

More than once, when he had met her on the stairs, he had lifted her with one hand and carried her all the rest of the way.

In fact, so little, and helpless, and delicate had the Dark Woman's page always appeared to that huge, ox-like Binks, that he had a sort of affection for the boy, as he thought him.

The young girl knew this well, and so had no fear of Binks.

She ran towards him.

"Ah!" she cried, "it is you! it is you! Get up, I pray you, for there has been danger here."

"Danger! What's amiss now, you little poll-parrot, eh?"

"Our mistress is taken."

"What?"

"She is a prisoner! Arrested—taken!"

"Took? Nabbed? No?"

Binks scrambled to his feet, somewhat sobered by the long sleep he had had on the doorstep in Hanover Square, and by the startling character of the intelligence just communicated to him by the page.

"Alas! yes. It is but too true. Do you not see that the door is broken down, Binks?"

"To be sure I do. But how did they nab her? She was usually too wide awake for that sort of thing."

The conscience of the young girl smote her at these words of Binks's. Had she not been the cause of the arrest of the Dark Woman, by preventing her from being, as Binks expressed it, sufficiently wide awake to take measures for her own safety?

Of course she had. The double opiate had done that.

The page was silent.

"Who took her?" asked Binks.

"I know not. There was some talk about a warrant, and there was a furious hammering at the door; and then, without more ado, they broke it down, as you see it, and took her away."

"Why didn't you floor 'em, eh?"

"I?"

"Oh, to be sure, how could you? If it had been a couple of canary birds you might have done so; but the traps were too much for such a little bit of a thing as you are. Well, I suppose she is in the Jug."

"The what?"

"The Stone Jug! Newgate I mean."

"I do not know."

"Well, I'll know soon, for I'll go and find out somehow."

"Ah! Binks, if you would only try to put the door to rights before you go."

"I will."

"I shall feel so much safer."

"But do you mean to stay here all alone, you little bit of a thing?"

"Yes—oh, yes. She may escape, you knew, and come back. Who shall say?"

"So she may. You are a sensible little thing, you are, though there ain't much of you. I'll put the door to rights. I don't say it will be as strong as it was, mind you, but it will look as strong."

"That will do, Binks; looks are so deceiving."

"Well, I suppose they is."

Binks was seldom without such a packet of housebreaking tools and implements that upon any occasion like the present he was as well provided with the means of putting a few screws into the wrenched off hinge of a door as if he carried a carpenter's shop about with him.

The accomplished housebreaker was a good workman; and in less than a quarter of an hour the outer door of that house of mystery, in Frith Street, Soho, was, to all appearance, as well secured as ever.

This was a great relief to the mind of the young girl. Her next hope was that Binks would leave the house as soon as possible.

In that hope, however, she was to a certain extent disappointed, for Binks was hungry, and it was not until he had devoured almost all the provisions in the house that he came down into the hall again, where the page had waited, and signified his intention to go and make some inquiries in regard to the fate of the Dark Woman.

"I'm off, little 'un," he said. "You keep house; and if anybody should come as you don't want, all you have got to do is to smash 'em."

"If I can."

"Very good. I'll come back again some time or another."

Binks let himself out of the house, to the great relief of the girl, and she made her way at once into the lower regions to see how Shucks was.

He was moaning, and seemed to have dropped into a kind of half sleep.

"He will die! He will die!" moaned the young creature. "He will surely die, and I shall be alone again!"

She sat down, resting her head upon her hands, and listened to the disturbed breathing of Shucks, which, for a time, was the only sound that broke the deep stillness of that melancholy abode.

But as the night deepened there were other sounds indicative of life in those vaults and cellars.

The rats and various things that for years had had an undisturbed home in the lower part of that house began to sally out on their nocturnal rambles.

There was the scrambling, scampering sound of their feet, and the page could see their eyes glaring upon her from each corner.

Terror took possession of the young girl, and she cried out aloud, "Father! father, awake! Let us make an effort to leave this terrible place."

"Yes, my dear," said Shucks.

The girl started at the sound of his voice. It was perfectly calm and collected.

"Oh, father! father! you are better!"

"Wonderfully better!"

"No pain—no agony now?"

"None! none! I cannot understand it, but the wound is quite easy."

"Oh, what joy! Thank heaven! You will soon be well now. Perhaps you can walk, father"

"Yes—no—I—don't feel quite—— Why have you put out the light so suddenly, dear!"

"The light! It is not out—it is here, Oh, heaven!"

The girl raised the light, and held it sufficiently close to her father's face. One glance was sufficient.

The aspect of approaching death was there.

The shadow of the wings of the destroyer was already over the features.

Shucks was dying. The absence of pain in his wound was the presence of mortification.

"Father! father, stay with me! stay with me! I am your own child!—I shall be so desolate, father. Oh, heaven, save my father! I have no mother, no brother, no sister—nothing to hold me to the world but this one poor father! Oh, spare him! spare him! spare him! spare him!—in mercy, spare him to this sad heart!"

"Hush! hush!"

Shucks placed his hand upon the brow of the young girl, and spoke gently.

"My dear—my own dear. I know it now. I feel certain of it now. I am going. God bless you, my child! Say—say that you forgive your bad, bad father."

"No; no! do not speak so to me, my dear, dear, good father! Oh, why can I not die for you?"

"Heaven forbid, my dear. You are young, innocent, and good. Do not weep for me. Do not shed tears for me. She has killed me, my dear. I thought she had, and it was only for a moment that I fancied myself so much better. Let me think where—where—where to——"

"Father! father! what would you say?"

"Yes! yes! Sixteen-stringed Jack. Find him out, dear. He is the man. God bless you, ever—ever—ever!"

Tears choked the utterance of the young girl as she tried to speak again now. Tears obscured her vision as she tried to look into the face of her dying father.

A fearful change came over the face of the expiring housebreaker, and yet he made a struggle to say something more which the page could not comprehend.

"A sister," he gasped. "Another. Go. The house by the river side. I wanted—wanted not to be known. Go—go—the Fearons. Oh, death! death!"

At the moment Shucks breathed his last the candle by some mysterious influence went out, and the young girl felt that she was alone with the dead.

The dismal lower regions of that house echoed to the cry of dismay that burst from her lips, and then terror took more entire possession of her.

It was terror of the dead. It was terror, too, of those reptile living things who seemed to inhabit those cellars in such troops, and who, now that the light was extinguished, seemed in reality or in imagination to swarm around her, and to be threatening her in all directions.

She felt that were she to attempt to remain there for any length of time, her reason would give way before the horrors of the place.

With frantic speed she fled from the cellars up the damp and slippery staircase. In her haste, more than once she partially slipped and fell; but, heedless of the hurts she gave herself, she rose again, and reached the passage.

Without the hesitation of another moment, she made her way to the street-door. To open it and to rush out into Frith Street, were the natural impulses of the disorder of her mind.

She left death, desolation, and terror behind her; and in a few minutes the page of the Dark Woman was half a mile from Soho.

Faint, then, and heated by the speed she had made, she half-staggered down a narrow turning, and found that it led her into St. James's Park.

There, upon one of those hard benches, which for so many years have served as the couches of the forlorn and the homeless, the young girl found refuge from her sorrows in a deep sleep.

It was such a sleep as only the young can hope for in the midst of mental distress.

The bright sun was shining upon the face of the page when she opened her eyes in the morning, and, confused and bewildered, she half rose and looked about her in the Park.

Memory was slow to bring to her mind again the recollection of the terrible scene she had gone through in the house in Soho.

Then, as, like a flash of summer electricity, the whole of those events came across her mind, she clasped her hands over her face, and uttered a cry of despair.

Two ladies, followed by several others, were slowly walking up the Mall, in the direction of that wooden bench in the occupation of the Dark Woman's page.

One of these ladies was of capacious dimensions, and wore a flowered silk dress of enormous size, the richness and costly character of which did not rescue it from the charge of vulgarity.

A profusion of light hair, with a bright tinge about it that was not without its effectiveness, hung about her plump and well-to-do-looking countenance.

The second lady was dark, almost to sallow-ness, in complexion, and was attired in a high dress of cloth. She wore a particularly ugly bonnet—or hat, as they were then called—in which were three feathers, arranged very much in the fashion of that called the Prince of Wales's plume.

It was tolerably evident that those ladies—to use a common expression—were somebody's, for the few persons who followed them took evident care to keep at an equal distance from them, and were clearly in attendance.

Not to make a mystery of that which need not partake of such a character, we may state at once that these ladies were the Princess Caroline of Brunswick, wife to the Regent, and the Marchioness of Sunningham.

Among the many mistakes and imprudent acts of the ill-fated Princess of Brunswick, one of the most notable was certainly the one of permitting the Marchioness of Sunningham to become an intimate and a *confidante*.

The slightest inquiry or the slightest discretion must have let the Princess of Brunswick know that such a woman could, if sincere in her expressions of regard, be nothing but a disgrace to her; while, if otherwise—which certainly was the case—she was playing the most treacherous, selfish, and dishonourable part that could possibly be imagined.

But at the cry of the Dark Woman's page, the Princess of Wales quickened her steps, and seeing what looked like a pretty young boy, sitting upon a bench, in the Park, and looking distressed and bewildered, she spoke at once.

"What is the matter? What is the matter? Whose boy are you; and what has happened to you?"

"Alas! alas! I know not—I cannot tell. What is to-day, madam? How long have I slept? Do you think it is all a dream?"

"What a dream? You are too pretty a boy to have bad dreams."

"Boy, your Royal Highness!" said the Marchioness of Sunningham. "I can see with half an eye it is a girl."

"Your Highness?" exclaimed the Dark Woman's page. "To whom am I speaking?"

"I am the Princess of Wales, and wife of the Regent."

The Princess of Brunswick was very often in the habit of thus describing herself since her separation from the Prince of Wales; but she was not a little surprised at the impulsive manner in which the page, whether girl or boy, replied to her.

"Ah, then, madam, you are the other wife of his Highness, and I think, as they have killed her who was Linda de Chevenaux, you will no longer be troubled with——Ah! what am I saying? It surely is sufficient that I leave her for ever—that by my means she has fallen into the hands of our enemies. I need not betray the confidence she has placed in me."

"What is the meaning of all this?" said the Princess of Wales aside to her companion.

"I think if your Royal Highness encourages the confidence of this girl in boy's clothes, we may make some important discoveries."

"Is this a girl in boy's clothes?"

"Does your Royal Highness think that with my experiences I can be deceived for a moment?"

The Princess of Wales turned to the page, and spoke kindly to her.

"My good boy, you spoke just now of having left your former mistress for ever. I am in want of a page, are you willing to accept such an office in my household?"

"Oh, yes, yes!" exclaimed the boy, clasping his hands together; "anything for employment—anything to shut out thought."

"Be it so, then," added the Princess of Wales. "I am about now to return to Brunswick House. Henceforth consider yourself as forming part of the household of her Royal Highness the Princess of Wales, wife of the Regent of England."

CHAPTER CXLIX.

THE DARK WOMAN IS CONVEYED TO THE TOWER AND FINDS HERSELF AN HISTORICAL PERSONAGE.

THE dissolute and unprincipled Colonel Hanger had every reason to be satisfied with his successes on that important evening when, by a series of lucky accidents, he found himself excessively useful to the Regent, and, at the same time, armed with power and authority to carry out the wishes of that exalted personage.

Promptly, and with an energy he seldom exhibited—for Hanger was one of those men who, waiting upon providence, generally allow things to take their own course, instead of attempting to direct them—he set about the arrest of the Dark Woman, and accomplished it with a success and a celerity quite unprecedented.

The audacity of this man's career had been such that, although, perhaps, he had never actually stooped to common criminality—a highwayman or a housebreaker—yet he seemed to have a tolerable knowledge of all the shifts and contrivances of such gentry.

Hanger armed himself with both sword and pistols; but the two Yeomen of the Guard, whom he took with him, he provided with a well-tempered crow-bar, of about three feet in length, which would not only be most formidable as a weapon of offence or defence, but before which no door or casement would stand for a moment.

The Colonel did not omit the precaution of sending a messenger to the Tower with a copy of the warrant, so that the lieutenant in command would be prepared to do his duty upon the almost unprecedented occasion of a prisoner being brought to the ancient fortress upon a Privy Council warrant.

It is to be presumed that Colonel Hanger was not destitute of courage, or he would scarcely have ventured to have attacked the house of the Dark Woman, in Frith Street, in the off-hand manner which characterised the assault.

That she was a woman of many resources, unexampled courage, and entire unscrupulousness in the means she adopted to carry out her object, or to defend herself, he well knew.

It did not seem to him, therefore, at all probable that she would be taken in her own stronghold, so to speak, without something approaching to a struggle.

There might be a chance shot or two—perhaps

a vigorous sword-thrust to contend with—but Colonel Hanger played for what he considered a heavy stake. The favour of the Regent and the reversion of the situation held by Sir Hinckton Moys were surely worth as much risk and danger as he would not have scrupled to encounter in a drunken brawl any evening of his life.

The private carriage which he took with him on the expedition was driven by a needy associate of his own; and the two Yeomen of the Guard, who seemed to be anything but pleased at the prospect of the dangers they were about to encounter, indefinite though they were, rode with him in the carriage.

Colonel Hanger rather congratulated himself upon the fact that the night was so unpropitious a one for out-door exercise.

The slight misly shower which had commenced early in the evening had increased to a steady, dogged, persevering kind of rain, into which no one, without some strongly inducing purpose, would willingly proceed.

Soho Square and its neighbouring streets are not lovely at the best of times; Frith Street, in particular, has a gloomy aspect particularly its own. The tall, grimy-looking houses were glistening with the dirty rain, which brought with it, as it passed through the fog-cloud that hovers over London, a tolerable infusion of soot.

The kennels were running with blackened water; and from the joints of all the drain-spouts there was kept up that ticking, trickling, pattering sound so incidental to continued rain in London.

As Colonel Hanger looked from the window of the coach, he was gratified to see that he and his assistants had Frith Street all to themselves.

Not a solitary passenger struck down the soddened thoroughfare.

Not a window was open.

Even those homeless, starving wretches who, upon such occasions and upon such nights, huddle up themselves and their rags in the shelter of some doorway, avoided Frith Street.

There were other thoroughfares where they had ten times the chance of attracting the eye of some compassionate passenger; and the most picturesque aspect of woe-by-gone poverty they well knew would be thrown away in the most gloomy street of Soho.

Colonel Hanger had considered with himself on his route whether to attempt the arrest of the Dark Woman by finesse or a sudden, violent, and noisy attack.

His feelings inclined to the latter course, and he, accordingly, adopted it.

"Halt!" he cried, from the window of the coach, as they reached the door of the Dark Woman's abode, which he, Hanger, knew very well as the house of the reputed astrologer, Astorath.

The coach stopped.

"Now, my men," added Hanger, as he sprung from the vehicle, "this is the place, and I hope to make short work of your duty to-night."

"You will certainly give an alarm, Colonel, if you speak so loud," said one of the Yeomen.

"Give an alarm!" shouted Hanger. "Why, that's just what I mean to do, my good fellow; and here goes to begin with. I like always to scare the enemy. He loses his wits in the midst of noise and confusion, and you come upon him with double effect. Lend me that crow-bar."

The two Yeomen shrunk back into the shadow of the coach, while Colonel Hanger commenced that furious attack upon the panels of the door of the Dark Woman's house which had so startled the page while attending upon the wounded Shucks in the cellar below.

There was no knocker on the door. The visitors to Astorath's house were supposed to be acquainted with the secret bell that announced their arrival, or they might tap with their knuckles for admission; but the crow-bar, in the hands of Colonel Hanger, was an alarming substitute for a knocker, and he hammered away with right good will.

He had calculated that in the excitement and alarm at such a racket at the door it would be suddenly opened; but when he found such was not the case, he got to the next part of the programme he had laid down in his own mind, and proceeded at once to force it.

"Now, my men," he said, "it's your time. Recollect that whatever we're doing is in the name of the law, the Privy Council, and the Regent. Prick your way in; never mind the lock, you'll find it as easy again by the hinges!"

The two Yeomen of the Guard had caught something of the excitement of the scene; and the careless, reckless audacity of Colonel Hanger seemed to be, to a certain extent, contagious.

They set to work with a will which soon made the door yield to their efforts, and then came that sudden crashing sound, which had let the page of the Dark Woman know that the assailants had gained an entrance.

Then Colonel Hanger drew his sword, and with a pistol in his other hand he dashed into the passage.

Had the Dark Woman but been in her ordinary state of preparation—had she but been in waking existence, it is probable enough that all the recklessness, and all the blind, headstrong courage of Colonel Hanger, would but have lured him to destruction.

But such was not the case.

She lay still on that couch above-stairs in dreamy unconsciousness, and though it is possible enough that even her sleeping senses conveyed to her brain some faint echoes of the tumult below, still that tumult was not sufficient to arouse her from the torpor which the powerful opiate had produced.

Her enemies were in the house, but yet she moved not.

Their footsteps were in the hall, and then on the staircase, but the Dark Woman slept.

All the resources of that well-arranged establishment seemed to sleep likewise. No trap-door opened beneath the feet of the foe, to hurl them headlong to destruction.

No fearful sounds smote upon their ears with accents of terror.

No sights met their eyes calculated to freeze the imagination with horror and shake the nervous system of the boldest.

All that the cunning of art and science, in its charlatanism and trickery, had assembled in that mansion, was still: the human agency that would have set in motion dangers and surprises for unwelcome visitors, was wanting.

The Dark Woman slept.

The page had practically renounced her service. Binks was absent.

And so that mysterious house in Frith Street, Soho, into which people were in the habit of stepping with bated breath and leaving with trembling limbs, became but a commonplace, dingy, gloomy, and deserted mansion.

The wires that traversed the walls and ceilings—the odd-looking handles, seeming to belong to nothing—and the gauzes and tapestries which here and there were hanging upon the walls, were all unheeded by Colonel Hanger; and yet they were curious, because they were portions of the apparatus by which the senses were deluded in that house of mystery.

With a lantern in his hand, through the lens of which there came a broad gleam of light, Colonel Hanger now ascended the staircase, followed by one of the Yeomen of the Guard. The other he left on duty in the hall below.

Hanger had sheathed his sword, but in his disengaged hand he held a pistol, and he repeated more than once in a loud voice as he ascended the stairs, "I will blow out the brains of the first person who impedes my progress, so help me heaven!"

There was no one to impede his progress. Those boisterous words sounded like an idle threat, and as the echo of them died away in the upper part of the mansion, the intense stillness that succeeded was a kind of mocking, contemptuous commentary upon them.

The first floor landing was reached; and with four more steps Colonel Hanger found himself in that large, mysterious apartment where Astorath, and afterwards the Dark Woman, were in the habit of receiving their imaginative dupes.

It was natural that even such a man as Hanger should pause for a moment or two to look about him in that place.

The lantern that he carried, by the broad beam of light that it produced, dissipated much of the darkness over the whole extent of the room; and where that radiating beam more particularly fell, the light was intense.

The apartment had a most dismal and funereal aspect, in consequence of the walls being hung with black cloth over the largest portion of their extent.

The floor presented only the bare boards; and if Colonel Hanger had looked down to them very scrutinisingly, he would have seen that in places they had very much the appearance of the stage of a theatre.

Here and there were small strips of metal; and the rectangular fashion in which some of the boards were cut, suggested the idea of trap-doors and communication with the rooms below.

Hanger turned twice round upon his heels with the lantern in his hand, so as to throw its rays into all the corners of the room.

"She is not here," he said.

"There is a door over yonder, sir," said the Yeoman of the Guard who was with him.

"I see—I see. Were you ever here before?"

"Never, sir."

"Then I have. And on that occasion Astorath, the fortune-teller, was in this room, and had the impertinence to make a prediction to me."

"Indeed, sir?"

"Yes. He said that I should be hanged. Ha! ha! Not very likely that! I wonder what on earth, though, has become of him, for this sort of gentry do not usually like their dens to be looked over in this careless fashion."

It was evident that the silence of the house and the lugubrious character of the hangings in that room were beginning to exercise an uncomfortable effect upon the nervous system of the Yeoman who was with Colonel Hanger.

"Don't you think, sir," he said, "we—we—had better go?"

"Yes."

"Come on, then, sir. Shall I carry the light?"

"What do you mean? Where are you off to now? You are going the wrong way."

"Oh, no, sir—this is the way back again."

"You mistake me. I am not going back again, but forwards through that door. You are surely not afraid?"

"Oh, no, sir, not afraid of—of—anything human."

'Then you need not be afraid here, for I came to arrest a woman, and that is the most human thing I know."

Colonel Hanger had satisfied his temporary curiosity in the slight examination he had made of that principal apartment in the house; and he now made his way at once through a narrow door which was at the further end of the large first-floor room.

That door was unfastened, and, indeed, was unlatched, so that not the least noise was made in opening it wide enough to pass through.

Never had that house, since it had been in the possession either of Astorath or the Dark Woman, been in such a state of defencelessness or neglect.

A dismal, narrow passage of about thirty feet in length now presented itself; and at the end of that there was another door which likewise yielded to a touch.

The room beyond was profoundly dark, for the shutters of the one window were closed.

The room, however, was small, so that the beam of light from the lantern was sufficient to penetrate to its full extent.

On a couch of dark-coloured velvet lay the Dark Woman.

"Ah!" said Colonel Hanger, "we are lucky. There's our prisoner, sound asleep."

The Dark Woman was sound asleep, but let sleep be ever so sound, it is in some respects amenable to changes in the atmosphere of the place in which lies the sleeper, and more particularly to accessions of light.

The Dark Woman moved slightly, and uttered some low moans, as the light from the lantern played upon her face.

The Yeoman of the Guard shrunk back.

He spoke in a whisper,

"This, Colonel Hanger," he said, "is the same person who made something like a riot in the Colour Court of St. James's."

"I know it."

"Some one fired at her from one of the windows."

"I know that, too."

Colonel Hanger indulged in a very sinister kind of laugh as he said this; for since he was the person who had so sought to be the death of the Dark Woman, no one could be better aware of the fact than himself.

The slumbering Linda de Chevenaux must at

that moment, even in her sleep, have had some dreamy notion of the danger she was in.

A kind of spasm seemed to come over her features, and she opened and shut her hands convulsively, while by the quiver of her lips it would appear that she was trying to utter some words.

The powerful opiate she had partaken of prevented her from entirely awaking, which these mental agitations must have otherwise brought about, but at length she did utter a word.

"Fire! Fire!"

"Ah!" said Colonel Hanger,—"that is the light in her eyes."

"Will you awaken her, sir?" said the Yeoman.

"Possibly. She is your prisoner. Her name is Linda de Chevenaux."

"Then, Linda de Chevenaux," said the Yeoman, as he laid his hand upon her shoulder, "I attach you of high treason."

The light flashing in her eyes had disturbed the Dark Woman. Nay, probably the very presence of strangers in the room had had some effect upon her repose, but it was reserved for that touch from the Yeoman of the Guard to break the deep slumber which sat upon her senses.

With a shrill cry, the Dark Woman awakened.

That was the cry which had been heard by the page, while listening below.

Colonel Hanger felt that the time for prompt action had come.

"Seize your prisoner!" he cried aloud.

At the same moment, he clasped Linda de Chevenaux by the wrist of one hand, and placed the point of the sword he carried to her throat.

Rage and surprise for a moment or two paralyzed the energies of the Dark Woman, and as her eyes were fixed with a sort of fascinated gaze during that short period of time upon those of Colonel Hanger, the Yeoman of the Guard had time to secure her with a cord he had brought with him, and with which he adroitly enough confined her arms by tying her elbows very nearly close together behind her back.

It was the sudden tightening of the slip-knot in this cord which let the Dark Woman know that she was truly a prisoner.

With another cry of rage, she sprang off the couch.

In doing so, she received a slight wound in the neck from the sword of Colonel Hanger, which he could only turn aside sufficiently to prevent its point from penetrating her throat. As it was, the sharp blade furrowed up the skin on the right side of the neck, and blood flowed.

"Ah, assassin!" cried the Dark Woman,—"you have, then, succeeded. It is murder you came to do."

"Not at all," replied Colonel Hanger. "That is just what I am expressly forbidden to do. Some wild animals are to be taken alive, and you are one of them, my lady."

"Villain! Vile tool of a tyrant!"

"That will do. I thought I should want it."

The Colonel had provided himself with a tolerably thick neck-shawl, which, in the helpless state of the Dark Woman, he had now no difficulty in placing over and into her mouth to a certain extent, and tying it securely at the back of her head, all further expression of her opinion upon what was taking place by word of mouth was quite out of the question.

"Now, bring her along!" said the Colonel; "and I think, take it for all in all, this capture has been made with the most singular success."

CHAPTER CL.

TRAITORS' GATE AT THE TOWER.

COLONEL HANGER had reason to congratulate himself upon the ease with which he had captured the Dark Woman. He had, in truth, more reason to be thankful to the good fortune which had befriended him in the enterprise than, probably, he was aware of.

It is likely enough, notwithstanding the fact that he, Hanger, had led a life so dissolute and unprincipled that it had been full of consequential dangers, never had he encountered at one time half the peril which this capture of the Dark Woman might have produced.

It was the young girl page who was, in reality, the conqueror of Linda de Chevenaux.

The double dose of the opiate which had been administered by the page it was that really captured the Dark Woman.

Colonel Hanger only, as is common enough in all the affairs of this world, came in second, and took away all the spoils of the victory.

The persevering rain that fell upon London kept Frith Street clear of passengers.

The Dark Woman was hurried down the staircase of the dismal house. The coach door was opened by the Yeoman who had been left on duty below, and in another minute the vehicle was in motion.

The Dark Woman made more than one terrible effort to free herself from the bonds that held her.

All was in vain.

Then her proud, disdainful heart seemed ready to break; and at that moment she would have been glad to die, so that she might escape the dreadful fate which she thought awaited her.

It was a natural enough thought of hers, that as she had before been consigned for safe keeping in a lunatic asylum, that would be her fate now.

Death by any means was, to her imagination, preferable to being compelled to wear out the remainder of her existence in such a place.

The half-stifled sobs and groans which she uttered should have melted a heart of stone; but it is quite clear that there are human hearts much harder than any primitive rock that has ever been discovered.

Colonel Hanger's heart must have been of that density, for the evident terrible suffering of the Dark Woman had no effect upon him whatever.

He had not thought it necessary now to take into the coach with him one of the Yeomen. The prisoner was bound and gagged. What could she do? Nothing whatever. Colonel Hanger felt himself perfectly at ease.

Still the Dark Woman uttered half-choked sobs, that seemed as if they would rend her heart in twain, and Colonel Hanger thought it as well to say a word or two to his prisoner.

Perhaps some feeling of curiosity, too, had come over him to know what account she would herself give of her connexion with the Regent.

As yet, he had only heard what the Prince himself chose to say about Linda de Chevenaux. It could do him no harm to hear her version of the story, provided she would tell it to him, and it might do him some good.

So Colonel Hanger, as the coach lumbered on towards London Bridge, where he proposed getting a boat to convey his prisoner by water to the Tower, settled himself comfortably on the seat opposite to her, and spoke.

"Hem! Well, madam, you know me, no doubt. At least, no doubt you have heard of me. I am Colonel Hanger, the faithful friend and intimate of the Regent."

The Dark Woman uttered some sound, of which he could make no sense.

"Well," he said, "I have been forced to gag you, to stop your tongue; but if I felt quite sure you would not try to breed a disturbance, I would not mind removing the gag—not that the disturbance would in the least help you."

The Dark Woman made another inarticulate sound; but Colonel Hanger thought, or chose to think, that it had an imploring tone about it.

"Well," he added, "you will quite comprehend that I am acting in the name of the law; and, therefore, any outcry you may make would not aid you in the least."

She nodded her head.

"You will be quiet, then, if I remove the gag?"

The Dark Woman had found out a mode of replying to him in the affirmative, and she nodded her head again repeatedly.

"Good! I will take your word so far, and the more willingly that I shall be able, if you break it, to restore affairs to their present position."

Colonel Hanger removed the gag.

The Dark Woman was able to speak again. It seemed to her that she was half-way towards freedom now that she was permitted the use of words once more.

The first word that the Dark Woman uttered, if it may be called a word, was a cry of half exultation, half despair.

"Silence!" said Hanger. "You forget."

"Oh, no—no!"

"You do, indeed, my lady. You were to be quiet if I removed the gag."

"Yes; I am quiet. But tell me one thing, or I will kill myself at once."

"What is it?"

"Am I to be removed to a madhouse?"

"Not that I know of."

"On your soul, you are speaking the truth?"

"On my word of honour!"

"But you have no honour!"

"That's polite."

"This is no time for politeness. I have heard of you, and know who and what you are. You are the infamous John Hanger, calling yourself Colonel Hanger."

"Oh, that's it! Well, my lady, I fancy the best plan will be to stop that tongue of yours again, for it is scarcely a civil one."

"No!—no!—no!"

"But, since I am the infamous Colonel Hanger, what else can you expect?"

"You are too practical and worldly a man to care that I speak the truth to you."

"Hem! I don't know."

"You do know. But, since it does not please

you, I will say no more in that strain. You might say things of me as harsh, and it is not for a man like you and a woman like me to waste time in mutual recriminations."

Colonel Hanger could not but acknowledge the truth in his own mind of what the Dark Woman said; but he did not like the turn the conversation had taken. He had lost the superiority which he wished to maintain over his captive; and he regretted he had removed the gag.

"Come, come, madam," he said, "you quite forget one thing, I fancy."

"What is that?"

"That you are in my power."

"No; you are in mine."

"I in your power?"

"Quite so."

"I should like to know how you make that out."

"Easily, John Hanger."

"Very good; I am all attention. Speak freely, Linda de Chevenaux; you interest me."

"The explanation is simple. I can buy you."

"Buy me?"

"Exactly so. You, and such men as you, have a price. It is only necessary to ascertain what it is, and then to pay it, and you are bought.'

"Hem! You are a bold woman."

"I know I am."

"And a clever one."

"I know that, too."

"Well, then," added Colonel Hanger, "just for argument's sake, and the amusement of the thing, what now do you consider should be my price—not that I agree with you that I am to be bought?"

"Do not seek to deceive me, Colonel Hanger. You are bargaining for yourself already."

"I? Oh, no, no! Why do you say that?"

"Because, when you ask me what price I will pay for you, you lower your tones."

"What then?"

"You don't want the men who are outside this coach to know the exact price at which John Hanger appraises himself."

Colonel Hanger was silent for a few moments, during which the Dark Woman gave him time to think. When he spoke again it was in still lower and more confident tones than before.

"Hark you, Linda de Chevenaux," he said. "If I were not the friend and confidante of the Regent, hang me if I would not be yours."

"You will be mine, notwithstanding."

"No, no—I cannot. Sink me! no, I cannot."

"Because the Regent will not know that you play the double game."

"He would be sure to know."

"Not so. And now that all that is settled, where are you about to take me?"

"All what is settled?"

"About your selling yourself to me."

"Ha! ha! That is cool! That is cool! Ha. ha! By heavens I begin to admire you, my lady. Come, now, since you say that it is all settled, pray let me know the price you put upon me, as you seem disposed to be both buyer and seller?"

"You are worth to me ten thousand pounds."

"Ten thousand!"

"I cannot give it to you in money."

"Oh!"

"But I can in jewels."

"Ah!"

"Which will be the same thing."

"Just the same thing."

"And now where are we going?"

"To the Tower."

"Impossible!"

"But true."

"To the Tower of London?"

"Just so!"

"But—but—no, you jest. It cannot be! On what pretence am I to be made a prisoner in the Tower?"

"High treason; that is all. You threatened and attempted the life of his Highness the Prince Regent."

"Ah!"

"Now you comprehend?"

"I do—I do."

"But," added Colonel Hanger, lowering his voice, "if you are prepared with that ten thousand pounds' worth of jewels, I rather think there

will be a sad story to tell the Regent of the escape of the Dark Woman."

"You shall have them."

"When?—when?"

'To-morrow. Set me free to-night, and you shall have them to-morrow."

Colonel Hanger laughed.

"No, my lady. Let me once get possession of the jewels, and I will find a means of letting you out of the Tower if you were in its deepest dungeons."

"How am I to trust you for my freedom?"

"How am I, then, to trust you for the jewels?"

"My word, which I never broke for good for evil."

"Hem! my honour!"

"It may not be. John Hanger, you must trust me, or you remain unsold."

"Then I cannot help it. But I will call on

you in a day or two, and if you should alter your mind I will find a means to liberate you. Here we are at London Bridge."

"Let my arms free!"

"Oh, no, no!"

"Then it is war between you and me! Beware!"

"Ha! ha! I have taken good care of myself hitherto, and will manage still to do so."

Linda was silent as, amid such a downfall of rain as was seldom seen in London, the coach drew up at the stairs close to London Bridge. The tide was ebbing; and they could hear it boiling, and bubbling, and rushing through the narrow arches of the old bridge like some impetuous torrent.

Colonel Hanger sprang from the coach.

"Look to your prisoner, my men," he cried. "On your lives, look to her! No, no! I cannot lose sight of her myself, even for a moment. Call for a boat! Call for a boat, one of you!"

"Boat! boat! boat ahoy!" shouted one of the Yeomen.

There was a little wretched public house close at hand from which there arose sounds of singing and jollity; but at the cry for a boat from the Yeoman, a Thames waterman issued out of the public-house, evidently not particularly sober, and shouted, "Who wants a boat? Ain't there the old bridge to cross over? Who wants a boat? How many are there of you, eh?"

"Come here, fellow!" cried Colonel Hanger. "Come here, fellow, if you want to earn a guinea!"

"Who talks about a guinea?"

"I do. A guinea to the old Tower!"

"Yes, your honour. Guineas ain't picked up so easy in the mud of the Thames, and so I says it—I, Ben Bolter."

"Come, then, Ben Bolter, where is your boat?"

"Hereaway, your honour, and a better wherry never swam on the Thames, though I say it, perhaps, as ought not; but so I says, and I'm Ben Bolter."

With a sudden dash, now, the rain, which had been pouring down so heavily, appeared to make up its mind to take no further trouble, but make an end of it by coming down all at once; for such an avalanche of water poured down upon the coach, the horses, the Yeomen of the Guard, and waterman, that it almost blinded them, and if it had continued, would have gone far towards sweeping them all, coach included, into the river.

The two Yeomen of the Guard cowed down close to the coach to shelter themselves as best they could, and Colonel Hanger withdrew into the vehicle again out of the cataract.

"Ya!" cried the waterman; "that's a cooler!"

"All the better for you," said Hanger; "you required one."

Even as Colonel Hanger spoke, the rain abruptly ceased, and before you could have counted ten, not a drop was falling. The hiss and roar of numerous drains and little streams which the rain had made in its progress from the upper ground, now mingled with the washing sound made by the tide of the river.

But the squall was over.

A narrow reft opened in the dim clouds that were sailing before a south-west wind overhead,

and the moon, about a week old, looked down upon the seething, frothy river.

"That's over," said Hanger.

The waterman was shaking his heavy coat.

"Well, he said, "it's about as heavy a downfall as ever I saw; and so I says it, and I'm Ben Bolter."

"Quick!" cried Hanger. "Where is your boat?"

"It should be hereaway if it ain't swamped."

The Dark Woman did not utter a word.

"Here you are!" added the waterman. "Here she is, but water-logged, or I'm a Frenchman."

The wherry was full of rain-water, but Ben Bolter soon tilted the greater portion of it out; and as the gap opened wider and wider in the clouds, the bright stars began to peep down upon the river and upon the old bridge with a sparkling luminosity, as if they, too, had been washed by the pelting shower which had left everything on that spot of earth bright and glistening.

One-half of the darkness which had shrouded every object vanished.

Colonel Hanger could see the river, the bridge, and the boats quite plainly. Ben Bolter was in one, which he was pushing, by the aid of a boat-hook, close to the little slippery steps by the side of the bridge.

"Now, your honour," he said, "here we are, all right and taut again."

"Come!" said Colonel Hanger to the Dark Woman. "Come, madam, it is time."

She stepped from the coach.

To resist would only have provoked a struggle, in which she must have been conquered. One-half of the terrible weight that had oppressed her mind on finding herself captured, was removed at the assurance that it was not to a lunatic asylum she was to be removed.

The Tower had but few terrors for her. If in truth it were intended to incarcerate her in the old world-renowned fortress, she would have abundant means of contriving an escape.

The Dark Woman would have been tranquil now but for a terrible throbbing pain in her temples, which was the result of the powerful opiate she had taken, and which had not been allowed to exhaust its influence over the nerves in sleep.

Without a word of inquiry or of remonstrance she stepped into the boat.

The Colonel had preceded her, and the two Yeomen of the Guard followed.

"Now push off," said Hanger.

"To the Tower, your honour?"

"Yes."

"The Tower Stairs?"

"No; the Traitors' Gate."

Ben Bolter, with an oar suspended in the air, stopped short in what he was about, and glared in the face of Colonel Hanger, who, with a haughty wave of his hand, said, "A State prisoner. You will get your guinea, my man. Ask no questions, but push off."

The waterman gave a long whistle, and then plunged his oars into the water, and began to pull slowly and deliberately through the turgid and troubled stream.

The small stairs were reflected from the water; and as the boat sped on, it seemed as if it broke them up into a thousand sparkling fragments.

The distance was so short that in a few moments

almost the historical White Tower became visible, and more and more visible, too, as the sky cleared and brightened beyond it.

It was then that the Dark Woman spoke once more to Colonel Hanger in a low voice, which could only reach his ears.

"Are you decided?"

"About what?"

"To accept my offer. So brilliant a night's work, even for Colonel Hanger, will not readily again present itself."

"It is you who must decide," said Colonel Hanger, in almost a lower tone than that in which the Dark Woman spoke. "It is you who are to decide. Show me the jewels—let me feel that I have them, and you are free."

"I cannot. It does not lie within the bounds of probability that I should have about me so large a sum, even in the portable form of jewels."

"Say, then, where I can get them—and I pledge myself that within four-and-twenty hours from that time you are free."

"As if I could trust you!" murmured the Dark Woman.

"That is just it," added Colonel Hanger, with a tone of suppressed vexation. "We cannot trust each other, and so the thing falls through. But you will think better of it, Linda de Chevenaux. The Tower is dark and gloomy, and full of uncomfortable associations. They may place you in the dreariest dungeon, and you may sigh in vain for the light of day; but even there I will visit you; and should you still feel inclined to pay me that price for your liberty, it shall be yours."

"And is it not possible," said the Dark Woman, "that I may make you pay a price for your suspicions?"

"As how? What mean you?"

"I may find a means of yet communicating with the Regent, and informing him that his intimate and friend—as you call yourself—has placed a price upon the freedom of his prisoner."

"Which I will deny. It is but word for word, and assertion for assertion. Where will be your proof, Linda de Chevenaux? Will the Prince believe you? No. Pull on, waterman! pull on! Why do you pause?"

"This is Traitors' Gate," said the waterman, as he not only ceased rowing down the river, but, on the contrary, made a backward movement with the sculls, or the wherry—tolerably loaded as it was—would have been carried past the Tower by the impetuosity of the ebbing tide.

CHAPTER CLI.

THE DARK WOMAN FINDS HERSELF IN AN APARTMENT OF GLOOM AND TERROR

THE tide of the Thames was at about half-ebb, and nothing could be imagined more gloomy and cavernous-like than the entrance of Traitors' Gate from the river.

This effect was rather heightened than decreased by a strange, dull, reddish-looking light, which came flickering, apparently from far away, within the gloomy arch that led to the Tower.

And now that rift among the dark clouds that had hung overhead—that rift which had widened temporarily to a gap some miles in extent, and through which the young moon and sparkling stars had looked down upon the earth—suddenly closed up, for a legion of clouds, like some advancing army, came with the south wind—but no rain fell, although the darkness became most intense.

The river, the bridge, the White Tower, were all obliterated in the blackness that reigned around.

But that dull, red glare, that came out of the cavernous depths beyond Traitors' Gate, increased in intensity.

The contrast with the darkness without did much for it; and if it oppressed the imagination of the Dark Woman, it likewise seemed, for a time, to have even a deadening effect upon the spirits of Colonel Hanger, who, half-standing in the boat, gazed earnestly through the cross-barred gateway, as if in doubt what next to do.

It was but for a fleeting moment or two, however, that that bold and reckless man was subdued into anything approaching reflectiveness by the magic or the mystery of the scene about him: starting suddenly, as if awakening from some painful and most unaccustomed reverie, he cried out, "A traitor prisoner for the Tower! a traitor prisoner for the Tower!"

Those words seemed as though they were an invocation, having the power of a spell with them, for no sooner were they spoken than the faint red light that had shone so mysteriously from the other or Tower side of Traitors' Gate, brightened and cast a broad glare upon the river.

That broad glare had, however, a peculiar character which was all its own.

The reflection came through the cross-barred entrance to the pool or well of water, just within Traitors' Gate; and as it fell upon the heaving tide of the river, it cast a huge shadow of these massive cross-bars along with it.

The effect was strange and startling.

"You see?" whispered Colonel Hanger to the Dark Woman.

"See what?"

"The bars of your State prison already environ you!"

The Dark Woman smiled scornfully.

"They environ you, too," she said; "and these two men who are the poor tools whose duty it has been to help you in this night's villany! It is for you to be afraid of shadows! They affect me not!"

Colonel Hanger bit his lips.

"You are bold!"

"I am."

"We shall see if the gloom of the Tower will not teach you a little humility!"

"Never! But——"

"But what? You speak in tones as though you had some proposition to make to me; and if so, you have but a short time in which to do so, for I can hear the plash of oars in the water, on the inner side of Traitors' Gate."

"Listen to me," whispered the Dark Woman, in hurried accents. "I am well aware that my imprisonment in the Tower will be kept a secret from all who could or would aid me. You say that you can save me?"

"If I please I can." •

"At a price——"

"Of ten thousand pounds, either in money or in jewels—sink me, if I care which!"

"Suppose I give you a written acknowledgment that I will pay you that amount so soon as you set me free?"

Colonel Hanger laughed.

"Am I a fool—an idiot—that I should trust to a memorandum or an acknowledgment for money from a person in your situation? How could I enforce it? How could I produce it or hope for a single moment to—to—— Stop! Yet, upon second thoughts, I do not know but I might feel inclined to accept such a guarantee as better than nothing, having so strong a desire to serve you."

It was quite evident that, even while he was speaking, commencing as he did to laugh to scorn the offer of the Dark Woman, some new thought had come over that insidious and politic brain of Colonel Hanger, so that the latter part of his speech bore no connexion whatever with the former.

"It seems," said the Dark Woman, "that your wish to serve me has come into sudden life."

"No, no! Let me think a moment—let me think."

Colonel Hanger had but very few moments in which to think, for the dusky red glare of light from the inner side of Traitors' Gate increased each moment; and there came upon the ears of the party in the wherry without the sound of dull, heavy blows, as of iron upon iron.

The heavy bar which secured Traitors' Gate within had rusted into its place, and that jarring sound was produced by a hammer upon the old iron stanchions for the purpose of releasing the bar which now for some years, amid the fogs, damps, and high tides of the river, had maintained its place.

Colonel Hanger thought it one of the most fortunate circumstances in the world that he was thus allowed a few minutes for the carrying out a plan which had suddenly darted across his brain, as if by inspiration, while he was declining the offer of the Dark Woman of anything in the shape of written acknowledgment for the heavy sum she proposed to give to him as a ransom.

The idea was this.

What a wonderful effect he might produce, and how great a claim he might have upon the purse of the Prince Regent, by bringing triumphantly before him such a document as a proof of how he had been tempted to play falsely by him, and betray the trust that had been reposed in him.

Such a document might not be worth ten thousand pounds, since the Prince of Wales's exchequer was not in such full flow as to enable him to play the generous potentate on so large a scale; but still Colonel Hanger reflected that, whenever he wanted money, the fact must be patent and present to the royal mind that he had resisted the temptation of so large a sum.

"Well?" said the Dark Woman, when she saw that some rapid revulsion of feeling had taken place in the mind of Colonel Hanger;—"well?"

"What would you say if I would accept your terms?"

"An acknowledgment for the money?"

"Just so."

"And upon that acknowledgment you will contrive my freedom?"

"On my head be it! Give me the acknowledg-ment now. Here is a pencil, and here paper. Moisten the lead with your lips, and press heavily. To-morrow I will set you free."

"And the next day you have the money."

"Agreed."

"Agreed; but you must set my hands at liberty."

"Certainly. There! Quick, my lady! quick! or, sink me! they will get the gates open."

As Colonel Hanger and the Dark Woman sat far aft in the boat, this conversation could easily be carried on, as, indeed, it was, in such low and rapid tones that the two Yeomen of the Guard and Ben Bolter, the waterman, heard nothing of it; but by the broad, red glare cast by the torches within Traitors' Gate, they saw, with some surprise, Colonel Hanger hastily release the arms of the Dark Woman from the cord that held them; then, placing before her an open pocket-book, he put a pencil in her hand, whispering, "Write—write it on that page. Do you think the Regent knows your handwriting, Linda de Chevenaux?"

He should know it! There was a time—but no matter, that has passed away, never to return.

"Write—write! By Jove! they'll have the gate open, and then it will be too late!"

"John Hanger, I thank you," said the Dark Woman, as she wrote rapidly; but the words she wrote on the blank leaf of the Colonel's pocket-book were anything but those he wished to see in order to show to the Regent. He had a plan—a scheme—a piece of tricky policy in furnishing the Dark Woman with the means of writing, and allowing her liberty of action to do so, but she had another.

It was diamond cut diamond, only that she was the keener, finer jewel of the two.

The Dark Woman did moisten the lead pencil with her lips. She did press heavily upon the blank page of the pocket-book, in order that the writing should not readily be effaced, and she wrote as follows:—

"My dear son Allan,—I am betrayed, made prisoner, and conveyed to the Tower by the villain Colonel Hanger. Whatever hands this pocket-book may fall into, carry it or this leaf of it to Allan Fearon, now residing in the last house abutting on the river in Buckingham Street, Strand, and ask for a reward in the name of

"LINDA DE CHEVENAUX."

The light from the torches from within Traitors' Gate came in a deceiving, dazzling, and tremulous fashion on the page of the pocket-book; so that, although Colonel Hanger made some efforts to read what the Dark Woman there wrote, he was puzzled to do so, and the difficulty was increased inasmuch as she took care that the shadow of one hand should be over the paper.

There could be no mistake, however, about the signature of Linda de Chevenaux.

That he saw plainly enough.

"You have written it!" he cried.

He stretched forth his hand to take the pocket-book; but before he could do so, the Dark Woman cried out, in a voice of exultation, as she held it above her head, and out of his reach, "You are foiled!—foiled still! This book may come back to you, but it will be in a different fashion to that you expected! For the present, I commit it to the tide of the Thames. I fancy it will float; and I hope it may, since it now contains a memorandum which will serve me into whosoever hands it may fall!"

"Fiend!—wretch! Let me have it! You know not what you do! Give me the book!"

The Dark Woman laughed scornfully as she threw the pocket-book far away into the heaving tide; and in the darkness of that night it seemed as though the pocket-book disappeared into illimitable space—being swallowed up, so to speak, in the black obscurity which confounded air and water into one indivisible and undistinguishable mass immediately outside the broad glare of light which came from the torches within Traitors' Gate.

"Confusion!" cried Colonel Hanger. "Tricked and fooled at last! Female fiend that you are! Do you know what you have done?"

"I do."

"Indeed you do not; but I'll be repaid for it. A note of twenty pounds value was in the pocket-book."

"It will pay my messenger."

"Your messenger?"

"Yes. Whoever is the fortunate finder of that pocket-book will have a message to deliver, and he will take the note for his pains."

For a few moments the rage of Colonel Hanger was so great that it seemed to be with difficulty that he could restrain himself from striking the Dark Woman; and probably he would not have refrained even from that unmanly act had he been alone with her in the boat.

All this happened, of course, in much less time than it has taken to relate; and by the time the little interlude was over, in which Colonel Hanger had proved so poor a match for the Dark Woman, in subtlety of intellect and fertility of resources, the bar had been removed from within Traitors' Gate.

Slowly, and with an ominous creaking sound, the two halves of the cross-barred portcullis-looking gate opened inwards, and then that strange reflection on the water of the river vanished.

A boat appeared manned by three persons.

Two of them were rowing it, and the third stood up, with a flaring flambeau in his hand, from which ignited resinous particles dropped into the river.

There was a regular form in the reception of any prisoner at Traitors' Gate; and since Colonel Hanger had obeyed strictly the injunctions of Sir John Scott—to send a messenger on beforehand with a copy of the warrant to the Tower—the proper official persons were there waiting to receive the prisoner.

"What traitor?" cried the man with the torch.

"Linda de Chevenaux," replied Colonel Hanger; and then he added, in a low voice, "and my bitterest maledictions go with her!"

"On what warrant," said the man with the torch, "do we receive Linda de Chevenaux as a prisoner in the Tower of London?"

"On the warrant of the Privy Council of England."

"Show your warrant."

"It is here!"

"Produce your prisoner."

"She is here!"

The boats ran alongside of each other; and the man with the torch placed his disengaged hand upon the shoulder of the Dark Woman.

"Linda de Chevenaux," he said, as if repeating some form, or reading from a book,—"Linda de Chevenaux, you are my prisoner—to hold firm and keep close in the name of the King—barring all rescue by force or fraud—dead or alive, until released by the high authority that has placed you here."

"Now, madam," said Colonel Hanger,—"now, madam, you and I part."

"But we shall meet again," said the Dark Woman.

The man with the torch, having only one hand at liberty, seemed rather confused in assisting the prisoner from the boat of Colonel Hanger to that which belonged to the Tower.

"Give me the torch, sir," said Hanger. "I will light you. Sink me! if I seem to like to come any further; the place smells like a dungeon, and looks like the bottom of a well."

The official of the Tower surrendered to Hanger the torch, and he stood up with one foot upon the gunwale of the boat; and holding the flambeau high above his head, he cast as much light as was possible from it into the stagnant pool which the waters of the river formed within Traitors' Gate.

The Dark Woman said not a word; but once only she clasped her hands over her face, as the boat shot along the inky-looking pool towards a flight of ancient-looking stone steps which seemed to descend deep into the tide.

A slippery, greasy moisture was upon the steps, and as the boat grated against them, the Dark Woman started, and half-rose in alarm.

"Be still, madam!" said the official of the Tower,—"be still, madam, or you will upset us!"

"Then I should drown."

"In good faith, madam, we should all drown, for this pool is of great depth."

If the Dark Woman had harboured for a single instant the faintest intention of putting an end to herself and all her sorrows in that picturesque and historical spot, the opportunity in another instant passed away; for one of the men in the boat secured the frail little craft to an iron ring, deeply embedded in the stone step, level with the surface of the water.

"Now, madam," said the official personage, as he assisted the Dark Woman from the boat.

She looked at him for a moment.

"May I ask, sir, who you are?"

"I am the Deputy Warden of the Tower."

"Do you know me, sir?"

"No, madam; but you must be some one of importance, or your crime must make you such; for I verily believe the last lady who ascended these steps was a royal princess."

"I, too—I, too," cried the Dark Woman, as she clasped her hands and spoke in screaming accents,—"I, too, am a royal princess; for am I not the wife of George Prince of Wales, and Regent of England?"

It was the depression of the place—the mystery of that strange entrance to the ancient Tower—the historical associations attached to the scene—and, perhaps, a certain amount of physical weakness arising still from the effects of the opiate she had so recently taken, that made the Dark Woman seem at that moment to lose all her firmness and ener y.

She turned when about half-way up those slippery and cankered steps, and stretching forth her arms towards the river, she cried out, "Oh, farewell, world!—farewell, world! Linda de Chevenaux will never look upon your sunny smiles again! Farewell for ever!"

She burst into a passion of tears.

The words she had uttered, and the sobs which succeeded them, reached the ears of Colonel Hanger, and he burst into a loud, brutal laugh.

"So, so!" he cried; "her ladyship's confidence forsakes her, and she shrieks and cries like a drab committed to Bridewell for a month. Ha! ha!"

The Dark Woman started. She drew herself up to her full height, and the old fiery flash, full of intellect and determination, came into her eyes.

"No!" she cried, "I will live! I will live yet, for I have debts to pay—debts of vengeance! Lead on, sir; I am your prisoner, and follow you! The old Tower is historical; but the residence of Linda, Princess of Wales, and wife of the Regent, shall add another page to its records."

CHAPTER CLII.

THE COUNTESS DE BLONDE REPLIES TO THE MARCHIONESS OF SUNNINGHAM, AND SENDS FOR SIR HINCKTON MOYS'S HEAD.

His Royal Highness the Regent, and Annie, Countess de Blonde, reached St James's Palace without being recognised by more than two or three people on their route there on foot from the Hanover Hotel.

The production of the two forged letters had thoroughly convinced the Regent of the good faith and the constancy of Annie towards him.

If Annie were innocent—and he did not now entertain a shadow of a doubt to the contrary—so was Allan Fearon; and to do him ample justice, with all his faults, it was an immense moral relief to him to find that he was not rivalled by his own son.

The Prince was quite gay and sportive as St. James's Palace came into view, and as he looked into the sweet face of Annie, he said with more earnestness than he usually threw into his tones, "Annie, I feel that I owe you some amends for the past! Tell me what I shall do to please you?"

"Do you mean that, pray?"

"On my faith, I do!"

Annie sighed.

"What is the matter? You sigh! I am afraid you fix your mind now upon something inaccessible."

"I do."

"What is it? The moon?"

"Oh, dear, no!"

"What then?"

"I want something ugly."

"Something ugly! Explain yourself?"

"I will. I mean the head of Sir Hinckton Moys."

The Regent laughed.

"My dear Annie, if I were the Caliph Haroun Al-Raschid, of whom we read in the 'Arabian Nights,' I would on the instant gratify you; but as I am only plain George, the Regent of England, I cannot."

"I know you cannot, so I must take some means of my own."

"Some means of your own, Annie, to get that man's head, do you say?"

"Oh, yes!"

"Come, come! Dismiss the absurd idea, and satisfy yourself of one thing—which is, that I have done with him for ever."

"That is well, George, because he is a bad man; and, although you are not a bad man at all when you are left alone, yet if you have one near you, he can generally make you as bad as himself."

"No, no, Annie! Don't say that—don't say that! But tell me now, since I cannot accommodate you with the head of Sir Hinckton Moys, is there anything else that I can do that will gratify you?"

"Let me think."

"I promise you beforehand anything you like."

"Oh, yes, I know it."

"What is it?"

"I want an emerald."

"You shall have one."

"A good large one!"

"As large an one as money can purchase—that is to say, as credit can procure."

"There is a shop, George."

Annie pointed to a jeweller's shop, which was at that time kept at the corner of Pall Mall and St. James's Street, by a person of the name of Worrell.

"There is a shop, George. Suppose, now, we go in and get one there. I will, when I have chosen it, tell you what I want to do with it!"

"Then it is not for yourself?"

"Not exactly, George."

"Who for, then?"

"A friend of mine, to whom I want you to do a good turn some of these odd days; but don't ask me anything else about it just now. Come in, and see if they have got one here."

"I am afraid they will know me."

"But they may trust you, nevertheless."

"Annie, you are a great deal too sharp and witty this morning. But there is no one but a ridiculous-looking young man in the shop, who seems as if all his leisure time was spent upon that remarkable odd-looking head of hair of his; so let us go in."

"George," said Annie, "you are brilliant to-day. Who, now, would have supposed you could have been so sarcastic about that poor creature's bundle of tow that he has on his head, and no doubt calls hair?"

The Regent was in high good humour, and they went into the jeweller's shop, where the foppish young man was admiring himself in a glass that was set in the wall in order to increase the appearance of the stock of gold and silver plate by reflection.

"Have you any emeralds?" asked the Regent.

"Yes, sir."

"He don't know me!" whispered the Prince to Annie.

"What beautiful air!" said Annie.

"Oh, madam—that is to say, miss—I—a—

nature has been bountiful. I—a—my hair is generally considered to be a—a——"

"Sir," said Annie, arching up her eyebrows, "I never mentioned your hair!"

"Eh?"

"I was remarking on the air of the morning. I don't admire ravelled string—which I believe is called oakum—in the least."

The jeweller's "young man" looked the picture of agony and anger.

"Come, sir," said the Regent, "if you have emeralds to show us, do so quickly."

A small drawer was produced, and with quite a disdainful look upon his face, the Adonis of the shop pointed out some emeralds.

"The best, I want!' said Annie.

"This one, madam, is our finest. It is sixty guineas!"

"Is that all?"

"That is all, madam."

"Very well. It will do. Now, George, do you think you will always know the emerald when you see it?"

"I think I should."

"Very well, then, it will do. Come a'ong."

"But—a—the—a—sixty guineas!" said the young man with the head of hair. "I cannot let the emerald go without the money!"

"Pay," said Annie.

The Regent felt in all his pockets. "I—I am afraid," he said, "that—I—that is, I begin to think I have no money about me just at present."

"No more have I."

The young man with the head of hair got red in the face, as he cried out, "I never met with such impudence in all my life. I have a good mind to call a constable."

"Do," said Annie; "he might know us."

"I have very little doubt that he would."

The Regent looked perplexed.

"Hark you, sir!" he said; "if you will send the emerald to the Palace in an hour, and ask for the Countess de Blonde, it will be paid for."

"I don't believe anything of the sort," exclaimed the shopman, as he eagerly counted the loose jewels in the drawer, to see that none were missing. "I don't believe it. I only wish I could see a 'runner,'—I would give you both in charge."

"What does he mean by a 'runner?'" said Annie.

"A Bow Street officer," said the Regent, laughing. "You refuse, then, sir, to send the emerald to St. James's?"

"Of course I do. Get out of the shop door quick as you can."

"We are turned out, Annie!"

"Come on then, George. Stop—I have but one question to ask. Is that extraordinary weed on your head real, or a wig to frighten people with as they come down St. James's Street?"

The shopman uttered a howl of despair as the Regent and Annie left the shop, for his faith in his head of hair was for ever shaken by the sarcasms of one with so much beauty and such sparkling eyes as belonged to Annie.

"There you are!" said the Regent. "It is quite absurd of us to go anywhere to buy anything. We are sure to be insulted, Annie."

"Never mind!"

"Oh, I don't mind, much; but it is provoking."

"I am hungry."

"We shall be at home directly."

"But those tarts——"

"Those what, Annie?"

"The tarts in that confectioner's window. Those raspberry puffs—I must have one!"

"Annie! Annie!"

"Oh, I must—whenever I see raspberry jam puffs, I must have some. You will have my death at your door, George, if you don't let me; and indeed I must and will, whether you let me or not!"

The Countess de Blonde disengaged herself from the arm of the Regent, and dashed into a confectioner's shop that was about two doors down Pall Mall; and, seating herself, she commenced an immediate attack upon some pastry that lay in an inviting pile upon the counter.

The Regent had no resource but to follow her.

"Beautiful!' said Annie; "and not at all fat. Why don't you try one, George?'

The Regent shook his head.

"Well, never mind!" added Annie; "I will take enough for two."

"You will make yourself ill, Annie!"

"I never was ill in my life. That will do—now come along."

"One and fourpence, sir, if you please,' said a female, with rather an unusual amount of colour at the end of her nose, who kept the shop; but then cherry brandy was one of the commodities sold, which, perhaps, accounted for the beacon the lady carried. "One and fourpence, if you please, sir!"

"Yes—oh, yes! Of course—one and—and—fourpence—one and—eh? Oh, to be sure! I will send it."

"Send it, sir?"

"Yes. I will send it—I said send it. Don't you hear?"

"We never give credit, sir."

"I knew it! I knew it!" said a voice, triumphantly, as the young man with the head of hair, from the jeweller's shop, dashed into the confectioner's. "Mrs. Boltpuppy, I knew it. I watched them round the corner. They have got no money. Of course—I knew it, Mrs Boltpuppy. Call a constable—call a constable. Ha! ha! my hair is oakum, and a wig is it? Ha! ha! Call a constable. They shan't go. Common cheats, out for a stroll, Mrs. Boltpuppy. I will give them in charge, and so can you. Ha! ha! my hair is bad-looking tow, is it? Oh, we shall see!"

"Gracious heaven, Mr. Whistler," said Mrs. Boltpuppy, "you don't say so?"

"Oh, yes, ma'am. Mr. Worrell has come home, so I was able to run out and follow them. Have they stolen anything here?"

"Only some raspberry puffs."

"And from our place an emerald."

"Stop, sir!" said the Regent. "Up to this moment, you amused me, and I thought you only a fool; but if you repeat your last words, I will knock you down."

"Bravo, George!" said Annie.

"Watch! Watch! A constable!" cried the shopman, as he ran into Pall Mall; for he did not like the looks of the Regent at all. "A constable! A constable! Thieves! Murder! Thieves!"

"This is too ridiculous!" said the Regent.

"Let us see the end of it," said Annie. "It's good fun. We won't go."

"No," said Mrs. Boltpuppy, "I will take care you don't go, ma'am, I can tell you!"

"What!" cried Annie, as with one rapid movement she upset the whole of the remainder of the raspberry puffs,—"what! You say you can, and will, prevent me going if I like?"

Another touch of Annie's hand sent the bottle of cherry brandy in fragments to the floor.

Mrs. Boltpuppy screamed; and at that moment the jeweller's shopman returned with a constable.

"Stop a moment!" said the Regent.

There was something about the tone and manner of the Prince which produced a momentary silence and lull in the tempest of indignation which was raging about him and Annie.

"Stop a moment!"

"Well, sir! and what now?" asked the shopman.

"Yes, sir, what now?" said Mrs. Boltpuppy.

"You see that gentleman opposite?"

"Yes, yes!"

"Who is he?"

"Why," said Mrs. Boltpuppy, "all the world knows that that is his Royal Highness the Duke of York!"

"In course, it is!" said the constable; "and it's like your impudence to point to him, it is."

"Call him over here!"

"Call the Duke of York?" cried Mrs. Boltpuppy.

"Call his Royal Highness?" exclaimed the shopman with the head of hair.

"Call one of the blessed royal family?" ejaculated the constable.

"Yes; he will pay for the tarts."

"To be sure he will!" said Annie.

The constable, Mr. Whistler, and Mrs. Boltpuppy looked at each other for a moment in speechless amazement. They never—no, they never had heard of such impudence.

But the Regent took advantage of this momentary confusion among his enemies, and pushing Mrs. Boltpuppy on one side, he reached the open door, and called out, "York! York!"

The Duke of York, who, in an undress military uniform, was quietly walking past Marlborough House, on the other side of the way, turned instantly, and looked over to the confectioner's shop.

"Come over here, York!" called out the Regent again.

"Gracious 'evens!" said Mrs. Boltpuppy,—"'imperence can go no further!"

"He will be hung, drawn, and quartered!" said the constable.

"I'm all over of a cold inspiration," said the jeweller's shopman.

But the Duke of York did not seem to be at all indignant at being asked to "Come over here" by a person who had not the money to pay for some raspberry puffs. He gave a good-humoured nod with his head, and straightway over the road he came.

"Have you got any money, York?" said the Regent. "One and fourpence will do."

"Oh, yes!"

Mrs. Boltpuppy turned red and white by turns.

The hair on the head of the jeweller' shopman began to move about as if it were alive.

The constable dropped his staff with the gilt crown at the end of it, and his knees knocked together.

The Duke of York produced two shillings, and laid them on the counter; and then—turning to Annie—he said, "I need not say I hope you are well, Countess, for you look charming, as usual."

"Thank you," said Annie, "I am quite well; but if you had not, fortunately, come by, we should have been locked up because we had not one and fourpence with us."

"Impossible!"

"And yet true," said the Regent. "Come now, Annie; I think we have had adventures enough for one morning."

Mrs. Boltpuppy dropped on to her knees amid the fragments of the raspberry puffs that Annie had thrown over, and cried out, in a howling voice, "Who? who? Oh, who is this—this gentleman?"

She pointed to the Prince of Wales, and she addressed the Duke of York.

"This gentleman," replied the Duke of York, "is my brother, and his Highness the Regent!"

Mrs. Boltpuppy fell flat among the raspberry puffs, and put an end, at once, to all hopes of restoring them to a saleable condition.

The jeweller's shopman and the constable both made a rush to escape, but they jammed each other in the doorway, and fought and kicked for two or three seconds, fiercely, before they both rolled out into the street, and made off in different directions.

The Regent and the Duke of York laughed heartily, and Annie almost swooned with delight.

"Well," said the Regent, as they entered St. James's Palace, "we had some amusement, Annie, by taking a walk from the Hanover Hotel. But now tell me what you intended to do with the emerald."

"I intended to give it to a friend of mine, and to make a condition with you that, upon his presenting it to you, you should grant him any favour asked."

"Any favour?"

"Oh, it would be an easy one."

"What would it be?"

"His life!"

"His life, Annie? I do not understand you?"

"I will explain. To do you but common justice, George, you have a kind heart."

"Thank you, Annie."

"And since you have been Regent, and have had the power—the—the——what do you call it?—of life and death in your hands in regard to condemned persons——"

"The royal prerogative of mercy."

"Yes; that's it. Since then you have put a stop to those terrible scenes at Newgate, when, almost every other Monday morning, some three or four poor creatures were brought out to die."

"I cannot bear to reflect on such scenes."

"Well, then, the emerald was meant to remind you, specially, to pardon one."

"Who is it?"

"A highwayman."

"And a friend of yours, Annie?"

"Just so—and a friend, too, of your Royal Highness's; inasmuch as, but for him, I should

not be with you now. When he is—as he may be—condemned to death, I want you to pardon him without arguing the matter with anybody, upon his sending you the emerald, so that you may know him to be the man I mean."

"I will do it."

"Thank you, George."

"What is his name? Who is he?"

"Sixteen-stringed Jack."

"Why, he is quite a noted knight of the road. But I will keep my word with you, Annie, as I am a gentleman; and I think I can do so without having an emerald sent to me to remind me of it. There is no risk of my forgetting his singular name of Sixteen-stringed Jack. And now, Annie, let me speak to you of some one else."

"Of whom, George?"

"Allan Fearon, as he calls himself; but who I wish to take the name of Fitz-George."

"That's right, George."

No. 70.—DARK WOMAN.

"I have wrongfully suspected him, and I would fain make him ample amends, Annie."

"Then send for him; and I would advise you, that you give him a commission in the Guards, which will just suit him. There is one person, though, whom I pity most sincerely, and that is his poor mother."

"She is mad! She is mad!"

"She may be so, George; and being so, is only the more to be pitied."

"Well, well, I will speak to Allan about her. And now, Annie, let us go to lunch; and never again will I do you and myself the injustice of allowing an unworthy suspicion to enter my mind concerning you; and to show you what complete confidence I have in you, I place in your hands this letter from the Marchioness of Sunningham."

"Yes, indeed!"

"Ah, Annie. The animus with which it is written shines forth in every line."

"'The what?'"

"The—the object."

"Then why did you not say so? You know what a poor, ignorant girl I am."

"No, Annie, you are not. There are times at which you perfectly amaze me by what you know. But read the letter, and judge for yourself."

Annie did read the letter; and then, as she and the Regent partook of lunch in that elegant boudoir he had fitted up for her, she said, "George, I want you to let me do something."

"What is it?"

"I want to answer the Marchioness of Sunningham's letter."

"With all my heart."

"That will do!—that will do! You may depend upon it, George, that such a letter, written by one woman, can only be properly answered by another."

"I think you are right, Annie," said the Regent. "These stewed woodcocks are delicious!"

———

CHAPTER CLIIL.

THE DARK WOMAN PASSES A NIGHT IN THE
TOWER, AND MEETS WITH AN ADVENTURE.

THAT ringing, insulting laugh of Colonel Hanger was still echoing in the brain of the Dark Woman, as she ascended the remainder of the steps that led to the Tower from the pool immediately within Traitors' Gate.

"Madam," said the warden, "will it please you to pause for a moment now, as I have to send a receipt to the person who brought you hither."

"A receipt?"

"Yes, madam,—a receipt for you."

"Oh, I understand. I will wait, sir."

It was not until the Dark Woman had so far ascended those stone steps as to be quite out of reach of the highest tide that had ever washed about them, that she was legally considered to be fairly in the Tower; and, consequently, the Warden, although he had the receipt for her all ready, did not tender it to Colonel Hanger until then.

The fact is, Colonel Hanger would, no doubt, have gone away without the important formal document, much to the distress of Sir John Scott, had not the boat of the Tower now been again rowed towards him, while the Warden called out, "There is your receipt, sir."

"Ah, that is well!" said Colonel Hanger, as he took the document. "This will show that I have done my duty. Now, my men, take me to Whitehall Stairs as quickly as you can."

As the boat containing Colonel Hanger shot out again into the tide of the river, the Dark Woman passed through an archway, at the top of the stone steps, which led her into a long, gloomy passage of the Tower.

The official personage who had received her in the ancient fortress preceded her a few paces, and she was followed by a warder of the Tower, who carried in one hand a huge bunch of keys, and in the other, one of those ancient weapons of offence and defence called a "partizan."

The Under Warden of the Tower seemed dis posed to perform his office gently; and it is probable enough—being, as he was, a man of ordinarily good disposition—that the bitterness with which Colonel Hanger had treated the unfortunate prisoner, predisposed him in her favour.

"Madam," he said, "there are no special directions where to place you; but if you do not object to an apartment of somewhat evil repute, you can occupy one that is high and dry, and well boarded, in the Tower."

"Place me where you will," said the Dark Woman; "and yet, believe me, I am not ungrateful for even this show of sympathy."

"Nay, madam, these warrants of the Privy Council carry people to the dungeons below the moat; but if you do not object to an apartment in what is called the 'Bloody Tower,' you shall have it, together with such attention as I can bestow upon you; for there is evidently some mystery and some oppression connected with your case, or that man who brought you here would not have done so with so much vicious personality."

"The Bloody Tower!" said the Dark Woman. "I do remember, it is that wherein tradition says the children of Edward the Fourth were murdered by their uncle, King Richard."

"I believe, madam, there is very little doubt of that. The old room remains much as it was, I fancy, at the period; and for all I knew to the contrary, you may sleep on the same couch on which reposed the murdered princes."

"I shall be content to do so, and thank you. I cannot say that I am well. I suffer yet from some strong potion that has been administered to me; but as I am somewhat of a physician where my own ailments are concerned, if you will permit me to send for such medicaments as I may require, I shall thank you."

"That, madam, I dare not do."

"Is it so?"

"I would with pleasure consent to your request, but it lies far beyond my duty to permit any State prisoner in the Tower to hold the slightest communication abroad. A physician and a surgeon are, however, attached to the royal fortress, and you have a right to see them at any time."

"No," said the Dark Woman, "I decline such services."

"They must visit you, madam, at stated periods, in accordance with their duty; for since the great plague of London, there has existed an order that one or other of the medical officers of the Tower shall see every one within its walls at stated periods, to be assured that they are not afflicted with any contagious disorder."

The Under Warden was inclined to be talkative, and but that the Dark Woman felt a heaviness of heart, which the very atmosphere of that gloomy place seemed to induce. she might have encouraged a garrulity by which she could lose nothing, but from which she might have acquired useful information.

The long gloomy passage in which they were branched off in several directions, but the Under Warden took one to the right, and as several doors had to be passed within the space they traversed, he paused whenever he came to one, and allowed the warder with the keys to step forward and unlock it.

The dull heavy rattle of the keys, and the dry

grating sound of the lock, as each of these doors were opened, produced a painful feeling in the mind of the Dark Woman. It was a great relief to her when the fourth of such doors were opened and she emerged at once into the open air, about midway between the Barbican Gate and the Bloody Tower.

The cool fresh air revived her much, and the fever in her brain seemed one-half to be wafted away by the night wind, as she looked up to the black and cloudy sky.

A sentinel was pacing the space immediately contiguous to the door through which they had emerged, and he challenged the party at once; but the Warden gave the password for the night, and in a few minutes they stood beneath the old time-worn gateway of the Bloody Tower.

There was a narrow door, reached by three slant steps, apparently cut in the thickness of the wall, and there the Under Warden paused, and spoke in a low tone to the men who followed him.

It took the trial of four or five different keys before the right one was found to open this long disused door; for although now that tower, with all its historical reminiscences, is inhabited, it was some years after the period of which we write before some officers of the guard on duty chose it as their quarters.

A narrow, winding staircase, steep and rugged, up which it would have been a matter of some difficulty for any two persons to walk abreast, presented itself the moment the door creaked on its rusted hinges.

The Warden ascended first, and the Dark Woman followed him for about thirty steps, until another door presented itself, low, arched, and studded with heavy nails.

This door presented, if possible, more difficulties in the way of opening it than the one below; but when at length it was thrown back upon its hinges, there appeared another, immediately within, of heavy rosewood, the mouldings of which appeared once to have been gilt. This door was secured by a latch of the very commonest construction, mechanically speaking, but made of brass, on which the faded gilding still remained, and which was heavily covered with ornamentation and rough chasing.

There seemed to be no means of fastening this inner door; and the Dark Woman's conductor, by a touch of the latch, opened it at once.

There then appeared a little ante-room, about eight feet square, which, in daytime, would be lighted by long, narrow slits in the walls of the Tower.

Immediately opposite the door they entered was another, and that likewise was secured by a latch only.

Probably both these doors, however, had fastenings on their inner sides, although the Dark Woman did not at that moment take sufficient notice of her prison to be sure of the fact.

"Here, madam," said the Under Warden, as he opened the second door,—"here, madam, is the chamber you can have if you please; although, I doubt, I have been hasty in offering it to you, for it seems heavily encumbered with dust."

"I care not," said the Dark Woman; "and will willingly stay here in preference to one of your damper dungeons."

The man who followed the Dark Woman with the "partizan" and the keys had a lighted lantern stuck into the belt which was round his waist; and now, perhaps, actuated as much by curiosity on his own part as by his desire to show the prisoner the extent and the accommodations of the prison-chamber to which she had been conducted, he held up the lantern, so that a feeble but still sufficient ray of light shone into all the corners of the Tower apartment.

It was a dull, heavy, depressing room.

There was nothing on the floor—although, at first, from the tread, the Dark Woman thought that a carpet had been there, and mouldered away.

But that was dust.

At the one narrow casement, the framework of which was almost as wide as the glass, there hung some tapestry; and about the height of six feet from the floor the walls had evidently been covered by similar hangings, for in some places they had remained, while in others they had fallen from their hooks, and lay in a confused heap upon the dirty boards.

There was a small, stunted bedstead, of perfectly black oak, richly carved, but mean in its proportions; and against one of the walls was a little escritoire, which seemed like the first idea of a modern chest of drawers, with that sloping top which, by some delusion, was supposed to combine the conveniences of the writing-desk with the wardrobe.

A broken high-backed chair, which was partially propped against one of the walls, completed the entire furnishing of the apartment; and it is probable enough, that with very little addition indeed, that was the amount of accommodation which the children of Edward the Fourth possessed in the Tower of London.

A glance sufficed to take in these particulars on the part of the Dark Woman; but as the official personage who had brought her there gazed about him, he evidently regretted that he had conducted his prisoner to so scantily appointed an apartment.

"It is years, madam, since I saw this place, and I really had forgotten what was in it. The impression upon my mind was certainly more favourable than I see it ought to have been."

"It will do," said the Dark Woman. "I prefer it much to one of your lower dungeons. Let me have some bed-clothing and a pillow, and I shall be content."

"That you shall have, madam, and welcome; and since you say you prefer this room, you shall have it, unless my superior officers in the Tower give contrary orders. It is proper, however, that I should now tell you that a sentinel will be at once placed at the foot of the staircase, and that any attempt to escape from this place will be perfectly futile."

The Dark Woman made no reply to this observation, which she considered was made within the strict line of his duty by her conductor to that historical apartment of the Bloody Tower.

The sensation which came over her when she was left alone in that apartment was very strange; and although the lantern was left with her, she felt as if at that moment she would almost have preferred the darkness to the faint light which gave the room, and everything in it, a ghost-like aspect.

It was a period of the night when the Tower

was profoundly silent, and the Dark Woman felt as though she were cut off from all communion with the world, at once and for ever.

It was a relief to her when, in about a quarter of an hour, she heard faintly the light rapping of a drum, and then listening intently, she heard—or fancied she heard—the regular tread of soldiers' feet.

There was the rattle of accoutrements and fire-locks, and then one sharp, clanging sound, which the Dark Woman translated to herself.

"The sentinel is posted," she said,—"he has taken up his position at the foot of the stairs—he has brought the butt of his fire-lock carelessly down upon the old stones, and stands at ease. I am indeed a prisoner!"

The Under Warden was as good as his word; and although he did not appear again himself, he sent an old woman, who had some duties in the Tower connected with the chapel, with the requisite bed-clothing to make something like an apology of a couch for the prisoner.

The Dark Woman said nothing to this new visitant; and from the frightened manner of the old woman, it was evident that her whole anxiety was to get out of the Bloody Tower as soon again as possible.

What she dreaded it would be difficult to conjecture. Perhaps the spectres of the murdered Princes, or of their two murderers, or of their crafty and cruel uncle Richard, or the grief-striken Edward the Fourth, or all together, were expected by the old woman to be hovering about the spot.

The Dark Woman was alone again.

No provisions had been brought her; but it was probably considered that her arrest had taken place at such an hour of the night that none were required: and, in fact, what she wanted now was sleep—a long, quiet sleep, which would free her mind and body both from the effects of the opiate which had been one of the chief causes of her arrest so easily.

She took but one more glance around the apartment, and then deferring all further thought concerning her own situation, or investigation of the place in which she was imprisoned, until the morrow, she cast herself upon the bed.

"I will sleep—I will sleep!" she said. "The light of a new day will send some of its straggling beams even through the gloomy casement of this chamber, and then I shall have power to think."

But if the Dark Woman, in that Bloody Tower, so full of terrible reminiscences, felt sad and lonely, not more so was she than the young girl who, by so strange a combination of circumstances, found herself for a time the undisputed mistress of Astorath's house, in Soho.

The girl-page of the Dark Woman would not have lain down to rest in that dreary mansion with half the composure that the Dark Woman exhibited when she sought repose on the bed of the murdered Princes in the Tower.

But that young heart was happily disposed of; and, perhaps, in her new situation in the household of the Princess of Wales, she may yet have an opportunity of hearing something concerning the fortunes of her late mistress, the Dark Woman.

And now there is an inanimate object to which it is necessary we should turn our attention for a few moments.

That inanimate object is the pocket-book, belonging to Colonel Hanger, which the Dark Woman had so adroitly cast into the Thames, after writing in it the memorandum which might, possibly, be of service to her.

The pocket-book might or might not float. Had there been coin in it, it would, in all probability, have sunk to the bottom of the river. But such was not the case; and the only portion of metal which entered into combination with it was the small thread of lead in the pencil, which Colonel Hanger had so kindly accommodated the Dark Woman with.

The pocket-book was light enough, therefore, to float upon the turgid waters of the river; and as the tide was so rapidly ebbing, although it was tossed to and fro upon the mimic waves of the large volume of waters, it still made rapid progress past the City, until, in a turn of the river, it was cast, in the strangest fashion, upon the lowest of a wooden flight of steps that formed one of the most ancient quays of the Thames, and communicated with a long, narrow, pestiferous-looking thoroughfare, that wound up into some gloomy region eastward of the City.

There Colonel Hanger's pocket-book lay, until the river was at its lowest ebb, at which period it was some ten or twelve feet above the surface of the water, lying high and dry upon the rugged wooden steps.

Some boys, whose faces, hands, and clothing bore perpetually the tinge of colour that characterized the river mud, came down the steps, on an expedition for such waifs and strays as the falling tide might have left behind it.

The pocket-book was seen by two or three of them at once, and welcomed by yells and screams of delight.

A pitched battle instantly ensued for its possession, which ended in one holding it up aloft, and attempting to make his escape up the aforesaid pestiferous thoroughfare with it; but he was turned by his companions, and in order to maintain his prize was compelled to descend the steps again.

The tide had begun to turn. There were some six or eight feet of water beneath the lowest step of the quay, and into this the whole party tumbled at once.

None of those ingenious youths were born to be drowned, so they scrambled out of the river; but the pocket-book, that had been the bone of contention, was left behind them, and the rapidly rising tide began to convey it back again to London in much the same fashion that it had brought it past the Tower to that outlying region.

The book still floated; and the next eyes that lit upon it were those of a waterman, who was skulling his wherry carelessly through one of the arches of old London Bridge.

"Look, master," said the waterman's apprentice, who was with him: "there's a book in the river. Shall I get it in with the hook?"

"In with it, boy. Who knows but there may be some good luck in it? It's hard times, these, for watermen, since the barges take down people for a groat apiece, and twenty at a time, to Greenwich."

The pocket-book was easily enough recovered, but its long immersion in the river, and the manner in which it had been washed to and fro by two tides, had, as may be supposed, produced an amount of saturation that made it difficult to handle.

"I'll take it home to the old woman, Bob," said the waterman; "it can go in the oven for half a day; and then mayhap we shall find whose it is, and get a shilling—or may be five shillings—and who shall say it mayn't be half-a-guinea, for giving it back again. Let's pull in, for there's nothing stirring on the river, and there's a sort of fog coming up the stream, or I'm much mistaken."

"Ay, ay, master," said the boy; "there's a fog: you could see the White Tower a little ago, and now it's gone right away into the mist."

"Pull away, Bob."

"Ay, ay, master!"

CHAPTER CLIV.

THE DARK WOMAN MAKES SOME IMPORTANT DISCOVERIES IN THE OLD TURRET OF THE TOWER OF LONDON.

LINDA DE CHEVENAUX, *alias* the Dark Woman, slept long and serenely in the Bloody Tower.

If any one, knowing nothing of the previous career of that vexed spirit, could have looked in upon the apparently calm and unruffled sleeper, they would hardly have supposed it possible that, in her, they saw the woman whose whole life had been a series of incidents transcending the wildest romance.

But exhausted nature will have its dues. The physical system of the Dark Woman wanted repose; so the sleep she fell into in the Tower of London almost resembled death, it was so profound.

And as she lay in that gloomy prison—with the brain, and all the warring passions and excitements at rest—much of the early beauty of Linda de Chevenaux returned to her; that is to say, she looked more like Linda de Chevenaux, and less like a Dark Woman.

She was then, in fact, no more than thirty-eight years of age. It was twenty, or rather more than twenty years before, that her girlish beauty had caught the fancy of the Prince of Wales.

She was then living in peace and in happiness at Dover Court—that home of her childhood which she had never dared to visit since she had known what she was.

In her waking moments she looked now much older than she was in reality.

Then it was that the agonies and sufferings she had passed through showed themselves upon her face.

Then it was that the wild revenges she nourished shone from her eyes.

But in this deep and dreamless sleep that came over her in the old Tower, all that suffering—all that agony was forgotten; and with the forgetfulness, the desire for vengeance was likewise extinguished.

And so the Dark Woman—so to speak—vanished, and Linda de Chevenaux only remained.

Oh, happy sleep!

How much—how very much happier would that poor belated spirit have been if it had never woke again?

But that was not to be.

In the great world's drama, Linda de Chevenaux had her part to play, and she had not yet reached its close.

Through the dust-begrimed and dim lattice of the Tower there struggled a faint ray of morning light; and after winding round the chamber which had echoed to the screams of the dying princes, it lit upon the brow of the Dark Woman.

A change at once came over the face.

The calm serenity left it. The new day was coming, and with it all the anxieties, all the passions, and all the warring interests that attached to the waking existence of that sufferer and that avenger.

A few moments more, and the Dark Woman was half-awake.

Some dream of the half-intelligent brain had suddenly come over the semi-sentient being, and she called out aloud, "Kill! kill! If it must be so, let me be numbered both as the avenger and the sufferer!"

The sound of her own voice thoroughly aroused her, and she sprang from the couch.

"What is this? what is this? Where am I? —oh, where am I?"

Then, at a second glance about her, she remembered all, and with a deep sigh she sat down on the side of the bed, and clasped her head with both her hands.

A bewildering, agonizing pain was darting like forked lightning through her temples.

If that pain had lasted, no human intellect could possibly have borne up against it, but it did not last.

With successive throbs, each one fainter than the other, it passed away.

Then the Dark Woman looked about her with some appearance of calmness.

All that happened to her on the preceding night came clearly to her memory.

"I know all, now," she said. "I am a prisoner again;—I am his prisoner;—the captive of the Regent! He has thought the Tower of London a safer place for me than one of those hideous asylums where intellect and sense are submerged in an atmosphere of insanity."

She shuddered as she spoke.

"I thank him! yes, I thank him for even so much consideration. It is war between us. I am his foe, and he is mine. He has captured me, and he has not done his worst; for he might have placed me in a far more horrible prison than even the deepest, dreariest dungeon of the old Tower of London."

While the Dark Woman uttered these words, she heard a slight sound which attracted her attention in the direction of the door of the chamber in which she was.

The latch was lifted, and the old woman who had appeared for a brief period the night before, made her appearance now again with a basket on her arm.

"If you please, marm, I brings your breakfast."

The look of the old dame, and the character of her language, were so little in accordance with the romantic associations of that historical old Tower, that they jarred upon the senses of the Dark Woman.

There was something terribly incongruous in

the aspect of an old charwoman of the nineteenth century with that apartment, that had scarcely been profaned by a footstep since the dead bodies of the two fair young princes had been carried from it.

"What do you want?" said the Dark Woman, sharply.

"Oh, if you please, ma'am, I don't want nothing; but if so be as your ladyship chooses to give anything to Deborah, it's purely welcome, my lady."

The curtsey the old woman accompanied these words with was fearfully modern.

The Dark Woman felt how much old Deborah was out of place in that romantic old Tower.

"And if you pleases, ma'am, I've brought your breakfast!"

"Set it down."

"Yes, ma'am, I'll sot it down. Hem!"

"That will do."

"Yes, ma'am. Hem!"

"What do you wait for?"

"Oh, nothin', ma'am, nothin'; only, if you die, be so good as to go for to think to give a poor lone woman a trifle, whose two sons have gone and been sogers: it's thankful I'd be, and the Lord——"

"Hush! I don't want to hear you speak in that way. I have nothing to give you."

"Nothin'?"

"I have said so."

"Well, I will say that some folks as give theirselves airs, and pretend to be gentlefolks, is worser——"

"Are you coming down, old 'un?" cried a man's voice at this moment. "I can't wait here all day with the keys for you."

"I'm a-coming, Mr. Knuckles—I'm a-coming! Then you haven't got nothin', ma'am, for poor old Deborah, with two sons sogers?"

"Nothing at all."

"Wus luck! I'm a-coming, Mr. Knuckles—I'm a-coming!"

It was quite a relief to the Dark Woman when the matter-of-fact old Deborah left her again to the solitude of the Bloody Tower.

At first, she had a disposition to disregard the breakfast, whatever it was, that had been brought to her, and she paced the narrow confines of the Tower in deep thought.

Gradually, that thought took a practical character; and as she paused and strove to look forth through the old grimy panes of the casement, she asked herself if the possibility of escape from the Tower might not fairly be entertained.

Escape! escape!

There is magic in the word to a prisoner.

But if she were from that moment to think of such a thing—if she were to turn all the wonderful energies of her heart and brain in such a direction, it would be necessary to keep up her strength.

She must take food.

So soon as this idea then found a home in her reflections, the Dark Woman examined the contents of the basket, which had been placed upon the floor by the old woman.

A loaf of pure, white bread—one-half of what looked like a rabbit-pie, and a tin case, containing about a pint of milk-and-water, made up a very tolerable repast for a prisoner.

The sight of the viands begat a kind of appetite, for then the Dark Woman breakfasted quite as well as she usually did.

Her next idea was to make a thorough survey and examination of the tower, so far as she was permitted to move about in it.

The room in which she had slept appeared to have no other outlet from it but the door at which she had entered.

That door had no fastening on the outer side, as we have before remarked; but on the inner side, there was one strong bolt about the centre of the door.

By the means of that bolt, the Dark Woman might certainly, for a time, shut out the authorities of the Tower; but an instant's reflection was sufficient to let her see how childish and futile such a course would be, so far as regarded it being of the slightest benefit to her.

The little ante-room at the top of the winding stairs had no furniture in it; and the door at the other end of it opened easily.

That heavy door, however, beyond, which was not above a foot from it, was secure.

The moment the Dark Woman put her hands upon it, she felt that she had reached the limits of the prison.

"Thus far shalt thou go, and no farther," that door seemed in its black strength to say to her.

Beyond it was the winding staircase; and at the foot of that was the strong door that opened upon the three stone steps leading from the arch of the tower where the sentinel was on her account specially posted.

The Dark Woman could not say that she was not well enough acquainted with the localities of her prison in that direction.

Having then so far satisfied herself, she returned to the large chamber, intending to thoroughly investigate it, but she was deterred for the present from that object, by hearing the clank of arms below, and she paused to listen to all the sounds which indicated a change of the guard.

Those sounds, however, did not cease where they seemed to begin: they approached the apartment in which she was a prisoner.

Then the Dark Woman felt certain that she was about to have a visitor.

She drew back as far as possible from the dim ray of light that came in through the grimy panes of the apartment, and waited.

She heard the strong door with the large iron nails unlocked, she heard the latches of the other two doors lifted one by one, and then a tall, gentlemanly-looking man presented himself.

The man was immediately followed by one of the Yeomen of the Guard with his halbert on his shoulder.

The Under Warden who had conducted the Dark Woman to the Bloody Tower appeared in another moment, with a bunch of keys in his hand.

"Is this the prisoner, Mr. Under Warden?" said the tall man, as he glanced at the Dark Woman.

"Yes, Lieutenant."

"Oh, very well. But this is far from being a proper place of confinement."

"I thought, sir, that I would place her here until you gave other orders."

"You know, Mr. Under Warden, that the penal portion of the Tower is not here."

The Dark Woman thought it time to speak. She had passed a night in the Bloody Tower, and she had a strange kind of feeling for that room, and dreaded it being exchanged for some other which might be gloomier still, without its interest.

"If, sir," she said, "the object of my being here is the security of my person until the Regent shall think proper to say what is the charge against me, I fancy this Tower is strong enough to hold a woman."

"I don't know that—I don't know that, madam; but I will see about it. I am the Deputy Lieutenant of the Tower."

The Dark Woman slightly inclined her head.

"And my duty is to visit any prisoners brought by proper warrant to the fortress."

The Dark Woman again inclined her head.

"Have you anything to say to me, madam?"

"No, sir. Not having the honour of your acquaintance, except as gaoler, I have nothing to say; because the only thing I could have to say would sound silly and puerile."

"What is it?"

"Let me go."

"Pho! pho! Is that all?"

"That is all."

"Very good. Now, Mr. Under Warden, we will go."

There was an empty-headed pomposity about the Deputy Lieutenant of the Tower which by no means prepossessed the Dark Woman in his favour, and she was glad to be left to the solitude of the chamber of the murdered princes again.

The Deputy Lieutenant had been officially accompanied by a guard; and the Dark Woman heard the tramp of their feet, and the clank of their weapons, as he left the Bloody Tower. She dreaded being removed from her present quarters; but as hour after hour passed away and no one came near her, she began to dismiss the fear, and turned her thoughts in the direction of her affairs in connexion with the outer world.

She wondered what had happened at the house in Frith Street, Soho. She speculated in her own mind as to what would become of the pocket-book of Colonel Hanger, which, with such a message written on one of its covers, she had committed to the Thames.

Would that message ever reach the eyes of him for whom it was intended? Would her son, Allan Fearon, ever look upon those words, and so learn that his mother, who had suffered so much for him, yet lived, and was in the Tower of London?

These and many similar reflections passed through the mind of the Dark Woman, until she received another visit from the old charwoman Deborah.

"Oh, if you please, ma'am, this is your dinner!"

Another basket was on the arm of the old woman, which she exchanged for the empty one.

"That will do," said the Dark Woman.

"Hem! hem! I'm a poor lone widow with two sons, sogers."

"I know—I know. You said all that before."

"Dear heart, did I? Well-a-day!—well-a-day! Perhaps, good lady, you wouldn't mind a trifle for a poor lone woman with two sons, sogers!"

"I have no money."

"No money?"

"Not one farthing."

The old charwoman was at the door in a moment, and her whining tone changed to one of defiance.

"In course I might have expectorated as much. No better than you should be, ma'am, and perhaps not half so good. No money, indeed! I wonder where you expectorates to go to?"

"Silence, woman."

"I won't silence, woman; and if you comes to that, I am no more a woman than you are. There, now!"

The Dark Woman was annoyed and disgusted, but she was a prisoner, and had no means of ridding herself of the intrusion of Mrs. Deborah, until a thought struck her that there must be some one at the iron-studded door who was waiting for her, since it was not at all likely that she would be entrusted with the keys.

The Dark Woman pursuing this line of thought, remembered that the name of this person, as it had been pronounced by old Deborah, was "Knuckles."

It came upon the old woman with all the shock of a surprise, when the prisoner—whose greatest possible fault in her eyes consisted in having no money—suddenly stepped past her, and called out aloud, "Mr Knuckles! Mr. Knuckles!"

"Gracious heavens!" cried old Deborah, "she knows Mr. Knuckles!"

"What is it?" said a Yeoman of the Guard, putting his head in at the door of the ante-room, adorned with the grotesque Elizabethan hat, which, as regards the Yeomen of the Guard, appears to be one of the institutions of the country.

"What is it? Who called me?"

"She knows Mr. Knuckles!" gasped the old woman. "How does she know Mr Knuckles?"

"I called you," said the Dark Woman, "to remove this person. If it be her duty to visit me with such provisions as are allowed me in this place, it cannot be a part of the afflictions of my imprisonment, because I have not the power, and probably not the will if I had, to bestow money upon her."

"Certainly not, certainly not," said the warder. "Clear out, old Mother Sly; and if I don't tell the Under Warden of you, I'm not a Christian."

"Oh, my dear Mr. Knuckles! Bless you, don't! I'll be even with you, marm! Dear heart, Mr. Knuckles, I didn't mean nothin'! I owes you one, marm, and old Deborah 'll take care to pay you! I'm a comin', Mr. Knuckles—I'm a comin'! Bless us, and save us! what things people will say about poor lone widows, who have two sons, sogers!"

"Clear out, I say, clear out!" cried the warder. "Don't mind her, my lady; she's the most cantankerous old dragon in all the Tower; only, you see, marm, the Under Warden thought you'd rather have a female come with your meals than one of us Yeomen of the Guard. Clear out with you, now, old Mother Sly!"

"Dear me, yes; I'm a goin'! I'll be one too many for her yet! No money, indeed! Marry come up! Fine folks brought to the Tower in the middle of the night, and no money! But we'll see to all that—we'll see to all that! I'm a comin', Mr. Knuckles!"

It was quite a relief to the Dark Woman when she found herself once more in the solitude of that ancient tower.

She blamed herself for a moment, however, that she had not inquired of the tolerably civil Yeoman of the Guard if her prison would be visited again before the following morning; for she wished to institute so rigid an examination of the chamber in which she had slept, and the adjoining ante-room, that any sudden interruption might be extremely inconvenient as regarded any projects of escape that might arise in her mind.

Still she considered that if she were visited again it would not be until nightfall; and so she resolved to take advantage of the faint gleams of daylight that came through the ancient casement, to satisfy herself if there were any discoveries or not to be made of concealed doors, or secret passages, in connexion with that ill omened and gloomy tower.

———

CHAPTER CLV.

THE POCKET-BOOK OF COLONEL HANGER AT LENGTH REACHES ITS DESTINATION AT ALLAN FEARON'S HOUSE.

WE left that rather important and mysterious book, that belonged to Colonel Hanger, in the hands of very honest people.

The boatman and his apprentice who had found it floating on the surface of the river, were both quite willing that its rightful owner should have it. The only difficulty lay in discovering who that rightful owner was.

Education had not descended quite down to the lower stratum of society, as it has in our day; and neither the honest waterman, nor the honest boy who was in due time to succeed him in command of the wherry, could read.

The wife, however,—as the waterman usually called her at home—had that accomplishment, and therefore was it that he considered the pocket-book would be of some good account, after it had been taken home and submitted to a drying process in the oven.

All this was done, as projected; and the good woman, whose literary powers were not great, put on her spectacles, and proceeded to carefully unfold the damp covers of the pocket-book: her husband and the apprentice stood by in mute admiration and expectation.

The twenty-pound note, the loss of which had so aggravated Colonel Hanger, was the first object that presented itself.

All three of them uttered exclamations of surprise at the sight of such a treasure; but a very few moments' reflection taught them to consider the prize not near so great as they had at first thought it.

The anxiety and embarrassment of those who find themselves in the possession of money to which they are not fairly entitled began to work its evil way into that peaceful and humble home.

"Twenty pounds!" exclaimed the waterman's wife: "we are rich people all at once; and Mrs. Snoggs, the ship-broker's wife, will no longer be able to turn up her nose at me on a Sunday."

"And I can have the wherry fresh painted," cried the waterman, "and corked, plugged, and coppered, and a new set of sculls."

"And I can have a new suit of clothes," cried the apprentice, "and needn't carry my boots in my hand for fear of wearing them out."

"Twenty pounds! twenty pounds!—what a sum! Twenty! twen——But I say, wife, it isn't ours, after all!"

"Not ours?" replied the good woman.

"Not ourn?" sighed the apprentice.

The waterman shook his head.

"I am afraid it isn't ours. You see, wife, there's nothing lost after it's found. The pocket-book was anybody's and everybody's as long as it was lost; but now that we've found it, you see it belongs to him who lost it."

"That's true," said the waterman's wife, with a sigh.

"It sounds all right," said the apprentice.

"And it is all right, because you see, wife, people don't fling away pocket-books with twenty pounds in them, and if so be we can find out who it belongs to, why, you see, we're bound, in a way of speaking, to take it back."

"But how are we to know who it belongs to?" said the wife, closing the pocket-book hurriedly, as though she dreaded that, by turning another leaf, the name and address of the owner might stare her in the face.

"That's true, wife; but then if we do keep the twenty-pound note——"

"Hush! hush, husband! Don't speak so loud! Shut the door! Pull the blind over the window, Bob!"

"What's the matter?"

"We mustn't let anybody hear—we mustn't let anybody know."

"You frigh'en me, wife!"

"And I'm getting all over hot," said Bob.

The waterman wiped his brow, upon which, for the first time in his life, there hung heavy drops, which were not the result of honest toil.

The good wife looked blanched and pale.

"I'm getting cold now," said Bob. "All down my back seems to be taking it by turns. Master—master, don't keep the note! What's twenty pounds if it makes us all ill, and frightens us so that we daren't speak out as we used to do when we didn't care a bit what we said?"

"You're right, Bob!" cried the waterman. "Open the door, wife, and draw the curtain on one side again; we can't live in this kind of way. It was bad times without the money; but we never felt all as we now feel, and look at each other as we now look. Let's speak out. Ha! Hem! We've found a pocket-book, and there's twenty pounds in it; but it ain't ours, and we don't want to keep it. Ha! Hem! And we ain't afraid a bit, and we don't care who knows it. Hem! Ha! And we're as poor as ever; and we've only got eighteen-pence in the world."

"One and threepence halfpenny," said the wife faintly, as she made a jingling in her pocket.

"Never mind—ha! hem!—we don't want anybody else's money."

"I'm ever so much better now, master," said Bob.

"To be sure you are, Bob; and so are you, wife?"

"I am—I am! I seem to breathe all the freer. And do you know, husband, I can't help thinking that somebody—it's just as well not to mention—must have put this money in our way as a temptation and a snare."

"A kind o' drag net, missus," said Bob.

"You don't say so?" cried the waterman. "But now you mention it, if I didn't think, when the door was shut, there was a strange smell of smoke and brimstone in the room.

"It was the Old'un, you may depend, master," said Bob,—"or the chimney."

"It always does smoke when the door's shut," ejaculated the good woman.

"Never mind, wife!—never mind! Take another look at the book, and see if you can find who owns it."

Colonel Hanger's pocket-book had been tolerably well dried in the oven of the waterman's humble home; but the leaves still stuck together, and it was with considerable difficulty that they were separated one by one. But still nothing could be made of the various memoranda which appeared upon the different pages.

The waterman's wife was but an indifferent

scholar, and as those memoranda chiefly consisted of items and speculations concerning horse-racing, games at cards and dice, together with various speculative diagrams concerning some games at tennis, to be played in the Haymarket,—the little party at the waterman's abode, which had had such a struggle with temptation, was for a considerable time none the wiser for the careful investigation of the pocket-book of Colonel Hanger.

"Dear me!" said the good wife; "what can this mean? Seven to one against the Maid of Athens—Juliana lame in the hind leg—and Polyphemus over weight?"

"Go on, wife; you'll come to something else next."

"Dear me! what's this? Here's something been written with a vengeance."

"A what?"

"A lead pencil with a vengeance, I mean; for

it's nearly gone through the leaf on to the next one. Gracious Providence! here's a secret. It'll go hard if we're not all hung, drawn, and transported!"

"Take it away, Bob!—take it away!" cried the waterman. "Scull out into the middle of the river, boy, and fling it in again—twenty pound and all. I won't be frightened and be made miserable about it any longer. Take it away, Bob—take it away!"

"But, master," said Bob, "we shall all be took up then for throwing it away."

"Yes," said the wife, "and nobody would believe that we threw the twenty-pound note away with it."

The waterman groaned and wiped his brow again, as he muttered in an under-tone, "Well, if ever I see twenty pocket-books in the river again, sailing along like a fleet, I won't meddle with one of them; for who's to say they mightn't each of them be full of bank notes: and if one twentypounder has made us all so miserable and frightened, what would hundreds do?"

"Smash us and swamp us!" said Bob, sententiously. "Down we'd go, master."

"Yes, Bob, down we'd go."

"Fifteen fathom, master."

"Ay, Bob, fifteen fathom, mayhap."

"Hold your tongues, both of you," cried the wife; "for deep as you think yourselves, you don't know what you're talking about. I begin to see it all now. The pocket-book's been thrown away on purpose that some honest, good Samaritans may find it."

"Sam who, wife?"

"Samaritan, husband—I'm ashamed of you. There's been some poor soul taken to the Tower, and she wants somebody to be let know of it. Get out the wherry at once, and let's be off to Buckingham Street; and who knows but after all it may be a good day's work?"

"Bravo!" cried Bob. "Missus, you knows a thing or two."

"Well, I will say, wife," added the waterman, "that you're a wonderful woman, and know how to put this and that together in such a way, that I sometimes think that you quite bemeaned yourself by marrying me."

The waterman's wife was a very good woman in the main, but she was not above some of the little weaknesses of human nature, and devoutly believed that she had—to use her husband's expression—bemeaned herself by an union with him; and upon these occasions, when, in the humility of his heart, the waterman gave utterance to such an opinion, his wife was in the habit of putting on a resigned, martyr-like kind of look for the rest of the day.

But, be all this as it may, another half-hour saw the whole party embarked on the Thames, with the mysterious pocket-book, and Bob and his master were pulling lustily towards Buckingham Street.

It was still early in the day when the boat's keel grated against the little ascent of stairs, up which once the powerful Dukes of Buckingham had trod in all their gallantry and splendour, little dreaming that their name and title would become a byword and reproach, and finally descend to the possession of an utilitarian trader.

But early as it was, Allan Fearon was abroad.

Deeply had he cogitated with himself and with his beloved Marian in regard to his condition.

The few words he had spoken to Sixteenstringed Jack probably afforded a fair enough indication of his state of mind as regarded the Regent.

Many of the early feelings with which Allan Fearon had encountered the first knowledge of the mystery of his birth had faded away, and he was enabled to look more calmly and rationally upon the inevitable past.

In his heart he must condemn the Regent; and with a deeper and wider feeling still, he must pity his mother, the unfortunate and wildly-straggling Linda de Chevenaux.

One of these feelings was materially softened, merely by the fact of his becoming accustomed to it; and while the other—that is to say, his sympathy for his mother—remained in full force, he felt that it was not for him to sit in judgment upon his father, the Regent, but to accept, without pride or irritation, the condition in which it had been the will of heaven to place him.

Moreover, if there were any means more likely than another to put him in a condition to throw a protecting shield over that mother, whatever were her crimes or errors, it would certainly be by his continuing to be on good terms with his father, the Prince of Wales.

There could be no doubt, now, but that whatever feelings of irritation possessed the Regent at his, Allan's, supposed treachery, must have completely subsided.

The exculpation of Annie was his exculpation.

Under the circumstances, therefore, Allan had no hesitation whatever in seeking another interview with the Regent.

He was glad to reflect, that under circumstances of disunion and almost quarrel, the Regent had permitted him to retain that ruby ring which was to be a passport to the royal presence.

Hence, then, was it that after some hours of the night even had been devoted to reflection and to earnest consultation with Marian upon this interesting subject, Allan had resolved to go to Carlton House, with the double object of entirely reconciling himself to his father, and of ascertaining, if possible, if anything was known there concerning the fate of the Dark Woman.

It was during this absence that the honest waterman and his wife reached that small house at the end of Buckingham Street, which had been now for some time in the occupation of the Fearons.

Marian received the visit with surprise and alarm, for she always dreaded that any hour might produce intelligence regarding the Dark Woman, which would plunge Allan into grief and perplexity.

Nothing was more likely than that Linda de Chevenaux would come to some violent and terrible end; and then Allan—with that natural feeling which always accompanies true generosity and nobleness of heart—she knew well would begin to accuse himself in a thousand different ways of neglects and omissions, none of which would have any real existence, except in his imagination.

No wonder, then, that Marian listened in terror to the confused story told by the waterman and his party, and considering that they all three spoke at once, the confusion was tolerably considerable.

The statement to Marian's ears sounded something in this strain:—

"Master—and—I, you—see, ma'am—my Bob and me, missus—if you please, ma'am, all of a sudden in the oven—comin' up with the tide; and master, says he, 'Bob!'—and so we handed it in, and a twenty-pound note—and after the door was shut, the smell of brimstone was awful!"

"For heaven's sake!" said Marian, "do one speak at a time, and tell me what it all means."

The next action of the party was to hold up with three hands the pocket-book, open at the identical leaf upon which the Dark Woman had written so impressively even in her hour of distress and danger, to the confusion and rage of Colonel Hanger.

"Ah!" said Marian; "I understand all this too well!"

"Do you really, marm?" said the waterman, and his wife, and Bob, all in a breath.

"I do, indeed. This memorandum is for my husband, who is now from home."

"And the twenty pounds?" said the waterman. "That's for him, too, I suppose?"

"Of that I know nothing; but if the pocket-book has belonged to the person who wrote these lines, my husband is the proper person to take possession of its contents."

"I'm glad of that, at any rate," said the waterman. "We've got rid of it, at all events, wife."

"But the lady is not sure.'

"Hush! Don't say a word! Let them get into a cold perspiration, and shut their doors and windows, and be afraid to speak above their breath, while the Old Gentleman comes down the chimney."

"But tell me," said Marian,—"have you no idea from whom this pocket-book comes?"

The waterman and his wife both shook their heads; but Bob brightened up as an idea darted into his brain, and he cried out aloud, "I know!"

"Tell me, then, at once."

"Juliana lame of the hind-leg, marm."

Marian was more puzzled by this intelligence than before; but the waterman's wife soon pointed out to her the memoranda upon which Bob founded his supposition; and then Marian had serious doubts, indeed, of the pocket-book belonging to the Dark Woman, for she had a better understanding than those simple-minded people—who might be said to live upon the river, with ideas limited by its breadth, its length, and its tides—of the nature of the memoranda in Colonel Hanger's pocket-book.

"Indeed, and in truth," she said, "I do not now think that this pocket-book belongs to the person who wrote these words in it."

"You don't, marm?"

"No; and I think I should do better and wiser merely to take out this leaf, which evidently concerns my husband, and is addressed to him, and return you all the rest."

It would have been impossible for Marian to have hit upon any proposition which would have produced such a panic in the mind of the honest waterman as this. He made a scrambling sort of rush back to his boat, dragging his wife and Bob with him, and calling out as he went, "No, no,

marm, we don't want it,—and we won't have it. Once caught, and never touch the bird again. No, no, marm, you don't catch us taking it back again. We don't want any more window-blinds drawn, and doors shut up, and smells of what's-his-name in the room. Good bye, marm! Keep it—keep it! and much good may it do you. Mayhap you'll find out who it really belongs to. But it isn't ours. Come along, wife! Come along, Bob!"

"Yes, husband! Push off!—push off! I wouldn't touch it again for all the world!"

"And I don't want my back hot and cold again," said Bob. "Push off, master! Here we are out of the shallows! Hurrah!"

Both Bob and his master cheered as they cleared Buckingham Street Quay, and Marian was left with the ill-fated pocket-book, containing the twenty-pound note, and that terrible memorandum, written by the Dark Woman in the midst of that lurid light which flashed from within the grated bars of Traitors' Gate, at the old Tower.

Perhaps, the most ardent hopes of Linda de Chevenaux would hardly have reached the length of supposing for a moment that so soon and so perfectly intact that pocket book—which, on the impulse of a moment, she had cast into the Thames—would reach its destination.

And now Marian had to ask herself what she should do, for she felt how important an element in the conversation which Allan Fearon was having with the Regent, this memorandum of the Dark Woman might have been.

And yet Marian was powerless to act, let her reflections take what shape they might.

She could not pursue Allan Fearon to the Palace. She had not even the means for obtaining admittance to the royal presence, even could she have brought herself to such a state of mind as to enable her to interrupt a conference between Allan and his father, the Regent.

"No," she said, "I can do nothing. I must wait Allan's return, and it will be for him to act; but much I fear that new perplexities are in store for him, unless the heart of the Regent should incline to a humility, which, alas, seems to be too foreign to his constitution!"

CHAPTER CLVI.

ALLAN FEARON HAS AN INTERVIEW BOTH WITH THE REGENT AND THE COUNTESS DE PLANDE AT ST. JAMES'S.

As Allan Fearon—on that morning which witnessed the arrival at the humble home at the river end of Buckingham Street, Strand, of the honest waterman, with Colonel Hanger's pocket-book—made his way towards St. James's, his mind became oppressed with gloomy forebodings.

So far as he was concerned, and so far as he had any knowledge of her movements, the Dark Woman had completely disappeared.

What had become of her? Was she living or dead? Had she given up the terrible struggle in which she had passed so large a portion of her life? and in giving it up had she sought for the peace and quietude of death?

These were the harassing questions which Allan put to his distracted imagination.

He had no means of replying to them; but he hoped that now the Regent would look upon him in a very different light to that which had appeared to surround him in their last interview, and so possibly he, Allan, might get some information from him regarding the unhappy Linda.

When Allan reached the Palace of the Regent, he doubted for a time if the Prince of Wales were there, so quiet and so silent did the royal residence appear to be.

Allan made his way to one of the side entrances, and, with that modest civility that was habitual to him, inquired if the Regent was stirring.

The stare of surprise with which he was met by a porter in a flaming scarlet coat, with the Prince of Wales's plume on its buttons, would, under any other circumstances, have amused Allan, but his mind was too much pre-occupied with graver matters, to take any note of small, ludicrous circumstances.

"I want to know," he added, "if the Regent is here, and yet up."

"Then you won't know."

"But I must know."

Bang! went the door shut in Allan's face.

For a moment or two the young man asked himself if he was to conclude that this reception was in accordance with any orders from the Regent.

If Allan could have come to such a conclusion, he would never again have troubled the repose of Carlton House.

But he could not feel any assurance that such was the case. It might only be the rough insolence of a pampered domestic, so Allan made up his mind to persevere.

There was one mode of testing the fact if the Regent had given orders to dismiss him in such a summary fashion; for if such was the case, the Palace porters, at all the entrances, would be simularly instructed; and in order to ascertain if such were the case, or not, all Allan had to do was to go to one of the other entrances and try his fortune.

Fearon was about to carry this mental suggestion into effect, when he had to step hastily aside, as a plain chariot drove up to Carlton House.

Curiosity did not hold a very large share of the mind of Allan, but he certainly could not help looking to see who alighted from the plain chariot.

A glance showed him that it was no other than Mr. Willes, the valet of the Regent.

Willes had not yet began to sport his title, which, in after years, he took good care should never be forgotten.

Indeed, Willes was quite disposed to leave the service of the Prince of Wales, and only stayed out of a sort of dignified complaisance to his royal master.

But there was the same air of crawling deference about the valet as ever, and when Allan stepped up to him and said, "I think, sir, you are of the household of his Highness the Regent?" Willes bowed low, and treated Allan with the greatest deference.

"Can you tell me," added Allan, "if the Regent s in Carlton House?"

Willes shook his head.

"His Highness is supposed to be in Carlton House, Mr. Fearon."

"Supposed to be?'

"Yes, sir. But he is in reality at St. James's."

"Oh, I think I comprehend!"

"I am sure you do, Mr. Fearon."

"How, then, shall I get an interview with him this morning?"

"I think, sir, that your best plan will be to follow me."

"I will do so, then, if you can pass me into the Palace."

"We will reach it by the private route, if you please, Mr. Fearon, from the garden of Carlton House. I feel quite sure that so soon as his Royal Highness is stirring, he will see you."

Willes made a sharp decisive application at the door from which Allan had been so recently repulsed, and it was opened in a moment.

The same surly porter appeared.

Willes made a low bow, and signified to Allan to precede him.

The porter's rubicund countenance began to assume a blue tint; and the idea began now to take a hold of his mind, such as it was, that he had made a grand mistake in regard to Allan.

"Pray walk in, sir," said Willes. "I follow you!"

Of course, the Regent's valet was perfectly well known, and no Minister of State had such easy right of ingress and egress, as regarded Carlton House, as he.

The porter staggered back till he supported himself by the wall.

"Mr. Willes—Mr. Willes," he said, in a half whisper to the valet, "who is that—that—gentleman?"

"Don't you know?"

"No—no!"

"Then I am afraid I am not justified in telling you!"

"Then he—he is somebody?"

"Oh, yes!"

"Good heavens! And I was as rude to him as could be, and slammed the door in his face!"

"You really did!"

"I did!"

"Then, my friend, I would not be in your shoes for any reward you could possibly name!"

Willes took a pleasure in awakening all the fears of the porter, and he certainly left him in a state of mind which, as the newspaper people say, may be easier imagined than described.

While this brief colloquy was taking place between the Regent's valet and the porter, it had occurred to Allan that Willes might know something of the Dark Woman. Seeing he was in so very courteous and affable a mood, so far as he, Allan, was concerned, the young man was resolved to question him.

Now Willes knew perfectly well what had happened, for he took care to keep himself always well informed in regard to all circumstances concerning the domestic life of the Regent, but he at the same time laid it down as a rule—and a very prudent one it was—never to know anything if questioned by any one.

From this rule he was not disposed even to except Allan Fearon, although he knew so well the intimate relation in which the young man stood to the Regent.

"Can you give me any information, Mr. Willes," said Allan, "of that unfortunate person who goes by the name of the Dark Woman?"

"Not the least, sir!"

"Then I fear even the Regent knows nothing of her."

Willes did not want to give an opinion one way or another on this point, as he was seized at the moment by a convenient cough, which saved him the necessity of speaking.

Perhaps Allan detected the little imposture, for he said no more on the subject. Reverting, however, to his wish to see the Regent, he held out his hand, on a finger of which was the ruby ring which was to be his passport to the royal presence, as he said, "You see, Mr. Willes, that the Regent has allowed me to retain this ring, which was to pass me to him whenever I desired to see him."

"Oh, yes, sir, and I shall have no hesitation whatever in announcing you to him!"

"I thank you. May I ask if the Countess de Blonde is in the Palace?"

"Yes; and firmer than ever in the good graces of the Regent!"

"I expected so; and—and—Mr. Willes, can you tell me what has become of Sir Hinckton Moys?"

"He is dismissed, with disgrace."

"He is a villain, and his very presence in the habitation of the Regent was a disgrace to the Prince of Wales!"

Willes again coughed.

By this time they had made their way through one of the wings of Carlton House, and out into the private flower garden, from which there was a shadowy walk that connected with a door in the wall, through which they made their way towards St. James's, which they reached by a route only used by the Regent himself, or those specially in his confidence.

"It is only his Royal Highness," said Willes, speaking in a low and deferential tone, "and myself who have keys to pass these doors."

Allan Fearon quite understood the state of affairs. The Regent was supposed to be at Carlton House, but was in reality at St. James's, occupying, with Annie, Countess de Blonde, the suite of magnificent rooms which had been fitted up for her residence in the old Palace.

Willes conducted Allan as far as that gallery which was immediately without those rooms, and there he desired him to wait.

"It is now twelve o'clock," he said; "and his Royal Highness's breakfast will soon be served. I will see him, and let him know you are here."

"I shall be much beholden to you."

Allan was left alone to his reflections, while the valet disappeared through a side door which he had a key to.

But it was not for long that Allan Fearon was left alone.

Willes had been absent about five minutes, when a hasty footstep sounded at the further end of the gallery, and a voice in not very measured accents cried out, "Very well—very well! His most gracious Highness is sure to pass this way, and his most obedient servant will wait for him."

With a swaggering gait, a tall man came along the gallery, dragging after him a chair, which he placed about the middle of the floor opposite to Annie's apartments. He then took off a roquelaire cloak, in which he had been wrapped from head to foot, and flung it carelessly over the arm of a statue of Hebe that was in the gallery. His hat, then, he placed on the head of the same statue; and then, with that sort of exclamation which a man who is fatigued is apt to make when he sits down, this somewhat coarse and presumptuous personage, in whom the reader has probably recognised Colonel Hanger, crossed one leg over the other, and began in low cadence to whistle a tune.

Probably, Colonel Hanger never before found himself so safe of a favourable reception from the Regent.

Had he not the intelligence to bring him of the successful capture of the Dark Woman, and her conveyance to the Tower of London? To be sure he had, and therefore he considered himself fairly placed as the confidante of the Prince of Wales.

Allan, with that sensitive loathing which such natures as his always feel for men like Colonel Hanger, had shrunk back into the deep recess of a window, when he saw the swaggering bully make his appearance in the gallery.

A touch to the heavy cloth hangings of the window brought them nearly close together, so that Allan was completely shrouded from Hanger's observation.

Had, however, Allan possessed the least idea that the man whom he was avoiding could give him all the information he wanted about Linda De Chevenaux, it would not have been his, Allan's fault if they were not soon face to face.

"Ah!" said Hanger, when he was, as he fancied, quite alone in the gallery, — "ah! John Hanger, I rather fancy, old boy that your fortune is made now. His Royal Highness the Regent will feel that you are the man to do him good service —a man who don't stick at trifles— no, sink me if I do! Ha! ha!"

Allan had felt an instinctive dislike to this man, and it was rapidly growing into abhorrence.

Still Hanger had said nothing which could give Allan any clue to who or what he was, or to the real secret of his seeming hold upon the Regent.

The delicacy of feeling of the young man began to be aroused for fear that this man should say something which he would fain not hear concerning the Prince of Wales, considering the relation in which he, Allan, stood to him; and he was upon the point of emerging from the recess of the window, just for the purpose of letting him see some one was there, when another footstep sounded in the gallery, and Allan shrunk back again to see who the new comer might be.

Whoever it was, it was evident some one was following him, and remonstrating about his presence there; and in a few seconds Allan heard that the voice of the remonstrant was that of Willes, the valet.

"Indeed, sir," he said, "I will not answer for the consequences of your presence here!"

"Nobody asked you!" was the reply. "So long as I am in possession of the pass-key of the back stairs, which his Highness handed to me himself, I have a right to admittance to St. James's. As soon as his Highness demands the key of me, I will go!"

"You are mad, Sir Hinckton Moys!"

"Ah!" said Allan. "Is it that villain?'

"Ah!" cried the man in the chair. "Sink me, but it's Moys!"

There was a flush of passion on the face of Sir Hinckton Moys as he strode up the gallery, followed by Willes, and he spoke loudly, as he said, "Sir, you follow me! If I wanted, now, a cur at my heels I might not find one!"

"Cur, sir? Did you say cur?"

"I did!"

"And—and—and did you mean me?"

"I did! I had a hope when I said it that the word might stir even your cowardly soul to action! I will meet you, although you are what you are, when and where you will!"

Sir Hinckton Moys touched the hilt of his sword as he spoke, and looked scornfully defiant at the valet.

Willes was choking with rage.

"Wretch!" he said. "I am, at all events, your equal! You are a Sir, but it was only a beggarly Lord-Lieutenant of Ireland who knighted you, while the Regent himself made me Sir Thomas!"

"You? you? Hound!"

"Thief! beast!"

"Bravo! bravo!" cried Colonel Hanger, as he clapped his hands. "Bravo! bravo! This is good! Ha! ha! Bravo!"

For the first time, Sir Hinckton Moys became aware of the presence of his hated foe and rival, Colonel Hanger, in the gallery. He turned towards him with a sound that was scarcely human, so full of passion was it.

Colonel Hanger half rose from the chair and confronted him.

"So," said Moyes, "I find you here!"

"Certainly! John Hanger, *vice* Moyes, discharged! Ha! ha!"

" Villain!"

"A hard word, Sir Hinckton, and one I am not used to! You scarcely expect me to put up with it?"

"If I thought it would goad you to fight, I would repeat it for an hour together!"

"You hear him! You hear him, Mr. Willes!" said Hanger. "He wants to draw swords in the Palace, so that the Prince may hear their clash even as he sits at breakfast; but, sink me! no—I know better than that!"

Willes was pale with rage, but he had had a few moments for reflection, and he was not at all sorry to transfer his own quarrel with Sir Hinckton Moys to Colonel Hanger. Perhaps for the first time in his life he felt a sort of affection for Hanger, arising from a community of feeling which made him defy Sir Hinckton Moys.

"Coward!" cried Moys, as he stamped his foot heavily upon the old oaken floor of the gallery,—"coward! I say, although you presume to name yourself by the title of a soldier; you know well that I had no intention even to tempt you to draw your sword within the precincts of the Palace! There are other places where those can meet who ever care to do so!"

"You challenge me, then?" said Colonel Hanger.

"I honour you by professing an intention of meeting you, as a man of honour and a gentleman!"

"And I'm sure," said Willes, "Colonel Hanger will meet you. It is, of course, impossible for an officer to look over your conduct and expressions! I'm sure I shall have great pleasure in seconding the Colonel, who I shall recommend to choose pistols, because it is well known that Sir Hinckton Moys once picked up a few stray guineas as a fencing master!"

Moys looked almost livid with rage as Willes uttered these words, and it evidently required all his self-control to save him from rushing forward, and committing some personal violence on the spot.

Probably Willes felt that he stood in such a position in the gallery as to be able to make a very hasty retreat, or he would scarcely have ventured this little biographical notice of Sir Hinckton Moys.

What would have been the result of the quarrel, had it proceeded much further, it is difficult to say, but the sudden, sharp, clear ringing of a bell startled Willes, if it did not any one else.

"The Regent has breakfasted!" he cried.

Sir Hinckton Moys tried to compose himself, and held the key in his hand, by virtue of which he had made his way into the Palace, fully prepared to give it up to the Regent the moment he should appear; for, after all, the presence of Moys on that occasion was but a foolish act of braggadocia, which in his cooler moments he would have rejected, since he might well know that the speech he had well conned to make to the Regent could have no possible effect upon his fortunes.

But Moys wanted to say something bitter—he wanted to relieve his surcharged heart and brain of the electric fire of passion with which they were filled.

Colonel Hanger had recovered his usual air of insolent satisfaction, and with one hand resting upon the back of the chair on which he had been sitting, he awaited the appearance of the Regent, and the certain discomfiture of Sir Hinckton Moys.

Willes had disappeared, and as regarded Allan Fearon, one of those sudden impulses, which overcome reason at the moment, and disarm reflection, came over him.

With a flush upon his brow, he suddenly appeared from behind the curtains which had shrouded him in the deep recess of the window, and gazing full into the eyes of Sir Hinckton Moys, who staggered back a pace or two at his appearance, he said, with calm and concentrated passion, " If Sir Hinckton Moys will tell me where he can be found, I will honour him so far as to send him a message, to which it will be well for him to attend.

"A challenge!" said Moys. "Ha! ha! It appears I shall have work enough upon my hands. A beggarly adventurer and bully—a wretched bad captain, calling himself a colonel, who, no doubt, some day will come to the gallows—for one opponent; a valet for another; and for the third——"

"Beware, sir!" said Allan. "I am patient to a degree, but I seem to see a word hovering upon your very lips, which if you dare to utter, look to yourself!"

Moys ran his eyes over the tall, athletic form of Allan Fearon, and discretion became at that moment the better part of valour.

"I cry you mercy, sir!" he said. "It's a wise child that knows it own father. I merely give utterance—casually, you hear—to a well-known proverb."

A door was at this moment flung open, and Willes, in much higher tones than he usually indulged in, cried out aloud, "His Highness the Regent!"

CHAPTER CLVII.

THE PRINCE OF WALES FORBIDS ONE DUEL, BUT SANCTIONS ANOTHER.—ALLAN'S PROMOTION.

At this announcement, certainly not expected on the part of any one there present in that old gallery of St. James's Palace, the war of words subsided, but the angry looks, the flashing eyes, and the hostile attitudes of those three men, still remained.

The Regent stopped short on the threshold of the doorway by which he was making his way from the apartments of the Countess de Blonde, and looked from one to the other of his unexpected guests in St James's Palace, with undissembled surprise.

A faint flush of anger came to the royal cheeks, and the handkerchief he held in his hand was crumpled up involuntarily as he looked from face to face.

That there had been some disturbance—some quarrel—the progress of which only his entrance had put a stop to, was only too evident.

Willes hovered behind the Regent, and was delighted. He looked now upon some signal discomfiture of Colonel Hanger as certain.

There was rather a long pause.

The Regent still looked from one to the other, as though he waited for some one to speak, and let him know what had happened.

But all were silent.

Allan Fearon bowed.

Colonel Hanger made rather an audacious military salute.

Sir Hinckton Moys bowed to the very floor.

The Regent saw that everybody was resolved to stand upon etiquette, and not say a word, until he broke the silence.

"Well, gentlemen," he said at length, "I suppose we ought to think ourselves highly honoured by so early an attendance, both of those we expect, and of those we do not."

"Your Royal Highness," said Colonel Hanger, "was pleased to give me leave to wait on you."

"And you, sir?" said the Regent, turning sharply to Sir Hinckton Moys.

"I have had the distinguished honour," said Moys, "to receive from your Royal Highness a key, which I did not think it consistent with my character, or your Royal Highness's dignity, to place in other hands than your own."

Moys knelt on one knee as he spoke, and tendered the key to the Regent.

That was decidedly the only possible plan that Moys could adopt to get out of the dilemma which this rash visit to St. James's had placed him in.

The attitude was one of respect, and it would almost appear as though the quarrel which Moys had had with Willes, the valet, with Colonel Hanger, and with Allan Fearon, had had the effect of cooling down his wrath, for he was certainly much more composed, calm, and master of himself, than he had been a short time previously.

Perhaps he began to perceive what a capital mistake he had made in coming to St. James's, under the circumstances, and was now self-possessed and politic enough to feel that nothing could get him even partially over it but an outward show of great respect for the Regent

And now the Prince, although he had rather fiercely put the question both to Sir Hinckton Moys and to Colonel Hanger regarding their presence there, abstained from even looking such an interrogation at Allan Fearon.

Allan was thankful and grateful for this mark of regard from the Regent—slender though it was.

The most noticeable person of the group was certainly the kneeling Sir Hinckton Moys, and to him it seemed necessary that the Regent should first attend.

Perhaps Moys hoped that he might, after all, be permitted to keep that key which in time to come might be a very desirable thing to possess; but as, since his dismissal, he had no other possible excuse for his presence there but to return it back to the Regent, he was compelled to do so.

And the Regent was, to a certain extent, compelled to accept the excuse—although it must be confessed he did so with a very bad grace.

"You need not have troubled yourself, sir," he said, "to attend personally upon so trivial an occasion; but, since you are here, and since you have thought the honour or credit of such a man as yourself concerned in the manner in which you might deliver up a key, place it where you will, sir, on the floor, and it shall be considered as surrendered."

"I place the key at your Highness's feet," replied Moys, "notwithstanding the unjust reproach with which the order has been accompanied; but I have a request to make to your Highness, which is, that as I still hold a commission in the service of the King, should your Highness hear that I have fought a duel, and spared my antagonist, you will still consider that it is a part of the devotion I shall always feel for your Highness's service in public, and your Highness's feelings in private!"

This speech was perfectly enigmatical to the Regent; and Sir Hinckton Moys fully intended it should be so. He meant it to provoke inquiry, and that that inquiry should result in a formal prohibition of a duel with Allan Fearon

It was not exactly that Sir Hinckton Moys feared the encounter from any ordinary sensations of cowardice—for he had fought several duels in his time, and although not a brave man, strictly speaking—for bravery and honour go together—he was not a poltroon.

But the lingering hope still clung to him that by some change of circumstances he might yet be useful to the Regent, and be restored to his old position. He could not but feel, however, that such a hope would be at once extinguished to its last spark should he ever place in jeopardy the life of one so nearly related to the Prince as Allan Fearon was.

"Hold, sir!" cried Allan, speaking for the first time. "I, at least, understand your words; and should you proceed further to speak of an affair which concerns us only, I shall doubt the courage as much as I doubt the honour of Sir Hinckton Moys!"

"Ah!" said the Regent, "now I see! It is you, Fitz-George, who have embroiled yourself with this man!"

That name sounded strangely in the ears of Allan, and yet he recollected that in that agitating interview with the Regent—when he had proclaimed himself his son, and the heart of the Prince had not been able to withstand the appeal made to him—that name had been used as one which the Regent had said he would be glad if Allan would bear.

Sir Hinckton Moys, too, heard it for the first time, and so did Colonel Hanger, and so, indeed, did Willes, the valet.

All these persons looked upon those few words from the Regent as a public acknowledgment of Allan Fearon as his son.

"Expressly," said the Regent, laying emphasis upon the word, — "expressly, Fitz-George, I forbid your meeting Sir Hinckton Moys in the field!"

Allan bowed.

"I leave my honour," he said, "in the keeping of the Regent!"

"And I," said Sir Hinckton Moys, "would rather die a thousand deaths than aim at the life of one so honoured and so near to your Royal Highness!"

"That sentiment," said Allan, "has not been always present to the mind of Sir Hinckton Moys!"

"But then, sir," said Moys, putting on a look of the most unexampled assurance,—"then, sir, I did not know you!"

Sir Hinckton felt that he had said and done all that was in his power to repair the mistake he had made in coming to St. James's Palace at all while the Regent's anger was fully in bloom against him; and, like some skilful actor who wishes to leave the stage while he can carry the suffrages of his audience with him, his anxious desire now was to back out of the royal presence without another word.

But there was another person who had yet something to say before Sir Hinckton Moys left.

That person was Colonel Hanger.

Hanger had no disposition in the world, at the very time in which he had been so fortunate as to supplant Sir Hinckton Moys in the royal service, to go out and risk his life in a duel with his discomfited opponent. It did not seem to him at all to be one of the pleasures of office that he should be obliged to fight the person who had been superseded to make room for him; and since the Regent had so expressly forbidden one duel, Colonel Hanger thought he might as well do the same as regarded another.

"I, too, your Royal Highness," he said, "have the honour to hold a commission in his Majesty's service; and, as now I feel some delicacy, after what your Royal Highness has said, in fighting a duel, I think it only ingenuous and proper to state that I, too, have one on the *tapis*"

"What! what!" cried the Regent, hurriedly. "What is the meaning of all this? How is it, Fitz-George, that both these men seem determined to fight with you? I will not—cannot have it!"

"Nay, your Royal Highness," said Allan; "I think it is with each other this time!"

"Oh, is that it? Well, we see no objection to that! Go, gentlemen, and good fortune to both of you!—we see no objection at all, and only feel somewhat surprised that you should trouble us with so needless a confidence! Come, Fitz-George, this way. We will speak with you."

"I attend your Highness."

"And I," said Colonel Hanger, "as it is quite possible I may not be in a condition to attend your Highness again, would be glad to report the success of a certain mission."

"Peace, sir!" cried the Regent, vehemently. "We have heard all that you have to tell!"

"And this is my reward?"

"Reward, sir! What reward?"

"Ha! ha!" laughed Sir Hinckton Moys, close to the ears of Colonel Hanger. "When you were a boy at school, John Hanger, had you never a copy which said, 'Put not your faith in princes?'"

Colonel Hanger bit his lips.

The Regent passed on frowningly, but he whispered to Willes, "Follow that rascal Hanger, and tell him I will see him this evening. A paltry scoundrel! to go on a secret mission, and then talk of it before everybody! Come, Fitz-George, come! What's that? what's that?"

"Stop, Sir Hinckton Moys!" cried a voice. "I thought I heard your sweet tones in the gallery, and wondered, for a moment, what business you could have here, until I recollected you had something to bring me."

It was Annie, the fair Countess de Blonde, who appeared at the same door by which the Regent had entered the gallery, and where, in all probability, she had been listening to the preceding scene.

Annie was entirely wrapped up in a cloak of that beautiful miniver fur, edged with its bolder brother ermine, and which is so regal in its aspect.

"Stop, Sir Hinckton Moys! You carry away something which no longer belongs to you!"

"Madam!—what?"

"Your head, sir!"

"My head, madam!"

"His head?" cried the Regent.

"Yes!" said Annie. "I'm only amazed that he has the assurance to carry it on his shoulders!"

"Oh, Countess," said Moys, with a sarcastic bow, "I do not forget our wager, but am not beaten yet! Be assured, that should I see the necessity for such a step, my last words will be that the stake shall be duly delivered to the fair Countess de Blonde!"

Sir Hinckton Moys touched his head as he spoke, and then vanished rapidly from the gallery.

"He's an impudent rascal!" cried the Regent.

"And uglier than ever!" added Annie. "Allan, is Marian well and happy?"

"Both, I hope and believe, Annie."

"That's all right; but, mind, if you dare to fight with that fellow, Moys, you will be the worst enemy of her who never should make an enemy, because she has been kind and good to all who ever came in contact with her. You do not belong to yourself, Allan—your life is another's—and it is not to be cast away because such a man as Sir Hinckton Moys feels angry and disappointed!"

"I've stopped all that, Annie!" said the Regent. "Come, Fitz-George, come!"

"Oh!" said Annie; "is that what you're going to call him?"

"I think so," said the Regent.

"It sounds odd! Fitz—Fitz! It puts me in mind of some sort of fireworks — or cats spitting!"

No. 72.—DARK WOMAN.

"My dear Annie, it means George—son of George—Fitz-George."

"Oh, does it? Then ain't you ashamed of yourself? Why don't you make him a duke, or a baron, or a colonel, or something of that sort?"

"Now, my dear Annie——"

"Now, my sweet George, didn't you turn Thomas Willes into Sir Thomas Willes, to please me; and here's my sister's husband plain Allan Fearon, or Fitz-George, as you call him! Can't you make him a duke at once?"

"Really, Annie, you don't understand, but there is no doubt but that in time to come I shall be able to do something for him that shall satisfy you all. In the meantime, a commission in the Guards shall be at his service, and I renew an offer I once made that from the privy purse he shall have the maintenance of a gentleman."

"Sir," said Allan "when that offer was made, my mind was full of distressful images. I knew

not what to think—I knew not what to say. Reflection and calmness have now come, and I accept, with the gratitude of a son, the benefac-
tions of a father."

"You please me very much," said the Regent,
extending his hand to Allan.

"And me, too," said Annie. "Come and kiss
me, Mr. Fitz——Now, don't be stupid and jealous,
George; it's all in the family; but mind, no duels
with Sir Hinckton Moys. If anybody is to fight
him, I'm the proper person; and I'm afraid I
shall never get his head till I take it, and I'm
determined to have it."

"Come—come, Annie," said the Regent;
"think no more of him. I hope that the shadow
of that man will never again darken the atmosphere of James's. His treachery to you has been
very great, but his best punishment from us will
be to forget him. As to you, Fitz-George, you
don't know how much you please me by your
ready acceptance of what I offer you. I would
wish you to be always near me; and who knows
but there may be some opportunity of you fully
returning to me every favour I may heap upon
you? Good bye, Annie, for the present. I shall
be back to lunch. You look like the Queen of
Muscovites in all that fur. Come, Fitz-George—
come!"

Colonel Hanger had had the discretion to take
his departure, after Willes had re-whispered to him
the message from the Regent, so that the latter
part of this interesting conversation might be
considered as strictly domestic.

And more than once had Allan opened his lips
to put the question to the Regent that had in
reality brought him to the Palace, but a something—he knew not what—had restrained him.
Perhaps it was the look of satisfaction on the face of
the Regent—perhaps it was the presence of Annie;
but he certainly did not speak until he and the
Prince of Wales had left the gallery, and reached
one of the smaller reception-rooms of St. James's
Palace.

Then, as if he almost dreaded the sort of answer
that might be made to him, Allan spoke.

"Father, permit me to address you upon another subject than that which concerns your
bounty to me, your wishes for my happiness, and
my gratitude to you."

"Another subject, Fitz-George? What? what?
what?"

"My mother!"

"Ah!"

From that moment the Regent did not look
into the eyes of his son; but although his face
was turned towards Allan, he seemed as if he
looked past him rather than at him.

"I know," said Allan, "that she has erred
greatly; but then she has suffered greatly. "Let
it be our task, then, father, to soothe the tortured
spirit, and make the decline of that life of anxiety
and turmoil serene, if not happy!"

"I—I—know not what you mean, boy."

"Oh, father, we shall both have a reflected joy
in feeling that we have saved her from herself.
Let us obliterate that being who was called the
Dark Woman from both our and her recollection,
and let Linda de Chevenaux, forgetting much of
the past and forgiving the remainder, live yet for
joy and hope in the time that is to come."

"You—you—know not what you say! She's

mad, I tell you, boy! She would destroy me—
you—every one who stands in the way of her
insatiable ambition. Do not speak of her—do
not speak of her!"

"I cannot help it—I must needs speak of her.
The thought of her, day and night, is on the surface of my heart. I think of her—I dream of
her! She clung to me with all a mother's fondness until my calmer reason clashed with the
wild dreams of ambition she had cherished—and
all for me; and then, although she loaded me
with reproaches, and banished me from her presence even, I knew that it was out of the very
frenzy of her affection for me that she spoke!"

"Peace! peace!" cried the Regent, as he paced
the room hurriedly. "Am I never to hear the
last of this Linda de Chevenaux?"

"You loved her once, father!"

"No more — no more! You're all leagued
against me! Now, look you here, Allan—you
see what strange shapes her persecutions take.
She aims at my life—haunts me at bed and board
with strange threats and sudden appearances! I
know not who to trust about me;—the most
smiling and devoted of my servants may be
some creature — some emissary of hers — paid
lavishly by her to betray me to her; and now,
you, with a different style of persuasion, try to—
to wring my heart, to—to annoy me—torment
me about that woman, who has forfeited all right
—all pretence——"

"Nay, father, you said that she was mad!"

"Madly wilful!'

"But you will be merciful!"

"Look you here, Allan——Tush! why do I
call you Allan? From this day you're Captain
Fitz-George! You shall have a majority next
week, and a colonelcy the week after! I will
knight you—make a baronet of you—you shall
be Sir—Sir Allan Fitz-George, I suppose it must
be; but do not speak to me of her!"

"Then, tell me, father, what is her fate? Let
mine be the task to soothe the remaining years of
one who has erred greatly, only from her wild and
extravagant affections! Tell me, father, what
has become of her? She has disappeared like an
exhalation of the morning, and no one can tell me
whither she is gone!"

"You know not where she is, Fitz-George?"

"Indeed, I do not!"

"You have no guess?"

"Indeed, I have not!"

"Nor have I; and now you can come with me
to Carlton House; and, since you know as much
as I do—and I as much as you—why—why, you
see, further discourse upon the subject is fruit-
less. I have quite a busy morning before me.
You can come and join the little Court of the
Regent!"

"No, father, I will come to you again to-morrow—I am too sad at present; but do not suppose
that I will always afflict you with a gloomy countenance. I will come again to-morrow."

Allan left the Palace. There was doubt and
uncertainty in his heart, and upon the face of the
Regent there was an expression of uncomfortable
anxiety which was not dispelled for the remainder
of the day.

CHAPTER CLVIII.

THE DARK WOMAN DISCOVERS A CONCEALED PASSAGE IN THE TOWER, AND HAS HOPES OF ESCAPE.

THE daylight, or rather that dim and uncertain portion of it that continued to make its way into the gloomy chamber of the Tower inhabited by the Dark Woman, faded away.

Black shadows began to cast themselves over the old black bedstead, over the ancient escritoire, and over the hangings, which now and then swayed to and fro upon the walls, as some current of air found its way into the prison-house.

The Dark Woman had often waited for night to come, when she was at the head of that gang of desperadoes known as "Paul's Chickens," but she had never waited for the cessation of daylight with one-half the anxiety that she now watched it as it slowly disappeared.

At length, accustomed as her eyes had become to the dim obscurity of that chamber, she could no longer distinguish the outlines of objects, and she told herself that the night had come.

No one had visited her since about mid-day, when old Deborah Sly had brought her her dinner, but the Dark Woman was decidedly of opinion that she would not be left alone for the whole of the night.

She was correct in her conjecture.

The darkness that made the chamber in the Bloody Tower look like a dungeon had lasted about an hour, when she heard the sounds that heralded the approach of some one.

The unlocking of the iron-studded door, at the top of the stairs, came plainly upon her ears, and then the latches of the other two doors were lifted.

A gleam of light streamed into the prison-chamber.

It was the Under Warden, who had first received the Dark Woman at Traitors' Gate, who now appeared.

Linda de Chevenaux had taught herself to think that this official was to a certain extent kindly disposed towards her, and she welcomed his presence.

"Ah," she said; "it is like two lights to see you with one!"

The man did not catch the meaning at the moment, and he replied, "Madam, I have but one light."

"That is so, but I feel you are humane and kind, and your appearance to me is equal to another light."

"Oh, I see! Well, madam, I thank you for your good opinion, and have brought you this lantern."

"Then I am not condemned to darkness?"

The Under Warden hesitated a moment before he replied, and then he said, "Prisoners are not allowed lights: I fancy if they had been, the old Tower would soon enough have been in a blaze; and if you had been imprisoned in one of the regular dungeons, I could not have brought you a lantern; but since you are here, in a tower chamber, I have taken leave to do so."

"For which accept my thanks."

"Oh, it is not much! But I ought to tell you that the light in the lantern will just last two hours, or thereabouts; and so, after that time, or before it, I hope you will go to sleep till the daylight comes again.

"I thank you, with all my heart."

The Warden placed the lantern on the top of the little, old carved escritoire, and it shed a bright light over the room, which he looked at for a few moments, as if with a feeling of great interest.

"There are few persons, madam," he said, "who would not, after all, rather be imprisoned in the lowest dungeon of the Tower, than in this apartment."

"Indeed! and why so?"

"Because of its ill-omened reputation!"

"You mean on account of the murder of the two young Princes?"

"I do."

"Ah!" said the Dark Woman; then, with a slight smile, "I was never afraid of the living, and I am not now going to begin to be afraid of the dead."

"It is not every one, madam, who can say so much!"

"Perhaps not; but my curiosity in regard to that shadowy and unknown region which lies beyond the grave,—that mystery of mysteries—

"'That bourne from whence no traveller returns,' is too great to be mingled with fear."

"Then I leave you with more composure in my own mind, for I was afraid the recollections attached to this apartment, and the whole of this tower, indeed, would tell upon your imagination, and I have been blaming myself for bringing you here at all."

"Think no more of it, then," replied the Dark Woman; "for I assure you that if it were possible that the murdered Princes could visit me in the deepest stillness of the night, I should esteem the visitation as a rare favour, rather than shrink from it with a vulgar terror."

"You are, indeed, madam, one among ten thousand, to use such words here, when you have to spend the long night alone in this place."

"I speak sincerely."

"I am sure you do, or you would not so speak at all; and so, good night."

"Good night, and many thanks."

The Warden was, in truth, not a little surprised at the courage of the Dark Woman,—a courage which he felt that his nerves would not permit him to imitate.

The two doors, which shut with latches only on the outer side, were closed.

The Dark Woman listened to the grating of the lock of the iron-studded door, and in a few more moments she felt she was indeed alone in the "Bloody Tower."

Alone, and at night, in that dismal place! But she felt a degree of exultation in the fact.

What transpired there deeply interested her.

She was one of those bold, inquiring spirits, who, for the privilege of knowing what others knew not,—of doing what others do not,—would encounter sights and sounds that would shake a more ordinary intellect to its foundation.

And yet the Dark Woman was, in her way, superstitious.

All powerful intellects are so.

But there is a vulgar, common superstition, and there is a refined superstition.

The one peoples darkness with ghosts, and such like nursery terrors.

The other takes night flights, and strives to be familiar, if it be possible, with the beings of another and an unknown world.

The Dark Woman spoke the exact truth when she told the Under Warden of the Tower that she would esteem it a favour if the spirits of the murdered Princes of the "Bloody Tower" could, and would, visit her there.

But it could not be said that she had any real expectation of such a visit.

If she had, she would have said the same thing; only she would have said it with much more interest than she did.

And now she had a sense of security that she would be alone for the remainder of the night.

She had completely slept off the lingering effects of the powerful opiate she had taken at the house in Frith Street.

The enforced repose in the Tower had braced her faculties both in mind and body; and she was ready for any enterprise that required skill and courage.

"Two hours or more," she said, as she looked at the lantern. "Will the light last me? I will economise it if I can."

A thought at that moment struck the Dark Woman that she ought to have asked the compassionate Under Warden for the means of re-lighting the lantern should it go out by any accident.

Upon examining it, she found that the light was produced by a wax candle, of about six inches in length—rather thick in wax, but very thin in the wick.

No doubt it would last her the time he had said; but the Dark Woman, while she was engaged in thought, and not in action, would have been glad to put it out, if she had had the means of relighting it.

Perhaps it was not too late to procure such means.

She resolved to try the experiment.

She hastily opened the door leading into the ante-room, and then the door from that again, which was so close to the heavy iron-studded one which was securely locked.

With the corner of the lantern, the Dark Woman made a sharp, knocking noise against the door.

In the silence of that tower, which was solely occupied by herself, the knocking was, no doubt, heard plainly.

In a few moments there came footsteps on to the stairs.

The appeal of the Dark Woman against the inside of the door was answered by some sharp blows on it without.

"What is the matter?" asked a voice.

"My light has gone out."

"We cannot help that. The Under-Warden has gone to his lodgings."

"No, no!" said another voice, which the Dark Woman recognised as that of the Under Warden. "No, no! I am here. What is it?"

Some words were now spoken in a low tone; and then the Dark Woman heard the key put into the lock of the door.

She blew out the wax-light in the lantern at once; for it would not do, after her declaration that the light had gone out, to be found with it burning quite brightly.

In another moment, the Under Warden made his appearance again.

"I thought to trim the lantern," said the Dark Woman, "and it went out."

"Relight it," said the Warden, to the Yeoman of the Guard, who was with him.

"If you would give me the means of relighting it," said the Dark Woman, "in case such an accident should again happen, I should be grateful."

"What's the use," growled the Yeoman. "Let it alone, and I'll warrant it won't go out."

"But suppose I want it to last till the morning by only lighting it at intervals?"

"Well, well, I understand what you mean," said the Warden. "It can do no harm. Go to the third Warden's lodgings, Yeoman, and get a tinder box and matches. I will take all the responsibility."

The Yeoman went grumbling on the errand, and the Dark Woman, to her satisfaction, found herself, in a few minutes, in possession of a tinder-box, flint and steel, and a bundle of matches.

The modern lucifer match had not then been invented.

The Dark Woman was glad to bid the Warden good night again; and, as she left the iron-studded door, she took the precaution to prevent the possibility of any sudden visit being made to her, by fastening one of the wooden-latched doors with the formidable ornamental bolt that was attached to it on the inner side.

So the Dark Woman shut out the rest of the Tower, and the world, from that historical chamber she occupied, and she smiled as she said, "Which now are the prisoners, they or I? There is a bolt on my side—a lock on theirs."

Then she looked carefully at the wax candle in the lantern, to note how much of it had decreased. The amount of consumption, as yet, was very small; and she held the lantern above her head, and looked curiously and carefully about the chamber.

There was nothing to discover about that old black carved bedstead. There it was in its entirety, and could possess no secrets.

But it might be far otherwise with the ancient escritoire.

That she approached with an interest, and almost an awe, which her imagination would be sure to surround it with.

Who should say but that the last hands that had rested on it, or opened it, were not the little ones of the murdered children of the King, Edward the Fourth?

Or it might be that the bloodstained fingers of Richard of Gloucester had tampered with the lock of that cabinet after his innocent victims had ceased to trouble his dreams by their existence.

The Dark Woman placed the lantern on the flat portion of the top of the escritoire, and then tried to open the slant front, within which would, no doubt, be a collection of small drawers.

It was fast.

It seemed, by the closeness with which it was made fast, as if it had never opened; and yet it must do so, for there was the old-fashioned key-hole, with a quantity of old brass-work, highly finished in chasing, about it.

Below this slanting portion of the escritoire there were three drawers.

They were all fast locked, to ordinary observation, but the Dark Woman thought that the lower one did not appear to be so close shut as the two others, and she made a more critical examination of it.

The result of that examination was that she became convinced that the lower drawer was not locked.

But, no doubt, the damps of so many winters, and the dust of so many summers, had had this effect upon the wood, and the drawer stuck to its place as though the whole escritoire had been one solid piece, and the key-holes and ancient handles had only been put on to draw the eye.

The Dark Woman had her weapon with her, and it was a rather strange thing that the authorities of the Tower had not thought proper to search their prisoner. Certainly, such a process had not been gone through, so that the Dark Woman still had in her possession a long, thin-bladed, poniard, which was made to fit into a sheath she had herself constructed for it in a portion of her apparel.

Now she felt that the poniard might be of far more service to her in the Bloody Tower than ever it could have been flimsy and slight as it was as a weapon of offence or defence.

It was just the thing she required now, for the purpose of making a way into that ancient escritoire in the Tower of the murdered princes.

She set to work on that lower drawer, which she felt certain was not locked.

After a little careful manipulation with the narrow blade of the poniard, the Dark Woman carefully set at rest all question in regard to whether that drawer was locked or not, for she easily succeeded in passing the dagger blade right along the top of it.

All she had to do, then, was to disengage it sufficiently to open it.

The handles showed a disposition to give way, if too great a pressure was put upon them, and the Dark Woman paused for a few moments to consider what to do.

Then a thought struck her, which she wondered had not struck her before.

It was to commence operations, with the aid of the poniard, at the back of the old piece of furniture, instead of at the front.

The Dark Woman instantly set about dragging the escritoire from the wall.

Something fell down with a rattling sound.

The Dark Woman redoubled her efforts. The old escritoire was heavy, but she succeeded in drawing it from the wall to a considerable angle, so that she could go behind it.

She hit upon something hard.

Another moment, and she held the lantern down to see what it was.

An ancient key!

The Dark Woman at once seized upon it as a treasure.

It was not until she had lifted it from quite a thick mass of dust on the floor, that she saw it was one of those old keys of the fifteenth century, which were two in one.

There were a set of wards at each end, connected by a strong shaft, from about the centre of which projected an ornamental cross-piece, both for strength and to give a strong hold to the hand.

Was this the key of the old escritoire?

That was the question.

The Dark Woman at once made the experiment.

The lock of the slanting portion yielded, after a few moments' gentle pressure, to one of the sets of wards of the old key.

No doubt the other set of wards would open the drawers.

The slanting portion of the ancient furniture opened, with a creaking noise, upon its hinges. The Dark Woman looked eagerly within.

Some folded papers—something that glittered, and some wrapped-up clothing, seemed to be the contents of the open part of the escritoire. But there was, as she expected, a number of small drawers, one of which she opened.

It was full of blackened coins.

How strange a discovery she had made! No doubt the Tower authorities had never thought it worth while to open that escritoire; and yet what treasures of antiquity might it not contain?

The Dark Woman lifted a piece of the clothing —it almost fell to pieces beneath her touch; but she could both see and feel that it was velvet, which had been embroidered.

From the size of the piece of apparel, it seemed as though it had belonged to some very young person; and, upon lifting up another faded bit of velvet, the Dark Woman saw portions of a collar of rich lace attached to it.

Were these pieces of clothing the sad memorials of those unfortunate princes who had lain down to sleep in that chamber only to awaken in eternity?

It would indeed seem so.

It was possible enough that no more furniture had been in that room than was now to be found there, on the occasion of the two children being sent there by their uncle, Richard.

Their clothing, when they retired to rest, might have been cast into the escritoire; and who shall say that the hand of the crook-backed tyrant himself might not have last used that key to lock up the cabinet, and then cast it behind the top, where it had lodged until the Dark Woman moved the piece of furniture, and it fell down to the accumulated dust of centuries, on the floor?

It might be so.

CHAPTER CLIX.

THE DARK WOMAN PURSUES HER INTERESTING DISCOVERIES IN THE OLD TOWER.

One by one, Linda de Chevenaux lifted those faded, time-rotted little garments, and her attention became speedily directed to the article that glittered when first she cast eyes on those truly sad memorials of the past.

That glittering object turned out to be a star, richly adorned, and apparently set with brilliants. It was fastened to a blue ribbon, but little of the colour of which remained, and which was so arranged, and shaped, as if it had been made to wear round the neck.

Could it be that this was the star which the little Prince of Wales had worn on his breast on the occasion of being lodged with his brother York in the Tower, by Richard?

The Dark Woman was disposed to think that such was, indeed, the case.

But now she had her curiosity strongly excited by the several small drawers, in one of which she had certainly found a considerable sum of money.

There were twelve of these drawers, and to the disappointment of the Dark Woman most of them were empty; but at length she came to one which contained a small piece of folded paper, on which was some faded writing.

It was with great difficulty she made out the following words:—

"Ye doore in ye walle to be closed for aye, and lette noe mane speke thereof, on paine of ye death of ane traitor to Richard, ye King."

There was a scrawling signature at the foot of this paper, which the Dark Woman made out to be "Richard Rex."

She had no doubt that this was a genuine autograph of the tyrant who ended his life and career upon the field of Bosworth.

"Alas!" said Linda de Chevenaux, "why is it that these sad memorials of the past interest me when I have so much to think of in the present Go back again, ye mournful evidences of the crimes and the ambitions of a generation that has passed away—I care not for you. I live for myself, and for the time that is to come!"

The Dark Woman huddled together the scraps of clothing and the written papers into the escritoire again composedly.

But she kept the star and the blue ribbon.

"Who knows," she said, "but that fate or Providence, let men call it which they may, has placed this glittering toy in my hands in order that I may yet attach it to the breast of my son? It has, doubtless, been the insignia of the rank of one Prince of Wales, and why may it not do the same duty by another?"

With the star in her hand, the Dark Woman sat down on the side of the bed to think; and as she did so a drowsiness came over her, which she only started from for a moment as she heard the sentinels change at ten o'clock.

Then, with a desire to preserve the power of illuminating her prison as often as possible, she extinguished the wax candle in the lantern, being satisfied that, should she require it before daylight, she had the means of relighting it.

If she should not awaken before the day shone once more into the Bloody Tower, she meant to preserve the end of the wax candle for future use, as it might possibly be of the greatest service to her.

And then the Dark Woman lay down, and fell into a deep sleep.

Darkness was upon the old Tower; and in every nook and corner of the ancient fortress, except the guard rooms.

It would be scarcely possible to suppose for a moment that any human imagination could at all subside into sleep and forgetfulness of the many exciting and strange discoveries made in the old escritoire by Linda de Chevenaux.

Certainly the brain of the Dark Woman was not of that order that could so readily shake off the impressions produced by those relics of the past.

It is not to be wondered at, therefore, although she seemed to sleep, an ever active fancy filled up all that was wanting in the remembrances of a past age.

One of the most singular dreams—if indeed it were a dream—that had ever vexed the slumbers of a human being, swept across the brain of the sleeper in that ill-omened apartment.

We will not say it was wholly a dream—for are there not

"More things in heaven and on earth
  Than are dreamt of in our philosophy?"

And who shall say that the visions of that night which presented themselves to the slumbers of the Dark Woman were all imaginary?

It appeared to her that, although she slept for a time, she then found it impossible to rest; and to her surprise, she saw that the wax candle in the lantern, which she had so carefully extinguished, was relighted.

The impression upon her mind that this was the case became so strong, that she thought she sat up in bed, and uttered an exclamation of surprise. Then the lantern—as if without the interposition of any human agency—slowly lifted itself, so to speak, from the dilapidated chair on which the Dark Woman had placed it, and seemed to sail away in a slant direction through the air, taking much the same route it would have done if carried by some one, until it placed itself on the level portion of the escritoire.

But no form was visible; no hand was there to direct the motions of the lantern; and the Dark Woman uttered another cry of surprise, perhaps mingled with some fear, as this phenomenon met her gaze.

This second cry from her lips seemed to be an invocation to some invisible being within the apartment; for although she still saw no one, yet a hissing sort of sound came through the air, terminating in the word "Hush! hush!" spoken in an under tone, and as if with difficulty, through the clenched teeth of some one who dreaded to hear the sound himself had made.

An undefined feeling of horror came over the Dark Woman—she tried to move, but her limbs seemed turned to lead: she tried to speak, but her voice was choked and dissipated before it reached her lips.

She could only gaze into the dim light around her; and she could only listen with a preternatural sense of hearing to the slightest sound indicative of the presence of unearthly beings in that chamber of mystery and murder.

It seemed to her as if the blood became almost stagnant in her veins. Her heart performed its functions laboriously; but at length, with a mighty effort, she did utter—or fancied she uttered—a sound.

"Hush! hush!" came that hissing demand for silence once again.

Then the Dark Woman bent her gaze again in the direction of the lantern; it seemed to her as if the atmosphere of the room was becoming opaque and thick before her eyes, and that a concentration of the invisible air, until it became an actual substance, was taking place exactly in front of the escritoire.

And soon this concentrated atmosphere assumed a human form—a form tall, gaunt, and hideous, on which the rays of light from the lantern fell obliquely—casting into strong relief such a countenance as the fiend himself might wear in looking upon the glory and beauty of that world he fain would destroy.

The light, too, fell upon a robe of purple velvet, heavily trimmed with ermine; it fell upon a steel breast-plate, around which the robe was huddled with one hand, as if half to hide it. A jewel, of amazing lustre, glittered in the cap that was worn by this thing of air.

And fain would the Dark Woman have questioned the apparition—fain would she have demanded who it was that made night-hideous in that place by such an appearance. Yet still she could not speak; she could only look—she could only listen. The blood then seemed to stop for a moment in her veins as the apparition spoke in hissing whispers.

"Keep them close!—keep them close! A coffin full of holes—and sink them deep in the Thames! Richard for England, and England for Richard! So perish Edward's accursed brood!"

These words seemed to ring through the apartment towards the conclusion of them, although they commenced in low accents, and they were followed by a yell which seemed as if it reached the innermost chambers of the brain of the Dark Woman.

"Keep off!—keep off!" cried the apparition. "I did not kill you—the blood upon your lips is none of my shedding! Keep off!—keep off! Why float you down upon me? Take them away!—take them away!—take them by the panel of the bed-head—the secret stair through the barred wall will guide you! Hush!—hush! Are their features swollen much? Would you know them for Edward's children? Put out the light!—put out the light! I shall find my way. Hush!—hush!—hush! Meet me to-morrow at Baynard's Castle."

The light in the lantern slowly faded away, and with it that same hideous figure, the head of which seemed to project forward on the neck in a most unnatural fashion; but as that material and yellow lustre, which the lighted lantern had produced, faded before the imagination of the Dark Woman, it was succeeded by a tender and delicate radiance in the Bloody Tower. A full blue ethereal tint banished the thick waves of darkness which a moment before seemed to be rolling over each other in endless confusion.

And with this beautiful light, which was a charm of itself to look upon, there came some faint sounds, as of music, afar off; but music so graceful and so enchanting, that it could never belong to this world.

And then the Dark Woman thought she saw—or really saw—that the source of this exquisite light which pervaded that dismal tower seemed to approach nearer and nearer; and as it seemed to advance in its progress, the figures of the two children, hand in hand, and with a look of unearthly beauty upon their faces, became visible to her eyes or imagination.

This sight, so different from that hideous figure which had turned to ice, as it were, every drop of blood in the veins of the unfortunate prisoner, was indeed a relief; and she stretched out her hands towards the two figures, as though imploring their protection and assistance.

Hand in hand they advanced—still walking upon the air—or, as it seemed to the Dark Woman, borne up upon that exquisite light which now seemed to irradiate and illumine every part of that hitherto gloomy apartment.

The Dark Woman tried to struggle to her feet, but was conscious of a leaden weight which seemed to crush her down upon that bed upon which the two innocent victims of an ambitious and wicked uncle had breathed their last breath, and taken their last look into each other's eyes.

Onward still they came, and as they neared the apartment the Dark Woman fancied that she heard the click of a lock, and immediately above the bed-head the two figures—still hand in hand —opened a panel, and advanced right into the Bloody Tower.

Joy, not fear, now took possession of the mind of Linda de Chevenaux.

Might not these two strange visitants have the means of setting her at liberty? Might they not show her a way of escape from a life-long imprisonment?

Again she made an effort to speak, and this time she succeeded in uttering, in imploring accents, "Stay!—stay! Oh, stay! Leave me not in loneliness, after having blest it so far beyond its deserts by appearing to give hope to an almost broken heart! Stay!—oh, stay!"

Even as she spoke, the Dark Woman fancied she saw the two children bend towards her with a look of ineffable pity upon their countenances, and in tones which sounded like the sighing of the south wind, whisper, "Hope—hope, and pray!"

"Alas! alas!" cried the Dark Woman, "I dare not!"—and she let her face fall upon her hands, which were clasped in agony of soul.

Still the two unearthly visitants for they were too lovely to belong to this world—passed, or rather glided, upon that pale blue light across the apartment; and in another moment they had disappeared through the opposite wall, noiselessly, even as they had entered.

The prisoner was left in darkness.

Linda de Chevenaux uttered a terrible cry, and wringing her hands, she sank back again upon the bed.

With that cry the Dark Woman awoke, and looking into the darkness with a wild and haggard look, she stretched out her hand to feel for the lantern.

She found it where she had left it, and the means of obtaining a light also.

In a few seconds the Dark Woman had relighted the wax candle, and now she began to ask herself whether what she had seen had merely been a trick of the imagination, or whether she had really beheld that wicked King and his two hapless victims.

Again she listened for that noise which had surely come from that far-off country from "whose bourne no traveller returns."

All was still; and the faint rays of the little end of wax candle did not succeed in dispelling the darkness.

The Dark Woman rose from her couch and approached the wall, through which had disappeared those two children who she fancied had whispered to her the word "Hope!" She searched minutely behind the tapestry, which still, in places, hung upon the walls, but could discover no outlet.

She clasped her hands over her eyes, and tried to collect her thoughts; then she said, aloud

'Yes! Above the bed's head, surely, I heard the click of a lock, and the panel opened! Heaven aid me now!"

With a strange, tottering step the Dark Woman mounted upon the bed, and drew aside, with her disengaged hand, the tapestry which covered that side of the apartment. Holding the lantern high above her head, she at length uttered a cry of joy.

She saw a spring; it represented the eye of some animal. She pressed it, but it was rusted by years of disuse, and she could not move it.

The Dark Woman now had recourse to the poniard she carried about her. Again she attacks the spring. Ah! the eye gives way! the spring acts! the panel flies open!

In the joy of her success, the Dark Woman was reckless of consequences; and fearing that she might be interrupted, she had been careless in her use of the sharp weapon which had stood her in such good stead.

When the Dark Woman found the panel yield to her wish, she paused in her work to take breath; and it was not until then that she was conscious that blood was flowing from her hand upon the coverlet of the bed, and staining in places the tapestry upon the wall.

Quick as thought, she descended from her elevated position; and binding a handkerchief tightly round the wounded hand, she again caught up the lantern, while a smile of triumph parted her lips—a smile which had not sat there for many a long day.

"I must be quick," she murmured, "or heaven will withdraw its protection."

Again she mounted the bed, and drew herself up through the panel, which led to what appeared to be a long—almost interminable it looked in the black darkness which reigned in it—corridor.

The Dark Woman, as soon as she had entered this corridor, turned to close the panel, so as to leave no indication of the means of her escape; and carefully arranging the tapestry over the head of the bed, she then closed the panel, which made a sharp, clicking noise—even as she had heard it make when those beautiful children closed it.

The Dark Woman closed the lantern, for the cold current of air from the corridor threatened to extinguish it every moment.

Slowly she now proceeded through that dismal corridor—fraught with so many terrible recollections; and as she walked with stealthy steps she became conscious of treading upon the dust which had not been disturbed for many long years—dust which had accumulated ever since that night when the young Princes were carried from the Bloody Tower—by the same route the Dark Woman was now taking—to their last resting-place beneath the dark waters of the river.

On—on she went, with hands outstretched. Now and then she could not avoid giving utterance to an expression of terror, as a bat would fly against her face, being startled by that unwonted light which emanated from the little wax candle, which the Dark Woman feared would scarcely serve her till she came to some outlet where she hoped the light of day would penetrate.

At length she reached a flight of stone steps—damp and slippery, and so accumulated with dust and creeping reptiles, that she shrunk back in horror.

But it was only for a moment that Linda de Chevenaux was discouraged. Was not life and liberty before her? If she now retraced her steps to the Bloody Tower, might she not linger a long lifetime a hopeless prisoner in that gloomy abode?

Then again there came to her recollection that low, soft whisper of the two children which bade her hope, and she took that as an earnest of her final success.

Gathering up her garments, so as to avoid as much as possible stepping upon the noisome creatures which hurried hither and thither as she approached, the Dark Woman continued her route; and so intent was she upon regaining her liberty, that in a short time she ceased to regard what at first had filled her with so much horror.

Step by step the Dark Woman descended the stone stairs without hesitation and without haste.

She had descended about thirty, when she became aware that she was in a lobby or ante-room; but as yet it was too dark for her to distinguish, with anything like accuracy, the kind of room she was in. She raised the lantern above her head, in order to take a better survey of the locality, but, in doing so, her hand struck against a projection in the wall, and, with an exclamation of pain, it fell from her hand.

The Dark Woman was in profound darkness.

For a time she felt as though death were preferable to the horrors of that moment, and it was with an undefined feeling of relief that she assured herself that she still possessed the poniard.

A gleam of lightning now furrowed the sky; and by its blue and livid light the Dark Woman saw, high above her head, a grated window.

"Ah!" sighed the Dark Woman,—"I am not, then, entirely abandoned of heaven! Another such a flash of lightning will surely enable me to discover some means of egress from this place."

It was evident that the Dark Woman, by means of that circuitous flight of stone steps, had traversed a much larger portion of ground than she had anticipated, and that she was nearer to some door or gateway which would lead to some of the outer courts of the Tower.

Just then a fearful peal of thunder seemed to shake the ground beneath the feet of the Dark Woman. A livid and sulphureous flash of lightning threw so dazzling a light upon the walls of the room, that she had no difficulty now in discovering what she hoped would prove a means of exit.

An iron grating, low down upon the ground, led out into the open air, the Dark Woman felt convinced, for she could feel the night air refreshing to her fevered brow.

"Courage! Courage, Linda de Chevenaux!" she whispered to herself. "Another moment, and you will be free!"

In an instant the Dark Woman was on her knees before the iron grating; but, at first, it resisted all her efforts, as she shook the iron bars with all the strength lent her by despair.

At length she had recourse to that weapon which had never failed her; and taking the poniard in her unwounded hand, she commenced to work diligently and skilfully.

A very short time sufficed to remove first one bar and then another, and, in less than a quarter of an hour, the Dark Woman had the satisfaction

of seeing that she had made an aperture sufficiently large to enable her to pass through.

The Dark Woman clasped her hands together,
and if ever a word of thanksgiving passed those
lips, it was surely when she looked out upon the
evening sky, and could whisper to herself the
assurance that she had indeed and in truth
escaped from the Bloody Tower.

Another moment, and Linda de Chevenaux
emerged from the little grating; but the sky was
cloudy, the moon was obscured, and it was impossible for her to ascertain in the darkness the precise locality in which she was.

She felt, however, that she was treading upon
grass, or herbage of some kind, for she could not
hear her own footsteps; and inasmuch as there
was no sentinel, she felt pretty certain that she
had made her way to some part of the old Tower
which was not used. She determined, therefore,
to wait—wait patiently, now that the free air of

No. 73.— DARK WOMAN.

heaven once more fanned her cheek—until daylight, and then might she not hope to distance all
pursuit?

As the Dark Woman thus waited, the clock of
St. Peter's Church struck the hour of one. She
then knew that she was standing upon the Tower
Green.

CHAPTER CLX.

ALLAN FEARON HAS A STORMY INTERVIEW WITH
THE REGENT AT ST. JAMES'S PALACE

THERE was an undefined something about the
tone and manner of the Prince Regent when he so
distinctly to Allan Fearon repudiated all knowledge of the whereabouts of Linda de Chevenaux,
which produced a very uncomfortable impression

upon the sensitive mind of that son, who was with such great anxiety inquiring for his mother.

It was, of course, impossible for Allan to look or insinuate a doubt on the subject, but still he was not satisfied.

The words of the Regent had not that kind of halo around them which, by some occult arrangement of Providence, ever seems to hover about the truth.

But Allan was obliged to leave the Palace with no further satisfaction than he had obtained, and that was poor enough.

The change that was about to take place in his own circumstances and position would, at any other time, have much affected him; but now he scarcely gave a passing thought to the fact that he was about to emerge from a position of poverty and dependence to one of rank and abundant means.

His thoughts were full of that poor belated heart which had suffered so much for him, and for his sake; and which, if its wild throbbing were not now quenched by death, was still suffering deeply.

In this frame of mind was it that Allan reached his humble home at the river end of Buckingham Street, in the Strand.

There, as the reader is aware, Marian was most anxiously waiting for him with the pocket-book that told so sad a tale of the fate of the Dark Woman.

At one moment Allan believed that he had no possible clue to what had become of his mother.

The next moment he knew exactly where she was, and could imagine all that had happened, when Marian met him on the very threshold of his home.

"Dear Allan! read this. I give it to you to read before you can tell me one word of what has passed at the Palace, between you and the Regent."

Allan's eyes devoured those few words that had been written for his observation by the Dark Woman.

The mystery as regarded her vanished in a moment.

"My mother in the Tower of London," he cried, "a state prisoner; and my father, the Regent of England, not know it!"

"Oh, Allan—Allan! has he denied it?"

Allan shook with emotion, and sat down for a few moments in silence, while he clasped his hands over his eyes.

Marian flung her arms around him, and pressed him to her heart.

"Do not grieve—oh, do not grieve, my Allan—my husband! Let those shed tears who have no one to love them."

These words at once reached the heart of Allan, and he uttered a cry of joy as he folded his own dear Marian to his heart.

"Ungrateful to you and to heaven, that I am," he said; "how dare I repine when I am indeed blessed with your unalterable affection, my Marian!"

Their tears now mingled for a few minutes, and they neither of them spoke.

It was Marian who then broke the silence by a proposition that Allan felt sprung from the goodness of her heart.

"As I understand you, dear Allan, your father

the Regent, has said that he does not know where your mother is?"

"He did say so, Marian," replied Allan, with a sigh.

"Well, Allan, it is not for you to doubt him."

"But this memorandum, dear?"

"That, too, you will believe, Allan."

"Ah, now I understand you, Marian. I must believe my mother when she says she is in the Tower, and I must believe my father when he says he knows not of it."

"Yes, Allan."

"It is hard to do so!"

"Undoubtedly, Allan, it will be more pain to your kind heart than to do otherwise."

"You are right, Marian—you are right, dearest, as you always are; because you take your heart into counsel with your understanding; but there is nothing to prevent me informing my father of the fact that my mother is in the Tower?"

"Nothing, Allan—nothing!"

"I will do so! I will go back to the Palace at once! I will see the Regent!"

"No—oh, no, Allan!"

"No, say you?"

"Not absolutely no; but no for a short time. Do you not go again to the Regent until you are cool, and calm, and collected, and have had time to think. If that unfortunate Linda de Chevenaux is in the Tower of London, remember that she is safe and well cared for. These are not the times when prisoners are made to suffer pain and hardships. The dungeon, the damp straw, and the clanking chains are banished now. She does not suffer in the Tower; and while you reflect and become composed, who shall say that a short period of even enforced inaction may not do much to calm the troubled intellects of Linda de Chevenaux?"

There was so much real, practical good sense in these words from Marian, that Allan looked at her with a sort of amazement and reverence, and wondered how it could be that, amid all the struggles of poverty she had gone through, she had been able to educate her intellect so to express herself.

"My Marian," he said, "you are my superior in all things but one. I will not let you say that you love me better than I love you; but in all else you are my guide and mentor."

Marian smiled.

"No, no, Allan—it is to you I look up; but you feel more acutely in regard to these affairs than any one else can, however deeply they may sympathise with all that concerns you. That is the sole difference. I am able to reason more calmly, that is all."

"I have promised," said Allan, as he again read the few words which the Dark Woman had written in Colonel Hanger's pocket-book,—"I have promised to see the Regent again to-morrow."

"Then be it so, Allan. Put off until the morrow all communication with him about your mother; and then, when you see him, tell him first that you have discovered where she is, and ask for her release."

"Which he will refuse."

"Perhaps not, upon conditions."

"What conditions, Marian?"

"Listen to me, Allan. There are two views to take of this terrible question between your mother and the Prince. No one can for a moment defend his conduct in the first instance, but what would you have him do?"

Allan could not reply.

"Can he make Linda de Chevenaux other than what she is?"

"Alas, no!"

"Can he undo the past? What is he to do to protect himself from the mad persecution of one who has no real claims but her betrayal and misfortunes, but who chooses to set up fictitious ones, which he—you—I—or any one must feel he cannot entertain for one passing moment."

"You are right, Marian."

"I do not defend the Regent, but there is a point at which even he who has done wrong must, and may, resist the consequences when they become irrational, and such as would destroy both him and others to give way to."

"Oh, yes, yes! Dear Marian, you clear my mind upon this subject."

"Suppose for a moment, Allan, that the Prince of Wales were to admit the legality of his marriage with the Dark Woman, what kind of justice would that be for the already sufficiently unfortunate Catherine of Brunswick, whom he really did marry in face of all the world?"

"You are right—you are right, Marian."

"And suppose, my Allan, he were, in compliance with the wild desires of Linda de Chevenaux, to acknowledge you as his son, what kind of justice would that be to the young Princess Charlotte, now just entering into life as the heiress, after him, to the English Crown."

"Say no more, Marian—say no more! I cannot defend my mother with arms gathered from my reason! It is my affection—the affection of a son only—that can speak for her. I will see the Regent to-morrow, and strain my utmost to heal the unhappy differences between him and Linda de Chevenaux."

"You will have to see her, too, Allan!"

"Yes—oh, yes!"

"It will lie with her to make, and keep, a peace which shall, while it leaves the Regent in security as regards her, leave her a contented and happy future."

"I will do all that man can do to effect such an object. And now, my Marian—Lady Marian Fitz George—let me talk to you of yourself."

"What do you mean, Allan?"

Allan Fearon now detailed to Marian all that had been said by the Regent, in regard to what he meant to do for him, and the station he meant him to occupy.

Marian listened with a slight flush of colour upon her cheeks, and then she flung herself into the arms of Allan, as she whispered, "For your sake, dear Allan, and for the sake of, perhaps, others who will be dearer to us than life itself, I welcome all this with joy!"

Ah! how different was the serene, happy atmosphere of that humble home in Buckingham Street, Strand, to the passion-fraught air of St. James's Palace or Carlton House.

Little did the Dark Woman, in the Bloody Tower chamber, where she chafed and moaned like some wild denizen of the woods, caught in the snares of the hunter, imagine that her son and his Marian enjoyed such true felicity, without the realisation of a single one of those dreams and visions of mad ambition which she had indulged in on his account.

But such is the history of human existence. The false lights which we follow, and which we in our inmost hearts believe to be the pioneers to happiness, leave us stranded in the quagmires of disappointment.

There were the elements, at all events, of serenity in the position of Linda de Chevenaux; but she fixed her attention upon some wandering star—the star of royalty—so far off, that the good which lay beneath her feet she trod down unmercifully, and would not have cast a thought upon.

Nor was the royal mind at St. James's Palace much more at ease than the heated imagination of the Dark Woman in the Tower of London. The Regent fully expected another visit from his son; and he had a presentiment that almost the first words that would come from that son's mouth would consist of a declaration that he had made a discovery of the place of imprisonment of the Dark Woman.

Over and over again, the Prince wished devoutly that he had avowed the fact of the imprisonment of Linda de Chevenaux, and boldly justified it.

But that was too late now.

Oh, those fearful words "too late!" How often during the progress of this most eventful history have the various people, whose actions we have detailed to the reader, been forced to utter them!

But as the day passed over, and Allan came not to the Palace, the Regent began to breathe more freely, and to think that, after all, the secret might be kept.

He was disposed almost to receive Colonel Hanger graciously when he should present himself; for the secret of the incarceration of the Dark Woman in the Tower was like the discovery of some hideous murder. If undiscovered for four-and-twenty hours, there was a fair prospect of it still remaining a secret for as many days; and if for as many days, why not for as many weeks—as many months—or as many years? And if so, why then—— The Regent paused at this point of his cogitation, for the idea that in as many years all human secrets and all human affairs would be to him as naught was an uncomfortable one.

He began to wish for the arrival of Colonel Hanger, just for the solace of being able to talk to somebody of an affair which he did not wish to make known to any other person than the man who had necessarily been an actor in it.

The Regent could almost have believed that his wishes had a necromantic power to ensure their own fulfilment, for scarcely had he uttered the words, "Confound that Hanger! why don't he come?" when a page announced the Colonel.

Hanger made his appearance with an audacious kind of familiarity—that kind of familiarity which a low mind always thinks its right as soon as it gets in possession of secrets belonging to a superior.

"Most gracious Regent," said Hanger, "be joyful and at peace. The scold is bridled—the termagant can only now rail through prison walls. Most lordly Regent, and King that shall be—your orders are obeyed."

"And you are drunk!" said the Regent.

Hanger held by the back of the chair. It was a little requisite that he should do so, to keep himself perfectly steady, although in his own estimation he was very far from the state which the Regent had so roughly designated.

"No, your Royal Highness—no! Jack Hanger can carry his three bottles with any man or with any prince; but the question is not whether Jack Hanger has had a glass too much or not, but whether the royalty of England is satisfied. I say the royalty of England—meaning your own most gracious Highness—for the Dark Woman is in the Tower of London; and sink me! if all is not serene."

"So you have caged the tigress?"

"Caged and cut her claws."

"I will not deny, Hanger, that you have done this thing well, and I shall not be disposed to forget it. Be as discreet in keeping the secret as you have been in creating it to keep I shall have money to-morrow. Come to me for a thousand pounds."

"To-morrow?—to-morrow?" said Hanger, as he dealt his forehead some sharp slaps with his open hand. "To-morrow? Oh! I recollect now. May it please your gracious Highness, if I fall, will you have me buried in the Abbey? The thousand pounds will raise a pretty monument to my memory. Let the design be pretty. Death, for instance, an angel with a trumpet, and he who is still a gentleman—although kicked out of good company and seldom mentioned—sitting at a table together. Let there be dice, cards, and half-a-dozen bottles; and amidst a thousand pieces of fanciful scroll-work, clouds, cherubim, and death's heads, let the words, 'Good night, old Jack Hanger,' be conspicuous."

"It seems to me," said the Regent, "that you're mad as well as drunk."

"No; but the fact is, your Highness, I've got to fight that rascal Moys at eight o'clock in Battersea Fields, and there is no knowing which way the luck may go."

"At eight?"

"Yes, your Highness—at eight precisely. He sent to me a fire-eating Major—what is his name? I cannot recollect it, but it's all the same. I was forced to accept the cartel; so who knows that Jack Hanger may be in life at mid-day, when your Highness rouses from rosy slumbers, to come for his thousand pounds?"

"In that case," said the Regent, "you won't want them."

"But, your Highness——"

"Oh, I can have nothing to do with your private quarrels. Go, and fight as much as you please."

"And this is the reward!"

"What mean you, sir? Do you want me to be your second? or do you inform me of this affair as some persons do their friends when they have an affair of honour on their hands, with the hope and expectation that some officious fool will send for the police?"

"No, your Highness, no. It shall never be said that Jack Hanger refused to meet his woman—I mean, his man."

"Very well," said the Regent sneeringly, as he moved towards the door; "very well—a thousand pounds are waiting for Jack Hanger, provided he makes his appearance here at one o'clock to-morrow

to claim them; but, for the present, I have the honour of bidding Jack Hanger good evening."

The Regent left the room.

"Now, that's scurvy," said Hanger, as he leant heavily upon the chair which had supported him during the interview. "That's what I call scurvy, now. He might have said 'Don't fight,' or 'I forbid the duel,' or something of that kind. He must want me again—he's sure to want me again —and yet he lets me go coolly and risk my life against that rascal Moys. And I must go, too— that's the worst of it, unless—unless—let me consider—unless I can think of some clever, cunning, out-of-the-way scheme to put it off. I must think —I must think; and that I may do so more clearly, I'll go to the 'Thatched House,' and have another bottle of the glorious claret. Who knows but I may imbibe an idea along with the bright ruby wine? I must think—I must think; and I'm half resolved already not to fight."

CHAPTER CLXI.

ALLAN FEARON PAYS ANOTHER VISIT TO THE REGENT, AND BY THE ASSISTANCE OF ANNIE PROCURES AN IMPORTANT DOCUMENT.

FROM the moment that Allan Fearon felt confident that his mother was an inmate of the Tower of London, he could know no rest until he had seen the Regent.

The morrow brought no change in the feelings with which Marian regarded the transaction. She still urged Allan not to quarrel with his father, but rather to assume that it would be a bit of intelligence to him to be informed that the Dark Woman was in the Tower.

There can be no doubt in the world but that this was by far the most judicious course to pursue.

Allan, therefore, found himself by twelve o'clock at St. James's Palace again, and this time he did not experience the difficulty he had done before in securing admission.

Probably the Regent's valet, now that he knew the position Allan was to occupy, and the new terms and status on which he would henceforth come either to Carlton House or to St. James's, had taken care that he should have facilities of ingress that he before could not pretend to.

Certainly Allan had not even to show the ruby ring which the Prince of Wales had given him as a passport to his presence.

One of the officers of the household respectfully saluted him, saying, "I believe I have the honour of speaking to Mr. Fitz George?"

That name sounded very odd and strange to Allan, but since it had been bestowed upon him by his father he was willing to answer to it.

"Yes, sir, I am Mr. Fitz George."

"Then, sir, if you please to wait in one of the private apartments, I think his Royal Highness will return by one o'clock."

"Return? Is he not in the Palace?"

"No, sir. His Royal Highness the Regent was summoned in haste to Windsor at an early hour this morning, on account of some alarming change in the health of his Majesty."

The Majesty mentioned by the officer of the

Palace was his grandfather, and it was just possible that his father, the Regent, might return to St. James's King of England.

It was not possible but that Allan should think what would have been his position if his mother, Linda de Chevenaux, could really have substantiated the dream of her life—namely, the legality of her marriage, or mock marriage, with the Prince of Wales.

Admitting that the old King might be dead and the Regent invested with the crown, he, Allan, would be the heir-apparent.

The position of the Princess Charlotte would then be most painful.

The marriage with Caroline of Brunswick would have to be declared null, and the most important changes would ensue in the descent of the crown of England.

But Allan felt that all these were but dreams of the imagination.

He started, and was alarmed to find himself indulging in them.

"No, no!" he said; "let me hope that those wild fancies of my mother will never be inherited by me."

The officer of the Palace, who had received him with so much amenity and respect, stood a few paces from him, and was, no doubt, rather surprised to see the rapid alternations in the countenance of Mr. Fitz George.

That officer, however, was far too well-bred, and too used to the Court, to take any notice of what was not intended for his observation, so he patiently waited until Allan chose to speak.

"I think, sir, I will avail myself of your kind offer, and wait for the Regent."

"If you please, sir. I will have the honour of conducting you, sir, to an apartment, and so soon as his Highness returns, he shall be informed of your presence."

"Sir, I thank you"

Allan soon found himself in a moderately-sized room, which was very splendidly furnished; and although the season did not now require such an indulgence, a bright fire of wood burnt on the hearth.

The Regent was fond of warmth, and both in Carlton House and St. James's, there were always apartments to be found all through the year in which wood fires were burning.

These wood fires were generally of cedar blocks, for the Prince had a particular liking for their odour while burning.

Such was the character of the fire in the room to which Allan Fearon was conducted by the polite officer of the Palace.

Allan—or Fitz George, as really we ought now to name him, since by that name he was known from that time—did not inherit the liking for the odour of cedar wood of his father.

To him the air of that apartment was close, sickly, and oppressive.

Fitz George, then, had his hand upon one of the windows to open it, when a door, which was not the one he had entered at, was suddenly opened, and some one cried out, "Oh! that is you?"

Fitz George turned and saw Annie with her usual look of pretty audacity, most superbly attired for the morning.

"Yes, Annie, I am here to see the Regent."

"That is right, Allan."

"I fancy, Annie, you must forget the old name of Allan, and call me by my new one of Fitz George."

"To be sure I will! Fitz George! I don't like it, though; and I told George I did not. By the bye, he has gone to Windsor, to see the old man."

This was the irreverent way in which the young and sparkling Countess De Blonde spoke of the old King, George the Third.

"So I have been told," replied Allan—we shall still, we find, now and then call him Allan—"so I am told; and for fear the news he brings back with him should be bad, I would not stay here, but that I must see him."

"Something has happened, I can see," said Annie, as she approached Fitz George, and looked him closely in the face.

"You are right, Annie."

"What is it? Is Marian well?"

"Oh, quite well, thank heaven!"

"I say thank heaven too. What is it then that makes you look so serious?'

"My mother."

"Oh, yes. It is of her?"

"It is, indeed."

"She is ill, I suppose—perhaps dead? Is it so, Allan?"

"I cannot say so; but by one of the strangest chances in the world, I have become aware that she is a prisoner in the Tower of London."

"No! no!"

"It is indeed so, Annie."

"The old Tower of London? Why, George once promised that he would have all the old keys found and take me over it, into the dungeons that nobody ever sees, and that nobody has ever been in for a thousand years."

"Not quite so long as that, Annie."

"Well, it was a good long time, however. But tell me all about it, Fitz George. I am glad George is not at home, because you will have time to tell me first, and I shall be able to help you when he does come back, you know."

"I am sure you will, Annie."

"To be sure. Come, now, sit down, and let me know all about it."

Allan himself was not at all sorry to have an opportunity of consulting Annie, in the first instance, in regard to what had happened to the Dark Woman, and he willingly related to her all he knew on the subject.

"Let me see the pocket-book," said Annie.

Fitz George handed it to her, but she could not take upon herself, any more than himself, to say to whom it had belonged.

The fact was, that Colonel Hanger had been particularly careful, like most persons connected with the "turf"—that is to say, gambling on horse-racing—to put no name in his pocket-book, so that if he lost it, or if his pocket were even picked of it, there would be no evidence of the way in which he meant to "make up his book."

"I don't know whose this is," said Annie, "but I will find out,"

"Can you?"

"Oh, yes! leave me alone for that."

"But what of my mother?"

Annie considered for an amazingly long time, taking into view how generally rapid she was in her conclusions. Then she spoke with a sound, solid sense that could scarcely have been expected from her.

"Look here, Fitz George: the Regent knows, of course, all about this?"

"You think so?"

"Oh, of course! And I can tell you who also, I think, knows all about it; and that is Colonel Hanger."

"I have heard of him."

"He is as great a rascal as Moys."

"Then he need not be a greater; for rascality, I fancy, can scarcely go further."

"That's true enough; but as you want to get your mother out of the Tower, it won't do to be too—too—what shall I say?—angry about it, because she has threatened the Regent, and led him a sad life, you know."

"That is true, Annie."

"Therefore, then, he must be secured in some way against her, or, do you see, she had better remain in the Tower."

It was quite impossible, amenable to reason as he was, that Fitz George could fail to see the justness of this reasoning, and he looked down with a sigh. He felt how utterly impossible it would be to extract anything like a promise from the Dark Woman to cease agitating for what she called her own and his rights.

"Then I fear," he said, "that she will have to remain in the Tower."

"We will see what can be done. But what does Marian say?"

"She says that the Regent ought to be let know that I am aware of where my mother is; but that it ought to be told him as if I did not think that he knew it already."

"That is right. He will pretend to be surprised; and then we shall be able to do just as we please. By the by, I wanted to see you, Allan."

"What for, Annie?"

"Wait a bit."

Annie flew from the room with her usual impetuosity, and, in a few moments, returned with a pair of very elegant pistols.

"Look here!" she said. "Tell me what you think of these, now?"

"Capital pistols, I should say. But what do you want with them, Annie?"

"A young friend of mine is going to fight a duel."

"Indeed!"

"Yes; and he has asked me to lend him a pair of pistols, and to get him a second. Now, if you think these pistols are really good, I will lend them to him, since they belong to the Regent; and what is his, you know, is mine."

"Annie! Annie! I would advise you to have nothing to do with such affairs."

"But I can't help having to do with this one, so you will be the second?"

"Who? I?"

"Just you."

"Impossible!"

"I don't see anything impossible in it. Of course, if you won't, you won't! People are very fond of saying things are impossible that they don't want to do."

"But, Annie!"

"But, Fitz George!"

"Let me reason with you."

"Don't!—oh, don't! The idea, now, of anybody wanting to reason with me! Come, Allan,—or Fitz George, whichever you like best to be called,—I ask you a favour; and if you wish to refuse it to me, why, of course, you can, and there is, then, no occasion to say another word about it."

"Annie, I will not refuse you."

"That's right!"

"But——"

"Now, if you go on saying 'but,' and 'if,' and all that sort of thing, I will get some one else to do the favour for my young friend; and then you will be sorry for it, perhaps, as long as you live."

"Well, I will say no more; but——"

"Hilloa! you said 'but' again!"

"I did not mean in the hesitating sense. And if——"

"Hoy! Stop! You said 'if!'"

"Annie! Annie! I was only going to say that I should like to know the name of your young friend."

"Cornet Dorville—Light Cavalry."

"And his opponent?"

"Sir Hinckton Moys."

"That villain?"

"Yes, that villain! And now, I suppose, you have no objection to be second to my young friend, the Cornet?"

"No; but do let me make one remark."

"Go on, then."

"Does the Regent know that you have a young friend, a cornet in the Light Dragoons?"

"That's an impertinent question, and I won't answer it. If you mean to ask anything further you can retract your promise; but otherwise you can come here at eleven o'clock to-night, and the little affair can come off."

"Here, Annie? Here, at eleven to-night?"

"Yes; in the old ball-room."

"Stop! stop!"

"I won't stop. The duel is to take place here, in the Palace. The old ball-room has not been opened since the marriage of George the Third to what's-her-name, the old Queen. I however, have the keys, and it is there my young friend, the Cornet, will, I hope, teach Sir Hinckton Moys a lesson."

"This is a mad-brained affair, Annie, altogether."

"No, it ain't. I cannot fight the rascal myself. The Regent won't let you fight him. Then who is to fight him, I should like to know, but some other friend of mine who is under no such restriction? I have the duel here in the Palace in case my young friend Dorville should be hurt; because, in that case, I can take care of him at once, you see. Come, now, don't look so serious. Will you come, or will you not?"

"I must."

"Of course you must. The Regent will be out till twelve o'clock to night, for he dines at Richmond, at the White Lodge, provided nothing has happened at Windsor of much consequence, so I shall expect you at eleven."

"I will come."

"That's right. Ah! I hear sounds that proclaim an arrival."

The rapid beating of the drums of the Guard announced, even to the unpractised ears of Fitz George, that some great personage had arrived at

St. James's; and in the course of a few minutes the principal door of the apartment in which Mr. Fitz George and Annie were was thrown open, and a gentleman usher announced—" His Highness the Regent."

The Prince entered the room with a quick step. He had on an overcoat, richly trimmed with sable, and there was haste and some excitement about his air and manner.

"Ah, Fitz George," he said, "you are here! Good morning, Annie. You look charming "

"Of course I do," said Annie. "It would be only difficult for me to look otherwise."

"I hope," said Fitz George, "that your Royal Highness brings good news from Windsor."

The Regent bent upon him a curious look, and Fitz George at once felt how equivocal must sound that expression "good news."

He meant that he hoped the old King was better, but the real good news to the Regent would be that he was much worse.

There was rather an awkward pause, and then the Regent said, hastily. "Good news, Fitz George? Oh, yes! The King is better."

"I am glad to hear it."

"But still a prisoner to his room."

"Ah, sir! that word prisoner is so suggestive to me just now that I cannot help repeating it, by informing you of what will, no doubt, surprise you; namely, that Linda de Chevenaux is a prisoner in the Tower."

The Regent staggered back a pace or two.

"Some officious persons," added Fitz George, "have placed her there.

"And properly enough," said Annie, "unless some security can be given that she will no longer torment or threaten the Regent."

The Prince looked at the Countess de Blonde gratefully, and it was evident he had expected she, too, would be against him, and it was quite a relief to find her arguing on his side of the question.

"In the Tower, say you?" he said.

It was quite evident from the tone of these words that the Regent meant to keep up the idea that it was news to him.

Fitz George was well content that the Regent should adopt this course, which was the best possible one for the object he had in view; since if the Prince professed ignorance of the incarceration of the Dark Woman in the Tower, it would be out of his power to justify the act.

"I was quite sure," said Fitz George, "that your Highness had but one object in view in regard to that unhappy person."

"Oh, of course! but one object — but one object—peace and quiet!"

"I will undertake that she shall not be liberated until I have received from her such assurances as shall satisfy your Highness. All I request is that you will arm me with authority to open her prison doors for her the moment I have such assurances; and I promise on my sacred word of honour that I will not open them upon any inducement short of perfect security to your Highness."

The Prince drew a long breath of relief, for, after all, the Dark Woman in the Tower was an embarrassment in more ways than one.

So long as she remained there, it placed him under a perpetual obligation to Colonel Hanger.

There was always the risk, too, of the affair getting into the newspapers; and at that period the Regent had a morbid kind of dread of the press.

Regents, princes, kings, and emperors have not been able to get rid of such a dread to the present day, but have rather found it increase upon them.

"That will do," said Annie, "capitally," interposing. "That will do capitally, you see, George. Neither he nor I wish that Linda de Chevenaux should worry your life out, because you're useful to me and useful to him. So now give him an order to take her out of the Tower when he pleases, and he will take care not to do so improperly."

"Oh, with pleasure—with pleasure!" said the Regent. "I am only too happy to meet your views, Fitz George; but you know it was impossible to continue exposed to the caprices of—of—one who—who——"

"Your Highness need say no more. The justification of self-defence is always complete."

"Come now, George," said Annie, "write an order for the release of Linda de Chevenaux at once, and let Fitz George have it on his promise to use it properly."

The Regent thought he was getting out of the affair very handsomely, and he wrote quite an unconditional order composed of two parts—one of which admitted Mr. Fitz George to the Tower at any time he pleased, as a visitor to Linda de Chevenaux, while another sentence gave him authority to take her away at his pleasure.

"That will do," said Annie; "and mind, now, Fitz George—dear me! I find I've got quite into the habit of calling you that Fitz—mind, now, I mean what I say—although I've helped you to get this document from George, I'm not going to have my property destroyed and worried by any Dark Woman, or light woman, or a woman of any other colour in the world! So if you let her free without any condition for the preservation of my property, I shall be against you!"

"What do you mean by your property?" said the Regent

"Why, you, to be sure!" cried Annie; "and now come and have some lunch, for I'm as hungry as a pig!"

CHAPTER CLXII.

FITZ GEORGE MEETS WITH A TERRIBLE SHOCK IN THE TOWER.

WHEN the intelligence first reached Fitz George that his mother was an inmate of the Tower, and he knew at the same time that his father, the Regent, had denied all knowledge of the fact, he might well be excused for thinking that he was on the eve of a painful scene between him and the Regent, which might possibly end in a complete rupture between them.

Thanks to the judicious advice of Marian, and the good management of Annie, Countess de Blonde, such painful scene had been entirely avoided, and Fitz George found that he had achieved his object without any needless irritation.

So anxious was he to have an interview with that poor, half-bewildered intellect, which he could not but feel had suffered more for his sake than for its own, that he hesitated with himself after leaving St. James's Palace, whether to proceed home or go at once to the Tower. But affection carried the day, and making what speed he could, he took his way to Buckingham Street, to inform Marian of the perfect success of the mode she had suggested of managing the Regent, and compassing the liberation of the Dark Woman.

Marian was well pleased to hear the report of what had taken place at the Palace; but she would not allow her husband to lose sight of the express conditions on which the order of liberation had been given.

"You, Allan," she said, "have a speciality of feeling in regard to Linda de Chevenaux which no one else can pretend to; and, therefore, you must not consider that either Annie or myself must allow you to forget for a moment that there is another party who must be considered in the matter. Reprehensible as the Regent's conduct in all respects may have been, he has still a kind of right to protect himself; and unless you quarrel with him definitively, and accept all the conditions which your mother lays down as those of her existence, you must admit that right, and you cannot liberate her until she solemnly promises to take a new view of the future."

"I am guided by you, Marian, and will continue to be so. Trust to my discretion. I will not now mar your fortunes by allowing feeling to get the better of reason; and for her own sake, too, my unhappy mother must oe coerced into some course which will dissipate those wild, ambitious dreams which have been the bane of her existence. So soon as daylight droops to-day I will repair to the Tower, for I feel that I must give myself some hours in which to think. And now, Marian, I have another strange affair on which to consult you, or rather of which I wish to inform you—for I have given a sort of promise to Annie which I cannot break."

Both surprise and consternation filled the breast of Marian when Allan informed her of Annie's mad project of engaging some one to fight a duel with Sir Hinckton Moys—since he, Allan, was forbidden to do so by the Regent, his father.

"I know not who it can possibly be," he said, "that she has taken into her confidence so far. She calls him Dorville, and speaks of his being a cornet in some light cavalry regiment. I know not what to think or what to hope. It is not either for you, or myself, Marian, to be rejoiced at her precarious connexion with the Regent; but yet, while she keeps up a sort of romantic constancy towards him, the affair assumes a different character to what it would wear if Annie were wild and fleeting in her affections. Indeed, and in truth, I know not what to do."

"You have promised her, Allan, and you must go to the Palace. I will not deny that I shall be full of fears and anxieties until your return; and yet about the whole conduct of Annie and her management with the Regent, there is so much discretion, so much apparent carelessness and abandonment, and yet at the same time so much tact and talent, that I have lost the sensation of believing that anything will ever go amiss with her."

Fitz George may now be said to have plenty to do and to think of. He had a faint sort of hope—but it was only a faint one—that the mono-tony of the Dark Woman's imprisonment in the Tower might have calmed her excitement and brought sager counsels to her mind.

And yet when he began to think how she had almost driven him from her presence when last he saw her in that house in Hanover Square, because he would not give himself up to her wild caprices, he began to think that, although he might see her in the Tower by virtue of the authority he had so to do, he might yet, in accordance with the promise by which he was bound, be compelled to leave her there.

The darkness set in early; and when Fitz George presented himself at the postern gate of the Tower, the night guards were placed, and the period had passed for the admission of strangers on casual business.

Fitz George had specially wished this to be the case, for his business was of that character at the ancient fortress that he did not wish it to excite the observation of strangers.

An uneasy feeling of apprehension came across him as he rapped at the postern.

Who exactly to ask for he knew not, and he took refuge in saying to the Yeoman who appeared at the small wicket, "I've an order, under the hand of the Regent, to see a prisoner. To whom should it be presented?'

This was an announcement which, of course, produced to Fitz George immediate admission.

"The Lieutenant-Governor, sir, you must see with such an order."

The Yeoman looked curiously by the light of a lantern, which was just within the postern gate, at the half-sheet of paper which Fitz George carried in his hand; and there was a kind of expression upon the face of the man which made Fitz George put a question to him.

He was the more inclined to put that question, inasmuch as, for the first moment that such an idea had taken possession of him, he thought it possible that Linda de Chevenaux's presence in the Tower might have been only a temporary measure, for the purpose of lulling suspicion in regard to some other and more real place of imprisonment, to which she might by this time have been removed.

"Do you know this name of Linda de Chevenaux?" said Fitz George to the Yeoman.

"We never know anything here, sir," was the reply; "but the Lieutenant knows everything."

Fitz George was compelled to be satisfied with this official reply. But still there was a look and manner about the man which filled him with an unknown dread.

A deep feeling of depression came over the spirits of Fitz George as he was conducted across the drawbridge of the moat, which at that period was half-full of stagnant water.

The lodgings of the Lieutenant abutted upon the Tower Green, not far from the chapel; and not a word passed between Fitz George and the Yeoman as the latter lighted him through the dreary fortress.

The password was given to the sentinels briefly; and it was a relief to the burdened imagination of Fitz George when the Yeoman paused at quite a modern door, and, turning to him, said, "Here, sir, are the lodgings of the Lieutenant, who will, no doubt, answer all your questions about Linda de Chevenaux."

There was something threatening and equivocal about these words, which struck forcibly upon the heart of Fitz George; but although the impulse was strong within him to ask another question of this man, he forbore to do so.

The Yeoman rang a bell sharply; and Fitz George had to pass several officials before he was shown into a small, well-lighted room, in which was seated a tall, elderly man, who rose to receive him.

The imagination of Fitz George had become excited, and, without uttering a word, he placed the order of the Regent before the Lieutenant of the Tower.

It seemed to Fitz George that the Lieutenant took a much longer time to read the document than was necessary; and he could only hazard, in his own mind, a supposition to account for that fact, that the Lieutenant was pretending to read, while, in reality, he was considering what answer

No. 74.—DARK WOMAN.

he should give to the bearer of that order of liberation.

Their eyes then met, and Fitz George could keep silent no longer. He spoke impatiently.

"Well, sir," he said, "you have read the order, and you seem to me to have well considered it; do you dispute it or obey it?"

"It is an autograph order, sir, from his Highness the Regent"

"You recognise it?"

"I do; although a little informal, on account of no seal being attached to it."

"But that informality, sir, I presume, is of little account when committed by the Regent himself."

"Of no account whatever."

"Then, sir——"

"Do not be impatient. You're a young man, and probably have some special feeling interested in this case, which is full of mystery."

"Sir," said Fitz George, "it is not to discuss with you the mystery of the case that I am here, but to see a certain prisoner, whose name you find on that order."

"Linda de Chevenaux?"

"Yes, sir—Linda de Chevenaux; and I beg of you to conduct me to her, or let some of your subordinates do so."

"That is just the difficulty."

"The difficulty?"

"Yes, sir; for we have not the slightest notion where she is."

"Good heavens! can that be possible?"

"Sit you down, sir, and I will tell you. To show as much courtesy as possible to a lady, this Linda de Chevenaux was not placed either in one of the prison towers, or one of the dungeons. She was accommodated in the Beauchamp—commonly known as the Bloody Tower."

"An ominous name, sir," said Fitz George, faintly.

"Oh, sir, a name is nothing! There are no sanguinary doings in the Tower of London now."

"Go on, sir, go on—tell me all you have to say."

"To that tower there is but one entrance, which was well guarded. The doors this morning were found locked and intact—the sentinels had been undisturbed—but the prisoner was gone."

"Gone, sir?"

"Vanished!"

"What can be the meaning of this? What am I to believe? What am I to think?"

The Lieutenant shrugged his shoulders, and elevated his eyebrows.

"I wish I could answer you, sir," he said; "but I have no theory upon the subject. The affair is a mystery to me. A prisoner is brought under warrant from the Privy Council—I take every precaution for her security—those precautions all remain undisturbed, but she vanishes. It has been my duty to make a report to the Constable of the Tower—that I have done—and, no doubt, it will be his duty again to report to the Privy Council, sir. I have nothing more to say."

Fitz George felt stupefied and bewildered for a moment. He could not doubt the good faith of the Lieutenant, who told him so plainly and distinctly all he knew himself upon the subject; and it was rather from a want of something to say, than that he really hoped to acquire any information by such a proceeding, that he said, "Could you do me the favour, sir, to show me the place in which the prisoner was confined?"

"With pleasure, sir."

"I will not trouble you personally."

"I shall not consider it a trouble—it is a duty. I am naturally desirous of showing every possible respect to this order from his Highness the Regent, and I am only very sorry that I have not the prisoner to surrender up to you, which I should have done at your request without the slightest hesitation."

The Lieutenant rung a bell as he spoke; and to the man who attended in answer to the summons, he said, "Let the Under Warden and two Yeomen attend me to the Bloody Tower immediately."

The man retired to execute the order, and Fitz George could only look in the face of the Lieutenant, totally at a loss what else to ask him. Perhaps the Lieutenant felt that this young man had more than an ordinary interest in the fate of the prisoner, and he rather now anticipated some natural question which might have arisen to the lips of Fitz George.

"I've made every possible search," he said. "I am convinced that there has been no breach of trust or treachery of any kind. The matter remains to me inexplicable. The keys of the doors were in the hands of the Under Warden. A sentinel was on special duty beneath the arch of the Tower, but still the prisoner has disappeared."

"There are no hiding places?"

"Oh, none whatever! But I wish to give you every satisfaction in my power. And now, sir, if you will follow me, I will conduct you to the chamber which was in the occupation of this Linda de Chevenaux, for I can hear that the Yeomen are without, and are waiting for us."

With a dreary feeling of disappointment, Fitz George followed the Lieutenant, and the party of five persons made their way to that tower from which the Dark Woman had so mysteriously disappeared.

Up the narrow, winding stairs Fitz George and the Lieutenant made their way. They reached that low, threatening-looking door, studded with iron, and the ponderous lock grated heavily and harshly to the key which the Under Warden produced.

Then came the ornamental door, with the brass latch; then the ante-room; the other door of similar construction; and then as the Lieutenant of the Tower held up a lantern, which he had taken from one of the Yeomen, Fitz George found himself in that dreary chamber which had been for so brief a space inhabited by the Dark Woman, and which either the dreams of imagination, or the reality of supernatural power, had peopled with such fearful and fanciful images.

There was the old, black, wooden bedstead, with its elaborate carvings.

There was the ancient escritoire in which the Dark Woman had made such strange discoveries.

There were the faded tapestries on the walls gently moving as the outer air forced its way into the chamber, as though that apartment of mystery and murder were instinct with a strange life, and the tapestries and the walls themselves breathed faintly.

"And this is the room?" said Fitz George, with a sigh.

"This was the apartment," said the Lieutenant, "in which Linda de Chevenaux was a prisoner."

Fitz George turned twice round upon his heels, and then, with a deep sigh, he acknowledged to himself the truth of what the Lieutenant had said—namely, that there was no hiding place in the tower.

At least, there was none that human eyes could see.

"Vanished! Vanished from here!" said Fitz George.

"Like a spirit," said the Lieutenant.

"It is more than strange, sir."

"I cannot pretend to comprehend it."

The Lieutenant happened to move the lantern at this moment in a particular direction, and some strange rays fell upon the ancient bed.

Fitz George uttered a cry.

"Here is blood!" he said.

The Lieutenant shook his head.

"I know there is," he said. "It only increases the mystery."

"But, sir!"

Fitz George faced the Lieutenant, almost threateningly.

"Sir! Do you not think—do you not suppose—does the terrible idea not grow up to the semblance of truth in your brain, that there has been some foul play here?"

"It is not possible, sir."

"But the blood?"

"I cannot comprehend it. I can say no more."

"Then I, sir, will know more some day and hour, and then I will say more. Oh, well is this tower called the Bloody Tower! It is a place for evil deeds—for blood and for murder."

The Lieutenant looked pale and anxious, but not at all angry, at the fierce conjectures raised by his visitor.

It was evident that he was to the full as much puzzled as Fitz George could be about the disappearance of the Dark Woman.

No person could possibly act the state of feeling that this official of the old fortress exhibited, and soon Fitz George began to be ashamed of a passion which, by its expression, seemed to accuse perhaps an innocent man.

"Sir," he said, in a much more gentle tone, "I have appeared here but as the messenger of his Highness the Regent in this affair; but I have a personal and special interest of my own in the matter, the acknowledgment of which, I hope, you will accept as some excuse for an expression of feeling which you may feel has done you an injustice."

"Say no more, sir," replied the Lieutenant. "I only wish I could unravel the mystery that besets this transaction."

"And I say 'Amen' to that wish."

"Should I be able to throw any new light upon it, where shall I address you, sir?"

"At St. James's Palace."

"And by the name on this order?"

"Yes; that is my name."

Fitz George felt that he could do no more in the Tower. The Dark Woman had disappeared; and he was about to leave the place with a heavy heart, when he bethought him that the Lieutenant would be able to tell him to a certainty who had conducted his mother to the State prison.

"Sir," he said, "you tell me that a sufficient warrant was brought here for the custody of Linda de Chevenaux."

"Most certainly."

"I have heard and read, then, that it is the custom to give a receipt to the person who brings a State prisoner."

"It is the custom."

"To whom, then, sir, was the receipt given for this unhappy and mysteriously-lost Linda de Chevenaux?"

The Lieutenant hesitated for a moment or two, as if he doubted the propriety of replying to this question; and Fitz George, seeing that such was the case, did not wish to press it.

"Pardon me, sir," he said. "I withdraw the inquiry."

"Nay, sir, I cannot see that I ought to hesitate to tell you, although for the moment I had a doubt upon the subject."

"I shall be glad, then, to know."

"It was a man who is known by the name of Colonel Hanger."

The blood seemed to retreat to the heart of poor Fitz George as he heard this name; for he knew Hanger by repute, and he doubted not but he was capable of quite as great a crime as might be involved in disposing of the Dark Woman, even by death.

When Fitz George left the Tower, his feelings were most painfully excited.

And yet he knew not what to do.

It was some time—so entirely engrossed was he with painful reflections concerning the mysterious disappearance of his mother—before he recollected his appointment with the fair Countess of Blonde, at the hour of eleven, at St. James's.

When that recollection did come to his mind, it brought with it a ray of hope.

"I will confide all to Annie," he said. "She will advise me. And it will be strange, too, if she should not find the power to aid me. Yes, I will take counsel of Annie, the Countess de Blonde."

CHAPTER CLXIII.

ANNIE, THE COUNTESS, PERPLEXES AND TERRIFIES SIR HINCKTON MOYS, AT ST. JAMES'S.

THERE was ample time for Fitz George to go home to his house at the river-end of Buckingham Street, in the Strand, before it would be necessary for him to repair to St. James's, to keep his appointment with the Countess de Blonde.

Fitz George, therefore, had the advantage of a conference with the calmer judgment of Marian as regarded the mystery of the Tower.

Marian's proposition at once was that the Dark Woman had escaped.

The reader knows how true an explanation that was of the whole affair; but the imagination of Fitz George was too much excited on the subject to enable him to look upon it with the calm eyes of reason, with which Marian regarded it.

He was satisfied, however, that she approved of his idea of consulting Annie; and so at about half-past ten that night Fitz George left his home again to take his way to the Palace.

It was a very strange thought and reflection to him that now he was a readily admitted and honoured visitor at the Palace of the Regent, when but a short time since he had been a nameless foundling, and his very life seemed to hang upon the will of such a man as Sir Hinckton Moys.

But such are the mutations of human existence; and no one could be said to experience them to a more graphic extent than Allan Fitz George.

But now we must leave him for a brief space, as he made his way across the Park to keep his appointment with the Countess de Blonde, while we step into the private apartments of that vivacious personage.

Annie was now in high spirits.

The Regent had departed from St. James's at about eight o'clock to go to the White Lodge at Richmond, where he was giving one of those suppers for which the modern Sardanapalus was famous.

It was not, however, that she had got rid of the

Prince of Wales until the morrow Annie was pleased and in high spirits, but because she had something to do which excited all her vivacity, and promised sport and pleasure.

What that something was we shall quickly see. Perhaps the sagacious reader, who knows Annie so well already, has a guess at it.

There was a young girl who was a native of the East Indies, who for a short time had been in the service of Annie, and the pleased devotion with which this young girl waited upon her made Annie take much notice of her, and like her attendance.

In what may be called Annie's dressing-room, was this young Hindoo girl and the Countess.

What the precise native name of the Indian girl was it is difficult to say, but it was some name that to Annie had sounded like Baby, and so she called the girl by that appellation, whenever she had occasion to address her by name.

"Baby," said the voice of Annie, "what is the time?"

"Half-past five, dear mistress!"

"That will do."

Now we have said the voice of Annie asked this question of Baby; but the person from whom that voice came was as different-looking from the fair Countess de Blonde as any one could very well be.

Standing in front of a tall cheval glass in the dressing-room, appeared a rather small, slim young man, nearly entirely equipped in a handsome Hussar uniform. The hair of this personage was of the darkest brown, and the slight moustache which graced the upper lip was only a shade or two lighter.

There was an elegance and a grace about the figure of the young Hussar which would have made it a very dangerous thing for him to have sauntered down the principal Mall of St. James's Park at the hour of fashionable lounging.

That is to say, it would have been dangerous for the hearts of any young ladies of a very susceptible disposition to have looked upon so much elegance, and almost feminine beauty.

And great would have been the delusion and great the disappointment of the aforesaid young ladies could they then have discovered that the seeming handsome young officer was no other than Annie, Countess de Blonde, in that startling and costly disguise.

But such was the fact.

It was Annie herself who stood before that cheval glass in the attire of a cavalry officer, and from that circumstance it will be surmised that it was she herself who meant to fight with Sir Hinckton Moys in the character of Cornet Dorville, of the Hussars.

"Well, Baby," said Annie, "what do you think of me now?'

"Beautiful!" said Baby.

"But that is not right."

"Dear mistress, what is not right?"

"I don't want to look beautiful."

"But it cannot be helped," said Baby, with the most innocent air in the world.

"I want to look like a man."

Baby shook her head.

"You don't think I do, then?"

"Perhaps to others, but to me who know you it is a difficult thing to fancy you other than my dear good mistress, let you put on what clothing you may."

"To be sure—to be sure," said Annie. "There is truth in that."

"But you always look beautiful."

"Oh! that is because you are dark and I am fair that you say that, Baby."

"You are like the fair and beautiful sunlight, while I am like the night."

"Well, never mind, Baby. Dark people, you know, admire fair ones, and fair people think nothing so handsome as darkness. What's o'clock now?"

"It is close to eleven."

A slight tap came to the door of the apartment as Baby spoke.

Annie stepped behind the cheval glass, which completely hid her, as she said to the Hindoo girl, "Baby, see who that is."

Some conversation in a low tone passed between Baby and another of Annie's attendants at the door; and then, when it was closed, the Hindoo girl said gently, "Mr. Fitz George is in the palace, and desires the honour of seeing you, dear mistress."

"All's right. He is punctual."

"But, dear mistress——."

"What now, Baby?"

"Will you see him in that dress?"

"Certainly; but he will not see me in it. Give me now that cloak with the ermine trimmings, and the hood that I can cover over my head. He will not now catch a glimpse of the uniform."

"But will he not think these rather strange?"

The Hindoo girl pointed to the slight moustache, which Annie had had a good deal of trouble to stick with gum to her upper lip.

"To be sure he would—to be sure he would! What a goose I am! Thank you, Baby—that would have ruined all. Some warm water, Baby. I must take them off now, and put them on again when I play the officer."

Annie disencumbered her pretty face from the mock moustache, and then folding the ermine cloak closely around her, and bringing the hood of it so far round her face that the dark wig beneath which it had cost her no little trouble to confine her really beautiful fair hair, she took a careful observation of herself in the mirror, and considered that there was nothing observable about her which could suggest to Fitz George her disguise.

"Baby!" she cried.

"Yes, dear mistress!"

"Put but one light in the small dining-room. Show Mr. Fitz George, then, into it, and say I will come to him."

Baby went to execute these orders, and Annie waited her return with some impatience.

"I will give the villain a fright," she said, "which shall make him fly from England with a precipitation he does not now dream of. Where can Willes be, I wonder. He dare not be out of the way when I have ordered him to attend me."

Annie listened to a slight scratching noise on the panel of the door.

"Ah!" she said, "that is Willes."

She opened the door about a couple of inches, and said sharply, "Wait in the breakfast-room."

"Yes, madam; but——'

"Be quiet; I don't want any advice."

"I was only going to say——"

"Don't say it, then. Be off."

Annie shut the door abruptly, and then again waited for Baby to return, which she soon did.

"Well, well?" said Annie.

"Mr. Fitz George waits, dear mistress; and I am told to say, by one of the ushers in waiting, that Sir Hinckton Moys is in the Old Throne Room."

"That is right. Now wait here for me; I shall soon come back."

The room into which Allan Fitz George had been shown by Baby was one of that brilliant suite which had been so gorgeously and lavishly decorated by the Regent for the Countess de Blonde.

The one solitary wax-light which the Hindoo girl had placed in it in pursuance of the orders of Annie scarcely permitted more than a dubious kind of twilight to irradiate the apartment.

That faint light, however, added rather than took away from the rich, gorgeous aspect of the room.

The gilding looked brighter and more glittering, and the heavy silken hangings more massive and imposing.

Fitz George could not but admire the beauty and repose of the room while he waited in it for a few minutes until Annie appeared.

He had, however, quite made up his mind to dissuade her, if possible, from the mad project she had conceived.

"Well!" said Annie. "Here you are, Allan."

"Yes, Annie, I am here, because I promised you that I would be."

"The best reason in the world."

"But, now, Annie——"

"Well, Allan?"

"Let me hope that calmer judgment——"

"What?"

"Calmer judgment."

Now, what *do* you mean by making game of me in that way? As if I was ever calmer in all my life, or ever had any judgment."

"You have plenty of judgment, Annie, when you please to exercise it."

"Stuff!'

"It is true."

"Well, now, Allan, I will give you a word of advice. Always praise women for their beauty; but don't say anything about their judgment. They don't care about it."

Fitz George shook his head.

"Come, come," added Annie, "don't be confusing your brains by shaking and rattling them about in your head. You know very well what you came here for. It is to be the second of my young friend, Cornet Dorville, in a duel with Sir Hinckton Moys, in the Old Throne Room."

"Annie! Annie!"

"Allan! Allan!"

"Are you quite mad?"

"Yes."

Fitz George found it rather difficult to say anything after this candid admission.

"Now are you satisfied?" added Annie.

"I cannot help it."

"Help what?"

"What you choose to do, Annie. But I had been much better pleased if you had let this man alone. Do you know that there is a piece of news

concerning him which places him in rather a strange position."

"What is it?"

"It is said that he killed Colonel Hanger this morning, in Hyde Park."

"No!"

"I am told so."

"By whom?"

"Willes, not five minutes ago, mentioned it to me."

"Indeed! Ah, that was what he wanted to tell me! Well, there is an ugly rascal the less in the world, if it be quite true, Allan."

"He was a villain!"

"No doubt about that. But you must now wait here, and I will send the Cornet to you. He is a dear fellow!"

"Annie! Annie! does the Regent approve of dear fellows—of cornets of light cavalry being in St. James's at this hour, while he is at the White Lodge?"

"Quite."

"Indeed!"

"Yes, indeed! And I can tell you, if he thought that Cornet was not here, the Regent would be very likely to rise from his supper table at the White Lodge and come post to London."

"Then I begin to suspect——"

"Suspect! What? What?"

"That the Prince of Wales himself has arranged all this affair."

"My dear Allan," laughed Annie, "you are quite a conjuror. But I will send the Cornet to you. He is young, but brave. He knows quite well the way about the Palace, and will conduct you to the Old Throne Room, where Sir Hinckton Moys is waiting."

"Then he has accepted this strange meeting?"

"I suppose so. Stop a moment. Here is a copy of the letter the Cornet wrote to him. You can amuse yourself by reading it, while I go and send him to you."

"I should like to see it."

"There it is, then. Read away. The Cornet will not be many moments, as he is only two or three rooms off."

The copy of a letter which Annie placed in the hands of Allan Fitz George, and which she had got Willes to write for her, ran as follows:—

"Guard Room, St. James's.
"To Sir Hinckton Moys, Knight.
  Sir,
"You are a villain!
"The key which you left on the floor of the Titian Gallery of St. James's is enclosed for your use again, since it will enable you to enter the Palace once more, in order, if you have the least spark of courage, and if you do not wish to be posted at Charing Cross to-morrow as a coward and a poltroon, that you may reach the Palace at a little after eleven o'clock to answer for your general conduct to,
  "Sir,
"Your most complete enemy and despiser,
      "AUGUSTUS DORVILLE,
          "Cornet, King's Hussars."

This note sounded on perusal a very strange one for any man to write to another; and perhaps Annie risked some discovery or suspicion of her little dramatic plot by letting Fitz George see it.

Allan had not, however, much time given him for reflection, for the door of the apartment was opened quietly, and a Hussar officer entered, saying rapidly as he did so, "I presume I have the pleasure to see Mr. Allan Fitz George?"

CHAPTER CLXIV.

SIR HINCKTON MOYS IS ALARMED, AND TAKES POST-HORSES FOR DOVER. — AN UNEXPECTED ARRIVAL.

A VERY important element of deception in the disguise in which Annie had enveloped herself consisted in the rapidity with which she appeared to change from one character to another.

It was quite impossible that the most accomplished actor or actress could have changed a costume so completely in so short a space of time as that which elapsed since the Countess de Blonde left the apartment in which Allan Fitz George was waiting, and the apparent young officer of Hussars entered it.

But then Annie had only to go to her apartment and fling off the ermine cloak and hood, and then slip her arms into the Hussar jacket, while the Hindoo girl assisted her in replacing the false moustache, and she was perfectly ready to carry out her part in the drama of the evening.

Allan Fitz George had no suspicion of the real truth of the transaction; and, to the intense delight of Annie, he bowed to the seeming young officer in a manner which convinced her that he was perfectly deceived, and had not the remotest conception on earth of her identity.

"Sir," said Fitz George, "I suppose it is too late now to reason with you about this affair, since you will, no doubt, consider your honour as a soldier and a gentleman pledged to carry out the wishes of the Countess de Blonde."

"Quite— quite!" said Annie, speaking a good couple of octaves lower than her ordinary voice.

"And, sir, you intend, then, to make St. James's Palace actually the arena of a conflict, which, if it took place at all, should certainly have been in some other place than under the roof of the Regent."

Annie was afraid to trust herself to speak much for fear some slight cadence of the voice—notwithstanding she took every possible pains to disguise it—should betray her identity to Fitz George.

But still she could not help replying to this observation which had been made by Allan, and she did so as shortly as possible.

"The whim of a pretty woman, sir," she said,— "the whim of a pretty woman, that is all I can say."

"But the anger of the Regent, sir?"

"That is not to be feared in the least."

From these last words, Allan Fitz George was more than ever inclined to believe that the Prince had actually given Annie leave to conduct this extraordinary affair according as her own fancy suggested.

He was reflecting for a few seconds only whether he could suggest any modification of its romantic character, but he gave up the idea; and stopping the young Hussar shortly as he was whistling a popular air—for that was an accomplishment in which Annie, Countess de Blonde, happened to be an adept—Fitz George put an end to all further argument on the question by saying, "Well, sir, I have promised the Countess de Blonde to second you in this affair. I should have been much better pleased to have been the principal; but, no doubt, she has informed you that the Regent has interdicted me from fighting with Sir Hinckton Moys?"

"Oh, yes—yes!" said Annie.

Regretting that interdiction extremely, I am not altogether so ill-pleased as I might be to adopt, at all events, the condition of being second to you, and to wish you every possible good fortune in the encounter."

"Thank you—thank you; I only fight for amusement."

"Sir!"

"Oh, that's all—that's all! Some people may think the Countess de Blonde pretty, but I don't. Some may think her worth fighting for, but I don't."

"Then, sir," said Allan Fitz George, with some warm, "give me leave to say, I differ from you on both these points. I am not given to flattery; but the word 'pretty,' to my mind, is far from being expressive of the fascinating beauty of the fair Countess de Blonde."

"Indeed! You think so?"

"Indeed, I do think so, sir! And as to her being worth fighting for, my opinion is, that although she now occupies a social position which grieves me to the soul, she has a thousand excellent and amiable qualities, an ingenuous feeling, and excellent intellect—a heart full of gentle and tender sensibilities, which should make it an honour for any man to draw a sword in her defence."

The seeming young Hussar for a moment placed his hands over his eyes, and, to the surprise of Allan Fitz George, he who had spoken so slightingly and disparagingly of Annie, was evidently shaken with a deep emotion at the words which he, Allan, had just uttered.

"Ah, sir!" cried Fitz George, "I can well perceive now that you were jesting with me when you spoke as you did of the Countess de Blonde."

"And are you, sir," said the young Hussar in low tones,—"are you, sir, not jesting with me when you speak of her in the way you do?"

"No, by heaven!"

There was a pause of a few moments' duration, and again that powerful emotion, which seemed to make him tremble in every limb, came over the young officer.

It seemed an effort to him to speak, as he then said suddenly, "Come, sir—follow me; and—for the honour of this Countess de Blonde, so fair and so good as you think her—I will see if good fortune may not permit me to punish the villain who has been her determined enemy, and sought her destruction by every possible means in his power."

"Lead on, sir. I will follow."

While Allan Fitz George is, with some confusion of mind—for he could not well make out who and what that young officer was—following his strange conductor to the Throne Room of old

St. James's Palace, it will be as well that we take a glance at Sir Hinckton Moys, who—in consequence of that letter a copy of which Annie had handed to Allan Fitz George to read—had once more found his way to St. James's Palace.

If Sir Hinckton Moys intended at all to remain in London society, and if he had the faintest idea of ever again permitting himself to be seen even in the gaming-houses of the metropolis, he dared not run the risk of exposing himself to the carrying out of the threat expressed in that letter.

Hence, if an appointment had been made with him under such circumstances in the lower regions themselves, and it had been possible for him to get there, he must have kept it.

The enclosure of the key, too, which he had surrendered to the Regent filled his mind with many conjectures.

He recollected perfectly well laying it down at the feet of the Prince of Wales; and he knew equally well who was present upon that occasion, any one of whom might have had an opportunity of picking it up.

There was a faint hope in his mind that even the Regent had relented, and was willing to think that he, Moys, might still be useful to him.

At all events, like some already singed moth, which hovers round a candle, heedless of all warnings of possible destruction, Moys felt constrained, so to speak, to seek his fortune as often at St. James's Palace as he possibly could.

And although the terms of the letter sent him were strange and peremptory, he scarely thought it possible that he should be coerced into a duel within the precincts of the Palace.

But Sir Hinckton Moys, before he could again be permitted to leave St. James's, was destined to have some strange experiences.

The private key he had let him into the old Palace by one of those gloomy little doors leading from the Colour Court, and thence by various intricate passages he knew he could reach the Titian Gallery, which was a sort of accredited place of waiting for all persons having a discretionary *entré* to the Palace, who had business with the Regent, and waited his leisure for an interview.

There it was, then, that Moys waited in no small surprise at the whole affair, which some presentiment seemed to tell him would not in its result be merely confined to a hostile meeting with the valorous Cornet Dorville.

Sir Hinckton had not been many minutes in the Titian Gallery when one of the lower domestics of the Palace came to him.

"Sir," he said, "I am commanded to show you into an apartment."

"I will follow you," replied Moys.

Now, it was, perhaps, only by accident that this servant used the word "commanded;" but accident or design, it had all its effect upon Moys, simply because it was the word always used in the Palace when an order of the Regent was spoken of.

Other orders from official persons were simply called orders, and nothing else.

The Regent's wishes were always commands.

Upon this very meagre and simple matter, Sir Hinckton Moys raised an airy superstructure of hope.

Surely, the Regent had thought better of his dismissal, and sought again to retain him in his service.

Moys trod the flooring of St. James's with a more confident manner than he had been able to assume on the occasions of his last two or three visits.

He began to feel himself again.

The servant said not another word, but, in pursuance of orders he had had from Willes, the Prince's valet, he led Sir Hinckton Moys to that large apartment in the Palace which went by the name of the Old Throne Room.

It was there, then, Annie, Countess de Blonde, *alias*—for that night only—Cornet Dorville, of the King's Hussars, meant to carry out the little comedy she had projected for the vexation, the humiliation, and the terror of Sir Hinckton Moys.

The room looked, in the dim light of only two wax candles, which the servant lighted, much larger than it really was; for, truth to say, there is not a positively handsome apartment in the whole of the Palace of St. James's.

One end had a raised portion of flooring, on which was the throne, covered with not very clean linen.

Over the throne was a canopy of crimson, about as high as the roof would permit it to go.

The apartment was carpeted with a crimson carpet, in the centre of which was, in a large, sprawling fashion, so as to take up as much room as possible, the royal arms.

Various couches and ottomans round the walls made up the other furniture of the room; but all were dusty, and bore the signs of neglect and long want of use.

It had been years since any king had sat upon that old, dingy, ricketty throne.

Into this room, then, was Sir Hinckton Moys shown; and there he was left.

"Ah!" he said, "I feel quite sure, now, that the Regent will come to me. He has, no doubt, heard that I have got rid of that rascal Hanger, whom I left in Hyde Park this morning, in, I sincerely hope, a bad way; and he cannot do without some one in the capacity in which I have served him,—and served him, I think I can say, best of all."

Sir Hinckton Moys paced the room to and fro as he spoke, and looked impatiently towards the door at which he had entered.

But minute after minute passed away, and no Regent made his appearance.

It was another door, at length, that opened behind the throne, and Sir Hinckton started, and placed his hand upon his sword at the slight creaking sound it made upon its long disused hinges.

Annie, the Countess, in her costume of Cornet Dorville, of the Hussars, made her appearance, accompanied by the unconscious Allan Fitz George.

The dim light was just sufficient to show Sir Hinckton Moys that there were two persons, one of whom was in the costume of a cavalry officer, but he could not at first see their faces.

It was Allan, then, who startled Moys, by the sound of his voice.

"Sir Hinckton Moys," he said, "I have proclaimed you a villain, and I proclaim you one still. The Regent has forbidden me to meet you in the field; but here is a gentleman and an office who defies and challenges you, and it pleases me to act as a second to him."

"It pleases many people," said Moys, in sneering tones, "to act as seconds who would not feel the same pleasure in acting as principals."

"Sir Hinckton Moys," replied Allan Fitz George calmly, "I have once been under the necessity of publicly chastising you for insolence. Beware, sir, that you do not provoke me to do so a second time."

"Insolent!"

Moys half-drew his sword, for he had come to the Palace in full Court costume.

"No, sir," said Allan, "I do not intend to fight with you; but if you draw that sword another inch from its scabbard in threat towards me, I will break the blade over your shoulders."

"Hold!" said Annie, stepping forward, and speaking in the assumed voice she had put on to deceive Allan. "Hold! It is on my account that this man Moys is here; and until my quarrel is settled with him, I cannot permit even such a wrangle as this."

"And who are you, sir?" cried Moys.

"My name is Dorville. Who I am is answered so far. What I am, you may see by my uniform."

"A boy cavalry subaltern."

"Truly, Sir Hinckton, I am not so old and hoary in iniquity as yourself."

"And what, sir, do you want with me?"

"A trifle."

"What, sir?"

"Your head!"

"My—head?"

"Just so, sir. The gay, charming, and witty Countess de Blonde has a desire for it; and not exactly seeing a ready way of procuring the ugly article, she said to me, 'My dear Dorville, you will oblige me by writing a note to Sir Hinckton Moys, asking him to come to St. James's. Send him this key, which I picked up from the floor. It will admit him. And when you see him, pray fight him, and kill him, and bring his head down into the Colour Court, that I may see it.'"

"Pshaw! This is folly!" cried Moys.

"'Most charming Countess,' said I, 'your wishes are my laws.' So I wrote the letter. You got it, of course, sir?"

"I did."

"Very well. And, now, all we have to do is to fight. I am rather pressed for time, and, therefore, wish to get the affair over. I have several appointments this evening yet; and there will be some fair ladies in despair if they do not see me before they sleep."

"Insufferable puppy!" said Sir Hinckton Moys, below his breath.

"Did you speak, sir?"

"I did; and it was to say that, as a gentleman and a man of honour, I never refuse a challenge."

"Very good, sir."

"But——"

"Ah! you are one of those fellows who have always a 'but' when it comes to real fighting."

"No, sir: I was going to say, that if I must kill you, I wish, for my own sake, to do it in the regular way. Send your friend to me, and I will send for a friend of mine, and then time and place can be arranged."

"That is all settled."

"How, sir?"

"The time is now. The place is here!"

"Here? In the Palace?"

"Just so. Here is my friend, Allan Fitz George; and as, surely, two witnesses are enough for a little affair of this sort, I have provided another, who, for the time being, you may call your friend, if you like."

"Who? Who? Oh, the Regent's valet!"

A door was opened, and Willes entered the Throne Room.

"Do you think for a moment," added Moys, "that I will accept as my second a man in his position."

"He is in as good a position as yourself, sir."

"Better," said Willes. "I am Sir Thomas Willes. I was knighted by the Prince of Wales; Sir Hinckton Moys was only knighted by the Lord Lieutenant of Ireland."

"What proof have I of this knighthood?" said Moys.

"My word," said Annie.

"Perhaps, sir, you saw it done?"

"I did."

Moys bit his lips.

"Well," he said, "I will not fight here."

"Then, to-morrow morning," said Annie, "there will be a placard at Charing Cross, proclaiming Sir Hinckton Moys a coward and a poltroon."

"Perdition catch you all!"

"After you, sir," said Annie. "We mean to go another way, if you please. Ah, what is that?"

"Twelve o'clock striking, sir," said Willes.

"Then we will lose no more time," added Annie. "You, my good friend, Mr. Allan Fitz George, be so good as to arrange matters with Mr.—I beg his pardon—Sir Thomas Willes on the account of Sir Hinckton Moys."

"Oh, this is too absurd!" cried Moys.

"Ah, but the Countess de Blonde wants it, nevertheless!"

"What do you mean?"

"You alluded to your head, did you not?"

"Now, by all the fiends——"

"Bravo!"

"By heaven, and the other place, I will fight you; and your death be upon your own head!"

"That's right. I'm ready."

The Countess de Blonde never for a moment forgot that she was playing a part. With admirable tact and discretion she kept up the assumed voice with which she had commenced the whole affair; and even Allan Fitz George was as much in the dark as regarded her identity as Sir Hinckton Moys.

Willes had his lesson previously from Annie, and knew exactly what she wished him to say and do.

Stepping forward towards Allan, he said quietly, "I propose pistols, sir."

"No, no!" cried Sir Hinckton Moys.

"I beg your pardon!" said Willes; "if I am to act for you, you must not interfere."

"Confound you all!"

"I agree, then," replied Allan, as he glanced at what he thought was Cornet Dorville, who signified assent by a nod.

"And as the light is rather deficient," said Willes, "I think each party had better hold a light in one hand, and the pistol in the other; in which case, they can take their stations, one at

each end of the room, and fire, upon the word being given so to do."

"I agree to that," said Allan; "since there is to be a duel in so strange a fashion."

Annie began to whistle an opera air.

Sir Hinckton Moys bit his lips with rage and vexation at being thus forced into a duel, after all his hopes on coming to the Palace.

There was something really provoking to him in the whole transaction; and along with all that was provoking, there was just a dim, glimmering perception on his mind that he was being hoaxed in some way.

How that was, however, he could not exactly see, so he made up his mind to shoot the supposed young Hussar, if he possibly could manage to do so.

CHAPTER CLXV.

BOTH THE REGENT AND ALLAN FITZ GEORGE RECEIVE A TERRIBLE ALARM.

SIR HINCKTON MOYS was getting decidedly angry.

If he were to fall before a pistol-shot in that Old Throne Room of St. James's Palace, who would pity him?

Not a human soul.

Who would avenge him?

No hand of all the great family of mankind would be raised to strike a blow for his memory.

No wonder, then, that, to Moys, this duel, that was so strangely forced upon him, should present itself to his mind in the most uncomfortable colours. But there he was.

He was like a bull in an amphitheatre. **Fight** he must.

He might have paraphrased the words of the tyrant, and cried out—

"They have tied me to a stake,
And I must, bear-like, fight the course"

There was positively no escape for the disgraced courtier, except through the smoke of the pistols, which would so soon awaken unwonted echoes in that old apartment.

"Come, gentlemen," cried Annie, "are you ready with your arrangements?"

"Quite," replied Willes.

"That is well; for I am impatient. As I say, I have appointments, and I don't like to keep fair ladies waiting."

"You will, perhaps, keep them waiting a little longer than you and they expect," muttered Sir Hinckton Moys through his clenched teeth.

"Come, sir," said Allan Fitz George, "if the combat is to take place, the sooner it is over the better."

"I am ready, sir."

"And I; as I told you before!" said Annie. "Really, Sir Hinckton Moys, this is the first time I ever saw you; and the fair Countess de Blonde told me I should find you ugly; but you transcend all my expectations!"

Moys growled out some words that were unintelligible at the moment; and then turning, with almost a fierceness of demeanour, to Willes, he said, "Since, sir, according to the phraseology in use in these affairs, it appears I must call you my friend, let me beg of you to get this affair over, now, with all reasonable expedition."

"Take your places, gentlemen," said Willes.

As he spoke, he handed one of the candlesticks, in which was a wax candle, to Sir Hinckton Moys.

Allan Fitz George placed the other in the hand of Annie.

"I wish you good fortune, sir," he said.

"Oh, have no fear for me!"

"I wish I could think so."

"I never miss my man," added Annie.

These words had the strangest tinge, so to speak, of Annie's natural voice in them, that she had allowed to appear during the whole scene in that ancient apartment.

Allan started at the familiar tone; but so entirely foreign to all his thoughts was the idea of identifying Annie, the Countess, with the young Hussar officer who was about to exchange shots with Sir Hinckton Moys, that he could not at the moment identify the sounds of the voice.

But Annie saw the start.

"What is the matter, sir?" she said, in tones now so well disguised that there was not a trace of her own voce left in them.

Allan thought he must have been mistaken.

"Nothing, sir! Nothing is the matter! Take your place, if you please."

"All's right!" said Annie.

The aspect of affairs in the Old Throne Room was now very curious and interesting.

The two combatants occupied positions facing each other, but as far off from each other as the walls of the apartment would allow them to be.

Willes had placed a chair to indicate the spot at which Sir Hinckton Moys was to stand; and Allan Fitz George had done the same for the so-called Count Dorville.

It looked strange to see the two opponents, each holding a light in the left hand, and looking fixedly at each other.

Moys was very pale. His face looked white and bloodless.

This was not all fear. It was, in good part, passion, mingled with a strange, superstitious kind of apprehension that something very calamitous to himself would surely happen.

Annie wore over the wig she had put on to conceal her own beautiful and luxuriant tresses the military shako of the light cavalry regiment to which she pretended to belong, but the small portion of the face that could be seen beneath was quite composed.

Annie had rubbed some rather coarse Venetian red over her delicate complexion, so that it looked much about the tint that some young man might be proud of, as an evidence of health and exercise.

Allan Fitz George, however, could not help being struck with the slim elegance of the rather *petite* figure of the young officer, as he thought him; and then came to his heart a pang of regret at the idea that he might see that fair, promising young form soon in the embrace of death.

It became an almost irresistible feeling in his mind to try once more to put an end to the contest that seemed about to begin.

"Hold, gentlemen!" he cried—"hold!"

"What is it?" said Annie.

"What now?" yelled Sir Hinckton Moys.

"Permit me to say that this is very singular," remarked Willes, the valet.

"It may be," said Allan. "But I have something to say even at this late hour."

"Some treachery," said Moys.

"You are a villain, sir," replied Allan; "and you speak from the constitution of your own mind."

"Come, come," said Annie, "give us the pistols!"

"No, no!" added Allan Fitz George, in a voice of some emotion—"no! I pray you to hear me. It is true that the Regent has forbidden me to fight with Sir Hinckton Moys, and it is true that I, of all other men, have reason to obey the Prince—a double reason."

"Your own fears and his commands. Ha, ha!" sneered Sir Hinckton Moys.

"No, sir, those are not the double reasons. In obeying him I obey a Prince and a father; but there are special circumstances, in which disobedience to both princes and fathers becomes a virtue."

"No, no!" said Annie.

Perhaps, with her sensitiveness and womanly instincts, she began to have a perception of what Allan Fitz George was about to say.

"Do not say no," he added. "But permit me to say that I think one of those special circumstances has arrived, and that I am justified now in disobeying the Prince and the father."

"What do you mean, sir?" said Annie.

"Only to try his hand at my life, in case you miss the taking it," said Moys.

"No, no!" resumed Allan. "I propose that you, Cornet Dorville, allow me now to take your place and finish this affair, since the quarrel with Sir Hinckton Moys is far more mine than yours."

"That cannot be," said Annie.

"I beg of you, sir, to let it be. As a favour

which, if I live, I shall always remember, I pray you to let it be. I would a hundred times rather stand in your place than act as your second. Give me the light, sir. You act for me as my friend, and let me feel that in becoming a principal in this affair, instead of a spectator, I am acting as I ought."

Annie shook her head.

"The Countess de Blonde," she said, "would lament you much if any accident should happen to you."

"I hope she would not, although——"

"Although what, sir?"

"I cannot help admitting that I have a great affection for her."

"It appears," sneered Sir Hinckton Moys, "that both of you mean to let pass away the opportunity of playing the gallant in favour of the Countess. It is, perhaps, more convenient for you, since, no doubt, you would both be deeply lamented, not to fight at all."

"Not so, sir," added Allan. "The Cornet will, I am sure, confer upon me the great favour of allowing me to take his place, and then you shall have no reason to complain of any further delays."

"I cannot do so," said Annie.

"I beg of you!"

"No, no, no!"

"You hear, Mr. Fitz George," said Willes; "the Cornet cannot do so."

"My honour forbids me," added Annie; "but you may be assured, Mr. Fitz George, that if I survive, both the Regent and the Countess de Blonde shall hear of your chivalry."

Allan sighed. He saw that it was of no use to urge his proposal further.

"Pray," said Sir Hinckton Moys, "how much longer am I to be expected to stand here with a candle in my hand?"

"No longer," cried Annie. "The pistols—the pistols!"

Willes produced the weapons, and paused for a moment, as if in doubt what to do with them.

"How am I to know," said Moys, "that there is not some foul play?"

"What do you mean, sir?" said Allan, firmly.

"Simply that there may be a great difference between those pistols."

Allan was about to make some very angry reply, but Annie stopped him by saying at once, "Let him choose—let him choose! I will take willingly the one he rejects"

To this proposal it was impossible that Sir Hinckton could say a word.

Willes stepped up to him with the pistols, one of which he snatched at quite in a random way; and hastily running the ramrod into the barrel to make sure there was a charge in it, he then held it in his hand ready for action.

"Will you give the word, Mr. Fitz George?" said Willes.

"No. You do so."

"Very well, gentlemen. You will understand that I shall count three, and then I will cry out 'Fire!' and you are neither of you to raise your pistols to a level until you hear that word 'Fire!' Then you can pull the trigger as soon as you like. Will that do, Mr. Fitz George?"

"Yes, yes!"

"Are you agreed to that, both, gentlemen?"

"Agreed!" said Annie.

"Agreed!" muttered Moys.

"And," added Annie, "I will trouble Mr. Fitz George to stand more out of the line of fire."

Allan could hardly at the moment have reasonably explained to himself why it was that he felt a kind of impulse or propensity to dash forward and cover with his own breast the position of the young officer, so as to protect him from the possible bullet that might seek his life.

Perhaps it was one of those occult but natural instincts of human existence which enabled the imagination and the feelings to penetrate the disguise of Annie, although the senses did not.

Fitz George, however, at once stepped back, now that his attention was called to the fact that he was actually in the line of fire.

"One!" said Willes.

It was a strange coincidence that at that moment the clock of St. James's struck one.

"Two!" said Willes.

There was a pause of a moment, during which all the persons in that ancient Throne Room could hear plainly enough the trampling of horses' feet in one of the court-yards of the Palace, and the rapid progress of carriage wheels.

Willes then put himself in an attitude of listening, and then he whispered, "It is the Regent!"

Annie uttered an exclamation of impatience.

"Ah!" said Moys. "Perhaps it is well arranged that his Royal Highness should be in at the death."

"Quick, sir!" cried Annie, addressing Willes. "Quick, sir! If the Regent has unexpectedly returned from the White Lodge at Richmond, we may be interrupted. Give the word, sir, and allow me to get this affair over."

"Three!" said Willes.

The tramp of horses' feet in the Colour Court, and the sound of carriage wheels, continued.

Then there came the beating of a drum. The guard was turned out.

The Regent had indeed most unexpectedly come from Richmond to the Palace.

"Fire!" cried Willes.

Bang! bang!

Two reports followed each other in rapid succession, and the Old Throne Room echoed loud and long to the concussions.

The air was full of blue smoke.

There was a clashing sound; and one of the candlesticks fell from the hand of one of the combatants, and rolled to the floor.

Annie sank back into the chair, close to which she had been standing.

Sir Hinckton Moys stood firm.

"By heaven!" cried Willes, "he has killed the Countess."

"Killed who?" shouted Allan.

"The Countess de Blonde, sir."

"Good heaven!"

Sir Hinckton Moys staggered back the few paces he had advanced, when he saw his antagonist fall, and drop the light and the pistol.

"Who?—who?—what?" he yelled.

"The Countess de Blonde," added Willes. "It is she whom you have shot, in the disguise of a young officer of Hussars."

"Then I am a dead man if I stay twelve hours longer in England!"

With these words, Sir Hinckton Moys made a rush to leave the apartment, but Allan Fitz George, who had just recovered from the terrible shock the words of Willes had given him, by a cross movement interrupted him.

"No, villain, no! Over my breast you may, but not otherwise."

"Way for the Regent!" shouted a voice close at hand.

"We are all lost!" said Willes.

Sir Hinckton Moys did not pause to say another word, but retreating two or three paces from one of the windows of the room, he did one of the most desperate things that, desperate as he was, it could ever have occurred to his imagination to do.

He took one fearful leap against the window, and carrying away the frame-work and the glass with him in one terrible wreck, he disappeared into the night air.

This movement on the part of Moys was by far too rapid and unexpected for it to be baulked by any one at the instant.

Willes was by the chair on which reclined Annie.

Allan had his back to the door by which Sir Hinckton Moys had first mediated his escape.

A rush of cold air came into the Old Throne Room through the destroyed casement.

Then there came a furious knocking at the door, against which Allan had his back.

"Way for the Regent!—way for the Regent!"

Fitz George moved aside.

The door was flung open.

A blaze of light came into the room, and the Regent crossed the threshold, looking pale and agitated. In his hand he held a scrap of paper, which looked like a portion of a letter.

"What has happened here?" he said. "There is the odour of gunpowder! What has happened here?"

"Oh, your, Highness," said Fitz George, "something has indeed happened!"

"What?—what?—what?"

"Lights—lights here!" added Allan. "Let us know the worst. Lights this way."

Fitz George flung his right arm round Annie, and lifted her up from the chair, partially.

The shako fell off.

The dark wig fell with it.

The beautiful hair of Annie escaped, and fell in waving masses over the uniform in which she was disguised, but disguised no longer.

"The Countess!" said the Regent.

"Yes, father—oh, yes! I did not know her. In this disguise she has fought a duel with Sir Hinckton Moys."

"And she is killed?"

"I fear it."

The Regent clasped his hands over his eyes.

"My poor Annie—my poor Annie! People call me cold and heartless, but I did love you. My poor, kind, good, dear girl, I shall miss you —my Annie!"

"No, you won't, George!" said Annie, suddenly starting up, and making one bound towards him, and clasping him round the neck—"no, you won't! Do you think I would let myself be killed, so long as you loved me? It is time enough for the wild, thoughtless Countess de Blonde to die when you no longer say you will miss me."

The Regent was bewildered.

Allan Fitz George rubbed his eyes, to make sure he was not dreaming.

"Why— why, good gracious, Annie!" said the Prince, "what does it all mean?"

"That I am alive."

"But—but——"

"Oh, I am, indeed! What paper is that you have?"

"A letter that came to me by a special messenger, to the White Lodge."

"Ah! I see. Hem! Who wrote this, now, I wonder?"

Annie read the paper.

"His Royal Highness the Regent is informed that S r Hinckton Moys has been challenged to meet a certain Cornet Dorville, a very dear friend of Annie, the mock Countess de Blonde, in the Old Throne Room of St. James's Palace. Let the Regent look to it."

Annie was puzzled.

Who could have betrayed her? Was it Moys himself? It was a mystery, but she looked up into the face of the Regent with a smile, as she said, "And so you came, George, to see——"

"How you got on."

"No, you didn't."

"Really, Annie."

"You wanted to know who this Cornet Dorville of the Hussars, was."

"Well, if I did?"

"Now I know."

"You are getting cunning and clever, George," said Annie.

The Regent shook his head.

"Is it either cunning or clever of you, Annie, to play these pranks?"

"Yes; with an object. I wanted to get rid of Moys at once and for ever. He has taken fright, and will be on the Continent by to-morrow, I dare say. Allan, can you forgive me, since his Highness has done so?"

"With all my heart," said Allan Fitz George. "I am too rejoiced to find you safe, to harbour any other feeling."

"But how came you here, Fitz George?" asked the Regent.

"I came to second Cornet Dorville."

"Whom he really thought to be Cornet Dorville," said Annie.

"On my honour, yes!" said Allan.

"What a wild, foolish child you are!" said the Regent. "What, now, if that rascal Moys had really killed you?"

"There were no bullets in the pistols."

The Regent smiled.

"And he has fled, you say?"

"Yes; through that window."

"The window?"

"Even so, George, and you will have a glazier's bill to pay, you see. But we have got rid of him, I fancy, for ever, as he will hardly show himself in England again after this, which is either a danger to him, or, what will be as bad, a laugh against him, which he will never be able to withstand. Come, now, I want some supper. You will stay to supper, Allan, I am sure?"

"I have something to say to his Highness," said Allan, "which I will stay to say, if his Highness will hear me."

"Come, then," said the Regent. "You sup with us."

"Pray pardon me," added Allan. "I am anxious to get home. If your Highness will allow me to speak—I—I——"

The hesitation of Fitz George was a pretty good indication to the Regent that what he had to say was something unpleasant.

A cloud came over the face of the Prince.

"Well, well," he said—"speak out. What is it, Fitz George, you have to say so solemnly?"

CHAPTER CLXVI.

THE DARK WOMAN REVISITS HER HOUSE IN FRITH STREET, SOHO, AND MAKES A DETERMINATION.

WE return to the Dark Woman, who had made so singular, and, in some respects, opportune, an escape from the Tower.

Let our readers think back for a few pages of this narrative, and they will see Linda de Chevenaux upon what is called the Tower Green of the old fortress—that open space upon which more judicial murders have been committed upon the high, the noble, and the patriotic, than upon any other spot of equal dimensions within the capital of England.

The feeling of liberty, the ecstatic impression of breathing the free, open air, after being imprisoned in one of those gloomy turret chambers, was of itself an exquisite enjoyment.

And as the Dark Woman there stood beneath the night sky she felt that, though alone in the world, she was still possessed with that terrible energy which had accredited her to society at large as a terror and a destroyer.

It seemed to the Dark Woman as if, from the moment that she felt the fresh night air upon her brow, and cooling the heat in her eye-balls, that she virtually commenced a completely new era in her existence.

Who had she now to bind her to life with that bond which should consist of a community of thought and an agreement of interests? No one.

The son for whom she toiled, schemed, and sinned, rejected the wild dream of rank, and name, and fortune, which her excited intellect suggested to him.

Allan took a calmer and more reasonable view of his position. He had not for twenty years nearly nursed a delusion until it had sapped his intellect and made a monomaniac of him.

The Dark Woman felt now that there was a gulf between her and her son, and it was gall and wormwood to that proud heart of hers to acknowledge her failure to herself.

Who had put her in the Tower?

The Regent, of course.

But with whose possible cognizance?

Allan's? Her son's?

The Dark Woman shuddered, as this idea came across her mind, and then she spoke bitterly: "Oh, fool—fool that I was!" she said. "I committed to the mimic waves of the river that pocket-book, with intelligence written upon one of its leaves, which, in all probability, would be no news to him to whom it was addressed."

The Dark Woman had spoken much too loudly for prudence, considering where she was, and was aroused from her dreamy imaginings by seeing the glimmer of a light not far from where she was on the Tower Green.

She shrunk back close to the old, time-worn wall, in the shadow of which she was standing.

The light slowly advanced.

It was carried by some one, who held it about breast high; and, in a few moments, the Dark Woman heard the tramp of feet, and the clank of arms.

Some party of the fortress were on some duty. It was one of the "night rounds," doubtless. She had but to keep close and still, and they would pass her.

The Dark Woman scarcely breathed as the sergeant's guard passed within about a couple of yards of where she was crouched up close against the old wall.

No one looked to the right or to the left.

Long impunity from danger and long established security had made those customs of watch and ward in the Tower things of mere form, to the spirit of which no one paid any attention; although, according to orders and custom, they were still carried out to the letter.

The light, the clank of the weapons, and the footsteps, died away.

The Dark Woman was alone again.

But this little interruption had had the effect of withdrawing her from her too imaginative thoughts and reflections. She was brought back again to the present—to the actual world, and all its hopes and fears.

"I must escape!" she said.

Up to that moment she had not considered how she was actually to leave the Tower. It had seemed to be all-sufficient that she should have found in so extraordinary a manner a means of escaping from her actual prison.

But now she began to reflect what obstacles still lay between her and actual freedom.

"The walls," she muttered, "and the moat."

Both of these obstacles were to be overcome.

The Dark Woman roused herself to action.

"If," she said, "I linger here until daylight, discovery is certain, and I shall only be consigned to some deeper dungeon, from which escape will be impossible."

This was a reflection that brought with it too keen a pang to allow it to grow into a certainty.

All was still now—so very still, that one might have supposed that ancient fortress only peopled by the dead, or by the flitting, noiseless ghosts of those who had suffered death or captivity within the gloomy walls.

The Dark Woman felt that this was her favourable opportunity.

"Now or never," she murmured. "I shall escape within the next hour, or I shall never again even have the chance of freedom."

She crept over the Tower Green, keeping herself bent down in a crouching attitude, so that by no accident should her moving form be detected as something blacker than the night sky.

She came to some stone steps.

One—two—three—four.

There were but four of them; and blocking up, to all appearance, the last one, was a low, thick door. That door was fast.

The Dark Woman could get no further in that direction; but she heard—or she fancied she heard—the low, washing, gurgling sound of water on the other side of that door.

"Oh, if I could but gain the other side of that moat!" she murmured.

But the door was as fast as though it had never moved, but formed a part of the solid stone rampart of the Tower.

The Dark Woman, then, reflecting upon her situation in the old fortress, began to think that if she should really succeed in leaving it it would have to be by the regular Barbican Gate.

"Be it so," she said. "Woe—woe to those who, at some critical moment, stay my progress!"

Linda de Chevenaux was not so well acquainted with the topography of the Tower of London that she could, from where she was, make her way by the most direct route to the outer gates, but she adopted the best plan she could.

She followed the wall—close to which she had emerged, by the old grating—until she came to its termination.

Then she saw, rising up before her in the night sky, the Bloody Tower.

The Dark Woman was surprised to find that she was so close to the place of her imprisonment; but the distance she had traversed, amid the gloomy passages within the Tower, appeared as nothing when in the open air.

No doubt, too, the route she had taken had been circuitous, as from the Bloody Tower to the Green, while now she saw it only as a right line from where she stood.

"Let me think," she said, softly; and she held her hands over her brow.

In a few moments the Dark Woman had made up her mind what to do. She had to pass, as best she might, the sentinel who kept watch and ward under the archway of the prison and murder tower.

She knew that if she could once pass him she had but to turn to the right to reach the drawbridge over the moat.

Then she would be close to the sally-port, and she might possibly escape.

"Now fortune favour me," she muttered.

Crawling along, so bent down that she almost imitated the motion of a serpent on the ground, the Dark Woman approached the dark, gloomy archway beneath the Bloody Tower.

She heard the measured tramp of the sentinel, as he paced to and fro on his lonely watch.

She watched, with eyes that had become, from long habit, familiar with darkness, the appearance of the man, as he reached the end of his walk nearest to where she was.

The soldier paused for a moment, and grounded his arms.

Hope died away in the breast of the Dark Woman.

While the soldier remained there, "standing at ease," there was no chance for her to pass him.

"Shall I kill him?" she whispered.

She grasped the long, thin-bladed poniard; but before the half formed suggestion could grow into a resolution, the sentinel shouldered his musket again, and resumed his walk in the archway.

The Dark Woman darted forward; and before he turned again, she had gained a position close to the arch, and in the shadow of an old buttress which very nearly hid her completely.

"I shall pass him," she said.

Another minute, and the soldier was again on the same spot where she had seen him ground his firelock; but this time he did not do so.

But he spoke.

"Confound this Tower duty! The relief, I am sure, ought to have been here before now."

Then he turned and resumed his walk through the dark arch.

The back of the sentinel was towards the Dark Woman. She crawled after him. He marched on towards the other end of his post; but before he turned again, the Dark Woman was crouching down in the old doorway that led up the narrow staircase to the tower chamber.

The fate of the Dark Woman hung now upon the events of the next half-minute.

The sentinel, when he turned to walk back again, might pass her; or he might cast a glance into the doorway.

If he did, he would be sure to see her.

"I will kill him,' she whispered to herself.

Tramp! tramp! tramp! came the soldier.

There was one anxious moment, and he had passed the doorway.

His back was towards the Dark Woman again. She flitted out of the arch like a ghost.

She had passed that sentinel's post, and entirely evaded his observation.

"Fool!" she said; "it is well that the fate of armies and of nations rest not upon such vigilance as yours."

But the Dark Woman was not yet out of the Tower.

No doubt, she was nearer to the postern gate; but was she on that account at all nearer to liberty? The question was one which she could not take upon herself to answer in the affirmative.

But still, since she had been so far successful, she had hope to support her.

It seemed to her to be a long walk to the drawbridge from the archway of the Bloody Tower; but, at length, she reached close to it.

Then she paused.

Another sentinel was there

How was it possible to pass him?

Murder even would not serve her turn; for, as she paused close to the shadow of the old, rough wall, she heard him speak to some one.

No doubt, one of the warders or Yeomen of the Guard was likewise at that post.

"I am lost!" said the Dark Woman.

As she uttered the words, she heard the voice either of the sentinel or of the person who had been talking to him more loudly.

"Well, mother," said the voice, "the next time you come in, bring me some tobacco."

"Give me the money, then," replied a female voice, in which the Dark Woman recognised the tones of the old woman who had temporarily waited upon her in her prison chamber of the old Tower.

"How suspicious you are," said the man's voice again. "There—there is the money."

"That will do."

"When shall you go out again?"

"Directly. I shall be back in a few moments."

"Very good."

The old woman came along from the direction

of the drawbridge directly towards where the Dark Woman was crouching down close to the wall.

Few persons beside Linda de Chevenaux could have made the sudden determination she did, and at the same moment almost carried it out.

Indeed, there was scarcely time to arrange anything; but the Dark Woman felt that her escape or non-escape from the Tower of London was now a question which the next few months must decide.

The old woman was upon the point of passing her, when the Dark Woman sprang upon her, and grappled her by the throat, while she said in a hissing, threatening whisper, "One word of alarm, and you are a corpse!"

"The Lord have mercy——"

"Hush!"

There was a faint, gurgling noise.

The old woman had fallen; and Linda de Chevenaux had her hand still upon her throat, and one knee upon her breast, as she lay close to the wall.

The Dark Woman was victorious; but she thought that fright had killed the old dame.

She relaxed her hold of her throat, and bending her face down, she said, "Speak, if you can!"

"Mercy!"

"That will do."

"Mer——"

"Silence! There is a dagger at your throat!"

The old woman was in a state of the most abject fear—so much so, indeed, that it was a wonder she understood what Linda de Chevenaux said to her in rapid whispers.

"Tell me if you have to use any pass-word as you leave the Tower."

"Oh, dear!—oh, dear!"

"Tell me, or die!"

"No, no!"

"On your soul, it is so?"

"Yes!—oh, dear, yes! They let me go in and out because they all know me."

"By your dress?"

"Yes; and they speak to me."

"What do they say?"

"Sometimes one thing, and sometimes another?"

This was not a very satisfactory answer; but Linda de Chevenaux thought, probably, it was the best one the old woman could give to her. After a pause of a few seconds, she spoke to her again.

"What do you usually say as you pass the warders and sentinels, if you say anything?"

"Nothing."

"Are you sure?"

"Oh, yes! My cough troubles me as I go over the moat. I think the moat is damp."

The Dark Woman thought it probable enough that the moat was damp.

"Cough slightly, now," she said.

The old woman coughed.

The Dark Woman thought she could easily imitate the tone of the cough.

"Now, listen to me," she said. "If you are prudent, you will live; if otherwise, your last hour has come."

"Yes, you! Oh, Lord, have mercy——"

"Silence!"

"I will!—I will!"

"I am escaping from the Tower. I will take this old cloak and this bonnet of yours; and you will remain where you are, in charge of the person who as assisted me, and who will kill you the moment you utter a sound."

"The person!" said the old woman. "Goodness gracious! What person?"

"You will only know who he is, and where he is, when the blow is struck."

"I won't speak a word."

The Dark Woman raised her head from the crouching position in which she had carried on this whispered dialogue with the old dame, and, placing her hand to her mouth funnelwise, she spoke as though addressing some other person.

"Let her live!—let her live!" she said, "if she will be prudent enough to preserve her life. Useless murder is worse than a crime. It is a mistake."

If anything could possibly have completed the bewilderment and fright of the old dame, these words were certainly calculated to accomplish that object.

"Mercy upon us!" she groaned; "don't let anybody kill me by mistake! I'm a poor old woman, and haven't long to live in the natural way; though, having my faculties, as the saying is——"

"Hush!" said the Dark Woman.

The old dame was terrified into silence.

"How long was it likely to be before you left the Tower again?"

"About ten minutes."

"That time has elapsed, then. Give me the cloak, and give me the bonnet."

The old dame was quite passive in the hands of Linda de Chevenaux; and the latter, with a full conviction that upon the next few minutes hung the question of her escape from the Tower or not, assumed the walk and gait of the old woman, and made her way slowly, but resolutely, towards the postern of the Tower.

CHAPTER CLXVII.

THE DARK WOMAN COMMENCES A NEW LIFE UPON HER OWN PRINCIPLES.

As Linda de Chevenaux approached the drawbridge, she heard that loquacious sentinel still conversing with some comrade, probably, or minor official of the Tower. That he would address her as she passed his post, believing her to be the old dame who had so recently entered the fortress—if, indeed, he did not detect her to be an impostor—she felt certain.

And so Linda de Chevenaux prepared herself to reply in as few words as possible.

She imitated the cough of the old woman as she approached the drawbridge; and then, as she expected, the sentinel cried out, "Don't forget the tobacco, mother!"

The Dark Woman coughed again as she replied, "How can I forget it when I've the money in my hand?"

"That's all right!—that's all right! Get along!"

The danger was passed, and Linda de Chevenaux had now but to clear the postern, when she would be safe upon Tower Hill. Yet the next few moments were probably as anxious ones a any she had passed in all her life, and she sadly feared that the more vigilant guard which must necessarily be kept at the outer gate of the Tower would detect her.

But in this particular, Linda de Chevenaux reasoned badly. It was perfectly true that the guard at the outer gate was vigilant; but that vigilance was directed against persons entering the fortress, and not against those who left it.

The outer guard knew perfectly well that upon them depended the first scrutiny into the character and authority of all persons entering the Tower; and that the sentinels and warders within the fortress would be rather inclined to take it for granted that none but one properly accredited would have been allowed to pass the postern gate.

This style of reasoning acted likewise in the contrary direction; and the guard at the postern might well believe that no person from the inner portion of the Tower could reach that point without passing the ordeal of a strict examination.

The danger, then, that the Dark Woman anticipated in leaving the fortress did not increase as she neared the portal; but, on the contrary, it decreased, and, to her surprise, she was allowed to pass out without a single word of question or comment.

In two minutes the Dark Woman was on Tower Hill.

She could hardly believe her senses.

"I am, indeed, free," she cried; "and let death rather be my portion than that I should be immured again within those gloomy walls."

There was a dim and dubious light upon Tower Hill; and as the Dark Woman glanced upwards, she felt certain that the dawn of the new day was close at hand, and, consequently, that it would be prudent to seek some place of refuge as speedily as possible.

But where was that refuge to be found for her?

Was she not a hunted, proscribed criminal?

Were not all men's hands lifted against her, because her hand had been lifted against all the world?

What was she to do?

But the Dark Woman, although she reasoned with herself, and although she doubted where to go, her heart at times sinking within her, as she felt how lonely she now was, and how utterly without aid and help from any human being, did not at the same time allow herself to linger in the shadow of the old Tower.

With a fleetness of foot which was lent to her by the excitement of the time, she had made her way up Thames Street, and, before half an hour had elapsed, she was far beyond any practicable pursuit, even should all the resources of the Tower be brought to bear upon it.

It was not with any fixed intention so to do that Linda de Chevenaux made her way towards her old residence in Frith Street, Soho. It seemed as if there were some mechanical movement both of mind and body which took her in that direction, and yet she started with all the feeling of a surprise when she found herself in the narrow and gloomy thoroughfare.

That cold, leaden looking light, which is the first indication of the dawn, was now spreading over London, and Linda de Chevenaux felt how hazardous it would be for her to remain in the streets; and yet she could hardly make up her mind to venture into the astrologer's house, although she had a special inclination so to do.

Taking her way stealthily and quietly along Frith Street, and keeping all her senses in the most strict state of observation, the Dark Woman reached the house exactly opposite her ancient residence, and in the deep doorway which was there she found a place of temporary refuge, where, at all events, she could make an observation more in detail of her old quarters.

It occurred to her likewise as somewhat improbable that her enemies would again look for her in the precise house where they had before taken her prisoner.

She began, indeed, to think that it would be a piece of admirable finesse to take up her abode in that house again, as the least likely place in which any one would seek her.

But still, in order to carry out such an idea, it became requisite for her to feel assured that the house was deserted—that no guard had been left in or about it—that no police spy was lurking about its gloomy chambers.

So the Dark Woman, as the dawn gradually brightened, bestowed upon the gloomy residence of Astorath, the astrologer, a fixed and earnest attention.

There was nothing in the world to indicate the presence of any one in the house. The shutters were all strictly closed; and even the somewhat shattered door was closely in its place, as though the last person who had left the house had been careful to give it as much as possible an aspect of safety and security.

Then the Dark Woman began to wonder if that young girl who had played the part of page to her so long might still be found in that gloomy residence; and as she reflected and still observed the house, the day brightened more and more, and she began to hear that peculiar sound which betokens the life of a new day in a great city.

The necessity for coming to some decision speedily was patent to her senses; but she thought she would first try an experiment, to ascertain if any one were within the house or not.

She picked a small pebble from the roadway, and cast it at one of the windows.

Many of the panes of glass in the astrologer's house were already broken, and the Dark Woman added another to the list.

"Surely," she said to herself, "if any one be within the house, there will be a natural impulse to make some show of their presence, even on this slight assault from without."

No, the house was as calm and still as before; and the Dark Woman felt the necessity of at once shrouding herself in its darksome recesses, or submitting to the scrutiny of some early passengers who with loud voices just entered into the street.

She was still in possession of a key, which, provided the door were not fastened on the inside, would procure her ready admission. She crossed the roadway at once. The door yielded too readily to her touch, for it was in a very dilapidated state; and, in another moment, the Dark Woman was in the passage of that gloomy residence, and had placed an iron bar across the door on the inner side, which seemed to be quite a necessary precaution, inasmuch as otherwise it

would appear as if the door itself, with a very slight impulse from without, would fall bodily into the passage.

The Dark Woman now stood near the foot of the staircase, and listened intently for full five minutes.

All was still.

"Felix! Felix! Felix!" she cried, increasing the volume of sound at each cry.

There was no response. That young girl who had played the part of page to the Dark Woman—under, at different times, the names of both Carlos and Felix—would never again answer to her summons.

The Dark Woman was more alone in the world even than she had thought herself.

Then she slowly ascended the staircase; and as she did so, the feeling of deep depression that came over her made her feel that she could never endure that place as an abode; and that what

No. 76.—DARK WOMAN.

she had to do within its walls, it would be well to do quickly, and then leave it for ever.

Familiar as she was with every apartment—with every door, secret and apparent, of the mansion—she made her way quickly and silently towards what had been the laboratory of Astorath, the alchemist. There she found the means of procuring a light; and she looked about her with a feeling of relief to see that no change had taken place in the disposition of the place or the various scattered apparatus and chemicals which the dead astrologer and charlatan had left behind him.

The Dark Woman then appeared to fear that she should meet with some interruption, for she carefully fastened the door of the laboratory, and proceeding to one of the furnaces, which was heavily built in with brickwork, she began to chip away a portion of the cement, and, finally, removing a loose brick, she disclosed a cavity, in which lay a bag of chamois leather, the heavy contents of which, and the musical jingle which they produced, sufficiently proclaimed that the Dark Woman had there secreted a considerable sum in gold, which, in a case of emergency like the present, she—and she only—could place her hands upon.

Linda de Chevenaux then took her way to those two apartments which she had been accustomed herself to occupy during the short and few periods when she might be said to be at home in domestic life.

Then from a wardrobe, which contained a multiplicity of apparel of all kinds and descriptions, she procured a suit of clothes, of somewhat antiquated fashion, but of very costly and excellent material, and which, when once she had donned, transformed her to the appearance of some well-to-do gentleman—not perhaps of the highest class of life, but something that looked between the wealthy tradesman and the educated professional man.

Linda de Chevenaux then turned to a glass, and removing from her head and hair some artfully-designed wrappings, she let fall those luxuriant and fair tresses, which, despite all the anxieties, all the dangers, and all the wild excitements she had passed through, still retained much of their original beauty.

And this Dark Woman—so called, who was fair in reality, and who, by that very fairness, had attracted the eyes of the Prince of Wales at a period when his pursuit of life was a pursuit of beauty—gazed at herself for a few minutes silently and sadly.

A slight tremour for a moment came across her frame; and then from a drawer she took a large and sharp pair of scissors.

"Perish!" she said. "What have I henceforth to do with charms that have lost their lustre and their power? Perish! Henceforth, I live for other objects and other purposes, and must run no useless risks for bygone sentiments. Alas! alas! there have been times when I have dreamt that these tresses would still look fair in the eyes of George, the Regent; but those dreams have passed away, and the time will never come again when Linda de Chevenaux, the Dark Woman, will ever wish for the power to show that she was once fair, and—to some eyes—beautiful. Perish! perish!"

Remorselessly, she closed the scissors upon the fair tresses one by one. They fell fluttering to her feet.

"Lie there!" she said; "remembrances of what I once was, but of what I shall be no more! So perish the last traces of earthly hope and earthly feeling! I will not die to please those who would glory in my death; but I will live for vengeance!"

The Dark Woman was so intent now upon a complete disguise, that the ordinary resource of a wig of a different colour to her own hair no longer sufficed; but from a vial—which she had to make another journey to the laboratory of Astorath to procure—she possessed herself of a dye of such potency, that the remains of her fair hair assumed, almost on the instant, a totally different tint; and so complete was the change produced in the appearance of Linda de Chevenaux, that she almost started at herself as she took another glance in the mirror.

"That is complete," she said. "Let my enemies now point at me, and call out aloud for my destruction, if they dare!"

Without, then, casting another glance about her at the room, which, she fully believed, she was leaving for ever, the Dark Woman hurried from the house of the astrologer, and, amid the full light of day, sauntered leisurely towards the West End of London.

It was, perhaps, an irresistible impulse that took her towards St. James's Palace, but she certainly did make her way in that direction; and, with great apparent ease and calmness, she set a watch which she had with her by the clock in the old turret above the gateway.

This perhaps, under the circumstances, was a piece of affectation on the part of the Dark Woman.

It was as if she wished to tell herself how calm and cool she was—and outwardly, indeed, she was calm and cool; but within her heart and brain there were thoughts and projects which would have set any ordinary intellect in a blaze.

Confident in her disguise, then, she had even the temerity to make her way into the Colour Court of St. James's, round which she slowly sauntered; and she was pleased to think that she attracted no more than ordinary attention from those persons who crossed her path.

"This will do—this will do!" she said. "Linda de Chevenaux has disappeared! This is the commencement of a new existence: what it shall be in its details and various ramifications, I cannot, as yet, precisely say; but it shall be startling, and it shall be dangerous. Let those to whom the danger will come, look to it. They have made me what I am, and they must take the consequences of their acts."

It was strange, now, that the Dark Woman never thought of seeking Allan Fitz George; but she seemed slowly to have made up her mind that he had leagued himself with the Regent against her.

There was a second-rate hotel in St. James's Street, at that period, called the Palace Hotel, in consequence of making a meretricious display of looking-glass; and into this the Dark Woman quietly walked.

Her appearance was respectable, not distinguished; and she just got the amount of attention she wished, no more.

"I shall stay here for a time," she said.

"Yes, sir," was the prompt reply.

"But I do not wish very expensive apartments."

"No, sir."

The "No, sir" was uttered in that tone which seemed to imply "You're a respectable man, but we know you don't want expensive apartments, although, perhaps, you might be very able to pay for them if you chose."

The Dark Woman was shown into a couple of rooms which answered her purpose well, inasmuch as they looked into St. James's Street.

She went to the window, and, resting her head upon her hand, she thought deeply.

Then she rose and paced the room, for her reflections were becoming of a more agitating character.

"And why not?" she cried,—"why not? Why not resume, at once, the position and the power which I forsook when I thought I saw the dearest objects of my life likely to be achieved? Why should I not again be the Dark Woman, whose reputation will easily assemble a party still stronger than that which I dispersed by death? What do new desperadoes care for the fate of the old?"

She paused for a few moments, and memory carried her back to that scene in which she had compassed the destruction of the whole of the band of Paul's Chickens, with the exception of two.

Following up the train of thought, she then added, "And they likewise are now no more. They are both dead, and with them have died the only hearts that cherished revenge against me, and possibly might have stirred up mutiny. Yes, I will have again my band about me. My name shall again be a terror; and I will accumulate, along with power, wealth, so that the time may come when I may be able to strike some blow which shall let even George the Regent see he has not yet crushed Linda de Chevenaux."

The Dark Woman uttered almost a cry at this moment; for, looking from the window, her eyes had caught sight of a figure on the opposite side of the way, which at one time she would almost have passed through a fiery furnace to behold, but the sight of which now filled her heart with bitterness.

It was her son Allan she saw.

That son she had dreamed of making a prince; and there he was, with ease and composure, pacing slowly the pavement of St. James's, in the direction of the Palace.

It was the costume in which Allan was now attired which excited wrath and anger in the breast of the Dark Woman.

The rank which the Regent had promised had been bestowed upon her son; and it was the rare fate of Linda de Chevenaux, by a singular combination of circumstances, to see Allan Fitz George in his uniform of an officer of the guard the very first hour he put it on.

She turned pale and flushed by turns.

She wrung her hands, and then clasped them over her face.

"By him, too!—by him, too!" she cried. "Condemned and forgotten!"

The Dark Woman was judging Allan from out the bitterness of her own heart; and she did not imagine that the slow step at which he was walking was because his was filled with sadness and reflective affection upon her account.

CHAPTER CLXVIII.

THE REGENT EXCUSES HIMSELF TO ALLAN FITZ GEORGE, AND MAKES A LIBERAL PROMISE.

WE left his Royal Highness the Prince of Wales in a state of rather dubious expectation in regard to what Allan Fitz George had to say to him, after declining the invitation to supper, and yet intimating that he had a communication to make which could not be delayed.

The Regent, no doubt, had a tolerably strong impression on his mind that that communication had something to do with the Dark Woman.

He did not like to meet the eyes of Allan Fitz George, but with averted gaze waited for him to speak.

"I have made a strange discovery," began Allan.

"Ah! Indeed!"

The Regent was decidedly fidgetty.

"Yes," added Allan. "My mother——"

"Oh! it is about her."

"It is."

"Well, well! What is it?—what is it? We should be oblceged to know at once what it is."

"She has been a prisoner in the Tower of London."

"Has been?"

The Regent turned full upon his son as he uttered these words, "Has been;"—for, to him, they were words of moment—inasmuch as, if they were to be taken in their grammatical sense, they implied that the Dark Woman was no longer a prisoner, and that all the pains he had taken to make her one had been thrown away.

"Has been? has been? What do you mean, Fitz George, by has been?"

"Because, sir, she is a prisoner in the Tower no longer."

"Ah! How?—how? How is that?"

"I know not; but such is the fact."

"Oh, of course! I comprehend. You went to release her, and you have done so on sufficient guarantees. That is what you mean?"

"No—no!"

"What then?—what then?"

"Her prison was empty, and there was blood upon the couch on which she had reposed."

The Regent moved two steps towards his son; and for the first time that he had ever thought so, Allan saw what might be called a look of dignity upon the face of his father.

No longer avoiding the gaze of Fitz George, the Prince spoke calmly and distinctly.

"Do you, for one moment, suppose me capable of the murder, in prison, of that unhappy person?"

"Oh! no, no!"

"That is well."

"But she is gone; and the officials of the Tower do not feel themselves possessed of sufficient information even to hazard a conjecture on the subject."

"I am sorry to hear it."

"Father!"

Allan uttered the name of father with an emotion that was quite sufficient to let the Regent feel certain something of a more than ordinary agitating nature was to follow it. He was profoundly still and silent as he looked inquiringly into the face of Fitz George. After a pause, then, Allan spoke.

"Father, will you on your word to me, not as a Prince, but as a father, tell me you do not know where Linda de Chevenaux is?"

"I do not know."

Allan bowed.

"That is sufficient," he said. "The mystery, then, is one that we are both interested in solving."

"It is, Fitz George, and I will say this much to you: do what you can and what you will in this affair. I give you full authority to act in the manner you shall think best. Find Linda de Chevenaux, and in my name make such arrange ments as you can for her peace and my security."

"I accept the trust, father."

"That is well; and, since you won't stay, why good night, and remember that from to-day your commission as an Ensign of the Guards—the Grenadiers—has been dated, and to-morrow you may put on the uniform, in which I expect you to present yourself to me before one o'clock."

"I shall obey you, father. Good night."

"Good night, Allan," said Annie. "Give my best and kindest love to Marian."

"I will—I will. Good night."

Allan Fitz George at once left the Palace.

That the Regent, although with a kind of justification which the intellect of Fitz George could not but admit, had put the Dark Woman in the Tower, it was tolerably evident he was ignorant of the mode by which she had left the fortress.

The question now paramount in the mind of Fitz George was, had she left the Tower voluntarily or involuntarily?

Had she managed, with some of those wonderful and unprecedented resources she possessed, to make an escape, or had those persons who surrounded the Regent, and made it their business to pander to the desires of a Prince, taken a kind of initiative in the business, and disposed of the Dark Woman in some way of which even he knew nothing?

This last idea tortured Fitz George.

It was a natural enough idea.

And yet, who could he suspect? Who could he charge with such an act?

Colonel Hanger? If any one was likely to be guilty of such an act, he was the man.

But then Allan Fitz George recollected that he had heard Hanger had fallen in a duel with Sir Hinckton Moys, and if so, he had in all probability carried the secret of what had become of the Dark Woman to the grave with him, if indeed he were at all burdened with such a secret.

At all events, Fitz George made up his mind that on the morrow he would make some special inquiries concerning Hanger, and if he were still in the land of the living, he would question him in such a fashion as should force the truth from him.

There was, in fact, some truth, accompanied by some exaggeration, about the statement made by Moys concerning the fate of Colonel Hanger.

The facts were simply these.

The rage that filled the soul of Sir Hinckton Moys against the man who had supplanted him in the royal favour was too great to permit him to sit down quietly under the infliction.

Hence, as we are aware, he had challenged Hanger, who was anything but in love with the encounter.

We left the Colonel attempting the vain project of clearing his wits for the discovery of some way of avoiding the duel, by muddling them still further with Burgundy.

That "other bottle" which Hanger had resolved to imbibe, in the hope of finding inspiration in its sparkling contents, was duly discussed; and then the Colonel, although certainly not intoxicated, yet a little under the influence of the wine, took his way to the old Tennis Court, which is still in existence, in a dull street close to the Haymarket Theatre.

There he knew he should find some one who, if necessary, would be his second in the contemplated duel, and he was not without a hope that that some one might be able to suggest some means of avoiding it.

There was a broken-down gamester and debauchee of the name of Lyon, who called himself by the convenient appellation of "Captain," who was just the sort of person to whom Hanger wished to apply in the emergency.

Colonel Hanger, too, was just the sort of person Captain Lyon wished to see on that occasion, for he wanted sadly to borrow a guinea from some one, and he thought it highly probable that Hanger had one.

These two men then shook hands with each other with a cordiality that was quite edifying to see.

They wanted each other.

"Ah!" cried Captain Lyon; "do I behold my noble friend Colonel Hanger?"

"The same, my excellent Captain. How goes the world with you?"

"Shabbily! shabbily! A word with you."

"A dozen, if you wish it."

"My excellent and noble friend, I am certain you will do me a favour if you can."

"With pleasure."

"Have you such a thing as a guinea about you?"

"Two."

"Eh?"

"Two, I say; and both at the service of my esteemed friend Captain Lyon."

The Captain was thoughtful. He felt quite certain that Colonel Hanger wanted something of him, or he would never be so liberal. In all probability, under ordinary circumstances, the request for the loan of the guinea would have been met by a prompt denial; but the surprising offer of two filled the imagination of the Captain with a thousand conjectures, as well as a thousand regrets.

The most prominent of those regrets was that he had not asked for a much larger sum.

Hence was it that curiosity and mortification both struggled for a mastery in the countenance of Captain Lyon.

"Come," said Colonel Hanger; "come and take a walk with me. I want you."

"I am ever at the service of my best of friends. But oh! oh! if you only knew——"

"Knew what?"

"Give me your hand. Oh, my friend!"

"What now?"

"If you only knew how much real service five guineas would do me——"

"Hark you, Captain Lyon! I have sought you out because I have ten spare guineas."

"Ten?—ten?"

"Exactly! And all at your service, if you can aid me in a little matter in which I want the assistance of a real friend—one who, in fact, will not be foolishly particular about what he does in the name of friendship and ten guineas."

"I'm your man!"

"I thought so!"

"Is it a heiress to run off with?—some troublesome, low fellow to get rid of?—some testimony in the shape of an eye-witness to something you want?"

"None of those things."

"Then, is it—is it——Eh?"

The Captain made a significant gesture with his finger across his throat, to signify his supposition that what Hanger wanted was some one's throat cut.

"No, no; I will tell you all in a few moments. I am challenged, and I don't want to fight."

"Hem!"

"Sir Hinckton Moys has challenged me, and I have been forced to accept; but I don't want to fight."

The Captain shook his head.

"How am I to avoid it?"

"No how. But I tell you what you can do. You can meet him safely enough, if pistols are the arms to be used."

"They are."

"Then it's all right; I can manage it!"

"But how?"

"Oh, the way it is often managed! I will take good care there is no bullet in your adversary's pistol."

"Can you do that?"

"Easily."

"In that case, then, Captain Lyon, I will make the ten guineas twenty!"

"You will?"

"On my honour!"

"Then you are as safe, Colonel, as if you were only fired at with a toy-gun from a children's toy-shop. Leave all to me! Who am I to communicate with on behalf of Sir Hinckton Moys?"

"That I know not at present; but I should not be in the least surprised at getting that information at my lodgings."

Colonel Hanger had made a shrewd guess when he thought he should find something in the shape of a hostile message in due form from Moys at his lodgings; for there, sitting by a very bad light, with grave patience, was a certain Major Wanstead, who was an acquaintance of Sir Hinckton Moys.

The errand of Major Wanstead was soon explained.

He had come to arrange time and place for a hostile meeting between Sir Hinckton Moys and Colonel Hanger.

The Colonel had sense enough left, notwithstanding the copious libations of Burgundy in which he had indulged, to step into an adjoining room, and leave the Captain and the Major to settle the preliminaries of the duel.

They were not long about it.

The Major took his departure; and Colonel Hanger was joined by the Captain, who cried out, "It's all settled, my excellent friend. Eight o'clock to-morrow morning—pistols—the bank of the Serpentine in Hyde Park."

"Thank you."

"And I will settle it all for you."

"I cannot see how."

"Trust to me; and I promise you a shot at Moys, while he shall only blaze away with powder at you."

"If you can arrange that, Captain, you are a cleverer fellow than I take you to be."

"You shall see."

Colonel Hanger and the Captain supped together; but not all the inducements he could present to him would induce Captain Lyon to tell Hanger how it was he meant to manage in regard to the pistols.

It was about three o'clock in the morning before Colonel Hanger lay down to get some rest; while the Captain made himself up an extemporaneous bed on a sofa in Hanger's lodgings.

At six the Colonel was aroused by his "friend" shaking him, and he started awake.

"Time," said Lyon, "for breakfast; and then to the field."

"What's o'clock?"

"Six."

"But it wants two hours yet to eight. What the deuce do you mean by rousing me up so soon?"

"Breakfast—breakfast! Would you go out in the raw morning air on an empty stomach? No! Perish the thought! A good jorum of mulled claret and a toast will steady your nerves."

"Well, perhaps you are right."

"I know I am."

Colonel Hanger felt, when he rose, that his nerves wanted some steadying; and he was not at all averse to the mulled claret and the dry toast, which he found did him a world of good.

It wanted about five-and-twenty minutes to eight when they both took their way towards Hyde Park, which was then the popular place for duels, although they were going out of fashion.

Hyde Park, in the time of the Regency, was by no means the frequented, popular place it is now. There were but one or two narrow field-paths across it; and the trees and shrubs were more numerous, so that it was not in places exposed to so much observation as at present.

Along the bank of the Serpentine was a very thick row of old trees, some of which still remained, but the majority of them have long since disappeared; and it was at that spot that several encounters similar to that projected between Colonel Hanger and Sir Hinckton Moys had recently taken place.

There was a disagreeable white mist upon the surface of the water.

That mist, as the wind took it, was rolled over in damp, chilling masses to the shore, and was excessively dispiriting and disagreeable.

Without the fortification of the mulled claret, Colonel Hanger felt that he would have been in anything but a good condition to meet his opponent with even the external appearance of courage and composure.

As it was, he kept up pretty well.

"By Jove!" he said, "we are first on the field."

"There they come!" said the Captain.

Two figures were to be seen slowly advancing among the trees.

Colonel Hanger felt a little uneasy.

"Look you here, Captain Lyon," he said. "I hope you have not some absurd idea in your head which will fail in the execution?"

"Oh, no!—oh, no!"

"Then I may depend upon you?"

"Most assuredly—most assuredly; but don't speak another word now. Look grave and cold, and walk a little apart."

"I will—I will!"

"Yet one moment. You may miss him, although you shall have a bullet in your pistol, and he none. In that case, as he is an obstinate fellow—and after a first shot people generally have a sort of maniacal propensity for a second, which might be awkward,—I would advise you to fall at the first, if he don't."

"You mean me to sham being hit?"

"Just so; they won't come near you. I will wave them off, and tell them you are badly hurt; and they will soon take themselves away, for fear of the possible consequences."

"I will do it. Here they are! I trust all to you."

Colonel Hanger was not without some trepidation, in the innermost recesses of his mind, about the character of the trust he put in Captain Lyon; but he felt that he could not do better; and, at all events, he gave himself a greater chance of safety than he could possibly have looked for under ordinary circumstances.

There was a hot and angry expression upon the countenance of Sir Hinckton Moys; and it was quite clear he was perfectly willing, if he could possibly contrive it, to get rid of the rival in iniquity who had taken his place with the Regent.

Sir Hinckton Moys's second made a formal bow to Captain Lyon; and, as if anticipating some objection which Lyon might make, he spoke rather rapidly, saying, "I hope, sir, that there will be no objection on the part of yourself or your principal to the use of these pistols I have with me, which belong to Sir Hinckton Moys? They are excellent weapons, and both alike in every respect."

"You must be aware, sir," said Captain Lyon, "that my principal may labour under considerable disadvantage in fighting with strange weapons, while, for all we know to the contrary, Sir Hinckton Moys may be acquainted with every trick and peculiarity of his pistols, from long practice with them."

"On my honour, sir, I assure you such is not the case."

"That assurance is quite sufficient and conclusive."

The two seconds bowed to each other in the most ceremonious manner; and an ignorant spectator to have seen them would have thought them the very mirrors of honour and chivalry,—although, in reality, two more disreputable individuals could scarcely have been found within the precincts of London.

CHAPTER CLXIX.

CAPTAIN LYON PROVES HIMSELF AN EXCELLENT FRIEND TO COLONEL HANGER.

WHILE this little discourse was taking place between the two seconds, the principals walked apart, and in different directions.

They assumed all that carelessness of manner and external *sang-froid* which is considered right and creditable under such circumstances.

The Major stole a glance at Sir Hinckton Moys when the question regarding the use of the pistols was settled, for he knew Moys would consider it a great point gained.

The fact was, that, notwithstanding the "ho-nour" of the Major had been pledged to the contrary, Sir Hinckton Moys was perfectly well acquainted with those pistols, and the use of them increased his chance of killing his opponent in a remarkable degree.

But the Major was no match for the Captain. It was, in truth, a game of "diamond cut diamond," Captain Lyon being much the keener, harder, and denser jewel of the two.

It mattered little what pistols Sir Hinckton used, provided Captain Lyon could prevent a bullet from being part of its charge.

And that was what he was confident of doing. The how remains to be seen.

In a careless manner, then, Captain Lyon spoke again to the Major.

"We will load our principal's respective weapons," he said, "if you please."

"Certainly—certainly! We are not likely to blunder upon our own side."

"And yet, Major, relying upon your honour as I do, I should have no hesitation whatever in allowing you to load the pistol to be used by my principal."

"Nor I the same as regards the Captain."

"But still, in these cases, custom gives laws."

"It does, indeed."

"And so, although we are both men of honour——"

They both bowed again.

"I say, although we are both men of honour, we will each load our principal's weapon."

The Major was profuse in his bows; and then there was a disagreeable little clicking-clacking sound, as the long duelling pistols, then in vogue, were loaded.

But Captain Lyon put no bullet in the one he was preparing, apparently, for the use of Colonel Hanger.

The Major took care that no such important omission should take place in the charge of the pistol he intended to place in the hands of Sir Hinckton Moys.

Then came the moment when all the tact and all the cleverness of Captain Lyon was required to get possession of the pistol with the bullet in it, and to foist upon the Major the one loaded with powder only.

It is said that most of the great tricks which are accomplished by the sleight-of-hand fraternity are, in reality, so very simple that it is a thousand wonders any one is deceived by them; and certainly, on this occasion, Captain Lyon carried out the principle.

"My dear sir," he said, "I hope, whatever may be the result of this encounter, you will readily bear witness to the fact that I, on the part of Colonel Hanger, behaved most liberally in consenting to use pistols belonging to his adversary."

"Certainly—most certainly."

"I have not a doubt but they are both alike——"

"My dear sir, examine them—examine them."

The Captain took the two pistols, and laying them together, looked at them with critical eyes.

Then he suddenly uttered an exclamation, and looked upward.

It was not in human nature but that the eyes of the Major should follow his. There was nothing to see—not even a bird upon the wing above the tops of the old trees; but Captain

Lyon was accustomed to that sort of prestidigitation which, before people's faces, changed one card or cube of dice for another.

The pistols were changed.

And yet there they were, apparently side by side, in the hand of Captain Lyon; and the Major would have taken his oath to the fact that neither of them had stirred an inch.

"What was it?" he said.

"I thought——"

"What?—what?"

"That there was some object in that tree darker than the leaves; but I see I was mistaken."

"It is only an odd-shaped bit of the trunk."

"I see now—I see now. Let us get this affair over, for it is nearly half-past eight, and we shall otherwise have a chance of interruption."

The Major thought he took the pistol back again that he himself had loaded for Sir Hinckton Moys; but, in reality, he took the one in which the Captain had only placed a charge of powder.

A few minutes more sufficed to step the ground, which was agreed to be sixteen paces, although Captain Lyon tried hard to reduce that distance, for he wanted to give Colonel Hanger the best possible chance of hitting Sir Hinckton Moys, so that he could never entertain a doubt of the fact that his pistol had a bullet in it.

The Major, however, was obstinate on that score, for Moys had been practising with the pistols, and found that, at that distance of sixteen paces, if he levelled at the foot of any object the bullet would rise to a height of about five feet, which would lodge it comfortably in the chest of his opponent.

What a revulsion of feeling would have taken place in the mind of Sir Hinckton Moys could any one have whispered to him, as he stood there, in Hyde Park, on that cold, raw morning, facing Colonel Hanger, that there was but one bullet in use between the two pistols, and it was to be found in that of his adversary.

But there was no such fiend or angel to give Sir Hinckton Moys such intelligence, and he stood there quietly to be shot at by a man whom he hated and despised, and whom he had been in two minds of assassinating instead of fighting him at all.

One glance—a meaning glance—passed between Captain Lyon and Colonel Hanger, and that glance said as plainly "I have done it," as if Lyon had placed a speaking trumpet to his lips and yelled out the intelligence.

A cold, ferocious smile curled the lip of Colonel Hanger, and he sincerely hoped that he would be able to put the bullet—which he alone could send on its winged flight of death or danger—deep in the heart of Moys.

With an elaborate courtesy, which went almost to the length of awakening some suspicions of he knew not what in the mind of the Major, Captain Lyon asked him to give the word. He consented to do so, and just as that white mist which had settled over the Serpentine began to get more thin and gauzy—as a pale ray of sunshine made its way through an opening in the slaty clouds above—the Major took a white handkerchief from his pocket, and crumpling it up, he said, with a loud voice, "Gentlemen, I will say one—two—and then I will throw down this handkerchief, upon which you will be so good as to fire."

This was the most polite and accredited form of duelling among gentlemen, and it was invented for the express purpose of preventing either party from taking aim and making any calculation or drawing any imaginary lines with the eye from the point of a pistol to the breast of an opponent.

It necessitated both parties to keep their eyes upon him who was about to give the signal, whereas if that signal had been merely by word of mouth, they need not have looked at him at all.

But both Sir Hinckton Moys and Colonel Hanger had their own secret felicitations in regard to the result of the duel.

Moys thought he ran the risk of a stray shot from a pistol which had peculiarities with which Hanger was perfectly unacquainted, but he made certain of hitting the Colonel by merely raising his hand so high as to level at his feet; and so he made up his mind to hear the ring of Hanger's pistol before he discharged his own, so that his eye might not be distracted or his aim disturbed by looking at the white handkerchief.

It was a singular and special thing as regarded this duel that both the principals had the same idea.

The Colonel was resolved not to fire until he heard the harmless discharge of the merely powder-loaded pistol of Sir Hinckton Moys.

Then he meant to take rapid but deliberate aim and shoot him.

And so, with these odd resolves, these two men —if by any means they could have put each other out of the world, there and then, and taken their two seconds with them, they would have conferred a great benefit on society—confronted each other, each believing the advantages all on his side, and that he had the other very much indeed in his power.

"Gentlemen, are you ready?" said the Major.

"Ready!" cried Hanger.

"Ready!" echoed Sir Hinckton Moys.

"One!" said the Major.

There was a pause of about twenty seconds in duration.

"Two!" said the Major.

He was, then, rather surprised to notice—which he could not help noticing—that neither of the combatants looked at him, whereas they should both have done, in order to keep their eyes on the handkerchief, which was to be the signal of firing.

However, he had nothing now to do but his straightforward duty.

He dropped the handkerchief.

There was a manifest pause, which rather astonished both the seconds, and which very much astonished Sir Hinckton Moys. It did not last many seconds, however—perhaps, really, not above six or seven.

Then Moys raised his pistol and fired.

"Missed, by Jove!" he said.

Then came the report of Colonel Hanger's pistol, and a streak of blood showed itself upon the side of the forehead of Sir Hinckton Moys, as if something red had been flung at him through the air.

He scarcely felt it; in fact, it was the slightest skin-wound that a passing bullet could possibly inflict.

And then Colonel Hanger, to his mortification,

192 THE DARK WOMAN.

saw that the only bullet used in the encounter had not done its deadly duty; and he saw at the same time, by the flashing, angry eyes of Sir Hinckton Moys, that another shot would certainly be demanded.

Who should say that Captain Lyon would be as lucky in effecting a change of pistols in the second instance as he was in the first?

Colonel Hanger thought he would leave well alone now, and not risk it.

He slowly sank to the ground. He uttered a groan, stretched out his legs convulsively, and then rolled over upon his face.

"By the fiends, I have hit him!" cried Moys.

Captain Lyon darted forward and knelt down by Hanger.

"You missed him!" he whispered.

"Confound him!—yes!"

"That's a pity."

"Get rid of them. Say I'm dead—dying—anything!"

"Gentlemen," cried Captain Lyon, "the Colonel is badly hit, and, I think, has not many moments to live. You will see the propriety of looking to yourselves."

"By Jove! yes!" said the Major. "Come, Sir Hinckton, it may be that we shall have to lie perdu until this affair blows over."

"Oh, no!" said Moys, as he put on his hat, after wiping the blood from the side of his forehead,—"oh, no! nobody will waste half a dozen words in inquiring after John Hanger. Come along! By Jove, I didn't think I'd hit him; although I could not make out how I'd possibly missed him. There is one rogue less in the world, at all events."

Colonel Hanger took care to lie still until Sir Hinckton Moys and his second were out of sight.

Then he assumed a sitting posture; and looking about him, he ground his teeth with rage as he said, "So that little affair is over. I've escaped with a whole skin, it is true, but I'm not pleased at it, for all that."

Captain Lyon shrugged his shoulders.

"My excellent friend, you ought to have aimed just two inches to the left, and then the bullet would have gone plump into his brain."

"Bah! I did the best I could. But I'm equally obliged to you, Captain."

"If he'd had a bullet in his pistol, you would really have been a dead man."

"It is possible enough—it is possible enough! Count upon me as a friend. But, sink me! if I'm not in a precious scrape now! How can I show myself to the Regent, or even anywhere, when I'm supposed to be lying dead in Hyde Park?"

"That's easily managed."

"I will trouble you to tell me how."

"Lie by for a day or two. Give out that you're wounded, but not so seriously as was at first comprehended. Then appear again, looking a little pale, and shamming a little weakness. You will have all the credit then of the duel, and none of the consequences."

"You're a capital fellow, Lyon! I will get home as quick as I can. I was to have been at the Palace to see the Regent to-day at one o'clock; but, sink me! I suppose a wounded man mustn't go, eh? It will be some amusement to hear what Moys says of the affair. I will lie by for a couple of days, at all events; and then who knows but I may persuade the Regent that, after all, I fought Moys on his account. I only wish I could persuade the Countess de Blonde of that. But she don't like me; so there's no help for it. Come on, Captain—come on! This little job's over."

"It is; and all we seem to have got by it at present is a pair of pistols, for here is not only the one you used, but Moys has flung down his own."

Hanger laughed; but the laughter had not much mirth in it, for he began to think now—rather too late, as such thoughts generally come—that he had placed himself very dangerously in the power of such a man as Captain Lyon.

Sir Hinckton Moys was quite persuaded in his own mind that he had killed Hanger.

The thought gave him no uneasiness as regarded merely the killing such a man; but, notwithstanding the bravado with which he had treated the transaction, and the easy way in which he had spoken of its consequences to the Major, he was not without some secret apprehensions, as he traversed Hyde Park, that some trouble might come of the affair.

Those were not exactly the days when killing was no murder, and although the law might take a lenient view of a casualty arising from a duel, yet Moys had a suspicion that even the Regent would not be sorry to see him involved in some serious perplexity which might necessitate his leaving England.

Full of these thoughts, Moys turned over in his mind how he could help himself; and it appeared to him that, under all the circumstances, he could not do better than seek counsel at Buckingham House.

If necessary, too, he could find concealment either there or at Warwick House, since he belonged to the party of Queen Caroline, and had to a certain extent suffered in that cause.

Moreover, was he not charged with a message to the Marchioness of Sunningham?

Had he not, then, at that moment in the breast of his apparel the letter which the Marchioness had sent to the Regent, and which the Regent had delivered open to him, Sir Hinckton Moys, requiring him to return it from whence it came?

Moys in his heart hated the Marchioness of Sunningham.

He knew perfectly well that if she could but reinstate herself in the Palace, so that her career of mendacity and plunder might recommence, she would soon get him turned adrift.

It was a gratification to him, therefore, that he had the means in his hands of submitting her to a serious mortification.

By the time Moys reached Grosvenor Gate, he had quite made up his mind to take the nearest route from that point to Buckingham House.

"My dear Major," he said, "I'm infinitely obliged to you. I do not think you need give yourself any trouble or uneasiness about the affair of this morning. But if you would like to go to Boulogne for a week——"

"I should."

"Then pray command my purse."

"I will avail myself of your kindness, Sir Hinckton; for, to tell the truth, my funds at the present instant are low."

Moys smiled.

"I perceive by your smiling that you would say 'That is not an unusual condition;' and, to

tell the truth, it happens much oftener than I like."

"If twenty guineas," added Moys, "will be of any use, they are at your service."

"I am much beholden to you."

It was rather a peculiar circumstance that this was the precise sum which Colonel Hanger had bestowed upon his second, the clever and unscrupulous Captain Lyon.

So it cost these two men between them forty guineas to fight a duel which did them both mischief, while, as regarded their rivalry and animosity one against the other, it left them just as they were.

Sir Hinckton Moys reached Buckingham House at far too early an hour to find any of its noble inmates stirring. But he was not sorry to avail himself of the hospitality of the establishment, and he breakfasted there before the Marchioness of Sunningham made her appearance.

No. 77.—DARK WOMAN.

Moys might have delivered to her the letter there and then, but in that case she would have kept the mortification to herself; so he waited until the Princess of Wales should be stirring, and as he really wished to hold a conference upon the altered state of affairs at the Palace, by his request, the little coterie, which was in the habit of meeting in solemn conclave to carry on the war against the Regent, was assembled in what was called the "Red Room" of Buckingham House.

The Princess of Wales looked jaded and vexed; but upon the fat and florid face of the Marchioness of Sunningham there was an air of serenity which Sir Hinckton Moys was highly pleas d to think he had in his pocket the instantaneous means of dispelling.

We have little to do with the other parties there assembled; and beyond the fa t that the Princess of Wales had the striking imprudence to go into an adjoining room, in order to consult with some hidden adviser, we do not wish to press hardly upon the imprudences of that unhappy Princess.

Sir Hinckton Moys was rather annoyed, however, to see that the Princess of Wales insisted upon having almost continually present with her a young girl, whose face he had not before seen at Buckingham House.

It was quite a peculiarity of the Princess of Wales that she took the most enthusiastic friendship and fondness for new faces.

There was always some one who was the prime favourite, and who for the time being could do nothing wrong.

Ingratitude, treachery, and absolute malice, which she frequently found was the result of these wild and vagrant fancies, had no effect in putting an end to them.

The great favourite now was the young girl whom she had found on a seat in the Park, and who the reader will recognise as late page to the Dark Woman.

CHAPTER CLXX.

SIR HINCKTON MOYS AND THE MARCHIONESS OF SUNNINGHAM LAY ANOTHER SNARE FOR THE COUNTESS DE BLONDE.

THE intelligence that Moys had to impart to the conclave at Buckingham House was by no means of the pleasantest description.

That intelligence mainly consisted of an account of the utter and complete failure of the whole plot which had been so elaborately, if not cleverly, constructed for the disgrace of Annie, and the destruction of the dawning fortunes of Allan.

If that plan of arousing the jealousy of the Regent past all bounds of reason or patience had been successful, no doubt, he would never again have looked upon either Annie, the Countess de Blonde, nor Allan Fitz George, as he now named him, again.

They were neither of them the sort of persons who would have thrust themselves upon the notice of the Regent if he had said or done anything to hurt their pride or their feelings to any great extent, so the plotters of Buckingham House would then have triumphed.

Such, however, was not to be the case.

The failure was as complete and as significant as it could possibly be.

And the worst of such a failure was, that it made future operations much more difficult, because it put all parties on their guard.

Allan Fitz George would now mistrust any letters or messages brought to him in urgent terms, in the name of the Countess de Blonde.

Annie would think twice before she stepped forth from the Palace upon any sudden incitement so to do.

The Regent, when anything should be intimated contrary to the good faith of Annie towards him, would think back at the plot which had just miscarried, and surmise that another was on the tapis.

He would be quite right in so thinking for before Sir Hinckton Moys left Buckingham House another plot was indeed on the tapis

Neither Moys, however, nor the female cabal at that house had the least idea that Moys was to pass through such a scene as he did that night at St James's Palace.

It will be recollected that although, in order to keep the events of our story in tolerable order, we have been compelled to anticipate the strange proceedings of that night in our narrative, we are but now filling up a hiatus in the career of Sir Hinckton Moys, by detailing what he did just before his duel with Annie in the old Throne Room.

There can be no doubt but that the Princess of Wales had been up to the time of their consultation at Buckingham House made a complete tool of by the unscrupulous Marchioness of Sunningham.

The Princess was persuaded that the fair and fascinating Countess de Blonde was the obstacle to her reconciliation to the Regent.

It suited the Marchioness to say so, while at the same time what she was aiming at was just to supplant Annie in her situation at the Palace.

Moys was quite explicit as regarded the failure of the whole plan for the destruction of Annie and of Allan Fitz George.

"And so, your Royal Highness and ladies," he said, when he got to an end of his narration, "all has failed and broken down."

"Then," said the Prince of Wales, "we are just where we were."

"I wish I could think so, your Highness," replied Moys, with a shake of the head.

"You do not, then, think so?"

"Indeed, I do not."

"What, then, has happened amiss, beyond the failure?"

"The experience of the Regent, and the suspicions of all who have been concerned in the plot."

The Princess looked vexed.

"We must try again," she said.

As she spoke, she glanced at the Marchioness of Sunningham, who was unusually silent, for her. Thus appealed to, however, by a look from the Princess, she was compelled to speak.

"I think," she said, "I would now counsel a short delay."

Sir Hinckton Moys shook his head.

"You do not agree with me, Moys?"

"I am sorry to say I do not."

"Nevertheless, I would wait a day or two, to give the Regent time to think."

Moys knew perfectly well what was in the mind of Lady Sunningham. As yet, she had received no answer to her letter to the Regent ; and as it had not been returned, she had begun to entertain a hope that it was under favourable consideration.

She little suspected that Moys had it in his pocket, and was only waiting the opportunity when he could mortify her most by its production to lay it on the table.

"It is a sad thing," said the Princess of Wales, "that my best friends generally differ in opinion."

"Your Highness," added Moys, "we are united on one point,—and that is the desire to do you all the service we can."

"What do you propose, then, Sir Hinckton?"

"War—still war——"

"Against the obstacle?"

"Decidedly."

The Princess of Wales had got into the habit, for the last few days, of calling the Countess de Blonde "the obstacle."

"Have you a plan?" asked the Marchioness.

"I have."

"We are all attention."

"It is this," added Moys : "Annie, the Countess de Blonde, must be provided with a real lover."

"A real lover?"

"Just so ; for we have found that a sham one has not answered the purpose."

"I do not comprehend you," said the Princess.

"I will explain, then. There will be no difficulty in finding some one who will fall in love with the Countess de Blonde, upon the instigation and presumption that the passion is reciprocated."

"Can that be done?"

"I know—that is, I have in my eye—such a man. He is at present employed in the Chamberlain's office, and is about to go into the Guards. He is most pre-eminently handsome——"

"Oh !" said the Marchioness.

"And most pre-eminently conceited," added Sir Hinckton Moys. "In fact, not to use too vulgar an expression, the man is a — a — a donkey."

The ladies smiled.

"And he fully and firmly believes that any lady he sees, or, I should rather put it, who sees him, is instantly and fatally in love with him."

"The wretch !" said the Marchioness.

"I shall find no difficulty in persuading him that the Countess de Blonde is in love with him, and that will flatter his vanity. I will then find a means of hiding him in her apartments, where the Regent will find him."

"That would be conclusive," said the Marchioness.

"And we should get rid of the obstacle," said the Princess of Wales.

"I hope and expect so."

The Marchioness of Sunningham seemed to be in deep thought for a few moments, and then she said, "The plan is a good one ; but still I would counsel two or three days' delay."

"Delays are dangerous."

"Not in this case. It would be well to lull the Countess de Blonde into a false security, and to calm in the mind of the Regent the first transports of a reconciliation with the fair object of his idolatry."

"Good !" said Moys.

"You agree with me?"

"Pardon me. I said good, but it was in admiration of the ability displayed in the few words you had just uttered."

"Oh, Sir Hinckton !"

"Nay, I seldom compliment. What I say I mean. But——"

"But what?"

"What?" said the Princess, seeing Moys pause as if he had something important to communicate.

"But I was going to say a something which I think will induce the Marchioness of Sunningham not to counsel delay."

"Indeed ?"

"Yes. When I last saw the Prince, he placed in my hands an open letter."

"Ah !"

"From a fair lady."

The Marchioness turned white.

"From a fair lady," added Moys. "And he ordered me to return it to her in such a way that the return was evidently the greatest expression of—of—what shall I say?—contempt that he could accord to the epistle."

The Marchioness turned pale.

"Who wrote the letter?" asked the Princess.

"Her ladyship the Marchioness of Sunningham—and there it is."

Sir Hinckton Moys placed the open letter of the Marchioness upon the table—that letter which, if the Princess of Wales had been allowed to read it, would have at once let her see the double game which the Marchioness was playing in regard to her and her hopes.

But Moys kept his hand on the letter.

The Princess, then, with all that curiosity with which she was so largely gifted, placed her hand on it likewise.

The third hand that was placed on the letter was the rather large and thick one of the Marchioness.

Then these three persons looked in each other's faces.

There was a lurking smile on the face of Sir Hinckton Moys.

Curiosity and suspicion were both exhibited on the countenance of the Princess.

Lady Sunningham was pale and excited.

"Your Royal Highness,' she said, "ought to know the contents of this letter."

"But I did not know of its existence."

"No. There was a reason."

"A reason, Marchioness?"

"Yes, your Royal Highness."

"What possible reason?'

"I—even I shrink from letting your Royal Highness know that I had attempted an appeal to the feelings of the Regent."

"You? An appeal?"

"To his feelings !" sneered Sir Hinckton Moys.

As Moys spoke, he very imprudently relinquished, to a certain extent, his hold on the letter. The Princess's hand only slightly touched one corner of it ; and the Marchioness, taking instant advantage of the favourable moment, made a vigorous snatch at it, which brought it entirely into her possession.

"Ah !" cried Moys.

"Marchioness !" said the Princess.

"I will, as in duty bound," said the Marchioness, "and occupying, as I do, the post of 'reader' to your Royal Highness, read you this letter."

The Princess was silent.

Moys looked amused in the midst of a little vexation. Perhaps, too, he was pleased to see that the Marchioness really had the tact and cleverness to pass off so very awkward a situation.

With a skill that really did some credit to her powers, the Marchioness pretended to read the letter ; but she really uttered very different words to those which the letter contained : —

"SIRE,

"The humble subject who addresses these lines

to you, does so in favour of a Princess who is entitled to all your esteem and affection. Take, Sire, the opinion of one woman upon another; and believe me when I tell you that in beauty, in ability, in excellence of heart and mind, the Princess, your wife, stands unrivalled. I urge you to add lustre to the crown which will so soon encircle your brows, and to make your domestic life a thing to be envied by at once forgetting all the past, and making such advances to her Royal Highness the Princess of Wales as shall induce her, too, to be forgiving, and to come to you at Carlton House.

"I am, with great respect, your Royal Highness's most humble and devoted subject,

"SARAH SUNNINGHAM."

"That is the letter," added the Marchioness; "and since it has failed in its object, let it perish!"

Quick as thought, she crumpled up the letter, and flung it into the fire.

A flame caught it, and it was consumed in a moment.

The Marchioness cast a triumphant look upon Sir Hinckton Moys.

He was beaten—foiled.

"Ah!" said the Princess of Wales; "you are, indeed, a true friend, Marchioness; but I am sorry you burnt the letter."

"So am I," said Moys.

"I should have liked to keep it as a memento of real and true friendship."

"So should I," said Moys.

"Think no more of it," cried the Marchioness: "it did not answer its purpose, and it is gone. Think no more of it, dear Princess; let the future, now, occupy us alone."

"Then," said the Princess, rising, "I agree to what has been proposed; for I think I am justified in doing anything that is possible to get rid of the obstacle."

The whole party rose as the Princess moved towards the door; and Sir Hinckton Moys darted forward, and held it open for her.

In five minutes more, Lady Sunningham and Moys were alone.

A flaming look came into the eyes of her ladyship as she said, "You tried to ruin me!"

"Impossible!" said Moys.

"What do you mean, wretch—what did you mean by producing that letter before the Princess?"

"A warning to you."

"Warning! What warning?"

The rather vulgar mind of the Marchioness of Sunningham heard that word "warning" much in the same way as it would have struck upon the ears of some pampered domestic, who might be suddenly informed that the career of extortion and insolence was at an end.

Sir Hinckton Moys smiled.

"I do not mean that!" he said. "But what I do mean is, that nothing can be more fatal to unity of purpose than the pursuit of mere individual objects by means kept secret from those who are acting with us."

"There was nothing in that letter," added the Marchioness petulantly,—"there was nothing in that letter that could possibly make any difference in your prospects, or in mine. It was quite an understood thing between us that the main object was for me to be reinstated as the favourite of the Regent. Then I was to get you a barony and the appointment of Chamberlain as quickly as possible."

"Precisely."

"And you know perfectly well that we were both making use of the Princess of Wales merely as a means to an end."

"That is just so."

"And yet you take some pains to entirely destroy my credit with her, which would have been the case, had she really seen the letter you so foolishly and ostentatiously displayed before her."

"My dear Marchioness," said Moys, "I never intended the Princess to see the letter."

"Then, why produce it before her?"

"For two objects."

"Pray, condescend to state them."

"The first was to give you a little fright; and the second was to convince myself that you were one of the cleverest women in existence."

"Oh, stuff! stuff!"

"I wanted to frighten you from taking any steps in all these matters of which I was not cognizant, and I wanted to see how cleverly you would get out of the seeming scrape in which I had placed you."

The Marchioness was not half satisfied, although the excuses of Sir Hinckton Moys partook very much of a compliment; but the impolicy of carrying on the dispute any further was evident enough, and she was so far smitten with the new enterprise which had been suggested by Moys for the destruction of Annie, Countess de Blonde, that she was willing to look over the past.

That was the more easily done, inasmuch as she was perfectly well aware that Sir Hinckton Moys never had any confidence in her, nor she in him; and although they seemed to act together for common objects, in reality they only looked to their own individual interests, and either one was quite willing to throw over the other at any moment that it might seem desirable so to do.

It was not until Sir Hinckton Moys reached his lodgings—after this little episode at Buckingham House—that he found that letter awaiting him from the sham Cornet Dorville, enclosing the key which would again admit him to St. James's Palace.

The reader is already aware of what passed on that occasion in the old Throne Room; and since we have followed the evil fortunes of Sir Hinckton Moys thus far, it may be as well to state what became of him before he again showed himself on the scene of active warfare in London.

The catastrophe which he thought had happened in the Throne Room of St. James's Palace was of a nature perfectly to stun and bewilder him; and when he made his way out of the window, the only wonder was that he did not break his neck, or, at all events, do himself some very serious injury.

Such men as Moys, however, appear to have a good luck peculiarly their own; and he alighted in one of the court-yards of St. James's, without really any serious hurt.

The impression upon his mind was full and complete that he had had the singular misfortune of at once putting an end to her career, by taking the life—although it was a mistake—of Annie, Countess de Blonde.

The vengeance of the Regent, he judged, would be of an implacable character; and all he saw before him in the future was that he would be a hunted fugitive throughout Europe, with a singularly heavy price set upon his head.

Again and again he raved at his own folly, in being induced to fight with the seeming Count Dorville under such circumstances.

"Where were my wits—where my judgment," he cried, "that I could not guess the whole affair was some wild freak of that mad-headed girl? What will become of me now? The Regent will be furious; and, now that she is gone, he will invest her with a thousand charms he never discovered before."

These disconsolate reflections did not prevent Sir Hinckton Moys from taking every possible measure to ensure his own safety.

He ran to his lodgings, and possessed himself quickly of all the money he had; and then, fearing each moment that the officers of justice would be upon his track, he made his way down to the river side, and hired a boat to convey him as far as the Medway.

There, in an obscure public-house—the very atmosphere of which seemed a compound of tar, tobacco, and new rum—the courtly Sir Hinckton Moys passed a few miserable hours, until the morning came, when he intended to take his passage in a miserable, little dirty sailing-boat, which was going to Boulogne.

Cold, wet, half famished, and wildly angry with himself and every one else, Sir Hinckton Moys reached Boulogne about the afternoon of the next day; but when there, his difficulties began to increase, for although it was at that period when one of those brief armistices between this country and the first Napoleon were taking place, any Englishman landing in a suspicious manner in France was sure to become an object of attention to the police.

It was with great difficulty that Sir Hinckton Moys got leave to re-embark from the port of Boulogne, in a Dutch fishing vessel which was bound for the Scheldt; and it was the evening of the second day before Sir Hinckton Moys landed at Antwerp, looking wofully dilapidated.

But he thought he had evaded pursuit for the present, and that he should have a little time to look around him.

CHAPTER CLXXI.

THE DARK WOMAN VISITS A MYSTERIOUS HAUNT OF CRIMINALITY.

WITH rage and anguish gnawing at her breast, Linda de Chevenaux, the Dark Woman, sat long at that window looking into St. James's Street, from which she had seen her son pass in the uniform of the Guards of that man who seemed to her to have denied his very existence.

The bitterness of her spirit increased hour by hour; and, although she did not certainly remain at that window the whole of the day, yet she lingered by it for the greater part of the hours

which intervened before the shadows of evening confused external objects.

Perhaps she had a hope of again seeing Allan pass; but, if she had, she was disappointed, for he came not that way again.

Then, when the twilight had deepened into darkness, Linda de Chevenaux, who had taken but a light repose during the day, retired from the window; and, dressed as she was in her male apparel, she cast herself upon the bed in the adjoining apartment, and, as if almost by an act of her own will, she fell into a deep sleep

The Dark Woman was accustomed to these snatches of repose; for, after all, they were but of that character, inasmuch as they seldom lasted beyond a couple of hours.

It was not much past seven o'clock when she sought to recruit exhausted nature by this sleep, and the step she meant to take that night could not be taken till near upon midnight.

The agitating occurrences that had taken place in the Tower of London had prevented her from having anything in the shape of regular repose while she was a prisoner in the fortress.

But now, if any one could have looked at her, they would scarcely for one moment have supposed that so wildly excited a heart and brain could be wrapped up in so soft and apparently so serene a slumber

The Dark Woman thought she could have slept only five minutes when she started awake.

She had left the door partially open between the two apartments, so that, if any of the persons connected with the hotel felt an officious desire to visit the rooms, they might see that the apparently respectable gentleman was reposing.

It was a gleam of light that shone upon her eyes that seemed to her the cause of her awakening; but such was not the fact; inasmuch as, although a gleam of light did come upon her eyes when she opened them, that gleam proceeded from a couple of lighted wax candles which had been burning for more than a couple of hours.

The Dark Woman started up, and entered the sitting-room. A glance at her watch let her see that it was ten minutes past eleven.

She was much refreshed by the sleep she had had.

But she felt a general tingling of the nervous system and an excitement of brain, which she felt she must allay, if possible.

Strong coffee, which to most persons would have produced the very symptoms she wished to repress, she knew well by experience would act as a sedative.

She rang the bell smartly, and was quickly served with the beverage in perfection.

Then she paced the room for a few seconds in silence.

"The time has come," she said; "the time has come. From this night forth I commence a new career; and before the world is four hours older, I ought to have power to make those who have injured me tremble. I will once again organize such a band, that the exploits and audacities of Paul's Chickens shall seem as nothing compared to that which I will now do!"

Situated as that hotel was in a populous and fashionable part of London, where late hours was a rule, the departure of the Dark Woman between eleven and twelve excited no remark whatever.

Probably there was no person in the whole extent of London who knew more of the criminal secrets of the great city than Linda de Chevenaux.

The reader may well surmise that her object was now to gather together, into a sort of association, some of those wandering spirits of evil who acted singly and without purpose,—those men whose lives are given up to depredation and a preying upon the community at large,—men who seemed with ease to be for ever acquiring plunder, and yet who, for the greater part of their time, are in want of the common necessaries of life.

This was for the want of system—the want of association—the want of some sort of government which should hold them together, and render their iniquities profitable.

The members of that band which was named Paul's Chickens were all individually better off, while they were under the authority of the Dark Woman, than they could have been if they had acted singly, and in an isolated fashion.

In addition to this an enormous sum remained in her hands at the time of the destruction of the band.

The distinct purpose of the Dark Woman now was to form such another association.

We shall see how she set about it.

It was not to the ordinary and common haunts of criminality in London that the Dark Woman bent her steps. One might have expected to find her burrowing among the cellars of St. Giles's, or seeking her recruits among the criminal purlieus of Whitechapel.

But the Dark Woman did no such thing.

She took an easy walk from St. James's Street towards Leicester Square, and there she paused.

There was a tall, dingy, gloomy-looking house —a house of many windows, and no doubt of many rooms—at the corner of one of the streets which led into the square.

The lower part of this house seemed, in a quiet, unpretending fashion, to be devoted to business; but it was not a shop.

In the parlour windows appeared some books, the binding of which was rich, although faded— the lettering on their backs was mostly in Latin —and it seemed, to look at that establishment, as though the lower part of it, at least, was occupied by some exceedingly quiet, exceedingly classical, and unobtrusive bookseller.

It was at this house that the Dark Woman stopped.

The outer door was open, late although it was; but another door, about twelve feet down the passage, looked strong and secure.

To the right, as you entered the house, was what had been the dining-room door in times when nothing in the shape of business profaned the establishment.

This door was half glazed, and covered within by a dwarf silken curtain.

Any one might pass out of Leicester Square, and turning the handle of this dining-room door, might find themselves in the bookseller's shop, the walls of which were covered with volumes, on which the dust of years lay thickly.

Linda de Chevenaux made her appearance before the bookseller, who was sitting at rather a massive circular table, apparently reading by the light of an oil reading-lamp, the sliding shade of which was pressed so low down that but a limited circle of bright light was thrown upon the table and the book before him.

A quiet, elderly, respectable-looking man was this bookseller; in fact, there was quite something of the old gentleman about him, as he there sat, looking through his gold spectacles, with just light enough reflected on his head to show that his hair had passed from the state of grey to white, and that he was far advanced in the winter of existence.

At the sound of Linda de Chevenaux's footsteps the respectable old bookseller looked up inquiringly.

"This is Friday night," said the Dark Woman.

The old bookseller raised the shade of the lamp, so that a much broader circle of light was spread round the table and the room.

He looked almost benevolently in the face of the Dark Woman, as he replied, "And well, sir, suppose it is Friday night?"

"You are up late," said the Dark Woman.

"Well, sir, and suppose I am up late?"

Linda de Chevenaux elevated both her arms in a peculiar fashion, and then clasped her hands above her head.

"Are you sick?" said the old man.

"Of the world? Yes."

"What world?"

Linda de Chevenaux made now a very peculiar movement with both her hands, clasping the fingers together in such a fashion that they formed the rough and rude imitation of a crown.

The old gentleman took off his spectacles, and made a low bow.

"You are one of us," he said.

"I command," said the Dark Woman; "and I ask you if there are those here to-night whom I can meet as brethren?"

"Most assuredly, sir,—most assuredly."

A sudden sharp noise behind the Dark Woman made her start.

"It is nothing," said the old bookseller; "I was but securing the door. I have a secret means, by a touch of the wall here, of dropping a heavy bolt into its socket. It is twelve o'clock: if it will please you to follow me, I will introduce you to the chamber, where probably you will find those you seek."

"I follow."

There did not seem to be any means of leaving that apartment, except by the door at which Linda de Chevenaux had entered it; but the old bookseller, by some secret mechanism, opened a door in one of the walls, the back of which was so covered with books, in regular continuation of those around it, that when closed it had no appearance of being a door.

The utmost darkness seemed to reign beyond.

"Will it please you," said the old bookseller, "to follow me, or precede me?"

"I will follow."

The old man bowed and passed through the doorway, the Dark Woman treading closely on his footsteps.

The door loaded with the books swung shut, and not the darkest cell in the dreariest prison that ever was constructed, nor the deepest of earth's caverns, could be darker than the narrow passage in which Linda de Chevenaux found herself.

it was not in human nature to tread onward with any feeling of ease and security in such a place.

She paused, and stretched forth her right arm to feel if she were near a wall on that side, and in an instant her wrist was grasped by an invisible hand, which held it as with a grip of iron.

It was difficult to avoid doing so; but the Dark Woman uttered no exclamation.

She stretched out her left hand, but it was instantly grasped in a similar manner, and then a harsh voice spoke abruptly.

"Who are you?"

"Your master!"

"Why the master?"

"Because I know you all, and your secrets!"

"From whom? and how?"

"In my possession is the vellum-book with the green binding. In my possession is the seal."

There was a dead stillness for a few seconds, and the Dark Woman felt the grasp that held her right wrist slightly relaxed. She heard whispers about her, as though some persons were consulting in a low tone, and then the harsh voice spoke again.

"We have had no master," it said, "for some time. He who was the master disappeared, and nominated no successor."

"He had a right to nominate, and he nominated me!"

"Light! light!" cried the voice.

A door was dashed open, and Linda de Chevenaux found herself confronted by a blaze of light, proceeding from a chandelier in an apartment which was very handsomely furnished.

But not a soul was to be seen. The mysterious hands that had held her wrists had suddenly been removed, and to all appearance she stood perfectly alone at the door of that room with the brilliant light.

But Linda de Chevenaux felt perfectly well aware that she was placed there to be the object of observation by persons, who, although they found means to hide themselves from her sight, were, nevertheless, enabled to indulge themselves with a fixed scrutiny of her.

The Dark Woman never wanted courage. It was only when her inmost heart was stirred with those wild aspirations and affections she had nourished so long that she occasionally trembled; but now she felt no tremour, and advancing slowly into the room, she placed her hand upon a table in its centre, and spoke in a low, earnest tone.

"The book and the seal were bequeathed to me. I am one who can lead and direct those who will follow me; and unless it be that among yourselves you have already found some one who can conduct you through the golden gates of fortune, trust to me to do so, and appear!"

The light went out.

The darkness became oppressive.

"Appear!—appear!" cried Linda de Chevenaux. "This is mummery!"

Several doors at that moment opened at different parts in the walls of the room, and eight or ten persons entered, each of whom carried in his hand a small lighted lantern.

These lanterns were, in the midst of profound silence, placed in a confused kind of heap on the table, and the aggregate illuminative power of them served to let the Dark Woman see that she was in the presence of men, all of whom seemed to be attired well, and even fashionably.

One of them spoke.

"We don't know who you are," he said; "but it is quite clear you know us, and have become possessed of the secret roll of the association, and the seal, which gives you authority over us all, or you never could have had the means of getting here. Who are you; and what do you propose?"

"Let me answer your second question first," said the Dark Woman. "I propose to be your leader. You are members of an association that has no name; but its purpose is to procure wealth for the individuals composing it by any and every means whatever."

A murmur of assent passed from mouth to mouth.

"From my experience, I have the means of directing your proceedings. I can penetrate even into the chambers of royalty itself; and many a fine booty that you would miss, owing to your not knowing of its existence, I shall be able to place within your grasp."

"We are gentlemen," said the voice that had first spoken. "We are gentlemen's younger sons —cashiered officers—men who have run a race with fortune and have lost it. But we must live; and that, too, in a manner which has become a fashion with us, and a part of our existence. We are willing to take any leader who will serve us and himself, and on whom we can always depend."

"I have power," said Linda de Chevenaux; "and should any of this fraternity in the cross accidents of life fall into danger, I have the highest and most peculiar power in this realm to set him free."

A murmur of surprise passed among the persons present.

"Yes," she added, speaking rather excitedly; "even were life itself at stake, I can present myself to those who dare not refuse such life at my asking. He upon whose brows the crown of England will soon descend would at any time purchase immunity from higher demands which I can make, by casting open any prison door which might shut in one whom I wished to be free."

"Who are you?—who are you?" cried several voices.

"It is fit that you should know."

"Speak! Your name—your name?"

"You shall know it. You may have heard it. I am Linda de Chevenaux, Princess of Wales!"

"The Dark Woman!" cried almost every voice.

"Yes, sirs, the Dark Woman! I am the Dark Woman, who, in association with men of coarse and brutal natures, whom I commanded, won a princely fortune. That is dissipated—scattered to the winds; but with you, who are gentlemen, I will take upon myself to say, that with strict obedience from every one of you—with courageous action when I order it, I will place in your hands a million before the next four seasons have passed over our heads."

"Agreed!" cried a voice.

"Agreed!" echoed another.

And so from voice to voice the word passed; and the Dark Woman, counting her subjects, found that she had eleven men, who were willing to obey her behests, and to trust in her brilliant promises for the time to come.

It was but by an accident that Linda de Chevenaux had discovered the history of this association. After the death of Astorath, the astrologer, in Frith Street, Soho, she had made a careful investigation of all the secret recesses of his laboratory, and in one of them she had discovered a small book, of green vellum, in which was inscribed the names of a number of persons composing a most singular association, formed for the purposes of plunder on an extensive scale.

The book contained a full description of the whole affair, together with those secret signs and words which enabled Astorath—who was, in reality, the head of the whole affair—to make himself known, at all times, and in all places, whatever might be his disguise, to any member of the fraternity.

Along with this book was a seal, which would be recognised as official, and would procure prompt obedience from any one in the pay of the association.

Linda de Chevenaux, when she found her son, and when she was full of the vain and wild idea that she would get him recognised as the legitimae child of the Prince of Wales, thought but little of this accidental discovery.

Now, however, she had brought it into use, and intended to work with it in the most formidable manner possible.

An hour's consultation with these men settled a plan of proceedings, which will quickly show itself in its results; and by about two o'clock in the morning the Dark Woman quietly walked back to the hotel in St. James's Street, pledged to commence a new career—full of danger, but at the same time full of triumph.

She was resolved, if possible, to inaugurate her reign over the confederates with some brilliant *coup* which should at once place in their possession extensive means.

She passed a great portion of the night in considering what this was to be; and about five o'clock in the morning she clasped her hands together, as she exclaimed, "I have it—I have it! A secret embassy from Persia, bringing with them untold wealt, shall arrive in London within the ensuing fortnight. Let the jewellers and goldsmiths of this great city look to it, for they will long remember the advent and disappearance of a Persian embassy."

What the Dark Woman meant by all this we shall speedily disclose to the reader.

CHAPTER CLXXII.

RETURNS TO SIXTEEN-STRINGED JACK, AND AN ADVENTURE WHICH HAPPENED TO HIM IN BOND STREET.

As in long journeys there are resting places, so are there in stories points at which it is necessary that both reader and author should pause for a moment to look about them.

Let us imagine that we have, in this eventful history of the Dark Woman, come upon one of those resting spots.

It will be seen that owing to the complexity of the incidents, it is our duty to record that our characters separate themselves, so to speak, into distinct groups.

It is worth while to take a glance at those separate groups as they at this juncture of our narrative exist.

First, then, on the principle of giving place to royalty, there is the Regent, full of perplexity and danger at the machinations and plots that emanated from Warwick and Buckingham Houses.

The Prince and the fair Countess de Blonde form of themselves one of the plots of our story, and with them may be considered as closely associated Willes, the valet. We really beg his pardon, for we ought to name him Sir Thomas Willes.

At the present time, it may be assumed that the atmosphere of St. James's, so far as regards the Regent and Annie the Countess, is fair and serene.

The jealousy that had inflicted such pangs on the Prince of Wales was dissipated. He had full faith in Annie's truth, and, if possible, he was more fascinated with her than ever.

To be sure, the Regent had his moments of depression and uneasiness.

The Dark Woman was at large, and, for all he knew, might at any moment make some appearance that would grossly disturb his peace.

Then the cabals of the Queen Caroline and her pretended friends kept him pretty constantly on the fret.

The Regent of England could no more escape the common lot of humanity in anxieties and tremours of the heart and brain, than when his time should come he could escape death!

Comfort, ye poor and lowly! You are, after all, perhaps as happy as a prince!

Then we come to another group of persons, who may be classed all together.

Sir Hinckton Moys, Colonel Hanger, and the party at Buckingham House, form a very curious assemblage of people.

Their motto was far from being "each for all and all for each." It was, on the contrary, a much more popular one, although one that is not so often avowed in polite society.

"Every one for himself" was the real guiding principle of these people.

The unfortunate and imprudent Princess of Wales wanted to be reconciled to the Regent.

The infamous Marchioness of Sunningham wanted to supplant her young rival, Annie, the Countess, in the affections of the Regent.

Sir Hinckton Moys wanted to resume his old post—or to get a better one—in the Palace.

Colonel Hanger was wondering what sort of reception he should get from the Regent, when next he presented himself.

Then there were Allan Fitz George and his amiable wife, Marian, neither of them self-seeking, but willing to find their own happiness in producing as much happiness for others as they possibly could.

And then there was the Dark Woman, in connexion with that dangerous association of unscrupulous persons she had assumed the control of.

Jack Singleton and his fortunes form another episode in this strange, eventful history; and it is our purpose now to devote a short space to a detail of what befel him in Bond Street, where

we left him, some time since, in circumstances of danger.

Several men pounced upon Jack, at the moment that Allan had uttered a few words of warning to him in regard to them.

"Ah!" cried Singleton. "That's the game, is it?"

Even as he spoke, he felled two of his assailants to the ground; but one of those was sufficiently alive to the circumstances of the case to adopt the best possible means of securing the prisoner.

This officer of the police—for such he was—did not attempt to get up, but he caught Sixteen-stringed Jack by the ankles.

"I have him!—I have him!" he cried.

Jack found further resistance useless, for one of the officers had flung open an over-coat that he wore, and drawn a cutlass which was concealed beneath it, with which he had it in his power to inflict a serious wound.

No. 78.—DARK WOMAN.

But Sixteen-stringed Jack did not see the necessity of making bad worse, and he suddenly ceased resistance.

"I surrender," he said.

"That's all right, Jack Singleton," said one of the officers. "There is plenty of help at hand, and resistance would be madness."

"So be it."

One of the officers had caught Allan by the arm, and was evidently inclined to arrest him, too, merely on the faith of his being in the company of Sixteen-stringed Jack.

"This gentleman," said Jack, "has nothing to do with my affairs, further than knowing me."

"We don't know that," said the officer, "and it will be the safest plan to put him in the Stone Jug along with you, Jack. for a time."

"At your peril," said Allan.

"Oh, we will chance that."

"Upon what charge, and upon what authority, do you take me prisoner?"

"Oh, bother him!" said the chief constable. "Let him go—I don't want him."

Allan was particularly anxious to be free, in order that he might be of service, as quickly as possible, to Sixteen stringed Jack.

"Depend upon me," he said, as he pressed Jack's hand. "I have, as you know, some interest, and will use it."

"Wait until you hear from me," was Jack's reply; and he uttered the words in so significant a manner, that Allan could not help thinking he had some meaning in them beyond what they themselves exactly seemed to imply.

And so he had.

"Farewell!" said Jack, then; and Allan thought, by the action of his hand, that he meant it would be better for him if he, Allan, left him as soon as possible.

The fact was, that a crowd was fast collecting, and the officers were beginning to get uneasy, and so was Sixteen-stringed Jack; for there was one thing he wished much to avoid, and that was being handcuffed, which measure he felt confident the officers would resort to if there was much more commotion in Bond Street about the capture.

"Come, now," said Jack. "There is no need to make me a public spectacle. I will pay for a hackney-coach."

"That's right, Jack. You are a sensible fellow, and I will not miss seeing you turned off, when the Monday morning comes."

"Much obliged," said Jack. "If it should happen to be inconvenient to you, I shall not be put out of my way much."

The officers laughed, and a hackney-coach at that moment lumbering up to the spot, Jack and two of his captors got inside, while the other two disposed themselves, one on the box with the driver, and the other on the foot-board behind.

Jack Singleton was certainly going in state to Newgate.

It remained to be seen whether he got there to the satisfaction of the officers.

Jack had an idea. It was a bold one, like most of Jack's ideas, but it only recommended itself more completely to him on that account.

After the coach had left Bond Street, and had proceeded some short distance towards the City, Jack addressed the officer who sat opposite to him calmly and civilly.

"I hope," he said, "you will get all the reward that is offered for me."

"Oh, no fear of that!"

"How much is it?"

"Well, I suppose it's about a couple of hundred guineas.'

"Is that all?"

"Well, that is about all."

"Why, it's only fifty for each of you!"

"That's about it."

"I always outbid the Government."

"What do you mean, Jack?"

"Why, if you had come quietly to me, I could have given you a hundred each."

"No?"

"Yes, most certainly. You know the 'Three Nags?'"

"The public-house in Long Acre?"

"The same."

"Well, what of that?"

"Only that the money is there."

The two officers in the coach looked at each other in a very comical fashion for a few moments; and Jack was not a little amused at watching the working of their countenances. He could perfectly comprehend what they were thinking of. It was not to let him off for the money he spoke of, but it was how they could get possession of it, and still lodge him in Newgate.

Cupidity was the only bait he could dangle with any degree of success before their eyes.

"Do you mean to say, Jack, that you have got so much as four hundred pounds at 'The Three Nags,' in Long Acre?"

"Oh, yes!"

"Humph!"

"Well, what say you both? Will you have the money, and set me free?"

"Oh, we are men of honour."

"Of course."

"And if so be that we took the money, why Jack, of course you would be free as air."

"Of course," said the other, with a wink at his companion.

"And so we will go to the 'Three Nags' and get it at once, Jack, if you like."

"I shall like nothing better," said Jack. "I hope you will keep faith with me?"

"Oh, honour—honour among—among——"

Thieves!" said the other.

"No, no! Gentlemen—gentlemen!"

The chief officer now pulled the check-string of the coach; and when it stopped, he called out at the window, "Drive to the 'Three Nags' in Long Acre!"

The horses' heads were turned in that direction, and the coach went lumbering along.

Now, Sixteen-stringed Jack had a very particular motive in getting to the "Three Nags," in Long Acre, for in the stable belonging to that hostel he had his horse.

How or by what manœuvres he was to get upon his horse's back, and bid good day to the officers, Jack, perhaps, had not a very clear notion; but he meant to try it, and to be guided by circumstances as regarded details.

If the constables had not been blinded very much by their cupidity, they might well have surmised that Sixteen-stringed Jack was considering some plan to escape from them; but the dust which is always most effectual in blinding human nature is certainly gold-dust.

The probability or the possibility of getting possession of the large sum which Jack had mentioned, was too tempting to be resisted.

The coach stopped with a jerk at the "Three Nags;" and as yet Sixteen-stringed Jack could not be said to have made up his mind what to do.

"Now, Jack," said one of the officers, who was a little more wary than his fellow,—"now, Jack, we don't mean to stand any nonsense."

The officer showed, significantly enough, what he meant, by producing one of those little, stumpy pistols with which the police of the period were generally armed.

Jack felt that whatever he did would not be wholly unattended by danger.

There was another difficulty, too, in the business, and that was, how to possess the landlord or the "Three Nags" with the circumstances of the case, so that he might assist him.

That landlord was actually standing at the door of the old hostel, with his hands in the pockets of a short, white apron he wore; and looking out at the hackney-coach, which so suddenly stopped at his door, with some curiosity, but no other feeling.

Jack Singleton then looked from the window; and from that moment, the landlord, as he afterwards said, in telling the story, knew that "something was up."

"Hilloa!" said Jack.

"Hilloa! is that you?" responded the landlord.

"To be sure it is; and in good company, too, as you may see."

The landlord saw then, in a moment, that Jack was in custody; but what he meant by coming there he could not divine.

Jack then turned to the two officers who were in the coach with him, and spoke in a low voice.

"The landlord of the 'Three Nags' is a good enough fellow; but when a man hides money, I don't think it does any good to say anything about it to any one. So he is not at all aware that, in my room which I occupied here, I have concealed the sum I offer to you to let me go."

"What is to be done, then, Jack?"

"You two had better come in with me, and I will get the money for you."

"Very well," said the principal officer. "Let it be so. We have no very particular wish, either, that anybody but ourselves should know of the affair."

The officer gave, what he thought, a remarkably cunning look to his comrade, as he spoke; for he fully intended to take Jack to Newgate, notwithstanding he agreed so willingly to take a bribe to set him free.

It was, at all events, something gained to have divided his four foes into two divisions; and Jack, although he was still rather undecided what precisely to do, felt that the affair was getting all the easier.

The officer who was on the coach-box remained there, and that one who had taken up his position on the footman's perch behind likewise continued to occupy that position.

Sixteen-stringed Jack and the two who were with him in the coach entered the "Three Nags" together.

The landlord was in a state of great perplexity, to guess what all this meant.

That there were four police officers, with Sixteen-stringed Jack in custody at his door, he could now easily see; but what they came there for, or how it was that they did not at once secure so important a prisoner, by conveying him to Newgate, the landlord could not make out.

But Jack hoped, by a few words, to give him a hint of what he wanted him to do.

"These gentlemen," he said, "will go with me to my room."

"Your room, Jack?" exclaimed the landlord. "What room do you mean?"

The officers looked suspicious.

"Come, come!" said Jack. "No harm will come of it, I am sure; so you may at once give me the key of the room at the back of the bar."

"Oh, no!" said the principal officer. "Jack Singleton and I understand each other."

The landlord—although not very sharp-witted, or he would have taken Jack's hint at once—now began to see that there was a something in the affair which it would be well for him to comprehend, and he said at once, "Oh, ah! To be sure! Your room, Jack."

The landlord had taken Jack's hints and meaning, but yet it was not exactly in a way that made the officers feel quite at their ease.

One of them, indeed, did seem rather inclined to draw back; and he looked at his companion with an expression of alarm.

Jack Singleton was not slow in observing this.

He put on a cool, determined, and slightly offended air and manner, as he said, "I am afraid you are suspicious of some foul play; and if so, I would rather you would not go any further in this matter."

"Oh, no, no!"

"Well, I was only going to add that I know a party, of influence, upon whom I have nothing to do but to dispose of the money I have hidden; and I am as safe as the Regent in his palace."

"Come, come, Jack!" added the officer who was the most grasping after money. "Come, come, Jack, let us see the 'glitter,' and all will be right."

The side touch and the wink which the officer bestowed upon his comrades were not in the least lost upon Sixteen-stringed Jack.

"They mean to betray me," thought Jack; "but many a woodman falls over his own snare."

"This way—this way!" cried the landlord of the "Three Nags," with an ostentatious alacrity and civility that ran the risk of being just a little over-acted.

Along a rather dark passage in the old hostel the party went, and entered a room at the back of the house.

Sixteen-stringed Jack seemed to linger a moment or two longer in the passage than was at all necessary, and the officer, who was suspicious, took hold of his left arm as he said, "Come, now, Jack, let us have all this affair above-board and honest. Don't deceive us."

"I deceive you!" cried Jack. "Perish the thought!"

But Sixteen-Stringed Jack had commenced letting the landlord of the public-house know what he wanted him to do.

Jack always carried in one of his pockets a small piece of white chalk, for it had served his purpose well once, when he was on a black horse and closely pursued.

On that occasion, Jack had made a white star on the forehead of the horse, and given him two white feet, and then tied the bridle to the railings of a house and hid himself close at hand. The officers who were in pursuit knew Jack's black horse so well, that when they saw a horse with a palpable white star on its forehead, and two white feet, they paid no attention to it, but rode on; and for that time Sixteen-Stringed Jack escaped, because he happened to have a piece of white chalk in his pocket.

Since then, he had always carried a piece, in case he should want it.

Now it stood him in good stead in the "Three Nags" public-house, for, as he lingered a moment in the narrow passage, he managed to write upon the wall the following words, "My horse in the passage here."

No sooner was Jack fairly in the room with the officers than he placed his finger on his lips, and assuming an air of great mystery, he said, in a low confidential tone of voice, "Hush! hush! hush!"

"What is it?"

"Who is listening?"

"No one, I hope, but I don't want the landlord to know where I hide my money."

"Oh, that's all right!"

"Certainly," said the other. "But, since we are to have it, I hope you have not the same objection in regard to us, Jack?"

"Certainly not. Which of you will go up?"

"Go where?"

"Up there."

"What do you mean, Jack?"

"Up the chimney."

"The chimney? You don't mean to say your money is up the chimney, do you?"

"I do."

The officers looked at each other, rather disconcerted at this statement, and for a few moments there was rather an awkward silence between Sixteen-stringed Jack and his captors.

———

CHAPTER CLXXIII.

JACK SINGLETON MAKES HIS ESCAPE, AND FINDS A REFUGE AT A MOMENT OF DANGER.

"COME, come, Jack," said one of the officers, "you are only joking with us, I take it."

"Not at all."

"Then," said the other, "those who hide may find; and as you know exactly whereabouts in the chimney the money is, why, you may as well get it, Jack."

"That's true. I will."

Sixteen-Stringed Jack approached the chimney and put the poker a long way up it, and then he gave a nod, and turned to the officers with a look of satisfaction.

"Do you see it?" he said.

"Why how the deuce should we?—and what is there to see?"

"The bag."

"With the money?"

"Just so."

One of the officers looked up the chimney, and a shower of soot came down into his eyes and face.

"Good gracious!" he said, "I am half-blinded."

"This won't do, Jack," said the other. "It seems to me that you are playing with us."

"Well, so I am."

"You are?"

"To be sure! I have altered my mind. Since I have had a little more time to think about it, I made up my mind not to show you the trap—Hem! No, no!—nothing. I mean not to show you the—the——Well, in a word, I won't let you know where my money is hidden."

Jack, as he spoke, made a scuffling on the floor with his feet, and pushed some of the sand which was liberally strewn upon it into a crack left by a square trap-door, which led from that room to the cellars beneath the ground floor.

"Then we are deceived!" cried one of the officers, "and we are only losing our time."

"Not exactly!" said the other, putting on a look which he thought was the most absolute sagacity and wisdom—"not exactly!"

"How do you mean?" asked his companion.

"Yes," said Jack, affecting an apprehension of manner he was far from feeling. "What do you mean?"

"Why, just that I can see there is a trap-door in the floor of this room, and that Jack Singleton is now standing on it, and don't want us to see it; for beneath it, I have no doubt, we shall really find the money?"

"Confusion!" said Jack.

"Ah! Is it so?" cried the other officer.

"See!" said the one who thought himself so clever, as he gave Jack a push which sent him a few paces from the spot,—"see! there is the outline of a trap-door, which, I dare say, we can manage to raise easily enough."

"You have been told of this," said Jack.

"No, no!"

"Then how on earth have you found it out?"

The officer placed a finger to his nose, and assumed such an aspect of preternatural cunning, that Sixteen-stringed Jack had the greatest difficulty to keep himself from laughing outright.

"Well," he said, "since, then, further concealment is useless, I will confess the truth."

"You had as well."

"I will. The money is really and truly underneath this room. There is the trap that leads to it. I have no more to say."

Jack assumed a look which might be called rather despairing, as he flung himself into a seat as if he really gave up now the whole affair to the two officers.

One of them, with the assistance of the thick, strong blade of a pocket-knife, managed to raise the trap in the floor.

All was dark beneath.

"Well, well," said Jack, "I will go and get it."

"Not exactly!"

"Then you go."

The officer was upon his knees on the floor, peering down the trap into the darkness below, and it required only a very slight impulse to send him headlong down the trap on to a cask or two of old ale and a quantity of empty bottles, which formed the contents of the cellar.

The other constable immediately flung himself upon Jack, as he cried out, "No, my fine fellow, this won't do!"

"Idiot!" said Jack.

"What for, eh?"

"To think that Jack Singleton is likely to let himself be taken by one man!"

"Then take that!"

The officer snatched from his pocket one of the little stumpy pistols they always had with them, and placing the muzzle of it right against the forehead of Jack, he pulled the trigger.

The pistol flashed only in the pan.

Jack's life was saved by one of those chances to which the fire-arms of those days were specially liable.

In another instant the pistol was wrenched from

the hand of the officer, and the brass-mounted butt of it came down upon his head, as Jack held it by the barrel, with a crack that no human skull could withstand.

The officer flung his legs from under him as if he were trying to see how soon he could get to the floor, and he lay like a dead man.

Jack was free!

It was, however, but for a moment that he felt himself rid of his foes.

The officer who had been precipitated down the trap-door was a man of resources. To be sure the fall confused him for the short space of time which Jack and the officer who was still above were settling matters, but that was all. He scrambled to his feet, and hastily placing a board upon end, he got on it and forced his head through the trap-door, as he cried out, "Hilloa, my fine fellow, I am not beat yet!"

"But now you are!" said Jack.

Jack caught the stunned officer by the arms, and swung him round so that his heels came with such force against the side of the head of his comrade, that down he went off the board with a celerity that was astonishing to see.

"Two are company," said Jack.

As he spoke, he precipitated the other officer down the trap, and closed it up.

There was but one table in that room, and that Jack turned completely over and placed it flatwise over the trap, with its legs in the air.

"Off and away, now!" he said. "I shall not have to trouble my friends now!"

Jack opened the door of the room, and the first object that presented itself to his notice outside was his horse.

The landlord had seen the little message on the wall, and had followed Jack's directions most implicitly.

"I think we shall do now," cried Jack, as he scrambled into the saddle—for the passage was too narrow and the ceiling was too low to permit him to mount otherwise than in rather an awkward position.

"Jack! Jack! What have you done?" asked the landlord, in an anxious whisper. "You haven't killed them?"

"Not I!"

"Where are they, Jack?"

"In the cellar."

"Ha! ha! Oh! Ha! ha! Capital! That's what I call capital, Jack!"

"What do you call capital?" cried a loud, harsh voice at this moment.

"Oh, Lord!"

"Who is that?" said Jack.

"Mr. Brand, the Bow Street runner."

"Ah, indeed!"

"Yes," said the new arrival. "What is all this about? I was passing the door here, and saw an officer I know minding a coach; and now I find a mounted man in the passage. Who are you, my friend?"

"Why, you see, Mr. Brand," said the landlord, "this is—a—that is—a - hem!—you see——"

"That's it!" cried Jack.

At the moment he spoke, he dashed his heels against the flanks of his horse, and gave it the rein.

With a rush that set all opposition at defiance, the horse dashed along the passage; and the well-known Bow Street runner, Thomas Brand, only saved himself from being knocked down and ridden over by jamming himself up so close to the wall that he occupied the smallest space possible.

As it was, the horse's tail gave him such a slash over the face that he was half-blinded by it, and, for the moment, bewildered.

Jack Singleton was out into Long Acre before you could have counted three.

The officer who had been left in charge of the coach, when he saw such an apparition as a man on horseback coming with such furious speed out of the public-house, could not but feel certain something had happened amiss with his comrades.

He raised a shout of surprise; and then yelled out, with the utmost power of his lungs, "Stop him! stop him! Stop thief! Stop him! He's a highwayman! Stop him!"

"Not so easy!" Jack cried. "Good day!"

Then was seen the odd sight of a hackney-coach pursuing a man on horseback; but the poor old horses who drew the coach had about as much chance of catching Jack as a tortoise really would have had of outrunning a hare, notwithstanding the proverb.

But Sixteen-stringed Jack's position was by no means destitute of peril. He was recognised; and he was in the midst of some of the narrowest thoroughfares of London, and there was a hue and cry at his heels.

Any obstruction to his progress, in the shape of a slip of his horse on the round stones, or the blocking up of a thoroughfare by some unwieldy caravan, would assuredly be fatal to him.

It was towards the North Road that Jack wanted to make his way—for, situated as he was in London, that was unquestionably the nearest route out of town. Therefore was it that, dashing down Long Acre, he dived down one of those long, narrow, tortuous thoroughfares which would lead him to Oxford Street—then called the Oxford Road,—and beyond which he would soon gain the open country. about the neighbourhood of where the Regent's Park now stands.

The most serious enemy that Sixteen-stringed Jack left behind him was the new arrival, at the "Nag's Head," in the person of Brand, the officer; and he, although without any more effectual means of pursuit than his own legs afforded him, rushed after Sixteen-stringed Jack, with the hope of at least keeping him in sight, and raising a hue and cry at his heels until good fortune should place a horse in his possession, or enable him to send other horsemen on the track of the fugitive.

Just as Brand darted over the way, keeping his eyes fixed upon Sixteen-stringed Jack and his horse, he saw, as he thought, a ready chance of enabling him effectually to pursue the flying highwayman.

A groom, riding one horse and leading another by the bridle, came trotting down Long Acre.

"Hold!" cried Brand. "Lend me this horse, on his Majesty's service! There'll be no harm done, and perhaps some good. Keep clear—keep clear!"

The horse swerved a little as Brand tried to mount it; but after two or three ineffectual attempts, he succeeded in getting on to the saddle; and the groom—being one of those slow-minded persons who, if taken by surprise, never know what to say or do—let him take possession of the horse, which was a fine animal, giving promise both of speed and courage.

The narrow turning down which Sixteen-stringed Jack had plunged was exactly opposite where Brand, the officer, had so fortunately found a steed ready to his hand, so that he had not to pause a moment to take thought of the route necessary to pursue ; but urging the horse forward, he flattered himself that he would soon be up with the highwayman, and add the most important achievement to his list of victories over those professional gentlemen with whom the police were supposed to be at war, but with whom, at the time of which we write, they were only too often in league.

We have stated that the thoroughfare was narrow, and we may add that for some distance down there was no turning on either side of the way.

All this seemed exceedingly favourable to the capture of Sixteen-stringed Jack, but in a very few seconds Mr. Brand found it necessary to pull up his horse, and to look about him with very great surprise and impatience.

A heavy waggon, of enormous width, hooped and canvassed so as to make it look like a moving house, was creeping along in the middle of the roadway; and just as well was it that this shapeless out-of-size vehicle should take the middle of the road, for had one of its wheels run in the kennel, there still would not have been space enough left for any moderate vehicle to pass.

A horseman, however, might get by by taking to the pavement, but that would produce a clatter which could not possibly escape some attention.

When, therefore, Mr. Brand drew rein, and called out in a loud voice to the boy who was driving the waggon, "Which way did a man on a dark bay horse go?" and the boy answered, " Drat me if I've seen a bay horse and a man ; they ain't come by me," he might well be excused for feeling a little at fault.

"Stop, my boy—stop !" he cried.

" Woa ! woa !"

The waggon-horses came to a stand-still, and Brand then, in still more imperious tones, called out, " Do you mean to tell me a man and a bay horse have not passed ahead of you and your team ?"

" No."

" What do you mean by no ?"

" 'Cos he hasn't."

Brand could see past the waggon, which was proceeding northward in the same direction Sixteen stringed Jack had taken, and there was not the slightest appearance of the flying man and horse.

What made the thing more puzzling was—or rather, we should say what made it puzzling at all—consisted in the fact that there was no turning, right or left, up to the point at which the waggon had stopped.

It was by a sort of instinctive impulse that the Bow Street runner looked up into the air, then into the windows of the houses on each side of the way, as though he hoped to catch some traces of Sixteen-stringed Jack.

Nothing was to be seen—not a door was open—and to all appearances it seemed as if both hors

and rider had exhaled into the atmosphere, leaving not a trace behind.

" He must have gone on," cried the officer; " and you are either a fool or a rogue, I don't know which."

" The same to you, sir," said the boy.

This answer, although it was well enough deserved, was perhaps all the more aggravating on that account ; and Brand, the officer, who, when he had mounted the spare horse led by the groom, had snatched a riding whip from the hands of the latter, made a savage cut at the boy with it as he trotted the horse on to the pavement to get past the vehicle.

Mr. Brand forgot at the moment that two persons could play at that kind of game, and the boy with the waggon was more efficiently set up for the pastime than he.

" Woa !" cried the boy.

Even as he spoke, the long elastic waggon whip twined round the shoulders of the officer with a close intimacy which was anything but delightful ; and the second slash fell partially upon the horse—which, being of high blood and mettle, and not used to such appeals, dashed off at a rate which no existing highwayman could possibly have equalled, and which, if Brand had really had Sixteen-stringed Jack in view, would soon have brought them face to face.

The boy with the waggon then went whistling on as if nothing had happened, and in a very few minutes turned down an archway which led into an old inn yard, at that period well known as the " Maltsters' Arms."

The yard presented one of those specimens of ancient English inns, several of which are still to be seen in London.

A gallery with balustrades ran round three sides at the height of the first floor—with crazy wooden steps here and there leading down into the thickly littered yard below.

This inn was the proper destination of the waggon, which had that morning delivered a heavy load at Covent Garden Market, and was to take passengers and goods to Watford in the evening at eight o'clock.

There was a look of great pride and exultation on the face of the boy as he now went to the tail of the waggon, and held aside for a moment the heavy flapping canvas which prevented anything like a connected view into the interior.

But a stream of daylight now made its way into the waggon; and lying on its side on the straw—which was there in abundance—might be seen a horse, with its fore-legs tied together by a silk handkerchief.

A man was kneeling close to the head of the horse, holding down its head, and patting its neck to keep it quiet.

That man was no other but Sixteen-stringed Jack, and the horse was the same which had carried him gallantly through many dangers, and which he had so recently mounted in the narrow passage at the " Three Nags " public-house in Long Acre.

————

CHAPTER CLXXIV.

SIXTEEN-STRINGED JACK BECOMES WITNESS TO
A CURIOUS MEETING IN THE OLD INN YARD.

JACK SINGLETON, throughout the whole of his
future life, never would be convinced that it was
mere chance that brought him and his horse on
that day, and the great part of the night following it, to the old inn yard whither the waggon
had conducted him.

Certainly the strange events that he was a
witness to in that place before he left it, might
well engender and encourage such an idea.

Those events we shall now in regular order
proceed to relate.

When the boy who drove the team of horses
that lumbered along with the waggon looked in
at the tail of the vehicle upon Sixteen-stringed
Jack, there was an expression of great gratification
on his face.

The boy nodded his head several times, and
then made a peculiar movement of his fingers
which rather astonished Jack.

"Is this lad a little out of his mind?" thought
Jack.

It was in accordance with that imitative faculty
which belongs to human nature that Jack made
a similar movement with his fingers to what the
boy had done, but Jack accompanied it by the
inquiry of "What do you mean by that, my lad?"

"Oh, you know!"

"Indeed I do not."

"That's right."

"What is right?"

"Why, to say you don't know; but you can
either stay where you are, or go into one of the
rooms from the old gallery up there. They won't
be here till nigh upon midnight."

"Who won't?"

"Come, come!—you know all about it better
than I do, I dare be bound."

The boy gave a nod and a wink to Jack, and
was about to leave him, when Jack cried out,
"No, no; I don't want to stay cooped up in a
waggon till night; while, at the same time, I think
if I could stay here till evening it would be all as
well."

"Of course you can."

"But the people of the inn? What will they
think and say? Can they be depended on?"

"Now, really!" said the boy. "Of course,
they can. Don't the old man and woman belong
to us?"

"Oh, do they?"

"Yes, to be sure."

"Well, that's satisfactory," said Jack; but although he said so, nothing could be well more
unsatisfactory, since he had not the remotest
idea of what the waggon boy meant by talking in
the mysterious manner he did.

After a pause, Jack jumped out of the waggon
and whistled to his horse, who scrambled to its
feet—for Jack had untied the silk handkerchief
which held its fore-legs together—and leaped out
of the waggon.

The boy opened the door of a stable that was
under the gallery, and ushered the horse into it,
as he said, "He will be all right there, and you
can come into the house, if you like, till they come."

"Who on earth," Jack was going to say—
"who on earth are they?" but he had made up
his mind to fathom the mystery, and he felt that
the only way to do that was to give in to the
boy's notion that he already knew all about it, so
he altered the sentence to "Who on earth do you
expect first?"

"Ah, that I don't know. They will come in
twos and threes, I dare say."

"Very likely," said Jack.

"But not till twelve o'clock strikes."

"You are sure of that?"

"Oh, quite."

"Hem! How did you know I belonged to
them?"

"You made the sign to me when you wanted
to leap your horse into the waggon."

"Did I?"

"You know you did."

Jack wondered how he had managed to do that,
as he knew of no sign; but he came to the correct
conclusion, in his own mind, that by some accident he had made some movement that to the boy
resembled a secret sign that was the property of
some fraternity, or of some confederation of which
this boy was an agent.

Jack was determined to humour this supposition.

"Well," he said, "you cannot blame me for
being very cautious and careful."

"To be sure not."

"I am sorry, though, that I cannot wait so late
as midnight, as I have some business on hand,
and I shall have to leave here at eleven o'clock at
the very latest."

"That is just as you please," replied the boy.

"Give my horse, then, a good feed, and see that
he is all ready for the road."

"I will, sir."

"Do you stay here with the waggon?"

"Oh, no! It's a common stage waggon, you
see, and comes and goes just in the usual way.
It starts at eight o'clock to-night, with passengers and goods to Watford, and I go with it.
You see, it would not do for the inn yard to
look as if it had no business at all; but I come
back here as soon as I meet some one to take
charge of the waggon."

"Ah, you do!"

"Oh, yes, because they want me sometimes."

"Who the deuce are 'they?'" thought Jack.
"I would give something to know who 'they'
were."

The impolicy of questioning the boy any further,
so as possibly to awaken a suspicion of his own
ignorance on the subject, was evident to Jack, so
he merely nodded his head.

"You understand?" said the boy.

"Oh, yes! Of course."

"The old couple get on very well."

"Do they?"

"Yes. The fact is, they are very comfortable,
with the whole inn to themselves—because the
two ostlers do not sleep on the premises, and are
only employed to start the waggon, to keep up
appearances, you see."

"I only wish I could see," thought Jack; but
he again nodded his head, although as far as regarded having any comprehension of what the
boy was talking about, that individual might as
well have spoken in some unknown tongue.

The full and clear explanation was, however, to come to Jack before he left the inn yard.

"Come this way," said the lad. "The old couple will dish us up something for dinner."

Jack Singleton had no objection to this proposition, but as he followed the boy he took care to feel that he had the butts of his pocket pistols handy for use in case of an emergency.

As they crossed the inn yard, towards a door that led into the house, there came lounging down the yard a couple of men, whose dress and appearance bespoke them to be horse helps, or under-ostlers, and they commenced attending to the horses in the waggon, who required feeding and looking to before they again left the inn.

"Those are the two helps," whispered the lad to Jack.

"Oh, are they?"

"Yes. But they know nothing."

"Indeed!"

"Not a word."

Jack was very much tempted to say, "Then they're about as wise as I am," but he restrained the impulse, and merely nodded his head—an action, by the by, which he found went a long way with the mysterious lad.

Immediately within the doorway through which they now passed was a wide passage, with rooms to the right and to the left.

One of those rooms had a sort of window in the wall, which served for a bar, and through which the interior could be seen.

That interior had a look of comfort about it. A bright fire burnt on the hearth, and the room was well enough furnished.

An old man was there whose white hair would, under ordinary circumstances, have commanded respect, but, as he rose and advanced to the bar, the malignant look of his face at once filled Jack with aversion.

"Servant, sir! Servant!" said the old man to Jack.

Jack nodded.

"It's all right," said the boy.

"Oh, that's satisfactory! Come in, sir—come in. Any news, sir, stirring?"

"None."

"The friend," said the boy, "will take something."

"To be sure—to be sure! Lucy Amelia! Where are you, Lucy Amelia?

Never was Sixteen-stringed so astonished as at the individual who answered to the feminine names of Lucy Amelia.

A hideous old hag hobbled into the room, and, with a high, cracked voice full of gall and passion, screamed out, "What do you want now, old wretch? What are you calling me for? Am I not to have a moment's rest, eh? What do you want now?"

The old man went deliberately to a corner of the room and picked up a stout stick, which, to the horror of Jack, he laid, with a sounding thwack, over the hag's back.

"Take that!" he said; "and keep a civil tongue in your head!'

The old woman raised an awful howl, but took no other notice of the transaction.

The boy laughed.

"That's the way he manages her," he said, appealing to Sixteen-stringed Jack.

"So I see."

"Lucy Amelia," said the old man, as if nothing had happened, "get something for the gentleman."

"It's all sopped up," whispered the hag. "I didn't think there could be so much blood in any one."

"What do you mean?"

"What—do—I—mean?"

The old hag looked suspiciously at Jack, who had listened to the words she had uttered with a creeping of the heart that almost made him sick.

"Yes," bellowed the old man, "what do you mean? Didn't you hear that the gentleman was one of us?"

"No, I didn't."

Thwack came the stick across her shoulders again, as the old man added, "Then you hear now!"

The old hag gave another howl, just as she had done before, and took no further notice of the little transaction. She bustled about the room; and, from a cupboard, procured a ham and some fine white bread. The old man placed a brown jug of delicious ale upon the table; and Jack, whatever might be his ideas of the party at the old inn, began to have great respect for the larder.

While he paid attention to the repast before him Jack had time to think.

That he had accidentally alighted upon the head-quarters, or upon one of the places of rendezvous, of persons who were carrying on some system of extensive criminality he could not doubt.

Indeed, from the horrible words that had escaped the old hag, he might reasonably come to the conclusion that murder was part of the practices of those persons.

Jack made up his mind, as he partook of the ham, the fine white bread, and the ale, that he would spare no pains to come at the heart of the mystery.

The day was fast fading away, and he considered that, when the dusk of evening arrived, he would have a good chance of making some arrangement that would suit his views.

What he wanted to succeed in doing, if it were possible, was to seem to leave the inn, but in reality to remain in it.

How this was to be done, he was not at that exact moment prepared to say.

"I must be guided by circumstances," thought Jack; "and I daresay I shall find some means of getting the better of the boy's caution."

There was soon quite a bustle in the inn yard, for the waggon was again getting ready to leave; and various packages of goods arrived to go by it, and some poor people who wanted to travel in the direction it went out of London, came to get a lift for the moderate sum charged in such a conveyance.

"They won't interfere with my horse?" said Jack.

"Oh, no, no!"

"I will just go and look at him."

"Number six," said the boy. "That's the stable he is in."

"All right!"

Sixteen-stringed Jack strolled out into the inn yard; and while all the bustle of getting the waggon and the waggon horses ready for de-

parture was taking place, he looked at his horse, which he found all safe, and with a full rack and manger.

There were about a dozen stables, all opening into the inn yard; and as Jack strolled along he saw that none of them were occupied.

It wanted yet some time to eight o'clock, when the waggon was to start; and Sixteen-stringed Jack employed his leisure in making such an examination of the premises as he could.

Feeling strongly tempted to ascend one of the staircases that led up to the gallery, frail and all aslant as they looked, he commenced doing so; but when he reached the gallery, he tried several doors opening into it, without finding any one that was not fastened.

Just as Jack was then about to descend again to the inn yard, he was transfixed to the spot on which he stood by hearing a very charming voice singing.

No. 79.—DARK WOMAN.

The sounds evidently came from within one of the rooms that opened from the gallery; but which door would lead to the singer, Jack could not very well decide.

The voice was young and fresh, and the words of the song were anything but suggestive of criminality, or even of any connivance in such awful deeds as had been hinted at so broadly by the old hag in the room below.

The enunciation of the singer was so perfect that Jack Singleton heard every word of the song.

It was as follows:—

"Oh, love is like the rainbow,
   That passes ere an hour:
Oh, love is like the beauty
   That decks the summer flower.
'Tis like the cameleon,
   Which never is the same;
'Tis like the timid antelope,
   So sweet, but hard to tame

Or like the gentle crescent moon,
Whose light so briefly shines;
Or like her sister stars that fade
When pensive night declines.
'Tis like the crystal of the lake
When rippled by the breeze;
'Tis like the perfumed zephyrs
That play among the trees;
'Tis like all beauteous sounds and sights,
Which this fair world supplies.
Yet, oh! I found it most complete
In my dear lady's eyes."

The voice ceased, and if Jack had heard those sweet and gentle tones anywhere else, or under any other circumstances, he would have been much more delighted than he was.

As it was, however, to listen to such melody in such a place had something jarring and revolting about it.

Jack shuddered, as the last notes died away upon the night air.

Who could be the singer? Who, in such a place, where crime, and possibly murder, in its most revolting aspect, found a home—who thus, in such sentimental strains, sang of love, and tenderness, and of beauty.

Truly, the mysteries of that old inn yard and the crumbling mass of buildings attached to it thickened about the imagination of Sixteen-stringed Jack, and made him at moments almost doubt if he were in his waking senses.

The room from which the sounds proceeded was no mystery, since the sweet strains of the singer's voice had lasted quite long enough for Jack Singleton to localise them.

That they came from one of the rooms leading from that old gallery, and that the particular door which opened upon that particular room had the number eight upon it, he was certain.

Cautiously Sixteen-Stringed Jack turned the handle of the lock.

The door was fast.

Whether it was locked from the inside or from the out, Jack was at first at a loss to discover. Had he been a "cracksman" instead of a "highwayman," he would probably much more quickly than he did, have come to some conclusion on that head.

As it was, it took Jack some few moments of thought before it occurred to him that he would try to ascertain if there were a key in the lock or not.

There was none.

Admitting, then, the door of the room to be locked, the fair singer—Jack called her "fair" in his own mind—was a prisoner.

The bustle in the inn yard consequent upon the departure of the waggon was now at its height, and if Jack wanted an opportunity of trying to hold communication with the singer, he could not have a better.

The shadows of evening were gathering about the old place.

Two or three lanterns were lit below in the inn yard, and they sent up to the gallery confusing shadows.

"Now is my time," said Jack. "I will try and speak to this young creature, be she whom she may."

Jack called the unknown singer a "young creature," since it did not stand to reason that a voice of such freshness and beauty could issue from other than youthful lips.

He tapped gently at the door.

There was no reply.

Jack tapped again, louder.

Then there came the low, mournful sound of a voice from within.

"No, no!" it said. "No more—no more! He will not come—he does not come!"

This speech was puzzling to Jack, and he thought as a "he" was spoken of, he might as well reply to it as if he had some comprehension of it.

"Yes," he said, "I am here."

"You?—you?"

"Yes; do you not hear my voice?"

There came from within the room a half-stifled cry, and some heavy body seemed to have been flung against the door.

"Speak! Oh, God! make him speak again!"

"Open the door," said Jack. "Open the door, if you can."

"No, it is not he!"

"Open the door."

"I cannot."

"I am a friend."

"I am a prisoner. You are not my Arthur Oh, no—no—no! You are not my Arthur!"

The sound of weeping came from within the room, but before Jack could now make up his mind what to do, there came across his eyes a flash of light, and he heard a grunting, growling kind of noise, that made him at first think some animal was on the gallery with him.

Upon looking, however, in the direction whence these noises proceeded, Jack saw that the old hag of a woman who officiated in the "bar" below had just ascended the flight of steps from the yard nearest to where he was.

The hag carried in her hand a lantern such as is used in stables, and over the other arm she had a basket, which appeared to be heavy, and Jack thought that it had clothing in it, by the glance he was able to take of it.

The old hag came on, grunting and grumbling, and wheezing and coughing, and stumbling upon the old worn-out boarding of the gallery, and muttering to herself, "Rich—oh, yes! I shall live to be rich yet. He! he! he! I shall be a rich woman—and then—then I—I—if it wasn't for my cough—and my—my rheumatiz, I should be quite happy—quite. Eugh! eugh!"

The idea took possession of Sixteen-stringed Jack's mind that the old woman was on a visit to that room in which was imprisoned the fair singer.

Curiosity to get at the heart of the mystery that shrouded these proceedings took a strong hold of him, and he resolved to watch the hag.

CHAPTER CLXXV.

THE MYSTERIES OF THE OLD INN BEGIN TO CLEAR.—JACK IN DANGER.

IN order that he might keep an eye upon the movements of the old hag who had ascended the gallery, without being himself seen, Jack Singleton had to adopt the readiest plan of concealment than presented itself to him.

He lay down at full length, and as flat as he

could, close to the balustrade of the gallery, so that he occupied as small a space as possible, and was in the shadow cast by that balustrade.

The presence of the lanterns in the inn yard below materially aided Sixteen-stringed Jack in hiding where he was, for they deepened the shadow of the balustrade on the gallery floor.

Not suspecting the presence of any one there, the old woman might very well overlook him.

Jack hoped she would.

"Yes," continued the hag, muttering to herself, —"yes; I shall be a rich woman yet, and then I will settle John, and begin a new life. Eh?—eh?"

Who John was that was to be "settled," Jack, at first, could not imagine, till he recollected he had heard the old man down below in the bar called by that name.

Considering the unfeeling manner in which John had laid a stick over the old woman's shoulders, Sixteen-stringed Jack was not surprised at her idea of "settling John."

She passed Jack without casting a glance even in the direction where he lay. The skirts of her ragged garments touched him, but he scarcely breathed as she hobbled past.

She stopped at the door of number eight.

There was then a great fumbling in some capacious pocket the hag wore for a key, and then she unlocked the door of the room.

"Now, poppet! Now, poppet!" she said. "Here's its good old granny, and Arthur will come to-night!"

"Oh, tell me so again and again!" replied a sweet voice. "Will he come? Will he come, and the two angels with him? I can hear them all three, at times, singing—singing, far up above, in the sunlight; and they are thinking of me, too! It is a long time since I died, you know, and it was hard that the silver cord should break and leave me here below, while they went up—up—up into the blue sky, to live in the golden clouds you may see any day at sunset! Oh, that was suffering—suffering for me; but, as he will come for me some day, I ought to be patient!"

"He, he, he! To be sure, poppet!" said the hag.

"The poor thing is mad!" murmured Jack to himself.

There could be no doubt whatever upon that point, after the extraordinary speech which the prisoner in that room had uttered.

What suffering and persecution had driven her to that sad state he had no means even of surmising.

"Come, come," added the old woman, as she stepped across the threshold of the room,—"come, come, ladybird. Here are your fine clothes; and you will take a pretty walk now by the King's Palace, and when the fine gentlemen speak to you you will be as cheerful as a bird, and bring one of them here; and then we will fetch Arthur, and all of us be as merry and happy as brides."

"What on earth does the old wretch mean?" thought Jack.

"No, no!—no more!" said the voice of the poor maniac. "I will go and smile no more, for you deceive me! Arthur does not come!"

"But, poppet!"

"I will not!"

"Then," said the hag, suddenly altering her tone to one of menace,—"then you will never see Arthur, your husband, nor your two children again!"

"Oh, do not say that!"

"I do say it!"

"Mercy! mercy! What am I to do?"

"You are to put on these fine clothes that make you look like a queen, and you are to go where you have gone before — opposite to the Palace—and you are to smile and look pretty; and when some fine gentleman speaks to you, you are to take him by the arm and bring him here, for there is one of those fine gentlemen who can tell us where your Arthur is, and some day you will bring home the right one!"

"Yes—oh, yes!"

"But if you say one word to him, before he gets here, about Arthur, he will shake you off and fly!"

"I know! I know!"

"You comprehend all that, poppet?"

"I will hold my head, for that keeps my poor brains together, and try to do so."

"To be sure you will—to be sure you will; and now put on the fine clothes."

The hag went into the room, and closed the door behind her.

Jack had been bewildered before, but certainly he was a little more confused now.

"I think," he said, "I shall have to hold my head to keep my brains together, in order to enable me to make out what all this means."

The rumbling of wheels down below in the inn yard now attracted Sixteen-stringed Jack's attention; and looking through the openings between the pillars of the balustrade he saw that the waggon was starting.

The old, steady horses were shaking their heads and jingling their bells.

The boy who had brought him (Jack) to that mysterious inn was cracking his whip.

The ostlers were putting out their lanterns.

The time for the waggon to go forth on its journey to Watford had come.

A confused Babel of voices arose from the passengers and their friends.

"Good bye, aunt!" "Look after Susey!" "Remember me to Uncle Samuel!" "I won't forget the gooseberries!" "All right!" "Back again on Tuesday!" "Be sure you write by the carrier!" "Good bye! good bye!"

The waggon lumbered out of the inn yard.

In five minutes more all was silence and darkness in the place.

Sixteen-stringed Jack would have risen from his place of concealment, but that he waited to see the old woman come out of number eight room again. He had not to wait very long.

The chimes of some neighbouring clock, probably that of St. Giles's-in-the-Fields, gave out the half-hour past eight.

Then the door of number eight opened; and in the light that came from the room itself, into which the hag had taken the lantern she had carried with her, Jack saw that two persons came out on to the balcony.

One was the hag.

Jack easily recognised her by her stooping gait, and the slightly tremulous motion of her head.

The other person stood a good head taller than

the hag; and even the dim light that shone upon her was sufficient to reveal the graceful contour and outlines of some youthful and handsome form.

"Go now, poppet," said the old woman; "and good luck go with you and come back with you."

"There is a shadow gone with me," said a soft, sweet voice.

"A shadow? What shadow?"

"The shadow of Death."

"Stuff—stuff! Be sure you say nothing of that sort to the fine gentleman, or you will never see Arthur again."

"I will not! I will not!

"'To-morrow is Saint Valentine's Day,
    All in the morn, betimes.'"

"Peace, peace, poppet!" cried the old woman. "Don't be singing here! Go your ways, and be sure you bring back some fine gentleman with a gold watch in his pocket and sparkling rings on his fingers, and we will make him tell us where Arthur is, if he is the right man to know; and if he is not, it is but to cry to him, 'Bid you good even, my pretty gentleman! Go your ways, for we want none of you.'"

Jack could see that the young person who was with the hag held both her hands for a moment together, as in the attitude of prayer.

"God bless my Arthur and my two little ones, and restore them to me this night," she said.

The old woman appeared to cower down until her head nearly touched the floor, as this prayer was uttered.

Sixteen-stringed Jack very nearly, on the impulse of the moment, cried out, "Amen!" but he controlled the desire so to do, for much he wanted to see the end of all these strange adventures.

"Now, poppet," said the hag, "go your ways."

"I go! I go!"

Slowly the charming-looking young woman now began the descent of the crazy steps that led down from the ancient gallery to the inn yard below; and as she did so, the old woman went back into the room, and brought out the lantern.

Jack still kept in hiding.

The hag tottered to the balustrade, just missing Sixteen-stringed Jack by about six inches of space, and held the lantern over the top of it, to watch the progress of the poor young creature, whose confused intellect she had been so cruelly practising on.

Then that poor demented one paused a moment, and turned.

She looked up.

A ray of light from the lantern fell upon her face, and Jack saw it.

Never had he looked upon anything half so beautiful and half so sad as was the fair young face that met his eyes.

The beauty was of that fascinating order that no one, with a human heart and with human feelings, could have looked upon unmoved; but the look of exquisite sadness and suffering about the eyes was enough to break any sensitive heart to behold.

It was but for a moment that Jack saw the face, but he felt that he should remember it to the latest hour of his life.

"Go on, poppet, go on!" cried the old woman.

The poor girl—for she looked little more—gathered, with an impatient action, more closely around her delicate form a rich silken cloak she wore, and then left the inn yard.

"He! he! he!" laughed the old hag.

Jack felt at that moment a vehement desire to fling the old woman over the balustrade into the yard below.

A touch would have done it, but he abstained from the act, and listened to her.

"He! he! he! She is too pretty not to attract some eyes, and there will be more plunder for me! I shall be a rich woman some day. I wonder what enamoured fool will follow her home to-night, little thinking that he is coming to his death! He! he!—eugh!—my cough is troublesome—to his death!—to his death! The old well will be too full at last, and then I must burn down the inn!—yes, then I must burn down the inn, and settle John, and get away with all my money! Eugh! eugh! eugh!"

Coughing and wheezing, the old woman now slowly descended the stairs, and crept along the inn yard, and was soon out of sight.

Jack rose up from his horizontal position.

He began to comprehend matters a little better.

"Let me think," he said. "Let me think."

Jack placed his hand upon his brow and reflected. He strove to make some connected story of all he had heard the old hag say, and of all he had heard her poor deranged victim say.

"I think I see it," said Jack. "The truth must be that, in some strange manner, this murderous old woman has got a hold of the imagination of that fair young creature, and makes her do her bidding, contrary to all the impulses of her own heart. She is sent out to decoy to this place —so lonely, desolate, and mysterious as it is— those persons who may be attracted by her more than mortal beauty; and then what becomes of them?"

Jack Singleton paused when he came to this point of his cogitations, and a kind of shudder came over him.

Putting together all the fragmentary expressions he had heard, so as to evolve from them something like a connected idea, he could come to no other possible conclusion than that whoever was brought home to that place—by the innocent fascinations of the poor insane girl—was murdered.

What a fearful place had chance, that evening, brought Sixteen-stringed Jack into!

The shuddering, shrinking horror that he began to feel at that inn yard, and at the rumbling old house which was attached to it, would have induced him to fly at once from the spot.

A kind of fascination, however, held him there; and it was no wonder that a feeling something akin to superstition came over him, to the effect that it was a duty upon his part to break up, if possible, such a den of iniquity, and rescue that fair young creature who, with her wandering intellect, was made subservient to criminality of the deepest dye.

The old hag had taken away the lantern, which was a great disappointment to Sixteen-stringed Jack, for he would gladly have examined the interior of that apartment—number eight—which seemed to be, during the day-time, a kind of prison for the young girl who had sallied out on so fearful an errand.

The result of Jack's reflections, however, after a few minutes, was that he had better now go and show himself in the inn, lest he should awaken suspicion that he was lurking about the premises more as a spy than as an associate.

Jack took good care, however, before he left the inn yard, to see that his horse was in good keeping; and finding such to be the case, he put on as careless an air as was possible under the circumstances, and strolled into the narrow passage which communicated with the bar-room of the old inn.

There was a very strange light in that passage, and Jack found that it proceeded from a lantern, which was placed upon the floor.

A glance showed him that the bar-parlour was empty; and the temptation came strongly upon Jack's mind to seize upon this lantern, and, by its aid, attempt an exploration of that chamber—number eight—leading from the gallery which had been in the occupation of the fair young creature whose fate filled him with commiseration.

Jack seized the lantern.

A glance at it showed him it was one of those which had a dark slide to it, and he immediately reduced it to a state which permitted the faintest possible gleam of light only to escape from it.

Jack had made up his mind to ascertain all the particulars he possibly could, in regard to the internal economy of that house of murder, before he left it.

Rapidly he made his way across the inn yard.

He reached the gallery. The door of number eight stood almost invitingly open.

With a presence of mind hardly to be expected under the circumstances of excitement into which he had been thrown, Sixteen-stringed Jack took the key from the outside of the lock, and transferred it to the inside.

Another moment, and he had locked the door upon himself, and, at all events, felt secure from immediate interruption.

Then he removed the darkening slide from the lens of the lantern, and, by the broad beam of light he thus procured, he, with the deepest interest, surveyed the apartment.

It was but an ordinary sitting-room, furnished in the most ordinary manner.

A few tables and chairs, of ancient and massive appearance, a faded carpet, and some very ancient prints, hanging in some old, blackened frames, that had once been gilt, upon the walls, completed, with one exception, the whole furnishing of the room.

That exception consisted of a piece of very beautiful and rich silken tapestry, which hung over the window.

That window looked out upon the gallery.

A feeling of disappointment came over the mind of Jack, at finding no more food for speculative curiosity in that room than, at the first glance, presented itself; but all his interest was soon aroused again, by observing a very narrow doorway in one corner.

Jack placed his hand upon a little brass handle, and found that this door opened without any trouble.

There was, in truth, no lock or fastening to it whatever, and it was only held in its place by fitting rather tightly in its framework.

There was a short space beyond this door, so narrow as only to admit of the passage of one person, and not above six feet in length.

Then there was another door, which yielded to a push; and Jack Singleton felt certain that he was in the next room to number eight, on the balcony.

That room would be number seven, or number nine—he knew not which.

It was, however, a much more interesting apartment than the one he had just quitted.

It was a bed-chamber.

Jack fancied that it was of larger dimensions than number eight, although the most noticeable article of furniture which it contained was a very large, old fashioned, four-post bedstead.

The draperies of this bedstead were very full and complete.

Very rich and costly, likewise, were they; and Jack had a confused notion, for a moment, on his mind, that he must have seen them somewhere else, as the texture and pattern appeared familiar to him.

It was a few moments before he could make up his mind whether this apparent reminiscence was a delusion or not; and then, all at once, it occurred to him that the costly piece of tapestry he had seen hanging by the window of number eight was of the same pattern and material as the rich and elaborate hangings to the massive bedstead.

It was in vain that Sixteen-stringed Jack tried to analyze a particular feeling which came over him while in this apartment.

It might be something in the air.

It might be something in his own constitutional sensations of the moment.

It might be merely imagination.

But, be it what it might, certainly the fact remained, that Jack drew his breath with difficulty; and there came a creeping, shuddering sensation at his heart, as he gazed about him.

He felt certain then that the air was loaded with some peculiar odour, which was intensely horrible; and yet he knew not why.

Thrice he turned completely round, and sent the broad, fan-shaped ray of light from the lantern into every corner of the apartment.

But there was nothing particularly to invoke either curiosity or apprehension.

All seemed still and calm enough; nor could he observe that there were any means of leaving that room, except by the way he had come into it.

Suddenly, then, Jack was startled by a slight creaking sound; and fixing his eyes in the direction from whence it came, he saw that one of the tall doors of an ancient-looking wardrobe had—apparently of its own accord—opened about a couple of inches.

Sixteen-stringed Jack knew very well that such a thing as that might happen from perfectly natural causes.

The merely coming into a room with a light will sometimes sufficiently agitate and alter the temperature of the air, as to induce some waves of it to act in such a manner upon wide, flat, and easily yielding surfaces.

But still there was a kind of mute invitation to a scrutiny of that wardrobe by the mere fact that one of its doors had opened this couple of inches before his eyes.

Jack accepted the invitation.

Striding forward, he opened the door fully.

The wardrobe was but a shell; the outline—the side-walls, so to speak, of such a piece of furniture.

Jack held the lantern before him, and then he recoiled with horror.

He understood in a moment whence came that peculiar odour in the air of the apartment.

It was the odour of blood!

Splashed upon the inner surface of this wardrobe—lying heavily upon the flooring of this imitation piece of furniture, lay blood in sufficient abundance to vitiate every breath of air that crossed it.

Jack felt at once that here was confirmation strong of all his worst surmises and suspicions in regard to the fearful practices of that hag, who herself, with one foot in the grave, played the part of a murderess, from a grasping cupidity that was as much a piece of insanity in her intellect as that affecting derangement of the head and brain which induced the fair young creature, who was the prisoner of number eight, to do her bidding.

Jack was at once puzzled, confounded, and horrified.

Whence came that blood—and if from the body of some murdered man, where was the body, and what could have been the object of placing it in that mock wardrobe, there to leave such ghastly evidences of its presence, while it had evidently been removed to some other place?

These were reflections that chased each other through the mind of Sixteen-stringed Jack; and it was some minutes ere, after recoiling from the fearful sight before him a second time, he could make up his mind to a more particular examination of the wardrobe.

Then Jack conquered his repugnance.

He carefully examined its interior.

If to discover terrible secrets, and to have the imagination infected with the recollection of deeds of blood, be rewards, then we may say, in common parlance, that Jack Singleton was rewarded for this closer examination by some discoveries.

He saw that there was an iron ring in the floor of the seeming wardrobe.

He saw that that ring belonged to a square trap-door, of quite sufficient width to admit the passage of a human body.

But for the coagulated blood which lay in a mass upon the ring, Jack would have liked to raise that trap-door, and look beneath it.

But he could not make up his mind to touch so ensanguined an object.

He was turning away, with a feeling of disgust and horror, when some peculiarity about one of the evident sides of the trap-door attracted his closer observation.

It was a piece of cloth, which seemed to have been nipped and held tight the last time the trap-door was closed.

This piece of cloth projected, in a straggling sort of manner, some two or three inches in height, and along nearly two-thirds of one side of the trap.

It looked like part of the skirt of a coat, and was either of dark crimson cloth originally, or was so dyed by the blood of him to whom it had belonged

Upon looking closer, Jack found that what held this piece of cloth so firmly was a rather large-sized gilt button.

The idea came across him that he would not leave that spot without possessing himself of such a memento—such an evidence of some fearful deed, which had been there enacted, and which, in the mysterious march of events, might possibly bring to human justice its perpetrators.

Jack searched in his pockets for a glove.

He did not like to touch that piece of cloth—dappled in blood as it was—with his hands. An invincible repugnance to do so restrained him; and finding that he had no glove with him, he looked about him for some means, in the room, of interposing between his actual hand and the object he wished to grasp.

Lying upon a chair was a cloak.

Its aspect, shape, make, and the brass clasp at its neck, suggested that it had belonged to some military costume.

There was a pocket in the side of the cloak, and from that Jack drew out a handkerchief and a pair of buff leather gloves.

Did that cloak, that handkerchief, and those gloves, belong to the unhappy person whose heart's blood splashed, with such hideous prodigality, the interior of the mock wardrobe?

Jack asked himself the question, and, at the same moment, could have taken his oath in the affirmative.

The gloves, however, answered his present purpose. He put them on, and again approached the wardrobe.

A hearty tug at the piece of cloth failed to disengage it.

"I must open the trap a short distance," said Jack Singleton, "however disagreeable it is to do so."

Without the gloves, he would not have ventured; but now, slightly averting his head—after placing the lantern on the floor, and just clear of the opening of the trap—he took hold of the iron ring.

The trap was stiff.

Perhaps it was that piece of cloth wedged in it which made it difficult to raise.

Perhaps its hinges were rusted with the terrible fluid that had flowed in and about them.

Jack was a strong man, but certainly it took him an effort to raise that trap.

He was not at all prepared for what happened the moment he did so.

The piece of cloth which had projected through the crevice, and was kept there so firmly by the button, disappeared with a suddenness and velocity that surprised him; and as it did so, he heard a sickening, crashing sound, and then a dull, heavy splash, as if some heavy object—after falling a considerable distance—had reached water.

Then all was still.

It was the stillness of death.

The stillness of consummated murder.

It needed little reflection, and no ingenuity, to comprehend what had happened.

The corpse of a murdered man had been attempted to be thrown down the trap, but in hastily closing it, that piece of cloth with the button attached to it had been caught, and the corpse had hung suspended until Jack Singleton released it, when it fell with that terrible sound into some profound and hideous depths below.

Was that the well which the old hag had feared at length would be full of victims?

Surely it was.

Jack staggered back and closed the wardrobe door.

He stood for a few moments in a state of irresolution. Then his impulse was to fly from that place, and adopt some immediate means for letting the authorities know that such a den of murder existed in the heart of London.

Before Jack, however, could take two steps towards leaving the apartment, he heard a violent knocking as if upon some wall close at hand.

He listened intently, and was convinced that it came from the direction of the first room he had entered—namely, number eight.

The door of that room he had locked on the inside. Some one, then, was in the gallery without, clamouring for admission.

Who could it be?

Was it that fair young creature returned with another victim?

Was it the hag herself?

What should he think?—what should he do?

Jack darkened his lantern.

He made his way creepingly and anxiously towards the outer room.

He stood by the door and listened.

It was the hag. She was coughing without.

"Engh! eugh! eugh! Where's the key?—what can have come of the key? I must go in, and put all to rights—for who knows but somebody may come? Where's the key?"

Jack heard her fumbling about and feeling on the floor of the gallery, close to the door, where she might suppose she had dropped the key; but, of course, that search was all in vain, inasmuch as it was at that moment in the lock of the door on the inner side.

"It's gone! it's gone!" said the old woman. "I'm afraid I'm getting old, and a little forgetful. But there's merry times coming yet, when I'm rich, as I shall be—oh, dear, yes!—as I shall be!"

Jack was afraid that she would adopt the same mode of ascertaining if the key were in the lock that he had, so he gently removed it.

The old woman spoke again.

"Well, well! It don't matter. I shall see it in daylight, for the key of number one opens all the doors."

"Oh, does it?" thought Jack. "That's a piece of information for me."

"But nobody knows that," added the old woman, "but me. John, even, don't know it. Ah! I do so look forward to settling John! And I wonder what's become of my lantern, too. That's some of John's doings, I'll be bound. So I'm forced to bring a candle; and if there was a breath of air a stirring, it would be blown out; but there isn't."

Jack heard the old woman hobbling along the gallery, no doubt to get the key of number one; and then he asked himself the very pertinent question of what he should do.

That there was something still to find out in that establishment, he fully believed. That there were tragic elements connected with that old inn, a knowledge of which would be at once interesting and terrible, he had every reason to anticipate.

If he were to seize upon the old hag and bring her career to a close, he probably would know no more than he had already acquired.

Jack was curious to know all.

He wanted to know—provided the fair young girl brought home a victim—what then exactly happened, and by whom that victim was disposed of.

He wanted to know how the death was accomplished, previous to the dead body being dragged into that mock wardrobe and precipitated down the trap.

Jack felt that he could only acquire this information by further observation, and that further observation he determined to enjoy.

He put out his lantern, and he waited for the old woman.

Soon he heard the grating of a key in the lock; and Jack had just time to crouch down behind a chair—which, to tell the truth, very inefficiently screened him—when the door opened, and the old woman entered, with a lighted candle in her hand.

"I suppose," she said, "he's gone out somewhere; for I haven't seen him for ever so long, though his horse is in the stable. But, as he's one of them, it don't matter."

Jack could very well understand that she alluded to him, and he congratulated himself again and again upon the mistake which the boy driving the waggon had made, in thinking him one of some fraternity with criminal objects and purposes, to whom that old inn and its arrangements belonged.

The old woman was a great deal too busy, in taking care of the candle from the draught of the door, to look about her; so that, badly as Jack was hidden, it answered all the purpose, and she passed him towards the inner room.

Jack was determined not to be foiled, and he crept after her.

Standing in the narrow passage, between those two doors, neither of which had any fastening or lock, Sixteen-stringed Jack was able, by holding the inner one open about a couple of inches, to keep an eye upon the movements of the old woman.

She placed the candle upon a table. She approached the bed, and drew aside the costly and beautiful hangings; and then what she was about completely and entirely puzzled Jack Singleton

Then came a sharp, clicking sound, and then the dull reverberation as of something soft—like a bed or mattress—falling. That was succeeded by a grinding noise, as if some pulley—or other apparatus, of a similar character—was being wound up; and then the old woman cried out, "All's right!"

She never went near the wardrobe, which Jack had closed. She just cast a casual glance about the apartment; but in that casual glance her eyes fell upon the cloak, from the pocket of which Jack had taken the gloves and the handkerchief.

"Dear me!" she said. "It's just as well not to leave this here. Perhaps it may be another officer. I wonder what it'll fetch? A guinea, I should say. Aaron will give a guinea. Ah! I shall certainly be a rich woman some day, and then I shall begin to enjoy life."

The hag hobbled off, with the cloak over her arm. Jack had retreated behind the chair again, and in a few moments more he was left to the undisturbed possession of those apartments so full of terrors and of mysteries.

The curiosity of Jack was so intensely excited, to know what the strange noises the old woman had produced, in connexion with the bedstead, could possibly mean, that he scarcely waited for her to get sufficient distance from the door of number eight, before he recommenced his inquiries.

He had blown out his lantern, in which there had been nothing but a piece of common candle; but he was provided with matches, which gentlemen of his profession were never without, and he soon relit it.

His curiosity overcame his repugnance to enter that bed-chamber again; and, without casting a single glance at the wardrobe, he advanced towards the massive bedstead, and commenced a critical examination of it.

The hangings were so voluminous—there were so many tassels, cords, valences, and extra pieces —that it was quite a confusing thing to get at the actual fabric of the bed itself.

Jack was persevering, however; and finally he was rewarded by observing a very curious piece of apparatus.

There was a small wheel embedded in one of the massive posts, and to this was attached a handle of wood, projecting about six inches, but which was easily lost and covered up by the heavy hangings.

Just above this was a little brass projection, something like a bell-pull—of that character which is worked by the finger, pulling it up, or pressing it down.

But Jack did not like to interfere with these contrivances, whatever they might mean, until he knew something more about them; so he took a good look at the bed.

There seemed to be a great weight of clothing upon it, and it presented a very flat appearance, as if some heavy weight had recently rested upon it. Up above, at what might be called the ceiling of the bedstead, appeared the same material of which the hangings were composed, but it had a tumbled, disarranged kind of look.

"What is the meaning of it all?" said Jack. "I should like to make out; and I will, too, before I leave it."

He set his lantern down upon a chair by the bed-side; but, owing to the disposition of the hangings, that left him in considerable darkness when he went round to the post where the curious apparatus was situated.

"I shall see better," he said, "if there's really anything to see, by placing the lantern on the bed."

Jack did this; and then he found that the whole affair was tolerably well illuminated; and considering that whatever had taken place when the old hag had worked the apparatus had done no harm to her, he thought he might as well place his finger upon that projecting piece of brass that looked like a bell-pull, and see what would come of it.

It was not in human nature to do otherwise than hesitate for a moment under such circumstances; and Jack kept his finger upon the bit of brass for a length of time, during which you might have counted ten, without pressure.

Then he exerted some force.

There was a grating sound for a moment, and then down came the whole ceiling of the bedstead with a heavy thud upon the bed below.

The lantern was smashed, and Sixteen-stringed Jack was in darkness.

CHAPTER CLXXVI

HIS ROYAL HIGHNESS THE REGENT BECOMES TIRED OF EVERYTHING AND OF EVERYBODY, AND WISHES A CHANGE.

THE Regent sat in his own dressing-room at Carlton House, in deep thought.

Some stewed lobsters—stewed in port wine, and then flavoured with a sauce, the invention of Mons. de Sautanville, the cook of Louis the Eighteenth of France, and whose loss the fat old Bourbon epicure regretted far more than that of the throne off which Napoleon kicked him—formed the Regent's repast.

De Sautanville died of sea-sickness, in crossing the Channel.

But he left the receipt of a sauce behind him which his Royal Highness the Regent liked amazingly.

But the sauce was so grateful to the royal palate that its use generally induced the Regent, however unromantic the statement may be, to eat too much.

Consequently, his Royal Highness felt uncomfortable.

Consequently, his Royal Highness was in a bad temper.

"Hilloa, Willes, Willes!"

"I have the honour to attend your Highness."

"Those lobsters were bad."

Willes shrugged his shoulders.

"The port wine was bad."

Willes gave another shrug.

"That French cook, who invented the sauce, was an idiot."

Willes bowed.

"What do you mean," cried the Regent, in a passion,—"what do you mean by bowing and grimacing there, when I want your opinion?"

"I have the honour of so entirely agreeing with what your Royal Highness has been pleased to say, that it would have been great presumption in me to attempt to put it in other words."

"Stuff!"

Willes bowed lower.

A door at this moment was dashed so suddenly and violently open, that it struck against the corner of a marble-topped console-table; and the concussion was sufficient to upset, and utterly destroy, one of those pretty-looking Louis Quatorze clocks, with their gilding and their little inlaid bits of Sevres china, which was on the table.

The Regent started.

"What is it? What is the matter?"

"It's only me!" said Annie, the Countess de Blonde.

Willes backed himself out of the room.

"Well, George, I wondered where you were!"

"And you seek me like a whirlwind, Countess!"

"Who?—I?"

"Yes, to be sure! Look what you have done!"

"What?"

"Broken the clock!"

"Oh, I see! A good job!"

"Why a good job? Is smashing the—the—a—goods of the Palace a good job?"

"Yes, to be sure!"

"You are incorrigible, Annie!"

"So are you; but I will prove to you, in a moment, George, that I have done a good thing by opening the door so sharply against that clock!"

"You cannot!"

"I will lay you a wager——"

"What about?"

"I will wager you five hundred pounds that I have, in breaking that clock, done what you wished!"

"What I wished? What do you mean?"

"I mean that I have accomplished one of your expressed desires."

"You are incomprehensible, Annie!"

"Shall I prove it?"

No. 80.— DARK WOMAN.

"Do. I shall be obliged."

"And you wager the five hundred pounds with me?"

"I do."

"Very well! You see the clock?"

"Of course I do! That is to say, I see all that remains of it. I see the wreck—the ruin of the clock."

"That is just it!"

"Well—go on."

"Have you not often said you wished that clock, which never would execute above half a dozen ticks without stopping, would go?"

"I have."

"Very well; I have done it now, and it is gone!"

"Annie, you are——"

"What?"

"A provoking little marmosette!"

"What's a marmosette?"

"A sort of monkey."

Annie laughed.

"Come, George," she said, "you are dull. You don't know what to do. Come and play at cards, or dice, or billiards; or will you go out for a walk?"

"A walk?"

"Yes. Why not? My dear George, before you knew me, I am told, you used often to go out for a walk, but now you seldom do so."

"Annie, I was afraid you would be jealous and unhappy!"

"No, no! I shall only be unhappy if you do not please yourself; and I can hardly be jealous so long as I can find a looking-glass in any of the rooms of the Palace!"

Annie turned and surveyed for a moment her pretty, piquant face and figure in a tall glass that was in the room; and the Regent, as he smiled, was half cured of his ill-temper by the vivacity and charming self-esteem of the fair Countess.

"Tell me, Annie," he said, "do you like Carlton House better than St. James's?"

"No."

"Really, now?"

"Really and truly, George, I like the old Palace, at St. James's, the best."

"Your reason, Annie?"

"Why, you see, this Carlton House is so new, so light, so bright, and so—so glaring. Now, in the old Palace there are many dear old dark rooms, and passages, and corridors, and galleries, and old nooks, and corners. One always expects to see a ghost, or a trap-door, or a secret panel in the wall, or something of that sort; while here there is not a shadow from one end of the place to the other!"

"Hem!" said the Regent.

"But if you like it, George, you know I will try to like it."

"My dear Annie, you are a good and a kind girl; but I only asked you because, in consequence of another disagreement between two members of my family, one of those members will come to live here, in Carlton House, and so you will have to go back to your old rooms."

"At St. James's?"

"Just so."

"I am glad of it."

"Then so am I, Annie. Now, Willes, what is it?"

The valet had tapped twice at the door, and then cautiously opened it and put in his head.

"Colonel Fox and Mr. Sheridan wait your Highness's pleasure."

"Oh, very well! Annie!"

"George!"

"You won't mind me leaving you for a few hours?"

"Not a bit."

The Regent did not exactly want Annie to say that she did not mind his leaving her a bit, but he could not very well quarrel with the leave of absence which, quite in the style of a family man, he had thus asked for and obtained.

"I will be back at twelve," he said.

"All right!"

Annie began to whistle. That, as the reader is aware, was one of the accomplishments of Annie, the Countess. She had acquired it of the boys in the street, when she resided in Martlett's Court, Bow Street.

"Willes, my coat and hat."

"They are here, your Highness?"

"Where are Fox and Sheridan?"

"They wait, your Highness, in the small cabinet."

"Very well. Annie, my dear, good evening; and be sure you amuse yourself in my absence; I am only going for a stroll."

"Good bye, George."

Willes pretended to be looking at the pattern of some gold and crimson paper on the wall while the Regent kissed Annie.

In another five minutes, the Prince, and Colonel Fox, and Sheridan were walking, arm-in-arm, up and down St. James's Street.

"Have either of you," asked the Regent, "heard anything of that rascal Moys?"

"Not I," said Colonel Fox.

"Nor I, much," added Sheridan; "except that, in fear that he will have the bloodhounds of the law on his track, he is flying over the Continent."

"Ha! ha! I have had a letter from Hanger."

"Who is alive?"

"Oh, yes! He has the assurance to congratulate me and himself upon getting rid of Moys, and to hope that he may ever continue my humble servant!"

"The Regent of England," said Colonel Fox, "cannot want the services of such a man."

"Certainly not," added Sheridan, "except when he is useful."

"He is a great rogue," added the Regent; "but he has a marvellous genius in finding out all the particulars of any affair."

"You must know, Fox," said Sheridan, "his Royal Highness, lately, has taken to making the English language subservient to his uses in an odd way."

"How so, Sherry? How so?"

"Why, your Highness strangely calls one of those an affair."

"One of what?"

"Those on in advance of us."

Two ladies had turned into a draper's shop as Sheridan spoke.

The Regent laughed.

"Well, I must own," he said, "that, what with cunning, and what with downright impudence, Hanger is the most useful fellow in the world in regard to such matters."

"No doubt. Ha!"

"What is it?"

"Hebe out for a walk."

"What? What?"

"Euphrosyne, unattended and in a silk cloak."

"By Jove!"

"Yes," added Sheridan; "and by all the celestial throng of gods and goddesses, there has just passed us the prettiest girl I ever saw in all my life!"

"No, no!"

"I have said it."

"Well, Sheridan," said the Regent, "I think I will leave you to entertain Colonel Fox—and, Colonel Fox, I think I will leave you to entertain Sheridan."

They both laughed.

The Regent had not taken his eyes off the young girl in the silk cloak who had passed them; and although he had missed actually seeing her face, of which it appeared that Sheridan had caught a glimpse—not the folds of the cloak nor the shadows of the evening could hide from the critical observation of the Regent the exquisite graceful figure of the young girl.

With a light but rapid step the Prince followed at once the fair unknown.

It did not seem as if the young girl in the silk cloak was at all aware that she had attracted the notice of the three gentlemen who, arm-in-arm, had passed her.

If she was aware of any such fact, she treated it with either perfect indifference or perfect tact.

She never slackened or increased her pace, nor did she look round for a moment. Quietly and serenely she made her way down St. James's Street, and then passed into Pall Mall.

The Regent followed.

The young girl then suddenly came to a standstill, and the Regent did so likewise. She then turned abruptly, and began to retrace her steps.

There was an oil-lamp close to the corner of Marlborough House, and inefficiently as it lighted that portion of the street, it was still sufficient to enable the Regent to catch a glimpse of the face of the young girl.

It was very lovely.

And yet, along with the loveliness, there was an air of sadness that made it painful, almost heartrending, to look upon.

Suffering, deep suffering of the heart, had left its traces upon that fair face.

The Regent almost felt sentimental as he looked for that fleeting moment into the face of the young creature.

"By Jove! yes," he muttered, "she is a rarity. Such a jewel as that is seldom out of a setting."

The young girl paused now for a moment at the corner of Marlborough House, where there was, up to twelve o'clock at night, a thoroughfare into the Park. Then, as if she had made up her mind that that was the way she wanted to take, she went into the Park.

The Regent, well satisfied that he should be able to make his first advances to her out of the actual street, followed closely.

The Park was gloomy.

The oil-lamps that in the streets, where their faint rays were confined by the houses, and aided by lights from shops and windows, scarcely succeeded in making much more than a dubious twilight in London, were almost completely lost in St. James's Park.

Except quite close to one of them, they shed no light upon any object.

The young girl who, upon the provocation of her light and airy figure and pretty face, the Prince of Wales was pursuing, looked like some spectre flitting among the old trees of the Mall.

But she did not quicken her pace.

The Regent, however, quickened his.

"Hem! hem! hem!" coughed the Prince.

The young girl took no notice.

"Hem! My dear!"

The young girl paused.

The Regent was by her side in a moment.

"My dear, are you not afraid?"

"Of what, sir?"

"That some dragon will seek to devour so much beauty?"

"Oh, no, no!"

"Well, I'm glad to hear that."

"Why so, sir?"

"Because you must know that I am a dragon."

"You, sir?"

"Yes, my charming creature; but I am not one of those fabulous dragons of antiquity, who took a pleasure in devouring young virgins. I am, on the contrary, a polite monster, and when I tell you that you are lovely—fascinating—that——"

"You love me?"

"With all my heart."

"Ah! then my task is done for this time."

The young girl put her arm familiarly within that of the Regent, and looked up in his face with so strange an expression that he did not know what to make of it.

"What do you mean, my dear, by your task being done this time?"

"I must not tell you that. Your name is not Arthur?"

"No—certainly not."

"But yet——Well, you say you love me?"

"I not only say it——"

"You mean, you not only say you love me, but you really do so?"

"That is just it."

"Come along, then."

The Regent hesitated. Never before had he met so much beauty in combination with so much eccentricity. He was not destitute of that feeling which is common to human nature—namely, that the rose which is too easily plucked, is not worth the plucking; and notwithstanding the faultless figure and the pretty face, his Highness the Regent was half inclined to give up this little adventure, and go again in search of his two friends, Colonel Fox and Richard Brinsley Sheridan, who, in all probability, would be still promenading in St. James's Street.

By this time, the Prince and his fair unknown companion had reached another of the lamps in the Park, and the critical eyes of the Regent again fell upon that sweet countenance, in which he could not find a blemish.

The slightly loosened chain which had entangled his fancy was again riveted.

No eccentricity of this young girl would now have been sufficient to induce her royal admirer to quit her.

"My dear girl," he said, "tell me at once who and what you are."

"I am a spirit!"

"A what?"

"A spirit!"

"You are a most incomprehensible one. But be you what you may, there can be no mistake about the substantiality of your beauty. This hand which I press, so warm and so soft, is not that of a spirit. These lips which——"

"Nay, sir! whether I be a spirit or not, you at least should be a gentleman."

"My dear, that is the very character in which I present myself to you; and when young ladies of your face and figure appear alone, at this hour of the night, in London streets, and after that take a stroll in St. James's Park, I fancy the meeting of a gentleman is something they may expect or anticipate."

"Come along, then," said the young girl.

"My dear, that is the second time you have said ‘Come along’ in that strange, brusque manner. May I ask where to?"

"With me. I will lead you."

"Nay, permit me rather to be your guide. I am quite certain that there must be something in modern fashions, which you have not yet added to your wardrobe. In Pall Mall, quite close at hand, resides a fashionable *modiste*, who will make you rich in all the requirements of the last Paris editions of shawls, cloaks, and bonnets, hats, robes, gloves, and all the *et ceteras* that the world of fashion projects for the adornment of the fairest specimens of humanity."

"No, no!"

"Nay; let me be your leader, and let me say to you, as you have said to me now, ‘Come along.’"

"Good night!"

"What do you mean by good night?"

"I mean farewell."

"Impossible!"

"It must be so. It is not to be. I have met you, and you have spoken to me. I was to take you with me, but you will not come; so farewell—farewell!"

"Nay, nay! If you are obstinate, I must needs accompany you; but, my dear girl, I hope you have good reasons for the course you adopt."

"I have—oh, I have! It gives me another hope!"

"You speak in riddles. But now that we have reached another lamp, and that by standing here I get its light, such as it is, full upon my face, I want you to tell me, truly and sincerely, if you know me?"

"I do not know you."

"If you say that you do, it will be nothing to your disadvantage."

There was no mistaking the look of perfect innocence and gentleness with which this fair young creature looked into the face of the Regent.

"No," she added; "I do not know you."

There was no actress in all the world who could have looked a part of such utter unconsciousness of his identity as she did, with, at the same time, the slightest knowledge of who and what he was.

The Regent was satisfied.

"Very well, my dear!" he said. "Since it must be so, I will go with you!"

CHAPTER CLXXVII.

RETURNS TO SIXTEEN-STRINGED JACK, IN THE MYSTERIOUS CHAMBER IN THE OLD INN.

THE descending ceiling of the bed smashed the lantern, and Sixteen-stringed Jack was in darkness.

He uttered an exclamation, which the rapidity and the peculiarity of the circumstance forced from him; and then it took but a moment's thought fully to comprehend the machinery which was attached to that massive old bedstead with its redundant hangings.

But Jack was in darkness!

The loss of the lantern was a calamity, and much he regretted that he had placed it on the bed, so that it had to sustain the shock of the suddenly falling ceiling.

There was no help for that, however, now; and, after a few moments' consideration, Jack was resolved to try an experiment with the small wooden handle that projected from the wheel embedded in the post of the bedstead.

"Surely," he said, "that will be the means by which this heavy mass of something, forming the ceiling or roof of the old bedstead, is raised up again."

The chamber was profoundly dark; but still, as Jack knew pretty well the position of the wooden handle and the wheel, he had no great difficulty in putting his hand upon the former.

Slowly, then, as he moved the handle, causing the wheel to revolve as he did so, he became confident that the mass of material which had fallen upon the bed was being elevated to its original position.

The work was very slow; and it took some hundreds of turns at the wheel before Jack felt certain the ceiling of the bedstead was in its place again.

From this, Jack came to the conclusion that, connected with the bedstead, there was some system of pulleys, artfully concealed, and constructed so that a considerable weight could be raised with a small amount of power; the mechanical consequence being that the motion was very slow.

Sixteen-stringed Jack had some hesitation now, in the darkness, to feel upon the bed for the lantern, for he did not know but that, experimenting merely with the machinery, he might meet with some accident.

Hopeless, however, as could be any idea that the lantern had survived the shock given to it, Jack felt curious to ascertain its precise condition; and, after a time, he cautiously felt on the bed for it.

It was literally smashed, so that he could have no doubt what would be the fate of any one who might have been lying on that treacherous couch on the occasion of the heavy weight above being released and permitted to fall, with that sickening thud, upon the bed below.

And now—as though he had seen the whole affair transacted before his eyes—Jack comprehended the secrets and mysteries of that old inn.

The fair young girl lured, by her beauty, victims who were destroyed by that fearful machinery connected with the bed; and then the half or wholly lifeless body was carried to the mock wardrobe, where, probably, in some fearful manner, death was made certain; and the smothered, mangled, bleeding corpse was dashed down the trap-door to keep company with previous victims.

A feeling of intense horror came over Jack.

Much had he heard and seen of the criminality of London, but all the war that he had been engaged in, and that his attention had been turned to, was against property.

Life he had never made a crusade against.

No man was more capable of crying "Stand!" upon the highway to a traveller than Sixteen-stringed Jack. He did not think much of a stray shot whistling past his ears—that was all in the way of business, and he could give and take.

But blood, murder, trap-doors, bedsteads with apparatus for smothering their occupants — all these things were new and hideous to the highwa man; and no wonder that for the moment they completely unnerved him.

Sixteen-stringed Jack felt positively and physically weak, as he felt about him for a chair on which to sit down and rest. He would have given something considerable at that moment for some stimulant that would have rallied the blood again about his heart, and enabled him to feel as strong, as capable, and as full of resources as he ordinarily did.

But the necessity for action presented itself so strongly to him that the mental energies began to rouse up the physical ones, and Sixteen-stringed Jack felt that he must do something to save probably another human life that night.

But what was he to do?

That was the question.

How sincerely he hoped that the fair young girl—who, with her intellect all astray, and lending herself to murder without the slightest idea of her participation in such fearful criminality—might fail that night in bringing a victim to that abode of death.

Jack almost uttered this hope and wish aloud; but no sooner had he done so, than he started to his feet, as if some hand had been suddenly laid upon him.

He heard footsteps and voices in the outer room.

Was it possible that the young girl had returned?

Did she bring some one with her, who, perhaps under the influence of some narcotic, was to be induced to lie down upon that fearful bed?

He flew to the door which opened into the outer apartment, for by this time his eyes had become so accustomed to the darkness that he could sufficiently detect its position.

To open it, and stand in that little narrow passage between the two doors, was the work of a moment; but any one who had been watching Jack Singleton would have been surprised at the rapidity with which he immediately turned again, and sought refuge in the chamber, hiding himself at the head of the old bedstead, in the midst of the massive folds of those costly hangings, the prodigality of which, as regarded quantity, he now so fully understood the reason of.

They concealed the machinery of death.

Jack had a reason for this sudden retreat.

No sooner had he reached the narrow passage between the two doors, than the one which led into the outer room was pushed open, and Jack must have escaped observation in the narrowest possible manner.

He felt that he could do nothing but what he was doing: for, after all, he could know little of the amount of force or power which might be at hand to resist any interference on his part with the murderous intentions of the hag, who, after all, might be but an executive of others near at hand, with more power of action than she herself possessed.

And, at all events, Jack was at the headquarters, so to speak, of the projected murder. He could stretch forth his hand at any moment to warn and save the victim.

Hardly for the space of half a minute had Jack been hidden, when a flash of light streamed into the room.

Then he heard the voice of the old woman.

There was an amazing attempt at jocularity and kindliness in the old hag's tones.

"This way, my pretty gentleman—this way! Dear heart, yes; I say it, perhaps, as shouldn't, there isn't a sweeter girl in all London. This way, my pretty gentleman! It's an old house, but a respectable one; and you might drop twenty pound upon the floor, and come for it the next day and not find one of them missing. We are poor, sir, but we're honest; and we wouldn't smother a fly, nor put a poor cat or dog into a well."

"What do you mean," said a man's voice, "about smothering flies, and putting cats and dogs into wells?"

Sixteen-stringed Jack nearly called out aloud, then he felt faint and sick, and nearly fell to the floor; and then, in a gasping sort of whisper, he said to himself, "By the heaven above us, that's the Regent!"

"Did you speak, my pretty gentleman?" added the hag, as she placed a light upon the table.

"Yes, I did speak," replied the Regent—for it was indeed no other than he who had been brought to that fearful place by the demented young girl he had met in St. James's Park—"yes, I did speak; and I would like to know why, having come here in the company of a young angel, I encounter an old——"

"He! he! he! Say it, my pretty gentleman—say it—an old devil! Bless you, she'll be here directly—she's only saying her prayers!"

"Her prayers? By Jove! I don't half like this place."

"It's a fine old place, my pretty gentleman, and a good many have been here that have never said a word agin it; and if so be, my pretty gentleman, you don't mind, I will fetch you a glass of wine that's so old and fusty that I don't like it—seeing as it was brought here, they do say, by the great Duke of Marlborough, and left and forgot in the cellars. We'd be glad to buy some new and fresh, but we can't afford it. Oh, dear—we can't afford it!"

The old hag must have found, or been told, that this description of the wines in the cellars of the old inn would be attractive to any one in the habit of imbibing such liquor, and it certainly was so to his Highness the Regent.

"Do you mean to say that you have wine in your cellars that has been there since Queen Anne's time?"

"So they say, and I'm very sorry."

"Pooh! pooh! Don't be sorry. Get a bottle—get a bottle! And by the time you bring it the young lady may have said her prayers. Get a bottle, at once."

"It will be five shillings."

"Pshaw! Stuff! There's a guinea! Be quick; I am cold—and—and—there seems to me a kind of strange—eh?—odour in this room!"

"It's the sweet marjoram," said the old woman.

"The sweet who?"

"The sweet marjoram! We keeps it in paper bags from summer to summer; and as my husband, poor dear John, often says, it makes an odour—it makes an odour! John looks forward to being settled, some day, my pretty gentleman;

but, as I often say, I wouldn't smother a fly; and as for cutting the throat of a tame rabbit, or putting a cat down a trap-door, I should be the last person——"

"Good gracious!" cried the Regent. "Hold your raving, and get the wine! What do I care for your putting flies down trap-doors and smothering cats?"

"He! he! he! He's a funny gentleman as well as a pretty gentleman!" said the hag. "A very funny gentleman, as ever I did see! I'll fetch the wine—I'll fetch the wine; and I hope it won't get into your head, that's all! He! he!"

The hag hobbled from the room.

Sixteen-stringed Jack was alone with the Regent; but the latter thought himself alone entirely.

What was Jack to do?

The most obvious thing was to step out from his place of concealment, and state at once that the house was a den of murder, from which instant escape was the most desirable thing to be accomplished.

But an almost overwhelming curiosity—a curiosity which was painful in its intensity—restrained Jack for the moment; and he determined to see, to the last moment that he could do so with safety, every incident in the life-drama that was presented before his eyes.

The Regent spoke.

"I don't half like this place. I'm afraid I've been imprudent; and yet who would not have been imprudent with such a temptation? Who on earth can the girl be? I never saw such beauty in my life! Such simplicity, too! She was not to be resisted; and yet I feel a kind of—I know not what,—a shuddering terror of this place; and I wish I were well out of it—provided I had never seen, and so should never regret, the more than mortal beauty that lured me here. But where is she? Why was I asked to walk in here, accompanied by that hideous old wretch who seems as mad as—as the girl herself."

The Regent looked about him, and kept turning round and round; so that Sixteen-stringed Jack, if he meant really to remain in concealment, was compelled to keep very quiet.

He let the folds of the heavy curtains fall completely before him, and only through the narrowest possible crevice permitted himself to peep out at the Regent, and at what might take place in that mysterious chamber.

It struck Jack that there was something peculiar in the speech that the old woman had made about the wine; and at all events he made up his mind to one thing—which was, that he would not allow the Regent to drink a drop of it.

But still Jack waited until it should be brought; and still the Regent muttered to himself, and kept looking round the room in a restless, disturbed fashion.

"No," said the Regent, again, "I don't like the place; but the beauty of the girl is marvellous. I will get her to come away from here, and have her well taken care of. Oh! here comes the old wretch, who is so full of talk about flies and cats."

"Here you are, my pretty gentleman; here's the wine. I had two thoughts of running over the way to the 'Cauliflower and Gridiron,' and asking them if they'd got anything to drink in the way of wine that is fresh and new."

"Why, you stupid old fool," said the Regent, "it's the age of wine gives it bouquet, fragrance, and value."

"Eh? Gives it what, my pretty gentleman?"

"There, there; that'll do. And so this bottle has been in the cellar a long while, has it?"

"Since the time of the Queen of Sheba."

"Stuff! stuff! Queen Anne, you said."

"I'm a poor woman;—do you want the change?"

"No, no! Give me that glass. Why, this is a crystal goblet, fit for a king. Where did you get this beautiful old cut glass from?"

"If you'd like a mug better——"

"Like a mug better, now, you mad old dolt! Where's the corkscrew?"

"Most of the pretty gentlemen knocks the neck off the bottle."

"Do they! Well, we might do worse. Get out of the way, witch!"

"He! he! he! The pretty gentleman's a funny gentleman."

"Now for it!" said the Regent, as he gave the neck of the bottle a blow upon the edge of the table, which sent it off at once.

"And now for it," thought Jack Singleton. "I won't let you take a drop of that, if I can help it."

The Regent poured out the wine.

"What is it?" he said. "Some sort of claret, I take it."

Jack Singleton crept softly along the side of the bedstead.

The Regent held up the glass.

Jack was close to his elbow. The Regent moved the glass towards his lips. Jack Singleton put his hand quietly over his shoulder: he stopped the glass within two inches of the mouth of the Regent, as he cried, in ringing accents, "Hold! There may be poison in the cup!"

The Regent dropped the glass, which fell into a thousand fragments, on the floor.

The old hag uttered a fearful yell, and tried to escape from the room; but Jack crossed her path, and she fell heavily to the floor.

The Prince of Wales staggered back until he came in contact with the mock wardrobe; and there he stood, with his arms out, in an attitude of defence.

"What's all this? What's all this?" he cried. "Help! Thieves! Murder! Guard!"

Now, Sixteen-stringed Jack thought it would be just as well not to proclaim the rank of the Regent, there and then, in presence of the hag; and he simply replied, "It all means, sir, that you are in a place of danger; and that I happily happened to be here to warn you."

"Warn me? Warn me of what?"

"Of murder!"

"Murder?—murder? Let me go! Open the door! Where's the window? Help! help! Treason!"

"I think, sir, the danger is past," added Jack; "but I was afraid to let you drink that wine, lest it contained some stupifying drug, which would have deprived you of the power of resistance."

"Let me get out! Clear the way! Come to me to-morrow! Who are you, eh? Who are you?"

"It matters not, sir, who I am; let it suffice

that I am armed, and that I assure you now that there is no danger. If you doubt my word, take these pistols. They are both well charged, and will not fail you."

The old hag was slowly tottering to her feet; the expression upon her face was something awful to look upon.

She made vain efforts to speak; and, as if it would aid her to do so, she kept grasping at her throat with her hands. Some spasmodic seizure seemed to have taken possession of her. The sudden fright at the frustration of all her plans by the appearance of Sixteen-stringed Jack had brought that criminal and revolting existence nearly to a close.

It was only by a great effort that she succeeded at last in articulating one word—" Mercy! mercy!"

"You hear, sir," said Jack. "By that word she confesses her guilt."

The old hag fell heavily upon her face.

"She is dead!" said the Regent. "Good heavens! what a night of horror! Sir—be you whom you may,—and I seem to have some slight recollection of you; although where, and under what circumstances, I have seen you I cannot call to mind at this present moment,—explain to me, if you can, the meaning of all this affair, for it passes my comprehension."

"And very nearly mine, too," replied Jack. "But still I fancy I do know something about it."

"Speak, then."

Jack Singleton made a respectful bow, which ought to have gone some way towards making the Regent suspect that the friend in need knew him; but the Prince of Wales was too used to bows, and to the outward semblances of respect, to take any notice of it.

"If," said Jack, "you will step this way, sir, I can show you something which need not now alarm you, but which will let you see that there was danger."

Jack lighted the candle from the table as he spoke, and took two steps towards the wardrobe.

The Regent hesitated.

"Are you sure there is no danger now?"

"Quite sure, sir.

"Then let me see what it is you have to show me."

Jack flung open the door of the wardrobe, and held the light low down, so that the Regent could have no difficulty in seeing the terrible, ensanguined condition of the interior of that mock piece of furniture.

He shuddered.

"Good heaven!"

"You see, sir?"

"I do—I do!"

Jack let the door of the wardrobe close again, which it did by its own impulse, to a certain extent; and then he once more turned his attention to the old hag, who had fallen to the floor.

Jack saw in a moment that the distance of the old woman from the door of the room was materially less than it had been.

She was only shamming insensibility, but, at the same time, slowly creeping out of the room.

That was a little manœuvre which Sixteen-stringed Jack was determined to put a stop to.

He went at once to the door, but there was no

fastening; so he felt the necessity of securing the old woman in some way.

"Get up! get up!" cried Jack, at the same time that he touched the murderous hag with his foot.

She did not stir.

"I fancy she is dead," said the Regent.

Jack smiled.

"Well," he said; "if so, I will place her on the bed; and, as it will do a dead person no harm, I will show you, sir, the sort of fate which was intended for you."

"No, no! Oh, no!" cried the hag, as she rose to her knees. "No—not that! Oh! have some mercy upon me, and I will tell all!"

"Ah! You see, sir!"

"I do, indeed!" said the Regent.

"I will tell all! I will confess all!" moaned the old woman.

"We know all!" said Jack.

"No, no! You do not know all! I can tell you something about the Dark Woman!"

"The who?" cried the Regent.

"The Dark Woman."

Jack whistled.

"So—so!" he said. "She is mixed up in this little affair, is she? I find that my accidental presence here grows more and more interesting."

<h2 style="text-align:center">CHAPTER CLXXVIII.</h2>

THE REGENT IS A SPECTATOR OF A STRANGE INCIDENT IN THE INN YARD.

SIXTEEN-STRINGED JACK looked curiously into the face of the Prince of Wales. It was pale and flushed by turns, as he muttered to himself, "That woman is still to be the bane of my existence. This is a deliberate attempt upon my life."

"Sir," said Jack, "this is the first mention I have heard of the Dark Woman since I have been in this house."

"Are you certain?"

"Quite so, sir. But since the mention of that name discomposes you, let us leave the place—I will conduct you in safety; and if you will accept of the loan of my horse, you may increase your speed from this ill-omened spot, and soon be in absolute safety."

"I thank you. I will go."

The old hag evidently thought now that she would escape further observation and be let alone. She crouched down on the floor into as small a space as possible, and did not utter a word. But Jack was not exactly going to be so careless of her share in the transactions of that evening as to leave her quite at liberty.

"As regards this old woman," he said; "what are your orders, sir?"

"Give her to the police."

"It shall be done."

"Oh, no, no, no! Do you forget that I have promised to tell you about the Dark Woman?"

"What of her? Speak, wretch!" said the Regent. "What have you to say of Linda de Chevenaux?"

"Linda who?"

"Ah! Perhaps you do not know her by that name, which is only too familiar to me."

"Hush!" said Jack.

"What? What is it?"

"Listen!"

There came upon the night air the faint tones of some musical instrument. It was either a bugle played very low and slow, or it was the soft wailing sound of a flute.

Whichever it was, it evidently came from the inn yard below.

"What does that mean?" said the Regent.

Jack shook his head.

"I am afraid I don't know, and cannot even guess."

"Spare my life!" whined the hag, "and I will tell you."

"Speak, then!"

"You promise?"

"Yes, yes!" cried the Regent, "we promise. What is the meaning of those sounds?"

"The Dark Woman!"

"Ah! She is here?"

"She will be."

"When—when?—and how?"

"She has seen much misfortune of late, and, owing to the malice of her enemies, she has suffered a great deal; but now she is collecting a new band, and means to be all, and more, too than she was before."

"Indeed!"

"Yes; and they all meet here to-night. I hear them coming! I hear their signals! Ah! if I could only—only——"

"Only what?"

The old hag was silent; but she commenced a stealthy movement towards the window of the chamber.

"She means," said Jack, "that if she could only let those who are without know what had happened here, she might soon turn the tables upon us."

"No, no!"

"I am certain of it."

"There! there!" cried the hag, as she suddenly seized the neck of the wine-bottle which the Regent had broken off, and which was lying on the floor, with the cork firmly embedded in it, and flung it with such force against the curtain that was over the window, that even the thickness of the hanging did not save a pane of glass from being broken by the blow.

"Now, you wretches!" cried the hag, "I shall get the better of you!"

She then commenced a series of shrieks, which were of the most alarming character; but Sixteen-stringed Jack, who was always rather happy at resources, caught up the Regent's hat, and, clapping it on the old woman's head, he gave it a blow upon the crown, which sent it in a moment right over her face down to her chin.

The cries she continued uttering were quenched and smothered.

The Regent turned as pale as death.

"Let me tell you, sir," he said, "whoever you are, that I have reason to believe the Dark Woman this old wretch has spoken of has some especial ill-will against me."

Jack bowed.

"And if it be indeed true that she has a band of desperadoes below, there will be nothing more welcome to them, nor gratifying to her, than my capture."

"That shall not happen, sir."

"Can you prevent it?"

"I will, if it cost me my life."

"You shall not find me ungrateful."

"Hush! I hear footsteps."

"Good gracious, we are lost!"

"Nobody is lost, so long as they rely upon themselves," added Jack.

As he spoke, he seized the old woman by the throat, and began to drag her towards the fatal bedstead; and she, with the hat wedged over her face, which she had made several attempts in vain to remove, could only know, from what Jack Singleton chose to say, in which direction she was going.

"At least," said Jack, "since there is no mode of escape for us, I will make this old murderess a victim by releasing the ceiling of the bedstead upon her."

"No, no! Oh, I will save you—I will save you! There is a secret door at the back of the wardrobe."

"I don't believe it."

"I will show you—I will show it to you. You seem to know all but that. You may cast me down the trap into the well, if you find that I deceive you."

"Come, then! Show us the door."

"I cannot see."

Sixteen-stringed Jack, by main force, removed the Regent's hat from over the head and face of the old woman; and then, with a bewildered look, she staggered towards the wardrobe, and opened it.

"Step on the trap-door, and over it," she said. "It is quite firm and strong; and push the panel at the other side."

"Be careful," said the Regent.

"I will," replied Jack. "Do you, sir, see that this old woman does not escape."

"I will shoot her without mercy, if she moves hand or foot."

The hag seemed to be instantly transfixed in the attitude she happened to be in, as the Regent presented one of Jack Singleton's loaded pistols at her head.

Jack took care not to rest much of his weight upon the trap-door, which led down, not only to an ancient well, some couple of hundred feet deep, but to some horribly ghastly company that inhabited it.

A tolerably hard push at the panel of the wall at the opposite side sufficed to make it give way, and it was evidently a door that creaked open.

Beyond that door, all was darkness the most profound.

"Where does this lead to?" asked Jack.

"To the bar parlour," replied the old woman, in a dejected tone.

"Sir! sir!" said the Regent at this moment. "I feel quite certain there are people coming this way."

"No! Ah, yes, I hear them!"

A clear, loud voice came now plainly to their ears from the outer room.

"Come, my good girl," it said; "what was the meaning of that broken window? Tell us?"

The poor insane young girl who had induced the Regent to put himself into a situation of so much danger, did not reply to the question addressed to her; but, in a high, wailing voice,

which, however, had much sweetness in it, she began to sing.

> "They bid me cease to think of thee;
>   They say that even now
> A wreath of fairest bridal flowers
>   Is resting on thy brow.
> And tear-drops fall from brightest eyes,
>   As o'er my couch of pain
> They bend, and whisper fearful words
>   Which rack my fevered brain."

It would seem that whoever those persons were who had left the inn yard below, and come up to the gallery on being alarmed by the broken window, they were not indifferent to the charms of melody.

The beautiful voice in which the demented young creature had sung the last few lines of the song which had darted into her brain had entranced their attention.

When she concluded, there was a clapping of

No. 81.—DARK WOMAN.

hands, which was only suddenly checked by a few words uttered in a voice which the Regent, as well as Sixteen-stringed Jack, knew quite well.

It was the voice of Linda de Chevenaux, the Dark Woman!

"What folly is this? Do we meet here to listen to ballads from a mad girl?"

All was still.

"By Jove!" said the Regent.

"You know that voice, sir?" whispered Jack.

"Too well!"

The Dark Woman spoke again, as it would appear from the words she uttered, in reply to something that had been said by some one who was with her.

"Search, then; but do so quickly. I will wait."

"Time!" said Jack.

"By Jove, yes!"

The Regent made a dart after Sixteen-stringed

Jack over the trap-door; but to do so, he released the old woman from the kind of surveillance in which he had kept her with the loaded pistol.

"This won't do," said Jack.

"What won't?"

"The hag."

The old woman had seen the opportunity, and she made a rush for the door. The bed and bedstead were in her way, and seeing that if she attempted to go to the right to skirt the massive old bedstead, she would inevitably be caught by Jack, she adopted the bolder expedient of scrambling over the bed to the door.

At that moment, too, the door of the room actually moved, as some one from the narrow passage beyond placed his hand upon it.

The situation was critical.

Jack had only handed one of his pistols to the Regent. The other was in a pocket of his breast, and to produce it, to level it, and to fire at the door, which was on the move, was the work of an instant.

The report in that small chamber was fearfully deafening.

There was a crashing sound, mingling with the loud, stunning shock to the air of the explosion of the pistol.

That was the bullet making its way through the upper panel of the door.

It was not in human nature for the persons on the other side to do otherwise than shrink back at this sudden assault from within.

That shrinking back gave Sixteen-stringed Jack just the few moments' time he wanted. To recapture the old hag, and carry her by main force over the trap-door, and through the secret door at the back of the wardrobe, would have required, probably, five times the time that Jack had at his disposal.

He did not attempt it.

But there was another resource which the old woman herself had suggested to him by the position in which she had placed herself.

She was on the bed still.

She was entangled in the bed-clothing, and she had encountered the remains of the crushed lantern, which at the moment terrified her.

Jack saw his opportunity, and, along with it, he saw that he had no other chance of securing the escape of himself and the Regent.

He pressed his finger on to the little brass projection in the bedpost.

With a rush, and a dull heavy sound, the ceiling came down on the bed.

The yell that the hag uttered when she saw it coming was awful to hear.

That yell was her last in this mortal life. She had no breath for another. Smothered—choked beneath that mass of material which, no doubt, she had ruthlessly let fall on many a poor, unsuspecting person, she lay hidden in the complications of the fearful machinery which, no doubt, she had long exulted in the possession of.

One hand and arm alone projected from beneath the ceiling of the bedstead.

The fingers opened and closed rapidly for two or three seconds, and then all was still.

The hand began to turn of a blueish black colour.

Sixteen-stringed Jack darted into the wardrobe, and pulled the door shut after him.

"Just in time, sir," he whispered to the Regent.

"Good heavens! what has happened?"

"Nothing particular, only that I think our friend the old lady has brought herself to a bad end; but as it was one she richly deserved, why we need not lament it."

"What end? what end has she brought herself to?"

"Smothered!"

The Regent made a grimace, which, however, Sixteen-stringed Jack could not see, as they were completely in the dark.

"It strikes me, my friend," he said, "that that must be a disagreeable death. But what are we to do now, and where are we?"

"I think we are safe. Listen!"

Two or three persons were evidently in the chamber; but they all spoke so confusedly and hurriedly together, that it was difficult to detect their exact numbers.

"What does it all mean?" cried one. "Something has been going on here."

"It is a something which concerns us not," said the Dark Woman. "The people in this place are faithful to me, now that they know me, and you have all agreed that they were faithful to you before I assumed the control of this association. It is to be supposed they have their own objects, and their own modes of carrying them out."

"Is this one of the objects?" said another voice. "What phenomenon is this? Look at the bed and bedstead! What does it mean? Here is a hand and arm swollen and blackened as in death!"

There was a general expression of surprise, and then Sixteen-stringed Jack whispered to the Regent, "I fancy, sir, it will be best for us to get away from this place as soon as possible."

"Yes—but the darkness here is suggestive of a thousand dangers. I don't like to move from the spot on which I stand."

"We will have a light," said Jack.

As he spoke, he ignited one of the matches he had with him, and by the slight flame which curled for a few moments round the splinter of wood of which the match was composed, he and the Regent could see tolerably well about them.

They stood exactly at the top of a nearly perpendicular flight of stairs, so that the caution of the Regent in not moving from the spot until he could see about him, was by no means superfluous.

Sixteen-stringed Jack, however, was interested in observing that there were a couple of strong bolts upon the side of the door, at the back of the wardrobe where they then stood.

To shoot these bolts into their sockets, and so to feel a sense of security, which before could not belong to their position, was Jack's first act; and then he breathed much more freely than he had done, since discovering the many dangers which surrounded him and the Regent in that house of mystery and of death.

The match then slowly went out, but Jack was too well aware, now, of the position of the staircase to require its aid; and still speaking in low tones, in order that the echo of his voice should not reach the apartment they had just left, he said, "If, sir, you will place your hand on my shoulder, I will precede you down the stairs, and no doubt we shall find ourselves in the lower part of the inn, and from thence we can find our way into the street."

"The sooner the better—the sooner the better," said the Regent. "I shall be only too delighted to see the street again, if it were the vilest and commonest thoroughfare in all London."

CHAPTER CLXXIX.

THE DARK WOMAN COMMENCES HER NEW LIFE WITH BOLDNESS AND PRECISION.

WE may safely leave his Royal Highness the Regent, accompanied by Sixteen-stringed Jack, to pursue their course down the narrow and nearly perpendicular staircase of the old inn, while we pay some attention to the proceedings of Linda de Chevenaux, the Dark Woman.

Darkness, black and profound, was in the old inn yard after the waggon had left it. The gates were closed, and even over a small wicket—which every one had to stoop to enter—a heavy bar was thrown.

Those premises were more like a fortified place than an ordinary inn in one of the commonplace streets of London.

It was the lad who had driven the waggon, and who had, by some strange accident, made so capital a mistake, in supposing that Sixteen-stringed Jack had given him the private signal of the iniquitous fraternity to which he belonged, when in reality Jack knew nothing about it, who had shut up the inn yard in that exact and close manner we have mentioned.

This lad had accompanied the waggon on its route to Watford but a very short distance, and had then given it up to an ordinary carter, while he returned to act as door-keeper to the persons who that night were to hold a meeting in the old inn yard.

The lad, from one of the stables, brought a dilapidated stool, which, upon three legs, each of unequal length, presented but a sorry substitute for something on which he could rest. Seated, however, upon that stool, he placed himself by the wicket-gate and waited.

The boy soliloquised, to while away the time before his masters should arrive.

"It's a very funny thing to me," he said, "and I can't a bit make it out—but that young girl the old woman calls Florella, goes out as fine as possible sometimes of an evening, about once a week, and she comes home with some gentleman at her heels, paying her all sorts of compliments, and telling her what a pretty girl she is, but I never see him go away again. Well, it's no business of mine, I suppose; and all I've got to do is to take care that nobody gets into the inn yard after eleven o'clock, but those who give me the signal. Ha! ha! What a capital fellow that is with the dark bay horse. How nicely he leaped, horse and all, into the waggon, after giving me the signal to let me know he was one of us. I thought at first it was only his hat tumbling off and that he was putting up his hand to save it; but when I happened to catch sight of Mr. Brand, the Bow Street runner, I knew he was escaping,

and that put me all right. I like that fellow, and I like his horse. Hilloa! somebody here!"

A succession of taps on the wicket, on the outer side, which the boy counted as nine in number, put an abrupt stop to his cogitations.

"I dare say it's all right," he said, "but I must do just what they told me."

With a pebble he had in his hand, which he had picked up from the inn yard, he now struck one sharp rap on the inner side of the wicket.

The applicant for admission without then struck eight times.

"That'll do," said the boy; "it makes two nines, all the world over."

He took down the bar, and opened the wicket.

A tall man, in shabby fashionable clothes, who had to stoop low to get through the narrow entrance, entered the inn yard.

This man cast his eyes rapidly about him in the darkness, as he said, abruptly, "Am I the first?"

"No, sir," said the boy, "there is one here."

"Only one?"

"That's all."

"Ah! I thought I was early. Is there any news stirring?"

"None that I know of."

"No alarm—no suspicion—no inquiries?"

"Oh, dear, no! It's all quiet enough."

"Very well—very well. I will go into the house and wait."

"There's another, sir."

Some other person from without knocked nine times on the wicket gate.

"I'll stop a moment," said the first comer, "and see who that is."

The boy then struck once again with the pebble.

Eight distinct raps then came from the outer side.

The boy opened the wicket, and another man entered the inn yard.

"Ah!" said the first comer, "that's you, Mountcashel, I think; but it's so plaguey dark, I can't see."

"Now, really," said the new arrival, "that's a little too bad. Here you call out my name, as if I wanted it to be perfectly well known to all the parish that I, the younger son of an Irish peer, kept bad company in the neighbourhood of Long Acre."

"Oh, we're all safe here. Come into the house, and see if old John has any of that Spanish wine left we sent in a stock of."

"Somebody else," said the boy, as again nine knocks from without demanded his attention.

"Say we're in the house—say we're in the house!" cried the man who was called Mountcashel.

They strolled across the inn yard, and entered the narrow passage by which Sixteen-stringed Jack had made his way at an earlier hour of the evening.

One by one, the boy at the wicket gate let in twelve men in this fashion, and, after a brief parley one with the other and with him, they all went into the house.

More than an hour had elapsed, during which these arrivals were taking place, and the boy evidently began to think that his duties for the night were over, when nine distinct blows upon the outer panel of the wicket, as if struck by some very sharp instrument, startled him into attention.

He responded with the one knock; the eight immediately followed, and he flung open the wicket.

A slight, active-looking person stepped into the inn yard, and, in a voice that was low and sweet, but at the same time had a tone of precision and command about it, this person asked, "How many have arrived?"

"About a dozen."

"Where are they?"

"They're all in the house, I fancy."

"Say that I wait."

This last-arrived personage then walked quietly to the very centre of the inn yard, and stood there still and motionless as a statue.

Down upon the ground, close to the three-legged stool upon which the boy had been sitting, was a dark lantern, the slide of which was impenetrably closed; but the boy now raised it, and, removing the slide, permitted a beam of light to escape from it, which fell upon the figure of this new arrival.

The costume of this person was as costly as it was peculiar.

Tall boots, of apparently the finest morocco leather, enveloped the lower limbs; the tops of the boots were just about met by the skirts of a coat of maroon velvet; a belt of milk-white leather crossed the breast, to which hung a sword, the hilt of which was sparkling with jewels.

A felt hat, perfectly plain, and a half-mask, which concealed all the upper part of the face, completed the costume of this somewhat singular personage.

"Who shall I say wants them all?" inquired the boy.

"Their master."

There was something in the tone which forbade another question; and the boy, placing the lantern at the feet of this imposing and imperious figure, ran across the inn yard into the house with the message he had been charged with.

There was something exceedingly picturesque and beautiful about the appearance of that solitary person in the middle of the inn yard, lighted up so strangely by the lantern at his feet.

The shadows, thrown upwards, gave a curious aspect to the figure and face; and when this person suddenly waved his right arm imperiously, the shadow of that arm fell upon the old inn, in huge, exaggerated dimensions, like the arm of a giant.

The mysterious person spoke.

"Once again—once again I will make myself known and dreaded; but not as before will I work with the sordid, ignorant souls, whose only motive was the acquisition of money, to expend again in riot and destruction. I now, with hawks of keener scent, fly at higher game. Boldly and openly—by force allied to cunning—I will make my name once more, in London, a wonder, a charm, and a terror! These men with whom I have newly associated myself have nearly all of them education and mental culture; and some of them have rank. They are debauchees—ruined gamesters—reckless younger sons of noble families, who have run through all their patrimony—men against whom the law has lifted its hand, and who are at war with all that makes up what is called the civilization of the world! They will aid me, and I will aid them. They have the power of force, recklessness and want of character, or regard of consequences. I shall be their directing genius, and, with scheme after scheme, plan after plan, and plot after plot, will show them the road to wealth and triumph! I am the Dark Woman; but the deeds that I have done hitherto, and which have earned me the title, shall be as blazing sunlight in comparison to the gloom which shall hang about those which are to come!"

The attitude and manner of Linda de Chevenaux, as she gave utterance to this harangue so threatening to the peace of many persons, may be easier imagined than described.

Her form seemed to dilate, and a wild fire shone in her eyes, which sufficiently indicated the brain disturbance that she endured.

For a moment, then, she clasped both her hands over her face.

A softer and a tenderer chord had been struck in her heart by a sudden recollection.

"My son! My son!" she murmured. "Oh, why is not his heart my heart? Why are we separated in feeling, in sentiment, and in interest?"

But this sudden sentiment died away before the stern resolves of her position. She heard the sound of footsteps, and upon looking again around her, she saw herself surrounded by those vicious, lawless spirits among whom she sought action, and whom she aspired to lead.

Another moment, and the Dark Woman was herself again.

"Ah!" she said, "you are here! Well met! There is work to do even to-night!"

A suppressed murmur of satisfaction passed from one to the other of the group around her.

"Yes," she added, "promise now and for ever that you will all be faithful to me, as you will be to each other, and this night I will lead you on an enterprise which will be to-morrow the talk of London, and which will enrich you all."

The dissolute men who had placed themselves under her control heard these words with satisfaction.

Their cupidity and their vanity alike felt flattered at such predictions and such promises.

"Speak—speak!" cried one. "We only desire to know whither you would lead us, and we are well content to follow you."

"Yes, yes!" said the other. "Well content! Well content!"

The Dark Woman smiled.

"Be it so! Be it so! I do not think that there is a traitor among us; although it is said that twelve men may not, according to a law of nature, get together without some one harbouring in his heart a design to betray his comrades."

There was an ominous silence among the band.

"No!" added the Dark Woman, after this silence had lasted a sufficient time to become painful,—"no, I will not doubt! All will be true!"

"All—all!" said the united voices of those present.

"I am certain," added one voice, "that if ever there should appear a traitor among us, it will be the general wish, and according to the general consent, that he should suffer death!"

"Yes! Death—death to a traitor!" said the others, as with one voice.

"That is well!" added the Dark Woman,—"that is well! I hear that with pleasure; and yet——"

"Yet what?" said the same voice that had just spoken in such strong terms as regarded the fate that ought to overtake any one false to the fraternity,—"yet what? It seems to me, brethren, that the leader we have chosen is suspicious."

"No," replied the Dark Woman, "I am not suspicious."

"Not suspicious? Wherefore, then. do you pause in action, and speak as you have spoken?"

"Because I am certain!"

"Ah!"

There was an uneasy movement among the band; but they closed closer together, and by the light of the lantern which was at the feet of the Dark Woman their excited faces could be seen, full of expressions of anxiety and expectation.

"I am certain," added Linda de Chevenaux, "there is a traitor!"

"Name! name! name!" burst from several lips, in anxious tones.

"I advise that the traitor leave us at once. I know him. I give him one minute more to leave this place in life. If he tarry beyond that minute, by the heaven above us, he dies!"

One tall, dusky-looking figure darted from among the throng around the Dark Woman, and made for the gate of the inn yard.

"There is the traitor!" cried the Dark Woman.

There was a clash of sword-blades, and every one was on the point of making after the flying figure, when Linda de Chevenaux rapidly drew a small pistol from the breast of her apparel.

There was a sharp report—a yell of pain—and the dark-looking figure fell within a couple of paces of the wicket-gate.

"Lead," said the Dark Woman, "is swifter than steel! You have none of you soiled your swords; and the traitor that was among you has met his deserved fate!"

A look of terrified inquiry passed from face to face now of the band, to discover who it was who had so unequivocally betrayed his base intentions, and so speedily met with their reward.

"It is the young Lord Nithsdale," said one.

"Hint not his name," added the Dark Woman; "but rejoice in the death of one who would assuredly have betrayed you all."

The throng of persons now gathered closer again round the Dark Woman; and she spoke in a low tone, and with animated gestures.

Close to her as were the members of the lawless fraternity who were prepared to carry out her bold and original suggestion, they had no difficulty whatever in hearing all that she said.

But there were two other persons who were silent spectators of that singular scene, who were too far off to hear her words now, but who would have given a good deal to know precisely what they were.

At least one of those persons would have promised a large sum for the information; for those two silent spectators were Sixteen-stringed Jack and His Royal Highness the Prince of Wales.

Finding the impossibility of escaping by the route he had taken, Jack had advised a return to the rooms opening on to the inn gallery.

From that position, then, the Regent, with his highwayman companion, were able to see and hear all that took place in the inn yard below, with the exception of the speech which the Dark Woman was now making—in so low and confidential a tone—to those about her.

The Regent, with the sensation of terrified bewilderment that a man might feel in some access of nightmare, when his senses are at the mercy of the disturbed imagination, had recognised Linda de Chevenaux.

Her voice was by far too familiar to his ears for him to have any doubt of her identity.

"Good heaven!" he whispered; "I know that woman!"

"So do I," replied Jack.

"You—you do?"

"I do, sir. That is the person who is so well known as the Dark Woman."

"It is! it is!"

"And dark and desperate, I fancy, will be her deeds in time to come!"

"I must escape—escape at once!"

"Impossible!"

"But, my good fellow—my good friend, as I may call you,—you do not know—you cannot know—how particularly desirable it is that I should keep out of the way of that desperate woman!"

Jack was silent for a few seconds. He knew perfectly well what urgent reasons the Regent had to keep out of sight of Linda de Chevenaux; but he did not like now, after for so long keeping up the delusion that the Prince was a stranger to him, to let him know that he had been aware of his identity all along.

"Sir," said Jack, after the pause, "permit me to say that I feel pretty sure we are all safe here."

"But—but, my good friend——"

"Nay, sir; consider only. The old hag, who could alone betray us, is no more. Those persons below meet here to arrange something that they will be off soon to carry out; and then the place will be clear for us, and there will be no difficulty in leaving the inn yard."

"You think so?"

"I do, indeed; and see, they are on the point of dispersing even now. I have a good horse below, in one of the stables, which shall be at your service."

"Oh, no, no! I don't think I shall want it. If I can only once get into the open streets I shall feel quite safe. Quite, quite!"

"Look, sir—look! They go!"

"Ah, yes! Thank heaven!"

The speech which the Dark Woman had uttered in such low tones consisted of the following startling words:—"I wish to commence my reign among you by an enterprise that shall convince you of my power and the fertility of my resources. The Regent has in that suite of private apartments which he occupies in St. James's Palace, a small cabinet of tortoise-shell and malachite, which was presented to George the Second from Russia. In that cabinet there are some costly jewels, which he would have long since parted with, but they belong to the Crown. Their value is about eighty thousand pounds."

The Dark Woman paused.

"Can it be possible," asked one, "to penetrate into the Palace?"

"To me it is possible."

"And," said another, "how, amid all the intricacies of old St. James's, are we to hope to make our way to the private apartments of the Prince?"

"St James's Palace, with all its intricacies, is as well known to me as this hand which I now hold before my eyes."

"Nay, comrades," said another. "If our new leader and captain will take us on this expedition, let us go, say I. By the fiends, I long to have the handling of some of those pretty gems!"

"And I, too! And I, too!" cried others.

The Dark Woman waved her arm with an imperious gesture.

"Follow me! follow me! and I will show you how easy it is to penetrate to the recesses of a palace!"

The movement that now ensued among the throng of persons in the inn yard was that movement which Sixteen-stringed Jack had drawn the attention of the Regent to, as indicative of their dispersion.

"See, sir—see!" he said. "They go!"

"By Jove, yes!" said the Regent.

In two minutes more the inn yard was left to solitude and to the dead.

The body of the detected spy still lay there, and was taken as little notice of as if it had been so much carrion. It was difficult to say what the Dark Woman thought was to become of such an evidence of a violent deed having been committed in that place.

CHAPTER CLXXX.

THE DARK WOMAN ATTACKS ST. JAMES'S PALACE, AND NEARLY FALLS BY THE HAND OF HER SON.

SIXTEEN-STRINGED JACK was well enough pleased to see the Dark Woman, and the gang of desperadoes who owned her as mistress, depart from the inn.

Turning to the Regent, he spoke in tones that showed he did not consider there was altogether so much need of caution.

"Now, sir," he said, "I propose that we descend at once to the yard below, and effect an exit from this place."

"Oh, yes, yes!—with pleasure!"

"Here are some steps."

"Yes. I see them—I feel them."

"Hush! One moment!"

Jack stopped the Regent from descending too hastily, for the boy who acted as gate-keeper to the fraternity at that moment made his appearance with a lantern, and proceeded to bar and bolt the wicket door.

This boy was an embarrassment to Sixteen-stringed Jack. That he was associated with that gang of marauders, who were perfectly unscrupulous in their actions, and to whom, in all probability, murder would come as little amiss as robbery, he, of course, knew.

But the boy had saved him.

It was a mistake; but, still, the boy had saved him from the active pursuit of one of the most energetic police-officers of London, and Sixteen-stringed Jack was not a person likely to forget such a transaction.

Hence Jack's embarrassment.

He did not want this boy sacrificed; but, still, self-preservation, and a kind of duty he owed the Regent, to see him clear of the dangers of that place, were considerations not to be slighted.

With exceeding care the boy secured the wicket gate; and then, lifting the lantern from the ground, he cast its broad, fan-shaped ray upon the dead body which lay upon the cold stones of the inn yard.

There did not seem to be any feeling of dread or regret on the boy's mind on account of this slaughter, which had taken place before his very eyes.

He looked upon the dead body with a cool indifference which went far to allaying those feelings in Sixteen-stringed Jack's mind which would have tended to the preservation of the boy from the dangers of his situation.

The Regent was getting impatient.

"My friend," he said, "whoever you are, permit me to ask if that lad is the only obstruction to our leaving this abominable place?"

"I scarcely know. Ah! he is calling some one!"

"John! John!" cried the boy, as he held the lantern above his head; "where are you? Old John, I say!"

"What is it now?" growled the man who had been, for so brief a space of time, seen by Sixteen-stringed Jack in what might be called the bar parlour of the inn.

"Come here! Come here!"

"What is it?"

"Why, they've settled one of them, and it won't do to leave him here."

Old John—whom the hag who superintended the murder well of that house had expressed her intention of "settling"—now made his way across the yard; and as the boy again threw the glare of the lantern upon the corpse, he saw what it was he was required for.

"Who is it? Who is it?" he cried.

"Oh, I don't know, and don't care; but it was somebody that they had to get rid of, or else he would have betrayed them all. So, you see, a pistol bullet has gone in at his back, but I don't see that it has come out again at his breast."

"Ah!" said the old man, with a hideous chuckle, "he won't be much heavier for that piece of lead. We must get him into one of the old stables, and dig a hole, and put him in at leisure. Help me to drag him along. Can't you put down the lantern and use both hands?"

"We shan't see our way if I do. But I'll do better than that. There now! What do you think of that?"

The boy dexterously tied the lantern, by a piece of twine, to the breast of the dead man, and then he and old John carried the body across the inn yard, towards the range of deserted stables on one side of it.

Old John laughed, chuckled, and coughed, and seemed to think it a good joke that the dead man should, in a manner of speaking, be carrying the lantern himself.

They disappeared into one of the stables; and then the Regent whispered to Sixteen-stringed Jack, "These people think nothing of murder. I never was in such a fearful place in my life. I never could have believed there was such a place in London."

"Nor I, either," replied Jack; "although, perhaps, I know more about it than you do, sir. But here is our opportunity."

"For flight?"

"Yes, certainly. Come down the stairs at once."

"They will see us. It will not do yet. They will come out of the stable before we are half-way across the yard; and then there will be a scuffle, perhaps a fight. Stop! stop! Good gracious! Where are you going?"

The floor of the balcony was about fifteen feet above the level of the inn yard. The balustrades were not above four feet in height; but suddenly, to the surprise of the Regent, Jack Singleton, without saying another word, swung himself over the balustrade, and hanging by his hands to the lower portion of them, he was able, lightly and actively, to drop the remainder of the distance without injury.

The stable into which old John and the boy had conveyed the dead body had two massive doors, closing together like a coach-house. Those doors could be secured on the outside by a long wooden bar, swinging on a centre, which, when placed horizontally, fell into iron staples prepared for its reception.

Jack had seen this little arrangement; and as, when old John and the boy carried in the body, the large square, heavy door by which they entered the stable swung after them—having a tendency to close of itself—he (Jack) made up his mind what to do.

He sprang across the yard; and, in an instant, placed the bar across the double door.

Old John, the boy, and the corpse of the traitor and spy were prisoners in the stable.

"Now," said Sixteen-stringed Jack, as he ran back to the part of the gallery where he had left the Regent, — "now, sir, descend; the coast is clear."

"Instantly!" cried the Regent.

For one moment only, in his haste, the Prince seemed inclined to follow Jack Singleton's example and get over the balustrade and drop into the yard; but he was by no means so light and active as the knight of the road, and he abandoned the idea as soon as it was formed.

To reach the nearest flight of steps took but a few brief seconds of time, and then the Regent was in the yard, by the side of Jack Singleton.

Jack had not been inactive while the Regent was making his way down the crazy old wooden stairs; for, by the time the Prince reached the yard, he had got his horse out of the stable in which he had been placed; and, holding the animal by the bridle, waited for the Regent.

"We're in no hurry now, sir," said Jack. "I think there is no one here to oppose our progress."

"Let us hurry, though. The very atmosphere of this place is full of murder."

A furious kicking at the double doors of the stable, from the inside, where old John and the boy were made prisoners, sufficiently testified to the fact that they were not only aware of their situation, but were determined to release themselves as quickly as possible.

Jack's horse took the alarm which such a noise was likely to engender, and it was with some difficulty he could hold it.

Certainly, Jack could not hold the animal at the same time that he undid the wicket gate.

The Regent saw the difficulty.

"Allow me," he said. "I will hold the horse."

"Thanks—thanks, sir!"

"Or, if you like to let it go, you shall have its full value, and more."

"It's an old friend," replied Jack; "and I would fain take it with me."

"Very well. I will hold it."

It was rather a curious spectacle, then, to see that proud, haughty Regent of England, who was accustomed to stand so much upon etiquette and the punctilious observances of his rank, carefully holding a highwayman's horse, and upon the best of possible terms with one of the most celebrated, perhaps we should say notorious, depredators of the King's highway.

It was much better, however, that the Regent should hold the horse and Jack undo the gate, for the bolts were numerous and the lock rather intricate.

"Good heavens!" said the Regent, as he saw Jack had some difficulty. "Are we never to get out of this dreadful place?"

"It is done," said Jack, as he flung the wicket-gate open. "Thank heaven, for that much!"

The horse had somewhat recovered his composure, although the furious knocking still continued from within the stable. Probably the creature had sagacity sufficient to know that when that wicket-gate was opened, it would leave the vicinity of those alarming sounds; but certain it was that the animal stooped its head, and stepped out into the open street with an alacrity and judgment that was pleasant to behold.

As for the Regent, he was on the other side of the way in a moment; and it gave Jack Singleton a certain kind of pang to think that the instant there was no more occasion for his services, and the danger had passed away, he was not thought worthy of another look or another word.

But Jack did some injustice to the Regent.

Certainly, the first impulse was to make the best of his way towards St. James's; but the second thought, that he was acting ungratefully and ungraciously, followed quickly that first impulse.

The Regent paused.

He retraced his steps.

Jack breathed more freely.

"I'm glad of that," he said to himself. "I should not have liked to have done for this man what I have, if he had gone off, as he seemed to be going."

"My good friend," said the Regent, "you have unquestionably saved my life to-night."

"It has given me pleasure to do so," said Jack; "because, for once in my life, I can say I have returned good for evil."

"Evil! What mean you?"

"It is an old story now, and has passed away; but if it should ever happen again that youth, and innocence, and beauty attract your eyes, and are coveted by your heart, pause, sir, and remember this night—when, but for me, death, in a hideous and awful form, would have fallen upon you. Shrink back then, sir, and let the contemplated victim escape, as you have escaped, and I shall consider myself as paid for this night's work!"

"I don't know what you mean," said the Regent—"you talk in riddles. But I beg that you will take this breast-pin, which I have been wearing this evening, and always keep it, until you shall wish to ask some favour, which none but the Prince of Wales can grant to you. You see, it is a peculiar Oriental topaz, and the only one of the colour, they say, that has been found."

"I see it, sir, and will carefully preserve it."

"Do so; and whatever you want at any time —be it money, protection, pardon, or what it may, —go to Carlton House with this, and ask for Mr. Willes, the Regent's valet. Say that you want to see Mr. George, and that will be enough. Good night! good night!"

The Regent, without another word, walked away as fast as he could go, flattering himself that he had amply provided for the debt of gratitude he owed Jack Singleton, while, at the same time, he had preserved his *incognito*.

Jack mounted his horse in a moment; and as he stooped low in the saddle, and set the animal in a canter, he said to himself, "I wonder, now, if the gratitude of George the Regent will last until I may want to put it to the test?"

The sharp report of a pistol-shot at this moment echoed through the silent street, and Jack heard a whistling sound pass his ears.

He glanced in the direction of the inn yard, and he saw projecting from the wicket gate a head and two hands.

One hand held a lantern.

The other hand held a pistol, pointed in the direction he was galloping.

"So—so!" said Jack, as he clapped spurs to his horse, "the boy has got out of the stable, and taken a long shot at me. So be it! A miss is as good as a mile. I owed that lad a favour; but I shall consider he has cancelled it, and we may meet again. What's the matter now, Charles?"

These words were addressed to a watchman, who had been wakened up by the pistol-shot; and not knowing what was the matter, thought it as well to alarm all the neighbourhood by springing his rattle.

"Who are you? Stop! stop!" cried the watchman. "Stop till I knock you down, and then take you up."

'Do you really want to know who I am?"

"In course I do."

"Then I'm Sixteen-stringed Jack, the highwayman! Look out, Charles!"

The watchman turned to fly, for he thought it much more likely that Sixteen-stringed Jack would knock him down without the after-process of taking him up, than that he should succeed in apprehending such a personage. But the watchman stumbled and fell into the roadway, to the great detriment of his lantern.

Jack's horse made a beautiful leap over the prostrate guardian of the night; and in five minutes more the highwayman was trotting quietly up the Oxford Road.

The Regent reached St. James's in great perturbation of spirit.

Willes was compelled to administer several restoratives, in the shape of small drops of brandy, before his royal master could recover sufficient composure to make up his mind whether to be communicative or not with regard to the night's adventures.

At one moment, he thought he would say nothing about them.

Then again, he thought it was absolutely necessary to do something to put a stop to the proceedings of such a gang of desperadoes as he had seen in the inn yard.

Then again, the presence of the Dark Woman— of that Linda de Chevenaux who was the bane of his existence—complicated the transaction fearfully.

The Regent sat on a chair, and groaned.

Willes stood by, rubbing his hands slowly one over the other, and wondering what had induced such a pertubation in the spirits of the Prince.

"May I humbly hope that your Royal Highness feels better?"

"No—worse."

Willes fetched up a sigh, and strove to look full of commiseration.

"Perhaps, if your Highness would condescend to inform the most faithful of your servants what has happened——"

"You ought to guess."

Willes looked more puzzled than before.

"It's that woman."

Now, this was a piece of very indefinite information from the Regent; and if Willes had not dreaded the royal displeasure for his want of perspicacity, he would have said "What woman?" As it was, however, he only bowed, and put on a look of deep interest.

"That woman!" added the Regent — "that wretched, infernal woman! What's to be done with her?"

Willes only bowed again.

"I ask you, what is to be done with her?"

Willes began to look dreadfully confused.

"Can't you speak? Have you lost your tongue? Am I surrounded by wretches, beasts, and dumb animals?"

"Oh, no, your Highness! I was thinking that the—a—female woman, whom your Highness mentions, is—a—that is, might be—a—respectable person."

"A murderess !'

"Decidedly a murderess, who is deserving of death — exceedingly deserving of death, your Highness."

"For vindication of the offended laws of the country."

"Very," said Willes.

"What do you mean by 'very,' idiot?"

"I was only thinking, your Royal Highness, that, as she was young and fair——"

"What?"

"Young and fair——"

"But she is no longer young, stupid; and as for being fair, when everybody calls her the Dark Woman——"

"Ah!" cried Willes, with a sensation of great relief—for now he knew who the Regent was speaking of. "I meant to say, your Highness, that she was once young and fair; but I hope no additional cause has arisen for your royal uneasiness on account of that female?"

"A mere trifle—ha, ha!—a mere trifle! I have only escaped by a miracle of being smothered first, and my throat cut afterwards. To follow which, my royal remains, as no doubt you would composedly call them, would have been flung down a well, and never heard of more."

"Goodness gracious!" said Willes. "Can such things be in this mortal world?"

CHAPTER CLXXXI.

THE DARK WOMAN ATTEMPTS A DEED OF DEATH AND OF DESPERATION.

WHEN Linda de Chevenaux left that dreary and suspicious inn yard, close to Long Acre, with the bold, daring, and reckless men who were ready and willing to obey her orders, and aid her in the perpetration of any iniquity her imagination could conceive, she paused beneath the piazzas close to Covent Garden Market.

The band gathered about her.

"It will be well," she said, "to separate now. No. 82.—DARK WOMAN.

The spot of rendezvous will be the narrow entrance to St. James's Park, by Spring Gardens."

"Permit me to make a remark," then said one.

"Speak!" cried the Dark Woman.

"Is it the intention to go into St. James's Park?"

"It is."

"Then that intention may be abandoned."

"I never abandon an intention."

"That is well. But it is now so late that the sentinel at the Park gate, not only at Spring Gardens, but elsewhere, will allow no one to pass."

"But us!" said the Dark Woman.

The band waited in silence some explanation of this expression of confidence, on the part of their new leader, in the fact that they would be permitted to pass a sentinel when all other persons would be stopped.

"Obstacles," added the Dark Woman, "are

but so many opportunities for action to those who are deserving of the rewards of success. One of you will assail the sentinel : a sharp poniard at once suffices to silence for ever, so far as he is concerned, his guard."

A shudder passed through the band.

"Do you shrink?" asked Linda de Chevenaux.

"No! no! no!"

"That is well! One—I care not which of you —will strike the blow; settle who it is to be among you. Another then will assume the great-coat, firelock, and cap of the sentinel, and hold guard until either it is four o'clock or I return with his friends."

"Why till four o'clock?"

"Because the guard is changed every two hours, and those hours are the regular ones of two, four, six, and so on. You might, whichever of you mounts guard, easily deceive any civilians who may see you, or even speak to you; but the sergeant's party, who will start at four o'clock to change the sentinels, would detect you in a moment."

"You think of everything," said one.

"I ought. It is my duty to you all to do so. Now separate; and remember that we all meet beneath the trees of the side mall of St. James's Park."

"Agreed! agreed!"

The Dark Woman did not utter another word, but folding closely about her that cloak which she wore on this occasion, she crossed the way, and was quickly lost to sight among the old, ruinous, broken-down sheds and dilapidated stalls which at that period formed Covent Garden Market.

There was a brief consultation now among the band, and then they scattered into individual parties, or parties of twos and threes.

Two, at as rapid a pace as they could walk, made their way down the first street that would lead them to Charing Cross.

This brief consultation which had taken place beneath the piazzas of Covent Garden had attracted but a slight amount of observation.

The few chance passengers who saw the assemblage of dark figures thought it by far the wisest plan not to interfere with them.

The one watchman who saw them was of exactly the same opinion, and he quietly got into his box, close to the church, and pulled his night-cap over his eyes.

The police of London, at the period of our tale, was so glaringly inefficient, that during the nights the whole city might be said to be left to take care of itself.

If people stayed out late, and were assailed or robbed, or even murdered in the streets, it was their own fault.

Everybody knew the insecurity of the public thoroughfares, and that the Bow Street officers did not at all consider it a part of their duty to act as the present police do as the preventives of crime.

Their business was to apprehend thieves after the crimes had been committed.

People, therefore, had to look to their own safety, and to carry arms for their own protection, as well in the streets as in their own houses.

As late as 1802, a man was found dead in Lincoln's Inn Fields. He had been shot through the head.

The next day a letter appeared in one of the daily papers, stating the writer of it was a gentleman, and that he had been thrice robbed in Lincoln's Inn Fields by a footpad, and that he had at length determined to protect himself, and on the fourth occasion had shot him. The writer of the letter went on to say that he withheld his name because he did not wish to lay himself open to the possible revenge of the robber's friends and associates.

From all this state of things, it may readily be supposed that the band of the Dark Woman were not likely to meet with any serious interruption in what they chose to set about.

We will now follow the proceedings of those two who were making such haste towards Charing Cross.

At the back of the Strand there still exists a straggling, not over reputable, thoroughfare, which leads to Trafalgar Square.

At the period of our story that thoroughfare led to the King's Mews, which then stood where the National Gallery now stands.

By going that way, these two men took the nearest route to Spring Gardens.

St. Martin's Church clock chimed the half-hour past two in the morning as they passed it.

Then one of these two men spoke in a low tone to the other.

"She has timed it well."

"She has. The sentinel will not be relieved for another hour and a half."

"Will he not? Ha, ha!"

"Oh, I comprehend you. He will individually be relieved, but the relief-guard will not come to the post till four."

"Just so. Let us hasten. Since I have promised to do this little piece of work, I am anxious to have it over."

"Oh, if you shrink, I will do it."

"Shrink? When did you ever know me shrink? Was it not I that ran my sword through two watchmen in Golden Square?"

"True! true! Come on!"

They crossed the roadway, and were in a few more moments at the commencement of the narrow way into the Park by Spring Gardens.

As they were passing a deep and shadowy doorway, a voice startled them.

"Do quickly, and do effectually," it said, "that which you have to do!"

It was the voice of the Dark Woman.

The two desperadoes made no reply, but they hurried forward. They felt that the observation of their new leader was upon them.

They wished to do their work well, to show their unscrupulous efficiency. They wished to excel. There was a pride even in wickedness—in murder!

The soldier on duty at the iron gate of Spring Gardens was enveloped in his grey great-coat. He stood "at ease," by the entrance to the sentry box.

Little dreamt he that his race was all but run— that the roll-call which summoned him to another world was about to be read.

With a slow but careless air, one of the two members of the Dark Woman's band, who came to do a deed of blood, strolled down to the gate.

"Stand!" cried the sentinel. "Who goes there?"

"A friend!" was the prompt reply.

"Stand, friend! You cannot pass here."

"I know that, my good fellow, ordinarily speaking; but I am an officer, and have a pass signed by your own Colonel."

"Show the pass, sir!"

The sentinel had a lantern in the sentry-box, which he promptly produced, and hung on a nail outside. He incautiously let his musket fall back into the hollow of his arm and shoulder, as the pretended officer with the pass advanced towards him.

Lightly as possible, the second member of the band had followed the first one; and while the doomed soldier was leaning forward to look at a scrap of paper—which the first one held before his eyes, to favour the delusion that he had a "pass" —the second assassin crept behind the unconscious victim.

"Is that a pass, sir? I don't see."

"But you will."

"Ah! Murder—mur——"

The sentinel fell forward, and would have reached the ground but that he was caught by the throat with one hand of the man before him, while the other hand grasped his musket, the rattle of the fall of which might make an alarm.

Indeed, the concussion might have discharged it.

"It is done!" said the assassin, who had crept so villanously behind the soldier.

"And well done!" said the other.

"Is he dead?"

"I think so. He does not move. He does not speak, move, or sigh. What is to be done with him?"

"Take the coat, firelock, and cap, and let us put him as far back as we can into the sentry-box."

"Ay, ay; that will do. What is that?"

"Three-quarters past two, by the clock of the Horse Guards."

"Then I will hold this post, at all events, for one hour, from now."

The great-coat, cap, and firelock of the murdered soldier were taken possession of. The dead body was thrust, in a doubled-up position, into the sentry-box; and the member of the Dark Woman's band, who had pretended to be an officer and to have a pass, took up a position in imitation of the sentinel at the entrance to the sentry-box.

"It is done!" said a voice.

The Dark Woman made her appearance, close at hand, with a startling suddenness.

She must have seen and heard all that had taken place in the perpetration of that cold-blooded murder.

"Put out that lantern," she said.

It was at once extinguished.

The Dark Woman then blew a long, wailing, faint note upon a silver whistle. It was so low a note that, but to the ears that would recognise it and comprehend its meaning, it would have been a thing to think and speculate about, but nothing further.

Indeed, by the art with which the tones were made to rise and fall, it would have been very difficult to say whether they were near at hand or coming upon the night air from a considerable distance.

But those notes were understood by the new band of the Dark Woman.

Down the narrow thoroughfare to the Park came the troop of dim and dusky-looking figures.

They halted at the iron gate.

The Dark Woman spoke.

"You will all follow me now as you are. In ten minutes more, you shall be in St. James's Palace."

She did not want to hear any remark that might be made, but dashed through the small iron gate into the Park.

The mock sentinel held the post.

The dead soldier was dyeing with his blood the floor of the sentry-box.

St. James's Park was profoundly dark.

Not a star could be seen in the heavens. Thick, heaving clouds hung between the earth and the bright constellations.

The forms of the band, as they followed the Dark Woman, looked like nothing more than blacker pieces of the darkness, cut out of the surrounding gloom.

But there was one lamp a little way beyond those few ricketty old sheds where, since the time of the first Charles, a couple of cows have been allowed to dispense milk to the children and nurse-maids who frequented the Mall on fine mornings.

It was of course one of the old miserable oil lamps, and the Dark Woman herself extinguished it.

The darkness thus had become very profound; for the next lamp was not nearer than the turnstile, which then was the mode of entrance to the Green Park from that of St. James's.

The Dark Woman did not purpose going so far as that.

In the wall of the old court-yard of St. James's Palace, which at that time was named the Ambassadors' Court, there was a small strong door.

The door was seldom, if ever, opened. The Regent usually made his way home from any nocturnal ramble by a private entrance to the gardens of Carlton House.

But the Dark Woman had a key to this door.

In earlier times, when her supremacy over the mind of Willes, the Regent's valet, was strong, she had made him procure for her this key.

It was useful to her now.

Not a soul witnessed the progress of the Dark Woman and her associates in St. James's Park. Truly might that time have been named

"The dead and waste hour of the night."

It would seem as if all London slept, so still was the great city.

The Dark Woman paused.

She made a gesture, which could be but faintly seen by those who were ready to obey her orders, but they did see it sufficiently to know that it meant they were to pause at the spot where she stood.

That was close to the little door in the wall which skirted the Ambassadors' Court of old St. James's Palace.

The Dark Woman was then about to speak, but she was interrupted by one of the band, who in an anxious whisper said, "Be it known that there is a footstep in the Park."

"Ah!"

"Yes. There is some one hastening in this direction from the Horse Guards."

"Down!—down!" said the Dark Woman. "Sit down, all of you, close to the wall, and the eyes of Argus would fail to see you in this darkness."

The dusky figures around her obeyed this order from the Dark Woman with alacrity, and the effect was as if they had all suddenly sunk down into the earth.

The disappearance was complete.

Then, from the position they all occupied close to the earth, they could hear the footstep of some one coming across the Park even more distinctly than before.

"You hear?" whispered the Dark Woman.

A murmured "Yes" was the response.

"No life must stand in our way. If that person, be he who he may, passes on and observes us not, he lives."

"If not, he dies," said one of the band. "I will do the deed. My hand is in for such work to-night."

"Yes—he dies! Wait, and watch!"

The footstep rapidly approached; and by the lightness with which it touched the earth, it was evidently that of a young man.

Ah! why did not some beneficent spirit at that time whisper to the Dark Woman the name of the person who was thus advancing to the danger which she had herself declared should surround him!

How little did it occur to her imagination that those footsteps betokened the arrival at that point of danger of the very person for whom she had so deeply sinned and suffered!

It was her own son—so long known to the reader as Allan Fearon, but now to be designated by his new name and title of Captain Fitz George, of the Guards.

It so happened that it was the duty of Fitz George to be the officer on guard for the night at St. James's; and he had only left for a brief space a subaltern on duty while he walked over to the Horse Guards on some regimental business.

He was now on his return, making what speed he could,—for his ideas of duty were precise and regular; and as little as the Dark Woman imagined it was her own son approaching her, did he for a moment dream his mother, with a band of assassins, was lying in ambush, and that his life depended upon the accident of which direction his eyes might be turned at a particular moment.

Fitz George rapidly neared the spot of danger.

The Dark Woman spoke again in a low tone.

"Shrink not!" she said. "What are human lives to us? Our road to success will be all the easier if we step over the dead!"

Nearer—nearer still—the footsteps came; and as the ground rose a little at that point, the impression on the part of the Dark Woman and her associates was that this person who approached was about to pause—possibly because he might have seen something suspicious beneath the wall of the Palace.

It was not certain, though, that such was the case.

The unscrupulous ruffian, however, who had murdered the sentinel at Spring Gardens' gate, and who had declared his hand to be "in" for such kind of work, would have been quite willing, on the bare suspicion and probability that the approaching stranger dimly saw them, to rush out and take his life.

He even whispered as much to the Dark Woman, crouched down as he was close to her.

"Shall I do it now? Shall I do it now? It is only another!"

"Wait!—wait!"

"See! He slackens his pace—he pauses—he fancies he sees something. I suppose we show up a little blacker than the wall."

"Do it!" said the Dark Woman.

The assassin began slowly to crawl forward, and as he did so Captain Fitz George approached diagonally, so that he would have passed the spot where they were lurking, leaving them some thirty paces or so on his right hand.

These movements both of the man who sought his life and of the young officer brought them rapidly nearer to each other.

It so happened, too, that the oil lamp at the turnstile leading into the Green Park began, in that precarious manner incidental to oil lamps, to burn with much greater brightness than before, and it sent a long, misty kind of ray right across the principal Mall of St. James's Park, fading away until it mingled itself with the darkness in the far distance.

Captain Fitz George just stepped into this ray of light, faint, dim, and uncertain as it was, as the assassin, crouching down, was within half-a-dozen yards of him.

The light, faint and uncertain as it was, flashed upon the uniform he wore. It borrowed a new lustre from the glittering epaulettes, and the gorget flashed like a jewel for a moment.

Then the assassin knew that he was an officer of the Guards, with his hand upon his sword-hilt, that he had to encounter.

And then the Dark Woman knew that it was that son for whom, at any moment, she would have given, even then, life for life.

The assassin shrank back, for the coward instinct was in his nature.

The Dark Woman uttered a piercing cry, which awakened echoes far and near about old St. James's and the Park.

CHAPTER CLXXXII.

CAPTAIN FITZ GEORGE APPEALS TO THE REASON AND AFFECTION OF HIS MOTHER.

THE young officer had seen nothing up to that moment of alarm. If permitted to do so, and undisturbed, he would have passed on his way without a thought that there were any lurking forms intent on mischief in his immediate vicinity.

But for the eagerness of that assassin, whose really cowardly nature shrank from a contest with an armed man, Captain Fitz George would have made his way quietly to one of the regular Park entrances to the Palace, and passed on to the guard room where it was his duty to remain.

But the eagerness to do a deed of blood was now nearly compromising the safety of that band led by the Dark Woman on this their first enterprise of daring criminality under her guidance.

Captain Fitz George still saw nothing of the dusky forms beneath the Palace walls. The faint ray of light he had stepped into, by glancing in his eyes, tended to throw that part of the Park into profounder gloom.

But he heard that piercing cry.

Starting back a pace he drew his sword half-way from the scabbard, for he could expect nothing else but an instant attack upon him, of which that cry was probably the precursor.

Then through the gloom there came swiftly a dim and dusky figure, and before Fitz George could wholly release his sword from its sheath, that figure had grasped him by the breast, had grasped him by the arm, and, in a voice which he had heard often enough never to forget, the seeming assailant spoke to him as though there were scarcely breath sufficient to give utterance to the words.

"Allan! Allan! my son! Once again—once again we meet!—we meet! You are not hurt? Your mother saves you! Oh, no, no! 'twas she condemned' Hush! I am mad! What am I saying? What am I saying?'

Captain Fitz George almost staggered back beneath the violence of the clutch she took of his breast and arm.

"Good heavens!" he said. "Is this possible? Mother! mother! you were in my thoughts—in my heart!"

"My son! my son! tell me that again!"

"I am bewildered—lost in a world of conjecture. For the last four-and-twenty hours I have thought and dreamt but of some mode of discovering you —some means of finding a clue to your retreat; and now, as if from the very clouds, you drop at my feet, and fill me with wonder and amazement!"

"Then you have still affection left for the poor heart that—that——"

"Oh, speak not thus! Affection left? When have I shown want of affection? When have I given you cause to doubt that I was willing, anxious, craving to show you all the affection of a son?"

The Dark Woman seemed to be half choked with emotion; but during the progress of this short dialogue she had contrived to drag Captain Fitz George some considerable distance up the Mall towards Buckingham House.

She wished to remove him from the immediate vicinity of the band of ruffians she had brought there that night on a deed of violence and murder.

Fitz George—whom she would still persist in calling Allan—could not understand the persistence with which she dragged him from the immediate vicinity of St. James's Palace.

"Mother! mother!" he said, "whither would you take me? Why do you hold me so convulsively?"

"To save you!"

"Save me? From what?"

"Ask me not—ask me not; but there has been danger."

"Alas! alas! mother, there will always be danger while your brain continues full of the mad projects which armed you almost with resentment against me when we last met."

"No, no, no!"

"Indeed it is a sad truth."

"No resentment—no resentment. My heart was full of bitterness."

"We will call it bitterness, then."

"And can you wonder at it when I found you willing to cast away your birthright? When I found that you—disregarding all that I have done and all that I have suffered—were willing to accept infamy and reproach instead of battling for a crown?"

"Mother! mother! this is madness! The irresistible logic of facts compel us all to accept that which is true."

"You are a prince!"

Captain Fitz George shook his head.

"You are a prince, I say. Who shall say nay to the proposition?"

"I—the Regent—the whole world will say nay to it. Oh, mother, mother, if you cannot be happy, why will you not strive for some serenity? That mock marriage with the Regent upon which you build your hopes can never be established."

"It is registered."

"Where, mother?"

"In heaven!'

"Alas! heaven's registers are closed to human justice. But I have found you now, and I will not again willingly part with you. Accident—or I will more willingly call it Providence—let me know that you were a prisoner in the Tower of London, and I hastened to procure from the Regent an order for your release."

"From him? From my persecutor?"

"Even so; if you choose to call him by that name. The Regent has no wish to persecute you, mother, if you do not goad him to retaliation for such a persecution on your part as surely no human being was ever tortured with before."

"You defend him?"

"No, no! I do not defend him. I defend you. It is for your sake I speak, not his; for your peace—your serenity."

"Perish the word!" cried the Dark Woman, passionately. "I hate the very sound of it!"

"What word?"

"That word serenity, which is, like the burden of some stale ballad, ever on your lips."

"I offend you, mother, but will love you still."

The Dark Woman made an impatient gesture.

"But tell me, now," added Captain Fitz George, —"tell me how and why it is I find you here, and in so strange a costume? If some new, wild project of vengeance or simple annoyance to the Regent has found a home in your heart, let me implore you to discard it as unworthy of you. Let me look upon this meeting as providential— as one that will enable me to save you, mother, from—from——"

"From what?"

"Will you be offended with me when I say from yourself?"

The Dark Woman was silent for a few moments, but still she kept a hold upon the arm of Captain Fitz George, as though she feared that—should she release him for a moment—he might fly from her, and she might never look upon his face again.

"Come, mother—come," he said. "Think better of the world. Have faith in happiness, and try to reach some portion of your wishes through the gates of forgiveness. This is a grievous subject to converse about, and to me a most distressing alternative is presented. I stand between you, my mother, and my father, the Regent. I do not defend him, but what would you have me do? It is not for me to be the avenger. We must leave things to a diviner justice than human nature can pretend to. Forgive, mother—forgive. It may not be possible to forget, but it is possible to forgive. Would you have me kill myself, because I am what I am?"

"No," replied the Dark Woman. "You have spoken, Allan, and now listen to me."

"I will—I will!" replied Fitz George, with a sigh, for it was not reason he expected to hear from his mother's lips.

"This meeting between us to-night, my son, has been arranged—arranged for us. It is fate. You and I must see the Regent; and before day-dawn he must—under his own hand and seal—declare the validity of the marriage, and your legitimacy."

"Dreams—dreams, mother!"

"There are some dreams that come true, and this is one. You have a sword by your side: come with me, and use it for yourself and for your mother."

"To speak more plainly, you wish me to draw my sword against the Regent."

"I wish you to show him that you have a sword, and the courage to use it. Since by fair and even paths we cannot accomplish our objects, we must do so by such forcible means as suggest themselves."

"Never!—never!"

"Think—oh, think again!"

"Never! Mother, were I to live a thousand years, and think the whole of that period, I would not draw my sword against the Regent, my father. It is he who, practically and virtually, has given me authority to wear it. There is a limit to retribution; after that it becomes revenge—a wild and evil passion. Mother, I will *not* side with you."

The Dark Woman did not speak, or if she did utter a word it was lost in the inarticulate cry which accompanied it.

Suddenly she disengaged her hold of Fitz George's arm; but he was prepared for such a contingency, fully believing that she would fly from him the moment she found it was impossible to move him to her purposes; and gradually, without her observation, he had contrived to take a firm grasp of the cloak she wore.

"Perish, then, with him!" cried the Dark Woman. "Perish, then, with that father whom you too much resemble! Vengeance shall still be mine!"

"No, mother. We will not perish, and we will, at the same time, save you."

She tried to dart from him, but was arrested by the cloak.

"Ah! You detain me? I am a prisoner?"

"Such a prisoner as never the world saw—a prisoner more for the benefit of the imprisoned than the captor. Mother, you shall not go."

The Dark Woman, by a rapid movement, unclasped the cloak from around her neck. She flung its heavy folds partially over the head and shoulders of Captain Fitz George, and before he could disentangle himself from it she was gone.

The young officer made a mistake in regard to the route she took, and she intended that he should do so; for Linda de Chevenaux ran, first of all, towards Buckingham House—then, crouch-

ing down, so as to avoid observation as much as possible, she rapidly crossed the Mall—and, under the shadow of the palings which surrounded the waste ground in the centre of the Park, she made her way again opposite to that door in the wall of St. James's Palace, where she had left her confederates.

Captain Fitz George was in despair.

It was the one drawback upon all the contentment of his existence, that his mother was in such a frame of mind as should induce her to scheme and plot against his father, the Regent.

He had hoped that if by some means he should discover where she was, and procure an interview with her, he might be able to awaken some more reasonable ideas in her mind.

That hope had now vanished.

He had felt, too, and the feeling had always come across his mind with a special pang, that if his mother were still to remain deaf to all reason, it would be his duty, both for her sake and for the sake of his father, to aid and assist in some steps to prevent her from becoming dangerous.

And what made Captain Fitz George feel all this so acutely, was that he was by no means unmindful of all his mother had suffered on his account.

His sensitive and noble heart was torn by contending emotions.

The escape of his mother from him on this occasion, when chance had thrown her in his way, was a source both of aggravation and affliction.

He had made up his mind to the necessity of detaining her.

Probably, then, on that night, in St. James's Park, he, Captain Fitz George, began to feel that it was far easier for him to hold a contest with his feelings, and finally make up his mind to a particular course of action as regarded his mother, than to carry that conclusion into effect.

The Dark Woman had baffled and defied the Regent, and she seemed to have the power to do the same to him, Fitz George.

The young officer ran for some distance in the direction of Buckingham House, but hearing no footsteps, he paused to listen.

All was still in that direction.

Then he turned and ran down the Mall in the other direction.

No, nothing could be seen or heard of the Dark Woman.

Captain Fitz George opened his lips for the purpose of calling to her.

What should he name her? How was he to call her?

Could he afford to bring ridicule upon himself by shouting out "Mother! mother!" in St. James's Park?

Was he to call to her by her name of Linda de Chevenaux, or by that of her far more terrible and popular name of the Dark Woman?

The result of these reflections was that the young officer did not call to her at all, feeling that it would be useless; as, if she were in hiding in the Park, she could easily rejoin him if she wished; and if she did not wish, all his calling to her would not make her.

With a heavy heart, he made his way towards the entrance to St James's, whither he was bound when the Dark Woman had sprung upon him from the shadow of the old Palace wall.

"The Regent must know of all this," said Captain Fitz George to himself. "So soon as he is stirring in the morning, it will be my duty to communicate to him what has happened."

Fitz George felt it was a double duty that was imposed upon him in this matter.

The duty of a son.

The duty of an officer.

And so he sought the old guard-room, where he was to pass the remainder of the night, in charge of the Palace.

The Dark Woman sunk down for a few moments close to one of the wooden seats in the Park.

She was exhausted at the moment both in mind and in body.

The clock of the Horse Guards struck three.

It was that sound that seemed to bring her back to the recollection of where she was, and of what she had determined that night to do.

She sprang to her feet.

"Three o'clock! I have but an hour!"

She made her way to the door in the Palace wall, where she had left the band.

They still occupied the same position.

"That is well," she said.

"We could not think," said one, "what had happened to you."

"It is needless to think."

"But you might have been in danger."

"I am always in danger. Let it be a rule of conduct with all of you, that, unless you know that I am killed or captured, you will always remain as you have now, where I left you, until my return."

The band, with murmured voices, signified their assent to this proposition, or rather command.

Then the Dark Woman produced the key which she had long ago got from Willes, the valet; and she opened with it the door in the wall of old St. James's Palace.

One by one, the dark figures of the band passed through that narrow, low doorway.

There were eleven.

One other was playing the part of the sentinel at the gate by Spring Gardens.

There was no sentry in the court-yard where the band of the Dark Woman now found themselves.

But well did Linda de Chevenaux know that they would not be able to leave that court and proceed to the next one without passing a post where a sentinel would be on duty.

It was her object, then, if possible, to penetrate into the Palace from that court, if it could be accomplished without much loss of time.

She had a key to one of the old doors that opened to the Colcur Court.

But, as we have remarked, there was always a sentinel on duty there.

Another murder, and another personation of a sentry in that court, so close to the guard-room, might not be so easy of accomplishment as the similar transaction at Spring Gardens had been.

The Dark Woman turned to the band, and spoke in low tones.

"Tell me," she said,—"can any of you climb to one of those three windows yonder?"

"I can," replied one. "I can, with a little help."

"What sort of help?"

"The shoulders of a comrade, if he will be so good as to allow me to place my feet upon them for a moment."

"So be it."

"Then you, Allanberg, will stand close to the wall for me."

"Ay, ay, Fitzpatrick, I will do it."

"Master," said the member of the band, who was then about to reach the window,—"Master, tell me what I am to do when I enter the Palace by that window."

The Dark Woman gave her directions in a low but distinct tone.

"Immediately within the window you will find one of those old window-seats which occupy the whole recess made by the thickness of the wall. You will alight upon that carefully and noiselessly."

"Yes—yes."

"Then you will find yourself in an old wainscoted room, from which there will either be a door which will lead you directly to a staircase, or through into another room, from which you will be able to make your way to the ground floor."

"And then?"

"Then you will hear a slight, tapping sound, which I will make from without at this door, which will be the one you will open from within."

"Good!"

"You comprehend fully?"

"I do."

With an agility and dexterity which went far towards the supposition that they must have studied the feat many a time before, the two dissolute young men who were to assist each other proceeded to do so.

One of them placed himself in a firm position close to the Palace; the other, with great activity, clambered up to his shoulders, and stood with a foot on each shoulder, so that he was quite up to the level of the window.

There was a slight creaking noise as he raised the window-sash.

Then he disappeared; for he had skilfully drawn himself through the opening.

The Dark Woman then approached the door that was nearly under the window, and made a slight tapping at it with her finger-nails.

There was the subdued sound of the grating of some rusted bolt in its socket, and then the door creaked open.

That door had not been opened for a good thirty years, or more.

"Come!" said the Dark Woman—"come! Follow me!"

She went first, and the ten men she had with her in the court-yard followed her.

As the last one disappeared within the doorway, the slight tap of a drum was heard close at hand.

The Dark Woman sprung past the band, and half emerged into the court again.

She held both hands close upon her heart, which began to throb painfully, as she whispered more to herself than to any one else's understanding—"What is that?—what is that?"

The tap-tap of the drum sounded again.

Then all was still.

One of the band approached the Dark Woman.

"I know what that is, master," he said.

By some strange whim they had all taken it into their heads to call her "Master."

"You know?"

"Oh, yes! It is the 'Palace rounds,' as it is called. It is the duty of the officer on guard to go round the courts at least once during the night, with a guard, to see that all is safe."

"Ah, yes! I had forgotten. I ought to know —I ought to know."

"So, master, we are, it appears, just housed in time."

"Just—just! Come in! Come in!"

They retired through the doorway, and the Dark Woman closed it.

CHAPTER CLXXXIII.

A TERRIBLE CRIME SUGGESTS ITSELF TO THE IMAGINATION OF THE DARK WOMAN.

LITTLE did Linda de Chevenaux suspect that the officer whose duty it was, on that eventful night at St. James's Palace, to go the 'rounds' was her own son.

It had not struck her that such was likely to be the case, owing to finding him in full uniform in the Park, although it might reasonably have done so.

The hurry and agitation of her spirits at so meeting him had put minor matters out of her head.

But it was Allan, as she still, in her mind, persevered in calling him.

The tap of the drum was merely a ceremony in the guard-room.

It was not intended that the "Palace rounds" should be a noisy demonstration; so after that slight summons to the soldiers on duty, Captain Fitz George, casting his cloak about him, drew his sword, and, preceded by a sergeant with a lantern, and followed by a guard of men, he went on the customary duty.

There was nothing to be seen.

The sentinel in the Colour Court "shouldered arms;" and, in reply to the sergeant's inquiry of "Is all well?" said, sharply, "All's well!"

The Ambassadors' Court was the next visited; and if the "Palace rounds" had made an appearance there only five minutes earlier, the proceedings of the Dark Woman and her band of unscrupulous ruffians might then and there have been put an end to.

As it was, not a sound disturbed the stillness of the court.

"All's well, sir!" said the sergeant.

At that moment Captain Fitz George felt something soft under his feet.

It was a glove.

A glove such as only a gentleman was likely to have worn, since it was of the most expensive material and make.

"How came this glove here, sergeant?" asked Fitz George, as he handed it to him.

The sergeant looked puzzled.

Now what puzzled the worthy sergeant was a little matter that did some credit to his thoughtfulness. There had been for the last hour or two a heavy dew falling—so heavy, indeed, that it almost resembled a very small rain—one of those small night rains that can be felt but not seen.

The flag-stones of the court-yard were damp with this falling moisture. The uniforms and firelocks of the guard were covered with it.

But that glove was perfectly dry.

A better evidence of the fact that it could not have been many minutes, nay, not many moments, in its position on the stones at the Ambassadors' Court, could not very well be.

"Captain," said the sergeant, "this glove has only just been dropped here."

"You think so?"

"It is quite dry, Captain."

Fitz George was puzzled. A cold feel came across his heart, for the idea that this glove was somehow connected with the appearance of his mother in the Park obtruded itself at once upon him.

How true that supposition was the reader is well aware; but Captain Fitz George dreaded to convince himself of it as a truth.

The glove belonged to one of the band, who had carelessly let it drop.

The Dark Woman would have been bitterly enraged could she have known it.

Captain Fitz George recollected, too, that his mother was disguised in male attire; and he felt sick at heart to think that she might possibly, with some terrible intent, be lurking about St. James's Palace.

But he could say nothing of these suspicions to the sergeant, although they thronged about his brain.

The worthy sergeant could not make out what made his superior so thoughtful.

The soldiers looked from one to the other anxiously.

"Yes," said Fitz George,—"yes, as you say, sergeant, this glove cannot have been here many minutes. I—I will keep it. Right about face! March! I will see to it—I will see to it."

The sergeant could not but perceive that there was more on the mind of his officer than the latter chose to impart to him; but, of course, he said nothing.

On the way back to the guard-room the young officer made up his mind what to do.

"It is my duty," he thought, "to unravel this mystery, and I shall be much more likely to do it alone than with the guard at my heels."

With this determination he dismissed the guard; and then, turning to the sergeant, he said, "Sergeant, see that the priming of my pistols is in good order."

"Yes, your honour."

The sergeant looked wistful, and, no doubt, would have been glad to accompany his officer; but it was not consistent with military discipline for him to suggest such a thing.

Captain Fitz George, then, placing a brace of pistols in his pocket, gathered his cloak about him, and prepared to investigate, by himself, and at his own individual risk, as far as it was possible, the mystery of the glove which he had found in the Ambassadors' Court.

Pocket pistols were not then, nor are they now, a part of the arms of the officers of the guard, but there was a sort of understood arrangement by which every officer possessed a brace of such

weapons, since it had been found in some of the recent campaigns that many an officer owed his life to the facility with which he could deliver a pistol shot, since the flimsy swords they wore were a great deal more for ornament than use.

It must not be supposed, however, for a moment that an idea had found a home in the brain of Captain Fitz George that such weapons were to be used against Linda de Chevenaux.

He could not believe it possible that his mother could make her way with such freedom as he had heard she was in the habit of doing into St. James's Palace, without having some accomplice within its walls.

That accomplice Captain Fitz George would have had no hesitation in shooting.

Such a man he would have considered not only a traitor to the Regent in whose service he was, but as one who, by the kind of assistance he lent to the Dark Woman, was really as great an enemy as he could possibly have.

No. 83.—DARK WOMAN.

Captain Fitz George reasoned that if he could get rid of such a person his mother would no longer find that facility of entrance to St. James's Palace which it was her boast to possess, and she would then, probably, listen to reason, which she had not hitherto done.

The young officer trod as lightly as foot could fall, and passing across the Colour Court he made his way into the next one where the glove had been found, and which he felt certain was the precise locality where any discoveries were to be looked for.

The darkness was tolerably profound in all parts of the Ambassadors' Court; but one side of it seemed more enveloped in gloom than the others; and there Captain Fitz George stationed himself to make his observations.

He made up his mind that not a single window or door that he could command a view of, from the place where he had stationed himself, should escape the most careful scrutiny.

For ten minutes he carried his eyes from one casement to another with a care and precision which made it impossible that anything unusual should elude his observation.

At the same time he kept his sense of hearing almost at a painful stretch, so that no sound of a suspicious character, however slight, should pass him unheeded.

But for some time he was not repaid for all this care and attention.

If St. James's Palace had been the abode of the dead it could not have presented a more intensely quiet and gloomy appearance.

If the whole world had been asleep, the silence could not have been more profound than that which reigned about the spot.

Had it not been for the discovery of that glove, lying so dry and so warm upon the damp stones of that court-yard, Captain Fitz George would have said to himself that nothing could be more improbable than the presence of an unaccredited person that night in St. James's Palace.

But he did not desert his post.

He had made up his mind to give an hour to the observation which he was bestowing so critically upon the windows and doors surrounding the Ambassadors' Court.

Another ten minutes elapsed.

Then he was rewarded for all his trouble and anxiety.

Suddenly, at one of the windows, there appeared a faint flush of light.

Captain Fitz George did not happen to be actually looking at the window at which this flush of light appeared; but amid the surrounding darkness it attracted his eyes instantly.

Then, as suddenly as it had appeared, it was gone.

The window was one of a row of six or seven, all fashioned so exactly alike, that it might well be presumed they belonged to some gallery, or large apartment, into which they all looked.

If this were the case, however, the light which appeared at one ought to have shed some radiance over the others.

Such, however, was not the case; and the young officer was coming to the conclusion, somewhat hastily, that his imagination had deceived him.

Or, perchance, the accidental reflection of some distant light on the panes of glass was the cause of the sudden illumination he fancied he saw.

He was wrong in both those conjectures.

About twenty seconds had elapsed, and then he saw the light appear at another window.

Twenty seconds more, and he saw it at a third —then at a fourth—and so on along the whole length of those windows, which now he felt certain belonged to some apartment, gallery, or corridor in the Palace.

That some person was pacing slowly past those windows, carrying a light, there could be no doubt, although that light was too faint to diffuse its rays over the space from one window to another.

"What shall I do?"

That is the question the young officer asked himself.

It was a puzzling one to answer.

What if he should make a sudden alarm—rousing the whole Palace from its repose and propriety—but to find that it was one of the attendants or inmates of the Palace, who harmlessly, and with a perfect right so to do, went past those windows with a light?

Would he not be considered a troublesome fellow—a suspicious kind of marplot—interfering in other persons' affairs for no object but the gratification of his own curiosity?

That was one side of the question.

But there was another.

Might not that light indicate that, in St. James's Palace, there was some one who not only had no right to be there, but whose presence indicated danger of the most unusual kind to the Regent.

Might not that person be the Dark Woman?

Might it not be that her imagination, inflamed by fresh passion on account of the interview she had had with him in the Park, was even then conceiving some terrible project which it was his duty to prevent, and which he had it in his power to put a stop to by an active alarm?

Yet he paused.

Again and again Captain Fitz George put to himself the question, "What shall I do? What shall I do?"

The light had disappeared.

It had traversed the whole space comprehended by the windows, and all was gloom, silence, and darkness again.

The suspense became intolerable. Captain Fitz George hardly knew upon what impulse he acted, but he crossed the court-yard, towards the door which was immediately opposite the post he had occupied.

What it was that induced him to push against that door he never could, in after times, tell himself; but he did so, and the door yielded at once.

If any confirmation were wanted of the fact that something strange and wrong was taking place in St. James's Palace on that night, there it was.

It was out of all question that a door should be left unfastened from within, unless by the special act and motive of some one who had a purpose in view inimical to the interests of the proper residents of the royal abode.

Was it left open by that person, whoever he was, who aided the Dark Woman in her designs upon the Regent; or was it left open by the Dark Woman herself, in order to facilitate her escape when she had perhaps carried out those designs to the full?

The young officer—who felt that it was his duty to defend a Sovereign, a benefactor, and a father—could not answer that question; but he drew his sword, and resolved that he would do that duty, and, if possible, at the same time, save his mother from the consequences of encountering any one less scrupulous of her safety than himself.

Fitz George then entered the Palace by that same door which had been opened from within to admit the Dark Woman and her associates.

He was but one man; and little could he guess that there were eleven desperadoes, well armed, and who had passed the threshold of that door before him, who would not scruple to take his life the moment they should see him.

Had he known as much, Captain Fitz George might no doubt have taken effective measures for their capture; but in his mind's eye, all he saw was his mother. Alone—full of desperation and the madness of grief and injury, seeking to do some deed of which she herself must bitterly repent when repentance was too late,—who was to save her but himself?

Her son was the proper person to interpose between her and her fighting soul.

He crossed the threshold of the door.

He closed it noiselessly behind him.

He stood, silent and dim as a spectre, in a small octagonal-shaped hall, which was the first apartment, if it may be called such, he came to.

Fitz George first listened—listened painfully—to catch the slightest sound which might indicate the presence of the Dark Woman, or the direction in which he was to seek for her.

But no such hints or indications met his ears.

He advanced slowly.

He held his sword with the point downwards, lest inadvertently, in that darksome place, he might inflict an injury upon the being he came to preserve.

With his left hand outstretched, he felt his way through the dark atmosphere; and then, after proceeding a dozen paces, he touched the wall.

He followed with that touch the wainscoting until it changed its character; and he felt convinced that his hand was upon one of those doors covered with crimson cloth, which were so common in St. James's Palace.

These doors he knew had no fastenings; they could either be pulled or pushed open, according to the side at which they were approached; some of them even swung both ways.

This one resisted pressure, but the young officer found the handle by feeling for it, and the door opened towards him easily.

He advanced a little too rapidly, and halfstumbled over the lowest of a flight of steps.

These he ascended slowly, and he thought it probable enough that those steps would lead him to the long gallery or corridor, at the successive windows of which he had seen the light appear.

Captain Fitz George could not have told why he counted the steps as he ascended them, but he recollected perfectly that they were twentyfour in number.

Another of the cloth-covered doors was at the top of these steps, and that, too, opened towards him.

He almost let it from his grasp as he opened it, for the moment he did so he saw at some distance before him a very faint ray of light, and he heard the confused whisper of voices.

That St. James's Palace was beleaguered in some way or shape by persons who had no right to be there, was now clear enough.

The young officer almost, too, began to doubt if his mother, after all, had anything to do with this burglarious entrance into the royal abode.

But yet, who but she would, in this mysterious manner, wish to enter St. James's? and who but she could succeed in doing so?

Again Captain Fitz George asked himself that pertinent question which shaped itself into the words, "What shall I do?"

Ah! how well he would have known what to do but for the dread that whatever he did must naturally have a tendency to compromise the safety, perhaps the life, of Linda de Chevenaux—that poor mother, whose mind had surely given way to some extent beneath the pressure of her wrongs, and the demolition of all her hopes.

CHAPTER CLXXXIV.

CAPTAIN FITZ GEORGE RESCUES THE COUNTESS DE BLONDE FROM A GREAT DANGER.

WE leave, for a short space of time, Captain Fitz George, who is placed in circumstances of painful difficulty, while we follow the more important progress and proceedings of the Dark Woman in St James's Palace.

That part of the royal habitation into which she and her myrmidons had so successfully made their way, was very seldom visited.

The apartments were not absolutely neglected, nor were they shut up and left to dust and to decay, but they were not among those which were in the ordinary use of the dwellers in the Palace.

The vast extent of the old building can only be appreciated by those who have the means and opportunity of wandering at will over it.

From the outside, but a very meagre idea can be formed of the suites of rooms, the galleries, the corridors, and the long passages which abound.

But they were all well known to Linda de Chevenaux, the Dark Woman.

She had, so to speak, made a study of Old St. James's.

No one, perhaps, with the exception of the official architect of the Palace, was so well acquainted with all its minor details as she was.

That knowledge now stood her in good stead.

Not only did it enable her to know exactly where she was, but it enabled her likewise to take the nearest route to where she wished to go.

Where that was, the reader already knows to some extent.

But the Dark Woman's mind had become gradually filled with the idea of a project of more desperate significance than was involved merely in the taking possession of a cabinet of jewels belonging to the Regent.

Linda de Chevenaux wanted now to make herself feared in another sense.

It was murder that had suggested itself to her heated brain.

The murder, not of the Regent, but of some one whose loss would wring his heart.

The murder of Annie, the fair Countess de Blonde, who had never done her, the Dark Woman, any injury, and, indeed, who was the last person in the world to willingly do any one harm, was the terrible thought that, minute after minute, grew into strength of purpose in the imagination of Linda de Chevenaux.

The jewels for those men who were with her, and the life of Annie, the Countess, for her!

Those were the objects of the Dark Woman.

We shall see how nearly they were both succeeding.

When the band of lawless men who on that occasion accompanied the Dark Woman reached, with her, the top of that short flight of steps which we have seen Captain Fitz George so recently tread, they paused for further instructions.

The Dark Woman spoke in one of those audible whispers which always, amid darkness and silence, sound so full of mystery.

"You will follow me, in such silence and with

such caution as you may well conceive is necessary in this place."

A murmured assent passed from lip to lip.

"But," added the Dark Woman, "there is one thing about which there must be no sort of misapprehension."

"What is that?" asked several of the band, in the same low tones in which she spoke.

"It is that, without scruple and without remorse, you will take the life of any one who impedes the work we have on hand here to-night."

"Is that all?" said one.

There was a light laugh among the others, at the tone in which this question was put.

"That is all," replied the Dark Woman.

There was then some whispering among them, and it appeared as if they were making some arrangements among themselves, as regarded who was to strike the fatal blow to any unfortunate Palace guard or domestic who might cross their path.

"Silence!" said the Dark Woman.

The whispering ceased.

"Continuous sounds," she added, "travel far. Let there be intervals of complete silence."

No one spoke.

The Dark Woman then, from means which she always now had about her, procured a light, and lit a small piece of wax taper.

The illuminating power was very small, and but slightly diffused.

As she held that lighted taper above her head, it no doubt flashed with that faint radiance upon the window panes which had been noticed by Captain Fitz George, as, in the darkness of the Ambassadors' Court below, he kept his silent and solitary watch.

The Dark Woman did not consider that there was any risk in the exhibition of so faint a light as that.

Little did she suspect that the eyes of her own son regarded it as an omen of danger.

"Wait for me," she said, in the same whispered tones.

The band gathered together in a throng of spectral-looking figures, and waited.

The Dark Woman slowly paced along the long gallery in which they were.

She held the lighted taper above her head as high as she could, and it was then that Captain Fitz George, from without, had seen this small, mysterious-looking light pass from window to window.

At the end of the gallery there was a door with faded gilding on its panels.

There the Dark Woman paused.

She set down the little taper light on the floor.

From a secret pocket, then, of her apparel she procured that master key which the fears of Willes had compelled him to give to her, and which consisted of a stout shaft of steel of about five inches long, with wards at each end of it.

One end or other of that key ought to open every door in the Palace.

The Dark Woman was about to try the experiment upon that door with the old and faded gilding upon it.

The lock was stiff with rust.

Dust had settled within it, and when compressed by the key became quite a solid obstruction.

It took all the strength Linda de Chevenaux could throw into her fingers to open that door.

But in a few seconds the lock did yield.

The door creaked.

"Who goes there?" cried a voice.

The Dark Woman in a moment put her foot upon the taper light.

All was darkness.

"Who goes there?" cried the voice again.

The Dark Woman did not move hand nor foot for more than a minute.

There was no other challenge; but she knew well that she was now close to a post of one of the Yeomen of the Guard.

She knew, too, that that post would have to be passed.

She knew, too, that it could only be passed over the dead body of the man who held it.

Did she feel remorse that she was, so to speak, strewing the path of her progress with the dead?

No, no! The heart of that woman was as cold as marble to any sentiment of pity, as it was cold to any sentiment of fear.

She closed the door gently.

Silently and slowly she made her way back to the spectral-looking band.

They could only dimly see her as she advanced, and they could only know that it was the Dark Woman by having never taken their eyes off her.

"Listen!" she said.

"We listen."

"At the end of this gallery there is a door. It conducts us the way which we must take."

"To the Regent's jewel casket?" asked one.

"Ay, to the Regent's jewel casket."

"Then, come on."

"Hold! One moment! On the other side of that door—some short distance to the left of it—there is one of the Yeomen of the Palace Guard on duty."

"Well, Master?"

"He must be removed!"

"By death?"

"You have said it. By death!"

"That is a small matter," said one of the band who seemed more disposed than any of the others to make remarks. "I only want to get near enough to him, and the deed is done."

"It must be done effectually and done silently," said the Dark Woman.

"Oh, leave me alone for that! He shall not complain of my doing my work in a bungling fashion!"

"Follow, then—follow!"

"All?"

"Ay, all!"

The Dark Woman led the way. The band followed her; but at the moment they did so, one of them lit a match.

That was the faint light which had flashed in the eyes of Captain Fitz George as he pulled open the cloth-covered door at the top of the short flight of stairs.

"Are you mad?" whispered the Dark Woman.

The light was let go out.

"I thought," began the man who had lighted it,—"I thought——"

"Peace!" added the Dark Woman. "No one is required to think but myself!"

It was this little transaction which, no doubt,

covered and rendered inaudible the slight noise which Captain Fitz George made as he entered the gallery.

The whispered sounds he had heard at that moment were those of the Dark Woman.

Then the band followed her in silence.

It was in vain that the young officer strove to pierce with his eyes the darkness of that place.

The nature and extent of the room, corridor, or gallery into which he had penetrated was quite unknown to him.

His eyes had not yet become sufficiently accustomed to the darkness to enable him even to distinguish that there were darker objects than the atmosphere itself in that place.

While, therefore, he stood in a pardonable state of irresolution, the Dark Woman and her associates reached the further end of the gallery, and only paused at her whispered order at the old gilt door.

"Halt!"

The band came to a stand-still.

The Dark Woman placed her hand on the handle of the door.

Then, before opening it, she spoke again in those low and hissing whispers which the faint echoes of the place brought to the ears of Captain Fitz George, although quite inarticulately.

"When I have summoned here the man who is to be slain, be sure that the hand which is to slay him is ready."

"Quite ready!" said one.

"The time, then, has come!"

The Dark Woman opened the door.

"Ah!" cried the Yeoman of the Guard who was on duty a short distance from the spot. "That strange noise again! Who goes there? Answer, or I alarm the Palace!"

"Hush!" said the Dark Woman,— "hush! You will oblige the Regent by silence!"

"But—but——"

"Make no alarm!"

"But my duty?"

"Your duty is to act as his Royal Highness the Regent would wish you."

"Who and what are you?"

"Do you not hear by my voice that I am a woman?"

The Dark Woman had spoken in her softest and most feminine tones.

"I do hear that. But——"

"You are strangely suspicious. Come this way, in the direction of the sound of my voice, and I will give you a good reason to be silent."

"Have you no light with you?"

"None. But you can easily find your way thither, can you not?"

"I can; but I would rather see my way. The oil lamp at this post was not properly fed, and has gone out."

"So much the better."

"You say 'So much the better,' but I would much rather see my way. However, I am feeling it along the wall."

"Time!" said Linda de Chevenaux.

The Yeoman of the Guard had reached the door. There was a slight scuffle—a deep groan—and then the fall of a heavy body.

"It is done!" said a voice.

"Forward! Follow me!" said the Dark Woman.

Captain Fitz George heard a door shut. The darkness seemed to his imagination to thicken around him.

Holding his sword stretched out before him, he made his way, step by step, along that gallery, but he could find no way out of it. The sounds he had so recently heard were so suggestive of murder, that he felt he should be acting criminally if he longer neglected taking some more active measures for the protection of the Palace and its inhabitants than merely stumbling about in the dark in its corridors and galleries.

What could he do, then, but retrace his steps, so as to get into the inhabited portion of the royal abode by some more readily accessible route?

After some trouble, he found the cloth-covered door again at the top of the flight of twenty-four steps.

This time he had to push it open, instead of pulling it; but in his agitation he forgot that change, and thought, for a few seconds that he failed to open it, that it had been made fast by some one on the other side, and he was a prisoner in that place.

Then, as by accident rather than design, he pushed it, and it readily opened, he nearly fell down the staircase.

The young officer, having overcome this difficulty, was soon in the Ambassadors' Court-yard.

From there to the guard-room was the next movement he made; and from the officers' guard-chamber there was easy access to the interior of the Palace.

In five minutes, Captain Fitz George was in the Titian Gallery, which is already known so well to the reader of these chronicles.

A Yeoman of the Guard, with his partizan over his shoulder, was on duty there.

At sight of the uniform of Captain Fitz George the man saluted him.

The oil night-lights in the Titian Gallery either did burn on that occasion more brightly than usual, or the contrast of that illuminated portion of the Palace with the gloomy region he had just left made the young officer think so.

"Can you tell me, sentry," he said, "where I can find Mr. Willes, the Regent's valet?"

"Yes, Captain. If you pass through yonder door, you will see a small passage to the right, at the extreme end of which are Mr. Willes's own apartments; but he may be at Carlton House."

"I thank you for your information. I will go and see if he is in his own rooms."

The Yeoman again saluted the officer, and Captain Fitz George walked rapidly in the direction which had been pointed out to him.

Not only the extraordinary occurrence of an officer of the Guard coming on his post at such an hour of the night, but the manner of Captain Fitz George as he spoke, was quite sufficient to convince the Yeoman of the Guard that something extraordinary had happened, or was about to happen.

But the wildest dreams of that man could scarcely have suggested to him that an actual armed force had penetrated into St. James's, and that one of his comrades had already fallen a victim.

Captain Fitz George soon reached the door of the apartment occupied by Willes, the valet.

He tapped, first lightly, and then more loudly,

upon the panel, and in a few seconds the door was flung open, and Willes appeared, with a light in his hand, looking pale and frightened, and with only a few articles of clothing huddled on to him.

"What is the matter?—what is the matter? Is anything amiss?"

"I'm afraid there is."

"Oh, Captain Fitz George, is that you? What a relief! I was afraid—afraid——"

"Afraid of what, Mr. Willes?"

"That it was some one else, sir. But what has happened, or what is going to happen? Surely, it is the middle of the night?"

"It is between three and four o'clock in the morning, Mr. Willes; but I have reason to know there are strangers in the Palace."

"Good gracious! no!"

"It is so; and, before alarming the Guard or the Regent, I thought it well to come to you, and take your advice."

Willes looked very frightened, and turned a shade paler. He seemed to find a difficulty almost in speaking, and he must have forgotten for a moment who it was who stood before him, when he laid his hand on Captain Fitz George's arm, and said, nervously, "Did you say you thought there were strangers in the Palace, sir?—that is to say, did you speak in the plural sense?"

"I certainly did."

"Then my mind is very much relieved."

"How so, Mr. Willes? Is there not more danger from many than from one?"

"Sir!—sir! I have no hesitation in speaking to you. You are what you are in relation to the Regent; and you know, sir, that I know all about it; therefore I'm sure that I may speak freely."

"You may do so; and partly because I can guess what you have to say."

"The—the—the Dark Woman, Captain Fitz-George!"

"Yes; it is of her you have to speak."

"It is—it is! Ah! what is that?"

A strange crashing sound, evidently from some distant part of the Palace, at the moment broke the stillness of the night, and interrupted the conversation between Captain Fitz George and Willes, the Regent's valet.

CHAPTER CLXXXV.

THE DARK WOMAN ACCOMPLISHES ONE OF HER OBJECTS AT ST. JAMES'S, BUT FAILS IN THE OTHER.

LINDA DE CHEVENAUX, in the midst of all her desire to carry out those special objects which interested her own feelings and passions, knew perfectly well that her hold upon the allegiance of those men who chose to call her master would soon be weak indeed if she did not show them that she could minister to their cupidity, and place in their grasp that amount of plunder which she had taught them to expect.

The speedy and successful possession of the casket of jewels which they had come expressly to St. James's to seek, she knew perfectly well would make them zealous in carrying out any other object she proposed.

After the murder of the Yeoman of the Guard, she did not anticipate that there would be any human obstruction to reaching the room where the cabinet containing the jewels would be found.

Easy entrance into that room the Dark Woman scarcely expected, for she knew that it was a strong and small apartment, which had been converted into a jewel room by George the Second.

Everything, then, that the ingenuity of the age could suggest had been done to render this room proof against any ordinary or extraordinary depredators.

The little likelihood, however, that any one would be able to penetrate through all the guards and attendants of royalty to such an apartment, had probably induced the architect to look to elegance as much as to strength.

That room would be visited, likewise, by noble, illustrious, and royal personages; therefore it was to be made worthy of such distinguished presences.

The Dark Woman had never been within the doors of that apartment, but from the accurate plan she had of St. James's Palace she knew perfectly well where it was situated.

"Halt!" she said again, to the dim, dusky, and gliding figures that followed on her footsteps.

The band paused.

The Dark Woman spoke with more confidence, and by no means in such low, whispered tones as she had found it necessary to use before, for she knew that she was in a completely uninhabited portion of St. James's Palace, and that any interruption to their proceedings now was almost out of the question.

"A light will be necessary," she said. "A light, however pale and feeble, will be necessary, and I have left the taper in the gallery."

"I can help you to that, master," said one of the band. "I am seldom without the means of seeing about me in a dark place."

"That is well," said the Dark Woman. "Union is strength—we help each other."

The man, who now ignited a match and lit up the flame of a small piece of green taper he took from his pocket, was of most ruffianly aspect.

He was just such a man who seemed to have run through the whole catalogue of crimes, while each one had left the traces of its presence upon his countenance.

"Here's the light, master," he said. "Shall I carry it, or will you?"

"Give it me. I lead the way. Follow quickly, but still with caution."

The Dark Woman now scarcely paused in her progress, except to open any door of communication from one room to another, that for a moment or two became an impediment.

The keys were in the locks of many of these doors, and the two or three that Linda de Chevenaux and her party had to pass through which were locked and the keys removed, easily yielded to one end or the other of that master key with which she was provided.

They at length came to a door, which was evidently of massive mahogany, and very richly carved.

The cipher of the Stuarts was emblazoned on one of the panels.

Then the Dark Woman had a little difficulty,

for an oval piece of brass seemed to be screwed over the key-hole of the door, for what purpose no one could guess.

One of the band immediately produced a small steel crow-bar, which, although not above four-een inches in length, was in truth a very formidable instrument—having at one end a hammer, and at the other being reduced to a flat edge, which would penetrate into the smallest crevices.

"Here is a weapon," he said, "that will soon clear the obstruction."

There was a slight cracking noise, and the oval plate flew from the key-hole of the door.

"Why, Lovemore," said one, "you're an adept at this sort of thing! Who would suppose, when you're disporting yourself in the Mall, or at Rane-lagh, or the sunny side of Bond Street, that you had such a weapon as that in your pocket?"

"Truly, no; but it is better than a sword—it is better than a brace of pistols, for it never fails you."

"Silence!" said the Dark Woman.

Those men, with all their insolence, and all that might be called their very pride of iniquity, obeyed her on the moment.

Not another word was spoken.

But the Dark Woman felt that she had spoken very harshly.

What she wanted was a character for firmness among them, not for insolence.

"You wonder," she said, "that this key-hole should be secured on the outer side, in such a fashion that it would be impossible to lock the door from where we stand. But there is a reason for all things."

"Do you know, master, the reason for this one?'

"I do."

"Is it curious?"

"No, it is only scandalous."

"Then it will be sure to please us."

A suppressed laugh passed through the band.

The Dark Woman was losing no time while engaged in this apparently frivolous discourse with the men who already that night had committed two murders under her guidance.

She was opening that heavy mahogany door with the master key; and when it yielded to her, she held her hand upon it for a moment, and assumed—despite the bitterness that was gnawing at her heart—a careless hilarity of manner, as she said, "We are now about to enter a suite of apartments, four in number, which were considered the special private rooms of the Spanish wife of Charles the Second."

"Indeed, master! They must needs be curious."

"It was by her orders, and under her own eyes, that that oval plate was screwed on the key-hole of the door on the outer side."

"And the reason?"

"It was simply this. Her royal and dissolute husband was in these rooms one day, when a note was brought him that an assignation had been made for him with one on whom his eyes had fallen with loving approbation. He rose to leave the Queen, but not before her sharp eyes had fallen upon the note. A slight altercation ensued, and she declared her intention of following him. She impetuously rushed into an adjoining chamber

to procure a cloak and hood, but the King took the opportunity of leaving the rooms, and in order that, at all events, he might have a good start of any pursuit, he locked the door and took the key with him."

"A wise precaution."

Again the suppressed laugh passed through the band.

"It was some time before the Queen could get released, and then she made a vow that, while she lived in St. James's, a key should never be placed in the lock of this door from the outer side. The oval plate was screwed on, and it has remained until to-night."

The Dark Woman ceased speaking, and, holding the green taper above her head, she entered the first of those four rooms of which she had given a perfectly accurate account.

The heavy draperies and the faded carpets remained, but the moveable portion of the furniture had been long since taken away.

Still the rooms looked gloomily magnificent, the only drawback to them being the common fault of all the apartments in St. James's Palace —namely, the lowness of the ceilings.

There was nothing to attract observation or curiosity in any of the four apartments.

The night, too, was waning fast.

The Dark Woman consulted her watch when the fourth of that suite of apartments was reached, and she was startled to find that it was nearly half-past three.

"We have much to do," she said, "and little time to do it in. Here is the door."

The door at which she paused was a peculiar one.

A narrow plate of looking-glass was inserted into each of the panels. The wood-work had been painted of a dead white colour, originally relieved by gilt mouldings.

There did not appear to be any lock whatever; but a large gilt plate covered nearly one-half the door, confined in its place by a clasp and padlock.

The Dark Woman moved the green taper up and down observantly, as she noted the peculiarities of this door.

"Is this the room, master?" asked the man who was called Lovemore.

"It is the room, I am certain; but, as I never penetrated so far as this in these apartments of St. James's, the fastening of the door has a singular and novel aspect to me."

"If I might venture to suggest, master, I should say that this plate must be removed at once, and beneath it we shall find a lock."

"It is more than probable. Remove it."

The finely-tempered crowbar did the work rapidly, and the gilt plate flew aside, disclosing— as might be expected—a lock beneath, which the Dark Woman hoped, yet scarcely expected, her master key to touch.

The experiment was a failure.

Neither end of the master key would produce the least impression upon the lock of that door.

The Dark Woman satisfied herself on that point, and then stepped aside.

"Force alone," she said, "will open it. Be resolute and quick."

Lovemore seemed well pleased that his services were called into requisition. He advanced instantly with the crowbar, and dashed its flat edge in at a small crevice left between the door and the wall.

There was a creaking noise, a loud crash, and the door opened.

That crash had reached the ears of Willes, the valet, and of Captain Fitz George.

The band of the Dark Woman pressed eagerly forward, to get a sight of the small apartment, which bore, for them, so attractive a name.

A jewel-room—provided it were not a casket without its contents—was, to them, the most attractive apartment they could set their feet in.

Their eagerness made them almost pass the Dark Woman; but she turned upon them, and the boldest of them shrunk back before the expression which gleamed from her eyes.

"You are eager for spoil," she said. "Take all. On this first adventure I reserve nothing for myself."

She stood in the middle of the small room, and held up the light.

At first sight, there did not appear to be much to reward the trouble that had been taken to reach the apartment. It was a five-sided room, without a window; some shelves were upon the walls, and the only furniture consisted of a couple of marble-topped tables.

The shelves were empty, but on one of the tables was the small cabinet, or casket, the Dark Woman had mentioned.

On the other table—tied loosely together with a crimson silk officer's sash—appeared to be some half dozen swords, of different shapes and lengths.

The associates of the Dark Woman cast scarcely a glance at the weapons; but they clustered round the little jewel-cabinet, as bees might round some blossom full of sweetness.

The casket was locked.

Impatience got the better of every other feeling. Not even the presence of the Dark Woman—not even her looks, so expressive of stern resolve and of haughty command—could restrain them. The man named Lovemore struck the casket one blow with the crow-bar, and shivered it to atoms.

A cry of joy burst from the band, for on to the table, and on to the floor, and amid the scattered relics of the casket itself, appeared its glittering contents.

Jewels, to all appearance of great size and value, glittered in the light of that small taper which the Dark Woman, with a certain appearance of contempt upon her features, held up so that they could easily see the glittering bait which had brought them to that place.

Those of the jewels that fell upon the floor were eagerly scrambled for; and, for a few moments, the Dark Woman herself was, no doubt, completely forgotten by those men for whom she was holding a light while they possessed themselves of wealth.

Then she spoke bitterly.

"If this is your discipline," she said—"if this is the mode and fashion in which you avail yourselves of the opportunities which I have promised to present to you, all will be lost, all will be confusion."

The band stood aghast in silence.

"One of our number," added the Dark Woman, "occupies the post of a sentinel in Spring Gardens. He is there for our convenience and the general good. Which of you will feel inclined to surrender some of these jewels to him as his portion of the spoil?"

"The master is right," cried one. "This won't do."

"Quite right," said another. "It must be share and share alike."

"Well, there's what I took," said a third; and placing his hand upon the marble top of the table, he unclasped it, and relinquished two or three bright jewels he had picked up from the floor.

Faint murmurs of assent to this proceeding ran through the whole group, and although it was evidently with some reluctance that two or three of the party gave up the jewels they had obtained possession of, still a goodly assemblage of bright and glittering gems appeared upon the marble table.

Then there was a solemn silence, and all eyes were bent upon the Dark Woman.

"These glittering crystals," she said, "should command a goodly sum. In themselves they are worthless; but when changed into money — cautiously and carefully—they will place you all in ample funds. It is my duty—if you choose to trust me—to change them into gold for you. I have the means of doing so within, perhaps, the next seven days; but since I disclaim, personally, participation in the sum these jewels may produce, you can deal with them yourselves if you are so minded."

"No, no!" cried every voice.

"Hush! Not so loud!"

"No, no!" then they all said again, in suppressed whispers.

"It is your will, then, that I take these jewels in charge for you?"

"It is—it is!"

The Dark Woman, without another word, gathered up the jewels and placed them in her pockets, while the eyes of some of the band followed them with a glistening longing.

"This part of our work is done," said the Dark Woman; "and now I call upon you to remember our compact."

"We do—we do!"

"Without question and without hesitation you are to obey my orders, always provided that I show you that the agreement between us is greatly to your benefit."

"Yes, yes!—it is so!"

"I fancy I have shown you that to-night."

"Command us. We obey you."

"It is my will and pleasure, then, to penetrate this night into the inhabited portion of St. James's Palace. I have an act to do, a blow to strike, which may appease this — this aching heart."

The band looked at each other's faces with a certain feeling of dismay; whispers passed from mouth to mouth; and then it was the reckless, careless Lovemore who addressed the Dark Woman.

"You're the master, and we will obey you, except in one thing. If your object be to take the life of the Regent, we must cry off from such an enterprise, since we have no ambition to be hanged, drawn, and quartered for such a paltry specimen of high treason."

"I do not aim at the life of the Regent."

"Oh, then we are with you, master. Only tell us what we have to do."

"It is simply this. I shall now conduct you to a well-known portion of St. James's, called the Titian Gallery. My business is with some one whom I shall find in a suite of apartments leading from that gallery; and your duty there will be, without hesitation and without remorse, at once to take the life of every human being who may set foot in that gallery until I rejoin you. We shall then retreat by the way we came, and our presence will only be known by the dead we shall leave behind us."

The band bowed their heads in assent; and then the Dark Woman turned, with a mocking kind of smile, to the table on which lay the bundle of swords tied together with the silken cord.

"I was not quite sure," she said, "that there was any other rich and valuable prize to be had in this apartment but the jewels we are in possession of."

The band looked all attention.

No. 84 —DARK WOMAN.

"But now I see there is such a prize."

"Where? where? What is it? What prize?"

"Those swords."

"What? These dingy-looking, worthless weapons, covered with rust and tarnish?"

The Dark Woman drew one of the swords from the bundle, and held up its hilt to the light.

"These weapons are forgotten," she said. "Behold!"

A cry of pleasure burst from the band.

The hilt of that sword was perfectly encrusted with diamonds and other precious stones.

"These are presentation swords," added the Dark Woman, "from different monarchs of Europe, and from some of the despots of the East, to different Kings of England. They have either been forgotten, or placed here by some one long ago, to be more readily plundered."

The band rushed upon the swords, and eagerly examined them from hilt to point. Many of the scabbards were of gold, and there was not one among the number less in value than at least a thousand pounds.

"Now follow me," said the Dark Woman. "You are well armed, and this night you have made a princely booty. Follow me, for I have now my own work to do; and, by the heaven above us, I will do it—I will do it!"

CHAPTER CLXXXVI.

THE DARK WOMAN COMMITS HIGH TREASON BOTH AGAINST MONARCHY AND INNOCENCE.

PROBABLY the associates of the Dark Woman would only have been too glad to leave St. James's Palace with the booty of which they now had possession, if they could have been permitted to do so.

That booty by far exceeded their utmost hopes and expectations; and they looked in each other's faces with an eagerness to be gone, which nothing but a prospect of still further chances of a similar character by their association with the Dark Woman could control.

They feared that the price of that plunder in jewels and in gold had yet to be paid.

They were perfectly correct in that supposition.

And so they followed the Dark Woman, not willingly, but still without any outward show of dissatisfaction.

There was a strange manner now about Linda de Chevenaux—a strange light in her eyes, which, if they could well have observed, those lawless men, would, perhaps, have really induced some effort on their part to bring the night's adventures to an end.

But they did not look so closely into the eyes of their powerful and mysterious leader to see the fire of excitement that was there raging.

The Dark Woman herself held the taper-light.

"Follow! follow! follow!" was now all she said, at intervals, in low tones.

The band crowded after her.

The splendid swords they had possession of glittered even in the faint rays from the little taper; and a more rich and dangerous assemblage surely had never before made its way through the solitary chambers of old St. James's Palace.

The Dark Woman evidently knew her way well among the intricate passages, corridors, and galleries of the ancient building.

She never paused for a moment in her progress until she reached a point where she considered it necessary to give some instructions to her band.

"Halt!"

She spoke in the faintest whisper; but at that still hour, and with no other voice to compete with hers, she was heard easily and distinctly.

The band came to a stand-still, and all waited for the next sounds of that voice, which, the more frequently they heard it, seemed to command only the more attention and obedience.

The Dark Woman pointed to a door close to which they were. She spoke in the same deep tones, which sounded something like the sighing and murmuring of the night wind.

"The time has come when I call upon you for a service, which you must render me without scruple——"

A murmur of assent ran through the band, and they could not imagine what service it could possibly be that the Dark Woman required at their hands, which she so evidently paused to name.

This uncertainty, however, did not last long.

The Dark Woman continued the sentence which they had thought finished, and its last words let them comprehend what was required of them.

"Without pity, and without remorse."

Those were the words with which the Dark Woman concluded her exhortation, and then the band that followed her guessed what she meant.

It was murder!

The murmur of assent came again; but it was not so hearty, nor so cheerfully given as before.

It was not that those men scrupled at the commission of murder—we have seen that they do not; but then if they did such a deed, they liked to see some immediate and present advantage from the act.

There was another reason, too, which had its effect in making them a little lukewarm in the affair: that was, that they had already achieved a large booty, and the Dark Woman did not even promise them a chance of adding to the plunder.

Perhaps Linda de Chevenaux saw that those new followers of hers would have been well pleased to depart at once, and leave undone the work she required of them; but she would not affect to see it.

There was a slightly sarcastic tone about the whisper in which she next spoke.

"I am rejoiced," she said, "that you all so willingly obey me, without the knowledge of what I am about to say; but, in fact, unless now every one who sees you in St. James's is prevented in the most effectual manner from giving an alarm, you are all dead men."

The murmur that passed through the band had quite a different tone about it now, and some of the faces of those men of crime blanched a little.

"Come," added the Dark Woman, "you have but to do as I direct you, and all will be well with us."

They felt then that their safety must lie in obeying her.

The Dark Woman placed her hand lightly upon the lock of the door at which she had paused. That door was fast.

Would the master-key open it?

There was a moment of anxiety, and then the lock yielded. Slowly the door opened. The Dark Woman at the same moment extinguished the taper, for there was a light in the space beyond that door, be it room, corridor, or gallery.

The light was but faint.

Those men, however, who were following the Dark Woman might well shrink back even from the slightest illumination of their secret and dangerous path through St. James's Palace. They had now everything to dread and nothing to gain, so that an approach towards the inhabited portion of the royal abode was to them full of peril.

True, the Dark Woman had pointed out to them a course of action which—should they succeed in carrying it out—would reduce that peril; but an intended victim might escape, and then their situation would be only so much the worse for the armed force, which would be summoned at once to the spot, could scarcely be expected to have any mercy upon men who marked their progress by death.

The Dark Woman, too, hung back for a moment, for she knew where that faint light on the other side of the door proceeded from.

She knew that she had reached the Titian Gallery of St. James's, and that she was in the immediate neighbourhood of those apartments in the occupation of Annie, Countess de Blonde, where she contemplated doing a deed that would strike terror into the heart of the Regent.

Should she succeed in the commission of that awful crime—for it was none other than the murder of Annie, the fair Countess, she intended—it could not be said that she felt quite clear as regarded the results.

Beyond that deed of violence and crime, the mind of the Dark Woman was misty and obscure. All she felt was, that inasmuch as previously she had been a terror to the Regent, she would then be a greater terror still.

Perhaps she hardly stopped to ask herself if sheer fright would have the effect of inducing the Regent to accede to her extravagant demands in the way of recognising the legality of a marriage which had in reality been but a mockery and a snare.

But the Dark Woman was in no mood to ask herself any questions at all, rational or irrational. All she felt was that it was necessary to strike some fearful blow at the peace of the Regent, and that the surest and the best way to reach him was through that young and faithful heart which certainly had fascinated George, Prince of Wales, not only to a far greater extent than any other had succeded in enchaining his fancy, but had without effort achieved a still more extraordinary feat.

The fair Annie, Countess de Blonde, had actually kept the Prince constant to her charms for a period of time that far exceeded his contentment with any other object of his affections.

It was the total absence of art that was Annie's power.

She succeeded in that for which she laid no plans—concocted no plots.

Had she done either of those things she would have, like others, failed.

But we return to the Dark Woman and her band of infamous associates.

Well might she pause for a moment at the door that would conduct her into the Titian Gallery, for it was there that all the danger would be found—if danger there were.

From that gallery none knew better than Linda de Chevenaux there opened the splendid suite of apartments in the occupation of Annie.

That those apartments would be merely tenanted by women she had a shrewd guess.

To be sure, what more likely place was there in which to find the Regent; but even if that were the case, the Dark Woman did not shrink from the idea of making him a spectator of the murder of the fair young girl to whom, if ever his cold, selfish heart had really known an affection in life, he was surely attached.

The door yielded to her touch.

She was in the Titian Gallery.

To her great surprise it was now in total darkness.

And yet she felt certain—she could have declared it to be a fact, that she had seen the faint glimmer of a light in that gallery almost at the moment she had opened the only door that divided her and her band from it.

The Dark Woman was right.

Up to that moment there had been a light in the Titian Gallery.

Little did Linda de Chevenaux guess by whose hand it had been extinguished.

It was by the hand of her own son.

Her own son, Captain Fitz George, for whose sake she would have said, had she been on her confession of her acts and deeds to heaven, she was doing all those fearful deeds which marked her career that night.

When the young officer had succeeded in rousing Willes, he felt that he had done all he could in that quarter.

Willes was in a state of fright, however, which almost benumbed his faculties; for notwithstanding what Captain Fitz George had said, he could not divest his mind of the idea that the Dark Woman must have a something to do with all the disturbances at St. James's Palace.

Perhaps these notions on the part of Willes arose more from his fears than from his reflections; but it was a very natural one, for all that.

"To you—to you," said Captain Fitz George, "I leave the task, Willes, of letting his Royal Highness the Regent know that there is danger in the Palace."

"Yes, yes! What? That is to say, how—— Oh, tell me again that you are sure it is not the —the—a——"

"No, no; I have no reason to think that Linda de Chevenaux has anything to do with what is taking place in the old Palace of St. James's this night."

"Thank heaven for that!"

"Rouse the Regent, Willes. I am now going to the Titian Gallery to hold guard there."

"Yes, yes!—oh, do, Captain Fitz George—do that, for there is the Regent!"

"Indeed!"

"Yes, there—in the apartments of the Countess de Blonde—you will find him."

"I have a double duty, then, at that part of the Palace. You know, or you ought to know, Mr. Willes, what to do in an emergency of this kind, so I shall leave you to act."

"Bless me!" said Willes; "what can I do but get together the Yeomen of the Guard? Although, perhaps, it would be better if you, Captain Fitz George, were to bring some of your men to the gallery."

This was an intelligible enough proposition on the part of Willes; and perhaps, at the moment it was made, the idea did occur to Captain Fitz George that he had been, to a certain extent, remiss in his duty.

He had but one excuse.

Anything in the shape of a premature alarm in St. James's Palace, or an alarm from possibly no cause at all, would justly have subjected him to censure.

It was too late now. All the possible mischief that could happen, might happen while he was making his way to the guard-house.

"You may be right, Mr. Willes," he said; "but I must remain here now, let the consequences be what they may. That there are persons in the Palace who have no right to be here, I feel assured. What the object of those persons may be, I cannot even conjecture. Plunder, murder, or treason may actuate them, but my station shall be the Titian Gallery, close to the door leading to the apartments of the Countess de Blonde; and there, with my sword in my hand, I will wait the issue of events."

"You shall not wait long without some assistance, Captain Fitz George," said Willes, who was now thoroughly awake.

"I am content—I am content. Be quite assured, Mr. Willes, that I shall be able to hold the post for any reasonable time."

Captain Fitz George left the valet of the Regent, and made his way as noiselessly, and with what expedition he could, to the Titian Gallery.

Feeling satisfied in his own mind that the people who had made their way into St. James's Palace were in numbers that would make a personal contest with them exceedingly hazardous, he thought his best plan was to shroud himself in darkness for a time, so that he might have the opportunity of observing them without being seen himself.

With this object he extinguished the oil-lamp, which always, during the night, stood upon a pedestal in the Titian Gallery.

It seemed as if a dense cloud had suddenly fallen upon that space, shrouding all things in its black obscurity; and for a few moments so confusing the eyes of the young officer that it seemed to him as if the darkness were a palpable something moving in huge masses about him, and against which, if he stirred with any precipitation, he was likely to do himself serious injury.

This feeling soon passed away. It was but the effect of the sudden transition from light to darkness.

In a few moments the eyes of Captain Fitz George became accustomed to the obscurity about him; and placing his back against the door of the suite of apartments in the occupation of Annie, Countess de Blonde, he stretched out his sword before him, and keeping strictly upon his guard, he waited the event.

Captain Fitz George was quite aware that when he stood up by that door he had given one of its panels an accidental rap with his sword hilt, but he was far from expecting that that rap at the door would have had any effect.

Precisely, however, at the moment that he saw a gleam of light appear at the further end of the Titian Gallery, the door against which he stood gave way, and a female voice, in very low, soft accents, sounded in his ears.

"Is that you, Mr. Whiffles? How very late you are?"

A warm air came from the apartment.

An air bringing with it delicate perfumes, as well as warmth. And as Captain Fitz George felt a soft hand upon his arm, he suspected that he was about—very unwillingly—to become a confidant in one of those little intrigues of a palace, of which he had heard so much but knew so little.

That he was mistaken for some one else, and that that accidental rap with his sword hilt at the panel of that door was the cause of that mistake, he had not the slightest doubt.

The room was as dark as the gallery beyond.

The young officer was puzzled to know what to do at the moment.

He did not doubt but that this was one of the Countess de Blonde's attendants who had some assignation with the Mr. Whiffles she mentioned, which name Fitz George recollected to have heard as belonging to one of the yeomen of the kitchen.

Under the circumstances, there was nothing he so much dreaded as a scream, which might, in all probability, arise from the terrified female should she be too hastily convinced of her mistake.

Moments were precious, because during those moments Willes, the valet, was no doubt gathering together such a force as would at once place the safety of the Regent, of the Countess de Blonde, and of the whole Palace beyond a doubt.

"Why, Whiffles, what's the matter now?" said the female voice; "why don't you speak?"

"A cold," said Captain Fitz George, huskily.

"Dear me! Why, where did you catch that? It has quite altered your voice!"

"Hem! hem!"

"What do you mean by saying 'hem?' I'll light the night-lamp in a moment."

"Silence! I'm not Whiffles."

"Ah!"

It was not a scream, but it was an exclamation sufficiently loud to reach any ears that might be awake to listen to it.

Captain Fitz George had not closed the door through which he had passed from the Titian Gallery, but of itself it had slowly moved upon its hinges, until it left an opening not above a foot in width; and now from the gallery, through that opening, there came an angular, narrow gleam of light.

"Forward!" cried a voice.

There was a rush of feet in the gallery. Captain Fitz George had just time to move sharply to the door and close it. Something cold touched his arm, succeeded instantly by a feeling of pain.

He was wounded.

A long, narrow sword-blade had been thrust through the opening of the door at the moment Fitz George closed it, and the blade was jammed sufficiently tight that the person without who held its hilt could not withdraw it.

The attendant upon the Countess de Blonde had the ready means of lighting the night-lamp; and now, looking pale and scared, she turned round with it in her hand, and seeing that the intruder was a young officer of the Guard, she exclaimed, "I'm lost! I'm betrayed!"

"Not at all," said Fitz George. "Keep your own counsel."

"But you—you—you are here! And what shall I do?"

"Peace! peace! Where is the Regent?"

The terrified attendant pointed in the direction of the suite of rooms in the outer one of which they were; but the whole attention of Captain Fitz George was now turned to the door, which creaked and shook upon its hinges as a powerful attempt was made from without to force it.

There was something awful and ominous in the silence that reigned in the Titian Gallery, while at the same time so much force was exerted to break open the door which kept those persons—be they whom they might—from the apartments in the occupation of the Countess de Blonde.

By the light which the trembling attendant held, Captain Fitz George saw that there were two brass bolts upon the door, both of which, the moment his eyes fell upon them, he shot into their sockets.

A sense and feeling of security came over him; but still never did benighted wanderer sigh for the dawn as he now sighed for those sounds which would indicate the approach of Willes with the Palace Guard.

Each passing second seemed minutes of time, each minute an hour; and it was not till the attendant uttered a few terrified words—calling his attention to the wound he had received—that he saw blood trickling from his arm on to the floor.

The sword-blade that had inflicted this hurt upon him was still firmly wedged between the door and the wall; but now it had a strange vertical movement about it which sufficiently showed that some one had hold of its hilt, and was endeavouring to work it out of its singular position.

An idea came across the mind of Captain Fitz George.

His own sword was one of those slim, courtly-looking weapons formerly in use by the officers of the Guard. The key-hole of the door was large, and the key had dropped to the floor—no doubt being forced out by some pick-lock from the outer side.

It was the impulse of the moment that induced Fitz George, when he saw the blood upon his arm, to suddenly pass his own sword-blade right up to the hilt through the key-hole of the door.

There was a cry of anger and pain from without.

It was evident that some one in the Titian Gallery had been wounded, in quite as singular a fashion as he, Captain Fitz George, had received a hurt within the apartment.

CHAPTER CLXXXVII.

THE DARK WOMAN'S BAND IS DEFEATED, BUT LEAVE A HOSTAGE BEHIND THEM.

THAT by that fortunate thrust through the keyhole of the door, he had inflicted, probably, a serious hurt upon one of the audacious intruders into St. James's Palace, Captain Fitz George could not entertain a doubt.

He had done more than that, too.

He had brought affairs to a kind of crisis.

No longer was the Dark Woman and her villainous associates to think that they were conducting the enterprise on which they were, amid secrecy and silence.

No longer was she to dream of striking the cruel blow she meditated, like some avenging fate which was to be felt, but not seen.

It was only too evident now that an alarm was given, and that some one was determined to defend, at the sword's point, that suite of apartments, into which Linda de Chevenaux thought she would be able to penetrate, amid the stillness of the night, like an apparition.

The man who was wounded by the sword of the young officer was that one of the Dark Woman's party for whom the least possible amount of sympathy could be felt.

It was the one whom she named Lovemore.

A most unscrupulous and murder-loving villain.

The thrust of Captain Fitz George's sword was tal.

With a deeep groan, after uttering the cry of pain, Lovemore sunk bleeding to the floor of the Titian Gallery, close to the feet of the Dark Woman herself.

Then she clasped both her hands upon her breast for a moment, as though she were nerving herself to the execution of some terrible resolve.

"Forward! forward!" she cried in a voice so distorted by passion, and so high and unnatural for a woman, that through the door, although he heard the voice, the gallant Captain Fitz George failed to recognise it as that of his mother.

"Forward! forward! Disguise, mystery, silence, and caution, are now alike useless. Rapidity of action can alone now accomplish the work that must be done this night in St. James's Palace, and ensure our safety when it shall be done."

The band recoiled from the door, from the other side of which so serious a wound had been inflicted on one of their members, but it was only for a moment or two that they so recoiled.

The Dark Woman added some words to her former ones, which let them know and feel that not only were they completely in her power, but that upon her they must depend for safety.

"I swear," she said—"I swear by the heaven above us, that if you shrink now from obeying me, and carrying out my designs in this place, I will give you all up to justice, and not one of you shall leave the Palace alive!"

They considered it was more than probable she had ample means of carrying out her threat, and that if crossed in her purpose she would do so, they could scarcely entertain a doubt.

The boldest of them retreated a few paces, and then made such a simultaneous rush at the door, that it would have needed to be made of something stronger than timber to withstand the shock.

There was a crash, and the door partially gave way.

"Again! again!" cried the Dark Woman.

And still she spoke in those high, strange, unnatural tones, which prevented Captain Fitz George from recognising them.

But before a second assault could be made upon the door, he, Fitz George, spoke.

"Treason! Treason! Treason! Awake! Awake! Arouse yourself, Regent of England, for murder is on the threshold of your chamber!"

There was nothing in the tones of Captain Fitz George which could so change them as to prevent the Dark Woman from recognising them at once.

No evil passion lurked in them—no wild principle of revenge was at work in his breast. She knew that it was her son who spoke.

She knew then that it was not the Regent—not the man who had made war upon her peace of mind, and destroyed it for ever—with whom she had to contend; but that son who—despite his defection from her—despite his condemnation of her purposes—she loved still dearer, oh, far, far dearer than life itself!

The Dark Woman uttered a shrill cry of dismay.

But still Captain Fitz George heard not in that cry any sound that could remind him of his mother.

"Awake! Awake! Treason! Treason! Treason!"

His voice rung like the sound of a trumpet through the suite of rooms in the occupation of the Regent, and of Annie, the fair Countess de Blonde.

The doors that led from that outer chamber to the next one were dashed open.

It was the Countess de Blonde who appeared.

Annie was completely wrapped up in a robe of pale green satin, edged with miniver. Her long and beautiful hair hung in disordered masses far below her waist.

There was alarm in her face, and as she clasped the rich robe about her, her hands trembled with apprehension.

"What is this?" she cried; "oh, what is this? What has happened, or what is about to happen?"

"Murder!" replied Captain Fitz George.

"Ah, that is you, dear friend, and all is well."

"No—all is not well, Annie. Where is the Regent? Arouse him, and tell him he must help me to defend his life and your life. All, else, will be lost. Moments are precious."

As he spoke, Captain Fitz George, with a promptitude that few persons would have had presence of mind enough to exhibit on such an occasion, kept seizing upon any portable article of furniture he could find in the room, and wheeling it or dragging it towards the half-broken down door.

It was astonishing with what rapidity he succeeded in constructing a kind of barricade against the panels of that door.

Not too soon was that barricade interposed between him and the assailants; for the second rush from those in the Titian Gallery, to break down the door, took place within some thirty seconds of the first one.

But for that barricade the door must have yielded.

It was off its hinges.

The two brass bolts were started from their fastenings.

The force with which those reckless men who were with the Dark Woman came against the door this second time actually projected several of the pieces of furniture that Fitz George had piled up against it right into the middle of the floor.

But the door still retained its place.

It was solely held up now artificially.

Annie, when she heard those last words which Captain Fitz George had addressed to her, turned at once, and made her way back in the direction whence she had come.

Fitz George heard her calling to the Regent.

"George!—George! It is time for fighting now! George!—George, I say! Where are you? A fight!—a fight!"

There was a scuffling of feet, and the Regent—looking pale and disordered, and with a crimson brocade dressing-gown hastily flung about him—appeared.

He had a long, straight, cavalry sword in his right hand, and in the other hand he carried a couple of very richly-mounted pistols.

"What, in the name of all that's terrible, is all this?" he asked.

"Treason and murder!" said Fitz George.

"Ah! You here?"

"Yes—to defend the life of my Sovereign and my father!"

The Regent gave one quick glance into the face of Annie, and a look of pain and anguish it was. For one moment the old feeling of jealousy which Sir Hinckton Moys had implanted in his heart, in regard to his son, came back to him.

But it was only for a moment.

"No, no!" he said. "No—not that! You are here to defend me, Fitz George; and you, Annie, are true as steel."

Neither the young officer nor the Countess de Blonde could comprehend what was passing in the mind of the Regent at that moment; and it was no time at which to speculate upon hidden meanings, or to ask curious questions.

Fitz George spoke rapidly.

"Take your place by my side, father," he said. "Help me to hold this post but for a few moments longer, and we shall have plenty of aid."

George, Prince of Wales, was not a coward.

We do not mean to say that he had that reckless kind of bravery that some people possess, which tempts them to court danger—to meet it even half-way, if it seems slow in approaching them—but he had that courage which would enable him to defend not only himself, but any one else in whom he felt an interest.

The Regent then did not hesitate to place himself by the side of Fitz George, and to hold the long cavalry sword in such an attitude that it was evident he intended and knew how to use it with effect.

"That's right, George," said Annie. "We will beat them yet."

As she spoke, the Countess de Blonde took the pistols from the left hand of the Regent.

"Mind, Annie—mind!" he said: "those pistols are loaded."

"Glad to hear it," said Annie. "Here goes!"

Two stunning reports immediately ensued.

The Countess de Blonde had fired both the pistols right through the upper panel of the door.

The room was full of the smoke of gunpowder.

The light was extinguished at once by the concussion of the air.

Then mingling with the echoes of the report of the pistols came a loud voice from the Titian Gallery.

"Charge!" cried the voice.

There was a rush of feet.

"Fire!" cried the voice again.

A rattling discharge of fire-arms ensued, which must have aroused the whole Palace.

A crash of glass then took place, for the windows of the Titian Gallery gave way to the disturbed air: the echoes died off like distant thunder.

Then there came a sharp knocking at the shattered door.

"Who knocks?" asked the Regent.

"I, your Royal Highness—I."

"Ah, that is Willes!"

"Then the affair is over," said Fitz George, "and I may open the door."

"I think so."

"Let me go out first," said Annie. "Don't you stir, George. They may want to kill you, which I suppose was the object of it all."

Little did Annie suppose that it was her life that was aimed at as a means of inflicting suffering on the Regent.

"No, Annie, no!" said the Regent. "You shall not expose yourself to any risk, my good girl. I will go out into the gallery myself."

Willes knocked again.

"Your Royal Highness may rest assured that there is no longer any danger."

Captain Fitz George moved the barricade he had made with the furniture of the room, and then the door showed an inclination to fall inwards.

Fitz George, however, gave it an outward impulse, and it went right over on to Willes, who for a moment had to support the whole weight of it until he could get away from it.

The gallery was in darkness.

"Do not go forth, father," said Fitz George: "do not leave this room until there is light in the gallery."

"There is a lamp in the next room," said Annie, as she darted away to fetch it.

The concussion of air, caused by the firing, had not reached beyond the Titian Gallery and that first apartment of the suite in possession of the Countess, so that Annie was able in a few moments to return with a lamp.

The scene that the Titian Gallery presented was curious.

A party of the Yeomen of the Guard, and a file of men from the guard-room—men from Captain Fitz George's regiment—were ranked across the gallery.

The Yeomen had their long partizans at the charge.

The soldiers had just reloaded their muskets, and the young subaltern who was with them stood a little on one side, with his drawn sword in his hand, and a look of perplexity upon his face.

But where was the enemy?

The Dark Woman and her band had most unaccountably and most mysteriously disappeared.

Annie, still attired in that most costly and beautiful robe of blue satin and miniver, held up the lamp at the shattered entrance to the room, and its rays sent a tolerably sufficient light over the gallery.

The assailants were certainly gone.

And so mysteriously and so suddenly had they disappeared, that but for the evidence of the shattered door, and the concurrent testimony of three persons, that there had been such assailants, the whole affair might have been set down as a dream.

The Regent stepped out into the Titian Gallery.

The subaltern of the Guard saluted, and the soldiers did so likewise

Willes was rubbing his head, upon which the door in its fall had raised a considerable bump.

"What is the meaning of all this?" asked the Regent.

Willes looked about him.

"Gone, your Royal Highness!"

"But who was it that was here to go?"

"I humbly submit to your Royal Highness that Captain Fitz George knows all about it."

"Something about it," said Fitz George, "but certainly not all."

"What is that?" said Annie, at this moment, as she pointed to a dark object some distance off in the semi-obscurity of the gallery.

"What, Annie—what?"

Captain Fitz George darted forward.

"A light! a light!" he cried.

Willes, with a low bow, took from the hand of the Countess de Blonde the lamp.

"Permit me——"

"More light here!" cried the Regent. "Some one go for lights!"

A couple of the Yeomen of the Guard immediately left the gallery.

Willes followed Captain Fitz George towards the dark object that Annie had seen.

A deep and awful groan came from it as he touched it with the point of his sword.

"A wounded man," he said.

"One of the villains!" said Willes.

"That is fortunate," said the Regent; "for now I fancy, we shall have a chance of discovering the meaning of all this affair."

Captain Fitz George beckoned to the Yeomen of the Guard as he said, "Raise this man. His Highness the Regent would question him."

"Curses on you all!" moaned the wounded man. "Let me die in peace!"

The Yeomen of the Guard shrunk back from the maledictions of the bleeding man.

"Heed not what he says," added Captain Fitz George, "but bring him along."

The Yeoman lifted Lovemore—for it was he—from the floor of the gallery, and brought him towards the Regent.

At that moment the two Yeomen who had gone in obedience to the Prince's orders for lights, returned, bearing flambeaux with them.

The whole of the Titian Gallery was brightly illuminated.

The Regent stepped right back within the doorway of Annie's apartments, and kept the sword at guard.

"What manner of man is this?" he asked, as the pale, bleeding ruffian was supported towards him by the two Yeomen who held him up.

CHAPTER CLXXXVIII.

THE WOUNDED RUFFIAN IS TRUE TO THE LAST, AND THE REGENT IS PERPLEXED.

WHEN the Regent and Captain Fitz George looked in the face of this man who was held up by the two Yeomen of the Guard, and from whom something in the shape of a revelation of the objects and motives of his presence in St. James's Palace was expected, they almost at once abandoned the intention of questioning him.

The dull glaze of death was in his eyes.

The pallor of the grave was spread over his face.

It was evident that that man was taking his last look at earthly things; and that whatever might have been his objects, his motives, or his crimes, a very few minutes more would dissolve *is* connexion with the world and all its concerns.

He had received two wounds.

The sword-thrust which Captain Fitz George had given through the key-hole of the door had been one.

A bullet from one of those pistols which Annie, the Countess, had discharged through the panel had likewise struck him.

And so it would appear that this man was on that night doomed to be the victim of Linda de Chevenaux's fearful and nefarious designs.

She had brought him there to death, and who would pity him?

The love of plunder—cupidity in its worst form—in order that he might obtain the means of riot and extravagance, had brought him into the train of the fearful and desperate mistress to whom he had sworn allegiance, and he took the consequences of the act.

There was the look of a gentleman about him—that indefinable something which speaks of physical and mental culture, which never can be assumed by those who have it not, and never can be wholly lost by those once possessing it.

"Speak to him, Fitz George," said the Regent,—"speak to him, and ask him what is the meaning of this disturbance, and how, in the name of all that's wonderful, he came here?"

"Your Royal Highness, he is dying!" said one of the Yeomen.

"Let him declare, then, with his last breath," said Captain Fitz George, "his purpose here in St. James's. Those whom he has sought to injure will accept that declaration as some expiation of his offence."

A smile—or rather a curl of the lip, which should have been a smile under happier auspices—appeared to convulse the countenance of the dying man for a moment. It was an expression of scorn and of defiance.

"Speak!" added Fitz George; "I implore you to speak—your time is short!"

"Never!" gasped the dying ruffian.

That one word was his last. His weight in the arms of the Yeomen of the Guard seemed to increase threefold. It was a dead man they held up, and they turned their eyes from his face with a shudder.

"Take him away—take him away!" cried the Regent. "I hate the sight of dead people—I don't like to think that there is such a thing as death in the world! I don't like sick people—wounded people and dead people! Take him away—take him away!"

The two Yeomen of the Guard dragged away the lifeless man, and the Regent, looking more pale and agitated than he had yet done since the moment he had been roused from his slumbers by those cries of murder and treason, hastily availed himself of an arm-chair, which Willes wheeled towards him, and sat down.

"There is no peace in the world!" he said,—"not a bit of peace! Never was anybody so harassed as I am; day or night, it's all the same! There's always some alarm—some riot; and here, when we have a chance of discovering what it is all about, the man who could tell us dies, and all is dark again."

"Dark?" said Annie. "That's it!"

"What's it?"

"That gives me an idea. I'm certain, George—certain as I stand here—that the Dark Woman——"

"Good gracious!" said the Regent, springing to his feet.

The Countess de Blonde happened to cast a glance upon the face of Captain Fitz George, and she saw there an expression of distress which induced her to pause in what she was saying.

"Never mind, George," she added,—"never mind! Perhaps I'm quite wrong. I daresay these were only thieves who attacked the Palace, and at all events one of them has gone to his last account. Don't think anything more of it. But I tell you what you must do, George."

"What? what?"

"Always have a—what do you call it?—a sergeant's guard in the Titian Gallery."

"I will—I will!"

Willes at this moment made a low bow to the Regent, and presented him with something on a gold salver.

The Regent looked gratified. The odour of the something which was contained in a wine-glass came upon the royal senses gratefully.

Willes said not a word.

The Regent took up the glass and drained it of its contents, which consisted of some of that choice liqueur brandy he was in the habit of considering at that time a specific for all disturbances, mental or physical.

The colour came back to the Prince's cheeks.

"Willes," he said, "you are attentive."

"I'm grateful for your Royal Highness's approbation."

"Yes, I say you're attentive, Willes; and—and——"

Willes bowed very low, with his hand upon his heart.

"Very attentive."

"Oh, your Royal Highness!" said Willes, in soft, silky, grateful accents.

"Exceedingly attentive; but as it is no more than you ought to be, no more need be said about it."

Willes looked blank.

The Countess de Blonde laughed.

"Come, George," she said; "that's not so bad for you!"

"I don't know what you mean, Annie. But it's quite clear that I, the Regent of England, Prince of Wales, and heir-apparent to the throne, run a risk of being murdered any night that a gang of assassins choose to make their way into St. James's Palace."

"It looks like it," said Annie; "only we've certainly got the better of them this time, George."

"Willes!"

"Your Royal Highness."

"Let everybody be discharged in the morning whose duty, either directly or indirectly, would be to keep watch and ward, and save us from attacks and intrusions of this character."

Willes bowed.

"Fitz George," added the Regent, "you breakfast with us in the morning."

"And in the meantime," said Captain Fitz George, "I will devote the remainder of this night to such a thorough search through old St.

THE COUNTESS DE BLONDE.

James's as I hope will throw some light on this extraordinary affair."

"Do so—do so! We give you full authority. Willes, you will see to that. Leave not a corner unsearched; get all the old keys you can find, and open every door. It is intolerable that we should be exposed to these attacks. Come, Annie, come;

No 85.—DARK WOMAN.

and Willes, I think we will have something to eat —something out of the ordinary way. Have that Frenchman roused up, that pretends to be such an extraordinary cook, and tell him to tax his ingenuity."

Leaning on the arm of the Countess de Blonde, the Regent passed through the door leading to the second of the suite of apartments; and as he did so, he whispered eagerly to her, "Annie, Annie, was it the Dark Woman? Was it Linda de Chevenaux?"

"Yes."

"You think so?"

"I know it; but it's a hard and an ungracious thing to speak of her now before poor Allan."

"Allan? Allan? Oh, I recollect! That was what Fitz George used to be called before we acknowledged him as our son. Oh, Annie, Annie! that woman will be the death of me yet!"

"I shouldn't wonder."

"You shouldn't wonder? Really now, how coolly you take it! Annie, Annie! you are like the rest of the world."

"Well, I suppose I am. There may be little differences; but cats are cats, and people are people."

The doors closed on the Regent and the Countess.

Every lamp that was in the Titian Gallery was lighted; the Yeomen of the Guard and the few soldiers from the guard-room still remained, awaiting the orders of Captain Fitz George, who was now the senior officer present.

Many painful rushing thoughts came through his mind, as he asked himself what he should do, and how he ought to act, under the circumstances in which he was placed?

The young subaltern who was with the few soldiers of the Guard, stepped up to him and spoke.

"Captain Fitz George," he said, "I took the precaution before I came here with our men to order Sergeant Armstrong—upon whom you know we can depend—to place trusty sentinels at every possible outlet of the Palace; so that, in truth, I don't think a mouse could leave St. James's without being seen."

"When was this done?"

"The moment Mr. Willes brought in the alarm."

"You did well—quite well!"

Captain Fitz George was evidently disturbed. He paced the Titian Gallery in silence for some seconds, during which he asked himself the pertinent question, "Shall I, on making this search through St. James's, find my mother? and if so, what am I to do?"

He did think of delegating the task of searching the Palace to the subaltern, but a shuddering dread came over him of what might be the consequences of a collision between the desperate and enraged Linda de Chevenaux and armed men, who might discover her in some retreat from which escape would be impossible.

"No, no!" he whispered to himself; "this is my duty—my duty, as regards both the Regent and Linda de Chevenaux—to father and to mother. O unhappy fate, that such an abyss should separate you!"

By a great effort he commanded his feelings sufficiently to address the young subaltern with something like composure.

"Sir," he said, "I shall ask you to be so good as to accompany me in the search I propose making, by the authority of the Regent, through the Palace."

"I am honoured by the order, Captain Fitz George. How many men shall we take with us?"

"When I say none, sir, do you still feel as inclined to accompany me?"

"Certainly; quite at your pleasure."

"Dismiss the men, then, and we will proceed together. What hour is that?"

St. James's clock struck four.

"The night is far advanced," said the subaltern; "in an hour and a half we shall have twilight. Perhaps, Captain Fitz George, relying, as you know we can, upon the sentinels that surround the Palace, it may be as well to put off this search until we have the dawn of the morning to help us. We shall then avoid the necessity of carrying with us artificial light."

"It will be better—much better! Wild and angry passions, too, will have time to cool."

These last words were not addressed to the young subaltern, and he was rather surprised to know what they could mean; but he did not remark upon them, seeing the troubled look that was upon the face of Captain Fitz George.

"At half-past five," added Fitz George,—"at half-past five meet me here in this gallery, and we will prosecute the search together."

The subaltern drew off his men; and as Willes had gone to obey the directions of the Regent in rousing up the new French cook, for the purpose of "taxing his ingenuity" to produce some little repast which would be tempting to the royal palate, Fitz George was left alone in the Titian Gallery of St. James's.

No—not quite alone.

The dead was with him!

Beneath one of the windows—far away out of sight of the Regent, and with an old grey cloak, that had been procured from the guard-chamber of the Yeomen, cast over him—lay the dead Lovemore.

After the tumult and excitement of the past hour the sort of silence that reigned in the Titian Gallery seemed more profound and complete than it had ever before struck upon the senses of Captain Fitz George.

That hour—it was about an hour that he had now to wait until the return of the young subaltern of the Guard—would be a weary one to him.

An hour, not so absolutely weary as regarded its lapse without activity, as on account of the sad thoughts that would only too surely belong to it.

What was he to think of the events of that night?

How was he to divest himself of the idea, painful as it was, that his mother was not only the instigator of them, but the prime agent and actor in them? Did he not recollect that meeting with her in the Park, when he would have gone the length even of arresting her, had she not so adroitly evaded him?—and could he doubt that she was then on the eve of effecting an entrance into the Palace?

And then came a more serious and painful thought still.

Who was Linda de Chevenaux now associated with?

Who were those men who were most certainly with her in St. James's, and one of whom lay so still in death only a few paces from him?

From all he had heard from time to time of the Dark Woman and her deeds, he had become well aware that the time had been when she was the head and leader of a band of desperadoes.

But he had heard likewise of how they had been dispersed—of how death had overtaken them—and therefore he was afflicted and pained beyond expression to think that again his mother had placed herself in communication with such a lawless band, and had had the audacity even to assail the Palace.

What was the object of that assault?

Captain Fitz George trembled as he asked himself that question.

The obvious answer to it, in his imagination, was that it was for the purpose of achieving the death of the Regent.

Could anything be more painful than the position of Fitz George between such a father and such a mother?

It was possible enough that, inflamed by rage and disappointment, the Dark Woman might meditate some terrible act of revenge; and what could be more terrible than the assassination of the Regent of England?

There was but one solitary argument against such a supposition, and the acute intellect of Captain Fitz George did not fail to seize upon it.

Nothing could be more unlikely than that she, the Dark Woman, would be able to prevail upon any band of lawless men with whom she might be associated to assist her in such an act.

What could be the object of following her as a party?

Plunder! nothing but plunder!

Would they then voluntarily, merely to please her evil passions, involve themselves in the consequences of a crime of such magnitude as the murder of the Regent?

It was not likely.

Captain Fitz George felt the strong improbability of the supposition; but then he asked himself if this appearance of the Dark Woman in the Palace was not for the purpose of being revenged upon the Regent, what was its real object?

It never occurred to him that his mother intended to strike the Prince of Wales through the breast of another, and that that other was Annie, the Countess de Blonde.

There was a natural chivalric feeling—a sensation of justice—in the mind of Fitz George, which completely precluded him from readily supposing any one would take measures to injure or destroy an innocent person, for no other object than to inflict a pang upon a guilty one.

In these sad reflections, however, the time he had to wait until the first dawn of the morning began to show itself, passed.

The lights in the Titian Gallery began to grow dim.

The struggle between them and the coming day was one in which they could not be the victor; and soon they began to assume that cold, sickly look which artificial light ever wears in the beams of the sun.

The chimes of the Palace clock struck the hour of half-past five, and then Captain Fitz George heard a rapid footstep in the gallery.

It was the young subaltern of the Guard, true to his appointment.

"I am in time, Captain Fitz George," he said, "am I not?"

"Quite so. Hush! some one comes! You are alone?"

"Quite alone."

A side door of the gallery opened, and Willes, the Regent's valet, made his appearance. He bore with him rather a large bunch of keys, and as he approached Fitz George, he said, "Captain, these keys will carry you through the whole Palace, but it will be useless."

"The search useless?"

"Quite—quite!"

Willes approached Fitz George closely, and added in a whisper, "You may depend, Captain, that she is acquainted with all the secret places in the old Palace; and although you may make your way easily enough from one suite of rooms to another, she has by this time made her escape."

"Shall I say I hope so, Willes?" replied Fitz George, in the same low tones.

Willes shook his head.

"There will be no peace until the Dark Woman is—is——"

"No, no! do not—oh, do not say dead!"

"I did not mean to say it, Captain Fitz George; but I did mean to say until she was secured in confinement somewhere, and prevented from doing further mischief."

"It may be so—it may be so. Give me those keys. I will at least, as a matter of form, make a search through the Palace."

CHAPTER CLXXXIX.

THE DARK WOMAN AND HER ASSOCIATES PROJECT AND CARRY OUT THE MOST AUDACIOUS SCHEME EVER IMAGINED.

WE need not follow Captain Fitz George and that young officer of the Guard in their researches through St. James's Palace: suffice it to say that they made no discoveries whatever.

It is with Linda de Chevenaux, the Dark Woman—who has made so extraordinary and unexpected an escape from the dangers which beset her in St. James's Palace—with whom we have now to do.

That this most unexampled and audacious attempt to take the royal residence by storm would have succeeded under ordinary circumstances, there cannot be a doubt.

The extraordinary and accurate knowledge which the Dark Woman had of the interior of the Palace, would have enabled her to penetrate successfully to that suite of apartments so magnificently and gorgeously decorated for the use and service of Annie, Countess de Blonde.

Whether or not her woman's heart would have failed her at the last moment, and whether or not, had she really succeeded in reaching her intended victim, she would have struck the blow which might have deprived Annie, the Countess de Blonde of her life, it is impossible to say.

Fortunately, the Dark Woman was spared that crisis of the passions, and that fearful mental struggle between right and wrong, which must have arisen in her breast at such a moment.

Practically, whenever an alarm was given in St. James's Palace, her enterprise was over.

It would have been absurd to remain another instant with the hope of waging successful warfare with the force that certainly would, in a very few minutes, be brought against her.

The discharge of those pistols which Annie had snatched from the hands of the Regent, and fired through the panel of the door, decided the matter.

The Dark Woman, in the midst of all her angry passions, and all her wild impulses of desperation and revenge, felt that it would be asking too much of those persons whom she had with her, were she to make the least attempt to induce them to remain any longer in so dangerous a position.

"It is over!" she said. "Escape—escape! Follow me, and escape!"

But one of the band had fallen. Lovemore, with the double wound from sword and pistol, was already in the embrace of death.

The Dark Woman cast but one glance at him, and seemed to see that he was past help.

Another of the band was bleeding from a wound which, however, was not serious.

Consternation sat on every face; for although that word "escape" sounded pleasantly enough in every ear as a most desirable thing to accomplish, yet it seemed a matter of very doubtful achievement.

"We are lost!" cried one.

"Taken and hanged, to a certainty!" said another.

"Like rats in a trap!" cried a third.

"Escape!" said the Dark Woman. "I have said, escape! Do you as yet all of you know so little of me as to imagine that I have not provided for such a contingency as this? Follow me, and escape! I answer for the safety of every one but the dead."

She cast one last glance at Lovemore, and then swift as a shadow she darted across the gallery.

Perhaps she was not sorry, since one of the band was to be sacrificed in this affair, that the lot had fallen to this man, Lovemore.

He was a reckless, heedless villain—dangerous alike to himself and to all his companions.

It was his glove that had been picked up in the court-yard of St. James's Palace by Captain Fitz George.

The Dark Woman felt that if she must spare to Death one of those men, who, for criminal purposes, had placed themselves under her guidance and control, Lovemore was the one that she would have picked out for any fate that presented itself.

Never had those lawless, unscrupulous men felt themselves so thoroughly dependent upon the Dark Woman as at this moment. Without her, they saw nothing but a prison, a trial, and the utmost penalties of the law awaiting them.

But she talked of escape, and they followed her with wonder and hopefulness, while St. James's Palace was ringing with alarm, and each moment they might expect to be surrounded by foes.

There was a small door, narrow and tall—not placed at all secretly in the panel that enclosed it, but rather ostentatiously ornamented and bedizened with brass-work about its locks and hinges.

It was but the door of a sort of cupboard or recess in the gallery, not above four feet in depth, and totally inadequate to hold the Dark Woman and her band, if she should be mad enough to suppose for a moment it would afford her shelter.

But still with the master-key she possessed to most of the locks of St. James's Palace she opened the door of this recess in the wall.

"Follow!—follow!" she said.

A gleam of light that at that moment appeared in the Titian Gallery betrayed to the eyes of the band how small a space it was into which she asked them to follow her.

A half-suppressed cry of despair burst from their lips.

It was at that moment that the young subaltern of the Guard, with a precipitation which defeated its own object, ordered his men to fire.

Then came that small volley of musketry in the Titian Gallery which produced so much confusion.

The noise and the smoke tended much more to assist the Dark Woman than to retard her.

Keeping the same master-key still in her hand, she turned abruptly to the right immediately on entering the recess in the Titian Gallery.

It would appear that two steps must bring her in contact with one of the side-walls of the recess, but that side-wall was a door of itself.

There was no key-hole to it, or it would have lost its character of secrecy; for it was the entrance to one of the hidden passages and tortuous winding ways of old St. James's Palace.

It opened by the pressure of a spring, and the object of the Dark Woman in still retaining the key in her hand was that she might the more readily by its means exert sufficient pressure upon the spring to make it act.

The door sprung open as if by magic.

"Follow!" she said.

The band uttered another cry; but it was now one of delight, for they saw escape before them.

Their faith in the resources of the Dark Woman became boundless; and, at that moment, it is probable that, even if she had asked them to return to the Titian Gallery—coupling the request with the promise of certain safety—they would have yielded to it.

But she had no such intention.

She felt that the object she had come to achieve that night was not to be accomplished.

The passage in which they were was narrow, and, by the depth of dust upon its flooring, it would seem probable that many a long year had elapsed since any human footstep had traversed its mysterious windings.

The smoke from the discharge of the muskets in the Titian Gallery had made its way into the recess—indeed, some few vapourous clouds had rolled into the secret passage, mingling with the close, damp, confined air of that narrow route, hollowed out of the thickness of the walls of the ancient building.

The Dark Woman had taken care that both the doors should be closed behind them; and, like a group of dismal-looking spectres, they followed her in single file, for the passage was too narrow for two to go abreast, and they began to wonder whither she would lead them, and where would be the end of that tortuous way—the confined, choking atmosphere of which began to produce disagreeable sensations.

The footfalls of the Dark Woman and her band produced a strange, murmuring sound behind the old wainscotings of the Palace.

No doubt they passed rooms in which persons were sleeping, or in which some wakeful official might start up and listen, fancying that legions of rats were making their way, from place to place, in the ancient building.

The distance traversed seemed to be considerable—perhaps it was really not so—but a few minutes of time spent in such a place would very likely, to the watchful imagination, become exaggerated to a considerable period.

Suddenly the Dark Woman paused.

"Halt!" she said in a suppressed whisper.

"Halt!—halt!" repeated several voices.

From mouth to mouth the word went like some dismal echo.

There was a slight noise as if metal had touched metal, but no means as yet presented itself of exit from the narrow passage.

"Who has a match?" asked the Dark Woman.

"Here! here!" repeated several voices.

"One only," she added.

The flicker of a match, burning with a dull, uncertain flame, lit up, for a moment or two, the ghastly-looking faces of those men, who followed their imperious task-mistress apparently from one danger to another.

The match was passed onward to the Dark Woman, who—although she knew she had come to the end of the passage—found it impossible without its aid to light upon the exact portion of the machinery that would open another secret door, similar to that from the recess from the Titian Gallery.

That slight gleam of artificial light, however, was sufficient.

She pressed the spring.

A door opened.

Then another door.

And then a cool rush of pleasant, vital air reached the senses of the Dark Woman and her band.

Every one uttered a sigh of relief, and although they could not see where they were—for darkness the most profound was around and about them—they felt like men who had emerged from some cavern into the upper air, and the consciousness that they were in some large apartment of the Palace came to their senses, although they had no accurate means of defining its extent.

"Where are we, master?" said one.

"Hush!" said the Dark Woman.

They scarcely breathed.

The silence continued for full five minutes, and then it was broken strangely and unexpectedly.

One of the band uttered a cry of terror, and in a voice not at all adapted to the secrecy of their situation and the dangers that surrounded them, he almost shouted aloud, "We are betrayed! we are betrayed! There are armed men in this apartment!"

A kind of panic took possession of the others, and in the darkness they rushed about in different directions, they knew not where.

The Dark Woman seemed paralysed for a moment, partly with indignation at this heedless folly, as well as with the thought that the disturbance would, in all probability, bring immediate danger upon them.

She adopted the only course she could to stay the tumult, and restore the band to their calmer senses.

"Lights! lights!" she said; "those of you who have matches, light them."

This was an order every one was eager to obey, for nothing as yet seemed to have come of the alarm except a clattering sound, as if some arms had fallen to the floor.

The flash of some half-dozen matches—those thieves' matches that had not become popular as articles of domestic use—lit up the apartment.

The mystery was solved.

Surprise was upon every countenance, but consternation vanished.

They were in the armoury of St. James's Palace.

An old-fashioned room of considerable extent, and with a domed roof, beneath which, at about twelve feet from the floor, ran a narrow gallery with gilt balustrades.

A rather large collection of ancient armour and weapons of offence and defence was here assembled.

The cause of the alarm of that member of the band who had shouted out in dismay was evident in a moment to them all, and created a general smile.

Some of the half-suits of armour were put upon lay figures, which stood upright close to the walls, and it was upon the face of one of these that the frightened member of the band happened to place his fingers. He felt what he thought was a human countenance, and hence the sudden dismay that had come over him.

The matches died out, and all was darkness again.

"We must have lights," said the Dark Woman. "Are any of you in possession of the means of producing a continued light, however feeble?"

"All's well," said one. "I'm the man for that, Here is a wax taper that will last a good hour, although it will look like a star-light only in this ample space."

"It is enough!" said the Dark Woman.

The taper was lit and placed upon the top of the helmet of the lay figure which had so much alarmed the band; and the little flame, feeble as it was, still sufficed to banish the darkness and to reflect many a bright gleam from the suits of armour around.

The Dark Woman examined the room attentively, and every eye was bent upon her as she did so, for there was a look of trouble upon her countenance.

"Master," said one, "what shall we do now?"

"Yes," added another; "the dawn is coming, and this armoury may have visitors, for aught we know to the contrary."

"It is not likely to have visitors," said the Dark Woman; "but we may yet find it difficult to make our way from it. Immediately beyond that door is one of the most public thoroughfares of the Palace."

The band shrank back from the door she indicated, as though some contagion had been immediately beyond it.

"We cannot retrace our steps," she said. "Let me think—let me think!"

"If we have to pass through that narrow passage again," murmured one, "I shall be choked outright. I yet seem to breathe an atmosphere of dust."

The Dark Woman pressed both her hands upon her brow.

"Let me think—let me think!" she said again.

"Silence! silence!" said the band one to another.

Some terrible reflections seemed to pass through the mind of the Dark Woman. By the little taper light which gleamed upon her face they saw that she seemed agitated by various impulses. She removed her hands from her brow, and her eyes wandered over the armoury and round the gallery with its gilt balustrades.

The band watched her for several minutes, and then they all drew nearer to her, as from the expression upon her countenance they guessed she had come to some determination.

She spoke in low, earnest tones.

"In less than an hour now the dawn of a new day will be upon us. To escape from this place it will be necessary to be alike daring as artful. There is one plan of operations, and one only, which I can recommend, since it has the advantage of open daring combined with finesse which no one would suspect."

The band looked at each other and listened, still in silence.

"You see around you in this place," added the Dark Woman, "plenty of costumes of the Yeomen of the Guard; and thanks to the conservative and antiquarian spirit of the monarchs of England, the colour, fashion, and cut of that costume has remained unchanged since the days of Henry the Eighth. Attire yourselves as completely as possible in those costumes. I will do so likewise. Let us assume, then, the port and bearing of a regular Guard of Yeomen of the Palace. There are the long partizans which make up the arms of such a guard. It will not be well to wait, probably, until the broad glare of daylight might direct critical glances at our getting up; but in the early dawn there will be nothing, I think, to prevent us marching boldly from the Palace through its most frequented ways and passages, and sallying forth into the open street."

A murmur of admiring assent came from the band.

"Who will stay to question a party of Yeomen of the Guard on special duty?"

"No one—no one!"

"We shall escape!" added the Dark Woman—"we shall yet escape!"

CHAPTER CXC.

THE DARK WOMAN AND HER BAND ESCAPE FROM ST. JAMES'S PALACE, AND CARRY A PRISONER WITH THEM.

THERE was no plan of operations which could so well have suited the imaginations of those men who had placed themselves under the control of the Dark Woman, as this which her prolific and scheming brain had devised.

There were costumes sufficient in that armoury for double their number; and, with an alacrity which showed with what heartiness they fell into the plan, they commenced attiring themselves—over their ordinary clothing—in those huge, grotesque surcoats so well known as the principal garment of the Yeomen of the Guard.

They adorned their necks with the huge ruffs—they put on the little shallow-crowned hats with the tufts of ribbon—they drew on the red stockings, and donned the rosetted shoes.

Each man possessed himself of one of the long formidable partizans, of which there was a great stock in the armoury.

The Dark Woman was not behindhand in similarly disguising herself, so that in the space of ten minutes, by the light of that small taper, a complete transformation was effected, and no one, without a hint to the contrary, would have suspected for a moment that this party assembled in the armoury of St. James's Palace was really and truly other than a guard of the Yeomen, at a most unusual hour, upon some special service.

The clock of St. James's now struck five.

The first faint indications of the coming dawn would be visible at that hour in the open air, but would be scarcely sufficient to penetrate into houses.

The Dark Woman paused a few moments, for she was in doubt whether it would be well to show herself and her party so very early, even on some supposed special service in the Palace.

That pause saved her, probably; for during the time that it ensued, the real party of the Yeomen of the Guard, that had been summoned by Willes, the valet, to the protection of the Regent and the Countess de Blonde, passed actually the door of the armoury.

The Dark Woman and her companions could hear the tramp of their footsteps and the slight jingle of their partizans, as by accident or carelessness they touched each other.

Not more still, for the brief period that these real Yeomen were passing, than the effigies in the armoury were the Dark Woman and her band.

You might have taken each man there for a statue, attired in that grotesque old dress merely for the purpose of its exhibition.

The footsteps died away in the distance, and a silence so profound crept over St. James's Palace, that it seemed as if all the alarm had subsided, and every person who had been aroused from slumber on that eventful night had retired to rest again, in the hope of snatching some short repose yet before the actual daylight.

"It is time!" said the Dark Woman.

She made a movement towards the door of the armoury, which she had no doubt of being able to unlock with the master-key she had in her possession.

Faint, then, and sick at heart felt for a moment the Dark Woman; and had she not possessed that control over her feelings which a life of danger and of difficulty had taught her, she must surely have screamed aloud.

The rattle of another key—a key from the outside—was in the lock of that door.

The lock was old, rusted, unyielding, and stiff in its wards, and the key did not readily perform its office.

The Dark Woman turned and faced her band, who, having all heard the noise, had assumed various attitudes of surprise and alarm.

"To the walls! to the walls!" she whispered. "Associate yourselves with these effigies in armour, and seem to be but statues of the past!"

They understood her.

With one accord they shrunk back to the walls of the armoury, and assuming different stations, they stood grim and silent.

The Dark Woman herself retired into a niche,

at the back of which hung a collection of ancient weapons.

But the little taper light burnt upon a table in the centre of the apartment.

For a moment they all forgot it, although its presence would be the means of at once awakening a suspicion that would most probably have been fatal to them.

The Dark Woman saw the omission.

She darted forward, and as the readiest means of extinguishing the taper, she placed over it the hat in which she had attired herself as one of the Yeomen of the Guard.

The action was only just in time, for the heavy door swung open, and a glare of light gleamed into the armoury.

The Dark Woman had not time to regain the niche from whence she had sprung: indeed, she could do nothing at the moment but crouch down and trust for concealment to the shadow of the massive oaken table which occupied the centre of the floor.

A more perilous situation for Linda de Chevenaux and her associates could not well be conceived.

Probably, never was the Dark Woman in such imminent danger of discovery and capture as upon this occasion; and the circumstances were such, too, as must have condemned her to some serious penalty.

Indeed it is doubtful if even the power of the Regent—provided he was willing to exercise it, and of that we will not entertain much doubt—could have saved her from that death which was the apportioned punishment of the offence to which she must have pleaded guilty.

A burglarious and night attack upon the Palace of St. James's—certainly with robbery for one of its objects, and possibly murder—could admit of no justification.

But sad—most sad and terrible would have been the reflection of Captain Fitz George if evil fortune had enforced upon him at that moment the necessity of being the means of surrendering his own mother up to justice.

But such, happily, was not the case.

One glance into that armoury was sufficient to show him what was the nature of the apartment; and as it happened that close to the door, which had been flung open in order that he might take a cursory glance within the armoury, there stood one of those effigies in armour with which the place was well supplied, Captain Fitz George directed no scrutiny towards the men of real flesh and blood, who stood so calmly and so still, in the costumes of the Yeomen of the Guard, against the walls.

But what a terrible moment that must have been to Linda de Chevenaux!

Crouching down behind that heavy oaken table, and looking from the darkness of the room towards the light, which, sending a broad gleam through the open doorway, threw the figure of Captain Fitz George into bold relief, how could she fail to know him?

There was her own son seeking her destruction, as she told herself; but most unjustly did she so tell herself. For, after all, he was but in the performance of a duty: and, in truth, he had taken that duty upon himself, rather than it should devolve upon another, who would feel

neither tenderness nor sympathy for the Dark Woman.

For the space of about half a minute Captain Fitz George gazed into that apartment.

Then he closed the door, and darkness fell upon the glittering arms, upon the suits of ancient mail, the buff coats and the costumes of the Yeomen of the Guard with which the armoury was crowded.

A darkness so profound that it seemed as if everything within the place had changed its hue to the most intense blackness.

Then the Dark Woman rose up from her crouching posture, and drew a deep breath.

"It is over!" she said. "That danger is past! We live again!"

Then there was a simultaneous movement on the part of the band, and the slight clash and clatter of arms resounded through the vaulted apartment.

"A light! a light!" said the Dark Woman. "We shall not be visited again, and the darkness in this place clings about one like a shroud."

A match soon lit up the scene, and the wax taper was again lighted.

The Dark Woman paced the armoury in thought. Then turning to her associates, she said, in that calm tone of command which admitted of neither dispute nor remonstrance, "It is unsafe, as yet, to make our way through the Palace. Researches and alarms are still rife about its passages and gloomy galleries. Remain here in peace and in security. I will return to you shortly."

There was a slight movement among the band, as though they would have stopped her from leaving the armoury; but if such an idea crossed their minds for a moment, it was as quickly abandoned.

Probably they looked with regret upon even a temporary separation from her; inasmuch as the pockets of her apparel were the depositories of those costly jewels which had been their temptation to make this assault upon St. James's Palace, and to the proceeds of which they looked forward for the means of leading, for some time, a life of riot and extravagance.

The Dark Woman did not seem to notice any of these impulses or sensations on the part of her band. It sufficed for her that she had given her orders and instructions; and, in good truth, her mind was too full of many thoughts to permit her to study very closely the caprices and changes of their reflections.

With a feeling of security in the disguise she wore—which was complete as a Yeoman of the Guard—she sallied forth from the armoury.

And then the Dark Woman became aware that the morning was further advanced than she had supposed.

A stream of tolerably white light came into the sort of corridor in which she found herself, through a large window which faced the east.

It is possible enough that Linda de Chevenaux had no very well defined idea of what she was about to do when she left that armoury alone; but the feverish wish and impulse to hear what was going on in the Palace, and her reliance upon chance to conduct her to the proximity of some of those persons in whom she felt interested, no doubt actuated her.

Familiar as she was with the inside of the royal residence, she found herself rather at fault to know in which direction to turn, in order to reach the more inhabited portion of the very ancient structure.

She turned mechanically to the right, and after proceeding for some distance along the corridor, she reached a staircase, the steps of which were covered with red cloth.

From this circumstance she came to the conclusion that occasionally the Regent must pass down those stairs, for she remembered to have heard that whenever any staircases occurred in the different routes by which he chose to enter or leave the Palace, they were so covered with that scarlet cloth.

The topography of the palace, so well known to the Dark Woman, must have escaped her at that moment, or she would have known that at the top of those stairs it was but necessary to pass through a suite of rooms, and she would reach that end of the Titian Gallery which was the farthest removed from the apartments in the occupation of Annie, Countess de Blonde.

The knowledge of where exactly she was at the moment she actually emerged into the Titian Gallery came like a flash of light upon the mind of the Dark Woman.

It was well that she did so soon discover her proximity to the inhabited portion of the Palace, for had she proceeded many paces further in the state of dreamy thought into which the events of the night had thrown her, she would have encountered a sentinel, really belonging to the Yeomen of the Guard, whose non-recognition of her as a comrade might have been troublesome.

The Dark Woman had just time to shrink back, and at the moment she thought she had been seen; for the Yeoman suddenly stopped in his careless march along the gallery, and drew himself up to an attitude of "attention."

"A life for a life!" muttered the Dark Woman to herself.

She seemed to feel at that moment the necessity of committing murder, but she was relieved from the action by seeing the true cause of the Yeoman's "attention."

A corporal of the Guard, with three men at his heels, came marching down the gallery.

These were regular soldiers of one of the regiments of Foot Guards; and the Dark Woman shrunk back into the shadow of the doorway from which she had emerged, as she came to the conclusion that the incident, which for a moment had alarmed her, was but a changing of the Guard.

The corporal said something which she could not catch, and the Yeoman then walked off with his partizan across his shoulder, while one of the soldiers assumed his post, and stood receiving apparently some instructions from the corporal.

A resolution, as bold as it was ingenious, sprung into the mind of the Dark Woman as if by inspiration.

She started out of the shadowy recess in which she was, and, with the partizan she had brought from the armoury, in the same attitude she had seen the Yeoman assume with that he carried, she approached the corporal and the three soldiers of the Foot Guards.

Then the Dark Woman saw what she had not before observed—namely, that this post at which a sentinel was placed was the broken door which led into the first of the suite of apartments in the occupation of the Countess de Blonde.

CHAPTER CXCI.

THE DARK WOMAN OVERHEARS AN INTERESTING CONVERSATION, AND FORMS A NEW RESOLUTION.

A STRANGE rush of feelings came over the mind of Linda de Chevenaux as she approached that spot which had so lately been the scene of so much tumult and confusion.

The door which had been battered down and forced from its hinges had been set upright in its place, and probably was kept there by the weight of some articles of furniture from within.

It was quite evident, however, that although the alarm in the Palace had subsided, and the audacious assailants who had sought to penetrate into those apartments were believed to be beaten off, the prudence of having a sentinel at that broken doorway was fully appreciated either by the Regent, by Captain Fitz George, or by the valet, Willes.

The idea of the Dark Woman partook of all that boldness and energy which characterized an intellect wasted for all beneficial purposes, but which, if properly directed, would have shone with a lustre that would have made it the delight and the ornament of an age.

Disguised as she was, she thought it possible to substitute herself for the sentinel which had just been placed at the door of that suite of rooms.

The probability that she would succeed in so doing was immensely increased by the fact that it was no longer one of the Yeomen of the Guard who held the post.

It was much more likely that she would succeed in imposing herself upon the corporal and the soldiers as a veritable member of that corps of Beef-eaters, as they were usually called, and which the military held in most especial contempt, than as if a real Yeoman had been there.

At all events, the effort was worth the trial, and it did not seem to the Dark Woman that it was possible to lose anything by its failure.

The sound of her footsteps came plainly enough upon the ear of the corporal and his men as they were moving off after placing one of their body on guard.

Now, the Dark Woman was in the costume of a captain of the band of Yeomen; and probably the corporal, although not, perhaps, very well versed in the details of the uniform, which he thought supremely ridiculous, had a suspicion that it was some sort of officer who addressed him, as the Dark Woman, in a tone of imperious command, cried "Halt!"

"Halt!" repeated the corporal—and the two soldiers he had with him obeyed the order.

"It is needless, corporal," said the Dark Woman,—"it is needless for you to place one of your men here. I have promised the Regent to hold this post for him myself until broad daylight, and have his gracious permission and command so to do."

There was a strong vein of superstition, and a tendency to fatalism, about the mind of the Dark Woman; and, indeed, upon reviewing some of the incidents of her eventful ilfe, it is scarcely to be wondered at that such should be the case.

But now, at the present moment, when she found herself actually keeping guard, and acting as a sentinel over that portion of St. James's Palace which contained all she once loved, and all she now hated, it is scarcely a matter of surprise that she should believe herself to be some instrument acting directly under the instigations of Providence, and destined to carry out purposes which should live in the history of the nation.

That terrible stillness, which seemed to come over the whole Palace, and which to her appeared unnatural, was but the ordinary quietude, which was more likely to be deep and profound at such an hour, than at any other of the four-and-twenty.

No. 86.—DARK WOMAN.

The Dark Woman took several turns in the Titian Gallery, with all the air and manner of a soldier on duty.

Then feeling convinced that she was quite alone —that no eye was observing her, and no ear listening to her words or to her actions, she turned her attention wholly to that broken-down door, which had been so temporarily replaced in its position, but which in reality could now form so slight an obstacle to any one who might really wish to make way into the royal apartments.

Linda de Chevenaux had got completely into her head the idea that Annie, Countess de Blonde, was a great obstacle in the way of her making some substantial terms with the Regent, which should place her in a very different position to that she now occupied.

Had the Regent himself taken a more logical view than he did of the whole affair, he would quickly have divested himself of all personal fears on account of the Dark Woman.

What would his death avail her?

Positively nothing; and, indeed, were it to happen either by her agency, or through the ordinary course of nature, there would be an end, at once and for ever, of all her hopes, wild and visionary as they were.

But she had the insane idea that, by striking at him through his predilections, his fancies, and his affections, she should succeed in her object.

To reside with him as his Queen when he ascended the throne, or to be acknowledged by him as Princess of Wales, so as to assume the social status of such a personage, she hardly imagined possible; because she could scarcely believe that, although above the ordinary action of the law as he was in consequence of his rank, he would like to proclaim himself a bigamist.

But what she thought exceedingly reasonable and rational was that he should acknowledge he had been married legally before his union with Caroline of Brunswick.

Following that acknowledgment, she wished him to take her son by the hand, and acknowledge him as his heir-presumptive.

The different view that Captain Fitz George had taken of the whole transaction, and the manner in which he had divided his interests and feelings from the wild and unreasonable objects of his mother, did not suffice to change her purpose.

She had suffered much from that defection on his part.

The common sense view he had taken of the matter was a severe blow to her; but inasmuch as the object she had set her life upon achieving had long since passed the bounds of reason, they were not amenable to ordinary circumstances of suppression; and after recovering from the first blow which her mind had received on finding that Allan Fearon did not go hand in hand with her in her purposes and objects, she felt a gloomy satisfaction in still adhering to those purposes, without which she had no aim in life.

If the Dark Woman were no longer to pursue and persecute the Regent of England, she felt that she might as well die, for the object of her existence would have passed away.

Life would have become a purposeless blank, and an encumbrance that she would gladly have been rid of on the first opportunity.

And so her intention distinctly was, by that midnight assault on St. James's Palace, not to injure a hair of the Regent's head, but to wring, with pain and regret, the fibres of his heart by the death of Annie, Countess de Blonde.

Yes, there can be no doubt whatever that, upon that occasion, the Dark Woman contemplated the deliberate murder of the innocent, unsophisticated, and really kind-hearted Countess de Blonde.

And now had not Providence itself seemed to place it in her power to carry out this fell and terrible purpose?

By a series of accidents, there she was—alone, unwatched, free to act, and with, apparently, nothing between her and her victim but a broken door, which it would require but a trifling amount of energy to displace from its temporary holding, and leave the passage free for the avenger.

The Dark Woman placed the long partizan she carried, in her capacity as a Yeoman of the Guard, against the wall of the Titian Gallery.

She then, by a gentle and sustained pressure, tried if the broken door would move.

Some heavy piece of furniture was on the other side supporting it, but that piece of furniture was not so heavy that it would not yield to a steadily sustained force from without.

The door moved.

The piece of furniture, whatever it was—probably one of the old inlaid cabinets, of which she knew there were several in the room—was pushed a few inches inwards.

The sound upon the floor was slight, and the Dark Woman, by continuing her efforts for about five minutes, established an opening which, though not above a foot in width, was sufficient to enable her, without much difficulty, to glide through.

She was in the apartments of the fair Annie, who could little suspect that one with such murderous designs had, by such a fortuitous train of circumstances, been enabled to penetrate so far towards her purposes.

A soft and delicate perfume was in the air of the apartment.

The Regent's fancy for odours and essences of all kinds and descriptions was well known to Linda de Chevenaux, and the mere sensation of that perfumed air was sufficient to assure her that he was present in that suite of rooms.

She paused a moment.

She asked herself a question.

Would the Regent defend Annie? Did he love her sufficiently to risk his life for hers? Would he seize upon some weapon and fight in her behalf?

These were questions which might well induce the Dark Woman to consider her position.

But answer them in her own mind how she might, she felt she had gone too far now to retreat, or she madly persuaded herself that she had done so.

To turn back now would be a piece of pusillanimity for which she should for ever reproach herself.

Crossing that outer apartment, she passed through an open door at its further extremity, and then she found herself in that small but exquisitely appointed dining-room, where the Regent so often partook of those little dinners and suppers with Annie, which, no doubt, in his mind, contributed not a little to the charm of their communication.

There was no light in the outer room, but a lamp was burning in this second apartment, the flame of which was covered with a ruby-tinted glass.

A soft, beautiful, rosy hue was diffused throughout the apartment; and here it was that upon the chimney-piece was slowly evolved from a silver censer that delicate and pleasant perfume which crept through the air of the rooms with a refreshing fragrance.

Some rare combination of flowers in which the odours had been confined but for awhile, to be diffused into the atmosphere as they smouldered to ashes in that silver censer, came most luxuriously upon the senses, and was anything but germane to the thoughts of death and destruction which filled the heart of the Dark Woman.

The lamp burnt low; and the glitter of the

gilded cornices, the soft, silken lustre of the gorgeous hangings, and the sparkle of the many rich and rare articles with which that room was adorned, all struck painfully upon the senses of Linda de Chevenaux.

"So much beauty," she murmured,—"so much grace—so much fragrance and costly magnificence wasted upon the frivolous heart of the minion of an hour; when one who could have been to him a wife, a Queen, emerges but from neglect and despair, with the smouldering fires of a thousand passions in her heart!"

Linda de Chevenaux knew that the next apartment to this was a bed-chamber, vying with it in magnificence, and only differing in the details of its costly treasures.

There was a door, the panels elaborately carved and gilt, while the flat portion of them were mirrors, in one of which she started to see herself.

So wan, so haggard did she look.

And then she sprung aside, and barely had time to hide herself behind one of the silken hangings, when that door of mirrors was suddenly opened.

"I'm sure, Annie, I heard something," said the Regent. "I'm certain I did."

The Dark Woman's heart almost stopped its beating.

Then she heard the voice of Annie—that voice which she had come there to still for ever, but which, in those careless, musical accents, which made it such a charm to listen to, called out from the inner apartment, "You're always fancying something, George. I hear all sorts of things at all sorts of times; but, as they come to nothing, I never disturb myself about them."

"But I'm sure, Annie, I heard somebody."

"A mouse!"

"Stuff—stuff, Annie!—nonsense! There's no mice here; but as I don't see anything or hear anybody, it was nothing."

"Ah, George," cried Annie, "you won't live long!"

"Not live long? Eh? What do you mean?"

"You're getting so dreadfully sensible!"

"Come, come, Annie! Nonsense, nonsense! Don't make any jokes about not living long. You know, of all things in the world that I dislike, it's anything about dying, and getting ill, and all that sort of bother."

The Regent withdrew his head, which he had projected from the door of mirrors into the dining-room, but he left the door about half an inch open.

The Dark Woman breathed again. She heard his voice distinctly, although it sounded in lower tones, as he said, "Well, now, go on, Annie. What were you saying? I have left that door a little way open, so that we shall get some advantage from the pastiles that are burning in the censer."

The Dark Woman stepped up close to the crevice in the door and listened.

Annie was speaking, and there was much more of emotion in her tones than she usually cared to exhibit.

The Dark Woman heard her with wonder and amazement; and as she so heard her, a cold tremor shook her frame, and the strength which had hitherto supported her seemed to pass away, so that she was constrained to lean against the side of the door to listen to those words which

sprung out of the generous disposition of Annie, Countess de Blonde.

"George," said Annie, "you will never be happy, nor I either, until something is done for the happiness or the peace of Linda de Chevenaux."

"There—there!" said the Regent. "Enough—enough, Annie. What can I do for the happiness or the peace of anybody, if they won't be happy nor peaceful? Good gracious, Annie, I ask you what can I do?"

"I hardly know, but it is very sad. Through all this poor woman's actions, and through all her wild, mad acts, I seem to see that bleeding, desolate heart!"

The Regent was silent.

"Betrayed, wrecked, and ruined! George—George, something must be done to restore peace to Linda de Chevenaux!"

"I wish to heaven," said the Regent, "she'd leave me a little peace! What can I do, Annie? The woman's mad! She's worse than a ghost! She haunts me—here, there, and everywhere, as you well know. But I can't please her. You know what she wants well enough. I'm to call her Princess of Wales; and Fitz George—for whom I'm doing all I can—Prince George, and heir apparent to the throne; for even at this moment, Annie, such is the precarious condition of a certain person at Windsor, that I may be King of England."

"That's nothing to do with it," said Annie.

"What has to do with it, then?"

"You must make an appointment with Linda de Chevenaux, and fairly meet her."

"Who? I? Ho! ho! Ha! ha!"

"Be quiet."

"Well, I am."

"I say, you must make an appointment with her, and fairly meet her. I confess——"

"Ho! ho! confess! A pretty father confessor! Ho! ho!"

"Do you know, George, you're uncommonly stupid? Who said anything about father confessors? Have you not told me over and over again what a wretch you are?"

"A wretch?"

"To be sure. Who knows that so well as I do, except yourself? There you go again! I know you're going to cry again! Ho! ho! No I won't—I won't!"

"You won't what?"

"I won't be stopped saying any more about it with a kiss."

"But how do you know I was going to do that?"

"I saw you screwing up your mouth."

"Well, well, Annie, say what you like, and I will listen to you."

"You told me that, in order to overcome the scruples of Linda de Chevenaux to a secret marriage, you had produced to her a written consent from the King, your father."

"Well, I—a——"

"Don't try to get out of it. You know you did. She was vain and credulous, and too readily permitted herself to fall into the snare."

"But, Annie——"

"You—a systematic deceiver——"

"Come, come! you'll say I've deceived you presently."

"Not a bit. I'm as bad as I can be, and I know it. But this Linda de Chevenaux was either foolish enough, or vain enough, to allow her judgment to go to sleep; and although she ought certainly to have taken some means to ascertain the real truth, she believed you, and there was a secret marriage; but the pretended consent of the King, your father, was written by yourself."

"No, by Jove!—no!"

"Who then?"

"Dead."

"What do you mean by *dead?*"

"Somebody that's dead. An old valet of mine. The fellow who preceded Willes. He wrote it. So you see, Annie, I had nothing to do with it, and am as innocent as a small babe."

"If you go on in that sort of way, George," said Annie, "I positively won't speak to you again. You call yourself innocent because you made another rascal write that paper?"

"Ho! ho! Treason! treason! Another rascal, indeed! I shall be *obleeged*, Annie, to send you to the Tower, on a charge of treason, for calling your Prince a rascal."

"Send me as soon as you like," said Annie. "I dare say I shall soon get out. Somebody will think me pretty. And as I'm sure to be obliging——"

"Now, Annie!—now, Annie! There—there! don't say any more about it!"

"Well, I won't about that. But what you must do, George, about this poor Linda de Chevenaux is just this."

"What? You've not done with her?"

"Certainly not. For your own sake, George—for my sake, and for her sake—for the sake of kindness, goodness, repentance of the past, and the poor, broken heart of that poor, lost, and betrayed Linda de Chevenaux—I say, for all these reasons, you must give her a meeting, George; and you must speak to her kindly and gently. You must confess the offence you have committed towards her, and convince her judgment, although you pain her heart. You must tell her that although the past cannot be recalled, that your earnest wish is that she should be happy for the future. You must show her that she is fighting for the shadow of greatness, while she is losing the substance of her life. Tell her that this consent of the King to your marriage with her was a delusion. Speak kindly and gently to her, and see if something cannot be done which will soothe—although you cannot eradicate wholly—the anguish of that desolate creature."

A deep silence ensued; then the Dark Woman could hear the rapid sound of footsteps as the Regent paced the room to and fro. He paused suddenly, and, in a voice which was struggling with vexation, he said, "Annie! Annie, you don't know her! If this marriage which she contracted with me had been one of real love on her part, I might hope, on a meeting with her, to awaken tender emotions. We might meet and part in kindness; but—but she never loved me."

"Is that so?"

"No; it was ambition. She thought she was exalting herself on a bubble blown into huge dimensions by her personal vanity and wish for rank, and rule, and power. She tried to soar aloft; but it collapsed, and she sank to such a depth that nothing was left to her but death or despair."

The Dark Woman struck her breast, and uttered a low moan.

For once—if only for once—she had heard a terrible truth from the lips of the Regent.

CHAPTER CXCII.

THE DARK WOMAN MAKES AN ILLUSTRIOUS PRISONER, AND PRODUCES CONSTERNATION IN THE PALACE.

THE resolution with which the Dark Woman had entered St. James's on that night vanished.

She no longer sought the life of Annie, Countess de Blonde.

Strangely excited and warped as was her intellect, she would have required to be incapable of the mental combinations we have seen she was so apt at, if she had been insensible to those words which Annie had uttered in reference to her condition and her ill-starred union with the Regent.

But while those words from the Countess de Blonde dissipated the resolution of the Dark Woman, they awakened another.

The proposition which Annie had made to the Regent to grant a real, confidential interview to the much-injured Linda de Chevenaux, was one which recommended itself very much to her mind.

It was perfectly true that more than once she had forced herself upon the Regent, and had held upon those occasions what might be called a discourse with him on their relative positions.

But then that discourse had always been carried on, as regarded the Regent himself, with anger and reluctance; and what was of more consequence, it had taken place under circumstances which had made the position of the Dark Woman precarious and dangerous.

But now the idea came across her mind that she would not only enforce such an interview as Annie, the Countess de Blonde, mentioned; but that it should be held at such a time and in such a place as should let the Regent see how impossible it would be to shorten its duration, or import into it any real danger to Linda de Chevenaux.

The Dark Woman stayed to hear no more.

She glided out of that magnificent apartment, where she had been so entirely an unsuspected listener to the most confidential words of the Regent, and made her way rapidly again to the Titian Gallery.

She did not pause there for a moment.

Her object now was to reach again with all the speed that was possible that armoury, where she had left her associates, no doubt, in a state of considerable anxiety on account of her prolonged absence.

She had work for them to do.

It was work they might object to, on account of its exceeding boldness and its possible consequences.

But the Dark Woman knew well she had a hold over them which was of a character they would scarcely seek to escape from.

She held in her possession those jewels of rare beauty—and, what was more to the purpose, of rare cost—which they had entered St. James's Palace expressly to seek.

No fond lover would be more attracted to follow in the footsteps of the idol of his heart than they would to keep her in view who was in possession of those magical bits of crystal which were convertible into bright and shining heaps of the current coin of the realm.

The Dark Woman met no one in her progress from the Titian Gallery to the armoury.

It was almost with a cry of delight she was welcomed by the band she had left there in great anxiety respecting her reappearance.

There was a simultaneous movement, and an exclamation of satisfaction from every voice.

The Dark Woman held up her hand as an indication of silence.

All was still again.

"You will now follow me," she said.

"Then the route of escape is easy?" asked one.

"It soon will be. But there is a something more to do."

"More plunder?"

"No!" replied the Dark Woman; and she enunciated the word clearly and distinctly, so that there could be no possible mistake regarding it.

A blank look of disappointment sat on every face.

"No!" she added again. "This time it is work—work for me; but not plunder. Remember your compact! It is through my knowledge and through my means that you will achieve resplendent booty; and, in return, you are to assist me in carrying out my purposes. Follow!"

No one thought of disputing these absolute commands; but, after a whisper had passed round among them, one stepped forward, and, speaking calmly and distinctly, said—"Master, we do not say that your orders are not to be obeyed; but what we wish is distinctly to understand them. What is it that you require that we should do?"

"So far as I think it necessary," replied the Dark Woman, "I explain my wishes. You will follow me to a gallery of St. James's Palace, where, indeed, you have been before, which communicates with a suite of private apartments, in one of which the Regent is at present."

The Dark Woman's associates looked uneasy.

"You will mount guard at the entrance of those apartments; and finding a means, which I will do, to induce the Regent to come forth, we will request him to attire himself, even as we are attired, in the costume of a Yeoman of the Guard."

"Impossible!" said several voices.

"Quite possible," added the Dark Woman; "for here are numerous spare costumes of that description, one of which we will take with us."

"But—but——"

"I have spoken. Dare you hesitate?"

A whispered consultation took place, but the Dark Woman spoke again before anything could come of it.

"You hesitate to take these steps," she said, "in the direction of my wishes, when, in order that the rich and unexpected booty you have made here in St. James's Palace should certainly be divided amongst you, I have taken pains, and incurred some danger, to place it in safety."

There was a start from every one of the band.

"Then," said several of them speaking together —"then, master, you have no longer those jewels about you?"

A cold smile of irony sat for a moment on the lips of the Dark Woman.

"No longer about me, as you say," she replied; "for I thought it dangerous, if I were taken, that the general welfare should be so far jeopardised."

Those lawless men saw at once that they were in her power; for since she no longer had the jewels about her, they must be entirely dependent upon her good-will and pleasure to tell them where they were.

"Master, we will follow you!"

"That is well! Your safety is my safety! Bring with you as complete a costume, similar to those we ourselves wear, as you can find."

There was no difficulty in obeying this injunction of the Dark Woman, for the armoury was well stocked with such apparel, and the necessary weapons belonging to it.

Then the Dark Woman flung open the door of the armoury. She placed herself at the head of her associates. They shouldered their partizans, and at the word "march," they followed her with a considerable show of boldness into the corridor beyond.

The morning had come.

Cold and grey, and without much light—for dense masses of clouds had gathered in the dawning sky—that morning presented itself.

But still it was morning.

The Dark Woman thought she heard a faint, indistinct sound in a distant portion of the Palace, as though some of the domestics were already astir.

She felt that what she had to do must be done quickly.

Keeping the step well—for some of these lawless young men who were with her had graduated in the army—this mock party of the Yeomen of the Guard followed their imperious and daring leader along the corridor, up that crimson cloth covered staircase, and so onward to the gallery which has been the scene of so many startling episodes in these memoirs.

But one person was met on the route.

That was an under-servant of the Palace, whose duty it was at daylight to extinguish the oil lamps that scattered the darkness out of the corridors and winding passages of old St. James's.

This man stood aside to allow the supposed party of Yeomen to pass him.

There was a look of surprise upon his face.

No doubt it was an unusual circumstance to see such a guard abroad at such a period; and the look of surprise increased to one of puzzled bewilderment, for this man failed to recognise a single countenance of any of these Yeomen; and, up to that time, he had thought himself familiar with the personal appearance of every member of the corps.

Coldly and sternly they passed him without a glance; and the lamp-lighter rubbed his eyes, as though he half suspected he was in a dream, or that this armed and accoutred party, none of whom he knew, were phantoms representing Yeomen, who had passed away from mortal life long before his appearance at the Palace.

Tramp, tramp—clank, clank—proceeded the

armed party, and then they emerged into the Titian Gallery.

"Halt!"

Two men were in the Titian Gallery. They carried something which looked suspicious.

It was the dead body of Lovemore, which had been left there until that period, but was now to be removed, lest its presence should offend the fine senses of the Regent.

Then the Dark Woman's heart nearly sank within her; for directing the removal of that dead body she saw an officer with a drawn sword in his hand.

That officer was Captain Fitz George.

The two men who were removing the dead body were a couple of the soldiers of his regiment in fatigue dresses.

Upon catching the sound of the footstep of the approaching party of seeming Yeomen of the Guard, Fitz George turned abruptly towards them, and then walking rapidly forward so as to meet them, he said in tones of some acerbity, "Who commands this party?—who commands this party?"

"I!" said the Dark Woman, in a deep, hollow voice.

"Then, sir, it is a very strange thing that a good hour ago a corporal of my regiment was prevented from placing a sentinel here, on the pretence that the post was to be occupied by one of the King's Yeomen, and now I find no sentinel here at all."

"By order of the Regent," replied the Dark Woman, in the same cold, disguised tones,—"by order of the Regent I hold this post, now and henceforth."

"That's all very well, sir, but for some time it has been held by nobody."

The Dark Woman made a slight inclination of her head, but returned no answer to Fitz George. Addressing her troop, however, she cried, "Forward!"

They followed her down the gallery.

Fitz George thought it strange that this officer of the Yeomen should press his hand so forcibly upon his breast.

The Dark Woman was compelled to do so to still the tumultuous beating of her heart.

Fitz George looked after them until he saw them halt at the door leading into the Countess de Blonde's apartments; and then he turned to follow his two men.

Not the slightest suspicion had crossed the mind of the young officer in regard to the genuine character of the armed party he saw.

He knew nothing of that mongrel race—half-door-keepers and servants, and half-soldiers—that were supposed to form the body-guard of the Sovereign; and any clumsiness they might exhibit was but in accordance with his preconceived notions in regard to them.

He left the gallery.

The Dark Woman was able to breathe freely again.

But little did those lawless men who followed her suppose that during the brief period of that young officer's presence their leader had passed through a period of terror, passion, tenderness, and grief which might well shake her to the soul.

"Remain!" she said. "I will return quickly; and, successful or non-successful, we leave St.

James's Palace in fifteen minutes from this time."

The Dark Woman passed through the broken doorway, and gliding over the soft carpet of the first apartment, she made her way to that exquisitely appointed dining-room, where she had so short a time before listened to the conversation of Annie, the Countess, and the Regent.

But the Dark Woman did not on this occasion pause for an instant to catch the meaning of any words that might be spoken by either of those personages.

She tapped lightly at the door of mirrors, which conducted to the bed-chamber.

"Who knocks?—who knocks?" cried the Regent.

"Officer on guard!" replied the Dark Woman.

"What is it?—what is it?"

"Will your Royal Highness——"

"What?"

"Will your Royal Highness——"

The Dark Woman purposely said no more, in order to awaken the curiosity of the Regent.

"Will I what?" he said impatiently as he opened the door.

"Now, George," cried Annie, "you might shut the door while people get their things on."

The Regent closed the door of mirrors, which was exactly what the Dark Woman wanted him to do.

"Well, sir?—well, sir?"

"Your Highness is in danger."

"Danger?—danger?"

"Great and immediate. But a guard of Yeomen occupy the gallery, in the midst of which your Royal Highness will be in perfect security; whereas a moment's delay in this room——"

It was not necessary for the Dark Woman to say a word more. The Regent, holding his dressing-gown tightly about him, rushed out of the dining-room, and crossing the outer apartment, found himself in another moment in the midst of the mock guard of Yeomen.

"Safe!—safe!" he cried. "Surely, I am safe now?"

"No, your Royal Highness," said the Dark Woman; "there is a plot!"

"A plot?"

"Yes, your Royal Highness, and against your royal person! It is intended to seize you, and carry you by force out of the Palace."

"Me?—me? Seize me?"

"Even so, your Highness!"

"Then it's that infernal—that—that——Hem! Linda de Chevenaux, the Dark Woman!"

"Your Royal Highness is perfectly correct. But if your Highness will take advice, the danger may be avoided by a stratagem, which, although it lurks in the very air we breathe, and although at any corner the hand of the assassin——"

"Assassin? Assassin? Does she contemplate our assassination?"

"She contemplates anything that her maddened heart suggests."

"Well, but—but—but——"

"Ah! your Highness, we don't know how or in what way the blow may be sought to be struck. It may be here—there—anywhere! At the opening of a door; at the foot or head of a staircase!"

"Gracious heaven!"

"And so, if your Royal Highness will but condescend rapidly to put on these garments, so as to assume the appearance of a common Yeoman of the Guard, and march along with my company, you may leave the Palace with perfect safety, since it is the Regent that is aimed at; and in this costume, those who lurk in old St. James's will avoid you rather than confront you."

The Dark Woman took care to keep her face in shadow; and the marvellous aptitude she had of changing her voice, enabled her completely to obliterate from it every tone that could remind he Regent of Linda de Chevenaux.

"Do you know, sir," said the Prince, "it appears to us that you are a very ingenious officer, and that you propose to do us a great service. The whole night in the Palace has been full of alarms, and what you say coincides but too well with an audacious attempt which has already been made to force their way into the most private and particular part of the Palace."

"I know it, your Highness!"

"Give me the uniform, and wait a moment."

"It is here!"

"We shall look very absurd; but safety, when combined with absurdity, is a great deal better than danger, if associated with the a——the a——"

"Trappings of a King!"

"Just so—just so! That is just what I was going to say. Wait a moment—wait a moment!"

The Regent took the costume which was handed to him and stepped back into those private apartments.

The Dark Woman faced her band, and placed her finger on her lips to enjoin silence. Every face was pale, and every heart probably beat laboriously, for they could not but feel in how precarious and dangerous a situation they stood; and how possible, and probable, indeed, it was that some real Yeomen of the Guard might make their appearance in the Titian Gallery and at once discover the imposture.

The Regent's voice was heard in high tones proceeding from the rooms.

He was speaking to the Countess de Blonde, and no doubt explaining to her the necessity which existed for him assuming a disguise.

Annie might or might not be convinced by the same style of reasoning which had awakened the fears of the Regent.

The few minutes of suspense that the Dark Woman endured in the dread that, after all, the finely woven plot might fail, were, indeed, minutes of the acutest possible suffering.

Then the Regent appeared in the full costume of a Yeoman of the Guard, and the Dark Woman felt as though she had been reprieved from death.

CHAPTER CXCIII.

THE REGENT BELIEVES THAT THE END OF HIS CAREER HAS ARRIVED.

THE appearance of the Prince of Wales in that disguise was a surprise to the associates of the Dark Woman; for up to that moment, although they had been listening to her proceedings, and

were fully cognisant of the specious manner in which she had seemed to prevail upon the Regent to adopt the course she had suggested, they had hardly believed it possible he would do so, until they actually saw him.

Then, of course, all doubt was out of the question, although their surprise continued.

But they had no means of knowing what Linda de Chevenaux knew so well,—namely, the state of mind in which he was in regard to anything that concerned the Dark Woman.

So active and continuous, and for so long a time, had been the persecutions he had endured, that the Regent's mind was certainly not in a healthy condition as regarded Linda de Chevenaux; hence was it that he fell into a suggestion which at any other time, and in regard to any other person, he would have treated with disdain.

"Now, sir," said the Regent, addressing the Dark Woman in her character of an officer in command of a party of the Yeomen of the Guard, —"now, sir, what is next to be done? You see we have yielded to your solicitations and followed your advice."

"It is well! Your Royal Highness will now be enabled to leave St. James's Palace in perfect safety, and in defiance of any lurking assassin that might be within its walls."

"And yet methinks," replied the Regent, "our Yeomen of the Guard might well protect us against not only an assassin, in the singular, but assassins, in the plural."

"A perfectly just remark, your Royal Highness, provided such assassin would show himself; but a stray bullet from some concealed corner is a thing that all your Highness's troops could not save you from."

"Certainly not—certainly not! Excuse me; I did not think of that. Of course, a King, or Prince, or Regent, may be proof against the knife of the assassin; but a bullet wings its way with destruction on its errand, and no man can stop it."

"Your Highness takes a proper view of the subject. May we have your royal permission to proceed?"

"Certainly—certainly!"

The Dark Woman was most anxious now to carry her project fully out, for she knew not but upon every passing moment might come some serious interruption that would not only destroy all her chances of success, but involve her and her associates in one common ruin.

"March!"

The Regent started, for it seemed so novel and odd to him to hear any order given in his presence. But he fell in along with the party with as good a grace as possible, and marched along by the side of Linda de Chevenaux without the shadow of a notion with regard as to who was his companion.

"Stop!" said the Regent, when they had reached the end of the gallery,—"stop! I have not quite made up my mind."

"Hesitation now, your Royal Highness, may be death!"

"No, no! I don't mean that! I mean that I have not exactly made up my mind where to go; and yet I fancy I'd better take my way to Carlton House, or across the Park to the Horse Guards. Surely I ought to be safe there!"

"Anywhere your Highness pleases."

"Come on, then! I will go to Carlton House. I wish I could see Willes! I wonder where Willes is?"

It will be remembered that at one end of the Titian Gallery there was a short flight of stairs which led to a guard-room usually in the occupa- of the Yeomen, and that very close to that was a door which led directly out into the Colour Court of St. James's Palace.

This was the route which the Dark Woman, accompanied by her associates and the Regent, took.

Linda de Chevenaux knew perfectly well the danger she had to encounter.

One or two of the real Yeomen would be sure to be in this guard-room, for it was one of the posts about the Palace never deserted by night or by day.

She could not but feel a well-grounded appre-hension that some obstruction would here take place; and if it did, as a last resource, the Regent would have to discover himself.

The stairs were descended, and the small guard-room was reached.

There were two Yeomen there, but one was lying asleep upon a bench, and the other was leaning upon his partizan.

The tramp of the Dark Woman and her party down the staircase had aroused this man's atten-tion, and he at once started into an attitude of vigilance.

He happened to be one of those persons of slow comprehension who are a good while taking in a fact; and in this case he was all the longer, inas-much as two facts came upon him at once, which jostled each other in his brain.

One fact was, that he saw the uniforms of his own corps; and the next was, that he did not know a single soul composing the party that approached his post.

The Dark Woman neither looked to the right nor to the left.

The Regent pulled his hat low down over his brow, and Linda de Chevenaux's band marched on like so many statues, paying not the remotest attention to the bewildered Yeoman.

The small, octagonal hall, immediately within the outer doorway, was reached. The door itself was flung open, and without even a challenge from the astonished Yeoman, the party passed out into the Colour Court.

It was a dull and cloudy morning.

The Yeoman shouldered his partizan, and ran to the door to look after the mysterious guard that had passed his post. His eyes were wider open than usual, and so was his mouth; but he had only as yet reached that state of surprise, and it would be some minutes before any action suggested itself to him.

Those few minutes were everything to the Dark Woman.

With the Regent at her side, she marched across the Colour Court. It did not take forty steps to reach the arched entrance so well known beneath the clock tower of St. James's Palace.

The sentinel there was a soldier of the Foot Guards, and from him neither surprise nor inquiry was to be expected.

All he did was to mutter to himself something about those stupid Beef-eaters being out rather early.

Linda de Chevenaux, the Regent, and her band were out in St. James's Street.

"Halt!" said the Prince. "Right face! We're not so bewildered as to forget that Carlton House lies in this direction!"

"Close up!" said the Dark Woman.

The band closed up so closely round the Regent and herself that they were both hidden from ob-servation: not, indeed, that there was anybody in particular to observe them, except the sentinel at the Palace gate, and a drowsy-looking watchman who had stopped at a post about three parts down St. James's Street, and was putting out his lantern, since the daylight was sufficiently strong that there was no further occasion for it.

The Dark Woman then faced the Regent, and raising to the level of his face a small pistol, the stock of which was entirely of silver richly inlaid with gold threads, she kept the muzzle steadily pointed at him as she spoke.

"George, Prince of Wales and Regent of Eng-land, the danger to which allusion has been made in the Palace only now commences. Raise the slightest alarm, or by word or gesture bring sus-picion upon what is going on here, and you die!"

The Regent was paralysed with terror.

"There is no wish, no desire, not the remotest intention to take your life or do you any injury; but you must place yourself at our disposal for the next two hours."

"Two hours?"

"About that."

"But who—what——"

"It is needless to make the inquiry who and what we are. You will never know. All you have to do is to march with us whither I please to lead you, and as gracefully and as calmly as the circumstances will allow, submit to an interview with one who adopts this mode of obtaining it."

"Betrayed!" said the Regent. "The Dark Woman!"

"Will you do this; or, as a lesser evil, will you think it better to be left a corpse here in the open street?"

"Lesser evil? By Jove! What do you mean, sir, by lesser evil? Don't speak of corpses to me!"

"Then you consent?"

The Regent was tall, so that he could see past the heads of some of the Dark Woman's com-panions; and before he replied he cast wistful glances about him, in the hope that something would occur to release him from his decidedly un-pleasant situation.

"It is in vain!" said the Dark Woman. "Your Highness wastes time."

"But if anybody interferes it is not my fault."

"The result will be the same."

"Result? What do you mean by result?"

"Death!"

The Regent had been trying, by various con-tortions of the countenance, to catch the attention of the sentinel at the gate of St. James's Palace; but upon these words of the Dark Woman he suddenly dropped his eyes, and rather shrunk from observation than courted it.

"Where—where," he said, "in the name of heaven do you want to take me?"

"To Hanover Square. There your Highness will find the lady who desires an interview with you."

"A dark lady?"

"I say no more. The interview will take place; and, fair or dark, your Highness will be able to judge for yourself. Are you content?"

"Not at all; but it seems I cannot help it."

"Just so! March!"

It was quite evident that although the Regent strove to assume a command over his fears, and to speak in tones as though he considered he was not in any danger, yet in reality he suffered from great trepidation.

In vain he looked about him for some succour. At that early hour no one appeared in the streets of a character to render him any assistance.

And, indeed, disguised as he was, and marching along with a party of the Yeomen of the Guard, it was not at all likely that any one would have thought proper to interfere unless from an absolute recognition of his features.

The order to march, which the Dark Woman

had given, was obeyed at once, and the party took the route which was nearest towards Hanover Square.

Linda de Chevenaux had noticed on the preceding evening that that same house she had previously occupied in the aristocratic square, and from which she had been compelled to beat so hasty a retreat, was without a tenant.

That probably some one was minding the mansion she could readily imagine, but upon that head she anticipated no difficulty; for she had made up her mind there to convey the Regent, and to hold with him the conversation which had been suggested by Annie, Countess de Blonde.

Perhaps nothing could be a bolder act on the part of the Dark Woman than to cross the threshold of that house again; but the very boldness of the proceeding brought with it its own safety.

Who would look there for the fine lady who had been compelled to leave the establishment so suddenly, and in pursuit of whom some of the most active police-officers of the metropolis were engaged?

It had occurred to the Dark Woman for a moment that it would be as well to convey the Regent to that mysterious house in Frith Street, Soho; but even to her imagination that place wore an aspect of gloom, and without some absolute necessity she wished never again to cross its threshold.

Through the few streets at the west-end of the town which intervened between St. James's Palace and Hanover Square the Dark Woman and her party made their way without the slightest interruption.

On the ample doorstep of the mansion which Linda de Chevenaux had so recently occupied with such grace, and state, and dignity, stood the foremost of the party.

She herself held the Regent by the arm.

"Whose house is this?—whose house is this?" asked the Prince of Wales; and he spoke now in more confident tones than before, because he was not conducted, as he expected to be, notwithstanding what the seeming officer of the Yeomen had said, to some dark and dismal region of the metropolis, where he would be removed from all aid.

"This is the house of the sufferer and of the avenger!" said the Dark Woman.

The Regent did not seem inclined to pursue a conversation which contained such ill-omened words; but he looked wistfully up and down the square, in the hope that somebody would appear who would step forward and ask some question concerning the meaning of the singular assemblage of which he formed a portion.

"I shall not be able to help it," he said,—"it will not be my fault if these outrageous proceedings are interrupted by some one."

"It will be your Royal Highness's misfortune."

"Misfortune?—my misfortune? I don't see that. It will be your misfortune, whoever you are; for it will probably end in your apprehension."

"Any interruption, from whatever cause, which compromises our safety, will be the signal of death to your Royal Highness."

"Good gracious! Is that just—is that reasonable?"

The Dark Woman made a sign to one of her associates, who, from previous experience, she knew was an adept at that kind of work, to open the door of the house.

This was quickly accomplished, so far as the lock was concerned, by an apparently slight-looking skeleton key.

The door yielded, but only to the extent of two or three inches; and then it was abruptly checked by a chain drawn across it on the inside.

The Dark Woman saw the obstruction at once.

Time was precious.

"Some one is in keeping of the house," she said; "descend—descend! There must be no delay. Make way through the basement and admit us."

These words she addressed to one of her party, who, leaving his partizan against the side of the door, began to climb over the area rails.

But all this took up time; and the Regent became hopeful, while the Dark Woman began to glare about her with an aspect of despair.

One of the band then spoke.

"See, master," he said, "the fan-light at the top of the door has been broken to pieces, and from the inner side it is merely pasted up with paper. I will open the door for you much quicker than any way can be made through the lower part of the house."

"Do so."

The man who suggested this mode of procedure was young, light, small, and active. Borrowing the shoulders of a comrade for a moment, he broke his way through the fan-light, very much after the fashion that that boy, who had been hired by the housebreaker upon a previous occasion, had accomplished the feat.

The door was flung open.

"Enter!" said the Dark Woman.

The Regent lingered for a moment; but the band closed up behind him, and he was half forced into the hall of the splendid mansion.

The Dark Woman kept her hand upon his arm. Perhaps she was scarcely conscious of the nervous clutch with which she held it; but she left there the mark of her fingers.

Across the hall, with its statuary and fading evergreens, for they were now neglected, and up the grand staircase, the Dark Woman took her way.

The followers seemed to understand, by signs, what she wished of them; and two stayed to keep guard in the hall.

Another opened the door, which led to the domestic regions of the house; and as they all felt assured that some one was minding the premises, he bent forward and listened intently.

The rest of the band followed the Dark Woman and the Regent.

They reached the landing of the first-floor, from whence opened those magnificent saloons, in one of which we have seen the Dark Woman on a previous occasion.

She flung the folding-doors open.

"Your Royal Highness will enter this apartment."

It was some satisfaction to the Regent to see that the drawing-room into which he was ushered was a costly one, and elaborately furnished

The folding-doors were closed, and the band kept watch without. The Dark Woman pointed to a chair of costly design, resplendent in gilding and crimson silk. The Regent sunk down upon it without a word; and then, as though she had been a spectre, who, having conducted him so far, had performed her errand on earth, the Dark Woman opened a single door of communication to the adjoining rooms, and disappeared.

The Regent was alone.

That is to say, to all appearance he was alone, although in his own mind he thought it very possible that such might not be the case.

He thought it prudent to sit still and look about him, and then he shook a little, partly with cold—for the atmosphere of the room had a damp and unoccupied feel about it,—and partly with apprehension with what was to happen next.

But as all continued so calm, so quiet, and so still about him, the Regent began to gather courage, and to think that after all it might want but some small effort on his part to rescue himself from the uncomfortable situation in which he was.

He rose from that crimson and gilt chair, which was as costly and as comfortable as any he could find in Carlton House, and made two steps towards the range of five windows that fronted Hanover Square

The moment he did so he was startled by a most significant admonition to be quiet.

There came a heavy crushing blow on one of the panels of the folding-doors that led from the landing at the top of the grand staircase into that saloon: and right through the splintered panel protruded a portion of the ancient, curiously-shaped steel mounting at the top of one of the partisans in use by the Yeomen of the Guard.

"Ah!" exclaimed the Regent.

He sank back into the depths of the magnificent chair again.

He was watched—that was quite clear. Some eye was upon him, and his every movement was undergoing a scrutiny at once provoking and subversive of any attempt to escape.

The Regent now gave up his position as hopeless.

"I can't help it!—I can't help it!" he said. "This woman has power that I cannot resist. But this can't go on. Something must happen either to her or to me which shall put an end to the intolerable persecution."

Then the Regent turned pale and grasped the arms of the chair. From the still and stagnant atmosphere of that house had come to his ears the faint echoes of a scream.

What was it? Was murder doing in that place, so rich, rare, and costly to look at, and yet with such an air of mystery about it?

The Regent lost his dread of the partizan and the broken panel. He sprang to his feet, and with a bound was at one of the windows.

"Hold!" cried a voice. "George, Regent of England, time was when Linda de Chevenaux was heard approaching by the pulsations of the heart that now scorns her."

The Regent's back was towards the voice that thus addressed him, but he turned rapidly as the well-remembered tones came upon his ears; and standing close to the gilt and crimson chair which he had just quitted, he saw a female form richly attired, dazzling with jewels, and perfectly brilliant in general appearance.

It was Linda de Chevenaux.

The Linda he had known and loved twenty years before, attired as she had been attired on that day when the nuptials had taken place which she fondly thought had made her Princess of Wales.

All was perfect as a repetition of the part but the youth and the beauty which had charmed the heart and the sight of the sybarite and the voluptuary.

Twenty years of scorn—twenty years of oppression and of suffering—twenty years of fierce and desperate passions, all wasted in the vain struggle against a destiny which was all but accomplished at the very commencement of that period of time —could not pass over the fairest face without leaving their traces behind them.

It was the Linda de Chevenaux he saw, but not the Linda of other years.

The rich robes had lost none of their lustre, the jewels sparkled as brilliantly as of old; but the once fair girl to whom they had scarce added a charm had vanished for ever.

CHAPTER CXCIV.

THE DARK WOMAN MAKES A PROPOSITION TO THE REGENT, AND THE HOUSE IN HANOVER SQUARE IS THE SCENE OF A CONFLICT.

THE appearance of Linda de Chevenaux was to the eyes of the Prince of Wales almost an apparition.

Associating her so long, as he had done in his own mind, by the terrible images conjured up by the name of the Dark Woman, he had forgotten what once she was.

He was not a man to dwell upon the reminiscences of the past, for they were to him full of broken vows; and the shadow of a present persecution was sufficient to him to obliterate every beauty and every excellence which had formed the charm of a past communion.

No wonder, then, that it came upon him with all the shock of a surprise that the Linda de Chevenaux of the past could even be so far presented to him again as she was presented by that image of beauty and luxury as to awaken even the memory of what she had been.

But vexation was mingled with that surprise, for he had heard among his associates a saying which was the invention of Sheridan, in one of those ribald moments, when, after the suppers at Carlton House, the riot of imagination mingled with the riot of drink.

The saying was to the effect that "an attempt to resuscitate an extinguished passion was like a feeble effort to re-cook a ragout;" and in fact nothing could be more obnoxious to George, Prince of Wales and Regent of England, than the repeated attempts which had been made from time to time to invest with a new life his forgotten passions.

An intrigue once over, he was apt to say, had all the flavour of an unsnuffed candle.

After, then, the first glance at Linda de Chevenaux, gorgeously attired as she was, and presenting to his sated eyes as she did the relic of her former beauty, a feeling of repulsion and abhorrence came over the heart of the Regent.

Linda de Chevenaux saw the look with which he regarded her.

She saw the facial expression of dislike.

She saw the slight movement of the hands which might have escaped a less acute observer, and she felt that the experiment had been tried, and had failed.

From the ashes of the Regent's former passion for her never again could the slightest approach to a flame be kindled.

And this Dark Woman—called dark on account of her deeds, and because she chose by such a name to mystify the perceptions of those who would otherwise have recognised her as who she once was—might still have been comely and pleasant to look upon, but for the wild storms of angry feeling which had passed over her heart.

Tempests of the soul which would surely leave their traces behind them.

And we must remember, too, that Linda de Chevenaux had suffered much by her long imprisonment in the cell of a madhouse.

Truly was she to be pitied; and probably to herself the change in her appearance was not so great as it appeared to the Regent.

Perhaps she thought that when she washed off the brown stain with which she obscured her complexion, and when she permitted to be released from their confinement the still handsome tresses of her long fair hair, she was still something of the Linda de Chevenaux of the years long fled.

That was a mistake.

The lines which passion and despair had traced upon the brow and face, the strange light that perpetual excitements had produced about the eyes, together with many changes which the hand of time had wrought in its own delicate and tender fashion, made her to the eyes of the Regent as different from the Linda de Chevenaux of twenty years ago as a piece of cut-glass could be to the brightest diamond in his princely crown.

The silence that ensued between these two persons was oppressive.

To the Dark Woman it seemed as though the atmosphere were thickening around her.

"You know me," she said.

The voice was harsh and grating.

The Regent's lips parted twice before he replied, and then if he had searched the whole vocabulary of the English language, he could not have hit upon a reply that would have touched her more keenly.

And yet, probably, the words he used were accidental.

"I did once."

That was the Regent's reply, and to the vivid perceptions of the Dark Woman they seemed to convey a world of meaning.

If ever for a moment she had cherished the dream that the Regent was to look upon her with the slightest remembrance of the affection of other years, that dream vanished.

She need ask no more questions—she need suggest nothing else of the past either to him or to herself.

It had all fled!

There remained but one congratulation in her mind, and that was, that whatever she now chose to say he was compelled to listen to.

She thrust back, so to speak, her heart into those cavernous recesses of pride and vengeful feeling from which it had for a moment emerged.

She had been Linda de Chevenaux for a moment.

Now she was the Dark Woman again.

And who shall say at this juncture what one kind word—one tender look from the Regent might have achieved for that wandering, bewildered soul?

But the opportunity was past.

There was the Dark Woman, and there was her prisoner.

She clutched the back of the chair close to which she stood until her nails sunk deep into the crimson silk covering.

"Tell me George, Regent of England," she said, "why am I thus defamed and persecuted because I had the misfortune to believe that you once loved me?"

The Regent now stood in a sidelong position close to one of the windows; and if he had one eye on the proceedings of the Dark Woman, he had certainly another directed into the open square, with the hope that he might see somebody coming to his rescue.

"That is good—that is good!" he said. "You, Linda de Chevenaux, talk of persecution; you who have never left me a quiet moment for years past; you who have brought upon yourself everything you have suffered, just because you would not leave me alone."

"And have I not suffered?"

"Yes, reflectively."

"Reflectively? What mean you by the use of that word? Do you believe me dead to all reflection?"

"No, no. You take it in the wrong sense. I mean to say that whatever you suffered was a kind of reflection of what you tried to make me suffer—that is to say, of your annoyances to me. In plain language, I mean if you had left me alone, I should have left you alone."

"I comprehend you."

"I'm glad of it."

"You mean to say that deceit, desertion, and a broken heart, were all nothing."

"I said no such thing; but if you want me to say what I really do think, I will say it."

"What is it?"

"Why, that nothing can be more profitless than this discussion."

"George, Regent of England and Prince of Wales, I'm not so sure of that."

"What's the use—what's the use? You certainly seem to have a gang of people about you who do your bidding, or you have suborned some of my people to do it. I suppose you don't want to murder me, or you would hardly seek the drawing-room of a house in Hanover Square for the purpose. What, then, do you seek?"

"I am dangerous."

"By Jove, I always thought so!"

"And consequently you are in danger. But I have a proposition to make to you."

"Oh, I guess it! I'll tell it to you beforehand. It is to proclaim you Princess of Wales; to tell the world I have committed a little genteel bigamy; brand with illegitimacy the Princess Charlotte, and to declare your son, Fitz George, the heir-apparent after me. That's the little proposal; and, for modesty, I must say it outbids anything I ever heard of."

"It would be just!"

"Ha, ha! Of course—of course! I knew it."

"Just because it is true!"

"Oh, yes; of course—of course!"

"But it was not that which I had to propose to you."

"Oh!"

"Although based upon these facts."

"Indeed?"

"No. It is this. Provided it should happen in the course of events that Caroline of Brunswick should depart from this life——"

The Regent uttered an exclamation, and shook his head.

"Some men are lucky," he said, "but I'm afraid it won't be my fate."

"If such should be the case, and if, likewise,

your daughter, the Princess Charlotte, should fall an early victim to the grave——"

"My daughter? No, no. So young—so—so full of life—on the threshold of her marriage with Leopold of Saxe-Coburg! No, Linda de Chevenaux—no! That daughter you mentioned is destined to be Queen of England when I am—that is to say, when I—for I suppose it cannot be avoided at some very, very distant period indeed —when I am—am dead. Well, there, I've said dead!"

The Dark Woman made an impatient gesture.

"If these two events should happen, would you then acknowledge him, whom you call Fitz George, to be your legitimate son?"

"And you the Princess of Wales," added the Regent, with a sarcastic bow.

"No. Look at this."

"At what?"

"This ring. You see, to all appearance, it presents a flat surface, and seems an ordinary signet-ring with a stone of little value. Touch this spring at the side, and the stone flies up on a concealed hinge."

"What then? I've half a dozen such rings. They hold scents and essences in a cavity, which, being subtle and volatile, find their way out, and cast a pleasant perfume."

"Yes; but in the cavity of this one lurks a deadly poison. I have but to touch it with my lip and it is instant death. Behold it!"

"Keep off!—keep off! Don't come near me with it! I don't want any of your deadly poisons! Keep away!—keep away! Who knows? Perhaps the very—very perfume of it may be dangerous! The air of the room may be half poisoned with it! I feel a sort of vertigo already!"

"I promise—I solemnly promise—I make a vow in the name of that heaven above us that now hears my words,—that on the day when you, in writing, acknowledge Fitz George to be your legitimate son, I will die!"

"Suicide?"

"Call it what you will. I remove an encumbrance from your path, as I remove encumbrances from my path."

The Prince of Wales clasped his hands, and uttered an exclamation of horror.

"Encumbrances?—encumbrances? You have mentioned two, Caroline of Brunswick, my—" the Regent made a grimace before he uttered the word—"wife; and my daughter Charlotte. Woman—woman, what do you mean? What do your words imply? Have you no conscience—no fears? Would you pursue your objects, and reach your purposes, by strewing your path to them with the corpses of murdered people?"

"Do you consent?"

"Consent to what?"

"To the terms I propose."

"Never! Of course not! Stuff!—stuff!"

A dark shade seemed to pass over Linda de Chevenaux's countenance. She compressed her lips until they became perfectly white, and then she said, in low, hissing tones, "Listen! I intend to be prophetic. That daughter, whom your selfish nature seems to feel some affection for, shall wed the man to whom she has given her wavering fancy; but ere one year has passed away a nation shall be in mourning, and the royal vault at Windsor shall receive the corpse of Charlotte of Wales."

"No, no! You are mad—mad! It is not in the course of nature but that even you—although murder might speak out of every action of your life—can be guarded against as something too dangerous to allow to breathe the common air with people who are masters of their actions."

The Dark Woman spoke again, in the same low, hissing tones.

"Caroline of Brunswick shall likewise prematurely drop into the grave; and when you find yourself a wifeless, childless man—unloving and unloved—we shall meet again!"

"Before that—long before that," cried the Regent, with passion, "I will have you arrested, if it costs me ten thousand pounds for the capture. I will pay—that is, I will owe—any amount of money to those who will secure you, and keep you from perpetrating the diabolical mischief you contemplate."

"And you?" said the Dark Woman.

"What of me?"

"You forget."

"What do I forget? Eh?"

"Where you are, and what I am. At a word from me, those men who brought you hither would commit an act that would convulse England and astonish Europe; while it at the same time altered the succession."

"Murder!"

"I did not say murder; but your life is in my hands."

The Regent struck his open left hand with his closed right, and in a voice which for energy rather astonished the Dark Woman, he exclaimed, "I don't believe it—I don't believe it. Those men you mention, disguised as Yeomen of the Guard, have assisted you for some great pecuniary bribe to bring me here; but I don't believe for a moment that they would every one of them voluntarily consign themselves to an ignominious death on the scaffold for the sake of carrying out your revenges."

This was so exactly the truth, that the Dark Woman shook a little as she heard the words.

"I did not threaten," she said. "I have the power, but I did not say that I would use it. Listen!"

With a clear, bell-like sound a clock in the room struck the hour of nine.

"You will remain here till mid-day," added the Dark Woman. "On your honour you will promise not to leave this room until the hands of that clock point to the hour of twelve."

"I will promise nothing of the sort."

"Shall it be war?" cried the Dark Woman, her eyes flashing with fury.

"War or not," said the Regent, "I will no longer put up with the indignity of being a prisoner here. Ah! a chance! This is fortune indeed! Help! help! help! Hilloa! Help! help! Treason! treason!"

The Regent had the whole time of this interview with Linda de Chevenaux kept himself tolerably close to one of the windows of the drawing-room, and from time to time—as we have before remarked—he had cast the most anxious glances into Hanover Square in the hope of seeing some one pass whom he knew, and to whom he could call for aid.

Fortune exceeded his expectations; for just at this crisis in his interview with the Dark Woman, when he began to think it just probable he might be compelled to remain in that house until the hour she had mentioned, he saw crossing obliquely at the corner of the square two officers of the Foot Guards in conversation.

It scarcely needed a second glance to convince him that one of these officers was Captain Fitz George.

Here was a chance not to be lightly thrown away

It might be dangerous to call for aid, but it might be just as dangerous—if not more so—to remain where he was; so the Regent seized a book which lay upon a small table near at hand, just within his reach, and dashing with it one of the panes of glass in the window to pieces—an act, which of itself, made some noise, and induced the two officers to look up—he shouted, as we have described, through the broken window for aid.

The Dark Woman immediately clapped her hands together, and the folding-doors of the saloon were flung open.

There was a look of excitement and terror upon the faces of the three or four of her band who there showed themselves, still in their dresses as Yeomen of the Guard, and with long steel-pointed partizans in their hands.

"Help! Hoy! Hilloa!" cried the Regent, still through the broken glass.

The Dark Woman pointed to him.

"Remove that man," she said.

The words were suspicious. They might mean simply take him away from the window—or, by a stretch of imagination, they might be construed into meaning "remove him from life to death."

The Regent took the alarm, and shutting his eyes and folding his arms about him, he went backward bodily through the window on to the balcony, which he reached amid the ruin of its framework, and in the midst of an avalanche of broken glass.

The Dark Woman uttered a shriek of rage, for she felt now that the danger of herself and of her associates was very great—simply because not intending the death of the Regent, he was therefore enabled to place her and her band in a most critical situation.

CHAPTER CXCV.

THE DARK WOMAN IS ARRESTED AND CONVEYED TO GILTSPUR STREET COMPTER.

WHEN the Regent broke that first pane of glass with the book, and called out so loudly for aid into Hanover Square that it was quite evident the royal lungs were not at all affected, Captain Fitz George, and the officer of the Guards who was walking with him, looked up to the house from whence the alarm proceeded in the most profound astonishment.

They were both as familiar as possible, not only with the voice of the Regent, but with every feature of his face.

Of his identity they could not have the slightest doubt; but they were for a few moments lost in astonishment at his presence there at such an hour in the morning.

Before the two officers could recover from their first surprise, although their intention was undoubtedly to assail the house, they saw that violent burst with which the Regent came through the entire window.

Situated where they were, they could not come to any defined conclusion as to whether the Regent had been thrust through the window or had voluntarily adopted that mode of getting on to the balcony.

Be that as it might, however, they had but one course to pursue, and that was to get into the house for the protection of the Regent as quickly as possible.

Such an enterprise, however, might have been fatal to the two young men, had it not been that, in perfect ignorance of who they were, the Dark Woman gave an order to her band, which she thought would necessarily make it so.

"Admit at once," she cried, "whoever knocks at the door of this house, but for your own safety's sake let them not live beyond its threshold."

Little did the Dark Woman suppose that in giving this order she was compromising the safety of one who was dearer to her than life itself.

But the Regent knew it.

From the many persecutions he had undergone, as well as from the conversation he had just had with Linda de Chevenaux, he was well aware how every hope—every aspiration of her existence was bound up in the life of Captain Fitz George.

We must not deny either to the Prince of Wales—even in the midst of all the selfishness of the voluptuary—some feeling for the young man he knew to be his own son.

And although, from all that had passed, he believed that his own life was perfectly safe, and that none of the associates of the Dark Woman would think of raising a hand against him, they might have no such tenderness as regarded Captain Fitz George, because the fears of the consequences were by no means so great.

The Regent felt that by keeping silence he might inflict a terrible blow upon the Dark Woman, for he might leave her son to be murdered in the hall of that house by her orders.

But the blow would recoil upon himself.

A few words would save Captain Fitz George, and it is doing him but common justice to say that the Regent uttered those words with all the precipitation and haste in his power.

"Hold!—hold! Forebear, Linda de Chevenaux!" he cried; "you know not what you say. It is Fitz George!—your own son, whom I have seen crossing the square, and to whom I have called for aid."

The Dark Woman uttered a scream.

"Would you sacrifice him to your wild insane rage?"

"No—no! Save him!—save him! Injure not one hair of his head! Save him!—save him!"

The Dark Woman rushed from that splendid apartment, and passing her bewildered associates, the mock Yeomen of the Guard, she flew down to the hall of the mansion upon the wings of fear.

The two young officers, however, had had time to reach the door-step and knock violently at the door; and as the first order of the Dark Woman to admit any one who knocked had been uttered in a voice which reached the hall, those of her associates who were there obeyed it.

The door was flung open.

Captain Fitz George, with his drawn sword in his hand, stood upon the topmost step for a moment, to be well upon his guard, and then made a rush into the hall.

One of the Dark Woman's band strove to strike him down with his partizan; but Fitz George eluded the blow by stooping, and the long, awkward, cumbrous weapon missed his head, but made a severe indentation in the shoulder of a marble statue that was in the hall.

It was at this juncture that the Dark Woman reached the scene of action.

She flung herself headlong into the conflict which Captain Fitz George was waging against such odds; and, indeed, the surprise he felt at seeing himself surrounded by those he thought Yeomen of the Guard, had for the moment almost paralysed his exertions, and certainly saved the life of the one who attacked him: for he could have run that man through the body with his sword, had he not paused a moment in his astonishment at the sight of the King's uniform on these persons.

The Dark Woman then flung herself—so to speak—on Fitz George.

With one hand she grasped his sword-blade, while she placed the other on his shoulder.

"Not hurt—not hurt?" she cried. "Say that you are not hurt, or all is lost!"

"My mother!" exclaimed Captain Fitz George.

"His mother?" echoed the Dark Woman's band.

It was evident that they had no knowledge of Linda de Chevenaux under the aspect she then wore.

No one of them had seen her in the costume befitting her sex, and deprived of this disguise of false hair and darkened complexion, which had assimilated her physically to the name her acts had obtained for her of the Dark Woman.

But they had little time to think, and certainly they had no time to make inquiries as to who and what this splendidly-dressed lady was who came like an apparition upon the scene, and was acknowledged by the young officer of the Guard, who had answered to the cries for help of the Regent, as his mother.

A far more dangerous state of things was to them rapidly ensuing.

The officer who had been walking with Fitz George was adopting a course of action which would very speedily make the position of the Dark Woman and her associates in that house untenable.

On the hasty recommendation of Fitz George this officer stood on the doorstep of the house, and called aloud, "Watch!—watch! Help!—help! Treason!—treason! The Regent is in danger! Treason!"

Windows began to open in many houses of the Square. Several chance passengers hurried to the spot; and then, from the opening doors of some of the houses, gentlemen, with such strong weapons as they could snatch up on the impulse of the moment, began to make their appearance.

The Regent had certainly appeared to be in danger, but the Dark Woman and her band were now in far greater peril.

"Fly!" she cried. "Fly and save yourselves! I am the master!"

That was the name they always gave her; and now that she spoke to them in the voice she usually assumed in addressing them, they began to recognise in this lady, sparking with jewels, and radiant in a costume which, although somewhat behind the fashion, was still magnificent, the bold, determined spirit to whom they owed allegiance.

They paused for a moment.

They looked hesitatingly at each other.

"Fly and save yourselves!" said the Dark Woman. "We shall meet again!"

They hesitated no longer.

One only cried out aloud, "The jewels!—the jewels!"

"Safe!" answered the Dark Woman.

They flung down their partizans in the hall, and while Linda de Chevenaux still held Captain Fitz George with a tenacity that would not be shaken off, or that he felt he could not shake off without doing her some personal injury, the whole of the band made a rush from the house, knocking down, right and left, every one who opposed them.

There was no practical pursuit of these men, —although there would have been but for the indiscreet conduct of the Regent himself.

He continued in the balcony of the house, making himself so prominent, and keeping up such a succession of shouts and outcries, that he detained everybody there upon the spot; and although he would have given something considerable—or perhaps owed something considerable, as he was in the habit of saying—for the capture of those mock Yeomen of the Guard, or any of them, yet was he the direct means of aiding in their escape.

Nothing, however, was really further from the intention of the Regent than to do this; but he was not cool, and calm, and collected enough to calculate the effect which his presence would have in the balcony of the house.

The morning was still young, and a throng of desperate men at that hour was not likely to meet with any very effective opposition.

They soon placed a few streets between them and Hanover Square, and there they separated, each one taking care of himself, until they were quickly lost in the awakening population of London.

But what was to become of the Dark Woman?

She did not think of herself at that moment.

Her only perception was that she had saved her son, and that she held him partially embraced; and so handsome, so brave, so noble did he look, that, for a few moments, she forgot the Regent—her own danger—the alarm which had echoed through Hanover Square — and the dozen or so persons that thronged the doorstep of the house.

"For the love of heaven, mother," cried Captain Fitz George, "tell me the meaning of all this? What wild, mad project have you been carrying out, that has brought you into this danger?"

"Danger?" cried the Dark Woman; "there is no danger for your sake!"

"Nay, mother, it is your danger that I speak of—not any of my own."

Linda de Chevenaux still held the arm of Captain Fitz George, but his last words seemed to arouse her to something like a sense of her position.

At that moment, too, there was a rush of several persons into the hall; and although those persons could not take upon themselves to say that the elegantly attired lady they saw was in any way implicated in what seemed to them to be some atrocious attempt upon the life of the Regent, yet any attempt of hers to leave the house at that juncture would necessarily excite suspicion.

Moreover, the Dark Woman was not attired for parading the streets of London.

She had no head-dress whatever, and her whole costume was far more fitted for a presentation at Court than a promenade in Hanover Square.

She began to feel the difficulties of her position.

She whispered to Fitz George, "A coach!—a coach! It is over. I have made an attempt for our sake, my son, and it has failed. Get me a coach, and let me leave this place. Your mother is in danger!"

Fitz George was torn by conflicting emotions. What should he do?

Had he not told himself, over and over again that he would devote every spare moment of his time to a discovery of his mother, and that then it would be his duty to place her somewhere in safety.

And now—now that chance, or accident, had brought him face to face with her—was he to surrender that idea, and leave her to wander out into the world again, the slave of her own wild passions and caprices?

Fitz George hesitated.

"You, too—you, too!" cried the Dark Woman, —"you impede me?"

"No, no; but—but——"

This brief conversation between the Dark Woman and her son was at this instant brought to a sudden termination; for the Regent, finding himself alone—and seeing, from his position on the balcony, that there was no one in the drawing-room to impede him—thought it advisable to make his way down stairs.

He appeared in the hall at the moment that the Dark Woman was looking with tender reproach into the eyes of her son.

"Seize that woman!—seize that woman!" cried the Regent. "A thousand pounds reward!"

Linda de Chevenaux made a movement to escape, but she saw that it was futile. She would have to make her way through a crowd of enemies, without the real means of repelling one.

Indeed, a sort of rush was made to lay hands upon her, but that was what Captain Fitz George would not permit; and as the Dark Woman shrank back from the open door—seeing how useless it was to attempt to pass through it—Captain Fitz George placed himself partially before her, with his drawn sword in his hand.

"Hold!" he said; "he who lays a hand on this lady is a dead man!"

There was something terribly in earnest about the looks of Captain Fitz George; and no one—even for the sake of the thousand pounds offered by the Regent—thought it worth while to risk the reception of some six inches of cold steel from the sword of that resolute young officer.

"Seize her!—seize her!" cried the Prince. "I command every one here present to aid and assist in the capture of that woman."

"Oh, your Royal Highness," said Captain Fitz George, in a voice of entreaty, "do not forget who and what she is?"

"By Jove! I'm not likely to forget it, after this morning, if my memory could have proved ever so treacherous before."

"But your Highness, she is—she is——."

"Linda de Chevenaux."

"And my mother!"

The Regent was shaken for a moment; but the idea of letting the Dark Woman go after the escapade of that morning, and the alarming events of the night in St. James's Palace, was something too much for the Regent to do on the mere score of sentiment.

"I cannot help it, Fitz George," he said; "I cannot help it! We will talk about it another time, and see what can be done; but Linda de Chevenaux must not be allowed to escape."

"Father!" said Fitz George, in a very low tone, so that none but the Regent could hear him.

The Regent placed his hand upon the young officer's arm, and replied in the same whispered tones.

"Your own reason, Fitz George, tells you I am right."

Fitz George felt that this was true.

"For her sake," added the Regent, "as well as for mine—for yours, for everybody's."

"Alas! it is too true."

"Then say no more—say no more!"

Fitz George lowered the point of his sword.

The Regent raised his voice.

"Is there a constable present?"

"Yes, your gracious honourable Majesty's worship," cried a man, elbowing his way through the crowd at the door, and exhibiting ostentatiously one of those small symbols of authority, in the shape of a constable's staff, with a little gilt crown at the end of it,—"yes your royal worship and majestic highness, I'm a constable."

"I give that woman into your custody."

"Now, mum."

"Hands off, sir!" said Fitz George. "Wherever it will be your duty to take this lady I shall accompany you—but touch her at your peril."

"It matters not!" said the Dark Woman.

Those were the only words she had spoken for some few minutes.

"Take her away—take her away!" said the Regent.

"Yes, your gracious worship, I will. I'm a constable of the Compter, your royal Majesty. I does duty on the lock sometimes, and sometimes I comes out on a nabbing lay."

"What does he mean?" said the Regent. "Is the man mad?"

"I grabs the knowin' ones, your splendid royalty; and when they sees me a comin' they *evaporates*."

"I don't understand a word you say, my man; but recollect this woman is in your charge, and you are to convey her to some place of security, on your head be it."

"My 'ed! Bless your royal worship, I won't let her go. Now, mum."

"Fetch a hackney coach," said Captain Fitz George; "let some one run for a hackney coach. There's a crown for the trouble."

A very few minutes sufficed to bring a vehicle to the door; and then the Dark Woman, who had still kept a grasp upon the arm of her son, turned slowly and faced the Regent.

"We shall meet again!" she said.

"I hope not."

"Oh, be assured that we shall meet again!"

"Take her away—take her away! We will communicate with the Governor of the Compter—if that's the prison she is to be consigned to—in the course of the day. In the meantime, at our charge, she is to be kept in safe custody."

The Dark Woman said not another word, but suffered herself to be handed into the coach; whatever were her intentions or schemes at that

No. 88.—DARK WOMAN.

moment—and there can be no doubt that she had plenty of both—it was evident that she considered her policy was silence and submission.

Despite a dissentient gesture from the Regent, Captain Fitz George entered the coach after his mother.

The constable, who was so profuse in his titles of honour to the Regent, would have followed them, but Fitz George prevented him.

"No," he said, "your prisoner will be quite safe, if you ride on the box with the coachman."

"I'd rayther not," said the constable; "when I don't git inside I git's up behind, and then I has the whole consarn before me, and can see what's goin' on."

"As you please—as you please."

The vehicle started, and how the Regent got home to St. James's Palace or to Carlton House, Captain Fitz George had not the remotest idea. The fact was that he walked back in the costume of a Yeoman of the Guard, being very much cheered as he went by a crowd of boys who followed him, and who were quite delighted to catch a "Beef-eater"—as they called him—abroad.

It was a melancholy drive, that of Captain Fitz George and the Dark Woman to the City; and before they had proceeded any distance Fitz George began to feel that he had taken upon himself a duty he had far better have left alone, since it was one in which his sense of what was right contended with his feelings.

It was clear that the Dark Woman looked upon herself as virtually at freedom, and during that drive from Hanover Square to the corner of Newgate Street she hoped to be able to win over what she could not but consider the plastic spirit of so young a man as her son to some of her objects and designs.

A terrible sense of depression came over the mind of Fitz George after the coach had made some little progress.

He clasped his hands despairingly, and spoke in tones of deep emotion to his mother.

"Oh, cease—cease," he said, "this insatiate struggle with the Regent. What can it end in, mother, but despair and perhaps—perhaps——"

"Perhaps what?"

"A death of infamy!"

"I live!"

"Yes, mother, you live now; but there are such things as laws in this country, and they are administered at times rather sharply. You affect to love me——"

"Affect to love you?"

"Yes; I say you affect to love me, and you compel me to use those words although they wring your heart. I say you affect to love me, mother, although by your acts you embitter my existence, and risk—by some terrible death you may come to—leaving me an inheritance of such shame, grief, and sorrow, that the world would no longer possess a charm to wean me from the despair that your remembrance will ever evoke."

"Be calm—be calm. You speak with the tongue of the Regent, and you think of me as one powerless alike to achieve or to avenge."

"There again!—there again! Achieve and avenge! Mother, you can achieve nothing but your own disgrace and destruction; and vengeance is like a sword, the hilt of which is sharper than the blade."

"You know me not."

"Oh, mother, mother, too well I know you! You have suffered much, and your fierce spirit is troubled by that suffering. You feel—you know that you have been mocked, betrayed, ruined, and undone."

"Well?"

"But can you recall the past? If you were to heap a thousand crimes upon your memory would it obliterate one pang or undo one duplicity of the time that is swept away into the ocean of eternity?"

"I like to hear you, George. You speak well. You are a good counsel for the Regent. You plead his cause glibly and eloquently. But still, is he guilty?"

"And what then, mother?"

"Retribution!"

"Retribution? Oh, how a vain word when used by those who would assume the aspects and powers of that providence which alone can inflict it!

Mother, I tell you you use that word retribution and you know not its meaning. Every act—every event in this life has its sequence—a something that follows it. That is retribution."

"It is in vain," said the Dark Woman. "You shall not—cannot turn me from my purpose. While I live I will contend, struggle, and fight with this man—this Regent of England. I may not accomplish my purpose. Accident or the common course of events in process of time may lay him and me both low; but to the last I will fight. I fancy now that the events of last night have made me rich beyond the utmost dreams of avarice."

"Mother, you rave."

"Think so, if it please you; but the time may come when you will have a deeper respect for the motives of your mother, the real Princess of Wales, when some glimmer of success dawns upon her exertions."

"Never!"

"Have you no ambition?"

"None—none of that kind which you would inculcate, and which is a false light to lure one to destruction. It is a false beacon which would lead the bark of one's fortune to a fearful wreck. Mother, I have not your ambition; but I have the ambition to be happy and contented, and to be at peace, and most of all at peace with him whom I must call father—let his conduct have been what it may—for has he not done for me all that his affection could suggest? He has picked me up from a low estate and made me what I am. Step by step I shall rise by his favour, and I rely upon his promises to compensate me as far as possible for every wrong."

Nothing could be a greater aggravation to the Dark Woman than to hear her son talk of gratitude to the Regent.

"You are mad," she cried, "and know not what you say. You are either mad or afflicted with such weakness of soul and heart that I can scarcely believe you to be really the son for whom I have sacrificed a life."

"Mother, let me entreat you," added Captain Fitz George—"let me entreat you to look upon these matters with calmer eyes. You say you are doing all these acts which bring trouble and disgrace upon you for me, and I believe you."

"Alas! alas! you may well believe me."

"I do from my heart, mother; but they will fail in their object. I am already on the road to honour, to preferment, and to happiness. Permit me to follow that path, and be yourself content."

"Never! Look at these, and these."

The Dark Woman from a pocket of her apparel took some of the costly jewels which had been taken from St. James's Palace.

A single glance at these gems of rare price was quite sufficient to convince Fitz George of their extreme value, but he could not conceive where his mother had procured them, and, therefore, he looked upon them with eyes rather of terror than of admiration.

The Dark Woman, in changing her apparel at the house in Hanover Square, had taken from the pockets of her male attire only some few of those jewels which rare good fortune had enabled her to discover secreted in the Palace.

It was these few with which she now tried to dazzle the eyes of her son, but as we have said

Captain Fitz George looked at them mournfully, and they had no effect upon his imagination, although they filled him full of fears.

CHAPTER CXCVI.

THE DARK WOMAN ESCAPES FROM GILTSPUR STREET COMPTER BY A VERY SIMPLE PROCESS, AND PARTS WITH TWO DIAMONDS OF GREAT PRICE.

LINDA de Chevenaux, when she exhibited the jewels to her son, looked into his eyes to see what effect their lustre had upon him.

She saw that they saddened him.

"Are you not human?" she said. "Are you, of the whole family of humanity, free from these glittering temptations?"

"No, mother; I admire all that is beautiful."

"Are not these jewels beautiful?"

"They are, indeed!"

"Behold how the morning light plays upon their glittering surfaces! See how it is shot forth again in sparks of fire! I tell you, my son, that all the rewards the Regent can give you, for being a traitor to your mother—a traitor to yourself—were they summed up together through your whole life—would not exceed the wealth I could place in your hands this morning."

Captain Fitz George shook his head.

"Tell me, mother, how that wealth came into your possession?"

"It is mine!"

"But how?"

"If these glittering jewels were in the hands of the Prince of Wales, they would be his. I am his wife, and I take them, therefore they are mine."

This was a kind of reasoning which Captain Fitz George might well be excused from feeling the force of.

"Mother!" he said, "you mean to say you took these jewels from St. James's Palace?"

"I did."

"Then am I surprised in every way, for the pecuniary difficulties of the Regent are so notorious, that I am truly astonished gems of such value should be accessible to you or any one."

"There was a tradition of their existence, but no one knew where to look for them. I only became aware of the secret place where they were deposited. How that knowledge came to me is of no moment. I have them, and I offer them all to you—for these are but a fraction of those I possess—if you will give up your attachment and dependence upon the Regent, and join your fortunes to mine."

"No, mother, I cannot."

"Think again—oh, think again! These jewels comprise in themselves a princely fortune."

The Dark Woman surely forgot at that moment that she was bound to divide among those men who had been her associates and assistants in her attack upon St. James's Palace, the glittering plunder she had there obtained.

But the jewels were in no danger.

Captain Fitz George was not tempted by their value or their beauty.

"No," he said; "I will not touch them. I will have none of them. I have made my election, mother, and I will abide the issue."

"Base! Degenerate!"

"Nay, hear me out, for what I say now is a sort of a confession of faith, to which, be assured, I shall adhere. I will stay by the side of the Regent, my father, and I will accept his bounty. I will not join with you, mother, in persecuting him; but I will never cease to conjure you to abandon all your wild resolutions, and to be at peace with him, with me, and with yourself."

"Never!"

"You say so now—you say so now; but I will pray to heaven the time may come when your determination will alter. Be assured, however, that although a prisoner now, the influence that I possess over the Regent shall ever be exerted in your favour."

"Prisoner!—influence!—favour! What expressions are these, my son, from you to me?"

"I cannot help them—they are very sad; but they spring out of circumstances which you, mother, have created."

"Stop!"

"I will say no more."

"I do not mean that—I mean that I will go no further. I see we are on the confines of the City, and that is not the route that I would take. Stop, I say!"

"Mother——"

"Do you not obey me?"

"Remember!"

"Remember what? You ask me to forget so much, that it is well that at times you should ask me to remember something."

"Remember you are a prisoner."

"Your prisoner?"

"Not entirely so; but in accompanying you I made myself answerable to the Regent for your safe keeping, and I must keep my word."

A deadly pallor came over the countenance of the Dark Woman, and for the first time she seemed clearly to understand that Captain Fitz George's motive in accompanying her was not for the purpose of deceiving the Regent, and setting her at liberty—but in reality to ensure her detention.

The revulsion of feeling was tremendous.

She seemed as if she could have struck him—killed him then and there in that coach; and then, by a violent effort, she controlled her feelings, and a preternatural calmness came over her.

"Be it so!" she said. "You conduct me to a prison, from which your father would conduct me to a scaffold."

"No, no!—a thousand times, no!"

"But I say a thousand times, yes! You sentence me to a gaol, and play the part of the tip-staff who conducts me thither. Now hear the sentence that I pass upon you."

"Mother, mother, say nothing rashly. These expressions are like curses—they ever recoil upon the heart that utters them."

"I sentence you to silence—silence from me; for from this moment never word will I speak to you."

The coach stopped.

The shadow of the gloomy-looking building in Giltspur Street, which went by the name of "the Compter," fell upon the Dark Woman and her son.

The constable leaped down from behind, where,

as he had said he would, he had taken his station, and a sharp appeal was made at the bell of the wicket-gate of the prison.

"Mother, mother," said Fitz George, "you know—you feel that I am only doing my duty—a duty to you as well as a duty to the Regent, my father. You may call my proceedings by as harsh terms as you please—they shall not offend me, nor will I take any exception at them; for in your own heart you know that I am only consenting you should be held in security in order that some arrangement should be made for your peace and happiness."

The Dark Woman answered not a word.

She looked cold and vacant, and as non-observant of what he said as if only some unusual current of wind had whistled through the carriage.

"Now, mum," said the constable, as he opened the door of the coach, "here we air! It's a nice comfortable crib, the old Compter, though I says it as oughtn't; 'cos you see, mum, in a manner o' speakin', I belongs to it."

Captain Fitz George sprung out of the coach.

He then offered his arm to assist his mother in alighting, but she rejected it with a look of cold disdain, and entered the prison.

Fitz George followed her.

"I wish to see the Governor of the prison," he said.

The constable had already communicated to the official persons on duty in the vestibule that the fine lady he had brought with him in the hackney-coach had been given into custody actually by the Regent himself; and that statement, combined with Captain Fitz George's uniform as an officer of the Guard, invested the whole proceeding with an aspect of peculiar importance to the minds of the officials of the prison.

Fitz George received numerous bows, and even the Dark Woman came in for a great share of respect, prisoner though she was and her offence unknown.

"What's the charge, sir?" said a man, with a pen behind his ear and a book in his hand.

This was a question to Captain Fitz George as embarrassing as it was unexpected.

What charge had he against the Dark Woman? And, indeed, he would have been puzzled to say upon what charge the Regent had given her into custody.

Fitz George turned to the constable, who was looking as confused as he.

"What's the charge?" asked the man with the book again.

"The charge?" replied the constable. "Well, the charge is—the—a—charge——"

"We can't lock up anybody without a charge."

The Dark Woman saw the difficulty, and made two steps towards the door.

It wrung the heart of Fitz George to interfere at such a moment; but he felt that if he allowed his mother to leave, that he should lose all power of attempting to accommodate matters between her and the Regent.

He recollected how she had eluded him when confined in the Tower; and from her whole conduct and the expressions she had made use of, he feared that her next act—were she at liberty—might be one that would place her beyond the reach of any exertions of his in her favour.

Far better was it that she should be detained for a time in the Compter on some slight charge, than permitted to go at large and perpetrate some much more serious offence.

"This lady," he said, "is given into custody for an assault on the Regent."

"That'll do," said the man with the book. "You give the charge, sir?"

"I do."

"Yes," cried the constable, "that's it. A salt on the Regent! A salt and battery on his majestic Grace, the Regent! His Majesty's Highness gave her in charge to me himself. We was quite familiar, me and the Regent, and got on capital. We understood each other, we did; and I shouldn't a bit wonder if I'm sent for to Court, and made a barrow-knight, or a turnspit, or something of that sort."

The Dark Woman said not a word.

Fitz George turned to her, and spoke in a low tone.

"You think this cruel—you think this terrible that I should be the person to ensure your detention here?"

She gazed at him with that kind of expression which looked *at* him, and yet at the same time seemed to look *past* him, or through him, into space.

He saw that it was useless to speak to her, and he turned aside with a sigh.

"Let me see the Governor at once," he said to one of the warders.

"This way, sir, if you please—this way."

Fitz George took one last look at his mother, and then followed the warder through some intricate passages until he reached the Governor's room.

It was the fashion at that period to appoint as governors of gaols, and even in some notable cases as police-magistrates, men who had been mere constables—ordinary Bow Street officers, who had exhibited superior intelligence or daring.

The long well-known Sir Richard Burney, chief magistrate of Bow Street, was selected from so humble an origin.

The Governor of Giltspur Street Compter had been what is called a Bow Street runner; and certainly for that position a man with such antecedents was much better suited than to sit upon the judicial bench.

The system of corruption, though, in the gaols, and connected with the whole administration of police, at that period was enormous.

Captain Fitz George was pretty well aware that a free use of money in any of the criminal gaols would purchase almost any indulgence short of actually opening the door and allowing the prisoner to walk out.

He was not aware, though, of what is now pretty generally known—that nearly all the wonderful escapes from Newgate and other prisons, which have been descanted upon and described at such length by novel-writers and romancists, were actually connived at by the authorities.

Captain Fitz George's object, however, in seeing the Governor was to bespeak what was technically called the "prison indulgences" for his mother.

And most of all he wished to bribe the Governor to forego the usual ceremony of having the prisoner searched; for he dreaded that those jewels she had exhibited to him should be found upon her, and that the slight charge upon which she was detained might by such means grow into magnitude.

The Governor was quite profuse in his civilities to Captain Fitz George.

The young officer laid a tolerably well-filled purse upon the table, as he said, "Mr. Governor, there are some matters which I trust will be explained between the lady who is your prisoner and his Royal Highness the Regent. Let me recommend to you that you treat her with every distinction and respect, and that no indignity be offered to her."

"Certainly, sir—certainly, sir," replied the Governor. "When people come into the Compter on horseback——"

"On horseback? What do you mean, sir?"

"Oh, that's our way of expressing when they are free and liberal in the way of garnish. You know what garnish is, I suppose, sir? Every foo—that is, everybody knows that."

"It is money, I presume; and in that purse I hope you will find a sufficiency."

"Quite, sir. I can see that with one eye shut and the other only open half a quarter the usual width."

"Do you search your prisoners?"

"Always."

"But in this case?"

Fitz George pointed to the purse.

"Oh, sir, if you and the lady have any objection——"

"It must be understood that no such process takes place as regards this prisoner."

The Governor made a jerking sort of bow.

"All's right, sir!"

"Keep faith, and that is but an instalment of what you will receive."

"Beg pardon, sir. What's her name?"

"That I am not at liberty to inform you. She may or may not herself give you her name; but I think you need not ask her, because——"

"Just so, sir—just so. We'll put her down in the books as Mrs. Bolt. My name's Bolt, you see, sir, and its always been thought a fine, bold sort of name. Bolt! Bolt! But we'll take care, sir, she don't bolt. Ha! ha! you take me, sir? A man can't help showing a little wit at times. Bolt, you see, sir—Bolt!"

"Good morning!" said Captain Fitz George.

He left the prison.

The Governor remained in a brown study.

"I wonder, now," he said, "what this is all about? That young chap's an officer—Captain in the Guards; and the prisoner, Mrs. Bolt—ha! ha! Mrs. Bolt!—she's as fine as a duchess, and his Royal Highness the Regent himself gave her in charge. I wonder what it all means, now? She's somebody, and he's somebody. Well, all I've got to do is to look out and see that I'm somebody, and that I make as much as I can out of the whole pack of them. So now I'll go and see Mrs. Bolt. Ha! ha! Mrs. Bolt!"

The Governor went to the door of his room and shouted out, "Figgins! Figgins!"

"Yes, your honour."

"Put Mrs. Bolt in number fourteen."

"Lor', your honour, I couldn't do it. She'd have my eyes out of my head before I was a minute older. Your honour ought to know what Mrs. Bolt is, with that scratch on your honour's nose!"

"Donkey! I don't mean my wife."

"Your honour said Mrs. Bolt."

"It's a curious circumstance, Figgins, but that fine lady who was brought in here for assaulting the Regent is likewise named Mrs. Bolt."

"Oh, I see!" said Figgins. "Bigamy!"

"Beast! No; only the same name."

"But I never heard it called anything but bigamy, your honour. The same name must be bigamy. I aint such a ass as not to know that."

The Governor rushed upon Figgins, and caught him by the hair of the head.

"It happens that the prisoner's name is Mrs. Bolt, the same as if somebody had been brought in here of the name of Figgins."

"Murder! Don't pull a feller's hair off his head. How can Bolt be the same as Figgins?"

"I didn't say so."

"You did; you know you did."

The enraged Governor kicked his subordinate all the way down the passage, and then himself gave the order for the Regent's prisoner to be put into the strong room, number fourteen.

This room was never used for criminal purposes; but as Giltspur Street Compter at that period was sometimes made use of as a debtors' prison, it was an apartment in which gentlemen in difficulties—provided they could pay a handsome gratuity for the accommodation—might wait the visits of their friends, and see their attorneys.

The Dark Woman suffered herself to be placed wherever they pleased without the slightest remark or opposition; and when the Governor visited her, she received him as coolly and as calmly as though she were not within the walls of a prison.

"Madam—your ladyship," he said, "I hope everything here is to your satisfaction. The young gentlemen has come down handsome, and we acts according."

"This evening," said the Dark Woman, giving not the slightest reply to what the Governor said, —"this evening, half an hour after dusk, I shall require an interview with you."

"Oh, very well, madam."

"I am usually called 'your ladyship;' and when people are ceremonious, they may say 'your Grace.'"

The Governor bowed lower still.

"I'm sure, your Grace, anything that I can do to make your stay in Giltspur Street Compter comfortable shall be done. There's a pretty bed-room overlooking a slaughter-house. To-morrow's killing day, and you may see it all."

"I shall not sleep in Giltspur Street Compter to-night."

"Not?"

"Certainly not. I have given you your orders, and now desire to be alone."

The Governor backed out of the room; and when he had closed the door upon the Dark Woman he muttered to himself, "By Jove! she's somebody, or she never would give herself such airs, or be half so impudent. Figgins! Figgins!"

"Yes, your honour."

CHAPTER CXCVII.

THE DARK WOMAN FINDS THE POTENCY OF
WEALTH, AND ESCAPES FROM THE COMPTER
WITH EASE.

THE Governor of the Compter was true to his
appointment—or rather, it might be said, he
obeyed the order which the Dark Woman had
given to him to make his appearance half an hour
after dusk in that apartment where she was made
a prisoner.

The Dark Woman had been eight hours in
Giltspur Street Compter, and it may be presumed
that during that period of time her son, Captain
Fitz George, had not been able to achieve anything
that would enable him to visit her with a proposal in the smallest degree acceptable.

What he had attempted, and how far he had
been able to get the Regent to agree with him,
must be the subject of another chapter.

At present we follow the special fortunes of the
Dark Woman herself.

"Now, madam," said the Governor, as he made
his appearance in number fourteen with not quite
the same amount of respect he had shown to her
in the morning, since the fact of the whole day
having passed away, and no notice having been
taken of her from St. James's Palace or from
Carlton House had somewhat blunted his notions
of her importance,—"now, madam, what can I
do for you?"

"A trifle," replied the Dark Woman; "but
for yourself, if you care for money, you can do
a great deal."

"If I care for money? Oh, my lady, that is
a commodity which we all care for!"

At the mere name of money the Governor was
getting a little more respectful.

"At present," added Linda de Chevenaux,
—"although it is necessary I should leave this
place, and therefore necessary that I should pay
you a handsome sum to allow me to do so—I have
no money."

"Well, marm," said the Governor, at once
dropping all titles, and assuming a rough
familiarity,—"well, marm, I will say that's
about the coolest speech as has ever been made to
me since I've been Governor of the Compter!"

"But," added the Dark Woman, not paying
the remotest attention to the rapid alteration of
manner in which the Governor addressed her,—
"but, as I cannot expect you to trust me to the
amount of the necessary bribe which you must
have before you will allow me to walk out of this
place, I must make some other arrangement with
you."

"Well, of all the cool, easy-going pieces of impudence that ever I came near, you beat them!
You seem to take it for granted that I'm to be
bribed without the least trouble or ceremony in
the world."

The Dark Woman took from her pocket one of
the diamonds she had procured at St. James's
Palace.

It was not that which she had shown in order
to dazzle the eyes of Captain Fitz George, but a
smaller one, and yet of considerable value and
beauty.

"You may take this," she said, "at once, to
some jeweller in the City. Sell it for its current
market value, and bring me back the money."

"Ah, my lady, that looks like a sparkler!"

"It is a diamond. Take it, and obey my
orders."

"Yes, your Grace; but—but——"

"Do you hesitate?"

"Not at all, your Grace; but the jeweller might
ask me how I came by it, and I shall hardly know
what to say to him."

"Say that it was given by the Regent of England to a lady who—in consequence of a slight
difference of opinion between her and the Regent—
desires to sell it."

"Oh! ah! I begin to see. That is, I think—
I feel pretty sure I begin to see. Report says
that the Regent is now madly in love with a lady,
whom he has created Countess, or Duchess, of
something. Perhaps, madam, I have the great
honour of speaking to that lady, who may have
had a little tiff with the Regent, but who may be
to-morrow morning on as excellent terms as ever
with him?"

The Dark Woman smiled bitterly.

"Exactly so," she said. "I can well perceive
you are a man of penetration, and your judgment
sanctions the ideas which a slight amount of evidence gives rise to."

"Oh, your Grace, I flatter myself I can see as
far through a mile-stone as my neighbours. The
whole affair is plain and straightforward to me
now; and I'm sure you will have so much in
your power when you make up the little matter
with the Regent, that you will be able to do a poor
fellow any good turn you please. This is not
much of a post—the Governor of Giltspur Street
Compter; and if I could only get something where
there was a good deal less to do, and a good deal
more to get for it, I should be much better pleased,
your Grace; and on that consideration—as for
letting you out of the Compter, why, I'll do that
for nothing."

"No; take the jewel. I myself want some of
its proceeds."

"Oh, that's quite another thing, my lady. I'm
your humble servant, and will be back quickly.
There's an acquaintance of mine in Bartholomew
Close who deals in these things, and who will give
the full value, which I will as faithfully bring
back to you, my lady, to the last farthing."

The Governor made two statements in these few
words, both of which were untrue.

His friend in Bartholomew Close was not at all
likely to give the full value for the diamond; but
then he was one of those convenient personages
who always had ready money for such little
matters, without asking impertinent questions as
to where they came from.

And the Governor of Giltspur Street Compter
was just as unlikely to bring back all the money
he got for the diamond to the Dark Woman, as his
friend was to give the full value for it.

Between the two, therefore, Linda de Chevenaux
was not at all in the way of receiving anything
like the market price for the jewel.

But what mattered that to her? Those gems,
after all, had come lightly enough into her possession.

The Governor was absent something over half
an hour, and when he returned he brought to
Linda de Chevenaux a sum of eighty guineas,

which he tendered to her with some misgivings in his own mind that she would think the price anything but sufficient.

He then felt all the pangs of an avaricious man upon finding that she made not the slightest remark, and that he might have abstracted another ten or twenty pounds of the money with perfect impunity.

Linda de Chevenaux carelessly picked up some ten or fifteen pieces of the gold, and then pushing the remainder over to him, she said, "Take that, and set me free at once."

"Oh, your Grace, that requires a little management. I must get some of my troublesome fellows out of the way, and I must put a man at the lock who, for a couple of guineas, would let out anybody. You will then have nothing to do but to put them into his hand, upon which he will open the wicket and shut his eyes, so that he will be able conscientiously to swear afterwards that he never saw you go out."

The Dark Woman betrayed some impatience at these details, and the Governor hastened his arrangements, which—considering the unlimited authority he had in the prison—were very easily and quickly effected.

At half-past eight o'clock exactly on that evening the Dark Woman—attired in a cloak and bonnet which belonged to the real Mrs. Bolt—found herself on Snow Hill, and perfectly free to go in what direction she would.

She had scarcely been able while within the walls of the prison to make up her mind in which direction she would proceed; and it was a sort of instinct which took her towards the neighbourhood of Soho Square, and to that gloomy house in Frith Street which she had not visited for so long.

She had no particular intention of avoiding her lodgings in St. James's Street, but she felt that it would be imprudent to make her appearance there until she had resumed carefully and fully the disguise under which she had taken them.

And it will be remembered that the Dark Woman had made several changes of apparel within the last four-and-twenty hours.

When she started on that romantic and criminal expedition to St. James's Palace—which had so fully succeeded in some respects and so signally failed in others—she was attired, as the reader is aware, in male apparel.

In fact, she wore the same suit of clothes in which she would have been recognised as the occupier of the lodgings she had had the audacity to take within a stone's throw of the very gate of St. James's.

Over that dress then she had worn the costume of a Yeoman of the Guard.

And then at that house in Hanover Square, whither she had succeeded with such wonderful address and effrontery in conveying the Regent, she had cast off the whole of that apparel, and had attired herself in the female robes and the glittering adornments, in which she had appeared before the astonished eyes of the Regent in the drawing-room of that mansion.

Brief as had been the occupancy of the Dark Woman of that house in Hanover Square, it had yet been sufficient to enable her to establish a secret depository in it.

She had herself carefully taken out one of the panels in the wainscoat of an upper room, and had manufactured a kind of recess which would hold every article she wished to conceal under any and every circumstance; and there it was she had kept the costume she had so hastily put on, and which had enabled her to appear before the Regent as the undoubted Linda de Chevenaux of past years.

The Dark Woman would probably have made her way at once to the mansion in Hanover Square again on leaving Giltspur Street Compton; but she had no means, as yet, of being perfectly aware of the state of affairs in that quarter, and she was not disguised sufficiently to make it safe even to institute the necessary inquiry.

That fearful languor and weariness, likewise, to which she had found herself amenable of late, began to creep over her.

She found that the physical system was not always at the command of the excited, wakeful, and stubborn intellect.

She had been many hours without rest—many hours without food; for although she had certainly beeen served with two meals at Giltspur Street Compter, she had scarcely touched either of them.

A mist seemed to be gathering before the eyes of the Dark Woman, as she made her way, rather by a kind of instinct than from any accurate observation of the path she took, towards Frith Street, Soho.

More than one person whom she met thought the staggering gait and uncertain footsteps were the results of intoxication; and by the time she reached the gloomy street in which Astorath, the astrologer's house was situated, she felt that if she had had another quarter of a mile to go, she must have fallen down then and there upon the pavement, and abandoned herself to despair.

She staggered up the steps.

It was with the greatest possible difficulty she could discover the secret spring by which she was accustomed to open that door.

It was long since she had visited the house, and the possibility that it might have been taken possession of by some one, and was consequently no longer a refuge for her, came with a cold, chilling sensation to her heart.

She could not find the spring.

It was either the trembling of her hand or some alteration that had taken place in the arrangement. At length, however, by accident, she pressed her finger on the necessary spot.

The door creaked open.

In a lumbering fashion—not easily and glibly upon its hinges—opened that door; for it will be recollected that it had been subjected to considerable violence.

But it was open.

Gloomy, dark, and cavernous appeared the passage beyond.

But the heart of the Dark Woman was more gloomy and cavernous than that dismal passage. She looked upon it at that time as a haven of safety; and summoning up all the strength that was left her to make the necessary effort, she closed the door.

"Safe! safe!" she said,—"I am safe! Rest—rest—I want rest! Rest for the brain, rest for the heart, and more than all, rest for the body, which keeps not pace with the fighting soul which inhabits it. Rest! oh, rest!"

The Dark Woman wanted food likewise, but she had reached that period of depression, that if the choicest viands could have been had by stretching out her hand to take them, she would have wanted energy to do so.

Besides, what food was to be found in that house, beyond perchance a mouldy crust, or some stimulant, which would have made her condition worse?

She staggered along the long, dark, gloomy, passage.

She reached the foot of the stairs.

She stumbled at the first one, for, in good truth, she had not strength sufficient to ascend them.

"Rest, rest, rest!" she kept repeating.

She had not energy to rise. She let her head drop upon the stairs, and as if death had there and then seized her—so still, so perfectly motionless was she—the Dark Woman fell into a deep sleep.

* * * * *

Slowly and cautiously that mysterious door was opened at the far end of the passage, which led down to the damp and cavernous recesses beneath the astrologer's house. A broad gleam of light played upon the passage walls, and a tall stalwart man emerged from those terrible regions of murder and of despair.

He raised the lantern which he carried above his head, so that the rays slowly traversed the whole passage, and at the same time they fell upon his own face, and disclosed the features of Sixteen-stringed Jack, the highwaymen.

CHAPTER CXCVIII.

CAPTAIN FITZ-GEORGE REMONSTRATES WITH THE REGENT; AND ANNIE, THE COUNTESS, PAYS A VISIT TO THE COMPTER.

THE anxiety of Captain Fitz George in regard to his mother, the Dark Woman, was most intense and painful. How difficult it was for him to hold the scales of justice even between Linda de Chevenaux and the Regent!

Feeling and sentiment dragged him in one direction.

Common sense in the other.

How could he justify his mother, and yet save his father, without compromising himself with one or with both? He felt for the time all those pangs and sensations of the scrupulously conscientious, who, in the vain endeavour to please every one, generally contrive to make a host of enemies.

And in this frame of mind he reached St. James's with but one fixed resolve and intention—which was to have an interview with his father, the Regent, and urge upon him the propriety, the feeling, the policy of making some concession, tender and gracious, which might still reach those submerged feelings which he thought might yet be found in the heart of the Dark Woman however deep they might lie.

But the young officer was doomed to disappointment.

Vexed, harrassed, tired, and exhausted, the Regent, immediately upon returning to the Palace, had gone to rest.

The strictest injunctions had been left not to disturb him on any account; and Captain Fitz George, in despair, sought out Willes, with the forlorn idea that he might gather sufficient from him to justify him in believing that the prohibition to break the royal slumbers might not extend to him.

Willes shrugged his shoulders.

"Captain Fitz George, it is impossible!" he said. "His Royal Highness's commands were positive, and I don't know what would be the consequence to any one who might infringe them."

Captain Fitz George hesitated for a moment. Nothing could be more repugnant to his feelings than to speak to any one of his mother: but Willes already knew so much upon the subject, that if any one one merited the treatment of a confidential friend, in regard to the doings and proceedings of Linda de Chevenaux, he was that person.

But for all this, Captain Fitz George was far from suspecting that he knew so much of his mother as he really did. He was quite ignorant of those earlier episodes in the career of the Dark Woman, during which she made Willes her abject slave, or perhaps the valet might have been the last person whom he would have consulted in regard to her fate or prospects.

"Mr. Willes," he said, with some hesitation, "you no doubt know something of what has occurred this morning?"

"I know," said Willes, with some asperity of manner, which he strove to correct by a very ceremonious bow,—"I know, sir, that the whole Palace has been in a state of confusion; and I know that his Royal Highness, the Regent, came home with a mob of boys at his heels, in the dress of a Yeoman of the Guard; but how he went out, and when, passes my comprehension. Since his return he has flung over a couple of tables, broken one chair, and flung a fragment of it in the centre of a looking-glass, so it may be presumed that the royal temper is just—just a little——"

Willes bowed again.

Captain Fitz George looked vexed.

"And all this," added the valet, "has been on account of the Dark Woman."

"She is now in prison."

"Ah!"

"Where she will remain, unless the Regent relent and make some terms with her which will put an end to this insensate struggle."

"Sir, may I make an observation?"

"Certainly, Willes—certainly!"

"Then, Captain Fitz George, the struggle will never be over so long as the lady is at liberty to continue it. If she be securely in prison, I would strongly advise that she remain there; for I feel convinced the only terms the Regent will decide upon would consist of an annuity, to be paid on condition that the lady resided in some foreign country and harassed him no more."

"Well, Willes—well, Willes—I cannot deny but you are right. Would to heaven that my— my——You know that she is my mother, Willes?"

The valet bowed again.

"Would to heaven she could be induced to accept such terms! Oh, that she would once become enamoured of piece and serenity! But I feel that that will never be. I cannot, however, leave

her in a common gaol, to herd with felons and the refuse of mankind. I must strive, at least, to be once more the messenger of peace. I must visit her with a conciliatory message from the Regent. Hours—nay, minutes are precious. I must see him, Willes, and brave even his displeasure."

"Captain Fitz George!"

"Well—well?"

"There is but one person in St. James's who would dare to disturb the Regent."

"And he?"

"Nay, it is no he at all. The Countess de Blonde might venture so far, but no one else."

"Annie!" cried Fitz George, clasping his hands. "Yes, Annie will aid me in this emergency. Her kind heart will overlook all that the excited passions of Linda de Chevenaux projected."

The voice of Captain Fitz George, insensibly to himself, lowered as he spoke, for he could not but recollect that he had almost heard enough on

No. 89.—DARK WOMAN.

the preceding night to convince him that one of the intentions of the Dark Woman had been to strike a blow at the heart of the Regent, through the life of the fair Countess de Blonde.

Was she then to be called upon to intercede for her would-be murderess? Could he fairly—and with anything like heart, soul, or judgment—call upon her to be the intercessor of a woman who would have swept her from the world, merely for the purpose of inflicting a pang upon another?

And yet something must be done; and what else presented itself to him in nearly so tangible a shape?

"I will seek the Countess de Blonde."

The valet bowed again.

"I shall, no doubt, find her in her own apartments."

Another bow.

"And so, thanking you, Mr. Willes, for your courtesy, I will not trouble you further."

The valet kept his body very nearly at right angles until Captain Fitz George was out of sight, and then, as he clenched his hands, he muttered to himself.

"Confound the Dark Woman! Bother take the Dark Woman! A plague upon her! I wish she were fifty fathoms under old London Bridge, with a couple of paving-stones round her neck. She'll get me into trouble yet. I'm sure she will. She cares for nobody—thinks for nobody—feels for nobody! What's the use of being Sir Thomas Willes, if that plague of a woman has it in her power, by half a dozen sentences, to ruin me with the Regent?"

Willes fenced with the air with both hands, and stamped with his feet, as he retired to the room which he called his own, and where he kept up a little sort of state and dignity, which was, as nearly as he could make it, an imitation of his imperious master, the Regent.

There Willes had his own attendant, who was forced to be a pattern of human humility.

If Willes was treated like a dog by the Regent, he was the dog that worried the cat, and the cat was his attendant.

There, in that apartment, the valet had scented handkerchiefs brought him, after the style of the Prince, on salvers of cedar wood.

There he burnt fumigating pastiles, one of which he kept smoking, like a little Vesuvius, between him and the cringing wretch who waited upon him.

But Willes was tired on this occasion, and feeling quite sure that the Regent was disposed of for a good six hours to come, he contented himself with flinging his boots at the head of his slave, and daring him to allow the slightest disturbance to approach him until dinner time.

Fitz George sought the apartments of Annie.

He tapped at that dilapidated door which led from the Titian Gallery to the apartments of the Countess, and was answered by a young girl whom he recognised as the favourite attendant upon Annie.

"I will not disturb your mistress if she is resting; but should she be up, will you kindly say that I would desire a few moments' conversation with her?"

There was an air of so much gentleness and sadness about Captain Fitz George, that the girl hesitated, although she knew that Annie was lying down.

"I will see, sir," she said, "if you will be seated for a moment."

"I thank you. I will wait."

The young officer's heart was sad as he sat in that splendid apartment which formed the first of the suite of rooms which had been fitted up for the fair Annie in the old Palace of St. James's.

But not for long, however, was he allowed to remain in reverie; for one of the doors, panelled with looking-glass, abruptly opened, and Annie, attired in that celebrated ermine cloak which she was wont to wear on hasty occasions, made her appearance.

"Allan—dear Allan, what has happened? My little maid, Maria, here, says you look as unhappy as you possibly can."

Fitz George smiled sadly.

"I'm afraid, Annie, that affairs have reached a crisis between two personages——"

"Ah! I know! You can go, Maria. Sit down, Allan, and tell me all about it. But, I believe, I ought not to call you Allan any more, since you are Captain Fitz George, and I dare say you're dreadfully offended."

"Not at all, Annie—not at all!"

"And you call me Annie, although I'm the Countess de Blonde. That's right; it puts me in mind of old times. Do you remember Martlett's Court, and how cold it used to be in winter when we couldn't afford to buy fuel? Ah, me! And George gave a hundred guineas for this ermine wrapper for me to put on occasionally. Is Marian well?"

"Quite well."

"And happy?"

"I hope and believe so, Annie."

"She ought to be—she ought to be! And—and does she think of me, and speak of me?"

"Often and often."

"And—and——"

"How, you would ask; and I can answer you that it is ever the same—loving, tender, affectionate, and true!"

Annie drew a long breath.

"How wicked and cruel!" she said. "It was some distress of your own you came to me to talk about, and here I've begun about my own affairs. What is it, Allan? If Marian is happy, the reflection of it is not on your face."

"My mother!"

"Ah! Yes, that's it. Linda de Chevenaux, the Dark Woman. What is to be done? What can be done? George is infuriated. This attack upon the Palace last night, and some adventure he has had with her since, has nearly driven him frantic. How can she be so ill-advised? What does she seek?—what does she want? All is hopeless—aimless. I tell you, Allan, that every step she takes with the wild idea of approaching nearer to the Regent only widens the breach between them. She is mad!"

"Think so, Annie—think so, in charity, and then you will forgive her!"

"Poor woman!"

"Listen to me, Annie. I want you to ask the Regent to empower me to try conciliation with her. I want him to go the length—not in writing, but verbally—to empower me to say how deeply he regrets the past, and that subsequent events prevent him from doing her justice. I want him, in fact, to *seem* to throw himself upon her consideration."

"I see—I see."

"But before you move in the matter, I feel that I ought not to conceal from you what was her motive in coming here last night."

"What was it? To assail the Regent?"

"Not personally; but to strike a blow at him through another. It was as if you knew some one whose heart and feelings you wished to touch most bitterly, possessed a fair jewel, upon which they set a store of affection, and in the dead hour of the night you should endeavour to reach the gem and splinter it to fragments."

"I'm dull," said Annie. "What's the application?"

"You are the jewel, Annie, by the destruction of which Linda de Chevenaux sought to pain the Regent."

"That's bad!"

"It is worse than bad—'tis madness!"

"Poor Linda de Chevenaux! Where is she, Allan?"

"In prison."

"Then I will go and see her."

"You, Annie?"

"And why not, I should like to know? She seeks my life, you tell me. Now that's a sad thing both for her and for me, and I must speak to her about it. And yet I think I will see George first; and if I can carry from him that message you speak of, who knows but, by adding to it my own sympathies, she may listen more even than she would to you?

"Annie, you are——"

"Hush! I won't be abused by you, or anybody else. I know I'm a good-for-nothing little wretch, and can't come to any good. That Sir Hinckton Moys was good enough to tell me I should die in a ditch, like Jane Shore—wasn't it Jane Shore?—but I don't believe it."

"No, Annie. If ever heaven looked with kindly eyes on human—human——"

"Wickedness," said Annie. "Go on."

"I cannot. Heaven bless you!"

"Amen! Have you had any breakfast? George is at Carlton House. There's the what's-his-name to pay between him and his daughter about something; and the people at Buckingham House are getting troublesome; and the old King is worse; and the Marchioness of Sunningham has written another letter; and I mean to put on my man's clothes and make an appointment with the old frump in the Park, and she'll be sure to come, thinking some wickedness is afloat; and they do say that Sir Hinckton Moys is come back, and has made up matters with that vagabond Hanger. Chocolate!—chocolate! Chocolate for two! Good gracious, I'm starved!"

"But, Annie!—Annie!"

"Well? Hot rolls!—hot rolls!"

"If you could see the Regent at once——"

"Can't do it! A lobster!—a lobster! Must wait till dinner time, Allan. Look you here! You don't know George half so well as I do. If you want to make him say 'no' to anything, just disturb his rest or put off his dinner. Now, we want him to say 'yes,' so you must leave it to me."

"Then it will be night?"

"Of course it will be before I can go to the prison, and see Linda de Chevenaux. But I will—here's my hand on it—don't squeeze; and now to breakfast."

With all his impatience—with all his desire to act speedily in an affair which might be one of life or death—Captain Fitz George could not but feel that the Countess de Blonde was right, and that nothing could be done until the evening.

The reader is well aware that by that time it was too late.

Too late to attempt to move the heart of the Dark Woman to softer impulses, for she had escaped from the Compter; and as that escape was her own act, and carried out with her own usual subtlety and ability, there was nothing in it which could in any way interfere with the steady, onward march of those wild passions, which surely were hurrying her to destruction.

Captain Fitz George breakfasted with the Countess de Blonde.

He left her then to resume his military duties, but the day passed with him nervously and depressingly.

Night was beginning to fall upon the great city before he again sought the interior of the Palace.

No one now ever attempted to obstruct him in his ingress or egress to the most private parts of St. James's, since it was by this time pretty well known who and what he was.

But it was with a heavy heart that he sought out Willes, the valet, to inquire if his Highness the Regent was yet stirring.

Willes was not in his own room, but the abject being who waited upon him was there; and this person, so humble—such a pattern of cringing subserviency as he usually appeared—Captain Fitz George found seated on a table, holding a miserable-looking boy by the hair of the head, while in imperious accents he issued his orders.

"Villain! bring me my best boots; and on your way run to one of the under clerks of the kitchen, and see if there's anything savoury that a gentleman may eat."

Captain Fitz George could not but smile at this exhibition of petty tyranny. In his mind's eye he saw perfectly well all the gradations of rule and power.

The Regent tyrannized over Willes—Willes tyrannized over the cringing man who was his domestic—and he again held a terrified boy by the hair of his head, while he thundered his commands in his ears.

Perhaps there was some lesser boy somewhere, over whom that now whimpering youth triumphed.

The appearance of Captain Fitz George, however, released the boy, and brought Willes's domestic almost to his knees.

"Most humbly, sir, I beg to state," he whined, "that Mr. Willes is in personal attendance upon his Royal Highness the Regent."

"Then his Highness is awake?"

"Certainly, sir."

Captain Fitz George turned from the room, and after hesitating for a moment, he thought he would seek Annie, in the hope that perhaps she had already had that conference with the Regent, which would enable her to visit the Dark Woman with a conciliatory message.

In the Titian Gallery Captain Fitz George was rather surprised to see a royal courier; but the idea then struck him that there must be bad news from Windsor, and he accosted the man at once.

"Tell me, sir, do you bring any calamitous intelligence from Windsor Castle?"

"His Majesty the King is much worse they say, sir; but I've sent in my despatches to his Highness the Regent."

It was quite evident from the manner of the courier that he meant, with all civility, to imply that he ought not to be questioned about the character of the information he brought from the Castle.

"You are quite right," said Captain Fitz George; "excuse me for troubling you."

The young officer, with his mind still sadly troubled about the possible fate of his mother, the Dark Woman, made two steps towards the door of the Countess de Blonde's apartments—that door which had so lately been so completely forced from its hinges, but which had now been completely repaired, and presented no traces of the injuries it had received.

Royal work is done well and quickly, at royal prices.

But Fitz George was still a few paces from the door when it was flung open, and closely buttoned up in a blue frock coat edged with fur, the Regent himself appeared.

Willes followed the Prince, carrying his hat in one hand and his gloves on a salver in the other.

A stream of light came from the room into the gallery, and through the open doorway Captain Fitz George saw Annie, the Countess, in a morning dress of very rich and beautiful fabric.

"Ah! Fitz George," said the Regent, "is that you? Are you on duty here?"

"No, your Highness; but I fear—that is to say, I hope——"

"Fear and hope, man? You are contradictory."

Fitz George spoke in a low tone, so that the courier, who was close at hand, should not hear him.

"I fear that bad news has come from Windsor, while at the same time I hope that the Countess de Blonde has said something to your Highness which will contribute to all our peace."

"Have it all your own way, and do as you like among you," said the Regent. "Annie, you settle it all with Fitz George, and I shall be content. The King is worse, and I must off to Windsor. Perhaps all is over, and I——"

The Regent drew a long breath.

Captain Fitz George knew as well as if he had uttered them the words that had been upon his lips.

"Perhaps, father," he said, "you are King of England!"

"Perhaps," said the Regent,—and there was a slight flush of colour upon his face; then as he took the gloves from Willes, he cried out, "Good night, Annie—good night! I shall sleep at the Castle, come what may."

"Good night, George! Take care of yourself."

"Way for the Regent!" cried Willes.

There was a clash of arms at the farther end of the gallery—a blaze of light down the short staircase that led to the Ambassadors' Court; and then the rush of carriage wheels and the tramp of four horses, showed that the Regent had gone post to Windsor.

"Come here, Allan," said Annie.

"I fear, Annie, it is all over with the old King."

"I don't know—but there's the despatch."

A large, open sheet lay on one of the tables, and Fitz George read the following words:—

"Doctor Hall respectfully intimates to his Royal Highness the Regent, that his Majesty's situation is critical."

"Well," said Fitz George, "this must have come sooner or later; but I would gladly have seen, before he went from this world, the old man who is the father of my father."

"Never mind," said Annie; "I'd rather be dead twenty times than mad. And now, Fitz George, will you go with me? Help me on with this cloak and hood. Here, Willes! Willes! Tommy! Tommy! Where are you?"

Willes looked aggravated as he appeared on the threshold of the room. Since he had been so sportively knighted by the Regent, nothing delighted him so much as to think of himself as Sir Thomas Willes.

The drop to Tommy, even from the fair lips of the capricious Countess, was anything but agreeable.

"Order my carriage at once," added Annie. "I'm going out."

"Out, your ladyship?"

"Yes, to be sure. To prison! Where is it, Fitz George? Newgate, eh?"

"No, Annie, another of the City prisons, called the Compter."

"A funny name for a prison. I served in a shop for a little while, and they made me sleep under the counter. How should you like that, Tommy?"

Willes made a grimace.

But the carriage was ordered, and during the quarter of an hour preceding its announcement, Annie informed Captain Fitz George that she had had the projected conversation with the Regent, who had given her—as indeed he, Fitz George, had heard—full power to act as she thought best in regard to the Dark Woman.

Giltspur Street Compter was reached within the hour, but the bird had flown.

With a pretended look of consternation, the Governor informed them that the lady had made her escape.

They asked no questions—they felt how useless they would be; but the heart of Fitz George was heavy, for he felt that all was lost for the present.

————

CHAPTER CXCIX.

SIXTEEN-STRINGED JACK HOLDS POSSESSION OF THE ASTROLOGER'S HOUSE IN FRITH STREET, AND THE DARK WOMAN FINDS HERSELF STILL A PRISONER.

WE left Linda de Chevenaux, the Dark Woman, fainting, exhausted, and torpid upon the lower steps of the gloomy staircase of that house of evil repute in Frith Street, Soho, where had been enacted some of the strangest events in her dramatic existence.

It was none other, indeed, than Sixteen-stringed Jack who emerged from the dark, pestiferous regions below that house into the passage, carrying the lantern which, for a few moments, shed a broad but sickly beam upon the prostrate and apparently lifeless form of the Dark Woman.

Sixteen-stringed Jack looked pale and excited.

There was a staring wildness about his eyes, while the colour seemed to have deserted his lips as well as his cheeks, so that he looked almost like a dead man revisiting the upper air, as he slowly came up from those terrible gloomy cellars beneath Astorath's house.

He had seen a sight there which might well shake the firmest nerves.

The pale gleam of that lantern he carried had fallen upon a spectacle of horror.

The decaying remains of the housebreaker lay

there, who might be in truth called the last of that gang of depredators, originally in the service of the Dark Woman, who went by the name of Paul's Chickens.

Sixteen-stringed Jack had sought that house expressly for the purpose of making what discoveries he could in regard to the fate of his old companion.

And awful indeed was the discovery he made!

It had required a stout heart to descend below the street surface of that gloomy mansion, but Sixteen-stringed Jack was just the man not to do things by halves.

So far as he was able to judge, he visited every room in the house, and then he descended to its cellars.

There he found the object of his search.

The problem was solved.

The last survivor of Paul's Chickens was no more.

A slight noise in the passage above had alarmed him, and hastily ascending, he brought with him that gleam of light that fell upon the form of the Dark Woman, as exhausted nature compelled her to sink into a state which was half swoon, half sleep, at the foot of the staircase.

The horror of Sixteen-stringed Jack had been great at the sight that met his eyes in the cellars, but his surprise now at this spectacle in the passage almost put the frightful object below out of his head.

The Dark Woman was still in the magnificent dress with which she had sought to awaken recollections of the past in the heart of the Regent at her interview with him in Hanover Square.

Over that costly robe, with all its rich adornments, she certainly wore those articles of apparel which she had so imperiously ordered the Governor of Giltspur Street Compter to procure for her.

But as she fell exhausted on the staircase, the common cloak and hood had partially fallen aside, disclosing the more costly material which truly formed her dress.

And there she lay before the wondering eyes of Sixteen-stringed Jack, an object of greater mystery than ever she had been before, although he had seen her in many circumstances which might well baffle the reason and afford abundant food for the imagination.

"The Dark Woman, by heaven!"

Those were his first words.

"Is she dead?"

That was his second exclamation.

He stooped and lowered the lantern to her face.

Her eyes were closed, her face was blanched; not the slightest movement of her lips betrayed the breath of life.

"Dead!" said Jack.

Then there was a slight quiver of the eyelashes.

The light had acted upon those sensitive organs; and although she still half slept, half swooned, the Dark Woman's senses were still not quite impervious to external emotions.

"No; she lives!" said Jack.

Then he recoiled from her with a sort of horror as he added the word, "Murderess!"

But what was he to do?

Jack Singleton never felt so puzzled in his life.

He set down the lantern on the curved end of the balustrades of the staircase, and folding his arms, he gazed on her for some moments in silence.

"Something has happened to her," he said. "She's been out in the rain, too, for I see drops still glitter on her hair and her clothes. Perhaps she is wounded, and has crept here, like some wild animal to its lair, that she may die in peace."

This idea quite took possession of Sixteen-stringed Jack, and he looked more carefully at her, to see if there were any traces of blood upon her garments.

No; there were none.

"What does it all mean?" said Jack. "Is it a trick?"

At this supposition he placed his hands upon his pistols and faced about, casting keen glances into the darkest recesses of the passage.

But all was still. Not the faintest noise disturbed the repose of that deserted house. It was too ill-omened to tempt any wandering mendicant even to take up his abode in it.

Jack Singleton himself seemed to be the only living, breathing thing within its walls; for he began to doubt again whether it was not the corpse of the Dark Woman he saw before him instead of the living likeness.

But she moaned lightly.

Jack started. A feeling of compassion crept over him.

"Guilty — guilty!" he said,—"although you are guilty to the very lips of rapine and of blood, I will not see even you die at my feet without some aid."

Jack Singleton had a small leather flask of spirits with him.

It was rather an unromantic thing, that Linda de Chevenaux—claiming to be Princess of Wales and possible Queen of England—should be indebted to a few drops of rum from a highwayman's flask for her continued existence.

But the stimulant, vulgar or romantic, did its duty.

Linda de Chevenaux opened her eyes, and they encountered the stern countenance of Sixteen-stringed Jack.

"Where am I? Oh, heaven! what has happened?"

Jack did not answer.

The Dark Woman, with a low moan, let her head droop again on the stairs, and again she closed her eyes.

She had not slept off the fearful fatigue which had seized upon every limb, upon every muscle, upon the heart, upon the brain, upon every sense.

"So, so!" said Jack; "something serious indeed has happened, when the iron frame of the Dark Woman yields in this fashion. I can afford to wait; for now that we have met once again, although in a strange fashion, you and I, my lady, don't part again quite so easily."

Jack Singleton raised the Dark Woman in his arms. Her weight was nothing to him; and carrying the lantern in one hand, he held her with the other, and slowly, but surely, ascended the staircase of the astrologer's house.

Little did the Dark Woman suppose that she was to be indebted to one whose life she had certainly more than once attempted, for her own preservation on that terrible occasion.

She moved not. She spoke not.

That fearful, death-like trance had come over

her again, and more than once Sixteen-stringed Jack, as he ascended the staircase, might well believe that he held in his arms the mortal remains of the Dark Woman.

The exploration he had made of the astrologer's house previous to her arrival stood him in good stead, for he now knew exactly where to go.

He knew, too, how to avoid one terrible danger which lay directly on his route.

In that large apartment on the first floor, where Astorath, the astrologer, was in the habit of receiving his dupes, and where the Dark Woman after his decease had received hers, there was a fearful-looking chasm in the floor.

A trap-door, which communicated with another immediately below it, and so conducted to the loathsome cellars below the house, was open; and it would have been a thousand chances to one that any intruder into that gloomy mansion, without a knowledge of the fact, or great care in picking his way, would have fallen into that dreary pit.

Destruction would have been certain.

But Sixteen-stringed Jack, when he visited that house and explored it for the purpose of ascertaining the fate of his friend and companion, the cracksman, had been too much upon his guard to fall into any such trap.

Well he knew that the place was one of danger and mystery, and therefore he had trodden cautiously over the creaking boards, and had taken care to make a full observation of what was before him, before he ventured to take a footstep in advance.

Into that large gloomy apartment on the first floor, Jack made his way with the Dark Woman, and carefully, by the light of his lantern, coasting that black and dismal-looking opening in the floor, he pushed open the door of the small apartment adjoining, from which the Dark Woman was wont to issue forth to utter her oracular responses.

Upon a couch there he laid her.

Then Jack spoke again: it was rather to himself that he uttered the following words, than to her.

"With much trouble and toil, and I fancy with some danger, I have found you, Linda de Chevenaux; and you shall do no more mischief, if I can help it."

The motion of being carried up the stairs, or the quietude of the recumbent posture in which she now was lying, had the effect of partially recovering the Dark Woman.

She could not be said to be fully mistress of her senses, but still she had a dreamy kind of perception of where she was, and that some one was with her, who, for good or for evil, had to a certain extent befriended her.

She spoke in a low, tremulous voice.

"Is this death? or is it but the slow approach of death?"

"It may be the latter," said Sixteen-stringed Jack; "and if so, I know of no one who should dread going to a long account so much as Linda de Chevenaux, the Dark Woman."

"Ah! you know me?"

"Too well."

The Dark Woman did not yet recognise him by his voice—her perceptions were still too confused; and when she tried to keep her eyes open for a few seconds, it seemed to her as if she had

to support a leaden weight with each of her eyelids.

"I must rest—I must rest," she said. "I cannot speak—I cannot think—I must rest."

These words were uttered in such a tone of anguish that Jack Singleton, who had always believed that there was a touch of mania in her conduct, was moved to some slight show of pity.

"Rest, then," he said, "but I will not leave you. When you have slept off this fearful exhaustion which oppresses you, I have something to say to you which shall be said, though it wring your heart to its inmost core."

"Speak again—speak again!" she said mournfully. "I surely know the voice."

"Look at me and name me," said Jack.

He held up the lantern as he spoke, so that its full rays fell upon his face, and the Dark Woman managed to keep her eyes open sufficiently long to recognise him.

"I know you now."

"Of course you do."

"Your name is Singleton."

"That's it. I'm Jack Singleton—*alias* Sixteen-stringed Jack. You have in vain sought more than once to bend me to your purposes, and to make a tool of me for your own objects—a tool to be cast aside when it was no longer wanted, to perish. But I tell you, Linda de Chevenaux, that all your arts, all your unscrupulous power, and all your vindictive resources——"

Jack Singleton stooped over her and looked in her face

The Dark Woman was in a profound sleep.

"Bah!" said Jack—"I'm talking to a shadow. She might as well be dead as in such a sleep as that. She don't hear a word I say."

It was singular that upon recognising Jack Singleton as the person in whose custody she might be said to be, the Dark Woman had given up all idea of being in any danger, and had at once resigned herself to that irresistible persuasion to sleep, which was pressing upon her senses.

Well she knew that Sixteen-stringed Jack was the friend of Allan, her son; and she conjectured that but little harm could come to her from an association with the highwayman, who, after all, was not in a condition to prove beyond a doubt that she was the murderess of either Shucks or Brada.

"Well, Linda de Chevenaux," said Jack, after a pause, "be it so; since you must sleep—sleep! and I at the same time feel confident that I have nothing better to do than to keep watch and ward over you."

Jack's idea was to give up the Dark Woman as speedily as possible to the custody of her son Allan, as he from habit still called him.

But he meant to do that upon a distinct understanding that Allan was to pledge himself to keep her out of mischief—in fact, by fair means or by foul, to put a stop to her career—which, otherwise, might sooner or later involve the death of every one who would not join with her.

The Dark Woman was like many other people who make some favourite project the object and study of their lives.

Every one who was not with her she considered

to be against her, and to be removed from her path in any manner most convenient.

Sixteen-stringed Jack drew a chair near to the door of the little apartment, and after placing his lantern upon the chimney-piece and calculating that it would probably last till daylight, he was about to sit down when a sound startled him, for the repetition of which he listened intently.

It was the continued ringing of a bell.

The incessant tinkling of some very small bell, which was pertinaciously agitated by some one whose patience perhaps had given way after repeated milder attempts to make it heard.

"What the deuce is that?" cried Jack.

He projected his head from the small apartment out into the large, mysterious room with the trap-door open in the floor, and listened.

He heard the bell plainer.

After a few seconds it ceased.

Then it began again.

"I have it," said Jack. "I recollect perfectly now. There is a bell, the means of ringing which is only known to what are called the initiated: that is to say, to persons who have been here before, and been shown the way. I wonder now if that is any one who is foolish enough to think they will get a peep into futurity by coming to this house?"

Jack Singleton cast another glance at the Dark Woman, in the expectation that possibly that continuous ringing of the bell, the sound of which must have been familiar to her, might arouse her.

Such was not the case.

She still slept profoundly.

Jack Singleton sallied out into the larger apartment, and held up his lantern.

Hanging down the wall, close by the side of each other, were two long, slender cords, each of which had a knot at its end by which it could be laid hold of securely.

Jack had scarcely made up his mind to experiment with these cords; or if he had, perhaps he would have hesitated a little before touching them.

It was by a sort of impulse that he gave one of them a violent jerk; and although he heard the jingling and scraping of wire through channels and orifices made for its reception, it was only by hearing the street door closed again, that he could come to the conclusion that he had opened it by the jerk he had given to the mysterious cord.

Nothing could be further from Sixteen-stringed Jack's intention than to do anything of this kind.

He certainly did not want company in the astrologer's house on that occasion.

"Confound them!" he said to himself. "Whoever they are, I must try and frighten them away by some means or another. But now I think of it, the passage is as dark as a pit. I will show a little light from the stair-head, and take my chance of frightening them out of the house in double quick time, as soon as they reach this room."

Jack crept slowly across the floor, and reaching the stair-head, he allowed a faint gleam of the lantern to show itself.

He heard voices in the passage.

The tones were decidedly feminine.

"Marchioness! Marchioness! I give it up!" said one of the voices. "There seems to me something terrible even in the atmosphere of this house."

"Hush, your Royal——I mean, Mrs. Smith. Do not call me Marchioness, or you will ruin all."

"Oh, indeed!" thought Sixteen-stringed Jack. "A Marchioness and a royal something! Now, is it not surprising that human credulity should soar so high?"

A whispered consultation now took place in the passage, but in so low a tone that Sixteen-stringed Jack could not catch the precise words.

He was quite satisfied, however, that the purpose of the two females in visiting that house was sufficiently strong, or, at all events, their curiosity was sufficiently excited, to induce them to persevere.

They began slowly and carefully to ascend the staircase.

The faint twilight which Sixteen-stringed Jack made at the head of the staircase with his lantern was quite a sufficient guide to them; and, no doubt, that light, small as it was, looked much brighter from the dark passage than it looked to Jack himself, who was at its source.

"What on earth shall I do?" he said to himself, in a low tone. "I cannot let these stupid women tumble down the trap-door in the floor. What evil genius has brought them here to-night? I thought this gloomy old house had been quite sufficiently long deserted to get rid of such folks."

Jack Singleton had no resource but to retreat into the large apartment, or to meet the two visitors face to face.

The latter was certainly what he did not wish to do, so he chose the former.

Jack Singleton hardly knew why it was that he felt an irresistible desire to pull that other cord which hung so quietly and invitingly beside the other that had opened the door.

It was one of those instinctive impulses which nobody attempts to resist which induced Jack to give this cord as good a jerk as he had given the other.

The effect was sudden and startling.

Down from the roof there came with a rush a heavy curtain of black cloth, which, if Jack had happened to look upwards a few minutes before, he would have seen coiled round a roller, and stretching the whole width of the room.

In Jack's first surprise—for he thought the house was coming about his ears—he nearly fell down the open trap-door; for the curtain, when it touched the floor, left that ugly-looking chasm along with Jack in that half of the room furthest from the staircase.

It was only for a moment, however, that Sixteen-stringed Jack was thus taken by surprise.

He then recollected perfectly well that he had seen such a curtain in that room, and that it was behind it, or before it, or in some way or another in connexion with it, that Astorath first, and afterwards the Dark Woman, had played their tricks.

"I'm in for it," said Jack. "It's quite clear that I'm to be the conjuror to-night."

Jack held up his lantern, and waved it to and fro as he looked at the curtain.

He was not at all aware of the effect he was producing on the other side.

That curtain was pierced in many places by minute holes, the edges of which were spangled with many-coloured, brilliant, sparking foil; so that, viewed from the other part of the room, it had an effect that was quite enchanting.

"Beautiful!" said one of the female voices.

"Beautiful?" muttered Jack. "What does she mean by that? She can't mean me, at all events, for I'm out of sight. What shall I do next, I wonder? I wish I saw some other string to pull. Oh! perhaps now they'll say what they've come about."

"If," said one of the females, raising her voice, —"if you can really read the stars, and the reputation which you have as an astrologer, soothsayer, and diviner of the future be well founded, you shall be amply rewarded by a favourable reply, if possible, to what we shall ask of you."

"That's good!" thought Jack. "She wants to bribe the stars."

Jack then thought he ought to say something, as there was rather a long pause; so pulling his hat entirely over his face, in order that his voice might sound hollow and distant, he said, "Speak! Oh! oh! oh! speak! What would you ask of the dog star and the moon in a fog?"

Both the females uttered exclamations, and Jack began to think he was very successful.

Then one of them spoke aloud.

"There is one test of your knowledge of the future, to which, if you have no objection, we should like to subject you."

"What the deuce does she mean?" thought Jack.

"That test," added the voice, "will consist of your knowledge of the present. Can you say who and what we are?"

"That's good!" thought Jack. "They forget their foolish tittle-tattle in the passage."

He put his hat over his face again, and spoke.

"Amid the starry host there is a Great Bear and a Little Bear, but they are both constellations——"

"What do you mean? We are not in a condition of life to understand such language."

"Gammon!" said Jack, in deep, hollow tones.

"Good gracious!" cried one of the females. "Come away!"

"No, no!" whispered the other; "since we are here, let us ascertain if report speaks true, when it says that this fortune-teller, for a valuable consideration, is willing to help out his own predictions."

"Oh, that's it!" thought Jack. "After all, that's it, is it? Now, I'll take good care, my fine ladies, that I'll know what you really do come about."

CHAPTER CC.

SIXTEEN-STRINGED JACK BECOMES PROTECTOR OF THE PRINCESS OF WALES, AND MEETS WITH AN ADVENTURE AT BUCKINGHAM HOUSE.

THERE was rather an ominous pause of some few minutes' duration after this last speech of one of the female visitors to the house of Astorath, the astrologer.

The probability was that they had come for the purpose of saying exactly what they had said, and were anxious to hear what sort of reply would be made to them.

There can be no doubt that quite up to this period, and even somewhat later, Caroline, Princess of Wales—in whom the observant reader has recognised one of these visitors to the house in Frith Street—was fully impressed with the opinion that the two great foes to her coming to a good understanding with the Regent, were Annie, Countess de Blonde, and favourite mistress and Sultana of the Prince, and Captain Fitz George, his natural son.

The Marchioness of Sunningham, who on this occasion was the companion of the Princess of Wales, had laboured indefatigably to convince her royal mistress that the Countess de Blonde was her mortal enemy.

Sir Hinckton Moys had done as much in regard to Fitz George.

And both Moys and the Marchioness had reasoned and acted with regard to their own hatreds and jealousies, making, as everybody did who called themselves of her party, a mere tool of the unfortunate Princess of Wales for their own purposes.

It was Jack Singleton who broke the silence that had ensued; and in doing so he paraphrased a sentence or two which he had heard the Dark Woman use on a former occasion.

"The oracles of fate," he said, "know not only perfectly well who and what you are, but what you come about. It is nevertheless necessary that you should speak plainly. What are your wishes? The oracles listen."

The two females whispered together for some seconds; and then it was the Marchioness of Sunningham who spoke, saying, "It will give us great confidence if we are convinced you really know who we are. Heaven knows we are not particularly proud of our position in the world, as the wives of respectable professional men; but if you can name us, do so."

"There's nothing to be particularly proud about," said Jack; "but I will consult a familiar."

"A what?" cried the Princess of Wales.

"A familiar spirit," added Jack.

The highwayman then made his hat into a smaller compass still, and farther muffled his voice by placing his hand before his mouth. Had he been aware of it, he would have easily found means of producing mysterious effects in that house much more readily than in the rough manner he sought to bring them about.

But still Jack's mode of operations answered the purpose very well; and the voice in which he spoke—a little aided by the imagination of those who were listening to him—seemed as though it went far away into the realms of space.

"Ho! my tricksy spirit," cried Jack, "whom have we here? Speak to your master!"

Sixteen-stringed Jack then made a low whistling sound, as though a rush of air were coming through a crevice.

Then all was still again.

Jack thought proper to wait for a few moments, in order that the solemnity of that stillness might have its effect upon the minds of the visitors, and then he spoke in a purposely assumed, anxious whisper.

"They tell me that Caroline, Princess of Brunswick and of Wales, is here?"

"Ah!" cried the Princess, "this is astonishing."

"It is clever," said the Marchioness of Sunningham, as she pressed the arm of her royal mistress, to prevent the mention of her own name and title,—"it is clever; but I wonder if the spirits can take upon themselves to say if your humble waiting woman—that is, myself—be married or single?"

"Both," said Jack.

"What mean you?"

"My familiar spirit intimates that the Marchioness of Sunningham, although married, takes upon herself all the privileges of a single life; and so——"

"Silence! Impertinent!"

"It is evident though, Marchioness," said the Princess of Wales, "that this fortune-teller, or

No. 90.—DARK WOMAN.

soothsayer, knows you—be he whom he may—as well as he knows me."

"Certainly," said Jack, who heard these words; "and now you will please to declare the precise object of your visit?"

The Marchioness was biting her lips with vexation, and as she did not seem inclined to utter one word, the Princess of Wales spoke in a voice of some agitation.

"I am assured," she said, "that there is one who is iniquitously and criminally nearer to the Regent than his own wife. Surely there must be something in the character of such a person to engender loathing rather than affection, could his Royal Highness be made aware of it."

"Princess——" said Jack.

But he had only time to utter that one word, when—as if something, or somebody, had descended from the clouds upon him—the lantern was dashed out of his hand, and he was himself so forcibly and rudely pushed aside that, standing close, as he did, to the trap-door in the floor, his feet slipped down it; and it was by the greatest miracle in the world that he contrived to grasp the edge of the aperture with both hands, and so save himself from a fall that might have had the most disastrous consequences.

But Sixteen-stringed Jack—although, for the moment, he was safe and uninjured—was perfectly incapable of being of the slightest assistance to anybody else.

He heard a wild, yelling, frantic voice above him, and in the tones, to his horror, he recognised those of the Dark Woman.

She must have awakened from that deep trance-like sleep; and, for aught he, Sixteen-stringed Jack, knew to the contrary, she might have been a listener to the conversation that had taken place between him and the imprudent visitors to that dangerous mansion.

"Vengeance—vengeance!" she cried. "Fate, destiny, or providence has delivered one into my hands, and the other will follow. I have prophesied this, and they shall both fall."

The darkness in the large apartment must have been profound, and no wonder neither the Princess of Wales nor the Marchioness of Sunningham could find their way readily to the door by which they had entered.

But if that darkness baffled them in their frantic attempts to escape, it likewise confused the Dark Woman, and prevented her from committing an act, which, although consonant to her ideas of equity and vengeance, must have handed her over to the utmost terrors of the law.

In her frantic rage to get past Sixteen-stringed Jack, and to prevent him from impeding her in her progress, she had dashed out the lantern, which, in truth, was the only light in the whole of that house.

How she was armed, and in what manner she intended to immolate the Princess of Wales to her blind fury, Jack could not conjecture; but in some manner, she had managed to make her way past the curtain, and was in the same compartment of the room with the terrified Princess of Wales and the Marchioness.

At the first shock and surprise at this meditated assault, they had both screamed aloud, and then surely some better judgment had come to their aid, and they felt that their only friend was the darkness that was about them—their only possible safety in complete silence.

But Jack Singleton's situation was critical.

He was a powerful, athletic man, and perhaps, under ordinary circumstances, or in sport, he could have raised himself well enough by his hands, and so scrambled out of the hole, into which he had been so nearly flung.

But unfortunately he had not done this at once, and the consequence was, he could not now do it at all.

His hands felt benumbed, and each moment growing more and more nerveless.

The horrible idea came across him that he must very soon perforce let go his hold, and fall to any depth that might happen to be beneath him.

Then he pictured to himself the fearful fate that would be his, provided that he went right down to the cellars of the old house, and was necessarily injured and maimed by the fall—the fearful fate of lying there in silence and in darkness, to die, with no companionship but the corpse of his old friend, the housebreaker, which had that evening met his horrified gaze.

A cold perspiration broke out upon the brow of Sixteen-stringed Jack.

He never thought himself so near his end in all his life before; and as death seemed momentarily to be approaching nearer and nearer, he made one last effort to save himself.

Jack knew that in the room below there was another trap-door immediately opposite to that by which he might be said to be suspended, and well he knew that if he were precipitated through this second trap, death, in a hideous form, was inevitable.

Horror at his impending fate lent him new strength for a moment, and finding that he could not succeed in raising himself from his present perilous position, he began to swing himself to and fro, and when he thought the moment had arrived, he allowed himself to drop through the yawning aperture.

The expedient had succeeded.

Jack found himself in the apartment below—but from having swung his body to and fro, instead of dropping through the second trap-door, only his feet had descended, which he took the precaution to raise as quickly as possible, and he found himself free once more.

An immediate revulsion of feeling took place in Sixteen-stringed Jack's mind.

The dread of death had passed away, and calm, cool, and collected, the highwayman was himself again.

There was nothing, certainly, in the character of Caroline of Brunswick, or in that of her ladyship, the Marchioness of Sunningham, which could specially call upon Sixteen-stringed Jack for warm sympathies; but at that moment he recollected nothing, thought of nothing, but that they were two defenceless females, almost at the mercy of one who might be considered little better than a maniac.

Their characters, antecedents, were objects of nothing to him; all he had to do was to save them from the wild rage of Linda de Chevenaux.

That he made up his mind to do.

As calmly and rapidly as possible in the dark, Jack examined his pistols, feeling the priming carefully, in order to be certain that the violent exertion he had recently gone through had not deranged its position.

Percussion caps were at that period unknown. All fire-arms were on the old flint and steel and pan full of powder principle, so that a miss-fire was a very frequent incident, unless the fire-arm were carefully looked to repeatedly.

It was not that Jack wanted to shoot the Dark Woman, but he had no other weapons with him, and it was natural that under the circumstances he should see to their efficiency.

He would not trust himself to leave the room in which he was exactly upon his feet, but he crouched down and crept upon his hands and knees, in order to save himself from the possibility of another tumble down the open trap which was there.

By going round the walls of the room in this way, Jack found the door.

It led him into the dark passage at once.

The cold air that blew from the street under the outer door, and likewise a lively current that came in through some broken panes in the fanlight above it, soon convinced him of where he was.

Besides, there were certain faint kinds of twilight which made their way into the passage through those broken panes, for the darkness in the gloomy street without was nothing to be compared with the darkness in the gloomy house within.

And now Sixteen-stringed Jack in half a dozen strides might have reached the street door, and in another moment he might have stood beneath the pure canopy of heaven free and unharmed from that house of fraud, iniquity, and murder.

But Jack never thought of escaping and leaving the Princess of Wales and the Marchioness of Sunningham to the fate which the ingenuity of the Dark Woman would surely, in a short time, enable her to inflict upon them

"I won't say I will save them," said Jack, to himself, "because I may not be able; but I will honestly try!"

He crept along the passage.

Slowly, cautiously, and silently he commenced the ascent of the stairs.

He wanted to reach the room above, without giving any indication of his presence; but the old stairs would creak a little beneath his weight, do what he might.

Jack found that the only way to reduce that slight creaking was to ascend two or three steps at a time, which he accordingly did so that he was much sooner on the landing-place, immediately outside the large apartment of mystery, than he would otherwise have been.

He was astonished at the stillness within the room.

It was awfully suggestive.

Suggestive of death—of murder—of some fearful catastrophe he was too late to prevent, and in the results and suspicions of which he might be fearfully implicated.

Jack placed his ear close to the panel of the door, and listened.

He heard something.

It was a sound like suppressed sobbing, mingled with praying; such a sound as might come from some one in hopeless agony, on board a doomed ship, from which there was no escape but into the wild waste of waters which was soon to submerge it.

With excessive caution Jack Singleton felt for the handle of the door.

Should he make any noise, or should the hinges creak, he had a strong impression upon his own mind that he would be a dead man.

But that door had been specially made to open and shut without the faintest indication of its movements.

It gave way like velvet, and the highwayman was able to look into the room—nay, scarcely to look—for he removed his eyes but from one darkness to another.

The pitchy obscurity of the staircase and the landing was only to be equalled by the pitchy obscurity of that large apartment.

"Mercy—mercy!" moaned a voice

"Hist!—hist!" whispered Jack; "I'm a friend. What has happened?"

"Nothing; but we are doomed—lost!"

"Not at all!"

"Oh, yes, yes! A fearful person has been here, who, with dreadful threats, has only left to procure a light, that she may see her way to our murder."

"All's right, then," said Jack.

He seemed to comprehend at once the state of affairs. The Princess of Wales and the Marchioness of Sunningham had had the prudence to keep so still about the middle of the floor of the apartment, that the Dark Woman, although she had felt her way once round the walls, had missed them.

Then, believing herself secure of them, she had left them to procure a light, muttering threats as she went.

No doubt Linda de Chevenaux was under the false impression that she had disposed of Sixteen-stringed Jack.

Had she not seen him fall down the open trap, at the moment she rushed against him, and dashed the lantern from his hands?

Certainly she had; and what could then save him from a fall of at least forty feet into those dismal regions below?

What could save him from an awful death, either immediate or of a lingering character, contingent upon the nature of the injuries he might receive?

Apparently that was, to the apprehensions of the Dark Woman, the inevitable doom of her old opponent, Sixteen-stringed Jack.

CHAPTER CCI.

JACK SINGLETON FINDS THAT IT IS HIS FATE TO BE ENTITLED TO THE GRATITUDE OF MORE THAN ONE ROYAL PERSONAGE.

THERE could be no doubt whatever of the real danger of the position of the Princess of Wales and the Marchioness of Sunningham.

At any moment the Dark Woman might return with a light, which, by enabling her to see her victims, would no doubt enable her to compass their destruction.

And in the frame of mind she was in, the probability was strong that nothing but the murder of the two unwelcome visitors would content her.

Bitterly, most bitterly might she regret and repent of such an act in quieter, calmer moments; but Linda de Chevenaux had gone through too much fatigue, turmoil, and excitement during the last twenty-four hours to be able to take a reasonable view of anything.

Jack Singleton strove in vain to find out exactly in what part of the room the Princess of Wales and the Marchioness of Sunningham were.

And they were both too much paralysed by fear to indicate to him their precise position.

They were in that state of mind in which the difficulty of distinguishing friends from foes becomes great.

"Speak—speak!" said Jack. "I come to save you. Tell me where you are."

"That's another," moaned the Princess. "Heaven have mercy upon our souls, for we are lost—lost!"

"Oh! why did I ever come here?" groaned the

Marchioness of Sunningham. "How mad I was to come here!"

"You will be worse than mad," said Sixteen-stringed Jack, "if you do not attend to what I say."

"I had every comfort," added the Marchioness. "I had plundered quite sufficient from the Regent to enrich my whole family, and to pay as many men ——No, I don't mean that! Oh, dear! what am I saying? I mean I had taken money and jewels enough to make us the richest family in England, and it would be easy for my sons to change their names. Oh, dear!—oh, dear!"

The Marchioness was making some imprudent revelations.

Probably the Princess of Wales heard enough on that occasion to account for the coolness that arose between her and the Marchioness of Sunningham so soon after the adventure of that night.

But the wailings and the lamentations of the Marchioness had one good effect; they enabled Sixteen-stringed Jack to come to a pretty accurate judgment as to where she and the Princess were in the room.

He moved cautiously forward.

"Ladies," he said, "it seems to me that the only chance for your lives is to get out of this place as soon as possible."

"Oh, yes," replied the Princess, "most willingly. But how is it to be done?"

"Follow me."

"I cannot see you."

"Keep still where you are, and let me in the darkness find you."

With his arms outstretched before him, Sixteen-stringed Jack moved slowly and cautiously across the floor.

The Marchioness of Sunningham uttered a scream of terror.

Jack had touched her head.

"Murder!—murder!"

"Let me recommend silence!" said Jack, in a sharp, firm voice.

"Who are you?—who are you?"

"A man!"

"A—a—man?"

"Yes, Marchioness; and I should have thought you the last person in the world to be alarmed at the information."

"You are a wretch!"

"Very likely. But if you, madam, decline to be saved from your present danger by a man, I am quite content to be the preserver of her Royal Highness the Princess of Wales."

"And I," said the Princess, "am content to trust to you."

"That is well."

"Where is your hand?"

"It is so dark, madam, that I can only wave my hand to and fro in the air; but if you will be so good as to do the same, we may meet."

"Yes, yes. I will—I do."

"Now, madam, trust to the hand that holds yours, and follow me."

"I follow."

"The Marchioness of Sunningham can stay, and fight her own battles."

"No! no!" screamed the Marchioness. "I will go, too—I will go with you."

She took a fair hold of the cloak in which the Princess of Wales was enveloped, so that she was guided along the floor towards the door of the room by the same movement that conducted the Princess in that direction.

Jack Singleton felt certain he was going right, although the darkness was so very profound and perplexing; and, according to his ideas, he must have nearly reached the door, and was holding out one arm in the expectation of touching it, when the Princess of Wales uttered a cry of dismay and terror.

The Marchioness of Sunningham screamed aloud.

A flash—a broad flash of light came into the room from the further end of it where the curtain was separated, and upon Jack Singleton hastily looking in that direction he saw the Dark Woman.

Linda de Chevenaux had a light in her left hand. It was some sort of oil lamp, which shed a bright ray about it as she held it a little above the level of her face.

In her right hand she had something which, at the first gleam, Jack thought was a formidable bludgeon.

But it scarcely required a second look to enable him to correct that opinion, and to come to a right conclusion in regard to what the Dark Woman held in her right hand.

It was a carbine!

A short, sturdy-looking carbine, such as cavalry soldiers wore at their saddles; and there could be no mortal doubt but that she meant mischief with it.

The situation was, in truth, a most critical one.

Jack found—when he could see about him by the lamp which the Dark Woman produced—that he was further from the door of the room than he had supposed.

The darkness had deceived him.

Linda de Chevenaux had time twice over to fire the carbine at him, and at the two helpless and apparently doomed females he had under his care.

Surprise at the sight of him was the only thing that made the Dark Woman pause for a moment.

That he had fallen down the trap, and was numbered with the dead, or with the dying, she had firmly believed; but now, to see him alive and well, and on the point of snatching her prey from her grasp, came upon her with a paralysing sense of surprise.

"Ah!" she cried, "the dead rise up to thwart me in my purposes and vengeance."

Jack thought then that his last hour was surely come.

Linda de Chevenaux placed the lamp upon a column close at hand, which was about the same height that she had held it.

She brought the carbine to the "present." Jack felt that there was but one resource. He had his pistols.

Self-preservation was the first law of nature. He levelled one of the pistols at the Dark Woman, but at the instant he did so the image of poor Allan Fearon seemed to rise up before his eyes, with his daughter Lucy by his side.

It seemed to Jack as if the voice of Allan sounded in his ears, saying, "And would you kill my mother?"

"No, by heaven!" cried Jack, in reply to this lightning-like freak of the imagination.

He altered the aim of the pistol.

He pulled the trigger.

The report was tremendous in that closely shut up apartment, and as Jack had intended, the couple of bullets with which the pistol was loaded, struck the lamp and dashed it to pieces.

The room was all darkness again on the instant.

"Stoop! Fall down—flat to the floor—for your lives' sake!" cried Jack.

The admonition was not one moment too soon.

The Dark Woman levelled the carbine, and fired.

There was a storm of shot and slugs upon the wall, beyond Jack, and the Princess of Wales, and the Marchioness.

But they had obeyed his injunctions to the letter, and had both flung themselves flat upon the floor.

He had done the same.

The leaden shower of death therefore passed over them unheeded.

"Lie still!" whispered Jack.

He then, himself, uttered a deep and awful groan.

The Dark Woman echoed it with a shriek of delight.

She made certain that she heard the death agony of one or more of her intended victims.

"A light!—a light!" she cried—"another light! We will soon illume this battle field! A light—a light!"

They heard her voice die away as she left the large apartment for the purpose, no doubt, of reaching Astorath's laboratory, where she would quickly be able to procure another light.

Jack Singleton felt that the time for escape had now really come.

The lamp which had enabled Linda de Chevenaux to see her enemies, had likewise enabled Sixteen-stringed Jack to note the exact position of the door of the room.

"Up—up, Princess, up, and follow me!" he cried.

He assisted the Princess of Wales to her feet. She was in a terrible state of agitation now, and could scarcely stand.

The Marchioness of Sunningham was terrified into absolute silence.

Jack could feel, as the Princes of Wales leant upon his arm, how she shook with fear.

"It is over," he said. "You are saved! Be under no further apprehensions. A little courage now, and a little exertion, and we shall reach the open air."

"Yes—yes! Oh, yes—the open air."

There was something promising and blessed about the idea of getting out of the atmosphere of that terrible house, and having nothing but the night sky of heaven above her head.

The Princess gathered strength and courage from the hope, and although she still leant upon the arm of Jack Singleton, she was not quite helpless.

Indeed, the principal obstructions to her progress consisted of the Marchioness of Sunningham, who clung to the clothes of the Princess with a persistence and a weight that was quite embarrassing.

And so they went out of the room.

Jack felt for the lock, and to his great joy, found the key in it.

To turn that key was the pleasantest thing he had done since he had been in that house, for he considered that, trifling as the obstacle might be to the Dark Woman, should she meditate pursuit of them, yet still it was an obstacle, and moments at that time carried with them human lives.

Down the dark staircase to the dark passage the fugitives made their way, and no alarm as yet followed them.

"Safe!" said Jack—"all is safe now!"

"Thank heaven and you!" said the Princess of Wales, in agitated terms.

At that moment the bell at the street door—that same bell which had alarmed Sixteen-stringed Jack some time before, and which had heralded the arrival of the Princess and the Marchioness—was rung violently.

The party were about half-way down the passage, towards the street door, when this demand for admission to Astorath's house took place.

The Princess of Wales only clung a little closer to Sixteen-stringed Jack.

But the Marchioness of Sunningham recovered from the torpor that had taken possession of her, and began to scream "Murder, murder!"

"Madam," said Jack, "this is intolerable. If you cannot be quiet, I shall save the Princess, and leave you to do the best you can, for you seem intent upon being the death of us all."

The ring at the door was repeated. Whoever was there, did not appear to be in the least repelled by the screams of the cowardly Marchioness of Sunningham.

"What shall we do now?" whispered the Princess to Jack Singleton.

"Leave the house at once; our danger is from within, not from without."

"But who can that be?"

"Some credulous person, who probably thinks it possible that they might get a peep into futurity by coming to this house."

The Princess of Wales felt the rebuke, for that was just what she had herself done, although, to tell the truth, she had been incited to the adventure by the Marchioness of Sunningham, who was anxious to find any means, or to engage any one who would, by fair means or by foul, aid her in displacing Annie, the Countess de Blonde, from her position in St. James's Palace.

The bell rang a third time.

But Jack had his hand on the door when this third application was made for admission to the house of the astrologer in Frith Street, Soho, and he opened it in the face of two men who stood on the doorstep.

These two men were muffled in those roquelaire cloaks so commonly worn at the period, and the fur collars of those cloaks were clasped over the lower part of their faces, so that combined with the fact that their hats were pulled low upon their brows, they were tolerably well concealed.

On the opening of the door these two men were stepping forward to cross the threshold of the house.

At sight of Jack Singleton and the two females with him they drew back.

"Hilloa!" cried one; "what game have we here, I wonder?"

At the moment the mind of Jack misgave him that they were police officers ; and if so, his position would be most critical.

Would the Princess of Wales save him? That was possible.

The light on the doorstep of that gloomy house was very faint, for it happened that the nearest lamp in the street was some fifty paces off, and that lamp was but a sorry one.

No wonder, then, that the Princess of Wales and the Marchioness of Sunningham were able to hide their faces tolerably completely in the hoods of the cloaks they wore.

Jack Singleton was forced to bear the brunt of such an examination as the dim light afforded and allowed.

"Gentlemen," he said, "do not interfere with us, and we will not interfere with you."

"Indeed !" said the other man. "Do you know, fair ladies, that we feel an uncommon degree of interest in whoever visits this house"

The Princess of Wales, at sound of this man's voice, uttered a slight exclamation, but at the same time she drew the folds of the hood of her cloak closer about her face to avoid recognition.

She knew the voice.

And so did the Marchioness of Sunningham.

And so, too, did Sixteen-stringed Jack, as far as feeling certain that he had heard it somewhere before, although he could not name the person to whom it belonged.

Both the Princess and the Marchioness, however, could have named him with ease.

The voice belonged to no other than the notorious Sir Hinckton Moys.

How he had discovered that it was safe for him to show himself in London again after his adventure with Annie, the Countess, it matters not.

Suffice it to say that his flight to the Continent had been a short one, and that from a miserable inn at Calais he had returned to London, having discovered that the Countess de Blonde was alive and well.

But who was his companion?

That, neither the Princess nor the Marchioness were able to say, for although that companion had spoken, it had been in suppressed and artificial tones.

If, however, they could have heard him speak in his own natural voice, they would have had little difficulty in naming him.

The companion of Sir Hinckton Moys in that visit to the astrologer's house in Frith Street, was his old opponent and rival, Colonel Hanger.

How two such repelling elements came to be associated together, we shall take an occasion of informing the reader. For the present, the fact must suffice that these two unscrupulous and villanous men thought it better to act in concert than to thwart each other, and so spoil the sport of each.

Moys was intent on discovering who the two ladies were that met him so oddly on the doorstep of the astrologer's house

A strange idea took possession of him, that the smaller one of the two—namely, the Princess of Wales—might be Annie, the Countess de Blonde.

It was a foolish notion, only engendered by the time and place, and the disguise of the cloak; for, to state the simple fact, the Princess of Wales was nearly twice the age of the young and somewhat *petite* Annie.

Of course he could make no such mistake about the Marchioness of Sunningham, who was of the coarse, big order of women, who by some strange infatuation are called fine by some men, when they are simply detestable, because, in so far as they are "fine," as it is called, they depart from the true feminine nature of women.

CHAPTER CCII.

JACK SINGLETON ESCORTS THE PRINCESS OF WALES TO BUCKINGHAM HOUSE AND HAS AN ENCOUNTER WITH A CERTAIN INFAMOUS PERSONAGE.

THE pause upon the doorstep of Astorath's house was an awkward one for all parties.

The first impulse of the Princess of Wales upon recognising the voice of Sir Hinckton Moys was to fly from the spot, but she had endured such an amount of terror in the house of the Dark Woman that she could not make up her mind to leave the protecting arm of Jack Singleton, who alone, she felt assured, had carried her in safety through it.

The Marchioness of Sunningham, on the contrary, was, after a moment's consideration, almost upon the point of disclosing who and what they were to Sir Hinckton Moys.

There had always been common cause between them ; and now that he had returned, she thought he still might be useful in carrying out the vengeance which she wished to concentrate wholly on the head of the Countess de Blonde.

A certain sort of respect, however, for the Princess, which she could not shake off, prevented her from taking such a step without her cognizance, so there was an awkward silence, which, however, was broken by Moys, as he exclaimed, "One cavalier to two fair dames is an unfair proportion of the goods of Providence. Madam, can I be of any service to you?"

He bowed to the Princess of Wales, and strove, by a gentle force, to push Sixteen-stringed Jack on one side.

But Sir Hinckton Moys was very much mistaken in his man if he thought that Jack was the sort of person to put up quietly with such treatment. He gave Moys a lurch which sent him spinning down the steps of the house and half-way into the road before he could stop himself.

"Scoundrel!" cried Moys, as he returned with a rush, "do you know who you dare treat in this fashion?"

"I neither know nor care." said Jack, calmly; "but I do know that the lady is under my protection, and as long as she chooses to remain so I shall not permit any interference."

"Indeed, sir! And do you claim the other lady, likewise?"

"Should she particularly wish it, I will; but, otherwise, let me inform you, you are particularly welcome to her."

The Marchioness of Sunningham was enraged; and, at that moment, if she could have hit upon any plan which would have ensured the destruction of Sixteen-stringed Jack she would gladly enough have embraced it.

But the Princess of Wales clu g still closer to him, and by the pressure of his arm seemed to implore him not to desert her.

Sir Hinckton Moys had probably by this time discovered that his opponent was unarmed, or appeared to be so; and as he had a sword under his roquelaire cloak, he considered that he had only to will it, and he could be amply avenged for the rude impetus that had been recently given to his movements.

Casting aside a portion of his cloak, he laid his hand upon the sword-hilt, and half drew it; but Sixteen-stringed Jack saw the movement, and, to the chagrin of Sir Hinckton Moys, the barrel of a pistol was presented within a few inches of his forehead.

Hanger, at these hostile demonstrations, immediately effected a retreat from the step, to keep out of harm's way.

It was a curious thing then to see those two men—one with fury in his eyes, afraid to draw his sword, and the other one keeping him so calmly and coolly in check with an empty pistol—for Sixteen-stringed Jack, in his haste, had laid hold of that one of his pistols which he had discharged, to the confusion of the Dark Woman, in the room above.

"Now, sir," said Jack, "what have you to say why I should not rid myself of an opponent who is evidently intent upon doing me some serious mischief?"

"Spare him!" whispered the Princess of Wales.

"Go your way, in the fiend's name," growled Moys, "and let me go mine. I don't know you now, but I hope to do so some day, for I have pretty well imprinted your features upon my remembrance."

"I don't think our meetings," said Sixteen-stringed Jack, "let them occur where they may, will be precisely satisfactory to both parties; but since I have, at all events, one lady with me, it is inconvenient at the present moment to take any further notice of you."

Moys's passion was excessive, but he was one of those men who always allowed discretion to be the better part of valour. He stepped aside, and allowed Sixteen-stringed Jack and the Princess of Wales to pass him.

The Marchioness of Sunningham brought up the rear, but she was so angry at the slighting manner in which Jack had spoken of her, and she was so desirous at the same time of renewing her intercourse with Moys, that, as she passed him, she touched his arm, and whispered, "Sunningham. Hush!"

"Ah!" exclaimed Moys. "I know all now."

The truth flashed across the mind of Sir Hinckton. The companion of the Marchioness of Sunningham, to whom she paid so much deference, could be no other than the Princess of Wales

Then he thought himself wonderfully stupid that he had not detected them both before.

But he was puzzled to know who Sixteen-stringed Jack was; for although he had had a tolerably good look at his face, he had not succeeded in recognising him as any of the well-known adherents of the unhappy Princess.

Moys little suspected who and what Jack really was, or that the acquaintance between him and the Princess of Wales had only arisen within the past half-hour.

The Marchioness of Sunningham, by the intimation she had given to Moys, was really, in all likelihood, the means of saving that individual's life; for had he entered the astrologer's house on that evening, the Dark Woman might very easily have found some means of sacrificing him to her blind, vindictive rage.

As it was, he spoke a few words apart with Hanger; and then, as Sixteen-stringed Jack, the Princess, and the Marchioness left Frith Street, the two worthies followed at a cautious distance.

"Confound you, John Hanger!" whispered Moys; "why did you not back me up with that fellow, instead of running away, which you incontestably did."

"Of course I did; only, Sir Hinckton Moys, most people call me by some title or another."

"Title?"

"Yes; Major, at the least."

"Notwithstanding you have lately promoted yourself to a colonelcy?" said Moys, in a sneering tone.

"If I did not promote myself, nobody else would."

"That's strictly true."

"It is; for his Royal Highness George the Regent has not been at all so grateful as he ought to have been for the eminent services I have rendered him."

"Eminent nonsense! The fact is, when I fled the country, after being tricked into the idea that I'd been the death of that little bundle of mischief, the Countess de Blonde, George had no resource but to fall back upon some such fellow as you"

"Hold! Hold, Sir Hinckton! Have a care! I understood that you and I had made an alliance, and that we were to play into each other's hands, and be good company and keep good companionship; but now you are as abusive as if I were thwarting you at every turn."

"I may well be hurt and annoyed."

"At what?"

"At your desertion of me just now."

"My dear friend, I did it to save your life. You don't know the fellow—now I do."

"Do you?"

"Ay, to be sure. I have seen him more than once. Did you never hear of Sixteen-stringed Jack, the famous highwayman?"

"Most certainly; but you do not mean to say —"

"Yes I do!" interrupted Colonel Hanger, "That's the man."

"A highwayman! and in close companionship with the Princess of Wales and the Marchioness of Sunningham!"

"Whew!" whistled Hanger. "That's the game, is it?"

Sir Hinckton Moys was vexed that he had so inadvertently let Hanger know who the two ladies were, but there was no help for it, and he made a merit of the error.

"Yes, Hanger, I was just going to tell you that I recognised in those two ladies Caroline of Brunswick and the somewhat notorious Marchioness of Sunningham, whose whole and sole object in life now is, I think, to supplant Annie, Countess de Blonde, in the affections of the Regent."

"Which she won't do," said Hanger, "while men have the sense to prefer a deer to an elephant."

"I don't know that. But there is one thing I do know."

"And that, Sir Hinckton?"

"That, Major, or Colonel, whichever you like to be called best, is that your friend the highwayman shall sleep to-night in Newgate."

"Don't be rash."

"Rash? Nonsense! I will keep my eyes upon him, and as soon as I can see sufficient assistance at hand, he shall be pounced upon, despite his fire-arms, and secured"

Hanger shook his head.

"Oh, I understand you," added Moys; "there is a sort of story afloat that you've been upon the road yourself; and, therefore, I suppose you have a kind of fellow-feeling with this highwayman."

"I have."

"Ha, ha! I thought as much!"

"What's a gentleman to do, when he's out at elbows, and nobody will trust him? What are Bagshot and Hounslow Heaths made for, I'd like to know?"

"Well, it's no business of mine—don't try to thwart me, and you may cry 'Stand and deliver!' to who you like. But here we are in Whitehall. I wonder if her Royal Highness will claim her privilege, and pass through the Horse Guards?"

"She may do so," said Hanger, "without claiming any privilege at all, since she is on foot, for the gates are not closed until twelve o'clock, and I fancy it wants a good hour of that time yet."

The Princess did pass through the Horse Guards. It was by far the nearer way to Buckingham House; and when fairly in the Park, she seemed to be able to breathe more freely, as if she felt herself in an atmosphere that more properly belonged to her.

Hardly, however, could the unhappy, although probably guilty enough, Caroline of Brunswick consider any spot of English ground as her home.

She was alien in heart, in habits, in hopes, and wishes.

"Sir," she said to Sixteen-stringed Jack, "you will permit me now to thank you for the great service you have rendered me, and to say that I do not think I need trouble you further."

"Dismiss me when you please, madam, but do not do so in ignorance of one fact which it is important you should know."

"What is that?"

"Simply that we are followed."

"Followed? Is that possible?"

"It is so, madam. Those two men whom we encountered on the door-step of the house in Frith Street, seem determined to see you to your home, and, in truth, there is no very ready way of preventing them from so doing."

"Then, sir, instead of asking you to leave me, I will rather beg you to be so good as to see me to the entrance of Buckingham House."

"That I will do, with pleasure."

"Surely, madam," said the Marchioness of Sunningham, "there can be no danger in St. James's Park, even at this time of the night?"

The Princess made no reply to the Marchioness of Sunningham. It was quite evident that the disfavour into which the Marchioness had been for some time gradually slipping, owing to a knowledge, bit by bit, which the Princess of Wales was acquiring of her real character, was reaching a height that would soon necessitate their separation.

The hour of the night by the time Sixteen-stringed Jack and his illustrious charge reached Buckingham House was getting late. Indeed, it was some time later than Sir Hinckton Moys and Colonel Hanger had thought it to be.

Twelve o'clock struck by the Horse Guards' clock as the Princess of Wales was on the threshold of her temporary home.

The moment the first stroke of the hour sounded, the bells of St. Martin's Church began to clang forth a merry peal.

That peal was taken up by other church bells; and in the course of the next two minutes, there was a clangour of joy-bells throughout the night air, which, as the Princess of Wales knew not its cause, filled her with amazement.

She paused just within the vestibule of Buckingham House, where a German domestic was in confidential attendance; and turning to Sixteen-stringed Jack she said, "Can you tell the cause of this ringing of surely all the bells of London?"

"I should have thought," replied Jack Singleton, "that your Royal Highness, of all persons, should have known the reason."

"Alas! how should I know?"

"It concerns your Highness."

"Concerns me?"

"Just so. It is well enough known through the whole town that to-morrow her Highness the Princess Charlotte is to be married to the Prince Leopold of Saxe-Coburg—or rather, I should say, to-day, since it is past the midnight hour."

The Princess of Wales burst into tears.

"They fool me! they fool me!" she sobbed. "They keep me in ignorance of everything that is passing that most interests me. I might as well be out of the world. I wish I were out of the world!"

Sixteen-stringed Jack really did not know what reply to make to this speech of the Princess, so he was silent; but she turned towards the Marchioness of Sunningham, and added, reproachfully, "You, Marchioness—you must have known this, and did not tell me."

"Nay, your Royal Highness; they who are your most faithful friends always act for the best, although they do not always get credit for their good intentions."

The Princess of Wales made no reply to this Jesuitical speech; but addressing herself to Sixteen-stringed Jack, she said, "Come, sir, follow us into our poor home, and we will at least find some token which you can keep in remembrance of this night, and of the unhappy Caroline of Brunswick."

"Madam! madam!" said the Marchioness of Sunningham, in a remonstrative tone.

"What now?" replied the Princess, sharply.

"Surely you will not take this stranger into Buckingham House at such an hour?"

"And why not?"

"Oh, madam!"

"I say, why not?"

"Your reputation!"

"Reputation? reputation? How can any reputation suffer which is in company with the pure and immaculate Marchioness of Sunningham?"

The bitter sarcasm of this speech struck home; and from that moment one of the most determined and relentless foes of Caroline of Wales was the woman who had already only made use of her as

a tool for the purpose of making her own way again to the coffers of the Regent.

But the Marchioness made no reply at the instant, and Sixteen-stringed Jack, who detested the woman, was too well pleased at her discomfiture to reflect upon what he was about, and followed the Princess of Wales into Buckingham House.

That house, although a royal residence, was but ill-supplied with the appurtenances of royalty.

The domestics were few; and as the Prince of Wales conducted Sixteen-stringed Jack up the grand staircase, no one appeared but the same grey-haired confidential German servant, who had shown himself in the vestibule.

The Marchioness of Sunningham did not follow Jack Singleton and the Princess. She had a little affair of her own to carry out. She wanted to see and to speak to Sir Hinckton Moys.

The scheming Marchioness had never really

given up the idea that Moys was the man who, in the long run, would be most useful to her, as regarded her hopes of gaining a settled supremacy over the Regent.

Now she thought so more than ever.

She saw that her little reign at Buckingham House was all but over.

Darting out from the vestibule of the royal abode into the kind of fore-court which shut it away from the Park, she looked eagerly for Moys and the person who was with him.

She did not, however, as yet know who that other person was.

The two dusky-looking figures stood close by some iron rails in front of the house.

The Marchioness saw that their attention was not directed towards her; and, for a few seconds, she did not see how so to direct it.

Then an idea struck her.

She picked up a couple of pebbles.

One she threw, with a bad aim, and missed her mark.

The other was more successful.

She hit Sir Hinckton Moys on the back, and he faced about instantly. Then he saw the Marchioness standing just in the shadow of the vestibule of Buckingham House, evidently waiting for him.

"Hunger," he said, "the Marchioness expects me. Wait for me here."

"All's right!"

Moys, in another moment, was by the side of her unscrupulous ladyship.

"I know you!" she said.

"No doubt. Who shall hide from the bright eyes of Sunningham?"

"Stuff!"

"Eh?"

"I say stuff! This is a time for action, not for foolish compliments."

"What action?"

"Meet me to-morrow."

"Where?"

"At your own lodgings. Where are they?"

"No. 2, Ryder Street, St. James's."

"I will be there at one o'clock. But how was it that you fled from England; and having so fled, how is it that you so soon find your way back again?"

"I was deceived."

"You?—you, the master of deceit?"

"Nay, it was a woman who deceived me. I flatter myself that no man could have done so; but your subtler sex, you know, my dear Marchioness——"

"Pho! pho! Don't talk rubbish. Good night! I will be with you to-morrow."

"And I shall expect you with all the impatience in the world. One word, though, now."

"What is it?"

"Who is that with the Princess of Wales?"

"I don't know."

"You don't know?"

"I certainly do not. But if you are the man I take you to be, you will take good care to know, if he should happen to leave Buckingham House alone."

"Alone?"

The Marchioness did not wait for any farther speech with Sir Hinckton Moys, but left him to make the most of what she had said, while she hastily made her way into the house.

CHAPTER CIII.

SIXTEEN-STRINGED JACK OVERCOMES TWO FOES, AND ESCAPES TO HIS HOUSE WITH A SLIGHT WOUND.

WHILE this little discourse was proceeding outside the gates of Buckingham House, between the Marchioness of Sunningham and Sir Hinckton Moys, Jack Singleton had followed the Princess of Wales up the grand staircase to the suite of rooms which she specially occupied.

"Clara! Clara!" cried the Princess as she opened a door. "Are you awake, child?"

"I am here, mistress," replied a voice.

That voice sounded strangely familiar to Jack Singleton. He had certainly heard it before; but where, he could not, at the time, for the life of him, determine.

The fact was, that the person who was now named Clara by the Princess of Wales, and spoken to with so much consideration and tenderness, was no other than the young girl who had been for so long a page and attached servant to the Dark Woman, under the name of Felix.

It will be in the memory of the reader how the Princess of Wales had found this young creature on once of the seats in the Park; and how, by one of those impulses which were so common with her, whether for good or evil, she had at once taken charge of her, and conceived for her a violent attachment.

That was an attachment which the grateful heart of the young girl most fully and entirely reciprocated.

A light flashed in the room; and then the Princess, turning to Jack, said, "It is not in the power of the wife of the Regent of England to be as grateful as she would wish, but you shall not go empty-handed from Buckingham House."

"Madam," said Sixteen-stringed Jack, "believe me, I desire nothing."

"Nay, I do not seek to pay you."

Jack bowed.

"My own keys, Clara. Give me my own keys, child."

A small bunch of keys was handed to the Princess, with one of which she opened a cabinet, from a drawer of which she took a ring, set with emeralds, in the centre of which was one opal.

"Take this," she said, "and when you look upon it remember that you have done a service to Caroline of Brunswick, and that you, or any one to whom you may present this ring, shall have a claim upon her gratitude."

"This is strange," thought Sixteen-stringed Jack. "I have already a ring from the Regent, for a similar service rendered to him. If I go on at this rate, I shall be able to ask for a dukedom, at the very least."

But Jack did not think it would be well to say anything to the Princess of Wales about the Regent or his ring, so he took the one that the Princess presented to him gratefully.

"Madam," he said, "I am only too well pleased to have been of service to you; and if you will consider that that fact gives me any right to advise you, I should certainly wish to say a word?"

"Say it freely."

"Let me, then, entreat you, as you value your life and safety, never again to be induced to visit the house in Frith Street, Soho."

At these words from Sixteen-stringed Jack, the young girl Clara, as she was now called, uttered a cry.

The Princess was alarmed.

Jack looked at her in surprise.

"Oh, that dreadful house!—oh, that dreadful house!" exclaimed Clara, as she covered her face with her hands, and seemed to be deeply affected.

"You know it?" said Jack.

"I do!—I do!"

"This is strange."

"Not so," said the Princess. "This young girl, who now is very near to my affections, was, for a long time, in the service of one Linda de Chevenaux."

"The Dark Woman!"

"Yes," said Clara with a shudder. "I was that unhappy girl who, for a long time, was her page."

"Then," said Sixteen-stringed Jack, "that accounts directly for how I thought your voice was familiar to me. I am sure I need say no more, for this girl, your Royal Highness, ought to be able to tell you quite sufficient of that house to prevent you from ever setting your foot across its threshold."

"Oh, mistress, dear mistress—dear, good, kind mistress!" said Clara, clasping her hands, and looking imploringly in the face of the Princess of Wales,—"you surely have not been to that dreadful house?"

"I have, my child."

"It is full of horrors!"

"It is, my dear."

The Princess of Wales trembled at the recollection of the fright she had endured at the house of the astrologer; and Sixteen-stringed Jack, feeling quite satisfied that she was not likely to repeat her visit, moved to the door of the room, saying, as he did so, "I have the honour to bid your Royal Highness farewell."

"Stop!—stop!"

Jack paused.

"One thing I was forgetting. You have not told me who and what you are?"

"My name is Singleton."

"Mr. Singleton?"

"Just so, your Royal Highness; so now, once more, farewell."

Jack was only too glad to get out of the room, without being more explicit in regard to what he was, for he would not exactly have liked to add, "And, madam, I am a highwayman!"

The Princess made a sign to the young girl, Clara, to show him out of the house; and she was on the landing-place almost as soon as Jack reached the top of the grand staircase.

Jack's senses were tolerably acute, and he fancied he saw the flash of a light, for a moment, in the hall below, and heard the scuffling of feet. But he could scarcely think those sounds, in such a place, were anything to him.

Clara, however, thought otherwise. She, too, heard something suspicious, for she knew that the whole household had retired long since to rest.

It was nearly one o'clock in the morning, and no one, with any good intention, was likely to be astir in the vestibule.

She laid her hand upon Jack's arm, as she whispered the one word "Wait."

Then Clara, crouching down quite low on the stairs, crept down about half-way, and listened.

She heard a voice that she knew perfectly well to belong to the Marchioness of Sunningham.

"Be careful," it said. "He must pass you."

Then another voice replied.

"Got, yes! Me shall be careful; me shall have von blood to him. Got, yes! Yah!"

That voice, with its bad grammar, English, and its coarse tones, the young girl likewise knew well.

It was the voice of that evil spirit of the Princess of Wales

The travelling servant and courier, Bergami.

That some mischief was intended she did not doubt.

She was back again by the side of Sixteen-stringed Jack in a moment.

"You are brave?"

"Well, I fancy, my good girl, that I am certainly no coward."

"That is well; but the bravest man, you know, cannot guard against one thing."

"What is that?"

"An assassin."

"Ah!"

"Yes—an assassin; and I think there is one down there waiting for you."

"He shall not wait long, then."

"Nay, pause. One moment."

"What for?"

"Have you arms?"

"Ah! that is well thought of. I have a pair of pistols with me, but one is without a charge. I will load it."

"Do so; but have you no sword?"

"Hardly."

"Then I will fetch you one. The moment you reach the last but three or four steps of the stairs make a leap into the vestibule as far as you can, and face about at once. By that means you will bring your foe to bay. Wait now for me half a minute."

Clara was scarcely gone the time she mentioned; and when she returned she placed a very costly Court sword in the hands of Sixteen-stringed Jack.

"Now go."

"A thousand thanks, my dear girl; but do tell me one thing?"

"What?"

"Who is the villain that seeks my life?"

"An Italian."

"His name?"

"Bergami."

"I shall not forget that, nor you either. Don't mind me. I have got a dear, good little girl of my own. You may take this kiss as a parting one, and now good night."

Jack kissed the brow of the young girl; and then, with the sword in his hand, he slowly descended the staircase in silence, to follow her instructions to the letter

It was the Marchioness of Sunningham who had taken upon herself to prepare this little surprise for Jack Singleton in the hall of Buckingham House.

The Princess of Wales had been imprudent enough to bring over from the Continent to England with her the cowardly Italian courier, who had managed to obtain so great an ascendancy over her; and she had had the further imprudence to allow him to lodge in Buckingham House.

When, therefore, the Marchioness of Sunningham had left Sir Hinckton Moys, she made her way at once to the room in the occupation of the infamous Bergami.

No feeling of gratitude for the service that Sixteen-stringed Jack had done her on that night at the house of the astrologer, in Frith Street, was sufficient to induce her to abstain from what she now meditated—which was revenge against him for the slights he had cast upon her, and his evident abhorrence of her.

Bergami was up, and paying his attentions to a hasty supper. He looked half stupid; for accompanying that hasty supper was some of the finest Tokay, which, at the expense of the Princess, who could scarcely afford any very good wines at her own table, he was drinking.

"Rouse yourself," said the Marchioness—"rouse yourself, or you are lost.

"Lost—lost! What?"

"The Princess has had a service done her to-night, which has saved her life, probably; and she is inclined to reward that service with such feelings as will make your longer stay here impossible."

Bergami turned yellower than he usually was with rage.

"I have overheard the man, who is an Englishman, speak to the Princess of you."

"Ob be?"

"Yes, of you. Are you curious to know what he said of you?"

"What? Got!—what?"

"He said he was surprised how any lady of the taste and discernment of her Royal Highness the Princess of Wales could ever look for half a moment with favourable eyes upon a dirty, yellow, greasy Italian like you."

Bergami uttered a howl.

He dived his hand into some secret pocket of his clothes, and produced a poniard.

"I will kill! kill! kill!"

"Oh, dear, no!"

"No? no? What shall hinder? I will kill!"

"You are not brave enough. By the by, he added that of you——"

"What ob be?"

"That, in addition to being a dirty, lazy, ugly foreigner, you are a linking, cowardly hound; and he would lay a horsewhip across your shoulders so soon as he could clap eyes on you."

Bergami howled again.

"But," added the Marchioness, "since you are by far too cowardly to interrupt him, he will walk out of the house in perfect safety the next half-hour."

"No! no!"

"He will."

"He shall not! I will—I—I—will fight him—openly fight him—defy him to his face—to his tooths! I will hide in the hall, and shot him in the back!"

A look of intense contempt set upon the face of the Marchioness of Sunningham; and that was a look which followed one of intense surprise.

The intense surprise was what had come over her mind at the first part of the speech of Bergami; for that part had been almost courageous, and so unlike him, that it had filled her with astonishment.

The conclusion of his speech, however, had restored him to his original character; and as the Marchioness of Sunningham, notwithstanding all her wickedness, was an English woman, she could not but feel the contempt she expressed at the Italian assassin.

Indeed, there can be no doubt whatever but that the false expressions she had put into the mouth of Sixteen-stringed Jack, as regarded Bergami, embodied her own opinion of that personage.

But, be all that as it may, she was succeeding in her object, which was to imperil the life of Sixteen-stringed Jack as he left Buckingham House, and so be revenged upon him for the slights he had put upon her, and the manner in which he had resisted her great friend and ally, Sir Hinckton Moys.

Bergami at once rose, and in the true assassin style set about his preparatins.

He rolled a cloak round his left arm, which was to serve the purpose of a shield, in case his victim should not fall at the first blow, and should manage to turn upon him.

With the poniard in his right hand, tucked securely up his sleeve, he was ready for action.

He looked yellower, uglier, and more vicious than ever; for the paint with which he was in the habit of bedaubing his countenance in the day time was no longer there.

Alas! that one who might, at least, have awakened all the respectable sympathies of Englishmen and Englishwomen, should sacrifice herself for all time to so despicable an object as Bergami, the Italian courier!

But such was the fate—such was the infatuation of Caroline of Brunswick!

Buckingham House was profoundly still.

The grey-haired domestic who had let in the Princess and Sixteen-stringed Jack, accompanied by the Marchioness of Sunningham, felt that his labours were over for the day, and had retired to rest.

Clara, the Princess, Bergami, and the Marchioness, were probably the only inhabitants of the royal residence who were awake, and Sixteen-stringed Jack was its only visitor.

The brief conversation which had taken place in the cabinet of the Princess, when Jack had warned her not again to risk her safety by a visit to that house of evil repute in Frith Street, Soho, had occupied about the same period of time as the conversation between the Marchioness of Sunningham and Bergami.

Those two periods of time being nearly equal, Bergami had, by another route down the grand staircase, accompanied by the Marchioness, reached the hall, which was very spacious, and very prettily adorned with statuary.

There were hiding places in it for twenty assassins, had they been so inclined to take up their position in the vestibule of that eminent residence.

One solitary lamp burned upon a pedestal; but Bergami was bent upon a deed which loved not light; and he and the Marchioness of Sunningham no sooner reached the hall than they took good care to extinguish that solitary lamp.

It was the slight flash that it made across the balustrades of the staircase, as it was moved from the column, that Jack and Clara had seen.

Another moment, and all was darkness.

Then had come the suspicions of the young girl, which had induced her to creep down the staircase and hear those ominous words which enabled her to put Jack Singleton upon his guard.

And now Jack, feeling himself armed, and caring, in truth, but little for any Italian assassin, or any half-dozen at once that might venture to cross his path, descended rapidly that principal staircase of Buckingham House.

He could just see sufficiently in the darkness to enable him to come to a standstill, about six steps from the bottom.

Then, in pursuance of the advice given him by

Clara, he took a leap which not only cleared those six steps, but carried him ten or twelve feet across the hall, completely clear of the lurking assassin Bergami, who was crouching down in a littlerecess, formed by an ornamental curl of the gilt balustrade of the staircase.

But so little did the assassin expect that his victim was going to slip through his fingers in such a fashion, that he sprang to his feet, and made a heavy plunge forward with the dagger.

He leant his whole weight and force to the blow, and had the poniard met with any resistance from a human form, there is very little doubt but it would have sheathed itself in that form up to the very hilt.

But the poniard only clove the innocent air.

Bergami, however, had made so furious an effort, and such a plunge forward, that he could not recover himself, but at the very moment Sixteen-stringed Jack turned to face him, the would-be assas-ins fell prostrate at his feet.

It was too dark for Jack to see anything, but the great lumbering form came tumbling down as though it had dropped from the clouds.

But he had not the smallest doubt about the facts of the case.

He felt perfectly certain that it was the foiled assassin who lay prostrate upon the marble pavement of the hall.

And such being the case, it was hardly in human nature that Sixteen-stringed Jack should walk quietly away, and leave his unscrupulous opponent with no mortifications but those that might arise from a failure of his dastardly attempt.

Jack had the sword in his hand that had been given to him by Clara.

His first impulse was to draw it from its sheath and sacrifice the infamous Bergami.

But then the Englishman's principle prevailed, and Bergami, although he did not know it—for he would not have had the slightest notion of such a feeling himself—owed his life at that moment to the fact that he was on the ground, and at the feet of the man he had sought to murder.

Sixteen-stringed Jack half drew his sword from its scabbard before this better impulse came over him.

Then he thrust it back again.

"No!" he said, "reptile as you are I will not kill you, but you shall not escape quite free, for all that."

With these words Jack commenced belabouring the prostrate Bergami with the sheathed sword, after a fashion that was likely to be exceedingly effective.

It was as if some machine was at work wielding a flail, and warranted to make so many strokes a minute.

In the darkness it was not possible for Jack to see where his blows fell; all he could do was to thrash away at the dark-looking mass before him.

Bergami howled, shrieked, raved, and roared.

He rolled over and over, but by some fatality he did not seem able to escape the blows that came raining upon him.

He cursed and swore in Italian, in German, in broken English, in Flemish, and in various other Continental jargons.

But he never attempted to rise to his feet.

The Marchioness of Sunningham had taken refuge in an apartment opening from the hall, in order that she might *enjoy* the assassination of the man who had slighted and offended her that night.

The treat—if it were one that she enjoyed—was quite of a different character.

She was eaten up with mortification.

Her rage was almost equal to Bergami's.

She could almost have rushed out into the hall and herself assailed Sixteen-stringed Jack, only that she thought it a little dangerous to do so.

She pulled violently at the bell-cord which was in the room.

She called "Help! murder! thieves!"

But nobody paid the least attention.

There could not be the slightest doubt but that the whole household was alarmed, but few people who are alarmed out of their sleep are able to make any quick movements.

The paralysis of fear, the loss of time of hurry, each have their effect, and Sixteen-stringed Jack, if he had felt so inclined, might have gone on belabouring Bergami for another five minutes at the least before meeting with any interruption.

But he was getting tired of the exercise.

Something between a yell and a scream, too, in a female voice smote upon his ears.

That arose from an accident.

As Sixteen-stringed Jack held the sword by its hilt, and so liberally used it as a threshing machine upon Bergami, the scabbard became loose.

That flying off of the scabbard was at an opportune moment, for the Marchioness of Sunningham had just made another violent appeal to the bell, and then had put her head out of her room of refuge to see how affairs were proceeding.

The scabbard at that moment flying from the sword blade, winged its way with a rush through the air of the hall, and inflicted one smart blow across the face of the vindictive Marchioness, leaving its mark behind it, and inducing that lady to fall at once prostrate in the room leading from the hall, in the full belief that she was killed outright.

Jack Singleton did not know of this last piece of retributive justice, which accident had brought about, but being satisfied with the punishment he had inflicted upon the Italian assassin, he dealt him one farewell kick, and then left Buckhingham House.

There was nothing to impede his departure.

He crossed the outer court, passed through the iron gates, and in a few seconds stood beneath the trees of the Park.

But Sixteen-stringed Jack had made more enemies than Bergami and the Marchioness of Sunningham on that night.

Sir Hinckton Moys and his new ally, Colonel Hanger, had been waiting his re-appearance from Buckingham House with some impatience.

Moys was determined to assail him.

Not exactly after the fashion of Bergami, the Italian, did he mean to make that assault, but he wished to take what advantage he could, and press so quickly upon Jack that he would not have time to avail himself of his pistols, but would fall a sacrifice to a sword thrust.

Moys reasoned with himself that this would be all fair, although the reasoning was false enough.

Sixteen stringed-Jack had overcome him in Frith Street, by presenting a pistol at his head, while he, Sir Hinckton Moys, had no pistols, and was taken too much by surprise to use his sword.

Now he considered that he would attack this unknown personage who had saved the Princess of Wales with a sword, thinking he had none, and too rapidly to enable him to make use of his fire-arms.

Moys tried to persuade himself that this was fair, although, in truth, it was quite the contrary, simply because Sixteen-stringed Jack, in the first instance, had acted in self-defence, and not as an assailant; and moreover, had it been otherwise, he could not tell whether Sir Hinckton Moys had fire-arms or not.

It was quite a chance that Jack had not flung down the sword that had done him such good service in the hall of Buckingham House, but some good genius surely restrained him, since it was to do him better service still.

So he carried it out in his hand into the Park, scarely knowing that he held it, or whether the sheath were on it or not.

He had not taken five paces under the shadow of the trees when Moys rushed out upon him with his drawn sword in his hand.

"Now, sir!" he cried. "You had me at a disadvantage awhile ago, but I fancy the odds have turned in my favour."

Jack stepped back a pace.

He instinctively held up his sword to guard himself from an attack, and great was the surprise of Sir Hinckton Moys to hear the dash of cold steel, as his sword blade rang upon the other.

He began to think he had made a serious mistake; and that, after all, the man who had issued from the house in Frith Street, Soho, along with the Princess of Wales, might be somebody of rank, and not at all the person Colonel Hanger had taken him to be.

But Moys was, after all, a man of courage; and certainly he was not likely to fly from an encounter which he himself, in so deliberate a manner, had courted.

He had warned Hanger to hold back, and not interfere—for in truth, he had expected an easy conquest; and Hanger, who had obeyed him literally, was some distance off under the trees.

Sixteen-stringed Jack, the highwayman, therefore, and Sir Hinckton Moys had the Park pretty well to themselves to finish their little differences in.

It was soon over.

Jack felt that he had received a slight wound in the arm.

He was not very well able, on the moment, to judge of its extent; but as it might bleed freely, and the loss of blood would weaken him, he felt the necessity of bringing the contest to an end as speedily as possible.

He pressed heavily upon Moys.

It was difficult for either of them to see by the dim night light what they were about, and several good opportunities were, no doubt, lost on both sides for inflicting mortal wounds.

Jack, however had the advantage, in height as well as in length of arm.

He made a dash forward, and, getting within the guard of Sir Hinckton Moys, he passed his sword, as he thought, right through his neck.

Moys uttered an exclamation, and fell.

"That'll do!" said Jack, as he withdrew his sword, and then flung it into the air.

It lodged in a tree.

Sixteen-stringed Jack then hastily strode down the Mall of the Park, and left it by the gate at Spring Gardens, without any challenge by the sentinel who stood there, and whose duty was only to call out to people entering the royal precincts, and not to those leaving them.

"A pretty night's work I've made of it!" said Jack, as he crossed hastily the open space in front of the King's Mews. "I'll get my horse now, and be off to Hounslow; for as I have ascertained the fate of my poor old comrade, who lies dead in the cellars of the house in Frith Street, Soho, I have nothing just now to linger for here.

In ten minutes more Sixteen-stringed Jack was mounted and riding rapidly out of London.

CHAPTER CCIV.

THE DARK WOMAN ATTEMPTS TO DISPOSE OF HER JEWELS, AND RISKS HER LIFE.

THE situation of Linda de Chevenaux was terrible.

She was scarcely able to reason with any coherence upon the position in which she found herself.

It seemed to her as if all her plans and projects only had the effect of heaping so much more confusion upon her head.

In everything she failed.

At the moment when least expected some serious obstacle seemed ever destined to rise up and mar whatever she was about.

And now she found herself again alone—alone in that terrible house, so full of memories of the past, that its very atmosphere seemed full of death and disaster. Alone, perhaps only for a short time; for whatever else could she expect now but that the officers of justice would quickly be upon her path, and she would find herself worse situated than ever, and with more tangible charges against her than had ever before been urged.

True, she had slept off some slight portion of the fatigue which had taken possession of her.

But still she was faint and weary.

Still she felt that she required rest, but there was no rest for her.

Action—action alone, was the atmosphere in which she would have to live, and in order to save herself from the consequences of her last mad attack upon the Princess of Wales and the Marchioness of Sunningham, she felt that that action must be immediate.

Henceforth, that house would surely be no place of refuge for her.

She must fly from it, and that at once.

But whither was she now to go?

The lodging that she had taken in St. James's Street would hardly receive her in her present costume, differing so largely as it did from the masculine suit in which she had taken it.

And yet it was there she felt she ought to go; for what option had she but to renew her intercourse with that band of desperate men who had accompanied her in her night attack, as it might be called, upon St. James's Palace?

Moreover, the whole plunder of that occasion

was in her possession; or rather, with the exception of the few jewels she had taken from the rest, and placed in the pockets of her female attire, that plunder was along with the suit of male habiliments she had left at the house in Hanover Square, when she had exchanged them for that rich and costly female attire by the aid of which she vainly hoped to awaken reminiscences in the heart of the Regent.

What was she to do?

She strove to think.

She strove to calm her agitated brow by outward pressure of her hands upon her head; and all the while she did so, she fancied that the minutes were flying fast, at the end of a certain number of which danger would seek her out, there and then, in that gloomy habitation, to hold her in its clutch.

In that idea the Dark Woman was mistaken.

No one who was aware of her presence there was likely to disturb her: in fact, Jack Singleton was the only one who might be said to be fully aware of the fact; and for Captain Fitz George's sake he would have condoned much more serious acts, on the part of Linda de Chevenaux, than those she had committed that night as against him.

She had no idea that Jack Singleton, wrapped up as he was in his affection for his daughter Lucy, spared her because he feared to inflict a pang upon Captain Fitz George, who, with Marian, his wife, had been so kind to that daughter.

These were sentiments and feelings which had long since been submerged in the whirl of angry passions awakened in the mind of the Dark Woman.

And so she strove to think exactly what she had to do; and amid all that striving of consecutive reason, the sense of danger kept rising up, and the one word "escape" came prominently before her.

She drew more carefully around her fanciful and rich dress the common cloak and hood which she had brought from Giltspur Street, Compter.

She crept down the gloomy staircase; she glided along the dark passage; and after listening for awhile, to assure herself that her foes were not actually upon the threshold, she opened the street-door, and sallied forth from that house of murder and iniquity, just as two o'clock sounded from the church spires of the vicinity.

The night air was cool and refreshing. It seemed like new life to Linda de Chevenaux to feel it blowing gustily upon her brow.

Her purpose then rose up clearly and distinctly before her. It was to make her way at once to that house in Hanover Square, and get possession again of the clothing which she had secreted here, and in the pockets of which so large a fortune was contained.

The Dark Woman had no fear whatever of finding that fortune tampered with, or appropriated in the slightest degree; for she had resided in that house quite long enough to enable her to establish one of those secret receptacles, which her perverse ingenuity contrived, wherever she thought proper to take up her abode for a time.

Nor did she, as her brain cooled and she became able to reason more calmly and discreetly upon her situation, anticipate that there would be either danger or difficulty in making her way into that mansion.

It had always been her custom to find safety in places which would be shunned by inferior intellects; and inasmuch as that house in Hanover Square would be about the last place in which any reasonable person would look for her, she considered it was the place of all others where she might go with the greatest amount of safety.

Moreover, she had been arrested there, and therefore there was no further inducement for the officers of justice to linger about the spot.

It was doubtful, even up to that hour, if her escape from Giltspur Street Compter was known.

And so, reasoning in this style, and feeling all the time the absolute necessity of getting possession, by fair means or by foul, of the male clothing which contained the costly jewels plundered by herself and her gang from St. James's Palace, she rather hastened than retarded her footsteps towards Hanover Square.

As she anticipated, at that hour of the night, the house was profoundly dark; but she was aware that it was in the keeping of a woman who resided in the kitchens; and it was necessary to attract the attention of this woman in order to obtain admittance.

The Dark Woman had an idea of climbing the area rails, and so enabling herself to make a much more direct appeal to the senses of the woman in charge of the house than she could hope to do by any appeal to the knocker or the bell.

It was with quite a forlorn hope in that direction that Linda de Chevenaux tried the lock of the area gate, and found that it opened readily to her touch.

She was down into the area of the house like a spectre; for she saw a watchman approaching, who, from his manner, she suspected had been desired to give some special observance to that mansion.

But Linda de Chevenaux was in the shadow of the outward wall of the area; and although the watchman waved his lantern to and fro, and made a sleepy kind of observation of the premises, he did not detect her, but passed on his way.

The Dark Woman listened to his retreating footsteps; and, when all was silent again, she tapped slightly at the first door leading into the kitchens.

The immediate sound as of something or somebody falling within the house, followed this appeal; and then a startled voice cried out from within, "Who knocks? Who is there? Gracious goodness, what do you want?"

"A messenger from his Royal Highness the Regent."

"Yes. His Highness is very well satisfied with the manner in which you discreetly remained in the lower part of the house, during the disturbance of to-day; and he sends you some gold, which I shall have the pleasure of handing to you."

The woman who had charge of the house was dazzled by the name of the Regent and the sound of gold—a juxtaposition of two such brilliant things that they completely confused her faculties; and she forgot to ask herself if it were at all reasonable to suppose that the Regent would send a special messenger in the middle of the night to bestow upon her a few guineas, and that

that special messenger would get easily down the area.

"Wait a moment," she cried, "and I'll get a light for your lordship."

The woman surely thought that everybody who ran errands for the Regent between two and three o'clock in the morning must be a lord at the very least.

Then the door was opened, and Linda de Chevenaux entered the kitchen.

She had neither time nor inclination to trifle with this woman any longer. It was easier for her now to exert the dominion of fear, and to use force if necessary.

"On your life," she cried, "stir not!"

The woman uttered a half cry. It was extorted from her by surprise and fear, and therefore was hardly a contravention of the orders of Linda de Chevenaux.

"Peace," she cried again,—"peace, woman, if you value your worthless existence. You shall have the gold I have mentioned, but it must be the price of your absolute silence, and of your absolute submission."

There was something about the tone and aspect of the Dark Woman which awed the poor trembling creature completely. Her strength seemed to desert her; and thinking, no doubt, that her last hour had come, she sunk upon her knees, and trembled in every limb.

The Dark Woman took but little notice of the abject fear she produced; but dashing upon the table some of the gold she had with her, she cried out, "You lose nothing by my presence, and gain much. Be discreet and silent; but, in order that I may avoid even a trifling inconvenience, I must make a prisoner of you for a time."

The Dark Woman glanced round the kitchen to see if there was any place in which she might bestow this woman in safety during the ten minutes or quarter of an hour which it would take her to repair to the upper rooms, and make the meditated change in her apparel.

But at the word "prisoner," the woman in charge of the house was so terrified, that the small remains of sense she had left departed from her.

She fell forward heavily to the floor in a swoon.

The Dark Woman took up the light that was upon the table, and holding it down, scanned her countenance.

She feared to be deceived.

A glance, however, was sufficient: the swoon was only too real.

"Be it so," said the Dark Woman: "that answers the purpose as well, if not better. Nature takes her senses prisoner, and she need be no captive of mine."

Taking the candle from the table, then, Linda de Chevenaux ascended to the upper portion of the house; she paused a moment before entering that magnificent drawing-room where some painful episodes in her history had taken place.

But then pushing open the door, she entered the large apartment; and as she gazed around her, with a sigh, at its large extent, so dimly lighted by the rushlight she carried, the scenes she had passsed through beneath that gilded roof came vividly before her imagination.

It was there, in that very apartment, that she

had specially and particularly explained to her son, then named Allan Fearon, the objects for which she had lived so long and suffered so much.

It was there, too, that he had repudiated those objects, and striven to convince her that they were the delusions and the snares which had beset her existence, and would, if not shaken off, like nightmares of the soul, bring her to destruction.

It was there, too, that she had been visited by the two housebreakers, Shucks and Brads, who had claimed acquaintance with her, and not only astonished her household by their coarse familiarity, but had let her see that while she remained there she would never be free from their demands.

And it was there, too, that she had had that last interview with the Prince of Wales, which had snapped asunder the last slender thread of hope that she could ever be to him other than a hated enemy.

No wonder that these recollections shook even the soul of the Dark Woman.

But they passed through her mind with the rapidity of the lightning's flash, and she seemed scarcely to have paused in the apartment, as she held the rushlight above her head, and took but one passing glance at the dim glitter of its costly furnishing.

She left the room by the same door she had entered it when she so astonished the Regent by her presence.

Ten minutes elapsed, and then a very different looking personage to that courtly and richly-attired lady, who had so lately left the drawing-room, re-entered it.

The Dark Woman had resumed her disguise, and nothing could be more dissimilar than the two appearances she had made that night.

In her male attire she looked much smaller; and the wig beneath which were concealed her luxuriant tresses, imparted quite a different expression to her features.

Once more she cast a glance around her; and then with an air of vexation she flung the lighted candle on the floor.

There was no special desire upon her mind to produce gratuitous mischief; and when she saw that the small flame of the rushlight was not extinguished, but that, on the contrary, it showed an inclination to communicate itself to the carpet, she stamped out the incipient conflagration.

"No," she said, "that would be folly. If Linda de Cheuenaux calls upon flame to aid her, it shall not be on the weak impulse or irritation of a moment."

She then made her way down the grand staircase with as much ease and promptitude as though it had been broad daylight.

Linda de Chevenaux had that faculty which some people possess of being wonderfully handy and at home in darkness.

Let the obscurity be what it would, she was never confused nor lost her way. This is a kind of extra sense, which is a gift of nature. Those have it upon whom it is bestowed, but it may not be acquired.

She had not lived so long in that house without being accurately informed in regard to the fastenings of its outer door, so that she was enabled

quietly and easily, by a touch or two, to open that outer door and leave the house.

She left the woman in the kitchen to recover from her swoon as best she might, and at the corner of the square she passed the watchman who had been specially desired to keep an eye upon No. 10.

The guardian of the night held up his lantern and looked at the gentleman, as he thought him, who was walking so staidly and so steadily from the Square, and whose footsteps he wondered he had not heard until they were almost close upon him.

"Good night, sir!" said the watchman.

"Good night!" replied the Dark Woman, and she passed on with Crown jewels to the amount of fifty thousand pounds in her pockets.

Linda de Chevenaux had now no hesitation whatever in seeking her lodgings in St. James's Street, for in that fashionable locality, even at such

No. 92.—DARK WOMAN.

an hour in the morning, it was not an occurrence likely to create any very intense surprise.

And thankful indeed did she feel that the distance was now so short between Hanover Square and St. James's Street; and when she fairly reached that lodging, and found herself in her own rooms, she could scarcely bear to think upon the physical fatigues and mental excitations of the last four-and-twenty hours.

She flung herself upon her couch, dressed as she was, and with a far greater sense of security than she had enjoyed when she sought a refuge from the lassitude and fatigue that had overcome her in the passage of the house in Frith Street, she sank into a deep sleep.

That sleep was uninterrupted.

A chequered gleam of sunshine through the Venetian blinds of the front windows of the apartment in which the Dark Woman lay, roused her to the consciousness that a new day had dawned.

So deep and dreamless had been her sleep for the last five or six hours, that it seemed to her as if she had but lain down the moment before on that couch.

She sprung to her feet.

She heard in a confused and dreamy fashion the thousand noises that made up the waking life of the great city.

The tramp of horses' feet, the rattle and grinding rush of carriage-wheels, the murmuring sound of foot-passengers, and that strange and universal agitation of the air, which can be compared to nothing but the restless motion of the sea.

It was between nine and ten o'clock.

The Dark Woman felt wonderfully refreshed by her repose, and for a few minutes she could hardly believe that all the strange incidents which had so recently befallen her were other than the suggestions of a morbid imagination.

But she had a means at hand of readily testing their truth and reality.

All she had to do was to produce from the pockets of her attire those jewels which she had taken from the casket in St. James's Palace, and their sight at once rescued her from the land of doubts, and of dreams, and brought her back most vividly to the realities of existence.

She drew up the blinds at the window of her apartment, and gazed out upon the moving throng of every day life before her.

Did she expect again to catch a sight of that son for whom she had already sacrificed so much, and for whom she was still willing to sacrifice a life?

If the Dark Woman had any such expectation she was mistaken.

Captain Fitz George was not again to be seen, as she had looked upon him once before from that window, taking his way to the Palace; for at that moment he was holding converse with the Regent, and she, Linda de Chevenaux, was the theme of the discourse.

She hurried from the window with a sigh.

The glittering jewels she had taken from her pockets remained upon the table.

She cast her handkerchief over them, and then she rang for breakfast and attendance

And there sat the Dark Woman, almost within sight of the passengers in St. James's Street, sipping her chocolate, and looking very much like a gentleman at ease, who might be seeking to while away some of the tedious hours of the morning, before it might be the accredited time to take a fashionable stroll in Bond Street or Pall Mall.

The mind, however, was busy within, although the Dark Woman schooled her countenance to calmness.

She had projects which, if they had been declared from the housetops, would have filled London with dismay.

But whatever those projects were, their contemplation was interrupted by a sound that made the Dark Woman start to her feet.

That sound was a salvo of artillery from the Park, and hardly had its echoes died away, when almost every church bell in London dashed into a joyous peal.

The Dark Woman then recollected that this was the wedding-day of the Princess Charlotte of Wales.

CHAPTER CCV.

THE DARK WOMAN SEEKS TO DISPOSE OF HER JEWELS, AND DISCOVERS A FEARFUL MYSTERY AT THE HOUSE OF THE LAPIDARY AND JEWELLER.

How agonizing must have been the feelings of the Princess of Wales on that morning of the nuptials of her daughter, at which she was not even allowed to be present !

How strange must have been the thoughts of the young and gallant Captain Fitz George, when he considered that the whole nation was so deeply interesting itself in the fortunes of one who in good truth was neither more nor less than his sister !

Listen ! The sound was so strange a one to him, who had always looked upon himself as in a state of forlorn orphanage.

And yet his sister the Princess Charlotte of Wales really was.

His sister, in nature.

But not his sister according to the laws of the land.

And so she knew him not; and he heard the roar of the cannon, and the pleasant jangle of the bells on her wedding-day, without taking any special part in the ceremony.

He was merely, on the occasion, "the officer on duty at St. James's Palace."

That was all.

But it is not with the marriage of Charlotte, Princess of Wales, with Leopold of Saxe-Coburg that we have now to do.

It is not with that bride of only a few short months before the grave closed upon her and her infant, that we have now to speak.

Darker episodes in our story, even, than that catastrophe, which put a nation into mourning, demand our attention.

Linda de Chevenaux commenced her work again.

Hope for anything like such terms with the Regent as would satisfy her ambition for herself or for her son, had now fairly deserted her heart.

It was the first time that such hopes had absolutely fled.

There had been periods when she had felt &c. spake.

There had been periods in her "life march" when she had felt as though she could "lie down and die by the way," but she had not yet wholly divested herself of hope.

That divinity that

"Springs eternal in the human breast,"

had always remained to her, persuading her that surely the time would come when all her perseverance would be rewarded.

But now that period was past.

She no longer lived in the expectation of achieving the desires of her life.

But she was resolved to exist for other objects and purposes.

The chief of those was comprehended in one word.

Revenge !

That was the word she kept now repeating to herself; and each time that she so repeated it, it sounded in her ear with a sombre cadence.

She felt that she had the two great resources for carrying out any schemes of violence or of vengeance that her active imagination might suggest.

Unscrupulous adherents and money.

With these two means of action, what was there that she need shrink from undertaking?

Nothing!

In the band of men who had so recently linked their fortunes to hers, and chosen her for their chief, she found the ready agents of any enterprise she could suggest.

The jewels she had taken from St. James's Palace furnished the means of carrying out any object, however expensive.

She had but one fear.

There was but one ingredient in the transaction that she dreaded.

It was this.

The plunder from the Palace was so extensive —so very valuable—that she dreaded it would engender habits of sloth and indulgence in the men who had assisted her in obtaining it.

If that were to be the case, so long as that plunder, or rather the gold that would be its produce, lasted, those men would be but of little use to Linda de Chevenaux.

But, after all, that was but a fear.

She dared not break faith with them on such a ground. On the contrary, she must let them see, and that quickly too, that she by no means repented of the liberal promises she had made them.

The jewels must be sold.

All or some of them must be sold forthwith, in order that she might be in a position on that evening to meet her band, with her hands full of gold.

It was, then, with the object of disposing of some of the most costly of those jewels, that Linda de Chevenaux, at about four o'clock in the afternoon, when she was thoroughly refreshed and rested, left her lodgings in St. James's Street.

She wore the male apparel, which she was always better pleased to attire herself in than in the troublesome robes of her own sex.

In male attire she had a freedom of action which suited her far better than a contemplation of all the troublesome finery of a woman.

And so perfect was the disguise of the Dark Woman that no one, without some hint of the fact, could possibly have suspected she was other than what she seemed.

Calmly and sedately she took her route up St. James's Street, and then she turned to the left, for she recollected to have some time since noticed a small shop kept by a jeweller and lapidary with a foreign name, in the window of which she had been struck by seeing some very rare and costly gems.

There was a dull air of quietude and mystery about the shop, which made the Dark Woman think that the sort of trade carried on there was not exactly an open one.

During her adventures in London, and during her connexion with her original band of "Paul's Chickens," she had learnt that many apparently quiet, respectable-looking shops in London are but the cloak, the disguise, the mask, behind which very different pursuits are carried on.

Linda de Chevenaux suspected this quiet, de-mure-looking jeweller's shop that she now made her way to.

The name over the door was a Dutch or Flemish one.

Vanden Becken.

There was nothing to attract the great, the rich, or the noble, to that dirty, dusty, rather repulsive-looking place.

And so it seemed to suit the Dark Woman admirably.

She tried the shop door.

It was fast.

At the corner of the window there was a small placard, on which was written the words, "Gold and jewels bought. Ring the bell."

This was, in the mind of the Dark Woman, conclusive.

The place was a "fence,"—that is, a place for the rapid conversion of stolen goods into cash.

It was just the kind of new connexion she wished to make.

At the East End of London, and in and about St. Martin's Lane and Field Lane, Linda de Chevenaux knew of plenty of places where property of any description whatever would be purchased, and "no questions asked."

But those were all places where the story of Paul's Chickens was rife.

What she wanted was to make some new arrangements; and this little mysterious shop close to the Green Park seemed to promise her every possible facility.

She found with difficulty a small bell-handle, which she pulled smartly.

The door opened with a creaking sound.

"Come in!"

The voice that spoke was not English.

The accent had all that laborious thickness about it of the inhabitants of the Low Countries.

She at once stepped into the shop.

"Shut the door!" said the voice.

The Dark Woman did so.

It closed with a sharp sound, and she felt quite certain it would not be easy to open it again without the consent of the shop proprietor.

The interior of the shop was very dark, so that coming out of the open air, Linda de Chevenaux had some difficulty for a few seconds in seeing about her.

"Number what, my dear?" asked the thick Jewish voice.

"I do not know what you mean," replied the Dark Woman.

"Ah! you don't know vat I means? Vat then you vants here, my dear?"

"I have something to sell."

"Vat? vat?"

"A diamond!"

"A bit of glass you means, my dear."

"Very well—good day."

"He! he! he! Ho! ho! Good day, you say. Ho! ho! my dear, if you have a diamond, you had better give it up at once!"

"Why so?"

"Because—he! he!—because——"

"Take your time," said the Dark Woman, coolly. "Because what?"

"Because, just by accident, you see, my dear, there is on the opposite side of the way Mr. Townshend, the vell-known—vat you call him?— Bow Street runner. He! he!"

" Well?"

" You say vell!"

" I do say well?"

" Don't you know if I vas to tap on the window-glass he would come over and take you, eh? Oh, my dear, you had better lay down the diamond, if it is a diamond—though it's only a bit of glass, I dare say—and be off at once!"

" I don't think so."

" Eh, my dear?"

" I say I don't think so; because, if Mr. Townshend the officer comes over here, I will tell him that this is a notorious receptacle for stolen goods, and give you at once into his custody."

" You will?"

" I will."

" My dear, I love you! Bless you!"

" Stuff! I came here to sell a diamond. I know what you are, and who you are, quite well, although you do not show yourself, and I only hear your voice."

" Then who are you, eh?"

" That's my business."

From behind a portion of the shop which was partitioned off lightly by a fragile wood frame-work, covered with paper, a man emerged.

His age was about sixty; and he had all the cunning, leering look of the lower class of Israelites, combined with the grasping expression of a dirty Fleming.

The shaggy white eyebrows nearly hid his eyes, and the black velvet skull-cap he wore suffered a quantity of either very grey or very dirty hair to fall upon his shoulders.

" Vell," he said, " I see you are a dear boy—a clever youth Mr. Townshend is not there. Bless you, I only said that to frighten you."

" You failed!"

" Vat?"

" I am never frightened."

" Vell, vell, my good friend, vere is the diamond? vere is it? A bit of glass, of course."

" If you say that again, you shall not see it at all."

" Well, well, I won't say it. How hasty you are, my dear! I won't say it. Where is the diamond?"

" There!"

Linda de Chevenaux laid one of the loose diamonds she had brought from the Palace before the jeweller; and the moment his eyes fell upon it, he said, " Ah, dear me!—ah, dear me! How clever—how very clever! Oh, dear me!"

" What's the matter?"

" Good! capital! It would almost take any-body in—anybody but me. Ah, dear!—ah, dear!"

" I again ask, what's the matter?"

The Flemish fence shook his head.

" It's an imitation, my dear."

" Indeed!"

" Oh, yes! Well done—beautifully done, but its an imitation. Oh, dear, yes—only an imita-tion."

" You don't say so?"

" I do, my dear—I do. I only wish it was not, that is all."

" And if it was, what would you give for it?"

" Von hundred pounds."

" Then that's the price."

" Eh?"

" That's the price, I say to you, of this jewel."

" But, my dear——"

" I have said——"

" But it's an imitation."

" That," said the Dark Woman, calmly,— " that is not of the slightest consequence."

" Vat?"

" Not of the slightest. I offer you this bit of stone for a hundred pounds. If you like to pay for it at once, you can have it; but, as my time is valuable, I shall put on ten pounds to the price for every five minutes you make me waste."

" Vat?"

" Ten pounds——"

" Ter teffel!"

" For every five minutes."

" Let me look at the stone again."

" Look!"

" It is an imitation; but as you seem a good young man, I—I will give you fifty pounds for it! There!"

" One hundred and ten pounds! Not one farthing less."

" Stop! stop! You agreed to one hundred."

" But you did not."

" But five minutes have elapsed."

" Donner and blitzen!"

" One hundred and twenty!"

The Dutch jeweller uttered a cry of despair. The diamond was well worth five hundred pounds, at the least; and he saw that he was losing at the rate of ten pounds for every five minutes.

" Stop! stop! You shall have the monies— you shall have the monies!"

" Quick!"

" In one moment!"

" One hundred and thirty pounds!"

" Dirty pounds?"

" Thirty."

" Von hundred and dirty pounds? Oh! oh! come this way. Step this way, my good young man. Vell, vell, be moderate, and you shall have the monies; but don't say any more—don't, now —don't."

" Since you have now bought it for one hundred and thirty pounds," said the Dark Woman, " I shall make no further advance upon it."

" Oh, dear—oh, dear! Von hundred and dirty —von hundred and dirty, ven I might have had him for von hundred!"

" You might," said Linda de Chevenaux, as she followed the stolen goods receiver from his shop into a dingy-looking but rather large apart-ment at the back of it, in which there was a lamp burning.

There was a window to the back parlour of the jeweller's shop, which, no doubt, would have ad-mitted light enough into it, but it was covered by a thick blind.

Nothing but artificial light, therefore, made ob-jects visible in that gloomy place.

There was a strange odour in the air.

What that odour was the Dark Woman could not possibly imagine.

" What is this," she said, " that taints the atmo-sphere of this room?"

The Dutch jeweller made a sniffing noise with his nose, and then he hastily set light to a pastile which was on the chimneypiece, and which soon began to send forth volumes of pale grey smoke and a sickly sort of perfume.

"It is the damps—the damps!" he said—"the damps and the fogs!"

"But there are none now."

"Oh, yes—yes! It is the damps and the fogs—the damps and the fogs! Sit down, young man, and you shall have your monies.'

Linda de Chevenaux knew not the sensation of fear, but she began to get suspicious.

Suspicious of what?

That she could not well define to herself; and yet she had an impression that she was in some danger.

Of that, however, she cared but little. She was well armed, and she felt fully competent to take good care of herself.

Nevertheless, she resolved that while she was in that place she would keep all her senses fully alive, and behave with the greatest caution.

"Now, young mans," said the Dutchman, "what will you have?"

"The money."

"But I means to drinks?"

"Nothing."

"Nothing? Oh, yes! some schnapps, now?"

"Certainly, not."

"Or some delicate Rhine wine, now, if your vat you call it—your stomach is von weak?"

"I want nothing. Pay me for the jewel, and then I will go."

"Oh, yes—yes! You will go! Quite sure to go! He! he! he!"

There was something truly hideous and repulsive about the laugh of this man; and had Linda de Chevenaux possessed one fragment less of the calm courage which was hers, she must have been alarmed to a degree.

The Dutchman went to a kind of bureau, that was in an obscure corner of the room, and brought out a long-necked bottle from it, and two tall, slender, and very elegant ruby-coloured glasses.

"Come, come!" he said; "we must drink to von better acquaintance, my goot friend, and I will call you Number Dirty."

"What?"

"Number Dirty. Dere is a young girl who comes here with what she can find at the theatres and public places, and I call her Number Twenty-nine; so mine, young friend, as you are the next, you must be Number Dirty, you see."

"I hear!"

"Come, come! you shall drink—you shall drink."

CHAPTER CCVI.

THE DARK WOMAN SHUTS UP THE SHUTTERS OF THE JEWELLER'S SHOP.

THE old Flemish receiver of stolen goods placed the tall bottle and the elegant ruby glasses on the table before Linda de Chevenaux; and then, looking as fully in her face as he well could by the dim light in that room, he said, "Young man, you are after mine own heart. You vas not one small bit frightened ven I spoke to you of Townshend, the officer."

"I know not fear."

"Vell, vell! That is vell! And now, my dear, this is some choice Rhine wine, from the cellar of Prince de Metternich, and you shall drink."

"And you?'

"Vell, I love the schnapps better; but I shall drink for von good fellowship, and von long to last friendship with you."

"Drink, then."

"I will—I will!"

The cork of the tall bottle was withdrawn, and the jeweller was about to pour out some of its contents into one of the ruby-coloured glasses, when he was interrupted by a sharp tinkle at that same bell which the Dark Woman had rang at for admittance to the shop.

"Ah! some von."

He set down the bottle.

The bell was rung a second time.

The jeweller cast a furtive glance around him, as though to see that if he left the room for a moment or two there would be nothing which he did not wish his customer to see exposed to observation; and then he said, "My good young man, help yourself; I shall be back in von half-minute."

The bell rang a third time.

Muttering the same Flemish oaths, the jeweller went into the shop.

The door of communication between it and the parlour closed with the same sort of snapping noise that the shop door had made.

The Dark Woman was alone.

That is to say, to all appearance she was alone.

The suspicions that had taken possession of her that some foul play was intended had almost deepened into certainty.

At all events, they had not decreased.

She felt that she might possibly not have more than a couple of minutes in which to look about her, but she was determined to make the most use of that time.

And yet what was she to discover?

What interest, indeed, could she have in any possible discoveries? For, after all, what had she to do in that place but to receive as quickly as possible the money she had now no doubt of receiving, and then to remove from it as quickly as possible?

But was she not in danger herself? Would she be permitted to take this cool and easy view of the circumstances? Did the Flemish jeweller—who, no doubt, drove a good trade in the reception of stolen property—intend that she should leave his premises in so free and easy a manner, without herself being implicated in some of its mysteries?

That was the question.

And it was from that motive and impulse that the Dark Woman felt it necessary, during the brief period she was left alone in that dingy parlour at the back of the jeweller's shop, to make what investigations might be in her power.

The pastile which had been lighted upon the chimney-piece was nearly expiring, but to a certain extent it had fulfilled its object, and the strange odour which had first of all assailed the senses of the Dark Woman had given way to the aromatic perfume of the burning ingredients of the pastile.

Still seated, when the Flemish jeweller had left her, the Dark Woman took as accurate visual survey of the apartment as she possibly could.

She felt certain that its corners contained closets or cupboards of considerable extent.

She hardly knew why it was that her attention was particularly directed towards one of these closets or cupboards, but so it was; and she felt impelled by an impulse she hardly chose to investigate, to make some researches specially in that direction.

And what was the sort of discovery she expected to make?

One of crime! One of possible murder!

Even the Dark Woman shook a little as the word suggested itself to her imagination.

Yet she had no precise grounds for her fears or for her surmises.

She could hear the Flemish fence-keeper's voice in the shop, conversing with some one; and she could gather from the tones that he was making what haste he could to dismiss the visitor.

There was not a moment to lose.

The Dark Woman, with a noiseless step, approached the closet that had attracted her attention.

A key was in the lock.

It was a simple enough process to turn that key, and the Dark Woman performed it instantly.

Then she retreated a step.

And well she might.

Well she might; for from within the cupboard came a sort of outward pressure, as if some one were there endeavouring to force the door open so soon as the turning of the key in the lock enabled it to move upon its hinges.

Linda de Chevenaux held the door fast.

The pressure from within did not increase, but it continued.

It was a nervous moment that.

No sound came from within the cupboard. There was no mode but actually opening the door by which the mystery could be elucidated.

And that she dreaded to do.

Then, while she paused irresolutely for a few seconds—and the whole transaction did not occupy the space of one whole minute—she heard the voices in the shop again.

"Not one farthing more," said the Flemish receiver of stolen goods.

"Then you don't get it," replied a voice angrily.

"Vell, go then."

There was now not another instant, surely, to expend in irresolution.

The Dark Woman opened the cupboard door.

She had seen too many terrible sights, and had led too adventurous a life herself, to be easily surprised into an exclamation; but seasoned, so to speak, as the Dark Woman was to deeds of horror, she nearly uttered a cry of dismay, as she found what it was that had seemed to be pushing the cupboard door outward.

The dead body of a young girl, evidently not above fifteen or sixteen years of age, fell out of the cupboard on to the floor at the feet of Linda de Chevenaux.

There was blood upon the lips, and the hue of death was upon the brow.

There could be no doubt whatever that the destroyer was there, although no precise wound presented itself.

The body had been propped up in the cupboard in a standing position, with the back against the edge of some shelves, so that it was kept there by the door.

So soon as the door yielded a little, the mere weight of the murdered girl exerted a pressure against it.

That was the pressure which had both astonished and alarmed the Dark Woman.

The mystery, however, was explained now.

She was in a den of murder.

That plausible-looking and soft-spoken Fleming took the lives of his victims.

From the tawdry and meretricious finery that was upon the young girl, the Dark Woman could very easily conceive the class of society to which she belonged.

It was all plain enough. No doubt she had come there to convert some jewel into cash, and the readiest mode of settling with her had been to take her life.

It was very horrible.

But so soon as the Dark Woman fully comprehended the situation, she was no longer anxious, or full of fears and doubts.

All her ordinary courage and self-possession came back to her on the instant.

She was equal to the emergency.

And now the first thing she did was to stoop over the dead body, and carefully to raise it, in order to replace it in the cupboard.

That was a task of some little difficulty.

It was only the door that would keep it in its place properly.

The difficulty, then, was to shut the door quickly enough to prevent the body from falling forward.

The Dark Woman had to make two attempts before she succeeded.

Then it was done.

The door was closed, and she turned the key in the lock and left it there, as she found it.

The object of the Dark Woman now was to get back to the chair on which she had been sitting before the departure of the Fleming to the front shop.

She just did this, with not the fraction of a second to spare.

Indeed, she could scarcely be said to be fairly seated, when the door of communication between the shop and that dark and gloomy parlour was opened, and the Fleming looked in.

There was a smile upon his face.

"Vell, my dear?"

"Well?" said Linda de Chevenaux, calmly.

"How do you like the Rhine wine?"

"I have not taken any of it."

"No?"

"Not a drop. You are my host and entertainer, and I waited for you."

"Vell, vell, that is all very vell; and so now we vill have one glass, and then I will get you your monies."

"Is the wine poisoned?" thought the Dark Woman.

She had every reason to think that it was. At all events, in such an establishment, it would certainly be running by far too great a risk to venture upon tasting it.

But how to avoid doing so without raising the suspicions of the jeweller was rather a difficulty.

It was not that the Dark Woman had any very great fears in regard to the issue of a contest with him, for she was well armed. But how could she as yet feel quite sure that he was alone in that house of murder?

It was to get at that fact the one way or the other that Linda de Chevenaux now spoke to her villainous entertainer.

"You came from Holland?" she said.

"Yah! Yes, I come from the Low Countries."

"And you find the presence of your family here make almost another home in this country?"

"Mine family?"

"Yes. You are not alone here?"

"I am."

"Quite alone?"

"Yah, my dear. I am quite alone in this country and in this house; but when I have, by honest industry, made von sum of the monies, I shall go back to mine own country, and be von burgomaster."

The Fleming almost looked affected as he spoke.

"Come, come, my dear!" he then added. "You do not drink."

The Dark Woman shook her head.

"I seldom, if ever, take wine so soon in the day."

"Never mind, you vill take some now."

"Excuse me."

"No, no! You must drink to our better acquaintance; and then I will show you some fine jewels I have that vill please your eyes, oh, so much!"

"Indeed?"

"Yah!"

"Where are they?"

"In von cupboard over there."

The Fleming pointed to the cupboard in which was the dead body that the Dark Woman had so recently look upon.

"Oh, in that cupboard!"

"Yah!"

"Show me, now."

"It is too soon."

"Why too soon?"

"Mine dear friend, you are not ready."

"I cannot comprehend what you mean by not ready."

"You will comprehend soon. Now drink of the Rhine wine It is good! Follow my example. Ah! It is good—good!"

The assassin poured himself out from the bottle a brimming glass of the pale yellow wine, and drank it off at once.

It was not the wine, then, that was poisoned.

For a moment or two the Dark Woman was puzzled.

Then she had an idea.

It was not the wine she had to dread, but it was the glass. That might have at the bottom of it some grains of poison, which, when the wine should be poured into it, would dissolve and make a potion that would at once lay hold of the springs of life.

She had heard of such things.

"Mine young friend, you don't drink."

"No—I—a—no!"

"Stuff! stuff! I shall pour out von glass for you."

"No—I—I——"

"Stuff! stuff!"

The murderer filled the glass which was placed next to the Dark Woman, but she made up her mind not to touch a drop of it.

"Drink! drink!" said the Fleming, as he again filled his own glass to the brim. "Yet stop von moment—stop von moment!"

The Dark Woman kept her eyes keenly fixed upon his face.

"In my country we have von fashion of drinking. You will take your glass, and you will touch my glass, and then we will——Ha! na! Yes, we will——"

"What? what?"

"We will change glasses."

All the conjectures and ideas of the Dark Woman were overthrown in a moment.

There was evidently no poison in the wine.

As certainly there was no poison in the glass which the jeweller had just drunk out of.

And if he now voluntarily took the other glass, there could as certainly be no poison in that.

What was she to do?

She still felt that she hovered on the point of death. She was certain that something was in progress which would be her destruction, if she were not wary enough to find it out.

But what could it be?

That was the question.

And for once in a way, the Dark Woman, with all her ingenuity, was at fault.

It was a question she could not find an answer to.

CHAPTER CCVII.

LINDA DE CHEVENAUX DISCOVERS THE SECRET OF THE FLEMISH JEWELLER, AND MAKES GOOD USE OF IT.

THERE was a secret.

There was some mode by which the astute and murderous Fleming was seeking the death of his visitor.

Linda de Chevenaux did not exactly see what it was; but she made up her mind that she would not let one drop of the wine, from either glass, pass her lips while those doubts remained.

That was a wise determination.

"Now, mine friend, we shall drink in mine own country fashion, and then you shall see vat you shall see. Ha! ha!"

There was an air of great triumph about the jeweller

He raised his glass.

"Come, now, come!"

The Dark Woman raised her glass likewise, for she was curious to know what he would really do; if he would really change the glasses, or only pretend to do so, and, by some sleight of hand, still make her keep the one she had.

That was what she began to suspect he would try to do.

But it was not so.

With great gravity the Fleming touched the edge of the Dark Woman's glass with his own, and then reaching out his other hand, he deliberately changed the glasses.

The act was done so openly that the Dark Woman felt quite certain she was not cheated.

Her eyes could not play her so very false as that.

She really and truly had the glass from which he had drunk with perfect safety of the wine from the same bottle from which her glass was filled.

The Dark Woman began almost to question the evidence of her own senses; and to ask herself if she had really seen a dead body in the cupboard, and if, after all, the old Flemish jeweller, with the exception that he was undoubtedly a receiver of stolen goods, might not be a very good sort of worthy personage.

But these doubts only lasted for the passing moment.

"Now we will drink," said the Fleming.

"Stop!"

"Eh? Vat?"

"Stop, I say. In the part of the country where I come from, which is a remote part of England, it is very strange, but we have the same fashion of changing the glasses that you have."

"Vell?"

"But in addition to that, we change them back again before actually drinking."

There was a slight quiver of the eyelids on the part of the jeweller.

"Yah! yah! Dat ish strange!"

"It is not so. I will now take my own, and you take yours."

The great coarse hand of the Fleming closed round the glass he held like a vice.

"No, no, mine young friend. That would be unlucky."

"Unlucky?"

"Very unlucky, indeed, and it cannot be done. Oh, dear, no!—oh, no!"

"But——"

What reply the jeweller was about to make was cut short by a smart ringing at the shop bell at this moment.

A look of vexation came over his face as he half rose from his chair, and then sat down again.

"Let them wait!—let them wait!" he said.

"Well!" said the Dark Woman, who now felt that all she had to do was to protract the time until the ringing at the bell should become an intolerable interruption that would enforce upon the Fleming the necessity of attending to it,—"well, if you have any objections, I, of course, do not persist."

"I have objections."

"That is quite sufficient."

The bell rang again.

"Donner and blitzen!"

The bell rang a third time.

The Fleming sprung to his feet, looking white with rage.

"I shall come back von moments."

He dashed into the shop.

The Dark Woman changed the glasses again with the quickness of thought, and as the jeweller popped his head into the parlour, she was holding the glass by the stem, a few inches from the table, exactly in the same attitude in which he had left her.

"Ah!"

"Who is it?" she said, calmly.

"Von thief."

"One of your customers, then."

"Yah! I have sent him away, to come agin in von quarter of von hour, when you will be gone!"

The tone in which the word "gone" was pronounced, was singularly suggestive to Linda de Chevenaux of the sort of departure he expected she would take.

"Come now," she said, "it is true that I will not press you to exchange glasses; but if you will let me have back what I may, while your guest, call my own, I would rather."

"Mine young friend, I have said it would be unlucky to me."

"But to me?"

"Drink, and you will not complain."

"Very well, since you will have it so, it is not for me to dispute your wishes. Mynheer, I drink to you."

"Yah! and I to you."

The jeweller tossed off about half the contents of his glass, and then he set it down on the table, with a force that broke it to atoms. His eyes seemed to be glaring out of his head, and his lips parted with a horrible expression, as he gasped out, "Vat? vat? Is—is this——"

"Retribution!"

"Yah! vat?"

"Retribution!" added the Dark Woman, as she rose from her chair, and flung the glass and its contents that she had in her hand, full in the face of the jeweller.

He tried to rise—he tried to shriek. He clutched at the table; his face turned livid; and then, with a deep groan, he fell backwards, carrying the chair with him.

He was dead!

"What can be the meaning of this?" said the Dark Woman. "Ah, fool that I was not to imagine it! A trick—a mere trick of sleight of hand. He did change the glasses, but, no doubt, he adroitly dropped something deadly into the one he thought I should drink out of. That was it. Ah, yes—that was it. I see it all plain enough now; and he is dead. I am in good company here—the company of the dead."

Before Linda de Chevenaux then could make up her mind what exactly to do, there came a ring at the bell again. It was more than probable that this was the return of the "customer," who had been sent away by the Fleming, until she, the Dark Woman, should, as he expected it, be "gone."

He was "gone" himself now, and in the same fashion that he had intended her to go.

The Dark Woman looked warily about her, and on a hook in one of the walls she saw some such a loose half over-coat, half cloak, as the Fleming wore.

To slip it on was the work of a moment, and the Dark Woman then, pulling her hat low down upon her brows, went into the shop.

She had a little difficulty in finding the mode of undoing the fastening of the shop door, but at length she did so, and then retreated to the back of the counter, which was a very shadowy kind of place.

The customer came in.

"Hilloa, old Ben what do you call yourself?" he cried. "Have you got through that little business you were about, and can you attend to a gentleman now?"

The Dark Woman was taken rather by surprise, for in this careless, loud, insolent voice, she recognised that of one of her own band.

The customer of the Flemish jeweller was one of the very men who had been with her on the perilous expedition to St. James's Palace so recently.

She was anxious to know what his precise business there could be.

She replied to him in a feigned voice, which was a good imitation of that of the Fleming.

"Vell, my dear, and vat do you want?"

"Vat do I want? Why gold! Gold is what I want, of course."

"And vat have you brought, my dear?"

"This sword hilt. It is a rare one, covered with jewels, as you will soon see; and to save chaffering, I tell you at once that I won't part with it under fifty gold pieces; so out with the money."

No. 93.—DARK WOMAN.

The Dark Woman was satisfied.

She had at first suspected that this member of her band might have secreted some of the jewels for his own purpose, for at the moment she had forgotten about the bundle of jewelled presentation swords that had been found at the Palace.

It was most unquestionably the hilt of one of them that the disreputable adventurer came to sell.

"Come in," said the Dark Woman. "Come in, and you shall have the money."

"I'll see you hanged first."

"What do you mean?"

"What do I mean, eh? Why, I mean that I won't trust myself into that wolf's den of yours. Hand out the gold here, and I will take it and be off."

"You may enter the wolf's den in safety," said the Dark Woman, "for the wolf is no more."

These words she spoke in her own ordinary

forces, so that she was at once and as easily recognised by that member of her band as he had been by her.

"Good heavens, master!" he cried; "is it possible that you are here?"

"I am here, and I am well pleased to meet you. Do you know aught of the man who kept this place?"

"Not much, master, except that he had an evil reputation. But you use the 'kept,' as though he were its owner no longer."

"He is its owner no longer, since he lies dead in the next apartment."

"Dead?"

"Even so. I seldom take life except in self-defence, and in this case it became matter of a few seconds of time whether he or I should be a corpse on the floor of that apartment. I naturally preferred that he should do so, and he lies there now."

"Naturally, indeed, master. Then he attempted your life?"

"He did. I came here seeking a market for some of those jewels which belong to you and to all of us. He invited me into the adjoining room, and then, with various expressions of pretended friendship, he tried to poison me in some Rhine wine."

"The old villain! I've often heard, master, that people have been invited further than the shop of this house, and that if they were unwary enough to accept the invitation, they never returned."

"I can well believe it. But the place now belongs to us. Come with me, and I shall be able to show you a sight which may even shake your resolution."

This member of the band, whose name was Lovat, had no hesitation now in entering what he called the wolf's den.

The shop door was secured easily, for the spring lock which fastened it fell into its place the moment it was closed. The only real difficulty was to undo it again, but that difficulty the Dark Woman had already surmounted, for she had admitted Lovat to the shop.

The feeling on both their minds was no doubt a strange one, to find themselves in quiet and undisturbed possession of an establishment which had so recently belonged to some one else.

The silence in the place had something about it that was depressing, and in itself almost suggestive of danger.

Both the Dark Woman and Lovat spoke low, as people unconsciously do when pacing down the aisle of some cathedral.

Was it the presence of death that had imparted a reverential air to that place?

It might be so; for to the knowledge of the Dark Woman there were certainly two dead bodies to be found in that inner room.

Lovat hesitated a moment on the threshold of the parlour, for he saw the dark object lying upon the floor, which only a short time before had been instinct with life, cunning, and the unscrupulous arrangements of murder.

"Enter!" said the Dark Woman; "all is peace here now."

"The peace of death!"

"Ay, the peace of death; and a deserved death, too. Would you have any further reason than the fact that this man had sought my life in the most treacherous, dastardly manner, to enable you to justify me for this deed?"

"None, master."

"And yet there is another reason."

The Dark Woman pointed to the cupboard in which she had discovered the murdered body.

"What is there there, master?"

"Death in another shape than this, if you would wish to look upon it."

"In good truth, not I," said Lovat, shrugging his shoulders. "I suppose you have discovered some victim of the old Flemish jeweller?"

"I have."

"Then I care not to look upon it, master, for I am one of those who take human life as I find it; and I would fain linger among its lightest shadows, if shadows I must have at all, than plunge into its deepest glooms. I came here for gold; and if gold is to be had, let me have it, since it is a medium of exchange for pleasure."

"There should be gold here. We are the victors, and we are entitled to the spoils of the field."

"A most unquestionably correct doctrine that, master."

"Let us search. But if, as you say, you are one of those who would avoid a sight of terror, lest it jar upon your capacities for enjoyment, approach not yonder cupboard with the key in the lock."

"Most assuredly I will not."

The Dark Woman and Lovat, perfectly heedless of the dead body of the jeweller, which lay upon the floor, commenced as active a search as possible in the parlour for such valuables as might fairly be supposed to be there.

Probably they missed a great deal; but from various secret receptacles which Lovat burst open without any ceremony, they took, not only a tolerable hoard of money, but a quantity of jewellery of price.

Lovat filled his pockets; and after the searching in the parlour had been carried on for a considerable period, and had ceased to be further productive, the Dark Woman laid her hand lightly on his arm as she said, "Now let us leave this place; the taint of murder is in its air."

"But, master, there is a house above us. Would it not be worth while to explore it?"

"Possibly; but yet I care not to do so. Be content. At each turn of fortune's wheel we become enriched. I will find some other mode of disposing of the jewels. Let us leave this place at once."

"Be it so, master."

Lovat's cupidity was very much excited, no doubt, by the plunder at the Flemish's jeweller's; but he was quite sufficiently under the command of the Dark Woman to comply with her wishes to leave the place when she expressed them decidedly.

There was likewise a certain amount of danger in remaining; for there was the chance every moment of some one calling, with whom it might be troublesome to deal.

And so the Dark Woman, accompanied by Lovat, reached the open street, closing the shop-door after them, leaving that establishment with its dead occupants to look after itself.

"To-night," said the Dark Woman, "we shall meet again."

"Where, master?"

"I have been thinking. It is necessary that we should have some place of assemblage, where, without suspicion, and at the same time with perfect safety to ourselves, we can meet from time to time."

"Do you know of such a place, master?"

"I am thinking. It should be at once convenient to us all—easy to reach and easy to leave."

"Such a place were difficult to find."

"Possibly; but I think I know of the precise spot that will suit us. In a narrow lane of the City, whither I can easily conduct you, there is a church—long anterior, in point of building, to those by which the City is adorned by the great architect of St. Paul's. It is ancient, dim, inconvenient, and dilapidated. No human footstep has trodden its gloomy aisles for many a long year. Its vaults are crowded with the dead; the spider and the rat alone divide the empire of that ancient church; and to the inhabitants of the few houses that crowd around it, it is an object rather of fear and of suspicion. It is said that strange sounds have been heard within its walls. We have but to feed the superstition of the neighbourhood, and, for as long as we may require it, the place will be all our own."

"It will do famously, master."

"You will meet me, then, at the eastern angle of St. Paul's to-night, when the clocks are striking twelve. Make it your business, between now and then, to warn our associates to be close at hand, and I will conduct you all to the church I have mentioned, so that in all time you may know it; for, from this moment, I devote myself to the business of life in two shapes. I must be a terror and a desolation!"

The manner in which the Dark Woman pronounced these words struck a cold chill even to the insensible heart of Lovat.

"A terror, master, and a desolation?" he said.

"Even so. I must be a terror to those upon whom I wish vengeance to alight, and I must spread desolation in another sense."

"In what sense?"

"I will deprive the rich and the great of so much of their earthly substance, which I will place at the disposal of those who aid me, that no man shall know when he lies down at night if it shall be his good fortune to arise in the morning, with the gold and the jewels he fondly supposed his own. Cling to me, you and all your comrades, and I will waft you over the stagnant lake of poverty to such a brilliant land of fortune, that the service you will do for me on the way shall seem weak and slight."

"We will all follow you, master, with heart and soul."

"Be it so. You have your instructions. Farewell!"

The Dark Woman left Lovat to cogitate over her words, and, secure in her disguise, she made her way to St. James's, where she was a witness to some of the festivities and rejoicings which closed that day of the Princess Charlotte's marriage.

That day which it was thought would be so important an one in the annals of England, but which turned out to be but a brief delusion, the results of which were to pass away like a dream.

CHAPTER CVIII.

THE DARK WOMAN MEETS HER ASSOCIATES IN ST. AUGUSTIN'S CHURCH, AND ATTACKS THE HOUSE OF THE LORD CHANCELLOR.

THE midnight hour is arrived.

It is a starlight and beautiful night; too light —far too light for those who come abroad after the eye of day is closed upon nefarious practices.

Far too light for the objects of the Dark Woman, and that mysterious band of men who own her as their chief and pioneer to fortune.

She had issued her orders, and they must be obeyed.

As the clock of St. Paul's struck the midnight hour, she herself stood carelessly leaning against the iron railings at the eastern corner of the vast area which contained the cathedral.

She made a slight gesture of impatience as the last stroke of the clock died away. But then, from the other side of the railings, where he had been concealed in the deep shadow of a tomb, a man made his appearance, and spoke in a low tone.

"Master!"

The Dark Woman strove to penetrate the darkness of the cathedral yard with a straining gaze, as she said, "It is you, Lovat!"

"It is, master."

"And the others?"

"They are all here."

"It is an ill-omened spot. Come away. I have no desire again to make St. Paul's an abiding place of mine for a moment."

"Nor I, master. So we will even follow you with what despatch we may."

The Dark Woman crossed to the other side of the way, and stood still as a statue; while Lovat and his associates clambered easily over the massive railings, and soon rejoined her.

The party was not a large one; but still it was sufficient to create some degree of attention if any one had been there at the time to bestow it.

London, however, at the time might have been almost believed to have been a city of the dead, so profoundly still was it.

But this stillness was only local, and peculiar to the City.

The day's life ceased there at a much earlier hour than it did at the West End of the town.

The absence of theatres and houses of entertainment within the City proper, made existence there a much more primitive thing than it was in the rest of London.

To be sure, at the corner of one of the courts leading into Paternoster Row, a watchman was dozing in his box; and it was well for him that he did so doze; for those men who were associated with the Dark Woman would have been perfectly unscrupulous about the mode in which they might dispense with the troublesome observation of any one.

"Follow me!" she said.

Without another word she took her way towards that mass of buildings which lies now between Cheapside and Cannon Street, but which, at the period of our story, extended in mazy, intricate thoroughfares right down to the bank of the river.

The Dark Woman walked swiftly, turning the corners with precision, and with an evident perfect knowledge of the route she was taking.

She paused in one of the narrowest and dingiest of the streets.

Nearly one-half the extent of one side of this street was occupied by an old grey-stone wall, in which there was but one ancient window at a considerable height.

Proceeding somewhat further on, where the wall terminated, there was an ancient gothic doorway, approached by three steps worn into hollows.

But the devout feet that had worn those steps had long since mingled with the dust.

The Dark Woman paused, and spoke in a scarcely audible tone, as she said, "This is the place."

"Somewhat public, master," suggested Lovat, who was close to her, as he looked up at the windows of the houses.

"Yes," replied the Dark Woman, "but we shall not enter here. I point this out to you as the church—the old, disused and deserted church of St. Augustin, which can always be a place of rendezvous for us. We shall enter it by a much more secret and private means. Follow!"

There was a narrow court; some houses falling to ruin were alone to be found within it; but at its further extremity there was an opening, or what would have been an opening but for some ancient iron rails, worn so thin that a child might have displaced them, which guarded one of those dreary little burial grounds so commonly attached to the old churches in the City.

In the wider and more open space of St. Paul's Churchyard that starlight night had looked down with something like brightness upon the Dark Woman and her band; but in the narrow and enclosed space in which they now were there reigned a perpetual gloom.

They looked like spectres just emerged from that dreary, little, old churchyard within the iron railings.

"This is the place," said the Dark Woman.

A kind of shudder passed through the band.

An ancient lime tree grew in the churchyard. One half of it was dead, but the other half had sent out its summer's vegetation, and the dingy, soot-begrimed leaves rustled gently in the night air.

"The removal," said the Dark Woman. "of one of those iron rails will afford space sufficient for us all with care."

"By my faith," cried one, "it's fortunate that we're of the young and active sort. When we get rich, and well to do, and portly like the citizens, we shall scarcely squeeze ourselves through such a space."

"True," said another; "and it's always been a marvel to me why these same portly citizens always made their pavements and streets so narrow. Fancy, now, an alderman, worthy of the name, trying to get between yonder post and the house corner."

"Peace!" said the Dark Woman; "the time has not yet come for jesting."

Lovat, in obedience to her orders, had removed one of the iron rails. There was no difficulty in doing so; in fact, so fragile was the whole affair, that the real difficulty consisted in not bringing the whole down at once.

This, however, was avoided, for it might have attracted some attention.

The Dark Woman stooped, and easily glided through the opening.

She was followed by her band, and they all stood amid the rank grass of the little burial place.

A dozen paces brought them to a narrow flight of stone steps, descending from the level; so that the total depth was over the head of an ordinary man.

At the foot of these steps was another such door as they had paused at in the open street.

The Dark Woman touched it with her hand.

"It is by this entrance," she said, "we make our way into the church of St. Augustin."

The door was worm-eaten and old. The massive nails which at one time had been an element of strength to it, now seemed dragging it to destruction. It was fastened from within, but it was quite evident that a small amount of violence from without would be sufficient to open it.

"Which of you," said the Dark Woman, "has the means about him to force a door?"

"I never come out after twelve o'clock," said one, "without my tools. Here is a crowbar of steel, small, portable, but efficient. It weighs but two pounds, and is but fifteen inches in length; but I should like to see the door that would say nay to it."

A slight crackling noise succeeded this speech, and then something fell from the door on the inner side, awakening a dismal echo in the old church.

It was the ancient massive lock, which had dropped completely off.

The old, rusted screws and fastenings stood no chance whatever against that modern polished weapon of destruction.

The entrance to the deserted church was free.

How cavernous it looked!

How damp and mouldy the air was!

No wonder the associates of the Dark Woman hesitated before availing themselves of the opening they had made into the dilapidated temple!

Then Linda de Chevenaux herself stepped forward and led the way; and, as she crossed the threshold, she said, in a low tone, "Let him who has the power produce a light. We must see that our foot-hold is safe within this ancient structure."

This was a suggestion which the band readily acted upon; and, indeed, none of them seemed very well disposed to plunge into the profound darkness of that old church after the Dark Woman.

But she made her way forward, although she was alone.

She knew perfectly well that she must be below the level of the pavement of the church, so she proceeded with great caution for four or five paces, until—according to her expectations—her foot struck against the lowest of another flight of steps, which no doubt would conduct her into the body of the church.

She ascended slowly and carefully, and by the time she had reached the topmost step one of her band had procured a light.

It was but a taper, small and star-like, but still it was sufficient to dissipate the intense darkness, and to enable the Dark Woman to see that she faced another door somewhat similar to that which had been broken open from without, but not nearly so much decayed.

The outer door had been exposed to wind and weather for a couple of hundred years.

The inner one had been sheltered.

There was no occasion to use force to this second door; it yielded to a touch.

And then the Dark Woman felt that she was with n the actual church, for the rays of the little taper seemed quenched in the larger expanse, and he who carried it appeared to be only walking about with a faint halo around him.

The whole area of the church was completely free from encumbrance of any kind. If, at any time, that area had been laid out in seats or pews, they had certainly been removed.

Indeed, there was nothing there but the bare walls, and that one window that looked into the narrow street.

The flag-stones which paved the church felt damp and mouldy; but the more evidences of desertion and decay that showed themselves in the ancient structure, the more fitted was it as a place of meeting for the Dark Woman and her band.

The one who carried the taper stood as nearly as might be in the centre of the church.

The others grouped themselves about him.

The Dark Woman had found a slightly elevated portion of the flooring. It was no doubt where the altar had once stood, and from that vantage ground she addressed her followers.

"I have work for you to do; and I have to propose to you to do it in a fashion that will recommend itself by its boldness, and ensure success. You know well that London at night is strangely and heedlessly enough consigned to the care of men who have not the power of protecting themselves against any attack accompanied by the slightest vigour. To these men, and to the accidental presence perhaps of a parish constable, is consigned the lives and property of thousands, whose riches lie for the first hand to grasp at and appropriate."

"True—true!" cried several members of the band.

"But how shall we proceed, master?" asked Lovat.

"I will tell you. We will decide—or rather I will decide, for you've made me your master, and the decision rests with me—upon what great, rich house is to be attacked on any given night; and on that night we will go and take possession of it step by step from its threshold to its attics by sheer force; and who shall prevent us? We will knock and ring for admission, and from the moment the door is opened the house is ours. You are thirteen now in all. Few houses in London hold so many males—that is, I mean houses of the class we shall attack; and as we shall go well armed and with a purpose—holding together, too, after the fashion of a disciplined force—what shall resist us—who shall overcome us?"

The tone of command and of absolute and entire confidence in her own powers and resources in which the Dark Woman spoke, imparted that confidence to her adherents.

A kind of enthusiasm took possession of them.

With one accord they burst out into exclamations of satisfaction.

The originality of the plan of operations delighted them.

It differed so largely from all vulgar housebreaking, that it just suited their views and their minds—gentlemen as they were, so far as regarded birth and education, but no better in morals than the poorest and lowest footpad who prowled about the streets at night, seeking to prey upon the unwary.

But there is an aristocracy in crime as in everything else.

"You consent, then?" added the Dark Woman. "You all of you comprehend and consent to this plan?"

"We do! We do!"

"And we like it immensely," said one.

"It just suits us," said another.

"And quite a gentlemanly way of doing things," added a third.

"Well, master," said Lovat, "since we are all so agreed and ready to follow you wherever you may lead, where shall it be?"

The Dark Woman paused for a few seconds, as though considering this question, and then she said, "To the Lord Chancellor's house in Bloomsbury Square."

"By Jove!" exclaimed one.

The exclamation attracted general attention.

"What is the objection?" asked the Dark Woman.

"None!"

"Then let it be to that house that we pay our first attentions."

"Bravo! bravo!"

"It is probably well known to you all," added the Dark Woman, "that the present Lord Chancellor has only been a few months in office, and that he has attained that office owing to marrying the daughter of one of the Royal Dukes, who for a long time has in vain sighed for a husband, until this most unscrupulous adventurer married her."

"Hem!"

This "hem" came from the same member of the band who had uttered the exclamation of "By Jove!" when first the Lord Chancellor's name was mentioned by the Dark Woman.

It was evident that he had a something to say on the subject.

"Speak," said the Dark Woman. "It seems to me that you know something of this Chancellor."

"I do."

"What is it."

"Just this—that the house in Bloomsbury Square in which he resides is quite familiar to me."

"That is well."

"And that in courtesy the Lord Chancellor is somewhat of a connexion of mine."

"How so?"

"I will tell you. He is my father's half brother, and so calls himself my uncle—or rather, he ought to do so; but as I want money, and don't want to get it in any of the ways that would seem pleasant to him, we are not on the best of terms."

"Is that all?"

"That is all. I merely mention it because, knowing the interior of the house well, I can be a very excellent guide to you all."

"That is so far fortunate. Can you tell us what likelihood of booty there may be?"

"I can. The most excellent likelihood in the world, I should say. We have only to go to the old rascal's—hem! I mean to my respected uncle's bedroom, and there we shall find a certain japan tin box, where he keeps his papers. If we can get off with that, the old villain—I mean the respected old gentleman will be happy to give a good round sum for its recovery."

"What does the box contain?"

"Papers, belonging mostly to other people. You must know that the ancient scoundrel—I mean my venerated uncle—was an attorney, but he went then to the bar; only he kept up his connexion among the bad set that he knew, and the little rascalities and forgeries by which he made money are, I think, pretty well all to be found in that tin box."

"Come, then," said the Dark Woman; "the night wears on apace, and we have our work before us. Are you all ready?

"Ready! ready!"

The voices of the band sounded hollow and sepulchral in that dismal old deserted church.

There was a rustling movement, such as when some outlying party of military makes, with all possible caution in the face of the enemy, some alteration in their position.

The band of the Dark Woman was preparing for the expedition.

That preparation consisted in each man looking carefully to the priming of his pistols, and then buttoning his coat right up to the throat.

Each one, too, produced a half mask, such as were in use by the knights of the road who at that period made the highways in the immediate vicinity of London so dangerous.

When those masks were on, and the whole of the preparations complete, the Dark Woman and her band certainly looked dangerous to the peace of the City.

A clock struck two.

They had been longer in the deserted church than she had anticipated; but still there was ample time to carry out the project of the night.

"Follow me," said the Dark Woman, "and obey me implicitly."

"We will—we will!"

"Put out the light, and leave it here"

All was darkness in another moment.

"Follow!"

The Dark Woman led the way; and although there was some stumbling at the stairs in the black darkness that covered them all up as with a pall, they succeeded in reaching the little wretched churchyard in safety.

The change from the darkness of the interior of the church itself, to only the darkness of the open air, was so great that the latter appeared light in comparison.

The band could see about them with tolerable ease.

The Dark Woman did not speak; but she led the way through the gap in the iron railings.

Then out of the dingy-looking old court, with its tumble-down houses, and then out of the narrow street into one of the wider—although that was not very wide—thoroughfares of the City.

Then an imprudent watchman, who happened to be awake, started out of a doorway.

He held up his lantern.

"Hilloa! Hilloa! What's all this? Who may you be, my masters?

"Down with him!" said the Dark Woman.

The watchman was the next instant lying sprawling in the kennel, perfectly insensible.

The Dark Woman walked on.

The band followed her, as if nothing particular had happened.

They understood now that everything was to be done by main force and assurance, and they felt a wild kind of excitement and pleasure in the idea that they were traversing London like conquerors whom none could resist.

The whole affair just suited them.

The Dark Woman led the way to St. Paul's Churchyard.

There was a hackney coach stand there: as luck would have it, there were but two vehicles on the stand, waiting for what fortune the night would bring to them.

It brought them a fortune they little expected.

<hr/>

CHAPTER CCIX.

THE DARK WOMAN AND HER BAND TAKE POSSESSION OF THE GREAT SEAL OF ENGLAND.

THE drivers of the two hackney coaches in St. Paul's Churchyard dozed upon the boxes of their vehicles.

The horses dozed in their wretched harness.

The Dark Woman paused at the corner of one of the narrow streets leading to Doctors' Commons, and gave her directions to the band.

"It is a long way to Bloomsbury Square, and will be more agreeable to ride than to walk, besides attracting less attention."

The band assented.

"Throw those two coachmen over the railings into the burial-yard of the Cathedral, and take possession of the coaches."

The band rushed forward.

The two drivers were torn down from their seats: a blow upon the head of each put them out of the world—at all events, for the time being.

Then they were flung bodily over the iron rails of the Cathedral.

The coaches were in possession of the Dark Woman and her band.

The driving-boxes of each were taken cool possession of, and into one of them got, with some little crowding, half a dozen of the band.

The door of the other coach was held obsequiously open by Lovat for the Dark Woman to enter.

"We will ride outside in some way, master," he said, "so as not to incommode you."

There were, counting the two who drove, and the six who were inside the other coach, still five of the band to be disposed of.

"No," said the Dark Woman, "let three more come in here; the other two can find places outside."

"Certainly, master."

The steps were put up, and the door of the coach was shut.

A man came running up to them from a court close at hand.

"Remember Water Jack, your honours," he

said, thinking the coaches had been hired in his temporary absence.

"Over with him!" said the Dark Woman.

There was a short scuffle, and then the fall of a heavy body, as the man was flung over the railings to keep company with the coachmen.

"It is done, master."

"Good! To Bloomsbury Square."

Off went the two coaches.

The Dark Woman, in these terribly violent proceedings, found a kind of solace for her perturbed feelings.

She had declared war now against all the world, and she cared not how savagely and ruthlessly she carried on the campaign.

The more violence there was, the calmer she became.

These two members of the band who assumed the places of coachmen for this occasion, urged the poor steeds in the hackney coaches to their utmost speed.

Probably they had never made such haste down Ludgate Hill before.

But as good fortune for the Dark Woman and her associates would have it, the horses did not fall, although they were on the point of doing so at least twenty times.

The reckless manner in which they were driven, and the hurry that was put into all their movements, probably really saved them from any dangerous slip.

Bloomsbury Square was reached.

"Stop!" said the Dark Woman.

The two coaches drew up at the corner of Southampton Street.

"What is the number of the Chancellor's house?"

"Four," replied his disreputable nephew. "Number four. I ought to know it."

"Come on, then."

"What is to be done with the coaches?" asked Lovat.

"Just leave them."

The two coaches remained where they had halted. The tired horses had no inclination to move.

Bloomsbury Square was quite deserted: not a soul, so far as could be judged, was up in any of the houses. It was close on to three o'clock now, and it may well be supposed that everybody who meant to go to bed had done so.

What had become of the watchman, whose special duty it was to keep watch and ward in that square, it is difficult to say. Perhaps he had had the good sense to go home, and leave the square to look after itself.

Certainly the so-called "guardian of the night" was not visible.

"Follow!" said the Dark Woman.

The band followed her.

Their footsteps, notwithstanding they trod lightly, made a strange sound in the silent square; but that sound gave no alarm.

Who could suppose that in the midst of London a band of fourteen persons would have the audacity to attempt to take a mansion by storm?

But such was to be the case.

And the audacity of the act was to bring with it its own safety.

Number four was reached.

The house was one of the largest, if not the largest in the square, which was then a fashion-able one, and not abandoned as it is now to some lodging-house keepers and bill-discounters.

"Halt!" said the Dark Woman.

She looked up at the Chancellor's house from the door-step.

A light was in the hall.

"Tell me," said the Dark Woman, as she turned to seek the nephew of the Chancellor, "is there a night-porter kept in the hall?"

"Yes."

"That is well. He is asleep."

The Dark Woman knocked lightly at the door; so lightly that the hall-porter ought to have heard the appeal, although it was not loud enough to disturb any one else in all the mansion.

But no notice was taken.

The hall-porter was fast asleep.

The Dark Woman knocked again somewhat louder.

This time there came a snuffling sort of sound from the passage.

"Master," said Lovat, "you want to get the door open quietly?"

"I do."

"Will you allow me to manage it?"

"Do so."

Lovat put his lips to the key-hole of the door.

"Hi! hi!" he said. "Porter! Hi! Are you awake? Hi! I'm the square watchman!"

"What's the matter?" asked a voice from within.

"Nothing!"

"Then what do you want?"

"Nothing. But I thought you wouldn't mind a drop of mulled eau de vie, and I'm a bad one to drink by myself?"

"What?"

"Don't you hear?"

"Yes, yes. Did you say you had something to drink?"

"I did."

"I'll open the door in a moment. No, I won't. Stop. How do I know you are the square watchman?"

"Nohow."

"How do I know you are not a thief?"

"Nohow."

"Then—then—what—what am I to—to do?"

"Nothing. I'm sitting on the step drinking the mull, and it's beau-ti-ful. You take a pint of fine old eau de vie, and you make it hot; then you take two tablespoonfuls of fine honey, and you put them in; then you beat up six eggs——"

"Stop! stop! Hang it man, don't drink it all —don't!"

The hall-porter flung the door open.

"Seize him!" said the Dark Woman.

He was caught in a moment by the throat.

"Don't let him speak."

The compression upon the throat of the hall-porter increased. A handkerchief was put across his mouth, like a horse's bit. He was nearly insensible.

"Throw him into the square garden."

"Yes, master."

The sentence was executed.

The Dark Woman and her band stepped into the hall of the Chancellor's house, and the last one quickly and quietly closed the door.

There was a sensation of warmth and comfort in the hall, at that hour of the night, after coming in out of the rather raw, open air.

A lamp was burning faintly, and the spacious hall was handsomely appointed.

Not the faintest sound could be heard from any part of the house.

The little fracas with the hall-porter had not had the effect of giving any alarm whatever.

It was quite evident that the Dark Woman and her band, so far, were eminently successful, and had all the place to themselves.

She turned and gave her orders.

"Three will remain here to guard the hall."

As she spoke, she indicated the three she intended for that duty.

They at once acquiesced, and took up their position like sentinels.

"All else will follow me," added the Dark Woman.

They did so.

Several doors opened from the hall; but the only thing the Dark Woman did of a particular character, as regarded those rooms, was to lock them one after the other, and possess herself of their keys.

Then she ascended the staircase, which was wide and handsome, and sprung from nearly the centre of the back of the hall.

Upon arriving at the head of the stairs, the Dark Woman turned to the Chancellor's nephew.

"Do you know," she asked, in a low voice that was scarcely a whisper even,—"do you know where the Chancellor sleeps?"

"Yes; above."

"And these rooms are but reception rooms?"

The Dark Woman pointed to three doors that opened from the first floor landing where they were.

"That is all."

"Follow, then. Or stay—you lead. We shall not lose time."

"Master, you intend, then, to seek the chamber of the Chancellor at once?"

"I do."

"This way."

The graceless nephew of the Lord Chancellor led the way up the next flight of stairs, and when they reached the top they would have been in darkness but that a second lamp was there burning, for the rays from that one in the hall did not penetrate so far up the house.

The Chancellor's nephew then pointed to a door, and whispered, "That is the bed-room of his lordship; and that," he added, pointing to another door, "is the room of his son."

"His son? A man?"

The nephew smiled.

"He looks like one, but he is a poltroon, as well as a fool."

Have you any objection to take charge of him?"

"None in the least."

"Very well, I will leave him to you. Your duty will be to take care that he does not create any alarm."

"He shall not."

"My business is with the Chancellor himself."

At this moment a grumbling, angry voice called out from the room that had been pointed out as that of the Chancellor, "What's that?

What's that? What's the matter? Eh, eh? What is it? Who's there?"

"Hush!" said the Dark Woman.

"Eh?"

"Hush!"

A lumbering sound was heard in the room.

Then another voice spoke.

That was a feminine voice, although the tones were neither very feminine nor very gentle.

"What ever is the matter now, you low-minded wretch? Is there is no such thing as peace and quiet to be had, you despicable beast?"

"Who is that?" asked the Dark Woman of the nephew.

"The Royal Duke's daughter."

"Indeed!"

"Yes, you hear that she is quite a lady."

"Hush!"

The Dark Woman now tapped on the panel of the Chancellor's bed-room door.

"What's that? Who's there?"

"My lord!"

"Well, well?"

"There are thieves in the house."

"Thieves?"

"Yes, my lord; but if your lordship makes a noise, we shall not be able to do comfortably what we are about."

"Ah! you are a constable?"

"Just so."

"Wait a moment—wait a moment. Bless my soul! where are my——I mean, where is my dressing-gown?"

"Fellow!" said the Duke's daughter, "I declare that to-morrow I will leave this low part of the town. Colonel Grimsby has often invited me to his nice little place at Richmond, and I intend to go there and stay a few weeks."

"Go to the devil as soon as you like," said the Chancellor.

The Duke's daughter uttered a slight scream, and then in a voice that seemed to be a concentration of vinegar, she added, "Was it for this I consented to marry you, you low lawyer? You know what a rogue you are, and always were. You know you have about as much pretension to be Lord Chancellor as to be the Archbishop of Canterbury, you low, hideous, common wretch!"

"Go on, my lady; let the watch and the constable hear you! Go on, do!"

The Chancellor opened his bed-room door.

The Dark Woman had stepped aside, and two of the band made a dash at his lordship.

One dealt him rather a bewildering rap on one side of the head; and the other, possibly with a charitable view of restoring the equilibrium of his brain, gave him a similar rap on the other side

The Chancellor staggered back.

He would have fallen but that he was clutched by the throat, and allowed more quietly to subside into a chair.

All this happened with such rapidity that the Royal Duke's daughter had not time to scream, but she was on the point of doing so when the Dark Woman stepped up to the side of the bed, and said, sternly, "Silence, woman! Utter word, or a cry, and your worthless life shall come to an end!"

The Royal Duke's daughter was struck as it by a mortal blow.

She had lived to be called a woman, and to be

told that her life was a worthless one! Surely the end of the world had come, or these were the premonitory symptoms of its speedy arrival.

She fell back upon the bed without a word, and lay perfectly still.

The Chancellor was in a state of great mental confusion.

He could hardly comprehend what had happened, except that he was in the hands of those who were not over scrupulous as to their acts.

But then he was not very scrupulous himself, so that on that score he certainly had no right to complain.

Nevertheless the Lord Chancellor was soon aroused to a sense of his true condition, for as he sat in the chair, with rather a bewildered look, while the two members of the band who had taken charge of him stood on either side like grim sentinels, the Dark Woman approached him.

No. 94.—DARK WOMAN.

"I told you," she said, "there were thieves in the house."

The Chancellor looked at her vacantly.

"Attend to me—and answer me."

There was something of menace in these tones, and the Chancellor roused his dormant faculties to listen to what was said to him, and attempt some reply.

"Do you hear me? There are thieves in the house."

"I hear."

"We are the thieves. Do you understand that?"

"Perfectly."

"I want a certain tin box that you generally keep under your own observation."

The Chancellor's eyes instinctively wandered to a corner of the room where that box was reposing, and the Dark Woman making a sign to her band one of them immediately took possession of it.

The Chancellor uttered a groan.

"Take all the money," he said, "that's in the house, but leave that box alone. It contains papers which are of no use to any one but—but—to the owner."

The Dark Woman paid no attention whatever to this appeal, but fixing her eyes sternly upon the face of the Chancellor, she said, "You are in possession of the Great Seal of England. I want it."

"No—no!"

"I say, I want it."

"I have it not—I cannot give it up—it's madness to expect it. I would be of no use to you, nor to any one."

The Dark Woman laid her hand upon the arm of one of her band, and said calmly, "Shoot this man. Never mind the noise."

"Yes, master."

"Hold!—hold!" cried the Chancellor; "I will give up the seal."

"Where is it?'

"In yonder cabinet."

The Dark Woman made a gesture of caution to ner band in regard to the accurate supervision which they were to keep over the Chancellor, and approaching the cabinet, she wrenched it open.

Exactly within it lay that gaudy-looking purse which contains the seal forming the real insignia of the authority of the Lord High Chancellor of Great Britain.

"Your money!" said the Dark Woman, as she turned abruptly from the bureau towards the Chancellor.

"All I have is upon that dressing-table. The property that is in that cabinet does not belong to me."

"We are not particular," replied the Dark Woman, "as to the ownership."

She beckoned to Lovat as she spoke.

"Secure what you can find here," she said, "and then we will leave the house. We have already the principal prizes of this expedition."

Lovat, with considerable dexterity, emptied the cabinet of about five hundred pounds, which formed its contents, and likewise bestowed about him a quantity of old-fashioned jewellery, which, no doubt, was the exclusive property of the Royal Duke's daughter.

There was a savage and angry look upon the face of the Chancellor as he saw all these proceedings going on, but he felt himself to be in the hands of those who were perfectly unscrupulous, and who, in a different manner, and in a different line of life, very much resembled himself.

The Dark Woman having accomplished her purposes, stepped up to him.

"On the third night from this," she said, "at the hour of twelve there will be a mounted man by the first milestone on the Great Western Road, past Tyburn Gate. That man will be in the possession of the Great Seal which I now take from you, and for the sum of a thousand pounds it will be delivered to you, or to any one whom you may send for it."

"I will send."

"As you please; but beware of treachery! Any attempt of such a character will recoil as surely upon your own head as you now see that your

house is taken by storm, and yourself completely at my mercy. Farewell!'

"Stop," said the Chancellor, "one moment."

"What would you say?"

"I should think that your audacity would almost extend as far as to induce you to tell me who you are."

"No," said the Dark Woman, "I am anonymous—and as that in itself is a kind of name, you may call me by it; and when you yourself, or whatever messenger you may send, accost at the milestone on the Western Road the man who will restore to you the Great Seal, it will be well to remember that name, or there may be some difficulty."

"I will remember it," said the Chancellor; "and it will go hard with me but—but——"

"Hold, sir! Is it wise to threaten?"

"Perhaps not. I say no more."

"Bind him," said the Dark Woman.

The Chancellor looked inexpressibly savage as, with the assistance of his own dressing-gown and a couple of stout bell-ropes that were cut down from the room, he was bound securely to a chair, and the chair itself to one of the massive carved posts of the bedstead.

"Gag him," said the Dark Woman.

"No—no! There is no occasion," cried the Chancellor.

But the Dark Woman had given the order, and protestations on his part were of no avail. He was gagged just in the same fashion that his own hall-porter had been; namely, by a twisted handkerchief placed in his mouth, and tied securely at the back of his head.

This mode of gagging did not much impede the breath, nor did it wholly prevent some sounds from being made; but it effectually prevented those sounds from being articulate, or loud enough to create anything like an extraordinary alarm.

The Dark Woman then made a gesture to her band, which indicated that their work was done.

She herself led the way from the Chancellor's bed-chamber.

The band followed, and the door was closed.

A serious tumult, however, appeared to arise in that apartment the moment the Dark Woman and her associates had left it.

The Royal Duke's daughter had remained perfectly quiescent while the proceedings we have recorded were taking place.

Had she not received morally a knock-down blow by being called a woman? And, moreover, was it not perfectly inconsistent with her dignity to make any movement whatever while the apartment was in the hands of its assailants?

But she had been grievously insulted, and told, for the first time, a home truth, to the effect that her life was worthless; and so it was not in human nature to exist without vengeance upon some one.

The sounds of tumult that arose in that room, therefore, consisted in a violent assault which the Royal Duke's daughter made upon the Chancellor, who was certainly not in a condition to defend himself.

The Dark Woman, from the few observations she had heard from the lips of the Royal Duke's daughter, was very well able to conceive what was taking place.

An expression of contempt, for a moment

hovered over her countenance, and then she rapidly descended the stairs.

Temporarily, she had forgotten to look for the Chancellor's nephew; and she feared at the moment that he might not be aware of their departure from the house.

She paused and glanced rapidly behind her, and was pleased to see that he was close at hand.

"How fared you," she said, "with the son of the Chancellor? I heard no noise."

"Oh, no! I told you that the fellow was a poltroon. He begged abjectly for his life, so I satisfied myself by making a sort of bundle of him, tying him up in a couple of sheets and a counterpane, and so leaving them half dead with fear in the middle of the floor of his own room, for any one to tumble over who may happen to go in."

A light, half-suppressed laugh passed through the band, but the Dark Woman checked the disposition to levity.

"Hush!" she said,—"hush! Remember where we still are."

The band was silent, and they descended the great staircase of the Chancellor's house like a throng of spectres.

All was still. If the servants who inhabited the upper portion of the mansion had really heard anything going on on the floor beneath them, they had, in all probability, attributed it to one of those little skirmishes which the Chancellor and the Royal Duke's daughter were accustomed to have at any period of the day or night when the elements for one rose to the surface.

And so this open and audacious assault upon the mansion of the highest dignity of the law, situated too in one of the most populous districts in London, was perfectly successful.

There was nothing complicated about it. The whole was simplicity itself; and it had been set about with but one principle of action to guide it —namely, to remove every possible obstruction that might arise by main force, and in the most unscrupulous manner.

The Dark Woman and her band stood upon the doorstep of the Chancellor's house, and listened to Bloomsbury Church clock striking four.

The expedition had lasted about one hour.

"Master," said Lovat "I can see the two hackney coaches waiting exactly where we left them, at the corner of Southampton Street."

"We are more than fortunate," said the Dark Woman. "One of them will be useful to me. Who will drive me to my lodgings in St. James's Street?"

"I, master," replied Lovat. "I drove one of the coaches here, and rather pride myself upon my dexterity."

The Dark Woman turned to the remainder of the band.

"Not to-morrow night," she said, "but the next after, we will meet at one o'clock at St. Augustin's Church. Between the present time and that, I shall be able to dispose of some of the jewels we took from St. James's Palace. Till then, farewell!"

"Farewell!" muttered the band, in low tones.

The Dark Woman walked rapidly up to one of the coaches, followed by Lovat, who, when they got to within three or four paces of it, preceded her and opened the door.

He had no sooner done so, however, than he started back with surprise; for a rough, burly-looking man leant forward from the interior of the coach, and holding a pistol in his hand, which was as rough and burly-looking as himself, he cried out, "Now, my fine fellows, I must know what all this is about. You have no difficulty in seeing what I am—a Bow Street officer, at your service; and finding a couple of coaches here abandoned, I guessed pretty well that something was up, and that somebody would soon make his appearance, and here you are! Now, what's it all about, eh?"

"A bullet!" said the Dark Woman.

She uttered not another word; but over the shoulder of Lovat she fired one of her pistols right in the face of the officer.

He fell back into the coach with a yell.

If his finger had happened to have been upon the trigger of the pistol he himself held, no doubt it would have been discharged, and in that case Lovat must have fallen.

But such was not the case. The Bow Street officers always carried those short, stumpy, murderous-looking pistols with them; but they were so accustomed to find everybody give in to their authority, that the necessity of firing one scarcely ever suggested itself to them.

In this case the Bow Street officer only held his pistol threateningly to prevent his intended prisoners from running away, which he fully believed it would be their first impulse to do.

But he little knew with whom he had to deal.

Lovat was somewhat startled at the rapidity of the whole affair; and, indeed, few human nervous systems could have stood with perfect impunity the passage of a pistol bullet so close to one of his ears, as that one which the Dark Woman had launched at the head of the unfortunate Bow Street runner.

The Dark Woman was cool and calm as possible.

"I think that will do, Lovat," she said. "I shall prefer the other coach now, and it will be as well to close the door of this one."

One of the officer's feet hung out, and interposed some difficulty in closing the door; but after a few efforts he succeeded in doing so.

Lovat approached the other coach with some caution and deliberation; for he thought it possible that that, too, might be tenanted by some one who would dispute their progress.

The Dark Woman saw that he hesitated, and she spoke a few words to re-assure him.

"There is no one there, Lovat; if there had been, he would have come forward to the assistance of his comrade."

"No, there is no one," cried Lovat; "the coach is empty."

The Dark Woman entered this second vehicle with all the deliberation in the world; and she carried with her the small tin box, as well as the Great Seal, which she had taken from the house of the Chancellor.

Lovat mounted the box and drove off, so that the last echoes which reverberated throughout Bloomsbury Square were those of the wheels of the vehicle which carried away, in safety and security, her who had planned and executed one of the most daring burglarious offences that modern times had known.

CHAPTER CCX.

THE DARK WOMAN PROJECTS A SPECIAL
JOURNEY TO WINDSOR ON AN ERRAND OF
DIFFICULTY AND DANGER.

LINDA DE CHEVENAUX sat alone in her apartments in St. James's Street. She felt no fatigue,
for during the last four-and-twenty hours she had
had rest.

She never wanted much.

And, moreover, now she was exceedingly
anxious to examine the contents of the tin box
she had brought from the Lord Chancellor's.

The examination, however, had very few
charms for her, since she found that the great
mass of papers consisted of legal documents, bills
of exchange, and such like matters, for which she
cared nothing.

Among the papers, however, were various documents to which the signature of the King was
attached; and the sight of that signature brought
to her recollection one all-important paper which
years and years ago had been presented to
her dazzled eye-sight by the Prince of Wales, for
it purported to be the consent of the King to his
marriage with her, Linda de Chevenaux.

How often had she condemned the folly which
had induced her to part with that document
again; for although the Prince had over and over
again declared it to be a forgery of his own, and
had attempted to justify it on the false and
flagitious principle that in love or war all
stratagems are fair, if she had still possessed it, it
would have been a powerful instrument in her
hands as against the Regent.

But there had always been a dreamy notion in
the mind of Linda de Chevenaux that it was possible the King had in a weak moment yielded to
the then mad passion of his son, and given his
consent to their union.

It had been many, many times a dream of her
existence that she would find a means of seeking
out the King and putting the question to him.

To be sure, such an enterprise was beset with
many difficulties; but was not her whole life a
struggle with difficulties?—and was she not
generally successful, by the impetuosity of her
character, in overcoming them?

Surely, yes.

And should she shrink now from any act which
would promise to arm her against the man who
had made her what she was?

Linda de Chevenaux leant her head upon her
hands and thought deeply. Then she sprung to
her feet.

"It shall be done," she said: "it is something
providential that I have made no appointment
with those men who call me their master, for to-
morrow night. I will go to Windsor Castle,
where the sick King lies nearly abandoned by all
who should be near him, and, by fair means or by
foul, I will find a means of putting to him the
question if twenty years ago he gave his consent
to the marriage of the Prince of Wales with the
daughter of a gentleman. Who shall say that
such may not have been the case; and that the
subsequent marriage of the Prince with Caroline
of Brunswick may not have been acquiesced in by
the King on the supposition that I was dead?"

The more the Dark Woman thought over this
extravagant proposition, the more it seemed to
recommend itself to her.

And whereas but a short time since she had
almost taught herself to believe that her hopes
were blighted for ever, and that she should never
make any real progress in establishing herself as
the wife of the Regent, now that hope seemed to
dawn again, and she was ready to engage in the
wildest schemes to give it realization.

Having come to this determination, Linda de
Chevenaux was able to turn her attention to the
more practical affairs of life.

One of the most urgent of those affairs, at that
time, was the disposal of the jewels that were still
in her possession.

That those gems were of great value she could
well imagine; but there was the usual difficulty
in disposing of such property, that the purchaser
required either to know something of how the
vendor became possessed of it, or would only give
a small price for it.

The thieves' price, in fact.

Certainly, the attempt that the Dark Woman
had already made to dispose of the jewels had not
been encouraging.

That attempt, as the reader is aware, had very
nearly cost her her life.

No wonder that she rather shrunk from repeating it.

But after some cogitation she thought of a
plan.

It was an ingenious one.

She collected the jewels all together, and placed
them in a foreign, antique-looking purse that she
had.

Then the Dark Woman left her lodgings, and
hiring a hackney coach, she directed that she
should be driven to the London Docks.

When there, she inquired if any vessel had
recently arrived from the Brazils; and ascertaining that one had reached the docks only the day
previously, which was named the Donna Maria,
she got into the coach again, and ordered the
driver to take her to a jeweller's in the City that
she named, and who was about the last person to
whom anything in the shape of stolen property
would be taken to dispose of.

But that was precisely the reason the Dark
Woman ordered herself to be driven to that establishment.

Indeed, the shop was one of those which had a
reputation for wealth, and for being able to execute
any order, however rich or exacting, that could
be given to it.

The jewels that Linda de Chevenaux had to
sell would be quite a godsend to them, at the fair
market price of the gems.

They were always in want of jewels, and always
ready to purchase them.

But they must know where they came from.

The Dark Woman had no fear of the jewels
being recognised.

Their existence in St. James's Palace had
evidently been forgotten, or they would long since
have found a destination in the liquidation of
some of the debts of the Regent.

They were for the most part loose stones, too, so
that their identity with any known ornaments
was out of the question.

The Dark Woman was hopeful.

When the coach stopped at the door of the jeweller's, she alighted with a grave and serious air, and inquired for one of the principals.

She was shown into a private counting-house, and waited upon by an elderly gentleman, with a bald head, who said not a word, but giving his head a jerk, as much as to intimate, "Here I am," waited for her to speak.

"I came to London yesterday, in the Donna Maria, from the Brazils."

"Well, sir?"

"I have brought some unset gems with me, on account of the firm of Jose Martinquez and Company."

"Don't know them."

"And I have the stones to sell."

"Don't buy of strangers."

"Very good."

The Dark Woman had taken out the antique, foreign-looking purse with the jewels, but she coolly put it back again into her pocket, and moved towards the door.

"Stop, sir!" said the bald-headed principal of the firm. "Stop, sir!"

"What is your pleasure?"

"Can you give me any reference?"

"What for?"

"Why, a—that—you—a—that is to say——"

"Oh, I comprehend, you are afraid——"

"Yes, rather."

"That you should be taken in, and that the jewels I speak of should not be real stones?"

"No, sir. Do you think I am such an old fool as not to know real stones from false, eh?"

"I don't know how that may be, but I bring from the Brazils certain gems to sell. I don't want your money without you have the jewels, and I will take good care you don't have them without, and you talk nonsense about references. Pray sir, have you any references?"

"Sir," he said, "have you any objection to show me the stones?"

"Yes."

"You have?"

"I certainly have, unless you feel inclined to purchase such articles. Why should I waste my time, and the time of Messrs. Jose and Martinquez, upon you?"

"Good! I like you."

"It's more than I do you."

"Capital! You speak your mind, and are a business man, sir. Show me the jewels, and if they suit me, I will buy them at once, sir—at once —at—at——"

The old jeweller was glancing at a newspaper that was on the table, and the Dark Woman saw that it was open at the "Shipping Intelligence."

"Oh!—ah!—to be sure! 'Arrived, the Donna Maria, from La Plata.'"

"There are the jewels," said the Dark Woman, when she saw that the old, suspicious jeweller had finished his verification of her statement, that such a ship as the Donna Maria had arrived the day previously from the Brazils.

"There are the jewels, sir."

She emptied the antique purse upon the table before her.

The old jeweller was not at all dazzled, although the sight was one of great beauty, for he had seen too many collections of rare gems in his lifetime to be struck by surprise by any.

He picked them up carefully, one after the other, and glanced at them, and then he said, "Sir, will you permit me to weigh the diamonds and the rubies?"

"Certainly."

The weighing process was carefully gone through, and then the jeweller said, "Now, sir, the price?"

"The price?"

"Yes. What do you, on account of your principals, ask for this little lot?"

"What will you give?"

The jeweller shook his head.

"If, sir, I buy these stones, I shall not ask any of my customers what they will give for them, you may be assured."

The Dark Woman was in a difficulty; she had had a very undefined idea of the net value of the jewels; she feared that she should undo all that she had done in engendering confidence in the jeweller if she should ask too little.

There was far less danger in asking too much.

But what would be too much?

That was the question.

The Dark Woman was silent.

"Well, sir," said the jeweller, "you talked awhile ago about wasting your time. Who wastes it now?"

"Eight thousand pounds!" said the Dark Woman, promptly.

"Too much!"

She was well pleased to hear these words, and better pleased still at the tone in which they were uttered; because, although the jeweller said "Too much!" he did not say so with an air or manner as if the sum named were preposterously too much.

The temporary anxiety of Linda de Chevenaux passed away.

She was safe again.

She felt that she now stood once more upon firm ground with the jeweller.

"Jewels," she said, "fetch a high price in the Brazils at present."

"Very likely."

"And we were told that they fetched a still higher one in London and Paris."

"True!"

"Eight thousand pounds, then, can scarcely be too much."

"Yes We cannot give it. Do you know the firm of Bandiera, Manuel, and Co., at La Plata?"

"No."

"You do not?"

"Certainly not."

The Dark Woman suspected from the tone in which the crafty old jeweller had asked this question that there was no such firm in existence.

He had slightly hesitated and faltered over the names, which gave Linda de Chevenaux the idea that he was inventing them even as he spoke.

"You are sure, sir, you don't know that firm?"

"Quite. I never heard even of it."

"Then, sir, I will give you six thousand pounds for the little lot of jewels?"

"Seven!"

"No!"

"Good day, sir."

"Stop! Six thousand five hundred, with an understanding that, if you can get together a similar lot, I will take them at a similar price?"

"Agreed!"

"Pray sit down a moment, Mr. a—a—Mr.——"

"Mr. Fernandez."

"A Spanish-American name; but you are surely English?"

"I am; but my father was a native of Cuba."

"Ah! that accounts for your name. You shall have your money, sir, at once, if you will make out a bill of sale to us from your firm for whom you act."

"I will sign such bill of sale if you will make it out." said the Dark Woman. "Our South American forms of business are not the same as yours"

"Very good, sir."

Every necessary formality was gone through, and the Dark Woman left the jeweller's with a draft on a banker for no less a sum than six thousand five hundred pounds, which draft she had exchanged within the hour for bank notes.

Linda de Chevenaux drew a long breath of relief when she once more sat down in her lodgings in St. James's Street.

The large sum of money she was possessed of lay on a table before her.

It was not hers. She had to divide it with those men who had helped her to possess it.

But that was not the thought that then took possession of her.

The woman who had disposed of the original band of desperadoes, who did her behests under the name of "Paul's Chickens," in the way, it will be recollected, she did dispose of them, was not likely now to be very scrupulous about her obligations to new associates.

So it was not of the band that the Dark Woman thought.

It was of herself.

Of her own life.

Her own lost life.

And, as she saw the sum of money before her, the thought occurred to her that then, if she chose to embrace it, was at once the opportunity of peace.

With that sum at her command she might retire at once and for ever from the turmoil, from all the heart-breaking events, from all the wild excitements, the dangers and the sufferings of the life she led, and in some peaceful, quiet home surround herself with every natural luxury, and give up the mad pursuit of the phantoms of her brain.

For a moment or two she seemed to see the cottage home—a cottage, in name, with the luxury of a mansion—which she might command either in England or in some clime more favoured by the liberal hand of nature.

The prospect was fascinating.

But it soon passed away.

She heard the tramp of horses' feet in the street.

A glance at the window showed a plumed troop of cavalry passing, and at the martial sight the proud heart of the Dark Woman resumed its sternness. "Why do they not escort a Royal Princess," she exclaimed, "whose name should be Linda?"

The dream of peace, and calmness, and content had fled.

The Dark Woman was herself again.

"To Windsor! To Windsor!" she said. "I will find a means of seeing the old King, and I will seek from his own lips an answer to the question I shall put to him."

The Dark Woman then set about her preparations.

She knew well that the servants who attended in the private apartments of royalty were in plain clothes, and it was as one of them she wished to pass into Windsor Castle.

At least, that was to her mind the most feasible mode she could adopt of carrying out her design.

But she meant to take with her what she called a golden key.

That consisted of some couple of hundred or more guineas in her pocket; so that, in case of any unexpected difficulty, she would be able to put the fidelity of the attendants upon the old sick monarch to rather a severe test.

That was the Dark Woman's golden key.

She was quite correct in giving the guineas that name; for few, indeed, would be the doors or the hearts that they would not unlock.

But she waited until the evening began to get shadowy before she left her lodgings, to proceed to Windsor.

She knew that she could reach there in a little over two hours, with post-horses, as she meant to pay the postilion.

And this she fully succeeded in doing, so that by nine o'clock the post-chaise she had ordered rattled into the little town of Windsor.

Linda de Chevenaux paid the postilion so liberally that the waiting for her was a pleasure, inasmuch as he looked forward to a similar liberality upon reaching London again.

Then the Dark Woman walked towards the Castle.

It looked huge, inaccessible, and frowningly down upon her.

She had a blind kind of reliance upon fortune to aid her in what she was about; for although she thought, if she could only once get into the interior of the Castle, she could manage very well, she had no well defined plan by which that first step could be gained.

Approaching the Castle by the domestic offices, the Dark Woman soon observed a man hurrying from the direction in which she was proceeding.

Quite upon the chance that he might be some one connected with the royal establishment, the Dark Woman arrested him.

"My friend, do you belong to the royal household?"

"Yes, sir."

"Then I am delighted to see you."

"You, sir?"

"Oh, yes, I belong to the *Evening Courant.*"

"The newspaper, sir?"

"Yes. There are five guineas to begin with."

What the gentleman who belonged to the *Evening Courant* meant by "five guineas to begin with," was beyond the comprehension of this man, who was one of the servants of the Castle; but five bright golden guineas were not to be despised on that account.

His hand closed over the coins.

"Sir," he said, "what can I have the pleasure to oblige you in?"

"How is the King?"

"Better, they say."

" Is he able to converse ?"

" They don't let him see anybody but the doctors and the Regent."

" Well, there are five more guineas to go on with."

The man was getting rather bewildered. Was the representative of the *Evening Courant* mad, or had he found a gold mine ?

But the second five guineas went into the same pocket as the first.

" Now, my good friend," said the Dark Woman, " I want to see the inside of the Castle."

The man shook his head.

" Nobody is allowed in the Castle but the household. I could not do it, sir."

" Hold out your hand ?"

" But—but, sir—I—a—another five guineas ? Well, sir, if you must get into the Castle, the only way is to come with me through the laundry."

" That will do."

" This way, Mr.—a—a——"

" *Courant*—I am the *Evening Courant*."

" Yes, sir—Mr. *Courant*—this way, if you please. And yet—yet——"

" Yet what ?"

" I am wrong to do it."

" So you are."

" You say so, sir ?"

" I do. I feel you are wrong, and so am I, merely for the satisfaction of an idle curiosity, to throw away the fifteen guineas I have given you, and the five more I was going to give you ; so let me have them back again."

" Back again ?"

" Yes ; and I will forego my intentions."

" Hem ! Well, I—a—don't see what harm there can be in it. I'm sure, sir, you are a gentleman ; and so, sir, I think you may as well, as you wish it, please yourself, and come into the Castle."

" Be it so, then."

The Dark Woman followed her guide, who led her through some intricate outbuildings, and then into the Castle at a small portal, which opened on to a narrow passage, at the end of which was a flight of stairs terminating in one of the galleries of the Castle.

" This," said the man, " is called the Blenheim Gallery, you see, sir."

" Yes. And where does the King stay ?"

" Oh, in his own rooms, you see, sir ; but we cannot go near that part of the Castle on any account."

" Of course not ; but where is it ?"

" You see that door, sir ?"

" I do."

" Well, sir, that leads to what is called the Queen's Drawing-room, and beyond that are the three rooms in the occupation of the King."

" Oh, indeed !"

" Yes, sir ; and if you come this way——"

" Stop, my friend. Hold out your hand."

" Oh, sir, you are too good ! '

" Not at all. There are ten guineas."

" Ten ?"

" I said ten. I am going to see the Queen's Drawing-room——"

" Sir ?"

" I say I am going to see the Queen's Drawing-room. which you tell me is through that door."

" Good gracious, sir ! you can't—you mustn't—indeed, you must not."

" I will. I have already opened the door."

" Opened—the—door ?"

" Yes, with a golden key, which has already cost me five-and-twenty guineas, and which will cost me five-and-twenty more, if a certain person is not blind to his own interest. You understand me ?"

" I do, sir ; and all I can say is that a gentleman like you ought to go where he likes."

" You are a sensible man."

" This way, sir. If you will be so good as to make as little noise as possible, of course it will be all the better."

" I will be careful."

The door leading to the Queen's Drawing-room was opened, and the servant preceded the Dark Woman, carrying a wax-light which he brought from one of the sconces in the Blenheim Gallery.

He spoke in a suppressed tone of voice, as he pointed to a door at the further end of the very beautiful apartment in which they were.

" That door, sir, which is locked, and is always kept so, leads to the King's apartments. The doctors, and the attendants, and his Royal Highness the Regent, always go the other way from the grand terrace, you comprehend, sir, so that this door is never opened by any one."

" Except by you, now."

" Sir !"

" I say except by you now."

" Oh, sir, you are pleased to be—to—to be quite funny."

" Not at all. The funny thing would be if a sensible man, such as you are most undoubtedly, were to raise any foolish scruples ; but I feel confident you will not do so, but will open the door at once."

The attendant looked perplexed, and not a little terrified ; but he happened, quite in the abstraction of the moment, to put his hand into the pocket where he had placed the various instalments of the five-and-twenty guineas he had already received from the Dark Woman.

The touch of the gold was enough.

It's pleasant jingle was more than enough.

The scruples of the royal attendant all vanished.

" I feel quite sure, Mr. a—a—*Courant*," he said, " that you don't mean any harm."

" None in the least."

" To—to the old King ?"

" On my soul, I do not."

The Dark Woman spoke with the most perfect sincerity. She did not mean any harm to the old King. What she meant was, if possible, some good to herself ; but whether or not she should be fortunate enough to accomplish it was quite another matter.

The attendant took a key, or rather two keys, from his pocket, for they were fastened loosely together, and with one of them he unlocked the door that led to the private and jealously-closed apartments of poor old George the Third, the insane King.

CHAPTER CCXI.

THE DARK WOMAN HAS AN AGITATING INTERVIEW WITH ROYALTY.

THE Castle attendant, after he had turned the key in the lock of the door, still lingered.

He trembled in every limb.

"Sir," he said, "Mr. *Evening Courant*, I almost begin to fancy—to think——"

"What?" said the Dark Woman, sharply.

"That one may pay too high a price for even fifty golden guineas."

"Indeed?"

"Yes. I feel quite ill, and I do think that I was never in such a fright before in all my life."

"You have nothing to be alarmed at. Come what may, I will never betray the means by which I have found my way into these rooms. You may rest easy on that score; and now that you have done all that I require of you, let me advise you to keep out of the way."

"I will—I must. But—but——"

"But what?"

"Do tell me. Do assure me over again that you don't mean any harm to the King."

"What can I say to assure you? I pledge my soul's safety. I will call upon heaven's thunders to crush me. I will say anything you please—take any oath you wish; because nothi g can be further from my thoughts than to contrive or think of any harm to that poor King, who should be rather an object of pity and commiseration."

The tone of the Dark Woman ought to have satisfied any one. It did satisfy the Castle attendant; and although he felt himself to be still in a perfect maze in regard to the object of Mr. *Evening Courant* in paying such a price for the opportunity merely of looking upon poor insane old King George, yet that was no business of his.

"I am satisfied," he said.

"And so, then, am I," said the Dark Woman. "I will keep these keys."

"I dare not part with them."

"But if you were to lose them?"

"Oh, then, indeed——"

"You could not help it, of course; although, perhaps, some superior in office here might accuse you of carelessness. Fancy that is the case, and you are none the worse off. Farewell!"

Linda de Chevenaux, as she spoke, possessed herself of the two keys, one of which she, at all events, knew was an important one to possess; and passing through the doorway, she closed it on the other side.

The terrified, but well-paid, attendant then hurried from the spot.

He felt that he had possibly done some mischief, but as he did not see the way to remedy it, except at his own cost, he let it alone.

Linda was in a small room, which had in it a powerful odour of aromatic drugs.

At first, she could not imagine from what that odour could proceed.

It was just that kind of composite odour which is usually to be found in a chemist's shop.

But there was sufficient light to enable her to look about her; and then she saw that there was a table, on which was placed all the paraphernalia of a druggist.

Scales, and weights, and bottles, and a variety of small drawers—such as might well have belonged to a chemist's shop, or a surgery, as those little apartments are called in which general practitioners keep a select assortment of drugs for their private patients.

And this was the ante-chamber of the rooms directly in the occupation of the mad King.

It did not require any very extraordin ry exercise of reasoning power to come to the conclusion that it was there, in the room she had reached, that the medical attendants of the King concocted their prescriptions.

She remembered to have heard that there was what was commonly called a doctor's shop in Windsor Castle.

But hardly had the Dark Woman had time to take note of these things about her when she was warned of some danger, by the sound of footsteps close at hand.

There came the sound, too, of voices.

Those indications of the neighbourhood of some persons, and probably of their near approach, were not to be mistaken or neglected.

The Dark Woman looked around her hurriedly for some place of hiding.

There was none that presented anything like perfect security.

The only place, indeed, that she could for a few minutes hope to conceal herself was behind the window curtain.

That curtain was of thick, heavy cloth, and it reached right down to the floor, where it lay, as regarded its extremity, in a confused heap.

To dash behind that curtain was the work of a moment to the Dark Woman; and, in good truth, she was not too soon in availing herself of its temporary shelter.

A door opened—not the one by which she had entered what may be called the doctor's shop of old Windsor Castle, but another one on the opposite side of that room—and three persons came in, slowly and deliberately.

Two of these three persons were conversing together as they entered.

It struck Linda de Chevenaux, at that moment, as strange that they should all three have creaking shoes on.

These little trivialities will strangely obtrude themselves upon the mind at moments when one might imagine that the thoughts were wholly occupied with objects of great importance.

"Well, Doctor," said one of the two persons who were talking together — "well, Doctor, I suppose you mean to go to the Duchess of Devonshire's to-night, yet?"

"Oh, yes!"

"Ah, I thought so! Maria Chetwynd is to be there, I suppose?"

"Come, come!" said the other, with a laugh. "If you say so much about Maria Chetwynd, I shall begin to think that you are yourself hit in that quarter."

"Ha, ha! Oh, no! I worship at another—and at what I think a still fairer—shrine."

"Ah! Dear me! this is tiresome!" said the third person who had come into the room.

"Very," said one of the others.

"Uncommonly tiresome," added the third person.

The Dark Woman managed to peep out from

her place of concealment, flimsy and fragile as it was; and she could see that these three persons were gentlemen, and that they were dressed, in the most scrupulous manner, in the costume of physicians.

Could it be possible that these were the three physicians who had the care of the royal patient?

Alas, it was but too true!

And this room was their consulting-room, to which they always retired after a visit—paid at the rate of fifty guineas each—to the poor, old, mad King.

But the nation paid that little expense; and while many a poor operative and his family were starving—for that happened to be a period of great national distress—the charlatans, under the name of physicians, who "attended" King George the Third made large fortunes.

But that was all to be expected.

And so the Dark Woman found herself, most

No. 95.—DARK WOMAN.

unexpectedly, an auditress of one of the medical consultations regarding the state of mind and body of the mad old King.

"I cannot help thinking." said one of the physicians, "that the *corps de ballet* at the little theatre in the Haymarket is one of the prettiest the metropolis ever saw."

"Oh, no, no!" said another. "Come, come! You quite forget the last spectacle at the Pantheon, in Oxford Street."

"Pantheon me no Pantheons!" cried the other. "You know, as well as I do, that it is now shut up."

"Oh, yes!"

"Yes," said the third physician; "and I can tell you why, if you don't know."

"Why?—why?"

"Well, you know, they were playing 'Don Giovanni.'"

"Yes, yes!"

"Well, then, you know, there are a lot of devils in the piece; and the manager had engaged seven, and got them up regardless of expense. But when they all assembled, just before they were wanted, an eighth appeared, bringing with him such a baneful odour of brimstone——"

"Oh, oh, oh!" cried the other two physicians. "Come, come! that won't do!"

"Well, as the old saying is:—

"'I know not how the truth may be,
But I tell the tale as told to me.'"

"The tail, you mean."

"Of the eighth devil!"

"Ha, ha!"

"Ha, ha, ha!"

The medical consultation on the state of the poor old King's health was going on in the most lively manner imaginable among the three Court physicians, who, for this kind of discourse, only got one hundred and fifty guineas among them.

Then one looked at his watch.

"By Jove, I must be off!"

"So must I."

"Well," said the third, "what is the bulletin to be?"

"Oh, you write it—any stuff will do!"

"Will this?

"'His Majesty has passed rather a restless night, but the symptoms remain the same.'"

"Oh, yes, yes!"

"Yes, to be sure—that will do; and let Adams, the apothecary, when he comes, make him up some of the old draught. It don't matter a fig whether he takes it, or not. By-the-bye, did you hear that story about the Regent and little Fanny Pierce?"

"No, no! What is it?"

"Oh, I will tell you as we go to town. It's the drollest thing, and will make you die with laughing. You must know that our fat friend, the Regent, was trotting down Pall Mall——"

What happened to our "fat friend," the Regent, while trotting down Pall Mall on the occasion referred to, the Dark Woman had no opportunity of ascertaining; for the three physicians left the room by the same door at which they had entered it, while one of their number, who was the most prolix of the three, was in full tide of telling the scandalous anecdote.

The Dark Woman was alone again.

The "medical consultation" on the state of the old mad King was over.

She emerged from her position behind the cloth curtain, and going to the door at which the physicians had left the room, she placed her ear close to it, and listened intently.

She thought she heard a groan.

But she could not be quite sure.

It might be some accidental singing of the wind through some narrow passage, for she could hear that it was blowing, in rather a gusty fashion, about the towers of old Windsor Castle.

She felt quite satisfied, however, that there was no one immediately on the other side of that door through which the physicians had passed.

And she felt quite satisfied, too, that it was not locked.

If it had been so, she must have heard the sound of the operation; therefore, she had but to gather confidence to turn the handle, and the door would be sure to yield to her.

Confidence was a quality which Linda de Chevenaux was, as the reader is well aware, not deficient in; and she gently turned the handle of the door, and opened it calmly and steadily.

It creaked a little upon its hinges, but not sufficiently so to create any alarm.

Linda found herself in a much larger apartment than that she had just left.

It was a bed-chamber.

A right royal-looking bedstead, above which was a gilt crown, and on the foot-board of which were the royal arms of England, occupied about a fourth of the whole space of the chamber.

Tall candelabra stood on each side of this bedstead, and the high chimney-piece had on it a quantity of very beautiful old china.

The Dark Woman recollected to have heard that Queen Charlotte had a fancy for old china, and this, no doubt, was some portion of her collection.

The floor was covered, not with a carpet, but with very thick crimson cloth.

Several tables and chairs, all in crimson velvet —that is to say, the chairs—were about the room, and on a large toilette-table there lay a mixed heap of properties, of various kinds.

That this was the King's sleeping-room she had no doubt; and the rapid survey she made of it took much less time than it has taken us, for the satisfaction of our readers, thus slightly to describe it.

There was a richly-gilt and elegantly-panelled door opposite to the one at which the Dark Woman had entered.

When she closed, however, that door that led to the doctors' shop, or consultation room, she saw that its panels on the side next to the royal bed-chamber were ornamented in the same way precisely as those of the door she saw facing her.

That door she had still to pass through.

At it she paused and listened, even as she had done at the other.

There could be no mistake now.

She heard palpable groans.

Then she knew that she was in the chamber exactly adjoining that in which she might expect to see the old King.

There was but one anxiety now oppressing her, and it resolved itself to one question:—"Was he alone?"

That was a question which the Dark Woman had no possible means of satisfactorily answering.

To be sure, no sound, as of any one moving, or of any human voice, came from the room, and no sound of life, with the exception of those groans of mental or bodily suffering, or of both combined; but yet the old King might not be alone.

He certainly ought not to be alone.

Surely, of all the cormorants who fattened and made money in the royal service, there ought to be found always some one to keep watch and ward in that chamber of affliction!

But, after what she had seen and heard in regard to the royal physicians, it would not surprise Linda de Chevenaux in the least to find the old mad King quite deserted, and left to his own devices.

And yet she paused.

And yet she listened at the door.

Listened with all the intentness in her power, throwing, as far as was possible, all her senses into that one of hearing.

The groans came at regular intervals.

But there was no other sound.

There certainly was no voice—no movement, as of any one in attendance on the monarch—there, in that royal residence, above which floated the flag of England.

Time was speeding on.

The Dark Woman felt that something must be left to chance.

She tried the door.

It was fast.

Fast, apparently, on the other side.

By what means, then, had the physicians left the royal apartments, for they had shown no disposition to lock doors behind them?

There seemed to be no other route.

Linda de Chevenaux carefully examined the lock of this door.

There was no key in it.

Her heart failed her. She was brought to an abrupt stand-still, if the door were locked upon the other side.

But one hope remained to her.

She had two keys.

One or the other of them might set the question at rest whether that door were locked, and the key that had locked it removed from the other side or not.

With some eagerness, which induced a slight rattling noise in the lock, the Dark Woman tried, not the key by which she had just obtained admittance to the "doctors' shop," but the other one that was loosely attached to it.

It was only her self-control which prevented her from uttering a cry of disappointment.

The door was not locked.

But it was fast.

"Bolted on the other side," said Linda to herself.

That was the inevitable conclusion that she came to; and yet, after a few moments' reflection, she thought that surely that door would not be left quite at the use and disposal of the mad King.

In fact, she scarcely knew what to think.

After a few moments, however, given to reflection, Linda de Chevenaux drew from its concealed sheath that narrow, flat-bladed dagger, which she always managed to have with her.

She tried carefully and cautiously if she could insinuate its blade between the door and the door-post.

Yes, that was possible.

Just possible.

But its possibility at all answered her intended purpose, which was to ascertain where the bolt was situated which held the door close.

Provided she could move the blade of the knife-like dagger she had down the narrow crevice behind the door and the jamb, or post, this was a matter that might be accomplished.

Yes.

She found the bolt.

It was exactly above the lock.

Then the Dark Woman set to work, not with the dagger, but with another implement that she

had with her in a case, that looked like a case of surgical instruments.

A fine saw was laid across the bolt.

There was a soft, grating sound.

The bolt was thin, circular, and of brass. It yielded almost as easily as a bit of wood might have done to the keen teeth of the fine and exquisitely tempered saw.

Then the Dark Woman felt that she had overcome what had threatened to be a great difficulty. She turned the handle of that door, and stepped over its threshold on to an extraordinary thick carpet which quite stood up from the floor.

The room was very dark.

At least, it seemed so to her upon first entering it; and it looked in that semi-darkness, at the first glance, more spacious than it really was.

It was the room in which was to be found King George the Third.

The atmosphere was warm. There was a large round table. There was a very large—in fact, quite out of all usual sized—easy chair.

Just above the back of it the Dark Woman saw some white, flossy-looking hair.

She felt convinced that there sat the King.

And he was alone.

Yet the Dark Woman heard, in a confused sort of way, the sound of voices not far off.

She could not exactly define where they came from, but she thought it essential to her security to make the discovery as quickly as possible.

CHAPTER CCXII.

THE DARK WOMAN ARMS HERSELF WITH THE ROYAL SIGN-MANUAL.

THE dull, heavy breathing of the old King in that massive easy chair proclaimed that he slept.

Linda de Chevenaux, as light as foot could fall, approached the chair.

But she need have had no caution in treading on that thick carpet.

The footstep of a horse would not have been heard upon it, and had she known that it had been placed there in consequence of the mad King having flung himself upon the floor, and tried to dash his head against it, she would not have wondered at its presence.

She did not notice another measure of precaution that was used in the royal chamber.

The walls were padded thickly to above seven feet from the floor.

But for some such precaution the life and the madness of George the Third would long since have come to an end at one and the same time.

And so the Dark Woman moved along the floor and faced the chair.

There sat the monarch.

A sad spectacle.

His long white hair and beard hung in wavy masses upon his breast and shoulders.

His face was ghastly pale. He looked old—old to a degree not at all warranted by his actual years; and, as he slept, there was an expression of pain and suffering upon his face that no one could do otherwise than pity.

Oh, what a contrast was the state of the mad King to that of his heir!

The Prince of Wales was rioting in extravagance and dissipation, surrounded by every possible luxury that money and credit could produce.

The King slept in pain and misery, neglected by all in that dreary chamber of Windsor Castle.

Waiting to die!

That surely was his best—his only hope!

Even the Dark Woman's heart was touched for a moment at the sad spectacle before her, and she nearly shed a tear for the mad King.

She was, however, still.

But she recollected that she had work to do.

And she recollected, too, that she stood there in that chamber on peril of, perhaps, her life.

She made a movement to awaken the King, but then she abstained from doing so.

In what mood would he awaken?

That was a question well worth the asking, if it were possible to procure any answer to it; which certainly, so far as regarded Linda de Chevenaux, was not possible, since she could not be in possession of the experience which would provide an answer.

And while she paused, doubtful of what exactly to do, there came again upon her ears faintly, but yet sufficiently distinctly for there to be no doubt about the sounds, the murmur of voices.

Loud laughter, too, accompanied those voices.

If the Dark Woman, considering where she was and the state of affairs at Windsor Castle, could have thought such a thing possible, she would have said there was some carousing, and wild feasting, and rioting going on within actual earshot of that chamber of distress and misery.

But surely that could not be. There might be indifference, scant attendance, and want of sympathy; but anything in the shape of riot of that description could surely, under no circumstances, be a part of the existence beneath the roof of Windsor Castle.

So close at hand, however, were those sounds that Linda de Chevenaux felt herself in a manner constrained to ascertain the cause before she should awaken the King.

There were several doors opening from the apartment in addition to that one at which she had entered.

No less than three, in fact, presented themselves in the panelling of the wall, immediately opposite the fire-place.

And from the disposition of their number it is more than probable that that room, in ancient times, had been a reception room of the monarch, to which persons could be introduced through one suite of aparments and shown out through another, without encountering other claimants to the royal countenance.

Accident alone determined the choice of Linda de Chevenaux, as she opened the one of these doors that lay most to the left hand.

Instantly upon doing so she felt inclined to close it again, for the sounds of riot, and that kind of physical enjoyment which consists of an unrestrained use of the wine-cup, came in a much fuller volume to her ears.

A second glance was sufficient to enable her to see the state of affairs.

The room was vacant itself into which this door opened, but there was another apartment immediately beyond it, the door of which was not closely shut, and it was in that other apartment that some rather noisy party was evidently in the full height of enjoyment.

The voices came pretty plainly to the ears of Linda de Chevenaux, and as she gently pushed the door close behind her, and then advanced a few paces into the outer room to that in which the revelry was going on, she could hear what was said with perfect distinctness.

The words had reference to card-playing.

"Confound my luck, I always lose! I've not had a good hand the whole evening. Pass that bottle, do! More glasses—more glasses! These nuts have nothing in them. Pay me that guinea now, or else you'll pretend to forget it. I wonder if old George is asleep or awake? Come now, shuffle—shuffle? Do you want to keep those cards in your hand all night, looking at them? Hurrah! this is rather jolly! Who wouldn't be a royal page?—lots to drink and nothing to do! Come, now, be quiet. If you play whist, play whist; but if you want to laugh and make a noise, do so. Hurrah!—ha! ha! ha!—the trump's a king! Is he mad?"

A roar of laughter followed this very mild jest.

The royal pages were enjoying themselves while in attendance upon their insane master.

A sensation of indignation came over Linda de Chevenaux.

She had that peculiarity of being perfectly alive to the misconduct and heartlessness of others, while, to carry on her own objects, who could be more unscrupulous than she?

Half inclined was she, suddenly, to present herself among that party of noisy, roystering pages, and to frghten them into something like propriety.

But if the notion ever held a place seriously in her mind, she gave it up as quickly as it was formed.

She stepped noiselessly back once more into the apartment of the King, and closing the door through which she had passed, she sought some means of fastening it, and found one of those small brass bolts which seemed so common on the doors of that part of Windsor Castle.

She shot this bolt into its socket, and then, with a feeling that she was tolerably free from the apprehension of interruption, she turned her attention to the aged and insane monarch.

The old King was muttering in his sleep, but far too unintelligibly for Linda de Chevenaux to make out what he said.

She spoke to him gently, and in a low, earnest voice, "King George, awake! awake! awake! It is a friendly voice which speaks to you."

The old King opened his eyes.

"Off! off!" he cried. "Yield me a prisoner to the Directory! Off! off!—not my head!—not my head! Where? where?—where's Wales, and York, and Clarence? Shoe the Horse Guards with felt, and then make no noise! Who are you? who are you?"

"A friend."

"No, no, no—oh, no! King George the Third has no friends. Never had—never will have; and since they caught him in that—that—what-do-you-call-it place, in Paris, where they set up the guillotine, and took off his head after that poor Louis the Sixteenth's, while the revolted provinces of America looked on and smiled—smiled—smiled to see the deed! He is—he is—what is he?"

"Will it please your Majesty to listen to me?"

"I can't help it," said the King, with a gleam of reason. "Am I not a prisoner?"

"Nay, not a prisoner."

"Yes, I say I am; and this is the Tower—the Tower to which they take captive kings."

"Alas, no! This is Windsor Castle."

"I tell you it is the Tower. Always contradicted—always contradicted! It is the Tower of London, reeking with blood—blood—blood! Who are you? Eh?—eh?—eh?"

"It has escaped your Majesty's recollection, that I said I was a friend."

"Ah, what?" cried the King, springing to his feet, and, so to speak, catching at a word which had accidentally fallen from Linda de Chevenaux's lips. "Eh?—what?—what is that you say? Escape?—escape?—escape?"

A look of animation came over his countenance.

A wild frenzied expression of insane joy shone in his eyes.

It was evident he must have brooded long over that word escape, for it to have such interest to him, and such power over his dormant intellect.

Linda de Chevenaux saw her advantage instantly. She felt that she had struck a chord which would be responsive in that poor mad brain; and she resolved, for her own purposes, to strike it again and again, until it produced the effect she desired.

"Yes," she said, "I have told your Majesty that I am a friend, and my errand here is to assist you to escape."

The old King tottered towards her, and grasped her arm with both hands.

"Let me—let me—look—look—look into your face, and see if you be an honest man!"

"I hope so."

"Do you mean escape—escape—escape from Willes—that rascal Willes?"

Linda de Chevenaux knew that one of the royal physicians was so named as well as the celebrated valet of the Regent, and she replied at once, "Yes, your Majesty; you shall escape from Willes, and all the rest of them who keep you here in most unworthy bondage."

"Why—why—why then, I'm a king again!"

There was something almost great in the manner in which George the Third uttered these words, and at the same moment raised both his arms above his head, and glared at Linda de Chevenaux. His white hair, which had not been trimmed or cut for years, floated wildly about his head and face, and the Dark Woman thought that a more living and startling picture of Old King Lear, in the midst of his deep afflictions from the unkindness of his daughters, could not have been found.

"Escape! escape! escape! Yes—yes—yes! I am a king again!"

"Every inch a king."

"Yes; every inch a king; and you shall be one of my great nobles. I have but to escape to London; and yet this London—for you know this is the Tower—tell me how we shall escape from the Tower?"

"Easily, your Majesty, with my assistance."

"Ah! How so? Speak—speak—speak! But every now and then keep using that word escape. My lords, you see before you your King—your rightful King, who has been badly used, but since he is a King again, why—why—why, my lords,

he must punish like a King. Did you say escape?"

"I did," replied Linda de Chevenaux, who had been revolving in her mind exactly how to manage the poor mad monarch. "I did say escape, and if your Majesty will be guided by me that escape will be a certainty; only it is necessary, your Majesty will comprehend, to answer me exactly and precisely something that I shall ask of you."

"Speak, worthy sir! Are you a duke or an earl?"

"I am whatever your Majesty pleases."

"Then I make you my minister. Name your colleagues, sir, and they shall meet with my approbation. Do you know my Lord North? Well, I'll have none of him. Now—now—now go on."

"Does your Majesty recollect if, about twenty years ago, his Royal Highness the Prince of Wales procured your sign manual to a leave and license that should enable him to marry where his affections were then fixed?"

"Wales?—Wales?—Wales? Our son Wales?"

"Yes; it is of him I speak."

"Affections?—affections? No—no—no!—he has no affections. Look here—look here, Duke! Would it not be well to spread a report through the Tower that the King was to be executed on the green—the green—the green, you know;—and then while all the crowd was there, couldn't we walk out of the gate? Eh! that's good—that's good! Eh!"

"A capital device."

"Thought you'd say so—thought you'd say so!"

"But can your Majesty charge your memory with an answer to my question? Did you, twenty years ago, give his Royal Highness the Prince of Wales, leave to marry?"

"Marry—marry? Marry who? What do you mean, my lord? Marry—marry—twenty years ago? Stuff! stuff! Royal Marriage Act, you know: didn't do it—couldn't do it! Cumberland, my brother, married—married—married low—beneath him. Stop! stop! Did you say escape?

"The lady's name was Linda de Chevenaux—the daughter of a gentleman."

"Stuff! Trash! Bah! Bo!"

The Dark Woman felt a pang at her heart.

This, then, was the result of her interview with the monarch. Epithets, both opprobrious and contemptuous, came, even from his shattered intellect, at the very idea of that consent to her marriage with the Regent, which she had cherished and lived upon for years.

That the Prince of Wales, to overcome her scruples at the period of their supposed union, had produced such a pretended consent from the King his father, there could be no doubt of; but he had pretty plainly told her the truth since, which was, that it was nothing but a forgery, sanctioned at the time, as he considered, by his ungovernable passion, and to be coolly avowed and repudiated whenever it might suit him so to do.

It would be wrong to say that Linda de Chevenaux was not prepared for some such reply as she had received from the old King.

But her politic brain had another resource.

"Your Majesty is perfectly right," she said,

"and what your Majesty has kindly said is quite satisfactory; so that now we turn our attention but to one subject, and that is your Majesty's escape."

"Good—good—a capital word that! escape—escape—escape from the Tower!"

"In order to accomplish that, I must have your Majesty's full authority to call upon all good subjects to assist us, and to overcome Willes."

"Rascal! rascal! Infernal rascal, Willes. Can't bear the sight of him! Will come, though, and intrude himself into our presence!"

"Your Majesty shall overcome him, and in order that you may do so, your royal signature to an authority, calling upon all loyal subjects to assist you, will be necessary."

"Yes, yes, yes! All right—all right! My royal signature, George Rex, you mean? They don't ask for that now. A man without a head, you know—without a head! It has been off, but it's grown on again! Do you see the seam? Do you see the seam?"

"Very slightly."

"Good—good—good! Slightly—only slightly! Go away altogether some day—won't it? won't it?"

"Certainly, your Majesty, and your royal signature to this paper will ensure your escape."

Linda de Chevenaux had provided herself with a written paper on which were the words, but without any date, that follow:—

"This certifies that whether lost, or still in existence, we executed a document at the proper period, giving our consent, as by law entitled to do, under the Royal Marriage Act, to the legal union of our son Wales, with Linda de Chevenaux."

The Dark Woman took care to fold this paper in such a manner that the old King saw the writing upon it but confusedly.

What she wanted, however, was, that he should sign his name—not at the foot of the writing—but across it.

She considered that by that means she might escape a most vexatious plea that the ingenuity of the advisers of the Prince of Wales would be sure to urge against her.

They might not be able to dispute the genuineness of the royal signature, but they might say that it had been procured in some surreptitious manner to a blank piece of paper.

By having the royal sign-manual over the writing, and in a different coloured ink—that is to say, ink of a different shade, although still black like the writing—she considered she avoided that difficulty.

She had often heard, and fully believed it, that there were people who, by careful analysis and microscopic observation, could pronounce most decidedly which line of writing—assuming one to be over the other—was written first.

It followed, therefore, that if the King's signature was proved to have been after the words implying the certificate of consent to the marriage, it would be difficult to gainsay it.

Truly the Dark Woman had a genius in these kind of things.

The absence of a date, likewise, upon the paper—although at first it would seem like a very fatal legal omission—was in reality a piece of *finesse* and greatly in its favour.

The old King had had frequent accessions of insanity during the last few years; and what Linda de Chevenaux wished to do, was to cut the ground of that objection from under her opponents' feet, so that they should not say, when the signature was proved beyond dispute, and when it was proved that it was written after and over the consent, that it must have been during one of the King's maniacal accesses.

The proof of that would remain with those who might dispute the document, since it was a well-known principle of English law that no one was called upon to prove a negative.

That is to say, Linda de Chevenaux could not be made to prove that the King was not insane when he affixed his sign manual to that paper.

And the Dark Woman had been provident and careful about every little particular.

She had with her a small bottle of ink and a pen.

She placed the paper upon the table, and George the Third, without looking where the ink or where the pen came from, took the latter as it was tendered to him by Linda de Chevenaux, and signed the paper—

"GEORGE REX."

"I triumph!" cried the Dark Woman.

"What? what? what? what?"

"I mean I shall triumph in your Majesty's escape."

"Hush! hush! That's Lutwych!"

The King had suddenly assumed an attitude of listening. Long residence in that room, and surrounded by the same people, had made him alive to the lightest sound, and able to detect at once their individual footsteps.

"Who does your Majesty mean?"

"Lutwych—Lutwych, one of the pages! Great rascal—great rascal! Comes here to insult his King! They take it turn, turn, and turn about! Thieves—thieves, and rascals all! Pretend they come to see if I'm safe—safe—safe! That's Lutwych; know his footstep—know his footstep!"

CHAPTER CCXIII.

THE MAD MONARCH MAKES A VACANCY IN THE CORPS OF GENTLEMEN PAGES AT WINDSOR.

THE Dark Woman felt all her danger.

With that sort of instinctive cleverness which belonged to her. combined by the slight hints dropped by the King, she could understand pretty well what was the meaning of the movement of one of the pages in that direction.

No doubt it was the duty of some one or other of them, at stated periods, to visit the insane King; and this one, whom he named and knew as Lutwych, had reluctantly risen from the card-table to perform his turn of duty.

The Dark Woman was never very scrupulous of human life.

The deaths of half a dozen pages would have seemed to her as nothing in comparison to her safe escape from Windsor Castle with the document, which she firmly believed would make her Princess of Wales and legal wife of the Regent.

She saw the fire of insanity in the eyes of the old King.

She heard the expressions of deep and bitter hatred which he kept muttering and associating with the name of Lutwych.

And the Dark Woman made her determination.

"Your Majesty must escape," she whispered; "but this man Lutwych will endeavour to prevent you, which will be treason."

"Treason! treason!" shouted the mad King, catching at the word.

"And so if necessary," added the Dark Woman, "your Majesty must sacrifice the traitor."

"Treason! treason!"

The Dark Woman flew to the fire-place, and from the fire-irons she selected the poker; for such weapons, dangerous as they were, were left in the power of the mad King, since up to that period he had manifested no desire whatever to make any aggressive use of them.

"Your Majesty is unarmed," added the Dark Woman, as she placed the poker in his hands, "but this will suffice."

"Treason! treason!"

The Dark Woman had just time to dart behind the great easy-chair in which the King usually sat when the door opened, and the Page Lutwych swaggered into the room.

There was an air of familiar and vulgar insolence about this young man which would have gone far to avert any scruples that the Dark Woman might have had concerning the fate that awaited him.

He spoke to the old, mad King with a coarse brutality, fancying himself alone with him, and that any complaint of the poor, afflicted monarch would be, of course, set down to the score of insanity.

"Well, old idiot," said Lutwych, "what are you at, now? A pretty thing when a fellow's forced to get up from his cards to come and look after you! Eh, old mad-brain?"

The King sprung upon him with a yell.

Lutwych just saw the poker brandished on high, and fear taking possession of him, he did the worst thing he could for his own safety.

Answering the yell of the mad King with a shout of terror, he turned to fly. His back was towards the King for a moment, and then down came the poker, crashing into his skull, and he fell a dead man at the feet of the mad monarch.

"Treason! treason! treason!" yelled the King. "Treason! treason! I'm a king again! Every inch a king!"

The Dark Woman's opportunity had come.

She must escape from Windsor Castle then or never.

In two bounds she reached the door at which she had entered that apartment, and dashing it open passed through it, and cleared the bed-chamber with a rush.

The doctor's shop was next passed through, and then, panting with the speed and the excitement of the moment, she turned the key again in the lock of that door where she had stood with the Castle attendant, and purchased it by more than its weight in gold.

Confused noises, cries, and shouts came from the King's apartments.

A terrible fight took place that night between the mad monarch and his attendants and pages.

Many of them had cause for the remainder of their lives never to forget that card and drinking party which they recklessly enjoyed within hearing of their poor afflicted master.

The newspapers of the period but darkly hinted at the scene that had taken place in Windsor Castle; but it was well known at the time that the King had been the death of one of the royal pages, and a tablet to the memory of this very Lutwych is now to be seen at the old church at Harrow, stating that he possessed every virtue under the sun—and, in fact, almost insinuating that he died of excessive amiability, being a great deal too good for this world, and so happily translated to a better.

The Dark Woman listened for a very few minutes to the sounds of strife in the apartments of the mad King, and then, feeling in her vest pocket, to be quite certain that she still had possession of the precious document she had been so very successful in obtaining, she turned all her attention to getting clear of the Castle.

A trembling figure appeared before her.

It was the man without whose assistance she certainly never could have reached the King's apartments. Linda de Chevenaux felt grateful to him, and she did not stop to consider the motives of sheer cupidity which had actuated him in so assisting her.

"Take this gold!" she said, as she handed him as many guineas as she could take from her pocket at a grasp. "Take this gold, and show me the shortest way out of the Castle!"

"Good gracious! What has happened?"

"Nothing!"

"But there is a disturbance. Oh! Mr. Evening Courant, what has happened to the King?"

"Nothing to the King. I swear it to you, by all that human nature can hold sacred, I left the King alive, and better than he was before I saw him."

"This way, then, sir—this way. There's an uproar about something, and the bells are ringing!"

"It is a tumult among the royal pages!"

"Ah! They are a bad lot."

"I agree with you."

"And the worst of them is that Mr. Lutwych. He is a real bad one, a brute, and a villain. He will come to some bad end, that's my prophesy."

"I give you credit for your prophetic genius; and so, now, as we are here in the open air, I take my leave of you, and you may comfort yourself in the thought that you have gained some gold by admitting me to the Castle, and done no sort of harm whatever."

"I hope so."

"Be sure of it. Good night!"

"Good night, Mr. Evening Courant! Good night!"

"Now," said Linda de Chevenaux, as she made her way into the open air; "now, I live again! Now, George of Wales, look to yourself. I am your wife—your Princess; and no one—not even the most unscrupulous and subtlest of your lawyers, will be able to set my claims aside."

The Dark Woman was in a state of great mental elation all the way to London, and when she reached her lodging in St. James's Street, she opened the most important document she had brought from Windsor, and felt half inclined to shout with exultation.

"I am now no longer the hunted, persecuted Dark Woman, but the Princess of Wales—her Royal Highness the Princess of Wales, and the wife—the lawful wife of the Regent! Who shall dispute it—dare he now do so? What will now become of the German Princess who aspires to the title that is really mine? What will now become of the young Princess who has merrily had the joy-bells of London jingled for her marriage with Leopold, the German adventurer? Ha! ha! I laugh—I laugh on them all!"

The Dark Woman was in that state, when it was quite out of the question that she could reason with anything like justice upon her true position. She fondly imagined, that, in getting so important an evidence as that which she now possessed, almost, if not quite, all her difficulties were overcome.

It was not until there had been repeated knockings at the door of her sitting-room, that she was aware some one was there demanding admission.

Hastily securing and secreting the precious signature of the King, she called out loudly, "Who is there? Who knocks?"

"It is I—it is I. Lovat! Lovat!"

The Dark Woman was taken disagreeably by surprise. She by no means wished to be hunted and followed to her private house by any members of that band with which she was associated.

But she had no good excuse for refusing to see this man whom she had, to a certain extent, taken into a kind of confidential favour.

"Come in! Come in!"

"I cannot. The door is fast."

The Dark Woman rose, and opened the door. The look of excitement had not left her face, and Lovat rather started at her appearance.

"Well?" said the Dark Woman.

"Nay, master, if I intrude upon you, I will take my leave; but accidentally seeing you enter this house, I thought I would call, if it were for nothing but to pay my dutiful respects to you."

The Dark Woman thought that she could detect a slight tone of irony in these words.

"Come in," she said; "I would speak with you, Lovat."

He entered the apartment; but it was in rather a hesitating sort of manner—at least, Linda thought so.

"Be seated."

Lovat sat down.

"You know me, as you think, Lovat; but you know me not at all as what I really am."

"I thought I did."

"What, then, do you suppose me to be?"

"The cleverest, the most remarkable woman of the age."

"What else?"

"I did not think of anything else."

The Dark Woman paced the room now twice in its entire length before she spoke again. Perhaps she still had some lingering doubts as to whether she should trust this man, Lovat, even so far as she meant to do, or not.

But her determination was made to do so. She felt the absolute necessity, now, of some one to work for her in such a confidential manner, that would leave her more at liberty for other great designs which were just dawning in her mind.

This young man, Lovat, always, provided she could say anything, or do anything, that would make him faithful, would be just the sort of person.

When she wanted nothing but brutality and strength — Binks, whom she had rescued from Newgate and from the gallows, was just the person that suited her.

But now she required education —finesse— a gentlemanly exterior—in fact, such a person as the scampish nephew of the Lord Chancellor.

But the real truth was, that let Lovat be as bad as he might be, he could not be such a disreputable man as his uncle, the Chancellor, really was.

Lovat might have some scruples of conduct, but the Chancellor had none.

"Listen to me with all the attention in your power," said the Dark Woman. "I wish to select you from the other members of the band as my confidential friend. Serve me well, honestly, and zealously, and your reward shall be a seat in the House of Peers."

Lovat looked amazed.

"A seat in the House of Peers!"

"I have said it."

"And—and—you—you——"

"I can redeem my promise. It will be but a junior barony, of course; but you shall have it, and along with it such a revenue that you shall have no occasion to blush for your new honour."

"Master, I am your very humble servant."

"Ever?"

"Ever, and ever."

"That is enough. I shall have to see your uncle, the Chancellor, privately and confidentially. Report says that he is a good enough lawyer, although a—a——"

"Bad enough, man," put in Lovat. "Don't mind me, I beg of you, in speaking of the old rogue. I know well what he is, and have no family prejudices, I assure you; but there is one thing that it is quite proper you should know."

"What is that?"

"He is Lord Chancellor now, but he will soon be Lord Chancellor no longer."

"Indeed!"

"It is so. His tenure of office depends upon the merest contingencies. The Regent has a strong personal dislike to him, and has been long preparing the way for his own great favourite lawyer, Sir John Scott (afterwards Earl of Eldon), to hold the great seal."

"Is that so?"

"You may depend upon this information. A change of Ministry is imminent, and my uncle will no longer be the Lord Chancellor."

"Why, then, that will be better still."

"Better—still?"

"Yes; for he will be the personal, as well as the political, enemy of the Regent."

"Of that there can be no possible doubt; and the enmities of my uncle, whether personal or political, are apt to be rather unscrupulous."

"Better and better still."

"You much surprise me, master."

"In time to come I shall surprise you more, Lovat; but, for the present, I pray you to think that you are attached to me entirely. I wish you to make the appearance of a gentleman. Take

No. 96.—DARK WOMAN.

lodgings near at hand to me. Spend money freely, but——"

"Yes—the—a—but——"

"Beware!"

"Beware of what, oh, master?"

"Beware of the wine cup! When the wine is in the wit is out; and the tongue blabs of that which, under other circumstances, it would not give utterance to for the wealth of worlds!"

Lovat turned pale and red by turns, as he turned his head and spoke in a low tone.

CHAPTER CCXIV.

THE DARK WOMAN IS LIBERAL TO THE BAND, AND WRITES TO HER SON.

IT was some few seconds before Lovat found courage to look up into the face of the Dark Woman, whom he called by the strange name of master.

Then he spoke in a low, subdued tone.

"Some one has maligned me! Some one has told you, master, that the wine cup—the—the flowing bowl, was my failing! Some one has said that of me, and—and, by the heaven above us, it was true!"

"Was true?"

"Yes, master, I speak of it in the past tense, because it is, and shall be, true no longer! Trust me!"

"Alas! alas!"

"Why do you cry 'Alas! alas!' master?"

"Because I am saddened and disappointed. No one told me that that was your failing. I only warned you in a general sense; but now I fear—I fear——"

"Ah, then it is time for me to cry alas!"

"It is very sad. I cannot—I dare not trust you, Lovat."

"I expected you to say as much; but still, surely, there is some faith and some dependence to be placed in human nature. Better—oh, far better, master, is it that you should trust me, knowing what I have been, and with the consciousness that I have resolved never to be that thing again, than to some one whom you may think immaculate, but who may deceive you at the hour of greatest need, by lapsing into the vice which, believe me, I am rescued from for ever and for ever!"

"If I could think so, Lovat——"

"Think so, I pray you, and all the rest is easy. Your confidence will give me strength; otherwise I sink, and am lost for ever!"

The Dark Woman lifted a candle from the table, and, approaching Lovat, she held it so that she was enabled to look fixedly in his face.

He did not shun her gaze this time, but endured it unflinchingly, painful though it probably was to him; but his anxiety was relieved when, after a pause of a few seconds, she said, "Lovat, I have determined to trust you. I play the game of life for high stakes. Assist me, and be assured that you shall gain by the adventure, and that too in the way I have mentioned, which seems to act vividly on your imagination."

"It does, indeed, master. I have always been declared a scamp and ne'er-do-well, and it would

please me much, I must own, to be able to give the lie to the prophetic wiseacres who have ever taken upon themselves to prophesy that Charles Lovat would come to no good. Trust me, then, master, entirely and completely. I will not betray your confidence, but work with you, and for you, in any way you may direct; but there is one thing which even I, Charles Lovat, being what I have been, and hoping to be what I shall be, would warn you against!"

"You warn me?"

The Dark Woman regarded him with surprise, a little mingled with indignation.

"Yes, master!" added Lovat, with a moral courage she barely expected from him—"yes, master, I want to warn you against something which is always very fatal"

"Speak! What would you say? What is it?"

"Half confidences!"

"Ah!" cried the Dark Woman, as she regarded Lovat with increased interest; "are you then as wise as that?"

"I hope I am!"

"Then I will, at the risk of seeming rashness, tell you all, Charles Lovat. I am Linda, Princess of Wales, and wife to the Regent!"

Lovat had risen to his feet when the Dark Woman lifted the candle to look at him, and now he staggered a few paces towards the door, as he said, only half aloud, "Oh! that's it, is it?—that's it! By heaven, how long you may know one of these people without a delusion dropping out! She is mad!—she is mad!"

"Is this my return," cried the Dark Woman, "for the full confidence you sought?"

"Master, I—I——"

"Hold, sir! Be still! I might say 'On your knees, and hear me;' for although not a sovereign princess, I am the wife of him who shall surely be a king. And, since you think this the delusion of some disordered brain—since you would leave this house thinking that the master whom you have followed through danger and difficulty, but who has always led you safely, is bereft of reason, behold the proof!"

The Dark Woman took from her pocket the important paper she had brought from Windsor Castle. She laid it upon the table, holding it down by both hands, but in such a manner that Lovat could read it.

He did so with unfeigned astonishment.

"And you, master—you——" he said.

"I am that Linda de Chevenaux!"

"And the—the wife, by leave and license of the King——"

"Of the Regent! This is the second document signed by his Majesty to this purport. The first was surreptitiously obtained from me by the Regent, when it became convenient for him, in order to get his debts paid by the British parliament and people, to contract an alliance with Caroline of Brunswick!"

"But this is conclusive!"

"It is conclusive!"

"And the King was just enough, notwithstanding all other circumstances, to give it you?"

"He was, as you see!"

"And the signature?"

"I am content to stand or fall by its genuineness, or otherwise!"

"And the—the—the interval in which he gave this paper was lucid?"

"Perfectly!"

The Dark Woman could not but feel at that moment but that she was doing what Lovat had emphatically warned her against—namely, making a half confidence; but she could not bring her mind to relate to any living soul the peculiar circumstances under which she had obtained the signature of the mad King to that most important paper.

"I perceive, master," said Lovat, "or I ought rather to say I perceive, your Royal Highness, that this paper is undated!"

There was rich perfume in the words Royal Highness to the senses of the Dark Woman.

"Yes," she replied, as she laid her hand upon the document,—"yes, the paper is undated, because his Majesty wished it to do for any time, and for all times!"

These words had a specious sound with them, but Charles Lovat could not but feel they had no meaning; yet, there was the document, and there was the royal signature across it, which, if it could not be disputed, stamped it with authenticity, and was worth a Queen's diadem.

He bowed low.

"Your Royal Highness has convinced me, and this frank revelation suffices at once to account for the extraordinary interest your Royal Highness took in our late inroad into St. James's Palace, as well as the mysterious interview which your Royal Highness contrived with the Regent, at the house in Hanover Square."

"You are right, Lovat. And now will your uncle assist me?"

"I have not the slightest doubt of it. He will do so with all his heart. No, by Jove, I am wrong there. He has no heart to do it with; but he will do so with all his head, and that will answer your Royal Highness's purpose a great deal better!"

"It will. And, now, Lovat, take this money, and make use of it for your own purposes. I have a very large sum on hand beyond it, which is the produce of some of the jewels we brought from the Palace. Let us now go at once to St. Augustin's Church, in the City, and satisfy your comrades that they are at least getting some portion of the spoil which they assisted to procure."

"Your presence will be welcome."

"Not a doubt—not a doubt."

"By what name will your Royal Highness for the future authorize me to call you?"

"Name me as you have ever done by that one word 'master.' Serve me but well and faithfully, and you will find me such a master and such a mistress combined as never mortal man had before. And now let us go at once to the old deserted church. Carry you this bag of gold; it will be divided among your comrades; and remember that, for the present, what I have told you is a state secret between you and me."

"It shall remain, master, hidden in the deepest recesses of my heart, and neither force nor fraud shall wrest it from me."

"I am content! I am more than content!"

The Dark Woman and Charles Lovat walked out into St. James's Street.

There was an elation of spirit and a stately kind of walk about the Dark Woman which rather surprised Lovat, since it could scarcely be that the mere communication to him of the secret of who she was could have had such an effect upon her imagination.

Had he been aware, however, that it was only within the last three hours that she had possessed the important document which seemed to make her the wife of the Regent, and Captain Fitz George his legitimate son and next heir to the throne of England, he would have found a reason for that elation of spirit.

Probably, too, the sweet and pleasant sound of "Royal Highness" contributed not a little to that feeling which showed itself in the manner of the Dark Woman. But certain it was that she could not have conducted herself more royally had she been the acknowledged Princess of Wales in the face of all the world.

A coach at the corner of Pall Mall, just opposite the gate of Marlborough House, was hailed by Lovat, and the strangely assorted pair made their way to that dismal, old, deserted church in the City together.

The band was assembled.

The Dark Woman ordered a taper, as on the former occasion of a visit to the old church, to be lit; and by its faint and dim light, as she stood on the spot which once had held the communion-table, she addressed the bold, reckless men who had yoked their fortunes to hers.

"With some difficulty I have disposed of some of the jewels we brought from St. James's Palace. A sum of money, which I am happy to say may be counted by thousands, is to be distributed among you."

A murmur of satisfaction passed among the band, and then the Dark Woman, turning to Lovat, added, "Produce the gold!"

The taper was taken to a bench, the flat top of which served admirably for the purpose of a table, and the clank, and jingle, and pleasant music of gold was heard in the old church above the bones of some one who little expected that so much of what the world, and perhaps he, coveted, should ever be jingling and jangling over his remains.

"And what for the master?" cried several voices.

"I have not parted with all the jewels," said the Dark Woman; "but I will appropriate to myself any sum, and no more than, you may please to name among you!"

"A thousand pounds!" said one.

"No," said another. "It will be fairer to say one-fourth of the whole!"

"Agreed—agreed!" cried every voice.

"Hush!" said the Dark Woman. "You speak rather loudly, considering that in silence, in shadow, and in secrecy we hold our meetings. I accept the terms freely and willingly, as they are offered, with a slight variation. I will take one-fifth!"

This was an offer that the band was quite willing to accede to, since it was one of a much more liberal character than that they themselves had contemplated; therefore they had every reason to be admirably satisfied.

Then the Dark Woman, when this business part of the meeting was over, spoke in a low but firm and self-assured voice: "Wait!" she said—"wait but for one week from now, and you shall all hear from me again. During that time I shall be able to mature some other plans which will add to your wealth, for that will be the proper term to apply to the means which I will place in your possession."

The dissolute young men who formed this new band of the Dark Woman were well enough pleased at this proposition.

They were decidedly of opinion that life without enjoyment was not a thing to be desired.

Hence they risked their lives to procure the means of enjoying it.

But they had no notion, while their pockets were full of money, of troubling themselves much to procure more.

Spend that first.

That was their maxim; and, consequently, they were well enough pleased that their "master," as they one and all called the Dark Woman, saw proper to give them a week's indulgence.

In the course of the next ten minutes the deserted church was left to solitude, and the rats and the rats and mice that infested it.

The Dark Woman got again into the hackney coach, and returned to her lodging in St. James's Street.

She again advised, and the advice came with the force of an order, Lovat to procure for himself fashionable lodgings close at hand.

"You know," she said, "that according to arrangement on the Friday night that is coming, I have to meet your uncle on the Western Road, in order to negotiate for the return of the Great Seal, which he will find it a difficult matter to account for the loss of, if he does not redeem it from me. You shall go with me on that occasion."

"I will attend you, master."

"And to-morrow, at the hour of twelve, let me see you, for I shall have other business for you to transact."

The Dark Woman was abundantly pleased with the respect that Lovat treated her.

Indeed, while in her presence he treated her so like the character she aspired to be—namely, the Princess of Wales—that she was half inclined to believe herself on those occasions the real and acknowledged wife of the Regent.

Linda de Chevenaux now felt all the importance of keeping up her health and strength.

She seemed to feel that she had something tangible to live for.

And that tangible something was a diadem—the crown of the Queen Consort!

Glittering bauble as it was, how it danced, and flashed, and glittered before the excited fancy of the Dark Woman.

She retired to rest at an early hour of that morning, with the hope and expectation either of sound repose or blissful dreams.

In that hope she was disappointed.

The visions that haunted her half slumbering brain were of the most distressful character. She thought herself hunted by bloodhounds, whose constant cry—for to her fancy they had human voices—was "Treason! treason! treason!"

No doubt the recollection of that word, as it had come pealing forth from the lips of the poor mad old King, at Windsor, influenced this dream, and made the imagination of the Dark Woman play her such a trick.

It was in vain she thought that she tried to escape from the fangs of those terrible dogs.

And then "a change came o'er the spirit of her dream." She thought that she was environed

by the ministers of the law, and that loud voice cried out, "Carry this traitress to the Tower!"

Very probably, the notion on the part of the King, at Windsor, that he was a prisoner in the Tower, had something to do with this notion of the vexed brain of the Dark Woman.

She thought that no sooner were these words uttered in such tones of authority than she was on the River Thames in a boat.

She found that rain was splashing down upon her, and the boat, and the guards, and constables who had charge of her, in torrents.

This was no fancy—that is to say, as regarded the rain—for it was in reality beating from without on the windows of the room in which she slept.

So it mingled with her dream, making up one of its accessory incidents, as external circumstances are so apt to do.

She thought then that she was conducted, even as she had been once before, through that dismal gate where so many illustrious captives had only to be afterwards conveyed to the scaffold.

So vivid was this dream, that she could see all the old stone-work of the Tower and the steps that led up from the water, the boat in which were the guards, and another boat in which stood a man with a blazing torch.

Then she thought she heard a voice cry out in loud accents, "Ye who enter here, at this portal, leave hope behind, for there is none in this place!"

That voice sounded to the Dark Woman so loud and so palpable, that it fairly awakened her from the troublous dream.

She started up with a cry of dismay.

There was a knocking at the door of her chamber.

"Sir! sir! sir!"

"Who knocks? What is it?"

"A gentleman, sir, desires to see you."

"Who is he? His name?"

"His name is Lovat, sir."

"Bid him wait—bid him wait! Can it be so late as twelve o'clock?"

The question was answered by the slow, measured strokes of the clock in the turret of St. James's Palace.

The Dark Woman counted the strokes. It was mid-day. She had slept, or half slept, about four hours, and was not refreshed.

"Be it so," she said,—"be it so. The cares of life may perhaps begin with the pressure of the diadem of a Queen. Be it so. I am content."

CHAPTER CCXV.

THE DARK WOMAN HOLDS A MEETING WITH HER SON, WHO VISITS THE PRINCESS CHARLOTTE.

LINDA DE CHEVENAUX had made a determination.

It was that she would communicate to her son, Captain Fitz George, the fact of her possession of so important a document as that which seemed to substantiate her claim to be the Regent's wife.

She could not believe it possible that human nature could be so destitute of ambition, but that if he saw his way as clearly as that document would seem to point it out, he would not go with her heart and hand.

With him to countenance her claims she fondly hoped that all would be easy.

And besides—and that was the bright and fair spot in the seared heart of poor Linda de Chevenaux—she loved him better, oh, far, far better than her life!

What, indeed, was life without him?

What was she striving for but to make him a Prince, and in all human likelihood, a King?

But for that hope she would have been content herself to give up the contest of life, and lie down in the security and the peace of death.

Alas, poor Linda de Chevenaux!

And so her determination was to communicate with her son.

She intended, as the first mission he should go upon, to send Lovat to Fitz George: and finding him, Lovat, in the breakfast-room, she invited him to partake of that meal, while she herself, after one cup of chocolate and a piece of dry toast, repaired to a table by the window that looked out into St. James's Street, and wrote the following letter to her son:—

"MY SON,—

"We write to you, and assume, as we may, the style royal.

"The messenger of this will conduct you to where you will meet the mother who still loves you. But it will be upon your honour as a gentleman, an officer, and a Prince, in no way to molest him if he should think fit not to conduct you, because he has his instructions only to do so upon your sacred word that you will betray the interview to no one, and that you will make no attempt to use it to the detriment of the liberty of   "YOUR MOTHER."

"Take this letter, Lovat, and go to the guard-room of the Palace, and ask for Captain Fitz George."

Lovat bowed.

"Read it first."

Lovat read it with no small surprise.

"Do you comprehend it?"

"Scarcely, master."

"Then I will make it clear to you, by telling you that this Captain Fitz George, who is beginning to be known about the Court of St. James's, and who is thought to be what is called the natural son of the Regent, is my son and his son truly and legitimately, and therefore next heir to the crown."

"You amaze me, master."

"I thought to do so. But you will comprehend that this young man—this Captain Fitz George—does not know of my possession of this conclusive evidence of my honour and of his legitimacy. He has been persuaded by the royal bigamist, his father, that our union is null and void; and so they consort together on different terms to those which must and will soon arise."

"I think I understand, master."

"I am sure you do."

"I am not to bring this young officer—this Captain Fitz George to you, except under the solemn promise dictated in this letter?"

"That is so; and even then you will not bring

him here. He must not know a place where he can come to again, nor must he see me again in this dress. Should he consent to the conditions under which he may have the interview with me, you will conduct him to the northern aisle of Westminster Abbey, and there both he and you will find me."

"Your orders shall be obeyed."

"Go now at once, good Lovat, and be assured that fortune and preferment both await you."

Lovat proceeded to St. James's Palace.

The moment he was gone, the Dark Woman repaired to her bed-room, and attired herself in feminine garments with great expedition.

A plain dress of rich, black silk, and a velvet mantle, with one of the extraordinary shaped bonnets then in fashion, completed the costume, which did not take her altogether a quarter of an hour to assume.

She then, quite regardless of the people of the lodgings, walked down stairs.

On the staircase she met one of the servants of the house, who looked at her with undisguised surprise, and seemed inclined to question her of her business in the house.

But the Dark Woman took the initiative.

"I perceive," she said, "that the gentleman who lodges in the first floor is not within."

"Oh, yes, madam, he was at home."

"No, he is out. Good morning."

There was something so lady-like and irreproachable in the dress of the Dark Woman, that the servant could not refrain from treating her with deference; and opening the street-door for her, she allowed her to leave the house in peace.

Linda de Chevenaux then made the best of her way across the Park to the old Abbey.

She knew not, nor cared she, whether that was a day on which the public had free admittance to any portion of the glorious old pile. She knew perfectly well that all doors in England, whether of church, prison, or palace, flew open to that golden key, which she had found open a path to her even to the privacy of the mad old King, at Windsor.

And so a small piece of gold was more than sufficient to enable the Dark Woman to procure admittance to the Abbey.

"A gentleman—perhaps two," she said to the verger, who she paid so handsomely, "will come here. Pray admit them, and consider that I have paid you for the service."

"Yes, my lady."

The verger involuntarily bestowed upon the Dark Woman a title. He thought that one who gave gold, where silver would very well have sufficed, must surely be somebody of importance.

The Dark Woman paced down the solemn and majestic aisle alone.

She went to its extreme end, where was a small, railed-in chapel, containing a few tombs. There was an ancient stone seat on the outside of it, all defaced—as, indeed, were the walls around—with rudely cut initials and dates, most of them as old as the Commonwealth; when for a time, until the Lord Protector, Cromwell, actively interfered, the Abbey was left to the good will and pleasure of the people.

There, then, Linda de Chevenaux sat alone.

Waiting for her son.

Waiting, as she thought, for a Prince, and at the

same time in the full belief that she would be able to substantiate her title to be a Princess.

And here we may remark how strange it was that Linda de Chevenaux began completely to ignore, if not completely to forget, the means by which she had obtained the signature of the King.

She never had chosen to permit herself to believe that the Regent spoke the truth when he told her that the pretended consent of the King, his father, which he had produced to her at the time of their marriage, was a forgery.

If she had ever told herself that that must be really so, she would have found herself like some ship at sea without a rudder.

The end and aim of her existence would have been lost.

And so deluding herself, and doing so with a kind of deliberation, determination, and a will to do so, with the belief that the Regent only accused himself of forgery to get rid of the crime of bigamy, she considered she was quite justified in the means she had adopted to defeat him.

And there she sat on that stone seat in the Abbey, which may still be seen by any of our readers curious enough to go and look for it.

Meanwhile, Lovat was not backward in performing his errand to Captain Fitz George.

The dissolute, but really well-educated, well-looking, and rather slim young man, had had ample time during the morning, before twelve o'clock, to make all the arrangements suggested to him by his patroness, the Dark Woman.

She had handed to him, he found, no less a sum than four hundred pounds.

To him it was an inexhaustible fund of pleasure and enjoyment.

More especially, too, was it such, since she had taken care to inform him that his finances could be recruited at any time by applying to her.

Lovat took a handsome suite of rooms in Pall Mall, close to Carlton House.

He managed to procure, at a fashionable tailor's in St James's Street, a suit of clothes which were just finished for a nobleman, but who could wait a day or two while the tailor disposed, for ready money, of the suit that was ready, to Mr. Charles Lovat, since they chanced to fit him to a nicety.

Indeed, they fitted him a great deal better than they would have done the nobleman for whom they were made; inasmuch as he, Lovat, was a good-looking, well-made young fellow, and the nobleman quite the reverse.

Presenting, then, the gentlemanly appearance that he did, young Lovat had no difficulty in making his way to the officers' guard-room of St. James's Palace.

He entered the royal abode now under very different circumstances than those which surrounded him on his late visit to it.

Then he was a midnight burglar.

Now he wore all the aspect of a gentleman visitor.

Lovat smiled to himself as the orderly sergeant saluted him respectfully.

"Is Captain Fitz George on duty?"

"Yes, sir."

"Will you kindly say that a gentleman wishes the honour of a few moments' conversation with him?"

"Yes, sir."

The sergeant, with military promptitude, turned on his heel, and sought Captain Fitz George. He returned in a few seconds to Lovat, saying, "If you will follow me, sir, the Captain will see you."

Lovat could not be said to feel quite at his ease as three or four doors closed behind him and the open air, as he knew what part he had so recently played in the transaction of a night at St. James's.

But he plucked up courage.

"Pshaw!" he whispered to himself. "Who is to recognise me? Who is even to suspect me? I am safe enough!"

And so he was.

Captain Fitz George was in a small apartment writing, and he rose, on the approach of his visitor, saying, with the courtesy natural to him, "Pray sir, be seated. That stupid fellow who announced you forgot your name."

Now Lovat had not given any name, so that this was only a polite way, he felt, on the part of Captain Fitz George of saying ' Who are you?'"

"My name, sir, is—is Lovat."

For the life of him, Charles Lovat could not think of any *alias* at the moment.

"Pray be seated, Mr. Lovat. In what can I be of any service to you, sir?"

Captain Fitz George was rather attracted by the appearance of his visitor, which, to tell the truth, was strikingly favourable; but he wondered what Mr. Lovat, of whom he knew nothing, could want with him.

"Sir," said Lovat, "I speak to a gentleman, an offic—c—c—a—man of honour?"

"I hope so, sir '"

" Will you promise me, then, sir, that whatever you may think, or whatever may be your ideas concerning me, after you know the object of my visit, you will in no way interfere with me or my free egress from St. James's Palace?"

Captain Fitz George was very much surprised at this speech, as well he might be.

His good opinion of his good-looking visitor was somewhat shaken, and he replied, " Sir, it appears to me that if you had any doubts upon that subject, it would have been better not to have come here at all."

"Perhaps so, Captain. But I trusted to your generosity as well as to your honour."

"It would be hard, indeed," said Fitz George, "for any man to be deaf to an appeal that comprehended both his generosity and his honour; so, sir, I give you the promise you ask."

"I thank you, Captain."

Fitz George thought it a very favourable part of the conduct of this Mr. Lovat that he accepted so frankly, without any question further on the point, his promise.

"Captain, there is a letter for you."

Fitz George took the letter, and opening it, he cast his eyes to the part of it where were those words "Your mother;" and then he at once felt that he had a key to the somewhat extraordinary conduct of his visitor.

He read the epistle through in silence.

"You bring this, Mr. Lovat, from a lady?"

"From a lady, Captain."

"Whom you know?"

"Whom I have the honour to know and to serve."

There was a something about the tone in which Lovat pronounced these words which surprised Captain Fitz George; and he looked at the visitor in wonder to know if he were the accomplice or the dupe of Linda de Chevenaux.

"And when, Mr. Lovat, may I meet my—I mean the lady?"

"That, Captain, I am only at liberty to disclose to you, if you will make the promise according to the terms conveyed in that letter."

"I have no resource, then, and make it freely."

"Then, Captain, I will conduct you to the aisle of Westminster Abbey, where, no doubt, by this time, the lady is waiting for you."

"This man is a gentleman," said Captain Fitz George to himself. "No one but a perfect gentleman could be so trustful of the word of another."

"Sir, I will follow you; and let me ask you one question as we go."

"What is it, sir?"

"Do you know who I am, and who the lady is, and have you seen more than the outside of this letter?"

"Yes, to all the questions," replied Lovat.

"Then," added Fitz George, "you must know and feel, unless you, too, are bitten by the same mania as my mother, that her truest interests lie in a very different direction to that in which she supposes."

"Do you ask my opinion, Captain?"

"Well, you can put it that way, if you please, Mr. Lovat."

"Then, Captain, I hardly feel justified in what I am about to say to you; but, as we are both young men, I suppose, we may talk to each other rather freely. I believe, then, your mother to be all that she says she is."

"By heaven, sir, you amaze me! What, in the name of all that's rational, could engender such a notion in your mind? Long suffering and much unmerited persecution may have had all its effect upon the imagination of poor, unhappy Linda de Chevenaux; but you, sir, like myself, stand but a few paces over the threshold of life—you cannot have suffered, and borne a load of anguish, until reason has been shaken on its throne?"

"Captain Fitz George," replied Lovat, "if you mean to tell me that, in your opinion, your mother is a maniac, I never saw such method in madness in all my life. But here we are at the Abbey, sir, and here my duty ends. I will wait, and heaven speed you!"

Captain Fitz George was bewildered.

It was not that he was particularly surprised at his mother desiring and contriving an interview with him; but what astonished him was that she had succeeded in so imposing upon the judgment of an evidently educated and intellectual young man, as to make him believe in the extravagant pretension.

With a look of anxiety upon his countenance, and with hasty footsteps, he entered the Abbey.

The Dark Woman could not see him from where she was; but, at his first step over the sacred threshold, she was certain he had come. There was a fine and exquisite sense, which enabled her to pronounce that he was there, even before any particularity in his footstep, if such there were, could have reached her ears.

She sprung from the stone seat on which she had been sitting, and advanced towards him.

They met about the centre of the long aisle of the cathedral, and, with emotion in every expression of his countenance, Captain Fitz George grasped her extended hands, as he exclaimed, "Mother! mother! do I indeed look upon you once again?"

"And I upon you, son of my heart?"

"Oh, let me hope that this meeting is the harbinger of happier times! Let me hope, mother, that you have cast aside, once and for all, hopes and expectations that can never be realized, and ideas that contain in themselves the very elements of despair!"

The Dark Woman looked at him for a few moments without speaking.

Pride and satisfaction beamed from every feature of her face.

"My Prince!"

"Oh, mother—mother!"

"And King that shall be!"

"Again! again!" cried Fitz George. "Again this fond, terrible, and fatal delusion! Oh, that I could banish it!"

The Dark Woman smiled. She placed her arm in that of her son, and, slowly pacing with him down the aisle of the cathedral, she spoke in tones in which were blended affection and triumph.

"Show me the man," she said, "who, with a kingly crown suspended as if in mid-air above his brows, will not please to allow it to descend upon them? Are you not human, oh, my son? Has the philosophy of the stoic and the cynic set up its altar in your young heart? Is it possible that you would introduce the romantic delusions of some pastoral drama into real life, and prefer the crook of a shepherd to the sceptic of a king?"

"No, mother, no," replied Fitz George; "that is not the question. I am human; and I hope I am beset by no such follies. I have philosophy enough to believe that human happiness is more equally distributed than people imagine. At all events, I am not infected with the delusion that princes and kings are more supremely blessed than other persons."

"And yet, my son—and yet——"

"Nay, mother, hear me out; that is not the question. I am not refusing rank, power, wealth, and earthly dignity."

"Indeed!"

"No, mother; but I am determined not to vex my soul with vain aspirations after that to which I have no title, and which has been the shadow and the blight of your existence."

"But, my son, listen to me!"

"Yes, mother; but, oh, speak reason!"

"If you were—if you felt and knew you were entitled to those earthly dignities, would you calmly surrender them to another?"

"Never!"

"Would you consent to sit down in obscurity, and with a stigma upon your name, if you felt yourself justly entitled to high state and perfect honour?"

"That question, mother, is needless; and its answer is one that would spring from every heart. Both question and answer but bring us back to what we were. You have been cruelly ill-used, but the legal validity of your marriage with the Regent is the question at issue, and not my hopes, feelings, or aspirations."

"Yes," replied the Dark Woman, and pleasure beamed from her eyes as she spoke,—"yes, that is the question; and how strange—how very strange it is."

"What is strange, mother?"

"Why, that I entrap you into becoming a Prince—a King!"

"Oh, this is raving."

"Not so. Time was when I might have raved, but that time has passed away, and I am calm and cool, because I am confident. They who win the game can afford to be serene. I do not speak to you as I have at times spoken to you, but I appeal to sober, calculating reason; and I tell you, my son, I have the proofs of the validity of that marriage now in my possession."

Fitz George was staggered.

"Do you think," added the Dark Woman, "you would prefer Marlborough House for a town residence? Or, perhaps, you have more rural tastes, and the White Lodge at Richmond would be more germane to your fancy?"

"Mad—quite mad!" thought Fitz George to himself.

"You were christened Allan," added his mother; "but that was in profound ignorance of your real state and dignity, and we will have a new and right royal christening. You shall take the name of some of the old kings of England—kings of the old, stately Plantagenet line!"

"Mother—mother!—do not—do not—do not speak in such a fashion! You make me sick with grief."

"Nay, the Regent shall be glad," added the Dark Woman; "since, at once and for ever, he gets rid of that Caroline of Brunswick, from whom, report says, he is eager to seek for a divorce on any possible terms, and on any possible pretence."

"I cannot, will not, hear this!"

"You must hear it, and shall. Let the first person to hold obedience to the Princess of Wales be her own son."

As she uttered these words, the Dark Woman produced the document she had brought from Windsor Castle; and with excitement and exultation beaming from her eyes, she held it with both her trembling hands before his face.

CHAPTER CCXVI.

CAPTAIN FITZ GEORGE HAS VARIOUS AGITATING INTERVIEWS WITH VARIOUS ROYAL PERSONAGES.

At almost the first glance Fitz George read the few words that were upon that important paper.

Then he tried to re-read them, as though doubting the evidence of his own senses.

But such was his mental agitation that they danced before him as though they were full of life.

The Dark Woman regarded him with eyes of intense gratification.

She saw him turn pale and then flushed by turns.

It pleased her to have to lead him to that stone seat on which she had waited his coming; and there, with one of his hands clasped in hers, she waited until the strange tide of feeling had passed away, and he was himself again.

"Speak—speak, my son!" she said. "What have you now to say to your mother?"

"Let me breathe—let me breathe for a few short moments more, and I will try to think."

"We have time," said Linda de Chevenaux. "We have time to deliberate—time to be just—time to be merciful!"

Captain Fitz George clasped his hands over his face, and let his head sink low down, as he sat there beside his mother.

He had felt at times very wretched.

But he had never felt so wretched as at that moment, when the possibility first dawned upon him that all his mother's wild assertions, and apparently mad fancies, might be true.

His thoughts flew back to the past, when he stood in London streets, homeless, friendless, and all but starving.

Then to the future flew the nimble spirits of the imagination, and he saw himself as what he might be, amid the confusion of a kingdom.

He saw the Regent overwhelmed with shame.

He saw that unhappy Princess of Brunswick lost and crushed for ever.

He saw, too, the Princess of Wales—the young Charlotte so lately married, and with all the prospect of a life of joy and happiness—for ever blasted in her youth.

And all for him!

To make him a Prince!

To make him a King!

It was with moans and sighs that Fitz George welcomed the possibility of these high dignities.

But the Dark Woman was getting impatient

She wanted to see the exultation—the triumphant looks and words; she wanted to see the happiness, and all the bounding hope and joy of the future, beaming in his face.

"Speak to me!—speak to me!" she cried. "You said that you were human, but is this the conduct of humanity? Speak to me, my son—my Prince!"

"Oh, mother, what shall I say? What shall I do?"

"Assume your right—your rank. Be true!"

"True?"

"Yes—to yourself! Think you for a moment that, if these circumstances were reversed, there is any mortal breathing who would hesitate to pull you down from whatever high estate you occupied, and take your place? No, not one! But you are not mad! Insanity has never had a place in your brain. Pity whom you will, and whom you may; be great, generous, and munificent; but barter not your birthright, because a few tears may flow from the eyes of those who have made your mother shed drops of blood!"

"It is fate!" said Fitz George.

"Ay, fate, or call it what you will! You are a Prince, and heir to the throne of England—once removed!"

"What shall I do?—what can I do?"

"I will tell you. I have thought of that. I have an appointment with the Chancellor of England, who will doubtless think proper to call upon the great lords of the kingdom, under these strange circumstances, to investigate your claim. The public voice will soon ring with it; and, in face of the facts, the Regent must bow down to the storm!"

"No, no—not so!" cried Fitz George, rising.

"Be quiet, mother! Take no such steps for the present! Let me show this paper to the Regent!"

The Dark Woman smiled.

"You are too simple, my son. The Regent is an epicure, but he would make a meal of this paper rather than leave it in existence."

"I have no right, then, to ask it of you, mother. It is yours, and, in the name of heaven, keep it! No human being, were he ten times your son, has the right to deprive you of it, nor even to dictate to you how you shall use it. But if you love me, mother, I implore you to grant me four-and-twenty hours' delay! Let me think—let me take counsel of myself, and of any other on whose judgment I may wish to found an opinion. Give me that time, and free warrant to say and do what I please, and I will meet you here again at this hour to-morrow."

"Be it so," said the Dark Woman. "I stand upon a rock! The petty waves of enmity may

No. 97.—DARK WOMAN.

dash around me, but they cannot dislodge me! Sleeping or waking, I never part from this paper; nor will I ever while life remains to me, unless it is placed in the hands of the Privy Council, to be solemnly lodged among the archives of England!"

Captain Fitz George bowed his head, and spoke faintly.

"I dare not say you are not right, mother. We shall meet again to-morrow. Where shall I conduct you now?"

"Nowhere. You will remain here until you hear the next chimes of the Abbey clock. Farewell, my son! Be happy in the remembrance of who and what you are!"

Poor Fitz George sat down again upon the stone bench, and watched the Dark Woman as, with a slow and stately step, she walked up the long aisle of the Abbey.

He saw her look right and left, as any indifferent person might do, upon the various tombs and tablets that she passed; and more and more he felt convinced that she was quite at ease as to the result of her future fortunes, and that it was the peace of mind of perfect confidence that now possessed her.

And there he sat.

Alone! alone!

A prince of the blood royal, for all he knew; and his Marian—the poor wardrobe maker to the theatres, whom he had married in poverty and almost want—to what earthly grandeur might he not now have the power to elevate her!

And he thought how happy she was already; and then he asked himself if he could possibly like to see any other expression upon her countenance than those smiles of serenity and contentment which now illumined it.

But what was he to do?

Was it right or just that, because his father, the Regent, had committed a great social crime, he was still to be branded with the name of bastard?

Was he to commit a great wrong against himself for fear some distress and misery should light upon others?

It was not he who had brought Caroline of Brunswick into the fearful position she would occupy.

It was not he who would be the blight and desolation to the young life of that Princess Charlotte of Wales, as she was called, who had so recently, amid the plaudits of a kingdom, asserted a will of her own by marrying the man of her choice.

If he were, indeed, the legitimate son of the Prince of Wales, how could he help it?

Was he to stand up in opposition to the fact of his own existence, because its substantiation would be inimical to the interests of other people?

Captain Fitz George was coming round to his mother's views rapidly.

But this conversion with him was very different to that which she had so often tempted him to avow.

It was only in accordance with positive proof, that would not only be convincing to him but to all the high authorities of the kingdom, that he would accord credence.

"If I am a prince," he said, as the chimes of the cathedral smote upon his ear, and he rose from the old stone bench on which he had been sitting, —"if I am a prince, there will be many eager to hail me as such; and so, now, I will consult with Marian, and on her calmer judgment, still, as ever, rest my hopes!"

Poor Marian was scarcely less bewildered at the vista opened before her than had been Fitz George himself.

"Oh, Allan, Allan," she said—for she still called him by that name—"Allan, Allan, we were happy in obscurity, and with the favour of your father, the Regent. Into what a sea of troubles may we not plunge, dragged forward by the mad ambition of your mother?"

"But there is one view of this subject, Marian, that we must not forget," said Fitz George. "Have I a right even to suggest to my mother to abstain from vindicating her name and honour because we are not ambitious?"

"No, Allan; we have no right. We must look upon ourselves as in the hands of Providence in this matter. What is to be, will be; but you should lose no time in communicating all that has passed to your father, the Regent. He may not be entitled to either our respect or our esteem, in any great degree; but it would be unfair, having accepted the benefits we have from him, to deal in any way disingenuously with him."

"That was spoken like my Marian," said Fitz George. "I will to the Palace now, and seek an interview with him at once."

"Do so It is a duty."

"And one that shall be instantly fulfilled. I am well pleased that I succeeded in leaving my mother without making any promise of secrecy as regards this matter."

"That, indeed, is well, Allan."

"Yes, Marian. I have four-and-twenty hours in which to act. If the claim she sets up in behalf of me and of herself be a just one, it can suffer nothing from any revelations I may make. If it be unjust, let it perish."

Perhaps it was the only alleviation which the excited feelings of Captain Fitz George could find under the circumstances, to determine upon perfect openness and ingenuousness with everybody concerned in regard to the important document his mother had shown him.

The oppression of the secret would have been otherwise too heavy to bear.

He repaired to the Palace at once, and seeking out Willes, the valet, eagerly desired to know how the Regent was occupied, in order that he might prefer a request for an interview.

"Captain Fitz George," said Willes, respectfully, "his Highness is at Windsor."

"At Windsor? That is unusual at this time in the day."

"Perfectly so. But his Highness has been summoned thither in hot haste. The King, they say, was much worse last night, and attacked his attendants, and it was thought necessary by his physicians that the Regent should be present at a consultation on that new aspect of the case."

"Hilloa! Is that you, Allan?" cried the Countess de Blonde, at this moment, as she was passing through the apartment in which Willis was speaking to him. "Hilloa! hilloa! Is that you? Come with me at once: I want somebody who has got a palace."

"A what, Annie?"

"A palate, to be sure; and then I want the confectioner of the kitchen discharged. He has sent me up some things he calls cheese-cakes, and cheesy enough they are in reality. George has gone off to see the old gentleman, your grandfather, you know; so come on. By the bye, Willis, are you any judge of cheese-cakes?"

"Whether I were or not," replied Willes, "I'd esteem it a duty, and an honour, entirely to agree with your ladyship."

"Then you're a donkey!"

"I am honoured by being a donkey, if your ladyship pleases."

"Very well. There's no accounting for tastes. Come on, Allan. Dear me, I'm always making a mistake; I ought to call you Fitz George. What can they mean by Fitz—Fitz, eh? But it don't matter. Come on, or else they'll say the cheese-cakes were bad because they got stale. Why, you've got a face a yard and a-half long. Whatever is the matter? Marian, eh? Is Marian ill?"

"Never was better in her life."

"Then what's the matter with you, eh?"

"I will tell you, Annie. I will follow you into your own apartments, and tell you, for I think you ought to know."

"Don't now—oh, don't!"

"Nay; why not?"

"Because I can guess it's something doleful, or you wouldn't wear such a woe-begone countenance about it; and I don't want to hear anything of that sort—I hear quite enough of it. There's all sorts of kind people, you know, continually saying things about me."

"About you, Annie?"

"Yes. There was a newspaper sent me the other day by some dear, kind friend, and a bit of it marked for my particular reading, where it said I should be sure to die on a dung-hill. Now, if I am, I am, and there's an end of it; but I don't want to be bothered with it beforehand. It's time enough when one feels one's feet sticking in it. So now, come and taste the cheesecakes."

Captain Fitz George had not determined upon telling Annie what had passed between him and his mother, but since the Regent was not there to hear the revelation, and she was—and since, so to speak, he had made up his mind to tell everybody nearly and remotely concerned, he thought he could not do better than begin with Annie.

Beneath all the carelessness of manner and levity of disposition of the Countess de Blonde, Fitz George knew likewise that there was to be found a deep mine of good feeling; and he had often heard her come to the most rapid conclusions about intricate matters, and give utterance to those conclusions in such well-selected words, that he had a high opinion of her natural abilities, uncultivated as she was.

To Annie, then, he related the whole circumstance; although, certainly, the gravity of his interview was a little marred by the manner in which she kept thrusting little bits of cheese-cake into his mouth, and demanding peremptorily his opinion.

Poor Fitz George's narration, therefore, was compounded of a dissertation on the qualities of cheese-cakes and the possibility of a social revolution in the royal family of England.

"Well, Annie," he said, when he had concluded, "what do you think of it all?"

"Stale and cheesy."

"But I mean this statement of my mother's?"

"Oh, about you being a prince, and all that sort of thing?"

"Yes, Annie."

"Fudge!"

"You don't believe it?"

"Not a bit. Bosh!"

"Well, but, Annie, the document?"

"Fiddle de dee!"

"I'm afraid fiddle de dee is not an argument, exactly."

"Yes, it is; and a very good one, too. Your mother is cracked—don't be offended, now—I say she's cracked in the upper storey; and that bit of paper she showed you, with poor, old George's name to it, she's either made herself, or got out of the old pump in one of his mad fits, and that's all about it."

"But Annie?"

"But Allan?"

"I know not what to think"

"I've just told you Fudge—bosh—and fiddle-de-dee! Hark! There's the drums beating. George is coming back. He'll want lunch, and you'd better stay and take some. Don't be stupid now, and don't you be thinking too much about that absurd bit of paper."

"I must speak to the Regent—to my father."

"Very well, then; do so. Here he is. Get it over at once, and ask him."

"Well, Countess," said the Regent, as he entered the room. "How is the fairest of the fair by this time? Glad to see you, Fitz George—glad to see you. I'm sorry to say his Majesty had a paroxysm last night, which has resulted in the death of one of the pages, young Lutwych; and another strange thing has taken place, too, which I can't make out at all."

"What is that, George?"

"Why, a member of the household—a—a kind of I don't know what—an under-groom of the chambers, or something of that sort, it appeared, got into a state of intoxication, and confessed that he had, for a bribe of fifty guineas, allowed some one, that in his maudlin state he called Mr. *Evening Courant*, to make way to the private apartments of the King."

Annie clapped her hands together, and shouted out at the top of her voice, "That's it! That's it! I have hit it!"

"Hit what, Annie?"

"You, George, with the cheese-cake."

The eccentric Countess de Blonde threw, as she spoke, one of the cheese-cakes so exactly in the mouth of the Regent, that it remained, for a moment or two, between his teeth.

"Good heaven, Annie, what do you mean by that? Have you taken leave of your senses, my good girl?"

"No, George, I have not; and for the best of all possible reasons—that I never had any to take leave of. But tell us some more about this mad or drunk fellow at the Castle."

"Oh, you know really as much as I do, now. I suppose there is nothing in it Doctor Willes says that he is labouring under an attack of what they call *delirium tremens*, which is a something that lays hold of the lower classes, I believe, when they drink too much; so it may be mere imagination."

"But George?"

"Well, Annie?"

"What does the King say?"

"My father?"

"Yes, George. Does he say anything about any one having been there?"

"Well, I—a—suppose he did; but you know we none of us place any account by what he says, and he may have heard the pages talking about it; but in his odd, mad way, he keeps talking of escape from the Tower, and of some Duke who is to assist him, to whom he has given an authority to call upon all good subjects to aid——"

"I have hit it again!" cried Annie.

"No, no! Don't, now, don't! I hate cheese-cakes; and if I liked them ever so, I should prefer them not thrown down my throat."

"I am not going to do. But now, George, you

are to listen to what Allan—I beg his pardon, I'm sure; I mean Fitz George—has to say; and if you want my opinion all about it afterwards, you shall have it and welcome. For the present, I leave you alone."

Fitz George could not but appreciate the delicacy of Annie, the Countess, in leaving him alone with his father, the Regent, to talk of a matter which was of so private and personal a character betwen that father and that son.

But he coloured and stammered as he would fain commence what he had to say; and although he felt some difficulty in connecting the circumstances together in his own mind, he could not help seeing that to the terse, natural intellect of Annie, the Countess, there was some visible connexion between the document which Linda de Chevenaux had with the signature of George the Third across it, and that circumstance at Windsor which was mentioned by the Regent.

CHAPTER CCXVII.

THE IMAGINATIVE VIEW WHICH CAPTAIN FITZ GEORGE HAD OF THE CROWN OF ENGLAND VANISHES INTO THIN AIR.

"WELL, Fitz George," said the Regent, "what is all this about, eh? Anything that I can do for you?"

"Yes, sir—yes, father."

"You are affected—you betray emotion. What has happened? Tell me in one word. Is *she* no more?"

"My mother?"

"Well, ay, — your mother and my plague. What—what has happened? I shall be *obleeged* by an immediate answer."

"She is alive!"

"Oh!"

"And she is well!"

"Oh, dear!"

"But she has had an interview with me, at which she has shown me a strange document."

"What document? What?—what?"

"A clear and distinct authority on the part of the King—a consent, couched in terms that admit not of ambiguity, to your marriage with her."

"Absurd! Pshaw, absurd! Some hair-brained forgery! Fitz George, what you say is simply impossible."

"Sir—father, I saw it."

"Ah, I see! You mistake me. I do not mean that you did not see such a document. Oh, no, no, no! Fitz George, from my soul I do not believe that you would stoop to deceive me in the slightest thing."

"I thank you for those words, sir."

"No, no," added the Regent, as he paced the room in some agitation,—"no, no; I have not the highest possible opinion of human nature—I believe that it is pretty well known that I have not; but the—the human mind would appear blacker to me than it has ever appeared, if the day were to come on which I doubted your truth and your honour."

"Father, I thank you. For the space of two hours I have been in possession of information which you ought to know. For the space of ten minutes I have had an opportunity of naming it to you, and you now know it. I have seen such a paper."

"Well?"

"Ah, sir, can it be true? Without your knowledge or cognisance, is it possible to be true?"

"Impossible! Bit by bit, Fitz George, you get the whole of this sad affair from me. It sounds strange for the father to say so to the son, but—but I was mad—I was infatuated with Linda de Chevenaux. I—I did show her such a paper, but it—it came again, no matter how, into my possession, and was destroyed."

Fitz George bowed his head.

He spoke in low, earnest tones.

"And now, sir, she exhibits a paper which does not pretend to be that paper."

"Good heaven, then what does it pretend to be?"

"A kind of certificate, under the sign manual of the King, to the effect that twenty years ago he did sign such a consent to your legal union with Linda de Chevenaux."

"A forgery!—a forgery!—a vile—that is—a —a—the—a—name of the King has been used for him."

The Regent could not forget that he, too, had committed the "forgery—the vile forgery" of that very King's name to the paper with which, twenty years ago, he had overcome the scruples of Linda da Chevenaux; and hence the latter part of his denunciation was so much milder than its commencement.

But poor Fitz George was in no mood to take any notice of these inconsistencies. All he wished was to arrive at the truth.

Was the document his mother had shown him a genuine one or not?

Would it avail to make the marriage legal, despite the repudiation of the Prince of Wales, provided it were genuine?

These were important questions.

But they were not the kind of interrogatories to put to the Regent.

So far as he was concerned, Fitz George was perforce compelled to be satisfied; but the Regent himself, now in the most voluntary manner, strove to put an end to all doubt upon the subject.

"Fitz George," he said, "I do not for an instant attempt to extenuate the past. What has been done twenty years ago, is done past all recall. This is a painful subject to both of us; but I declare to you, upon my word and honour, that I never asked the King for any such consent, and that, therefore, none such existed; and it is, therefore, again impossible that he could give a certificate to the effect you have mentioned."

This was conclusive.

The third question arose in the mind of poor Captain Fitz George.

Was his mother herself deceived, or was she trying to deceive him and others?

No wonder that he uttered a groan as he asked that question of himself.

"Come, come, Fitz George," said the Regent; "it is better as it is. You shall, I hope, be able to say that, so far as it was in his power, your father, the Regent, was mindful of your fortunes. You know that I love you; and—and if it had pleased heaven that I had had a son like you, who would really have been my legitimate successor, instead of—of the daughter, who is not exactly all that a daughter——Well, well, I hope she will be happy. I think you comprehend what I mean—I hope you do, Fitz George."

The Regent, for once in a way, was much affected, and tears actually stood in his eyes.

"Oh, my father!" said Fitz George, as half kneeling on one knee, he took the hand of the Regent, and pressed it to his lips,—"oh, my father, say no more upon this painful subject, and never—never again shall it be mentioned by me. I will be content to be the son of your affections for ever and ever!"

"God bless you, boy! God bless you! Hoy! hoy! My dear! Countess! Annie! Annie! Where are you? She is a good girl, Fitz George, and I almost think at times that she loves me."

"What now?" said Annie, as she made her appearance,—"what now? Talking scandal of me, George, behind my back, are you?"

"No, Annie," said Fitz George; "his Highness, the Regent, was only praising you, and saying that he almost thought you loved him."

"Does he want me to love him?"

"Yes, Annie," said the Regent. "I have been a better man, if a worse Prince, since I knew you, my good girl."

"Then I am quite content if I do die on that dunghill they mention. Get away, do!"

Annie's heart was easily touched. Tears ran down her face, mingling with the smiles that dimpled her pretty mouth.

It was quite April weather.

Sunshine and a shower.

Fitz George quietly took his leave, and neither the Regent nor Annie missed him at the moment. She was beginning really to love the Regent; and perhaps of all those who had shared his smiles and his gold, Annie, the Countess, was the only one who imparted any real feeling into the transaction.

"Now, what am I to do?" said Captain Fitz George, as he drew a long breath and walked hurriedly down the Titian Gallery,—"now, what am I to say to my mother?"

That was rather a puzzling question.

But it was one that required to be met and answered, and that, too, as quickly as possible; for the four-and-twenty hours that he had begged of her for consideration were rapidly passing away.

"Sir! Captain!" said a voice.

It was the voice of Willes, the Regent's valet.

"Yes, Willes; what would you of me?"

"Here are three letters, sir, for you."

"For me? Surely not; I have no correspondence."

"Hem! They are strange letters."

"Why strange?"

"Because, Captain, they are all three sealed with the arms of the royal family."

"That is strange, indeed!"

Captain Fitz George took the letters, which Willes handed to him on a gold salver with perfect ceremony, and as much respect as he would or could have awarded to the Regent himself.

Willes rather liked Captain Fitz George; and, moreover, he had found out how much attached to him the Regent was.

Hastily opening the first letter that came to his hand, Captain Fitz George found that it only contained the following words:—

"Courage—courage! My Prince, courage!
"LINDA."

That, then, was from his mother.

The second letter was somewhat longer:—

"SIR,—
"Upon the subject-matter of this note, I think that an autograph letter may be excused. I have received a communication of so extraordinary a nature that I should be glad, along with his Royal Highness the Prince, my husband, to see you at the Hunting Lodge, at Claremont, at your convenience, letting me know by note when that may be. "CHARLOTTE.

"Claremont."

That was from the Princess Charlotte, the wife of the Prince Leopold of Saxe-Coburg.

The third note remained to be opened.

It ran as follows:—

"To CAPTAIN FITZ GEORGE.
"SIR,—
"A kindly visit, as from a gentleman of honour to an unhappy lady, at Buckingham House, will be esteemed by, sir,
"Your well-wisher,
"CAROLINE OF WALES."

That was from the wife of the Regent.

Fitz George was astonished. What could all this mean? Why did these high people write to him? What steps had his mother been taking that had spread such alarm among the royal family? He justly enough attributed it all to her.

That she had been adopting energetic proceedings was sufficiently evidenced by these letters; and they would hardly have been addressed to him if she had not used his name in a manner to point to him as the powerful person concerned in an affair that must deeply interest every member of the royal family.

Willes, the valet, was not a little curious to know what these three royal letters could possibly be about; for, probably, as regards two of them, he had sufficient cunning and instinct to know from whom they came.

The letter of the Dark Woman was, perhaps, the only one of the three of which he knew nothing; but it was not possible that he should ask a direct question of Captain Fitz George; and he could only follow him with his eyes as he walked down the Titian Gallery, holding the letters in his hand, and looking both bewildered and perplexed.

"There is something very particular going on," thought Willes, "and I should like to know what it is."

At this moment one of the Regent's household appeared in the gallery, carrying something on a salver; and seeing Willes and Captain Fitz George, he said respectfully, "A letter for you, sir, by a special messenger from Frogmore House."

"Good gracious!" cried Willes—"that's from the Duke of York! What on earth can they be all writing to this young man for?"

Captain Fitz George opened the letter mechanically, and glanced at its contents:—

"The Duke of York presents his compliments to Captain Fitz George, and would be pleased to see him at his convenience, at any time between one and four o'clock to-morrow."

"Another!" said Captain Fitz George, with surprise in his tones and looks.

"And yet another!" exclaimed Willes, as a second member of the Regent's household approached, bearing another salver.

"A letter for Captain Fitz George."

"I shall burst," said Willes, "if I don't know what all this is about. I must know. Sir — Captain, if you please, sir, may I humbly ask if I can be of any service to you?"

"None in the least, I thank you," replied Fitz George, as he opened this fresh letter:—

"The Duke of Clarence will be at the Admiralty to-morrow morning at half-past nine, where, if convenient to Captain Fitz George, he will be pleased to see him."

Poor Allan—we cannot help calling him poor Allan sometimes—held these five letters in his hand, and turned twice round in the Titian Gallery, wondering what he should do with such a mass of royal appointments pressing upon him.

Then he recollected how he had almost praised himself to the Regent, his father, for the ingenuous manner in which he behaved in regard to all matters appertaining to Linda de Chevenaux.

This, then, certainly was not the period for anything in the shape of concealment or secrecy.

"I will show these letters at once to the Regent," he said, "and he shall decide for me. I will place myself entirely in his hands, for I implicitly believe the statements he has made to me. It is not for me now to act, but it is for him to direct. Oh, unhappy — unhappy mother! into what an intricate web of plotting and scheming are you not plunging yourself! Would that I could extricate you from it; but I cannot—I dare not be your partner in these affairs, which can bring nothing but dishonour and despair."

Fitz George had no doubt but that he should find the Regent still with Annie, the Countess; and in fact, in the middle of the day the Regent seldom left home.

Probably at night he might sally forth on a visit with some of his old associates; but that state of things was gradually passing away, since the Regent was then no longer a young man, and was beginning to outlive some of the follies of his youth.

"Willes," said Fitz George, "will you kindly announce me to his Royal Highness?—stating, as an excuse for the intrusion, that something has happened which I feel it my duty to communicate to him."

"Certainly—certainly, sir," said Willes. "I will do so with pleasure; and if, at the same time, Captain, I can be of any service to you——"

"Thank you—thank you; not in the least."

"Confound him!" muttered Willes; "he won't tell me anything. But I must try and ferret it all out for myself: and I will too, or my name is not Willes—Sir Thomas Willes."

In a very few minutes Captain Fitz George was admitted to that small dining-room where the Regent was wont to partake of those little elegant repasts he so much admired, in the lively society of Annie, Countess de Blonde.

He was engaged at that moment in the discussion of a particular kind of pie, the principal peculiarity of which certainly consisted in the fact that it was by far too rich to agree with any stomach of lighter digestive powers than that of an ostrich; and for hours after partaking of it the Regent was compelled to be continually putting himself to rights with little drops of brandy.

"Well, Fitz George—well, Fitz George—here you are again; back again, as the King used to say to Lord Granville, like a bad shilling."

"He means penny," said Annie, "only he thinks coppers are vulgar. I recollect finding a penny once in Vinegar Yard, Drury Lane, and buying a polony with it."

"Now, Annie!" cried the Regent, laying down his knife and fork. "Good gad! What on earth is a polony? I'd be *obleeged* to you, Annie, to tell me what a polony is? The horrid idea, too, of picking up a penny! In what yard did you say?"

"Vinegar Yard, by the side of Drury Lane; and you'd have picked up one, too, George, if you'd been half as hungry as I was sometimes. I saw that the man who sold it me hadn't washed his hands for a month, so I pumped on the polony before I ate it, at the pump at the corner of Russell Court."

"There, now, you've done it!"

"Done what?"

"Spoilt the gout pie."

"And a good job, too. I'm glad to hear you call it that. I tell you what he means by that, Fitz George. Old Doctor Jolliffe attended on him once, and coming in one day he saw him eating one of those pies; so the next time he saw him he cried out, 'Well, your Royal Highness, have you had any more gout pie?'—and he said he'd warrant any one to have a smart fit of the gout after three pies of this description."

"Oh, stuff—stuff! Willes, a drop of brandy! Well, Fitz George, my boy, what is it now?"

"These letters, sir."

"Letters—letters! One, two, three, four, five! Why—why, what do they all mean? One from Charlotte—one from Clarence—York, too; and one from——Oh!"

The Regent made a wry face, and then added, "Willes, another drop of brandy."

"Will you be so good, sir," said Captain Fitz George, "as to run your eye over all these letters—they are short—and give me your kind directions concerning them? I place myself entirely in your hands as regards them, and will act as you direct."

The Regent hesitated, and looked distressed; then, turning to Annie, he said, in that tone of voice which showed that he thought it a relief to lift the responsibility of action off his shoulders on to somebody else's, "Annie—Annie! you know all about this. It's quite plain that—that—well, I suppose I must pronounce her name—Linda de Chevenaux has been communicating with all these persons, and mentioning Fitz George. What ought he to do, Annie? You see he has very properly come to me; and I must say, from first to last, his conduct has been most ingenuous."

"If," said Annie, "Fitz George is convinced, as I am, and as you are, that all this turmoil of Linda de Chevenaux's is as baseless as a bit of sea-foam, he cannot do better than see these folks and tell them so."

"Yes," said the Regent; "and by so doing, Fitz George, you will stand between me and any complication of this kind; and at once, and for ever, put an end to these absurd claims, which could only become respectable were you to countenance them."

"It is my duty," said Fitz George, "to do as you wish, and I will keep these appointments. The result of the meetings shall be duly communicated to you; and I have but one favour to ask in return—which is, from this time forward, assuming that no actual act is committed of which the law must take cognizance, the future fate of —of my mother shall be left in my hands."

"Certainly!" cried Annie; "and, up to this moment, I'm quite sure that George will hold her harmless for anything whatever."

"But——" said the Regent.

"Just so," interrupted Annie. "George is going to say that, being invested with all the power of a king, although called a regent, he will exercise the royal prerogative at any time in favour of Linda de Chevenaux. There, now! I got that long word prerogative out of the same newspaper that promised me the dunghill."

"But, Annie, I really——'

"Now, can't you be off, Fitz George? You've got all you want, unless you want some of the gout pie."

Fitz George bowed and took his leave, feeling perfectly sure that the promise which Annie had made for the Regent was quite as good as if the Prince himself had sworn to it with half-a-dozen oaths.

It was very irksome to him to have to call on all those people who had written to him, but perhaps the most irksome of all the visits was that one which he was called upon to make at Buckingham House.

Captain Fitz George was not prepossessed in favour of Caroline of Brunswick, the wife of the Regent.

Without believing all the scandalous chronicles of the day, which made so free with her name and fame, he could not acquit her of a great amount of indiscretion in her mode of life, and of a culpable disregard of public opinion as regarded the favourites with whom she surrounded herself.

He had a special horror, too, of the Marchioness of Sunningham; but he might have divested himself of that feeling in connexion with his visit to Buckingham House, for a decided and furious quarrel had taken place between the Marchioness and the Princess of Wales.

The unhappy Caroline had discovered of the Marchioness of Sunningham what, in time, she discovered of every one around her, and more especially of those who paid her the most assiduous court—namely, that they only used her as a sort of political puppet or stalking-horse for their own ambition, and that, while pretending to be actuated by the sincerest sympathies for her, they were wholly intent upon their own nefarious plans and projects.

The circumstances that had attended the visit, foolish as it was, of the Princess of Wales to the house of the astrologer, in Frith Street, Soho, had materially tended to open the eyes of the wife of the Regent to the real character of the infamous Marchioness of Sunningham.

With disgrace and contumely she had left Buckingham House, to engage in the series of intrigues which at length brought her again to the notice of the Prince of Wales.

But all this Captain Fitz George knew nothing of; and it was with a great dislike to the job, if we may be allowed the expression, that he crossed the Palace Yard, and entered St. James's Park, on his route to old Buckingham House, to obey the summons of the Prince of Wales.

CHAPTER CCXVIII.

DETAILS A CONSULTATION THAT TOOK PLACE BETWEEN SIR HINCKTON MOYS AND COLONEL HANGER, AND SHOWS HOW THEY BECAME AGAIN ADVISERS OF THE PRINCESS OF WALES.

IN rather a shabby room in one of the back streets of St. James's sat two men.

A bottle and two glasses were before them. Some preserved fruits were on a dish; but, from the quantity that was there of the preserved fruits, and the lightness of the bottle, it was pretty evident that these two men had paid no attention at all to the former, and a great deal to the latter.

One of these men had a bandage round his neck that was somewhat thicker in dimensions than a cravat, and it was evident that he moved his head with difficulty.

After this, the reader need hardly be informed that this man was Sir Hinckton Moys, and that he was still suffering from the wound in the neck that Sixteen-stringed Jack had given him in St. James's Park.

That wound had not been a dangerous one; but it was annoying, inasmuch as, until it had gone some length towards healing, Sir Hinckton Moys was compelled to keep his head wonderfully steady, and in one position.

It was like a stiff neck, warranted to last some three weeks or more.

The other person who sat in that rather dreary room, and who, by the look of his eyes, had evidently paid a great deal of attention, not only to that bottle that was before him, but to another empty one that was upon the floor under a sideboard, was Colonel Hanger.

It would be, indeed, a difficult and invidious task to say which was the greater scoundrel of these two men.

Their fates, however, were very different.

Colonel, or Major Hanger, as he was named, was, in due time, hanged.

But Moys played his cards better, and ultimately amassed a considerable fortune in the service of the Regent, which his descendants enjoy to the present day, and the mode by which it was acquired is all but forgotten.

Similar is the case of the Marchioness of Sunningham, who, while we write these pages, has but just "shuffled off her mortal coil," ridding the world of all her grossness and all her iniquity.

By the bye, we read a glowing panegyric of this female in a gentle paper only the last week; and her descendants, the Lords Bondesborough, enjoy to this day the plunder of George the Fourth's cabinet.

But this is all by the way, and we now once more attend to the proceedings of those two nefarious men, Sir Hinckton Moys and Colonel Hanger.

The Colonel spoke.

"Come, Moys; hang care—it killed a cat, and it is well known that they have nine lives. Pass the bottle!"

"Bah! You said all that before, Hanger. I am very nearly sick of everything and everybody."

"So am I, with one exception."

"And pray who may that be?"

"One Jack Hanger."

"Pshaw!"

"Well, if you won't drink, I must. Now you can do as you like; I have filled my own glass, and left the bottle with you. Come, what do you propose? How is the game to be carried on? How is the enemy to be routed, and our sweet selves installed in his place?"

"I hardly know. There will be no chance whatever of our getting again into the favour of the Regent while that girl, Annie, Countess de Blonde, as he chooses to call her, is his favourite."

"That's true."

"If we could only get rid of her, and instal the Marchioness of Sunningham in her place, all would be well."

"Of course it would."

"I never did know, in all my life, the Regent to be so enslaved; and I—even I—fool that I was—I was the person who originally brought to his notice this little piece of pink and white humanity."

"Ah! that's a pity."

"But I had a fancy for her myself, you see, Hanger; and I thought it a capital thing to have my *cher amie* likewise the favourite of the Regent."

"Good! Let me tell you, Moys, that was not at all a bad idea of yours if it could have been carried out; but, failing, it became a very bad job, indeed."

"Yes; for I found I could make no way with her, at all. She had the coolness and impudence to tell me that I was her greatest aversion, and that she thought me so positively ugly that she hated the sight of me."

"You are not handsome."

"Oh, stuff—stuff! So long as a man don't frighten a horse by his looks, he ought to do for any woman under the sun."

"That is a matter of opinion, Moys, altogether. Recollect, old fellow, that the bottle stands with you."

"I don't want any. It impedes the healing of this scratch in the neck, which, although it only went skin deep, seems as if it would never get well. And you, Hanger—you, if you had not been a coward, might have settled that fellow easily."

"I glory in it."

"In what?"

"In being a coward."

"Then you are glorious, indeed, for a more infernal coward I never met with; but I suppose you have, as the old country proverb says, 'eaten shame and drunk after it,' so it is of no use to say more to you on that head."

"Not a bit."

"Then the question is, what is to be done next?"

"I have an idea."

"Well; what is it?"

"The Regent is accessible to only one feeling in regard to this Countess de Blonde."

"Ah! I know what you mean—jealousy—jealousy! It has been tried, and failed as well, you know—most signally failed, I tell you; and that game will not do."

"Yes, it will."

"How—how will it do?"

"I will ruin her with him in ten days."

"Absurd! You are drunk!"

"That is profoundly true, and that is why I have such capital ideas, Moys. When I am sober I am apt to be rather slow, but in contradistinction—(hang it, that's a precious long word!)—in contra—dis—dis——Well, you know what I mean. When the wine is in, they say, the wit is out, but it is not so with John Hanger. When the wine is out there is no wit, but wit flows in along with ruby streams.

"'Flow, thou regal, ruby stream,
In my goblet sparkling rise;
Tinctured by the solar breeze,
Cheer my heart, and glad my eyes.'

Drink, Moys, drink! This is good wine! Drink—drink! Hang care!—it killed a cat. But I said that before. Never mind! I must be Jack Hanger. I know a plan, by which the Regent, believing his own eyes and his own senses, will be so extravagantly jealous that he will never speak to Annie, the Countess de Blonde, again."

"Then she will die on a dunghill."

If Annie had heard the words from Moys she would have had no difficulty in detecting from whence the inspiration of the newspaper had come which prophesied that fate for her.

"Listen!" said Hanger, making an effort to overcome the fumes of the wine he had had almost all to himself—"listen, Moys, and I will put you up to the dodge."

"Well?—well?"

"In a shop in Long Acre—a shop where they sell coach-linings and lamps, and all that sort of thing, rosettes for horses' heads, and——"

"Good gracious, Hanger, what, in the name of all that's infernal, do I care what they sell, so that they can and will sell me revenge and success?"

"That's it."

"What's it?"

"That is what you will be able to buy at that shop in Long Acre."

"You are mad!"

"Oh, no! not in the least. I am steadily drunk, that is all, but I know what I say, and I know what I mean. In that shop there is a young girl; she serves in it, and is a kind of distant cousin of the proprietor; but she is such an extraordinary likeness, although not so pretty, of Annie, Countess de Blonde, that she might, if dressed like her, be mistaken for her by any one."

"Ah!"

"You begin to see?"

"I fancy I do."

"And you don't think Jack Hanger quite such a fool, do you?"

"Quite the contrary—quite the contrary! It is a good idea—a glorious idea—if it can be carried out; but sometimes you meet with so many scruples, so much infernal questioning, and what the great, stupid, addle-headed world calls conscience and virtue, and all that sort of trash, that you are foiled in the very best schemes and combinations the human brain is capable of."

"Pooh!—pooh! That won't be the case in this instance. Moys. I have sounded the party. A handful of gold, unlimited credit at a milliner's and dressmaker's, and a couple of ponies, with a new drag, after the Barrymore fashion, will do the business, and purchase the nymph of the coach-lining shop.

"If you'd win the tender fair,
With gold and follies test her;
If you'd fix her yours for aye,
Why, then, my good sir, beat her.'

Ha! ha! That's the way to manage, eh? Who's

No. 98.—DARK WOMAN.

that? I rather think some one is knocking for admittance."

"Come in!" cried Sir Hinckton Moys.

The servant of the house brought in a letter. It was addressed to Moys, and opening it impatiently, he cried out in some surprise, "Ah! this is from the Princess of Wales. It is almost incoherent. What can have happened to make her write in such a style as this?"

"Read—read!" cried Hanger—"read—read!"

Moys only hesitated sufficiently long to make himself carefully master of the epistle first, and then he read as follows:—

"Buckingham House.

"The Princess of Wales desires to see Sir Hinckton Moys; and if there is any truth and sincerity in his recent professions of attachment to her cause and fortunes, he will only suffer sufficient time to elapse to compass the distance between him and Buckingham House before he presents himself to the Princess."

"Hem!" said Moys; "what can this mean?"

"It means, my dear fellow, that Caroline of Brunswick is in a deuce of a hurry."

"I will go to Buckingham House at once."

"And I with you."

"No, no! You have had too much. Stay here, and finish the bottle, Hanger. I will come back to you, and you shall know all; for I am sufficiently pleased with your suggestion about the girl at the shop in Long Acre, to take you fully and entirely into my confidence."

Moys took his sword from a corner of the room, and hastily buckling it on as he left the room, he hastened to Buckingham House.

Colonel Hanger was not sorry to be left to finish the bottle, which he not only intended to do, but to make some progress in another, if he could get it before, Moys could have time to return to him.

Upon reaching Buckingham House, Sir Hinckton Moys was at once ushered to the Princess of Wales, whom he found alone, and in a state of great agitation.

Without a word, she lifted up a heavy, gilt inkstand that was on the table before her, and handed him a letter, which had been crushed beneath it.

Moys took the letter with some surprise, and holding it in his hand, he said, "Have I your Royal Highness's order to read this letter?"

"Yes—oh, yes! At once—at once!"

Moys did read it.

"To her Serene Highness the Princess Caroline of Brunswick.

"MADAM,—

"As a matter of courtesy of one lady to another, I beg to inform you that the long-questioned proofs of the Prince of Wales's marriage, twenty years ago, with the daughter of a gentleman of the name of Chevenaux are now forthcoming.

"A young officer of the Guard, now known as Captain Fitz George, is the son of that union; and, consequently, next heir to the throne of England, after the Regent.

"I beg to say that one of my first acts will be to take care to secure you an ample private provision.

"I am, madam,
"LINDA, PRINCESS OF WALES."

"Well?—well?" cried the Princess, with impatience, when she found that Moys had got through this epistle, and which was, no doubt, pretty nearly similar to what the Dark Woman had addressed to the Princess Charlotte—"well? well? What am I to think of this?"

"Nothing! nothing!"

"Nothing? But—but——"

"Oh, your Royal Highness, I know all about this Linda de Chevenaux. There can be no reasonable doubt but that the semblance of a marriage some twenty years ago took place between her and the Prince of Wales; and I suppose there is no doubt that this young officer, Captain Fitz George, who is here mentioned is her and his son; but she is mad, and has no such proofs as she has spoken of."

"You relieve my mind greatly, Sir Hinckton Moys."

"Think nothing of it, madam—think nothing of it. A mere idle threat, that can only be of any importance if your Royal Highness should make it so. But there is one thing I would advise."

"What is it?"

"That you see this young man, Captain Fitz George, upon this affair. That you send for him to visit you here, and get from him some information as to what this mad mother of his is about. It may be that it will be wise to make some use of this affair to bring the Regent to reason in regard to yourself. I do not exactly say that I see my way to any such result at present; still it would be satisfactory if you were to send for Captain Fitz George, and hear his version of the affair."

"I will—I will, at once"

And thus was it that Fitz George received the letter, of which the reader is already aware, from the Princess.

————

CHAPTER CCXIX.

SIR HINCKTON MOYS CONCERTS A MURDER WITH THE VILLAIN BERGAMI.

MOYS remained for some time longer in consultation with that unhappy Princess, in whose confidence he had succeeded in completely re-establishing himself.

She always had had advisers.

It was either such an infamous person as the Marchioness of Sunningham.

Or such a weak-headed individual as Alderman Dood.

Or some scheming lawyer, looking for preferment, like Henry Dooem.

But, by some unfortunate fatality, the Princess of Wales never had one really sincere, and at the same time capable, friend about her.

And that fatality was her ruin.

After bringing the consultation to a close, Sir Hinckton Moys left the room in which he had seen the Princess, and inquired for the "Baron."

That was the name by which the ex-valet, courier, and public robber, Bergami, went by in the household of the Princess. He held the assumed post of her private secretary, when, in reality, he could do little more, educationally, than write his own name, and that was a recent acquisition.

This individual Moys found seated at a card-table, playing with a low Italian servant. Bergami was well aware of the value of the services of such a man as Sir Hinckton Moys, for there was a kind of instinct on his part in such matters, which made him recognise in Moys an intellect like his own, that would not stop at any rascality to compass its ends.

Bergami, therefore, left his game unfinished, and, at the request of Moys, took him to an apartment in Buckingham House where they could converse at leisure.

That the Italian was a poltroon and coward of the first order Moys believed, but what he had to propose to him was not an act of courage.

It was, on the contrary, an act of cowardice,

and so just the sort of thing he was likely to do well.

It was an assassination!

Perhaps no feeling had rankled deeper in the mind of Moys than his hatred of Captain Fitz George. He was angry and maddened at Annie, the Countess; but she was, after all, a woman, and Moys could not feel altogether so desperately infuriated against her as he did against Captain Fitz George.

Him he would have seen go to any kind of death, and the more painful the better, with pleasure.

And now he thought he saw an opportunity of compassing his revenge through the instrumentality of another; and that other was the cowardly, burly ruffian, Bergami.

"You are aware, Baron, no doubt," said Moys, 'that the Princess has received a letter, which, if its contents be true, places her in such a position that she will neither have rank nor wealth?"

Bergami uttered a string of oaths in Dutch, German, and Italian, and then signified that he was aware of such a letter.

"Well, then, Baron," added Moys, "it may be true, or it may not, but the shortest way of settling the affair is to get rid of the only two persons who agitate it."

"Vat? Vat you beans, Sir Boys?"

"The female who pretends to be the wife of the Regent, to the exclusion of the illustrious lady who has made you a Baron, is a bold, scheming, artful woman. I, however, will charge myself with the task of disposing of her."

"Dispose of her? Oh, mine friend, I understands! Eh? eh?"

Bergami drew his fingers across his throat, to signify that that would be the best way of disposing of Linda de Chevenaux.

"You may safely leave her to me," added Moys. "But in regard to her son, the Captain Fitz George, as he is called, you are the man to settle accounts with him."

"Be? Be the ban?"

"Yes, Baron! You, most unquestionably."

"Oh, do, do! I ain't the ban!"

"Permit me, Baron, to explain."

"You bay go on explaining as long as you like, bine friend, but I ain't the ban!"

"I do not mean you to fight him!"

"Oh, vell, explain, then—explain."

"I have advised the Princess to write a note to him to come here; and I do think that, with common good will to the work, and good management, he need never go home again, Baron!"

"Ah! Vell? vell?"

"What say you?"

"If I can get behind him——"

"That is it."

"Mine friend, then I ab the ban!"

"I thought you were."

"Yes, I ab the ban!"

"I was sure you were. What do you say to enticing him into this, or some other convenient room which you can name, as you know the house well, and there doing the job?'

"One body?"

"What?"

"One body? It was difficult to do away with one body in one house. Show me what is to be done with one body, and I ab the ban!"

"Oh, keep it here till midnight, and then fetch it out into the Green Park. I will help you in that; but be sure you kill him."

"Yes, I will be sure. I ab the ban!—I ab the ban for that! I have done one job like that before. I ab the ban!"

"I do not doubt you for a moment. I will be with you again in about a couple of hours, and then I will stay the evening, in case he comes."

"Tanks, tanks—much tanks! It shall be done. I will tink how it shall be done easy; but it shall be done, mine good friend, Sir Boys!"

Moys left Buckingham House, convinced that, at all events, he had laid a dangerous trap for Captain Fitz George, should he come there.

He was much too cautious a man to mix himself up with such an affair actively and personally, but he had not the slightest objection to suggest its commission to such a man as Bergami.

Nor did he think he ran any personal risks of after consequences in the matter; for, let what would come of the act, it would be too idle and frivolous for Bergami to say that he was told to commit a murder, and so committed it; and, if it were legally true that the instigator to a deed of that description could be made to bear part of the penalty, certainly the unsupported evidence of the man who did the deed would not be sufficient to entail such consequences upon any one.

Sir Hinckton Moys was a villain of the deepest dye, but he was an artful one; and, as we have already intimated, he contrived to keep his own neck out of the noose, while he at the same time accomplished almost all his nefarious designs.

The wily Italian set about his preparations for the assassination of Captain Fitz George, with a coolness and heartlessness which sufficiently betrayed what must originally have been his profession.

Several members of the Bergami family were in—what was called—the service of the Princess of Wales, and resided at Buckingham House.

There is too much reason to suppose that one, if not more, of them knew perfectly well what Bergami himself was about.

A very large screen, composed of six divisions hinged together, was brought into that same room where the conference had taken place between the Italian and Sir Hinckton Moys.

This screen, when opened, converted the room almost into two; only the space that it shut off in one direction was not more than two feet in width.

Into that space another door opened, communicating with a couple of rather handsome apartments in the special occupation of Bergami.

These little preparations completed, the Italian sat down in his own rooms, and waited with the patience of some noxious reptile expecting its prey, for the arrival of the brave and noble-hearted Fitz George.

Bergami had made his arrangements well, but there was one fatal mistake.

He had told one of the attendants of Buckingham House to be sure to inform him if a gentleman of the name of Fitz George arrived and asked for the Princess of Wales.

Now Bergami knew perfectly well that this attendant was not likely to be either curious or scrupulous as regarded what he was about; but he omitted to warn him that the matter was one of secrecy and caution. Therefore, this man, who had involved himself in an intrigue in Westminster, and who wished on that evening to leave Buckingham House, deputed the task of letting the Baron know when Captain Fitz George should arrive, to his wife, who likewise belonged to the household.

And then again, if this wife had performed the mission entrusted to her, Bergami's plans would not have suffered.

But they were all Italians together, and this woman's southern blood was in a flame with the suspicion that her husband was about to leave Buckingham House on some errand inimical to her peace.

She resolved to follow him; and so Bergami's orders went through another hand, and reached the very worst person—as far as he was concerned —into whose keeping they could get.

The Italian servant's wife happened to encounter that young girl who had been picked up in the Park by the Princess of Wales, after she had left the service of the Dark Woman.

The young girl who, it will be remembered, played the part of page to Linda de Chevenaux, and served her so faithfully, until her horror and affliction at the deed of murder which had been committed at the house in Frith Street, Soho, induced her rather to throw herself upon the wide world to seek her fortune, than to remain longer in such fearful companionship.

A character for kindness, good-nature, and willingness to oblige every one had been acquired among the household of the Princess by this young girl; and therefore was it that the Italian servant's wife did not hesitate to request her to do the duty deputed to her by her husband.

And the young girl promised.

She was called Fidele, now, in the house of the Princess of Wales; for Caroline of Brunswick always had some fantastic name for her favourites.

It was but a little matter, then, that Fidele was asked to do. It was only to let the Baron, as Bergami was called, know when Captain Fitz George came.

That name thrilled through the mind of the newly-christened Fidele; and a sensation that there was danger to him, and, indeed, to any one who advocated truth and justice, and who might come to Buckingham House for such a purpose, came strongly over her.

She could not forget what had happened in relation to Bergami and Sixteen-stringed Jack on the occasion of his visit to Buckingham House.

The possibility of a repetition of such a scene of terror blanched her cheek; and this young girl made a determination which had been hovering in her mind for some time—and which was, to leave an establishment in which assassination seemed to lurk in the very atmosphere.

She could not, however, quite make up her mind to leave Buckingham House without a last interview with the Princess of Wales, who certainly had treated her with every kindness and indulgence.

This faithful and brave-hearted young girl, too —whom we may call Clara or Fidele, as we please, since she had held both those names in the household of the Princess—felt that it was her duty to let that indulgent mistress know that Bergami, the Baron, who she, in her simplicity and innocence, really believed to be the secretary of her mistress, had a soul intent on murder.

With this object, and feeling that there might be no time to lose, Fidele availed herself of the permission which had been given her to approach the Princess whenever she pleased, and presented herself before her.

There was so much evident agitation in the young girl's looks, that the Princess of Wales, whose thoughts were fixed upon the precarious character of her own affairs, exclaimed at once, "Ah, my Fidele! You, too, come with evil tidings? I can see them in your face. What more have I to hear this night that should invade the peace of the Princess of Wales?"

"Madam," replied the young girl, showing by the eagerness of her gestures how deeply interested she felt in what she was saying,—"madam, it is true that I come to speak of evil, but it is in order that good may come. You are kind and gentle, and full of many charities; but there is one here, who seems to enjoy your confidence, who is so unworthy——"

A flush came over the countenance of the Princess of Wales.

"Child! child!" she cried, "what do you mean? Beware of calumny!"

"Oh, madam, I will beware of calumny, but it is of the Baron I wish to speak!"

"Even as I supposed," said the Princess, sternly, "and I will not hear you. Oh, how sad—how sad it is that there is not one heart about me who will look with indulgence, or who—who will put the best, instead of the worst, construction upon my actions!"

"Then, madam, I will abstain from pressing this communication upon you; and leaving it unuttered, I bid you farewell for ever."

"Farewell, girl? You bid me farewell, after all my kindness towards you?"

"Ah, that is indeed the affliction!"

The young girl could contain her sorrow no longer, and she sobbed most bitterly.

None of the enemies of the Princess of Wales— and heaven knows she had enough of them—ever denied her sensibility and feeling; so when she saw the tears of this poor creature flowing so abundantly, she could not but cry in sympathy.

"Ah, Fidele," she said, "you shall tell me what you please, and I will listen to you; but it is hard when we think ourselves beloved, and for our own sakes, to have the delusion dispelled, even though it be by the words of truth."

This was a great practical truth as regarded human nature, although the Princess of Wales, when she uttered it, hardly knew that it was so.

"And yet, good, kind, and gracious mistress," said Fidele, "I must—indeed and in truth, I must tell you."

"Speak, child! I will listen."

"The Baron——"

"Oh, are you sure of what you say? Are you certain that the evil of which you are about to speak concerns the Baron as the author of it?"

"Certain!"

"Let me look at you!"

The Princess of Wales removed the light upon the table to such a position that it shone fully upon the fair, delicate face of this young girl.

With a look of gentleness, and candour, and grief, poor Fidele met the gaze of her mistress.

"Shall I still speak, madam?" she asked quietly.

"Yes, yes—now."

"Then, madam, for the second time, the Baron has made his arrangements in this house—in this palace—this home of yours, to commit a murder!"

"No, no!"

"Madam, it is true!"

There was a wonderful courage about that young girl when courage was necessary—a moral courage, which was as rare as it was beautiful; and she looked into the eyes of the Princess of Wales as undauntedly, and spoke as unflinchingly, as it was possible for right to do in the face of prejudice.

"Shall I go on, madam?"

"Yes, tell me all."

"A man protected your Royal Highness and the Marchioness of Sunningham from some danger, or from some misfortune, I know not exactly which, and that man came into this house."

"He did, and left it with thanks and honour."

"No, madam!"

"No, say you? No?"

"Certainly not, madam. He left it in the midst of a broil in which he had to fight for his life, assailed by the Baron. He easily overcame him; but had he not been the strong, vigorous, courageous man that he was, he must have fallen beneath the blows of the assassin."

"This is horrible!"

"It is horrible, madam."

"Horrible to hear such words spoken. You cannot know this, girl! It is impossible that you should know; and you should shrink from repeating such—such calumnious stories. Even if they were true, it does not become us to be so censorious of others. Calumny and—and what you call in England, back-biting—oh, no, no! it should not be repeated."

"I have done, madam."

"That is well—that is well, girl!"

"But, madam, permit me to say that it appears to me you are by far more shocked that these crimes should be spoken of, than at their commission."

With these words, the young creature left the room, for she was quite convinced that the fears and the weakness of the Princess of Wales would keep her there for an indefinite period.

And during that time Captain Fitz George might easily fall a victim to the assassin!

To save him!

To preserve that precious life!

At the same time, too, to remove herself once and for all from that house, which contained such a man as the villain Bergami.

Such were the determinations of the courageous girl, who so well merited the name of Fidele.

Faithful she was to truth, to courage, to honour, to gratitude, and to humanity.

When she crossed the threshold of the room in which she had held this brief conversation with the Princess of Wales, she felt that she had crossed it for ever.

She put on a light hat, destitute of all feather plumes or ornaments, and without being particularly observed by any one, she left Buckingham House.

There was a group of very stately elm trees not above fifty paces from the entrance-gate, and in the deep shadow of those elms Fidele disposed herself.

"I will wait!—I will wait!" she said,—"wait and warn him, if the whole night should pass away before I see him."

A broad gleam of light at this moment fell over the space that lay between her and the entrance of the mansion of royalty.

That is to say, a beam, broad comparatively speaking, although it was not above, in reality, six feet in width. It came from a light that was at one of the upper windows of St. James's Palace, and found its way right across the Park.

Through a gap in the trees it crossed the Mall, and fell slantways over the blackness, which else would have confounded Buckingham House with the night air.

Through and across that beam of light the faithful Fidele knew that any one must needs pass who should attempt to reach Buckingham House.

And so she crouched down and watched.

Watched for Captain Fitz George, towards whom she had a gentle and kindly feeling.

And another watched for him, too.

That other was the assassin!

The Baron Bergami!

In the room to which he intended Fitz George to be shown, behind the screen he had had removed, there he, too, watched for a visitor.

And little did he dream that providence had appointed one of its purest spirits to warn that intended victim of his danger, and to save him.

There was a third watcher, likewise, on that night.

Sir Hinckton Moys.

He lingered about the Park entrance to St. James's Palace, in the hope that he should see Captain Fitz George go forth to meet his doom.

It was a curious position that the young girl now occupied.

She was about mid-way between Sir Hinckton Moys and the Baron Bergami.

Upon one cry of her gentle voice being heard depended the life of Fitz George. Nay, probably, upon the continuance, for half an hour longer, of that light in one of the upper windows of St. James's, depended that life.

If that light were extinguished, the ray that it sent into the darkness of the Park would vanish, and it would be difficult for the young sentinel of life to be sure that any person she might see approaching the gate of Buckingham House was really him she sought to save.

But the light continued.

CHAPTER CCXX.

CAPTAIN FITZ GEORGE TAKES FIDELE TO MARIAN, WHO WELCOMES THE PRESERVER OF HER HUSBAND'S LIFE.—A CATASTROPHE AT BUCKINGHAM HOUSE.

IT was a weary and an anxious time that the young girl had to wait, measured as it was by her anxieties.

How lightly and easily half an hour—a whole hour passes away on the wings of pleasure, or even in that vacuity of mind and action, which is neither pleasure nor pain! '

But what terrible half-hours there are in this life to those who are compelled to measure time's pulses by some fearful human feeling!

The young Fidele thought that Fitz George would never come, or that he had come and she had not seen him, and was even then lying dead in that room where he was waited for by the Italian assassin.

The horrible idea took possession of her mind that she must have closed her eyes for a moment, and that, during that moment, he had, with the quick, elastic step of youth, passed her post, and entered Buckingham House.

This was too positively painful a thought for her to think for long.

She must rather dissipate it as a mere illusion of the over-excited imagination, or she must go back to the house itself, and assure her mind that it was not so.

Or that it was so.

Terrible alternative!

The beam of light was still there, but the eyes of Fidele were getting pained and confused: there were moments when she thought it was gone.

More than once, too, she started forward from her post of observation with a half cry, which was partly compounded of the name of Fitz George; because her fancy conjured up his figure crossing that ray of light towards the fatal threshold.

This could not last.

It was a mercy to Fidele that it did not last any longer. The reality of a footstep—the reality of a human form approaching Buckingham House—at once set to flight all the fancied appearances. Now there was a something tangible about the fact that some one was there. A figure, wrapped up in a blue cloth cloak, such as was worn by the officers of the Guard, passed before her eyes.

It was the man she watched for.

She sprung forward.

She called out, "Stop—stop!"

He did not hear her. He was almost on the threshold of Buckingham House. She bethought herself of a plan that she felt sure would attract his attention—of a word she was certain would reach his ears, and as certainly meet with the most immediate attention.

"Help—help! Oh, help!"

That was the word. It was one that never appealed to the senses of Captain Fitz George in vain.

He heard it, and paused instantly. He turned in the direction from where the sounds came, with his hand on his sword, he approached the noble group of elm trees.

He was saved.

"Thank heaven! oh, thank heaven!" exclaimed Fidele, as she clung to his arm; and then she fell into a passion of tears, for her feelings had been highly wrought by the suspense that had occurred.

Captain Fitz George could neither comprehend what all this emotion meant, nor why he had been summoned to render some aid where none, to all appearance, was required.

"Calm yourself, my good girl," he said, " and tell me who you are, and what it is that alarms you."

"Ah, sir! you do not know me."

"I cannot name you, or recollect where I have heard your voice before, although I certainly have heard it."

"Do you recollect a page that was in the service of—of one who—who——"

"My mother?"

"Yes, in the service of your mother. I was that page, but something occurred more terrible than usual, at that terrible house in Frith Street, Soho. I could remain there no longer; and, although friendless and destitute, I left it. In that sad extremity of my fortunes I was seen by the Princess of Wales, who took me into her service. I have not one word to say of her that should not breathe the spirit of gratitude, but there is one in that mansion she inhabits whose soul is that of a murderer."

"Ah!"

"Yes; I think you begin to see that when I cried 'Help!' it was not for myself?"

"You would tell me, then, that I was in danger by going to Buckingham House?"

"In peril of your life; why should I conceal it? The villain Bergami intended to assassinate you."

"Gracious heaven! and has the unhappy Caroline of Brunswick sunk so low that she can employ such arts as these to carry out her purposes?"

"Oh, no, no! A thousand times, no! Do not accuse her. If she errs at all, it is in not being able to give credence to the existence of so much wickedness."

Captain Fitz George half drew his sword from its scabbard.

And then Fidele clung to his arm.

"What would you do?—oh, what would you do?"

"I would still cross the threshold of that mansion, but it would be with my sword in my hand; and I would seek out the assassin, and confront him with the keen blade and the knowledge of his baseness."

"No, no! Be content! For the sake of the unhappy Princess of Wales, be content; but never, on any pretence whatever, cross the threshold of a house within which is to be found Bergami, the assassin. Now farewell; I am very happy that I have saved you."

Fidele turned away with a sigh, but it was not likely that Captain Fitz George was going to part with her in such a fashion as that.

He gently detained her.

"Say, my dear good girl," he said—"say, what are your intentions, and whither are you going now?"

"Alas! I do not know."

"Then let me know. You shall come with me."

"With you?"

"Yes, so far as my home, where I can introduce you to my wife as the dear friend who has saved her husband's life. She will love, and I shall esteem you."

The frank manner in which Fidele placed both her hands in those of Captain Fitz George charmed him much, and he hastened with her from the Park, satisfied, on reflection, that it was indeed far better to be content with having foiled the assassin than to go across the threshold of Buckingham House in search of him.

And Fitz George was not weary in promising to Clara, which name he preferred to Fidele, a kindly welcome.

Inexpressibly shocked as he was at the perfidy

which was intended to be perpetrated against him at Buckingham House, yet Captain Fitz George was well pleased that he had taken the advice of Clara, and not made any knight errant-like attempt to bring the villain Bergami to account for his rascally design.

But he resolved that the Regent should no longer be a stranger to the kind of business which was hatched at the residence of the Princess of Wales.

Fitz George and Clara were both aware, as they passed through the Park, that they were dogged by some one, who kept nearly pace by pace with them, but, at the same time, took good care to conceal himself among the trees.

That was Sir Hinckton Moys.

More than once Fitz George felt inclined to loosen his sword in the scabbard, and turn in pursuit of this, to him, mysterious person; but Clara clung to his arm, and he dreaded to leave her, even for an instant, unprotected in the Mall.

For all he knew, the repeated dim appearances of this figure might be for the very purpose of provoking him to such an act, and then some serious calamity might befall Clara.

That idea settled the matter in the mind of Fitz George at once.

Had he known it, Sir Hinckton Moys might have conducted his espial upon Clara and the young officer more openly than he did.

As he did conduct it, however, it was quite sufficient to astonish him—for his impression was that Captain Fitz George, with the levity of youth, had got into conversation with some fair nymph of the Mall; so that when he found the young Captain took the young girl direct to his own house he was perfectly astonished.

We should have before this time informed the reader that, owing to the munificence of the Regent to his son, the latter had been able to please himself by taking a very pretty, small house for his Marian, close to the Green Park.

There, in peace, happiness, and comfort, Marian resided, with Sixteen-stringed Jack's daughter as a companion; and a dear and attached companion she was—for the better Marian knew her, the more good and gentle qualities she found in her.

It was to this peaceful and happy abode, then, that Fitz George took poor sobbing Clara.

"Marian, dear," he said, "I bring you, not a visitor, but an inmate. Will you receive her for my sake?"

"Yes, dear Allan—yes, with joy!"

Marian still loved the old name of Allan.

The smile that was upon his lips let Marian see that he had some story to tell, and that the introduction of the fair young girl, almost a child in years as she was, who rested on his arm, was not to be wholly confined to the few words he had spoken.

But it was Clara herself who then spoke, before Fitz George could say another word.

"Ah, dear, dear madam! if you will be so kind to me as to afford shelter, and the name of a home, to a poor orphan girl, until she can find a new mistress, she and heaven will bless your goodness."

"No, no!" interposed Fitz George, as he took Clara by the hand—"no, no! that is not fair."

Marian looked from one to the other of them in surprise.

"No, Marian; I must introduce this young person to you as she should be introduced. Know in her the preserver of my life!"

Clara made a deprecating gesture, as though she did not wish Fitz George to tell that.

"Yes," he added; "this night would have been, I do believe, my last upon earth, but for this young girl, Marian!"

"Your life? Oh, Allan—Allan!"

The dismal image thus conjured up was too much for Marian, and she sunk sobbing upon the breast of her husband, who briefly told her all that had occurred.

Do you not suppose, dear reader, with what affection and grateful feeling Marian then greeted Clara?

And Lucy, too, the daughter of Jack Singleton—she took the hand of Clara, and in her soft, sweet way, asked that she might be a sister to her.

They were a happy party that night at the pretty little house by the Green Park.

And while they wept and smiled by turns, there was one who might be literally said to be gnashing his teeth with rage without.

Sir Hinckton Moys had missed his victim.

There was another, too, whose poniard waited in vain, at Buckingham House, for one of the noblest hearts in all the world as a sheath.

That was the dastardly Bergami.

But we will take a glance at the state of affairs at that royal residence.

So assured was Bergami that Captain Fitz George would make his appearance at Buckingham House, that he took up his position behind the window screen in waiting for him, expecting each moment to hear his footstep.

The Princess of Wales had been both alarmed and shocked at what the young girl whom she fancifully named Fidele had said to her.

It was true she had disputed the point with her, and affected to disbelieve the tale to the prejudice of Bergami, but there was a still small voice at her heart which told her it might be true.

In a state of great agitation, after Fidele had left, and when she really found the young girl did not return, she sent for an Italian servant, who was a cousin of Bergami.

This man was named Ugolio.

To him the Princess spoke with some agitation: "You are to bring the Baron here to me at once, Ugolio—at once, you comprehend me. You are to tell him that no excuse will avail. I must, and will, see him here, in this room."

"Madam's orders shall be obeyed." said Ugolio, who was tolerably civil to the poor Princess, since he was, by one peculation and another, making such a fortune in her service that he could afford to purchase both an estate and a title in his own native Tuscany — "Madam's orders shall be obeyed."

"Quick—quick!"

Ugolio almost flew from the room.

"Diable!" he said to himself. "What a fortunate man is the Baron to be wanted in such a hurry!"

Through Buckingham did Ugolio make his way, eagerly inquiring for the Baron Bergami.

But no one whom he met could, for some time, tell him where he was to be found. It was at length a young lad who was one of the favourites of the Princess of Wales, because he had a soft, flute-like voice and could play the guitar, who, in answer to Ugolio's inquiries, said, "Ah, yes, Master Ugolio, I saw the Baron go into that room."

He indicated the door of the apartment with the screen as he spoke.

"This room, you say?"

"Yes. Let me open the door for you. You will find the Baron there."

All that Bergami heard was the opening of the door, and the voice of some one saying, "You will find the Baron there," and then the footstep—the footstep of the unconscious Ugolio.

Imagination does wonders.

Bergami had so worked himself to the idea that Captain Fitz George, the son of the Regent—and the possibly legitimate son, too—would be shown into that apartment, that he almost thought, through the screen, he could see the young officer's uniform.

He gave the sharp, short yell which the Roman assassins usually use when they rush upon a victim, and the next moment his poniard was in the heart of Ugolio.

Bergami committed this deed after the manner of the professional bravos and man-slayers of Italy. That is to say, he reached his arm over the left shoulder of his victim, and so dashed the dagger into his heart.

Ugolio uttered a yell, and fell dead upon his face.

"That's done!" said Bergami, as he wiped the poniard with a double action, right and left, upon his sleeve: "that's done—and well done, too!"

The next word that was uttered by Bergami was a strange one to hear in the eighteenth century in England.

"Sanctuary!"

The commission of that assassination had taken him back to his old habits and his old associations, and for the moment he forgot that he was in England.

It was only for the moment, however, that this oblivious condition of mind came over him, and then he laughed at himself.

"No, no! This is no country of 'sanctuary!' I shall wait for my friend Moys to come."

Bergami shut the door of the room in which the dead man was, and went coolly walking along the passage beyond it.

He was unexpectedly met by the Princess of Wales. There was disorder in her looks, and it was evident to Bergami that she suffered under some great agitation.

She seized his arm, and looked fixedly in his face by the light of a chandelier that hung in that passage, or corridor, as it might be called.

"Baron—Bergami—speak! What is this I hear? What have you thought of doing? What have you attempted to do? Speak to me, or I shall go mad!"

Bergami put on a look, and assumed an attitude of fawning subservience to the Princess of Wales; and she, seeming to see that he was on the point of uttering some common-place expression, that no doubt he intended for a compliment, interrupted him almost fiercely.

"No, Bergami—no; you shall answer me. What have you done? What have you tried to do?"

"It is done!" said Bergami.

The Princess of Wales fell at his feet in a swoon.

CHAPTER CCXXI.

COLONEL HANGER TAKES SIR HINCKTON MOYS TO THE SHOP OF THE COACH-TRIMMING SELLER IN LONG ACRE.

THERE was a deathlike pallor upon the face of Sir Hinckton Moys, and blood upon his lip, for he had bitten it in his rage, as he dashed into the room where he had left Colonel Hanger enjoying himself with the wine; and, striking the table with his fist, he cried out, "The fellow has a charmed life—nothing will kill him! Angels or devils interpose to save him! Something that looked female—human—delicate almost as a child, but slim and stately as a woman, seemed to rise up from the very earth on which he trod, and, taking him almost in her arms, led him away from danger—away from death!"

"Permit me to remark," said Colonel Hanger, with a sleepy look, "that that's decidedly odd."

"Pshaw! If that is all the remark you have to make about it, pray keep it to yourself. I am foiled—foiled—baffled again by that Captain Fitz George, alias Allan Fearon, alias the fiend knows what; who, I thought, this night would surely have slept the sleep that knows no awaking!"

Sir Hinckton Moys flung himself heavily into a chair.

Colonel Hanger glared at him in a kind of stupid surprise. It was evident that he, Hanger, had taken a great deal too much wine; and, although he was well-seasoned to deep potations, he was gradually getting into that stolid condition of mind which precedes complete intoxication.

"Wine, wine!" cried Moys, as he struck the table again heavily, making the glasses and bottles jingle again,—"wine, wine, I say!"

"Allow me to remark, my friend," said Hanger, "that that is the most sensible word you have uttered since you have been here. You are getting rational, Moys—decidedly rational!"

"And you the reverse!"

"Eh? What do you say? And you the reverse? Who's the reverse? I'll fight any man who says I'm the reverse! What do you mean, eh? You are the reverse yourself!"

"Idiot!"

"Oh, you may call me an idiot as long as you like! Jack Hanger don't mind being called an idiot, but he won't be called the reverse; so don't do that again."

Moys rose and paced the room with hurried strides.

"I don't know what'll come of it all," he muttered; "and yet it's a game worth playing. I have played the fool with Fortune once; and if I could but get her in my grasp again, the slippery jade should not escape me so easily."

"Oh, I see what it is!" said Hanger: "he has been jilted, and is taking it to heart. Bless you, my dear fellow, there's as good fish in the sea as ever came out of it! Don't you recollect the old song?"

"Go to the deuce!"

"'What care I how fair she be
If she be not kind to me.'"

"Silence!" roared Moys. "You don't know what you're talking about!"

"How should I, when it's a woman? Ain't they everything by turns, and nothing long?"

"Hanger!"

"Well, I say hang her, too! I don't know who she is, but hang her!"

"You misunderstand me. I speak to you Colonel—Major—Jack, whatever you call yourself. I speak to you."

"Oh, that's quite another affair!"

"Are you sober enough, or do you think you will be sober enough soon, or have you any means of making yourself sober enough, to attend to business?"

"Stop—now stop a bit! You said sober enough three times over, and I'm only a little bit gone once. What do you mean by it? They say a fellow sees double when he's had a drop too much. Perhaps he sees treble, and perhaps he hears treble! Did you say I was sober enough

three times over? Because, if you did, I never was quite so sober as that in my life!"

"There's nothing to be got out of this fool to-night but quibbles and insane jests," muttered Sir Hinckton Moys.

"Oh, but there is, though," said Hanger; "and, if there's anything really to do, give me a wine-glass of good malt vinegar and a pitcher of cold water—I shall soon be right then! I haven't taken much. It was the solitude—the solitude! I was all alone. Oh, I shall be all right again!"

Moys was quite willing to try the experiment; for he was in that state of irritation, anxiety, and anger, that he felt he should have no rest until he had accomplished something of a favourable character towards the completion of his designs.

It had been rather a collateral desire upon his part to destroy Captain Fitz George; but his principal object was the displacement of Annie, the Countess, from the strong position she held in the favour of the Regent.

He and the Marchioness of Sunningham had made a regular compact, that the fortunes of one should be the fortunes of the other.

But Annie was the obstacle.

She once removed, they both fully believed in the possibility of inducing the Regent to return to his old flame; and history, indeed, tells us that such was the fact, although no history but this is able to tell us how it came about.

Colonel Hanger tried his sobering process with the vinegar and the cold water.

The former he took a copious draught of, and the latter he dashed over his head and face in such profusion that he succeeded, at least for a time, in completely chilling the sense of intoxication.

"Now, Moys," he said, "I'm your man. What is to be done?"

"I want you to take me to Long Acre."

"Ah, to be sure—I recollect now! That is to be the plot. Come with me, and I will show you the pattern divinity at once."

"Are you certain about this likeness you speak of, or is it a mere fancy?"

"Certain as that I stand here, Moys. By some accident, or freak of nature, the girl is so like Annie, the Countess de Blonde, that you could not know one from the other. Mind you, I don't mean to say that if they were together there might not be points of difference, as there might be between two peas; but apart, it would puzzle a conjuror to decide which was which."

"You give me new hope."

"I thought I should. It would be a rare game if it could be brought about."

"Yes; and if the girl has no foolish scruples, and will give credit."

"Bah to the scruples! But what do you mean by the credit?"

"Why, I take it, Hanger, that both you and I are in rather low water financially."

"Oh, there's no doubt about that."

"I did not doubt it, or we should not be talking in such a vile hole as this. At Buckingham House, too, there is no money. The Princess of Wales has been trying to raise a loan, but her City friends, although backed by an alderman, are shy. They say money is tight. Curses on them! it always is tight when you want it. The Marchioness of Sunningham, however, I know, has money, but she is niggardly."

"Always was," said Hanger, sententiously.

"Yes; it is not with her 'lightly come, lightly go,' but lightly come, and hold fast. Nevertheless she must provide the sinews of war. But when I spoke of credit, I meant would this girl, who bears so wonderful a resemblance to Annie the Countess, consent to play the part we require of her upon promise of a large reward in perspective?"

"We will try her, Moys. Come along, and I will show her to you."

"But how—how! You don't mean she is stuck up in a shop as a kind of public spectacle, for anybody to come and look at her that pleases?"

"Oh, dear, no; but I'm an old campaigner, and have made my approaches. She is a niece of the proprietress of the shop. I say proprietress, although there is the proprietor, but he's nobody;

one of your jerry-sneak sort of men, who cannot call his soul his own. Well, you see, Moys, the aunt of the extraordinary likeness frequents a conventicle in one of the off-streets of Long Acre, and there's where I picked up her acquaintance."

"You, Hanger?—you at such a place?"

"To be sure. I had matrimonial thoughts. I don't know exactly what has become of the last Mrs. Hanger, and I don't intend to inquire. A man may as well be hanged for a sheep as a lamb. Censorious people pretend I have committed bigamy already; so, under those circumstances, I thought I would marry again; and, bearing in mind the advice of the man in the play it was to the meeting-house, the conventicle, that I went, in order to look for a wife, warranted not to last too long, but with plenty of money."

"I see—I see!"

"Of course you do. Well, there I saw the aunt, and there I saw the niece; and, struck with the extraordinary likeness of the latter to our fair Countess de Blonde, spoke to them, and escorted them home. I supped with them upon tripe, sheep's trotters, and sausages, made endurable by drops of burnt brandy."

"Then you are quite an acquaintance?"

"Oh, quite—quite!"

"And who do they think you?"

"Once a Major—always a Major. I called myself Major Brown, and am willing to introduce you as Captain Smith. And here we are—this is the shop!"

Colonel Hanger and Sir Hinckton Moys, during the latter part of this conversation, had made their way to Long Acre, and they paused opposite a shop which, although the hour was late, was not closed, although but a glimmering sort of light was in its window.

Moys looked up, and saw the rather singular name of Monday over the door.

"So that is the name," he said: "it is one not likely to be forgotten. Now, Hanger, I have only one question to put to you, and that is just this. Is all you've said really true; or are you about, with your usual impudence, to get me into some ridiculous scrape? If so, tell me at once, for I can forgive it now, although not afterwards."

"Stuff, stuff! Business—business, Moys! I never joke about business. But I must confess I'm rather surprised to see the shop open yet. I hope nothing has happened to poor Monday."

Sir Hinckton Moys laughed, for it was tolerably evident that Major Hanger cared about as much whether anything had happened to poor Monday, as he called him, or not, as he cared for the domestic affairs of the King of the Sandwich Islands.

What amused Moys, however, particularly, was the quiet, serious look which Hanger put on as he tapped at the shop door.

"Remember, Moys," whispered Hanger, then. "Don't make any blunder!"

"What do you mean? You are much more likely to blunder than I am."

"Pho! pho! Don't be so short and curt. I mean in regard to the names. Remember, you are Captain Smith, and I am Major Brown."

"Yes, yes!"

"Your pious female dearly loves a military man. But hush! Some one comes!"

The shop door was opened. A tall, lank-looking female appeared, and in a nasal tone inquired their business.

"Don't you know me, Susannah?" asked Major Hanger.

"Oh, is it you, sir?"

"Even so. There you are!"

It was evident that Major Hanger placed a piece of money in the ready and open hand of the tall, gaunt female who rejoiced in the name of Susannah, which she as adroitly transferred to her pocket.

"At home?" asked the Major.

"Yes, sir. Supper is ordered for three."

"Then I was expected?"

"I think you was, sir," replied Susannah, without being at all particular about her grammar,—"I think you was; but he is rather obstropulous to-night."

"He? Monday?"

"Yes, sir. Missus has twice ordered him to go out, and once has told him he shall stay all night in the cellar if he don't mind what he is about; but he is rather obstropulous."

"Never mind. Come in, Captain Smith."

"Oh, bless us! have you brought another millingtary gentleman with you, Major Brown?"

"Yes, an old friend of mine—Captain Smith, of the Three Hundred and Forty-second Cavalry."

"Lor'!"

Susannah retreated before Hanger and Moys towards the back parlour of the shop, which movement on her part Hanger chose to construe into an invitation to follow.

"Come in," he whispered to Moys,—"come in, and you shall see both the aunt and the niece."

"A queer place!" muttered Moys.

"Where's the odds, if it answer our purpose? Come on—come on!"

A screaming voice at this moment came from the back parlour.

"You wretched object, how often am I to speak to you, and tell you I have the vapours, and that the sight of your horrid pudding-face makes me a great deal worse, eh?"

"My dear, really——"

The reply was in a weak, hesitating stammer, which Moys conjectured rightly enough proceeded from the unfortunate Monday.

"Don't speak to me, wretch!—don't! don't! I know quite well what you want to say; it is something impudent and aggravating, you horrid, ill-looking tyrant!"

"Oh, oh! Me a tyrant?"

"Yes, you. But I have found you out!—oh, yes! I have found you out!"

"Found—me—out?"

"To be sure I have! Didn't I see you looking at that charity school of girls, passing down the Acre, only last Monday was a fortnight? Oh, I saw you!"

"My dear!"

"Don't 'my dear!' me! Monster! Blue Beard! I know you well!"

"My love!"

"Don't 'my love!' me! I say, Mr. Monday, will you go into the cellar?"

"Really, I—I——"

"Or will you go out of the house?"

"Well, well! Don't scream so! Of the two,

I would rather, of course, go out of the house, than into the cellar."

"Oh, you would!"

"Well, my dear——"

Mrs. Monday began to scream, and drum on the floor with her feet; and the unhappy Monday made a rush to get out of the house, passing Colonel Hanger and Sir Hinckton Moys, in the semi-darkness of the shop, without seeing them, or taking the least notice of them.

"Ha, ha!" laughed Hanger.

"What a spectacle!" said Moys. "So much, Hanger, for matrimony."

"Yes, in this instance. But come on!"

"Mum! mum!—if you please, mum," said Susannah, "here is Major Brown, and another millingtary gent—a Capting Smith, if you please, mum!"

The incipient hysterics of Mrs. Monday stopped on the instant.

"The dear Major, did you say, Susannah?"

"Yes, mum, and a Capting."

"Oh, dear!—oh, dear! Maria Jane, do settle my comb—do! Am I fit to be seen?"

"Oh, yes, aunt! Did you say another gentleman, Susannah?"

"Yes, Miss Maria Jane—a Capting."

"Ladies," said Major Hanger, as he put one foot and his head into the room—"ladies, can you pardon the presumption of your most humble and devoted servant, who has presumed to bring with him a friend, because he wished him, too, to be a sharer in the delight of gazing on youth and loveliness?"

"Oh, Major!"

Moys thought it scarcely possible that coarse flattery of the description which Major Hanger was administering could be acceptable; but he was quite of a different opinion soon, and took up the same style of discourse.

"Allow me," added the Major—"allow me, ladies, to introduce to you my friend Captain Smith."

Moys bowed.

"Captain Smith, this is the lovely Mrs. Monday, fairest of the fair at her age, which you will see is about twenty-eight."

"Oh, Major Brown!" simpered Mrs. Monday. "You flatterer! I am older—much older."

"No?"

"Yes, alas! I—I am twenty-nine."

Mrs. Monday was thirty-nine, at the least.

"Twenty-nine!" exclaimed Sir Hinckton Moys, taking his cue from Hanger. "Is it possible that you are so much? I should have said twenty-four, at the utmost."

"Oh, Captain!"

"And here," added Major Hanger—"here is the fair and incomparable Miss Maria Jane Alltuch, who is just sweet seventeen."

This was near the fact; and as Moys turned to Maria Jane, and then looked up, just as Susannah came into the room with a couple of lighted candles, he was able to see how far Major Hanger was right in the account he had given of the likeness of the niece of Mrs. Monday to Annie, Countess of Blonde.

Moys was perfectly startled at the resemblance. It was one of those accidental likenesses which sometimes occur, although they are rarely so perfect as in this case

To be sure, there was, perhaps, an absence of the candid, ingenuous expression which was always present about the eyes of Annie; but, apart from that, certainly the young girl at the coach-trimming shop in Long Acre was wonderfully like the Countess.

All that Moys could possibly have suggested would have been some little alteration in the mode of wearing her hair, and then Maria Jane would have passed well for Annie to any one who was not most specially intimate with the latter.

We mean she would have imposed upon any such person, even in a room.

But it would not be necessary that so severe a test as that would have to be encountered.

Moys was delighted.

Fully comprehending, then, that Major Hanger was expected to pay almost exclusive attention to Mrs. Monday, he sat down by the side of Maria Jane Allsuch, and engaged her in conversation.

He found a frivolous, rather ignorant, and decidedly ill-formed mind.

"I am afraid," he said, "you don't see so much of the world as you ought, in this rather gloomy shop and street?"

"Oh, no— indeed I don't!" was the reply. "Aunt don't, either; and although we would like to go out a little now and then, it is so very awkward without a beau."

Maria Jane bent her eyes upon Moys as she spoke, in a fashion which said as plainly as looks could stand for actual words, "You may be the beau, if you like."

Moys then spoke up at once.

"Mrs. Monday," he said, "the Major and I are very anxious that you and your lovely niece should have the charity to accompany us to the Pantheon on Saturday."

"Oh, my!" exclaimed Maria Jane, "how finely pleasant that would be!"

Major Hanger took the hint at once, and added, "Yes, Captain Smith and I talked it over, and if you will be ready at eight o'clock, we will bring a coach for you."

"I am afraid," sighed Mrs. Monday, "that the Pantheon is hardly a proper place for seriously-disposed persons to go to; but, since you are so pressing, gentlemen, I cannot—oh, dear! I feel that I cannot say no. We will be ready on Saturday; and now we will take a bit of supper."

CHAPTER CCXXII.

THE DARK WOMAN MEETS THE LORD CHANCELLOR, AND MAKES SOME MAGNIFICENT PROPOSALS.

WAS Linda de Chevenaux any the happier now that she seemed to have taken so important a step forwards towards the accomplishment of her designs?

Alas, no!

By one of those strange divarications of the human mind, which are as singular as they are common, she had almost succeeded in persuading herself that the document she had procured, by a trick that had the most unbounded audacity as its principal element, from the old King, was a real and genuine document, which she could hold to and stand upon as upon some irrefragable right; but she was not happy, for all that.

The time was rapidly passing away, and she had several things to do, each one of which was a source of disquietude to her.

She had her son, Captain Fitz George, to meet again, to hear his determination in regard to the new aspect of affairs.

And she had that appointment she had made with the Lord Chancellor to keep. Him she hoped to make a partisan, if it were possible, by painting the most brilliant and seductive picture to any human mind to stultify its real convictions.

Until she had carried out, then, these two appointments, and satisfied herself about the results of each, she could do nothing.

Lovat still remained in close attendance upon her, as a kind of private secretary; and so powerful was the hold that her intellect got of his imagination, that with all his knowledge of the world, and with all his real practical good sense, he found himself looking upon her, and truly believing her to be what she represented herself.

The veritable Princess of Wales!

That was the power of the strong mind over the weaker.

Not that his was a weak mind, properly so called, but hers had about it those firm resolves that few could contend with.

And so the Dark Woman, at all events, triumphed over that one intellect, and to Lovat was all the Princess!

It was a relief to her to be able to get the appointment with the Lord Chancellor over before she should again be compelled to see her son Fitz George.

She thought that if she could see him, and be at the same time armed with a favourable opinion and the high legal authority of the Lord High Chancellor of England, it would surely have some weight with him.

That the high legal functionary would keep his appointment in some shape or another the Dark Woman did not doubt, and she was resolved to take some steps to prevent any treachery on his part.

Those steps were clear and effectual enough.

A few hours before the time when, in order to meet her, he ought to be close to the spot appointed, she, by the aid of Lovat, who, in that particular, was well able to be of essential assistance to her, caused to be delivered to the Chancellor the following note:—

"Private and confidential.

"The Princess of Wales presents her compliments to the Lord Chancellor, and particularly requests him to meet her at Tyburn Gate about ten minutes before twelve o'clock to-night.

"The Princess of Wales will be there in a plain green chariot with plain panels."

That this letter would place the Chancellor in a difficulty Linda de Chevenaux well knew, because he would have to be at Tyburn Gate just about the time she had mentioned, in order to keep the appointment that concerned the safety of the Great Seal of England.

Of course she had so timed it, that on his route to that appointment he could meet the "Princess of Wales," who, no doubt, he would fancy was Caroline of Brunswick, at Tyburn Gate; and as it was pretty well known he had been, so to speak, coquetting with the Princess's party, there was very little doubt but that he would be both willing and anxious to hear what she had to say to him so secretly.

Little did he imagine that it was the Dark Woman, of whom he had heard frequently, who, in her assumption of the title of Princess of Wales, made that appointment with him.

The bait, then, succeeded. At least a quarter of an hour before the time appointed, the Lord High Chancellor of England might have been seen in the Bayswater Road, or Oxford Road, as it was then termed, looking very anxious, and very undignified indeed.

There was no carriage.

No obsequious officials, well paid by the nation to do honour to the office, if none were due, in reality, to the man.

With nothing but an umbrella to protect him from the inclemency of rather a squally and uncomfortable evening, the Chancellor hovered about the spot appointed in the mysterious letter he had received.

That spot ought to have brought with it some salutary reflections.

It was close to the gallows upon which so many depredators had suffered the dread penalty of death, which is, and always will be, the most dreaded penalty, and a terrible necessity, for crimes of really deep dye, let philanthropists and weak-minded "abolition of the punishment of death" societies say what they may.

And this Chancellor must surely—or he ought, if he did not—have reflected how many persons must have suffered on that spot for crimes against property, who were not half such—what shall we say?—the direct common word is surely the best —so we will say, persons who were not half such thieves as he was.

He ought to have reflected upon that fact, which no one could know better than himself, or one half so well; and he ought to have felt uncomfortable accordingly, but it is doubtful if he did.

Then, just as he began to have an idea that he might possibly have been hoaxed, and that some political enemy might have written the letter that had brought him to that spot, he saw a carriage approaching.

A plain, dark-green carriage, with nothing on the panels to denote the rank or the position of its owner.

"She comes!" said the Chancellor—"she comes! I shall now be able to settle in my own mind the question that has long agitated it—namely, whether it will be more to my advantage, or not, to join the party of the Princess of Wales, or pretend to be an out-and-out supporter of his Highness the Regent!"

The carriage stopped.

The Chancellor furled up his umbrella.

He approached it, and coughed.

A hand was slightly projected from the window; and the Chancellor's eyes—albeit, they were used enough to magnificence—were perfectly dazzled by the beauty and brilliancy of the gems that sparkled on the finger of the hand.

If he had had any doubts before about the apparent fact that it was, indeed, the poor Princess of Wales who favoured him with this interview, that doubt vanished in the blaze of those diamonds.

He made a low bow to the coach and the supposed royal occupant.

Then the hand opened the door.

"Step in!" said a voice.

The Chancellor entered the coach.

By the dim light within it, he could see a lady. She was closely wrapped up in a cloak, the fur collar of which hid two-thirds of her face, and the rim of a hat-and-feathers came so low down over her eyes, that it completed the state of mystification in which her whole countenance was kept.

The Chancellor was a gallant kind of man in his way, and he now spoke in his blandest and most courtly tones.

"Madam—most illustrious madam, may I hope that I may be favoured with your commands, since you see before you one who sincerely feels for your position, and who would only be too happy to be of service to you."

As they were quite alone, the Chancellor was by no means particular what promises or what protestations he made.

By such means he thought he would secure the confidence of the unhappy Princess of Wales, whom he supposed to be his companion in the coach.

It would be time enough afterwards, he considered, to decide upon whether it would answer his purpose best to stand by her or to betray her.

"You received a note?" said the female.

"I did, madam—I had that honour."

"And you can spare an hour?"

"Easily."

"You have no other engagement to-night?"

"None. It is true that I had one, if I had chosen to keep it, but I have made some little arrangements which put it aside."

"Without being considered impertinently curious, my lord, may I ask what that engagement was?"

"Oh, certainly! My house, in Bloomsbury Square, was attacked by burglars some few nights since, and among other things stolen was the seal of office, which, I need scarcely tell your Royal Highness, is a very sacred possession to the Chancellor for the time being."

"So I should suppose."

"It is so, indeed. But these ruffians took it with them, and have had the unparalleled assurance to hope that I shall meet one or more of them this night to negotiate for its return, by means, no doubt, of a large reward."

"Indeed!"

"Oh, yes, your Highness; but, upon reflection, I have adopted a course which will be very uncomfortable."

"To you, my lord?"

"Oh, no, no!—to the robbers!"

"You are quite right, no doubt; and I can well perceive that it would require no common subtlety of intellect to overmatch you."

"Hem! Well, your Royal Highness only does me, so far, justice. I have seen a good deal of the world—a good deal of—of—its worst side."

"No doubt."

"And so I am not easily deceived, as your Royal Highness justly remarks."

"May I still further ask what are the means you have taken to catch these persons in their own snare?"

"Oh, yes! I have no less than twenty persons, officers of the police and their assistants, secreted about the spot where I was to meet the chief of the burglarious gang."

"Ah! that is well."

"I hope and trust so; and even as I have the honour now to speak to your Highness, I am in momentary expectation of the arrival of my men with a prisoner, or perhaps with several prisoners."

"Well, my lord, I am more than ever pleased, then, that I have made this appointment with you."

"Oh, your Highness does me great honour."

"And I do myself some pleasure."

"May I then ask upon what point your Highness wishes to consult me?"

"Yes; I am in possession of some very strange facts in regard to a very mysterious person, who calls herself by the same title which I have so many reasons, although some of them are sad enough, to consider my own."

"The same title?"

"Yes, the title of Princess of Wales. Only the person of whom I speak signs herself Linda, Princess of Wales—not Caroline."

The Dark Woman—for it was in truth none other than herself who was conversing thus with the Chancellor in that coach—spoke these words with great deliberation, and as narrowly as she could watched their effect upon him.

"Pho! pho!" he said. "We know quite well all about that!"

"All about what, my lord?"

"This Linda de Chevenaux!"

"Indeed!"

"Oh, yes, your Highness. That is her name. It appears that some twenty years ago the Prince of Wales became enamoured of her, and there was a kind of mock marriage, which it has suited her to try and transform into a real one."

"And you know her?"

"Not personally, but she has made herself rather notorious of late by her exploits under the name of the Dark Woman!"

"And the marriage was a mock one?"

"Yes—permit me to explain."

"I shall be grateful."

"By the Royal Marriage Act, no marriage of any royal member of the royal family can be legal without the consent of the Crown."

"I am aware of that."

"Well, your Highness, no such consent was given in the case of the Prince of Wales and this Linda de Chevenaux; so that the marriage, let it have been performed how or under what circumstances it may, is illegal."

"That is the whole question, my lord."

"Nay, your Royal Highness, permit me to say that it is no question. It is the law."

"Your lordship misunderstands me"

"I beg ten thousand pardons."

"What I mean is, that the whole question turns upon the fact of whether the Crown did give its consent to the marriage or not."

"Oh, there can be no doubt upon that point"

"None, whatever!"

"Your Highness!"

"None, whatever, I repeat, because I have seen the consent."

"Some impudent forgery!"

"No, no!"

"Then some document procured from the old King while not in his right senses, and so not capable of giving it."

Linda de Chevenaux was not at all pleased at these remarks from the Lord Chancellor, because they so exactly fitted the case, and were so true. The pretended consent of the King to the marriage of the Dark Woman, then Linda de Chevenaux, had taken two phases.

In the first instance, twenty years ago that pretended consent had been produced by the enamoured Prince, for the purpose of overcoming the scruples of the young girl whom he wished to make his own on any terms.

That, as the wily Chancellor had characterized it, was "an impudent forgery."

The second phase of the subject consisted in the verification of that consent which the Dark Woman had procured of the poor old mad King at Windsor Castle.

She was silent now for some few moments, and then the Chancellor, who still believed that he was speaking to the Prince Caroline of Brunswick, the foolish and unhappy wife of the Regent, thought he could not possibly do better than argue fully and completely against the pretended claims of Linda de Chevenaux; and he said, with quite a decided and judicial tone of voice, "Your Royal Highness must not give yourself one moment's uneasiness on the subject. This Linda de Chevenaux, or Dark Woman, as she is called, has no power to harm you; and it is very probable that she has brooded over her wrongs, real and imaginary, until she is a little deranged."

"It may be so. It may be so, indeed and in truth," said the Dark Woman. "But yet, my Lord Chancellor, I have one more most important question to ask of you."

The Chancellor bowed.

CHAPTER CCXXIII.

LINDA DE CHEVENAUX PROCURES ANOTHER SIGNATURE TO THE MAD KING'S DOCUMENT, AND PLACES THE CHANCELLOR IN AN AWKWARD SITUATION.

THE Dark Woman spoke now in low, earnest tones to the Chancellor, as she said, "The important question I have to put to you, my lord, is simply this. Supposing that this person, this—this——"

"Linda de Chevenaux?"

"Yes. Supposing that she should succeed in substantiating the fact that a sufficient royal consent was given to her marriage twenty years ago with the Prince of Wales, in what position would Caroline of Brunswick be?"

"Hem! A very awkward one!"

"And what would be the condition of the Princess Charlotte of Wales, now the wife of the Prince Leopold of Saxe-Coburg?"

"Perhaps a more awkward one still."

"Well, let us, as we are here alone, assume for one moment that such were the case — what would you do?"

"I?—I?"

"Yes; you, as a man, a peer, and the highest legal authority in the kingdom?"

"Well, madam, I admire the Persians in some things."

"As how? What do you mean?"

"They worship the rising sun. But at the same time I must say that I should be actuated by the sincerest commiseration for you, madam."

"Yet you would consider this Linda de Chevenaux to be the rising sun?"

"I do not know that I could take any other view of her position."

"Well, my lord, what if I were to tell you that she is in possession of a paper signed by the King himself, which states that he did give his royal consent to the marriage of the Prince of Wales with Linda de Chevenaux?"

"I should not think much of it."

"Because why?"

"Because the King is mad."

"But if it were dated before his madness?"

"Then it would be more important; and it would be more important still if witnessed, and verified to be the signature of the King by some high officer of State."

"Such as a Secretary of State?"

"Exactly."

"Or the Chancellor?"

"Better still, your Highness."

"That will just do, then."

The Dark Woman made some signal, and the plain green chariot without any arms on its panels began to move off.

The Chancellor slightly started.

"May I presume to ask, madam, whither we are now going; although anywhere in the company of your Royal Highness must, of course, be a pleasure?"

The pace at which the carriage moved on increased. It had turned, too, and was making its way towards London.

"My lord," said the Dark Woman, "I cannot be sufficiently grateful for the high legal opinions I have had from your lordship. Moreover, I am greatly pleased at one expression that has fallen from your politic and learned lips."

"What—what may that be?"

"Your lordship said that you admired the Persian system of worshipping the rising sun?"

"I did; but—but——"

"Oh, my lord, do not seek to qualify the pretty simile, I pray you, because I am the rising sun!"

"Your Highness!"

"Yes—I am Linda de Chevenaux!"

The Chancellor uttered a cry of terror, and made an effort to open the coach-door; failing in which, he turned upon the Dark Woman, and stretching forth his hand to clutch her by the throat, he said, "I arrest you, in the name of the law!"

"And I scatter your brains upon the ceiling of this carriage, in the name of the Dark Woman!"

"Ah!"

The pistol which the Dark Woman presented exactly between the eyes of the Chancellor had a beautifully bright and polished barrel; and as the coach at that moment happened to pass one of the oil lamps in the Oxford Road, there shot a gleam of light over that barrel, which dazzled the eyes of the Chancellor.

He saw all his danger.

"A slight pressure of my finger," said the Dark Woman—"for this pistol has what is called a 'hair trigger'—a slight pressure of my finger, and you are a dead man!"

"Don't — don't! What—what good will a murder do you?"

"None!"

"Then do not threaten me."

"Except in self-defence."

"I am still. Oh, fool! fool! fool!"

"You mean yourself, of course?"

"I do. Thrice-soddened fool that I have been, to forget that Caroline of Brunswick could not speak English as you spoke it; and here have I been conversing with you for half an hour, and never discovered the cheat!"

"I must say," replied the Dark Woman, "that that circumstance does not say much for your penetration, my lord; but if you are wise now, although rather late, you are safe."

The Chancellor looked from the coach window, and saw that he was now in the lower part of the Oxford Road, now named Oxford Street.

But the hour was not one at which many passengers were to be seen in the streets; and the miserable and inefficient police of that period, in the shape of wretched old paupers from the workhouses, as watchmen, afforded him no hope of assistance.

He came reluctantly to the conclusion that he was completely in the power of Linda de Chevenaux, the Dark Woman.

If he were in any way to better his position, it would be by *finesse*, now.

Violence, he felt certain, would be useless, and might end in his own destruction.

"Well, madam," he said, assuming a coolness he was far from feeling,—"well, madam, since you have been so far successful, may I inquire what is your further purpose?"

"That you will learn in due time."

"Then I suppose I must have patience?"

"Assuredly."

The Chancellor sank back on the cushions of the coach, and resigned himself to the guidance of the Dark Woman.

The vehicle, which was driven by Lovat, went directly towards the City. Its destination was that little gloomy, desolate church, where the Dark Woman and her associates had met lately to concoct their nefarious designs, and to divide their spoil.

When the coach approached the back street in which the church was situated, the Dark Woman spoke to the Chancellor again.

"Listen!" she said. "And, if you please, profit by what you hear!"

"I am infinitely well disposed so to do!" was the reply of the discomfited Chancellor.

"You are at present, then, enjoying the emoluments of an office which you hold at the pleasure of a man who is on the eve of disgrace?"

"Hem!"

"You know what I say to be perfectly true. The Ministry is in a tottering condition, and must soon fall, when you will fall with it!"

" Well ?"

" You are deeply in debt !"

" Indeed !"

" You seem surprised that I can know so much of your private affairs; but when you left practice as a solicitor, and went to the bar, you had to compromise some disagreeable episodes in your life by promises to pay such large sums of money, that you are not yet out of debt and out of danger !"

The Dark Woman surprised the Chancellor by this intimacy with his private affairs; but the fact was, that she had obtained such particulars from Lovat, who, of course, was acquainted with them in all their ramifications.

The Chancellor, as well he could, now looked keenly in the face of the Dark Woman as he said, " What do you propose ?"

" Ten thousand a year, and the Chancellorship of the Duchy of Cornwall, which my son will confer on you !"

" Your son ?"

" Yes, my son, the Prince of Wales; but who is now known as Captain Fitz George. That is to say, he will be Prince of Wales so soon as it shall please Providence to release my father-in-law, the old King, from his troubles."

The Dark Woman uttered these words, claiming a near kindred with the Royal Family, with such perfect ease and assurance, that the Chancellor, who admired audacity, perhaps, as much as any man breathing, was quite struck by them.

" You surprise me !" he said.

" Perhaps so; but the service you can render to me and to my son will be so great, that no reward we have it in our power to offer you can be too much for it !"

" What service ?"

" You will witness the document which has been signed by the King, and which states that he did, twenty years ago, give his consent to the marriage of the Prince of Wales to Linda de Chevenaux."

" Witness it ?"

" Yes; I said so."

" I ?—I ?"

" Even you, my Lord Chancellor !"

" But a witness to the signing of a document requires to see it signed."

" Ten thousand a year, and the Chancellorship of the Duchy of Cornwall !" said the Dark Woman, with a cold precision.

" Let me see the paper in question."

" Halt !"

The coach stopped.

A faint light from one of the City lamps shone in at the window from the street adjoining that in which was the old Church of St. Augustine, and which was their place of destination.

By the light of that lamp the Chancellor was able to read the paper which the Dark Woman handed to him; and the moment he had done so, he crushed it up in his hand, and flung it from the coach, saying, " Now, madam, what will you do ?"

" Nothing."

" But you have no longer the document upon which you built such high hopes and expectations !"

" Yes. That was only a copy !"

" A—a—copy ?"

" Certainly. That is all. Do you think I do not know you ? Can you imagine for one half moment that I would trust such a man as you are ?"

The Chancellor was confounded.

All his spirits seemed to desert him at once, and it was in a subdued tone that he said, " I own that you have a genius which deserves high fortune. I wish you were the Princess of Wales, and that I were your devoted servant."

" Ah !" said Linda de Chevenaux, " I now perceive that we begin to understand each other."

The coach had gone on in obedience to a request she had made, and now it stopped not far from the court where the old dilapidated wood railings were that led through the ancient grave-yard to the deserted church.

" Come," said the Dark Woman, " I would fain make you my friend in the only way, not to flatter you, in which I have any idea that you may become such—by the tie of your own self interest. Follow me, and no harm will befall you; but recollect that this evening you have the refusal of ten thousand a-year, and the Chancellorship of the Duchy of Cornwall."

The Dark Woman led the way, and the Lord Chancellor followed her through the old grave-yard, and into the ancient church.

A dim sepulchral kind of light was in it, and by that light he saw some spectral-looking faces hovering about the gloomy aisles.

" Is all ready ?" asked the Dark Woman.

" Ready !" replied a deep, hollow voice.

" The vault is open ?"

" It is open," replied the voice.

" And the old leaden coffin cleared of its ancient occupant, so that it may receive a more modern guest ?"

" Ay, master !" replied the voice again.

" It is well," said the Dark Woman.

" What is the meaning of all this ?" asked the rather startled Chancellor.

" It simply means that if it should be necessary to dispose of you, that all the preparations so to do are complete."

" Oh !"

" And now sign !"

The Dark Woman spread out upon the tomb, that occupied rather a conspicuous place in the old church, the veritable paper which had been signed by the old mad King at Windsor.

By the dim light he could see that pens and ink were before him; and he could see, too, another thing which rather surprised him—and that was the signature of the King, which he knew so well, that he had not the least doubt of its genuineness.

Still he was loth to append his name to that paper.

" If I refuse ?" he said.

" You die !"

" A harsh judgment that !"

" Very."

" You admit it is so ?"

" With all my heart I do, and I much regret it; but it is a sentence passed, and it cannot now be recalled, so all argument concerning it is useless. Will you sign ?"

" By compulsion, I do."

" Any way."

The Chancellor signed the paper with the word

"Attested," and then his name—or rather, we should say, the title of his barony.

"And now the oath," said the Dark Woman.

"Oath? what oath?"

"The oath which binds you not to disclose what has taken place between you and me this night; and which further binds you to the service of Linda, the true Princess of Wales, and her son, now known as the Captain Fitz George."

"And if I refuse that oath?"

"I shall deeply regret to stain the termination of our conference with blood."

"Blood?"

"Ay, with blood!"

"But—but——"

"It is enough. He refuses the oath. Advance, headsman. A peer of England should die by the axe. Spread the sawdust, and be calm, and cool, and steady."

"No, no! Good gracious! No; I will swear!"

No. 100.—DARK WOMAN.

The terrified Chancellor had seen a sort of commotion in the dim distance of the old church, and a dash of sawdust was scattered across the old stones, almost to his feet.

"Back! back!" said the Dark Woman. "He will swear!"

"Swear! swear! swear!" said three distinct voices, in deep and awful accents.

"I will then, since I needs must, on pain of death. I swear that I will not reveal the—the secrets of this night. Is that sufficient?'

"It is!"

The Chancellor drew a long breath of relief.

"But," added the Dark Woman, "do not, for a moment, deceive yourself with the fancy that, when you are at home, or at the Privy Council, away from me, you can break this oath at your pleasure. You will be surrounded by those who, at a word or sign from me, will be ready to avenge the perjury, by taking your life.

You will never be safe but by keeping this oath inviolate"

The Chancellor shuddered.

The little dim light in the old church went out, and then some one took him by the arm, and led him out into the open street. He was whirled round, then, rapidly, three or four times, by some powerful arms; and then, as he nearly fell, he heard the sound of retreating footsteps, and then the wheels of the coach, rattling over the old paving-stones.

He was alone.

But he had witnessed the important paper for Linda de Chevenaux, the Dark Woman, and he had taken rather a perilous oath to keep secret the mode by which he had been made to do so.

And, after all, too, he had not got back the seal of the Chancellor, so that he was disappointed in all ways.

―――

CHAPTER CCXXIV.

SIR HINCKTON MOYS BEGS AND OBTAINS AN AUDIENCE OF THE REGENT.

SIR HINCKTON MOYS was completely delighted with the scheme that had been elaborated in the politic brain of Major Hanger for the destruction of Annie, Countess de Blonde.

This was not the first time that Moys had made an attempt of this description, but it was the first time that he had really had sanguine hopes of success.

He almost wondered at himself when he came to consider his previous attempts to instil jealousy of Annie into the mind of the Regent.

The failure of those attempts enabled him to see what elements of hazard had surrounded them.

But this scheme of Major Hanger's he considered perfect.

It was as if chance—luck—Providence—call it what he might—had resolved, in the most extraordinary manner, to assist him in carrying out his designs.

And although so recently he had signally failed in compassing the destruction of Captain Fitz George by the aid of the infamous Bergami, he thought that some other scheme might be well considered which would have that object in view, and which it would be much easier to carry out when the Countess de Blonde should be removed from the scene of action.

Full of new hopes and impulses, then, Sir Hinckton Moys wrote the following letter to the Regent.

It was a letter so Jesuitical in its construction, and so eminently calculated to produce an effect upon the perpetually suspicious mind of the Prince of Wales, that while Moys deserved all the discredit that could possibly appertain to his rascally practices, he certainly might have been congratulated by any mind as unscrupulous as his own upon the production.

"MAY IT PLEASE YOUR ROYAL HIGHNESS,—

"A glance at the foot of this letter will let your Highness see that it is the production of one who in former times had the happiness to enjoy your royal favour.

"He feels that those times have passed away never to return, and as he is about to leave England for ever—his principal motive for so doing being that he should never be accused of a desire to trouble your Royal Highness—he feels that he ought not to do so without one word of warning, for which he asks neither fee, reward, nor recognition.

"There is one who always has been loaded with your Royal Highness's favour, and who to all her personal attractions adds the most consummate finesse, and an ability to deceive which exceeds all description.

"I allude to the fair Countess de Blonde.

"She is sufficiently clever to appear innocence itself; but if your Highness really wishes to see how she disposes of her time in your absence, you have but to induce her to believe that, on Saturday night next, you are called to Windsor urgently; and then, disguising yourself, if you will appear at the masked ball at the Pantheon, your eyes will be opened to proceedings on the part of Annie, the Countess de Blonde, which it has never entered into your royal imagination to conceive. I have the honour to be

"Your Royal Highness's most devoted and humble servant,
"HINCKTON MOYS."

Sir Hinckton Moys and Hanger were in that shabbily-appointed lodging where we so lately introduced them to the reader, when this precious epistle was concocted.

Moys read it to Hanger with extreme unction, and the latter, with the bowl of a pipe, beat time, so to speak, to the cadences of its various sentences.

"Well," said Moys, "what do you think of that, Hanger? Will it touch the Regent?"

"Assuredly."

"You really think so?"

"I'm quite certain of it. If you'd asked him for a guinea, the case might have been different; but, as it is, it looks so deuced disinterested."

"I flatter myself it does; and, I must say, I feel confident as to the result—as confident as I can be even of any physical phenomenon—so that I would lay even the most ridiculous wager on my own success."

"Would you? I like a wager. What shall it be?"

"Well, you see that bottle?"

"Stop! that's well said. I've seen nothing but that bottle for these two hours, and have the most ardent longing and desire to see another."

"Pshaw!" cried Moys, as he rose and put on his hat; "you've given yourself too much to drinking of late, Hanger, and you'll come to the bad. I will now set about finding a trusty and private friend, who will see that this letter is put in good train to meet the eyes of the Regent."

"But the other bottle, Moys? You won't go away without ordering the other bottle?"

"Stuff! stuff! You will find more wine in yonder cellaret; but remember, Hanger, although it is all very well to drink deeply now, if it so please you, you must be as sober as a judge on Saturday."

"Which judge?"

"Now—now, there you go again! Upon my word, Hanger, you're brilliant to-night!"

"Well, I happen to know that two or three of the judges drink rather deeply. But be off with you, and good luck attend you. I shall pay my attentions to the cellaret, while you lay the train which is to explode in old St. James's Palace, and blow Annie, the Countess de Blonde, to confusion!"

"Hush!—hush! Don't talk of trains and explosions! If we were overheard, such language would be sufficient to cause us to be apprehended as incendiaries."

Moys left the house, and he certainly did succeed in getting his letter transmitted to the Regent; and it had all its desired effect, apparently—for the next morning he received a note, signed by Willes, ordering him to be in attendance at Carlton House by twelve o'clock.

Moys was ready to leap into the air with joy on the reception of this billet; and as he was not kept waiting for more than half an hour, in one of the small apartments adjoining the Gold Room, before he was joined by the Regent, he began to consider that he was get ng into high favour again.

There was a old and uncomfortable look, however, upon the face of the Prince of Wales, as he just came so far into the room as to show himself, but held the door in his hand.

"Oh, your Royal Highness," cried Moys, in tones of affected deep emotion—"oh, your Royal Highness! the sight of your royal countenance again is worth ten years of life to your devoted servant."

"Going to leave the country?" said the Prince curtly.

"Ye-ye-s. I thought of so doing, your Royal Highness; but——"

"Oh, carry it out—carry it out by all means! Where did you think of going?"

Moys was vexed and confounded, but it was necessary to say something.

"I had an idea," he stammered, "of—of——"

"Well, well! of what?"

"Of going to the North American colonies."

"Very well—I shall be so delighted to hear that you are gone, that if you are poor, and the passage money is any object, you can come to me for it. Willes has orders to give it to you."

All the hopes of Sir Hinckton Moys were crushed in a moment.

He felt thoroughly beaten down and humiliated.

"Your Royal Highness," he said, "I had hoped that it was on the subject of my letter that you had condescended to see me."

"Oh, that don't concern me a bit! If you want any answer to that, the proper person to give it, I presume, is the Countess de Blonde."

"The Countess?"

"Oh, yes! Annie! Annie! come here. Here's your old friend Moys!"

"Confusion!" cried Sir Hinckton Moys, as he turned his back very unceremoniously on the Regent, and darted out of the room.

He heard a peal of shrill laughter close upon his flight, and he felt convinced that the sounds were the musical ones that came from the lips of Annie, the Countess.

Discomfited — enraged — bitterly disappointed, and full of the most malignant ideas and thoughts, Sir Hinckton Moys fled from Carlton House into the Park.

"Foiled! — foiled again!" he cried. "The man's besotted! Nothing will turn him from her; and I do believe that were an angel from heaven to come and tell him she was false, he would doubt the radiant messenger."

Sir Hinckton Moys quite forgot that he was not an angel from heaven, as well as that the accusations that he was bringing against Annie were perfectly false, and but the coinage of his own brain.

He argued and declaimed, as he stamped furiously on the gravelled Mall of the Park, as though he were the injured party; and in that state of mind he reached the gates of Buckingham House, without being well aware that he had taken that direction.

"I will see the Marchioness of Sunningham," he muttered, "and consult with her upon this unexpected evil turn."

We have already stated that since his return from the Continent, Sir Hinckton Moys had made a strict alliance with the unscrupulous Marchioness; so that upon the mention of his name he was admitted to a private conference with her immediately.

She could see by the disorder of Sir Hinckton Moys's looks that something was amiss; and he soon, in a most vociferous manner, began to inform her of the particulars.

"You know, Marchioness," he said, "we agreed upon two objects. One was the destruction of this Allan Fearon, now called Captain Fitz George; and the other a similar fate for the audacious and interloping Countess de Blonde."

"Exactly. But are you not surprised?"

"At what, Marchioness?"

"To find me here at Buckingham House?"

"By Jove, yes!"

Moys clasped his hands over his brows for a moment, and then he added, "I fancy I am not half sharp to-day. Of course, now I come to think of it, I am surprised, since you and the Princess of Wales are no longer on terms of intimacy. How is it, my dear Marchioness, then, that you are here?"

"Simply because Caroline of Brunswick is no longer here. She has gone to Warwick House."

"Indeed!"

"Yes. There has been some little diplomatic arrangement between her and the Regent, by which she is to inhabit Warwick House for a time; and I fancy the better understanding has been brought about by the very person you just now were mentioning."

"The Countess de Blonde?"

"Just so!"

"Confound her!"

"With all my heart; but, from your tone and manner, I can gather that you have been trying to confound her, and have not succeeded."

"That is just it. Listen!"

"With all my ears."

Moys then related the whole of the plot which he and Major Hanger had got up for the destruction of poor Annie, and concluded by a graphic description of his late interview with the Regent.

The Marchioness of Sunningham laughed in a most uproarious fashion.

"And is that all?" she cried; "is that all which has so discomfited the ingenious and practical Sir Hinckton Moys?"

"All?" he repeated. "In good truth, Marchioness, I know not what more you would have. They actually laughed at me, to my face!"

"Ha, ha!"

"Well, Marchioness, you may laugh likewise; but my opinion is, that if I had not escaped as I did, I should scarcely have done so with a whole skin."

"And so," said the Marchioness, in a tone of raillery—"so you really believe you have failed?"

"Most incontestably."

"Then I am of a different opinion."

"Different opinion, Marchioness? Why, it is not a matter of opinion at all, but one of fact. A different opinion, say you? Why, there cannot be two opinions on the subject."

"Yes, there may be! You fancy you know the Prince of Wales well—as you men always do fancy you know each other—but you do not know him as I know him; and I tell you that, notwithstanding he showed your letter at once to this Countess de Blonde, as he calls her, that it will rankle—rankle, I say!"

"Rankle?" repeated Moys.

"Yes; when he is alone he will think of it. And I would almost go to the length of wagering my life that, between this and Saturday night, he will thoroughly make up his mind to go to the masked ball at the Pantheon."

"Marchioness, you give me new life, by giving me new hope!"

"I am quite surprised that ever you abandoned hope! Take my advice, Sir Hinckton, and make all your preparations, just the same as if the Regent had received you with open arms."

"I will!—I will!"

"Take this girl with you to the ball, at the Pantheon—this girl of whom you speak as such an extraordinary likeness of Annie, the Countess—although, I must confess, I should have liked to have seen her first—for we women are better judges of such things than you men."

"Nay, but Marchioness, you, in your turn, now forget that this extraordinary likeness is not to be submitted to the inspection of a woman, but of a man."

"True, Sir Hinckton—true! I am rejoiced to find that you are not near so stupid as I feared you were getting. Now, go about your preparations; and if you succeed, believe me, a brilliant future awaits us both; for no sooner shall this pert, insolent minx of a girl lose the favour of the Regent, than he will feel the void in his—his heart, I was going to say, only he does not possess such an article."

"At all events, Marchioness, you will fill up the void, whether in heart or brain."

"I hope and expect so; and you may be sure that my first care shall be to advance your fortunes. But recollect, when next you wish to see me, that it must be at Sunningham House, in Pall Mall; for I'm only here to take away some things that belong to me, and which I brought to Buckingham House when I was in confidential attendance upon the Princess of Wales."

Moys laughed.

"Unconsidered trifles, I presume, Marchioness," he said, "which yet may come to some account?"

The Marchioness tried to put on a severe look of reprehension at this insinuation on the part of Sir Hinckton Moys; but it was a failure, and she laughed aloud.

"Well, Moys," she said, "be it so. And you may rest perfectly assured that you will have the share in full of the 'unconsidered trifles' that may come into my hands, when, by your help, I am——"

"The mistress of the Regent!" added Moys; "and, practically, the Queen of England!"

"Be it so; I do not quarrel with the former title, if it be the road to the latter."

"Then, Marchioness, all is arranged between us. I am quite willing to accept your judgment, as regards what the Regent is likely to do on account of the letter I have sent him; and there is only one thing more I can wish."

"What is that?"

"It is that you should be present at the ball at the Pantheon, to see with your own eyes what is going on, and possibly to assist by your advice in some emergency."

"I will be there, Moys, you may rest assured; and so good morning."

———

CHAPTER CCXXV.

ANNIE DREAMS NOT OF THE DANGER THAT SURROUNDS HER.

IT did rankle.

That expression, on the part of the wicked and designing Marchioness of Sunningham, was strictly applicable to the state of mind produced in the Regent by the infamous letter that had been sent him from Sir Hinckton Moys.

Deep in his heart—for, notwithstanding the doubts on the part of the Marchioness, the Prince of Wales had a heart—deep in that heart, then, did the contents of that letter rankle, even as she had said they would.

It has often been seen, during the course of this narrative, that the Regent, with all his faults, was, now and then, capable of a generous action.

Now and then, too, he acted nobly and as became a Prince.

But that is to say nothing more than that he was human.

Any being destitute of all generous impulses and feelings would be a monster.

And any being who was all goodness, nobleness, truth, and virtue, would be something more than human.

So, in the mixed woof of the structure of the mind of the Prince of Wales we find those motives and impulses which belong to the same humanity of which is composed the brain and the heart of the humblest peasant.

He did love Annie.

And it was because he did love her, and had confidence in her, that he, on the impulse of the moment, behaved so well on the occasion of the reception of the infamous letter from Sir Hinckton Moys.

But still—still it rankled.

And when he was alone—when the bright, fair eyes of Annie no longer beamed upon him, the Regent more than once asked himself if it were possible there could be any truth in that odious epistle.

Pacing one of the reception-rooms of Carlton House, he cogitated the matter over and over.

That was the "rankling."

"If," he said—"if I only knew that she was false to me, in any shape or way, I would, as Othello says,

"'Whistle her down the wind,
To prey at fortune.'

But no, no, no!—a thousand times, no! I cannot, must not think it! She is so perfectly artless—she has been so perfectly faithful to me—and she is so sincere—too sincere, indeed, sometimes—that I can never believe anything wrong of her; and so—and so it will do no harm to go to the ball at the Pantheon, if it is only for the purpose of confounding her enemies, so that they should not have to say, at some future time, that if I had gone I should have found out something or another."

That was the specious reason which the Regent gave to himself for obeying the injunctions contained in the letter of Sir Hinckton Moys.

He knew he was deceiving himself.

He knew perfectly well that it was because a feeling of jealousy had been awakened in his mind that he resolved upon going to the ball.

But he chose to shut his eyes to that fact, and to affect to believe that he went there to justify Annie, and not to find materials with which to accuse her.

It was late on the day when the ball was to take place that he spoke to the fair Countess de Blonde with reference to the subject.

"Oh, by the bye, Annie, what did you do with that absurd letter from Moys?"

"Here it is."

"Where?"

"In my hair."

"In your hair?"

"Oh, yes! There is one terrible long curl of hair at the back of my head, which I put in paper till supper-time; so I used that letter."

"Oh, that is it!"

"That's it, George."

"Ha, ha! And—and, Annie—and—and—Ha, ha!"

"What's the matter now, George? You look like a cat with somebody hold of its tail."

"Do I? Well, Annie, I cannot help saying that, at times, your comparisons are not dignified."

"Of course not. You don't expect them to be, do you? But come, now! What is the matter, and what were you laughing in that odd sort of way for, like a hyæna in fits—eh?"

"Now, Annie!"

"Now, Georgy!"

"Come, come! I was thinking that, after all—eh?—you might like to go to that ball at the Pantheon."

"Then don't think it any more."

"You would rather not?"

"I don't mean——"

"Decidedly?"

"Now don't be provoking, George, if you please. I have said that I don't mean to go, and I never thought of going, I tell you; and I can't think what put it into your head that I would."

"Annie, I am glad you are not going."

"What for?"

"Because I feel sure that some of your and my foes will be there."

"Very well—let them go. What does it matter to us? Just nothing at all. And now come to dinner."

"Alas!"

"Eh?"

"Alas, I am forced to go to Windsor! Don't you know it? The tenth of the month, Annie?"

"What of that?"

"Why, I have agreed to go to Windsor always on the tenth."

"Very well, go there; but I suppose you can dine first?"

"Oh, yes, I can dine; and I shall be back by twelve o'clock here. You won't leave the Palace, of course?"

"Certainly not."

The Regent had succeeded in what he was about, although he could hardly be said to have set himself deliberately to catch Annie in a promise that she would not leave the Palace that night.

One word, however, had begot another, and he had made all the necessary arrangements to satisfy himself of, as he thought, the truth or the falsehood of Annie, by going to the ball at the Pantheon himself, and assuring his own eyes that she was or was not there.

There was that evening on the mind of Annie an undefined sense of peril, and yet she knew not what it could be.

It was in vain that she strove to shake it off. As the evening went on, the feeling rather increased than diminished; and perhaps for the first time in her life, Annie, the fair Countess de Blonde, felt sentimentally unhappy.

She had some cause to do so, although she knew it not.

She was in the toils, so to speak, of those implacable foes who had as yet spared no pains to compass her destruction.

The Prince of Wales apparently started for Windsor, but in reality he remained in town, and met Sheridan at a house in Piccadilly, which they were both in the habit of frequenting.

It was from there that the Regent meant to go to the ball at the Pantheon.

That was the same Pantheon in Oxford Street which is now a bazaar. It was then a theatre.

The Regent communicated to Sheridan the secret uneasiness that was upon his mind as regarded Annie; but the clever and witty dramatist only ridiculed the idea of attaching any weight to anything that such a man as Moys might say.

"I am not one," he said, "as your Highness well knows, who has a very exalted opinion of women; but I would not suspect or condemn a female sparrow upon the word of such a man as Sir Hinckton Moys."

"Nor I—nor I! By Jove, nor I! That is, not condemn, I mean."

"But you might suspect?"

"Well, a—I—a——"

"Then come to the ball, by all means. It is to be a fancy dress one, I think?"

"Yes—oh, yes!"

"Then it will be easy to adopt some disguises. Come with me to Drury Lane Theatre, and let me fit you out. A wig, a slight alteration in the size and shape of the nose, and a new complexion, will effect far more concealment than any mask would do."

The Regent agreed to this proposition, and he and Sheridan went to the theatre, of which

Sheridan was then the lessee; and by ten o'clock at night the disguises were effected.

The Regent was attired in an Oriental costume, of great richness, which, owing to its flowing, robe-like character, concealed in a great measure the growing rotundity of his figure.

Sheridan went in a very plain dress, but in a wig which made it difficult to recognise him.

A private carriage conveyed them both to the Pantheon.

The letter of Sir Hinckton Moys was therefore so far successful.

In fact, up to that point it was as successful as he had even hoped, or dared to expect, it would be.

At the very moment that the Prince of Wales and Sheridan reached the door of the Pantheon Theatre, Annie was retiring to rest.

She had not felt quite well on that evening, and as she did not expect the return of the Regent for at least two hours, she determined upon trying to get a sleep for that period, even if she had to get up to sup with him afterwards.

Annie had a habit, when she went to rest by herself, of saying " Good night " when she put out the night-lamp, which she always did when alone; as she very wisely, as far as the preservation of her eyes were concerned, preferred to sleep in as absolute darkness as possible.

It so happened, then, that Annie, the Countess de Blonde, went to rest at the moment that the coach with the Regent and Sheridan reached the door of the Pantheon.

As they crossed the threshold, Annie put out her light.

" Good night!" said Annie, and composed herself to sleep.

CHAPTER CXXVI.

SIR HINCKTON MOYS IS QUITE CONFIDENTIAL WITH THE YOUNG LADY FROM THE SHOP IN LONG ACRE.

MRS. MONDAY and Maria Jane were on the tenter hooks of expectation for the hour to come on Saturday, which would bring to them the gallant Major Brown, *alias* Major Hanger, and the no less gallant Captain Smith, *alias* Sir Hinckton Moys.

Mrs. Monday had been unusually amiable for the whole of that day to the wretched and subdued Mr. Monday.

But not a word concerning the projected visit to the ball at the Pantheon had been suffered to reach his ears.

To be sure, for the whole of the day before, and for the whole of that Saturday, poor Monday had been surprised to catch glimpses of bright and gay female apparel such as he seldom saw in the house.

There were stray bits of silk and satin, and ends of ribbons, and sprays of artificial flowers; and, now and then, mysterious-looking bundles and band-boxes would be brought into the house by as mysterious-looking females, so that Monday could not but be aware that something unusual was going on.

What it was, however, he could not divine, nor had he the least suspicion.

Curiosity, however, is not solely a mental characteristic of the softer sex. We have known such Paul Prys of men, that no woman's curiosity could possibly equal them.

In the same way, too, we have known men who would, and could, out-talk any three women who ever existed, notwithstanding the ladies have a reputation for the use of their tongues—bless them!

Mr. Monday had, therefore, a curiosity to know what all the preparation, evidently going on, meant.

Towards the latter part of the day, he mustered up courage to speak.

"My love! are you going anywheres with Maria Jane?"

Well would it have been for Monday if he had held his tongue, and obeyed the injunction often given to children, that they should hear, see, and say nothing.

The moment he made that unlucky inquiry, Mrs. Monday and Maria Jane uttered two screams of such ear-piercing intensity, that Monday slipped off his chair—he always sat on the extreme edge—on to the floor.

The two screams were then repeated, just because both the ladies saw the capital effect they produced.

Monday, then, felt criminal, although he could not say exactly what he had done; but remonstrances or demands, however humbly couched, for explanation, were, he knew, quite useless, so he gathered himself up, did that unhappy Monday.

He gathered himself up, and fled.

That was just what Mrs. Monday and Maria Jane wanted.

The preparations for the ball went on with rapidity, and without concealment, so that when, at about half-past nine o'clock, Sir Hinckton Moys and Major Hanger arrived, the ladies were

" In gorgeous array."

The Major was in a military uniform, and in his pocket he had a pair of large, false whiskers and moustachios, which he meant to put on at the theatre.

Sir Hinckton Moys was in private dress; but he had decided upon carrying a mask with him, and deliberately putting it on at the Pantheon, in defiance of all regulations to the contrary.

The ball was advertised to be a fancy dress one; but, as upon all such occasions, the fancy dressing was quite optional, and there were sure to be many persons there merely in evening costume.

Masks were, however, prohibited on the occasion.

Who was there to interfere, though, with Moys, if, to suit his own purposes, he at any moment chose to put one on?

In the coach that conveyed these two persons to Long Acre, there was a small parcel, which Moys and Hanger both considered bore an important part in the night's proceedings.

Now, it will be recollected that Sir Hinckton Moys had said to Hanger that he had the means of getting a letter safely carried to the Regent.

That is to say, he could get it placed on the table in the small room, named the " Italian Cabinet," where the Regent's letters were placed, after they had passed the scrutiny of Willes, the confidential valet.

The way by which Moys was thus enabled to communicate directly with the Regent was this.

Attached to the household of the Palace, there was a woman who had been an old, and not very respectable, acquaintance of Sir Hinckton Moys. In fact, he got her the situation she held in the royal household; and in due time she had married one of the Yeoman of the Guard.

Moys had, during the period when he was in favour with the Regent, been very liberal to this couple; and now he reaped the fruits of the liberality, for they were both willing—no doubt being incited thereto by the prospect of favours to come, should Moys again creep into the favour of the Regent—to do anything they could for him.

It was this Yeoman of the Guard who placed Sir Hinckton Moys's letter along with the others that would reach the Regent safely, on the table in the "Italian Cabinet."

But the wife of the Yeoman performed a more important service still.

This woman, at the instigation of Moys, stole from the wardrobe of Annie, the Countess, a cloak made of extremely fine velvet, and edged with narrow lace of the most costly character, as regarded its fineness and texture.

It was this cloak that Moys had in the mysterious little bundle he brought with him in the coach to Long Acre.

That such an article of Annie's apparel would be well known to the Regent he did not doubt for a moment.

The Prince had a talent and taste for observation in clothing.

Hence he, Moys, considered, if the likeness which Maria Jane bore to Annie could be aided by some article well known to be hers, in the shape of dress, the delusion would be perfect.

Mrs. Monday welcomed Major Brown with a languishing look.

Maria Jane was all smiles and sweetness to Captain Smith.

"Ladies," said Hanger, " I hope we are true to our time. Punctuality becomes the brave, when they have enlisted in the service of the fair."

"Oh, Major, you are so gallant!"

"Not at all, madam—not at all. I am, on the contrary, a selfish man, and a public benefactor; at least, on this occasion."

"Indeed, Major!"

"Yes, madam, I bestow on myself a reflected ray of your beauty by taking you to the ball, and I delight the sight of all beholders with your wondrous charms."

"Oh, Major!—oh! oh!"

"He speaks nothing but the truth," said Moys; "and as I feel myself to be quite a new acquaintance here in comparison with the Major, I have taken upon myself to hope that the fair Maria Jane will not be offended if I make her an humble offering."

"Oh, dear sir!" simpered Maria Jane.

"It is this cloak."

The velvet cloak belonging to Annie was displayed by Moys.

The two ladies were in raptures with it, and Maria Jane, with the assistance of Mrs. Monday, at once put it on.

"By Jove!" muttered Moys to Hanger, "the likeness is complete."

"It is wonderful."

"We shall succeed, if the Prince be but there."

"Of course we shall. Hush!"

Mrs. Monday had rather a cloud upon her brow, for the magnificent cloak certainly cast her ball preparations into the shade.

"Well, I'm sure, Maria Jane," she said, "you are fortunate, for there are few such polite men as Captain Smith."

This was intended as a hit at Major Hanger, but he would not take it: he knew perfectly well that Mrs. Monday would not let her envy go so far as to deprive her of the visit to the ball; and if it had, he would have been all the better pleased, since she was not wanted there at all, and was only taken as a kind of necessity in the arrangement which conducted Maria Jane to the festive scene.

The fact was, that the circumstances of Sir Hinckton Moys and Major Hanger were not in a very flourishing condition; and although they were both working for the purposes of the Marchioness of Sunningham, that personage was not sufficiently liberal to supply her myrmidons with cash.

Had the Marchioness filled the pockets of Sir Hinckton Moys, which it certainly would have been wise to do, Mrs. Monday would have had no reason to complain of any want of liberality on the part of Captain Smith.

But all that could not be helped, and the anticipation of approaching pleasure at the ball overcame every other consideration.

By ten o'clock the little party started, and the short distance was traversed amid so much laughter and delight on the part of the ladies, and so many gallant speeches from the Major and the Captain, that they never had been so well pleased in their lives.

Poor Monday was entirely forgotten; and, in fact, so far as he was concerned, he might have hidden himself deep in the centre of the earth.

The scene of gaiety and excitement in Oxford Street, on the occasion of this ball at the Pantheon, carried with it all the charms of bustle and excitement which were sure to be pleasing to minds constituted as were those of Mrs. Monday and Maria Jane.

A throng of coaches blocked the entrance.

Link-boys, porters, footmen, and visitors in gay dresses, seemed to be all mingled together in one scene of confusion.

The road traffic in Oxford Street was not at that period anything like what it is now in some of the second-rate streets of London.

The few hundred spectators, therefore, that had collected to see the guests of the ball arrive in their fancy costumes, were scarcely incommoded by the few passing vehicles that lumbered along the thoroughfare.

Mrs. Monday was in ecstacies.

Maria Jane almost screamed with delight.

The portals of the theatre were passed.

A few more seconds, and amid a blaze of light, and a dazzling sensation of many colours, the party made their way into the ample space produced by the pit of the theatre being boarded over level with the stage.

The music struck up a lively measure, and all seemed gaiety and excitement.

How much treachery may be hidden by the beauty and glitter of such a scene!

Moys and Hanger found an opportunity to whisper to each other.

"You must get the old one out of the way," said Sir Hinckton. "If the Prince should come, it will be within the next hour."

"You think so?" replied Hanger, drily.

"I certainly do. But what do you mean?—you speak doubtingly."

"Then I will speak certainly."

"You are quite enigmatical, Hanger. What on earth do you mean?"

"Nothing particular, only that he is here!"

"The Regent?"

"Exactly so, in his own proper person."

"Alone? Where?"

"Over there, in the corner of that private box; but not alone—some one is with him. Ah! I see now—it is Sheridan."

"By Jove, yes! There is no mistaking the contour of his head and shoulders. I see him, Hanger."

"Of course you do! And now I should say it's all plain sailing with us. Leave me to amuse the female Monday; and then, the moment you see the eyes of any one tolerably young and tolerably good-looking directed with admiration upon Maria Jane, make an excuse to leave her alone for a few minutes. She will be sure, then, to be accosted; and I don't think she's a young lady born to be cruel. Leave the rest to chance and good luck. I feel a presentiment that all will go well."

"Hanger," muttered Moys, "you're a far cleverer fellow than I took you to be. We shall succeed now, without a doubt; and I seem to feel as if a new fortune were within my grasp—a fortune which you shall share."

"All's right! Now for the ladies!"

Major Hanger turned to Mrs. Monday, and assuming the blandest possible manner, he said, "I really don't see what we have to do, now, with my friend Captain Smith and Maria Jane. Let them take their own course. We shall easily meet in a few hours."

"Oh, certainly, Major Brown! Maria Jane is a girl who can take care of herself· and yet we poor, sensitive women are so weak!"

"Nay, Mrs. Monday, do not say that! It is we men who are weak, when we fall a victim to the charms of your delightful sex! Will you dance, or shall we have some refreshment?"

The word "refreshment" always had a pleasant sound with it to Mrs. Monday.

"I think, Major Brown, we will have some refreshment first, and dance afterwards."

"That is precisely my opinion, dear madam! This way, if you please."

While Major Hanger was thus drawing off the attention of Mrs. Monday, Sir Hinckton Moys, with his usual tact and discretion, was making the fair Maria Jane entirely subservient to his purposes—purposes so treacherous and so dastardly, that, with all her frivolity of character, love of admiration, and want of reflective power, she would have shrunk aghast from playing the part she was unwittingly playing in that drama of real life, had she but comprehended its full purport.

CHAPTER CCXXVII.

THE REGENT IS ASTONISHED AND AFFLICTED AT THE SUPPOSED PERFIDY OF THE COUNTESS DE BLONDE.

THE likeness of Maria Jane to Annie was certainly marvellous.

There were differences, no doubt; and had they been together in that ball-room, and similarly attired, those differences would have been seen at a glance.

Maria Jane was a trifle larger, take her for all in all, than Annie, who had no pretensions to being what is called a fine woman.

But the difference was very trifling indeed.

A mere line or two in height, and a shade in width.

That was all.

The colour of the hair was as exact as could be.

The shape of the face, too, and the complexion; and, along with those particulars, there was the accidental movement and carriage—which, it is to be presumed, belong to certain physical organizations—which were so like Annie's, that the delusion was quite wonderful.

Sir Hinckton Moys kept his eyes upon that private box, as if by a species of fascination, for there he felt confident he still saw the Regent, notwithstanding the artful manner in which Sheridan had had him disguised, from the ample resources of Drury Lane Theatre.

It was the object of Moys gradually to get Maria Jane to proceed in the direction of what might be called, on that occasion, the royal box; and then he fully intended to carry out the plan of operations laid down by Major Hanger.

"Well, this is delightful!" he said, looking into her eyes with a pleased smile.

"Oh, it's all beautiful!" exclaimed Maria Jane.

"You mean the ball, and the scene around us; and there I perfectly agree with you; but what I meant to allude to was the departure of Mrs. Monday. I am so pleased to have you all to myself—and surprised, as well as pleased; for between you and I, my dear, I cannot imagine what my friend Major Brown can see in Mrs. Monday."

Maria Jane laughed immensely.

"Nor I either, Captain Smith—nor I either; but there's no accounting for tastes in love."

"Not in the least—not in the least; only there can be no dispute concerning the admiration with which all eyes must behold the lovely Maria Jane."

Insensibly to herself, and by slow degrees, Sir Hinckton Moys had led the young girl to the immediate neighbourhood of the private box in which were ensconced so snugly the Regent and Sheridan.

Then he looked about for some admirer into whose hands he could transfer Maria Jane; for he did not like exactly to trust to the chance of recognition, when the eyes of the Regent or of Sheridan should actually fall upon that excellent imitation of the Countess de Blonde, and, at the same time, upon whoever might be her companion.

Chance favoured him.

A gentlemanly-looking young man, dressed in

an Albanian costume, and with a profusion of glossy, dark hair—either natural, or acquired by a visit to the *perruquier*—was evidently regarding Maria Jane with admiration.

It was not at all a matter of surprise that such should be the case; for, as may be presumed, she could not possibly be so very like Annie, without being, at the same time, very fair to look upon.

Sir Hinckton Moys made up his mind what to do in a moment.

Turning to Maria Jane, he whispered in soft accents, "In order that we should fully enjoy all that is here to be enjoyed, and participate in all the gratifications with which this place abounds, it is necessary that I should speak to the master of the ceremonies."

"Oh, yes, certainly! Let us see everything and enjoy everything."

"Then you will not be offended if I leave you for a few minutes in the care of that gentleman?"

No. 101.—DARK WOMAN.

"Which? which?"

"There—with the black hair."

"Oh, gemini! what a beautiful dress! I declare, Captain Smith, you may leave me as long as you like—that is, no—I don't mean exactly——"

"Pray make no excuses. I like that natural candour, which adorns you as much as it does your beauty."

There certainly could be no comparison whatever between Sir Hinckton Moys and the gentleman with the glossy hair and Albanian costume, in regard to personal appearance.

But Moys was not at all afflicted at the evident preference which the representative of Annie, the Countess, gave to the stranger over himself.

It was just what he desired; and as he did not care a button about her, he was quite ready and willing to resign her to the glittering and handsome Albanian.

Stepping up to this strange gentleman, with something of the well-bred, courtly air which the atmosphere of St. James's had taught him, Sir Hinckton Moys, with a slight bow, addressed him.

"Sir," he said, "would you have any objection, as a matter of courtesy from one gentleman to another, to take charge of this young lady for a short time?"

"That young lady with the velvet cloak and the fair hair?"

"That is the lady, sir."

"None in the least, sir, I can assure you. On the contrary, I—that is to say, I am very happy to oblige you, sir."

Sir Hinckton Moys smiled and bowed.

The gentleman in the Albanian costume smiled and bowed likewise.

Moys then made his way among the throng of dancers and guests, while the handsome young man with the glossy dark hair made his way up to the side of the delighted and pleased Maria Jane.

"Your protector," he said—"the gentleman who was recently with you—has deputed to me the pleasing task of remaining with you until his return."

"Oh, sir, you are too good!"

"Not at all—I am only too fortunate. Will you accept my arm?"

Maria Jane readily enough accepted it.

A handsome, pleasant, radiant-looking couple they looked: she so fair, and we might almost say beautiful; and he presenting so striking a contrast, in the real or artificial sun-tint which was upon his face, and that raven black hair which waved about it.

Surely Fate was propitious to Sir Hinckton Moys and Major Hanger, for every accident in the whole of that evening favoured their designs.

Maria Jane had not been one minute resting upon the arm of the handsome young man in the Albanian costume, before the eyes of both the Regent and Sheridan fell upon her.

Exclamations burst from their lips at the same moment; and the Regent, as he almost fell backward, trod on the toes of Sheridan with such force, that he extorted from him a shout of pain.

"By heaven!" cried the Prince, "it is she!"

"Corns! corns!" cried Sheridan; "and your Highness is no light weight."

"Eh? What's the matter?"

"If your Royal Highness will condescend to take your royal foot off my toe——"

"Oh! ah!—very good! But I feel sick. Sheridan — Sheridan, are your eyes better, or worse, than mine? Tell me—for the love of peace, and of heaven, and by Jove!—if that is Annie?"

The Regent was rather profane in his language, but he was in a state of excitement at that moment, which made it excusable.

Sheridan answered him promptly.

"I have had the honour of seeing the young lady who has recently had the felicity of attracting your Royal Highness's regards; and having had that honour, I have no hesitation in saying that I behold her now."

The Regent drew a long breath, and sunk back into a corner of the box.

"Your Royal Highness is indisposed."

"I am—I am! Oh, Annie, Annie! nothing but my own eyesight would convince me that you could serve me in this fashion! And the very cloak, too, that I always admired so much! Annie! Annie! Annie!"

"Your Royal Highness is worse."

"Much worse," replied the Regent, with a groan.

"Shall I try and get a glass of brandy?"

"No, no, no!"

"Then I'm sure your Royal Highness is worse than ever I knew you to be; for I never heard of your being near so bad, but that that was a specific."

"Alas! alas! Why could she not be happy and contented as she was? I'm sure I was liberal to her; and she had everything she wanted. There never were such suppers as she had. Look again, Sheridan—look again!"

"It's of no use, your Royal Highness, looking again—once is enough."

"But the beast?—the beast?"

"The what?"

"The beast in the Greek dress?"

"Oh, the fellow?"

"Yes! Do you know him?"

"No—yes! Let me look again! Ah, to be sure! It's the young Marquis of Bristol—about as good-looking a fellow, I should say, as you'll find here or there."

The Regent uttered three awful groans.

"Really, your Highness," interposed Sheridan. "I would not take this so much to heart. A pretty girl like this fair Annie, whom you call Countess de Blonde, will be sure to have her little vagaries now and then; and whoever advised you to come here to watch her—and who, I recollect now, your Highness informed me, was that fellow Moys—certainly does not deserve to be ranked among your Highness's friends."

"That's all very well," said the Regent sadly; "but there she is, after solemnly assuring me that she was going to stay at home; and here I see her in company with a young man notorious for his amours, and who I did not think she was in the slightest degree acquainted with. O falsehood! O duplicity, duplicity! thy name is Annie!"

There was something of the pathetic, as well as something of the ludicrous, in the style in which the Regent uttered these words.

Sheridan, the thorough man of the world and lively and accomplished dramatist, was just the person to appreciate and enjoy this serio-comic distress of the Prince of Wales.

Biting his lips to suppress his laughter, he replied as seriously as he could, "Ah, your Highness! it is the old story, from the beginning of the world to the end. Women will always be after the forbidden fruit, I fancy."

"Yes, yes! Oh, Annie, what can you see in that fellow?"

By this time the young Marquis of Bristol had succeeded—no difficult task—in making himself specially agreeable to Maria Jane.

We have said that in regard to personal advantages he had every possible reason to feel satisfied with himself; and it was not likely that the fair Maria Jane would be quite blind to the difference between the very handsome young nobleman and the faded middle-aged roue, Sir Hinckton Moys.

Accordingly her inclinations chimed in very well with not only the solicitations of the Marquis, but likewise the hopes of Moys, who seriously wished that the young nobleman would be so obliging as to take her off his hands, since he had done with her, and did not wish to be troubled with her any longer.

"I presume," said the Marquis of Bristol, in most insinuating terms,—"I presume that was your father who left you in my care just now?"

"Oh, no, no!"

"Your uncle, then?"

"No—he is—he—he—is——"

"Good heavens! you do not mean to say that he is your husband?"

"No, no! I have no husband."

"What a relief!"

"But—but——"

"But what, fairest of the fair?"

The Marquis hazarded that bit of flattery, just to see how anything in such a strain would be received.

He had every possible reason to be satisfied with the result.

"He is a gentleman who wishes—that is to say, who is paying attention to me."

"Oh! is that all?"

"Yes, that is all."

"And do you like him? I may use a stronger term, and say, do you—can you love him?"

Maria Jane stole a glance at the fine eyes of the gay Marquis, and sighed.

"Ah, tell me," he added, "tell me, fair, beautiful girl—tell me that that man, who, by the bye, is quite old enough to be your grandfather, has not possession of your young heart?"

"Certainly not!"

"Oh, joy!"

"And, if I ever love——"

"Well, dear one? If you ever love?"

"It will be some one who is young and handsome, and with dark, glossy hair, and such sweet eyes!"

The Marquis smiled.

He pressed the hand of Maria Jane.

The pressure was returned.

"Now, my dear girl," he said, "who is this elderly beau of yours?"

"Captain Smith."

The Marquis shook his head.

"Are you sure of that?"

"He says he is Captain Smith; and he was introduced by his friend, Major Brown."

"Are you sure Major Brown is a Major Brown, my dear?"

"No, I know nothing of him."

"Then, you may depend upon it, they are a couple of adventurers—perhaps sharpers, swindlers, or pickpockets!"

"Oh, gracious!"

"And I would advise you to have nothing more to do with either of them."

"But what can I do? They come to our house: they know—that is to say, they have picked up an acquaintance with Mrs. Monday."

"Never mind, Mrs. Monday, or Mrs. Tuesday, or any day of the week. Place yourself under my protection, and you will be happy. I am a gentleman; my fortune is ample, and I love you."

"Oh, my!"

"Indeed, I may tell you—since you will find out the fact soon—that I am a nobleman."

"Oh, gracious!"

"Don't be alarmed. I love you, and would make you mine."

"Yours? Your—your lady-wife?"

"Better than that."

"Better? How? how?"

The young Marquis was an adept in affairs of the heart; and he bent down until his glossy locks brushed the fair cheek of Maria Jane, and his lips just touched her brow, as he whispered, in honied accents, "You shall be my lady-love!"

The victory was won. Maria Jane yielded to the fascinations of the passion which love had lit up in her bosom, and from that hour she belonged to the young Marquis of Bristol.

Now, the Regent could not but see all this acted so palpably—although, to his observation, in pantomime, since he was too far off to hear what was said; and he felt quite sure that he saw the proof before his eyes of the perfidy of Annie.

"Sherry," he said, "I will go now."

"I am at your Highness's service; but if I might venture to suggest——"

"What, Sherry?"

"I would revenge myself upon this fickle fair one after her own fashion."

"How do you mean?"

"I would descend to the parterre, and pick out the fairest form and face I could see, and console myself for the loss of one by the acquisition of another."

The Regent shook his head.

"No, no! I cannot do that just now. The time perhaps will come; but the real truth is, that I never did care for any one half so much as for Annie. But I will get rid of her. She shall not sleep in St. James's Palace another night. On that point I am quite clear and resolved."

"As your Royal Highness pleases."

"So come along, Sherry. And—and yet I would fain—I would like——"

"What, your Highness?"

"That she should see me—that she should hear me speak—before I go."

"That is easily accomplished."

"You think so?"

"Oh, yes! Your Highness has but to come down to the parterre——Ah, there they go!"

"Who? Where?"

"The Marquis of Bristol, and the Countess de Blonde. There they go!"

"Ah, yes!"

CHAPTER CCXXVIII.

THE REGENT IS ASTONISHED AT THE AUDACITY OF ANNIE, AND LISTENS TO AN EXPENSIVE SUGGESTION FROM SHERIDAN.

THE mock Annie, but the real Maria Jane, had been with the young Marquis of Bristol to the refreshment saloon, where her judgment was not made any the clearer by imbibing some strong waters, which the Marquis took upon himself to recommend.

It was, then, evident to him that Maria Jane dreaded to meet with Captain Smith, so that, taking advantage of that apprehension, he had no difficulty in persuading her to leave the theatre with him.

He pressed her hand tenderly as he made the proposition, and, without a word of opposition, Maria Jane consented.

They were making their way evidently towards the doors, when Sheridan called the attention of the Regent towards them.

The expression on the face, then, of the Prince of Wales was one of concentrated fury.

"I will go down now, Sherry," he said. "I will go down to the parterre, and meet them face to face. I will go at once."

"Nay, your Highness. Would not that be rather a serious compromise of your dignity?"

"Yes, you are right; and yet——"

"And yet, your Highness would say, you do not like to let them go off in triumph in that easy fashion?"

"Just so!—just so!"

"Then, as I am tolerably familiar with the internal arrangements of this theatre, in common with all others in London,—I can, if your Royal Highness pleases, take you by a short cut to the lobby, where you can interrupt them as they pass out."

"The very thing, Sherry!—the very thing! Do so, at once. There is not a moment to lose. I don't know what I should have done to-night without you, Sherry."

"Your Royal Highness does me much honour."

Sheridan led the Prince, then, through a private door, of which he had a pass-key, and so on by some of those intricate passages which are to be found in all theatres, to the outer lobby.

They just reached it as the Marquis of Bristol and the fair Maria Jane were about to pass through it.

The Regent darted forward. He caught Maria Jane by the velvet cloak which he knew so perfectly well belonged to Annie, and, giving it rather a vigorous pluck, he cried out, "Ingrate! —ingrate!"

Maria Jane turned half round only, so that the Regent did not see all her face. If he had, perhaps even then he might have detected some of those differences between her and the real Annie, which would have, at the last moment, jeopardised the success of the plot of Sir Hinckton Moys and Major Hanger.

But it seemed as if, on that night, everything was to work successfully for the conspiracy against Annie, the Countess, and the Regent.

So small a portion, then, of Maria Jane's face was visible, that the Prince could not doubt her identity, close as he was to her.

"Ingrate! ingrate!" he cried again.

The Marquis of Bristol turned, and in rather a menacing manner, said, "What do you mean, sir?"

"What does the man mean?" said Maria Jane.

"Wretch!" said the Regent, again plucking at the cloak.

"My dear," said the Marquis, "do you know this person?"

"Certainly not."

The Regent stepped forward two steps, so that he was close to the left ear of Maria Jane.

"Annie, Annie!" he whispered; "you know my voice, although I am disguised!"

"Get along, ugly!" said Maria Jane.

The Regent recoiled.

Another moment, and the young Marquis of Bristol had led his prize from the lobby, and they were gone.

"This," said the Regent,—"this, Sherry, is the very height of assurance!"

"It was cool."

"I have done with her for ever and for ever!"

"So I suppose."

"I will go to the Palace, and wait for her; and when she does come in——"

"No, your Royal Highness, no! Let me, as a true, and, I hope, trusted friend, advise you not to do any such thing. Let to-night pass away, and in the cool judgment and daylight of to-morrow it will be time to act. To-night, you might for a moment forget the proper dignity of the Prince in the natural feelings of the man."

Sheridan knew perfectly well that any appeal to his dignity was sure of a favourable reception from the Regent.

"Be it so—be it so, then!" he said, with a sigh. "I will sleep at Carlton House; and to-morrow I will act. Sleep, did I say? Alas! I am afraid I shall not sleep to-night!"

"Then my sincere counsel to your Royal Highness is not to go to bed."

"Where can I go, then?"

"Your Highness is well disguised. Come to Crockford's, and pass away a few hours till the morning, in the saloons. We are sure of high company there; and perhaps since Venus has taken it into her head to be adverse to you to-night, who knows but the as fickle Goddess of Fortune may take you into favour, and you may win a few thousands?"

This suggestion was only too much in accordance with the taste of the Regent; and relying upon his disguise, he accompanied Sheridan to the notorious and historical gaming-house.

There it was, and that was the occasion on which the Regent lost the forty-two thousand pounds which were made such a rant about in the House of Commons, on the occasion of the Bill that was introduced that session by Mr. Walpole, to pay the Royal debts.

There were two persons who had been deeply interested spectators from one of the darkest of the private boxes of the Pantheon, of all that had taken place.

Those persons were Sir Hinckton Moys and Major Hanger.

The Major had got rid of Mrs. Monday. He had in the coolest possible manner deserted her in the throng of persons about the doors of the refreshment saloon.

Then, by previous arrangement, he joined Moys in the dark private box.

They smiled at each other.

"All's well!" said Moys.

"Charming!"

"Ha! ha! What a comedy!"

"It may end in a tragedy!"

"Oh, no, no! Only a domestic drama of startling interest and situations—that is all."

They continued from this same post of espial to watch the proceedings of Maria Jane and the Marquis of Bristol.

They kept an eye, too, on that box in which were Sheridan and the Regent.

But a feeling of alarm took possession of them both, when they saw the Regent and Sheridan abruptly retire from the box, as the Marquis of

Bristol and the fair Maria Jane made their way towards the doors from the parterre.

They felt that a critical moment, in all probability, had arrived.

"We must see this," said Moys.

'Certainly."

"Come on—come on, Major !"

They both reached the lobby at the moment that the Regent made that pluck at the velvet cloak of the supposed Annie; and they both saw and heard the little scene that took place.

"Good, Moys ! That will do !"

"Capitally ! And now, Moys, I think we may go to supper."

"With all my heart !"

"Where shall we go ?"

"Where our news will be most welcome, to be sure."

"And where is that ?"

"At Sunningham House. There, you may be assured, we shall find the Marchioness up and stirring, and the information we bring her will assure us a hearty welcome."

"Come on, then, Moys; and I am all the more pleased that you yourself propose this, because you would not introduce me to Sunningham House if you did not intend to keep faith with me."

"Did you doubt me ?"

"No, no !—I cannot say I did; but still every little circumstance that makes me feel certain that our fortunes hang together is pleasing."

"Let us take a coach, then, at once. I suppose you are out of cash, Hanger ?"

"Quite."

"Well, the Marchioness shall lend us, or give us, a couple of hundred guineas to-night; and you shall share them."

Moys felt quite confident that the news he took with him to Sunningham House would suffice even to open the purse of the sordid Marchioness.

He was quite right in his idea that she would be up. Indeed, he had felt a good deal of surprise not to see her at the Pantheon; but, although she had fully intended to be there, she had, upon second thoughts, considered it advisable not to show herself, as the Regent could hardly overlook her, and the sight of her might have had the effect of engendering in his mind some suspicions of a plot.

She knew so well the constitution of his mind, that anything in the shape of throwing herself in his way she felt certain would defeat her objects.

What he most ardently always sought after was what seemed to him inaccessible.

Truly might he have said—

"The flower that is easily plucked
Is not worth the plucking for me."

And the Marchioness was plotting and planning in her mind of many schemes, how, provided he sent Annie from the Palace, he could be persuaded that it would be very difficult to get her, the Marchioness of Sunningham, to supply the vacant place.

Her ladyship was in the midst of these cogitations and reflections when Sir Hinckton Moys "and another gentleman" were announced.

The smile upon the face of Moys spoke volumes to the Marchioness.

"All is well ?" she said.

"Better than well."

"You take away my breath," Sir Hinckton."

"Be calm, dear Marchioness. Annie, the Countess de Blonde, will not sleep another night at St. James's."

A flush of triumph was upon the somewhat large face of the Marchioness, as she said, "I hope she will never sleep anywhere again, the hussey !"

"Nay, madam," interposed Major Hanger. "She is decidedly pretty, and I know where I should like her to sleep."

"Ah !" who are you ?"

"Jack Hanger, my lady."

"Allow me," interposed Moys. "This is Major Hanger, Marchioness, of whom you have heard, no doubt, often."

"I have heard of him, and nothing to—to——"

Hanger laughed.

"Say it out, my lady. Nothing to his credit, you mean. I admit that the world gives me a bad name, but I don't quite deserve it—at least, no more than others. I am called a sad dog; but, if I am a dog at all, I at least have the one canine quality of being faithful to the hand that feeds me and uses me well."

"He is quite right," said Moys; "and I hope, Marchioness, you will take into your special favour the Major. It was at his suggestion that this affair, which I trust and hope will be the destruction of the Countess de Blonde, was set about."

The Marchioness smiled graciously on Major Hanger.

"Be it so," she said. "I will take good care of all who have helped me."

"A thousand thanks, madam !"

Moys then related to the gratified Marchioness all that had taken place at the Pantheon; and when he had concluded, the Marchioness fairly clapped her hands together with joy, as she cried out, "Then the reign of that girl is over ?"

"Yes, Marchioness; and yours will soon begin."

"I will hope so."

"Be sure of it; but just now we, your faithful friends, want a little accommodation."

"Certainly—beds and a supper ?"

Moys smiled.

"Something else, Marchioness. We want the sinews of war—money !"

"Money ?"

"Yes, Marchioness; and I make bold to ask you for a couple of hundred guineas to-night !"

The Marchioness frowned.

"So soon," she said, "as I am installed at the Palace, and have the private purse of the Regent in my hands, come to me for double the amount."

Moys laughed.

Hanger echoed the laugh.

"No, no, Marchioness !" said Moys. "We cannot wait. Our present necessities cry out aloud. What sum, now, my dear Marchioness, do you suppose Annie, the Countess de Blonde, would give for a real and faithful relation of all the events of to-night at the Pantheon Theatre ?"

The Marchioness turned pale.

"Wait here a few moments, Sir Hinckton Moys, and I will fetch you the money."

"A thousand thanks !"

CHAPTER CCXXIX.

A STRANGE SCENE TAKES PLACE IN THE TITIAN
GALLERY OF OLD ST. JAMES'S PALACE.

IT was about half-past ten o'clock on the morning following the ball at the Pantheon, that Annie was handed, in her own private apartments, a note from the Regent.

The note was sealed, and addressed to Annie.

The contents were short, but very much to the purpose:—

"St. James's, Sunday morning.

"The person named Annie, and at times called, in sport, the Countess de Blonde, will, by order of his Royal Highness the Regent, leave St. James's Palace before sunset.

"His Royal Highness will, at any time that he may be convinced the person named Annie, and called in sport the Countess de Blonde, is leading a quiet and respectable life, alone, grant her an annuity, from the privy purse, of one thousand pounds per annum."

There was a slight quiver upon the lips of Annie, as she read this note.

She turned, and looked at the attendants who were in the room.

"Pack——" she began to say; and then she checked herself, and added, "No, I have nothing to pack—I will take nothing."

She clasped her hands over her face for a few seconds, and then she asked herself, in a whisper, "What does it mean? What is the cause of this? What have I done or said? Or is it but the cruel exhibition of the caprice of which I have heard so much, but never till now believed to be true?"

The attendants saw that something serious was the matter; and one girl, who had been specially attentive to Annie, and treated by her in return with great kindness, burst into tears as she approached her, saying, "Oh, dear, dear madam! what has happened?"

"Nothing particular," replied Annie. "I am going—that is all."

"Going?"

"Going?" repeated the other attendants.

"Yes. The Regent is tired of me."

No sooner had Annie uttered these ominous words, than she was left completely alone, with the exception of that one girl, who was really attached to her.

Annie smiled.

"Mary," she said, "pray get some one to send or go for Captain Fitz George."

"Yes, madam—yes."

The girl flung herself upon her knees at the feet of Annie.

"What's the matter, Mary? What do you want?"

"To go with you, madam—to wait on you—to be your servant still, wherever you may be—wherever you may go."

"So you shall; and yet I am afraid——Well, never mind. We won't part yet."

The girl was delighted, and hastened upon her errand to find Captain Fitz George, who happened to be on guard at the Palace.

In less than half an hour he was with Annie.

She handed him the Regent's letter, which he read with surprise; and yet there was, along with that surprise, some faint feeling of satisfaction.

Why was that?

It arose simply from this one feeling.

Situated as he was—the son of the Regent, and the husband of Annie's sister—it was not an agreeable thing for him to feel that it was well known to every one so near a connexion of his by marriage was the mistress of the Regent.

He had always looked forward, likewise, to the time when some such incident as that which now fell upon Annie like a thunder-clap should take place.

But still he was so far from expecting it on that occasion, that he looked all the surprise that he really felt, and was quite incapable for some time of answering Annie's inquiring glances.

"Well," she said, "what do you think of that, Allan?"

She still frequently called him Allan, from old association with the name.

"I know not what to think of it, Annie. It is cruelly precise and formal, and forces from me the question of 'What do you mean to do?'"

"Do?" cried Annie, while the colour mounted to her cheek, and even to her brow—"do, Allan? Go, of course. I shall remain not another hour in St. James's, feeling that I am unwelcome."

"You are perfectly right, Annie."

"I'm quite sure of that. And now, Allan, for what I sent for you. You must do me a favour, and do it at once."

"Do you think I would hesitate? No, Annie. I can guess the favour you require, if it may be called such; and you may look upon it as done—or rather, I should say, unnecessary to do. You wish me to go to Marian, and prepare her for your arrival at our home; but be assured, Annie, that that is unnecessary. You will be welcome, come when and how you will; and I myself will accompany you."

Annie rose, and paced the room twice. She then, for some few seconds, looked from the window into one of the court-yards of St. James's. There was a determination upon her mind that she would not betray the emotion which was struggling from her heart to her eyes and to her lips.

By a great effort, she succeeded.

She was enabled to speak to Captain Fitz George with apparent composure.

"No, Allan—that was not what I wanted to say to you."

"I am glad to hear it, Annie."

"Indeed!"

"Yes; because it shows me you put faith in our affection for you, by considering it unnecessary to send me on such a message to Marian."

"Oh, you mistake me still—you mistake me still! Do you believe—can you believe that I would disgrace your happy and peaceful home by my presence?"

"Hush, Annie—hush! Not a word of that!"

"Yes, Allan—there must be a word of that. I say, and ought to say, that such a notion never came into my head. No, Allan! I am what I am; and I will take my shame, be assured, far away from your threshold."

"Oh, Annie, Annie! do not speak in that

fashion! I will not say—because it would be to falsify the truth—that your position, as regards the Regent, has not been deeply and painfully regretted both by Marian and by myself. I may, indeed, go so far as to add that the knowledge of that position has been the one cloud in the otherwise bright sky of her happiness; but still I will say that, if you would add to that distress, it will be by refusing to come to us, and by withdrawing yourself from an affection that is ever ready to receive you."

"No," said Annie; "it can't be—it can't be, and it ought not to be. You will feel that some day, and so will Marian. Don't talk about it any more, because it only, you see, distresses me. But what I want you to do is this:—go to Marian, and tell her what has happened, and ask her to send me some clothes; for, as I live, I'll take nothing from St. James's Palace that the Regent can call his own."

"Nay, Annie, you are entitled——"

"Hush!—don't plague me! I've made up my mind, and there's an end of it. Go to Marian, and ask her to send me some things."

"But, Annie——"

"Do you want me to walk out without any, which I must do if you won't go?"

"I will do as you wish, Annie, in every way; while I still will not abandon the hope that you may take up your abode with us."

"Stuff! stuff!" cried Annie. "Now be off, at once!"

Captain Fitz George left the private and luxurious apartments of Annie, the Countess; but before he repaired to Marian to inform her of what had occurred, and to communicate to her the message with which Annie had charged him, he felt an irresistible desire to solicit an interview with the Regent.

That desire grew upon him momentarily, as he walked the length of the Titian Gallery; and yet his reason and his feelings did not sanction it, but, on the contrary, battled with it in every possible way.

What was he to say to his father, the Regent, on the subject?

Was he to ask him to continue a connexion which he ought to feel gratified at his discontinuing?

Was he to demand from him reasons for putting an end to a state of things which, in themselves, were well put an end to in any way?

Such was the mode in which Captain Fitz George must reasonably view the affair; but still the ardent desire to see the Regent upon the subject clung to him, and the conviction grew upon his mind each moment that the Prince was acting under some delusion, and that Annie and he were separating as a consequence of the successful completion of some plot of the real enemies of both.

It was this latter consideration, probably, that stirred up Captain Fitz George more than any other, to try and fathom the mystery that surrounded the whole affair.

The day was young—there was plenty of time—he had never yet been denied an audience of his father; and accordingly, seeking Willes, the valet, who was generally the medium of his requests to see the Regent, he, with as much calmness as he could muster, solicited the interview.

There was an anxious and confused look upon the face of Willes.

Without being fully aware of all that had happened, the valet knew, from some disjointed expressions that had fallen from his royal master, that the dismissal of Annie was a fact accomplished.

In that dismissal Willes saw imminent danger to himself.

Who might be the successor of the Countess de Blonde was a matter that concerned him very materially.

He looked most wistfully in the face of Captain Fitz George, as though he would gladly talk over the matter with him, if he were so permitted.

Willes, however, met with no encouragement, and he was fain to go at once to the Regent with the message of the young officer, soliciting to see him.

The reply was a refusal.

"Be it so," said Fitz George: "no one, less than myself, would wish to intrude upon the Regent."

Captain Fitz George then, with hasty strides, was taking his way through the Titian Gallery, as being the nearest route from the Palace, when a door that was seldom used suddenly opened, and in a morning dress the Regent appeared.

At sight of Fitz George he seemed inclined to retreat, but then immediately checking the inclination, he accosted him with his usual friendliness.

"Oh, Fitz George, that's you, is it? Sorry—very sorry we're so busy this morning. Come to us to-morrow—come to us to-morrow. What you have to say will keep, eh?"

"As long as your Highness pleases."

"Very good—very good! Ah!"

The door of Annie's apartments had suddenly opened, and she looked out, exclaiming "Are you not gone yet, Allan? I'm sure I've heard you walking about here ever so long."

The Regent made a blundering attempt to get through the doorway from which he had just emerged, but in the confusion of the moment he ran against the wall of the gallery, striking himself rather sharply; and then, as if to add to the complication of the scene, a groom of the chambers approached, and bowing low to the Regent, spoke in soft, silken accents.

"May it please your Royal Highness, Sir Hinckton Moys waits your pleasure."

"That's it!" cried Annie, as she clapped her hands together. "Now I know all about it. George, you're an idiot! Moys has set another trap for you, and caught you this time! What was on the hook, eh? Toasted cheese?"

The Regent made a wry face as he repeated the words, "toasted cheese;" but before any one could make any further remark, Sir Hinckton Moys, in a rich, costly, new Court suit, advanced slowly up the gallery, and at sight of the Regent, bowed low, almost to the very floor.

Willes then committed an act of audacity—perhaps the greatest he had ever committed; but he was urged to it by the circumstances of the moment, and by the conviction that if things were let go on as they were proceeding, his tenure of office in St. James's Palace must very soon come to a close.

It appeared that he had been immediately behind the Regent, when he issued forth from that seldom used doorway into the Titian Gallery; and now, as several persons were there assembled, Willes suddenly wheeled out a gilt arm-chair, which he stopped abruptly immediately behind his royal master, and he cried out, "His Royal Highness will be seated."

The Regent turned, and looked at Willes with amazement. Not that he could see much of the valet, for the latter executed so low a bow, that the Prince would have had to look right over the back of the chair to see him.

Willes then disappeared into the apartment from whence he had issued, but he returned with extraordinary quickness, carrying a gold salver in his hand, on which was a small exquisitely cut glass, the contents of which sent the unmistakable aroma of brandy over the Titian Gallery.

The offering was irresistible.

In all difficulties. whether mental or physical, a glass of brandy was a favourite specific of the Regent.

And now that he seemed by a series of extraordinary accidents compelled to hold a sort of court in the Titian Gallery, and give audience to several persons, he felt that he could not have a better preparation than the tempting glass ef *eau de vie*, which Willes so respectfully handed to him.

The Regent lifted the glass.

He drank the brandy.

He sank down then in a chair, with a sigh of relief, and seemed to prepare himself for some scene, which perhaps might require yet another glass of the same stimulant before he could get successfully through with it.

Perhaps the most embarrassed person there present was Sir Hinckton Moys. He had been sent for by the Regent, who had repented somewhat of his manner towards him on the previous day, after finding, or fancying he had found, that the information conveyed to him in the letter was true.

The very last person, however, that Moys was desirous of encountering in St. James's was Annie, the Countess; and but that he feared something might be said or done in his absence, which he might by his presence counteract, he would gladly have fled from the scene.

As it was, however, he summoned all his assurance to his aid, and remained

The Regent looked from one to the other in rather a confused manner, as though he expected somebody to begin to say something which would produce a scene of recrimination. But no one spoke for some seconds.

Annie, the Countess, then seemed to nave made up her mind what to do.

She stepped close up to the Regent, and looked him in the face.

"I've had your letter," she said; "and of course the only answer you want to it—or are likely to get—will consist in my absence. Make your mind easy—such as it is—I'm going."

The Regent drew back his head as far as he could to the back of the chair, as if he feared some assault from Annie.

"I can very well understand," she added, "why you're sitting there. You want to see that I don't make away with anything that don't belong to me; and that's very right and prudent of you, George, indeed."

"No, no!" said the Regent—"no such thing! Take all—everything!"

"Oh, nonsense! All I hope is, that you'll be as watchful of other people. I don't know what has become of the clothes I brought here with me Stop! Yes, I do! Bless us! Hurrah!"

The Regent drew back again a little further.

"Hurrah!" again shouted Annie. "They're in a drawer! I'll take off these, and put on the others in half a minute."

The Regent looked hurt and mortified.

It was strange how very sensitive that royal personage was, on many occasions, when his own feelings were concerned; and how entirely regardless he was usually of those of other people.

Captain Fitz George now lost some of his temper, some of his patience, and some of his discretion. He took two steps towards Sir Hinckton Moys, as he said, "I feel well convinced that, whatever may be the sort of misunderstanding that has taken place, this bold, bad man is at the bottom of it."

Moys looked savage.

"And," added Captain Fitz George, "he may be assured that, if I live and he live for the next four-and-twenty hours, he shall render to me an account of his actions."

"Peace—peace, Fitz George!" said the Regent. "Is this proper before me?"

Captain Fitz George bowed, and spoke in a low, gentle tone of voice.

"No, your Royal Highness; but at the moment I forgot myself, in the thought that this man should have succeeded in poisoning your ears against one who has been as true to you as steel."

CHAPTER CCXXX

ANNIE, THE COUNTESS, LEAVES THE PALACE, AND SIR HINCKTON MOYS QUARRELS WITH MAJOR HANGER.

CAPTAIN FITZ GEORGE, as he uttered those words to the Regent with which the last chapter concluded, quite forgot all his prudent ideas about Annie, and he found himself unwittingly advocating a continuance of her residence in St. James's as the mistress of the Prince.

But Sir Hinckton Moys was by no means oblivious of that fact.

A cold, sneering smile came over his face, and he spoke with an acid bitterness which showed deep resentment against Fitz George.

"Captain Fitz George does well to advocate the cause of the lady who, to him, fulfils the two conditions of sister to his wife and mistress to his father."

If ever any man deeply repented of uttering a few imprudent words, Sir Hinckton Moys was that man, so soon as that little acrimonious speech had passed his lips.

He had been sent for by the Regent on that morning, and had looked upon his restoration to power, and to place, and favour, and fortune, as things all but settled.

But what had he done now?

Dashed at one rash, fell blow all those fair and glittering prospects to the dust.

The look that the Regent gave him could not be mistaken.

So far as the royal favour was concerned, Sir Hinckton Moys was a doomed and a lost man from that minute.

Captain Fitz George placed his hand upon his sword-hilt, and the colour flew from his heart to his cheeks, and then as rapidly retreating, left him of a death-like paleness.

What he would have said—what he would have done—under the sting of that taunt from Sir Hinckton Moys, we cannot tell, for the Regent immediately rose and placed a hand upon his arm.

"No, Fitz George—no! It is our province and our right to speak."

Fitz George bowed.

Sir Hinckton Moys looked livid with rage and apprehension.

The Regent turned slowly towards him. He spoke in tones of suppressed passion.

"Sir Hinckton Moys, henceforward, if you are

No. 102.—DARK WOMAN.

ever found within the doors, or beneath the roof, of any dwelling that can call me its master, I will have you treated as a common felon, who has made his way there for purposes of theft. Now, sir, go!"

"Your Highness!"

"Go, sir!"

Moys drew himself up to his full height, and he cast a withering look about him, which would speedily have been fatal, if looks could by any means have killed any one.

First at the Regent, then at Annie, and then at Captain Fitz George, he cast that look; and then he burst into a hideous, mocking laugh, as he cried aloud, "Be it so—be it so, then! I accept a banishment from the dignified and moral Court of St. James's, uttered with so much precision by the modern Sardanapalus Ha! ha! Perhaps it may be possible to exist somewhere else, since the free air of heaven blows quite as sweetly, and perhaps more so, than about the purlieus of a Court!"

The Regent looked almost dignified as he called out, "Now, Sir Hinckton Moys, the door!"

"Oh, your Royal Highness, I am going! Pray do not trouble yourself with any ceremonies! I am going; but I leave a few legacies behind me. Ha! ha!"

Moys slowly retreated backwards along the length of the gallery as he spoke.

"Yes, a few legacies behind me! To you, O Regent of England, I leave the prospect of a life of disease and remorse! To you, Annie—sometimes called Countess de Blonde—I leave the fate which will sooner or later follow the career you have chosen—a death of destitution and despair, when the beauty that tempted men to think you a divinity shall have faded away and be seen no more."

"Oh, thank you!" said Annie. "Of course one must grow old and plain; but still it is a dreadful thing to begin by being such a fright as you must always have been!"

"To you, young sir," added Moys, addressing himself to Fitz George, "I will leave a different legacy. You comprehend me?"

Moys slightly touched the hilt of the Court sword he wore.

"I do comprehend you!" replied Captain Fitz George; "I comprehend you perfectly, and——'

"No," interposed the Regent, — "no, Fitz George! I place a solemn interdict upon any duel with that man. Fitz George, it must not—cannot be!"

The young officer bowed.

"You hear, sir," he said. "I am in a position which makes obedience to the commands of the Regent a double duty."

"And a convenient one, too!" said Moys. "Ha! ha!"

He turned, and left the gallery.

"Oh, father! Prince!" said Captain Fitz George, in a low, plaintive tone—"I pray you to permit me to chastise the insolence of that man."

"No, no—I have said it! No, Fitz George, I will not permit it."

Captain Fitz George bowed with a sigh.

"And now," added the Regent, "I will say one thing to you, Annie."

"Go on, George!"

"It is just this, Annie——"

"Well, why don't you say it? What a time you are about it, to be sure!"

"If you will confess all——"

"Oh, yes!"

"You will?"

"Of course I will, as soon as I know what it is. One likes to know what one has got to confess. Come, now, what is it?"

"If you will confess where you went last night between the hours of ten and eleven——"

"Oh, is that all?"

"If, I say, you will confess, and promise that for the future no such thing shall ever happen, I will forget and forgive all!"

"That's very kind, but I can't!"

"You cannot?"

"Certainly not. I don't mind the confessing part a bit!"

"Oh, oh, Annie!"

"Oh, oh, George!"

"Alas—alas! Is it possible that you do not care about the exposure of your acts, and yet that you will not even promise to avoid their repetition?"

"That's it!"

Captain Fitz George looked from the Regent to Annie, and from Annie to the Regent, in surprise and bewilderment as to what all this could mean.

The fair Countess de Blonde was as much in the dark as regarded it as he was, and she looked inquiringly at the Regent.

"Confess!" he said,—"confess, then!"

"Oh, that's easy! I went——"

"Ah, I know!"

"You mean, you guess?"

"No; I saw you."

"Then you must have been in the cupboard, and looking through a keyhole. I'm ashamed of you, George—it's mean! At ten o'clock, I confess, I went——"

"Yes, yes!"

"To bed!"

"To bed?"

"Exactly; and shall I tell you why? Or, perhaps, you have heard it before. I went to bed, because—because, you see, the bed would not come to me!"

"Annie, Annie, this frivolity is dreadful! Do you persist in that statement?"

"I do."

"Then—then——"

"Well, what then?"

"We part for ever!"

"Indeed! And all because I won't promise never to go to bed again! Very well. If you are mad, I am not!"

"Annie, I would believe no one, and nothing, but the evidence of my own eyes. Farewell, once and for ever!"

The Regent turned hastily, and darted from the Titian Gallery.

Annie, and Captain Fitz George, and Willes, the valet, were the only persons now in that part of the Palace, and they looked at each other, for some few moments, in silence.

It was Annie who broke the spell that seemed to have come over them, by saying, "Do you know, Willes, what all this means?"

"Not exactly, Countess."

"But do you know at all, Willes?" said the young Captain Fitz George.

"I know just this much, sir—that his Royal Highness has an impression on his mind that he actually saw the Countess de Blonde at a ball given at the Pantheon last night."

"Saw me?"

"Yes, Countess—I heard him say so; and he keeps on appealing, as against all his other convictions, to the evidence of his own senses."

"This is some singular delusion, Annie," said Fitz George.

"Well, I don't know anything about it, but I shall go at once. Will you be so good as to wait here for me, Allan?"

"I will, Annie."

"Very good."

With all the apparent composure in the world—for Annie had a brave heart—she went into that suite of rooms opening from the Titian Gallery, which she was to look upon for the last time.

After an absence of about a quarter of an hour, she returned.

Captain Fitz George uttered an exclamation of surprise, and, despite all he could do to prevent them, tears rushed to his eyes.

There was Annie, in the same dress that she had worn at the masquerade—the dress of a "Folly," so fanciful, and so theatrical; and she held in her hand the little Phrygian cap, with its tinkling bells.

"Come, Allan," she said. "This is clothing that, at all events, I can take with me. I will call upon Marian, with you, and she will lend me some other clothes. Come!"

Captain Fitz George took Annie on his arm.

"Good bye, Willes—good bye, old fellow! I wish you all sorts of luck."

"No, no! I——God—bless—you!"

Willes actually cried.

Annie shook her little cap and bells, and walked along the gallery with Captain Fitz George, who called out, when he got to the little hall at the foot of the stairs, "Will some one get me a coach?"

Some one did so, and he and Marian, in another five minutes, left St. James's Palace.

Two men stood close to the clock-turret, as the coach passed out; and one of them uttered a loud, dissonant laugh, and pointed at the vehicle.

It was Sir Hinckton Moys.

The person with him was Major Hanger.

Annie only shook her cap and bells.

The coach took its course, and in another quarter of an hour Annie was in the arms of her sister—her still loving, tender-hearted sister Marian.

Moys and Hanger regarded each other for some few seconds in silence, and then it was the former who spoke.

"You see, Hanger, she is gone!"

"Yes; and much good it is to us!"

"Pho! pho!"

"It's all very well for you to say 'Pho! pho!' but it is quite clear that you have allowed your most abominable temper to get the better of you, and to embarrass everything."

"Indeed!"

"Yes, indeed, and in truth, too!"

"My dear Hanger, you are mistaken."

"Am I?"

"To be sure you are. Nothing is embarrassed at all. All is as clear as possible. The Regent has banished me from his presence and from the Court, once and for ever!"

"The deuce he has!"

"Just so. All the hold we have now is upon the gratitude of the Marchioness of Sunningham."

"The what?"

"The gratitude."

"Then we are dished—cleared out—trumped—bilked and done for?"

"I should not wonder."

"You should not wonder? And you talk so coolly as all that about it, after giving me so much trouble and making such magnificent promises?"

"Exactly!"

"Then you are worse than a fool!"

"Beware!"

"Beware of you?—of you, you old, rascally-looking thief!"

Major Hanger was far from being choice in his language, and Sir Hinckton Moys's mind at that time was like a slumbering volcano, which might at any moment burst into a state of furious ignition, and scatter destruction around it.

He turned upon Major Hanger with all the fury of some wild animal, and uttering a yell of rage, he struck him to the ground, and left him on the stone flags, close to the Colour Court of St. James's Palace, in a state of partial insensibility.

Then Moys, as he strode from the spot, bit his lip, and muttered between his clenched teeth, "What have I to live for?—what have I to live for, now? Ha! ha! One word—one short word of two syllables, comprises all that is left to bind me to life! Revenge! revenge! Yes, I still live for revenge!"

———

CHAPTER CCXXXI.

THE DARK WOMAN TAKES SOME IMPORTANT STEPS TO RENDER HER ATTESTED ROYAL SIGNATURE OF SERVICE.

It is morning again.

The morning after those events which had made so great a change in the state of affairs at St. James's Palace.

The Dark Woman sits alone in that room of her apartments in St. James's Street where we have already seen her holding consultations with Lovat.

The ascendancy she had acquired over the mind of that young man was now so great, that he attended upon her as though she had been an acknowledged sovereign princess.

He was in the same room with her, but at a table close to a window, at a distant part of it from where she was.

That table was covered with letters and papers, some of which bore ducal and other coroneted seals.

The Dark Woman herself was in a morning dress of great richness—a dress, indeed, quite in accordance with her assumed character of Princess of Wales.

A silver cup, in which was some exquisitely fine mocha coffee, the aroma of which impregnated the air of the apartment, was before her, on a small table.

She seemed to be in deep thought.

Were they happy thoughts that had possession of that teeming brain?

Alas! who shall say that they were? And yet Linda de Chevenaux felt herself, perhaps, nearer to the accomplishment of all her wishes than she had ever been.

That is to say, she thought she was nearer.

She thought she had made some onward progress, although, in truth, that apparent success was but a delusion.

It was as if some one in a boat were fagging hard at the oars, and fancying that they were nearing some distant and much-desired point, while all the time a strange current was carrying the little barque two feet to one in an opposite direction.

The young man who had been elected to be the private secretary of Linda de Chevenaux—or Linda, Princess of Wales, as she now named

... of ... only now and then looked up to her respectfully

... ... to expect some orders from her.

At length, she spoke.

Lovat, with an air of extreme deference, bent forward to listen.

"Lovat, is that the lost letter?"

"Yes, madam."

"From Lord Sidmouth?"

"Yes, madam—or—or I should say, from Lord Sidmouth's secretary, rather."

"Read it."

Lovat took up one of the letters that lay on the table before him, and read, in a low, deferential tone:—

"MADAM,

"I am directed by Lord Sidmouth to acknowledge receipt of a letter, signed 'Linda Princess of Wales;' and to say that his lordship declines any answer to the communication.

"I am, madam,

"Your obedient servant,

"AUGUSTUS GREY."

"Is that all?"

"It is, madam."

"Well, be it so. We will try to recollect the scant courtesy with which we have been treated by Lord Sidmouth."

A faint flush of colour was upon the face of the Dark Woman. And here we should state that she had assumed a very different style of dress to that which she had lately adopted.

The male habiliments were discarded, and she wore a very handsome robe of velvet, trimmed with that fine and beautiful fur which was then rather scarce, but which is now well known, and common enough, by the name of miniver.

She had made up her mind to a dangerous and a desperate game.

The next few days, she considered, would either mar or make for her fortune and position.

She had ceased to care for the Regent. All she wished now was to get some kind of acknowledgment of what she considered to be her real rank.

Then she would retire to some continental city, and leave the world to go on as it pleased; but she would have the satisfaction of knowing that, even in despite of what might be considered his own active opposition to the measure, she had made her son a prince.

What dreams they were in which the Dark Woman indulged!

"Enough, Lovat—enough!" she said, suddenly. "I write no more letters. The whole of the Privy Council, I think, have now been addressed?"

"They have, madam."

"And about twenty have replied?"

"Twenty-one, madam; and all in much the same terms as my Lord Sidmouth."

"Be it so!—be it so! Now I will pay this visit to Warwick House that I have resolved upon, and see what view the Princess Caroline of Brunswick takes of her position."

The secretary rose and approached the window, which commanded a view of the street.

"Madam," he said, "the carriage your Highness ordered has just arrived."

"That is well. Is it—is it fit for a person of my rank?"

"I think so, madam. The liveries of the servants appear to be perfect."

The colour deepened upon the face of poor Linda de Chevenaux; she hesitated for a few seconds whether to compromise her dignity or show her strength of mind.

In the former case, she would go to the window and look at the carriage.

In the latter, she would remain where she was.

But curiosity prevailed.

The Dark Woman rose, and paced slowly towards one of the windows, which looked fully and fairly out into St. James's Street.

Immediately opposite to the door of the house there was a handsome plain chariot, such as the royal family might use when they went in privacy somewhere.

On the panels the royal arms were, however, to be seen in miniature.

The coachman and footman wore the well-known bright scarlet livery of the royal household; and slowly gathering about the carriage was a knot of curious idlers, who supposed, if they only waited long enough, they would see some great personage come out of that house.

Perhaps the Regent himself.

Who should say?

The Dark Woman smiled faintly.

"Why, Lovat," she said, "you have done all this well—admirably well!"

"Madam, I had the wand of an enchanter," replied Lovat.

"Indeed?"

"Yes, madam; you supplied me with an unlimited amount of gold, and that smoothed all difficulties, overcame all scruples, and put an end to all questioning."

"Yes, yes; it is true, Lovat. As we ascend higher and higher in the scale of human civilization, gold becomes more and more the enchanter."

"It does, madam."

"Wait for me here—I shall be ready to go in ten minutes."

Linda de Chevenaux retired into another room to make some change in her apparel, and the moment she had done so there came a low, gentle tap at the door of the sitting-room.

"Come in," said Lovat.

The landlord and landlady of the house, with wonder on their faces, appeared.

"Well?" asked the secretary.

"Oh! sir, if you please—what—who—who—what, if you please, is Mr. Brown a—a——That is to say, what and who is Mr. Brown, for there is one of the royal carriages at the door?"

Lovat smiled; but what reply he would have made was anticipated by the Dark Woman, who—still in the velvet dress, but with the addition of a hat and feathers, such as were then the fashion—came suddenly from the inner room.

"The Mr. Brown," she said, "to whom you let these lodgings, is no more; but in his place you have the Princess of Wales."

The landlord and landlady looked petrified with astonishment. Involuntarily, they turned their eyes towards Lovat, as if they would ask of him if what they had just heard could be indeed true.

He answered the mute appeal.

" Yes; that lady is the Princess of Wales—the true wife of the Regent, and the future Queen of England."

The landlady—who was a very loyal woman, and thought that royal personages must perforce be made of superior clay to the rest of humanity—at once dropped to her knees.

The landlord, who—happy man!—considered his wife a great authority, imitated the action; and Linda de Chevenaux felt, for the first time in her life, her proud heart swell with delight, at the homage that was paid to her supposed royal state.

Delight beamed from her eyes.

She looked ten—ay, twenty years younger; and if the Regent had at that moment seen her, he would have more easily recognised the Linda of former years, for whom he had entertained so ungovernable a passion, than he had done in the house in Hanover Square, where she had adopted every means of recalling herself, as once she was, to his memory.

" Rise, my good people," said the Dark Woman. " This homage is quite unnecessary."

" Oh, your Majesty!" said the landlady, " I do hope everything has been to your Majesty's satisfaction, since your Majesty has been here. I'll discharge that wretched Jane, the cook, at once, your Majesty, for I know she spoilt those cutlets yesterday."

" But," chimed in the landlord, " we did not know yesterday that your Majesty was your Majesty."

" Certainly not," added the landlady.

" Enough! enough!" said the Dark Woman. " Say no more, and discharge no one on my account. Come, Lovat, to Warwick House."

Lovat bowed low, and, as he reached the top of the stairs, he cried out, " Way for her Royal Highness the Princess of Wales !"

The whole house was in commotion, from kitchen to attics.

The landlord made a rush into the dining-room, to get the table-cover, to lay it over the door-step; but the landlady was quicker, both in action and in perception, and got hold of a piece of uncut scarlet cloth—of which she had intended to construct a very elaborate petticoat—and that she flung over the steps.

The crowd outside thickened.

Some small boys shouted and cheered immensely.

Linda de Chevenaux stepped out of her house—or rather her lodgings—with all the state, all the pride, all the dignity of a princess.

And she looked the character.

Her costume was splendid. The jewels she wore glittered in the morning sun, and dazzled the eyes of all beholders.

She stepped into the carriage.

" To Warwick House," said Lovat, as he respectfully took his place on the opposite seat.

The carriage drove off.

Truly, the Dark Woman was playing a bold and adventurous part.

She might be said to have set her fortunes on a cast, and to be prepared and willing to

" Stand the hazard of the die."

But she had well thought of what she was about.

For the whole of the day and the night pre-vious to this exhibition of royal state, Linda de Chevenaux had well considered her position, and the result was that she had thoroughly made up her mind to risk everything to try to accomplish everything.

The important document, signed by the mad King, and countersigned by the Lord Chancellor, was in her possession—a small gold box, which she had instructed Lovat to purchase for her, contained it.

That box, with its precious contents, she carried in a fold of the breast of her apparel; and it was further secured by a gold chain, in the links of which a thread of stout silken cord was entwined and passed round her throat.

There was no moment of her existence, now, that she did not feel the presence of that small gold box.

Without it she would be lost.

With it, she deluded herself into the idea that she was all-powerful.

And so we now see the Dark Woman fairly launched upon a most perilous career, which, within the next four-and-twenty hours, must either make or mar her fortunes for ever.

The visit to Warwick House was for the purpose of endeavouring to convince Caroline of Brunswick that all opposition to her, Linda's, claims would be useless.

If she could but make a convert of that unfortunate Princess, and induce her to leave the field open to her, Linda de Chevenaux, a great point would surely be gained; and the production of the signed and attested document she had with her ought, she considered, to go a long way towards such a result.

We shall see how far the calculations of the Dark Woman were founded on sound reasonings, or otherwise.

CHAPTER CCXXXII.

WARWICK HOUSE PRESENTS THE SINGULAR SPEC-TACLE OF THREE QUEENS-CONSORT PRESUMP-TIVE OF ENGLAND.

THE distance from St. James's Street to Warwick House was but short.

Soon the seeming royal carriage rolled up to the door of that temporary abode of the unhappy Caroline of Brunswick.

At sight of the royal liveries, the small household of the Princess of Wales were all astir. The impression was that one of the royal dukes had come to pay a visit.

Or, possibly, some member of the family, who was on the opposition as regarded the Regent.

But be it whom it might, the liveries and the royal arms on the carriage were at once passports for the visitor.

No question was asked, but Linda de Chevenaux was received with the greatest respect.

A major-domo, however, stepped up to Lovat, with an inquiring air, and whispered, " Who am I to announce ?"

Now, this was a point which had not escaped the consideration of the Dark Woman, and she had felt that it would not do to go to the house inhabited by the Princess Caroline of Brunswick,

and announce herself to be the Princess of
Wales.

Lovat having then his instructions, replied to
the inquiry of the major-domo at once.

"Her Royal Highness the Princess Linda!"

The major-domo looked bewildered and distressed.

He was one of those small-souled people who
pride themselves upon knowing the titles, names,
family descents, &c., of all royal and noble personages.

And now to find that there was actually a
Royal Highness by the name of Linda, whom he
had never heard of, was quite a shocking affair.

The major-domo turned pale.

"The—the—a—her Royal Highness the Princess Linda, did you say, sir?"

"I did."

"I never heard of her!"

"I cannot help that, sir."

There was just time for this brief colloquy between Lovat and the major-domo, before Linda de
Chevenaux entered the hall of Warwick House,
and then her appearance silenced all questioning
and all opposition.

Such a magnificent dress!

Such a blaze of jewels!

So commanding an air!

All conspired to produce an effect upon the
major-domo, which induced him to bow to the
very floor, and to speak in his most courtly accents, as he said, "I will have the honour of
guiding your Royal Highness to the state reception-room."

The Dark Woman, by a slight movement of
the hand, signified her assent, and followed the
major-domo.

Lovat walked a few paces behind her, and then
paused in an apartment which formed a kind of
ante-room to what was called the state reception-
room of Warwick House.

The major-domo ostentatiously placed an arm-
chair, all crimson silk and gold, for Linda de Chevenaux, and then he bowed low again, and waited
her gracious commands.

At least, that was to all intents and purposes
just what his countenance expressed.

"I would request the honour," said the Dark
Woman, "of an interview with the Princess Caroline."

The major-domo bowed himself out of the room
backwards.

Linda de Chevenaux thought she was alone.

She compressed her lips, and looked about her
with vivacious eyes, as she muttered, in the lowest
of all possible low tones, "Shall I lodge here, when
this unfortunate Caroline of Brunswick, with her
blighted name and her ruined hopes, returns to
Germany?"

The Dark Woman started.

Some sound had come upon her ears.

It was surely a sob.

Surely some one in an agony of heart-distress,
and in that apartment, too.

At one end of the state reception-room was a
gilded screen, and the eyes of the Dark Woman
were at once directed towards it, for it seemed to
her that, without doubt, the sob of distress had
come from behind it.

"Who is there?" she asked. "Who is it that
suffers amid all this splendour?"

There was an agitation of the screen. Then a
voice replied to Linda.

"Madam! Princess! you who are a Princess
without the necessity of filching from another the
sacred right to that title, oh, forgive me for this
intrusion, and hear me!"

Linda de Chevenaux was astonished at these
words, and well she might be.

Who could it be that thus addressed her as
a Princess, and so earnestly besought her forgiveness for she knew not what?

"Come forth," said the Dark Woman. "Come
forth, and let me see who and what you are!"

"At your commands, madam, I will," added
the voice.

The screen was then further agitated, and there
came forth from behind it a lady, in an elegant
and neat, becoming dress of violet-coloured silk,
and approached Linda de Chevenaux with tears
in her eyes.

The Dark Woman knew her at once.

She had only seen that face upon one occasion,
but she had not forgotten it.

The person who emerged from behind the screen
was no other than the well-known Mrs. Fitzherbert, about whose marriage with the Prince of
Wales there had been so much controversy.

A sharp pang shot through the heart of the
Dark Woman.

In Mrs. Fitzherbert she saw another claimant
to the hand of the Regent.

She put on a look of cold disdain.

The circumstances were those under which one
woman never could look for a single instant ami-
ably at another.

Mrs. Fitzherbert saw the look, and it did more
to restore her courage, which appeared to have
failed her greatly, than anything else could have
done.

But still the mystery of her presence there was
unexplained.

Still, Linda de Chevenaux could not conceive
how or why it was she addressed her.

We can, however, in a very few words, put an
end to this mystery as regards the reader.

Mrs. Fitzherbert on that very morning had
made up her mind to an interview for the first
time, and probably the last, with the Princess of
Wales.

Bribery and sympathy among some of the
female servants of the household at Warwick
House, one of whom had been previously lady's-
maid to Mrs. Fitzherbert, had procured for her
a secret introduction to the mansion, and to that
very room where it was known that the Princess
of Wales was in the habit of sitting for about an
hour each morning.

All this had gone well enough with Mrs. Fitzherbert up to the appearance of Linda de Chevenaux, whom she mistook for the real Princess of
Wales.

Hence, then, the manner in which she addressed,
and hence the mystification of the mind of the
Dark Woman, to find herself so addressed.

But this delusion was not likely to last long on
the mind of Mrs. Fitzherbert. She had only to
get one good look at Linda de Chevenaux to feel
convinced that she was not Caroline of Brunswick.

When people are impressed with the truth of
any appearance, it is perfectly marvellous how, for

a time, even the senses will aid in the deception, if it be one.

And so it was in this case.

Mrs. Fitzherbert felt so perfectly sure that she was addressing the Princess Caroline of Wales, that she had to look twice into the face of Linda de Chevenaux to convince herself that she was in error.

"Madam," she said, speaking under the delusion that she addressed Caroline of Brunswick,—"madam, you may feel surprised at a visit from me ; but the cause of it is that I would make one last effort to get justice from the Regent, and hope even for your assistance——"

Mrs. Fitzherbert had got thus far before she saw that she was addressing some one who was to her a stranger.

She shrunk back.

"Pardon me, madam—I find I have made a foolish mistake."

"What mistake?" said the Dark Woman, coldly.

"I thought I was addressing the Princess of Wales."

"You are !"

"Madam !"

"I say you are addressing the wife of the Regent of England, and consequently the Princess of Wales !"

Mrs. Fitzherbert rubbed her eyes.

She began to think that insanity had come over her, for there was not the shadow of a likeness, even, between the richly-attired lady before her, and the Princess Caroline.

The latter was decidedly plain.

The Dark Woman in every feature still bore the impress of her former beauty.

The silence that ensued had the appearance of being embarrassing to both parties; but, probably, it was only so to one—that one being Mrs. Fitzherbert.

The Dark Woman was self-possessed enough, for she could see very well the mistake that had been committed; and, in fact, from the moment that she started upon the enterprise of that morning, it might be said she was fully prepared for any contingencies, and was not likely to be startled or surprised at anything that might happen.

One thing she rapidly determined upon, and that was, that she would not pretend to recognise Mrs. Fitzherbert, but would treat her and her pretensions completely as novelties.

The Dark Woman, therefore, looked coldly in the face of that unhappy victim of the Regent; and Mrs. Fitzherbert, gathering, we may say, courage from the coldness of that very look, spoke to her with more firmness and decision than had as yet characterized her.

"Madam," she said, "I perceive that I have made an error. You may be, and probably are, some lady of rank here on a visit to the Princess of Wales; but it is as cruel of you as it is useless to attempt to impose upon me that you are that personage."

"As you please," said the Dark Woman. "I neither know nor care who or what you may be !"

"And yet, madam," said Mrs. Fitzherbert, drawing herself up with an appearance of dignity which was far from being pleasing to Linda de Chevenaux,—"and yet, madam, although you say you know not who I am, I may tell you that it is I who should be seated where you are, and you who should be assuming a respectful attitude before me."

"Indeed !" replied the Dark Woman, while a cold smile played about her lips.

"Yes, madam ; for, be you whom you may, and whatever your titles and difficulties may be, I am the true and veritable wife of the Regent !"

"It is false !" cried the Dark Woman, as she sprang to her feet.

"It is as true," said Mrs. Fitzherbert, "as heaven can make a truth !"

As she spoke, Mrs. Fitzherbert adroitly took a chair, and, by rapidly seating herself, thus reversed the relative positions of the two parties.

Linda de Chevenaux then found herself standing in that state reception-room, and speaking to Mrs. Fitzherbert, who was seated, at the very moment that a couple of doors were thrown open, and the major-domo, who had already officiated in the introduction of the Dark Woman to that apartment, called out, "Her Royal Highness the Princess of Wales !"

Attired in a loose morning-wrapper, a good deal the worse for wear, and looking old, plain, worn, Caroline of Brunswick made her appearance.

She paused almost upon the threshold of the state reception-room, and looked in surprise from one to the other of the two women who occupied it.

That apartment presented, then, a strange spectacle.

The three persons who were in it each claimed the title of Princess of Wales, and to be wife to the Regent.

Perhaps, the bitterest enemies of the Prince could scarcely have wished him a worse fate than to be there upon that occasion, shut up in that apartment without the power of leaving it, and exposed to the reproaches of those three women, with each of whom he had as certainly gone through the ceremony of marriage as that he was a living man.

Mrs. Fitzherbert recognised the Princess of Wales at once.

And so did Linda de Chevenaux.

They both made two steps towards her; and then they both essayed to speak at the same moment—both pausing instantly to listen to what the Princess herself said, as she exclaimed, in a tone of anger, "What is the meaning of all this? Am I to have no peace? Am I ever to be intruded upon, without the slightest regard to my feelings or my rank?"

"No, madam," said the Dark Woman. "I come to you not as an intruder, but as a visitor, whose business is of that essential nature that it requires your instant attention and your serious regards."

"And I, too," said Mrs. Fitzherbert—"I come to appeal to you—not as a princess, but as a woman, with a human heart—a human soul, which must some day render an account of its acts. I come to you to ask for justice—I come to you, madam, to convince you that I am the wife of the Regent."

"You ?"

"Even I, madam. Known as I am to the

world as Mrs. Fitzherbert, I declare to you—and I fancy I have the means of proving it—that, in the face of heaven, and with all the ceremonies of the Church, I became the wife of the Prince of Wales!"

The Dark Woman stepped back a pace or two, and leant her hand upon a table. She seemed curious to know what the Princess of Wales would say, in answer to this attack upon her position.

For a few moments Caroline of Brunswick made no reply whatever. Then it was a practical one, for she retreated to the chimney-piece, and laid her hand on a bell-rope.

"If," she said—"if you do not leave Warwick House at once, I will order the servants to turn you from its doors."

Mrs. Fitzherbert advanced a pace or two.

"Can it be possible," she said, "that your courage, considering your own position, is so great? I would have you look to yourself, and your own shameless life, as the mistress of a servant."

Fury flashed from the eyes of the Princess of Wales, at this ambiguous speech from Mrs. Fitzherbert—a speech, indeed, so ambiguous, that if she had had the coolness and the wisdom to affect not to understand it, she might very well have done so.

That it alluded to her supposed criminal connexion with Bergami, the courier and valet, there was, of course, no doubt; but the Princess of Wales was none the more indiscreet on that account, in replying to it as she did.

"An accusation of that sort," she said, "comes well from the woman who is the discarded mistress of the greatest libertine in Europe!"

The Dark Woman was rather pleased than otherwise at this discussion.

Mrs. Fitzherbert, apparently coming there on an errand that very much resembled her own, might be considered an enemy; so the more she was damaged, the better.

The Princess of Wales, in a passion, would likewise be much more likely to fall a prey to the cool and more calculating judgment of Linda de Chevenaux.

But the scene was doomed to be interrupted, or there is no knowing what length it might have gone to.

CHAPTER CCXXXIII.

THE DARK WOMAN PRODUCES CONSTERNATION IN TWO ROYAL BREASTS.

SINCE the removal of the Princess of Wales from Buckingham House to Warwick House, it was known that the Regent no longer absolutely prohibited his daughter, the Princess Charlotte, from visiting her mother.

Those visits did not exceed, in the whole, more than three in number; for the tempers of the mother and the daughter were never in unison, and they soon disagreed.

This visit was the first of the three.

Perhaps the sort of concession which the Regent had made, in regard to the visiting, on the part of the Princess Charlotte, at Warwick House, was all but compulsory.

Since her marriage to the Prince Leopold, th

Princess Charlotte had told her father, the Regent, that she recognised any authority from him just so far as it happened to square with her own wishes and inclinations.

It followed therefore that it was wise, although probably irksome, to pretend to be agreeable to what the young Princess and young wife chose to do.

There was what might be called a cross look upon the face of the Princess Charlotte as she made her appearance in the state reception-room at Warwick House.

At sight of two persons there beside her mother, she paused a few paces within the room, and half put down from her hat, over her face, a white lace veil.

That was a habit of hers when she saw people she did not wish to speak to.

"Oh, you are come in good time, Charlotte!" said the Princess of Wales. "Your mother is insulted in what, for the present, at least, should be considered her own house."

"And," said Mrs. Fitzherbert, turning to the Princess Charlotte, —" and allow me to add, that your mother can be as insulting, in what she calls for the present her own house, as the lowest of her sex."

The Princess of Wales was only partially acquainted with the English language—that is to say, she spoke it well enough, and could express very correctly whatever she wanted to say, but there were times when she did not precisely comprehend involved and parenthetical sentences from other people.

This was one of those times.

She thought that Mrs. Fitzherbert called her "the lowest of her sex."

Anger got the better of all prudence, and she lost command of her temper.

An inkstand of silver stood close to her, on a small side table; and it seemed a positive relief to her, for she uttered a scream of pleasure as she did so, to fling it in the face of Mrs. Fitzherbert.

The inkstand did not do much damage, but the ink made a show.

A slight graze on the right temple was all the wound that Mrs. Fitzherbert received, but the ink streamed down her face; and had it been red instead of black, she would have had the appearance of being very seriously wounded.

Mrs. Fitzherbert staggered back under the first shock of this attack. Then, by the manner in which she looked about her, it would seem that she was upon the point of catching up some missile, which would enable her to retaliate the attack upon the Princess of Wales.

The latter, however, pulled the bell-rope furiously, and several of the servants of Warwick House appeared.

In fact, these servants appeared so quickly, that had either of the persons in the room been sufficiently unabsorbed in what was going on there to reflect about it, they might have come to the conclusion that those servants must have been wonderfully close at hand.

"Remove that woman!" cried the Princess of Wales, pointing to Mrs. Fitzherbert.

"I am going," said the discomfited and undaunted wife of the Regent—"I am going; and I can well afford to forgive one who has, by far, more misery in store for her than can ever fall

to my lot. The time will come, and that soon, when disgrace and contumely will surround you, and if you have a heart at all, it will break with the pressure of despair."

Mrs. Fitzherbert left the room.

It was upon that occasion that she met several members of the House of Lords, and complained that, calling upon the Princess of Wales, as one woman might upon another, she had been grossly assailed, and would perhaps have been killed, but for the presence of other people.

The little episode, with many additions and colourings, got into the newspapers, and was known at the time by the quaint heading of "The Tragedy of the Inkstand, at Warwick House."

It did the unfortunate Princess of Wales a great deal of harm.

And now the only persons in that state reception-room at Warwick House were the Princess of

Wales, the Princess Charlotte, and Linda de Chevenaux.

They both looked at her with evident surprise, as to who she was, and how she came there.

The Dark Woman did not allow them to remain for long in ignorance on those points. Stepping forward, she assumed that cool, calm, and commanding manner which she had so frequently found to have its full effect upon higher intellects than those of the Princess Charlotte and her mother.

"My visit here," she said, "is one of charity or of defiance. You may make it which you will."

"Pray, madam," said the Princess Charlotte, "who are you, may I ask?"

"I am the Princess Linda."

"Linda?"

"Linda?" repeated the Princess Caroline. "Linda of what? Is it Russian?"

"No, madam, it is English. I am the wife of his Royal Highness the Regent!"

Both the Princess Charlotte and her mother looked astonished and incredulous. The Princess Charlotte slightly touched her forehead and glanced at the bell-rope.

The Dark Woman, with that quickness of perception that characterized her, understood instantly what she meant.

"No, Princess," she said,—"no, I am not mad; and it is not at all necessary to ring for the servants, unless you and the Princess, your mother, particularly wish that they should be witnesses of this interview."

"What do you mean?" cried the Princess of Wales. "Are you another Fitzherbert?"

"Oh, no, madam, I am quite a different person; and I look upon it as a rare chance, and a most fortunate one, that your daughter is here present. You have supposed yourself the wife of the Regent now for eighteen years?"

"Supposed myself?"

"Yes; I say 'supposed,' because it is only a supposition; and you, Charlotte, calling yourself Princess of Wales, but who ought now to be named the Princess Leopold—you suppose yourself to be the legitimate child of the Regent?"

"Suppose myself, madam?"

"I have said it. Suppose now, for an instant, getting rid of all anger and of all irritation upon the subject—suppose, I say, that you were both convinced that the Regent was, some two years or so before his marriage with you, Caroline of Brunswick, actually and truly married with the royal consent to another?"

"Impossible!"

"An idle tale!"

"Perhaps so; but, I say, suppose such a thing to be true, what course would you two adopt?"

The Princess of Wales looked at the Princess Charlotte, and the latter looked at her mother, but they were both silent.

"Try," added the Dark Woman,—"try to realize in imagination such a state of things, and then tell me what you would do?"

"No!" cried the Princess Charlotte, as she saw her mother was about to speak. "No, I will not tell you what I would do; nor will you, mother, be so indiscreet as to say one word on such a subject to a stranger."

"Who," added the Princess of Wales,—"who will oblige us by leaving Warwick House at once."

"Exactly so. Now, madam, we do not wish to know any more about you, or to hear anything more you have to say; so be so good as to go."

"Soon, I will," said the Dark Woman. "But you must hear me!"

"Must?"

"Ay, must! Do you think that I am so weak as to allow either of you, or both of you, to interfere with my intentions?"

As she spoke, the Dark Woman, with that boldness and rapidity of action which her adventurous life had made familiar to her, suddenly turned the key in the lock of the door leading to the ante-room, and then adroitly placing herself between the Princess of Wales and the bell-rope, she seemed to be mistress of the situation.

"Be not alarmed," she added. "No harm is intended; but, on the contrary, much good, if you will have it so."

There was now a subdued sweetness and tenderness in the tones of the Dark Woman which struck forcibly upon the ears of both the Princess of Wales and her daughter.

It would, probably, have been quite possible for them to have made an outcry, and so procured assistance, but they did not show any symptoms of a desire to do so.

"Ah! I now see," added Linda de Chevenaux,—"I now see that you will both listen to me!"

"Say what you have to say," cried the Princess Charlotte—"for you have now awakened my curiosity."

"And mine, too," said the Princess of Wales.

The Dark Woman smiled faintly. She no longer stood on guard, so to speak, over the bell-rope; and she spoke in the same low, soft accents which had characterized her last words.

"You are both, most surely, to be pitied. Every one is to be pitied who innocently has to suffer for the establishment of the right of any other person; and yet your reason will point out to you how more than unjust it would be if the right of that other person were to be denied on account of that innocent suffering."

The Dark Woman could scarcely tell if either or both of her auditors followed her reasoning, for they neither of them spoke, and she continued; "But if the person whose right is to be so established can in any way, and by making some sacrifice of a portion of that right, mitigate the suffering of the innocent persons, it would be well to do so."

Again she paused; and then the Princess Charlotte said, with some vivacity, "Pray, what does all this lead to?"

"This!" said the Dark Woman.

As she spoke, she placed plainly and fairly on the table the real and original paper she had procured the signature of the old mad King to at Windsor, and which she had made the Lord Chancellor attest.

Both the Princess of Wales and her daughter stepped forward to look at the paper.

Both were sufficiently familiar with the signature of the King to have no doubt about its genuineness.

The attestation of the Chancellor, too, was a serious item in the affair.

They looked at each other, perplexed and confounded.

"You see," said the Dark Woman, "this paper establishes a fact of the most serious character as regards you both!"

"My God!" said the Princess of Wales.

"Hush!" said the Princess Charlotte. "Surely, the original consent of the King, dated at the period of this—this pretended marriage, would be a better document than this?"

"Infinitely better!" replied the Dark Woman. "But the Prince of Wales, when he tired of Linda de Chevenaux, was anxious to be rid of her; and he got possession of that original consent, and, no doubt, destroyed it. This, then, became at once necessary as secondary evidence."

There was so much calm, cool reasoning in these words, that it was impossible to gainsay them; and the two Princesses looked at each other in consternation and confusion.

"I can well perceive," said the Dark Woman, "that your reason is too strong to be submerged either by your fears or your anger; and therefore, I will say to you, at once, that I have a proposal to make, which will save the Princess of Wales, and permit of the legitimacy of the Princess Charlotte remaining, as at present, perfectly unquestioned."

"What proposal?"

"It is simply this. If this Linda de Chevenaux——"

"That is yourself?" cried the Princess Charlotte.

"Myself! If, then, I had died within the two years that elapsed between the marriage of the Prince of Wales with me, and his public espousal with you, Caroline of Brunswick, you would have been his legal wife, and you, Charlotte, his legitimate daughter."

"But you live?"

"I live—I do live; but who shall know, if I will consent to be supposed to have died in that interval, and I will so effectually disappear, that no one shall know of my whereabouts?"

"You will do that?" said the Princess of Wales.

"You will?" cried Charlotte. "And yet you are in possession of such a document as this?"

"I will."

"It is too generous!"

"It is too incredible!"

"No—because there is a reason."

"Ah, a reason?"

"Yes; I have a son!"

The Princess Charlotte uttered a cry.

"Now," she said, "I recollect—now I know all about it. I have heard things said—I have had a letter. All this is for the purpose of depriving me of my succession to the throne, and setting up this Captain Fitz George, who is said to be a son of the Regent!"

"He is your brother!"

A look of pride and scorn came over the face of the Princess Charlotte.

"Your brother!" added the Dark Woman. "And what I propose is this. The legality of my marriage with the Regent to be admitted by you two, so that my son, now called Captain Fitz George, shall be able to assume his proper position. Then it may be given out that I died before the Regent's marriage with you, Caroline of Brunswick; the effect of all which will be that you still remain Princess of Wales."

"And I?" cried the Princess Charlotte.

"You escape!"

"Escape? escape? What do you mean by escape?"

"You escape the brand of illegitimacy!"

"Ha! ha! ha! The brand of illegitimacy, indeed! And I lose the throne of England, in order that your son should sit on it?"

"Just so."

"And my children, too?"

"Your children, too!"

"Then I declare the whole thing an impudent imposture, and will fight it out to the last!"

"Your mother is of a different opinion."

"Pho! pho! What do I care about the opinions of any one else? I never did, and I am not going to begin now. Ha! ha! A precious proposition, truly! Ha! ha! Well, madam—

well, Mrs., or Miss, Linda de Chevenaux, is that all you have to say?"

"It is all"

"Then there is the door; and you may thank yourself that we do not call the constables."

"Indeed!"

"Oh, yes; for, if report speaks truth, you have another name besides that of Linda de Chevenaux, which would be very well known at a police-office."

"No," said the Dark Woman, as she pressed one hand upon her breast,—"no, I have made up my mind that I will not be angry—no, no!"

"Please yourself," said the Princess Charlotte, scornfully — "please yourself about that; but please us by leaving this house at once."

The Princess of Wales looked bewildered and perplexed. Perhaps the proposal made by Linda de Chevenaux was not so distasteful to her as it was to her daughter; but she totally wanted moral force sufficient to stem the tide of indignation of Charlotte, who had it all her own way.

"I go," said the Dark Woman, as she carefully replaced the important document in the gold box, and secured it round her neck by its chain of silk and gold—"I go now; and it is to proclaim, to all who choose to hear me, the story of my wrongs, so do not blame me if it carry with it your disgrace."

She turned to the door.

"Stop!" said the Princess of Wales.

"No!" cried the Princess Charlotte. "And yet, perhaps, an arrest——"

The Dark Woman cast a scornful look upon her, and left the state reception-room.

"Stop, and detain, that woman!" cried the Princess Charlotte.

A couple of servants stepped forward.

"Try it!" said the Dark Woman.

The servants recoiled, tumbling, in their haste, over each other, for she had a bright, long-barrelled pistol in each hand.

And so she passed out of Warwick House without hindrance, and found Lovat in the hall. He could well see that there were traces of agitation on her face, but he was alarmed at the order she gave as she stepped into the carriage with the royal liveries.

"To St. James's Palace!"

"Was she mad? Had anything happened at Warwick House to drive her reason from its throne?"

Such were the questions that Lovat asked himself with deep anxiety.

"Madam," he whispered, "have I heard you aright?"

"To the Palace!"

Lovat sighed deeply.

"Oh, madam, consider!"

"I have considered! Fear nothing; it is all well considered, Lovat. Do not think that I act without pre-arrangement and ample consideration. Boldness and openness are now my weapons. To the Palace!"

"Yes, madam! To St. James's Palace!"

Lovat took his place again on the opposite seat of the coach to that occupied by Linda de Chevenaux; and as she looked at him, she could see, by the heightened colour on his face, that he was really excited.

"Be calm—be calm, Lovat!" she said. "There is little danger."

"Oh, madam! if they should choose to arrest you as—as—the—a—Dark Woman, who may be amenable to the law?"

Linda de Chevenaux smiled.

"I happen to be able to prove that I am the Princess of Wales; and therefore, as a consequence of my rank, I am not amenable to the jurisdiction of the ordinary tribunals, let them accuse me as an individual of what they may. It is the King, or the Regent, sitting in Privy Council, who can alone deal with me."

"Yes, yes! But——"

"Nay, fear nothing. I am sick of delay—I famish for the state and dignity to which I aspire. This is not a country in which one can be slaughtered, as in the palace of an Eastern despot. There is no amount of publicity which can hurt one who has strength to abide inquiry. In four-and-twenty hours, now, the whole of London—the whole of England, I may say—will ring with my story, and I shall have hundreds of thousands of partisans. Fear nothing, Lovat, and all may yet go well. This day is the crisis of the fate of the Dark Woman."

The coach, with its royal arms, and the royal liveries of its attendants, was suffered by the guard to roll into the Colour Court of old St. James's Palace.

CHAPTER CCXXXIV.

THE LORD CHANCELLOR HOLDS A MEETING OF PEERS IN THE PAINTED CHAMBER OF ST. JAMES'S, AND THE REGENT MAKES A ROYAL SPEECH.

THE Dark Woman spoke truly. A crisis approached in her fate, which was to make an indelible impression upon all who had any connexion with her.

In order that the reader should fully comprehend how this crisis and catastrophe was brought about, we must, for a brief space, leave the Dark Woman in the court-yard of St. James's Palace, while we follow the proceedings of that scheming, cunning, unscrupulous man who was then the Lord Chancellor of England.

Well was that man aware that his fate, as regarded his political career and the high office he held, hung on the chances of the next few days.

He knew that he was particularly obnoxious to the Regent.

He knew that the unfortunate Caroline of Brunswick could have no faith in him, for he had broken faith with her on more than one occasion.

In fact, he was a man neither esteemed nor trusted by any party, because he had in turns pretended to belong to all, and had been faithless to all.

Under these circumstances, he thought that amid the general gloom of his position he saw a light shining, or beginning to shine, which would lead him into a harbour of safety.

He thought he saw that a new party, and one which might find favour with many persons, and was almost sure to be the party of the people, was about to arise in strength and power.

That party was the party of Linda de Chevenaux, the legitimate wife of the Regent.

That is to say, if the authenticity of the document she possessed, with the royal sign manual attached to it, could be substantiated, and no fatal flaw be found in the proceedings.

Like some mariner swimming in a wide ocean, without a hope of rescue, might hail a boat which would be possibly wafted by the wind and the tide towards him, the sinking Chancellor hailed Linda de Chevenaux and her claims.

The more he reflected upon the strange and most unprecedented circumstances that had taken place in regard to himself and to her, the more his imagination became interested in her favour.

The cold, hard, cruel, unscrupulous man of the world began almost to believe that a special Providence had interfered, to save him from utter ruin and despair.

Within the four-and-twenty hours after his singular interview with Linda de Chevenaux, when she had threatened and cajoled him in the manner the reader is already aware of, he had made up his mind to attach himself to her, and to her cause and claims.

The moment he had so made up his mind he set to work with energy.

It would be difficult to say if the Chancellor really, at the bottom of his heart, believed that Linda de Chevenaux was the legitimate wife of the Regent.

Probably that was a question that he never asked himself.

He cared not a rush about the truth.

What he cared for was his own interest; and what he asked himself was—could he prove those facts which were most likely to advance it?

That was all.

And he thought he could prove sufficient to place Linda de Chevenaux in a very strong position indeed—a position so strong that the opposite party (that is to say, the Regent) would either have to give in entirely, and agree to the fact—or supposed fact—of his real and indefeasible marriage with Linda, or make such terms with him, the Chancellor, to abandon her, as would satisfy all his ambition and all his avarice.

That he was quite open to offers of that kind there can be no doubt whatever.

Alas, poor Linda de Chevenaux! Were you never to find one heart that was truly attached to you—one tongue that would speak to you the truth, besides that one to which you would not listen?

Fitz George had in vain sought, as we are aware, to turn his mother from her career of mad ambition into peaceful and serene paths; but to him she would not listen.

She would not listen to him, because it was for him she fought.

After long cogitation, then, the Chancellor made up his mind to a course of action which was at once bold and perilous.

But he thought that the boldness counteracted the peril.

He had it in his power, by the high office he held, to summon a private and special meeting of the Privy Council.

It was a bold step to take, but the exceptional nature of the circumstances urged him on.

He did summon such a meeting, for four o'clock,

at St. James's Palace, on that very day when the Dark Woman had assumed the royal arms and the royal liveries.

On that very day when she had paid the memorable visit to the Princess Caroline of Brunswick, and offered the last and only compromise which she would stoop to.

That compromise rejected, all was open war.

The Chancellor, then, had summoned this meeting of the Privy Council without the cognizance or the consent of the Regent.

This, of itself, was a most important step to take.

It certainly, according to the constitution of the country, was not absolutely necessary that the King, or the person who, by the name of Regent, exercised the royal functions, should be apprized of a meeting of the Council, or that such meeting should only be held on the royal command.

Yet, as a matter of usage and courtesy, such was always the case.

The Chancellor then took a bold and perilous step by ignoring the Regent on this occasion.

If he were successful, and the Lords of the Council should decide in favour of Linda de Chevenaux's claims, that step would bring with it its own excuse, and its own justification.

Somebody says that "there is nothing so successful as success."

If then, the movement in favour of Linda de Chevenaux were successful, the Chancellor had nothing to fear.

If otherwise, why he was not much worse off than before.

The crimson room at St. James's, where the meetings of the Council were often held, was a square apartment, the walls of which were hung with crimson cloth.

Heavy draperies were over the one window, which was a very wide one, and embayed or built out a considerable distance, with side lights.

The floor was covered with a rich carpet of tapestry, the prevailing colour of which was crimson.

Down the centre of the room was a massive table of oak, so old that it had assumed almost the colour of mahogany.

Upon the table was a velvet cover, thick and massive, of a deep sea-green colour.

Chairs were ranged on each side of the table—one was at the top, with a small gilt crown on the top of the back of it.

That was the King's chair.

No one intruded into that seat, even when it was known that royalty would not be present at the council board on any occasion.

The President of the Council sat in the centre of one of the sides of the table, so that it could not be said that when the monarch took his seat the President was at the bottom of the table.

Some cabinets, which would open in the shape of writing desks, were in the room, at one of which usually sat the clerk of the Council.

The table was strewn with pens, paper, and writing materials of all kinds and descriptions.

This room was one of a suite—the last, in fact; and there was a door, seldom used, which opened from the front of the suite into the Titian Gallery.

It was at half-past three o'clock on that day when the Dark Woman presented all the outward insignia of royalty in her carriage, her dress, and her attendants, that the door of the crimson room was opened, and two gentlemen appeared.

Each of these personages had a drawn sword in his hand.

They had come there to perform a ceremony which is always gone through before a meeting of the Privy Council.

That ceremony was to institute a strict search in the room, to see that no person was concealed in it.

With their swords they examined every corner, and behind the hangings and draperies, and beneath the table, in quite a systematic way.

This ceremony over, one of these persons took up his station at one of the doors opening into the crimson room, and the other at the door that led from it to the private rooms of the Regent.

The Palace clock struck the hour of four.

In rapid succession nine carriages rolled into the Ambassadors' Court of St. James's Palace.

Nine gentlemen, the first in rank and consideration in all England, alighted from those carriages, and took their way to the Council chamber.

By a private door, the Chancellor himself entered the Palace, and sought the crimson room.

He was pale; but, although there were traces of some agitation upon his face, his lips were firmly compressed, and he was evidently in a state of mind that evinced the firmest determination.

The clock chimed the quarter past four.

With a sharp, clanging sound, the doors of the Council chamber were closed.

The lords took their seats.

But the chair of the King was vacant.

The chair, too, of the President of the Council was unoccupied.

The wily Chancellor had omitted to summon him, as well as some of the members of the Council, who he knew would side with the Regent, and whom he more than suspected would be difficult to manage.

What he meant to say in excuse of all his breaches of custom and etiquette was, that the affair was so domestic in some of its aspects, that he thought it was delicate in the first instance not to trouble the personal friends of the Regent with it.

And what he wanted to do was, to get a vote for inquiry by these nine Privy Councillors whom he had summoned.

The Regent was at Windsor.

The Dark Woman was speaking those last words, which we have recorded, to the Prince of Wales at Warwick House.

Captain Fitz George was on guard at the gate of the Palace.

Annie, the fair Countess de Blonde, was in the arms of her sister Marian; for, although she had declared she would not make one of the happy little family circle of Allan, she had called to see Marian; and when the latter had placed in her arms a little rosy-cheeked child, and had welcomed her with so much affection, how could Annie leave her?

The Marchioness of Sunningham was anxiously expecting some notice from the Regent.

Sir Hinckton Moys, and his rascally associate, Major Hanger, were anything but happy.

Such, then, was the state of affairs when those nine lords of the Privy Council held the most extraordinary meeting which, perhaps, since the deposition of King James the Second, had ever l een held beneath the roof of the royal residence.

The Chancellor just sat down for a moment, and then, looking white as it was possible for any human face to look, and still preserve its vitality, he rose again.

He spoke.

"My lords, I am a guilty man—guilty against the usages and the etiquettes of your lordships' high position, and my own office; but I have an excuse, of the validity of which your lordships will judge; and I hope that you will say that the highest legal officer of the realm, and the keeper of the conscience of the King, has done that which will be not only best for the peace and happiness of the Regent, but likewise for the welfare of the country!"

The lords looked at each other in surprise.

There was one member of the Council of which the Chancellor knew but little. He was the youngest present, and was the representative of one of the most ancient families in the kingdom.

We will name him the Marquis of Forchamp, which, while we admit it not to be his real title, will be recognisable by those conversant with the history of the Regency.

It was this Marquis, then, who said drily, "Perhaps we had better wait for his Royal Highness the Regent, before we discuss any important matter."

"I think not, my lords," said the Chancellor. "His Royal Highness is very nearly concerned in what will be the subject-matter of our deliberations, and it is more delicate towards him not to discuss those matters in his royal presence."

"Then, my Lord Chancellor," said another of the Council,—"it needs no great wit to come to the conclusion that it is something that concerns the Princess of Wales?"

"Your lordship is right."

A roll of drums at this moment came with a muffled sound upon the ears of the Council.

The Chancellor, from white, turned of a dingy yellow colour, for too well he knew what those sounds meant.

The Regent had most unexpectedly returned from Windsor, or he had never been there.

The plot thickened.

CHAPTER CCXXXV.

THE CONCLUSION.

THE phenomenon of the return of the Regent so unexpectedly from Windsor can be easily explained.

The young Marquis of Forchamp, who was quite new in the political world, had only a few months before attracted the attention of the Regent.

The young nobleman was not slow to perceive that a brilliant Court career was open to him, based on the personal favour of one who soon would be the actual King of England.

The summonses, then, that the wily Chancellor had sent to the nine lords of the Council had included him as one, simply because the Chancellor knew nothing about him but that he was young,

and he thought, from that circumstance alone, he might be easily moulded to his views.

There he was mistaken.

The Marquis of Forchamp no sooner got the summons, than he felt certain something unusual was on the *tapis* because he had taken leave of the Regent only the hour before, as he, the Prince, was going to Windsor.

An extraordinary express had reached Carlton House, signifying that a very unfavourable change had taken place in the condition of the King, and hence the projected hasty visit of the Regent.

That visit never took place.

The Marquis of Forchamp was one of the best horsemen in England. He had an Arabian horse that he named "The Prophet," and upon it he could make extraordinary speed.

Upon that steed, then, he overtook the Regent at Staines, and showed him the summons to the Council, which was headed, "Strictly private."

The Prince of Wales hesitated a few moments, and then he cried out, "Very well! It's a plot! Back to London!—back to London, at once!"

The Marquis preceded him, and reached the Council, cool, calm, and collected, about half an hour before the post-horses of the Regent could, at a half-gallop, bring the royal carriage to St. James's.

Then came the roll of the drums as Captain Fitz George called out the guard.

The Regent took a circuitous route through the Palace to the crimson room, preceded by the principal officers of the household. A couple of folding-doors were thrown open that had not been used for half a century; they opened from the throne-room into that Council chamber; and, with an angry flush upon his brow, the Regent appeared before the eyes of the Council.

The Chancellor turned decidedly yellow.

It is said that Charles the First, on his route across the Park to execution, changed in colour from his habitual sallow paleness to a strange golden sort of tint.

It was the same sort of physical distinction which took place in the Chancellor, and he looked golden and strange in the face as he bowed to the Regent.

The lords all rose.

The Regent looked from one to the other, and the colour deepened on his brow, as he slowly sat down in the chair with the gilt crown at the back of it.

He spoke in a mocking, sarcastic tone of voice.

"We are afraid, my lords, that our memory has been signally at fault to-day, for we were halfway to Windsor, when we recollected there was a private and confidential meeting of the Council at four o'clock."

The Chancellor turned a shade yellower.

"But," added the Regent, with a ghastly kind of smile, "all's well that end's well. What, my Lord Chancellor, is this most urgent and private business that calls us together?"

They all looked at the Chancellor.

Out of the depths of his despair he then gathered a wild sort of courage.

He spoke, and as he spoke he looked right into the eyes of the Regent.

"I would fain have made a communication to

these good lords of the Council in the absence of your Royal Highness, because——"

"It would have suited you much better," interrupted the Regent. "Oh, I quite comprehend that. Come to the matter, my lord."

"I will, your Royal Highness; but I had hoped that we should have seen some way of sparing your Royal Highness's feelings."

"That's kind!"

"It was intended to be so."

"Well, never mind that, my lord; just assume for once that we have no feelings to be tried."

The Chancellor, if his life had depended upon it, could not have resisted saying what he did in reply.

"That, your Royal Highness, will not be a difficult task, by any means."

The Regent felt the sting of the retort, and the look that he cast upon the Chancellor showed that he was politically doomed.

Had the Regent been Sultan of Turkey, or some Indian satrap, the Lord High Chancellor would not have lived another five minutes.

But kings and regents in England can only be vicious and revengeful in polite ways.

The Chancellor's head was safe enough, but his career, politically and socially, was over.

The knowledge of the fact gave him all the strength he wanted.

He looked bold and defiant, and he spoke in a tone and with a manner that, in a better cause, before an irritated monarch, would have done him a world of honour.

"I summoned this Council together, in order to inform it that evidence had been placed in my hands which is quite conclusive of the fact that his Royal Highness the Prince of Wales and Regent of England forgot that even princes and regents in this country cannot have two wives at one and the same time!"

"What?" cried the Regent.

The Council half rose again from their seats.

"Two royal marriages," added the Chancellor, "and both with the consent of the Crown, are likely to produce confusion."

"Mad!" cried the Regent.

"Yes—most mad confusion!" added the Chancellor, audaciously adopting the word.

"My lords," said the Regent, "this is very sad. Our poor Chancellor is bereft of his senses."

"No, your Royal Highness—I have come to them; and shall teach these noble lords to whom their respect is due. There is a lady——"

The Regent turned his head aside, and listened. A confused murmuring noise was in the Palace. It approached nearer and nearer—it reached the throne-room, which was only separated from the Council chamber by those folding-doors. Voices, apparently in contention, sounded without. The lords of the Council laid their hands upon their swords. The Regent looked flushed and excited.

"Way for her Royal Highness the Princess of Wales!" shouted a voice.

There was a clashing sound as of swords crossed, and the folding-doors were flung open.

Lovat appeared with a drawn sword in his hand.

There was blood upon his breast.

"Way for her Royal Highness Linda, Princess of Wales!" he cried again.

Then he fell to the floor.

The guard at the Council door had run him through the breast with the thin Court sword he had in his hand.

The Dark Woman stepped over the body of her young secretary, and presented herself before the astonished eyes of the Regent and the Council.

Then there was another rush of footsteps; and from the further end of the throne-room, the whole of which could now be seen, there appeared a party of the Guard, headed by an officer.

His sword was in his hand.

Some affrighted civilian officers of the household were urging him on; and they all pointed towards the Dark Woman and Lovat, the secretary, who was evidently breathing his last.

The Regent half drew the gold-hilted sword he wore.

Two of the Council stepped between him and the apparent danger, and crossed their swords over him to protect him.

The Chancellor saw what a crisis things had come to; and he called out, in a loud voice, so that all might hear, "Councillors, attendants, soldiers, and every one present, either in the throne-room or beyond it,—I declare, as Chancellor of England, that this lady, sometime known as Linda de Chevenaux, is the lawful, and the only lawful, wife of the Prince of Wales, our illustrious Regent!"

"Linda!" gasped the Regent.

"Mother!" exclaimed Captain Fitz George,—for he was the young officer who had been summoned in hot haste to protect the Regent.

"Traitor!" shouted the Marquis of Forchamp, as he howled in the face of the Chancellor.

"Traitor in your teeth, my Lord Forchamp!" cried the Chancellor. "I say again this lady is the true Princess of Wales."

The Dark Woman looked brilliant.

Her fair hair hung in wavy folds from her head-dress, and the robe she wore was resplendent with jewels. Once, and once only, she turned her eyes to the Regent; but all was cold disdain and hatred there.

Then she looked at Fitz George.

One gloved hand was over his eyes, and the other trailed his sword upon the floor. The most profound grief appeared to have taken possession of him.

The Dark Woman sighed.

"Cheer up, Prince of Wales that shall be," she said, in a soft, low voice. "Out of all this seeming confusion shall arise order, and regularity, and right. My lords——"

"Oh, mother! mother!" cried Fitz George. "This is despair!—this is death!"

"No—it is a new life!"

"Remove that woman!" said the Regent. "From this hour I throw aside all lenity. I prosecute Linda de Chevenaux, for treason to the Crown. It is treason, I believe, my lords, to dispute the succession?"

"Rank treason!" cried several.

"Unless," said the Chancellor, his voice rising like a bell over all the others,—"unless there should be good proof adduced."

"Where is the proof?"

"Here! here! here!" cried the Dark Woman, as she placed upon the Council table the real original document, which she had procured from the mad old King at Windsor. "Here is the proof; and, as I am among noblemen and gentlemen, I trust this paper to their sacred honour!"

The Chancellor raised the paper from the table, and read it:—

"'Windsor Castle, February 1, 1818.

"'This certifies that, whether lost or still in existence, we executed a document, at the proper period, giving our consent, as by law entitled to do, under the Royal Marriage Act, to the legal union of our son Wales with Linda de Chevenaux.

"'GEORGE REX.'"

A death-like stillness followed the reading of this document, to every word of which the Chancellor took care to give due emphasis.

Then the Dark Woman spoke.

"My lord, the period of the marriage can be easily proved, and my identity likewise. I believe that will be all that can be required."

"Infamous!" cried the Regent. "A delusion! —a wild delusion!—a forgery!"

"I, for one," said the Chancellor, "declare this signature to be that of the King."

"But the writing has been added."

"Nay, your Royal Highness, the royal sign-manual is across the writing."

"But no such consent of the Crown was given at the time of the—a—the—a—surreptitious ceremony which was gone through, twenty years ago, to satisfy the religious scruples of this lady!"

"It was given," said the Dark Woman. "I saw it, and this is the confirmation of it."

The Regent opened his mouth to speak again. He was about to say that the apparent consent of the King which he had shown her at that time was but a ruse on his part to overcome her scruples, but he shrank from making such a declaration before the lords of the Council.

The Marquis of Forchamp then entitled himself to the utmost gratitude of his royal master, by stepping in to the rescue.

"Will your Royal Highness permit me," he said, "to ask some questions of this lady?"

"Yes. Oh, yes, Forchamp—oh, yes!"

"And will the lady condescend to reply to me?"

"That will depend upon whether the questions are such as may be answered by the Princess of Wales," replied Linda de Chevenaux.

"They will be such, madam. Their sole object will be to substantiate your statement, if it be capable of real substantiation."

"Say on, sir."

A sneering smile sat upon the face of the Chancellor.

"My Lord Chancellor," added Lord Forchamp, "will you oblige me with that very important document?"

"Certainly, my lord—I trust it to your honour!"

"And I, too," said the Dark Woman.

"Oh, it is perfectly safe!"

"Mother, mother!" whispered Fitz George; "oh, give up this insensate struggle!"

"Peace, peace! Let us hear this lord."

"Madam," said the Marquis, "does it not strike you that it must strike us this document may have been procured from his Majesty while in that unhappy state of health which would prohibit him from knowing what he signed?"

"Nay, my Lord Forchamp," cried the Chancellor. "His Majesty, on the first of February, last year, was perfectly himself, and in good health. Several important State papers were signed after that. Recollect, we are now in the year 1819."

"Just so. Now, madam, did you get this paper signed by the King on the date you mention?"

"I did."

It will be in the recollection of the reader that there was no date to the paper which the Dark Woman had got the old mad King's signature to at Windsor. She had put that date to it of the previous year afterwards.

"And his Majesty saw you there?"

"He did."

"And knew what he was doing?"

"Perfectly."

"That this document would render the marriage of his Royal Highness the Regent with the Princess Caroline of Brunswick null and void?"

"Perfectly so."

"And the Princess Charlotte consequently illegitimate?"

"Just so!"

"Did his Majesty not feel the stupendous character of those startling events?"

"He did. But he considered that the truth was of greater importance still."

"That is quite right. And now will you let me ask you one more question, which appears to me the most important and curious of all?"

"Ask it, my lord!"

"How did you manage to get a document signed on the 1st of February, 1818, on paper that, as all their lordships will see when I hold it up to the light, *bears the water-mark of* 1819, *with the name of its maker?*"

The Dark Woman uttered a terrible cry.

The Regent sprung to his feet.

"By God!" he shouted, "she is foiled at last!"

The Lord Chancellor staggered back, and fell into a chair, with a deep groan.

All lost!—all lost by such a piece of folly!— by such a miserable oversight as that!

"Ruin! Ruin! Ruin!" he gasped.

Boom! boom! boom! boom! came, at that moment the sound of cannon from the Park.

Boom! boom! boom!

The reports shook the windows of the Palace.

The lords of the Council looked significantly at each other.

The Regent turned quite white.

He grasped nervously at the arm of his chair.

Boom! boom! boom! came the thundering reports of the cannon.

Then a voice cried out aloud in the throne-room, "Long live his Majesty King George the Fourth!"

The Regent—Regent no longer—made an effort to rise, but he sank back again, as he said, "My lords—I—we—my lords—we think that our royal father is no more."

The lords of the Council all bowed low.

The Dark Woman had remained with her hands clasped over her face, but now she recovered, and uttered shriek upon shriek.

Those shrieks were terrible to hear.

"Save me! Oh, heaven, save me! No, no! I am a princess! Oh, God, have mercy on this poor heart. I am a queen—the Queen-Consort of England—I, Linda de Chevenaux! I command—I reign—I feel the crown upon my brow! Oh, what is this? what darkness?"

She staggered back through the folding doors.

Captain Fitz George caught her in his arms.

The nearest seat to her was the throne itself. He gently placed her upon it.

"Mother! Oh, mother, look up! It is your son—your own son, who speaks to you!"

"My—my boy!"

"Yes, mother. It is your own boy. You will be very happy yet. Father, father, forgive her! Oh, forgive her! She was mad—mad!"

An awful change came over the face of the Dark Woman. She felt about with her jewel-decked hands, and spoke faintly.

"George — George! I did love you. Can

No. 104.—DARK WOMAN.

you, at this dread hour, say, 'Linda, I forgive you?'"

The Regent—the King approached and took her hand.

"Linda, I am very, very sorry; and forgive all."

She burst into tears, and sobbed like a child.

"Where—where am I?"

"On the throne," said the King.

A faint smile illumined her face for a moment, and she said, gently, "Kiss me, dear one!"

Fitz George clasped her in his arms, and kissed her. When he unclasped them again, she was dead.

And so ended the strange and troubled career of Linda de Chevenaux, the Dark Woman.

———

The chronicles from which we have succeeded

in extracting the strange and eventful history of the unhappy and persecuted Linda de Chevenaux, *alias* the Dark Woman, are exceedingly voluminous; but they do not in all cases supply us with information such as we should like to have, concerning the fate of all the subordinate persons who have figured in this strange drama of the Court of England.

Such information, however, as we do possess, we freely communicate to our readers.

But first, we feel bound to do common justice to one who, if he had a few more of the faults of humanity than all possess, yet had to thank a faulty education for many of the mental impulses that held possession of him.

We allude to his Royal Highness the Prince of Wales, afterwards King George the Fourth.

That he was a voluptuary, and fond to excess of self-gratification in every form and shape, cannot be denied; but that he was so utterly destitute of heart, as he has by some writers been represented, cannot be substantiated by facts.

The conduct of the Regent, or, we should say, of the King, on the death of Linda de Chevenaux, was creditable, if nothing more.

When poor Captain Fitz George looked up from his mother's corpse, it was with flashing eyes, which he intended should meet those of his father, the Regent, in one look of reproach which he should never forget.

But the Regent was not at the moment amenable to that look.

Stepping back until he came to a chair, he had seated himself, and was rocking to and fro in an apparent excess of grief, which no reproaches could add to.

Perhaps at that moment he had looked back through all the busy period of twenty years, and seen Linda de Chevenaux as she then was, the fairest of the fair—a gentle, happy girl, without a cloud upon her brow—and now what was she?

Even as the clod of the valley, or the storm-drift that is seen for a moment, and then vanishes for ever.

A deep silence reigned in the apartment.

None of the lords of the Privy Council felt qualified or courageous enough to break the stillness.

It was the stillness of death.

Then, one man, with a soft and noiseless step, went from the room, and gently closed the door behind him.

That was the Marquis of Forchamp.

He could not, after the active part he had taken against the poor, dead thing that lay upon the throne as a terrible reproach to its real possessor, look into the face of the Regent—the King!

And less than all could he bear to look into the face of Captain Fitz George.

He had done quite right, no doubt; but the memory of that day was the blight upon the life and the spirits of the young nobleman.

It was the King at last, as it was proper it should be, who broke the silence.

"Fitz George!" he said gently.

"Father!" was the reply.

The lords of the Privy Council looked at each other with uneasy and inquiring eyes.

"Fitz George, your poor mother thought herself my wife, and she shall rest in the royal vault at Windsor. There, at least, she will know the peace which in this world was denied to her."

The King's voice was broken by emotion.

Fitz George then stepped up to him, and bending on one knee, kissed his hand.

Then, rising, the young man turned to the lords of the Council, and spoke firmly, although sadly.

"I can well perceive, my lords, that there is some perplexity, as well as some regret, in your minds, about what has just now happened; and I, as the sole heir and living representative of my poor mother, think it right to state that I make none of the pretensions the pursuit of which has consumed her existence. I am the son of the King, but my mother was not legally his wife. Let me, then, put an end, by these few words, to all doubt—all perplexity. I am a nameless——"

"No, no!" cried the King, as he stepped up to Fitz George, and cast his left arm about him,—"no—by heaven, no! There is no rank below the throne that you may not aspire to, and that you would not grace."

The lords of the Council, then, would all shake hands with the young officer, but his heart was very full; and at that time, he would have given all he possessed to be alone with that still corpse on the throne, and to have relieved his bosom of the load of tears that seemed to fill it.

The Regent and King was as good as his word; and at midnight, on that same evening night, the royal vault at Windsor was opened, and in a niche in one of the walls a plain coffin was deposited.

On the coffin was the one name—"LINDA."

There were but two mourners present on the occasion.

One was the King.

The other his son.

It was, in truth, a strange spectacle, that midnight funeral of the Dark Woman.

As if the elements had felt that one in whose heart there had raged worse storms than ever they in their wildest moments could have produced, was now no more, there arose around Windsor Castle at that hour of midnight a fierce tornado of wind, which appeared to do battle about the ancient pile with victorious clamour.

A storm raged through the royal domain such as had been seldom witnessed.

Huge trees were torn up in Windsor Park, and in that part of it which was particularly wild, and which went by the name of Windsor Chase.

Even in the royal vault, in which, as yet, so few who belonged to the reigning family of England had found a place, the uproar of the elements was heard distinctly.

"Father," whispered Fitz George, "my poor mother led but a stormy and troublous life; and now that we consign her to the tomb, the warring elements of nature sing in fervent tones her requiem."

"Get it over—oh, get it over as soon as possible!" said the Regent. "All this is terrible!"

One of the domestic chaplains had been hastily summoned to perform the solemn service of the dead for the Dark Woman.

The few attendants whose services were absolutely necessary had been pledged to silence by Captain Fitz George.

There was but one solitary flambeau lighted in

the royal vault; and now, as that Regent so lately, but now King of England, sat on one of the richly-covered Gothic seats in the vault, which in some of its details resembled a chapel, he leant his head upon his hands, and perhaps reflected more in that ten minutes than he had done in twenty years before.

Once, only, he looked up—and then he saw the tall form of his son—the son of the Dark Woman, arrayed in the long, solemn cloak befitting the occasion, and gazing with pale face and tearful eyes at the proceedings of that sad and awful hour.

The King shrank back a little.

He wondered that Fitz George did not hate him as the actual destroyer of his mother.

The service then proceeded, and the solemn and affecting conclusion was come to.

One of the men there present had brought a small quantity of earth, which he had at the proper moment handed to Fitz George, who had cast it upon the coffin.

The sad receptacle of the poor heart that had suffered so much was then placed in the horizontal niche that had been hewn in the wall.

The funeral was virtually over.

Fitz George touched the King on the arm.

"Father!"

"Yes, yes, my son! Can you—oh, can you ever, really and truly——"

The King's voice faltered.

"What would you say to your son, oh, my father!"

"Can you forget?"

"Forget?"

Captain Fitz George pointed to the coffin in the wall, and the gesture was too significant to be mistaken. He meant that he could never forget the poor soul that was still for ever, and which had inhabited that body, and which had made such war on all the world for his sake.

"No! no!" added the King, "I do not mean that you should forget her; but can you forget all that has taken place in relation to her in which I have been an actor?"

"All, father, but this one night's act, when you have stood as a mourner by the side of her coffin."

The King pressed the hand of Fitz George, and rose from the Gothic chair.

"Come now, my dear boy!"

That was the first time his royal father had ever used so endearing an expression towards him, and Captain Fitz George was very glad and thankful that it had been used at such a time.

"One moment, father," he said.

"Yes, I will wait."

Fitz George saw that the coffin containing the remains of his mother would soon be out of sight, and probably for ever.

He stepped forward, and taking from his breast, where it had been concealed, a small coronal of flowers, he placed it on the coffin-lid. Then he placed there a folded paper.

That attracted the attention of the King.

"What was it?" he asked, sadly.

"Only an epitaph, father."

"An epitaph?"

"Yes; but it will soon moulder away—sooner than the poor remains it accompanies now. It is the dirge from 'Cymbeline.' I copied it for the purpose of laying it upon the coffin of my poor, dear, lost mother. You remember it, father?"

"Yes, yes. This is very strange."

"What, father?"

"You know, Fitz George, that it is popularly believed the death of my father's, the old King's, favourite daughter Amelia, had much to do with that mental aberration from which he suffered?"

"Yes, I have heard as much."

"On the night of her death he, too, copied out that melancholy dirge from 'Cymbeline,' and placed it on her tomb."

"It is a strange coincidence, father; and yet I cannot think it quite applicable to—to your sister Amelia. How melancholy and how sweet the words are, and what a world of heart-breaking tenderness breathes through every line!—

"'Fear no more the heat of the sun,
Nor the furious winter's rages;
Thou thy earthly task hast done,
Hence art gone, and ta'en thy wages!
Fear no more the frown of the great,
Thou art past the tyrant's stroke.
Care no more to clothe and eat,
To thee the reed is as the oak;
Fear no more the lightning's flash,
Nor the all-dreaded thunder stone;
Fear not slander—censure rash—
Thou hast finished joy and moan.'"

The King clasped his hands over his face while Captain Fitz George spoke; and when he had uttered the last word of the dirge, he slowly, leaning heavily upon the arm of his son, left the vault.

The niche in the wall was carefully closed up, and great pains were taken to give it the appearance of never having been opened.

Perhaps, in future years, some researches in that royal vault may discover the coffin with the name of Linda upon it, when the history and the existence of the Dark Woman may both be forgotten.

And now, we will say what we can of the other persons in whom we hope the reader has felt an interest; some on account of their virtues and their excellencies, although blended with follies and human frailties; and others on account of their crimes.

First, we speak of Annie, the fair Countess de Blonde.

There is a letter extant which was written to her by the King, dated the 21st of the month in which his father died. That letter runs as follows:—

"ANNIE,

"I am called fickle, capricious, and uncertain. Am I so to you, when, by this, I say to you, come back to me, and give me no explanation whatever of the past, for I still love you? Go to the Pavilion at Brighton—it will be yours. You will find those there who will acknowledge you as their mistress. I will come to you.

"GEORGE."

Annie's reply was characteristic:—

"GEORGE,
"I won't.

"Good-bye!
"ANNIE."

After this, Annie continued to reside with her sister; and her memory will be long cherished by many a poor heart that rejoiced at her bounty; for after about a year she was prevailed upon to accept a pension of one thousand per annum from the King, all of which she distributed in charity, with the exception of what she could persuade Marian to take for her board and lodging.

But she died young.

Alas, poor Annie! But only in this world were you misconceived and maligned. There is another, in which your true feminine heart will be appreciated.

Major Hanger was hanged for forgery, after carrying on a career of great profligacy for some time, and escaping the consequences of many criminal acts.

The girl from the shop in Long Acre had married him some time before his disgraceful death; and after that event she became somewhat notorious in the metropolis for her intemperance.

Sir Hinckton Moys, who was a villain of a higher grade, if there be grades in villany, than Hanger, managed to "carry on the war," as he called it, for some years, as the owner of a gaming-house; but as his notions of honesty and fair play were of the loosest, he was detected by an Irish baronet in some trick at cards, and knocked down.

A hostile meeting was the result, and Moys was shot through the brain.

The Irish baronet and the two seconds fled; and it was not until two days afterwards that the dead body of Sir Hinckton Moys was found lying amid a clump of trees in Kensington Gardens.

No one took the trouble to pursue the aforesaid Irish baronet on account of the transaction, and the general verdict of society was that it was well rid of such a man as Sir Hinckton Moys.

The band of the Dark Woman, finding themselves without a leader, were appalled at the dangerous position in which they were.

The story of the robbery of the jewels in St. James's Palace got by some means abroad, and the whole of the police energies of London were set to work to discover the culprits.

It was then that one of the band turned against his fellows, and sought to betray them at a meeting they had arranged at the old church in the City.

Before, however, the officers made their appearance, the members of the band who were present had discovered the intended treachery.

When the officers entered the church, all they found there was the traitor, dead from some wounds in the breast.

The others, it is supposed, at once left the country, for they were heard of no more.

Sixteen-stringed Jack continued his career on the road for some time, and was at length captured in an extraordinary manner.

He had stopped a post-chaise upon Hampstead Heath, and appropriated the valuables belonging to two gentlemen who occupied it, but in Pancras Vale he was met by a party of nine officers, all of whom knew him well.

To contend against such odds were madness, and flight seemed to be out of the question, for his horse had fallen lame during his ride down the hill.

It was early in the evening, and Sixteen-stringed Jack, as a last resource, took to the green lanes which then were to be found in abundance on both sides of the high road to Hampstead.

For the space of time of about four minutes only, he continued to get out of sight of his pursuers, and leaped bodily, horse and all, into a waggon, the huge canvas top of which completely hid him.

This stratagem might have succeeded, for the officers, after talking to the terrified waggoner, were about to ride on, when one of their horses took it into his head to neigh in a peculiar manner.

Sixteen-stringed Jack's horse immediately replied, and a search in the waggon resulted in his capture.

Tried and condemned to death, he lay in Newgate, and everybody expected his execution; but there was a mystery about the affair which was never cleared up, although he was reported to have escaped.

The fact was, that Jack had taken special good care of the ruby ring that the Regent had given him, and he got Captain Fitz George to present it to the King.

That saved him. He did escape, but it was with the connivance of the authorities.

Jack then emigrated to the American colonies.

In due time Fitz George became an earl, and although we do not choose exactly to blazon forth the title by which he was known, and which his son now bears, yet there are those who will readily recognise him when we state that he was the nobleman who, exhausted by fatigue, had only just fallen asleep in the Palace when George the Fourth expired in the arms of one of the royal pages, and that he prevented the Marchioness of Sunningham from taking the rings from the fingers of the dead King, and turned her out of the chamber.

And now, of all our characters, perhaps, we should say that Marian had been the most equably and serenely happy.

From first to last, she, and she only, with her husband, had pursued the even course of rectitude and justice. Truth was their motto, and they had never, for one moment, allowed themselves to deviate from it.

In their happy household, to which those two young girls were attached—namely, the daughter of Sixteen-stringed Jack, whom he would not take across the seas with him, and that faithful, gentle-hearted creature, who had been the page to Linda de Chevenaux, and then filled a similar capacity in the household of the Princess of Wales—they tasted of that serenity which the turmoils of the great world, and the agonies of ambition, would have denied them.

Shall we say that, of their family of five little ones, the girls inherited their mother's charms, both of body and mind, and the boys their father's true and noble gentleness and courage.

Their Aunt Annie was the idol of their young affections. Little did they guess that that Aunt Annie had at one time been the inmate of a palace, and had at her control almost the destinies of a kingdom.

And now, perhaps, we ought to say some few words in regard to the unhappy Princess Caroline of Brunswick, the wife of the Regent, afterwards King.

She lived just long enough to make one of the most terrible of discoveries

The discovery of the hollowness and the fickleness of all about her.

She found that the politicians—the lawyers—ay, even the divines that had thronged Buckingham House, and offered her lip-homage—were all false as the mirage of the desert, which looks all things to men's eyes, but is in reality nothing but a vapour.

Deserted by all, she alone made the memorable attempt to be present at the coronation of the King—of George the Fourth!

Spurned from the banquet hall at Westminster, she retired, but to die of a broken heart.

There are such things as broken hearts in the world, let sceptics in such matters say what they may.

And so ended the troubles, the indiscretions, and the follies of one who ought to have sat upon the throne of England as Queen Consort.

The calculations, selfish as they were, and carried out with audacity and with infamous means, of the Marchioness of Sunningham, were successful.

She did manage to enthral the King; and with little intermission, until the day of her death she was the cold, selfish, calculating, and imperious mistress of the private apartments in Carlton House and the Pavilion at Brighton.

No one loved her.

No one admired her.

But all feared her except one, and that was a young page of the household, who on all occasions thwarted her as far as he was able.

It was that page who stopped her from a robbery of the King's dressing-case after his decease.

But one other character of our varied *dramatis personæ* requires to be mentioned, and her fate was one of great singularity.

We allude to the Princess Charlotte, the wife for a year of the Prince Leopold.

It was discovered, after her sudden and most untimely death, that some few weeks before that event she had received a letter written evidently by a foreigner, and to the following purport:—

"Milan.

"If the Princess Charlotte of Wales desires a happy issue to the event which is about to occur, and which may have so remarkable an effect upon the succession to the English crown, she is invited to read carefully a book which she will find in the library of her mother, and which was sent to her along with many others, which is entitled, 'A Treatise on the Mineral Waters of Carlsbad.'

"This comes from a true friend."

It was well known that in the mind of the Princess there was a vein of superstition, and although she at first laughed at the letter, it was said that she had sought for the book, and was reading it with difficulty some three days only before she lay in death at Claremont.

We say she read it with difficulty, because the leaves adhered, in places, so closely together, that it was by no means an easy task to separate them.

To facilitate that process, the Princess very heedlessly damped the leaves with her lips.

There was some subtle poison upon them, which the slightest contact with was death.

The arts of the Borgias had descended to some one, and the name of Bergami, half erased, upon the cover of the book pointed to the author of the deed.

And this ends the strange, eventful history of Linda de Chevenaux, the Dark Woman.

THE END.